D1431695

AN ANTHOLOGY

OF FAMOUS

AMERICAN STORIES

AN ANTHOLOGY

OF FAMOUS

AMERICAN STORIES

>>

EDITED BY

ANGUS BURRELL

AND

BENNETT CERF

>>

THE MODERN LIBRARY
NEW YORK

THE MODERN LIBRARY

IS PUBLISHED BY

RANDOM HOUSE, INC.

BENNETT A. CERF · DONALD S. KLOPFER · ROBERT K. HAAS

Manufactured in the United States of America
By H. Wolff

* Contents *

★ *Acknowledgements* ★

FULLY eighty per cent of the material contained in this volume is copyrighted, and the collection is made possible only by the gracious permissions extended by the authors' publishers, authors' representatives, or holders of the copyrights listed below. In many instances they allowed the editors to reprint stories that have never before appeared in an anthology. Two of the stories were written so recently that they appear in book form in this collection for the first time. The result, the editors believe, is a book of American stories of wider scope and greater variety than has ever been issued before.

The editors also gratefully acknowledge valuable suggestions from Christopher Morley, H. C. Moriarty, Raymond Weaver, and especially Blanche Coton Williams.

Permissions:

A.&C. BONI, INC.: for *An Occurrence at Owl Creek Bridge* by Ambrose Bierce; *The Boarded Window* by Ambrose Bierce.

BRANDT AND BRANDT: for *Silent Snow, Secret Snow* by Conrad Aiken; *Little Gentleman* by Booth Tarkington (published by Doubleday, Doran and Company); *The Body of an American* by John Dos Passos (published by Harcourt, Brace and Company).

DOUBLEDAY, DORAN AND COMPANY: for *The Furnished Room* by O. Henry; *A Blackjack Bargainer* by O. Henry; *A Municipal Report* by O. Henry; *Effie Whittlesy* by George Ade; *A Deal in Wheat* by Frank Norris; *The Arrow* by Christopher Morley.

EDNA FERBER: for *The Afternoon of a Faun* by Edna Ferber (published by Doubleday, Doran and Company).

HAMLIN GARLAND: for *The Return of a Private* by Hamlin Garland.

SUSAN GLASPELL: for *A Jury of Her Peers* by Susan Glaspell.

HARCOURT, BRACE AND COMPANY, INC.: for *María Concepción* by Katherine Anne Porter, copyright, 1930, 1935; *The Hitch-Hikers* by Eudora Welty, copyright, 1941.

HARPER AND BROTHERS: for *The Celebrated Jumping Frog of Calaveras County* by Mark Twain; *The Man that Corrupted Hadleyburg* by Mark Twain; *Big Dan Reilly* by Harvey O'Higgins; *A New England Nun* by Mary E. Wilkins; *Editha* by William Dean Howells.

THE ESTATE OF JOEL CHANDLER HARRIS: for *Brer Rabbit, Brer Fox, and the Tar Baby* by Joel Chandler Harris.

HOUGHTON MIFFLIN COMPANY: for *The Outcasts of Poker Flat* by Francis Bret Harte; *The Author of Beltraffio* by Henry James; *The Courting of Sister Wisby* by Sarah Orne Jewett; *Marjorie Daw* by Thomas Bailey Aldrich.

THE ESTATE OF WILLIAM DEAN HOWELLS (MILDRED HOWELLS AND JOHN MEAD HOWELLS): for *Editha* by William Dean Howells.

ALFRED A. KNOPF, INC.: for *The Open Boat* by Stephen Crane; *Paul's Case* by Willa Cather; *Wild Oranges* by Joseph Hergesheimer; *Tact* by Thomas Beer; *A Cycle of Manhattan* by Thyra Samter Winslow.

LITTLE, BROWN & COMPANY: for *The Great Pancake Record* from *The Prodigious Hickey* by Owen Johnson; *Pretty Mouth and Green My Eyes* from *Nine Stories* by J. D. Salinger, copyright, 1951.

THE ESTATE OF JACK LONDON: for *To Build a Fire* by Jack London.

THE MACMILLAN COMPANY: for *The Real Thing* by Henry James.

ROBERT M. McBRIDE AND COMPANY: for *Porcelain Cups* by James Branch Cabell.

THE MODERN LIBRARY, INC.: for *The Good Anna* by Gertrude Stein.

RANDOM HOUSE: for *The Portable Phonograph* by Walter Van Tilburg Clark; *A Rose for Emily* by William Faulkner; *Do You Like It Here?* by John O'Hara; *The Daring Young Man on the Flying Trapeze* by William Saroyan; *My Christmas Carol* by Budd Schulberg; *Act of Faith* by Irwin Shaw.

CHARLES SCRIBNER'S SONS: for *The Lady, or the Tiger?* by Frank R. Stockton; *The Mission of Jane* by Edith Wharton; *The Bar Sinister* by Richard Harding Davis; *Some Like Them Cold* by Ring Lardner; *The Golden Honeymoon* by Ring Lardner; *The Rich Boy* by F. Scott Fitzgerald; *The Killers* by Ernest Hemingway; *The Gambler, the Nun, and the Radio* by Ernest Hemingway; *A Portrait of Bascom Hawke* by Thomas Wolfe.

SIMON & SCHUSTER, INC.: for *The Lost Phœbe* by Theodore Dreiser.

WILBUR DANIEL STEELE: for *The Man Who Saw Through Heaven* b. Wilbur Daniel Steele (published by Harper and Brothers).

FREDERICK A. STOKES COMPANY: for *The Pearls of Loreto* by Gertrude Atherton.

JAMES THURBER: for *The Secret Life of Walter Mitty* by James Thurber.

THE VIKING PRESS, INC.: for *I'm a Fool* by Sherwood Anderson; *I Want to Know Why* by Sherwood Anderson; *Big Blonde* by Dorothy Parker; *Kneel to the Rising Sun* by Erskine Caldwell; *The Red Pony* by John Steinbeck.

ANN WATKINS, INC.: for *Night Club* by Katharine Brush (published by Farrar and Rinehart).

Of the stories in this collection the following appeared originally in *The New Yorker:* "The Secret Life of Walter Mitty" by James Thurber; "Do You Like It Here?" by John O'Hara; "Act of Faith" by Irwin Shaw and "Pretty Mouth and Green My Eyes" by J. D. Salinger.

* Introduction *

I̶T might be interesting to under-
take here a history of the evolution of the short story in the United States
in terms of the parallel development of the country itself and the short
story as its most characteristic literary manifestation. The evidence for
this inseparable growth lies before you in this volume of short stories
that by popular consensus have survived the floods and back-washes of
American literary history. True to that history, this collection begins
with Washington Irving and continues chronologically to the present.

History books have said that Columbus discovered America; and
though Columbus is now reputed to have been a wretched navigator
with much imagination, there is no question that he did cross the
Atlantic. Columbus wrote a journal—and with that American fiction
might take a start. Later, Doctor Johnson said that as for emigration to
America he could urge no argument against it for "a man of mere
animal life." "But," he continued, "a man of any intellectual enjoyment
will not easily go and immerse himself and his posterity for ages in
barbarism." Yet even at the time of this pontifical dictum, prose of considerable vitality, occasionally of distinction, was being written in America. What concerned those writers of the eighteenth century were politics,
economics, and moral preachments. So that we might, if this had not
been conceived of as a collection strictly of novelettes and short stories,
have included one or two "curiosities" of the imaginative literature of
the period; Jonathan Edwards' character sketch *Sarah Pierrepont,* or
Parson Weems' best-seller pamphlet *God's Revenge Against Gambling,*
or something from Benjamin Franklin might have been included:
Reflexions on Courtship and Marriage, or *The Glory of Eternity, Treating of Immortality and Perpetual Peace of the Soul.* Then there was
William Austin (1778–1841) with his long and unique story, *Peter
Rugg, the Missing Man.* Peter Rugg left Boston and "spent the rest of
his life frantically trying to find it." The story is rambling and bad, and
its chief value lies in the fact (so say the scholars) that it influenced both
Hawthorne and Poe.

No satisfactory definition of the short story is possible: the form is
immediately recognized, even though it cannot be neatly and simply
defined. On the border-line is the "tale," which, according to a statement

xiii

used by Blanche Colton Williams, "may lack proportion, may show no progressive heightening, no nice adjustment to scale, and it may fail to produce a single emotional effect." *The Legend of Sleepy Hollow* and *Rip Van Winkle* might seem to be tales. *The Man Without a Country* and *Billy Budd* fall beyond definition, unless they are placed in the category of the novelette—defined in the French dictionary as *une composition littéraire qui tient le milieu entre le conte et le roman*—which keeps the middle course, literally, between the short story and the novel.

Many readers, we are aware, are sure to ask: But why, when they included this, did they omit that? There are a few answers and they are usually easy. Certain fine stories and novelettes have been left out because there is not space to include them. Others are omitted because it has been impossible to get permission from the publishers to reprint them. In a collection that tries to bring together so many stories that have been regarded for many years as masterpieces, it seems almost fatal not to include Edith Wharton's *Ethan Frome,* or Willa Cather's *A Lost Lady.* Their publishers, however, will not permit any anthologist to use them. Nor do we blame them. We must offer other stories from the pens of these gifted authors.

Another question likely to arise is: What are our criteria of judgment? One basis for judgment that is often used to the annoyance of the sceptical and impatient is that of age. We are told that *Rip Van Winkle* is a classic *because* it has survived all these years. It is not, we know, an infallible criterion. Yet there may be enough truth in it for us to trust it, for we believe that if the succeeding generations read this tale with pleasure, it must contain a deep current of vitality. And it does. About 1930, such a discerning critic as Ludwig Lewisohn wrote: "The two subdued but still unfaded little masterpieces *Rip Van Winkle* and *The Legend of Sleepy Hollow* come to enrich, in their minute degree, the imagination of the world." But the final answer to this question is personal taste.

Returning now to the short stories themselves.

Twenty years ago, writing in the *Dial,* Mary Colum said: "Those of us who take an interest in literary history will remember how particular literary forms at times seize hold of a country: in Elizabethan England it was the verse drama; in the eighteenth century it was the essay. . . At present America is in the grip of the short story—so thoroughly in its grip indeed that, in addition to all the important writers, nearly all the literate population . . . are writing or are about to write short stories." If that was true twenty years ago, it is even truer now. And as a matter of historical fact, it has been true from the beginning of our literary history. But Mrs. Colum continued to deplore the quality of short stories then bulging the American magazines. "Why a vivid people

like the American should be so dusty and dull in their short stories is
a lasting puzzle to the European, who knows that America has produced a large proportion of the great short stories of the world." We
have quoted this because, about 1915, hers was a charge against short
fiction in the United States that no intelligent person would deny. And
it is a further pleasure to recall that arid period in order to find satisfaction in the considerably improved quality of the short stories that
have been appearing in the last few years.

There have been, of course, throughout our literary history, fine artists
—Irving, Poe, Hawthorne, Melville, Henry James—whose emphasis in
fiction has always been upon truth in characterization. (An exception
to this might be made against Poe, because, as everyone knows, Poe's
people are not the people of actual life, but rather the fantastic people
of his own macabre imagination. At the same time his characters often
represent essential truths about human beings.) But the great writers
always realize that fiction—short or long—is an attempt to "render the
visible world." They would go all the way with Conrad when he said:
"My task which I am trying to achieve is, by the power of the written
word, to make you hear, to make you feel—it is, before all to make you
see—that, and no more: and it is everything!"

It was after the form of the short story had been set by Poe that many
writers with not very much to say mastered the form and poured into
it vapid and ephemeral subject matter. Their emphasis was upon incident, upon climax: they seemed to forget that stories to be living must
be about living men and women. That is why it is difficult to find stories
after Mark Twain and until comparatively recent years that have the
ring of truth. A transfusion of great talent put new life into the short story
when O. Henry took hold of it. Since O. Henry's day the form itself has
seemed to become an empty shell that our very contemporary writers
avoid.

Beginning really with Chekhov in Russia, and working back to the
United States in roundabout ways, came a change in the short story
form. When Chekhov wrote to a friend that he thought story writers
should cut off the beginnings and ends of stories because that was
where they were most inclined to lie; and more than that, when he
practiced what he preached, he managed to demolish the carefully built
scaffolding. In his own form, there was more resilience, more yielding
—yielding to the characters' needs. He believed, furthermore, that the
truth about people lies in carefully chosen, significant moments, and
these moments might not be at all those that we had been taught to
believe were revealing. Having selected such moments, it was his problem to explore them, and to make them reveal character. Whatever
may be the imperfections of the method, as practiced by mediocre writ-

ers, the fact is that in the hands of Chekhov and Katherine Mansfield, the story took on a new life. And, of course, precisely the same thing happened in the work of Henry James, and years later in that of Sherwood Anderson, particularly in his book *Winesburg, Ohio*. It is not extravagant to say that, under all of these impacts, the short story in the United States began to breathe again with the breath of life.

We have demanded of the stories in this anthology that they measure up to a high standard of truthful characterization. We could not, even if there were space, go into the problem of why certain characters are true to some people and not to others. We know also that some of these stories are less alive in this regard than others; but where this is true, the story is reprinted for one of several reasons: for its being representative of a genre, as with both Poe and Bierce, for its cleverness, even though it be a 'trick' story, as *The Lady, or the Tiger?*, etc. The characters in *The Outcasts of Poker Flat* are more representational than real. Then occasionally, the milieu may be so well worked out that the truth of the local color tends to give the character, who is only sketched, reality through our own creative reading, as in Frank Norris' *A Deal in Wheat*. Our demand has been that we feel concern for the people involved even more than we feel astonished or excited by the events in which they find themselves caught. We would like to follow their lives into other adventures. We leave such a story as *A New England Nun* wondering about the life of the heroine after her happy renunciation. We figure out for ourselves Effie Whittlesy's life before and after the immediate episode of the story under that name by George Ade.

This matter of truthful characterization is, especially in the short story, a relative virtue; but it is very illuminating to observe how deeply our best contemporary short story writers are concerned with creating character. From Sherwood Anderson and Conrad Aiken right down to William Faulkner and Erskine Caldwell and William Saroyan, it is always manifest. They will sacrifice almost everything in the way of formulas or rules to make their people live. They all know, as Arnold Bennett says, that everything counts in fiction. "Style counts, plot counts, originality of outlook counts. But none of these counts anything like so much as the convincingness of the characters. . . . The foundation of good fiction is character-creating and nothing else. . . ." It makes no difference how an author achieves this truth; each must do it in his own way. But achieve it he must, if his work is to be anything but ephemeral.

It is interesting to note the gradual quickening of tempo as the stories in this collection come closer and closer to the day in which we are living. The manner of telling a story becomes more staccato when dealing with violent subject-matter; more intense in stories which attempt to dig below the surface and reveal the deeply hidden motivations of human character. But in either event, there is a manner of telling based, not upon conventional formulas, but upon the demands of the subject-matter itself.

We completed the volume only after many months of selection, replacement, indecision, consultation with friends (everybody has his own ideas about what stories should be included in an anthology of this sort!), and arguments with each other. Re-reading the final selection in proper sequence, we were struck anew by the extraordinary scope and mood of the different stories—covering as they do every section of the country and every walk of life.

All this, we say, we noticed when we re-read the finished volume. But we never intended that the reader should follow any such course. We were, in truth, compiling a "Bedside Book"—one that a tired reader, just before turning in for a night's sleep, might open at random and round out his day by reading one of the gems of the short story literature of our country.

ANGUS BURRELL
BENNETT A. CERF

AN ANTHOLOGY OF
FAMOUS AMERICAN
STORIES

The Legend of Sleepy Hollow

BY WASHINGTON IRVING

A pleasing land of drowsy head it was,
Of dreams that wave before the half-shut eye;
And of gay castles in the clouds that pass,
For ever flushing round a summer sky.

CASTLE OF INDOLENCE

IN the bosom of one of the spacious coves which indent the eastern shore of the Hudson, at that broad expansion of the river denominated by the ancient Dutch navigators the Tappan Zee, and where they always prudently shortened sail, and implored the protection of St. Nicholas when they crossed, there lies a small market-town or rural port, which by some is called Greensburgh, but which is more generally and properly known by the name of Tarry Town. This name was given, we are told, in former days, by the good housewives of the adjacent country, from the inveterate propensity of their husbands to linger about the village tavern on market days. Be that as it may, I do not vouch for the fact, but merely advert to it, for the sake of being precise and authentic. Not far from this village, perhaps about two miles, there is a little valley, or rather lap of land, among high hills, which is one of the quietest places in the whole world. A small brook glides through it, with just murmur enough to lull one to repose; and the occasional whistle of a quail or tapping of a woodpecker, is almost the only sound that ever breaks in upon the uniform tranquillity.

I recollect that, when a stripling, my first exploit in squirrel-shooting was in a grove of tall walnut-trees that shades one side of the valley. I had wandered into it at noon time, when all nature is peculiarly quiet, and was startled by the roar of my own gun, as it broke the Sabbath still ness around, and was prolonged and reverberated by the angry echoes. If ever I should wish for a retreat, whither I might steal from the world and its distractions, and dream quietly away the remnant of a troubled life, I know of none more promising than this little valley.

From the listless repose of the place, and the peculiar character of its inhabitants, who are descendants from the original Dutch settlers, this sequestered glen has long been known by the name of SLEEPY HOLLOW, and its rustic lads are called the Sleepy Hollow Boys throughout all the neighboring country. A drowsy dreamy influence seems to hang over the land, and to pervade the very atmosphere. Some say that the place was bewitched by a high German doctor, during the early days of the settlement; others, that an old Indian chief, the prophet or wizard of his tribe, held his powwows there before the country was discovered by Master Hendrick Hudson. Certain it is, the place still continues under the sway of some witching power, that holds a spell over the minds of the good people, causing them to walk in a continual reverie. They are given to all kinds of marvelous beliefs; are subject to trances and visions; and frequently see strange sights, and hear music and voices in the air. The whole neighborhood abounds with local tales, haunted spots, and twilight superstitions; stars shoot and meteors glare oftener across the valley than in any other part of the country, and the nightmare, with her whole nine fold, seems to make it the favorite scene of her gambols.

The dominant spirit, however, that haunts this enchanted region, and seems to be commander-in-chief of all the powers of the air, is the apparition of a figure on horseback without a head. It is said by some to be the ghost of a Hessian trooper, whose head had been carried away by a cannon-ball, in some nameless battle during the Revolutionary War; and who is ever and anon seen by the country folk, hurrying along in the gloom of night, as if on the wings of the wind. His haunts are not confined to the valley, but extend at times to the adjacent roads, and especially to the vicinity of a church at no great distance. Indeed, certain of the most authentic historians of those parts, who have been careful in collecting and collating the floating facts concerning this specter, allege that the body of the trooper, having been buried in the churchyard, the ghost rides forth to the scene of battle in nightly quest of his head; and that the rushing speed with which he sometimes passes along the Hollow, like a midnight blast, is owing to his being belated, and in a hurry to get back to the churchyard before daybreak.

Such is the general purport of this legendary superstition, which has furnished materials for many a wild story in that region of shadows; and the specter is known at all the country firesides by the name of the Headless Horseman of Sleepy Hollow.

It is remarkable that the visionary propensity I have mentioned is not confined to the native inhabitants of the valley, but is unconsciously imbibed by everyone who resides there for a time. However wide awake they may have been before they entered that sleepy region, they are sure, in a little time, to inhale the witching influence of the air, and begin to grow imaginative—to dream dreams, and see apparitions.

I mention this peaceful spot with all possible laud; for it is in such little retired Dutch valleys, found here and there embosomed in the great state of New York, that population, manners, and customs remain fixed; while the great torrent of migration and improvement, which is making such incessant changes in other parts of this restless country, sweeps by them unobserved. They are like those little nooks of still water which border a rapid stream; where we may see the straw and bubble riding quietly at anchor, or slowly revolving in their mimic harbor, undisturbed by the rush of the passing current. Though many years have elapsed since I trod the drowsy shades of Sleepy Hollow, yet I question whether I should not still find the same trees and the same families vegetating in its sheltered bosom.

In this by-place of nature there abode, in a remote period of American history, that is to say, some thirty years since, a worthy wight of the name of Ichabod Crane; who sojourned, or, as he expressed it, "tarried," in Sleepy Hollow, for the purpose of instructing the children of the vicinity. He was a native of Connecticut; a state which supplies the Union with pioneers for the mind as well as for the forest, and sends forth yearly its legions of frontier woodmen and country schoolmasters. The cognomen of Crane was not inapplicable to his person. He was tall, but exceedingly lank, with narrow shoulders, long arms and legs, hands that dangled a mile out of his sleeves, feet that might have served for shovels, and his whole frame most loosely hung together. His head was small, and flat at top, with huge ears, large green glassy eyes, and a long snipe nose, so that it looked like a weather-cock, perched upon his spindle neck, to tell which way the wind blew. To see him striding along the profile of a hill on a windy day, with his clothes bagging and fluttering about him, one might have mistaken him for the genius of famine descending upon the earth, or some scarecrow eloped from a corn-field.

His school-house was a low building of one large room, rudely constructed of logs; the windows partly glazed, and partly patched with leaves of old copy-books. It was most ingeniously secured at vacant hours, by a withe twisted in the handle of the door, and stakes set against the window-shutters; so that, though a thief might get in with perfect ease, he would find some embarrassment in getting out; an idea most probably borrowed by the architect, Yost Van Houten, from the mystery of an eel-pot. The school-house stood in a rather lonely but pleasant situation, just at the foot of a woody hill, with a brook running close by, and a formidable birch-tree growing at one end of it. From hence the low murmur of his pupils' voices, conning over their lessons, might be heard in a drowsy summer's day, like the hum of a bee-hive; interrupted now and then by the authoritative voice of the master, in the tone of menace or command; or, peradventure, by the appalling sound of the birch, as he urged some tardy loiterer along the flowery path of knowledge. Truth to say, he was a conscientious man, and ever bore in mind the golden maxim, "Spare the rod and spoil the child." Ichabod Crane's scholars certainly were not spoiled.

I would not have it imagined, however, that he was one of those cruel potentates of the school, who joy in the smart of their subjects; on the contrary, he administered justice with discrimination rather than severity; taking the burthen off the backs of the weak, and laying it on those of the strong. Your mere puny stripling, that winced at the least flourish of the rod, was passed by with indulgence; but the claims of justice were satisfied by inflicting a double portion on some little tough, wrong-headed, broad-skirted Dutch urchin, who sulked and swelled and grew dogged and sullen beneath the birch. All this he called "doing his duty by their parents"; and he never inflicted a chastisement without following it by the assurance, so consolatory to the smarting urchin, that "he would remember it and thank him for it the longest day he had to live."

When school-hours were over, he was even the companion and play-mate of the larger boys; and on holiday afternoons would convoy some of the smaller ones home, who happened to have pretty sisters, or good housewives for mothers, noted for the comforts of the cupboard. Indeed, it behoved him to keep on good terms with his pupils. The revenue arising from his school was small, and would have been scarcely sufficient to furnish him with daily bread, for he was a huge feeder, and though lank, had the dilating powers of an anaconda; but to help out his maintenance, he was, according to country custom in those parts, boarded and lodged at the houses of the farmers, whose children he instructed. With these he lived successively a week at a time; thus going the rounds of the neighborhood, with all his worldly effects tied up in a cotton handkerchief.

That all this might not be too onerous on the purses of his rustic patrons, who are apt to consider the costs of schooling a grievous burden, and schoolmasters as mere drones, he had various ways of rendering himself both useful and agreeable. He assisted the farmers occasionally in the lighter labors of their farms; helped to make hay; mended the fences; took the horses to water; drove the cows from pasture; and cut wood for the winter fire. He laid aside, too, all the dominant dignity and absolute sway with which he lorded it in his little empire, the school, and became wonderfully gentle and ingratiating. He found favor in the eyes of the mothers by petting the children, particularly the youngest; and like the lion bold, which whilom so magnanimously the lamb did hold, he would sit with a child on one knee, and rock a cradle with his foot for whole hours together.

In addition to his other vocations, he was the singing-master of the neighborhood, and picked up many bright shillings by instructing the young folks in psalmody. It was a matter of no little vanity to him, on Sundays, to take his station in front of the church gallery, with a band of chosen singers; where, in his own mind, he completely carried away the palm from the parson. Certain it is, his voice resounded far above all the rest of the congregation; and there are peculiar quavers still to be heard in that church, and which may even be heard half a mile off, quite to the opposite side of the mill-pond, on a still Sunday morning, which are said to be legitimately descended from the nose of Ichabod Crane. Thus, by divers little make-shifts, in that ingenious way which is commonly denominated "by hook and by crook," the worthy pedagogue got on tolerably enough, and was thought, by all who understand nothing of the labor of head-work, to have a wonderfully easy life of it.

The schoolmaster is generally a man of some importance in the female circle of a rural neighborhood; being considered a kind of idle gentleman-like personage, of vastly superior taste and accomplishments to the rough country swains, and, indeed, inferior in learning only to the parson. His appearance, therefore, is apt to occasion some little stir at the tea-table of a farm-house and the addition of a supernumerary dish of cakes or sweetmeats, or peradventure the parade of a silver tea-pot. Our man of letters, therefore, was peculiarly happy in the smiles of all the country damsels. How he would figure among them in the churchyard between services on Sundays! gathering grapes for them from the wild vines that overran the surrounding trees; reciting for their amusement all the epitaphs on the tombstones; or sauntering with a whole bevy of them along the banks of the adjacent mill-pond; while the more bashful country bumpkins hung sheepishly back, envying his superior elegance and address.

From his half-itinerant life, also, he was a kind of traveling gazette, carrying the whole budget of local gossip from house to house; so that his appearance was always greeted with satisfaction. He was, moreover, esteemed by the women as a man of great erudition, for he had read several books quite through, and was a perfect master of Cotton Mather's *History of New England Witchcraft,* in which, by the way, he most firmly and potently believed.

He was, in fact, an odd mixture of small shrewdness and simple credulity. His appetite for the marvelous, and his powers of digesting it, were equally extraordinary; and both had been increased by his residence in this spell-bound region. No tale was too gross or monstrous for his capacious swallow. It was often his delight, after his school was dismissed in the afternoon, to stretch himself on the rich bed of clover, bordering the little brook that whimpered by his school-house, and there con over old Mather's direful tales, until the gathering dusk of the evening made the printed page a mere mist before his eyes. Then, as he wended his way by swamp and stream and awful woodland, to the farm-house where he happened to be quartered, every sound of nature, at that witching hour, fluttered his excited imagination: the moan of the whip-poor-will* from the hill-side; the boding cry of the tree-toad, that harbinger of storm; the dreary hooting of the screech-owl, or the sudden rustling in the thicket of birds frightened from their roost. The fire-flies, too, which sparkled most vividly in the darkest places, now and then startled him, as one of uncommon brightness would stream across his path; and if by chance a huge blackhead of a beetle came winging his blundering flight against him, the poor varlet was ready to give up the ghost, with the idea that he was struck with a witch's token. His only resource on such occasions, either to drown thought or drive away evil spirits, was to sing psalm tunes;—and the good people of Sleepy Hollow, as they sat by their doors of an evening, were often filled with awe at hearing his nasal melody, "in linked sweetness long drawn out," floating from the distant hill, or along the dusky road.

Another of his sources of fearful pleasure was to pass long winter evenings with the old Dutch wives, as they sat spinning by the fire, with a row of apples roasting and spluttering along the hearth, and listen to their marvelous tales of ghosts and goblins, and haunted fields, and haunted brooks, and haunted bridges, and haunted houses, and particularly of the headless horseman, or Galloping Hessian of the Hollow, as they sometimes called him. He would delight them equally by his anecdotes of witchcraft, and of the direful omens and portentous sights and sounds in the air, which prevailed in the earlier times of Connecticut; and would frighten them woefully with speculations upon comets and shooting stars; and with the alarming fact that the world did absolutely turn round, and that they were half the time topsy-turvy!

But if there was a pleasure in all this, while snugly cuddling in the chimney-corner of a chamber that was all of a ruddy glow from the crackling wood fire, and where, of course, no specter dared to show its face, it was dearly purchased by the terrors of his subsequent walk homewards. What fearful shapes and shadows beset his path amidst the

---

* The whip-poor-will is a bird which is only heard at night. It receives its name from its note, which is thought to resemble those words.

dim and ghastly glare of a snowy night!—With what wistful look did he eye every trembling ray of light streaming across the waste fields from some distant window!—How often was he appalled by some shrub covered with snow, which, like a sheeted specter, beset his very path!—How often did he shrink with curdling awe at the sound of his own steps on the frosty crust beneath his feet! and dread to look over his shoulder, lest he should behold some uncouth being tramping close behind him!—and how often was he thrown into complete dismay by some rushing blast, howling among the trees, in the idea that it was the Galloping Hessian on one of his nightly scourings!

All these, however, were mere terrors of the night, phantoms of the mind that walk in darkness; and though he had seen many specters in his time, and been more than once beset by Satan in divers shapes, in his lonely perambulations, yet daylight put an end to all these evils; and he would have passed a pleasant life of it, in despite of the devil and all his works, if his path had not been crossed by a being that causes more perplexity to mortal man than ghosts, goblins, and the whole race of witches put together, and that was—a woman.

Among the musical disciples who assembled one evening in each week to receive his instructions in psalmody, was Katrina Van Tassel, the daughter and only child of a substantial Dutch farmer. She was a blooming lass of fresh eighteen; plump as a partridge; ripe and melting and rosy-cheeked as one of her father's peaches, and universally famed, not merely for her beauty, but her vast expectations. She was, withal, a little of a coquette, as might be perceived even in her dress, which was a mixture of ancient and modern fashions, as most suited to set off her charms. She wore ornaments of pure yellow gold, which her great-great-grandmother had brought over from Saardam; the tempting stomacher of the olden time; and withal a provokingly short petticoat, to display the prettiest foot and ankle in the country round.

Ichabod Crane had a soft and foolish heart towards the sex, and it is not to be wondered at that so tempting a morsel soon found favor in his eyes, more especially after he had visited her in her paternal mansion. Old Baltus Van Tassel was a perfect picture of a thriving, contented, liberal-hearted farmer. He seldom, it is true, sent either his eyes or his thoughts beyond the boundaries of his own farm; but within those, everything was snug, happy, and well-conditioned. He was satisfied with his wealth, but not proud of it; and piqued himself upon the hearty abundance, rather than the style in which he lived. His stronghold was situated on the banks of the Hudson, in one of those green, sheltered, fertile nooks, in which the Dutch farmers are so fond of nestling. A great elm-tree spread its broad branches over it, at the foot of which bubbled up a spring of the softest and sweetest water, in a little well formed of a barrel, and then stole sparkling away through the grass to a neighboring brook that bubbled along among alders and drawf willows. Hard by the farm-house was a vast barn that might have served for a church, every window and crevice of which seemed bursting forth with the treasures of the farm; the flail was busily resounding within it from morning to night; swallows and martins skimmed twittering about the eaves; and rows of pigeons, some with one eye turned up, as if watching the weather, some with their heads under their wings, or buried in their bosoms, and others swelling, and cooing, and bowing about their dames, were enjoying the sunshine on the roof. Sleek unwieldy porkers were grunting in the repose and abundance of their pens, whence sallied forth now and then troops of sucking pigs, as if to snuff the air. A stately squadron of snowy geese were riding in an adjoining pond, convoying whole fleets of ducks; regiments of turkeys were gobbling through the farm-yard, and guinea-fowls fretting about it, like illtempered house-wives, with their peevish, discontented cry. Before the barn door strutted the gallant cock, that pattern of a husband, a warrior, and a fine gentleman, clapping his burnished wings, and crowing in the pride and gladness of his heart—sometimes tearing up the earth with his feet, and then generously calling his ever-hungry family of wives and children to enjoy the rich morsel which he had discovered.

The pedagogue's mouth watered as he looked upon his sumptuous promise of luxurious winter fare. In his devouring mind's eye he pictured to himself every roasting-pig running about with a pudding in his belly, and an apple in his mouth; the pigeons were snugly put to bed in a comfortable pie, and tucked in with a coverlet of crust; the geese were swimming in their own gravy; and the ducks pairing cozily in dishes, like snug married couples, with a decent competency of onion sauce. In the porkers he saw carved out the future sleek side of bacon and juicy relishing ham; not a turkey but he beheld daintily trussed up, with its gizzard under its wing, and, peradventure, a necklace of savory sausages; and even bright chanticleer himself lay sprawling on his back in a side dish, with uplifted claws, as if craving that quarter which his chivalrous spirit disdained to ask while living.

As the enraptured Ichabod fancied all this, and as he rolled his great green eyes over the fat meadow-lands, the rich fields of wheat, of rye, of buckwheat, and Indian corn, and the orchards burthened with ruddy fruit, which surrounded the warm tenement of Van Tassel, his heart yearned after the damsel who was to inherit these domains, and his imagination expanded with the idea, how they might be readily turned into cash, and the money invested in immense tracts of wild land, and shingle palaces in the wilderness. Nay, his busy fancy already realized his hopes, and presented to him the blooming Katrina, with a whole family of children, mounted on the top of a wagon loaded with household trumpery, with pots and kettles dangling beneath; and he beheld himself bestriding a pacing mare, with a colt at her heels, setting out for Kentucky, Tennessee, or the Lord knows where.

When he entered the house, the conquest of his heart was complete. It was one of those spacious farm-houses, with high-ridged, but lowly sloping roofs, built in the style handed down from the first Dutch settlers; the low projecting eaves forming a piazza along the front, capable of being closed up in bad weather. Under this were hung flails, harness, various utensils of husbandry, and nets for fishing in the neighboring river. Benches were built along the sides for summer use; and a great spinning-wheel at one end, and a churn at the other, showed the various uses to which this important porch might be devoted. From this piazza the wondering Ichabod entered the hall, which formed the center of the mansion and the place of usual residence. Here rows of resplendent pewter, ranged on a long dresser, dazzled his eyes. In one corner stood a huge bag of wool ready to be spun; in another, a quantity of linsey-woolsey just from the loom; ears of Indian corn, and strings of dried apples and peaches, hung in gay festoons along the wall, mingled with the gaud of red peppers; and a door left ajar gave him a peep into the best parlor, where the claw-footed chairs and dark mahogany tables shone like mirrors; and irons, with their accompanying shovel and tongs, glistened from their covert of asparagus tops; mock oranges and conch-shells decorated the mantel-piece; strings of various colored birds' eggs were suspended above it; a great ostrich egg was hung from the center of the room, and a corner-cupboard, knowingly left open, displayed immense treasures of old silver and well-mended china.

From the moment Ichabod laid his eyes upon these regions of delight, the peace of his mind was at an end, and his only study was how to gain the affections of the peerless daughter of Van Tassel. In this enterprise, however, he had more real difficulties than generally fell to the lot of a knight-errant of yore, who seldom had anything but giants, enchanters, fiery dragons, and such like easily conquered adversaries, to contend with; and had to make his way merely through gates of iron and brass, and walls of adamant, to the castle keep, where the lady of his heart was confined; all which he achieved as easily as a man would carve his way to the center of a Christmas pie, and then the lady gave him her hand as a matter of course. Ichabod, on the contrary, had to win his way to the heart of a country coquette, beset with a labyrinth of whims and caprices, which were forever presenting new difficulties and impediments; and he had to encounter a host of fearful adversaries of real flesh and blood, the numerous rustic admirers who beset every portal to her heart, keeping a watchful and angry eye upon each other, but ready to fly out in the common cause against any new competitor.

Among these the most formidable was a burly, roaring, roistering blade, of the name of Abraham, or, according to the Dutch abbreviation, Brom Van Brunt, the hero of the country round, which rang with his feats of strength and hardihood. He was broad-shouldered and double-jointed, with short curly black hair, and a bluff but not unpleasant countenance, having a mingled air of fun and arrogance. From his Herculean frame and great powers of limb, he had received the nick-name of BROM BONES, by which he was universally known. He was famed for great knowledge and skill in horsemanship, being as dexterous on horseback as a Tartar. He was foremost at all races and cock-fights, and, with the ascendency which bodily strength acquires in rustic life, was the umpire in all disputes, setting his hat on one side, and giving his decisions with an air and tone admitting of no gainsay or appeal. He was always ready for either a fight or frolic, but had more mischief than ill-will in his composition; and, with all his overbearing roughness, there was a strong dash of waggish good humor at bottom. He had three or four boon companions, who regarded him as their model, and at the head of whom he scoured the country, attending every scene of feud or merriment for miles round. In cold weather he was distinguished by a fur cap, surmounted with a flaunting fox's tail; and when the folks at a country gathering descried this well-known crest at a distance, whisking about among a squad of hard riders, they always stood by for a squall. Sometimes his crew would be heard dashing along past the farm-houses at midnight, with hoop and halloo, like a troop of Don Cossacks, and the old dames, startled out of their sleep, would listen for a moment, till the hurry-scurry had clattered by, and then exclaim, "Ay, there goes BROM BONES and his gang!" The neighbors looked upon him with a mixture of awe, admiration, and good-will; and when any mad-cap prank or rustic brawl occurred in the vicinity, always shook their heads and warranted Brom Bones was at the bottom of it.

This rantipole hero had for some time singled out the blooming Katrina for the object of his uncouth gallantries, and though his amorous toyings were something like the gentle caresses and endearments of a bear, yet it was whispered that she did not altogether discourage his hopes. Certain it is, his advances were signals for rival candidates to retire, who felt no inclination to cross a lion in his amours; insomuch that when his horse was seen tied to Van Tassel's paling on a Sunday night, a sure sign that his master was courting, or, as it is termed, "sparking," within, all other suitors passed by in despair, and carried the war into other quarters.

Such was the formidable rival with whom Ichabod Crane had to contend, and, considering all things, a stouter man than he would have shrunk from the competition, and a wiser man would have despaired. He had, however, a happy mixture of pliability and perseverance in his nature; he was in form and spirit like a supple-jack,—yielding, but tough; though he bent, he never broke; and though he bowed beneath the slighest pressure, yet, the moment it was away—jerk! he was as erect, and carried his head as high as ever.

To have taken the field openly against his rival would have been madness; for he was not a man to be thwarted in his amours, any more than that stormy lover, Achilles. Ichabod, therefore, made his advances in a quiet and gently insinuating manner. Under cover of his character of singing-master, he made frequent visits at the farm-house; not that he had anything to apprehend from the meddlesome interference of parents, which is so often a stumbling-block in the path of lovers. Balt Van Tassel was an easy, indulgent soul; he loved his daughter better even than his pipe, and, like a reasonable man and an excellent father, let her have her way in everything. His notable little wife, too, had enough to do to attend to her housekeeping, and manage her poultry; for, as she sagely observed, ducks and geese are foolish things, and must be looked after, but girls can take care of themselves. Thus, while the busy dame bustled about the house, or plied her spinning-wheel at one end of the piazza, honest Balt would sit smoking his evening pipe at the other, watching the achievements of a little wooden warrior, who, armed with a sword in each hand, was most valiantly fighting the wind on the pinnacle of the barn. In the meantime, Ichabod would carry on his suit with the daughter by the side of the spring under the great elm, or sauntering along in the twilight, that hour so favorable to the lover's eloquence.

I profess not to know how women's hearts are wooed and won. To me they have always been matters of riddle and admiration. Some seem to have but one vulnerable point, or door of access; while others have a thousand avenues, and may be captured in a thousand different ways. It is a great triumph of skill to gain the former, but a still greater proof of generalship to maintain possession of the latter, for a man must battle for his fortress at every door and window. He who wins a thousand common hearts is therefore entitled to some renown; but he who keeps undisputed sway over the heart of a coquette, is indeed a hero. Certain it is, this was not the case with the redoubtable Brom Bones; and from the moment Ichabod Crane made his advances, the interests of the former evidently declined; his horse was no longer seen tied at the palings on Sunday nights, and a deadly feud gradually arose between him and the preceptor of Sleepy Hollow.

Brom, who had a degree of rough chivalry in his nature, would fain have carried matters to open warfare, and have settled their pretensions to the lady, according to the mode of those most concise and simple reasoners, the knights-errant of yore—by single combat; but Ichabod was too conscious of the superior might of his adversary to enter the lists against him; he had overheard a boast of Bones, that he "would double the school-master up, and lay him on a shelf of his own school-house"; and he was too wary to give him an opportunity. There was something extremely provoking in this obstinately pacific system; it left Brom no alternative but to draw upon the funds of rustic waggery in his disposition, and to play off boorish practical jokes upon his rival. Ichabod became the object of whimsical persecution to Bones and his gang of rough riders. They harried his hitherto peaceful domains; smoked out his singing-school, by stopping up the chimney; broke into the school-house at night, in spite of his formidable fastenings of withe and window stakes, and turned everything topsy-turvy; so that the poor schoolmaster began to think all the witches in the country held their meetings there. But what was still more annoying, Brom took all opportunities of turning him into ridicule in the presence of his mistress, and had a scoundrel dog whom he taught to whine in the most ludicrous manner, and introduced as a rival of Ichabod's to instruct her in psalmody.

In this way matters went on for some time, without producing any material effect on the relative situation of the contending powers. On a fine autumnal afternoon, Ichabod, in pensive mood, sat enthroned on the lofty stool whence he usually watched all the concerns of his little literary realm. In his hand he swayed a ferule, that scepter of despotic power; the birch of justice reposed on three nails behind the throne, a constant terror to evil-doers; while on the desk before him might be seen sundry contraband articles and prohibited weapons, detected upon the persons of idle urchins; such as half-munched apples, pop-guns, whirligigs, fly-cages, and whole legions of rampant little paper game-cocks. Apparently there had been some appalling act of justice recently inflicted, for his scholars were all busily intent upon their books, or slyly whispering behind them with one eye kept upon the master; and a kind of buzzing stillness reigned throughout the school-room. It was suddenly interrupted by the appearance of a Negro, in tow-cloth jacket and trousers, a round-crowned fragment of a hat, like the cap of Mercury, and mounted on the back of a ragged, wild, half-broken colt, which he managed with a rope by way of halter. He came clattering up to the school door with an invitation to Ichabod to attend a merry-making, or "quilting frolic," to be held that evening at Mynheer Van Tassel's; and having delivered his message with that air of importance and effort at fine language which a Negro is apt to display on petty embassies of the kind, he dashed over the brook, and was seen scampering away up the hollow, full of the importance and hurry of his mission.

All was now bustle and hubbub in the late quiet school-room. The scholars were hurried through their lessons without stopping at trifles; those who were nimble skipped over half with impunity, and those who were tardy had a smart application now and then in the rear, to quicken their speed, or help them over a tall word. Books were flung aside without being put away on the shelves; inkstands were overturned, benches thrown down, and the whole school was turned loose an hour before the usual time, bursting forth like a legion of young imps, yelping and racketing about the green in joy at their early emancipation.

The gallant Ichabod now spent at least an extra half-hour at his toilet, brushing and furbishing up his best, and indeed only suit of rusty black, and arranging his locks by a bit of broken looking-glass that hung up in the school-house. That he might make his appearance before his mistress in the true style of a cavalier, he borrowed a horse from the farmer with whom he was domiciliated, a choleric old Dutchman, of the name of Hans Van Ripper, and, thus gallantly mounted, issued forth like a knight-errant in quest of adventures. But it is meet I should, in the true spirit of romantic story, give some account of the looks and equipments of my hero and his steed. The animal he bestrode was a broken-down plough-horse that had outlived almost everything but his viciousness. He was gaunt and shagged, with a ewe neck and a head like a hammer; his rusty mane and tail were tangled and knotted with burrs; one eye had lost its pupil, and was glaring and spectral; but the other had the gleam of a genuine devil in it. Still he must have had fire and mettle in his day, if we may judge from the name he bore of Gunpowder. He had, in fact, been a favorite steed of his master's, the choleric Van Ripper, who was a furious rider, and had infused, very probably, some of his own spirit into the animal; for, old and broken-down as he looked, there was more of the lurking devil in him than in any young filly in the country.

Ichabod was a suitable figure for such a steed. He rode with short stirrups, which brought his knees nearly up to the pommel of the saddle; his sharp elbows stuck out like grasshoppers; he carried his whip perpendicularly in his hand, like a scepter, and, as his horse jogged on, the motion of his arms was not unlike the flapping of a pair of wings. A small wool hat rested on the top of his nose, for so his scanty strip of forehead might be called; and the skirts of his black coat fluttered out almost to the horse's tail. Such was the appearance of Ichabod and his steed, as they shambled out of the gate of Hans Van Ripper, and it was altogether such an apparition as is seldom to be met with in broad daylight.

It was, as I have said, a fine autumnal day, the sky was clear and serene, and nature wore that rich and golden livery which we always associate with the idea of abundance. The forests had put on their sober brown and yellow, while some trees of the tenderer kind had been nipped by the frosts into brilliant dyes of orange, purple, and scarlet. Streaming files of wild ducks began to make their appearance high in the air; the bark of the squirrel might be heard from the groves of beech and hickory nuts, and the pensive whistle of the quail at intervals from the neighboring stubble field.

The small birds were taking their farewell banquets. In the fulness of their revelry, they fluttered, chirping and frolicking, from bush to bush and tree to tree, capricious from the very profusion and variety around them. There was the honest cock-robin, the favorite game of stripling sportsmen, with its loud, querulous note; and the twittering blackbirds flying in sable clouds; and the golden-winged woodpecker, with his crimson crest, his broad black gorget, and splendid plumage; and the cedar-bird, with its red-tipt wings and yellow-tip tail, and its little monteiro cap of feathers; and the blue jay, that noisy coxcomb, in his gay light-blue coat and white underclothes; screaming and chattering, nodding and bobbing and bowing, and pretending to be on good terms with every songster of the grove.

As Ichabod jogged slowly on his way, his eye, ever open to every symptom of culinary abundance, ranged with delight over the treasures of jolly autumn. On all sides he beheld vast stores of apples; some hanging in oppressive opulence on the trees; some gathered into baskets and barrels for the market; others heaped up in rich piles for the cider-press. Further on he beheld great fields of Indian corn, with its golden ears peeping from their leafy coverts, and holding out the promise of cakes and hasty-pudding; and the yellow pumpkins lying beneath them, turning up their fair round bellies to the sun, and giving ample prospects of the most luxurious of pies; and anon he passed the fragrant buckwheat fields breathing the odor of the bee-hive, and as he beheld them, soft anticipations stole over his mind of dainty slapjacks, well buttered, and garnished with honey or treacle, by the delicate little dimpled hand of Katrina Van Tassel.

Thus feeding his mind with many sweet thoughts and "sugared suppositions," he journeyed along the sides of a range of hills which look out upon some of the goodliest scenes of the mighty Hudson. The sun gradually wheeled his broad disc down into the west. The wide bosom of the Tappan Zee lay motionless and glassy, except that here and there a gentle undulation waved and prolonged the blue shadow of the distant mountain. A few amber clouds floated in the sky, without a breath of air to move them. The horizon was of a fine golden tint, changing gradually into a pure apple-green, and from that into the deep blue of the mid-heaven. A slanting ray lingered on the woody crests of the precipices that overhung some parts of the river, giving greater depth to the dark-gray and purple of their rocky sides. A sloop was loitering in the distance, dropping slowly down with the tide, her sail hanging uselessly against the mast; and as the reflection of the sky gleamed along the still water, it seemed as if the vessel was suspended in the air.

It was towards evening that Ichabod arrived at the castle of the Heer Van Tassel, which he found thronged with the pride and flower of the adjacent country. Old farmers, a spare leathern-faced race, in homespun coats and breeches, blue stockings, huge shoes, and magnificent pewter buckles. Their brisk withered little dames, in close crimped caps, long-waisted short gowns, homespun petticoats, with scissors and pincushions, and gay calico pockets hanging on the outside. Buxom lasses, almost as antiquated as their mothers, excepting where a straw hat, a fine riband, or perhaps a white frock, gave symptoms of city innovation. The sons, in short square-skirted coats with rows of stupendous brass buttons, and their hair generally queued in the fashion of the times, especially if they could procure an eel-skin for the purpose, it being esteemed throughout the country as a potent nourisher and strengthener of the hair.

Brom Bones, however, was the hero of the scene, having come to the gathering on his favorite steed Daredevil, a creature like himself, full of mettle and mischief, and which no one but himself could manage. He was, in fact, noted for preferring vicious animals, given to all kinds of tricks, which kept the rider in constant risk of his neck, for he held a tractable, well-broken horse as unworthy of a lad of spirit.

Fain would I pause to dwell upon the world of charms that burst upon the enraptured gaze of my hero, as he entered the state parlor of Van Tassel's mansion. Not those of the bevy of buxom lasses, with their luxurious display of red and white; but the ample charms of a genuine Dutch country tea-table in the sumptuous time of autumn. Such heaped-up platters of cakes of various and almost indescribable kinds, known only to experienced Dutch housewives! There was the doughty dough-nut, the tenderer oly koek, and the crisp and crumbling cruller; sweet-cakes and short-cakes, ginger-cakes and honey-cakes, and the whole family of cakes. And then there were apple-pies and peach-pies and pumpkin-pies; besides slices of ham and smoked beef; and, moreover, delectable dishes of preserved plums, and peaches, and pears, and quinces; not to mention broiled shad and roasted chickens; together with bowls of milk and cream, all mingled higgledy-piggledy, pretty much as I have enumerated them, with the motherly tea-pot sending up its clouds of vapor from the midst—Heaven bless the mark! I want breath and time to discuss this banquet as it deserves, and am too eager to get on with my story. Happily, Ichabod Crane was not in so great a hurry as his historian, but did ample justice to every dainty.

He was a kind and thankful creature, whose heart dilated in proportion as his skin was filled with good cheer; and whose spirits rose with eating as some men's do with drink. He could not help, too, rolling his large eyes round him as he ate, and chuckling with the possibility that he might one day be lord of all this scene of almost unimaginable luxury and splendor. Then he thought, how soon he'd turn his back upon the old school-house, snap his fingers in the face of Hans Van Ripper and every other niggardly patron, and kick any itinerant pedagogue out of doors that should dare to call him comrade!

Old Baltus Van Tassel moved about among his guests with a face dilated with content and good humor, round and jolly as the harvest moon. His hospitable attentions were brief, but expressive, being confined to a shake of the hand, a slap on the shoulder, a loud laugh, and a pressing invitation to "fall to, and help themselves."

And now the sound of the music from the common room or hall summoned to the dance. The musician was an old gray-headed Negro, who had been the itinerant orchestra of the neighborhood for more than half a century. His instrument was as old and battered as himself. The greater part of the time he scraped on two or three strings, accompanying every movement of the bow with a motion of the head; bowing almost to the ground, and stamping with his foot whenever a fresh couple were to start.

Ichabod prided himself upon his dancing as much as upon his vocal powers. Not a limb, not a fiber about him was idle; and to have seen his loosely hung frame in full motion, and clattering about the room, you would have thought Saint Vitus himself, that blessed patron of the dance, was figuring before you in person. He was the admiration of all the Negroes; who, having gathered, of all ages and sizes, from the farm and the neighborhood, stood forming a pyramid of shining black faces, at every door and window, gazing with delight at the scene, rolling their white eye-balls, and showing grinning rows of ivory from ear to ear. How could the flogger of urchins be otherwise than animated and joyous? the lady of his heart was his partner in the dance, and smiling graciously in reply to all his amorous oglings; while Brom Bones, sorely smitten with love and jealousy, sat brooding by himself in one corner.

When the dance was at an end, Ichabod was attracted to a knot of the sager folks, who, with old Van Tassel, sat smoking at one end of the piazza, gossiping over former times, and drawing out long stories about the war.

This neighborhood, at the time of which I am speaking, was one of those highly favored places which abound with chronicle and great men. The British and American line had run near it during the war; it had, therefore, been the scene of marauding, and infested with refugees, cow-boys, and all kinds of border chivalry. Just sufficient time had elapsed to enable each story-teller to dress up his tale with a little becoming fiction, and, in the indistinctness of his recollection, to make himself the hero of every exploit.

There was the story of Doffue Martling, a large bluebearded Dutchman, who had nearly taken a British frigate with an old iron ninepounder from a mud breastwork, only that his gun burst at the sixth discharge. And there was an old gentleman who shall be nameless, being too rich a mynheer to be lightly mentioned, who, in the battle of White Plains, being an excellent master of defense, parried a musketball with a small sword, insomuch that he absolutely felt it whiz round the blade, and glance off at the hilt; in proof of which he was ready at any time to show the sword, with the hilt a little bent. There were several more that had been equally great in the field, not one of whom but was persuaded that he had a considerable hand in bringing the war to a happy termination.

But all these were nothing to the tales of ghosts and apparitions that succeeded. The neighborhood is rich in legendary treasures of the kind. Local tales and superstitions thrive best in these sheltered long-settled retreats; but are trampled under-foot by the shifting throng that forms the population of most of our country places. Besides, there is no encouragement for ghosts in most of our villages, for they have scarcely had time to finish their first nap, and turn themselves in their graves, before their surviving friends have traveled away from the neighborhood; so that when they turn out at night to walk their rounds, they have no acquaintance left to call upon. This is perhaps the reason why we so seldom hear of ghosts except in our long-established Dutch communities.

The immediate cause, however, of the prevalence of supernatural stories in these parts, was doubtless owing to the vicinity of Sleepy Hollow. There was a contagion in the very air that blew from that haunted region; it breathed forth an atmosphere of dreams and fancies infecting all the land. Several of the Sleepy Hollow people were present at Van Tassel's, and, as usual, were doling out their wild and wonderful legends. Many dismal tales were told about funeral trains, and mourning cries and wailings heard and seen about the great tree where the unfortunate Major André was taken, and which stood in the neighborhood. Some mention was made also of the woman in white, that haunted the dark glen at Raven Rock, and was often heard to shriek on winter nights before a storm, having perished there in the snow. The chief part of the stories, however, turned upon the favorite specter of Sleepy Hollow, the headless horseman, who had been heard several times of late, patrolling the country; and, it was said, tethered his horse nightly among the graves in the churchyard.

The sequestered situation of this church seems always to have made it a favorite haunt of troubled spirits. It stands on a knoll surrounded by locust-trees and lofty elms, from among which its decent white-washed walls shine modestly forth, like Christian purity, beaming through the shades of retirement. A gentle slope descends from it to a silver sheet of water, bordered by high trees, between which peeps may be caught at the blue hills of the Hudson. To look upon its grass-grown yard, where the sunbeams seem to sleep so quietly, one would think that there at least the dead might rest in peace. On one side of the church extends a wide woody dell, along which raves a large brook among broken rocks and trunks of fallen trees. Over a deep black part of the stream, not far from the church, was formerly thrown a wooden bridge; the road that led to it, and the bridge itself, were thickly shaded by overhanging trees, which cast a gloom about it, even in the daytime; but occasioned a fearful darkness at night. Such was one of the favorite haunts of the headless horseman, and the place where he was most frequently encountered. The tale was told of old Brouwer, a most heretical disbeliever in ghosts, how he met the horseman return-ing from his foray into Sleepy Hollow, and was obliged to get up be-hind him; how they galloped over bush and brake, over hill and swamp, until they reached the bridge; when the horseman suddenly turned into a skeleton, threw old Brouwer into the brook, and sprang away over the tree-tops with a clap of thunder.

This story was immediately matched by a thrice marvelous adventure of Brom Bones, who made light of the Galloping Hessian as an arrant jockey. He affirmed that, on returning one night from the neighboring village of Sing-Sing, he had been overtaken by this midnight trooper; that he had offered to race with him for a bowl of punch, and should have won it too, for Daredevil beat the goblin horse all hollow, but, just as they came to the church bridge, the Hessian bolted, and van-ished in a flash of fire.

All these tales, told in that drowsy undertone with which men talk in the dark, the countenances of the listeners only now and then receiv-ing a casual gleam from the glare of a pipe, sank deep in the mind of Ichabod. He repaid them in kind, with large extracts from his invaluable author, Cotton Mather, and added many marvelous events that had taken place in his native state of Connecticut, and fearful sights which he had seen in his nightly walks about Sleepy Hollow.

The revel now gradually broke up. The old farmers gathered to-gether their families in their wagons, and were heard for some time rattling along the hollow roads, and over the distant hills. Some of the damsels mounted on pillions behind their favorite swains, and their light-hearted laughter, mingling with the clatter of hoofs, echoed along the silent woodlands, sounding fainter and fainter until they gradually died away—and the late scene of noise and frolic was all silent and deserted. Ichabod only lingered behind, according to the custom of country lovers, to have a *tête-à-tête* with the heiress, fully convinced that he was now on the high road to success. What passed at this interview I will not pretend to say, for in fact I do not know. Something, I fear me, must have gone wrong, for he certainly sallied forth, after no very great interval, with an air quite desolate and chop-fallen. Oh, these women! these women! Could that girl have been playing off any of her coquettish tricks?—Was her encouragement of the poor pedagogue all a mere sham to secure her conquest of his rival?—Heaven only knows, not I!—Let it suffice to say, Ichabod stole forth with the air of one who had been sacking a hen-roost, rather than a fair lady's heart. Without looking to the right or left to notice the scene of rural wealth on which he had so often gloated, he went straight to the stable, and with several hearty cuffs and kicks, roused his steed most uncourteously from the comfortable quarters in which he was soundly sleeping, dreaming or mountains of corn and oats, and whole valleys of timothy and clover.

It was the very witching time of night that Ichabod, heavy-hearted and crest-fallen, pursued his travels homewards, along the sides of the lofty hills which rise above Tarry Town, and which he had traversed so cheerily in the afternoon. The hour was as dismal as himself. Far below him the Tappan Zee spread its dusky and indistinct waste of waters, with here and there the tall mast of a sloop riding quietly at anchor under the land. In the dead hush of midnight he could even hear the barking of the watch-dog from the opposite shore of the Hudson; but it was so vague and faint as only to give an idea of his distance from this faithful companion of man. Now and then, too, the long-drawn crowing of a cock, accidentally awakened, would sound far, far off, from some farm-house away among the hills—but it was like a dreaming sound in his ear. No signs of life occurred near him, but occasionally the melancholy chirp of a cricket, or perhaps the guttural twang of a bull-frog, from a neighboring marsh, as if sleeping un-comfortably, and turning suddenly in his bed.

All the stories of ghosts and goblins that he had heard in the afternoon now came crowding upon his recollection. The night grew darker and darker; the stars seemed to sink deeper in the sky, and driving clouds occasionally hid them from his sight. He had never felt so lonely and dismal. He was, moreover, approaching the very place where many of the scenes of the ghost-stories had been laid. In the center of the road stood an enormous tulip-tree, which towered like a giant above all the other trees of the neighborhood, and formed a kind of landmark. Its limbs were gnarled and fantastic, large enough to form trunks for ordinary trees, twisting down almost to the earth, and rising again into the air. It was connected with the tragical story of the unfortunate André, who had been taken prisoner hard by; and was universally known by the name of Major André's tree. The common people regarded it with a mixture of respect and superstition, partly out of sympathy for the fate of its ill-starred namesake and partly from the tales of strange sights and doleful lamentations told concerning it.

As Ichabod approached this fearful tree, he began to whistle; he thought his whistle was answered; it was but a blast sweeping sharply through the dry branches. As he approached a little nearer, he thought he saw something white hanging in the midst of the tree—he paused and ceased whistling; but on looking more narrowly, perceived that it was a place where the tree had been scathed by lightning, and the white wood laid bare. Suddenly he heard a groan—his teeth chattered, and his knees smote against the saddle; it was but the rubbing of one huge bough upon another, as they were swayed about by the breeze. He passed the tree in safety, but new perils lay before him.

About two hundred yards from the tree a small brook crossed the road, and ran into a marshy and thickly wooded glen, known by the name of Wiley's Swamp. A few rough logs, laid side by side, served for a bridge over this stream. On that side of the road where the brook entered the wood, a group of oaks and chestnuts, matted thick with wild grapevines, threw a cavernous gloom over it. To pass this bridge was the severest trial. It was at this identical spot that the unfortunate André was captured, and under the covert of those chestnuts and vines were the sturdy yeomen concealed who surprised him. This has ever since been considered a haunted stream, and fearful are the feelings of the schoolboy who has to pass it alone after dark.

As he approached the stream, his heart began to thump; he summoned up, however, all his resolution, gave his horse half a score of kicks in the ribs, and attempted to dash briskly across the bridge; but instead of starting forward, the perverse old animal made a lateral movement, and ran broadside against the fence. Ichabod, whose fears increased with the delay, jerked the reins on the other side, and kicked lustily with the contrary foot: it was all in vain; his steed started, it is true, but it was only to plunge to the opposite side of the road into a thicket of brambles and alder-bushes. The schoolmaster now bestowed both whip and heel upon the starveling ribs of old Gunpowder, who dashed forward, snuffling and snorting, but came to a stand just by the bridge, with a suddenness that had nearly sent his rider sprawling over his head. Just at this moment a plashy tramp by the side of the bridge caught the sensitive ear of Ichabod. In the dark shadow of the grove, on the margin of the brook, he beheld something huge, mis-shapen, black and towering. It stirred not, but seemed gathered up in the gloom, like some gigantic monster ready to spring upon the traveler.

The hair of the affrighted pedagogue rose upon his head with terror. What was to be done? To turn and fly was now too late; and besides, what chance was there of escaping ghost or goblin, if such it was, which could ride upon the wings of the wind? Summoning up, therefore, a show of courage, he demanded in stammering accents—"Who are you?" He received no reply. He repeated his demand in a still more agitated voice. Still there was no answer. Once more he cudgelled the sides of the inflexible Gunpowder, and, shutting his eyes, broke forth with involuntary fervor into a psalm tune. Just then the shadowy object of alarm put itself in motion, and with a scramble and a bound, stood at once in the middle of the road. Though the night was dark and dismal, yet the form of the unknown might now in some degree be ascertained. He appeared to be a horseman of large dimensions, and mounted on a black horse of powerful frame. He made no offer of molestation or sociability, but kept aloof on one side of the road, jogging along on the blind side of old Gunpowder, who had now got over his fright and waywardness.

Ichabod, who had no relish for this strange midnight companion, and bethought himself of the adventure of Brom Bones with the Galloping Hessian, now quickened his steed, in hopes of leaving him behind. The stranger, however, quickened his horse to an equal pace. Ichabod pulled up, and fell into a walk, thinking to lag behind—the other did the same. His heart began to sink within him; he endeavored to resume his psalm tune, but his parched tongue clove to the roof of his mouth, and he could not utter a stave. There was something in the moody and dogged silence of this pertinacious companion that was mysterious and appalling. It was soon fearfully accounted for. On mounting a rising ground, which brought the figure of his fellow-traveler in relief against the sky, gigantic in height, and muffled in a cloak, Ichabod was horror-struck on perceiving that he was headless!— but his horror was still more increased on observing that the head, which should have rested on his shoulders, was carried before him on the pommel of the saddle: his terror rose to desperation; he rained a shower of kicks and blows upon Gunpowder, hoping, by a sudden movement, to give his companion the slip—but the specter started full jump with him. Away then they dashed, through thick and thin; stones flying and sparks flashing at every bound. Ichabod's flimsy garments fluttered in the air, as he stretched his long lank body away over his horse's head, in the eagerness of his flight.

They had now reached the road which turns off to Sleepy Hollow; but Gunpowder, who seemed possessed with a demon, instead of keeping up it, made an opposite turn, and plunged headlong down the hill to the left. This road leads through a sandy hollow, shaded by trees for about a quarter of a mile, where it crosses the bridge famous in goblin story, and just beyond swells the green knoll on which stands the white-washed church.

As yet the panic of the steed had given his unskilful rider an apparent advantage in the chase; but just as he had got half way through the hollow, the girths of the saddle gave way, and he felt it slipping from under him. He seized it by the pommel, and endeavored to hold it firm, but in vain; and had just time to save himself by clasping old Gunpowder round the neck, when the saddle fell to the earth, and he heard it trampled under-foot by his pursuer. For a moment the terror of Hans Van Ripper's wrath passed across his mind—for it was his Sunday saddle; but this was no time for petty fears; the goblin was hard on his haunches; and (unskilful rider that he was!) he had much ado to maintain his seat; sometimes slipping on one side, sometimes on the other, and sometimes jolted on the high ridge of his horse's back-bone, with a violence that he verily feared would cleave him asunder.

An opening in the trees now cheered him with the hopes that the church bridge was at hand. The wavering reflection of a silver star in the bosom of the brook told him that he was not mistaken. He saw the walls of the church dimly glaring under the trees beyond. He recollected the place where Brom Bones' ghostly competitor had disappeared. "If I can but reach that bridge," thought Ichabod, "I am safe." Just then he heard the black steed panting and blowing close behind him; he even fancied that he felt his hot breath. Another convulsive kick in the ribs, and old Gunpowder sprang upon the bridge; he thundered over the resounding planks; he gained the opposite side; and now Ichabod cast a look behind to see if his pursuer should vanish, according to rule, in a flash of fire and brimstone. Just then he saw the goblin rising in his stirrups, and in the very act of hurling his head at him. Ichabod endeavored to dodge the horrible missile, but too late. It encountered his cranium with a tremendous crash—he was tumbled headlong into the dust, and Gunpowder, the black steed, and the goblin rider passed by like a whirlwind.

The next morning the old horse was found without his saddle, and with the bridle under his feet, soberly cropping the grass at his master's gate. Ichabod did not make his appearance at breakfast—dinner-hour came, but no Ichabod. The boys assembled at the school-house, and strolled idly about the banks of the brook; but no schoolmaster. Hans Van Ripper now began to feel some uneasiness about the fate of poor

Ichabod and his saddle. An inquiry was set on foot, and after diligent investigation they came upon his traces. In one part of the road leading to the church was found the saddle trampled in the dirt; the tracks of horses' hoofs deeply dented in the road, and evidently at furious speed, were traced to the bridge, beyond which, on the bank of a broad part of the brook, where the water ran deep and black, was found the hat of the unfortunate Ichabod, and close beside it a shattered pumpkin.

The brook was searched, but the body of the schoolmaster was not to be discovered. Hans Van Ripper, as executor of his estate, examined the bundle, which contained all his worldly effects. They consisted of two shirts and a half; two stocks for the neck; a pair or two of worsted stockings; an old pair of corduroy small clothes; a rusty razor; a book of psalm tunes, full of dog's ears; and a broken pitch-pipe. As to the books and furniture of the school-house, they belonged to the community, excepting Cotton Mather's *History of Witchcraft,* a New England Almanac, and a book of dreams and fortune-telling; in which last was a sheet of foolscap much scribbled and blotted in several fruitless attempts to make a copy of verses in honor of the heiress of Van Tassel. These magic books and the poetic scrawl were forthwith consigned to the flames by Hans Van Ripper; who from that time forward determined to send his children no more to school, observing that he never knew any good come of this same reading and writing. Whatever money the schoolmaster possessed, and he had received his quarter's pay but a day or two before, he must have had about his person at the time of his disappearance.

The mysterious event caused much speculation at the church on the following Sunday. Knots of gazers and gossips were collected in the churchyard, at the bridge, and at the spot where the hat and pumpkin had been found. The stories of Brouwer, of Bones, and a whole budget of others, were called to mind; and when they had diligently considered them all, and compared them with the symptoms of the present case, they shook their heads, and came to the conclusion that Ichabod had been carried off by the Galloping Hessian. As he was a bachelor, and in nobody's debt, nobody troubled his head any more about him: the school was removed to a different quarter of the Hollow, and another pedagogue reigned in his stead.

It is true, an old farmer, who had been down to New York on a visit several years after, and from whom this account of the ghostly adventure was received, brought home the intelligence that Ichabod Crane was still alive; that he had left the neighborhood, partly through fear of the goblin and Hans Van Ripper, and partly in mortification at having been suddenly dismissed by the heiress; that he had changed his quarters to a distant part of the country; had kept school and studied law at the same time; he had been admitted to the bar, turned politician, election-eered, written for the newspapers, and finally had been made a justice of the Ten-pound Court. Brom Bones, too, who shortly after his rival's disappearance conducted the blooming Katrina in triumph to the altar, was observed to look exceedingly knowing whenever the story of Icha-bod was related, and always burst into a hearty laugh at the mention of the pumpkin; which led some to suspect that he knew more about the matter than he chose to tell.

The old country wives, however, who are the best judges of these matters, maintain to this day that Ichabod was spirited away by super-natural means; and it is a favorite story often told about the neighbor-hood round the winter evening fire. The bridge became more than ever an object of superstitious awe, and that may be the reason why the road has been altered of late years, so as to approach the church by the border of the mill-pond. The school-house, being deserted, soon fell to decay, and was reported to be haunted by the ghost of the unfortunate peda-gogue; and the plough-boy, loitering homeward of a still summer evening, has often fancied his voice at a distance, chanting a melancholy psalm tune among the tranquil solitudes of Sleepy Hollow.

Postscript

FOUND IN THE HANDWRITING OF MR. KNICKERBOCKER

The preceding tale is given, almost in the precise words in which I heard it related at a Corporation meeting of the ancient city of Man-hattoes, at which were present many of its sagest and most illustrious burghers. The narrator was a pleasant, shabby, gentlemanly old fellow, in pepper-and-salt clothes, with a sadly humorous face; and one whom I strongly suspected of being poor—he made such efforts to be enter-aining. When his story was concluded, there was much laughter and approbation, particularly from two or three deputy aldermen, who had been asleep the greater part of the time. There was, however, one tall, dry-looking old gentleman, with beetling eyebrows, who maintained a grave and rather a severe face throughout: now and then folding his arms, inclining his head, and looking down upon the floor, as if turning a doubt over in his mind. He was one of your wary men, who never laugh, but upon good grounds—when they have reason and the law on their side. When the mirth of the rest of the company had subsided, and silence was restored, he leaned one arm on the elbow of his chair, and sticking the other akimbo. demanded. with a slight but exceedingly sage motion of the head, and contraction of the brow, what was the moral of the story, and what it went to prove?

The story-teller, who was just putting a glass of wine to his lips, as a refreshment after his toils, paused for a moment, looked at his inquirer with an air of infinite deference, and, lowering the glass slowly to the table, observed that the story was intended most logically to prove:—

"That there is no situation in 'ife but has its advantages and pleasures —provided we will but take a joke as we find it:

"That, therefore, he that runs races with goblin troopers is likely to have rough riding of it.

"Ergo, for a country schoolmaster to be refused the hand of a Dutch heiress is a certain step to high preferment in the state."

The cautious old gentleman knit his brows tenfold closer after this explanation, being sorely puzzled by the ratiocination of the syllogism: while, methought, the one in pepper-and-salt eyed him with something of a triumphant leer. At length he observed that all this was very well; but still he thought the story a little on the extravagant—there were one or two points on which he had his doubts.

"Faith sir," replied the story-teller, "as to that matter, I don't believe one half of it myself."

D. K.

2

Rip Van Winkle

BY WASHINGTON IRVING

THE following Tale was found among the papers of the late Diedrich Knickerbocker, an old gentleman of New York, who was very curious in the Dutch history of the province, and the manners of the descendants from its primitive settlers. His historical researches, however, did not lie so much among books as among men; for the former are lamentably scanty on his favorite topics, whereas he found the old burghers, and still more their wives, rich in that legendary lore so invaluable to true history. Whenever, therefore, he happened upon a genuine Dutch family, snugly shut up in its low-roofed farm-house, under a spreading sycamore, he looked upon it as a little clasped volume of black letter, and studied it with the zeal of a book-worm.

The result of all these researches was a history of the province during the reign of the Dutch governors, which he published some years since. There have been various opinions as to the literary character of his work, and, to tell the truth, it is not a whit better than it should be. Its chief merit is its scrupulous accuracy, which indeed was a little questioned on its first appearance, but has since been completely established; and it is now admitted into all historical collections as a book of unquestionable authority.

The old gentleman died shortly after the publication of his work, and now that he is dead and gone, it cannot do much harm to his memory to say, that his time might have been much better employed in weightier labors. He, however, was apt to ride his hobby his own way; and though it did now and then kick up the dust a little in the eyes of his neighbors, and grieve the spirit of some friends, for whom he felt the truest deference and affection; yet his errors and follies are remembered "more in sorrow than in anger," and it begins to be suspected that he never intended to injure or offend. But however his memory may be appreciated by critics, it is still held dear by many folk whose good opinion is well worth having, particularly by certain biscuit-bakers, who have gone so far as to imprint his likeness on their new-year cakes, and have thus given him a chance for immortality, almost equal to the being stamped on a Waterloo medal or a Queen Anne's farthing.

By Woden, God of Saxons,
From whence comes Wensday, that is Wodensday.
Truth is a thing that ever I will keep
Unto thylke day in which I creep into
My sepulchre—

CARTWRIGHT

WHOEVER has made a voyage up the Hudson must remember the Kaatskill mountains. They are a dismembered branch of the great Appalachian family, and are seen away to the west of the river, swelling up to a noble height, and lording it over the surrounding country. Every change of season, every change of weather, indeed, every hour of the day, produces some change in the magical hues and shapes of these mountains, and they are regarded by all the good wives, far and near, as perfect barometers. When the weather is fair and settled, they are clothed in blue and purple, and print their bold outlines on the clear evening sky; but sometimes, when the rest of the landscape is cloudless, they will gather a hood of gray vapors about their summits, which, in the last rays of the setting sun, will glow and light up like a crown of glory.

At the foot of these fairy mountains, the voyager may have descried the light smoke curling up from a village, whose shingle-roofs gleam among the trees, just where the blue tints of the upland melt away into the fresh green of the nearer landscape. It is a little village, of great antiquity, having been founded by some of the Dutch colonists, in the early times of the province, just about the beginning of the government of the good Peter Stuyvesant (may he rest in peace!) and there were some of the houses of the original settlers standing within a few years, built of small yellow bricks brought from Holland, having latticed windows and gable fronts, surmounted with weathercocks.

In that same village and in one of these very houses (which, to tell the precise truth, was sadly time-worn and weather-beaten), there lived many years since, while the country was yet a province of Great Britain, a simple good-natured fellow, of the name of Rip Van Winkle. He was a descendant of the Van Winkles who figured so gallantly in the chivalrous days of Peter Stuyvesant, and accompanied him to the siege of Fort Christina. He inherited, however, but little of the martial character of his ancestors. I have observed that he was a simple good-natured man; he was, moreover, a kind neighbor, and an obedient hen-pecked husband. Indeed, to the latter circumstance might be owing that meekness of spirit which gained him such universal popularity; for those men are most apt to be obsequious and conciliating abroad, who are under the discipline of shrews at home. Their tempers, doubtless, are rendered pliant and malleable in the fiery furnace of domestic tribulation, and a curtain lecture is worth all the sermons in the world for teaching the virtues of patience and long-suffering. A termagant wife may, therefore, in some respects, be considered a tolerable blessing; and if so, Rip Van Winkle was thrice blessed.

Certain it is that he was a great favorite among all the good wives of the village, who, as usual with the amiable sex, took his part in all family squabbles; and never failed, whenever they talked those matters over in their evening gossipings, to lay all the blame on Dame Van Winkle. The children of the village, too, would shout with joy whenever he approached. He assisted at their sports, made their playthings, taught them to fly kites and shoot marbles, and told them long stories of ghosts, witches, and Indians. Whenever he went dodging about the village, he was surrounded by a troop of them hanging on his skirts, clambering on his back, and playing a thousand tricks on him with impunity; and not a dog would bark at him throughout the neighborhood.

The great error in Rip's composition was an insuperable aversion to all kinds of profitable labor. It could not be from the want of assiduity or perseverance; for he would sit on a wet rock, with a rod as long and heavy as a Tartar's lance, and fish all day without a murmur, even though he should not be encouraged by a single nibble. He would carry a fowling-piece on his shoulder for hours together, trudging through woods and swamps, and up hill and down dale, to shoot a few squirrels or wild pigeons. He would never refuse to assist a neighbor even in the roughest toil, and was a foremost man at all country frolics for husking Indian corn, or building stone fences; the women of the village, too, used to employ him to run their errands, and to do such little odd jobs as their less obliging husbands would not do for them. In a word, Rip was ready to attend to anybody's business but his own; but as to doing family duty, and keeping his farm in order, he found it impossible.

In fact, he declared it was of no use to work on his farm; it was the most pestilent little piece of ground in the whole country; everything about it went wrong, and would go wrong, in spite of him. His fences were continually falling to pieces; his cow would either go astray, or get among the cabbages; weeds were sure to grow quicker in his fields than anywhere else; the rain always made a point of setting in just as he had some outdoor work to do; so that though his patrimonial estate had dwindled away under his management, acre by acre, until there was little more left than a mere patch of Indian corn and potatoes, yet it was the worst conditioned farm in the neighborhood.

His children, too, were as ragged and wild as if they belonged to nobody. His son Rip, an urchin begotten in his own likeness, promised to inherit the habits, with the old clothes, of his father. He was generally seen trooping like a colt at his mother's heels, equipped in a pair of his father's cast-off galligaskins which he had much ado to hold up with one hand, as a fine lady does her train in bad weather.

Rip Van Winkle, however, was one of those happy mortals, of foolish, well-oiled dispositions, who take the world easy, eat white bread or brown, whichever can be got with least thought or trouble, and would rather starve on a penny than work for a pound. If left to himself, he would have whistled life away in perfect contentment; but his wife kept continually dinning in his ears about his idleness, his carelessness, and the ruin he was bringing on his family. Morning, noon, and night, her tongue was incessantly going, and everything he said or did was sure to produce a torrent of household eloquence. Rip had but one way of replying to all lectures of the kind, and that, by frequent use, had grown into a habit. He shrugged his shoulders, shook his head, cast up his eyes, but said nothing. This, however, always provoked a fresh volley from his wife; so that he was fain to draw off his forces, and take to the outside of the house—the only side which, in truth, belongs to a hen-pecked husband.

Rip's sole domestic adherent was his dog Wolf, who was as much hen-pecked as his master; for Dame Van Winkle regarded them as companions in idleness, and even looked upon Wolf with an evil eye, as the cause of his master's going so often astray. True it is, in all points of spirit, befitting an honorable dog, he was as courageous an animal as ever scoured the woods—but what courage can withstand the ever-during and all-besetting terrors of a woman's tongue? The moment Wolf entered the house, his crest fell, his tail drooped to the ground, or curled between his legs, he sneaked about with a gallows air, casting many a side-long glance at Dame Van Winkle, and at the least flourish

of a broomstick or ladle, he would fly to the door with yelping precipitation.

Times grew worse and worse with Rip Van Winkle as years of matrimony rolled on; a tart temper never mellows with age, and a sharp
tongue is the only edged tool that grows keener with constant use. For
a long while he used to console himself, when driven from home, by
frequenting a kind of perpetual club of the sages, philosophers, and
other idle personages of the village; which held its sessions on a bench
before a small inn, designated by a rubicund portrait of His Majesty
George the Third. Here they used to sit in the shade through a long
lazy summer's day, talking listlessly over village gossip, or telling
endless sleepy stories about nothing. But it would have been worth any
statesman's money to have heard the profound discussions that sometimes took place, when by chance an old newspaper fell into their hands
from some passing traveler. How solemnly they would listen to the
contents, as drawled out by Derrick Van Bummel, the schoolmaster, a
dapper learned little man, who was not to be daunted by the most
gigantic word in the dictionary; and how sagely they would deliberate
upon public events some months after they had taken place.

The opinions of this junto were completely controlled by Nicholas
Vedder, a patriarch of the village, and landlord of the inn, at the door
of which he took his seat from morning till night, just moving sufficiently to avoid the sun and keep in the shade of a large tree; so that
the neighbors could tell the hour by his movements as accurately as by
a sundial. It is true he was rarely heard to speak, but smoked his pipe
incessantly. His adherents, however (for every great man has his adherents), perfectly understood him, and knew how to gather his opinions. When anything that was read or related displeased him, he was
observed to smoke his pipe vehemently, and to send forth short, frequent, and angry puffs, but when pleased he would inhale the smoke
slowly and tranquilly, and emit it in light and placid clouds; and sometimes, taking the pipe from his mouth, and letting the fragrant vapor
curl about his nose, would gravely nod his head in token of perfect
approbation.

From even this stronghold the unlucky Rip was at length routed by
his termagant wife, who would suddenly break in upon the tranquillity
of the assemblage and call the members all to naught; nor was that
august personage, Nicholas Vedder himself, sacred from the daring
tongue of this terrible virago, who charged him outright with encouraging her husband in habits of idleness.

Poor Rip was at last reduced almost to despair; and his only alternative, to escape from the labor of the farm and clamor of his wife, was
to take gun in hand and stroll away into the woods. Here he would

sometimes seat himself at the foot of a tree, and share the contents of his wallet with Wolf, with whom he sympathized as as a fellow-sufferer in persecution. "Poor Wolf," he would say, "thy mistress leads thee a dog's life of it; but never mind, my lad, whilst I live thou shalt never want a friend to stand by thee!" Wolf would wag his tail, look wistfully in his master's face, and if dogs can feel pity, I verily believe he recipro-cated the sentiment with all his heart.

In a long ramble of the kind on a fine autumnal day, Rip had uncon-sciously scrambled to one of the highest parts of the Kaatskill mountains. He was after his favorite sport of squirrel-shooting, and the still solitudes had echoed and re-echoed with the reports of his gun. Panting and fatigued, he threw himself, late in the afternoon, on a green knoll, covered with mountain herbage, that crowned the brow of a precipice. From an opening between the trees he could overlook all the lower country for many a mile of rich woodland. He saw at a distance the lordly Hudson, far, far below him, moving on its silent but majestic course, with the reflection of a purple cloud, or the sail of a lagging bark, here and there sleeping on its glassy bosom, and at last losing itself in the blue highlands.

On the other side he looked down into a deep mountain glen, wild, lonely, and shagged, the bottom filled with fragments from the im-pending cliffs, and scarcely lighted by the reflected rays of the setting sun. For some time Rip lay musing on this scene; evening was gradually advancing; the mountains began to throw their long blue shadows over the valleys; he saw that it would be dark long before he could reach the village, and he heaved a heavy sigh when he thought of en-countering the terrors of Dame Van Winkle.

As he was about to descend, he heard a voice from a distance, halloo-ing, "Rip Van Winkle! Rip Van Winkle!" He looked round, but could see nothing but a crow winging its solitary flight across the mountain. He thought his fancy must have deceived him, and turned again to descend, when he heard the same cry ring through the still evening air: "Rip Van Winkle! Rip Van Winkle!"—at the same time Wolf bristled up his back, and, giving a loud growl, skulked to his master's side, look-ing fearfully down into the glen. Rip now felt a vague apprehension stealing over him; he looked anxiously in the same direction, and per-ceived a strange figure slowly toiling up the rocks, and bending under the weight of something he carried on his back. He was surprised to see any human being in this lonely and unfrequented place; but supposing it to be some one of the neighborhood in need of his assistance, he hastened down to yield it.

On nearer approach he was still more surprised at the singularity of the stranger's appearance. He was a short, square built old fellow, with thick bushy hair and a grizzled beard. His dress was of the antique Dutch fashion—a cloth jerkin, strapped round the waist—several pair of breeches, the outer one of ample volume, decorated with rows of buttons down the sides, and bunches at the knees. He bore on his shoulder a stout keg, that seemed full of liquor, and made signs for Rip to approach and assist him with the load. Though rather shy and distrustful of this new acquaintance, Rip complied with his usual alacrity; and mutually relieving each other, they clambered up a narrow gully, apparently the dry bed of a mountain torrent. As they ascended, Rip every now and then heard long rolling peals, like distant thunder, that seemed to issue out of a deep ravine, or rather cleft, between lofty rocks, towards which their rugged path conducted. He paused for an instant, but supposing it to be the muttering of one of those transient thunder-showers which often take place in mountain heights, he proceeded. Passing through the ravine, they came to a hollow, like a small amphitheater, surrounded by perpendicular precipices, over the brinks of which impending trees shot their branches, so that you only caught glimpses of the azure sky and the bright evening cloud. During the whole time Rip and his companion had labored on in silence, for though the former marveled greatly what could be the object of carrying a keg of liquor up this wild mountain; yet there was something strange and incomprehensible about the unknown, that inspired awe and checked familiarity.

On entering the amphitheater, new objects of wonder presented themselves. On a level spot in the center was a company of odd-looking personages playing at nine-pins. They were dressed in a quaint outlandish fashion; some wore short doublets, others jerkins, with long knives in their belts, and most of them had enormous breeches, of similar style with that of the guide's. Their visages, too, were peculiar; one had a large head, broad face, and small piggish eyes; the face of another seemed to consist entirely of nose, and was surmounted by a white sugar-loaf hat, set off with a little red cock's tail. They all had beards, of various shapes and colors. There was one who seemed to be the commander. He was a stout old gentleman, with a weather-beaten countenance; he wore a laced doublet, broad belt and hanger, high-crowned hat and feather, red stockings, and high-heeled shoes, with roses in them. The whole group reminded Rip of the figures in an old Flemish painting, in the parlor of Dominie Van Shaick, the village parson, and which had been brought over from Holland at the time of the settlement.

What seemed particularly odd to Rip was, that though these folks were evidently amusing themselves, yet they maintained the gravest faces, the most mysterious silence, and were, withal, the most melancholy party of pleasure he had ever witnessed. Nothing interrupted the stillness of the scene but the noise of the balls, which, whenever they were rolled, echoed along the mountains like rumbling peals of thunder.

As Rip and his companion approached them, they suddenly desisted from their play, and stared at him with such fixed, statue-like gaze, and such strange, uncouth, lack-luster countenances, that his heart turned within him, and his knees smote together. His companion now emptied the contents of the keg into large flagons, and made signs to him to wait upon the company. He obeyed with fear and trembling; they quaffed the liquor in profound silence, and then returned to their game.

By degrees Rip's awe and apprehension subsided. He even ventured, when no eye was fixed upon him, to taste the beverage, which he found had much of the flavor of excellent Hollands. He was naturally a thirsty soul, and was soon tempted to repeat the draught. One taste provoked another; and he reiterated his visits to the flagon so often, that at length his senses were overpowered, his eyes swam in his head, his head gradually declined, and he fell into a deep sleep.

On waking, he found himself on the green knoll whence he had first seen the old man of the glen. He rubbed his eyes—it was a bright sunny morning. The birds were hopping and twittering among the bushes, and the eagle was wheeling aloft, and breasting the pure mountain breeze. "Surely," thought Rip, "I have not slept here all night." He recalled the occurrences before he fell asleep. The strange man with a keg of liquor— the mountain ravine—the wild retreat among the rocks—the woebegone party at nine-pins—the flagon—"Oh! that flagon! that wicked flagon!" thought Rip; "what excuse shall I make to Dame Van Winkle?"

He looked round for his gun, but in place of the clean well-oiled fowling-piece, he found an old firelock lying by him, the barrel incrusted with rust, the lock falling off, and the stock worm-eaten. He now suspected that the grave roysters of the mountain had put a trick upon him, and, having dosed him with liquor, had robbed him of his gun. Wolf, too, had disappeared, but he might have strayed away after a squirrel or partridge. He wistled after him, and shouted his name, but all in vain; the echoes repeated his whistle and shout, but no dog was to be seen.

He determined to revisit the scene of the last evening's gambol, and, if he met with any of the party, to demand his dog and gun. As he rose to walk he found himself stiff in the joints, and wanting in his usual activity. "These mountain beds do not agree with me," thought Rip; "and if this frolic should lay me up with a fit of the rheumatism, I shall have a blessed time with Dame Van Winkle." With some difficulty he got down into the glen: he found the gully up which he and his companion had ascended the preceding evening; but, to his astonishment, a mountain stream was now foaming down it—leaping from rock to rock, and filling the glen with babbling murmurs. He, however, made shift to scramble up its sides, working his toilsome way through thickets of birch, sassafras, and witch-hazel, and sometimes tripped up or entangled by the wild grape-vines that twisted their coils or tendrils from tree to tree, and spread a kind of network in his path.

At length he reached to where the ravine had opened through the cliffs to the amphitheater; but no traces of such opening remained. The rocks presented a high impenetrable wall, over which the torrent came tumbling in a sheet of feathery foam, and fell into a broad, deep basin, black from the shadows of the surrounding forest. Here, then, poor Rip was brought to a stand. He again called and whistled after his dog; he was only answered by the cawing of a flock of idle crows, sporting high in air about a dry tree that overhung a sunny precipice; and who, secure in their elevation, seemed to look down and scoff at the poor man's perplexities. What was to be done?—the morning was passing away, and Rip felt famished for want of his breakfast. He grieved to give up his dog and his gun; he dreaded to meet his wife; but it would not do to starve among the mountains. He shook his head, shouldered the rusty firelock, and, with a heart full of trouble and anxiety, turned his steps homeward.

As he approached the village he met a number of people, but none whom he knew, which somewhat surprised him, for he had thought himself acquainted with everyone in the country round. Their dress, too, was of a different fashion from that to which he was accustomed. They all stared at him with equal marks of surprise, and, whenever they cast their eyes upon him, invariably stroked their chins. The constant recurrence of this gesture induced Rip, involuntarily, to do the same—when, to his astonishment, he found his beard had grown a foot long!

He had now entered the skirts of the village. A troop of strange children ran at his heels, hooting after him, and pointing at his gray beard. The dogs, too, not one of which he recognized for an old acquaintance, barked at him as he passed. The very village was altered; it was larger and more populous. There were rows of houses which he had never seen before, and those which had been his familiar haunts had disappeared. Strange names were over the doors—strange faces at the windows —everything was strange. His mind now misgave him; he began to doubt whether both he and the world around him were not bewitched. Surely this was his native village, which he had left but the day before. There stood the Kaatskill mountains—there ran the silver Hudson at a distance—there was every hill and dale precisely as it had always been. Rip was sorely perplexed. "That flagon last night," thought he, "has addled my poor head sadly!"

It was with some difficulty that he found the way to his own house, which he approached with silent awe, expecting every moment to hear the shrill voice of Dame Van Winkle. He found the house gone to decay —the roof fallen in, the windows shattered, and the doors off the hinges. A half-starved dog that looked like Wolf, was skulking about it. Rip called him by name, but the cur snarled, showed his teeth, and passed on. This was an unkind cut indeed—"My very dog," sighed poor Rip, "has forgotten me!"

He entered the house, which, to tell the truth, Dame Van Winkle had always kept in neat order. It was empty, forlorn, and apparently aban- doned. The desolateness overcame all his connubial fears—he called loudly for his wife and children—the lonely chambers rang for a mo- ment with his voice, and then all again was silence.

He now hurried forth, and hastened to his old resort, the village inn— but it too was gone. A large, rickety, wooden building stood in its place, with great gaping windows, some of them broken and mended with old hats and petticoats, and over the door was painted, "The Union Hotel, by Jonathan Doolittle." Instead of the great tree that used to shelter the quiet little Dutch inn of yore, there was now reared a tall naked pole, with something on the top that looked like a red nightcap, and from it was fluttering a flag, on which was a singular assemblage of stars and stripes—all this was strange and incomprehensible. He recognized on the sign, however, the ruby face of King George, under which he had smoked so many a peaceful pipe; but even this was singularly meta- morphosed. The red coat was changed for one of blue and buff, a sword was held in the hand instead of a scepter, the head was decorated with a cocked hat, and underneath was painted in large characters, GENERAL WASHINGTON.

There was, as usual, a crowd of folks about the door, but none that Rip recollected. The very character of the people seemed changed. There was a busy, bustling, disputatious tone about it, instead of the accustomed phlegm and drowsy tranquillity. He looked in vain for the sage Nicholas Vedder, with his broad face, double chin, and fair long pipe, uttering clouds of tobacco-smoke instead of idle speeches; or Van Bummel, the schoolmaster, doling forth the contents of an ancient newspaper. In place of these, a lean, bilious-looking fellow, with his pockets full of hand- bills, was haranguing vehemently about rights of citizens—elections— members of Congress—liberty—Bunker's Hill—heroes of seventy-six —and other words, which were a perfect Babylonish jargon to the bewildered Van Winkle.

The appearance of Rip, with his long grizzled beard, his rusty fowling- piece, his uncouth dress, and an army of women and children at his heels, soon attracted the attention of the tavern politicians. They crowded round him, eyeing him from head to foot with great curiosity. The orator bustled up to him, and, drawing him partly aside, inquired "on which side he voted?" Rip stared in vacant stupidity. Another short but busy little fellow pulled him by the arm, and, rising on tiptoe, inquired in his ear, "Whether he was Federal or Democrat?" Rip was equally at a loss to comprehend the question; when a knowing, self-important old gentleman, in a sharp cocked hat, made his way through the crowd, putting them to the right and left with his elbows as he passed, and planting himself before Van Winkle, with one arm akimbo, the other resting on his cane, his keen eyes and sharp hat penetrating, as it were, into his very soul, demanded in an austere tone, "What brought him to the election with a gun on his shoulder, and a mob at his heels, and whether he meant to breed a riot in the village?"—"Alas! gentlemen," cried Rip, somewhat dismayed, "I am a poor quiet man, a native of the place, and a loyal subject of the king, God bless him!"

Here a general shout burst from the bystanders—"A tory! a tory! a spy! a refugee! hustle him! away with him!" It was with great difficulty that the self-important man in the cocked hat restored order; and, having assumed a tenfold austerity of brow, demanded again of the unknown culprit, what he came there for, and whom he was seeking? The poor man humbly assured him that he meant no harm, but merely came there in search of some of his neighbors, who used to keep about the tavern.

"Well—who are they?—name them."

Rip bethought himself a moment, and inquired, "Where's Nicholas Vedder?"

There was a silence for a little while, when an old man replied in a thin piping voice, "Nicholas Vedder why, he is dead and gone these eighteen years! There was a wooden tombstone in the churchyard that used to tell all about him, but that's rotten and gone too."

"Where's Brom Dutcher?"

"Oh, he went off to the army in the beginning of the war; some say he was killed at the storming of Stony Point—others say he was drowned in a squall at the foot of Antony's Nose. I don't know—he never came back again."

"Where's Van Bummel, the schoolmaster?"

"He went off to the wars too, was a great militia general, and is now in Congress."

Rip's heart died away at hearing of these sad changes in his home and friends, and finding himself thus alone in the world. Every answer puzzled him too, by treating of such enormous lapses of time, and of matters which he could not understand; war—Congress—Stony Point; —he had no courage to ask after any more friends, but cried out in despair, "Does nobody here know Rip Van Winkle?"

"Oh, Rip Van Winkle!" exclaimed two or three. "Oh, to be sure! that's Rip Van Winkle yonder, leaning against the tree."

Rip looked, and beheld a precise counterpart of himself, as he went up the mountain: apparently as lazy, and certainly as ragged. The poor fellow was now completely confounded. He doubted his own identity, and whether he was himself or another man. In the midst of his bewilderment, the man in the cocked hat demanded who he was, and what was his name?

"God knows," exclaimed he, at his wits' end; "I'm not myself—I'm somebody else—that's me yonder—no—that's somebody else got into my shoes—I was myself last night, but I fell asleep on the mountain, and they've changed my gun, and everything's changed, and I'm changed, and I can't tell what's my name, or who I am!"

The bystanders began now to look at each other, nod, wink significantly, and tap their fingers against their foreheads. There was a whisper, also, about securing the gun, and keeping the old fellow from doing mischief, at the very suggestion of which the self-important man in the cocked hat retired with some precipitation. At this critical moment a fresh comely woman pressed through the throng to get a peep at the gray-bearded man. She had a chubby child in her arms, which, frightened at his looks, began to cry. "Hush, Rip," cried she, "hush, you little fool; the old man won't hurt you." The name of the child, the air of the mother, the tone of her voice, all awakened a train of recollections in his mind.

"What is your name, my good woman?" asked he.

"Judith Gardenier."

"And your father's name?"

"Ah, poor man, Rip Van Winkle was his name, but it's twenty years since he went away from home with his gun, and never has been heard of since—his dog came home without him; but whether he shot himself, or was carried away by the Indians, nobody can tell. I was then but a little girl."

Rip had but one question more to ask; but he put it with a faltering voice,—

"Where's your mother?"

"Oh, she too had died but a short time since; she broke a blood-vessel in a fit of passion at a New-England pedlar."

There was a drop of comfort, at least, in this intelligence. The honest man could contain himself no longer. He caught his daughter and her child in his arms. "I am your father!" cried he—"Young Rip Van Winkle once—old Rip Van Winkle now!—Does nobody know poor Rip Van Winkle?"

All stood amazed, until an old woman, tottering out from among the crowd, put her hand to her brow, and peering under it in his face for a moment, exclaimed, "Sure enough! it is Rip Van Winkle—it is himself! Welcome home again, old neighbor—Why, where have you been these twenty long years?"

Rip's story was soon told, for the whole twenty years had been to him but as one night. The neighbors stared when they heard it; some were seen to wink at each other, and put their tongues in their cheeks: and the self-important man in the cocked hat, who, when the alarm was over, had returned to the field, screwed down the corners of his mouth, and shook his head—upon which there was a general shaking of the head throughout the assemblage.

It was determined, however, to take the opinion of old Peter Vander-donk, who was seen slowly advancing up the road. He was a descendant of the historian of that name, who wrote one of the earliest accounts of the province. Peter was the most ancient inhabitant of the village, and well versed in all the wonderful events and traditions of the neighbor-hood. He recollected Rip at once, and corroborated his story in the most satisfactory manner. He assured the company that it was a fact, handed down from his ancestor the historian, that the Kaatskill mountains had always been haunted by strange beings. That it was affirmed that the great Hendrick Hudson, the first discoverer of the river and country, kept a kind of vigil there every twenty years, with his crew of the *Half-moon;* being permitted in this way to revisit the scenes of his enterprise, and keep a guardian eye upon the river, and the great city called by his name. That his father had once seen them in their old Dutch dresses playing at nine-pins in a hollow of the mountain; and that he himself had heard, one summer afternoon, the sound of their balls, like distant peals of thunder.

To make a long story short, the company broke up, and returned to the more important concerns of the election. Rip's daughter took him home to live with her; she had a snug, well-furnished house, and a stout cheery farmer for her husband, whom Rip recollected for one of the urchins that used to climb upon his back. As to Rip's son and heir, who was the ditto of himself, seen leaning against the tree, he was employed to work on the farm; but evinced an hereditary disposition to attend to anything else but his business.

Rip now resumed his old walks and habits; he soon found many of his former cronies, though all rather the worse for the wear and tear of time; and preferred making friends among the rising generation, with whom he soon grew into great favor.

Having nothing to do at home, and being arrived at that happy age when a man can be idle with impunity, he took his place once more on the bench at the inn door, and was reverenced as one of the patriarchs of the village, and a chronicle of the old times "before the war." It was some time before he could get into the regular track of gossip, or could be made to comprehend the strange events that had taken place during his torpor. How that there had been a revolutionary war—that the country had thrown off the yoke of Old England—and that, instead of being a subject of His Majesty George the Third, he was now a free citizen of the United States. Rip, in fact, was no politician; the changes of states and empires made but little impression on him; but there was one species of despotism under which he had long groaned, and that was —petticoat government. Happily that was at an end; he had got his neck out of the yoke of matrimony, and could go in and out whenever he pleased without dreading the tyranny of Dame Van Winkle. Whenever her name was mentioned, however, he shook his head, shrugged his shoulders, and cast up his eyes; which might pass either for an expression of resignation to his fate, or joy at his deliverance.

He used to tell his story to every stranger that arrived at Mr. Doolittle's hotel. He was observed at first to vary on some points every time he told it, which was, doubtless, owing to his having so recently awaked. It at last settled down precisely to the tale I have related, and not a man, woman, or child in the neighborhood but knew it by heart. Some always pretended to doubt the reality of it, and insisted that Rip had been out of his head, and that this was one point on which he always remained flighty. The old Dutch inhabitants, however, almost universally gave it full credit. Even to this day they never hear a thunder-storm of a summer afternoon about the Kaatskill, but they say Hendrick Hudson and his crew are at their game of nine-pins; and it is a common wish of all hen-pecked husbands in the neighborhood, when life hangs heavy on their hands, that they might have a quieting draught out of Rip Van Winkle's flagon.

NOTE: The foregoing tale, one would suspect, had been suggested to Mr. Knickerbocker by a little German superstition about the Emperor Frederick *der Rothbart*, and the Kypphaüser mountain; the subjoined note, however, which he had appended to the tale, shows that it is an absolute fact, narrated with his usual fidelity:—

The story of Rip Van Winkle may seem incredible to many, but nevertheless I give it my full belief, for I know the vicinity of our old Dutch settlements to have been very subject to marvelous events and appearances. Indeed, I have heard many stranger stories than this in the villages along the Hudson, all of which were too well authenticated to admit of a doubt. I have even talked with Rip Van Winkle myself, who, when I last saw him was a very venerable old man, and so perfectly rational and consistent on every other point, that I think no conscientious person could refuse to take this into the bargain; nay, I have seen a certificate on the subject, taken before a country justice, and signed with a cross, in the justice's own handwriting. The story, therefore, is beyond the possibility of doubt.

D. K.

Postscript

THE FOLLOWING ARE TRAVELING NOTES FROM A
MEMORANDUM-BOOK OF MR. KNICKERBOCKER

The Kaatsberg, or Catskill Mountains, have always been a region full of fable. The Indians considered them the abode of spirits, who influenced the weather, spreading sunshine or clouds over the landscape, and sending good or bad hunting seasons. They were ruled by an old squaw spirit, said to be their mother. She dwelt on the highest peak of the Catskills, and had charge of the doors of day and night, to open and shut them at the proper hour. She hung up the new moons in the skies, and cut up the old ones into stars. In times of drought, if properly propitiated, she would spin light summer clouds out of cobwebs and morning dew, and send them off from the crest of the mountain, flake after flake, like flakes of carded cotton, to float in the air, until, dissolved by the heat of the sun, they would fall in gentle showers, causing the grass to spring, the fruits to ripen, and the corn to grow an inch an hour. If displeased, however, she would brew up clouds black as ink, sitting in the midst of them like a bottle-bellied spider in the midst of its web; and when these clouds broke, woe betide the valleys!

In old times, say the Indian traditions, there was a kind of Manitou or Spirit, who kept about the wildest recesses of the Catskill Mountains, and took a mischievous pleasure in wreaking all kinds of evils and vexations upon the red men. Sometimes he would assume the form of a bear, a panther, or a deer, lead the bewildered hunter a weary chase through tangled forests and among ragged rocks, and then spring off with a loud ho! ho! leaving him aghast on the brink of a beetling precipice or raging torrent.

The favorite abode of this Manitou is still shown. It is a great rock or cliff on the loneliest part of the mountains, and, from the flowering vines which clamber about it, and the wild flowers which abound in its neighborhood, is known by the name of the Garden Rock. Near the foot of it is a small lake, the haunt of the solitary bittern, with water-snakes basking in the sun on the leaves of the pond-lilies which lie on the surface. This place was held in great awe by the Indians, insomuch that the boldest hunter would not pursue his game within its precincts. Once upon a time, however, a hunter who had lost his way penetrated to the Garden Rock, where he beheld a number of gourds placed in the crotches of trees. One of these he seized and made off with, but in the hurry of his retreat he let it fall among the rocks, when a great stream gushed forth, which washed him away and swept him down precipices, where he was dashed to pieces, and the stream made its way to the Hudson, and continues to flow to the present-day, being the identical stream known by the name of the Kaaters-kill.

3

The Great Stone Face

BY NATHANIEL HAWTHORNE

ONE afternoon, when the sun was going down, a mother and her little boy sat at the door of their cottage, talking about the Great Stone Face. They had but to lift their eyes, and there it was plainly to be seen, though miles away, with the sunshine brightening all its features.

And what was the Great Stone Face?

Embosomed amongst a family of lofty mountains, there was a valley so spacious that it contained many thousand inhabitants. Some of these good people dwelt in log-huts, with the black forest all around them, on the steep and difficult hill-sides. Others had their homes in comfortable farm-houses, and cultivated the rich soil on the gentle slopes or level surfaces of the valley. Others, again, were congregated into populous villages, where some wild, highland rivulet, tumbling down from its birthplace in the upper mountain region, had been caught and tamed by human cunning, and compelled to turn the machinery of cotton-factories. The inhabitants of this valley, in short, were numerous, and of many modes of life. But all of them, grown people and children, had a kind of familiarity with the Great Stone Face, although some possessed the gift of distinguishing this grand natural phenomenon more perfectly than many of their neighbors.

The Great Stone Face, then, was a work of Nature in her mood of majestic playfulness, formed on the perpendicular side of a mountain by some immense rocks, which had been thrown together in such a position as, when viewed at a proper distance, precisely to resemble the features of the human countenance. It seemed as if an enormous giant, or a Titan, had sculptured his own likeness on the precipice. There was the broad arch of the forehead, a hundred feet in height; the nose, with

44

its long bridge; and the vast lips, which, if they could have spoken, would have rolled their thunder accents from one end of the valley to the other. True it is, that if the spectator approached too near, he lost the outline of the gigantic visage, and could discern only a heap of ponderous and gigantic rocks, piled in chaotic ruin one upon another. Retracing his steps, however, the wondrous features would again be seen; and the farther he withdrew from them, the more like a human face, with all its original divinity intact, did they appear; until, as it grew dim in the distance, with the clouds and glorified vapor of the mountains clustering about it, the Great Stone Face seemed positively to be alive.

It was a happy lot for children to grow up to manhood or womanhood with the Great Stone Face before their eyes, for all the features were noble, and the expression was at once grand and sweet, as if it were the glow of a vast, warm heart, that embraced all mankind in its affections, and had room for more. It was an education only to look at it. According to the belief of many people, the valley owed much of its fertility to this benign aspect that was continually beaming over it, illuminating the clouds, and infusing its tenderness into the sunshine.

As we began with saying, a mother and her little boy sat at their cottage-door, gazing at the Great Stone Face, and talking about it. The child's name was Ernest.

"Mother," said he, while the Titanic visage smiled on him, "I wish that it could speak, for it looks so very kindly that its voice must needs be pleasant. If I were to see a man with such a face, I should love him dearly."

"If an old prophecy should come to pass," answered his mother, "we may see a man, some time or other, with exactly such a face as that."

"What prophecy do you mean, dear mother?" eagerly inquired Ernest. "Pray tell me all about it!"

So his mother told him a story that her own mother had told to her, when she herself was younger than little Ernest; a story, not of things that were past, but of what was yet to come; a story, nevertheless, so very old, that even the Indians, who formerly inhabited this valley, had heard it from their forefathers, to whom, as they affirmed, it had been murmured by the mountain streams, and whispered by the wind among the tree-tops. The purport was, that, at some future day, a child should be born hereabouts, who was destined to become the greatest and noblest personage of his time, and whose countenance, in manhood, should bear an exact resemblance to the Great Stone Face. Not a few old-fashioned people, and young ones likewise, in the ardor of their hopes, still cherished an enduring faith in this old prophecy. But others, who had seen more of the world, had watched and waited till they were weary, and had beheld no man with such a face, nor any man that proved to be much greater or nobler than his neighbors, concluded it to be nothing but an idle tale. At all events, the great man of the prophecy had not yet appeared.

"O mother, dear mother!" cried Ernest, clapping his hands above his head, "I do hope that I shall live to see him!"

His mother was an affectionate and thoughtful woman, and felt that it was wisest not to discourage the generous hopes of her little boy. So she only said to him, "Perhaps you may."

And Ernest never forgot the story that his mother told him. It was always in his mind, whenever he looked upon the Great Stone Face. He spent his childhood in the log-cottage where he was born, and was dutiful to his mother, and helpful to her in many things, assisting her much with his little hands, and more with his loving heart. In this manner, from a happy yet often pensive child, he grew up to be a mild, quiet, unobtrusive boy, and sun-browned with labor in the fields, but with more intelligence brightening his aspect than is seen in many lads who have been taught at famous schools. Yet Ernest had had no teacher, save only that the Great Stone Face became one to him. When the toil of the day was over, he would gaze at it for hours, until he began to imagine that those vast features recognized him, and gave him a smile of kindness and encouragement, responsive to his own look of veneration. We must not take upon us to affirm that this was a mistake, although the Face may have looked no more kindly at Ernest than at all the world besides. But the secret was that the boy's tender and confiding simplicity discerned what other people could not see; and thus the love, which was meant for all, became his peculiar portion.

About this time there went a rumor throughout the valley, that the great man, foretold from ages long ago, who was to bear a resemblance to the Great Stone Face, had appeared at last. It seems that, many years before, a young man had migrated from the valley and settled at a distant seaport, where, after getting together a little money, he had set up as a shopkeeper. His name—but I could never learn whether it was his real one, or a nickname that had grown out of his habits and success in life—was Gathergold. Being shrewd and active, and endowed by Providence with that inscrutable faculty which develops itself in what the world calls luck, he became an exceedingly rich merchant, and owner of a whole fleet of bulky-bottomed ships. All the countries of the globe appeared to join hands for the mere purpose of adding heap after heap to the mountainous accumulation of this one man's wealth. The cold regions of the North, almost within the gloom and shadow of the Arctic Circle, sent him their tribute in the shape of furs; hot Africa sifted for him the golden sands of her rivers, and gathered up the ivory tusks of her great elephants out of the forests; the East came bringing him the rich shawls, and spices, and teas, and the effulgence of diamonds, and the gleaming purity of large pearls. The ocean, not to be behindhand with the earth, yielded up her mighty whales, that Mr. Gathergold might sell their oil, and make a profit on it. Be the original commodity what it might, it was gold within his grasp. It might be said of him, as of Midas, in the fable, that whatever he touched with his finger immediately glistened, and grew yellow, and was changed at once into sterling metal, or, which suited him still better, into piles of coin. And, when Mr. Gathergold had become so very rich that it would have taken him a hundred years only to count his wealth, he bethought himself of his native valley, and resolved to go back thither, and end his days where he was born. With this purpose in view, he sent a skilful architect to build him such a palace as should be fit for a man of his vast wealth to live in.

As I have said above, it had already been rumored in the valley that Mr. Gathergold had turned out to be the prophetic personage so long and vainly looked for, and that his visage was the perfect and undeniable similitude of the Great Stone Face. People were the more ready to believe that this must needs be the fact, when they beheld the splendid edifice that rose, as if by enchantment, on the site of his father's old weather-beaten farm-house. The exterior was of marble, so dazzlingly white that it seemed as though the whole structure might melt away in the sunshine, like those humbler ones which Mr. Gathergold, in his young play-days, before his fingers were gifted with the touch of trans-mutation, had been accustomed to build of snow. It had a richly orna-mented portico, supported by tall pillars, beneath which was a lofty door, studded with silver knobs, and made of a kind of variegated wood that had been brought from beyond the sea. The windows, from the floor to the ceiling of each stately apartment, were composed, respec-tively, of but one enormous pane of glass, so transparently pure that it was said to be a finer medium than even the vacant atmosphere. Hardly anybody had been permitted to see the interior of this palace; but it was reported, and with good semblance of truth, to be far more gorgeous than the outside, insomuch that whatever was iron or brass in other houses was silver or gold in this; and Mr. Gathergold's bedchamber, especially, made such a glittering appearance that no ordinary man would have been able to close his eyes there. But, on the other hand, Mr. Gathergold was now so inured to wealth, that perhaps he could not have closed his eyes unless where the gleam of it was certain to find its way beneath his eyelids.

In due time, the mansion was finished; next came the upholsterers, with magnificent furniture; then, a whole troop of black and white servants, the harbingers of Mr. Gathergold, who, in his own majestic person, was expected to arrive at sunset. Our friend Ernest, meanwhile, had been deeply stirred by the idea that the great man, the noble man, the man of prophecy, after so many ages of delay, was at length to be made manifest to his native valley. He knew, boy as he was, that there were a thousand ways in which Mr. Gathergold, with his vast wealth, might transform himself into an angel of beneficence, and assume a control over human affairs as wide and benignant as the smile of the Great Stone Face. Full of faith and hope, Ernest doubted not that what the people said was true, and that now he was to behold the living likeness of those wondrous features on the mountain-side. While the boy was still gazing up the valley, and fancying, as he always did, that the Great Stone Face returned his gaze and looked kindly at him, the rumbling of wheels was heard, approaching swiftly along the winding road.

"Here he comes!" cried a group of people who were assembled to witness the arrival. "Here comes the great Mr. Gathergold!"

A carriage, drawn by four horses, dashed round the turn of the road. Within it, thrust partly out of the window, appeared the physiognomy of the old man, with a skin as yellow as if his own Midas-hand had transmuted it. He had a low forehead, small, sharp eyes, puckered about with innumerable wrinkles, and very thin lips, which he made still thinner by pressing them forcibly together.

"The very image of the Great Stone Face!" shouted the people. "Sure enough, the old prophecy is true; and here we have the great man come, at last!"

And, what greatly perplexed Ernest, they seemed actually to believe that here was the likeness which they spoke of. By the roadside there chanced to be an old beggar-woman and two little beggar-children, stragglers from some far-off region, who, as the carriage rolled onward, held out their hands and lifted up their doleful voices, most piteously beseeching charity. A yellow claw—the very same that had clawed together so much wealth—poked itself out of the coach-window, and dropped some copper coins upon the ground; so that, though the great man's name seems to have been Gathergold, he might just as suitably have been nicknamed Scattercopper. Still, nevertheless, with an earnest shout, and evidently with as much good faith as ever, the people bellowed:

"He is the very image of the Great Stone Face!"

But Ernest turned sadly from the wrinkled shrewdness of that sordid visage, and gazed up the valley, where, amid a gathering mist, gilded by the last sunbeams, he could still distinguish those glorious features which had impressed themselves into his soul. Their aspect cheered him. What did the benign lips seem to say?

"He will come! Fear not, Ernest; the man will come!"

The years went on, and Ernest ceased to be a boy. He had grown to be a young man now. He attracted little notice from the other inhabitants of the valley; for they saw nothing remarkable in his way of life, save that, when the labor of the day was over, he still loved to go apart and gaze and meditate upon the Great Stone Face. According to their idea of the matter, it was a folly, indeed, but pardonable, inasmuch as Ernest was industrious, kind, and neighborly, and neglected no duty for the sake of indulging this idle habit. They knew not that the Great Stone Face had become a teacher to him, and that the sentiment which was expressed in it would enlarge the young man's heart, and fill it with wider and deeper sympathies than other hearts. They knew not that thence would come a better wisdom than could be learned from books, and a better life than could be molded on the defaced example of other human lives. Neither did Ernest know that the thoughts and affections which came to him so naturally, in the fields and at the fireside, and wherever he communed with himself, were of a higher tone than those which all men shared with him. A simple soul,—simple as when his mother first taught him the old prophecy,—he beheld the marvelous features beaming adown the valley, and still wondered that their human counterpart was so long in making his appearance.

By this time poor Mr. Gathergold was dead and buried; and the oddest part of the matter was, that his wealth, which was the body and spirit of his existence, had disappeared before his death, leaving nothing of him but a living skeleton, covered over with a wrinkled, yellow skin. Since the melting away of his gold, it had been very generally conceded that there was no such striking resemblance, after all, betwixt the ignoble features of the ruined merchant and that majestic face upon the mountain-side. So the people ceased to honor him during his lifetime, and quietly consigned him to forgetfulness after his decease. Once in a while, it is true, his memory was brought up in connection with the magnificent palace which he had built, and which had long ago been turned into a hotel for the accommodation of strangers, multitudes of whom came, every summer, to visit that famous natural curiosity, the Great Stone Face. Thus, Mr. Gathergold being discredited and thrown into the shade, the man of prophecy was yet to come.

It so happened that a native-born son of the valley, many years before, had enlisted as a soldier, and, after a great deal of hard fighting, had now become an illustrious commander. Whatever he may be called in history, he was known in camps and on the battle-field under the nickname of Old Blood-and-Thunder. This war-worn veteran, being now infirm with age and wounds, and weary of the turmoil of a military life, and of the roll of the drum and the clangor of the trumpet, that had so long been ringing in his ears, had lately signified a purpose of return-

ing to his native valley, hoping to find repose where he remembered to
have left it. The inhabitants, his old neighbors and their grown-up
children, were resolved to welcome the renowned warrior with a salute
of cannon and a public dinner; and all the more enthusiastically, it
being affirmed that now, at last, the likeness of the Great Stone Face had
actually appeared. An aid-de-camp of Old Blood-and-Thunder, traveling
through the valley, was said to have been struck with the resemblance.
Moreover the schoolmates and early acquaintances of the general were
ready to testify, on oath, that, to the best of their recollection, the afore-
said general had been exceedingly like the majestic image, even when
a boy, only that the idea had never occurred to them at that period. Great,
therefore, was the excitement throughout the valley; and many people,
who had never once thought of glancing at the Great Stone Face for
years before, now spent their time in gazing at it, for the sake of knowing
exactly how General Blood-and-Thunder looked.

On the day of the great festival, Ernest, with all the other people of
the valley, left their work, and proceeded to the spot where the sylvan
banquet was prepared. As he approached, the loud voice of the Rev.
Dr. Battleblast was heard, beseeching a blessing on the good things set
before them, and on the distinguished friend of peace in whose honor
they were assembled. The tables were arranged in a cleared space of the
woods, shut in by the surrounding trees, except where a vista opened
eastward, and afforded a distant view of the Great Stone Face. Over
the general's chair, which was a relic from the home of Washington,
there was an arch of verdant boughs, with the laurel profusely inter-
mixed, and surmounted by his country's banner, beneath which he had
won his victories. Our friend Ernest raised himself on his tiptoes, in
hopes to get a glimpse of the celebrated guest; but there was a mighty
crowd about the tables anxious to hear the toasts and speeches, and to
catch any word that might fall from the general in reply; and a volunteer
company, doing duty as a guard, pricked ruthlessly with their bayonets
at any particularly quiet person among the throng. So Ernest, being of
an unobtrusive character, was thrust quite into the background, where
he could see no more of Old Blood-and-Thunder's physiognomy than
if it had been still blazing on the battle-field. To console himself, he
turned towards the Great Stone Face, which, like a faithful and long-
remembered friend, looked back and smiled upon him through the
vista of the forest. Meantime, however, he could overhear the remarks
of various individuals, who were comparing the features of the hero
with the face on the distant mountain-side.

" 'T is the same face, to a hair!" cried one man, cutting a caper for joy.
"Wonderfully like, that's a fact!" responded another.

"Like! why, I call it Old Blood-and-Thunder himself, in a monstrous looking-glass!" cried a third.

"And why not? He's the greatest man of this or any other age, beyond a doubt."

And then all three of the speakers gave a great shout, which communicated electricity to the crowd, and called forth a roar from a thousand voices, that went reverberating for miles among the mountains, until you might have supposed that the Great Stone Face had poured its thunder-breath into the cry. All these comments, and this vast enthusiasm, served the more to interest our friend; nor did he think of questioning that now, at length, the mountain-visage had found its human counterpart. It is true, Ernest had imagined that this long-looked-for personage would appear in the character of a man of peace, uttering wisdom, and doing good, and making people happy. But, taking an habitual breadth of view, with all his simplicity, he contended that Providence should choose its own method of blessing mankind, and could conceive that this great end might be effected even by a warrior and a bloody sword, should inscrutable wisdom see fit to order matters so.

"The general! the general!" was now the cry. "Hush! silence! Old Blood-and-Thunder's going to make a speech."

Even so; for, the cloth being removed, the general's health had been drunk, amid shouts of applause, and he now stood upon his feet to thank the company. Ernest saw him. There he was, over the shoulders of the crowd, from the two glittering epaulets and embroidered collar upward, beneath the arch of green boughs with intertwined laurel, and the banner drooping as if to shade his brow! And there, too, visible in the same glance, through the vista of the forest, appeared the Great Stone Face! And was there, indeed, such a resemblance as the crowd had testified? Alas, Ernest could not recognize it! He beheld a war-worn and weather-beaten countenance, full of energy, and expressive of an iron will; but the gentle wisdom, the deep, broad, tender sympathies, were altogether wanting in Old Blood-and-Thunder's visage; and even if the Great Stone Face had assumed his look of stern command, the milder traits would still have tempered it.

"This is not the man of prophecy," sighed Ernest to himself, as he made his way out of the throng. "And must the world wait longer yet?"

The mists had congregated about the distant mountain-side, and there were seen the grand and awful features of the Great Stone Face, awful but benignant, as if a mighty angel were sitting among the hills, and enrobing himself in a cloud-vesture of gold and purple. As he looked, Ernest could hardly believe but that a smile beamed over the whole visage, with a radiance still brightening, although without motion of the

lips. It was probably the effect of the western sunshine, melting through
the thinly diffused vapors that had swept between him and the object that
he gazed at. But—as it always did—the aspect of his marvelous friend
made Ernest as hopeful as if he had never hoped in vain.

"Fear not, Ernest," said his heart, even as if the Great Face were
whispering him,—"fear not, Ernest; he will come."

More years sped swiftly and tranquilly away. Ernest still dwelt in his
native valley, and was now a man of middle age. By imperceptible degrees, he had become known among the people. Now, as heretofore, he
labored for his bread, and was the same simple-hearted man that he had
always been. But he had thought and felt so much, he had given so many
of the best hours of his life to unworldly hopes for some great good to
mankind, that it seemed as though he had been talking with the angels,
and had imbibed a portion of their wisdom unawares. It was visible in
the calm and well-considered beneficence of his daily life, the quiet
stream of which had made a wide green margin all along its course. Not
a day passed by, that the world was not the better because this man,
humble as he was, had lived. He never stepped aside from his own path,
yet would always reach a blessing to his neighbor. Almost involuntarily,
too, he had become a preacher. The pure and high simplicity of his
thought, which, as one of its manifestations, took shape in the good deeds
that dropped silently from his hand, flowed also forth in speech. He
uttered truths that wrought upon and molded the lives of those who
heard him. His auditors, it may be, never suspected that Ernest, their
own neighbor and familiar friend, was more than an ordinary man;
least of all did Ernest himself suspect it; but, inevitably as the murmur
of a rivulet, came thoughts out of his mouth that no other human lips
had spoken.

When the people's minds had had a little time to cool, they were
ready enough to acknowledge their mistake in imagining a similarity
between General Blood-and-Thunder's truculent physiognomy and
the benign visage on the mountain-side. But now, again, there were
reports and many paragraphs in the newspapers, affirming that the
likeness of the Great Stone Face had appeared upon the broad shoulders of a certain eminent statesman. He, like Mr. Gathergold and Old
Blood-and-Thunder, was a native of the valley, but had left it in his
early days, and taken up the trades of law and politics. Instead of the
rich man's wealth and the warrior's sword, he had but a tongue, and
it was mightier than both together. So wonderfully eloquent was he,
that whatever he might choose to say, his auditors had no choice but to
believe him; wrong looked like right, and right like wrong; for when
it pleased him, he could make a kind of illuminated fog with his mere
breath, and obscure the natural daylight with it. His tongue, indeed,

was a magic instrument: sometimes it rumbled like the thunder; sometimes it warbled like the sweetest music. It was the blast of war,—the
song of peace; and it seemed to have a heart in it, when there was no
such matter. In good truth, he was a wondrous man; and when his
tongue had acquired him all other imaginable success,—when it had
been heard in halls of state, and in the courts of princes and potentates,
—after it had made him known all over the world, even as a voice crying from shore to shore,—it finally persuaded his countrymen to select
him for the Presidency. Before this time,—indeed, as soon as he began
to grow celebrated,—his admirers had found out the resemblance between him and the Great Stone Face; and so much were they struck by
it, that throughout the country this distinguished gentleman was known
by the name of Old Stony Phiz. The phrase was considered as giving
a highly favorable aspect to his political prospects; for, as is likewise the
case with the Popedom, nobody ever becomes President without taking
a name other than his own.

While his friends were doing their best to make him President, Old
Stony Phiz, as he was called, set out on a visit to the valley where he
was born. Of course, he had no other object than to shake hands with
his fellow-citizens, and neither thought nor cared about any effect which
his progress through the country might have upon the election. Magnificent preparations were made to receive the illustrious statesman; a
cavalcade of horsemen set forth to meet him at the boundary line of
the State, and all the people left their business and gathered along the
wayside to see him pass. Among these was Ernest. Though more than
once disappointed, as we have seen, he had such a hopeful and confiding
nature, that he was always ready to believe in whatever seemed beautiful
and good. He kept his heart continually open, and thus was sure to catch
the blessing from on high when it should come. So now again, as buoyantly as ever, he went forth to behold the likeness of the Great Stone
Face.

The cavalcade came prancing along the road, with a great clattering
of hoofs and a mighty cloud of dust, which rose up so dense and high
that the visage of the mountain-side was completely hidden from
Ernest's eyes. All the great men of the neighborhood were there on
horseback; militia officers, in uniform; the member of Congress; the
sheriff of the county; the editors of newspapers, and many a farmer, too,
had mounted his patient steed, with his Sunday coat upon his back. It
really was a very brilliant spectacle, especially as there were numerous
banners flaunting over the cavalcade, on some of which were gorgeous
portraits of the illustrious statesman and the Great Stone Face, smiling
familiarly at one another, like two brothers. If the pictures were to be
trusted, the mutual resemblance, it must be confessed, was marvelous.

We must not forget to mention that there was a band of music, which made the echoes of the mountains ring and reverberate with the loud triumph of its strains; so that airy and soul-thrilling melodies broke out among all the heights and hollows, as if every nook of his native valley had found a voice, to welcome the distinguished guest. But the grandest effect was when the far-off mountain precipice flung back the music; for then the Great Stone Face itself seemed to be swelling the triumphant chorus, in acknowledgment that, at length, the man of prophecy was come.

All this while the people were throwing up their hats and shouting, with enthusiasm so contagious that the heart of Ernest kindled up, and he likewise threw up his hat, and shouted, as loudly as the loudest, "Huzza for the great man! Huzza for Old Stony Phiz!" But as yet he had not seen him.

"Here he is, now!" cried those who stood near Ernest. "There! There! Look at Old Stony Phiz and then at the Old Man of the Mountain, and see if they are not as like as two twin brothers!"

In the midst of all this gallant array came an open barouche, drawn by four white horses; and in the barouche, with his massive head uncovered, sat the illustrious statesman, Old Stony Phiz himself.

"Confess it," said one of Ernest's neighbors to him, "the Great Stone Face has met its match at last!"

Now, it must be owned that, at his first glimpse of the countenance which was bowing and smiling from the barouche, Ernest did fancy that there was a resemblance between it and the old familiar face upon the mountain-side. The brow, with its massive depth and loftiness, and all the other features, indeed, were boldly and strongly hewn, as if in emulation of a more than heroic, of a Titanic model. But the sublimity and stateliness, the grand expression of a divine sympathy, that illuminated the mountain visage and etherealized its ponderous granite substance into spirit, might here be sought in vain. Something had been originally left out, or had departed. And therefore the marvelously gifted statesman had always a weary gloom in the deep caverns of his eyes, as of a child that has outgrown its playthings or a man of mighty faculties and little aims, whose life, with all its high performances, was vague and empty, because no high purpose had endowed it with reality.

Still, Ernest's neighbor was thrusting his elbow into his side, and pressing him for an answer.

"Confess! confess! Is not he the very picture of your Old Man of the Mountain?"

"No!" said Ernest, bluntly, "I see little or no likeness."

"Then so much the worse for the Great Stone Face!" answered his neighbor; and again he set up a shout for Old Stony Phiz.

But Ernest turned away, melancholy, and almost despondent: for this was the saddest of his disappointments, to behold a man who might have fulfilled the prophecy, and had not willed to do so. Meantime, the cavalcade, the banners, the music, and the barouches swept past him, with the vociferous crowd in the rear, leaving the dust to settle down, and the Great Stone Face to be revealed again, with the grandeur that it had worn for untold centuries.

"Lo, here I am, Ernest!" the benign lips seemed to say. "I have waited longer than thou, and am not yet weary. Fear not; the man will come."

The years hurried onward, treading in their haste on one another's heels. And now they began to bring white hairs, and scatter them over the head of Ernest; they made reverend wrinkles across his forehead, and furrows in his cheeks. He was an aged man. But not in vain had he grown old: more than the white hairs on his head were the sage thoughts in his mind; his wrinkles and furrows were inscriptions that Time had graved, and in which he had written legends of wisdom that had been tested by the tenor of a life. And Ernest had ceased to be obscure. Unsought for, undesired, had come the fame which so many seek, and made him known in the great world, beyond the limits of the valley in which he had dwelt so quietly. College professors, and even the active men of cities, came from far to see and converse with Ernest; for the report had gone abroad that this simple husbandman had ideas unlike those of other men, not gained from books, but of a higher tone,—a tranquil and familiar majesty, as if he had been talking with the angels as his daily friends. Whether it were sage, statesman, or philanthropist, Ernest received these visitors with the gentle sincerity that had characterized him from boyhood, and spoke freely with them of whatever came uppermost, or lay deepest in his heart or their own. While they talked together, his face would kindle, unawares, and shine upon them, as with a mild evening light. Pensive with the fulness of such discourse, his guests took leave and went their way; and passing up the valley, paused to look at the Great Stone Face, imagining that they had seen its likeness in a human countenance, but could not remember where.

While Ernest had been growing up and growing old, a bountiful Providence had granted a new poet to this earth. He, likewise, was a native of the valley, but had spent the greater part of his life at a distance from that romantic region, pouring out his sweet music amid the bustle and din of cities. Often, however, did the mountains which had been familiar to him in his childhood lift their snowy peaks into the clear atmosphere of his poetry. Neither was the Great Stone Face forgotten, for the poet had celebrated it in an ode, which was grand enough to have been uttered by its own majestic lips. This man of genius, we may say, had come down from heaven with wonderful endowments. If he sang of a mountain, the eyes of all mankind beheld a mightier grandeur reposing on its breast, or soaring to its summit, than had before been seen there. If his theme were a lovely lake, a celestial smile had now been thrown over it, to gleam forever on its surface. If it were the vast old sea, even the deep immensity of its dread bosom seemed to swell the higher, as if moved by the emotions of the song. Thus the world assumed another and a better aspect from the hour that the poet blessed it with his happy eyes. The Creator had bestowed him, as the last best touch to his own handiwork. Creation was not finished till the poet came to interpret, and so complete it.

The effect was no less high and beautiful, when his human brethren were the subject of his verse. The man or woman, sordid with the common dust of life, who crossed his daily path, and the little child who played in it, were glorified if they beheld him in his mood of poetic faith. He showed the golden links of the great chain that intertwined them with an angelic kindred; he brought out the hidden traits of a celestial birth that made them worthy of such kin. Some, indeed, there were, who thought to show the soundness of their judgment by affirming that all the beauty and dignity of the natural world existed only in the poet's fancy. Let such men speak for themselves, who undoubtedly appear to have been spawned forth by Nature with a contemptuous bitterness; she having plastered them up out of her refuse stuff, after all the swine were made. As respects all things else, the poet's ideal was the truest truth.

The songs of this poet found their way to Ernest. He read them after his customary toil, seated on the bench before his cottage-door, where for such a length of time he had filled his repose with thought, by gazing at the Great Stone Face. And now as he read stanzas that caused the soul to thrill within him, he lifted his eyes to the vast countenance beaming on him so benignantly.

"O majestic friend," he murmured, addressing the Great Stone Face, "is not this man worthy to resemble thee?"

The face seemed to smile, but answered not a word.

Now it happened that the poet, though he dwelt so far away, had not only heard of Ernest, but had meditated much upon his character, until he deemed nothing so desirable as to meet this man, whose untaught wisdom walked hand in hand with the noble simplicity of his life. One summer morning, therefore, he took passage by the railroad, and, in the decline of the afternoon, alighted from the cars at no great distance from Ernest's cottage. The great hotel, which had formerly been the palace of Mr. Gathergold, was close at hand, but the poet, with his carpetbag on his arm, inquired at once where Ernest dwelt, and was resolved to be accepted as his guest.

Approaching the door, he there found the good old man, holding a volume in his hand, which alternately he read, and then, with a finger between the leaves, looked lovingly at the Great Stone Face.

"Good evening," said the poet. "Can you give a traveler a night's lodging?"

"Willingly," answered Ernest; and then he added, smiling, "Methinks I never saw the Great Stone Face look so hospitably at a stranger."

The poet sat down on the bench beside him, and he and Ernest talked together. Often had the poet held intercourse with the wittiest and the wisest, but never before with a man like Ernest, whose thoughts and feelings gushed up with such a natural feeling, and who made great truths so familiar by his simple utterance of them. Angels, as had been so often said, seemed to have wrought with him at his labor in the fields; angels seemed to have sat with him by the fireside; and, dwelling with angels as friend with friends, he had imbibed the sublimity of their ideas, and imbued it with the sweet and lowly charm of household words. So thought the poet. And Ernest, on the other hand, was moved and agitated by the living images which the poet flung out of his mind, and which peopled all the air about the cottage-door with shapes of beauty, both gay and pensive. The sympathies of these two men instructed them with a profounder sense than either could have attained alone. Their minds accorded into one strain, and made delightful music which neither of them could have claimed as all his own, nor distinguished his own share from the other's. They led one another, as it were, into a high pavilion of their thoughts, so remote, and hitherto so dim, that they had never entered it before, and so beautiful that they desired to be there always.

As Ernest listened to the poet, he imagined that the Great Stone Face was bending forward to listen too. He gazed earnestly into the poet's glowing eyes.

"Who are you, my strangely gifted guest?" he said.

The poet laid his finger on the volume that Ernest had been reading.

"You have read these poems," said he. "You know me, then,—for I wrote them."

Again, and still more earnestly than before, Ernest examined the poet's features; then turned towards the Great Stone Face; then back, with an uncertain aspect, to his guest. But his countenance fell; he shook his head, and sighed.

"Wherefore are you sad?" inquired the poet.

"Because," replied Ernest, "all through life I have awaited the fulfilment of a prophecy; and, when I read these poems, I hoped that it might be fulfilled in you."

"You hoped," answered the poet, faintly smiling, "to find in me the likeness of the Great Stone Face. And you are disappointed, as formerly with Mr. Gathergold, and Old Blood-and-Thunder, and Old Stony Phiz. Yes, Ernest, it is my doom. You must add my name to the illustrious three, and record another failure of your hopes. For—in shame and sadness do I speak it, Ernest—I am not worthy to be typified by yonder benign and majestic image."

"And why?" asked Ernest. He pointed to the volume. "Are not those thoughts divine?"

"They have a strain of the Divinity," replied the poet. "You can hear in them the far-off echo of a heavenly song. But my life, dear Ernest, has not corresponded with my thought. I have had grand dreams, but they have been only dreams, because I have lived—and that, too, by my own choice—among poor and mean realities. Sometimes, even—shall I dare to say it?—I lack faith in the grandeur, the beauty, and the goodness, which my own works are said to have made more evident in Nature and in human life. Why, then, pure seeker of the good and true, shouldst thou hope to find me, in yonder image of the divine?"

The poet spoke sadly, and his eyes were dim with tears. So, likewise, were those of Ernest.

At the hour of sunset, as had long been his frequent custom, Ernest was to discourse to an assemblage of the neighboring inhabitants in the open air. He and the poet, arm in arm, still talking together as they went along, proceeded to the spot. It was a small nook among the hills, with a gray precipice behind, the stern front of which was relieved by the pleasant foliage of many creeping plants that made a tapestry for the naked rock, by hanging their festoons from all its rugged angles. At a small elevation above the ground, set in a rich framework of verdure, there appeared a niche, spacious enough to admit a human figure, with freedom for such gestures as spontaneously accompanying earnest thought and genuine emotion. Into this natural pulpit Ernest ascended, and threw a look of familiar kindness around upon his audience. They stood, or sat, or reclined upon the grass, as seemed good to each, with the departing sunshine falling obliquely over them, and mingling its subdued cheerfulness with the solemnity of a grove of ancient trees, beneath and amid the boughs of which the golden rays were constrained to pass. In another direction was seen the Great Stone Face, with the same cheer, combined with the same solemnity, in its benignant aspect.

Ernest began to speak, giving to the people of what was in his heart and mind. His words had power, because they accorded with his thoughts; and his thoughts had reality and depth, because they harmonized with the life which he had always lived. It was not mere breath that this preacher uttered; they were the words of life, because a life of good deeds and holy love was melted into them. Pearls, pure and rich, had been dissolved into this precious draught. The poet, as he listened, felt that the being and character of Ernest were a nobler strain of poetry than he had ever written. His eyes glistening with tears, he gazed reverentially at the venerable man, and said within himself that never was there an aspect so worthy of a prophet and a sage as that mild, sweet, thoughtful countenance, with the glory of white hair diffused about it. At a distance, but distinctly to be seen, high up in the golden light of the setting sun, appeared the Great Stone Face, with hoary mists around it, like the white hairs around the brow of Ernest. Its look of grand beneficence seemed to embrace the world.

At that moment, in sympathy with a thought which he was about to utter, the face of Ernest assumed a grandeur of expression, so imbued with benevolence, that the poet, by an irresistible impulse, threw his arms aloft and shouted:

"Behold! Behold! Ernest is himself the likeness of the Great Stone Face!"

Then all the people looked and saw that what the deep-sighted poet said was true. The prophecy was fulfilled. But Ernest, having finished what he had to say, took the poet's arm, and walked slowly homeward, still hoping that some wiser and better man than himself would by and by appear, bearing a resemblance to the GREAT STONE FACE.

4

Rappaccini's Daughter

(FROM THE WRITINGS OF AUBÉPINE)

BY NATHANIEL HAWTHORNE

W̲E do not remember to have seen any translated specimens of the productions of M. de l'Aubépine—a fact the less wondered at, as his very name is unknown to many of his own countrymen as well as to the student of foreign literature. As a writer, he seems to occupy an unfortunate position between the Transcendentalists (who, under one name or another, have their share in all the current literature of the world) and the great body of pen-and-ink men who address the intellect and sympathies of the multitude. If not too refined, at all events too remote, too shadowy, and unsubstantial in his modes of development to suit the taste of the latter class, and yet too popular to satisfy the spiritual or metaphysical requisitions of the former, he must necessarily find himself without an audience, except here and there an individual or possibly an isolated clique. His writings, to do them justice, are not altogether destitute of fancy and originality; they might have won him greater reputation but for an inveterate love of allegory, which is apt to invest his plots and characters with the aspect of scenery and people in the clouds, and to steal away the human warmth out of his conceptions. His fictions are sometimes historical, sometimes of the present day, and sometimes, so far as can be discovered, have little or no reference either to time or space. In any case, he generally contents himself with a very slight embroidery of outward manners,—the faintest possible counterfeit of real life,—and endeavors to create an interest by some less obvious peculiarity of the subject. Occasionally a breath of Nature, a raindrop of pathos and tenderness, or a gleam of humor, will find its way into the midst of his fantastic imagery, and make us feel as if, after all, we were yet within the limits of our native earth. We will only add to this very cursory notice that M. de l'Aubépine's productions, if the reader chance to take them in precisely the proper point of view, may amuse a leisure hour as well as those of a brighter man; if otherwise, they can hardly fail to look excessively like nonsense.

Our author is voluminous; he continues to write and publish with as much praiseworthy and indefatigable prolixity as if his efforts were crowned with the brilliant success that so justly attends those of Eugene Sue. His first appearance was by a collection of stories in a long series of volumes entitled "Contes deux fois racontées." The titles of some of his more recent works (we quote from memory) are as follows: "Le Voyage Céleste à Chemin de Fer," 3 tom., 1838; "Le nouveau Père Adam et la nouvelle Mère Eve," 2 tom., 1839; "Roderic; ou le Serpent à l'estomac," 2 tom., 1840; "Le Culte du Feu," a folio volume of ponderous research into the religion and ritual of the old Persian Ghebers, published in 1841; "La Soirée du Château en Espagne," 1 tom., 8 vo, 1842; and "L'Artiste du Beau; ou le Papillon Mécanique," 5 tom., 4to, 1843. Our somewhat wearisome perusal of this startling catalog of volumes has left behind it a certain personal affection and sympathy, though by no means admiration, for M. de l'Aubépine; and we would fain do the little in our power towards introducing him favorably to the American public. The ensuing tale is a translation of his "Beatrice; ou la Belle Empoisonneuse," recently published in "La Revue Anti-Aristocratique." This journal, edited by the Comte de Bearhaven, has for some years past led the defense of liberal principles and popular rights with a faithfulness and ability worthy of all praise.

A young man, named Giovanni Guasconti, came, very long ago, from the more southern region of Italy, to pursue his studies at the University of Padua. Giovanni, who had but a scanty supply of gold ducats in his pocket, took lodgings in a high and gloomy chamber of an old edifice which looked not unworthy to have been the palace of a Paduan noble, and which, in fact, exhibited over its entrance the armorial bearings of a family long since extinct. The young stranger, who was not unstudied in the great poem of his country, recollected that one of the ancestors of this family, and perhaps an occupant of this very mansion, had been pictured by Dante as a partaker of the immortal agonies of his Inferno. These reminiscences and associations, together with the tendency to heartbreak natural to a young man for the first time out of his native sphere, caused Giovanni to sigh heavily as he looked around the desolate and ill-furnished apartment.

"Holy Virgin, signor!" cried old Dame Lisabetta, who, won by the youth's remarkable beauty of person, was kindly endeavoring to give the chamber a habitable air, "what a sigh was that to come out of a young man's heart! Do you find this old mansion gloomy? For the love of Heaven, then, put your head out of the window, and you will see as bright sunshine as you have left in Naples."

Guasconti mechanically did as the old woman advised, but could not quite agree with her that the Paduan sunshine was as cheerful as that of Southern Italy. Such as it was, however, it fell upon a garden beneath the window and expended its fostering influences on a variety of plants, which seemed to have been cultivated with exceeding care.

"Does this garden belong to the house?" asked Giovanni.

"Heaven forbid, signor, unless it were fruitful of better pot herbs than any that grow there now," answered old Lisabetta. "No; that garden is cultivated by the own hands of Signor Giacomo Rappaccini, the famous doctor, who, I warrant him, has been heard of as far as Naples. It is said that he distils these plants into medicines that are as potent as a charm. Oftentimes you may see the signor doctor at work, and perchance the signora, his daughter, too, gathering the strange flowers that grow in the garden."

The old woman had now done what she could for the aspect of the chamber; and, commending the young man to the protection of the saints, took her departure.

Giovanni still found no better occupation than to look down into the garden beneath his window. From its appearance, he judged it to be one of those botanic gardens which were of earlier date in Padua than elsewhere in Italy or in the world. Or, not improbably, it might once have been the pleasure-place of an opulent family; for there was the ruin of a marble fountain in the center, sculptured with rare art, but so woefully shattered that it was impossible to trace the original design from the chaos of remaining fragments. The water, however, continued to gush and sparkle into the sunbeams as cheerfully as ever. A little gurgling sound ascended to the young man's window, and made him feel as if the fountain were an immortal spirit that sung its song unceasingly and without heeding the vicissitudes around it, while one century embodied it in marble and another scattered the perishable garniture on the soil. All about the pool into which the water subsided grew various plants, that seemed to require a plentiful supply of moisture for the nourishment of gigantic leaves, and, in some instances, flowers gorgeously magnificent. There was one shrub in particular, set in a marble vase in the midst of the pool, that bore a profusion of purple blossoms, each of which had the luster and richness of a gem; and the whole together made a show so resplendent that it seemed enough to illuminate the garden, even had there been no sunshine. Every portion of the soil was peopled with plants and herbs, which, if less beautiful, still bore tokens of assiduous care, as if all had their individual virtues, known to the scientific mind that fostered them. Some were placed in urns, rich with old carving, and others in common garden pots; some crept serpent-like along the ground or climbed on high, using whatever means of ascent was offered them. One plant had wreathed itself round a statue of Vertumnus, which was thus quite veiled and shrouded in a drapery of hanging foilage, so happily arranged that it might have served a sculptor for a study.

While Giovanni stood at the window he heard a rustling behind a screen of leaves, and became aware that a person was at work in the garden. His figure soon emerged into view, and showed itself to be that of no common laborer, but a tall, emaciated, sallow, and sickly looking man, dressed in a scholar's garb of black. He was beyond the middle term of life, with gray hair, a thin, gray beard, and a face singularly marked with intellect and cultivation, but which could never, even in his more youthful days, have expressed much warmth of heart.

Nothing could exceed the intentness with which this scientific gardener examined every shrub which grew in his path: it seemed as if he was looking into their inmost nature, making observations in regard to their creative essence, and discovering why one leaf grew in this shape and another in that, and wherefore such and such flowers differed among themselves in hue and perfume. Nevertheless, in spite of this deep intelligence on his part, there was no approach to intimacy between himself and these vegetable existences. On the contrary, he avoided their actual touch or the direct inhaling of their odors with a caution that impressed Giovannia most disagreeably; for the man's demeanor was that of one walking among malignant influences, such as savage beasts, or deadly snakes, or evil spirits, which, should he allow them one moment of license, would wreak upon him some terrible fatality. It was strangely frightful to the young man's imagination to see this air of insecurity in a person cultivating a garden, that most simple and innocent of human toils, and which had been alike the joy and labor of the unfallen parents of the race. Was this garden, then, the Eden of the present world? And this man, with such a perception of harm in what his own hands caused to grow,—was he the Adam?

The distrustful gardener, while plucking away the dead leaves or pruning the too luxuriant growth of the shrubs, defended his hands with a pair of thick gloves. Nor were these his only armor. When, in his walk through the garden, he came to the magnificent plant that hung its purple gems beside the marble fountain, he placed a kind of mask over his mouth and nostrils, as if all this beauty did not conceal a deadlier malice; but, finding his task still too dangerous, he drew back, removed the mask, and called loudly, but in the infirm voice of a person affected with inward disease:

"Beatrice! Beatrice!"

"Here am I, my father. What would you?" cried a rich and youthful voice from the window of the opposite house—a voice as rich as a tropical sunset, and which made Giovanni, though he knew not why, think of deep hues of purple or crimson and of perfumes heavily delectable. "Are you in the garden?"

"Yes, Beatrice," answered the gardener, "and I need your help."

Soon there emerged from under a sculptured portal the figure of a young girl, arrayed with as much richness of taste as the most splendid of the flowers, beautiful as the day, and with a bloom so deep and vivid that one shade more would have been too much. She looked redundant with life, health, and energy; all of which attributes were bound down and compressed, as it were, and girdled tensely, in their luxuriance, by her virgin zone. Yet Giovanni's fancy must have grown morbid while he looked down into the garden; for the impression which the fair stranger made upon him was as if here were another flower, the human sister of those vegetable ones, as beautiful as they, more beautiful than the richest of them, but still to be touched only with a glove, nor to be approached without a mask. As Beatrice came down the garden path, it was observable that she handled and inhaled the odor of several of the plants which her father had most seduously avoided.

"Here, Beatrice," said the latter, "see how many needful offices require to be done to our chief treasure. Yet, shattered as I am, my life might pay the penalty of approaching it so closely as circumstances demand. Henceforth, I fear, this plant must be consigned to your sole charge."

"And gladly will I undertake it," cried again the rich tones of the young lady, as she bent towards the magnificent plant and opened her arms as if to embrace it. "Yes, my sister, my splendor, it shall be Beatrice's task to nurse and serve thee; and thou shalt reward her with thy kisses and perfumed breath, which to her is as the breath of life."

Then, with all the tenderness in her manner that was so strikingly expressed in her words, she busied herself with such attentions as the plant seemed to require; and Giovanni, at his lofty window, rubbed his eyes and almost doubted whether it were a girl tending her favorite flower, or one sister performing the duties of affection to another. The scene soon terminated. Whether Dr. Rappaccini had finished his labors in the garden, or that his watchful eye had caught the stranger's face, he now took his daughter's arm and retired. Night was already closing in; oppressive exhalations seemed to proceed from the plants and steal upward past the open window; and Giovanni, closing the lattice, went to his couch and dreamed of a rich flower and beautiful girl. Flower and maiden were different, and yet the same, and fraught with some strange peril in either shape.

But there is an influence in the light of morning that tends to rectify whatever errors of fancy, or even of judgment, we may have incurred during the sun's decline, or among the shadows of the night, or in the less wholesome glow of moonshine. Giovanni's first movement, on starting from sleep, was to throw open the window and gaze down into the garden which his dreams had made so fertile of mysteries. He was surprised and a little ashamed to find how real and matter-of-fact an affair it proved to be, in the first rays of the sun which gilded the dew-drops that hung upon leaf and blossom, and, while giving a brighter beauty to each rare flower, brought everything within the limits of ordinary experience. The young man rejoiced that, in the heart of the barren city, he had the privilege of overlooking this spot of lovely and luxuriant vegetation. It would serve, he said to himself, as a symbolic language to keep him in communion with Nature. Neither the sickly and thoughtworn Dr. Giacomo Rappaccini, it is true, nor his brilliant daughter, were now visible; so that Giovanni could not determine how much of the singularity which he attributed to both was due to their own qualities and how much to his wonder-working fancy; but he was inclined to take a most rational view of the whole matter.

In the course of the day he paid his respects to Signor Pietro Baglioni, professor of medicine in the university, a physician of eminent repute, to whom Giovanni had brought a letter of introduction. The professor was an elderly personage, apparently of genial nature, and habits that might almost be called jovial. He kept the young man to dinner, and made himself very agreeable by the freedom and liveliness of his conversation, especially when warmed by a flask or two of Tuscan wine. Giovanni, conceiving that men of science, inhabitants of the same city, must needs be on familiar terms with one another, took an opportunity to mention the name of Dr. Rappaccini. But the professor did not respond with so much cordiality as he had anticipated.

"Ill would it become a teacher of the divine art of medicine," said Professor Pietro Baglioni, in answer to a question of Giovanni, "to withhold due and well-considered praise of a physician so eminently skilled as Rappaccini; but, on the other hand, I should answer it but scantily to my conscience were I to permit a worthy youth like yourself, Signor Giovanni, the son of an ancient friend, to imbibe erroneous ideas respecting a man who might hereafter chance to hold your life and death in his hands. The truth is, our worshipful Dr. Rappaccini has as much science as any member of the faculty—with perhaps one single exception —in Padua, or all Italy; but there are certain grave objections to his professional character."

"And what are they?" asked the young man.

"Has my friend Giovanni any disease of body or heart, that he is so inquisitive about physicians?" said the professor, with a smile. "But as for Rappaccini, it is said of him—and I, who know the man well, can answer for its truth—that he cares infinitely more for science than for mankind. His patients are interesting to him only as subjects for some new experiment. He would sacrifice human life, his own among the rest, or whatever else was dearest to him, for the sake of adding so much as a grain of mustard seed to the great heap of his accumulated knowledge."

"Methinks he is an awful man indeed," remarked Guasconti, mentally recalling the cold and purely intellectual aspect of Rappaccini. "And yet, worshipful professor, is it not a noble spirit? Are there many men capable of so spiritual a love of science?"

"God forbid," answered the professor, somewhat testily; "at least, unless they take sounder views of the healing art than those adopted by Rappaccini. It is his theory that all medicinal virtues are comprised within those substances which we term vegetable poisons. These he cultivates with his own hands, and is said even to have produced new varieties of poison, more horribly deleterious than Nature, without the assistance of this learned person, would ever have plagued the world withal. That the signor doctor does less mischief than might be expected with such dangerous substances is undeniable. Now and then, it must be owned, he has effected, or seemed to effect, a marvelous cure; but, to tell you my private mind, Signor Giovanni, he should receive little credit for such instances of success,—they being probably the work of chance,—but should be held strictly accountable for his failures, which may justly be considered his own work."

The youth might have taken Baglioni's opinions with many grains of allowance had he known that there was a professional warfare of long continuance between him and Dr. Rappaccini, in which the latter was generally thought to have gained the advantage. If the reader be inclined to judge for himself, we refer him to certain black-letter tracts on both sides, preserved in the medical department of the University of Padua.

"I know not, most learned professor," returned Giovanni, after musing on what had been said of Rappaccini's exclusive zeal for science,— "I know not how dearly this physician may love his art; but surely there is one object more dear to him. He has a daughter."

"Aha!" cried the professor, with a laugh. "So now our friend Giovanni's secret is out. You have heard of this daughter, whom all the young men in Padua are wild about, though not half a dozen have ever had the good hap to see her face. I know little of the Signora Beatrice save that Rappaccini is said to have instructed her deeply in his science, and that, young and beautiful as fame reports her, she is already qualified to fill a professor's chair. Perchance her father destines her for mine! Other absurd rumors there be, not worth talking about or listening to. So now, Signor Giovanni, drink off your glass of lachryma."

Guasconti returned to his lodgings somewhat heated with the wine he had quaffed, and which caused his brain to swim with strange fantasies in reference to Dr. Rappaccini and the beautiful Beatrice. On his way, happening to pass by a florist's he bought a fresh bouquet of flowers.

Ascending to his chamber, he seated himself near the window, but within the shadow thrown by the depth of the wall, so that he could look down into the garden with little risk of being discovered. All beneath his eye was a solitude. The strange plants were basking in the sunshine, and now and then nodding gently to one another, as if in acknowledgment of sympathy and kindred. In the midst, by the shattered fountain, grew the magnificent shrub, with its purple gems clustering all over it; they glowed in the air, and gleamed back again out of the depths of the pool, which thus seemed to overflow with colored radiance from the rich reflection that was steeped in it. At first, as we have said, the garden was a solitude. Soon, however,—as Giovanni had half hoped, half feared, would be the case,—a figure appeared beneath the antique sculptured portal, and came down between the rows of plants, inhaling their various perfumes as if she were one of those beings of old classic fable that lived upon sweet odors. On again beholding Beatrice, the young man was even startled to perceive how much her beauty exceeded his recollection of it; so brilliant, so vivid, was its character, that she glowed amid the sunlight, and, as Giovanni whispered to himself, positively illuminated the more shadowy intervals of the garden path. Her face being now more revealed than on the former occasion, he was struck by its expression of simplicity and sweetness,— qualities that had not entered into his idea of her character, and which made him ask anew what manner of mortal she might be. Nor did he fail again to observe, or imagine, an analogy between the beautiful girl and the gorgeous shrub that hung its gemlike flowers over the fountain, —a resemblance which Beatrice seemed to have indulged a fantastic humor in heightening, both by the arrangement of her dress and the selection of its hues.

Approaching the shrub, she threw open her arms, as with a passionate ardor, and drew its branches into an intimate embrace—so intimate that her features were hidden in its leafy bosom and her glistening ringlets all intermingled with the flowers.

"Give me thy breath, my sister," exclaimed Beatrice; "for I am faint with common air. And give me this flower of thine, which I separate with gentlest fingers from the stem and place it close beside my heart."

With these words the beautiful daughter of Rappaccini plucked one of the richest blossoms of the shrub, and was about to fasten it in her bosom. But now, unless Giovanni's draughts of wine had bewildered his senses, a singular incident occurred. A small orange-colored reptile, of the lizard or chameleon species, chanced to be creeping along the path, just at the feet of Beatrice. It appeared to Giovanni,—but, at the distance from which he gazed, he could scarcely have seen anything so minute, —it appeared to him, however, that a drop or two of moisture from the broken stem of the flower descended upon the lizard's head. For an instant the reptile contorted itself violently, and then lay motionless in the sunshine. Beatrice observed this remarkable phenomenon, and crossed herself, sadly, but without surprise; nor did she therefore hesitate to arrange the fatal flower in her bosom. There it blushed, and almost glimmered with the dazzling effect of a precious stone, adding to her dress and aspect the one appropriate charm which nothing else in the world could have supplied. But Giovanni, out of the shadow of his window, bent forward and shrank back, and murmured and trembled.

"Am I awake? Have I my senses?" said he to himself. "What is this being? Beautiful shall I call her, or inexpressibly terrible?"

Beatrice now strayed carelessly through the garden, approaching closer beneath Giovanni's window, so that he was compelled to thrust his head quite out of its concealment in order to gratify the intense and painful curiosity which she excited. At this moment there came a beautiful insect over the garden wall; it had, perhaps, wandered through the city, and found no flowers or verdure among those antique haunts of men until the heavy perfumes of Dr. Rappaccini's shrubs had lured it from afar. Without alighting on the flowers, this winged brightness seemed to be attracted by Beatrice, and lingered in the air and fluttered about her head. Now, here it could not be but that Giovanni Guasconti's eyes deceived him. Be that as it might, he fancied that, while Beatrice was gazing at the insect with childish delight, it grew faint and fell at her feet; its bright wings shivered; it was dead—from no cause that he could discern, unless it were the atmosphere of her breath. Again Beatrice crossed herself and sighed heavily as she bent over the dead insect.

An impulsive movement of Giovanni drew her eyes to the window. There she beheld the beautiful head of the young man—rather a Grecian than an Italian head, with fair, regular features, and a glistening of gold among his ringlets—gazing down upon her like a being that hovered in mid air. Scarcely knowing what he did, Giovanni threw down the bouquet which he had hitherto held in his hand.

"Signora," said he, "there are pure and healthful flowers. Wear them for the sake of Giovanni Guasconti."

"Thanks, signor," replied Beatrice, with her rich voice, that came forth as it were like a gush of music, and with a mirthful expression half childish and half woman-like. "I accept your gift, and would fain recompense it with this precious purple flower; but if I toss it into the air it will not reach you. So Signor Guasconti must even content himself with my thanks."

She lifted the bouquet from the ground, and then, as if inwardly ashamed at having stepped aside from her maidenly reserve to respond to a stranger's greeting, passed swiftly homeward through the garden. But few as the moments were, it seemed to Giovanni, when she was on the point of vanishing beneath the sculptured portal, that his beautiful bouquet was already beginning to wither in her grasp. It was an idle thought; there could be no possibility of distinguishing a faded flower from a fresh one at so great a distance.

For many days after this incident the young man avoided the window that looked into Dr. Rappaccini's garden, as if something ugly and monstrous would have blasted his eyesight had he been betrayed into a glance. He felt conscious of having put himself, to a certain extent, within the influence of an unintelligible power by the communication which he had opened with Beatrice. The wisest course would have been, if his heart were in any real danger, to quit his lodgings and Padua itself at once; the next wiser, to have accustomed himself, as far as possible, to the familiar and daylight view of Beatrice—thus bringing her rigidly and systematically within the limits of ordinary experience. Least of all, while avoiding her sight, ought Giovanni to have remained so near this extraordinary being that the proximity and possibility even of intercourse should give a kind of substance and reality to the wild vagaries which his imagination ran riot continually in producing. Guasconti had not a deep heart—or, at all events, its depths were not sounded now; but he had a quick fancy, and an ardent Southern temperament, which rose every instant to a higher fever pitch. Whether or no Beatrice possessed those terrible attributes, that fatal breath, the affinity with those so beautiful and deadly flowers which were indicated by what Giovanni had witnessed, she had at least instilled a fierce and subtle poison into his system. It was not love, although her rich beauty was a madness to him; nor horror, even while he fancied her spirit to be imbued with the same baneful essence that seemed to pervade her physical frame; but a wild offspring of both love and horror that had each parent in it, and burned like one and shivered like the other. Giovanni knew not what to dread; still less did he know what to hope; yet hope and dread kept a continual warfare in his breast, alternately vanquishing one another and starting up afresh to renew the contest. Blessed are all simple emotions, be they dark or bright! It is the lurid intermixture of the two that produces the illuminating blaze of the infernal regions.

Sometimes he endeavored to assuage the fever of his spirit by a rapid walk through the streets of Padua or beyond its gates: his footsteps kept time with the throbbings of his brain, so that the walk was apt to accelerate itself to a race. One day he found himself arrested; his arm was seized by a portly personage, who had turned back on recognizing the young man and expended much breath in overtaking him.

"Signor Giovanni! Stay, my young friend!" cried he. "Have you forgotten me? That might well be the case if I were as much altered as yourself."

It was Baglioni, whom Giovanni had avoided ever since their first meeting, from a doubt that the professor's sagacity would look too deeply into his secrets. Endeavoring to recover himself, he stared forth wildly from his inner world into the outer one and spoke like a man in a dream.

"Yes; I am Giovanni Guasconti. You are Professor Pietro Baglioni. Now let me pass!"

"Not yet, not yet, Signor Giovanni Guasconti," said the professor, smiling, but at the same time scrutinizing the youth with an earnest glance. "What! did I grow up side by side with your father? and shall his son pass me like a stranger in these old streets of Padua? Stand still, Signor Giovanni; for we must have a word or two before we part."

"Speedily, then, most worshipful professor, speedily," said Giovanni, with feverish impatience. "Does not your worship see that I am in haste?"

Now, while he was speaking there came a man in black along the street, stooping and moving feebly like a person in inferior health. His face was all overspread with a most sickly and sallow hue, but yet so pervaded with an expression of piercing and active intellect that an observer might easily have overlooked the merely physical attributes and have seen only his wonderful energy. As he passed, this person exchanged a cold and distant salutation with Baglioni, but fixed his eyes upon Giovanni with an intentness that seemed to bring out whatever was within him worthy of notice. Nevertheless, there was a peculiar quietness in the look, as if taking merely a speculative, not a human, interest in the young man.

"It is Dr. Rappaccini!" whispered the professor when the stranger had passed. "Has he ever seen your face before?"

"Not that I know," answered Giovanni, starting at the name.

"He *has* seen you! he must have seen you!" said Baglioni, hastily. "For some purpose or other, this man of science is making a study of you. I know that look of his! It is the same that coldly illuminates his face as he bends over a bird, a mouse, or a butterfly, which, in pursuance of some experiment, he has killed by the perfume of a flower; a look as deep as Nature itself, but without Nature's warmth of love. Signor Giovanni, I will stake my life upon it, you are the subject of one of Rappaccini's experiments!"

"Will you make a fool of me?" cried Giovanni, passionately. "*That,* signor professor, were an untoward experiment."

"Patience! patience!" replied the imperturbable professor. "I tell thee, my poor Giovanni, that Rappaccini has a scientific interest in thee. Thou hast fallen into fearful hands! And the Signora Beatrice,—what part does she act in this mystery?"

But Guasconti, finding Baglioni's pertinacity intolerable, here broke away, and was gone before the professor could again seize his arm. He looked after the young man intently and shook his head.

"This must not be," said Baglioni to himself. "The youth is the son of my old friend, and shall not come to any harm from which the arcana of medical science can preserve him. Besides, it is too insufferable an impertinence in Rappaccini, thus to snatch the lad out of my own hands, as I may say, and make use of him for his infernal experiments. This daughter of his! It shall be looked to. Perchance, most learned Rappaccini, I may foil you where you little dream of it!"

Meanwhile Giovanni had pursued a circuitous route, and at length found himself at the door of his lodgings. As he crossed the threshold he was met by old Lisabetta, who smirked and smiled, and was evidently desirous to attract his attention; vainly, however, as the ebullition of his feelings had momentarily subsided into a cold and dull vacuity. He turned his eyes full upon the withered face that was puckering itself into a smile, but seemed to behold it not. The old dame, therefore, laid her grasp upon his cloak.

"Signor! signor!" whispered she, still with a smile over the whole breadth of her visage, so that it looked not unlike a grotesque carving in wood, darkened by centuries. "Listen, signor! There is a private entrance into the garden!"

"What do you say?" exclaimed Giovanni, turning quickly about, as if an inanimate thing should start into feverish life. "A private entrance into Dr. Rappaccini's garden?"

"Hush! hush! not so loud!" whispered Lisabetta, putting her hand over his mouth. "Yes; into the worshipful doctor's garden, where you may see all his fine shrubbery. Many a young man in Padua would give gold to be admitted among those flowers."

Giovanni put a piece of gold into her hand.

"Show me the way," said he.

A surmise, probably excited by his conversation with Baglioni, crossed his mind, that this interposition of old Lisabetta might perchance be connected with the intrigue, whatever were its nature, in which the professor seemed to suppose that Dr. Rappaccini was involving him. But such a suspicion, though it disturbed Giovanni, was inadequate to restrain him. The instant that he was aware of the possibility of approaching Beatrice, it seemed an absolute necessity of his existence to do so. It mattered not whether she were angel or demon; he was irrevocably within her sphere, and must obey the law that whirled him onward, in ever-lessening circles, towards a result which he did not attempt to foreshadow; and yet, strange to say, there came across him a sudden doubt whether this intense interest on his part were not delusory; whether it were really of so deep and positive a nature as to justify him in now thrusting himself into an incalculable position; whether it were not merely the fantasy of a young man's brain, only slightly or not at all connected with his heart.

He paused, hesitated, turned half about, but again went on. His withered guide led him along several obscure passages, and finally undid a door, through which, as it was opened, there came the sight and sound of rustling leaves, with the broken sunshine glimmering among them. Giovanni stepped forth, and, forcing himself through the entanglement of a shrub that wreathed its tendrils over the hidden entrance, stood beneath his own window in the open area of Dr. Rappaccini's garden.

How often is it the case that, when impossibilities have come to pass and dreams have condensed their misty substance into tangible realities, we find ourselves calm, and even coldly self-possessed, amid circumstances which it would have been a delirium of joy or agony to anticipate! Fate delights to thwart us thus. Passion will choose his own time to rush upon the scene, and lingers sluggishly behind when an appropriate adjustment of events would seem to summon his appearance. So was it now with Giovanni. Day after day his pulses had throbbed with feverish blood at the improbable idea of an interview with Beatrice, and of standing with her, face to face, in this very garden, basking in the Oriental sunshine of her beauty, and snatching from her full gaze the mystery which he deemed the riddle of his own existence. But now there was a singular and untimely equanimity within his breast. He threw a glance around the garden to discover if Beatrice or her father were present, and, perceiving that he was alone, began a critical observation of the plants.

The aspect of one and all of them dissatisfied him; their gorgeousness seemed fierce, passionate, and even unnatural. There was hardly an individual shrub which a wanderer, straying by himself through a forest, would not have been startled to find growing wild, as if an unearthly face had glared at him out of the thicket. Several also would have shocked a delicate instinct by an appearance of artificialness indicating that there had been such commixture, and, as it were, adultery, of various vegetable species, that the production was no longer of God's making, but the monstrous offspring of man's depraved fancy, glowing with only an evil mockery of beauty. They were probably the result of experiment, which in one or two cases had succeeded in mingling plants individually lovely into a compound possessing the questionable and ominous character that distinguished the whole growth of the garden. In fine, Giovanni recognized but two or three plants in the collection, and those of a kind that he well knew to be poisonous. While busy with these contemplations he heard the rustling of a silken garment, and, turning, beheld Beatrice emerging from beneath the sculptured portal.

Giovanni had not considered with himself what should be his deportment; whether he should apologize for his intrusion into the garden, or assume that he was there with the privity at least, if not by the desire, of Dr. Rappaccini or his daughter; but Beatrice's manner placed him at his ease, though leaving him still in doubt by what agency he had gained admittance. She came lightly along the path and met him near the broken fountain. There was surprise in her face, but brightened by a simple and kind expression of pleasure.

"You are a connoisseur in flowers, signor," said Beatrice, with a smile, alluding to the bouquet which he had flung her from the window. "It is no marvel, therefore, if the sight of my father's rare collection has tempted you to take a nearer view. If he were here, he could tell you many strange and interesting facts as to the nature and habits of these shrubs; for he has spent a lifetime in such studies, and this garden is his world."

"And yourself, lady," observed Giovanni, "if fame says true,—you likewise are deeply skilled in the virtues indicated by these rich blossoms and these spicy perfumes. Would you deign to be my instructress, I should prove an apter scholar than if taught by Signor Rappaccini himself."

"Are there such idle rumors?" asked Beatrice, with the music of a pleasant laugh. "Do people say that I am skilled in my father's science of plants? What a jest is there! No; though I have grown up among these flowers, I know no more of them than their hues and perfume; and sometimes methinks I would fain rid myself of even that small knowledge. There are many flowers here, and those not the least brilliant, that shock and offend me when they meet my eye. But pray, signor, do not believe these stories about my science. Believe nothing of me save what you see with your own eyes."

"And must I believe all that I have seen with my own eyes?" asked Giovanni, pointedly, while the recollection of former scenes made him shrink. "No, signora; you demand too little of me. Bid me believe nothing save what comes from your own lips."

It would appear that Beatrice understood him. There came a deep flush to her cheek; but she looked full into Giovanni's eyes, and responded to his gaze of uneasy suspicion with a queenlike haughtiness.

"I do so bid you, Signor," she replied. "Forget whatever you may have fancied in regard to me. If true to the outward senses, still it may be false in its essence; but the words of Beatrice Rappaccini's lips are true from the depths of the heart outward. Those you may believe."

A fervor glowed in her whole aspect and beamed upon Giovanni's consciousness like the light of truth itself; but while she spoke there was a fragrance in the atmosphere around her, rich and delightful, though evanescent, yet which the young man, from an indefinable reluctance, scarcely dared to draw into his lungs. It might be the odor of the flowers. Could it be Beatrice's breath which thus embalmed her words with a strange richness, as if by steeping them in her heart? A faintness passed like a shadow over Giovanni and flitted away; he seemed to gaze through the beautiful girl's eyes into her transparent soul, and felt no more doubt or fear.

The tinge of passion that had colored Beatrice's manner vanished; she became gay, and appeared to derive a pure delight from her communion with the youth not unlike what the maiden of a lonely island might have felt conversing with a voyager from the civilized world. Evidently her experience of life had been confined within the limits of that garden. She talked now about matters as simple as the daylight or summer clouds, and now asked questions in reference to the city, or Giovanni's distant home, his friends, his mother, and his sisters—questions indicating such seclusion, and such lack of familiarity with modes and forms, that Giovanni responded as if to an infant. Her spirit gushed out before him like a fresh rill that was just catching its first glimpse of the sunlight and wondering at the reflections of earth and sky which were flung into its bosom. There came thoughts, too, from a deep source, and fantasies of a gemlike brilliancy, as if diamonds and rubies sparkled upward among the bubbles of the fountain. Ever and anon there gleamed across the young man's mind a sense of wonder that he should be walking side by side with the being who had so wrought upon his imagination, whom he had idealized in such hues of terror, in whom he had positively witnessed such manifestations of dreadful attributes,—that he should be conversing with Beatrice like a brother, and should find her so human and so maidenlike. But such reflections were only momentary; the effect of her character was too real not to make itself familiar at once.

In this free intercourse they had strayed through the garden, and now, after many turns among its avenues, were come to the shattered fountain, beside which grew the magnificent shrub, with its treasury of glow-ing blossoms. A fragrance was diffused from it which Giovanni recognized as identical with that which he had attributed to Beatrice's breath, but incomparably more powerful. As her eyes fell upon it, Gio-vanni beheld her press her hand to her bosom as if her heart were throbbing suddenly and painfully.

"For the first time in my life," murmured she, addressing the shrub, "I had forgotten thee."

"I remember, signora," said Giovanni, "that you once promised to reward me with one of these living gems for the bouquet which I had the happy boldness to fling to your feet. Permit me now to pluck it as a memorial of this interview."

He made a step towards the shrub with extended hand; but Beatrice darted forward, uttering a shriek that went through his heart like a dagger. She caught his hand and drew it back with the whole force of her slender figure. Giovanni felt her touch thrilling through his fibers.

"Touch it not!" exclaimed she, in a voice of agony. "Not for thy life! It is fatal!"

Then, hiding her face, she fled from him and vanished beneath the sculptured portal. As Giovanni followed her with his eyes, he beheld the emaciated figure and pale intelligence of Dr. Rappaccini, who had been watching the scene, he knew not how long, within the shadow of the entrance.

No sooner was Guasconti alone in his chamber than the image of Beatrice came back to his passionate musings, invested with all the witchery that had been gathering around it ever since his first glimpse of her, and now likewise imbued with a tender warmth of girlish womanhood. She was human; her nature was endowed with all gentle and feminine qualities; she was worthiest to be worshipped; she was capable, surely, on her part, of the height and heroism of love. Those tokens which he had hitherto considered as proofs of a frightful pecu-liarity in her physical and moral system were now either forgotten, or, by the subtle sophistry of passion transmitted into a golden crown of enchantment, rendering Beatrice the more admirable by so much as she was the more unique. Whatever had looked ugly was now beautiful; or, if incapable of such a change, it stole away and hid itself among those shapeless half ideas which throng the dim region beyond the daylight of our perfect consciousness. Thus did he spend the night, nor fell asleep until the dawn had begun to awake the slumbering flowers in Dr. Rappaccini's garden, whither Giovanni's dreams doubtless led him. Up rose the sun in his due season, and, flinging his beams upon the young man's eyelids, awoke him to a sense of pain. When thoroughly aroused, he became sensible of a burning and tingling agony in his hand—in his right hand—the very hand which Beatrice had grasped in her own when he was on the point of plucking one of the gemlike flowers. On the back of that hand there was now a purple print like that of four small fingers, and the likeness of a slender thumb upon his wrist.

Oh, how stubbornly does love,—or even that cunning semblance of love which flourishes in the imagination, but strikes no depth of root into the heart,—how stubbornly does it hold its faith until the moment comes when it is doomed to vanish into thin mist! Giovanni wrapped a handkerchief about his hand and wondered what evil thing had stung him, and soon forgot his pain in a reverie of Beatrice.

After the first interview, a second was in the inevitable course of what we call fate. A third; a fourth; and a meeting with Beatrice in the garden was no longer an incident in Giovanni's daily life, but the whole space in which he might be said to live; for the anticipation and memory of that ecstatic hour made up the remainder. Nor was it otherwise with the daughter of Rappaccini. She watched for the youth's appearance, and flew to his side with confidence as unreserved as if they had been playmates from early infancy—as if they were such playmates still. If, by any unwonted chance, he failed to come at the appointed moment, she stood beneath the window and sent up the rich sweetness of her tones to float around him in his chamber and echo and reverberate throughout his heart: "Giovanni! Giovanni! Why tarriest thou? Come down!" And down he hastened into that Eden of poisonous flowers.

But, with all this intimate familiarity, there was still a reserve in Beatrice's demeanor, so rigidly and invariably sustained that the idea of infringing it scarcely occurred to his imagination. By all appreciable signs, they loved; they had looked love with eyes that conveyed the holy secret from the depths of one soul into the depths of the other, as if it were too sacred to be whispered by the way; they had even spoken love in those gushes of passion when their spirits darted forth in articulated breath like tongues of long-hidden flame; and yet there had been no seal of lips, no clasp of hands, nor any slightest caress such as love claims and hallows. He had never touched one of the gleaming ringlets of her hair; her garment—so marked was the physical barrier between them—had never been waved against him by a breeze. On the few occasions when Giovanni had seemed tempted to overstep the limit, Beatrice grew so sad, so stern, and withal wore such a look of desolate separation, shuddering at itself, that not a spoken word was requisite to repel him. At such times he was startled at the horrible suspicions that rose, monster-like, out of the caverns of his heart and stared him in the face; his love grew thin and faint as the morning mist, his doubts alone had substance. But, when Beatrice's face brightened again after the momentary shadow, she was transformed at once from the mysterious, questionable being whom he had watched with so much awe and horror; she was now the beautiful and unsophisticated girl whom he felt that his spirit knew with a certainty beyond all other knowledge.

A considerable time had now passed since Giovanni's last meeting with Baglioni. One morning, however, he was disagreeably surprised by a visit from the professor, whom he had scarcely thought of for whole weeks, and would willingly have forgotten still longer. Given up as he had long been to a pervading excitement, he could tolerate no companions except upon condition of their perfect sympathy with his present state of feeling. Such sympathy was not to be expected from Professor Baglioni.

The visitor chatted carelessly for a few moments about the gossip of the city and the university, and then took up another topic.

"I have been reading an old classic author lately," said he, "and met with a story that strangely interested me. Possibly you may remember it. It is of an Indian prince, who sent a beautiful woman as a present to Alexander the Great. She was as lovely as the dawn and gorgeous as the sunset; but what especially distinguished her was a certain rich perfume in her breath—richer than a garden of Persian roses. Alexander, as was natural to a youthful conqueror, fell in love at first sight with this magnificent stranger; but a certain sage physician, happening to be present, discovered a terrible secret in regard to her."

"And what was that?" asked Giovanni, turning his eyes downward to avoid those of the professor.

"That this lovely woman," continued Baglioni, with emphasis, "had been nourished with poisons from her birth upward, until her whole nature was so imbued with them that she herself had become the deadliest poison in existence. Poison was her element of life. With that rich perfume of her breath she blasted the very air. Her love would have been poison—her embrace death. Is not this a marvelous tale?"

"A childish fable," answered Giovanni, nervously starting from his chair. "I marvel how your worship finds time to read such nonsense among your graver studies."

"By the by," said the professor, looking uneasily about him, "what singular fragrance is this in your apartment? Is it the perfume of your gloves? It is faint, but delicious; and yet, after all, by no means agreeable. Were I to breathe it long, methinks it would make me ill. It is like the breath of a flower; but I see no flowers in the chamber."

"Nor are there any," replied Giovanni, who had turned pale as the professor spoke; "nor, I think, is there any fragrance except in your worship's imagination. Odors, being a sort of element combined of the sensual and the spiritual, are apt to deceive us in this manner. The recollection of a perfume, the bare idea of it, may easily be mistaken for a present reality."

"Ay; but my sober imagination does not often play such tricks," said Baglioni; "and, were I to fancy any kind of odor, it would be that of some vile apothecary drug, wherewith my fingers are likely enough to be imbued. Our worshipful friend Rappaccini, as I have heard, tinctures his medicaments with odors richer than those of Araby. Doubtless, likewise, the fair and learned Signora Beatrice would minister to her patients with draughts as sweet as a maiden's breath; but woe to him that sips them!"

Giovanni's face evinced many contending emotions. The tone in which the professor alluded to the pure and lovely daughter of Rappaccini was a torture to his soul; and yet the intimation of a view of her character, opposite to his own, gave instantaneous distinctness to a thousand dim suspicions, which now grinned at him like so many demons. But he strove hard to quell them and to respond to Baglioni with a true lover's perfect faith.

"Signor professor," said he, "you were my father's friend; perchance, too, it is your purpose to act a friendly part towards his son. I would fain feel nothing towards you save respect and deference; but I pray you to observe, signor, that there is one subject on which we must not speak. You know not the Signora Beatrice. You cannot, therefore, estimate the wrong—the blasphemy, I may even say—that is offered to her character by a light or injurious word."

"Giovanni! my poor Giovanni!" answered the professor, with a calm expression of pity, "I know this wretched girl far better than yourself. You shall hear the truth in respect to the poisoner Rappaccini and his poisonous daughter; yes, poisonous as she is beautiful. Listen; for, even should you do violence to my gray hairs, it shall not silence me. That old fable of the Indian woman has become a truth by the deep and deadly science of Rappaccini and in the person of the lovely Beatrice."

Giovanni groaned and hid his face.

"Her father," continued Baglioni, "was not restrained by natural affection from offering up his child in this horrible manner as the victim of his insane zeal for science; for, let us do him justice, he is as true a man of science as ever distilled his own heart in an alembic. What, then, will be your fate? Beyond a doubt you are selected as the material of some new experiment. Perhaps the result is to be death; perhaps a fate more awful still. Rappaccini, with what he calls the interest of science before his eyes, will hesitate at nothing."

"It is a dream," muttered Giovanni to himself; "surely it is a dream."

"But," resumed the professor, "be of good cheer, son of my friend. It is not yet too late for the rescue. Possibly we may even succeed in bringing back this miserable child within the limits of ordinary nature, from which her father's madness has estranged her. Behold this little silver vase! It was wrought by the hands of the renowed Benvenuto Cellini, and is well worthy to be a love gift to the fairest dame in Italy. But its contents are invaluable. One little sip of this antidote would have rendered the most virulent poisons of the Borgias innocuous. Doubt not that it will be as efficacious against those of Rappaccini. Bestow the vase, and the precious liquid within it, on your Beatrice, and hopefully await the result."

Baglioni laid a small, exquisitely wrought silver vial on the table and withdrew, leaving what he had said to produce its effect upon the young man's mind.

"We will thwart Rappaccini yet," thought he, chuckling to himself, as he descended the stairs; "but, let us confess the truth of him, he is a wonderful man—a wonderful man indeed; a vile empiric, however, in his practice, and therefore not to be tolerated by those who respect the good old rules of the medical profession."

Throughout Giovanni's whole acquaintance with Beatrice, he had occasionally, as we have said, been haunted by dark surmises as to her character; yet so thoroughly had she made herself felt by him as a simple, natural, most affectionate, and guileless creature, that the image now held up by Professor Baglioni looked as strange and incredible as if it were not in accordance with his own original conception. True, there were ugly recollections connected with his first glimpses of the beautiful girl; he could not quite forget the bouquet that withered in her grasp, and the insect that perished amid the sunny air, by no ostensible agency save the fragrance of her breath. These incidents, however, dissolving in the pure light of her character, had no longer the efficacy of facts, but were acknowledged as mistaken fantasies, by whatever testimony of the senses they might appear to be substantiated. There is something truer and more real than what we can see with the eyes and touch with the finger. On such better evidence had Giovanni founded his confidence in Beatrice, though rather by the necessary force of her high attributes than by any deep and generous faith on his part. But now his spirit was incapable of sustaining itself at the height to which the early enthusiasm of passion had exalted it; he fell down, grovelling among earthly doubts, and defiled therewith the pure whiteness of Beatrice's image. Not that he gave her up; he did but distrust. He resolved to institute some decisive test that should satisfy him, once for all, whether there were those dreadful peculiarities in her physical nature which could not be supposed to exist without some corresponding monstrosity of soul. His eyes, gazing down afar, might have deceived him as to the lizard, the insect, and the flowers; but if he could witness, at the distance of a few paces the sudden blight of one fresh and healthful flower in Beatrice's hand, there would be room for no further question. With this idea he hastened to the florist's and purchased a bouquet that was still gemmed with the morning dew-drops.

It was now the customary hour of his daily interview with Beatrice. Before descending into the garden, Giovanni failed not to look at his figure in the mirror,—a vanity to be expected in a beautiful young man, yet, as displaying itself at that troubled and feverish moment, the token of a certain shallowness of feeling and insincerity of character. He did gaze, however, and said to himself that his features had never before possessed so rich a grace, nor his eyes such vivacity, nor his cheeks so warm a hue of superabundant life.

"At least," thought he, "her poison has not yet insinuated itself into my system. I am no flower to perish in her grasp."

With that thought he turned his eyes on the bouquet, which he had never once laid aside from his hand. A thrill of indefinable horror shot through his frame on perceiving that those dewy flowers were already beginning to droop; they wore the aspect of things that had been fresh and lovely yesterday. Giovanni grew white as marble, and stood motionless before the mirror, staring at his own reflection there as at the likeness of something frightful. He remembered Baglioni's remark about the fragrance that seemed to pervade the chamber. It must have been the poison in his breath! Then he shuddered—shuddered at himself. Recovering from his stupor, he began to watch with curious eye a spider that was busily at work hanging its web from the antique cornice of the apartment, crossing and recrossing the artful system of interwoven lines —as vigorous and active a spider as ever dangled from an old ceiling. Giovanni bent towards the insect, and emitted a deep, long breath. The spider suddenly ceased its toil; the web vibrated with a tremor originating in the body of the small artisan. Again Giovanni sent forth a breath, deeper, longer, and imbued with a venomous feeling out of his heart: he knew not whether he were wicked, or only desperate. The spider made a convulsive gripe with his limps and hung dead across the window.

"Accursed! accursed!" muttered Giovanni, addressing himself. "Hast thou grown so poisonous that this deadly insect perishes by thy breath?"

At that moment a rich, sweet voice came floating up from the garden.

"Giovanni! Giovanni! It is past the hour! Why tarriest thou? Come down!"

"Yes," muttered Giovanni again. "She is the only being whom my breath may not slay! Would that it might!"

He rushed down, and in an instant was standing before the bright and loving eyes of Beatrice. A moment ago his wrath and despair had been

so fierce that he could have desired nothing so much as to wither her by
a glance; but with her actual presence there came influences which had
too real an existence to be at once shaken off: recollections of the delicate
and benign power of her feminine nature, which had so often enveloped
him in a religious calm; recollections of many a holy and passionate out-
gush of her heart, when the pure fountain had been unsealed from its
depths and made visible in its transparency to his mental eye; recollections which, had Giovanni known how to estimate them, would have assured him that all this ugly mystery was but an earthly illusion, and that,
whatever mist of evil might seem to have gathered over her, the real
Beatrice was a heavenly angel. Incapable as he was of such high faith,
still her presence had not utterly lost its magic. Giovanni's rage was
quelled into an aspect of sullen insensibility. Beatrice, with a quick
spiritual sense, immediately felt that there was a gulf of blackness between them which neither he nor she could pass. They walked on
together, sad and silent, and came thus to the marble fountain and to its
pool of water on the ground, in the midst of which grew the shrub that
bore gemlike blossoms. Giovanni was affrighted at the eager enjoyment
—the appetite, as it were—with which he found himself inhaling the
fragrance of the flowers.

"Beatrice," asked he, abruptly, "whence came this shrub?"

"My father created it," answered she, with simplicity.

"Created it! created it!" repeated Giovanni. "What mean you,
Beatrice?"

"He is a man fearfully acquainted with the secrets of Nature," replied
Beatrice; "and, at the hour when I first drew breath, this plant sprang
from the soil, the offspring of his science, of his intellect, while I was
but his earthly child. Approach it not!" continued she, observing with
terror that Giovanni was drawing nearer to the shrub. "It has qualities
that you little dream of. But I, dearest Giovanni,—I grew up and blossomed with the plant and was nourished with its breath. It was my
sister, and I loved it with a human affection; for, alas!—hast thou not
suspected it?—there was an awful doom."

Here Giovanni frowned so darkly upon her that Beatrice paused and
trembled. But her faith in his tenderness reassured her, and made her
blush that she had doubted for an instant.

"There was an awful doom," she continued, "the effect of my father's
fatal love of science, which estranged me from all society of my kind.
Until Heaven sent thee, dearest Giovanni, oh, how lonely was thy poor
Beatrice!"

"Was it a hard doom?" asked Giovanni, fixing his eyes upon her.

"Only of late have I known how hard it was," answered she, tenderly.
"Oh, yes; but my heart was torpid, and therefore quiet."

Giovanni's rage broke forth from his sullen gloom like a lightning flash out of a dark cloud.

"Accursed one!" cried he, with venomous scorn and anger. "And, finding thy solitude wearisome, thou hast severed me likewise from all the warmth of life and enticed me into thy region of unspeakable horror!"

"Giovanni!" exclaimed Beatrice, turning her large bright eyes upon his face. The force of his words had not found its way into her mind; she was merely thunderstruck.

"Yes, poisonous thing!" repeated Giovanni, beside himself with passion. "Thou hast done it! Thou hast blasted me! Thou hast filled my veins with poison! Thou hast made me as hateful, as ugly, as loathsome and deadly a creature as thyself—a world's wonder of hideous monstrosity! Now, if our breath be happily as fatal to ourselves as to all others, let us join our lips in one kiss of unutterable hatred, and so die!"

"What has befallen me?" murmured Beatrice, with a low moan out of her heart. "Holy Virgin, pity me, a poor heart-broken child!"

"Thou,—dost thou pray?" cried Giovanni, still with the same fiendish scorn. "Thy very prayers, as they come from thy lips, taint the atmosphere with death. Yes, yes; let us pray! Let us to church and dip our fingers in the holy water at the portal! They that come after us will perish as by a pestilence! Let us sign crosses in the air! It will be scattering curses abroad in the likeness of holy symbols!"

"Giovanni," said Beatrice, calmly, for her grief was beyond passion, "why dost thou join thyself with me thus in those terrible words? I, it is true, am the horrible thing thou namest me. But thou,—what hast thou to do, save with one other shudder at my hideous misery to go forth out of the garden and mingle with thy race, and forget that there ever crawled on earth such a monster as poor Beatrice?"

"Dost thou pretend ignorance?" asked Giovanni scowling upon her. "Behold! this power have I gained from the pure daughter of Rappaccini."

There was a swarm of summer insects flitting through the air in search of the food promised by the flower odors of the fatal garden. They circled round Giovanni's head, and were evidently attracted towards him by the same influence which had drawn them for an instant within the sphere of several of the shrubs. He sent forth a breath among them, and smiled bitterly at Beatrice as at least a score of the insects fell dead upon the ground.

"I see it! I see it!" shrieked Beatrice. "It is my father's fatal science! No, no, Giovanni; it was not I! Never! never! I dreamed only to love thee and be with thee a little time, and so to let thee pass away, leaving but thine image in mine heart; for, Giovanni, believe it, though my body be nourished with poison, my spirit is God's creature, and craves love as its daily food. But my father,—he has united us in this fearful sympathy. Yes; spurn me, tread upon me, kill me! Oh, what is death after such words as thine? But it was not I. Not for a world of bliss would I have done it."

Giovanni's passion had exhausted itself in its outburst from his lips. There now came across him a sense, mournful, and not without tenderness, of the intimate and peculiar relationship between Beatrice and himself. They stood, as it were, in an utter solitude, which would be made none the less solitary by the densest throng of human life. Ought not, then, the desert of humanity around them to press this insulated pair closer together? If they should be cruel to one another, who was there to be kind to them? Besides, thought Giovanni, might there not still be a hope of his returning within the limits of ordinary nature, and leading Beatrice, the redeemed Beatrice, by the hand? O, weak, and selfish, and unworthy spirit, that could dream of an earthly union and earthly happiness as possible, after such deep love had been so bitterly wronged as was Beatrice's love by Giovanni's blighting words! No, no; there could be no such hope. She must pass heavily, with that broken heart, across the borders of Time—she must bathe her hurts in some fount of paradise, and forget her grief in the light of immortality, and *there* be well.

But Giovanni did not know it.

"Dear Beatrice," said he, approaching her, while she shrank away as always at his approach, but now with a different impulse, "dearest Beatrice, our fate is not yet so desperate. Behold! there is a medicine, potent, as a wise physician has assured me, and almost divine in its efficacy. It is composed of ingredients the most opposite to those by which thy awful father has brought this calamity upon thee and me. It is distilled of blessed herbs. Shall we not quaff it together, and thus be purified from evil?"

"Give it me!" said Beatrice, extending her hand to receive the little silver vial which Giovanni took from his bosom. She added, with a peculiar emphasis, "I will drink; but do thou await the result."

She put Baglioni's antidote to her lips; and, at the same moment, the figure of Rappaccini emerged from the portal and came slowly towards the marble fountain. As he drew near, the pale man of science seemed to gaze with a triumphant expression at the beautiful youth and maiden, as might an artist who should spend his life in achieving a picture or a group of statuary and finally be satisfied with his success. He paused; his bent form grew erect with conscious power; he spread out his hands over them in the attitude of a father imploring a blessing upon his children; but those were the same hands that had thrown poison into the stream of their lives. Giovanni trembled. Beatrice shuddered nervously, and pressed her hand upon her heart.

"My daughter," said Rappaccini, "thou art no longer lonely in the world. Pluck one of those precious gems from thy sister shrub and bid thy bridegroom wear it in his bosom. It will not harm him now. My science and the sympathy between thee and him have so wrought within his system that he now stands apart from common men, as thou dost, daughter of my pride and triumph, from ordinary women. Pass on, then, through the world, most dear to one another and dreadful to all besides!"

"My father," said Beatrice, feebly,—and still as she spoke she kept her hand upon her heart,—"wherefore didst thou inflict this miserable doom upon thy child?"

"Miserable!" exclaimed Rappaccini. "What mean you, foolish girl? Dost thou deem it misery to be endowed with marvelous gifts against which no power nor strength could avail an enemy—misery, to be able to quell the mightiest with a breath—misery, to be as terrible as thou art beautiful? Wouldst thou, then, have preferred the condition of a weak woman, exposed to all evil and capable of none?"

"I would fain have been loved, not feared," murmured Beatrice, sinking down upon the ground. "But now it matters not. I am going, father, where the evil which thou hast striven to mingle with my being will pass away like a dream—like the fragrance of these poisonous flowers, which will no longer taint my breath among the flowers of Eden. Farewell, Giovanni! Thy words of hatred are like lead within my heart; but they, too, will fall away as I ascend. Oh, was there not, from the first, more poison in thy nature than in mine?"

To Beatrice,—so radically had her earthly part been wrought upon by Rappaccini's skill—as poison had been life, so the powerful antidote was death; and thus the poor victim of man's ingenuity and of thwarted nature, and of the fatality that attends all such efforts of perverted wisdom, perished there, at the feet of her father and Giovanni. Just at that moment Professor Pietro Baglioni looked forth from the window, and called loudly, in a tone of triumph mixed with horror, to the thunderstricken man of science,—

"Rappaccini! Rappaccini! and is *this* the upshot of your experiment!"

The Murders in the Rue Morgue

BY EDGAR ALLAN POE

*What song the Syrens sang, or what name Achilles
assumed when he hid himself among women, although
puzzling questions, are not beyond all conjecture.*

SIR THOMAS BROWNE, *Urn-Burial*

THE mental features discoursed of as the analytical, are, in themselves, but little susceptible of analysis. We appreciate them only in their effects. We know of them, among other things, that they are always to their possessor, when inordinately possessed, a source of the liveliest enjoyment. As the strong man exults in his physical ability, delighting in such exercises as call his muscles into action, so glories the analyst in that moral activity which *disentangles.* He derives pleasure from even the most trivial occupations bringing his talents into play. He is fond of enigmas, of conundrums, of hieroglyphics; exhibiting in his solutions of each a degree of *acumen* which appears to the ordinary apprehension preternatural. His results, brought about by the very soul and essence of method, have, in truth, the whole air of intuition. The faculty of re-solution is possibly much invigorated by mathematical study, and especially by that highest branch of it which, unjustly, and merely on account of its retrograde operations, has been called, as if *par excellence,* analysis. Yet to calculate is not in itself to analyze. A chess-player, for example, does the one without effort at the other. It follows that the game of chess, in its effects upon mental character, is greatly misunderstood. I am not now writing a treatise, but simply prefacing a somewhat peculiar narrative by observations very much at random; I will, therefore, take occasion to assert that the higher powers of the reflective intellect are more decidedly and more usefully tasked by the unostentatious game of draughts than by all the elaborate frivolity of chess. In this latter, where the pieces have different and *bizarre* motions, with various and variable values, what is only complex is mistaken (a not unusual error) for what is profound. The *attention* is here called powerfully into play. If it flag for an instant, an oversight is committed, resulting in injury or defeat. The possible moves being not only manifold but involute, the chances of such oversights are multiplied; and in nine cases out of ten it is the more concentrative rather than the more acute player who conquers. In draughts, on the contrary, where the moves are *unique* and have but little variation, the probabilities of inadvertence are diminished, and the mere attention being left comparatively unemployed, what advantages are obtained by either party are obtained by superior *acumen*. To be less abstract—Let us suppose a game of draughts where the pieces are reduced to four kings, and where, of course, no oversight is to be expected. It is obvious that here the victory can be decided (the players being at all equal) only by some *recherché* movement, the result of some strong exertion of the intellect. Deprived of ordinary resources, the analyst throws himself into the spirit of his opponent, identifies himself therewith, and not unfrequently sees thus, at a glance, the sole methods (sometimes indeed absurdly simple ones) by which he may seduce into error or hurry into miscalculation.

Whist has long been noted for its influence upon what is termed the calculating power; and men of the highest order of intellect have been known to take an apparently unaccountable delight in it, while eschewing chess as frivolous. Beyond doubt there is nothing of a similar nature so greatly tasking the faculty of analysis. The best chess-player in Christendom *may* be little more than the best player of chess; but proficiency in whist implies capacity for success in all these more important undertakings where mind struggles with mind. When I say proficiency, I mean that perfection in the game which includes a comprehension of *all* the sources whence legitimate advantage may be derived. These are not only manifold but multiform, and lie frequently among recesses of thought altogether inaccessible to the ordinary understanding. To observe attentively is to remember distinctly; and, so far, the concentrative chess-player will do very well at whist; while the rules of Hoyle (themselves based upon the mere mechanism of the game) are sufficiently and generally comprehensible. Thus to have a retentive memory, and to proceed by "the book," are points commonly regarded as the sum total of good playing. But it is in matters beyond the limits of mere rule that the skill of the analyst is evinced. He makes, in silence, a host of observations and inferences. So, perhaps, do his companions; and the difference in the extent of the information obtained, lies not so much in the validity of the inference as in the quality of the observation. The necessary knowledge is that of *what* to observe. Our player confines himself not at all; nor, because the game is the object, does he reject deductions from things external to the game. He examines the countenance of his partner, comparing it carefully with that of each of his opponents. He considers the mode of assorting the cards in each hand; often counting trump by trump, and honor by honor, through the glances bestowed by their holders upon each. He notes every variation of face as the play progresses, gathering a fund of thought from the differences in the expression of certainty, of surprise, of triumph, or chagrin. From the manner of gathering up a trick he judges whether the person taking it can make another in the suit. He recognizes what is played through feint, by the air with which it is thrown upon the table. A casual or inadvertent word; the accidental dropping or turning of a card, with the accompanying anxiety or carelessness in regard to its concealment; the counting of the tricks, with the order of their arrangement; embarrassment, hesitation, eagerness or trepidation—all afford, to his apparently intuitive perception, indications of the true state of affairs. The first two or three rounds having been played, he is in full possession of the contents of each hand, and thenceforward puts down his cards with as absolute a precision of purpose as if the rest of the party had turned outward the faces of their own.

The analytical power should not be confounded with simple ingenuity; for while the analyst is necessarily ingenious, the ingenious man is often remarkably incapable of analysis. The consecutive or combining power, by which ingenuity is usually manifested, and to which the phrenologists (I believe erroneously) have assigned a separate organ, supposing it a primitive faculty, has been so frequently seen in those whose intellect bordered otherwise upon idiocy, as to have attracted general observation among writers on morals. Between ingenuity and the analytic ability there exists a difference far greater, indeed, than that between the fancy and the imagination, but of a character very strictly analogous. It will be found, in fact, that the ingenious are always fanciful, and the *truly* imaginative never otherwise than analytic.

The narrative which follows will appear to the reader somewhat in the light of a commentary upon the propositions just advanced.

Residing in Paris during the spring and part of the summer of 18—, I there became acquainted with a Monsieur C. Auguste Dupin. This young gentleman was of an excellent—indeed of an illustrious family, but, by a variety of untoward events, had been reduced to such poverty that the energy of his character succumbed beneath it, and he ceased to bestir himself in the world, or to care for the retrieval of his fortunes. By courtesy of his creditors, there still remained in his possession a small remnant of his patrimony; and, upon the income arising from this, he managed, by means of a rigorous economy, to procure the necessaries of life, without troubling himself about its superfluities. Books, indeed, were his sole luxuries, and in Paris these are easily obtained.

Our first meeting was at an obscure library in the Rue Montmartre, where the accident of our both being in search of the same very rare and very remarkable volume, brought us into closer communion. We saw each other again and again. I was deeply interested in the little family history which he detailed to me with all that candor which a Frenchman indulges whenever mere self is the theme. I was astonished, too, at the vast extent of his reading; and, above all, I felt my soul enkindled within me by the wild fervor, and the vivid freshness of his imagination. Seeking in Paris the objects I then sought, I felt that the society of such a man would be to me a treasure beyond price; and this feeling I frankly confided to him. It was at length arranged that we should live together during my stay in the city; and as my worldly circumstances were somewhat less embarrassed than his own, I was permitted to be at the expense of renting, and furnishing in a style which suited the rather fantastic gloom of our common temper, a time-eaten and grotesque mansion, long deserted through superstitions into which we did not inquire, and tottering to its fall in a retired and desolate portion of the Faubourg St. Germain.

Had the routine of our life at this place been known to the world, we should have been regarded as madmen—although, perhaps, as madmen of a harmless nature. Our seclusion was perfect. We admitted no visitors. Indeed the locality of our retirement had been carefully kept a secret from my own former associates; and it had been many years since Dupin had ceased to know or be known in Paris. We existed within ourselves alone.

It was a freak of fancy in my friend (for what else shall I call it?) to be enamored of the Night for her own sake; and into this *bizarrerie,* as into all his others, I quietly fell; giving myself up to his wild whims with a perfect *abandon.* The sable divinity would not herself dwell with us always; but we could counterfeit her presence. At the first dawn of the morning we closed all the massy shutters of our old building; lighted a couple of tapers which, strongly perfumed, threw out only the ghastliest and feeblest of rays. By the aid of these we then busied our souls in dreams—reading, writing, or conversing, until warned by the clock of the advent of the true Darkness. Then we sallied forth into the streets, arm and arm, continuing the topics of the day, or roaming far and wide until a late hour, seeking, amid the wild lights and shadows of the populous city, that infinity of mental excitement which quiet observation can afford.

At such times I could not help remarking and admiring (although from his rich ideality I had been prepared to expect it) a peculiar analytic ability in Dupin. He seemed, too, to take an eager delight in this exercise—if not exactly in its display—and did not hesitate to confess the pleasure thus derived. He boasted to me, with a low chuckling laugh, that most men, in respect to himself, wore windows in their bosoms, and was wont to follow up such assertions by direct and very startling proofs of his intimate knowledge of my own. His manner at these moments was frigid and abstract; his eyes were vacant in expression; while his voice, usually a rich tenor, rose into a treble which would have sounded petulantly but for the deliberateness and entire distinctness of the enun-ciation. Observing him in these moods, I often dwelt meditatively upon the old philosophy of the Bi-Part Soul, and amused myself with the fancy of a double Dupin—the creative and the resolvent.

Let it not be supposed, from what I have just said, that I am detailing any mystery, or penning any romance. What I have described in the Frenchman was merely the result of an excited, or perhaps of a diseased, intelligence. But of the character of his remarks at the periods in question an example will best convey the idea.

We were strolling one night down a long dirty street, in the vicinity of the Palais Royal. Being both, apparently, occupied with thought, neither of us had spoken a syllable for fifteen minutes at least. All at once Dupin broke forth with these words:

"He is a very little fellow, that's true, and would do better for the *Théâtre des Variétés.*"

"There can be no doubt of that," I replied unwittingly, and not at first observing (so much had I been absorbed in reflection) the extraordinary manner in which the speaker had chimed in with my meditations. In an instant afterwards I recollected myself, and my astonishment was profound.

"Dupin," said I, gravely, "this is beyond my comprehension. I do not hesitate to say that I am amazed, and can scarcely credit my senses. How was it possible you should know I was thinking of ———?" Here I paused, to ascertain beyond a doubt whether he really knew of whom I thought.

——— "of Chantilly," said he, "why do you pause? You were remarking to yourself that his diminutive figure unfitted him for tragedy."

This was precisely what had formed the subject of my reflections. Chantilly was a *quondam* cobbler of the Rue St. Denis, who, becoming stage-mad, had attempted the *rôle* of Xerxes, in Crébillon's tragedy so called, and been notoriously Pasquinaded for his pains.

"Tell me, for Heaven's sake," I exclaimed, "the method—if method there is—by which you have been enabled to fathom my soul in this matter." In fact I was even more startled than I would have been willing to express.

"It was the fruiterer," replied my friend, "who brought you to the conclusion that the mender of soles was not of sufficient height for Xerxes *et id genus omne.*"

"The fruiterer!—you astonish me—I know no fruiterer whomsoever."

"The man who ran up against you as we entered the street—it may have been fifteen minutes ago."

I now remembered that, in fact, a fruiterer, carrying upon his head a large basket of apples, had nearly thrown me down, by accident, as we passed from the Rue C—— into the thoroughfare where we stood; but what this had to do with Chantilly I could not possibly understand.

There was not a particle of *charlatanerie* about Dupin. "I will explain," he said, "and that you may comprehend all clearly, we will first retrace the course of your meditations, from the moment in which I spoke to you until that of the *rencontre* with the fruiterer in question. The larger links of the chain run thus—Chantilly, Orion, Dr. Nichols, Epicurus, Stereotomy, the street stones, the fruiterer."

There are few persons who have not, at some period of their lives, amused themselves in retracing the steps by which particular conclusions of their own minds have been attained. The occupation is often full of interest; and he who attempts it for the first time is astonished by the apparently illimitable distance and incoherence between the starting-point and the goal. What, then, must have been my amazement when I heard the Frenchman speak what he had just spoken, and when I could not help acknowledging that he had spoken the truth. He continued:

"We had been talking of horses, if I remember aright, just before leaving the Rue C——. This was the last subject we discussed. As we crossed into this street, a fruiterer, with a large basket upon his head, brushing quickly past us, thrust you upon a pile of paving-stones collected at a spot where the causeway is undergoing repair. You stepped upon one of the loose fragments, slipped, slightly strained your ankle, appeared vexed or sulky, muttered a few words, turned to look at the pile, and then proceeded in silence. I was not particularly attentive to what you did; but observation has become with me, of late, a species of necessity.

"You kept your eyes upon the ground—glancing, with a petulant expression, at the holes and ruts in the pavement (so that I saw you were still thinking of the stones), until we reached the little alley called Lamartine, which has been paved, by way of experiment, with the overlapping and riveted blocks. Here your countenance brightened up, and, perceiving your lips move, I could not doubt that you murmured the word 'stereotomy,' a term very affectedly applied to this species of pavement. I knew that you could not say to yourself 'stereotomy' without being brought to think of atomies, and thus of the theories of Epicurus; and since, when we discussed this subject not very long ago, I mentioned to you how singularly, yet with how little notice, the vague guesses of that noble Greek had met with confirmation in the late nebular cosmogony, I felt that you could not avoid casting your eyes upwards to the great *nebula* in Orion, and I certainly expected that you would do so. You did look up; and I was now assured that I had correctly followed your steps. But in that bitter *tirade* upon Chantilly, which appeared in yesterday's *'Musée,'* the satirist, making some disgraceful allusions to the cobbler's change of name upon assuming the buskin, quoted a Latin line about which we have often conversed. I mean the line

Perdidit antiquum litera prima sonum

I had told you that this was in reference to Orion, formerly written Urion; and, from certain pungencies connected with this explanation, I was aware that you could not have forgotten it. It was clear, therefore, that you would not fail to combine the two ideas of Orion and Chantilly. That you did combine them I saw by the character of the smile which passed over your lips. You thought of the poor cobbler's immolation. So far, you had been stooping in your gait; but now I saw you draw yourself up to your full height. I was then sure that you reflected upon the diminutive figure of Chantilly. At this point I interrupted your meditations to remark that as, in fact, he *was* a very little fellow—that Chantilly —he would do better at the *Théâtre des Variétés.*"

Not long after this, we were looking over an evening edition of the "Gazette des Tribunaux," when the following paragraphs arrested our attention.

"EXTRAORDINARY MURDERS.—This morning, about three o'clock, the inhabitants of the Quartier St. Roch were aroused from sleep by a succession of terrific shrieks, issuing, apparently, from the fourth story of a house in the Rue Morgue, known to be in the sole occupancy of one Madame L'Espanaye, and her daughter, Mademoiselle Camille L'Espanaye. After some delay, occasioned by a fruitless attempt to procure admission in the usual manner, the gateway was broken in with a crowbar, and eight or ten of the neighbors entered, accompanied by two *gendarmes*. By this time the cries had ceased; but, as the party rushed up the first flight of stairs, two or more rough voices, in angry contention, were distinguished, and seemed to proceed from the upper part of the house. As the second landing was reached, these sounds, also, had ceased, and everything remained perfectly quiet. The party spread themselves, and hurried from room to room. Upon arriving at a large back chamber in the fourth story (the door of which, being found locked, with the key inside, was forced open), a spectacle presented itself which struck every one present not less with horror than with astonishment.

"The apartment was in the wildest disorder—the furniture broken and thrown about in all directions. There was only one bedstead; and from this the bed had been removed, and thrown into the middle of the floor. On a chair lay a razor, besmeared with blood. On the hearth were two or three long and thick tresses of gray human hair, also dabbled in blood, and seeming to have been pulled out by the roots. Upon the floor were found four Napoleons, an earring of topaz, three large silver spoons, three smaller of *métal d'Alger,* and two bags, containing nearly four thousand francs in gold. The drawers of a *bureau,* which stood in one corner, were open, and had been, apparently, rifled, although many articles still remained in them. A small iron safe was discovered under the *bed* (not under the bedstead). It was open, with the key still in the door. It had no contents beyond a few old letters, and other papers of little consequence.

"Of Madame L'Espanaye no traces were here seen; but an unusual quantity of soot being observed in the fireplace, a search was made in the chimney, and (horrible to relate!) the corpse of the daughter, head downwards, was dragged therefrom; it having been thus forced up the narrow aperture for a considerable distance. The body was quite warm. Upon examining it, many excoriations were perceived, no doubt occasioned by the violence with which it had been thrust up and disengaged. Upon the face were many severe scratches, and, upon the throat, dark bruises, and deep indentations of finger-nails, as if the deceased had been throttled to death.

"After a thorough investigation of every portion of the house, without farther discovery, the party made its way into a small paved yard in the rear of the building, where lay the corpse of the old lady, with her throat so entirely cut that, upon an attempt to raise her, the head fell off. The body, as well as the head, was fearfully mutilated—the former so much so as scarcely to retain any semblance of humanity.

"To this horrible mystery there is not as yet, we believe, the slightest clue."

The next day's paper had these additional particulars.

"*The Tragedy in the Rue Morgue.* Many individuals have been examined in relation to this most extraordinary and frightful affair" (the word '*affaire*' has not yet, in France, that levity of import which it conveys with us), "but nothing whatever has transpired to throw light upon it. We give below all the material testimony elicited.

"*Pauline Dubourg,* laundress, deposes that she has known both the deceased for three years, having washed for them during that period.

The old lady and her daughter seemed on good terms—very affectionate towards each other. They were excellent pay. Could not speak in regard to their mode or means of living. Believed that Madame L. told fortunes for a living. Was reputed to have money put by. Never met any persons in the house when she called for the clothes or took them home. Was sure that they had no servant in employ. There appeared to be no furniture in any part of the building except in the fourth story.

"*Pierre Moreau*, tobacconist, deposes that he has been in the habit of selling small quantities of tobacco and snuff to Madame L'Espanaye for nearly four years. Was born in the neighborhood, and has always resided there. The deceased and her daughter had occupied the house in which the corpses were found, for more than six years. It was formerly occupied by a jeweler, who under-let the upper rooms to various persons. The house was the property of Madame L. She became dissatisfied with the abuse of the premises by her tenant, and moved into them herself, refusing to let any portion. The old lady was childish. Witness had seen the daughter some five or six times during the six years. The two lived an exceedingly retired life—were reputed to have money. Had heard it said among the neighbors that Madame L. told fortunes—did not believe it. Had never seen any person enter the door except the old lady and her daughter, a porter once or twice, and a physician some eight or ten times.

"Many other persons, neighbors, gave evidence to the same effect. No one was spoken of as frequenting the house. It was not known whether there were any living connections of Madame L. and her daughter. The shutters of the front windows were seldom opened. Those in the rear were always closed, with the exception of the large back room, fourth story. The house was a good house—not very old.

"*Isidore Musèt, gendarme,* deposes that he was called to the house about three o'clock in the morning, and found some twenty or thirty persons at the gateway, endeavoring to gain admittance. Forced it open, at length, with a bayonet—not with a crowbar. Had but little difficulty in getting it open, on account of its being a double or folding gate, and bolted neither at bottom nor top. The shrieks were continued until the gate was forced—and then suddenly ceased. They seemed to be screams of some person (or persons) in great agony—were loud and drawn out, not short and quick. Witness led the way upstairs. Upon reaching the first landing, heard two voices in loud and angry contention—the one a gruff voice, the other much shriller—a very strange voice. Could distinguish some words of the former, which was that of a Frenchman. Was positive that it was not a woman's voice. Could distinguish the words '*sacré*' and '*diable.*' The shrill voice was that of a foreigner. Could not be sure whether it was the voice of a man or of a woman. Could not make out what was said, but believed the language to be Spanish. The state of the room and of the bodies was described by this witness as we described them yesterday.

"*Henri Duval,* a neighbor, and by trade a silversmith, deposes that he was one of the party who first entered the house. Corroborates the testimony of Musèt in general. As soon as they forced an entrance, they reclosed the door, to keep out the crowd, which collected very fast, notwithstanding the lateness of the hour. The shrill voice, the witness thinks, was that of an Italian. Was certain it was not French. Could not be sure that it was a man's voice. It might have been a woman's. Was not acquainted with the Italian language. Could not distinguish the words, but was convinced by the intonation that the speaker was an Italian. Knew Madame L. and her daughter. Had conversed with both frequently. Was sure that the shrill voice was not that of either of the deceased.

"——— *Odenheimer restaurateur.* This witness volunteered his testimony. Not speaking French, was examined through an interpreter. Is a native of Amsterdam. Was passing the house at the time of the shrieks. They lasted for several minutes—probably ten. They were long and loud—very awful and distressing. Was one of those who entered the building. Corroborated the previous evidence in every respect but one. Was sure that the shrill voice was that of a man—of a Frenchman. Could not distinguish the words uttered. They were loud and quick—unequal —spoken apparently in fear as well as in anger. The voice was harsh— not so much shrill as harsh. Could not call it a shrill voice. The gruff voice said repeatedly '*sacré,*' '*diable*' and once '*mon Dieu.*'

"*Jules Mignaud,* banker, of the firm of Mignaud et Fils, Rue Deloraine. Is the elder Mignaud. Madame L'Espanaye had some property. Had opened an account with his banking house in the spring of the year ——— (eight years previously). Made frequent deposits in small sums. Had checked for nothing until the third day before her death, when she took out in person the sum of 4000 francs. This sum was paid in gold, and a clerk sent home with the money.

"*Adolphe Le Bon,* clerk to Mignaud et Fils, deposes that on the day in question, about noon, he accompanied Madame L'Espanaye to her residence with the 4000 francs, put up in two bags. Upon the door being opened, Mademoiselle L. appeared and took from his hands one of the bags, while the old lady relieved him of the other. He then bowed and departed. Did not see any person in the street at the time. It is a byestreet—very lonely.

"*William Bird,* tailor, deposes that he was one of the party who entered the house. Is an Englishman. Has lived in Paris two years. Was one of the first to ascend the stairs. Heard the voices in contention. The gruff voice was that of a Frenchman. Could make out several words, but cannot now remember all. Heard distinctly *'sacré'* and *'mon Dieu.'* There was a sound at the moment as if of several persons struggling—a scraping and scuffling sound. The thrill voice was very loud—louder than the gruff one. Is sure that it was not the voice of an Englishman. Appeared to be that of a German. Might have been a woman's voice. Does not understand German.

"Four of the above-named witnesses, being recalled, deposed that the door of the chamber in which was found the body of Mademoiselle L. was locked on the inside when the party reached it. Everything was perfectly silent—no groans or noises of any kind. Upon forcing the door no person was seen. The windows, both of the back and front room, were down and firmly fastened from within. A door between the two rooms was closed, but not locked. The door leading from the front room into the passage was locked, with the key on the inside. A small room in the front of the house, on the fourth story, at the head of the passage, was open, the door being ajar. This room was crowded with old beds, boxes, and so forth. These were carefully removed and searched. There was not an inch of any portion of the house which was not carefully searched. Sweeps were sent up and down the chimneys. The house was a four-story one, with garrets (*mansardes*). A trap-door on the roof was nailed down very securely—did not appear to have been opened for years. The time elapsing between the hearing of the voices in contention and the breaking open of the room door, was variously stated by the witnesses. Some made it as short as three minutes—some as long as five. The door was opened with difficulty.

"*Alfonzo Garcio,* undertaker, deposes that he resides in the Rue Morgue. Is a native of Spain. Was one of the party who entered the house. Did not proceed upstairs. Is nervous, and was apprehensive of the consequences of agitation. Heard the voices in contention. The gruff voice was that of a Frenchman. Could not distinguish what was said. The shrill voice was that of an Englishman—is sure of this. Does not understand the English language, but judges by the intonation.

"*Alberto Montani,* confectioner, deposes that he was among the first to ascend the stairs. Heard the voices in question. The gruff voice was that of a Frenchman. Distinguished several words. The speaker appeared to be expostulating. Could not make out the words of the shrill voice. Spoke quick and unevenly. Thinks it the voice of a Russian. Corroborates the general testimony. Is an Italian. Never conversed with a native of Russia.

"Several witnesses, recalled, here testified that the chimneys of all the rooms on the fourth story were too narrow to admit the passage of a human being. By 'sweeps' were meant cylindrical sweeping-brushes, such as are employed by those who clean chimneys. These brushes were passed up and down every flue in the house. There is no back passage by which any one could have descended while the party proceeded up stairs. The body of Mademoiselle L'Espanaye was so firmly wedged in the chimney that it could not be got down until four or five of the party united their strength.

"*Paul Dumas,* physician, deposes that he was called to view the bodies about daybreak. They were both then lying on the sacking of the bedstead in the chamber where Mademoiselle L. was found. The corpse of the young lady was much bruised and excoriated. The fact that it had been thrust up the chimney would sufficiently account for these appearances. The throat was greatly chafed. There were several deep scratches just below the chin, together with a series of livid spots which were evidently the impression of fingers. The face was fearfully discolored, and the eyeballs protruded. The tongue had been partially bitten through. A large bruise was discovered upon the pit of the stomach, produced, apparently, by the pressure of a knee. In the opinion of M. Dumas, Mademoiselle L'Espanaye had been throttled to death by some person or persons unknown. The corpse of the mother was horribly mutilated. All the bones of the right leg and arm were more or less shattered. The left *tibia* much splintered, as well as all the ribs of the left side. Whole body dreadfully bruised and discolored. It was not possible to say how the injuries had been inflicted. A heavy club of wood, or a broad bar of iron—a chair—any large, heavy, and obtuse weapon would have produced such results, if wielded by the hands of a very powerful man. No woman could have inflicted the blows with any weapon. The head of the deceased, when seen by witness, was entirely separated from the body, and was also greatly shattered. The throat had evidently been cut with some very sharp instrument—probably with a razor.

"*Alexandre Etienne,* surgeon, was called with M. Dumas to view the bodies. Corroborated the testimony, and the opinions of M. Dumas.

"Nothing farther of importance was elicited, although several other persons were examined. A murder so mysterious, and so perplexing in all its particulars, was never before committed in Paris—if indeed a murder has been committed at all. The police are entirely at fault—an unusual occurrence in affairs of this nature. There is not, however, the shadow of a clue apparent."

The evening edition of the paper stated that the greatest excitement still continued in the Quartier St. Roch—that the premises in question had been carefully re-searched, and fresh examinations of witnesses instituted, but all to no purpose. A postscript, however, mentioned that Adolphe Le Bon had been arrested and imprisoned—although nothing appeared to criminate him, beyond the facts already detailed.

Dupin seemed singularly interested in the progress of this affair—at least so I judged from his manner, for he made no comments. It was only after the announcement that Le Bon had been imprisoned, that he asked me my opinion respecting the murders.

I could merely agree with all Paris in considering them an insoluble mystery. I saw no means by which it would be possible to trace the murderer.

"We must not judge of the means," said Dupin, "by this shell of an examination. The Parisian police, so much extolled for *acumen,* are cunning, but no more. There is no method in their proceedings, beyond the method of the moment. They make a vast parade of measures; but, not unfrequently, these are so ill adapted to the objects proposed, as to put us in mind of Monsieur Jourdain's calling for his *robe-de-chambre— pour mieux entendre la musique.* The results attained by them are not unfrequently surprising, but, for the most part, are brought about by simple diligence and activity. When these qualities are unavailing, their schemes fail. Vidocq, for example, was a good guesser, and a persevering man. But, without educated thought, he erred continually by the very intensity of his investigations. He impaired his vision by holding the object too close. He might see, perhaps, one or two points with unusual clearness, but in so doing he, necessarily, lost sight of the matter as a whole. Thus there is such a thing as being too profound. Truth is not always in a well. In fact, as regards the more important knowledge, I do believe that she is invariably superficial. The depth lies in the valleys where we seek her, and not upon the mountain-tops where she is found. The modes and sources of this kind of error are well typified in the contemplation of the heavenly bodies. To look at a star by glances—to view it in a side-long way, by turning towards it the exterior portions of the *retina* (more susceptible of feeble impressions of light than the interior), is to behold the star distinctly—is to have the best appreciation of its luster—a luster which grows dim just in proportion as we turn our vision *fully* upon it. A greater number of rays actually fall upon the eye in the latter case, but, in the former, there is the more refined capacity for comprehension. By undue profundity we perplex and enfeeble thought; and it is possible to make even Venus herself vanish from the firmament by a scrutiny too sustained, too concentrated, or too direct.

"As for these murders, let us enter into some examinations for ourselves, before we make up an opinion respecting them. An inquiry will afford us amusement" (I thought this an odd term, so applied, but said nothing), "and, besides, Le Bon once rendered me a service for which I am not ungrateful. We will go and see the premises with our own eyes. I know G——, the Prefect of Police, and shall have no difficulty in obtaining the necessary permission."

The permission was obtained, and we proceeded at once to the Rue Morgue. This is one of those miserable thoroughfares, which intervene between the Rue Richelieu and the Rue St. Roch. It was late in the afternoon when we reached it; as this quarter is at a great distance from that in which we resided. The house was readily found; for there were still many persons gazing up at the closed shutters, with an objectless curiosity, from the opposite side of the way. It was an ordinary Parisian house, with a gateway, on one side of which was a glazed watch-box, with a sliding panel in the window, indicating a *loge de concierge*. Before going in we walked up the street, turned down an alley, and then, again turning, passed in the rear of the building—Dupin, meanwhile, examining the whole neighborhood, as well as the house, with a minuteness of attention for which I could see no possible object.

Retracing our steps, we came again to the front of the dwelling, rang, and, having shown our credentials, were admitted by the agents in charge. We went upstairs—into the chamber where the body of Mademoiselle L'Espanaye had been found, and where both the deceased still lay. The disorders of the room had, as usual, been suffered to exist. I saw nothing beyond what had been stated in the "Gazette des Tribunaux." Dupin scrutinized everything—not excepting the bodies of the victims. We then went into the other rooms, and into the yard: a *gendarme* accompanying us throughout. The examination occupied us until dark, when we took our departure. On our way home my companion stopped in for a moment at the office of the daily papers.

I have said that the whims of my friend were manifold, and that *Je les ménageais:*—for this phrase there is no English equivalent. It was his humor, now, to decline all conversation on the subject of the murder, until about noon the next day. He then asked me, suddenly, if I had observed anything *peculiar* at the scene of the atrocity.

There was something in his manner of emphasizing the word "peculiar," which caused me to shudder, without knowing why.

"No, nothing *peculiar*," I said; "nothing more, at least, than we both saw stated in the paper."

"The 'Gazette,'" he replied, "has not entered, I fear, into the unusual horror of the thing. But dismiss the idle opinions of this print. It appears to me that this mystery is considered insoluble, for the very reason which should cause it to be regarded as easy of solution—I mean for the *outré* character of its features. The police are confounded by the seeming absence of motive—not for the murder itself—but for the atrocity of the murder. They are puzzled, too, by the seeming impossibility of reconciling the voices heard in contention, with the facts that no one was discovered upstairs but the assassinated Mademoiselle L'Espanaye, and that there were no means of egress without the notice of the party ascending. The wild disorder of the room; the corpse thrust, with the head downwards, up the chimney; the frightful mutilation of the body of the old lady; these considerations, with those just mentioned, and others which I need not mention, have sufficed to paralyze the powers, by putting completely at fault the boasted *acumen,* of the government agents. They have fallen into the gross but common error of confounding the unusual with the abstruse. But it is by these deviations from the plane of the ordinary, that reason feels its way, if at all, in its search for the true. In investigations such as we are now pursuing, it should not be so much asked 'what has occurred,' as 'what has occurred that has never occurred before.' In fact, the facility with which I shall arrive, or have arrived, at the solution of this mystery, is in the direct ratio of its apparent insolubility in the eyes of the police."

I stared at the speaker in mute astonishment.

"I am now awaiting," continued he, looking towards the door of our apartment—"I am now awaiting a person who, although perhaps not the perpetrator of these butcheries, must have been in some measure implicated in their perpetration. Of the worst portion of the crimes committed, it is probable that he is innocent. I hope that I am right in this supposition; for upon it I build my expectation of reading the entire riddle. I look for the man here—in this room—every moment. It is true that he may not arrive; but the probability is that he will. Should he come, it will be necessary to detain him. Here are pistols; and we both know how to use them when occasion demands their use."

I took the pistols, scarcely knowing what I did, or believing what I heard, while Dupin went on, very much as if in a soliloquy. I have already spoken of his abstract manner at such times. His discourse was addressed to myself; but his voice, although by no means loud, had that intonation which is commonly employed in speaking to some one at a great distance. His eyes, vacant in expression, regarded only the wall.

"That the voices heard in contention," he said, "by the party upon the stairs, were not the voices of the women themselves, was fully proved by the evidence. This relieves us of all doubt upon the question whether the old lady could have first destroyed the daughter, and afterward have committed suicide. I speak of this point chiefly for the sake of method; for the strength of Madame L'Espanaye would have been utterly unequal to the task of thrusting her daughter's corpse up the chimney as it was found; and the nature of the wounds upon her own person entirely preclude the idea of self-destruction. Murder, then, has been committed by some third party; and the voices of this third party were those heard in contention. Let me now advert—not to the whole testimony respecting these voices—but to what was *peculiar* in that testimony. Did you observe anything peculiar about it?"

I remarked that, while all the witnesses agreed in supposing the gruff voice to be that of a Frenchman, there was much disagreement in regard to the shrill, or, as one individual termed it, the harsh voice.

"That was the evidence itself," said Dupin, "but it was not the peculiarity of the evidence. You have observed nothing distinctive. Yet there *was* something to be observed. The witnesses, as you remark, agreed about the gruff voice; they were here unanimous. But in regard to the shrill voice, the peculiarity is—not that they disagreed—but that, while an Italian, an Englishman, a Spaniard, a Hollander, and a Frenchman attempted to describe it, each one spoke of it as that *of a foreigner.* Each is sure that it was not the voice of one of his own countrymen. Each likens it—not to the voice of an individual of any nation with whose language he is conversant—but the converse. The Frenchman supposes it the voice of a Spaniard, and 'might have distinguished some words *had be been acquainted with the Spanish.'* The Dutchman maintains it to have been that of a Frenchman; but we find it stated that *'not understanding French this witness was examined through an interpreter.'* The Englishman thinks it the voice of a German, and *'does not understand German.'* The Spaniard 'is sure' that it was that of an Englishman, but 'judges by the intonation' altogether, *'as he has no knowledge of the English.'* The Italian believes it the voice of a Russian, but *'has never conversed with a native of Russia.'* A second Frenchman differs, moreover, with the first, and is positive that the voice was that of an Italian; but, *not being cognizant of that tongue,* is, like the Spaniard, 'convinced by the intonation.' Now, how strangely unusual must that voice have really been, about which such testimony as this *could* have been elicited!—in whose *tones,* even, denizens of the five great divisions of Europe could recognize nothing familiar! You will say that it might have been the voice of an Asiatic—of an African. Neither Asiatics nor Africans abound in Paris; but, without denying the inference, I will now merely call your attention to three points. The voice is termed by one witness 'harsh rather than shrill.' It is represented by two others to have been 'quick and *unequal.'* No words—no sounds resembling words—were by any witness mentioned as distinguishable.

"I know not," continued Dupin, "what impression I may have made, so far, upon your own understanding; but I do not hesitate to say that legitimate deductions even from this portion of the testimony—the portion respecting the gruff and shrill voices—are in themselves sufficient to engender a suspicion which should give direction to all farther progress in the investigation of the mystery. I said 'legitimate deductions'; but my meaning is not thus fully expressed. I designed to imply that the deductions are the *sole* proper ones, and that the suspicion arises *inevitably* from them as the single result. What the suspicion is, however,

I will not say just yet. I merely wish you to bear in mind that, with myself, it was sufficiently forcible to give a definite form—a certain tendency—to my inquiries in the chamber.

"Let us now transport ourselves, in fancy, to this chamber. What shall we first seek here? The means of egress employed by the murderers. It is not too much to say that neither of us believe in præternatural events. Madame and Mademoiselle L'Espanaye were not destroyed by spirits. The doers of the deed were material, and escaped materially. Then how? Fortunately, there is but one mode of reasoning upon the point, and that mode *must* lead us to a definite decision.—Let us examine, each by each, the possible means of egress. It is clear that the assassins were in the room where Mademoiselle L'Espanaye was found, or at least in the room adjoining, when the party ascended the stairs. It is then only from these two apartments that we have to seek issues. The police have laid bare the floors, the ceilings, and the masonry of the walls, in every direction. No *secret* issues could have escaped their vigilance. But not trusting to *their* eyes, I examined with my own. There were, then, *no* secret issues. Both doors leading from the rooms into the passage were securely locked, with the keys inside. Let us turn to the chimneys. These, although of ordinary width for some eight or ten feet above the hearths, will not admit, throughout their extent, the body of a large cat. The impossibility of egress, by means already stated, being thus absolute, we are reduced to the windows. Through those of the front room no one could have escaped without notice from the crowd in the street. The murderers *must* have passed, then, through those of the back room. Now, brought to this conclusion in so unequivocal a manner as we are, it is not our part, as reasoners, to reject it on account of apparent impossibilities. It is only left for us to prove that these apparent 'impossibilities' are, in reality, not such.

"There are two windows in the chamber. One of them is unobstructed by furniture, and is wholly visible. The lower portion of the other is hidden from view by the head of the unwieldy bedstead which is thrust close up against it. The former was found securely fastened from within. It resisted the utmost force of those who endeavored to raise it. A large gimlet-hole had been pierced in its frame to the left, and a very stout nail was found fitted therein, nearly to the head. Upon examining the other window, a similar nail was seen similarly fitted in it; and a vigorous attempt to raise this sash, failed also. The police were now entirely satisfied that egress had not been in these directions. And, *therefore,* it was thought a matter of supererogation to withdraw the nails and open the windows.

"My own examination was somewhat more particular, and was so for the reason I have just given—because here it was, I knew, that all apparent impossibilities *must* be proved to be not such in reality.

"I proceeded to think thus—*à posteriori*. The murderers *did* escape from one of these windows. This being so, they could not have re-fastened the sashes from the inside, as they were found fastened;—the consideration which put a stop, through its obviousness, to the scrutiny of the police in this quarter. Yet the sashes *were* fastened. They *must,* then, have the power of fastening themselves. There was no escape from this conclusion. I stepped to the unobstructed casement, withdrew the nail with some difficulty, and attempted to raise the sash. It resisted all my efforts, as I had anticipated. A concealed spring must, I now knew, exist; and this corroboration of my idea convinced me that my premises, at least, were correct, however mysterious still appeared the circumstances attending the nails. A careful search soon brought to light the hidden spring. I pressed it, and, satisfied with the discovery, forbore to upraise the sash.

"I now replaced the nail and regarded it attentively. A person passing out through this window might have reclosed it, and the spring would have caught—but the nail could not have been replaced. The conclusion was plain, and again narrowed in the field of my investigations. The assassins *must* have escaped through the other window. Supposing, then, the springs upon each sash to be the same, as was probable, there *must* be found a difference between the nails, or at least between the modes of their fixture. Getting upon the sacking of the bedstead, I looked over the head-board minutely at the second casement. Passing my hand down behind the board, I readily discovered and pressed the spring, which was, as I had supposed, identical in character with its neighbor. I now looked at the nail. It was as stout as the other, and apparently fitted in the same manner—driven in nearly up to the head.

"You will say that I was puzzled; but, if you think so, you must have misunderstood the nature of the inductions. To use a sporting phrase, I had not been once 'at fault.' The scent had never for an instant been lost. There was no flaw in any link of the chain. I had traced the secret to its ultimate result,—and that result was *the nail*. It had, I say, in every respect, the appearance of its fellow in the other window; but this fact was an absolute nullity (conclusive as it might seem to be) when compared with the consideration that here, at this point, terminated the clue. 'There *must* be something wrong,' I said, 'about the nail.' I touched it; and the head, with about a quarter of an inch of the shank, came off in my fingers. The rest of the shank was in the gimlet-hole, where it had been broken off. The fracture was an old one (for its edges were incrusted with rust), and had apparently been accomplished by the blow of a hammer, which had partially imbedded, in the top of the bottom sash, the head portion of the nail. I now carefully replaced this head portion in the indentation whence I had taken it, and the resemblance to a perfect nail was complete—the fissure was invisible. Pressing the spring, I gently raised the sash for a few inches; the head went up with it, remaining firm in its bed. I closed the window, and the semblance of the whole nail was again perfect.

"The riddle, so far, was now unriddled. The assassin had escaped through the window which looked upon the bed. Dropping of its own accord upon his exit (or perhaps purposely closed), it had become fastened by the spring; and it was the retention of this spring which had been mistaken by the police for that of the nail,—farther inquiry being thus considered unnecessary.

"The next question is that of the mode of descent. Upon this point I had been satisfied in my walk with you around the building. About five feet and a half from the casement in question there runs a lightning-rod. From this rod it would have been impossible for any one to reach the window itself, to say nothing of entering it. I observed, however, that the shutters of the fourth story were of the peculiar kind called by Parisian carpenters *ferrades*—a kind rarely employed at the present day, but frequently seen upon very old mansions at Lyons and Bordeaux. They are in the form of an ordinary door (a single, not a folding door), except that the upper half is latticed or worked in open trellis—thus affording an excellent hold for the hands. In the present instance these shutters are fully three feet and a half broad. When we saw them from the rear of the house, they were both about half open—that is to say, they stood off at right angles from the wall. It is probable that the police, as well as myself, examined the back of the tenement; but, if so, in looking at these *ferrades* in the line of their breadth (as they must have done), they did not perceive this great breadth itself, or, at all events, failed to take it into due consideration. In fact, having once satisfied themselves that no egress could have been made in this quarter, they would naturally bestow here a very cursory examination. It was clear to me, however, that the shutter belonging to the window at the head of the bed, would, if swung fully back to the wall, reach to within two feet of the lightning-rod. It was also evident that, by exertion of a very unusual degree of activity and courage, an entrance into the window, from the rod, might have been thus effected.—By reaching to the distance of two feet and a half (we now suppose the shutter open to its whole extent) a robber might have taken a firm grasp upon the trellis-work. Letting go, then, his hold upon the rod, placing his feet securely against the wall, and springing boldly from it, he might have swung the shutter so as to close it, and, if we imagine the window open at the time, might even have swung himself into the room.

"I wish you to bear especially in mind that I have spoken of a *very* unusual degree of activity as requisite to success in so hazardous and so difficult a feat. It is my design to show you, first, that the thing might possibly have been accomplished:—but, secondly and *chiefly,* I wish to impress upon your understanding the *very extraordinary*—the almost præternatural character of that agility which could have accomplished it.

"You will say, no doubt, using the language of the law, that 'to make out my case' I should rather undervalue, than insist upon a full estimation of the activity required in this matter. This may be the practice in law, but it is not the usage of reason. My ultimate object is only the truth. My immediate purpose is to lead you to place in juxtaposition that *very unusual* activity of which I have just spoken, with that *very peculiar* shrill (or harsh) and *unequal* voice, about whose nationality no two persons could be found to agree, and in whose utterance no syllabification could be detected."

At these words a vague and half-formed conception of the meaning of Dupin flitted over my mind. I seemed to be upon the verge of comprehension, without power to comprehend—as men, at times, find themselves upon the brink of rememberance, without being able, in the end, to remember. My friend went on with his discourse.

"You will see," he said, "that I have shifted the question from the mode of egress to that of ingress. It was my design to suggest that both were effected in the same manner, at the same point. Let us now revert to the interior of the room. Let us survey the appearances here. The drawers of the bureau, it is said, had been rifled, although many articles of apparel still remained within them. The conclusion here is absurd. It is a mere guess—a very silly one—and no more. How are we to know that the articles found in the drawers were not all these drawers had originally contained? Madame L'Espanaye and her daughter lived an exceedingly retired life—saw no company—seldom went out—had little use for numerous changes of habiliment. Those found were at least of as good quality as any likely to be possessed by these ladies. If a thief had taken any, why did he not take the best—why did he not take all? In a word, why did he abandon four thousand francs in gold to encumber himself with a bundle of linen? The gold *was* abandoned. Nearly the whole sum mentioned by Monsieur Mignaud, the banker, was discovered, in bags, upon the floor. I wish you, therefore, to discard from your thoughts the blundering idea of *motive,* engendered in the brains of the police by that portion of the evidence which speaks of money delivered at the door of the house. Coincidences ten times as remarkable as this (the delivery of the money, and murder committed within three days upon the party receiving it), happen to all of us every

hour of our lives, without attracting even momentary notice. Coincidences, in general, are great stumbling-blocks in the way of that class
of thinkers who have been educated to know nothing of the theory of
probabilities—that theory to which the most glorious objects of human
research are indebted for the most glorious of illustration. In the present
instance, had the gold been gone, the fact of its delivery three days before would have formed something more than a coincidence. It would
have been corroborative of this idea of motive. But, under the real circumstances of the case, if we are to suppose gold the motive of this outrage, we must also imagine the perpetrator so vacillating an idiot as to
have abandoned his gold and his motive together.

"Keeping now steadily in mind the points to which I have drawn
your attention—that peculiar voice, that unusual agility, and that
startling absence of motive in a murder so singularly atrocious as this
—let us glance at the butchery itself. Here is a woman strangled to
death by manual strength, and thrust up a chimney, head downwards.
Ordinary assassins employ no such modes of murder as this. Least of all,
do they thus dispose of the murdered. In the manner of thrusting the
corpse up the chimney, you will admit that there was something *excessively outré*—something altogether irreconcilable with our common
notions of human action, even when we suppose the actors the most depraved of men. Think, too, how great must have been that strength
which could have thrust the body *up* such an aperture so forcibly that
the united vigor of several persons was found barely sufficient to drag
it *down!*

"Turn, now, to other indications of the employment of a vigor most
marvelous. On the hearth were thick tresses—very thick tresses—of gray
human hair. These had been torn out by the roots. You are aware of the
great force necessary in tearing thus from the head even twenty or
thirty hairs together. You saw the locks in question as well as myself.
Their roots (a hideous sight!) were clotted with fragments of the flesh
of the scalp—sure token of the prodigious power which had been exerted
in uprooting perhaps half a million of hairs at a time. The throat of the
old lady was not merely cut, but the head absolutely severed from the
body: the instrument was a mere razor. I wish you also to look at the
brutal ferocity of these deeds. Of the bruises upon the body of Madame
L'Espanaye I do not speak. Monsieur Dumas, and his worthy coadjutor
Monsieur Etienne, have pronounced that they were inflicted by some
obtuse instrument; and so far these gentlemen are very correct. The
obtuse instrument was clearly the stone pavement in the yard, upon
which the victim had fallen from the window which looked in upon
the bed. This idea, however simple it may now seem, escaped the police
for the same reason that the breadth of the shutters escaped them—

because, by the affair of the nails, their perceptions had been hermetically sealed against the possibility of the windows having ever been opened at all.

"If now, in addition to all these things, you have properly reflected upon the odd disorder of the chamber, we have gone so far as to combine the ideas of an agility astounding, a strength superhuman, a ferocity brutal, a butchery without motive, a *grotesquerie* in horror absolutely alien from humanity, and a voice foreign in tone to the ears of men of many nations, and devoid of all distinct or intelligible syllabification. What result, then, has ensued? What impression have I made upon your fancy?"

I felt a creeping of the flesh as Dupin asked me the question. "A madman," I said, "has done this deed—some raving maniac, escaped from a neighboring *Maison de Santé.*"

"In some respects," he replied, "your idea is not irrelevant. But the voices of madmen, even in their wildest paroxysms, are never found to tally with that peculiar voice heard upon the stairs. Madmen are of some nation, and their language, however incoherent in its words, has always the coherence of syllabification. Besides, the hair of a madman is not such as I now hold in my hand. I disentangled this little tuft from the rigidly clutched fingers of Madame L'Espanaye. Tell me what you can make of it."

"Dupin!" I said, completely unnerved; "this hair is most unusual—this is no *human* hair."

"I have not asserted that it is," said he; "but, before we decide this point, I wish you to glance at the little sketch I have here traced upon this paper. It is a *facsimile* drawing of what has been described in one portion of the testimony as 'dark bruises, and deep indentations of fingernails,' upon the throat of Mademoiselle L'Espanaye, and in another (by Messrs. Dumas and Etienne), as a 'series of livid spots, evidently the impression of fingers.'

"You will perceive," continued my friend, spreading out the paper upon the table before us, "that this drawing gives the idea of a firm and fixed hold. There is no *slipping* apparent. Each finger has retained —possibly until the death of the victim—the fearful grasp by which it originally imbedded itself. Attempt, now, to place all your fingers, at the same time, in the respective impressions as you see them."

I made the attempt in vain.

"We are possibly not giving this matter a fair trial," he said. "The paper is spread out upon a plane surface; but the human throat is cylindrical. Here is a billet of wood, the circumference of which is about that of the throat. Wrap the drawing around it, and try the experiment again."

I did so; but the difficulty was even more obvious than before.

"This," I said, "is the mark of no human hand."

"Read now," replied Dupin, "this passage from Cuvier."

It was a minute anatomical and generally descriptive account of the large fulvous Orang-Outang of the East Indian Islands. The gigantic stature, the prodigious strength and activity, the wild ferocity, and the imitative propensities of these mammalia are sufficiently well known to all. I understood the full horrors of the murder at once.

"The description of the digits," said I, as I made an end of reading, "is in exact accordance with this drawing. I see that no animal but an Orang-Outang, of the species here mentioned, could have impressed the indentations as you have traced them. This tuft of tawny hair, too, is identical in character with that of the beast of Cuvier. But I cannot possibly comprehend the particulars of this frightful mystery. Besides, there were *two* voices heard in contention, and one of them was unquestionably the voice of a Frenchman."

"True; and you will remember an expression attributed almost unanimously, by the evidence, to this voice,—the expression, '*mon Dieu!*' This, under the circumstances, has been justly characterized by one of the witnesses (Montani, the confectioner), as an expression of remonstrance or expostulation. Upon these two words, therefore, I have mainly built my hopes of a full solution of the riddle. A Frenchman was cognizant of the murder. It is possible—indeed it is far more than probable —that he was innocent of all participation in the bloody transactions which took place. The Orang-Outang may have escaped from him. He may have traced it to the chamber; but, under the agitating circumstances which ensued, he could never have recaptured it. It is still at large. I will not pursue these guesses—for I have no right to call them more—since the shades of reflection upon which they are based are scarcely of sufficient depth to be appreciable by my own intellect, and since I could not pretend to make them intelligible to the understanding of another. We will call them guesses then, and speak of them as such. If the Frenchman in question is indeed, as I suppose, innocent of this atrocity, this advertisement, which I left last night, upon our return home, at the office of 'Le Monde' (a paper devoted to the shipping interest, and much sought by sailors), will bring him to our residence."

He handed me a paper, and I read thus:

CAUGHT—*In the Bois de Boulogne, early in the morning of the — inst.* (the morning of the murder), *a very large, tawny Orang-Outang of the Bornese species. The owner (who is ascertained to be a sailor, belonging to a Maltese vessel), may have the animal again, upon identifying it satisfactorily, and paying a few charges arising from its capture*

*and keeping. Call at No. —, Rue —, Faubourg St. Germain — au troi-
sième.*

"How was it possible," I asked, "that you should know the man to be
a sailor, and belonging to a Maltese vessel?"

"I do *not* know it," said Dupin. "I am not *sure* of it. Here, however,
is a small piece of ribbon, which from its form, and from its greasy appearance, has evidently been used in tying the hair in one of those long
queues of which sailors are so fond. Moreover, this knot is one which
few besides sailors can tie, and is peculiar to the Maltese. I picked the
ribbon up at the foot of the lightning-rod. It could not have belonged
to either of the deceased. Now if, after all, I am wrong in my induction
from this ribbon, that the Frenchman was a sailor belonging to a Maltese vessel, still I can have done no harm in saying what I did in the
advertisement. If I am in error, he will merely suppose that I have been
misled by some circumstance into which he will not take the trouble to
inquire. But if I am right, a great point is gained. Cognizant although
innocent of the murder, the Frenchman will naturally hesitate about
replying to the advertisement—about demanding the Orang-Outang.
He will reason thus:—'I am innocent; I am poor; my Orang-Outang
is of great value—to one in my circumstances a fortune of itself—why
should I lose it through idle apprehensions of danger? Here it is, within
my grasp. It was found in the Bois de Boulogne—at a vast distance from
the scene of that butchery. How can it ever be suspected that a brute
beast should have done the deed? The police are at fault—they have
failed to procure the slightest clue. Should they even trace the animal,
it would be impossible to prove me cognizant of the murder, or to im-
plicate me in guilt on account of that cognizance. Above all, *I am known.*
The advertiser designates me as the possessor of the beast. I am not sure
to what limit his knowledge may extend. Should I avoid claiming a
property of so great value, which it is known that I possess, I will render
the animal, at least, liable to suspicion. It is not my policy to attract attention either to myself or to the beast. I will answer the advertisement,
get the Orang-Outang, and keep it close until this matter has blown
over.'"

At this moment we heard a step upon the stairs.

"Be ready," said Dupin, "with your pistols, but neither use them nor
show them until at a signal from myself."

The front door of the house had been left open, and the visitor had
entered, without ringing, and advanced several steps upon the staircase.
Now, however, he seemed to hesitate. Presently we heard him descending. Dupin was moving quickly to the door, when we again heard him

coming up. He did not turn back a second time, but stepped up with decision and rapped at the door of our chamber.

"Come in," said Dupin, in a cheerful and hearty tone.

A man entered. He was a sailor, evidently,—a tall, stout, and muscular-looking person, with a certain dare-devil expression of countenance, not altogether unprepossessing. His face, greatly sunburnt, was more than half hidden by whisker and *mustachio*. He had with him a huge oaken cudgel, but appeared to be otherwise unarmed. He bowed awkwardly, and bade us "good evening," in French accents, which, although somewhat Neufchatelish, were still sufficiently indicative of a Parisian origin.

"Sit down, my friend," said Dupin. "I suppose you have called about the Orang-Outang. Upon my word, I almost envy you the possession of him; a remarkably fine, and no doubt a very valuable animal. How old do you suppose him to be?"

The sailor drew a long breath, with the air of a man relieved of some intolerable burthen, and then replied, in an assured tone:

"I have no way of telling—but he can't be more than four or five years old. Have you got him here?"

"Oh no; we had no conveniences for keeping him here. He is at a livery stable in the Rue Dubourg, just by. You can get him in the morning. Of course you are prepared to identify the property?"

"To be sure I am, sir."

"I shall be sorry to part with him," said Dupin.

"I don't mean that you should be at all this trouble for nothing, sir," said the man. "Couldn't expect it. Am very willing to pay a reward for the finding of the animal—that is to say, anything in reason."

"Well," replied my friend, "that is all very fair, to be sure. Let me think!—what should I have? Oh! I will tell you. My reward shall be this. You shall give me all the information in your power about these murders in the Rue Morgue."

Dupin said the last words in a very low tone, and very quietly. Just as quietly, too, he walked towards the door, locked it, and put the key in his pocket. He then drew a pistol from his bosom and placed it, without the least flurry, upon the table.

The sailor's face flushed up as if he were struggling with suffocation. He started to his feet and grasped his cudgel; but the next moment he fell back into his seat, trembling violently, and with the countenance of death itself. He spoke not a word. I pitied him from the bottom of my heart.

"My friend," said Dupin, in a kind tone, "you are alarming yourself unnecessarily—you are indeed. We mean you no harm whatever. I pledge you the honor of a gentleman, and of a Frenchman, that we intend you no injury. I perfectly well know that you are innocent of the atrocities in the Rue Morgue. It will not do, however, to deny that you are in some measure implicated in them. From what I have already said, you must know that I have had means of information about this matter—means of which you could never have dreamed. Now the thing stands thus. You have done nothing which you could have avoided— nothing, certainly, which renders you culpable. You were not even guilty of robbery, when you might have robbed with impunity. You have nothing to conceal. You have no reason for concealment. On the other hand, you are bound by every principle of honor to confess all you know. An innocent man is now imprisoned, charged with that crime of which you can point out the perpetrator."

The sailor had recovered his presence of mind, in a great measure, while Dupin uttered these words; but his original boldness of bearing was all gone.

"So help me God," said he, after a brief pause, "I *will* tell you all I know about this affair;—but I do not expect you to believe one half I say—I would be a fool indeed if I did. Still, I *am* innocent, and I will make a clean breast if I die for it."

What he stated was, in substance, this. He had lately made a voyage to the Indian Archipelago. A party, of which he formed one, landed at Borneo, and passed into the interior on an excursion of pleasure. Himself and a companion had captured the Orang-Outang. This companion dying, the animal fell into his own exclusive possession. After great trouble, occasioned by the intractable ferocity of his captive during the home voyage, he at length succeeded in lodging it safely at his own residence in Paris, where, not to attract towards himself the unpleasant curiosity of his neighbors, he kept it carefully secluded, until such time as it should recover from a wound in the foot, received from a splinter on board ship. His ultimate design was to sell it.

Returning home from some sailors' frolic on the night, or rather in the morning of the murder, he found the beast occupying his own bed-room, into which it had broken from a closet adjoining, where it had been, as was thought, securely confined. Razor in hand, and fully lathered, it was sitting before a looking-glass, attempting the operation of shaving, in which it had no doubt previously watched its master through the keyhole of the closet. Terrified at the sight of so dangerous a weapon in the possession of an animal so ferocious, and so well able to use it, the man, for some moments, was at a loss what to do. He had been accustomed, however, to quiet the creature, even in its fiercest moods, by the use of a whip, and to this he now resorted. Upon sight of it, the Orang-Outang sprang at once through the door of the chamber, down the stairs, and thence, through a window, unfortunately open, into the street.

The Frenchman followed in despair; the ape, razor still in hand, occasionally stopping to look back and gesticulate at its pursuer, until the latter had nearly come up with it. It then again made off. In this manner the chase continued for a long time. The streets were profoundly quiet, as it was nearly three o'clock in the morning. In passing down an alley in the rear of the Rue Morgue, the fugitive's attention was arrested by a light gleaming from the open window of Madame L'Espanaye's chamber, in the fourth story of her house. Rushing to the building, it perceived the lightning-rod, clambered up with inconceivable agility, grasped the shutter, which was thrown fully back against the wall, and, by its means, swung itself directly upon the headboard of the bed. The whole feat did not occupy a minute. The shutter was kicked open again by the Orang-Outang as it entered the room.

The sailor, in the meantime, was both rejoiced and perplexed. He had strong hopes of now recapturing the brute, as it could scarcely escape from the trap into which it had ventured, except by the rod, where it might be intercepted as it came down. On the other hand, there was much cause for anxiety as to what it might do in the house. This latter reflection urged the man still to follow the fugitive. A lightning-rod is ascended without difficulty, especially by a sailor; but, when he had arrived as high as the window, which lay far to his left, his career was stopped; the most that he could accomplish was to reach over so as to obtain a glimpse of the interior of the room. At this glimpse he nearly fell from his hold through excess of horror. Now it was that those hideous shrieks arose upon the night, which had startled from slumber the inmates of the Rue Morgue. Madame L'Espanaye and her daughter, habited in their night clothes, had apparently been arranging some papers in the iron chest already mentioned, which had been wheeled into the middle of the room. It was open, and its contents lay beside it on the floor. The victims must have been sitting with their backs toward the window; and, from the time elapsing between the ingress of the beast and the screams, it seems probable that it was not immediately perceived. The flapping-to of the shutter would naturally have been attributed to the wind.

As the sailor looked in, the gigantic animal had seized Madame L'Espanaye by the hair (which was loose, as she had been combing it), and was flourishing the razor about her face, in imitation of the motions of a barber. The daughter lay prostrate and motionless; she had swooned. The screams and struggles of the old lady (during which the hair was torn from her head) had the effect of changing the probably pacific purposes of the Orang-Outang into those of wrath. With one determined sweep of its muscular arm it nearly severed her head from her body. The sight of blood inflamed its anger into frenzy. Gnashing its teeth, and flashing fire from its eyes, it flew upon the body of the girl, and imbedded its fearful talons in her throat, retaining its grasp until she expired. Its wandering and wild glances fell at this moment upon the head of the bed, over which the face of its master, rigid with horror, was just discernible. The fury of the beast, who no doubt bore still in mind the dreaded whip, was instantly converted into fear. Conscious of having deserved punishment, it seemed desirous of concealing its bloody deeds, and skipped about the chamber in an agony of nervous agitation; throwing down and breaking the furniture as it moved, and dragging the bed from the bedstead. In conclusion, it seized first the corpse of the daughter, and thrust it up the chimney, as it was found; then that of the old lady, which it immediately hurled through the window headlong.

As the ape approached the casement with its mutilated burthen, the sailor shrank aghast to the rod, and, rather gliding than clambering down it, hurried at once home—dreading the consequences of the butchery, and gladly abandoning, in his terror, all solicitude about the fate of the Orang-Outang. The words heard by the party upon the staircase were the Frenchman's exclamations of horror and affright, comingled with the fiendish jabberings of the brute.

I have scarcely anything to add. The Orang-Outang must have escaped from the chamber, by the rod, just before the breaking of the door. It must have closed the window as it passed through it. It was subsequently caught by the owner himself, who obtained for it a very large sum at the *Jardin des Plantes*. Le Bon was instantly released, upon our narration of the circumstances (with some comments from Dupin) at the *bureau* of the Prefect of Police. This functionary, however well disposed to my friend, could not altogether conceal his chagrin at the turn which affairs had taken, and was fain to indulge in a sarcasm or two, about the propriety of every person minding his own business.

"Let them talk," said Dupin, who had not thought it necessary to reply. "Let him discourse; it will ease his conscience. I am satisfied with having defeated him in his own castle. Nevertheless, that he failed in the solution of this mystery, is by no means that matter for wonder which he supposes it; for, in truth, our friend the Prefect is somewhat too cunning to be profound. In his wisdom is no *stamen*. It is all head and no body, like the pictures of the Goddess Laverna,—or, at best, all head and shoulders, like a codfish. But he is a good creature after all. I like him especially for one master stroke of cant, by which he has attained his reputation for ingenuity. I mean the way he has '*de nier ce qui est, et d'expliquer ce qui n'est pas.*' "*

* Rousseau. *Nouvelle Héloïse.*

The Pit and the Pendulum

BY EDGAR ALLAN POE

Impia tortorum longos hic turba furores
Sanguinis innocui, non satiata, aluit.
Sospite nunc patriâ, fracto nunc funeris antro,
*Mors ubi dira fuit vita salusque patent.**

I WAS sick—sick unto death with
that long agony; and when they at length unbound me, and I was permitted to sit, I felt that my senses were leaving me. The sentence—the
dread sentence of death—was the last of distinct accentuation which
reached my ears. After that, the sound of the inquisitorial voices seemed
merged in one dreamy indeterminate hum. It conveyed to my soul the
idea of *revolution*—perhaps from its association in fancy with the burr
of a mill-wheel. This only for a brief period; for presently I heard no
more. Yet, for a while, I saw; but with how terrible an exaggeration!
I saw the lips of the black-robed judges. They appeared to me white—
whiter than the sheet upon which I trace these words—and thin even
to grotesqueness; thin with the intensity of their expression of firmness
—of immovable resolution—of stern contempt of human torture. I saw
that the decrees of what to me was Fate, were still issuing from those
lips. I saw them writhe with a deadly locution. I saw them fashion the
syllables of my name; and I shuddered because no sound succeeded. I
saw, too, for a few moments of delirious horror, the soft and nearly imperceptible waving of the sable draperies which enwrapped the walls
of the apartment. And then my vision fell upon the seven tall candles

* Quatrain composed for the gates of a market to be erected upon the site of the Jacobin
club house at Paris.

upon the table. At first they wore the aspect of charity, and seemed white slender angels who would save me; but then, all at once, there came a most deadly nausea over my spirit, and I felt every fiber in my frame thrill as if I had touched the wire of a galvanic battery, while the angel forms became meaningless specters, with heads of flame, and I saw that from them there would be no help. And then there stole into my fancy, like a rich musical note, the thought of what sweet rest there must be in the grave. The thought came gently and stealthily, and it seemed long before it attained full appreciation; but just as my spirit came at length properly to feel and entertain it, the figures of the judges vanished, as if magically, from before me; the tall candles sank into nothingness; their flames went out utterly; the blackness of darkness supervened; all sensations appeared swallowed up in a mad rushing descent as of the soul into Hades. Then silence, and stillness, and night were the universe.

I had swooned; but still will not say that all of consciousness was lost. What of it there remained I will not attempt to define, or even to describe; yet all was not lost. In the deepest slumber—no! In delirium —no! In a swoon—no! In death—no! Even in the grave all *is not* lost. Else there is no immortality for man. Arousing from the most profound of slumbers, we break the gossamer web of *some* dream. Yet in a second afterward (so frail may that web have been), we remember not that we have dreamed. In the return to life from the swoon there are two stages; first, that of the sense of mental or spiritual; secondly, that of the sense of physical, existence. It seems probable that if, upon reaching the second stage, we could recall the impressions of the first, we should find these impressions eloquent in memories of the gulf beyond. And that gulf is—what? How at least shall we distinguish its shadows from those of the tomb? But if the impressions of what I have termed the first stage, are not, at will, recalled, yet, after long interval, do they not come unbidden, while we marvel whence they come? He who has never swooned, is not he who finds strange palaces and wildly familiar faces in coals that glow; is not he who beholds floating in mid-air the sad visions that the many may not view; is not he who ponders over the perfume of some novel flower—is not he whose brain grows bewildered with the meaning of some musical cadence which has never before arrested his attention.

Amid frequent and thoughtful endeavors to remember, amid earnest struggles to regather some token of the state of seeming nothingness into which my soul had lapsed, there have been moments when I have dreamed of success; there have been brief, very brief periods when I have conjured up remembrances which the lucid reason of a later epoch assures me could have had reference only to that condition of seeming unconsciousness. These shadows of memory tell, indistinctly, of tall figures that lifted and bore me in silence down—down—still down—till a hideous dizziness oppressed me at the mere idea of the interminableness of the descent. They tell also of a vague horror at my heart, on account of that heart's unnatural stillness. Then comes a sense of sudden motionlessness throughout all things; as if those who bore me (a ghastly train!) had outrun, in their descent, the limits of the limitless, and paused from the wearisomeness of their toil. After this I call to mind flatness and dampness; and then all is *madness*—the madness of a memory which busies itself among forbidden things.

Very suddenly there came back to my soul motion and sound—the tumultuous motion of the heart, and, in my ears, the sound of its beating. Then a pause in which all is blank. Then again sound, and motion, and touch—a tingling sensation pervading my frame. Then the mere consciousness of existence, without thought—a condition which lasted long. Then, very suddenly, *thought,* and shuddering terror, and earnest endeavor to comprehend my true state. Then a strong desire to lapse into insensibility. Then a rushing revival of soul and a successful effort to move. And now a full memory of the trial, of the judges, of the sable draperies, of the sentence, of the sickness, of the swoon. Then entire forgetfulness of all that followed; of all that a later day and much earnestness of endeavor have enabled me vaguely to recall.

So far, I had not opened my eyes. I felt that I lay upon my back, unbound. I reached out my hand, and it fell heavily upon something damp and hard. There I suffered it to remain for many minutes, while I strove to imagine where and *what* I could be. I longed, yet dared not to employ my vision. I dreaded the first glance at objects around me. It was not that I feared to look upon things horrible, but that I grew aghast lest there should be *nothing* to see. At length, with a wild desperation at heart, I quickly unclosed my eyes. My worst thoughts, then, were confirmed. The blackness of eternal night encompassed me. I struggled for breath. The intensity of the darkness seemed to oppress and stifle me. The atmosphere was intolerably close. I still lay quietly, and made effort to exercise my reason. I brought to mind the inquisitorial proceedings, and attempted from that point to deduce my real condition. The sentence had passed; and it appeared to me that a very long interval of time had since elapsed. Yet not for a moment did I suppose myself actually dead. Such a supposition, notwithstanding what we read in fiction, is altogether inconsistent with real existence;—but where and in what state was I? The condemned to death, I knew, perished usually at the *autos-da-fé,* and one of these had been held on the very night of the day of my trial. Had I been remanded to my dungeon, to await the next sacrifice, which would not take place for many months? This I at once saw could not be. Victims had been in immediate demand. Moreover, my dungeon, as well as all the condemned cells at Toledo, had stone floors, and light was not altogether excluded.

A fearful idea now suddenly drove the blood in torrents upon my heart, and for a brief period, I once more relapsed into insensibility. Upon recovering, I at once started to my feet, trembling convulsively in every fiber. I thrust my arms wildly above and around me in all directions. I felt nothing; yet dreaded to move a step, lest I should be impeded by the walls of a *tomb*. Perspiration burst from every pore, and stood in cold big beads upon my forehead. The agony of suspense grew at length intolerable, and I cautiously moved forward, with my arms extended, and my eyes straining from their sockets, in the hope of catching some faint ray of light. I proceeded for many paces; but still all was blackness and vacancy. I breathed more freely. It seemed evident that mine was not, at least, the most hideous of fates.

And now, as I still continued to step cautiously onward, there came thronging upon my recollection a thousand vague rumors of the horrors of Toledo. Of the dungeons there had been strange things narrated— fables I had always deemed them—but yet strange, and too ghastly to repeat, save in a whisper. Was I left to perish of starvation in this subterranean world of darkness; or what fate, perhaps even more fearful, awaited me? That the result would be death, and a death of more than customary bitterness, I knew too well the character of my judges to doubt. The mode and the hour were all that occupied or distracted me.

My outstretched hands at length encountered some solid obstruction. It was a wall, seemingly of stone masonry—very smooth, slimy, and cold. I followed it up; stepping with all the careful distrust with which certain antique narratives had inspired me. This process, however, afforded me no means of ascertaining the dimensions of my dungeon; as I might make its circuit, and return to the point whence I set out, without being aware of the fact; so perfectly uniform seemed the wall. I therefore sought the knife which had been in my pocket, when led into the inquisitorial chamber; but it was gone; my clothes had been exchanged for a wrapper of coarse serge. I had thought of forcing the blade in some minute crevice of the masonry, so as to identify my point of departure. The difficulty, nevertheless, was but trivial; although, in the disorder of my fancy, it seemed at first insuperable. I tore a part of the hem from the robe and placed the fragment at full length, and at right angles to the wall. In groping my way around the prison, I could not fail to encounter this rag upon completing the circuit. So, at least I thought: but I had not counted upon the extent of the dungeon, or upon my own weakness. The ground was moist and slippery. I staggered onward for some time, when I stumbled and fell. My excessive

fatigue induced me to remain prostrate; and sleep soon overtook me as
I lay.

Upon awaking, and stretching forth an arm, I found beside me a loaf
and a pitcher with water. I was too much exhausted to reflect upon this
circumstance, but ate and drank with avidity. Shortly afterward, I
resumed my tour around the prison, and with much toil, came at last
upon the fragment of the serge. Up to the period when I fell I had
counted fifty-two paces, and upon resuming my walk, I had counted
forty-eight more;—when I arrived at the rag. There were in all, then,
a hundred paces; and, admitting two paces to the yard, I presumed the
dungeon to be fifty yards in circuit. I had met, however, with many
angles in the wall, and thus I could form no guess at the shape of the
vault; for vault I could not help supposing it to be.

I had little object—certainly no hope—in these researches; but a vague
curiosity prompted me to continue them. Quitting the wall, I resolved
to cross the area of the enclosure. At first I proceeded with extreme
caution, for the floor, although seemingly of solid material, was treacherous with slime. At length, however, I took courage, and did not hesitate
to step firmly; endeavoring to cross in as direct a line as possible. I had
advanced some ten or twelve paces in this manner, when the remnant
of the torn hem of my robe became entangled between my legs. I stepped
on it, and fell violently on my face.

In the confusion attending my fall, I did not immediately apprehend
a somewhat startling circumstance, which yet, in a few seconds afterward, and while I still lay prostrate, arrested my attention. It was this
—my chin rested upon the floor of the prison, but my lips and the upper
portion of my head, although seemingly at a less elevation than the chin,
touched nothing. At the same time my forehead seemed bathed in a
clammy vapor, and the peculiar smell of decayed fungus arose to my
nostrils. I put forward my arm and shuddered to find that I had fallen
at the very brink of a circular pit, whose extent, of course, I had no means
of ascertaining at the moment. Groping about the masonry just below
the margin, I succeeded in dislodging a small fragment, and let it fall
into the abyss. For many seconds I harkened to its reverberations as it
dashed against the sides of the chasm in its descent; at length there was
a sudden plunge into water, succeeded by loud echoes. At the same
moment there came a sound resembling the quick opening, and as rapid
closing of a door overhead, while a faint gleam of light flashed suddenly
through the gloom, and as suddenly faded away.

I saw clearly the doom which had been prepared for me, and congratulated myself upon the timely accident by which I had escaped.
Another step before my fall, and the world had seen me no more. And
the death just avoided, was of that very character which I had regarded

as fabulous and frivolous in the tales respecting the Inquisition. To the victims of its tyranny, there was the choice of death with its direst physical agonies, or death with its most hideous moral horrors. I had been reserved for the latter. By long suffering my nerves had been un-strung, until I trembled at the sound of my own voice, and had become in every respect a fitting subject for the species of torture which awaited me.

Shaking in every limb, I groped my way back to the wall; resolving there to perish rather than risk the terrors of the wells, of which my imagination now pictured many in various positions about the dun-geon. In other conditions of mind I might have had courage to end my misery at once by a plunge into one of these abysses; but now I was the veriest of cowards. Neither could I forget what I had read of these pits—that the *sudden* extinction of life formed no part of their most horrible plan.

Agitation of spirit kept me awake for many long hours; but at length I again slumbered. Upon arousing, I found by my side, as before, a loaf and a pitcher of water. A burning thirst consumed me, and I emptied the vessel at a draught. It must have been drugged; for scarcely had I drunk, before I became irresistibly drowsy. A deep sleep fell upon me— a sleep like that of death. How long it lasted of course, I know not; but when, once again, I unclosed my eyes, the objects around me were visible. By a wild sulphurous luster, the origin of which I could not at first determine, I was enabled to see the extent and aspect of the prison.

In its size I had been greatly mistaken. The whole circuit of its walls did not exceed twenty-five yards. For some minutes this fact occa-sioned me a world of vain trouble; vain indeed! for what could be of less importance, under the terrible circumstances which environed me, than the mere dimensions of my dungeon? But my soul took a wild in-terest in trifles, and I busied myself in endeavors to account for the error I had committed in my measurement. The truth at length flashed upon me. In my first attempt at exploration I had counted fifty-two paces, up to the period when I fell; I must then have been within a pace or two of the fragment of serge; in fact, I had nearly performed the circuit of the vault. I then slept, and upon awaking, I must have re-turned upon my steps—thus supposing the circuit nearly double what it actually was. My confusion of mind prevented me from observing that I began my tour with the wall to the left, and ended it with the wall to the right.

I had been deceived, too, in respect to the shape of the enclosure. In feeling my way I had found many angles, and thus deduced an idea of great irregularity; so potent is the effect of total darkness upon one arousing from lethargy or sleep! The angles were simply those of a few slight depressions, or niches, at odd intervals. The general shape of the prison was square. What I had taken for masonry seemed now to be iron, or some other metal, in huge plates, whose sutures or joints occasioned the depression. The entire surface of this metallic enclosure was rudely daubed in all the hideous and repulsive devices to which the charnel superstition of the monks has given rise. The figures of fiends in aspects of menace, with skeleton forms, and other more really fearful images, overspread and disfigured the walls. I observed that the outlines of these monstrosities were sufficiently distinct, but that the colors seemed faded and blurred, as if from the effects of a damp atmosphere. I now noticed the floor, too, which was of stone. In the center yawned the circular pit from whose jaws I had escaped; but it was the only one in the dungeon.

All this I saw indistinctly and by much effort: for my personal condition had been greatly changed during slumber. I now lay upon my back, and at full length, on a species of low frame-work of wood. To this I was securely bound by a long strap resembling a surcingle. It passed in many convolutions about my limbs and body, leaving at liberty only my head, and my left arm to such extent that I could, by dint of much exertion, supply myself with food from an earthen dish which lay by my side on the floor. I saw, to my horror, that the pitcher had been removed. I say to my horror; for I was consumed with intolerable thirst. This thirst it appeared to be the design of my persecutors to stimulate: for the food in the dish was meat pungently seasoned.

Looking upward, I surveyed the ceiling of my prison. It was some thirty or forty feet overhead, and constructed much as the side walls. In one of its panels, a very singular figure riveted my whole attention. It was the painted figure of Time as he is commonly represented, save that, in lieu of a scythe, he held what, at a casual glance, I supposed to be the pictured image of a huge pendulum such as we see on antique clocks. There was something, however, in the appearance of this machine which caused me to regard it more attentively. While I gazed directly upward at it (for its position was immediately over my own) I fancied that I saw it in motion. In an instant afterward the fancy was confirmed. Its sweep was brief, and of course slow. I watched it for some minutes, somewhat in fear, but more in wonder. Wearied at length with observing its dull movement, I turned my eyes upon the other objects in the cell.

A slight noise attracted my notice, and, looking to the floor, I saw several enormous rats traversing it. They had issued from the well, which lay just within view to my right. Even then, while I gazed, they came up in troops, hurriedly, with ravenous eyes, allured by the scent of the meat. From this it required much effort and attention to scare them away.

It might have been half an hour, perhaps even an hour (for I could take but imperfect note of time), before I again cast my eyes upward. What I then saw confounded and amazed me. The sweep of the pendulum had increased in extent by nearly a yard. As a natural consequence, its velocity was also much greater. But what mainly disturbed me was the idea that it had perceptibly *descended*. I now observed—with what horror it is needless to say—that its nether extremity was formed of a crescent of glittering steel, about a foot in length from horn to horn; the horns upward, and the under edge evidently as keen as that of a razor. Like a razor also, it seemed massy and heavy, tapering from the edge into a solid and broad structure above. It was appended to a weighty rod of brass, and the whole *hissed* as it swung through the air.

I could no longer doubt the doom prepared for me by monkish ingenuity in torture. My cognizance of the pit had become known to the inquisitorial agents—*the pit* whose horrors had been destined for so bold a recusant as myself—*the pit,* typical of hell, and regarded by rumor as the Ultima Thule of all their punishments. The plunge into this pit I had avoided by the merest of accidents, and I knew that surprise, or entrapment into torment, formed an important portion of all the grotesquerie of these dungeon deaths. Having failed to fall, it was no part of the demon plan to hurl me into the abyss; and thus (there being no alternative) a different and a milder destruction awaited me. Milder! I half smiled in my agony as I thought of such application of such a term.

What boots it to tell of the long, long hours of horror more than mortal, during which I counted the rushing vibrations of the steel! Inch by inch—line by line—with a descent only appreciable at intervals that seemed ages—down and still down it came! Days passed—it might have been that many days passed—ere it swept so closely over me as to fan me with its acrid breath. The odor of the sharp steel forced itself into my nostrils. I prayed—I wearied heaven with my prayer for its more speedy descent. I grew frantically mad, and struggled to force myself upward against the sweep of the fearful scimitar. And then I fell suddenly calm, and lay smiling at the glittering death, as a child at some rare bauble.

There was another interval of utter insensibility; it was brief; for, upon again lapsing into life there had been no perceptible descent in the pendulum. But it might have been long; for I knew there were demons who took note of my swoon, and who could have arrested the vibration at pleasure. Upon my recovery, too, I felt very—oh, inexpressibly sick and weak, as if through long inanition. Even amid the agonies of that period, the human nature craved food. With painful effort I outstretched my left arm as far as my bonds permitted, and took possession of the small remnant which had been spared me by the rats. As I put a portion of it within my lips, there rushed to my mind a half-formed thought of joy—of hope. Yet what business had *I* with hope? It was, as I say, a half-formed thought—man has many such which are never completed. I felt that it was of joy—of hope; but I felt also that it had perished in its formation. In vain I struggled to perfect—to regain it. Long suffering had nearly annihilated all my ordinary powers of mind. I was an imbecile—an idiot.

The vibration of the pendulum was at right angles to my length. I saw that the crescent was designed to cross the region of the heart. It would fray the serge of my robe—it would return and repeat its operations—again—and again. Notwithstanding its terrifically wide sweep (some thirty feet or more) and the hissing vigor of its descent, sufficient to sunder these very walls of iron, still the fraying of my robe would be all that, for several minutes, it would accomplish. And at this thought I paused. I dared not go farther than this reflection. I dwelt upon it with a pertinacity of attention—as if, in so dwelling, I could arrest *here* the descent of the steel. I forced myself to ponder upon the sound of the crescent as it should pass across the garment—upon the peculiar thrilling sensation which the friction of cloth produces on the nerves. I pondered upon all this frivolity until my teeth were on edge.

Down—steadily down it crept. I took a frenzied pleasure in contrasting its downward with its lateral velocity. To the right—to the left —far and wide—with the shriek of a damned spirit; to my heart with the stealthy pace of the tiger! I alternately laughed and howled as the one or the other idea grew predominant.

Down—certainly, relentlessly down! It vibrated within three inches of my bosom! I struggled violently, furiously, to free my left arm. This was free only from the elbow to the hand. I could reach the latter, from the platter beside me, to my mouth, with great effort, but no farther. Could I have broken the fastenings above the elbow, I would have seized and attempted to arrest the pendulum. I might as well have attempted to arrest an avalanche!

Down—still unceasingly—still inevitably down! I gasped and struggled at each vibration. I shrunk convulsively at its every sweep. My eyes followed its outward or upward whirls with the eagerness of the most unmeaning despair; they closed themselves spasmodically at the descent, although death would have been a relief, oh! how unspeakable! Still I quivered in every nerve to think how slight a sinking of the machinery would precipitate that keen, glistening axe upon my bosom. It was *hope* that prompted the nerve to quiver—the frame to shrink. It was *hope*—the hope that triumphs on the rack—that whispers to the death-condemned even in the dungeons of the Inquisition.

I saw that some ten or twelve vibrations would bring the steel in actual contact with my robe, and with this observation there suddenly came over my spirit all the keen, collected calmness of despair. For the first time during many hours—or perhaps days—I *thought*. It now occurred to me that the bandage, or surcingle, which enveloped me, was *unique*. I was tied by no separate cord. The first stroke of the razor-like crescent athwart any portion of the band, would so detach it that it might be unwound from my person by means of my left hand. But how fearful, in that case, the proximity of the steel! The result of the slightest struggle how deadly! Was it likely, moreover, that the minions of the torturer had not foreseen and provided for this possibility? Was it probable that the bandage crossed my bosom in the track of the pendulum? Dreading to find my faint, and, as it seemed, my last hope frustrated, I so far elevated my head as to obtain a distinct view of my breast. The surcingle enveloped my limbs and body close in all directions—*save in the path of the destroying crescent.*

Scarcely had I dropped my head back into its original position, when there flashed upon my mind what I cannot better describe than as the unformed half of that idea of deliverance to which I have previously alluded, and of which a moiety only floated indeterminately through my brain when I raised food to my burning lips. The whole thought was now present—feeble, scarcely sane, scarcely definite,—but still entire. I proceeded at once, with the nervous energy of despair, to attempt its execution.

For many hours the immediate vicinity of the low framework upon which I lay, had been literally swarming with rats. They were wild, bold, ravenous; their red eyes glaring upon me as if they waited but for motionlessness on my part to make me their prey. "To what food," I thought, "have they been accustomed in the well?"

They had devoured, in spite of all my efforts to prevent them, all but a small remnant of the contents of the dish. I had fallen into an habitual seesaw, or wave of the hand about the platter: and, at length, the unconscious uniformity of the movement deprived it of effect. In their voracity the vermin frequently fastened their sharp fangs in my fingers. With the particles of the oily and spicy viand which now remained, I thoroughly rubbed the bandage wherever I could reach it; then, raising my hand from the floor, I lay breathlessly still.

At first the ravenous animals were startled and terrified at the change —at the cessation of movement. They shrank alarmedly back; many sought the well. But this was only for a moment. I had not counted in vain upon their voracity. Observing that I remained without motion, one or two of the boldest leaped upon the framework, and smelt at the surcingle. This seemed the signal for a general rush. Forth from the well they hurried in fresh troops. They clung to the wood—they overran it, and leaped in hundreds upon my person. The measured movement of the pendulum disturbed them not at all. Avoiding its strokes they busied themselves with the anointed bandage. They pressed—they swarmed upon me in ever accumulating heaps. They writhed upon my throat; their cold lips sought my own; I was half stifled by their thronging pressure; disgust, for which the world has no name, swelled my bosom, and chilled, with a heavy clamminess, my heart. Yet one minute, and I felt that the struggle would be over. Plainly I perceived the loosening of the bandage. I knew that in more than one place it must be already severed. With a more than human resolution I lay *still*.

Nor had I erred in my calculations—nor had I endured in vain. I at length felt that I was *free*. The surcingle hung in ribands from my body. But the stroke of the pendulum already pressed upon my bosom. It had divided the serge of the robe. It had cut through the linen beneath. Twice again it swung, and a sharp sense of pain shot through every nerve. But the moment of escape had arrived. At a wave of my hand my deliverers hurried tumultuously away. With a steady movement—cautious, sidelong, shrinking, and slow—I slid from the embrace of the bandage and beyond the reach of the scimitar. For the moment, at least, *I was free*.

Free!—and in the grasp of the Inquisition! I had scarcely stepped from my wooden bed of horror upon the stone floor of the prison, when the motion of the hellish machine ceased and I beheld it drawn up, by some invisible force, through the ceiling. This was a lesson which I took desperately to heart. My every motion was undoubtedly watched. Free!—I had but escaped death in one form of agony, to be delivered unto worse than death in some other. With that thought I rolled my eyes nervously around on the barriers of iron that hemmed me in. Something unusual—some change which, at first, I could not appreciate distinctly—it was obvious, had taken place in the apartment. For many minutes of a dreamy and trembling abstraction, I busied myself in vain, unconnected conjecture. During this period, I became aware, for the first time, of the origin of the sulphurous light which illumined the cell. It proceeded from a fissure, about half an inch in width, extending entirely around the prison at the base of the walls, which thus appeared, and were, completely separated from the floor. I endeavoured, but of course in vain, to look through the aperture.

As I arose from the attempt, the mystery of the alteration in the chamber broke at once upon my understanding. I have observed that, although the outlines of the figures upon the walls were sufficiently distinct, yet the colors seemed blurred and indefinite. These colors had now assumed, and were momentarily assuming, a startling and most intense brilliancy, that gave to the spectral and fiendish portraitures an aspect that might have thrilled even firmer nerves than my own. Demon eyes, of a wild and ghastly vivacity, glared upon me in a thousand directions, where none had been visible before, and gleamed with the lurid luster of a fire that I could not force my imagination to regard as unreal.

Unreal!—Even while I breathed there came to my nostrils the breath of the vapor of heated iron! A suffocating odor pervaded the prison! A deeper glow settled each moment in the eyes that glared at my agonies! A richer tint of crimson diffused itself over the pictured horrors of blood. I panted! I gasped for breath! There could be no doubt of the design of my tormentors—oh! most unrelenting! oh! most demoniac of men! I shrank from the glowing metal to the center of the cell. Amid the thought of the fiery destruction that impended, the idea of the coolness of the well came over my soul like balm. I rushed to its deadly brink. I threw my straining vision below. The glare from the enkindled roof illumined its inmost recesses. Yet, for a wild moment, did my spirit refuse to comprehend the meaning of what I saw. At length it forced—it wrestled its way into my soul—it burned itself in upon my shuddering reason.—Oh! for a voice to speak!—oh! horror—oh! any horror but this! With a shriek, I rushed from the margin, and buried my face in my hands—weeping bitterly.

The heat rapidly increased, and once again I looked up, shuddering as with a fit of the ague. There had been a second change in the cell—and now the change was obviously in the *form*. As before, it was in vain that I, at first, endeavored to appreciate or understand what was taking place. But not long was I left in doubt. The Inquisitorial vengeance had been hurried by my twofold escape, and there was to be no more dallying with the King of Terrors. The room had been square. I saw that two of its iron angles were now acute—two, consequently, obtuse. The fearful difference quickly increased with a low rumbling or moaning sound. In an instant the apartment had shifted its form into that of a lozenge. But the alteration stopped not here—I neither hoped nor desired it to stop. I could have clasped the red walls to my bosom as a garment of eternal peace. "Death," I said, "any death but that of the pit!" Fool! might I have not known that *into the pit* it was the object of the burning iron to urge me? Could I resist its glow? or, if even that, could I withstand its pressure? And now, flatter and flatter grew the lozenge, with a rapidity that left me no time for contemplation. Its center, and of course, its greatest width, came just over the yawning gulf. I shrank back—but the closing walls pressed me resistlessly onward. At length for my seared and writhing body there was no longer an inch of foothold on the firm floor of the prison. I struggled no more, but the agony of my soul found vent in one loud, long, and final scream of despair. I felt that I tottered upon the brink—I averted my eyes—

There was a discordant hum of human voices! There was a loud blast as of many trumpets! There was a harsh grating as of a thousand thunders! The fiery walls rushed back! An out-stretched arm caught my own as I fell, fainting, into the abyss. It was that of General Lasalle.

The French army had entered Toledo. The Inquisition was in the hands of its enemies.

The Purloined Letter

BY EDGAR ALLAN POE

Nil sapientiæ odiosius acumine nimio.

SENECA

AT Paris, just after dark one gusty evening in the autumn of 18—, I was enjoying the twofold luxury of meditation and a meerschaum, in company with my friend C. Auguste Dupin, in his little back library, or book-closet, *au troisième, No. 33, Rue Dunôt, Faubourg St. Germain*. For one hour at least we had maintained a profound silence; while each, to any casual observer, might have seemed intently and exclusively occupied with the curling eddies of smoke that oppressed the atmosphere of the chamber. For myself, however, I was mentally discussing certain topics which had formed matter for conversation between us at an earlier period of the evening. I mean the affair of the Rue Morgue, and the mystery attending the murder of Marie Rogêt. I looked upon it, therefore, as something of a coincidence, when the door of our apartment was thrown open and admitted our old acquaintance, Monsieur G——, the Prefect of the Parisian police.

We gave him a hearty welcome; for there was nearly half as much of the entertaining as of the contemptible about the man, and we had not seen him for several years. We had been sitting in the dark, and Dupin now arose for the purpose of lighting a lamp, but sat down again, without doing so, upon G——'s saying that he had called to consult us, or rather to ask the opinion of my friend, about some official business which had occasioned a great deal of trouble.

"If it is any point requiring reflection," observed Dupin, as he forebore to enkindle the wick, "we shall examine it to better purpose in the dark."

"That is another of your odd notions," said the Prefect, who had a fashion of calling everything "odd" that was beyond his comprehension, and thus lived amid an absolute legion of "oddities."

"Very true," said Dupin, as he supplied his visitor with a pipe, and rolled towards him a comfortable chair.

"And what is the difficulty now?" I asked. "Nothing more in the assassination way, I hope?"

"Oh no; nothing of that nature. The fact is, the business is *very* simple indeed, and I make no doubt that we can manage it sufficiently well ourselves; but then I thought Dupin would like to hear the details of it, because it is so excessively *odd*."

"Simple and odd," said Dupin.

"Why, yes; and not exactly that, either. The fact is, we have all been a good deal puzzled because the affair *is* so simple, and yet baffles us altogether."

"Perhaps it is the very simplicity of the thing which puts you at fault," said my friend.

"What nonsense you *do* talk!" replied the Prefect, laughing heartily.

"Perhaps the mystery is a little *too* plain," said Dupin.

"Oh, good heavens! who ever heard of such an idea?"

"A little *too* self-evident."

"Ha! ha! ha!—ha! ha! ha!—ho! ho! ho!"—roared our visitor, profoundly amused, "oh, Dupin, you will be the death of me yet!"

"And what, after all, *is* the matter on hand?" I asked.

"Why, I will tell you," replied the Prefect, as he gave a long, steady, and contemplative puff, and settled himself in his chair. "I will tell you in a few words; but, before I begin, let me caution you that this is an affair demanding the greatest secrecy, and that I should most probably lose the position I now hold, were it known that I confided it to any one."

"Proceed," said I.

"Or not," said Dupin.

"Well, then; I have received personal information, from a very high quarter, that a certain document of the last importance, has been purloined from the royal apartments. The individual who purloined it is known; this beyond a doubt; he was seen to take it. It is known, also, that it still remains in his possession."

"How is this known?" asked Dupin.

"It is clearly inferred," replied the Prefect, "from the nature of the document, and from the non-appearance of certain results which would at once arise from its passing *out* of the robber's possession;—that is to say, from his employing it as he must design in the end to employ it."

"Be a little more explicit," I said.

"Well, I may venture so far as to say that the paper gives its holder a certain power in a certain quarter where such power is immensely valuable." The Prefect was fond of the cant of diplomacy.

"Still I do not quite understand," said Dupin.

"No? Well; the disclosure of the document to a third person, who shall be nameless, would bring in question the honor of a personage of most exalted station; and this fact gives the holder of the document an ascendancy over the illustrious personage whose honor and peace are so jeopardized."

"But this ascendancy," I interposed, "would depend upon the robber's knowledge of the loser's knowledge of the robber. Who would dare—"

"The thief," said G——, "is the Minister D——, who dares all things, those unbecoming as well as those becoming a man. The method of the theft was not less ingenious than bold. The document in question—a letter, to be frank—had been received by the personage robbed while alone in the royal *boudoir*. During its perusal she was suddenly interrupted by the entrance of the other exalted personage from whom especially it was her wish to conceal it. After a hurried and vain endeavor to thrust it in a drawer, she was forced to place it, open as it was, upon a table. The address, however, was uppermost, and, the contents thus unexposed, the letter escaped notice. At this juncture enters the Minister D——. His lynx eye immediately perceives the paper, recognizes the handwriting of the address, observes the confusion of the personage addressed, and fathoms her secret. After some business transactions, hurried through in his ordinary manner, he produces a letter somewhat similar to the one in question, opens it, pretends to read it, and then places it in close juxtaposition to the other. Again he converses, for some fifteen minutes, upon the public affairs. At length, in taking leave, he takes also from the table the letter to which he had no claim. Its rightful owner saw, but, of course, dared not call attention to the act, in the presence of the third personage who stood at her elbow. The minister decamped; leaving his own letter—one of no importance—upon the table."

"Here, then," said Dupin to me, "you have precisely what you demand to make the ascendancy complete—the robber's knowledge of the loser's knowledge of the robber."

"Yes," replied the Prefect; "and the power thus attained has, for some months past, been wielded, for political purposes, to a very dangerous extent. The personage robbed is more thoroughly convinced, every day, of the necessity of reclaiming her letter. But this, of course, cannot be done openly. In fine, driven to despair, she has committed the matter to me."

"Than whom," said Dupin, amid a perfect whirlwind of smoke, "no more sagacious agent could, I suppose, be desired, or even imagined."

"You flatter me," replied the Prefect; "but it is possible that some such opinion may have been entertained."

"It is clear," said I, "as you observe, that the letter is still in possession of the minister; since it is this possession, and not any employment of the letter, which bestows the power. With the employment the power departs."

"True," said G——; "and upon this conviction I proceeded. My first care was to make thorough search of the minister's hotel; and here my chief embarrassment lay in the necessity of searching without his knowledge. Beyond all things, I have been warned of the danger which would result from giving him reason to suspect our design."

"But," said I, "you are quite *au fait* in these investigations. The Parisian police have done this thing often before."

"Oh yes; and for this reason I did not despair. The habits of the minister gave me, too, a great advantage. He is frequently absent from home all night. His servants are by no means numerous. They sleep at a distance from their master's apartment, and, being chiefly Neapolitans, are readily made drunk. I have keys, as you know, with which I can open any chamber or cabinet in Paris. For three months a night has not passed, during the greater part of which I have not been engaged, personally, in ransacking the D—— hotel. My honor is interested, and, to mention a great secret, the reward is enormous. So I did not abandon the search until I had become fully satisfied that the thief is a more astute man than myself. I fancy that I have investigated every nook and corner of the premises in which it is possible that the paper can be concealed."

"But is it not possible," I suggested, "that although the letter may be in possession of the minister, as it unquestionably is, he may have concealed it elsewhere than upon his own premises?"

"This is barely possible," said Dupin. "The present peculiar condition of affairs at court, and especially of those intrigues in which D—— is known to be involved, would render the instant availability of the document—its susceptibility of being produced at a moment's notice—a point of nearly equal importance with its possession."

"Its susceptibility of being produced?" said I.

"That is to say, of being *destroyed*," said Dupin.

"True," I observed; "the paper is clearly then upon the premises. As for its being upon the person of the minister, we may consider that as out of the question."

"Entirely," said the Prefect. "He has been twice waylaid, as if by footpads, and his person rigorously searched under my own inspection."

"You might have spared yourself this trouble," said Dupin. "D——,

I presume, is not altogether a fool, and, if not, must have anticipated these waylayings, as a matter of course."

"Not *altogether* a fool," said G——, "but then he's a poet, which I take to be only one remove from a fool."

"True," said Dupin, after a long and thoughtful whiff from his meer-schaum, "although I have been guilty of certain doggerel myself."

"Suppose you detail," said I, "the particulars of your search."

"Why, the fact is, we took our time, and we searched *everywhere*. I have had long experience in these affairs. I took the entire building, room by room; devoting the nights of a whole week to each. We exam-ined, first, the furniture of each apartment. We opened every possible drawer; and I presume you know that, to a properly trained police agent, such a thing as a *secret* drawer is impossible. Any man is a dolt who permits a 'secret' drawer to escape him in a search of this kind. The thing is *so* plain. There is a certain amount of bulk—of space—to be accounted for in every cabinet. Then we have accurate rules. The fiftieth part of a line could not escape us. After the cabinets we took the chairs. The cushions we probed with the fine long needles you have seen me employ. From the tables we removed the tops."

"Why so?"

"Sometimes the top of a table, or other similarly arranged piece of furniture, is removed by the person wishing to conceal an article; then the leg is excavated, the article deposited within the cavity, and the top replaced. The bottoms and tops of bedposts are employed in the same way."

"But could not the cavity be detected by sounding?" I asked.

"By no means, if, when the article is deposited, a sufficient wadding of cotton be placed around it. Besides, in our case, we were obliged to proceed without noise."

"But you could not have removed—you could not have taken to pieces *all* articles of furniture in which it would have been possible to make a deposit in the manner you mention. A letter may be compressed into a thin spiral roll, not differing much in shape or bulk from a large knitting-needle, and in this form it might be inserted into the rung of a chair, for example. You did not take to pieces all the chairs?"

"Certainly not; but we did better—we examined the rungs of every chair in the hotel, and, indeed, the jointings of every description of furni-ture, by the aid of a most powerful microscope. Had there been any traces of recent disturbance we should not have failed to detect it in-stantly. A single grain of gimlet-dust, for example, would have been as obvious as an apple. Any disorder in the gluing—any unusual gaping in the joints—would have sufficed to insure detection."

"I presume you looked to the mirrors, between the boards and the

plates, and you probed the beds and the bedclothes, as well as the curtains and carpets."

"That of course; and when we had absolutely completed every particle
of the furniture in this way, then we examined the house itself. We
divided its entire surface into compartments, which we numbered, so
that none might be missed; then we scrutinized each individual square
inch throughout the premises, including the two houses immediately
adjoining, with the microscope, as before."

"The two houses adjoining!" I exclaimed; "you must have had a great
deal of trouble."

"We had; but the reward offered is prodigious."

"You include the *grounds* about the houses?"

"All the grounds are paved with brick. They gave us comparatively
little trouble. We examined the moss between the bricks, and found it
undisturbed."

"You looked among D——'s papers, of course, and into the books of
the library?"

"Certainly; we opened every package and parcel; we not only opened
every book, but we turned over every leaf in each volume, not contenting
ourselves with a mere shake, according to the fashion of some of our
police officers. We also measured the thickness of every book-*cover,* with
the most accurate admeasurement, and applied to each the most jealous
scrutiny of the microscope. Had any of the bindings been recently med-
dled with, it would have been utterly impossible that the fact should
have escaped observation. Some five or six volumes, just from the hands
of the binder, we carefully probed, longitudinally, with the needles."

"You explored the floors beneath the carpets?"

"Beyond doubt. We removed every carpet, and examined the boards
with the microscope."

"And the paper on the walls?"

"Yes."

"You looked into the cellars?"

"We did."

"Then," I said, "you have been making a miscalculation, and the letter
is *not* upon the premises, as you suppose."

"I fear you are right there," said the Prefect. "And now, Dupin, what
would you advise me to do?"

"To make a thorough research of the premises."

"That is absolutely needless," replied G——. "I am not more sure
that I breathe than I am that the letter is not at the hotel."

"I have no better advice to give you," said Dupin. "You have, of course,
an accurate description of the letter?"

"Oh yes!"—And here the Prefect, producing a memorandum book, proceeded to read aloud a minute account of the internal, and especially of the external appearance of the missing document. Soon after finishing the perusal of this description, he took his departure, more entirely depressed in spirits than I had ever known the good gentleman before.

In about a month afterwards he paid us another visit, and found us occupied very nearly as before. He took a pipe and a chair and entered into some ordinary conversation. At length I said:

"Well, but G——, what of the purloined letter? I presume you have at last made up your mind that there is no such thing as overreaching the minister?"

"Confound him, say I—yes; I made the re-examination, however, as Dupin suggested—but it was all labor lost, as I knew it would be."

"How much was the reward offered, did you say?" asked Dupin.

"Why, a very great deal—a *very* liberal reward—I don't like to say how much, precisely; but one thing I *will* say, that I wouldn't mind giving my individual check for fifty thousand francs to any one who could obtain me that letter. The fact is, it is becoming of more and more importance every day; and the reward has been lately doubled. If it were trebled, however, I could do no more than I have done."

"Why, yes," said Dupin, drawlingly, between the whiffs of his meerschaum, "I really—think, G——, you have not exerted yourself—to the utmost in this matter. You might—do a little more, I think, eh?"

"How?—in what way?"

"Why—puff, puff—you might—puff, puff—employ counsel in the matter, eh?—puff, puff, puff. Do you remember the story they tell of Abernethy?"

"No; hang Abernethy!"

"To be sure! hang him and welcome. But, once upon a time, a certain rich miser conceived the design of sponging upon this Abernethy for a medical opinion. Getting up, for this purpose, an ordinary conversation in a private company, he insinuated his case to the physician, as that of an imaginary individual.

"'We will suppose,' said the miser, 'that his symptoms are such and such; now, doctor, what would *you* have directed him to take?'

"'Take!' said Abernethy, 'why, take *advice,* to be sure.'"

"But," said the Prefect, a little discomposed, "I am *perfectly* willing to take advice, and to pay for it. I would *really* give fifty thousand francs to any one who would aid me in the matter."

"In that case," replied Dupin, opening a drawer, and producing a check-book, "you may as well fill me up a check for the amount mentioned. When you have signed it, I will hand you the letter."

I was astounded. The Prefect appeared absolutely thunder-stricken. For some minutes he remained speechless and motionless, looking incredulously at my friend with open mouth, and eyes that seemed starting from their sockets; then, apparently recovering himself in some measure, he seized a pen, and after several pauses and vacant stares, finally filled up and signed a check for fifty thousand francs, and handed it across the table to Dupin. The latter examined it carefully and deposited it in his pocketbook; then, unlocking an *escritoire,* took thence a letter and gave it to the Prefect. This functionary grasped it in a perfect agony of joy, opened it with a trembling hand, cast a rapid glance at its contents, and then, scrambling and struggling to the door, rushed at length unceremoniously from the room and from the house, without having uttered a syllable since Dupin had requested him to fill up the check.

When he had gone, my friend entered into some explanations.

"The Parisian police," he said, "are exceedingly able in their way. They are persevering, ingenious, cunning, and thoroughly versed in the knowledge which their duties seem chiefly to demand. Thus, when G—— detailed to us his mode of searching the premises at the Hôtel D——, I felt entire confidence in his having made a satisfactory investigation—so far as his labors extended."

"So far as his labors extended?" said I.

"Yes," said Dupin. "The measures adopted were not only the best of their kind, but carried out to absolute perfection. Had the letter been deposited within the range of their search, these fellows would, beyond a question, have found it."

I merely laughed—but he seemed quite serious in all that he said.

"The measures, then," he continued, "were good in their kind, and well executed; their defect lay in their being inapplicable to the case, and to the man. A certain set of highly ingenious resources are, with the Prefect, a sort of Procrustean bed, to which he forcibly adapts his designs. But he perpetually errs by being too deep or too shallow for the matter in hand; and many a schoolboy is a better reasoner than he. I knew one about eight years of age whose success at guessing in the game of 'even and odd' attracted universal admiration. This game is simple, and is played with marbles. One player holds in his hand a number of these toys, and demands of another whether that number is even or odd. If the guess is right, the guesser wins one; if wrong, he loses one. The boy to whom I allude won all the marbles of the school. Of course he had some principle of guessing; and this lay in mere observation and admeasurement of the astuteness of his opponents. For example, an arrant simpleton is his opponent, and, holding up his closed hand, asks, 'Are they even or odd?' Our schoolboy replies, 'odd' and loses; but upon the second trial he wins, for he then says to himself, 'the simpleton had them even upon the first trial, and his amount of cunning is just sufficient to make him have them odd upon the second; I will therefore guess odd';—he guesses odd, and wins. Now, with a simpleton a degree above the first, he would have reasoned thus: 'This fellow finds that in the first instance I guessed odd, and, in the second, he will propose to himself upon the first impulse, a simple variation from even to odd, as did the first simpleton; but then a second thought will suggest that this is too simple a variation, and finally he will decide upon putting it even as before. I will therefore guess even';—he guesses even, and wins. Now this mode of reasoning in the schoolboy, whom his fellows termed 'lucky,'—what, in its last analysis, is it?"

"It is merely," I said, "an identification of the reasoner's intellect with that of his opponent."

"It is," said Dupin; "and, upon inquiring of the boy by what means he effected the *thorough* identification in which his success consisted, I received answer as follows: 'When I wish to find out how wise, or how stupid, or how good, or how wicked is any one, or what are his thoughts at the moment, I fashion the expression of my face, as accurately as possible, in accordance with the expression of his, and then wait to see what thoughts or sentiments arise in my mind or heart, as if to match or correspond with the expression.' This response of the schoolboy lies at the bottom of all the spurious profundity which has been attributed to Rochefoucauld, to La Bougive, to Machiavelli, and to Campanella."

"And the identification," I said, "of the reasoner's intellect with that of his opponent, depends, if I understand you aright, upon the accuracy with which the opponent's intellect is admeasured."

"For its practical value it depends upon this," replied Dupin; "and the Prefect and his cohort fail so frequently, first, by default of this identification, and, secondly, by ill-admeasurement, or rather through non-admeasurement, of the intellect with which they are engaged. They consider only their *own* ideas of ingenuity; and, in searching for anything hidden, advert only to the modes in which *they* would have hidden it. They are right in this much—that their own ingenuity is a faithful representative of that of *the mass;* but when the cunning of the individual felon is diverse in character from their own, the felon foils them, of course. This always happens when it is above their own, and very usually when it is below. They have no variation of principle in their investigations; at best, when urged by some unusual emergency—by some extraordinary reward—they extend or exaggerate their old modes of *practice,* without touching their principles. What, for example, in this case of D——, has been done to vary the principle of action? What is all this boring, and probing, and sounding, and scrutinizing with the microscope, and dividing the surface of the building into registered square inches—what is it all but an exaggeration *of the application* of the one principle or set of principles of search, which are based upon the one set of notions regarding human ingenuity, to which the Prefect, in the long routine of his duty, has been accustomed? Do you not see he has taken it for granted that *all* men proceed to conceal a letter,—not exactly in a gimlet-hole bored in a chair-leg—but, at least, in *some* out-of-the-way hole or corner suggested by the same tenor of thought which would urge a man to secrete a letter in a gimlet-hole bored in a chair-leg? And do you not see also, that such *recherchés* nooks for concealment are adapted only for ordinary occasions, and would be adopted only by ordinary intellects; for, in all cases of concealment, a disposal of the article concealed—a disposal of it in this *recherché* manner,—is, in the very first instance, presumable and presumed; and thus its discovery depends, not at all upon the acumen, but altogether upon the mere care, patience, and determination of the seekers; and where the case is of importance—or, what amounts to the same thing in the political eyes, when the reward is of magnitude,—the qualities in question have *never* been known to fail. You will now understand what I mean in suggesting that, had the purloined letter been hidden anywhere within the limits of the Prefect's examination—in other words, had the principle of its concealment been comprehended within the principles of the Prefect— its discovery would have been a matter altogether beyond question. This functionary, however, has been thoroughly mystified; and the remote source of his defeat lies in the supposition that the minister is a fool, because he has acquired renown as a poet. All fools are poets; this the Prefect *feels;* and he is merely guilty of a *non distributio medii* in thence inferring that all poets are fools."

"But is this really the poet?" I asked. "There are two brothers, I know; and both have attained reputation in letters. The minister I believe has written learnedly on the Differential Calculus. He is a mathematician, and no poet."

"You are mistaken; I know him well; he is both. As poet *and* mathematician, he would reason well; as mere mathematician, he could not have reasoned at all, and thus would have been at the mercy of the Prefect."

"You surprise me," I said, "by these opinions, which have been contradicted by the voice of the world. You do not mean to set at naught the well-digested idea of centuries. The mathematical reason has long been regarded as *the* reason *par excellence.*"

" '*Il y a à parier,*' " replied Dupin, quoting from Chamfort, " '*que toute idée publique, toute convention reçue, est une sottise, car elle a convenu au plus grand nombre.*' The mathematicians, I grant you, have done their best to promulgate the popular error to which you allude, and which is none the less an error for its promulgation as truth. With an art worthy a better cause, for example, they have insinuated the term 'analysis' into application to algebra. The French are the originators of this particular deception; but if a term is of any importance—if words derive any value from applicability—then 'analysis' conveys 'algebra' about as much as, in Latin, *ambitus* implies 'ambition,' *religio* 'religion,' or *homines honesti,* a set of *honorable* men."

"You have a quarrel on hand, I see," said I, "with some of the algebraists of Paris; but proceed."

"I dispute the availability, and thus the value, of that reason which is cultivated in any special form other than the abstractly logical. I dispute, in particular, the reason educed by mathematical study. The mathematics are the science of form and quantity; mathematical reasoning is merely logic applied to observation upon form and quantity. The great error lies in supposing that even the truths of what is called *pure* algebra, are abstract or general truths. And this error is so egregious that I am confounded at the universality with which it has been received. Mathematical axioms are *not* axioms of general truth. What is true of *relation* —of form and quantity—is often grossly false in regard to morals, for example. In this latter science it is very usually *un*true that the aggregated parts are equal to the whole. In chemistry also the axiom fails. In the consideration of motive it fails; for two motives, each of a given value, have not, necessarily, a value when united, equal to the sum of their values apart. There are numerous other mathematical truths which are only truths within the limits of *relation*. But the mathematician argues, from his *finite truths,* through habit, as if they were of an absolutely general applicability—as the world indeed imagines them to be. Bryant, in his very learned 'Mythology,' mentions an analogous source of error, when he says that 'although the Pagan fables are not believed, yet we forget ourselves continually, and make inferences from them as existing realities.' With the algebraists, however, who are Pagans themselves, the 'Pagan fables' *are* believed, and the inferences are made, not so much through lapse of memory, as through an unaccountable addling of the brains. In short, I never yet encountered the mere mathematician who could be trusted out of equal roots, or one who did not clandestinely hold it as a point of his faith that $x^2 + px$ was absolutely and unconditionally equal to q. Say to one of these gentlemen, by way of experiment, if you please, that you believe occasions may occur where $x^2 + px$ is *not* altogether equal to q, and, having made him understand what you mean, get out of his reach as speedily as convenient, for, beyond doubt, he will endeavor to knock you down.

"I mean to say," continued Dupin, while I merely laughed at his last observations, "that if the minister had been no more than a mathematician, the Prefect would have been under no necessity of giving me this check. I knew him, however, as both mathematician and poet, and my measures were adapted to his capacity, with reference to the circumstances by which he was surrounded. I knew him as a courtier, too, and as a bold *intrigant*. Such a man, I considered, could not fail to be aware of the ordinary policial modes of action. He could not have failed to anticipate—and events have proved that he did not fail to anticipate—the waylayings to which he was subjected. He must have foreseen, I reflected, the secret investigations of his premises. His frequent absences from home at night, which were hailed by the Prefect as certain aids to his success, I regarded only as *ruses,* to afford opportunity for thorough search to the police, and thus the sooner to impress them with the conviction to which G——, in fact, did finally arrive—the conviction that the letter was not upon the premises. I felt, also that the whole train of thought, which I was at some pains in detailing to you just now, concerning the invariable principle of policial action in searches for articles concealed—I felt that this whole train of thought would necessarily pass through the mind of the minister. It would imperatively lead him to despise all the ordinary *nooks* of concealment. *He* could not, I reflected, be so weak as not to see that the most intricate and remote recess of his hotel would be as open as his commonest closets to the eyes, to the probes, to the gimlets, and to the microscopes of the Prefect. I saw, in fine, that he would be driven, as a matter of course, to *simplicity,* if not deliberately induced to it as a matter of choice. You will remember, perhaps, how desperately the Prefect laughed when I suggested, upon our first interview, that it was just possible this mystery troubled him so much on account of its being so *very* self-evident."

"Yes," said I, "I remember his merriment well. I really thought he would have fallen into convulsions."

"The material world," continued Dupin, "abounds with very strict analogies to the immaterial; and thus some color of truth has been given to the rhetorical dogma, that metaphor, or simile, may be made to strengthen an argument, as well as to embellish a description. The principle of the *vis inertiæ,* for example, seems to be identical in physics and metaphysics. It is not more true in the former, that a large body is with more difficulty set in motion than a smaller one, and that its subsequent *momentum* is commensurate with this difficulty, than it is, in the latter, that intellects of the vaster capacity, while more forcible, more constant, and more eventful in their movements than those of inferior grade, are yet the less readily moved, and more embarrassed and full of hesitation in the first few steps of their progress. Again: have you ever noticed which of the street signs, over the shop doors, are the most attractive of attention?"

"I have never given the matter a thought," I said.

"There is a game of puzzles," he resumed, "which is played upon a map. One party playing requires another to find a given word—the name of town, river, state or empire—any word, in short, upon the motley and perplexed surface of the chart. A novice in the game generally seeks to embarrass his opponents by giving them the most minutely-lettered names; but the adept selects such words as stretch, in large characters, from one end of the chart to the other. These, like the over-largely lettered signs and placards of the street, escape observation by dint of being excessively obvious; and here the physical oversight is precisely analogous with the moral inapprehension by which the intellect suffers to pass unnoticed those considerations which are too obtrusively and too palpably self-evident. But this is a point, it appears, somewhat above or beneath the understanding of the Prefect. He never once thought it probable, or possible, that the minister had deposited the letter immediately beneath the nose of the whole world, by way of best preventing any portion of that world from perceiving it.

"But the more I reflected upon the daring, dashing, and discriminating ingenuity of D——; upon the fact that the document must always have been *at hand,* if he intended to use it to good purpose; and upon the decisive evidence, obtained by the Prefect, that it was not hidden within the limits of that dignitary's ordinary search—the more satisfied I became that, to conceal this letter, the minister had resorted to the comprehensive and sagacious expedient of not attempting to conceal it at all.

"Full of these ideas, I prepared myself with a pair of green spectacles, and called one fine morning, quite by accident, at the ministerial hotel. I found D—— at home, yawning, lounging, and dawdling, as usual, and pretending to be in the last extremity of *ennui.* He is, perhaps, the most really energetic human being now alive—but that is only when nobody sees him.

"To be even with him, I complained of my weak eyes, and lamented the necessity of the spectacles, under cover of which I cautiously and thoroughly surveyed the apartment, while seemingly intent only upon the conversation of my host.

"I paid special attention to a large writing-table near which he sat, and upon which lay confusedly, some miscellaneous letters and other papers, with one or two musical instruments and a few books. Here, however, after a long and very deliberate scrutiny, I saw nothing to excite particular suspicion.

"At length my eyes, in going the circuit of the room, fell upon a trumpery filigree card-rack of pasteboard, that hung dangling by a dirty blue ribbon, from a little brass knob just beneath the middle of the mantelpiece. In this rack, which had three or four compartments, were five or six visiting cards and a solitary letter. This last was much soiled and crumpled. It was torn nearly in two, across the middle—as if a design, in the first instance, to tear it entirely up as worthless, had been altered, or stayed, in the second. It had a large black seal, bearing the D—— cipher *very* conspicuously, and was addressed, in a diminutive female hand, to D——, the minister, himself. It was thrust carelessly, and even, as it seemed, contemptuously, into one of the upper divisions of the rack.

"No sooner had I glanced at this letter, than I concluded it to be that of which I was in search. To be sure, it was, to all appearance, radically different from the one of which the Prefect had read us so minute a description. Here the seal was large and black, with the D—— cipher; there it was small and red, with the ducal arms of the S—— family. Here, the address, to the minister, was diminutive and feminine; there the superscription, to a certain royal personage, was markedly bold and decided; the size alone formed a point of correspondence. But, then, the *radicalness* of these differences, which was excessive; the dirt; the soiled and torn condition of the paper, so inconsistent with the *true* methodical habits of D——, and so suggestive of a design to delude the beholder into an idea of the worthlessness of the document; these things, together with the hyperobtrusive situation of this document, full in the view of every visitor, and thus exactly in accordance with the conclusions to which I had previously arrived; these things, I say, were strongly corroborative of suspicion, in one who came with the intention to suspect.

"I protracted my visit as long as possible, and, while I maintained a most animated discussion with the minister, on a topic which I knew well had never failed to interest and excite him, I kept my attention really riveted upon the letter. In this examination, I committed to memory its external appearance and arrangement in the rack; and also fell, at length, upon a discovery which set at rest whatever trivial doubt I might have entertained. In scrutinizing the edges of the paper, I observed them to be more *chafed* than seemed necessary. They presented the *broken* appearance which is manifested when a stiff paper, having been once folded and pressed with a folder, is refolded in a reversed direction, in the same creases or edges which had formed the original fold. This discovery was sufficient. It was clear to me that the letter had been turned, as a glove, inside out, redirected, and resealed. I bade the minister good morning, and took my departure at once, leaving a gold snuff-box upon the table.

"The next morning I called for the snuff-box, when we resumed, quite eagerly, the conversation of the preceding day. While thus engaged, however, a loud report, as if of a pistol, was heard immediately beneath the windows of the hotel, and was succeeded by a series of fearful screams, and the shoutings of a mob. D—— rushed to a casement, threw it open, and looked out. In the meantime, I stepped to the card-rack, took the letter, put it in my pocket, and replaced it by a *facsimile* (so far as regards externals), which I had carefully prepared at my lodgings; imitating the D—— cipher, very readily, by means of a seal formed of bread.

"The disturbance in the street had been occasioned by the frantic behavior of a man with a musket. He had fired it among a crowd of women and children. It proved, however, to have been without ball, and the fellow was suffered to go his way as a lunatic or a drunkard. When he had gone, D—— came from the window, whither I had followed him immediately upon securing the object in view. Soon afterwards I bade him farewell. The pretended lunatic was a man in my own pay."

"But what purpose had you," I asked, "in replacing the letter by a *facsimile*? Would it not have been better, at the first visit, to have seized it openly, and departed?"

"D——," replied Dupin, "is a desperate man, and a man of nerve. His hotel, too, is not without attendants devoted to his interests. Had I made the wild attempt you suggest, I might never have left the ministerial presence alive. The good people of Paris might have heard of me no more. But I had an object apart from these considerations. You know my political prepossessions. In this matter, I act as a partisan of the lady concerned. For eighteen months the minister has had her in his power. She has now him in hers; since, being unaware that the letter is not in his possession, he will proceed with his exactions as if it was. Thus will he inevitably commit himself, at once, to his political destruction. His downfall, too, will not be more precipitate than awkward. It is all very well to talk about the *facilis descensus Averni;* but in all kinds of climb-ing, as Catalani said of singing, it is far more easy to get up than to come down. In the present instance I have no sympathy—at least no pity—for him who descends. He is that *monstrum horrendum,* an unprincipled man of genius. I confess, however, that I should like very well to know the precise character of his thoughts, when, being defied by her whom the Prefect terms 'a certain personage,' he is reduced to opening the letter which I left for him in the card-rack."

"How? Did you put anything particular in it?"

"Why—it did not seem altogether right to leave the interior blank—that would have been insulting. D——, at Vienna once, did me an evil turn, which I told him, quite good-humoredly, that I should remember. So, as I knew he would feel some curiosity in regard to the identity of the person who had outwitted him, I thought it a pity not to give him a clue. He is well acquainted with my MS., and I just copied into the middle of the blank sheet the words—

'——Un dessein si funeste,
S'il n'est digne d'Atrée, est digne de Thyeste.'

They are to be found in Crébillon's 'Atrée.'"

8

Billy Budd, Foretopman

WHAT BEFELL HIM IN THE YEAR OF THE GREAT MUTINY

BY HERMAN MELVILLE

DEDICATED TO JACK CHASE, ENGLISHMAN
WHEREVER THAT GREAT HEART MAY NOW BE HERE ON
EARTH OR HARBORED IN PARADISE. CAPTAIN OF THE
MAINTOP IN THE YEAR 1843 IN THE U. S. FRIGATE
"UNITED STATES"

Preface

THE year 1797, the year of this narrative, belongs to a period which, as every thinker now feels, involved a crisis for Christendom not exceeded in its undetermined momentousness at the time by any other era whereof there is record. The opening proposition made by the Spirit of that Age * involved rectification of the Old World's hereditary wrongs. In France, to some extent, this was bloodily effected. But what then? Straightway the Revolution itself became a wrongdoer, one more oppressive than the kings. Under Napoleon it enthroned upstart kings, and initiated that prolonged agony of continual war whose final throe was Waterloo. During those years not the wisest could have foreseen that the outcome of all would be what to some thinkers apparently it has since turned out to be—a political advance along nearly the whole line for Europeans.

Now, as elsewhere hinted, it was something caught from the Revolutionary Spirit that at Spithead emboldened the man-of-war's men to rise against real abuses, long-standing ones, and afterwards at the Nore to

* Crossed out; was one hailed by the noblest men of it. Even the dry tinder of a Wordsworth took fire.

make inordinate and aggressive demands—successful resistance to which was confirmed only when the ringleaders were hung for an admonitory spectacle to the anchored fleet. Yet in a way analogous to the operation of the Revolution at large—the Great Mutiny, though by Englishmen naturally deemed monstrous at the time, doubtless gave the first latent prompting to most important reforms in the British navy.

IN the time before steamships, or then more frequently than now, a stroller along the docks of any considerable seaport would occasionally have his attention arrested by a group of bronzed marines, man-of-war's men or merchant-sailors in holiday attire ashore on liberty. In certain instances they would flank, or, like a bodyguard, quite surround some superior figure of their own class, moving along with them like Aldebaran among the lesser lights of his constellation. That signal object was the "Handsome Sailor" of the less prosaic time, alike of the military and merchant navies. With no perceptible trace of the vainglorious about him, rather with the off-hand unaffectedness of natural regality, he seemed to accept the spontaneous homage of his shipmates. A somewhat remarkable instance recurs to me. In Liverpool, now half a century ago, I saw under the shadow of the great dingy street-wall of Prince's Dock (an obstruction long since removed) a common sailor, so intensely black that he must needs have been a native African of the unadulterated blood of Ham. A symmetric figure, much above the average in height. The two ends of a gay silk handkerchief thrown loose about the neck danced upon the displayed ebony of his chest; in his ears were big hoops of gold, and a Scotch Highland bonnet with a tartan band set off his shapely head.

It was a hot noon in July, and his face, lustrous with perspiration, beamed with barbaric good-humor. In jovial sallies right and left, his white teeth flashing into view, he rollicked along, the center of a company of his shipmates. These were made up of such an assortment of tribes and complexions as would have well fitted them to be marched up by Anacharsis Cloots before the bar of the first French Assembly as Representatives of the Human Race. At each spontaneous tribute rendered by the wayfarers to this black pagod of a fellow—the tribute of a pause and stare, and less frequent an exclamation—the motley retinue showed that they took that sort of pride in the evoker of it which the Assyrian priests doubtless showed for their grand sculptured Bull when the faithful prostrated themselves. To return—

If in some cases a bit of a nautical Murat in setting forth his person ashore, the Handsome Sailor of the period in question evinced nothing of the dandified Billy-be-Damn—an amusing character all but extinct now, but occasionally to be encountered, and in a form yet more amusing than the original, at the tiller of the boats on the tempestuous Erie Canal or, more likely, vaporing in the groggeries along the towpath. Invariably a proficient in his perilous calling, he was also more or less of a mighty boxer or wrestler. It was strength and beauty. Tales of his prowess were recited. Ashore he was the champion; afloat the spokesman; on every suitable occasion always foremost. Close-reefing topsails in a gale, there he was—astride the weather yard-arm-end, foot in "stirrup," both hands tugging at the "earring" as at a bridle, in very much the attitude of the young Alexander curbing the fiery Bucephalus. A superb figure, tossed up as by the horns of Taurus against the thunderous sky, cheerily ballooning to the strenuous file along the spar.

The moral nature was seldom out of keeping with the physical make. Indeed, except as toned by the former, the comeliness and power, always attractive in masculine perfection, hardly could have drawn the sort of homage the Handsome Sailor, in some examples, received from his less gifted associates.

Such a cynosure, at least in aspect, and something such too in nature, though with important variations made apparent as the story proceeds, was welkin-eyed Billy Budd, or Baby Budd—as more familiarly, under circumstances hereafter to be given, he at last came to be called—aged twenty-one, a foretopman of the fleet towards the close of the last decade of the eighteenth century. It was not very long prior to the time of the narration that follows, that he had entered the King's Service, having been impressed on the Narrow Seas from a homeward-bound English merchantman into a seventy-four outward-bound, H.M.S. *Indomitable*; which ship, as was not unusual in those hurried days, had been obliged to put to sea short of her proper complement of men. Plump upon Billy at first sight in the gangway the boarding officer, Lieutenant Ratcliffe, pounced, even before the merchantman's crew formally was mustered on the quarter-deck for his deliberate inspection. And him only he elected. For whether it was because the other men when ranged before him showed to ill advantage after Billy, or whether he had some scruples in view of the merchantman being rather short-handed; however it might be, the officer contented himself with his first spontaneous choice. To the surprise of the ship's company, though much to the Lieutenant's satisfaction, Billy made no demur. But indeed any demur would have been as idle as the protest of a goldfinch popped into a cage.

Noting this uncomplaining acquiescence, all but cheerful one might say, the shipmates turned a surprised glance of silent reproach at the sailor. The shipmaster was one of those worthy mortals found in every vocation—even the humbler ones—the sort of person whom everybody agrees in calling "a respectable man." And—nor so strange to report as it may appear to be—though a ploughman of the troubled waters, life-long contending with the intractable elements, there was nothing this honest soul at heart loved better than simple peace and quiet. For the rest, he was fifty or thereabouts, a little inclined to corpulence, a prepossessing face, unwhiskered, and of an agreeable color—a rather full face, humanely intelligent in expression. On a fair day with a fair wind and all going well, a certain musical chime in his voice seemed to be the veritable unobstructed outcome of the innermost man. He had much prudence, much conscientiousness, and there were occasions when these virtues were the cause of overmuch disquietude in him. On a passage, so long as his craft was in any proximity to land, there was no sleep for Captain Graveling. He took to heart those serious responsibilities not so heavily borne by some shipmasters.

Now, while Billy Budd was down in the forecastle, getting his kit together, the *Indomitable's* Lieutenant—burly and bluff, nowise disconcerted by Captain Graveling's omitting to proffer the customary hospitalities on an occasion so unwelcome to him; an omission simply caused by preoccupation of thought—unceremoniously invited himself into the cabin, and also to a flask from the spirit locker, a receptacle which his experienced eye instantly discovered. In fact, he was one of those sea-dogs in whom all the hardship and peril of naval life in the great prolonged wars of his time never impaired the natural instinct for sensuous enjoyment. His duty he always faithfully did; but duty is sometimes a dry obligation, and he was for irrigating its aridity whensoever possible with a fertilizing decoction of strong waters. For the cabin's proprietor there was nothing left but to play the part of the enforced host with whatever grace and alacrity were practicable. As necessary adjuncts to the flask he silently placed tumbler and water-jug before the irrepressible guest. But excusing himself from partaking just then, he dismally watched the unembarrassed officer deliberately diluting his grog a little, then tossing it off in three swallows, pushing the empty tumbler away, yet not so far as to be beyond easy reach, at the same time settling himself in his seat and smacking his lips with high satisfaction, looking straight at the host.

These proceedings over, the Master broke the silence; and there lurked a rueful reproach in the tone of his voice: "Lieutenant, you are going to take my best man from me, the jewel of 'em."

"Yes, I know," rejoined the other, immediately drawing back the tumbler preliminary to a replenishing. "Yes, I know. Sorry."

"Beg pardon, but you don't understand, Lieutenant. See here now. Before I shipped that young fellow, my forecastle was a rat-pit of quarrels. It was black times, I tell you, aboard the *Rights* here. I was worried to that degree my pipe had no comfort for me. But Billy came; and it was like a Catholic priest striking peace in an Irish shindy. Not that he preached to them or said or did anything in particular; but a virtue went out of him, sugaring the sour ones. They took to him like hornets to treacle; all but the bluffer of the gang, the big shaggy chap with the fire-red whiskers. He, indeed, out of envy perhaps of the newcomer, and thinking such a "sweet and pleasant fellow," as he mockingly designated him to the others, could hardly have the spirit of a game-cock, must needs bestir himself in trying to get up an ugly row with him. Billy forebore with him and reasoned with him in a pleasant way—he is something like myself, Lieutenant, to whom aught like a quarrel is hateful—but nothing served. So, in the second dog-watch one day the Red-Whiskers, in the presence of the others, under pretense of showing Billy just whence a sirloin steak was cut—for the fellow had once been a butcher—insultingly gave him a dig under the ribs. Quick as lightning Billy let fly his arm. I dare say he never meant to do quite as much as he did, but anyhow he gave the burly fool a terrible drubbing. It took about half a minute, I should think. And, Lord bless you, the lubber was astonished at the celerity. And will you believe it, Lieutenant, the Red-Whiskers now really loves Billy—loves him, or is the biggest hypocrite that ever I heard of. But they all love him. Some of 'em do his washing, darn old trousers for him; the carpenter is at odd times making a pretty little chest of drawers for him. Anybody will do anything for Billy Budd; and it's the happy family here. Now, Lieutenant, if that young fellow goes—I know how it will be aboard the *Rights*. Not again very soon shall I, coming up from dinner, lean over the capstan smoking a quiet pipe—no, not very soon again, I think. Ay, Lieutenant, you are going to take away the jewel of 'em; you are going to take away my peacemaker." And with that the good soul had really some ado in checking a rising sob.

"Well," answered the Lieutenant, who had listened with amused interest to all this, and now waxing merry with his tipple, "well, blessed are the peacemakers, especially the fighting peacemakers! And such are the seventy-four beauties, some of which you see poking their noses out of the portholes of yonder warship lying-to there for me," pointing through the cabin window at the *Indomitable*. "But courage! don't look so down-hearted, man. Why, I pledge you in advance the royal approbation. Rest assured that His Majesty will be delighted to know that in a time when his hard-tack is not sought for by sailors with such avidity as should be; a time also when some shipmasters privily resent the borrowing from them of a tar or two for the service; His Majesty, I say, will be delighted to learn that *one* shipmaster, at least, cheerfully surrenders to the King the flower of his flock: a sailor who with equal loyalty makes no dissent.—But where's my beauty? Ah," looking through the cabin's open door, "here he comes; and, by Jove—lugging along his chest—Apollo with his portmanteau! My man," stepping out to him, "you can't take that big box on board a warship. The boxes there are mostly shot-boxes. Put up your duds in a bag, lad. Boot and saddle for the cavalryman, bag and hammock for the man-of-war's man."

The transfer from chest to bag was made. And, after seeing his man into the cutter, and then following him down, the Lieutenant pushed off from the *Rights-of-Man*. That was the merchant ship's name; though by her master and crew abbreviated in sailor fashion into the *Rights*. The hard-headed Dundee owner was a staunch admirer of Thomas Paine, whose book in rejoinder to Burke's arraignment of the French Revolution had then been published for some time and had gone everywhere. In christening his vessel after the title of Paine's volume, the man of Dundee was something like his contemporary shipowner, Stephen Girard of Philadelphia, whose sympathies alike with his native land and its liberal philosophies he evinced by naming his ships after Voltaire, Diderot, and so forth.

But now, when the boat swept under the merchantman's stern, and officer and oarsmen were noting—some bitterly and others with a grin —the name emblazoned there; just then it was that the new recruit jumped up from the bow where the coxswain had directed him to sit, waving his hat to his silent shipmates sorrowfully looking over at him from the taffrail, and bade the lads a genial good-by. Then making a salutation as to the ship herself, "And good-by to you too, old *Rights-of-Man!*"

"Down, Sir," roared the Lieutenant, instantly assuming all the rigor of his rank, though with difficulty repressing a smile.

To be sure, Billy's action was a terrible breach of naval decorum. But in that decorum he had never been instructed; in consideration of which the Lieutenant would hardly have been so energetic in reproof but for the concluding farewell to the ship. This he rather took as meant to convey a covert sally on the new recruit's part—a sly slur at impressment in general, and that of himself in especial. And yet, more likely, if satire it was in effect, it was hardly so by intention, for Billy (though happily endowed with the gayety of high health, youth and a free heart) was yet by no means of a satirical turn. The will to it and the sinister dexterity were alike wanting. To deal in double meaning and insinuations of any sort was quite foreign to his nature.

As to his enforced enlistment—that he seemed to take pretty much as he was wont to take any vicissitude of weather. Like the animals, though no philosopher, he was, without knowing it, practically a fatalist. And, it may be, that he rather liked this adventurous turn in his affairs which promised an opening into novel scenes and martial excitements.

Aboard the *Indomitable* our merchant-sailor was forthwith rated as an able seaman, and assigned to the starboard watch of the foretop. He was soon at home in the service, not at all disliked for his unpretentious good looks and his rather genial happy-go-lucky air. No merrier man in his mess; in marked contrast to certain other individuals included like himself among the impressed portions of the ship's company; for these when not actively employed were sometimes—and more particularly in the last dog-watch, when the drawing near of twilight induced reverie—apt to fall into a saddish mood which in some partook of sullenness. But they were not so young as our foretopman, and no few of them must have known a hearth of some sort, others may have had wives and children left, too probably, in uncertain circumstances, and hardly any but must have acknowledged kith and kin; while for Billy, as will shortly be seen, his entire family was practically invested in himself.

II

Though our new-made foretopman was well received in the top and on the gun-decks, hardly here was he that cynosure he had previously been among those minor ship's companies of the merchant marine, with which companies only had he hitherto consorted.

He was young; and despite his all but fully developed frame, in aspect looked even younger than he really was. This was owing to a lingering adolescent expression in the as yet smooth face, all but feminine in purity of natural complexion, but where, thanks to his seagoing, the lily was quite suppressed and the rose had some ado visibly to flush through the tan.

To one essentially such a novice in the complexities of factitious life, the abrupt transition from his former and simpler sphere to the ampler and more knowing world of a great warship—this might well have abashed him had there been any conceit or vanity in his composition. Among her miscellaneous multitude, the *Indomitable* mustered several individuals who, however inferior in grade, were of no common natural stamp: sailors more signally susceptive of that air which continuous martial discipline and repeated presence in battle can in some degree impart even to the average man. As the "Handsome Sailor" Billy Budd'•

position aboard the seventy-four was something analogous to that of a rustic beauty transplanted from the provinces and brought into competition with the high-born dames of the court. But this change of circumstances he scarce noted. As little did he observe that something about him provoked an ambiguous smile in one or two harder faces among the blue-jackets. Nor less unaware was he of the peculiar favorable effect his person and demeanor had upon the more intelligent gentlemen of the quarter-deck. Nor could this well have been otherwise. Cast in a mold peculiar to the finest physical examples of those Englishmen in whom the Saxon strain would seem not at all to partake of any Norman or other admixture, he showed in face that humane look of reposeful good nature which the Greek sculptor in some instances gave to his heroic strong man, Hercules. But this again was subtly modified by another and pervasive quality. The ear, small and shapely, the arch of the foot, the curve in mouth and nostril, even the indurated hand dyed to the orange-tawny of the toucan's bill, a hand telling of the halyards and tar-buckets. But, above all, something in the mobile expression, and every chance attitude and movement, something suggestive of a mother eminently favored by Love and the Graces; all this strangely indicated a lineage in direct contradiction to his lot. The mysteriousness here became less mysterious through a matter of fact elicited when Billy at the capstan was being formally mustered into the service. Asked by the officer, a small, brisk little gentleman as it chanced, among other questions, his place of birth, he replied, "Please, Sir, I don't know."

"Don't know where you were born? Who was your father?"

"God knows, Sir."

Struck by the straightforward simplicity of these replies, the officer next asked, "Do you know anything about your beginning?"

"No, Sir. But I have heard that I was found in a pretty silk-lined basket hanging one morning from the knocker of a good man's door in Bristol."

" 'Found,' say you? Well," throwing back his head and looking up and down the new recruit; "well it turns out to have been a pretty good find. Hope they'll find some more like you, my man; the fleet sadly needs them."

Yes, Billy Budd was a foundling, a presumable by-blow, and, evidently, no ignoble one. Noble descent was as evident in him as in a blood horse.

For the rest, with little or no sharpness of faculty or any trace of the wisdom of the serpent, nor yet quite a dove, he possessed that kind and degree of intelligence which goes along with the unconventional rectitude of a sound human creature—one to whom not as yet had been proffered the questionable apple of knowledge. He was illiterate. He could not read, but he could sing, and like the illiterate nightingale was some-times the composer of his own song.

Of self-consciousness he seemed to have little or none, or about as much as we may reasonably impute to a dog of St. Bernard's breed.

Habitually being with the elements, and knowing little more of the land than as a beach, or, rather, that portion of the terraqueous globe, providentially set apart for dance-houses, doxies and tapsters, in short what sailors call a "fiddlers' green," his simple nature remained un-sophisticated by those moral obliquities which are not in every case incomparable with that manufacturable thing known as respectability. But are sailors, frequenters of fiddlers' greens, without vices? No; but less often than with landsmen do their vices, so called, partake of crook-edness of heart, seeming less to proceed from viciousness than from exuberance of vitality after long restraint, frank manifestations in ac-cordance with natural law. By his original constitution aided by the co-operating influences of his lot, Billy in many respects was little more than a sort of upright barbarian, much such perhaps as Adam presum-ably might have been ere the urbane Serpent wriggled himself into his company.

And here be it submitted that, apparently going to corroborate the doctrine of man's fall—a doctrine now popularly ignored—it is observ-able that where certain virtues pristine and unadulterate peculiarly char-acterize anybody in the external uniform of civilization, they will upon scrutiny seem not to be derived from custom or convention but rather to be out of keeping with these, as if indeed exceptionally transmitted from a period prior to Cain's City and citified man. The character marked by such qualities has to an unvitiated taste an untampered-with flavor like that of berries, while the man thoroughly civilized, even in a fair specimen of the breed, has to the same moral palate a questionable smack as of a compounded wine. To any stray inheritor of these primi-tive qualities found, like Caspar Hauser, wandering dazed in any Chris-tian capital of our time, the poet's famous invocation, near two thousand years ago, of the good rustic out of his latitude in the Rome of the Cæsars, still appropriately holds:—

> *"Faithful in word and thought,*
> *What has Thee, Fabian, to the city brought."*

Though our Handsome Sailor had as much of masculine beauty as one can expect anywhere to see; nevertheless, like the beautiful woman in one of Hawthorne's minor tales, there was just one thing amiss in him. No visible blemish, indeed, as with the lady; no, but an occasional liability to a vocal defect. Though in the hour of elemental uproar or peril, he was everything that a sailor should be, yet under sudden provocation of strong heart-feeling his voice, otherwise singularly musical, as if expressive of the harmony within, was apt to develop an organic hesitancy—in fact more or less of a stutter or even worse. In this particular Billy was a striking instance that the arch interpreter, the envious marplot of Eden, still has more or less to do with every human consignment to this planet of earth. In every case, one way or another, he is sure to slip in his little card, as much as to remind us—I too have a hand here.

The avowal of such an imperfection in the Handsome Sailor should be evidence not alone that he is not presented as a conventional hero, but also that the story in which he is the main figure is no romance.

III

At the time of Billy Budd's arbitrary enlistment into the *Indomitable* that ship was on her way to join the Mediterranean fleet. No long time elapsed before the junction was affected. As one of that fleet the seventy-four participated in its movements: though at times on account of her superior sailing qualities, in the absence of frigates, despatched on separate duty as a scout—and at times on less temporary service. But with all this the story has little concernment, restricted as it is to the inner life of one particular ship and the career of an individual sailor.

It was the summer of 1797. In April of that year had occurred the commotion at Spithead followed in May by a second and yet more serious outbreak in the fleet at the Nore. The latter is known, and without exaggeration in the epithet, as the Great Mutiny. It was indeed a demonstration more menacing to England than the contemporary manifestoes and conquering and proselyting armies of the French Directory.

To the Empire, the Nore Mutiny was what a strike in the fire-brigade would be to London threatened by general arson. In a crisis when the Kingdom might well have anticipated the famous signal that some years later published along the naval line of battle what it was that upon occasion England expected of Englishmen; *that* was the time when at the mastheads of the three-deckers and seventy-fours moored in our own roadstead—a fleet, the right arm of a Power then all but the sole free conservative one of the Old World, the blue-jackets, to be numbered by thousands, ran up with hurrahs the British colors with the union and cross wiped out; by that cancellation transmuting the flag of founded law and freedom defined, into the enemy's red meteor of unbridled and unbounded revolt. Reasonable discontent growing out of practical grievances in the fleet had been ignited into irrational combustion as by live cinders blown across the Channel from France in flames.

The event converted into irony for a time those spirited strains of Dibdin—as a song-writer no mean auxiliary to the English Government

—at the European conjuncture, strains celebrating, among other things, the patriotic devotion of the British tar:

> *"And as for my life, 'tis the King's!"*

Such an episode in the Island's grand naval story her naval historians naturally abridge; one of them (G. P. R. James) candidly acknowledging that fain would he pass it over did not "impartiality forbid fastidiousness." And yet his mention is less a narration than a reference, having to do hardly at all with details. Nor are these readily to be found in the libraries. Like some other events in every age befalling states everywhere, including America, the Great Mutiny was of such character that national pride along with views of policy would fain shade it off into the historical background. Such events cannot be ignored, but there is a considerate way of historically treating them. If a well-constituted individual refrains from blazoning aught amiss or calamitous in his family, a nation in the like circumstance may without reproach be equally discreet.

Though after parleyings between Government and the ringleaders, and concessions by the former as to some glaring abuses, the first uprising—that at Spithead—with difficulty was put down, or matters for a time pacified; yet at the Nore the unforeseen renewal of insurrection on a yet larger scale, and emphasized in the conferences that ensued by demands deemed by the authorities not only inadmissible but aggressively insolent, indicated, if the red flag did not sufficiently do so, what was the spirit animating the men. Final suppression, however, there was, but only made possible perhaps by the unswerving loyalty of the marine corps, and a voluntary resumption of loyalty among influential sections of the crews. To some extent the Nore Mutiny may be regarded as analogous to the distempering *irruption* of contagious fever in a frame constitutionally sound, and which anon throws it off.

At all events, of these thousands of mutineers were some of the tars who not so very long afterwards—whether wholly prompted thereto by patriotism, or pugnacious instinct, or by both—helped to win a coronet for Nelson at the Nile, and the naval crown of crowns for him at Trafalgar. To the mutineers those battles, and especially Trafalgar, were a plenary absolution; and a grand one; for all that goes to make up scenic naval display is heroic magnificence in arms. Those battles, especially Trafalgar, stand unmatched in human annals.

IV

Concerning *"The greatest sailor since the world began"*—TENNYSON.

In this matter of writing, resolve as one may to keep to the main road, some bypaths have an enticement not readily to be withstood. Beckoned by the genius of Nelson, I am going to err into such a bypath. If the reader will keep me company I shall be glad. At the least we can promise ourselves that pleasure which is wickedly said to be in sinning, for a literary sin the divergence will be.

Very likely it is no new remark that the inventions of our time have at last brought about a change in sea warfare in degree corresponding to the revolution in all warfare effected by the original introduction from China into Europe of gunpowder. The first European firearm, a clumsy contrivance, was, as is well known, scouted by no few of the knights as a base implement, good enough peradventure for weavers too craven to stand up crossing steel with steel in frank fight. But as ashore knightly valor, though shorn of its blazonry, did not cease with the knights, neither on the seas, though nowadays in encounters there a certain kind of displayed gallantry be fallen out of date as hardly applicable under changed circumstances, did the nobler qualities of such naval magnates as Don John of Austria, Doria, Van Tromp, Jean Bart, the long line of British admirals and the American Decaturs of 1812 become obsolete with their wooden walls.

Nevertheless, to anybody who can hold the Present at its worth without being inappreciative of the Past, it may be forgiven, if to such an one the solitary old hulk at Portsmouth, Nelson's *Victory,* seems to float there, not alone as the decaying monument of a fame incorruptible, but also as a poetic reproach, softened by its picturesqueness, to the *Monitors* and yet mightier hulls of the European ironsides. And this not altogether because such craft are unsightly, unavoidably lacking the symmetry and grand lines of the old battleships, but equally for other reasons.

There are some, perhaps, who while not altogether inaccessible to that poetic reproach just alluded to, may yet on behalf of the new order be disposed to parry it; and this to the extent of iconoclasm, if need be. For example, prompted by the sight of the star inserted in the *Victory's* deck, designing the spot where the Great Sailor fell, these martial utilitarians may suggest considerations implying that Nelson's ornate publication of his person in battle was not only unnecessary, but not military, nay, savored of foolhardiness and vanity. They may add, too, that at Trafalgar it was in effect nothing less than a challenge to death; and death came; and that but for his bravado the victorious admiral might possibly have survived the battle, and so, instead of having his sagacious dying injunction overruled by his immediate successor in command, he himself when the contest was decided might have brought his shattered fleet to anchor, a proceeding which might have averted the deplorable loss of life by shipwreck in the elemental tempest that followed the martial one.

Well, should we set aside the more disputable point whether for various reasons it was possible to anchor the fleet, then plausibly enough the Benthamites of war may urge the above.

But it *might have been* is but boggy ground to build on. And certainly in foresight as to the larger issue of an encounter, and anxious preparation for it—buoying the deadly way and mapping it out, as at Copenhagen—few commanders have been so painstakingly circumspect as this reckless declarer of his person in fight.

Personal prudence, even when dictated by quite other than selfish considerations, is surely no special virtue in a military man; while an excessive love of glory, exercising to the uttermost heartfelt sense of duty, is the first. If the name of *Wellington* is not so much a trumpet to the blood as the simpler name of *Nelson*, the reason for this may be inferred from the above. Alfred in his funeral ode on the victor of Waterloo ventures not to call him the greatest soldier of all time, though in the same ode he invokes Nelson as "the greatest sailor since the world began."

At Trafalgar, Nelson, on the brink of opening the fight, sat down and wrote his last brief will and testament. If under the presentiment of the most magnificent of all victories, to be crowned by his own glorious death, a sort of priestly motive led him to dress his person in the jeweled vouchers of his own shining deeds; if thus to have adorned himself for the altar and the sacrifice were indeed vainglory, then affectation and fustian is each truly heroic line in the great epics and dramas, since in such lines the poet but embodies in verse those exaltations of sentiment that a nature like Nelson, the opportunity being given, vitalizes into acts.

V

The outbreak at the Nore was put down. But not every grievance was redressed. If the contractors, for example, were no longer permitted to ply some practices peculiar to their tribe everywhere, such as providing shoddy cloth, rations not sound, or false in the measure; not the less impressment, for one thing, went on. By custom sanctioned for centuries, and judicially maintained by a Lord Chancellor as late as Mansfield, that mode of manning the fleet, a mode now fallen into a sort of abeyance but never formally renounced, it was not practicable to give up in those years. Its abrogation would have crippled the indispensable fleet, one wholly under canvas, no steam-power, its innumerable sails and thousands of cannon, everything, in short, worked by muscle alone; a fleet the more insatiate in demand for men, because then multiplying its ships of all grades against contingencies present and to come of the convulsed Continent.

Discontent foreran the Two Mutinies, and more or less it lurkingly survived them. Hence it was not unreasonable to apprehend some return of trouble, sporadic or general. One instance of such apprehensions: In the same year with this story, Nelson, then Vice-Admiral Sir Horatio, being with the fleet off the Spanish coast, was directed by the Admiral in command to shift his pennant from the *Captain* to the *Theseus;* and for this reason: that the latter ship having newly arrived in the station from home where it had taken part in the Great Mutiny, danger was apprehended from the temper of the men; and it was thought that an officer like Nelson was the one, not indeed to terrorize the crew into base subjection, but to win them by force of his mere presence back to an allegiance, if not as enthusiastic as his own, yet as true. So it was that for a time on more than one quarter-deck anxiety did exist. At sea precautionary vigilance was strained against relapse. At short notice an engagement might come on. When it did, the lieutenants assigned to batteries felt it incumbent on them in some instances to stand with drawn swords behind the men working the guns.

But on board the seventy-four in which Billy now swung his hammock, very little in the manner of the men and nothing obvious in the demeanor of the officers would have suggested to an ordinary observer that the Great Mutiny was a recent event. In their general bearing and conduct the commissioned officers of a warship naturally take their tone from the commander, that is if he has that ascendancy of character that ought to be his.

Captain the Honorable Edward Fairfax Vere, to give his full title, was a bachelor of forty or thereabouts, a sailor of distinction, even in a time prolific of renowned seamen. Though allied to the higher nobility, his advancement had not been altogether owing to influences connected with that circumstance. He had seen much service, been in various engagements, always acquitting himself as an officer mindful of the welfare of his men, but never tolerating an infraction of discipline; thoroughly versed in the science of his profession, and intrepid to the verge of temerity, though never injudiciously so. For his gallantry in the West Indian waters as flag-lieutenant under Rodney in that Admiral's crowning victory over De Grasse, he was made a post-captain.

Ashore in the garb of a civilian, scarce anyone would have taken him for a sailor, more especially that he never garnished unprofessional talk with nautical terms, and grave in his bearing, evinced little appreciation of mere humor. It was not out of keeping with these traits that on a passage when nothing demanded his paramount action, he was the most undemonstrative of men. Any landsman, observing this gentleman not conspicuous by his stature and wearing no pronounced insignia, emerging from his retreat to the open deck, and noting the silent deference of the officers retiring to leeward, might have taken him for the King's guest, a civilian aboard the King's ship, some highly honorable discreet envoy on his way to an important post. But, in fact, this unobtrusiveness of demeanor may have proceeded from a certain unaffected modesty of manhood sometimes accompanying a resolute nature, a modesty evinced at all times not calling for pronounced action, and which shown in any rank of life suggests a virtue aristocratic in kind.

As with some others engaged in various departments of the world's more heroic activities, Captain Vere, though practical enough upon occasion, would at times betray a certain dreaminess of mood. Standing alone on the weather-side of the greater deck, one hand holding by the rigging, he would absently gaze off at the black sea. At the presentation to him then of some minor matter interrupting the current of his thoughts, he would show more or less irascibility; but instantly he would control it.

In the navy he was popularly known by the appellation—Starry Vere. How such a designation happened to fall upon one who, whatever his sturdy qualities, was without any brilliant ones, was in this wise: a favorite kinsman, Lord Denton, a free-handed fellow, had been the first to meet and congratulate him upon his return to England from the West Indian cruise: and but the day previous turning over a copy of Andrew Marvell's poems had lighted, not for the first time, however, upon the lines entitled "Appleton House," the name of one of the seats of their common ancestor, a hero in the German wars of the seventeenth century, in which poem occur the lines,

> "This 'tis to have been from the first
> In a domestic heaven nursed,
> Under the discipline severe
> Of Fairfax and the starry Vere."

And so, upon embracing his cousin fresh from Rodney's victory, wherein he had played so gallant a part, brimming over with just family pride in the sailor of their house, he exuberantly exclaimed, "Give ye joy, Ed; give ye joy, my starry Vere!" This got currency, and the novel prefix serving in familiar parlance readily to distinguish the *Indomitable's* Captain from another Vere, his senior, a distant relative, an officer of like rank in the navy, it remained permanently attached to the surname.

VI

In view of the part that the commander of the *Indomitable* plays in scenes shortly to follow, it may be well to fill out that sketch of him outlined in the previous chapter. Aside from his qualities as a sea-officer Captain Vere was an exceptional character. Unlike no few of England's renowned sailors, long and arduous service with signal devotion to it had not resulted in absorbing and *salting* the entire man. He had a marked leaning towards everything intellectual. He loved books, never going to sea without a newly replenished library, compact but of the best. The isolated leisure, in some cases so wearisome, falling at intervals to commanders even during a war-cruise, never was tedious to Captain Vere. With nothing of that literary taste which less heeds the thing conveyed than the vehicle, his bias was towards those books to which every serious mind of superior order occupying any active post of authority in the world, naturally inclines; books treating of actual men and events, no matter of what era—history, biography and unconventional writers, who, free from cant and convention, like Montaigne, honestly, and in the spirit of common sense, philosophize upon realities.

In this love of reading he found confirmation of his own more reserved thoughts—confirmation which he had vainly sought in social converse, so that as touching most fundamental topics, there had got to be established in him some positive convictions which he forefelt would abide in him essentially unmodified so long as his intelligent part remained unimpaired. In view of the humbled position in which his lot was cast, this was well for him. His settled convictions were as a dyke against those invading waters of novel opinion social, political, and otherwise, which carried away as in a torrent no few minds in those days, minds by nature not inferior to his own. While other members of that aristocracy to which by birth he belonged were incensed at the innovators mainly because their theories were inimical to the privileged classes, Captain Vere disinterestedly opposed them because they seemed to him incapable of embodiment in lasting institutions, but at war with the peace of the world and the good of mankind.

With minds less stored than his and less earnest, some officers of his rank, with whom at times he would necessarily consort, found him lacking in the companionable quality, a dry and bookish gentleman as they deemed. Upon any chance withdrawal from their company one would be apt to say to another something like this: "Vere is a noble fellow, Starry Vere. 'Spite the gazettes, Sir Horatio is at bottom scarce a better seaman or fighter. But between you and me now, don't you think there is a queer streak of the pedantic running through him? Yes, like the King's yarn in a coil of navy-rope!"

Some apparent ground there was for this sort of confidential criticism; since not only did the Captain's discourse never fall into the jocosely familiar, but in illustrating any point touching the stirring personages and events of the time, he would cite some historic character or incident of antiquity with the same easy air that he would cite from the moderns. He seemed unmindful of the circumstance that to his bluff company such remote allusions, however pertinent they might really be, were altogether alien to men whose reading was mainly confined to the journals. But considerateness in such matters is not easy to natures constituted like Captain Vere's. Their honesty prescribes to them directness, sometimes far-reaching, like that of a migratory fowl that in its flight never heeds when it crosses a frontier.

VII

The lieutenants and other commissioned gentlemen forming Captain Vere's staff it is not necessary here to particularize nor needs it to make mention of any of the warrant-officers. But among the petty officers was one who, having much to do with the story, may as well be forthwith introduced. This portrait I essay, but shall never hit it.

This was John Claggart, the Master-at-arms. But that sea-title may to landsmen seem somewhat equivocal. Originally, doubtless, that petty-officer's function was the instruction of the men in the use of arms, sword, or cutlass. But very long ago, owing to the advance in gunnery making hand-to-hand encounters less frequent—and giving to niter and sulphur the pre-eminence over steel—that function ceased; the master-at-arms of a great warship becoming a sort of Chief of Police charged, among other matters, with the duty of preserving order on the populous lower gun-decks.

Claggart was a man of about five-and-thirty, somewhat spare and tall yet of no ill figure upon the whole. His hand was too small and shapely to have been accustomed to hard toil. The face was a notable one; the features, all except the chin, cleanly cut as those on a Greek medallion; yet the chin, beardless as Tecumseh's, had something of the strange protuberant heaviness in its make that recalled the prints of the Rev. Dr. Titus Oates, the historical deponent with the clerical drawl in the time of Charles II, and the fraud of the alleged Popish Plot. It served Claggart in his office that his eye could cast a tutoring glance. His brow was of the sort phrenologically associated with more than average intellect; silken jet curls partly clustering over it, making a foil to the pallor below, a pallor tinged with a faint shade of amber akin to the hue of time-tinted marbles of old.

This complexion singularly contrasting with the red or deeply bronzed visages of the sailors, and in part the result of his official seclusion from the sunlight, though it was not exactly displeasing, nevertheless seemed to hint of something defective or abnormal in the constitution and blood. But his general aspect and manner were so suggestive of an education and career incongruous with his naval function, that when not actively engaged in it he looked like a man of high quality, social and moral, who for reasons of his own was keeping incog. Nothing was known of his former life. It might be that he was an Englishman; and yet there lurked a bit of accent in his speech suggesting that possibly he was not such by birth, but through naturalization in early childhood. Among certain grizzled sea-gossips of the gun-decks and forecastle went a rumor perdue that the master-at-arms was a chevalier who had volunteered into the King's navy by way of compounding for some mysterious swindle whereof he had been arraigned at the King's bench. The fact that nobody could substantiate this report was, of course, nothing against its secret currency. Such a rumor once started on the gun-decks in reference to almost any one below the rank of a commissioned officer would, during the period assigned to this narrative, have seemed not altogether wanting in credibility to the tarry old wiseacres of a man-of-war crew. And indeed a man of Claggart's accomplishments, without prior nautical experience entering the navy at mature life, as he did, and necessarily allotted at the start to the lowest grade in it; a man, too, who never made allusion to his previous life ashore; these were circumstances which in the dearth of exact knowledge as to his true antecedents opened to the invidious a vague field for unfavorable surmise.

But the sailors' dog-watch gossip concerning him derived a vague plausibility from the fact that now, for some period, the British Navy could so little afford to be squeamish in the matter of keeping up the muster-rolls, that not only were press gangs notoriously abroad both afloat and ashore, but there was little or no secret about another matter, namely, that the London police were at liberty to capture any able-bodied suspect, and any questionable fellow at large, and summarily ship him to the dockyard or fleet. Furthermore, even among voluntary enlistments, there were instances where the motive thereto partook neither of patriotic impulse nor yet of a random desire to experience a bit of sea-life and martial adventure. Insolvent debtors of minor grade, together with the promiscuous lame ducks of morality, found in the navy a convenient and secure refuge. Secure, because once enlisted aboard a King's-Ship, they were as much in sanctuary, as the transgressor of the Middle Ages harboring himself under the shadow of the altar. Such sanctioned irregularities, which for obvious reasons the Government would hardly think to parade at the time—and which consequently, and as affecting the least influential class of mankind, have all but dropped into oblivion—lends color to something for the truth whereof I do not vouch, and hence have some scruple in stating; something I remember having seen in print, though the book I cannot recall; but the same thing was personally communicated to me now more than forty years ago by an old pensioner in a cocked hat, with whom I had a most interesting talk on the terrace at Greenwich, a Baltimore Negro, a Trafalgar man. It was to this effect: In the case of a warship short of hands, whose speedy sailing was imperative, the deficient quota, in lack of any other way of making it good, would be eked out by drafts called direct from the jails. For reasons previously suggested it would not perhaps be very easy at the present day directly to prove or disprove the allegation. But allowed as a verity, how significant would it be of England's straits at the time, confronted by those wars which, like a flight of harpies, rose shrieking from the din and dust of the fallen Bastille. That era appears measurably clear to us who look back at it, and but read of it. But to the grandfathers of us graybeards, the thoughtful of them, the genius of it presented an aspect like that of Camoen's "Spirit of the Cape," an eclipsing menace, mysterious and prodigious. Not America even was exempt from apprehension. At the height of Napoleon's unexampled conquests, there were Americans who had fought at Bunker Hill, who looked forward to the possibility that the Atlantic might prove no barrier against the ultimate schemes of this portentous upstart from the revolutionary chaos, who seemed in act of fulfilling the judgment prefigured in the Apocalypse.

But the less credence was to be given to the gun-deck talk touching Claggart, seeing that no man holding his office in a man-of-war can ever hope to be popular with the crew. Besides, in derogatory comments upon any one against whom they have a grudge, or for any reason or no reason mislike, sailors are much like landsmen: they are apt to exaggerate or romance it.

About as much was really known to the *Indomitable's* tars of the Master-at-arms' career before entering the service as an astronomer knows about a comet's travels prior to its first observable appearance in the sky. The verdict of the sea *guid nunc's* has been cited only by way of showing what sort of moral impression the man made upon rude uncultivated natures whose conceptions of human wickedness were necessarily of the narrowest, limited to ideas of vulgar rascality—a thief among the swinging hammocks during a night watch, or the man-brokers and land-sharks of the seaports.

It was no gossip, however, but fact, that though, as before hinted, Claggart upon his entrance into the navy was, as a novice, assigned to the least honorable section of a man-of-war's crew, embracing the drudges, he did not long remain there.

The superior capacity he immediately evinced, his constitutional sobriety, his ingratiating deference to superiors, together with a peculiar ferreting genius manifested on a singular occasion, all this capped by a certain austere patriotism, abruptly advanced him to the position of Master-at-arms.

Of this maritime Chief of Police the ship's-corporals, so called, were the immediate subordinates, and compliant ones; and this—as is to be noted in some business departments ashore—almost to a degree inconsistent with entire moral volition. His place put various converging wires of underground influence under the Chief's control, capable when astutely worked through his understrappers of operating to the mysterious discomfort, if nothing worse, of any of the sea-commonalty.

VIII

Life in the foretop well agreed with Billy Budd. There, when not actually engaged on the yards yet higher aloft, the topmen, who as such had been picked out for youth and activity, constituted an aërial club, lounging at ease against the smaller stun'sails rolled up into cushions, spinning yarns like the lazy gods, and frequently amused with what was going on in the busy world of the decks below. No wonder then that a young fellow of Billy's disposition was well content in such society. Giving no cause of offense to anybody, he was always alert at a call. So in the merchant service it had been with him. But now such punctiliousness in duty was shown that his topmates would sometimes good-naturedly laugh at him for it. This heightened alacrity had its cause, namely, the impression made upon him by the first formal gangway-punishment he had ever witnessed, which befell the day following his impressment. It had been incurred by a little fellow, young, a novice, an after-guardsman absent from his assigned post when the ship was being put about, a dereliction resulting in a rather serious hitch to that maneuver, one demanding instantaneous promptitude in letting go and making fast. When Billy saw the culprit's naked back under the scourge gridironed with red welts, and worse; when he marked the dire expression in the liberated man's face, as with his woolen shirt flung over him by the executioner, he rushed forward from the spot to bury himself in the crowd, Billy was horrified. He resolved that never through remissness would he make himself liable to such a visitation, or do or omit aught that might merit even verbal reproof. What then was his surprise and concern when ultimately he found himself getting into petty trouble occasionally about such matters as the stowage of his bag, or something amiss in his hammock, matters under the police oversight of the ship's-corporals of the lower decks, and which brought down on him a vague threat from one of them.

So heedful in all things as he was, how could this be? He could not understand it, and it more than vexed him. When he spoke to his young topmates about it, they were either lightly incredulous, or found something comical in his unconcealed anxiety. "Is it your bag, Billy?" said one; "well, sew yourself up in it, Billy boy, and then you'll be sure to know if anybody meddles with it."

Now there was a veteran aboard who, because his years began to disqualify him for more active work, had been recently assigned duty as mainmast-man in his watch, looking to the gear belayed at the rail round about that great spar near the deck. At off-times the foretopman had picked up some acquaintance with him, and now in his trouble it occurred to him that he might be the sort of person to go to for wise counsel. He was an old Dansker long anglicized in the service, of few words, many wrinkles and some honorable scars. His wizened face, time-tinted and weather-stormed to the complexion of an antique parchment, was here and there peppered blue by the chance explosion of a gun-cartridge in action. He was an *Agamemnon*-man; some two years prior to the time of this story having served under Nelson, when but Sir Horatio, in that ship immortal in naval memory, and which, dismantled and in part broken up to her bare ribs, is seen a grand skeleton in Hayden's etching. As one of a boarding-party from the *Agamemnon* he had received a cut slantwise along one temple and cheek, leaving a long pale scar like a streak of dawn's light falling athwart the dark visage. It was on account of that scar and the affair in which it was known that he had received it, as well as from his blue-peppered complexion, that the Dansker went among the *Indomitable's* crew by the name of "Board-her-in-the-smoke."

Now the first time that his small weazel eyes happened to light on Billy Budd, a certain grim internal merriment set all his ancient wrinkles into antic play. Was it that his eccentric unsentimental old sapience, primitive in its kind, saw, or thought it saw, something which in contrast with the warship's environment looked oddly incongruous in the Handsome Sailor? But after slyly studying him at intervals, the old Merlin's equivocal merriment was modified. For now when the twain would meet, it would start in his face a quizzing sort of look, but it would be but momentary, and sometimes replaced by an expression of speculative query as to what might eventually befall a nature like that, dropped into a world not without some man-traps and against whose subtleties simple courage lacking experience and address and without any touch of defensive ugliness, is of little avail; and where such innocence as man is capable of does yet, in a moral emergency, not always sharpen the faculties or enlighten the will.

However it was, the Dansker in his ascetic way rather took to Billy. Nor was this only because of a certain philosophic interest in such a character. There was another cause. While the old man's eccentricities, sometimes bordering on the ursine, repelled the juniors, Billy, undeterred thereby, would make advances, never passing the old *Agamemnon*-man without a salutation marked by that respect which is seldom lost on the aged, however crabbed at times, or whatever their station in life. There was a vein of dry humor, or what not, in the mast-man; and whether in freak of patriarchal irony touching Billy's youth and athletic frame, or for some other and more recondite reason, from the first in addressing him he always substituted Baby for Billy. The Dansker, in fact, being the originator of the name by which the foretopman eventually became known aboard ship.

Well then, in his mysterious little difficulty going in quest of the wrinkled one, Billy found him off duty in a dog-watch ruminating by himself, seated on a shot-box of the upper gun-deck, now and then surveying with a somewhat cynical regard certain of the more swaggering promenaders there. Billy recounted his trouble, again wondering how it all happened. The salt seer attentively listened, accompanying the foretopman's recitals with queer twitchings of his wrinkles and problematical little sparkles of his small ferret eyes. Making an end of his story, the foretopman asked, "And now, Dansker, do tell me what you think of it."

The old man, shoving up the front of his tarpaulin and deliberately rubbing the long slant scar at the point where it entered the thin hair, laconically said, "Baby Budd, *Jimmy Legs*" (meaning the master-at-arms) "is down on you."

"*Jimmy Legs!*" ejaculated Billy, his welkin eyes expanding; "what for? Why he calls me *the sweet and pleasant young fellow,* they tell me."

"Does he so?" grinned the grizzled one; then said, "Ay, Baby Lad, a sweet voice has *Jimmy Legs.*"

"No, not always. But to me he has. I seldom pass him but there comes a pleasant word."

"And that's because he's down upon you, Baby Budd."

Such reiteration, along with the manner of it (incomprehensible to a novice), disturbed Billy almost as much as the mystery for which he had sought explanation. Something less unpleasingly oracular he tried to extract. But the old sea-chiron, thinking perhaps that for the nonce he had sufficiently instructed his young Achilles, pursed his lips, gathered all his wrinkles together, and would commit himself to nothing further.

Years, and those experiences which befall certain shrewder men subordinated lifelong to the will of superiors, all this had developed in the Dansker the pithy guarded cynicism that was his leading characteristic.

IX

The next day an incident served to confirm Billy Budd in his incredulity as to the Dansker's strange summing up of the case submitted.

The ship at noon going large before the wind was rolling on her course, and he, below at dinner and engaged in some sportful talk with the members of his mess, chanced in a sudden lurch to spill the entire contents of his soup-pan upon the new scrubbed deck. Claggart, the master-at-arms, official rattan in hand, happened to be passing along the battery, in a bay of which the mess was lodged, and the greasy liquid streamed just across his path. Stepping over it, he was proceeding on his way without comment, since the matter was nothing to take notice of under the circumstances, when he happened to observe who it was that had done the spilling. His countenance changed. Pausing, he was about to ejaculate something hasty at the sailor, but checked himself, and pointing down to the streaming soup, playfully tapped him from behind with his rattan, saying, in a low musical voice, peculiar to him at times, "Handsomely done, my lad! And handsome is as handsome did it, too!" and with that passed on. Not noted by Billy as not coming within his view was the involuntary smile, or rather grimace, that accompanied Claggart's equivocal words. Aridly it drew down the thin corners of his shapely mouth. But everybody taking his remark as meant for humorous, and at which therefore as coming from a superior they were bound to laugh, "with counterfeited glee" acted accordingly; and Billy tickled, it may be, by the allusion to his being the handsome sailor, merrily joined in; then addressing his messmates exclaimed, "There now, who says that Jimmy Legs is down on me!"

"And who said he was, beauty?" demanded one Donald with some surprise. Whereat the foretopman looked a little foolish, recalling that it was only one person, Board-her-in-the-smoke, who had suggested what to him was the smoky idea that this Master-at-arms was in any peculiar way hostile to him. Meantime that functionary resuming his path must have momentarily worn some expression less guarded than that of the bitter smile and, usurping the face from the heart, some distorting expression perhaps—for a drummer-boy, heedlessly frolicking along from the opposite direction, and chancing to come into light collision with his person was strangely disconcerted by his aspect. Nor was the impression lessened when the official, impulsively giving him a sharp cut with the rattan, vehemently exclaimed, "Look where you go!"

x

What was the matter with the Master-at-arms? And, be the matter what it might, how could it have direct relation to Billy Budd, with whom prior to the affair of the spilled soup he had never come into any special contact, official or otherwise? What indeed could the trouble have to do with one so little inclined to give offense as the merchant-ship's *peacemaker*, even him who in Claggart's own phrase was "The sweet and pleasant young fellow"? Yes, why should *Jimmy Legs,* to borrow the Dansker's expression, be *down* on the Handsome Sailor?

But at heart and not for nothing, as the late chance encounter may indicate to the discerning, down on him, secretly down on him, he assuredly was.

Now to invent something touching the more private career of Claggart—something involving Billy Budd, of which something the latter
should be wholly ignorant, some romantic incident implying that Claggart's knowledge of the young blue-jacket began at some period anterior
to catching sight of him on board the seventy-four—all this, not so
difficult to do, might avail in a more or less interesting way to account
for whatever enigma may appear to lurk in the case. But, in fact, there
was nothing of the sort. And yet the cause, necessarily to be assumed
as the sole one assignable, is in its very realism as much charged with
that prime element of Radcliffian romance, *the mysterious*, as any that
the ingenuity of the author of the "Mysteries of Udolpho" could devise.
For what can more partake of the mysterious than an antipathy spontaneous and profound such as is evoked in certain exceptional mortals
by the mere aspect of some other mortal, however harmless he may be?
—if not called forth by that very harmlessness itself.

Now there can exist no irritating juxtaposition of dissimilar personalities comparable to that which is possible aboard a great warship fully
manned and at sea. There, every day, among all ranks, almost every
man comes into more or less of contact with almost every other man.
Wholly there to avoid even the sight of an aggravating object one must
needs give it Jonah's toss, or jump overboard himself. Imagine how all
this might eventually operate on some peculiar human creature the direct
reverse of a saint?

But for the adequate comprehending of Claggart by a normal nature,
these hints are insufficient. To pass from a normal nature to him one
must cross "the deadly space between," and this is best done by indirection.

Long ago an honest scholar, my senior, said to me in reference to one
who like himself is now no more, a man so unimpeachably respectable
that against him nothing was ever openly said, though among the few
something was whispered, "Yes, X—— is a nut not to be cracked by the
tap of a lady's fan. You are aware that I am the adherent of no organized
religion, much less of any philosophy built into a system. Well, for all
that, I think that to try and get into X——, enter his labyrinth and get
out again, without a clue derived from some source other than what is
known as *knowledge of the world*—that were hardly possible, at least
for me."

"Why," said I, "X——, however singular a study to some, is yet
human, and knowledge of the world assuredly implies the knowledge
of human nature, and in most of its varieties."

"Yes, but a superficial knowledge of it, serving ordinary purposes.
But for anything deeper, I am not certain whether to know the world
and to know human nature be not two distinct branches of knowledge,

which while they may coexist in the same heart, yet either may exist with little or nothing of the other. Nay, in an average man of the world, his constant rubbing with it blunts that fine spiritual insight indispensable to the understanding of the essential in certain exceptional characters, whether evil ones or good. In a matter of some importance I have seen a girl wind an old lawyer about her little finger. Nor was it the dotage of senile love. Nothing of the sort. But he knew law better than he knew the girl's heart. Coke and Blackstone hardly shed so much light into obscure spiritual places as the Hebrew prophets. And who were they? Mostly recluses."

At the time my inexperience was such that I did not quite see the drift of all this. It may be that I see it now. And, indeed, if that lexicon which is based on Holy Writ were any longer popular, one might with less difficulty define and denominate certain phenomenal men. . . . As it is, one must turn to some authority not liable to the charge of being tinctured with the Biblical element.

In a list of definitions included in the authentic translation of Plato, a list attributed to him, occurs this: "Natural Depravity: a depravity according to nature." A definition which though savoring of Calvinism by no means involves Calvin's dogma as to total mankind. Evidently its intent makes it applicable but to individuals. Not many are the examples of this depravity which the gallows and jails supply. At any rate, for notable instances—since these have no vulgar alloy of the brute in them, but invariably are dominated by intellectuality—one must go elsewhere. Civilization, especially if of the austerer sort, is auspicious to it. It folds itself in the mantle of respectability. It has its certain negative virtues serving as silent auxiliaries. It never allows wine to get within its guard. It is not going too far to say that it is without vices or small sins. There is a phenomenal pride in it that excludes them from anything. Never mercenary or avaricious. In short, the depravity here meant partakes nothing of the sordid or sensual. It is serious, but free from acerbity. Though no flatterer of mankind it never speaks ill of it.

But the thing which in eminent instances signalizes so exceptional a nature is this: though the man's even temper and discreet bearing would seem to intimate a mind peculiarly subject to the law of reason, not the less in his soul's recesses he would seem to riot in complete exemption from that law, having apparently little to do with reason further than to employ it as an ambidexter implement for effecting the irrational. That is to say: towards the accomplishment of an aim which in wantonness of malignity would seem to partake of the insane, he will direct a cool judgment sagacious and sound.

These men are true madmen, and of the most dangerous sort, for their lunacy is not continuous, but occasional; evoked by some special object; it is secretive and self-contained: so that when most active it is, to the average mind, not distinguished from sanity, and for the reason above suggested that whatever its aims may be (and the aim is never disclosed) the method and the outward proceeding is always perfectly rational.

Now something such was Claggart, in whom was the mania of an evil nature, not engendered by vicious training or corrupting books or licentious living, but born with him and innate, in short, "a depravity according to nature."

Can it be this phenomenon, disowned or not acknowledged, that in some criminal cases puzzles the courts? For this cause have our juries at times not only to endure the prolonged contentions of lawyers with their fees, but also the yet more perplexing strife of the medical experts with theirs? And why leave it to them? Why not subpoena as well the clerical proficients? Their vocation bringing them into peculiar contact with so many human beings, and sometimes in their least guarded hour, in interviews very much more confidential than those of physician and patient; this would seem to qualify them to know something about those intricacies involved in the question of moral responsibility; whether in a given case, say, the crime proceeded from manias in the brain or rabies of the heart. As to any differences among themselves which clerical proficients might develop on the stand, these could hardly be greater than the direct contradictions exchanged between the remunerated medical experts.

Dark sayings are these, some will say. But why? It is because they somewhat savor of Holy Writ in its phrase "mysteries of iniquity."

The point of the story turning on the hidden nature of the Master-at-arms has necessitated this chapter. With an added hint or two in connection with the incident at the mess, the resumed narrative must be left to vindicate as it may, its own credibility.

XI

(Pale ire, envy and despair)

That Claggart's figure was not amiss, and his face, save the chin, well molded, has already been said. Of these favorable points he seemed not insensible, for he was not only neat but careful in his dress. But the form of Billy Budd was heroic; and if his face was without the intellectual look of the pallid Claggart's, not the less was it lit, like his, from within, though from a different source. The bonfire in his heart made, luminous the rose-tan in his cheek.

In view of the marked contrast between the persons of the twain, it is more than probable that when the Master-at-arms in the scene last

given applied to the sailor the proverb *Handsome is as handsome does*
he there let escape an ironic inkling, not caught by the young sailors
who heard it, as to what it was that had first moved him against Billy,
namely, his significant personal beauty.

Now envy and antipathy, passions irreconcilable in reason, nevertheless in fact may spring conjoined like Chang and Eng in one birth. Is
Envy then such a monster? Well, though many an arraigned mortal
has in hopes of mitigated penalty pleaded guilty to horrible actions, did
ever anybody seriously confess to envy? Something there is in it universally felt to be more shameful than even felonious crime. And not
only does everybody disown it, but the better sort are inclined to incredulity when it is in earnest imputed to an intelligent man. But since
its lodgment is in the heart, not the brain, no degree of intellect supplies
a guarantee against it. But Claggart's was no vulgar form of the passion.
Nor, as directed towards Billy Budd, did it partake of that streak of
apprehensive jealousy which marred Saul's visage perturbedly brooding
on the comely young David. Claggart's envy struck deeper. If askance
he eyed the good looks, cheery health and frank enjoyment of young
life in Billy Budd, it was because these happened to go along with a
nature that, as Claggart magnetically felt, had in its simplicity never
willed malice or experienced the reactionary bite of that serpent. To
him, the spirit lodged within Billy, and looking out from his welkin eyes
as from windows—that ineffability it was which made the dimple in
his dyed cheeks, suppled his joints, and dancing in his yellow curls made
him pre-eminently the Handsome Sailor. One person excepted, the
Master-at-arms was perhaps the only man in the ship intellectually capable of adequately appreciating the moral phenomenon presented in
Billy Budd, and the insight but intensified his passion, which, assuming
various secret forms within him, at times assumed that of cynic disdain
—disdain of innocence. To be nothing more than innocent! Yet in an
æsthetic way he saw the charm of it, the courageous free-and-easy temper
of it, and fain would have shared it, but he despaired of it.

With no power to annul the elemental evil in himself, though readily
enough he could hide it; apprehending the good, but powerless to be
it; a nature like Claggart's, surcharged with energy as such natures
almost invariably are, what recourse is left to it but to recoil upon itself
and, like the scorpion for which the Creator alone is responsible, act out
to the end the part allotted it.

Passion, and passion in its profoundest, is not a thing demanding a
palatial stage whereon to play its part. Down among the groundlings,
among the beggars and rakers of the garbage, profound passion is
enacted. And the circumstances that provoke it, however trivial or mean,
are no measure of its power. In the present instance the stage is a scrubbed

gun-deck, and one of the external provocations a man-of-war's man's spilled soup.

Now when the Master-at-arms noticed whence came that greasy fluid streaming before his feet, he must have taken it—to some extent wilfully perhaps—not for the mere accident it assuredly was, but for the sly escape of a spontaneous feeling on Billy's part more or less answering to the antipathy on his own. In effect a foolish demonstration he must have thought, and very harmless, like the futile kick of a heifer, which yet were the heifer a shod stallion would not be so harmless. Even so was it that into the gall of envy Claggart infused the vitriol of his contempt. But the incident confirmed to him certain tell-tale reports purveyed to his ear by *Squeak,* one of his more cunning corporals, a grizzled little man, so nicknamed by the sailors on account of his squeaky voice and sharp visage ferreting about the dark corners of the lower decks after interlopers, satirically suggesting to them the idea of a rat in a cellar.

Now his chief's employing him as an implicit tool in laying little traps for the worriment of the foretopman—for it was from the Master-at-arms that the petty persecutions heretofore adverted to had proceeded —the corporal, having naturally enough concluded that his master could have no love for the sailor, made it his business, faithful understrapper that he was, to ferment the ill blood by perverting to his chief certain innocent frolics of the good-natured foretopman, besides inventing for his master sundry contumelious epithets he claimed to have overheard him let fall. The Master-at-arms never suspected the veracity of these reports, more especially as to the epithets, for he well knew how secretly unpopular may become a Master-at-arms—at least a Master-at-arms of those days, zealous in his function—how the blue-jackets shot at him in private their raillery and wit; the nickname by which he goes among them (*Jimmy Legs*) implying under the form of merriment their cherished disrespect and dislike.

But in view of the greediness of hate for provocation, it hardly needed a purveyor to feed Claggart's passion. An uncommon prudence is habitual with the subtler depravity, for it has everything to hide. And in case of any merely suspected injury its secretiveness voluntarily cuts it off from enlightment or disillusion; and not unreluctantly, action is taken upon surmise as upon certainty. And the retaliation is apt to be in monstrous disproportion to the supposed offense; for when in anybody was revenge in its exactions aught else but an inordinate usurer? But how with Claggart's conscience? For though consciences are unlike as foreheads, every intelligence, not including the Scriptural devils who "believe and tremble," has one. But Claggart's conscience being but the lawyer to his will, made ogres of trifles, probably arguing that the motive imputed to Billy in spilling the soup just when he did, together with the epithets alleged—these, if nothing more, made a strong case against him; nay, justified animosity into a sort of retributive righteousness. The Pharisee is the Guy Fawkes prowling in the hid chambers underlying some natures like Claggart's. And they can really form no conception of an unreciprocated malice. Probably, the Master-at-arms' clandestine persecutions of Billy were started to try the temper of the man; but they had not developed any quality in him that enmity could make official use of, or ever pervert into even plausible self-justification; so that the occurrence at the mess, petty if it were, was a welcome one to that peculiar conscience assigned to be the private mentor of Claggart; and for the rest, not improbably it put him upon new experiments.

XII

Not many days after the last incident narrated, something befell Billy Budd that more gravelled him than aught that had previously occurred.

It was a warm night for the latitude; and the foretopman, whose watch at the time was properly below, was dozing on the uppermost deck whither he had ascended from his hot hammock—one of hundreds suspended so closely wedged together over a lower gun-deck that there was little or no swing to them. He lay as in the shadow of a hillside stretched under the lee of the *booms,* a piled ridge of spare spars, and among which the ship's largest boat, the launch, was stowed. Alongside of three other slumberers from below, he lay near one end of the booms which approached from the foremast; his station aloft on duty as a foretopman being just over the deck station of the forecastlemen entitling him according to usage to make himself more or less at home in that neighborhood.

Presently he was stirred into semi-consciousness by somebody, who must have previously sounded the sleep of the others, touching his shoulder, and then as the foretopman raised his head, breathing into his ear in a quick whisper, "Slip into the lee fore-chains, Billy; there is something in the wind—don't speak. Quick. I will meet you there;" and disappeared.

Now Billy—like sundry other essentially good-natured ones—had some of the weakness inseparable from essential good nature; and among these was a reluctance, almost an incapacity of plumply saying *no* to an abrupt proposition not obviously absurd, on the face of it, nor obviously unfriendly, nor iniquitous. And being of warm blood he had not the phlegm to negative any proposition by unresponsive inaction. Like his sense of fear, his apprehension as to aught outside of the honest and natural was seldom very quick. Besides, upon the present occasion, the drowse from his sleep still hung upon him.

However it was, he mechanically rose and, sleepily wondering what could be *in the wind,* betook himself to the designated place, a narrow platform, one of six, outside of the high bulwarks and screened by the great dead-eyes and multiple columned lanyards of the shrouds and back-stays; and, in a great warship of that time, of dimensions commensurate to the ample hull's magnitude; a tarry balcony, in short, overhanging the sea, and so secluded that one mariner of the *Indomitable,* a non-conformist old tar of serious turn, made it even in daytime his private oratory.

In this retired nook the stranger soon joined Billy Budd. There was no moon as yet; a haze obscured the starlight. He could not distinctly see the stranger's face. Yet from something in the outline and carriage, Billy took him to be, and correctly, for one of the afterguard.

"Hist, Billy!" said the man; in the same quick cautionary whisper as before. "You were impressed, weren't you? Well, so was I;" and he paused as to mark the effect. But Billy, not knowing exactly what to make of this, said nothing. Then the other: "We are not the only impressed ones, Billy. There's a gang of us. Couldn't you—help—at a pinch?"

"What do you mean?" demanded Billy, here shaking off his drowse.

"Hist, hist!" the hurried whisper now growing husky, "see here;" and the man held up two small objects faintly twinkling in the night light. "See, they are yours, Bill, if you'll only—"

But Billy here broke in, and in his resentful eagerness to deliver himself his vocal infirmity somewhat intruded; "D-D-Damme, I don't know what you are d-driving at, or what you mean, but you had better g-g-go where you belong!" For the moment the fellow, as confounded, did not stir; and Billy, springing to his feet, said, "If you d-don't start, I'll t-t-toss you back over the r-rail!" There was no mistaking this, and the mysterious emissary decamped, disappearing in the direction of the mainmast in the shadow of the booms.

"Hallo, what's the matter?" here came growling from a forecastleman awakened from his deck-doze by Billy's raised voice. And as the foretopman reappeared and was recognized by him; "Ah, *Beauty,* is it you? Well, something must have been the matter for you st-st-stuttered."

"Oh," rejoined Billy, now mastering the impediment; "I found an afterguardsman in our part of the ship here and I bid him be off where he belongs."

"And is that all you did about it, foretopman?" gruffly demanded another, an irascible old fellow of brick-colored visage and hair, and who was known to his associate forecastlemen as *Red Pepper.*

"Such sneaks I should like to marry to the gunner's daughter!" by that expression meaning that he would like to subject them to disciplinary castigation over a gun.

However, Billy's rendering of the matter satisfactorily accounted to these inquirers for the brief commotion, since of all the sections of a ship's company the forecastlemen, veterans for the most part, and bigoted in their sea-prejudices, are the most jealous in resenting territorial encroachments, especially on the part of any of the afterguard, of whom they have but a sorry opinion, chiefly landsmen, never going aloft except to reef or furl the mainsail, and in no wise competent to handle a marlingspike or turn in a *dead-eye,* say.

XIII

This incident sorely puzzled Billy Budd. It was an entirely new experience—the first time in his life that he had ever been personally approached in underhanded intriguing fashion. Prior to this encounter he had known nothing of the afterguardsman, the two men being stationed wide apart, one forward and aloft during his watch, the other on deck and aft.

What could it mean? And could they really be guineas, those two glittering objects the interloper had held up to his (Billy's) eyes? Where could the fellow get guineas? Why, even buttons, spare buttons, are not so plentiful at sea. The more he turned the matter over, the more he was nonplussed, and made uneasy and discomfited. In his disgustful recoil from an overture which, though he but ill comprehended, he instinctively knew must involve evil of some sort—Billy Budd was like a young horse fresh from the pasture suddenly inhaling a vile whiff from some chemical factory and by repeated snortings trying to get it out of his nostrils and lungs. This frame of mind barred all desire of holding further parley with the fellow, even were it but for the purpose of gaining some enlightenment as to his design in approaching him. And yet he was not without natural curiosity to see how such a visitor in the dark would look in broad day.

He espied him the following afternoon in his first dog-watch below, one of the smokers on that forward part of the upper gun-deck allotted to the pipe. He recognized him by his general cut and build, more than by his round freckled face and glassy eyes of pale blue, veiled with lashes all but white. And yet Billy was a bit uncertain whether indeed it were he—yonder chap about his own age, chatting and laughing in a free-hearted way, leaning against a gun—a genial young fellow enough to look at, and something of a rattle-brain, to all appearance. Rather chubby, too, for a sailor, even an afterguardsman. In short the last man in the world—one would think—to be overburthened with thoughts, especially those perilous thoughts that must needs belong to a conspirator in any serious project, or even to the underling of such a conspirator.

Although Billy was not aware of it, the fellow, with one sidelong watchful glance had perceived Billy first, and then noting that Billy

was looking at him, thereupon nodded a familiar sort of friendly recognition as to an old acquaintance, without interrupting the talk he was
engaged in with the group of smokers. A day or two afterwards, chancing in the evening promenade on a gun-deck, to pass Billy, he offered a
flying word of good-fellowship, as it were, which by its unexpectedness,
and equivocalness under the circumstances, so embarrassed Billy that
he knew not how to respond to it, and let it go unnoticed.

Billy was now left more at a loss than before. The ineffectual speculations into which he was led were so disturbingly alien to him that he
did his best to smother them. It never entered his mind that here was a
matter, which, from its extreme questionableness, it was his duty as a
loyal blue-jacket to report in the proper quarter. And, probably, had such
a step been suggested to him, he would have been deterred from taking
it by the thought—one of novice-magnanimity—that it would savor
overmuch of the dirty work of a tell-tale. He kept the thing to himself.
Yet upon one occasion he could not forbear a little disburthening himself to the old Dansker, tempted thereto perhaps by the influence of a
balmy night when the ship lay becalmed; the twain, silent for the most
part, sitting together on deck, their heads propped against the bulwarks.
But it was only a partial and anonymous account that Billy gave—the
unfounded scruples above referred to preventing full disclosure to
anybody. Upon hearing Billy's version, the sage Dansker seemed to
divine more than he was told; and after a little meditation, during
which his wrinkles were pursed as into a point—quite effacing for the
time that quizzing expression his face sometimes wore—answered:
"Didn't I say so, Baby Budd?"

"Say what?" demanded Billy.

"Why, *Jimmy Legs* is *down* on you."

"And what," rejoined Billy in amazement, "has *Jimmy Legs* to do
with that cracked afterguardsman?"

"Ho, it was an afterguardsman, then: a cat's-paw, only a cat's-paw!"
And with that exclamation, which, whether it had reference to a light
puff of air just then coming over the calm sea, or subtler relation to the
afterguardsman, there is no telling. The old Merlin gave a twisting
vrench with his black teeth at his plug of tobacco—vouchsafing no reply
to Billy's impetuous question, though now repeated, for it was his
wont to relapse into grim silence when interrogated in sceptical sort as
to any of his sententious oracles, not always very clear ones, but rather
partaking of that obscurity which invests most Delphic deliverances
from any quarter.

XIV

Long experience had very likely brought this old man to that bitter prudence which never interferes in aught, and never gives advice.

Yes, despite the Dansker's pithy insistence as to the Master-at-arms being at the bottom of these strange experiences of Billy on board the *Indomitable*, the young sailor was ready to ascribe them to almost anybody but the man who, to use Billy's own expression, "always had a pleasant word for him." This is to be wondered at. Yet not so much to be wondered at. In certain matters, some sailors even in mature life, remain unsophisticated enough. But a young seafarer of the disposition of our athletic foretopman is yet very much of a child-man. And yet a child's utter innocence is but its blank ignorance, and the innocence more or less wanes as intelligence waxes. But in Billy Budd intelligence, such as it was, had advanced, while yet his simple-mindedness remained for the most part unaffected. Experience is a teacher indeed; yet did Billy's years make his experience small. Besides, he had none of that intuitive knowledge of the bad which in natures not good or incompletely so, foreruns experience, and therefore may pertain, as in some instances it too clearly does pertain, even to youth.

And what could Billy know of man except of man as a mere sailor? And the old-fashioned sailor, the veritable man-before-the-mast—the sailor from boyhood up—he, though indeed of the same species as a landsman, is in some respects singularly distinct from him. The sailor is frankness, the landsman is finesse. Life is not a game with the sailor, demanding the long head; no intricate game of chess where few moves are made in straightforwardness, and ends are attained by indirection; an oblique, tedious, barren game hardly worth that poor candle burnt out in playing it.

Yes, as a class, sailors are in character a juvenile race. Even their deviations are marked by juvenility. And this more especially holding true with the sailors of Billy's time. Then, too, certain things which apply to all sailors, do more pointedly operate here and there upon the junior one. Every sailor, too, is accustomed to obey orders without debating them; his life afloat is externally ruled for him; he is not brought into that promiscuous commerce with mankind where unobstructed free agency on equal terms—equal superficially, at least—soon teaches one that unless upon occasion he exercises a distrust keen in proportion to the fairness of the appearance, some foul turn may be served him. A ruled, undemonstrative distrustfulness is so habitual, not with businessmen so much, as with men who know their kind in less shallow relations than business, namely certain men-of-the-world, that they come at last to employ it all but unconsciously; and some of them would very likely

feel real surprise at being charged with it as one of their general characteristics.

XV

But after the little matter at the mess Billy Budd no more found himself
in strange trouble at times about his hammock or his clothes-bag, or
what not. While, as to that smile that occasionally sunned him, and the
pleasant passing word: these were, if not more frequent, yet if anything
more pronounced than before.

But for all that, there were certain other demonstrations now. When
Claggart's unobserved glance happened to light on belted Billy rolling
along the upper gun-deck in the leisure of the second dog-watch, exchanging passing broadsides of fun with other young promenaders in
the crowd; that glance would follow the cheerful Sea Hyperion with a
settled meditative and melancholy expression—his eyes strangely suffused with incipient feverish tears. Then would Claggart look like the
man of sorrows. Yes, and sometimes the melancholy expression would
have in it a touch of soft yearning, as if Claggart could even have loved
Billy but for fate and ban. But this was an evanescence, and quickly
repented of, as it were, by an immitigable look, pinching and shrivelling
the visage into the momentary semblance of a wrinkled walnut. But
sometimes, catching sight in advance of the foretopman coming in his
direction, he would, upon their nearing, step aside a little to let him
pass, dwelling upon Billy for the moment with the glittering dental
satire of a Guise. Yet, upon an abrupt unforeseen encounter, a red light
would flash forth from his eye, like a spark from an anvil in a dusky
smithy. That quick fierce light was a strange one, darted from orbs
which in repose were of a color nearest approaching a deeper violet, the
softest of shades.

Though some of these caprices of the pit could not but be observed
by their object, yet were they beyond the construing of such a nature.
And the thews of Billy were hardly comparable with that sort of sensitive spiritual organization which in some cases instinctively conveys
to ignorant innocence an admonition of the proximity of the malign.
He thought the Master-at-arms acted in a manner rather queer at times.
That was all. But the occasional frank air and pleasant word went for
what they purported to be—the young sailor never having heard as yet
of the "too fair-spoken man."

Had the foretopman been conscious of having done or said anything
to provoke the ill will of the official, it would have been different with
him, and his sight might have been purged if not sharpened.

So was it with him in yet another matter. Two minor officers, the
Armorer, and Captain of the Hold, with whom he had never ex-

changed a word, his position on the ship not bringing him into contact with them; these men now for the first began to cast upon Billy—when they chanced to encounter him—that peculiar glance which evidences that the man from whom it comes has been some way tampered with, and to the prejudice of him upon whom the glance lights. Never did it occur to Billy as a thing to be noted, or a thing suspicious—though he well knew the fact that the Armorer and Captain of the Hold, with the ship's yeomen, apothecary, and others of that grade, were by naval usage, messmates of the Master-at-arms; men with ears convenient to his confidential tongue.

But the general popularity that our Handsome Sailor's manly forwardness upon occasion, and irresistible good nature, indicating no mental superiority tending to excite an invidious feeling; this good will on the part of most of his shipmates made him the less to concern himself about such mute aspects toward him as those whereto allusion has just been made.

As to the afterguardsman, though Billy for reasons already given, necessarily saw little of him, yet when the two did happen to meet, invariably came the fellow's off-hand cheerful recognition, sometimes accompanied by a passing pleasant word or two. Whatever that equivocal young person's original design may really have been, or the design of which he might have been the deputy, certain it was from his manner upon these occasions, that he had wholly dropped it.

It was as if his precocity of crookedness (and every vulgar villain is precocious) had for once deceived him, and the man he had sought to entrap as a simpleton had, through his very simplicity, baffled him.

But shrewd ones may opine that it was hardly possible for Billy to refrain from going up to the afterguardsman and bluntly demanding to know his purpose in the initial interview, so abruptly closed in the fore-chains. Shrewd ones may also think it but natural in Billy to set about sounding some of the other impressed men of the ship in order to discover what basis, if any, there was for the emissary's obscure suggestions as to plotting disaffection aboard. The shrewd may so think. But something more, or rather, something else than mere shrewdness is perhaps needful for the due understanding of such a character as Billy Budd's.

As to Claggart, the monomania in the man—if that indeed it were —as involuntarily disclosed by stars in the manifestations detailed, yet in general covered over by his self-contained and rational demeanor; this, like a subterranean fire was eating its way deeper and deeper in him. Something decisive must come of it.

XVI

After the mysterious interview in the fore-chains—the one so abruptly ended there by Billy—nothing especially germane to the story occurred until the events now about to be narrated.

Elsewhere it has been said that owing to the lack of frigates (of course better sailors than line-of-battle ships) in the English squadron up the Straits at that period, the *Indomitable* was occasionally employed not only as an available substitute for a scout, but at times on detached service of more important kind. This was not alone because of her sailing qualities, not common in a ship of her rate, but quite as much, probably, that the character of her commander—it was thought—specially adapted him for any duty where, under unforeseen difficulties, a prompt initiative might have to be taken in some matter demanding knowledge and ability in addition to those qualities employed in good seamanship. It was on an expedition of the latter sort, a somewhat distant one, and when the *Indomitable* was almost at her furthest remove from the fleet, that in the latter part of an afternoon-watch she unexpectedly came in sight of a ship of the enemy. It proved to be a frigate. The latter—perceiving through the glass that the weight of men and metal would be heavily against her—invoking her light heels, crowded on sail to get away. After a chase urged almost against hope—and lasting until about the middle of the first dog-watch she signally succeeded in effecting her escape.

Not long after the pursuit had been given up, and ere the excitement incident thereto had altogether waned away, the Master-at-arms, ascending from his cavernous sphere, made his appearance (cap in hand) by the mainmast: respectfully awaiting the notice of Captain Vere—then solitary walking the weather-side of the quarter-deck—doubtless somewhat chafed at the failure of the pursuit. The spot where Claggart stood was the place allotted to the men of lesser grades when seeking some more particular interview either with the officer-of-the-deck or the Captain himself. But from the latter it was not often that a sailor or petty-officer of those days would seek a hearing; only some exceptional cause, would, according to established custom, have warranted that.

Presently, just as the Commander, absorbed in his reflections, was on the point of turning aft in his promenade, he became sensible of Claggart's presence, and saw the doffed cap held in deferential expectancy. Here be it said that Captain Vere's personal knowledge of this petty-officer had only begun at the time of the ship's last sailing from home, Claggart then for the first, in transfer from a ship detained for repairs, supplying on board the *Indomitable* the place of a previous Master-at-arms disabled and ashore.

No sooner did the Commander observe who it was that now so deferentially stood awaiting his notice, than a peculiar expression came over him. It was not unlike that which uncontrollably will flit across the countenance of one at unawares encountering a person, who, though known to him, indeed, has hardly been long enough known for thorough knowledge, but something in whose aspect nevertheless now, for the first time, provokes a vaguely repellent distaste. Coming to a stand and resuming much of his wonted official manner, save that a sort of impatience lurked in the intonation of the opening word, he said, "Well? what is it, Master-at-arms?"

With the air of a subordinate grieved at the necessity of being a messenger of ill tidings, and while conscientiously determined to be frank, yet equally resolved upon shunning overstatement, Claggart at this invitation, or rather summons to disburthen, spoke up. What he said, conveyed in the language of no uneducated man, was to the effect following if not altogether in these words, namely, that during the chase and preparations for the possible encounter he had seen enough to convince him that at least one sailor aboard was a dangerous character in a ship mustering some who not only had taken a guilty part in the late serious trouble, but others also who, like the man in question, had entered His Majesty's service under another form than enlistment.

At this point Captain Vere, with some impatience, interrupted him: "Be direct, man; say impressed men."

Claggart made a gesture of subservience and proceeded. Quite lately he (Claggart) had begun to suspect that some sort of movement prompted by the sailor in question was covertly going on, but he had not thought himself warranted in reporting the suspicion so long as it remained indistinct. But from what he had that afternoon observed in the man referred to, the suspicion of something clandestine going on had advanced to a point less removed from certainty. He deeply felt— he added—the serious responsibility assumed in making a report involving such possible consequences to the individual mainly concerned, besides tending to augment those natural anxieties which every naval commander must feel in view of the extraordinary outbreak so recent as those which, he sorrowfully said it, it needed not to name.

Now at the first broaching of the matter Captain Vere, taken by surprise, could not wholly dissemble his disquietude, but as Claggart went on, the former's aspect changed into restiveness under something in the testifier's manner in giving his testimony. However, he refrained from interrupting him. And Claggart, continuing, concluded with this:

"God forbid, your honor, that the *Indomitable's* should be the experience of the—"

"Never mind that!" here peremptorily broke in the superior, his face altering with anger instantly, divining the ship that the other was about to name, one in which the Nore Mutiny assumed a singularly tragical character that for a time jeopardized the life of its Commander. Under the circumstances he was indignant at the purposed allusion. When the commissioned officers themselves were on all occasions very heedful how they referred to the recent events—for a petty-officer unnecessarily to allude to them in the presence of his Captain, this struck him as a most immodest presumption. Besides, to his quick sense of self-respect, it even looked under the circumstances something like an attempt to alarm him. Nor at that was he without some surprise that one who, so far as he had hitherto come under his notice, had shown considerable tact in his function, should in this particular evince such lack of it.

But these thoughts and kindred dubious ones flitting across his mind were suddenly replaced by an intuitional surmise, which though as yet obscure in form, served practically to affect his reception of the ill tidings. Certain it is that, long versed in everything pertaining to the complicated gun-deck life (which like every other form of life has its secret mines and dubious side; the side popularly disclaimed), Captain Vere did not permit himself to be unduly disturbed by the general tenor of his subordinate's report. Furthermore, if in view of recent events prompt action should be taken at the first palpable sign of recurring insubordination—for all that, not judicious would it be, he thought, to keep the idea of lingering disaffection alive by undue forwardness in crediting an informer, even if his own subordinate, and charged with police surveillance of the crew. This feeling would not perhaps have so prevailed with him were it not that upon a prior occasion the patriotic zeal officially evinced by Claggart had somewhat irritated him as appearing rather supersensible and strained. Furthermore, something even in the official's self-possessed and somewhat ostentatious manner in making his specifications strangely reminded him of a bandsman, a perjured witness in a capital case before a court-martial ashore of which when a lieutenant he, Captain Vere, had been a member.

Now the peremptory check given to Claggart in the matter of the arrested allusion was quickly followed up by this: "You say that there is at least one dangerous man aboard. Name him."

"William Budd, a foretopman, your honor—"

"William Budd," repeated Captain Vere with unfeigned astonishment, "and mean you the man our Lieutenant Ratcliffe took from the merchantman not very long ago—the young fellow who seems to be so popular with the men—Billy, the Handsome Sailor, as they call him?"

"The same, your honor; but for all his youth and good looks, a deep one. Not for nothing does he insinuate himself into the good will of his shipmates, since at the least they will at a pinch say a good word for him at all hazards. Did Lieutenant Ratcliffe happen to tell your honor of that adroit fling of Budd's jumping up in the Cutter's bow under the merchantman's stern when he was being taken off? It is even masqued by that sort of good-humored air that at heart he resents his impressment. You have but noted his fair cheek. A man-trap may be under his fine ruddy-tipped daisies."

Now the *Handsome Sailor,* as a signal figure among the crew, had naturally enough attracted the Captain's attention from the first. Though in general not very demonstrative to his officers, he had congratulated Lieutenant Ratcliffe upon his good fortune in lighting on such a fine specimen of the *genus homo* who, in the nude, might have posed for a statue of young Adam before the fall.

As to Billy's adieu to the ship *Rights-of-Man,* which the boarding lieutenant had indeed reported to him, Captain Vere—but in a deferential way—more as a good story than aught else—though mistakenly understanding it as a satiric sally, had but thought so much the better of the impressed man for it; as a military sailor, admiring the spirit that could take an arbitrary enlistment so merrily and sensibly. The foretopman's conduct, too, so far as it had fallen under the Captain's notice had confirmed the first happy augury, while the new recruit's qualities as a *sailor-man* seemed to be such that he had thought of recommending him to the executive officer for promotion to a place that would more frequently bring him under his own observation, namely, the captaincy of the mizzen-top, replacing there in the starboard watch a man not so young whom partly for that reason he deemed less fitted for the post. Be it parenthesized here that since the mizzen-top-men have not to handle such breadths of heavy canvas as the lower sailors on the mainmast and foremast, a young man if of the right stuff not only seems best adapted to duty there, but, in fact, is generally selected for the captaincy of that top, and the company under him are light hands, and often but striplings. In sum, Captain Vere had from the beginning deemed Billy Budd to be what in the naval parlance of the times was called a *"King's bargain,"* that is to say, for His Britannic Majesty's navy a capital investment at small outlay or none at all.

After a brief pause—during which the reminiscences above mentioned passed vividly through his mind—he weighed the import of Claggart's last suggestion, conveyed in the phrase, "pitfall under the clover," and the more he weighed it the less reliance he felt in the informer's good faith. Suddenly he turned upon him: "Do you come to me, Master-at-arms, with so foggy a tale? As to Budd, cite me an act or spoken word of his confirmatory of what you here in general charge against him. Stay," drawing nearer to him, "heed what you speak. Just now and in a case like this, there is a yard-arm-end for the false-witness."

"Ah, your honor!" sighed Claggart mildly shaking his shapely head as in sad deprecation of such unmerited severity of tone. Then bridling —erecting himself as in virtuous self-assertion, he circumstantially alleged certain words and acts, which collectively if credited, led to presumptions mortally inculpating Budd, and for some of these averments, he added, substantiating proof was not far.

With gray eyes now impatient and distrustful, essaying to fathom to the bottom Claggart's calm violet ones, Captain Vere again heard him out; then for the moment stood ruminating. The mood he evinced, Claggart—himself for the time liberated from the other's scrutiny— steadily regarded with a look difficult to render:—a look curious of the operation of his tactics, a look such as might have been that of the spokesman of the envious children of Jacob deceptively imposing upon the troubled patriarch the blood-dyed coat of young Joseph.

Though something exceptional in the moral quality of Captain Vere made him, in earnest encounter with a fellow-man, a veritable touchstone of that man's essential nature, yet now as to Claggart and what was really going on in him his feeling partook less of intuitional conviction than of strong suspicion clogged by strange dubieties. The perplexity he evinced proceeded less from aught touching the man informed against —as Claggart doubtless opined—than from considerations how best to act in regard to the informer. At first, indeed, he was naturally for summoning that substantiation of his allegations which Claggart said was at hand. But such a proceeding would result in the matter at once getting abroad—which—in the present stage of it, he thought, might undesirably affect the ship's company. If Claggart was a false witness —that closed the affair. And therefore, before trying the accusation, he would first practically test the accuser; and he thought this could be done in a quiet undemonstrative way.

The measure he determined upon involved a shifting of the scene— a transfer to a place less exposed to observation than the broad quarterdeck. For although the few gun-room officers there at the time had, in due observance of naval etiquette, withdrawn to leeward the moment Captain Vere had begun his promenade on the deck's weather side; and though during the colloquy with Claggart they of course ventured not to diminish the distance; and though throughout the interview Captain Vere's voice was far from high, and Claggart's silvery and low; and the wind in the cordage and the wash of the sea helped the more to put them beyond earshot; nevertheless, the interview's continuance already had attracted observation from some topmen aloft, and other sailors in the waist or further forward.

Having now determined upon his measures, Captain Vere forthwith took action. Abruptly turning to Claggart he asked, "Master-at-arms, is it now Budd's watch aloft?"

"No, your honor." Whereupon—"Mr. Wilkes," summoning the near est midshipman, "tell Albert to come to me." Albert was the Captain's hammock-boy, a sort of sea-valet in whose discretion and fidelity his master had much confidence. The lad appeared. "You know Budd the foretopman?"

"I do, Sir."

"Go find him. It is his watch off. Manage to tell him out of earshot that he is wanted aft. Contrive it that he speaks to nobody. Keep him in talk yourself. And not till you get well aft here, not till then, let him know that the place where he is wanted is my cabin. You understand. Go.—Master-at-arms, show yourself on the decks below, and when you think it time for Albert to be coming with his man, stand by quietly to follow the sailor in."

XVII

Now when the foretopman found himself closeted, as it were, in the cabin with the Captain and Claggart, he was surprised enough. But it was a surprise unaccompanied by apprehension or distrust. To an immature nature, essentially honest and humane, forewarning intimations of subtler danger from one's kind come tardily, if at all. The only thing that took shape in the young sailor's mind was this: "Yes, the Captain, I have always thought, looks kindly upon me. I wonder if he's going to make me his coxswain. I should like that. And maybe now he is going to ask the Master-at-arms about me."

"Shut the door there, sentry," said the commander. "Stand without and let nobody come in.—Now, Master-at-arms, tell this man to his face what you told of him to me;" and stood prepared to scrutinize the mutually confronting visages.

With the measured step and calm collected air of an asylum physician approaching in the public hall some patient beginning to show indications of a coming paroxysm, Claggart deliberately advanced within short range of Billy, and mesmerically looking him in the eye, briefly recapitulated the accusation.

Not at first did Billy take it in. When he did the rose-tan of his cheeks looked struck as by white leprosy. He stood like one impaled and gagged. Meanwhile the accuser's eyes, removing not as yet from the blue, dilated ones, underwent a phenomenal change, their wonted rich violet color blurring into a muddy purple. Those lights of human intelligence losing human expression, gelidly protruding like the alien eyes of certain un cataloged creatures of the deep.

The first mesmeric glance was one of surprised fascination; the last was the hungry lurch of the torpedo-fish.

"Speak, man!" said Captain Vere to the transfixed one, struck by his aspect even more than by Claggart's, "Speak! defend yourself." Which appeal caused but a strange, dumb gesturing and gurgling in Billy; amazement at such an accusation so suddenly sprung on inexperienced nonage; this, and it may be horror at the accuser, serving to bring out his lurking defect, and in this instance for the time intensifying it into a convulsed tongue-tie; while the intent head and entire form straining forward in an agony of ineffectual eagerness to obey the injunction to speak and defend himself, gave an expression to the face like that of a condemned vestal priestess in the moment of her being buried alive, and in the first struggle against suffocation.

Though at the time Captain Vere was quite ignorant of Billy's liability to vocal impediment, he now immediately divined it, since vividly Billy's aspect recalled to him that of a bright young schoolmate of his whom he had seen struck by much the same startling impotence in the act of eagerly rising in the class to be foremost in response to a testing question put to it by the master. Going closer up to the young sailor, and laying a soothing hand on his shoulder, he said. "There is no hurry, my boy. Take your time, take your time." Contrary to the effect intended, these words, so fatherly in tone, doubtless touching Billy's heart to the quick, prompted yet more violent efforts at utterance—efforts soon ending for the time in confirming the paralysis, and bringing to the face an expression which was as a crucifixion to behold. The next instant, quick as the flame from a discharged cannon at night—his right arm shot out and Claggart dropped to the deck. Whether intentionally, or but owing to the young athlete's superior height, the blow had taken effect full upon the forehead, so shapely and intellectual-looking a feature in the Master-at-arms; so that the body fell over lengthwise, like a heavy plank tilted from erectness. A gasp or two and he lay motionless.

"Fated boy," breathed Captain Vere in a tone so low as to be almost a whisper, "what have you done! But here, help me."

The twain raised the felled one from the loins up into a sitting position. The spare form flexibly acquiesced, but inertly. It was like handling a dead snake. They lowered it back. Regaining erectness, Captain Vere with one hand covering his face stood to all appearance as impassive as to the object at his feet. Was he absorbed in taking in all the bearings of the event, and what was best not only now at once to be done, but also in the sequel? Slowly he uncovered his face; forthwith the effect was as if the moon, emerging from eclipse, should reappear with quite another aspect than that which had gone into hiding. The father in him, manifested towards Billy thus far in the scene, was replaced by the military disciplinarian. In his official tone he bade the foretopman retire to a stateroom aft (pointing it out), and there remain till thence summoned. This order Billy in silence mechanically obeyed. Then, going to the cabin door where it opened on the quarter-deck, Captain Vere said to the sentry without, "Tell somebody to send Albert here." When the lad appeared his master so contrived it that he should not catch sight of the prone one. "Albert," he said to him, "tell the surgeon I wish to see him. You need not come back till called."

When the surgeon entered—a self-poised character of that grave sense and experience that hardly anything could take him aback—Captain Vere advanced to meet him, thus unconsciously interrupting his view of Claggart and interrupting the other's wonted ceremonious salutation, said, "Nay, tell me how it is with yonder man," directing his attention to the prostrate one.

The surgeon looked, and for all his self-command, somewhat started at the abrupt revelation. On Claggart's always pallid complexion, thick black blood was now oozing from mouth and ear. To the gazer's professional eyes it was unmistakably no living man that he saw.

"Is it so, then?" said Captain Vere intently watching him. "I thought it. But verify it." Whereupon the customary tests confirmed the surgeon's first glance, who now looking up in unfeigned concern, cast a look of intense inquisitiveness upon his superior. But Captain Vere, with one hand to his brow, was standing motionless. Suddenly, catching the surgeon's arm convulsively, he exclaimed pointing down to the body, —"It is the divine judgment of Ananias! Look!"

Disturbed by the excited manner he had never before observed in the *Indomitable's* Captain, and as yet wholly ignorant of the affair, the prudent surgeon nevertheless held his peace, only again looking an earnest interrogation as to what it was that had resulted in such a tragedy.

But Captain Vere was now again motionless, standing absorbed in thought. Once again starting, he vehemently exclaimed—"Struck dead by an angel of God. Yet the angel must hang!"

At these interjections, incoherences to the listener as yet unapprised of the antecedent events, the surgeon was profoundly discomfited. But now, as recollecting himself, Captain Vere in less harsh tone briefly related the circumstances leading up to the event.

"But come; we must despatch," he added, "help me to remove him (meaning the body) to yonder compartment"—designating one opposite where the foretopman remained immured. Anew disturbed by a request that, as implying a desire for secrecy, seemed unaccountably strange to him, there was nothing for the subordinate to do but comply.

"Go now," said Captain Vere, with something of his wonted manner. "Go now. I shall presently call a drum-head court. Tell the lieutenants what has happened, and tell Mr. Morton"—meaning the Captain of Marines. "And charge them to keep the matter to themselves."

Full of disquietude and misgivings, the surgeon left the cabin. Was Captain Vere suddenly affected in his mind, or was it but a transient excitement brought about by so strange and extraordinary a happening? As to the drum-head court, it struck the surgeon as impolitic, if nothing more. The thing to do, he thought, was to place Billy Budd in confinement, and in a way dictated by usage, and postpone further action in so extraordinary a case to such time as they should again join the squadron, and then transfer it to the Admiral. He recalled the unwonted agitation of Captain Vere and his exciting exclamations so at variance with his normal manner. Was he unhinged? But assuming that he was, it were not so susceptible of proof. What then could he do? No worse trying situation is conceivable than that of an officer subordinated under a Captain whom he suspects to be, not mad indeed, but yet not quite unaffected in his intellect. To argue his order to him would be insolence. To resist him would be mutiny. In obedience to Captain Vere he communicated to the lieutenants and Captain of Marines what had happened; saying nothing as to the Captain's state. They stared at him in surprise and concern. Like him they seemed to think that such a matter should be reported to the Admiral.

Who in the rainbow can draw the line where the violet tint ends and the orange tint begins? Distinctly we see the difference of the color, but where exactly does the first one visibly enter into the other? So with sanity and insanity. In pronounced cases there is no question about them. But in some cases, in various degrees supposedly less pronounced, to draw the line of demarcation few will undertake, though for a fee some professional experts will. There is nothing namable but that some men will undertake to do for pay. In other words, there are instances where it is next to impossible to determine whether a man is sane or beginning to be otherwise.

Whether Captain Vere, as the surgeon professionally surmised, was really the sudden victim of any degree of aberration, one must determine for himself by such light as this narrative may afford.

XVIII

The unhappy event which has been narrated could not have happened at a worse juncture. For it was close on the heel of the suppressed insurrections, an after-time very critical to naval authority, demanding from every English sea-commander two qualities not readily interfusable— prudence and rigor. Moreover, there was something crucial in the case.

In the jugglery of circumstances preceding and attending the event on board the *Indomitable* and in the light of that martial code whereby it was formally to be judged, innocence and guilt, personified in Claggart and Budd, in effect changed places.

In the legal view the apparent victim of the tragedy was he who had sought to victimize a man blameless; and the indisputable deed of the latter, navally regarded, constituted the most heinous of military crimes. Yet more. The essential right and wrong involved in the matter, the clearer that might be, so much the worse for the responsibility of a loyal sea-commander, inasmuch as he was authorized to determine the matter on that primitive legal basis.

Small wonder then that the *Indomitable's* Captain, though in general a man of rigid decision, felt that circumspectness not less than promptitude was necessary. Until he could decide upon his course, and in each detail; and not only so, but until the concluding measure was upon the point of being enacted he deemed it advisable, in view of all the circumstances, to guard as much as possible against publicity. Here he may or may not have erred. Certain it is, however, that subsequently in the confidential talk of more than one or two gun-rooms and cabins he was not a little criticized by some officers, a fact imputed by his friends, and vehemently by his cousin Jack Denton, to professional jealousy of Starry Vere. Some imaginative ground for invidious comment there was. The maintenance of secrecy in the matter, the confining all knowledge of it for a time to the place where the homicide occurred—the quarter-deck cabin; in these particulars lurked some resemblance to the policy adopted in those tragedies of the palace which have occurred more than once in the capital founded by Peter the Barbarian, great chiefly by his crimes.

The case was such that fain would the *Indomitable's* Captain have deferred taking any action whatever respecting it further than to keep the foretopman a close prisoner till the ship rejoined the squadron, and then submitting the matter to the judgment of his Admiral.

But a true military officer is, in one particular, like a true monk. Not with more of self-abnegation will the latter keep his vows of monastic obedience than the former his vows of allegiance to martial duty.

Feeling that unless quick action were taken on it, the deed of the foretopman, as soon as it should be known on the gun-decks, would tend to awaken any slumbering embers of the Nore among the crews—a sense of the urgency of the case overruled in Captain Vere all other considerations. But though a conscientious disciplinarian, he was no lover of authority for mere authority's sake. Very far was he from embracing opportunities for monopolizing to himself the perils of moral responsibility, none at least that could properly be referred to an official superior, or shared with him by his official equals or even subordinates. So thinking, he was glad it would not be at variance with usage to turn the matter over to a summary court of his own officers, reserving to himself, as the one on whom the ultimate accountability would rest, the right of maintaining a supervision of it, or formally or informally interposing at need. Accordingly a drum-head court was summarily convened, he electing the individuals composing it, the First Lieutenant, the Captain of Marines, and the Sailing Master.

In associating an officer of marines with the sea-lieutenants in a case having to do with a sailor, the Commander perhaps deviated from general custom. He was prompted thereto by the circumstances that he took that soldier to be a judicious person, thoughtful and not altogether incapable of gripping with a difficult case unprecedented in his prior experience. Yet even as to him he was not without some latent misgiving, for withal he was an extremely good-natured man, an enjoyer of his dinner, a sound sleeper, and inclined to obesity. The sort of man who, though he would always maintain his manhood in battle, might not prove altogether reliable in a moral dilemma involving aught of the tragic. As to the First Lieutenant and the Sailing Master, Captain Vere could not but be aware that though honest natures, of approved gallantry upon occasion, their intelligence was mostly confined to the matter of active seamanship, and the fighting demands of their profession. The court was held in the same cabin where the unfortunate affair had taken place. This cabin, the Commander's, embraced the entire area under the poop-deck. Aft, and on either side, was a small stateroom—the one room temporarily a jail, and the other a dead-house—and a yet smaller compartment leaving a space between, expanding forward into a goodly oblong of length coinciding with the ship's beam. A skylight of moderate dimension was overhead, and at each end of the oblong space were two sashed porthole windows, easily convertible back into embrasures for short cannonades.

All being quickly in readiness, Billy Budd was arraigned, Captain Vere necessarily appearing as the sole witness in the case, and as such temporarily sinking his rank, though singularly maintaining it in a matter apparently trivial, namely, that he testified from the ship's weather side, with that object having caused the court to sit on the lee side. Concisely he narrated all that had led up to the catastrophe, omitting nothing in Claggart's accusation and deposing as to the manner in which the prisoner had received it. At this testimony the three officers glanced with no little surprise at Billy Budd, the last man they would have suspected, either of mutinous design alleged by Claggart, or of the undeniable deed he himself had done. The First Lieutenant, taking judicial primacy and turning towards the prisoner, said, "Captain Vere has spoken. Is it or is it not as Captain Vere says?" In response came syllables not so much impeded in the utterance as might have been anticipated. They were these:

"Captain Vere tells the truth. It is just as Captain Vere says, but it is not as the Master-at-arms said. I have eaten the King's bread and I am true to the King."

"I believe you, my man," said the witness, his voice indicating a suppressed emotion not otherwise betrayed.

"God will bless you for that, your honor!" not without stammering said Billy, and all but broke down. But immediately was recalled to self-control by another question, with which the same emotional difficulty of utterance came: "No, there was no malice between us. I never bore malice against the Master-at-arms. I am sorry that he is dead. I did not mean to kill him. Could I have used my tongue I would not have struck him. But he foully lied to my face, and in the presence of my Captain, and I had to say something, and I could only say it with a blow. God help me!"

In the impulsive above-board manner of the frank one the court saw confirmed all that was implied in words which just previously had perplexed them, coming as they did from the testifier to the tragedy, and promptly following Billy's impassioned disclaimer of mutinous intent— Captain Vere's words, "I believe you, my man."

Next it was asked of him whether he knew of or suspected aught savoring of incipient trouble (meaning a mutiny, though the explicit term was avoided) going on in any section of the ship's company.

The reply lingered. This was naturally imputed by the court to the same vocal embarrassment which had retarded or obstructed previous answers. But in main it was otherwise here; the question immediately recalling to Billy's mind the interview with the afterguardsman in the fore-chains. But an innate repugnance to playing a part at all approaching that of an informer against one's own shipmates—the same erring sense of uninstructed honor which had stood in the way of his reporting the matter at the time; though as a loyal man-of-war man it was incumbent on him and failure so to do charged against him and, proven, would have subjected him to the heaviest of penalties. This, with the blind feeling now his, that nothing really was being hatched, prevailing with him. When the answer came it was a negative.

"One question more," said the officer of marines now first speaking and with a troubled earnestness. "You tell us that what the Master-at-arms said against you was a lie. Now why should he have so lied, so maliciously lied, since you declare there was no malice between you?"

At that question unintentionally touching on a spiritual sphere wholly obscure to Billy's thoughts, he was nonplussed, evincing a confusion indeed that some observers, such as can be imagined, would have construed into involuntary evidence of hidden guilt. Nevertheless he strove some way to answer, but all at once relinquished the vain endeavor, at

the same time turning an appealing glance towards Captain Vere as
deeming him his best helper and friend. Captain Vere, who had been
seated for a time, rose to his feet, addressing the interrogator. "The
question you put to him comes naturally enough. But can he rightly
answer it?—or anybody else? unless indeed it be he who lies within
there," designating the compartment where lay the corpse. "But the
prone one there will not rise to our summons. In effect though, as it
seems to me, the point you make is hardly material. Quite aside from
any conceivable motive actuating the Master-at-arms, and irrespective
of the provocation of the blow, a martial court must needs in the present
case confine its attention to the blow's consequence, which consequence
is to be deemed not otherwise than as the striker's deed!"

This utterance, the full significance of which it was not at all likely
that Billy took in, nevertheless caused him to turn a wistful, interroga-
tive look towards the speaker, a look in its dumb expressiveness not unlike that which a dog of generous breed might turn upon his master,
seeking in his face some elucidation of a previous gesture ambiguous to
the canine intelligence. Nor was the same utterance without marked
effect upon the three officers, more especially the soldier. Couched in it
seemed to them a meaning unanticipated, involving a prejudgment on
the speaker's part. It served to augment a mental disturbance previously
evident enough.

The soldier once more spoke, in a tone of suggestive dubiety addressing at once his associates and Captain Vere: "Nobody is present—none
of the ship's company, I mean, who might shed lateral light, if any is to
be had, upon what remains mysterious in this matter."

"That is thoughtfully put," said Captain Vere; "I see your drift. Ay,
there is a mystery; but to use a Scriptural phrase, it is 'a mystery of iniquity,' a matter for only psychologic theologians to discuss. But what
has a military court to do with it? Not to add that for us any possible
investigation of it is cut off by the lasting tongue-tie of him in yonder,"
again designating the mortuary stateroom. "The prisoner's deed. With
that alone we have to do."

To this, and particularly the closing reiteration, the marine soldier,
knowing not how aptly to reply, sadly abstained from saying aught.
The First Lieutenant, who at the outset had not unnaturally assumed
primacy in the court, now overrulingly instructed by a glance from
Captain Vere (a glance more effective than words), resumed that primacy. Turning to the prisoner: "Budd," he said, and scarce in equable
tones, "Budd, if you have aught further to say for yourself, say it now."

Upon this the young sailor turned another quick glance towards
Captain Vere; then, as taking a hint from that aspect, a hint confirming

his own instinct that silence was now best, replied to the Lieutenant, "I have said all, Sir "

The marine—the same who had been the sentinel without the cabin-door at the time that the foretopman, followed by the Master-at-arms, entered it—he, standing by the sailor throughout their judicial proceed-ings, was now directed to take him back to the after compartment orig-inally assigned to the prisoner and his custodian. As the twain disap-peared from view, the three officers, as partially liberated from some inward constraint associated with Billy's mere presence—simultaneously stirred in their seats. They exchanged looks of troubled indecision, yet feeling that decide they must, and without long delay; for Captain Vere was for the time sitting unconsciously with his back towards them, apparently in one of his absent fits, gazing out from a sashed porthole to windward upon the monotonous blank of the twilight sea. But the court's silence continuing, broken only at moments by brief consulta-tions in low earnest tones, this seemed to assure him and encourage him. Turning, he to-and-fro paced the cabin athwart; in the returning ascent to windward, climbing the slant deck in the ship's lee roll; without knowing it symbolizing thus in his action a mind resolute to surmount difficulties even if against primitive instincts strong as the wind and the sea. Presently he came to a stand before the three. After scanning their faces he stood less as mustering his thoughts for expression, than as one in deliberating how best to put them to well-meaning men not intellectually mature—men with whom it was necessary to demonstrate certain principles that were axioms to himself. Similar impatience as to talking is perhaps one reason that deters some minds from addressing any popular assemblies; under which head is to be classed most legis-latures in a Democracy.

When speak he did, something both in the substance of what he said and his manner of saying it, showed the influence of unshared studies, modifying and tempering the practical training of an active career. This, along with his phraseology now and then, was suggestive of the grounds whereon rested that imputation of a certain pedantry socially alleged against him by certain naval men of wholly practical cast, captains who nevertheless would frankly concede that His Majesty's Navy mustered no more efficient officers of their grade than "Starry Vere."

What he said was to this effect: "Hitherto I have been but the witness, little more; and I should hardly think now to take another tone, that of your coadjutor, for the time, did I not perceive in you—at the crisis too—a troubled hesitancy, proceeding, I doubt not, from the clashing of military duty with moral scruple—scruple vitalized by compassion. For the compassion, how can I otherwise but share it. But, mindful of para-mount obligation, I strive against scruples that may tend to enervate decision. Not, gentlemen, that I hide from myself that the case is an exceptional one. Speculatively regarded, it well might be referred to a jury of casuists. But for us here, acting not as casuists or moralists, it is a case practical and under martial law practically to be dealt with.

"But your scruples! Do they move as in a dusk? Challenge them. Make them advance and declare themselves. Come now—do they import something like this: If, mindless of palliating circumstances, we are bound to regard the death of the Master-at-arms as the prisoner's deed, then does that deed constitute a capital crime whereof the penalty is a mortal one? But in natural justice is nothing but the prisoner's overt act to be considered? Now can we adjudge to summary and shameful death a fellow-creature innocent before God, and whom we feel to be so?— Does that state it aright? You sign sad assent. Well, I, too, feel that, the full force of that. It is Nature. But do these buttons that we wear attest that our allegiance is to Nature? No, to the King. Though the ocean, which is inviolate Nature primeval, though this be the element where we move and have our being as sailors, yet as the King's officers lies our duty in a sphere correspondingly natural? So little is that true, that in receiving our commissions we in the most important regards ceased to be natural free-agents. When war is declared, are we the commissioned fighters previously consulted? We fight at command. If our judgments approve the war, that is but coincidence. So in other particulars. So now, would it be so much we ourselves that would condemn as it would be martial law operating through us? For that law and the rigor of it, we are not responsible. Our vowed responsibility is in this: That however pitilessly that law may operate, we nevertheless adhere to it and administer it.

"But the exceptional in the matter moves the heart within you. Even so, too, is mine moved. But let not warm hearts betray heads that should be cool. Ashore in a criminal case will an upright judge allow himself when off the bench to be waylaid by some tender kinswoman of the accused seeking to touch him with her tearful plea? Well, the heart here is as that piteous woman. The heart is the feminine in man, and hard though it be, she must here be ruled out."

He paused, earnestly studying them for a moment; then resumed.

"But something in your aspect seems to urge that it is not solely that heart that moves in you, but also the conscience, the private conscience. Then, tell me whether or not, occupying the position we do, private conscience should not yield to that imperial one formulated in the code under which alone we officially proceed?"

Here he three men moved in their seats, less convinced than agitated by the course of an argument troubling but the more the spontaneous conflict within. Perceiving which, the speaker paused for a moment; then abruptly changing his tone, went on:

"To steady us a bit, let us recur to the facts.—In war-time at sea a man-of-war's man strikes his superior in grade, and the blow kills. Apart from its effect, the blow itself is, according to the Articles of War, a capital crime. Furthermore—"

"Ay, Sir," emotionally broke in the officer of marines, "in one sense it was. But surely Budd purposed neither mutiny nor homicide."

"Surely not, my good man. And before a court less arbitrary and more merciful than a martial one that plea would largely extenuate. At the Last Assizes it shall acquit. But how here? We proceed under the law of the Mutiny Act. In feature no child can resemble his father more than that Act resembles in spirit the thing from which it derives—War. In His Majesty's service—in this ship indeed—there are Englishmen forced to fight for the King against their will. Against their conscience, for aught we know. Though as their fellow-creatures some of us may appreciate their position, yet as Navy officers, what reck we of it? Still less recks the enemy. Our impressed men he would fain cut down in the same swath with our volunteers. As regards the enemy's naval conscripts, some of whom may even share our own abhorrence of the regicidal French Directory, it is the same on our side. War looks but to the frontage, the appearance. And the Mutiny Act, War's child, takes after the father. Budd's intent or non-intent is nothing to the purpose.

"But while, put to it by those anxieties in you which I cannot but respect, I only repeat myself—while thus strangely we prolong proceedings that should be summary, the enemy may be sighted and an engagement result. We must do; and one of two things must we do—condemn or let go."

"Can we not convict and yet mitigate the penalty?" asked the junior Lieutenant here speaking, and falteringly, for the first time.

"Lieutenant, were that clearly lawful for us under the circumstances, consider the consequences of such clemency. The people" (meaning the ship's company) "have native sense; most of them are familiar with our naval usage and tradition; and how would they take it? Even could you explain to them—which our official position forbids—they, long molded by arbitrary discipline, have not that kind of intelligent responsiveness that might qualify them to comprehend and discriminate. No, to the people the foretopman's deed, however it be worded in the announcement, will be plain homicide committed in a flagrant act of mutiny. What penalty for that should follow, they know. But it does not follow. *Why?* they will ruminate. You know what sailors are. Will they not revert to the recent outbreak at the Nore? Ay, they know the well-founded alarm—the panic it struck throughout England. Your clement sentence they would account pusillanimous. They would think that we flinch, that we are afraid of them—afraid of practising a lawful rigor singularly demanded at this juncture lest it should provoke new troubles. What shame to us such a conjecture on their part, and how deadly to discipline. You see then whither, prompted by duty and the law, I steadfastly drive. But I beseech you, my friends, do not take me amiss. I feel as you do for this unfortunate boy. But did he know our hearts, I take him to be of that generous nature that he would feel even for us on whom in this military necessity so heavy a compulsion is laid."

With that, crossing the deck, he resumed his place by the sashed porthole, tacitly leaving the three to come to a decision. On the cabin's opposite side the troubled court sat silent. Loyal lieges, plain and practical, though at bottom they dissented from some points Captain Vere had put to them, they were without the faculty, hardly had the inclination to gainsay one whom they felt to be an earnest man—one, too, not less their superior in mind than in naval rank. But it is not improbable that even such of his words as were not without influence over them, less came home to them than his closing appeal to their instinct as sea-officers, in the forethought he threw out as to the practical consequences to discipline (considering the unconfirmed tone of the fleet at the time)—should a man-of-war's man's violent killing at sea of a superior in grade be allowed to pass for aught else than a capital crime, demanding prompt infliction of the penalty?

Not unlikely they were brought to something more or less akin to that harassed frame of mind which in the year 1842 actuated the commander of the U.S. brig-of-war *Somers* to resolve (under the so-called Articles of War—Articles modeled upon the English Mutiny Act) to resolve upon the execution at sea of a midshipman and two petty officers as mutineers designing the seizure of the brig. Which resolution was carried out, though in a time of peace and within not many days' sail of home. An act vindicated by a naval court of inquiry subsequently convened ashore—history, and here cited without comment. True, the circumstances on board the *Somers* were different from those on board the *Indomitable*. But the urgency felt, well-warranted or otherwise, was much the same.

Says a writer whom few know, "Forty years after a battle it is easy for a non-combatant to reason about how it ought to have been fought. It is another thing personally and under fire to direct the fighting while involved in the obscuring smoke of it. Much so with respect to other emergencies involving considerations both practical and moral, and when it is imperative promptly to act. The greater the fog, the more it imperils the steamer, and speed is put on though at the hazard of running somebody down. Little ween the snug card-players in the cabin of the responsibilities of the sleepless man on the bridge."

In brief, Billy Budd was formally convicted and sentenced to be hung at the yardarm in the early morning watch, it being now night. Otherwise, as is customary in such cases, the sentence would forthwith have been carried out. In war-time on the field or in the fleet, a mortal punishment decreed by a drum-head court—on the field sometimes decreed by but a nod from the General—follows without a delay on the heel of conviction without appeal.

XIX

It was Captain Vere himself who, of his own motion, communicated the finding of the court to the prisoner; for that purpose going to the compartment where he was in custody, and bidding the marine there to withdraw for the time.

Beyond the communication of the sentence, what took place at this interview was never known. But, in view of the character of the twain briefly closeted in that state-room, each radically sharing in the rarer qualities of one nature—so rare, indeed, as to be all but incredible to average minds however much cultivated—some conjectures may be ventured.

It would have been in consonance with the spirit of our Captain Vere should he on this occasion have concealed nothing from the condemned one—should he indeed have frankly disclosed to him the part he himself had played in bringing about the decision, at the same time revealing his actuating motives. On Billy's side it is not improbable that such a confession would have been received in much the same spirit that prompted it. Not without a sort of joy indeed he might have appreciated the brave opinion of him implied in his Captain making such a confidant of him. Nor as to the sentence itself could he have been insensible that it was imparted to him as to one not afraid to die. Even more may have been. Captain Vere in the end may have developed the passion sometimes latent under an exterior stoical or indifferent. He was old enough to have been Billy's father. The austere devotee of military duty, letting himself melt back into what remains primeval in our formalized humanity, may in the end have caught Billy to heart, even as Abraham may have caught young Isaac on the brink of resolutely offering him up in obedience to the exacting behest. But there is no telling the sacrament—seldom if in any case revealed to the gadding world wherever under circumstances at all akin to those here attempted to be set forth—two of great Nature's nobler order embrace. There is privacy at the time, inviolable to the survivor, and holy oblivion (the sequel to each diviner magnanimity) providentially covers all at last.

The first to encounter Captain Vere in the act of leaving the compartment was the senior Lieutenant. The face he beheld, for the moment one expressive of the agony of the strong, was to that officer, though a man of fifty, a startling revelation. That the condemned one suffered less than he who mainly had effected the condemnation, was apparently indicated by the former's exclamation in the scene soon perforce to be touched upon.

Of a series of incidents within a brief term rapidly following each other, the adequate narration may take up a term less brief, especially if explanation or comment here and there seem requisite to the better understanding of such incidents. Between the entrance into the cabin of him who never left it alive, and him who when he did leave it left it as one condemned to die; between this and the closeted interview just given, less than an hour and a half had elapsed. It was an interval long enough, however, to awaken speculations among no few of the ship's company as to what it was that could be detaining in the cabin the Master-at-arms and the sailor, for it was rumored that both of them had been seen to enter it and neither of them had been seen to emerge. This rumor had got abroad upon the gun-decks and in the tops; the people of a great warship being in one respect like villagers, taking microscopic note of every untoward movement or non-movement going on. When therefore in weather not at all tempestuous all hands were called in the second dog-watch, a summons under such circumstances not usual in those hours, the crew were not wholly unprepared for some announcement extraordinary, one having connection, too, with the continued absence of the two men from their wonted haunts.

There was a moderate sea at the time; and the moon, newly risen and near to being at its full, silvered the white spar-deck wherever not blotted by the clear-cut shadows horizontally thrown of fixtures and moving men. On either side of the quarter-deck the marine guard under arms was drawn up; and Captain Vere, standing up in his place surrounded by all the wardroom officers, addressed his men. In so doing his manner showed neither more nor less than that properly pertaining to his supreme position aboard his own ship. In clear terms and concise he told them what had taken place in the cabin; that the Master-at-arms was dead; that he who had killed him had been already tried by a summary court and condemned to death; and that the execution would take place in the early morning watch. The word *mutiny* was not named in what he said. He refrained, too, from making the occasion an opportunity for any preachment as to the maintenance of discipline, thinking, perhaps, that under existing circumstances in the Navy the consequence of violating discipline should be made to speak for itself.

Their Captain's announcement was listened to by the throng of standing sailors in a dumbness like that of a seated congregation of believers in Hell listening to the clergyman's announcement of his Calvinistic text.

At the close, however, a confused murmur went up. It began to wax all but instantly, then, at a sign, was pierced and suppressed by shrill whistles of the Boatswain and his mates piping "Down one watch."

To be prepared for burial Claggart's body was delivered to certain petty officers of his mess. And here, not to clog the sequel with lateral matters, it may be added that at a suitable hour, the Master-at-arms was committed to the sea with every funeral honor properly belonging to his naval grade.

In this proceeding, as in every public one growing out of the tragedy, strict adherence to usage was observed. Nor in any point could it have been at all deviated from, either with respect to Claggart or Billy Budd, without begetting undesirable speculations in the ship's company, the sailors, and more particularly the men-of-war's men, being of all men the greatest sticklers for usage.

For similar cause all communication between Captain Vere and the condemned one ended with the closeted interview already given, the latter being now surrendered to the ordinary routine preliminary to the end. This transfer under guard from the Captain's quarters was effected without unusual precautions—at least no visible ones.

If possible, not to let the men so much as surmise that their officers anticipate aught amiss from them, is the tacit rule in a military ship. And the more that some sort of trouble should really be apprehended, the more do the officers keep that apprehension to themselves; though not the less unostentatious vigilance may be augmented.

In the present instance the sentry placed over the prisoner had strict orders to let no one have communication with him but the Chaplain. And certain unobtrusive measures were taken absolutely to insure this point.

XX

In a seventy-four of the old order the deck known as the upper gun-deck was the one covered over by the spar-deck, which last, though not without its armament, was for the most part exposed to the weather. In general it was at all hours free from hammocks; those of the crew swinging on the lower gun-deck, and berth-deck, the latter being not only a dormitory but also the place for the stowing of the sailors' bags, and on both sides lined with the large chests or movable pantries of the many messes of the men.

On the starboard side of the *Indomitable's* upper gun-deck, behold Billy Budd under sentry lying prone in irons in one of the bays formed by the regular spacing of the guns comprising the batteries on either side. All these pieces were of the heavier caliber of that period. Mounted on lumbering wooden carriages, they were hampered with cumbersome harness of breeching and strong side-tackles for running them out. Guns and carriages, together with the long rammers and shorter lintstocks lodged in loops overhead—all these, as customary, were painted black; and the heavy hempen breechings, tarred to the same tint, wore the like livery of the undertakers. In contrast with the funereal tone of these surrounding the prone sailor's exterior apparel, white *jumper* and white duck trousers, each more or less soiled, dimly glimmered in the obscure light of the bay like a patch of discolored snow in early April lingering at some upland cave's black mouth. In effect he is already in his shroud or the garments that shall serve him in lieu of one. Over him, but scarce illuminating him, two battle-lanterns swing from two massive beams of the deck above. Fed with the oil supplied by the war-contractors (whose gains, honest or otherwise, are in every land an anticipated portion of the harvest of death), with flickering splashes of dirty yellow light they pollute the pale moonshine all but ineffectually struggling in obstructed flecks through the open ports from which the tompined cannon protrude. Other lanterns at intervals serve but to bring out somewhat the obscurer bays which, like small confessionals or side-chapels in a cathedral, branch from the long, dim-vasted, broad aisle between the two batteries of that covered tire.

Such was the deck where now lay the Handsome Sailor. Through the rose-tan of his complexion, no pallor could have shown. It would have taken days of sequestration from the winds and the sun to have brought about the effacement of that young sea-bloom. But the skeleton in the cheek-bone at the point of its angle was just beginning delicately to be defined under the warm-tinted skin. In fervid hearts self-contained some brief experiences devour our human tissue as secret fire in a ship's hold consumes cotton in the bale.

But now, lying between the two guns, as nipped in the vise of fate, Billy's agony, mainly proceeding from a generous young heart's virgin experience of the diabolical incarnate and effective in some men—the tension of that agony was over now. It survived not the something healing in the closeted interview with Captain Vere. Without movement, he lay as in a trance, that adolescent expression previously noted as his, taking on something akin to the look of a slumbering child in the cradle when the warm hearth-glow of the still chamber of night plays on the dimples that at whiles mysteriously form in the cheek, silently coming and going there. For now and then in the gyved one's trance, a serene happy light born of some wandering reminiscence or dream would diffuse itself over his face, and then wane away only anew to return.

The Chaplain coming to see him and finding him thus, and perceiving no sign that he was conscious of his presence, attentively regarded him for a space, then slipping aside, withdrew for the time, peradventure feeling that even he, the minister of Christ, though receiving his stipend from wars, had no consolation to proffer which could result in a peace transcending that which he beheld. But in the small hours he came again. And the prisoner, now awake to his surroundings, noticed his approach, and civilly, all but cheerfully, welcomed him. But it was to little purpose that in the interview following the good man sought to bring Billy Budd to some godly understanding that he must die, and at dawn. True, Billy himself freely referred to his death as a thing close at hand; but it was something in the way that children will refer to death in general, who yet among their other sports will play a funeral with hearse and mourners. Not that like children Billy was incapable of conceiving what death really is. No, but he was wholly without irrational fear of it, a fear more prevalent in highly civilized communities than those so-called barbarous ones which in all respects stand nearer to unadulterated Nature. And, as elsewhere said, a barbarian Billy radically was; as much so, for all the costume, as his countrymen the British captives, living trophies made to march in the Roman triumph of Germanicus. Quite as much so as those later barbarians, young men probably, and picked specimens among the earlier British converts to Christianity, at least nominally such, and taken to Rome (as today converts from lesser isles of the sea may be taken to London), of whom the Pope of that time, admiring the strangeness of their personal beauty —so unlike the Italian stamp, their clear, ruddy complexions and curled flaxen locks, explained, "Angles" (meaning in English the modern derivative)—"Angels do you call them? And is it because they look so like *angels?*" Had it been later in time one would think that the Pope had in mind Fra Angelico's seraphs, some of whom, plucking apples in gardens of Hesperides, have the faint rose-bud complexion of the more beautiful English girls.

XXI

If in vain the kind Chaplain sought to impress the young barbarian with ideas of death akin to those conveyed in the skull, dial and cross-bones on old tombstones; equally futile to all appearances were his efforts to bring home to him the thought of salvation and a Savior. Billy listened, but less out of awe or reverence, perhaps, than from a certain natural politeness; doubtless at bottom regarding all that in much the same way which most mariners of his class take any discourse abstract or out of the common tone of the workaday world. And this sailor way of taking clerical discourse is not wholly unlike the way in which the pioneer of Christianity—full of transcendant miracles—was received long ago on tropic isles by any superior *savage* so called: a Tahaitian, say of Captain Cook's time or shortly after that time. Out of natural courtesy he received but did not appreciate. It was like a gift placed in the palm of an outstretched hand upon which the fingers do not close.

But the *Indomitable's* Chaplain was a discreet man possessing the good sense of a good heart. So he insisted not in his vocation here. At the instance of Captain Vere, a lieutenant had apprised him of pretty much of everything as to Billy; and since he felt that innocence was even a better thing than religion wherewith to go to judgment, he reluctantly withdrew; but in his emotion not without performing an act strange enough in an Englishman, and under the circumstances yet more so in any regular priest. Stooping over, he kissed on the fair cheek his fellow-man, a felon in martial law, one who, though in the confines of death, he felt he could never convert to a dogma; nor for all that he did fear for his future.

Marvel not that, having been made acquainted with the young sailor's essential innocence, the worthy man lifted not a finger to avert the doom of such a martyr to martial discipline. So to do would not only have been as idle as invoking the desert, but would also have been an audacious transgression of the bounds of his function—one as exactly prescribed to him by military law as that of any other naval officer. Bluntly put, a chaplain is the minister of the Prince of Peace serving in the host of the God of War—Mars. As such, he is as incongruous as a musket would be on the altar at Christmas. Why then is he there? Because he indirectly subserves the purpose attested by the cannon; because, too, he lends the sanction of the religion of the meek to that which practically is the abrogation of everything but force.*

XXII

The night so luminous on the spar-deck, but otherwise on the cavernous ones below—levels so very like the tiered galleries in a coal-mine—the luminous night passed away. Like the prophet in the chariot disappearing in heaven and dropping his mantle to Elisha, the withdrawing night transferred its pale robe to the peeping day. A meek shy light appeared in the East, where stretched a diaphanous fleece of white furrowed vapor. That light slowly waxed. Suddenly *one bell* was struck aft, responded to by one louder metallic stroke from forward. It was four o'clock in the morning. Instantly the silver whistles were heard summoning all hands to witness punishment. Up through the great hatchway rimmed with racks of heavy shot, the watch below came pouring, overspreading with the watch already on deck the space between the

* Melville notes on this passage: "An irruption of heretic thought hard to suppress."

mainmast and foremast, including that occupied by the capacious *launch* and the black booms tiered on either side of it—boat and booms making a summit of observation for the powder boys and younger tars. A different group comprising one watch of topmen leaned over the side of the rail of that sea-balcony, no small one in a seventy-four, looking down on the crowd below. Man or boy, none spake but in whisper, and few spake at all. Captain Vere—as before, the central figure among the assembled commissioned officers—stood nigh the break of the poop-deck, facing forward. Just below him on the quarter-deck the marines in full equipment were drawn up much as at the scene of the promulgated sentence.

At sea in the old time, the execution by halter of a military sailor was generally from the fore-yard. In the present instance—for special reasons —the main yard was assigned. Under an arm of that yard the prisoner was presently brought up, the Chaplain attending him. It was noted at the time, and remarked upon afterwards, that in this final scene the good man evinced little or nothing of the perfunctory. Brief speech indeed he had with the condemned one, but the genuine gospel was less on his tongue than in his aspect and manner towards him. The final preparations personal to the latter being speedily brought to an end by two boatswain's-mates, the consummation impended. Billy stood facing aft. At the penultimate moment, his words, his only ones, words wholly unobstructed in the utterance, were these—"God bless Captain Vere!" Syllables so unanticipated coming from one with the ignominious hemp about his neck—a conventional felon's benediction directed aft towards the quarters of honor; syllables, too, delivered in the clear melody of a singing-bird on the point of launching from the twig, had a phenomenal effect, not unenhanced by the rare personal beauty of the young sailor, spiritualized now through late experiences so poignantly profound.

Without volition, as it were, as if indeed the ship's populace were the vehicles of some vocal electric current, with one voice, from alow and aloft, came a resonant echo—"God bless Captain Vere!" And yet, at that instant, Billy alone must have been in their hearts, even as he was in their eyes.

At the pronounced words and the spontaneous echo that voluminously rebounded them, Captain Vere, either through stoic self-control or a sort of momentary paralysis induced by emotional shock, stood erectly rigid as a musket in the ship-armor's rack.

The hull, deliberately recovering from the periodic roll to leeward, was just regaining an even keel—when the last signal, the preconcerted dumb one, was given. At the same moment it chanced that the vapory fleece hanging low in the East, was shot through with a soft glory as of the fleece of the Lamb of God seen in mystical vision; and simultaneously therewith, watched by the wedged mass of upturned faces, Billy ascended; and ascending, took the full rose of the dawn.

In the pinioned figure, arrived at the yard-end, to the wonder of all no motion was apparent save that created by the slow roll of the hull, in moderate weather so majestic in a great ship heavy-cannoned.

A DIGRESSION

When, some days afterwards, in reference to the singularity just mentioned, the Purser (a rather ruddy, rotund person, more accurate as an accountant than profound as a philosopher) said at mess to the Surgeon, "What testimony to the force lodged in will-power," the latter, spare and tall, one in whom a discreet causticity went along with a manner less genial than polite, replied, "Your pardon, Mr. Purser. In a hanging so scientifically conducted—and, under special orders, I myself directed how Budd's was to be effected—any movement following the completed suspension and originating in the body suspended, such movement indicates mechanical spasm in the muscular system. Hence the absence of that is no more attributable to will-power, as you call it, than to horse-power—begging your pardon."

"But this muscular spasm you speak of—is not that, in a degree, more or less invariable in these cases?"

"Assuredly so, Mr. Purser."

"How then, my good sir, do you account for its absence in this instance?"

"Mr. Purser, it is clear that your sense of the singularity in this matter equals not mine. You account for it by what you call will-power, a term not yet included in the lexicon of science. As for me, I do not with my present knowledge pretend to account for it at all. Even should one assume the hypothesis that, at the first touch of the halyards, the action of Budd's heart, intensified by extraordinary emotion at its climax, abruptly stopped—much like a watch when in carelessly winding it up you strain at the finish, thus snapping the spring—even under that hypothesis, how account for the phenomenon that followed?"

"You admit, then, that the absence of spasmodic movement was phenomenal?"

"It was phenomenal, Mr. Purser, in the sense that it was an appearance, the cause of which is not immediately to be assigned."

"But tell me, my dear sir," pertinaciously continued the other, "was the man's death effected by the halter, or was it a species of euthanasia?"

"*Euthanasia,* Mr. Purser, is something like your will-power; I doubt its authenticity as a scientific term—begging your pardon again. It is at once imaginative and metaphysical; in short, Greek. But," abruptly changing his tone, "there is a case in the sick-bay which I do not care to leave to my assistants. Begging your pardon, but excuse me." And rising from the mess he formally withdrew.

XXIIl

The silence at the moment of execution, and for a moment or two con-tinuing thereafter (but emphasized by the regular wash of the sea against the hull, or the flutter of a sail caused by the helmsman's eyes being tempted astray), this emphasized silence was gradually disturbed by a sound not easily to be here verbally rendered. Whoever has heard the freshet-wave of a torrent suddenly swelled by pouring showers in tropical mountains, showers not shared by the plain; whoever has heard the first muffled murmur of its sloping advance through precipitous woods, may form some conception of the sound now heard. The seem-ing remoteness of its source was because of its murmurous indistinctness, since it came from close by, even from the men massed on the ship's open deck. Being inarticulate, it was dubious in significance further in that it seemed to indicate some capricious revulsion of thought or feeling such as mobs ashore are liable to—in the present instance possibly imply-ing a sullen revocation on the men's part of their involuntary echoing of Billy's benediction. But ere the murmur had time to wax into clamor it was met by a strategic command, the more telling that it came with abrupt unexpectedness.

"Pipe down the starboard watch, Boatswain. and see that they go."

Shrill as the shriek of the sea-hawk the whistles of the Boatswain and his Mates pierced that ominous low sound, dissipating it; and yielding to the mechanism of discipline the throng was thinned by one half. For the remainder most of them were set to temporary employments connected with trimming the yards and so forth, business readily to be found upon occasion by any officer-of-the-deck.

Now each proceeding that follows a mortal sentence pronounced at sea by a drum-head court is characterized by a promptitude not per-ceptibly merging into hurry, though bordering that. The hammock— the one which had been Billy's bed when alive, having already been ballasted with shot and otherwise prepared to serve for his canvas coffin—the last offices of the sea-undertakers, the Sail-maker's Mates, were now speedily completed. When everything was in readiness, a second call for all hands, made necessary by the strategic movement before mentioned, was sounded: and now to witness burial.

The details of this closing formality it needs not to give. But when the tilted plank let slide its freight into the sea, a second strange human murmur was heard—blended now with another so inarticulate sound proceeding from certain larger sea-fowl, whose attention having been attracted by the peculiar commotion in the water resulting from the heavy sloped dive of the shotted hammock into the sea, flew screaming to the spot. So near the hull did they come, that the stridor or bony creak of their gaunt double-jointed pinions was audible. As the ship under light airs passed on, leaving the burial spot astern, they still kept circling it low down with the moving shadow of their outstretched wings and the cracked requiem of their cries.

Upon sailors as superstitious as those of the age preceding ours—all men-of-war's men, too, who had just beheld the prodigy of repose in the form suspended in air and now foundering in the deeps; to such mariners the action of the sea-fowl, though dictated by a mere animal greed for prey, was big with no prosaic significance. An uncertain movement began among them, in which some encroachment was made. It was tolerated but for a moment. For suddenly the drum beat to quarters—which familiar sound, happening at least twice every day, had upon the present occasion some signal peremptoriness in it. True martial discipline long continued superinduces in an average man a sort of impulse of docility, whose operation at the official tone of command much resembles in its promptitude the effect of an instinct.

The drum-beat dissolved the multitude, distributing most of them along the batteries of the two covered gun-decks. There, as wont, the gun crews stood by their respective cannon erect and silent. In due course the First officer, sword under arm and standing in his place on the quarter-deck, formally received the successive reports of the sworded Lieutenants commanding the sections of batteries below; the last of which reports being made, the summed report he delivered with the customary salute to the Commander. All of this occupied time, which, in the present case, was the object of beating to quarters at an hour prior to the customary one. That such variance from usage was authorized by an officer like Captain Vere (a martinet as some deemed him), was evidence of the necessity for unusual action implied in what he deemed to be temporarily the mood of his men. "With mankind," he would say, "forms, measured forms, are everything; and that is the import couched in the story of Orpheus, with his lyre, spell-binding the wild denizens of the woods." And this he once applied to the disruption of forms going on across the Channel and the consequence thereof.

At this unwonted muster at quarters, all proceeded as at the regular hour. The band on the quarter-deck played a sacred air. After which the Chaplain went through with the customary morning service. That done, the drum beat the retreat, and toned by music and religious rites subserving the discipline and purpose of war, the men in their wonted, orderly manner dispersed to the places allotted them when not at the guns.

And now it was full day. The fleece of low-hanging vapor had vanished, licked up by the sun that late had so glorified it. And the circumambient air in the clearness of its serenity was like smooth white marble in the polished block not yet removed from the marble-dealer's yard.

XXIV

The symmetry of form attainable in pure fiction cannot so readily be achieved in a narration essentially having less to do with fable than with fact. Truth uncompromisingly told will always have its ragged edges; hence the conclusion of such a narration is apt to be less finished than an architectural finial.

How it fared with the Handsome Sailor during the year of the great mutiny has been faithfully given. But though properly the story ends with his life, something in way of a sequel will not be amiss. Three brief chapters will suffice.

In the general re-christening under the Directory of the craft originally forming the navy of the French Monarchy, the *St. Louis* line-of-battle ship was named the *Athéiste*. Such a name, like some other substituted ones in the Revolutionary fleet, while proclaiming the infidel audacity of the ruling power, was yet (though not so intended to be) the aptest name, if one consider it, ever given to a warship; far more so, indeed, than the *Devastation* or the *Eritus* (the Hell) and similar names bestowed upon fighting ships.

On the return passage to the full English fleet from the detached cruise during which occurred the events already recorded, the *Indomitable* fell in with the *Athéiste*. An engagement ensued; during which Captain Vere, in the act of putting his ship alongside the enemy with a view of throwing his boarders across the bulwarks, was hit by a musket-ball from a porthole of the enemy's main cabin. More than disabled, he dropped to the deck and was carried below to the same cockpit where some of his men already lay. The senior Lieutenant took command. Under him the enemy was finally captured, and though much crippled, was by rare good fortune successfully taken into Gibraltar, an English fort not very distant from the scene of the fight. There Captain Vere with the rest of the wounded was put ashore. He lingered for some days, but the end came. Unhappily he was cut off too early for the Nile and Trafalgar. The spirit that, in spite of its philosophic austerity, may yet have indulged in the most secret of all passions—ambition—never attained to the fulness of fame.

Not long before death, while lying under the influence of that magical drug which, in soothing the physical frame, mysteriously operates on the subtler element in man, he was heard to murmur words inexplicable to his attendant—"Billy Budd, Billy Budd." That these were not the accents of remorse, would seem clear from what the attendant said to the *Indomitable's* potent senior officer of marines, who, as the most reluctant to condemn of the members of the drum-head court, too well knew (though here he kept the knowledge to himself) who Billy Budd was.

XXV

Some few weeks after the execution, among other matters under the main head of *News from the Mediterranean*, there appeared in one naval chronicle of the time, an authorized weekly publication, an account of the affair. It was doubtless for the most part written in good faith, though the medium, partly rumor, through which the facts must have reached the writer, served to deflect and in part to falsify them. The account was as follows:—

"On the tenth of the last month a deplorable occurrence took place on board *H.M.S. Indomitable.* John Claggart, the ship's Master-at-arms, discovering that some sort of plot was incipient among an inferior section of the ship's company, and that the ringleader was one William Budd, he, Claggart, in the act of arraigning the man before the Captain was vindictively stabbed to the heart by the suddenly drawn sheath-knife of Budd.

"The deed and the implement employed sufficiently suggest that, though mustered into the service under an English name, the assassin was no Englishman but one of those aliens adopting English cognomen whom the present extraordinary necessities of the Service have caused to be admitted into it in considerable numbers.

"The enormity of the crime and the extreme depravity of the criminal, appear the greater in view of the character of the victim—a middle-aged man, respectable and discreet, belonging to that minor official grade, the petty officers, upon whom, as none know better than the commissioned gentlemen, the efficiency of His Majesty's Navy so largely depends. His function was a responsible one—at once onerous and thankless—and his fidelity in it the greater because of his strong patriotic impulse. In this instance, as in so many other instances in these days, the character of the unfortunate man signally refutes, if refutation were needed, that peevish saying attributed to the late Dr. Johnson, that patriotism is the last refuge of a scoundrel.

"The criminal paid the penalty of his crime. The promptitude of the punishment has proved salutary. Nothing amiss is now apprehended aboard the *H.M.S. Indomitable.*"

The above item appearing in a publication, now long ago superannuated and forgotten in all that hitherto has stood in human record, to

attest what manner of men respectively were John Claggart and Billy
Budd.*

XXVI

Everything is for a season remarkable in navies. Any tangible object
associated with some striking incident of the service is converted into a
monument. The spar from which the foretopman was suspended was
for some few years kept trace of by the bluejackets. Then knowledge followed it from ship to deck-yard, and again from deck-yard to ship, still
pursuing it even when at last reduced to a mere deck-yard boom. To
them a chip of it was as a piece of the Cross. Ignorant though they were
of the real facts of the happening, and not thinking but that the penalty
was unavoidably inflicted from the naval point of view, for all that they
instinctively felt that Billy was a sort of man as incapable of mutiny as
of wilful murder. They recalled the fresh young image of the Handsome
Sailor, that face never deformed by a sneer or subtler vile freak of the
heart within! This impression of him was doubtless deepened by the fact
that he was gone, and in a measure mysteriously gone. On the gun-decks
of the *Indomitable* the general estimate of his nature and its unconscious
simplicity eventually found rude utterance from another foretopman,
one of his own watch, gifted as some sailors are with an artless poetic
temperament. Those tarry hands made some lines which, after circulat-
ing among the shipboard crew for a while, finally were rudely printed
at Portsmouth as a ballad. The title given to it was the sailor's own:

BILLY IN THE DARBIES

> *Good of the Chaplain to enter Lone Bay*
> *And down on his marrow-bones here and pray*
> *For the likes just o' me, Billy Budd,—But look:*
> *Through the port comes the moon-shine astray!*
> *It tips the guard's cutlass and silvers this nook;*
> *But 'twill die in the dawning of Billy's last day.*
> *A jewel-block they'll make of me tomorrow,*
> *Pendant pearl from the yard-arm-end*
> *Like the eardrop I gave to Bristol Molly—*
> *O, 'tis me, not the sentence, they'll suspend.*
> *Ay, Ay, all is up; and I must up too*
> *Early in the morning, aloft from alow.*
> *On an empty stomach, now, never it would do.*
> *They'll give me a nibble—bit o' biscuit ere I go.*
> *Sure, a messmate will reach me the last parting cup;*

---

* An author's note, crossed out, here appears in the original MS. It reads: Here ends a
story not unwarranted in this incongruous world of ours—innocence and infirmity,
spiritual depravity and fair respite.

But, turning heads away from the hoist and the belay,
Heaven knows who will have the running of me up!
No pipe to those halyards—but aren't it all sham?
A blur's in my eyes, it is dreaming that I am.
A hatchet to my panzer? all adrift to go?
The drum roll to grog, and Billy never know?
But Donald he has promised to stand by the plank;
So I'll shake a friendly hand ere I sink.
But—no! It is dead then I'll be, come to think.—
I remember Taff the Welshman when he sank.
And his cheek it was like the budding pink.
But me, they'll lash me in hammock, drop me deep
Fathoms down, fathoms down, how I'll dream fast asleep.
I feel it stealing now. Sentry, are you there?
Just ease these darbies at the wrist.
And roll me over fair.
I am sleepy, and the oozy weeds about me twist.

April 19, 1891

9

The Man Without a Country

BY EDWARD EVERETT HALE

I SUPPOSE that very few casual readers of the *New York Herald* of August 13th observed, in an obscure corner, among the "Deaths," the announcement:

"NOLAN. Died, on board U. S. Corvette *Levant*, Lat. 2° 11" S., Long. 131° W., on the 11th of May, Philip Nolan."

I happened to observe it, because I was stranded at the old Mission-House in Mackinac, waiting for a Lake Superior steamer which did not choose to come, and I was devouring, to the very stubble, all the current literature I could get hold of, even down to the deaths and marriages in the *Herald*. My memory for names and people is good, and the reader will see, as he goes on, that I had reason enough to remember Philip Nolan. There are hundreds of readers who would have paused at that announcement, if the officer of the *Levant* who reported it had chosen to make it thus: "Died, May 11th, The Man Without a Country.'" For it was as "The Man Without a Country" that poor Philip Nolan had generally been known by the officers who had him in charge during some fifty years, as indeed, by all the men who sailed under them. I dare say there is many a man who has taken wine with him once a fortnight, in a three years' cruise, who never knew that his name was "Nolan," or whether the poor wretch had any name at all.

There can now be no possible harm in telling this poor creature's story. Reason enough there has been till now, ever since Madison's Administration went out in 1817, for very strict secrecy, the secrecy of honor itself, among the gentlemen of the navy who have had Nolan in successive charge. And certainly it speaks well for the *esprit de corps* of the profession and the personal honor of its members, that to the press this man's story has been wholly unknown,—and, I think, to the country at large also. I have reason to think, from some investigations I made in the Naval Archives when I was attached to the Bureau of Construction, that every official report relating to him was burned when Ross burned the public buildings at Washington. One of the Tuckers, or possibly one of the Watsons, had Nolan in charge at the end of the war; and when, on returning from his cruise, he reported at Washington to one of the Crowninshields,—who was in the Navy Department when he came home,—he found that the Department ignored the whole business. Whether they really knew nothing about it, or whether it was a *Non mi ricordo,* determined on as a piece of policy, I do not know. But this I do know, that since 1817, and possibly before, no naval officer has mentioned Nolan in his report of a cruise.

But, as I say, there is no need for secrecy any longer. And now the poor creature is dead, it seems to me worth while to tell a little of his story, by way of showing young Americans of today what it is to be

A MAN WITHOUT A COUNTRY

Philip Nolan was as fine a young officer as there was in the "Legion of the West," as the Western division of our army was then called. When Aaron Burr made his first dashing expedition down to New Orleans in 1805, at Fort Massac, or somewhere above on the river, he met, as the Devil would have it, this gay, dashing, bright young fellow, at some dinner party, I think. Burr marked him, talked to him, walked with him, took him a day or two's voyage in his flat-boat, and, in short, fascinated him. For the next year barrack-life was very tame to poor Nolan. He occasionally availed of the permission the great man had given him to write to him. Long, high-worded, stilted letters the poor boy wrote and re-wrote and copied. But never a line did he have in reply from the gay deceiver. The other boys in the garrison sneered at him, because he sacrificed in this unrequited affection for a politician the time which they devoted to Monongahela, sledge, and high-low-jack. Bourbon, euchre, and poker were still unknown. But one day Nolan had his revenge. This time Burr came down the river, not as an attorney seeking a place for his office, but as a disguised conqueror. He had defeated I know not how many district attorneys; he had dined at I know not how many public dinners; he had been heralded in I know not how many Weekly Arguses; and it was rumored that he had an army behind him and an empire before him. It was a great day—his arrival—to poor Nolan. Burr had not been at the fort an hour before he sent for him. That evening he asked Nolan to take him out in his skiff, to show him a cane-brake or a cottonwood tree, as he said,—really to seduce him; and by the time the sail was over, Nolan was enlisted body and soul.

From that time, though he did not yet know it, he lived as "A Man Without a Country."

What Burr meant to do I know no more than you, dear reader. It is none of our business just now. Only, when the grand catastrophe came, and Jefferson and the House of Virginia of that day undertook to break on the wheel all the possible Clarences of the then House of York, by the great treason-trial at Richmond, some of the lesser fry in that distant Mississippi Valley, which was farther from us than Puget's Sound is today, introduced the like novelty on their provincial stage, and, to while away the monotony of the summer at Fort Adams, got up, for *spectacles,* a string of court-martials on the officers there. One and another of the colonels and majors were tried, and, to fill out the list, little Nolan, against whom, Heaven knows, there was evidence enough—that he was sick of the service, had been willing to be false to it, and would have obeyed any order to march anywhither with anyone who would follow him, had the order only been signed, "By command of His Exc. A. Burr." The courts dragged on. The big flies escaped,—rightly for all I know. Nolan was proved guilty enough, as I say; yet you and I would never have heard of him, reader, but that, when the president of the court asked him at the close, whether he wished to say anything to show that he had always been faithful to the United States, he cried out, in a fit of frenzy:

"Damn the United States! I wish I may never hear of the United States again!"

I suppose he did not know how the words shocked old Colonel Morgan, who was holding the court. Half the officers who sat in it had served through the Revolution, and their lives, not to say their necks, had been risked for the very idea which he so cavalierly cursed in his madness. He, on his part, had grown up in the West of those days, in the midst of "Spanish plot," "Orleans plot," and all the rest. He had been educated on a plantation, where the finest company was a Spanish officer or a French merchant from Orleans. His education, such as it was, had been perfected in commercial expeditions to Vera Cruz, and I think he told me his father once hired an Englishman to be a private tutor for a winter on the plantation. He had spent half his youth with an older brother, hunting horses in Texas; and, in a word, to him, "United States" was scarcely a reality. Yet he had been fed by "United States" for all the years since he had been in the army. He had sworn on his faith as a Christian to be true to "United States" which gave him the uniform he wore, and the sword by his side. Nay, my poor Nolan, it was only because "United States" had picked you out first as one of her own confidential men of honor, that "A. Burr" cared for you a straw more than for the flat-boat men who sailed his ark for him. I do not excuse Nolan; I only explain to the reader why he damned his country, and wished he might never hear her name again.

He never did hear her name but once again. From that moment, September 23, 1807, till the day he died, May 11, 1863, he never heard her name again. For that half century and more he was a man without a country.

Old Morgan, as I said, was terribly shocked. If Nolan had compared George Washington to Benedict Arnold, or had cried, "God save King George," Morgan would not have felt worse. He called the court into his private room, and returned in fifteen minutes, with a face like a sheet, to say,—

"Prisoner, hear the sentence of the Court. The Court decides, subject to the approval of the President that you never hear the name of the United States again."

Nolan laughed. But nobody else laughed. Old Morgan was too solemn and the whole room was hushed dead as night for a minute. Even Nolan lost his swagger in a moment. Then Morgan added: "Mr. Marshal, take the prisoner to Orleans in an armed boat, and deliver him to the naval commander there."

The marshal gave his orders, and the prisoner was taken out of court.

"Mr. Marshal," continued old Morgan, "see that no one mentions the United States to the prisoner. Mr. Marshal, make my respects to Lieutenant Mitchell at Orleans, and request him to order that no one shall mention the United States to the prisoner while he is on board ship. You will receive your written orders from the officer on duty here this evening. The court is adjourned without day."

I have always supposed that Colonel Morgan himself took the proceedings of the court to Washington City, and explained them to Mr. Jefferson. Certain it is that the President approved them,—certain, that is, if I may believe the men who say they have seen his signature. Before the *Nautilus* got round from New Orleans to the Northern Atlantic coast with the prisoner on board, the sentence had been approved, and he was a man without a country.

The plan then adopted was substantially the same which was necessarily followed ever after. Perhaps it was suggested by the necessity of sending him by water from Fort Adams and Orleans. The Secretary of the Navy—it must have been the first Crowninshield, though he is a man I do not remember—was requested to put Nolan on board a Government vessel bound on a long cruise, and to direct that he should be only so far confined there as to make it certain that he never saw or heard of the country. We had few long cruises then, and the navy was very much out of favor; and as almost all of this story is traditional, as I have explained, I do not know certainly what his first cruise was.

But the commander to whom he was intrusted—perhaps it was Tingey or Shaw, though I think it was one of the younger men,—we are all old enough now—regulated the etiquette and the precautions of the affair, and according to his scheme they were carried out, I suppose, till Nolan died.

When I was second officer of the *Intrepid* some thirty years after, I saw the original paper of instructions. I have been sorry ever since that I did not copy the whole of it. It ran, however, much in this way:

"Washington," (with the date, which must have been late in 1807.)

"Sir,—You will receive from Lt. Neale the person of Philip Nolan, late a Lieutenant in the United States Army.

"This person on his trial by court-martial expressed with an oath the wish that he might never hear of the United States again.

"The court sentenced him to have his wish fulfilled.

"For the present, the execution of the order is intrusted by the President to this department.

"You will take the prisoner on board your ship, and keep him there with such precautions as shall prevent his escape.

"You will provide him with such quarters, rations, and clothing as would be proper for an officer of his late rank, if he were a passenger on your vessel on the business of his Government.

"The gentlemen on board will make any arrangements agreeable to themselves regarding his society. He is to be exposed to no indignity of any kind, nor is he ever unnecessarily to be reminded that he is a prisoner.

"But under no circumstances is he ever to hear of his country or to see any information regarding it; and you will especially caution all the officers under your command to take care that, in the various indulgences which may be granted, this rule, in which his punishment is involved, shall not be broken.

"It is the intention of the Government that he shall never again see the country which he has disowned. Before the end of your cruise you will receive orders which will give effect to this intention.

"Resp'y yours,
"W. SOUTHARD, for the
"Sec'y of the Navy."

If I had only preserved the whole of this paper, there would be no break in the beginning of my sketch of this story. For Captain Shaw, if it was he, handed it to his successor in the charge, and he to his, and

I suppose the commander of the *Levant* has it today as his authority for keeping this man in his mild custody.

The rule adopted on board the ships on which I have met "The Man Without a Country" was, I think, transmitted from the beginning. No mess liked to have him permanently, because his presence cut off all talk of home or of the prospect of return, of politics or letters, of peace or of war,—cut off more than half the talk men like to have at sea. But it was always thought too hard that he should never meet the rest of us, except to touch hats, and we finally sank into one system. He was not permitted to talk with the men unless an officer was by. With officers he had unrestrained intercourse, as far as they and he chose. But he grew shy, though he had favorites: I was one. Then the captain always asked him to dinner on Monday. Every mess in succession took up the invitation in its turn. According to the size of the ship, you had him at your mess more or less often at dinner. His breakfast he ate in his own stateroom,—he always had a stateroom,—which was where a sentinel, or somebody on the watch, could see the door. And whatever else he ate or drank he ate or drank alone. Sometimes, when the marines or sailors had any special jollification, they were permitted to invite "Plain-Buttons," as they called him. Then Nolan was sent with some officer, and the men were forbidden to speak of home while he was there. I believe the theory was, that the sight of his punishment did them good. They called him "Plain-Buttons," because, while he always chose to wear a regulation army uniform, he was not permitted to wear the army button, for the reason that it bore either the initials or the insignia of the country he had disowned.

I remember, soon after I joined the navy, I was on shore with some of the older officers from our ship and from the *Brandywine*, which we had met at Alexandria. We had leave to make a party and go up to Cairo and the Pyramids. As we jogged along (you went on donkeys then) some of the gentlemen (we boys called them "Dons," but the phrase was long since changed) fell to talking about Nolan, and some one told the system which was adopted from the first about his books and other reading. As he was almost never permitted to go on shore, even though the vessel lay in port for months, his time, at the best, hung heavy; and everybody was permitted to lend him books, if they were not published in America and made no allusion to it. These were common enough in the old days, when people in the other hemisphere talked of the United States as little as we do of Paraguay. He had almost all the foreign papers that came into the ship, sooner or later; only somebody must go over them first, and cut out any advertisement or stray paragraph that alluded to America. This was a little cruel sometimes, when the back of what was cut out might be as innocent as Hesiod. Right in the midst of one of Napoleon's battles, or one of Canning's speeches, poor Nolan would find a great hole, because on the back of the page of that paper there had been an advertisement of a packet for New York, or a scrap from the President's message. I say this was the first time I ever heard of this plan, which afterwards I had enough, and more than enough, to do with. I remember it because poor Phillips, who was of the party, as soon as the allusion to reading was made, told a story of something which happened at the Cape of Good Hope on Nolan's first voyage; and it is the only thing I ever knew of that voyage. They had touched at the Cape, and had done the civil thing with the English Admiral and the fleet, and then, leaving for a long cruise up the Indian Ocean, Phillips had borrowed a lot of English books from an officer, which, in those days, as indeed in these, was quite a windfall. Among them, as the Devil would order, was the "Lay of the Last Minstrel," which they had all of them heard of, but which most of them had never seen. I think it could not have been published long. Well, nobody thought there could be any risk of anything national in that, though Phillips swore old Shaw had cut out the "Tempest" from Shakespeare before he let Nolan have it because he said "the Bermudas ought to be ours and, by Jove, should be one day." So Nolan was permitted to join the circle one afternoon when a lot of them sat on deck smoking and reading aloud. People do not do such things so often now, but when I was young we got rid of a great deal of time so. Well, so it happened that in his turn Nolan took the book and read to the others; and he read very well, as I know. Nobody in the circle knew a line of the poem, only it was all magic and Border chivalry, and was ten thousand years ago. Poor Nolan read steadily through the fifth canto, stopped a minute and drank something, and then began, without a thought of what was coming,—

> "Breathes there the man, with soul so dead,
> Who never to himself hath said"—

It seems impossible to us that anybody ever heard this for the first time; but all these fellows did then, and poor Nolan himself went on, still unconsciously or mechanically,—

> "This is my own, my native land!"

Then they all saw something was to pay; but he expected to get through, I suppose, turned a little pale, but plunged on,—

> "Whose heart hath ne'er within him burned,

As home his footsteps he hath turned
    From wandering on a foreign strand?—
    If such there breathe, go, mark him well."

By this time the men were all beside themselves, wishing there was any way to make him turn over two pages; but he had not quite presence of mind for that; he gagged a little, colored crimson, and staggered on:

"For him no minstrel raptures swell;
    High though his titles, proud his name,
    Boundless his wealth as wish can claim,
    Despite these titles, power and pelf,
    The wretch, concentered all in self,"—

and here the poor fellow choked, could not go on, but started up, swung the book into the sea, vanished into his stateroom, "and by Jove," said Phillips, "we did not see him for two months again. And I had to make up some beggarly story to that English surgeon why I did not return his Walter Scott to him."

That story shows about the time when Nolan's braggadocio must have broken down. At first, they said, he took a very high tone, considered his imprisonment a mere farce, affected to enjoy the voyage, and all that; but Phillips said that after he came out of his state-room he never was the same man again. He never read aloud again, unless it was the Bible or Shakespeare, or something else he was sure of. But it was not that merely. He never entered in with the other young men exactly as a companion again. He was always shy afterwards, when I knew him,—very seldom spoke, unless he was spoken to, except to a very few friends. He lighted up occasionally,—I remember late in his life hearing him fairly eloquent on something which had been suggested to him by one of Fléchier's sermons,—but generally he had the nervous, tired look of a heart-wounded man.

When Captain Shaw was coming home,—if, as I say, it was Shaw,—rather to the surprise of everybody they made one of the Windward Islands, and lay off and on for nearly a week. The boys said the officers were sick of salt-junk, and meant to have turtle soup before they came home. But after several days the *Warren* came to the same rendezvous; they exchanged signals; she sent to Phillips and these homeward-bound men letters and papers, and told them she was outward bound, perhaps to the Mediterranean, and took poor Nolan and his traps on the boat back to try his second cruise. He looked very blank when he was told to get ready to join her. He had known enough of the signs of the sky to know that till that moment he was going "home." But this was a distinct evidence of something he had not thought of, perhaps,—that there was no going home for him, even to a prison. And this was the first of some twenty such transfers, which brought him sooner or later into half our best vessels, but which kept him all his life at least some hundred miles from the country he had hoped he might never hear of again.

It may have been on that second cruise—it was once when he was up the Mediterranean—that Mrs. Graff, the celebrated Southern beauty of those days, danced with him. They had been lying a long time in the Bay of Naples, and the officers were very intimate in the English fleet, and there had been great festivities, and our men thought they must give a great ball on board the ship. How they ever did it on board the *Warren* I am sure I do not know. Perhaps it was not the *Warren,* or perhaps ladies did not take up so much room as they do now. They wanted to use Nolan's state-room for something, and they hated to do it without asking him to the ball; so the captain said they might ask him, if they would be responsible that he did not talk with the wrong people, "who would give him intelligence." So the dance went on, the finest party that had ever been known, I dare say; for I never heard of a man-of-war ball that was not. For ladies they had the family of the American consul, one or two travelers who had adventured so far, and a nice bevy of English girls and matrons, perhaps Lady Hamilton herself.

Well, different officers relieved each other in standing and talking with Nolan in a friendly way, so as to be sure that nobody else spoke to him. The dancing went on with spirit, and after a while even the fellows who took this honorary guard of Nolan ceased to fear any *contretemps.* Only when some English lady—Lady Hamilton, as I said, perhaps—called for a set of "American dances," an odd thing happened. Everybody then danced contra-dances. The black band, nothing loath, conferred as to what "American dances" were, and started off with "Virginia Reel," which they followed with "Money-Musk," which, in its turn in those days, should have been followed by "The Old Thirteen." But just as Dick, the leader, tapped for his fiddlers to begin, and bent forward, about to say, in true Negro state. " 'The Old Thirteen,' gentlemen and ladies!" as he had said, " 'Virginny Reel, if you please!' " " 'Money-Musk,' if you please!" the captain's boy tapped him on the shoulder, whispered to him, and he did not announce the name of the dance; he merely bowed, began on the air, and they all fell to,—the officers teaching the English girls the figure, but not telling them why it had no name.

But that is not the story I started to tell.—As the dancing went on, Nolan and our fellows all got at ease, as I said,—so much so that it seemed quite natural for him to bow to that splendid Mrs. Graff, and say,—

"I hope you have not forgotten me, Miss Rutledge. Shall I have the honor of dancing?"

He did it so quickly, that Shubrick, who was by him, could not hinder him. She laughed and said,—

"I am not Miss Rutledge any longer, Mr. Nolan; but I will dance all the same," just nodded to Shubrick, as if to say he must leave Mr. Nolan to her, and led him off to the place where the dance was forming.

Nolan thought he had got his chance. He had known her in Philadelphia, and at other places had met her, and this was a godsend. You could not talk in contra-dances, as you do in cotillions, or even in the pauses of waltzing; but there were chances for tongues and sounds, as well as for eyes and blushes. He began with her travels, and Europe, and Vesuvius, and the French; and then, when they had worked down, and had that long talking-time at the bottom of the set, he said boldly,— a little pale, she said, as she told me the story, years after,—

"And what do you hear from home, Mrs. Graff?"

And that splendid creature looked through him. Jove! how she must have looked through him! "Home!! Mr. Nolan!!! I thought you were the man who never wanted to hear of home again!"—and she walked directly up the deck to her husband, and left poor Nolan alone, as he always was.—He did not dance again.

I cannot give any history of him in order; nobody can now; and, indeed, I am not trying to. These are the traditions, which I sort out, as I believe them, from the myths which have been told about this man for forty years. The lies that have been told about him are legion. The fellows used to say he was the "Iron Mask"; and poor George Pons went to his grave in the belief that this was the author of "Junius," who was being punished for his celebrated libel on Thomas Jefferson. Pons was not very strong in the historical line. A happier story than either of these I have told is of the War. That came along soon after. I have heard this affair told in three or four ways,—and, indeed, it may have happened more than once. But which ship it was on I cannot tell. However, in one, at least, of the great frigate-duels with the English, in which the navy was really baptized, it happened that a round shot from the enemy entered one of our ports square, and took right down the officer of the gun himself, and almost every man of the gun's crew. Now you may say what you choose about courage, but that is not a nice thing to see. But as the men who were not killed picked themselves up, and the surgeon's people were carrying off the bodies, there appeared Nolan, in his shirt-sleeves, with the rammer in his hand, and, just as if he had been the officer, told them off with authority,—who should go to the cockpit with the wounded men, who should stay with him,—perfectly cheery, and with that way which makes men feel sure all is right and is going to be right. And he finished loading the gun with his own hands, aimed it, and bade the men fire. And there he stayed, captain of that gun, keeping those fellows in spirits, till the enemy struck,—sitting on the carriage while the gun was cooling, though he was exposed all the time —showing them easier ways to handle heavy shot,—making the raw hands laugh at their own blunders,—and when the gun cooled again, getting it loaded and fired twice as often as any other gun on the ship. The captain walked forward, by way of encouraging the men, and Nolan touched his hat and said,—

"I am showing them how we do this in the artillery, sir."

And this is a part of the story where all the legends agree: that the Commodore said,—

"I see you do, and I thank you, sir; and I shall never forget this day, sir, and you never shall, sir."

And after the whole thing was over, and he had the Englishman's sword, in the midst of the state and ceremony of the quarter-deck, he said,—

"Where is Mr. Nolan? Ask Mr. Nolan to come here."

And when Nolan came, the captain said,—

"Mr. Nolan, we are all very grateful to you today; you are one of us today; you will be named in the dispatches."

And then the old man took off his own sword of ceremony, and gave it to Nolan, and made him put it on. The man told me this who saw it. Nolan cried like a baby, and well he might. He had not worn a sword since that infernal day at Fort Adams. But always afterwards on occasions of ceremony, he wore that quaint old French sword of the Commodore's.

The captain did mention him in the dispatches. It was always said he asked that he might be pardoned. He wrote a special letter to the Secretary of War. But nothing ever came of it. As I said, that was about the time when they began to ignore the whole transaction at Washington, and when Nolan's imprisonment began to carry itself on because there was nobody to stop it without any new orders from home.

I have heard it said that he was with Porter when he took possession of the Nukahiwa Islands. Not this Porter, you know, but old Porter, his father, Essex Porter,—that is, the old Essex Porter, not this Essex. As an artillery officer, who had seen service in the West, Nolan knew more about fortifications, embrasures, ravelins, stockades, and all that, than any of them did; and he worked with a right good will in fixing that battery all right. I have always thought it was a pity Porter did not leave him in command there with Gamble. That would have settled all the question about his punishment. We should have kept the islands, and at this moment we should have one station in the Pacific Ocean. Our French friends, too, when they wanted this little watering place, would have found it was preoccupied. But Madison and the Virginians, of course, flung all that away.

All that was near fifty years ago. If Nolan was thirty then, he must have been near eighty when he died. He looked sixty when he was forty. But he never seemed to me to change a hair afterwards. As I imagine his life, from what I have seen and heard of it, he must have been in every sea, and yet almost never on land. He must have known, in a formal way, more officers in our service than any man living knows. He told me once, with a grave smile, that no man in the world lived so methodical a life as he. "You know the boys say I am the Iron Mask, and you know how busy he was." He said it did not do for anyone to try to read all the time, more than to do anything else all the time; but that he read just five hours a day. "Then," he said, "I keep up my note-books, writing in them at such and such hours from what I have been reading; and I include in them my scrap-books." Those were very curious indeed. He had six or eight, of different subjects. There was one of History, one of Natural Science, one which he called "Odds and Ends.' But they were not merely books of extracts from newspapers. They had bits of plants and ribbons, shells tied on, and carved scraps of bone and wood, which he had taught the men to cut for him, and they were beautifully illustrated. He drew admirably. He had some of the funniest drawings there, and some of the most pathetic, that I have ever seen in my life. I wonder who will have Nolan's scrap-books.

Well, he said his reading and his notes were his profession, and that they took five hours and two hours respectively of each day. "Then," said he, "every man should have a diversion as well as a profession. My Natural History is my diversion." That took two hours a day more. The men used to bring him birds and fish, but on a long cruise he had to satisfy himself with centipedes and cockroaches and such small game. He was the only naturalist I ever met who knew anything about the habits of the house-fly and the mosquito. All those people can tell you whether they are *Leipidoptera* or *Steptopotera*; but as for telling how you can get rid of them, or how they get away from you when you strike them,—why Linnaeus knew as little of that as John Foy, the idiot, did. These nine hours made Nolan's regular daily "occupation." The rest of the time he talked or walked. Till he grew very old, he went aloft a great deal. He always kept up his exercise and I never heard that he was ill. If any other man was ill, he was the kindest nurse in the world; and he knew more than half the surgeons do. Then if anybody was sick or died, or if the captain wanted him to on any other occasion, he was always ready to read prayers. I have remarked that he read beautifully.

My own acquaintance with Philip Nolan began six or eight years after the War, on my first voyage after I was appointed a midshipman. It was in the first days after our Slave-Trade treaty, while the Reigning House, which was still the house of Virginia, had still a sort of sentimentalism about the suppression of the horrors of the Middle Passage, and something was sometimes done that way. We were in the South Atlantic on that business. From the time I joined, I believe I thought Nolan was a sort of lay chaplain,—a chaplain with a blue coat. I never asked about him. Everything in the ship was strange to me. I knew it was green to ask questions, and I suppose I thought there was a "Plain-Buttons" on every ship. We had him to dine in our mess once a week, and the caution was given that on that day nothing was to be said about home. But if they had told us not to say anything about the planet Mars or the Book of Deuteronomy, I should not have asked why; there were a great many things which seemed to me to have as little reason. I first came to understand anything about "the man without a country" one day when we overhauled a dirty little schooner which had slaves on board. An officer was sent to take charge of her, and after a few minutes he sent back his boat to ask that some one might be sent him who could speak Portuguese. We were all looking over the rail when the message came, and we all wished we could interpret, when the captain asked who spoke Portuguese. But none of the officers did; and just as the captain was sending forward to ask if any of the people could, Nolan stepped out and said he should be glad to interpret, if the captain wished, as he understood the language. The captain thanked him, fitted out another boat with him, and in this boat it was my luck to go.

When we got there, it was such a scene as you seldom see, and never want to. Nastiness beyond account, and chaos run loose in the midst of the nastiness. There were not a great many of the Negroes; but by way of making what there were understand that they were free, Vaughan had had their handcuffs and ankle-cuffs knocked off, and, for convenience sake, was putting them upon the rascals of the schooner's crew. The Negroes were, most of them, out of the hold, and swarming all round the dirty deck, with a central throng surrounding Vaughan and addressing him in every dialect and *patois* of a dialect, from the Zulu click up to the Parisian of Beledeljereed.

As we came on deck, Vaughan looked down from a hogshead, on which he had mounted in desperation, and said,—

"For God's love, is there anybody who can make these wretches understand something? The men gave them rum, and that did not quiet them. I knocked that big fellow down twice, and that did not soothe him. And then I talked Choctaw to all of them together; and

I'll be hanged if they understood that as well as they understood the English."

Nolan said he could speak Portuguese, and one or two fine-looking Kroomen were dragged out, who, as it had been found already, had worked for the Portuguese on the coast at Fernando Po.

"Tell them they are free," said Vaughan; "and tell them that these rascals are to be hanged as soon as we can get rope enough."

Nolan "put that into Spanish," * that is, he explained it in such Portuguese as the Kroomen could understand, and they in turn to such of the Negroes as could understand them. Then there was such a yell of delight, clinching of fists, leaping and dancing, kissing of Nolan's feet, and a general rush made to the hogshead by way of spontaneous worship of Vaughan as the *deus ex machina* of the occasion.

"Tell them," said Vaughan, well pleased, "that I will take them all to Cape Palmas."

This did not answer so well. Cape Palmas was practically as far from the homes of most of them as New Orleans or Rio Janeiro was; that is, they would be eternally separated from home there. And their interpreters, as we could understand, instantly said, *"Ah, non Palmas,"* and began to propose infinite other expedients in most voluble language. Vaughan was rather disappointed at this result of his liberality, and asked Nolan eagerly what they said. The drops stood on poor Nolan's white forehead as he hushed the men down, and said,—

"He says, 'Not Palmas.' He says, 'Take us home, take us to our own country, take us to our own house, take us to our own pickaninnies and our own women.' He says he has an old father and mother, who will die, if they do not see him. And this one says he left his people all sick, and paddled down to Fernando to beg the white doctor to come and help them, and that these devils caught him in the bay just in sight of home, and that he has never seen anybody from home since then. And this one says," choked out Nolan, "that he has not heard a word from his home in six months, while he has been locked up in an infernal barracoon."

Vaughan always said he grew gray himself while Nolan struggled through his interpretation. I, who did not understand anything of the passion involved in it, saw that the very elements were melting with fervent heat, and that something was to pay somewhere. Even the

---

* The phrase is General Taylor's. When Santa Ana brought up his immense army at Buena Vista, he sent a flag of truce to invite Taylor to surrender. "Tell him to go to hell," said old Rough-and-Ready. "Bliss, put that into Spanish." "Perfect Bliss," as this accomplished officer, too early lost, was called, interpreted liberally, replying to the flag, in exquisite Castilian, "Say to General Santa Ana that, if he wants us, he must come and take us." And this is the answer which has gone into history.

Negroes themselves stopped howling as they saw Nolan's agony, and Vaughan's almost equal agony of sympathy. As quick as he could get words, he said,—

"Tell them yes, yes; tell them they shall go to the Mountains of the Moon, if they will. If I sail the schooner through the Great White Desert, they shall go home!"

And after some fashion Nolan said so. And then they all fell to kissing him again and wanted to rub his nose with theirs.

But he could not stand it long; and getting Vaughan to say he might go back, he beckoned me down into our boat. As we lay back in the stern-sheets and the men gave way, he said to me: "Youngster, let that show you what it is to be without a family, without a home, and without a country. And if you are ever tempted to say a word or to do a thing that shall put a bar between you and your family, your home, and your country, pray God in His mercy to take you that instant home to His own heaven. Stick by your family, boy; forget you have a self, while you do everything for them. Think of your home, boy; write and send, and talk about it. Let it be nearer and nearer to your thought, the farther you have to travel from it; and rush back to it, when you are free, as that poor black slave is doing now. And for your country, boy," and the words rattled in his throat, "and for that flag," and he pointed to the ship, "never dream a dream but of serving her as she bids you, though the service carry you through a thousand hells. No matter what happens to you, no matter who flatters you or who abuses you, never look at another flag, never let a night pass but you pray God to bless that flag. Remember, boy, that behind all these men you have to do with, behind officers and government, and people even, there is the Country Herself, your Country, and that you belong to her as you belong to your own mother. Stand by Her, boy, as you would stand by your mother, if those devils there had got held of her today!"

I was frightened to death by his calm, hard passion; but I blundered out that I would, by all that was holy, and that I had never thought of doing anything else. He hardly seemed to hear me; but he did, almost in a whisper say, "Oh, if anybody had said so to me when I was of your age!"

I think it was this half-confidence of his, which I never abused, for I never told this story till now, which afterward made us great friends. He was very kind to me. Often he sat up, or even got up, at night to walk the deck with me when it was my watch. He explained to me a great deal of my mathematics, and I owe to him my taste for mathematics. He lent me books, and helped me about my reading. He never alluded so directly to his story again; but from one and another officer I have learned, in thirty years, what I am telling. When we parted from him in St. Thomas harbor, at the end of our cruise, I was more sorry than I can tell. I was very glad to meet him again in 1830; and later in life, when I thought I had some influence in Washington, I moved heaven and earth to have him discharged. But it was like getting a ghost out of prison. They pretended there was no such man, and never was such a man. They will say so at the Department now! Perhaps they do not know. It will not be the first thing in the service of which the Department appears to know nothing!

There is a story that Nolan met Burr once on one of our vessels, when a party of Americans came on board in the Mediterranean. But this I believe to be a lie; or rather, it is a myth, *ben trovato*, involving a tremendous blowing-up with which he sunk Burr,—asking him how he liked to be "without a country." But it is clear, from Burr's life, that nothing of the sort could have happened; and I mention this only as an illustration of the stories which get a-going where there is the least mystery at bottom.

So poor Philip Nolan had his wish fulfilled. I know but one fate more dreadful; it is the fate reserved for those men who shall have one day to exile themselves from their country because they have attempted her ruin, and shall have at the same time to see the prosperity and honor to which she rises when she has rid herself of them and their iniquities. The wish of poor Nolan, as we all learned to call him, not because his punishment was too great, but because his repentance was so clear, was precisely the wish of every Bragg and Beauregard who broke a soldier's oath two years ago, and of every Maury and Barron who broke a sailor's. I do not know how often they have repented. I do know that they have done all that in them lay that they might have no country,—that all the honors, associations, memories, and hopes which belong to "country" might be broken up into little shreds and distributed to the winds. I know, too, that their punishment, as they vegetate through what is left of life to them in wretched Boulognes and Leicester Squares, where they are destined to upbraid each other till they die, will have all the agony of Nolan's, with the added pang that every one who sees them will see them to despise and to execrate them. They will have their wish, like him.

For him, poor fellow, he repented of his folly, and then, like a man, submitted to the fate he had asked for. He never intentionally added to the difficulty or delicacy of the charge of those who had him in hold. Accidents would happen; but they never happened from his fault. Lieutenant Truxton told me that when Texas was annexed, there was a careful discussion among the officers, whether they should get hold of Nolan's handsome set of maps, and cut Texas out of it,—from the map of the world and the map of Mexico. The United States had been cut out when the atlas was bought for him. But it was voted, rightly enough, that to do this would be virtually to reveal to him what had happened, or, as Harry Cole said, to make him think Old Burr had succeeded. So it was from no fault of Nolan's that a great botch happened at my own table, when, for a short time, I was in command of the *George Washington* corvette, on the South American Station. We were lying in the La Plata, and some of the officers, who had been on shore, and had just joined again, were entertaining us with accounts of their misadventures in riding the half-wild horses of Buenos Aires. Nolan was at table, and was in an unusually bright and talkative mood. Some story of a tumble reminded him of an adventure of his own, when he was catching wild horses in Texas with his brother Stephen, at a time when he must have been quite a boy. He told the story with a good deal of spirit,—so much so, that the silence which often follows a good story hung over the table for an instant, to be broken by Nolan himself. For he asked, perfectly unconsciously,—

"Pray, what has become of Texas? After the Mexicans got their independence, I thought that province of Texas would come forward very fast. It is really one of the finest regions on earth; it is the Italy of this continent. But I have not seen or heard a word of Texas for near twenty years."

There were two Texan officers at the table. The reason he had never heard of Texas was that Texas and her affairs had been painfully out of his newspapers since Austin began his settlements; so that, while he read of Honduras and Tamaulipas, and, till quite lately, of California, this virgin province, in which his brother had traveled so far and, I believe, had died, had ceased to be with him. Waters and Williams, the two Texas men, looked grimly at each other, and tried not to laugh. Edward Morris had his attention attracted by the third link in the chain of the captain's chandelier. Watrous was seized with a convulsion of sneezing. Nolan himself saw that something was to pay, he did not know what. And I, as master of the feast, had to say,—

"Texas is out of the map, Mr. Nolan. Have you seen Captain Back's curious account of Sir Thomas Roe's Welcome?"

After that cruise I never saw Nolan again. I wrote to him at least twice a year, for in that voyage we became even confidentially intimate; but he never wrote to me. The other men tell me that in those fifteen years he aged very fast, as well he might indeed, but that he was still the same gentle, uncomplaining, silent sufferer that he ever was, bearing as best he could his self-appointed punishment,—rather less social, perhaps, with new men whom he did not know, but more anxious, apparently, than ever to serve and befriend and teach the boys, some of them fairly seemed to worship him. And now the dear old fellow is dead. He had found a home at last, and a country.

Since writing this, and while considering whether or no I would print it, as a warning to the young Nolans and Vallandighams and Tatnalls of today of what it is to throw away a country, I have received from Danforth, who is on board the *Levant,* a letter which gives an account of Nolan's last hours. It removes all my doubts about telling this story.

To understand the first words of the letter, the non-professional reader should remember that after 1817 the position of every officer who had Nolan in charge was one of the greatest delicacy. The government had failed to renew the order of 1807 regarding him. What was a man to do? Should he let him go? What, then, if he were called to account by the Department for violating the order of 1807? Should he keep him? What, then, if Nolan should be liberated some day, and should bring an action for false imprisonment or kidnapping against every man who had had him in charge? I urged and pressed this upon Southard, and I have reason to think that other officers did the same thing. But the Secretary always said, as they so often do at Washington, that there were no special orders to give, and that we must act on our own judgment. That means, "If you succeed, you will be sustained; if you fail, you will be disavowed." Well, as Danforth says, all that is over now, though I do not know but I expose myself to a criminal prosecution on the evidence of the very revelation I am making.

Here is the letter:

"Levant, 2° 2″ S. @ 131° W.

"DEAR FRED,—I try to find heart and life to tell you that it is all over with dear old Nolan. I have been with him on this voyage more than I ever was, and I can understand wholly now the way in which you used to speak of the dear old fellow. I could see that he was not strong, but I had no idea that the end was so near. The doctor had been watching him very carefully, and yesterday morning came to me and told me that Nolan was not so well, and had not left his state-room,—a thing I never remember before. He had let the doctor come and see him as he lay there,—the first time the doctor had been in the state-room, and he said he should like to see me. Oh, dear! do you remember the mysteries we boys used to invent about his room, in the old *Intrepid* days? Well, I went in, and there, to be sure, the poor fellow lay in his berth, smiling pleasantly as he gave me his hand, but looking very frail. I could not help a glance round, which showed me what a little shrine he had made of the box he was lying in. The stars and stripes were triced up above and around a picture of Washington, and he had painted a majestic eagle, with lightnings blazing from his beak and his foot just clasping the whole globe, which his wings overshadowed. The dear old boy saw my glance, and, said, with a sad smile, 'Here, you see, I have a country!' And then he pointed to the foot of his bed, where I had not seen before a great map of the United States, as he had drawn it from memory, and which he had there to look upon as he lay. Quaint, queer old names were on it, in large letters: 'Indiana Territory,' 'Mississippi Territory,' and 'Louisiana,' as I supposed our fathers learned such things; but the old fellow had patched in Texas, too; he had carried his western boundary all the way to the Pacific, but on that shore he had defined nothing.

" 'Oh, Danforth,' he said, 'I know I am dying. I cannot get home. Surely you will tell me something now?—Stop! stop! Do not speak till I say what I am sure you know, that there is not in this ship, that there is not in America,—God bless her!—a more loyal man than I. There cannot be a man who loves the old flag as I do, or prays for it as I do, or hopes for it as I do. There are thirty-four stars in it now, Danforth. I thank God for that, though I do not know what their names are. There has never been one taken away; I thank God for that. I know by that, that there has never been any successful Burr. Oh, Danforth, Danforth,' he sighed out, 'how like a wretched night's dream a boy's idea of personal fame or of separate sovereignty seems, when one looks back on it after such a life as mine! But tell me,—tell me something,—tell me everything, Danforth, before I die!'

"Ingham, I swear to you that I felt like a monster that I had not told him everything before. Danger or no danger, delicacy or no delicacy, who was I that I should have been acting the tyrant all this time over this dear, sainted old man, who had years ago expiated, in his whole manhood's life the madness of a boy's treason? 'Mr. Nolan,' said I, 'I will tell you everything you ask about. Only, where shall I begin?'

"Oh, the blessed smile that crept over his white face! and he pressed my hand and said, 'God bless you! Tell me their names,' he said, and he pointed to the stars on the flag. 'The last I know is Ohio. My father lived in Kentucky. But I have guessed Michigan and Indiana and Mississippi,—that was where Fort Adams is,—they make twenty. But where are your other fourteen? You have not cut up any of the old ones, I hope?'

"Well, that was not a bad text, and I told him the names, in as good order as I could, and he bade me take down his beautiful map and draw them in as I best could with my pencil. He was wild with delight about Texas, told me how his brother died there; he had marked a gold cross where he supposed his brother's grave was; and he had guessed at Texas. Then he was delighted as he saw California and Oregon;—that, he said, he had suspected partly, because he had never been permitted to land on that shore, though the ships were there so much. 'And the men,' said he, laughing, 'brought off a good deal besides furs.' Then he went back —heavens, how far!—to ask about the Chesapeake, and what was done to Barron for surrendering her to the Leopard, and whether Burr ever tried again,—and he ground his teeth with the only passion he showed. But in a moment that was over, and he said, 'God forgive me, for I am sure I forgive him.' Then he asked about the old war,—told me the true story of his serving the gun the day we took the *Java*,—asked about dear old David Porter, as he called him. Then he settled down more quietly, and very happily, to hear me tell in an hour the history of fifty years.

"How I wished it had been somebody who knew something! But I did as well as I could. I told him of the English war. I told him about Fulton and the steamboat beginning. I told him about old Scott and Jackson; told him all I could think about the Mississippi, and New Orleans, and Texas, and his own old Kentucky. And do you think he asked who was in command of the 'Legion of the West.' I told him it was a very gallant officer, named Grant and that, by our last news, he was about to establish his headquarters at Vicksburg. Then, 'Where was Vicksburg?' I worked that out on the map; it was about a hundred miles, more or less, above his old Fort Adams; and I thought Fort Adams must be a ruin now. 'It must be at old Vick's plantation,' said he; 'well that is a change!'

"I tell you, Ingham, it was a hard thing to condense the history of half a century into that talk with a sick man. And I do not now know what I told him,—of emigration, and the means of it,—of steamboats and railroads and telegraphs,—of inventions and books and literature,—of the colleges and West Point and the Naval School,—but with the queerest interruptions that ever you heard. You see it was Robinson Crusoe asking all the accumulated questions of fifty-six years!

"I remember he asked, all of a sudden, who was President now; and when I told him, he asked if Old Abe was General Benjamin Lincoln's son. He said he met old General Lincoln, when he was quite a boy himself, at some Indian treaty. I said no, that Old Abe was a Kentuckian like himself, but I could not tell him of what family; he had worked up from the ranks. 'Good for him!' cried Nolan; 'I am glad of that. As I have brooded and wondered, I have thought our danger was in keeping up those regular successions in the first families.' Then I got talking about my visit to Washington. I told him of meeting the Oregon Congressman, Harding; I told him about Smithsonian and the exploring Expedition; I told him about the Capitol,—and the statues for the pediment,—and Crawford's Liberty,—and Greenough's Washington: Ingham, I told him everything I could think of that would show the grandeur of his country and its prosperity; but I could not make up my mouth to tell him a word about this infernal Rebellion! *

"And he drank it in, and enjoyed it as I cannot tell you. He grew mor? and more silent, yet I never thought he was tired or faint. I gave him glass of water, but he just wet his lips, and told me not to go away. The\. he asked me to bring the Presbyterian 'Book of Public Prayer,' which lay there, and said, with a smile, that it would open at the right place,— and so it did. There was his double red mark down the page; and I knelt down and read, and he repeated with me, 'For ourselves and our country, O gracious God, we thank Thee, that, notwithstanding our manifold transgressions of Thy holy laws, Thou hast continued to us Thy marvelous kindness,'—and so to the end of that thanksgiving. Then he turned to the end of the same book, and I read the words more familiar to me: 'Most heartily we beseech Thee with Thy favor to behold and bless Thy servant, the President of the United States, and all others in authority,'—and the rest of the Episcopal collect. 'Danforth,' said he, 'I have repeated those prayers night and morning, it is now fifty-five years.' And then he said he would go to sleep. He bent me down over him and kissed me; and he said, 'Look in my Bible, Danforth, when I am gone.' And I went away.

"But I had no thought it was the end. I thought he was tired and would sleep. I knew he was happy, and I wanted him to be alone.

"But in an hour, when the doctor went in gently, he found Nolan had breathed his life away with a smile. He had something pressed close to his lips. It was his father's badge of the Order of Cincinnati.

"We looked in his Bible, and there was a slip of paper, at the place where he had marked the text,—

"'They desire a country, even a heavenly: wherefore God is not ashamed to be called their God: for he hath prepared for them a city.'

"On this slip of paper he had written,—

"'Bury me in the sea; it has been my home, and I love it. But will not someone set up a stone for my memory at Fort Adams or at Orleans, that my disgrace, may not be more than I ought to bear? Say on it,—

IN MEMORY OF

PHILIP NOLAN,

LIEUTENANT

IN THE ARMY OF

THE UNITED STATES.

He loved his country as no other man has loved her; but no man deserved less at her hands.' "

* This story was written in 1863.—EDITOR.

10

The Diamond Lens

BY FITZ-JAMES O'BRIEN

I. THE BENDING OF THE TWIG

FROM a very early period of my life the entire bent of my inclinations had been towards microscopic investigations. When I was not more than ten years old, a distant relative of our family, hoping to astonish my inexperience, constructed a simple microscope for me, by drilling in a disk of copper a small hole, in which a drop of pure water was sustained by capillary attraction. This very primitive apparatus, magnifying some fifty diameters, presented, it is true, only indistinct and imperfect forms, but still sufficiently wonderful to work up my imagination to a preternatural state of excitement.

Seeing me so interested in this rude instrument, my cousin explained to me all that he knew about the principles of the microscope, related to me a few of the wonders which had been accomplished through its agency, and ended by promising to send me one regularly constructed, immediately on his return to the city. I counted the days, the hours, the minutes, that intervened between that promise and his departure.

Meantime I was not idle. Every transparent substance that bore the remotest resemblance to a lens I eagerly seized upon, and employed in vain attempts to realize that instrument, the theory of whose construction I as yet only vaguely comprehended. All panes of glass containing those oblate spheroidal knots familiarly known as "bull's-eyes" were ruthlessly destroyed, in the hope of obtaining lenses of marvelous power. I even went so far as to extract the crystalline humor from the eyes of fishes and animals, and endeavored to press it into the microscopic service. I plead guilty to having stolen the glasses from my Aunt

Agatha's spectacles, with a dim idea of grinding them into lenses of wondrous magnifying properties,—in which attempt it is scarcely necessary to say that I totally failed.

At last the promised instrument came. It was of that order known as Field's simple microscope, and had cost perhaps about fifteen dollars. As far as educational purposes went, a better apparatus could not have been selected. Accompanying it was a small treatise on the microscope, —its history, uses, and discoveries. I comprehended then for the first time the "Arabian Nights Entertainments." The dull veil of ordinary existence that hung across the world seemed suddenly to roll away, and to lay bare a land of enchantments. I felt towards my companions as the seer might feel towards the ordinary masses of men. I held conversations with nature in a tongue which they could not understand. I was in daily communication with living wonders, such as they never imagined in their wildest visions. I penetrated beyond the external portal of things, and roamed through the sanctuaries. Where they beheld only a drop of rain slowly rolling down the window-glass, I saw a universe of beings animated with all the passions common to physical life, and convulsing their minute sphere with struggles as fierce and protracted as those of men. In the common spots of mold, which my mother, good housekeeper that she was, fiercely scooped away from her jam pots, there abode for me, under the name of mildew, enchanted gardens, filled with dells and avenues of the densest foliage and most astonishing verdure, while from the fantastic boughs of these microscopic forests hung strange fruits glittering with green, and silver, and gold.

It was no scientific thirst that at this time filled my mind. It was the pure enjoyment of a poet to whom a world of wonders has been disclosed. I talked of my solitary pleasures to none. Alone with my microscope, I dimmed my sight, day after day and night after night, poring over the marvels which it unfolded to me. I was like one who, having discovered the ancient Eden still existing in all its primitive glory, should resolve to enjoy it in solitude, and never betray to mortal the secret of its locality. The rod of my life was bent at this moment. I destined myself to be a microscopist.

Of course, like every novice, I fancied myself a discoverer. I was ignorant at the time of the thousands of acute intellects engaged in the same pursuit as myself, and with the advantage of instruments a thousand times more powerful than mine. The names of Leeuwenhoek, Williamson, Spencer, Ehrenberg, Schultz, Dujardin, Schact, and Schleiden were then entirely unknown to me, or if known, I was ignorant of their patient and wonderful researches. In every fresh specimen of cryptogamia which I placed beneath my instrument I believed that I discovered wonders of which the world was as yet ignorant. I remember well the thrill of delight and admiration that shot through me the first time that I discovered the common wheel animalcule (*Rotifera vulgaris*) expanding and contracting its flexible spokes, and seemingly rotating through the water. Alas! as I grew older, and obtained some works treating of my favorite study, I found that I was only on the threshold of a science to the investigation of which some of the greatest men of the age were devoting their lives and intellects.

As I grew up, my parents, who saw but little likelihood of anything practical resulting from the examination of bits of moss and drops of water through a brass tube and a piece of glass, were anxious that I should choose a profession. It was their desire that I should enter the counting-house of my uncle, Ethan Blake, a prosperous merchant, who carried on business in New York. This suggestion I decisively combated. I had no taste for trade; I should only make a failure; in short, I refused to become a merchant.

But it was necessary for me to select some pursuit. My parents were staid New England people, who insisted on the necessity of labor; and therefore, although, thanks to the bequest of my poor Aunt Agatha, I should, on coming of age, inherit a small fortune sufficient to place me above want, it was decided that, instead of waiting for this, I should act the nobler part, and employ the intervening years in rendering myself independent.

After much cogitation I complied with the wishes of my family, and selected a profession. I determined to study medicine at the New York Academy. This disposition of my future suited me. A removal from my relatives would enable me to dispose of my time as I pleased without fear of detection. As long as I paid my Academy fees, I might shirk attending the lectures if I chose; and, as I never had the remotest intention of standing an examination, there was no danger of my being "plucked." Besides, a metropolis was the place for me. There I could obtain excellent instruments, the newest publications, intimacy with men of pursuits kindred with my own,—in short, all things necessary to insure a profitable devotion of my life to my beloved science. I had an abundance of money, few desires that were not bounded by my illuminating mirror on one side and my object-glass on the other; what, therefore, was to prevent my becoming an illustrious investigator of the veiled worlds? It was with the most buoyant hope that I left my New England home and established myself in New York.

II. THE LONGING OF A MAN OF SCIENCE

My first step, of course, was to find suitable apartments. These I obtained, after a couple of days' search, in Fourth Avenue; a very pretty second floor unfurnished, containing sitting room, bedroom, and a smaller apartment which I intended to fit up as a laboratory. I furnished my lodgings simply, but rather elegantly, and then devoted all my energies to the adornment of the temple of my worship. I visited Pike, the celebrated optician, and passed in review his splendid collection of microscopes,—Field's Compound, Hingham's, Spencer's, Nachet's Binocular (that founded on the principles of the stereoscope), and at length fixed upon that form known as Spencer's Trunnion Microscope, as combining the greatest number of improvements with an almost perfect freedom from tremor. Along with this I purchased every possible accessory,—draw tubes, micrometers, a *camera-lucida,* lever stage, achromatic condensers, white cloud illuminators, prisms, parabolic condensers, polarizing apparatus, forceps, aquatic boxes, fishing tubes, with a host of other articles, all of which would have been useful in the hands of an experienced microscopist, but, as I afterwards discovered, were not of the slightest present value to me. It takes years of practice to know how to use a complicated microscope. The optician looked suspiciously at me as I made these wholesale purchases. He evidently was uncertain whether to set me down as some scientific celebrity or a madman. I think he inclined to the latter belief. I suppose I was mad. Every great genius is mad upon the subject in which he is greatest. The unsuccessful madman is disgraced and called a lunatic.

Mad or not, I set myself to work with a zeal which few scientific students have ever equalled. I had everything to learn relative to the delicate study upon which I had embarked,—a study involving the most earnest patience, the most rigid analytic powers, the steadiest hand, the most untiring eye, the most refined and subtle manipulation.

For a long time half my apparatus lay inactively on the shelves of my laboratory, which was now most amply furnished with every possible contrivance for facilitating my investigations. The fact was that I did not know how to use some of my scientific implements,—never having been taught microscopics,—and those whose use I understood theoretically were of little avail, until by practice I could attain the necessary delicacy of handling. Still, such was the fury of my ambition, such the untiring perseverance of my experiments, that, difficult of credit as it may be, in the course of one year I became theoretically and practically an accomplished microscopist.

During this period of my labors, in which I submitted specimens of every substance that came under my observation to the action of my lenses, I became a discoverer,—in a small way, it is true, for I was very young, but still a discoverer. It was I who destroyed Ehrenberg's theory that the *Volvox globator* was an animal, and proved that his "monads" with stomachs and eyes were merely phases of the formation of a vegetable cell, and were, when they reached their mature state, incapable of the act of conjugation, or any true generative act, without which no organism rising to any stage of life higher than vegetable can be said to be complete. It was I who resolved the singular problem of rotation in the cells and hairs of plants into ciliary attraction, in spite of the assertions of Mr. Wenham and others, that my explanation was the result of an optical illusion.

But notwithstanding these discoveries, laboriously and painfully made as they were, I felt horribly dissatisfied. At every step I found myself stopped by the imperfections of my instruments. Like all active microscopists, I gave my imagination full play. Indeed, it is a common complaint against many such, that they supply the defects of their instruments with the creations of their brains. I imagined depths beyond depths in nature which the limited power of my lenses prohibited me from exploring. I lay awake at night constructing imaginary microscopes of immeasurable power, with which I seemed to pierce through all the envelopes of matter down to its original atom. How I cursed those imperfect mediums which necessity through ignorance compelled me to use! How I longed to discover the secret of some perfect lens, whose magnifying power should be limited only by the resolvability of the object, and which at the same time should be free from spherical and chromatic aberrations, in short from all the obstacles over which the poor microscopist finds himself continually stumbling! I felt convinced that the simple microscope, composed of a single lens of such vast yet perfect power was possible of construction. To attempt to bring the compound microscope up to such a pitch would have been commencing at the wrong end; this latter being simply a partially successful endeavor to remedy those very defects of the simple instrument, which, if conquered, would leave nothing to be desired.

It was in this mood of mind that I became a constructive microscopist. After another year passed in this new pursuit, experimenting on every imaginable substance,—glass, gems, flints, crystals, artificial crystals formed of the alloy of various vitreous materials,—in short, having constructed as many varieties of lenses as Argus had eyes, I found myself precisely where I started, with nothing gained save an extensive knowledge of glass-making. I was almost dead with despair. My parents were surprised at my apparent want of progress in my medical studies (I had not attended one lecture since my arrival in the city), and the expenses of my mad pursuit had been so great as to embarrass me very seriously.

I was in this frame of mind one day, experimenting in my laboratory on a small diamond,—that stone, from its great refracting power, having always occupied my attention more than any other,—when a young Frenchman, who lived on the floor above me, and who was in the habit of occasionally visiting me, entered the room.

I think that Jules Simon was a Jew. He had many traits of the Hebrew character: a love of jewelry, of dress, and of good living. There was something mysterious about him. He always had something to sell, and yet went into excellent society. When I say sell, I should perhaps have said peddle; for his operations were generally confined to the disposal of single articles,—a picture, for instance, or a rare carving in ivory, or a pair of duelling pistols, or the dress of a Mexican *caballero*. When I was first furnishing my rooms, he paid me a visit, which ended in my purchasing an antique silver lamp, which he assured me was a Cellini, —it was handsome enough even for that,—and some other knickknacks for my sitting room. Why Simon should pursue this petty trade I never could imagine. He apparently had plenty of money, and had the *entrée* of the best houses in the city,—taking care, however, I suppose, to drive no bargains within the enchanted circle of the Upper Ten. I came at length to the conclusion that this peddling was but a mask to cover some greater object, and even went so far as to believe my young acquaintance to be implicated in the slave trade. That, however, was none of my affair.

On the present occasion, Simon entered my room in a state of considerable excitement.

"*Ah! mon ami!*" he cried, before I could even offer him the ordinary salutation, "it has occurred to me to be the witness of the most astonishing things in the world. I promenade myself to the house of Madame —— How does the little animal—*le renard*—name himself in the Latin?"

"Vulpes," I answered.

"Ah! yes,—Vulpes. I promenade myself to the house of Madame Vulpes."

"The spirit medium?"

"Yes, the great medium. Great heavens! what a woman! I write on a slip of paper many of questions concerning affairs the most secret,— affairs that conceal themselves in the abysses of my heart the most profound; and behold! by example! what occurs? This devil of a woman makes me replies the most truthful to all of them. She talks to me of things that I do not love to talk of to myself. What am I to think? I am fixed to the earth!"

"Am I to understand you, M. Simon, that this Mrs. Vulpes replied to questions secretly written by you, which questions related to events known only to yourself?"

"Ah! more than that, more than that," he answered, with an air of some alarm. "She related to me things— But," he added, after a pause, and suddenly changing his manner, "why occupy ourselves with these follies? It was all the biology, without doubt. It goes without saying that it has not my credence.—But why are we here, *mon ami*? It has occurred

to me to discover the most beautiful thing as you can imagine,—a vase
with green lizards on it, composed by the great Bernard Palissy. It is in
my apartment; let us mount. I go to show it to you."

I followed Simon mechanically; but my thoughts were far from
Palissy and his enamelled ware, although I, like him, was seeking in the
dark a great discovery. This casual mention of the spiritualist, Madame
Vulpes, set me on a new track. What if this spiritualism should be really
a great fact? What if, through communication with more subtile organisms than my own, I could reach at a single bound the goal, which
perhaps a life of agonizing mental toil would never enable me to attain?

While purchasing the Palissy vase from my friend Simon, I was
mentally arranging a visit to Madame Vulpes.

III. THE SPIRIT OF LEEUWENHOEK

Two evenings after this, thanks to an arrangement by letter and the
promise of an ample fee, I found Madame Vulpes awaiting me at her
residence alone. She was a coarse-featured woman, with keen and rather
cruel dark eyes, and an exceedingly sensual expression about her mouth
and under jaw. She received me in perfect silence, in an apartment on
the ground floor, very sparely furnished. In the center of the room,
close to where Mrs. Vulpes sat, there was a common round mahogany
table. If I had come for the purpose of sweeping her chimney, the
woman could not have looked more indifferent to my appearance. There
was no attempt to inspire the visitor with awe. Everything bore a simple
and practical aspect. This intercourse with the spiritual world was evidently as familiar an occupation with Mrs. Vulpes as eating her dinner
or riding in an omnibus.

"You come for a communication, Mr. Linley?" said the medium, in
a dry, business-like tone of voice.

"By appointment,—yes."

"What sort of communication do you want?—a written one?"

"Yes,—I wish for a written one."

"From any particular spirit?"

"Yes."

"Have you ever known this spirit on this earth?"

"Never. He died long before I was born. I wish merely to obtain from
him some information which he ought to be able to give better than any
other."

"Will you seat yourself at the table, Mr. Linley," said the medium,
"and place your hands upon it?"

I obeyed,—Mrs. Vulpes being seated opposite to me, with her hands
also on the table. We remained thus for about a minute and a half, when
a violent succession of raps came on the table, on the back of my chair,

on the floor immediately under my feet, and even on the windowpanes. Mrs. Vulpes smiled composedly.

"They are very strong tonight," she remarked. "You are fortunate." She then continued, "Will the spirits communicate with this gentleman?"

Vigorous affirmative.

"Will the particular spirit he desires to speak with communicate?"

A very confused rapping followed this question.

"I know what they mean," said Mrs. Vulpes, addressing herself to me; "they wish you to write down the name of the particular spirit that you desire to converse with. Is that so?" she added, speaking to her invisible guests.

That it was so was evident from the numerous affirmatory responses. While this was going on, I tore a slip from my pocketbook, and scribbled a name, under the table.

"Will this spirit communicate in writing with this gentleman?" asked the medium once more.

After a moment's pause, her hand seemed to be seized with a violent tremor, shaking so forcibly that the table vibrated. She said that a spirit had seized her hand and would write. I handed her some sheets of paper that were on the table, and a pencil. The latter she held loosely in her hand, which presently began to move over the paper with a singular and seemingly involuntary motion. After a few moments had elapsed, she handed me the paper, on which I found written, in a large, uncultivated hand, the words, "He is not here, but has been sent for." A pause of a minute or so now ensued, during which Mrs. Vulpes remained perfectly silent, but the raps continued at regular intervals. When the short period I mention had elapsed, the hand of the medium was again seized with its convulsive tremor, and she wrote, under this strange influence, a few words on the paper, which she handed to me. They were as follows:—

"I am here. Question me.

"LEEUWENHOEK."

I was astounded. The name was identical with that I had written beneath the table, and carefully kept concealed. Neither was it at all probable that an uncultivated woman like Mrs. Vulpes should know even the name of the great father of microscopics. It may have been biology; but this theory was soon doomed to be destroyed. I wrote on my slip— still concealing it from Mrs. Vulpes—a series of questions, which, to avoid tediousness, I shall place with the responses, in the order in which they occurred:—

I.—Can the microscope be brought to perfection?

SPIRIT.—Yes.

I.—Am I destined to accomplish this great task?

SPIRIT.—You are.

I.—I wish to know how to proceed to attain this end. For the love which you bear to science, help me!

SPIRIT.—A diamond of one hundred and forty carats, submitted to electromagnetic currents for a long period, will experience a rearrangement of its atoms *inter se,* and from that stone you will form the universal lens.

I.—Will great discoveries result from the use of such a lens?

SPIRIT.—So great that all that has gone before is as nothing.

I.—But the refractive power of the diamond is so immense, that the image will be formed within the lens. How is that difficulty to be surmounted?

SPIRIT.—Pierce the lens through its axis, and the difficulty is obviated. The image will be formed in the pierced space, which will itself serve as a tube to look through. Now I am called. Good night.

I cannot at all describe the effect that these extraordinary communications had upon me. I felt completely bewildered. No biological theory could account for the *discovery* of the lens. The medium might, by means of biological *rapport* with my mind, have gone so far as to read my questions, and reply to them coherently. But biology could not enable her to discover that magnetic currents would so alter the crystals of the diamond as to remedy its previous defects, and admit of its being polished into a perfect lens. Some such theory may have passed through my head, it is true; but if so, I had forgotten it. In my excited condition of mind there was no course left but to become a convert, and it was in a state of the most painful nervous exaltation that I left the medium's house that evening. She accompanied me to the door, hoping that I was satisfied. The raps followed us as we went through the hall, sounding on the balusters, the flooring, and even the lintels of the door. I hastily expressed my satisfaction, and escaped hurriedly into the cool night air. I walked home with but one thought possessing me,—how to obtain a diamond of the immense size required. My entire means multiplied a hundred times over would have been inadequate to its purchase. Besides, such stones are rare, and become historical. I could find such only in the regalia of Eastern or European monarchs.

IV. THE EYE OF MORNING

There was a light in Simon's room as I entered my house. A vague impulse urged me to visit him. As I opened the door of his sitting room unannounced, he was bending, with his back towards me, over a carcel lamp, apparently engaged in minutely examining some object which he held in his hands. As I entered, he started suddenly, thrust his hand into his breast pocket, and turned to me with a face crimson with confusion.

"What!" I cried, "poring over the miniature of some fair lady? Well, don't blush so much; I won't ask to see it."

Simon laughed awkwardly enough, but made none of the negative protestations usual on such occasions. He asked me to take a seat.

"Simon," said I, "I have just come from Madame Vulpes."

This time Simon turned as white as a sheet, and seemed stupefied, as if a sudden electric shock had smitten him. He babbled some incoherent words, and went hastily to a small closet where he usually kept his liquors. Although astonished at his emotion, I was too preoccupied with my own idea to pay much attention to anything else.

"You say truly when you call Madame Vulpes a devil of a woman," I continued. "Simon, she told me wonderful things tonight, or rather was the means of telling me wonderful things. Ah! if I could only get a diamond that weighed one hundred and forty carats!"

Scarcely had the sigh with which I uttered this desire died upon my lips, when Simon, with the aspect of a wild beast, glared at me savagely, and, rushing to the mantelpiece, where some foreign weapons hung on the wall, caught up a Malay creese, and brandished it furiously before him.

"No!" he cried in French, into which he always broke when excited. "No! you shall not have it! You are perfidious! You have consulted with that demon, and desire my treasure! But I shall die first! Me! I am brave! You cannot make me fear!"

All this, uttered in a loud voice trembling with excitement, astounded me. I saw at a glance that I had accidentally trodden upon the edges of Simon's secret, whatever it was. It was necessary to reassure him.

"My dear Simon," I said, "I am entirely at a loss to know what you mean. I went to Madame Vulpes to consult her on a scientific problem, to the solution of which I discovered that a diamond of the size I just mentioned was necessary. You were never alluded to during the evening, nor, so far as I was concerned, even thought of. What can be the meaning of this outburst? If you happen to have a set of valuable diamonds in your possession, you need fear nothing from me. The diamond which I require you could not possess; or, if you did possess it, you would not be living here."

Something in my tone must have completely reassured him; for his expression immediately changed to a sort of constrained merriment, combined, however, with a certain suspicious attention to my movements. He laughed, and said that I must bear with him; that he was at certain moments subject to a species of vertigo, which betrayed itself in incoherent speeches, and that the attacks passed off as rapidly as they came. He put his weapon aside while making this explanation, and endeavored, with some success, to assume a more cheerful air.

All this did not impose on me in the least. I was too much accustomed to analytical labors to be baffled by so flimsy a veil. I determined to probe the mystery to the bottom.

"Simon," I said, gayly, "let us forget all this over a bottle of Burgundy. I have a case of Lausseure's *Clos Vougeot* downstairs, fragrant with the odors and ruddy with the sunlight of the Côte d'Or. Let us have up a couple of bottles. What say you?"

"With all my heart," answered Simon, smilingly.

I produced the wine and we seated ourselves to drink. It was of a famous vintage, that of 1848, a year when war and wine throve together, —and its pure but powerful juice seemed to impart renewed vitality to the system. By the time we had half finished the second bottle, Simon's head, which I knew was a weak one, had begun to yield, while I remained calm as ever, only that every draught seemed to send a flush of vigor through my limbs. Simon's utterance became more and more indistinct. He took to singing French *chansons* of a not very moral tendency. I rose suddenly from the table just at the conclusion of one of those incoherent verses, and, fixing my eyes on him with a quiet smile, said: "Simon, I have deceived you. I learned your secret this evening. You may as well be frank with me. Mrs. Vulpes, or rather one of her spirits, told me all."

He started with horror. His intoxication seemed for the moment to fade away, and he made a movement towards the weapon that he had a short time before laid down. I stopped him with my hand.

"Monster," he cried, passionately, "I am ruined! What shall I do? You shall never have it! I swear by my mother!"

"I don't want it," I said; "rest secure, but be frank with me. Tell me all about it."

The drunkenness began to return. He protested with maudlin earnestness that I was entirely mistaken,—that I was intoxicated; then asked me to swear eternal secrecy, and promised to disclose the mystery to me. I pledged myself, of course, to all. With an uneasy look in his eyes, and hands unsteady with drink and nervousness, he drew a small case from his breast and opened it. Heavens! How the mild lamplight was shivered into a thousand prismatic arrows, as it fell upon a vast rose-diamond that glittered in the case! I was no judge of diamonds, but I saw at a glance that this was a gem of rare size and purity. I looked at Simon with wonder, and—must I confess it?—with envy. How could he have obtained this treasure? In reply to my questions, I could just gather from his drunken statements (of which, I fancy, half the incoherence was affected) that he had been superintending a gang of slaves engaged in diamond-washing in Brazil; that he had seen one of them secrete a diamond, but, instead of informing his employers, had quietly watched the Negro until he saw him bury his treasure; that he had dug it up and fled with it, but that as yet he was afraid to attempt to dispose of it publicly,—so valuable a gem being almost certain to attract too much attention to its owner's antecedents,—and he had not been able to discover any of those obscure channels by which such matters are conveyed away safely. He added, that, in accordance with the oriental practice, he had named his diamond with the fanciful title of "The Eye of Morning."

While Simon was relating this to me, I regarded the great diamond attentively. Never had I beheld anything so beautiful. All the glories of light, ever imagined or described, seemed to pulsate in its crystalline chambers. Its weight, as I learned from Simon, was exactly one hundred and forty carats. Here was an amazing coincidence. The hand of destiny seemed in it. On the very evening when the spirit of Leeuwenhoek communicates to me the great secret of the microscope, the priceless means which he directs me to employ start up within my easy reach! I determined, with the most perfect deliberation, to possess myself of Simon's diamond.

I sat opposite to him while he nodded over his glass, and calmly revolved the whole affair. I did not for an instant contemplate so foolish an act as a common theft, which would of course be discovered, or at least necessitate flight and concealment, all of which must interfere with my scientific plans. There was but one step to be taken,—to kill Simon. After all, what was the life of a little peddling Jew, in comparison with the interests of science? Human beings are taken every day from the condemned prisons to be experimented on by surgeons. This man, Simon, was by his own confession a criminal, a robber, and I believed in my soul a murderer. He deserved death quite as much as any felon condemned by the laws: why should I not, like government, contrive that his punishment should contribute to the progress of human knowledge?

The means for accomplishing everything I desired lay within my reach. There stood upon the mantelpiece a bottle half full of French laudanum. Simon was so occupied with his diamond, which I had just restored to him, that it was an affair of no difficulty to drug his glass. In a quarter of an hour he was in a profound sleep.

I now opened his waistcoat, took the diamond from the inner pocket in which he had placed it, and removed him to the bed, on which I laid him so that his feet hung down over the edge. I had possessed myself of the Malay creese, which I held in my right hand, while with the other

I discovered as accurately as I could by pulsation the exact locality of the heart. It was essential that all the aspects of his death should lead to the surmise of self-murder. I calculated the exact angle at which it was probable that the weapon, if levelled by Simon's own hand, would enter his breast; then with one powerful blow I thrust it up to the hilt in the very spot which I desired to penetrate. A convulsive thrill ran through Simon's limbs. I heard a smothered sound issue from his throat, precisely like the bursting of a large air-bubble, sent up by a diver, when it reaches the surface of the water; he turned half round on his side, and, as if to assist my plans more effectually, his right hand, moved by some mere spasmodic impulse, clasped the handle of the creese, which it remained holding with extraordinary muscular tenacity. Beyond this there was no apparent struggle. The laudanum, I presume, paralyzed the usual nervous action. He must have died instantly.

There was yet something to be done. To make it certain that all suspicion of the act should be diverted from any inhabitant of the house to Simon himself, it was necessary that the door should be found in the morning *locked on the inside.* How to do this, and afterwards escape myself? Not by the window; that was a physical impossibility. Besides, I was determined that the windows *also* should be found bolted. The solution was simple enough. I descended softly to my own room for a peculiar instrument which I had used for holding small slippery substances, such as minute spheres of glass, etc. This instrument was nothing more than a long slender hand-vise, with a very powerful grip, and a considerable leverage, which last was accidentally owing to the shape of the handle. Nothing was simpler than, when the key was in the lock, to seize the end of its stem in this vise, through the keyhole, from the outside, and so lock the door. Previously, however, to doing this, I burned a number of papers on Simon's hearth. Suicides almost always burn papers before they destroy themselves. I also emptied some more laudanum into Simon's glass,—having first removed from it all traces of wine,—cleaned the other wine glass, and brought the bottles away with me. If traces of two persons drinking had been found in the room, the question naturally would have arisen, Who was the second? Besides, the wine-bottles might have been identified as belonging to me. The laudanum I poured out to account for its presence in his stomach, in case of a *post-mortem* examination. The theory naturally would be, that he first intended to poison himself, but, after swallowing a little of the drug, was either disgusted with its taste, or changed his mind from other motives, and chose the dagger. These arrangements made, I walked out, leaving the gas burning, locked the door with my vise, and went to bed.

Simon's death was not discovered until nearly three in the afternoon.

The servant, astonished at seeing the gas burning,—the light streaming on the dark landing from under the door,—peeped through the keyhole and saw Simon on the bed. She gave the alarm. The door was burst open, and the neighborhood was in a fever of excitement.

Everyone in the house was arrested, myself included. There was an inquest; but no clue to his death beyond that of suicide could be obtained. Curiously enough, he had made several speeches to his friends the preceding week, that seemed to point to self-destruction. One gentleman swore that Simon had said in his presence that "he was tired of life." His landlord affirmed that Simon, when paying him his last month's rent, remarked that "he should not pay him rent much longer." All the other evidence corresponded,—the door locked inside, the position of the corpse, the burnt papers. As I anticipated, no one knew of the possession of the diamond by Simon, so that no motive was suggested for his murder. The jury, after a prolonged examination, brought in the usual verdict, and the neighborhood once more settled down into its accustomed quiet.

V. ANIMULA

The three months succeeding Simon's catastrophe I devoted night and day to my diamond lens. I had constructed a vast galvanic battery, composed of nearly two thousand pairs of plates,—a higher power I dared not use, lest the diamond should be calcined. By means of this enormous engine I was enabled to send a powerful current of electricity continually through my great diamond, which it seemed to me gained in luster every day. At the expiration of a month I commenced the grinding and polishing of the lens, a work of intense toil and exquisite delicacy. The great density of the stone, and the care required to be taken with the curvatures of the surfaces of the lens, rendered the labor the severest and most harassing that I had yet undergone.

At last the eventful moment came; the lens was completed. I stood trembling on the threshold of new worlds. I had the realization of Alexander's famous wish before me. The lens lay on the table, ready to be placed upon its platform. My hand fairly shook as I enveloped a drop of water with a thin coating of oil of turpentine, preparatory to its examination,—a process necessary in order to prevent the rapid evaporation of the water. I now placed the drop on a thin slip of glass under the lens, and throwing upon it, by the combined aid of a prism and a mirror, a powerful stream of light, I approached my eye to the minute hole drilled through the axis of the lens. For an instant I saw nothing save what seemed to be an illuminated chaos, a vast luminous abyss. A pure white light, cloudless and serene, and seemingly limitless as space itself, was my first impression. Gently, and with the greatest care, I depressed

the lens a few hair's breadths. The wondrous illumination still continued, but as the lens approached the object a scene of indescribable
beauty was unfolded to my view.

I seemed to gaze upon a vast space, the limits of which extended far
beyond my vision. An atmosphere of magical luminousness permeated
the entire field of view. I was amazed to see no trace of animalculous
life. Not a living thing, apparently, inhabited that dazzling expanse. I
comprehended instantly that, by the wondrous power of my lens, I had
penetrated beyond the grosser particles of aqueous matter, beyond the
realms of infusoria and protozoa, down to the original gaseous globule,
into whose luminous interior I was gazing, as into an almost boundless
dome filled with a supernatural radiance.

It was, however, no brilliant void into which I looked. On every side
I beheld beautiful inorganic forms, of unknown texture, and colored
with the most enchanting hues. These forms presented the appearance
of what might be called, for want of a more specific definition, foliated
clouds of the highest rarity; that is, they undulated and broke into vegetable formations, and were tinged with splendors compared with which
the gliding of our autumn woodlands is as dross compared with gold.
Far away into the illimitable distance stretched long avenues of these
gaseous forests, dimly transparent, and painted with prismatic hues of
unimaginable brilliancy. The pendent branches waved along the fluid
glades until every vista seemed to break through half-lucent ranks of
many-colored drooping silken pennons. What seemed to be either fruits
or flowers, pied with a thousand hues, lustrous and ever varying, bubbled from the crowns of this fairy foliage. No hills, no lakes, no rivers, no
forms animate or inanimate, were to be seen, save those vast auroral
copses that floated serenely in the luminous stillness, with leaves and
fruits and flowers gleaming with unknown fires, unrealizable by mere
imagination.

How strange, I thought, that this sphere should be thus condemned
to solitude! I had hoped, at least, to discover some new form of animal
life,—perhaps of a lower class than any with which we are at present
acquainted, but still, some living organism. I found my newly discovered
world, if I may so speak, a beautiful chromatic desert.

While I was speculating on the singular arrangements of the internal
economy of Nature, with which she so frequently splinters into atoms
our most compact theories, I thought I beheld a form moving slowly
through the glades of one of the prismatic forests. I looked more attentively, and found that I was not mistaken. Words cannot depict the
anxiety with which I awaited the nearer approach of this mysterious
object. Was it merely some inanimate substance, held in suspense in the
attenuated atmosphere of the globule? or was it an animal endowed

with vitality and motion? It approached, flitting behind the gauzy, colored veils of cloud-foliage, for seconds dimly revealed, then vanishing. At last the violet pennons that trailed nearest to me vibrated; they were gently pushed aside, and the form floated out into the broad light.

It was a female human shape. When I say human, I mean it possessed the outlines of humanity,—but there the analogy ends. Its adorable beauty lifted it illimitable heights beyond the loveliest daughter of Adam.

I cannot, I dare not, attempt to inventory the charms of this divine revelation of perfect beauty. Those eyes of mystic violet, dewy and serene, evade my words. Her long, lustrous hair following her glorious head in a golden wake, like the track sown in heaven by a falling star, seems to quench my most burning phrases with its splendors. If all the bees of Hybla nestled upon my lips, they would still sing but hoarsely the wondrous harmonies of outline that enclosed her form.

She swept out from between the rainbow-curtains of the cloud-trees into the broad sea of light that lay beyond. Her motions were those of some graceful naiad, cleaving, by a mere effort of her will, the clear, unruffled waters that fill the chambers of the sea. She floated forth with the serene grace of a frail bubble ascending through the still atmosphere of a June day. The perfect roundness of her limbs formed suave and enchanting curves. It was like listening to the most spiritual symphony of Beethoven the divine, to watch the harmonious flow of lines. This, indeed, was a pleasure cheaply purchased at any price. What cared I, if I had waded to the portal of this wonder through another's blood? I would have given my own to enjoy one such moment of intoxication and delight.

Breathless with gazing on this lovely wonder, and forgetful for an instant of everything save her presence, I withdrew my eye from the microscope eagerly,—alas! As my gaze fell on the thin slide that lay beneath my instrument, the bright light from mirror and from prism sparkled on a colorless drop of water! There, in that tiny bead of dew, this beautiful being was forever imprisoned. The planet Neptune was not more distant from me than she. I hastened once more to apply my eye to the microscope.

Animula (let me now call her by that dear name which I subsequently bestowed on her) had changed her position. She had again approached the wondrous forest, and was gazing earnestly upwards. Presently one of the trees—as I must call them—unfolded a long ciliary process, with which it seized one of the gleaming fruits that glittered on its summit, and, sweeping slowly down, held it within reach of Animula. The sylph took it in her delicate hand and began to eat. My attention was so entirely absorbed by her, that I could not apply myself to the task of determining whether this singular plant was or was not instinct with volition.

I watched her, as she made her repast, with the most profound attention. The suppleness of her motions sent a thrill of delight through my frame; my heart beat madly as she turned her beautiful eyes in the direction of the spot in which I stood. What would I not have given to have had the power to precipitate myself into that luminous ocean, and float with her through those groves of purple and gold! While I was thus breathlessly following her every movement, she suddenly started, seemed to listen for a moment, and then cleaving the brilliant ether in which she was floating, like a flash of light, pierced through the opaline forest, and disappeared.

Instantly a series of the most singular sensations attacked me. It seemed as if I had suddenly gone blind. The luminous sphere was still before me, but my daylight had vanished. What caused this sudden disappearance? Had she a lover or a husband? Yes, that was the solution! Some signal from a happy fellow-being had vibrated through the avenues of the forest, and she had obeyed the summons.

The agony of my sensations, as I arrived at this conclusion, startled me. I tried to reject the conviction that my reason forced upon me. I battled against the fatal conclusion,—but in vain. It was so. I had no escape from it. I loved an animalcule!

It is true that, thanks to the marvelous power of my microscope, she appeared of human proportions. Instead of presenting the revolting aspect of the coarser creatures, that live and struggle and die, in the more easily resolvable portions of the water-drop, she was fair and delicate and of surpassing beauty. But of what account was all that? Every time that my eye was withdrawn from the instrument, it fell on a miserable drop of water, within which, I must be content to know, dwelt all that could make my life lovely.

Could she but see me once! Could I for one moment pierce the mystical walls that so inexorably rose to separate us, and whisper all that filled my soul, I might consent to be satisfied for the rest of my life with the knowledge of her remote sympathy. It would be something to have established even the faintest personal link to bind us together,—to know that at times, when roaming through those enchanted glades, she might think of the wonderful stranger, who had broken the monotony of her life with his presence, and left a gentle memory in her heart!

But it could not be. No invention of which human intellect was capable could break down the barriers that nature had erected. I might feast my soul upon her wondrous beauty, yet she must always remain ignorant of the adoring eyes that day and night gazed upon her, and, even when closed, beheld her in dreams. With a bitter cry of anguish I fled from the room, and, flinging myself on my bed, sobbed myself to sleep like a child.

VI. THE SPILLING OF THE CUP

I arose the next morning almost at daybreak, and rushed to my microscope. I trembled as I sought the luminous world in miniature that contained my all. Animula was there. I had left the gas-lamp, surrounded by its moderators, burning, when I went to bed the night before. I found the sylph bathing, as it were, with an expression of pleasure animating her features, in the brilliant light which surrounded her. She tossed her lustrous golden hair over her shoulders with innocent coquetry. She lay at full length in the transparent medium, in which she supported herself with ease, and gambolled with the enchanting grace that the nymph Salmacis might have exhibited when she sought to conquer the modest Hermaphroditus. I tried an experiment to satisfy myself if her powers of reflection were developed. I lessened the lamplight considerably. By the dim light that remained, I could see an expression of pain flit across her face. She looked upward suddenly, and her brows contracted. I flooded the stage of the microscope again with a full stream of light, and her whole expression changed. She sprang forward like some substance deprived of all weight. Her eyes sparkled and her lips moved. Ah! if science had only the means of conducting and reduplicating sounds, as it does the rays of light, what carols of happiness would then have entranced my ears! what jubilant hymns to Adonïs would have thrilled the illumined air!

I now comprehended how it was that the Count de Gabalis peopled his mystic world with sylphs,—beautiful beings whose breath of life was lambent fire, and who sported forever in regions of purest ether and purest light. The Rosicrucian had anticipated the wonder that I had practically realized.

How long this worship of my strange divinity went on thus I scarcely know. I lost all note of time. All day from early dawn, and far into the night, I was to be found peering through that wonderful lens. I saw no one, went nowhere, and scarce allowed myself sufficient time for my meals. My whole life was absorbed in contemplation as rapt as that of any of the Romish saints. Every hour that I gazed upon the divine form strengthened my passion,—a passion that was always overshadowed by the maddening conviction, that, although I could gaze on her at will, she never, never could behold me!

At length, I grew so pale and emaciated, from want of rest, and continual brooding over my insane love and its cruel conditions, that I determined to make some effort to wean myself from it. "Come,"

I said, "this is at best but a fantasy. Your imagination has bestowed on Animula charms which in reality she does not possess. Seclusion from female society has produced this morbid condition of mind. Compare her with the beautiful women of your own world, and this false enchantment will vanish."

I looked over the newspapers by chance. There I beheld the advertisement of a celebrated *danseuse* who appeared nightly at Niblo's. The Signorina Caradolce had the reputation of being the most beautiful as well as the most graceful woman in the world. I instantly dressed and went to the theater.

The curtain drew up. The usual semicircle of fairies in white muslin were standing on the right toe around the enamelled flower-bank, of green canvas, on which the belated prince was sleeping. Suddenly a flute was heard. The fairies start. The trees open, the fairies all stand on the left toe, and the queen enters. It was the Signorina. She bounded forward amid thunders of applause, and, lighting on one foot, remained poised in air. Heavens! was this the great enchantress that had drawn monarchs at her chariot-wheels? Those heavy muscular limbs, those thick ankles, those cavernous eyes, that stereotyped smile, those crudely painted cheeks! Where were the vermeil blooms, the liquid expressive eyes, the harmonious limbs of Animula?

The Signorina danced. What gross, discordant movements! The play of her limbs was all false and artificial. Her bounds were painful athletic efforts; her poses were angular and distressed the eye. I could bear it no longer; with an exclamation of disgust that drew every eye upon me, I rose from my seat in the very middle of the Signorina's *pas-de-fascination,* and abruptly quitted the house.

I hastened home to feast my eyes once more on the lovely form of my sylph. I felt that henceforth to combat this passion would be impossible. I applied my eye to the lens. Animula was there,—but what could have happened? Some terrible change seemed to have taken place during my absence. Some secret grief seemed to cloud the lovely features of her I gazed upon. Her face had grown thin and haggard; her limbs trailed heavily; the wondrous luster of her golden hair had faded. She was ill!—ill, and I could not assist her! I believe at that moment I would have gladly forfeited all claims to my human birthright, if I could only have been dwarfed to the size of an animalcule, and permitted to console her from whom fate had forever divided me.

I racked my brain for the solution of this mystery. What was it that afflicted the sylph? She seemed to suffer intense pain. Her features contracted, and she even writhed, as if with some internal agony. The wondrous forests appeared also to have lost half their beauty. Their hues were dim and in some places faded away altogether. I watched

Animula for hours with a breaking heart, and she seemed absolutely to wither away under my very eye. Suddenly I remembered that I had not looked at the water-drop for several days. In fact, I hated to see it; for it reminded me of the natural barrier between Animula and myself. I hurriedly looked down on the stage of the microscope. The slide was still there,—but, great heavens! the water-drop had vanished! The awful truth burst upon me; it had evaporated, until it had become so minute as to be invisible to the naked eye; I had been gazing on its last atom, the one that contained Animula,—and she was dying!

I rushed again to the front of the lens, and looked through. Alas! the last agony had seized her. The rainbow-hued forests had all melted away, and Animula lay struggling feebly in what seemed to be a spot of dim light. Ah! the sight was horrible: the limbs once so round and lovely shrivelling up into nothings; the eyes—those eyes that shone like heaven—being quenched into black dust; the lustrous golden hair now lank and discolored. The last throe came. I beheld that final struggle of the blackening form—and I fainted.

When I awoke out of a trance of many hours, I found myself lying amid the wreck of my instrument, myself as shattered in mind and body as it. I crawled feebly to my bed, from which I did not rise for months.

They say now that I am mad; but they are mistaken. I am poor, for I have neither the heart nor the will to work; all my money is spent, and I live on charity. Young men's associations that love a joke invite me to lecture on Optics before them, for which they pay me, and laugh at me while I lecture. "Linley, the mad microscopist," is the name I go by. I suppose that I talk incoherently while I lecture. Who could talk sense when his brain is haunted by such ghastly memories, while ever and anon among the shapes of death I behold the radiant form of my lost Animula!

11

The Lady, or the Tiger?

BY FRANK R. STOCKTON

IN the very olden time, there lived a semi-barbaric king, whose ideas, though somewhat polished and sharpened by the progressiveness of distant Latin neighbors, were still large, florid, and untrammelled, as became the half of him which was barbaric. He was a man of exuberant fancy, and, withal, of an authority so irresistible that, at his will, he turned his varied fancies into facts. He was greatly given to self-communing; and, when he and himself agreed upon anything, the thing was done. When every member of his domestic and political systems moved smoothly in its appointed course, his nature was bland and genial; but whenever there was a little hitch, and some of his orbs got out of their orbits, he was blander and more genial still, for nothing pleased him so much as to make the crooked straight, and crush down uneven places.

Among the borrowed notions by which his barbarism had become semified was that of the public arena, in which, by exhibitions of manly and beastly valor, the minds of his subjects were refined and cultured.

But even here the exuberant and barbaric fancy asserted itself. The arena of the king was built, not to give the people an opportunity of hearing the rhapsodies of dying gladiators, nor to enable them to view the inevitable conclusion of a conflict between religious opinions and hungry jaws, but for purposes far better adapted to widen and develop the mental energies of the people. This vast amphitheater, with its encircling galleries, its mysterious vaults, and its unseen passages, was an agent of poetic justice, in which crime was punished, or virtue rewarded, by the decrees of an impartial and incorruptible chance.

When a subject was accused of a crime of sufficient importance to interest the king, public notice was given that on an appointed day the

248

fate of the accused person would be decided in the king's arena,—a structure which well deserved its name; for, although its form and plan were borrowed from afar, its purpose emanated solely from the brain of this man, who, every barleycorn a king, knew no tradition to which he owed more allegiance than pleased his fancy, and who ingrafted on every adopted form of human thought and action the rich growth of his barbaric idealism.

When all the people had assembled in the galleries, and the king, surrounded by his court, sat high up on his throne of royal state on one side of the arena, he gave a signal, a door beneath him opened, and the accused subject stepped out into the amphitheater. Directly opposite him, on the other side of the enclosed space, were two doors, exactly alike and side by side. It was the duty and the privilege of the person on trial, to walk directly to these doors and open one of them. He could open either door he pleased: he was subject to no guidance or influence but that of the aforementioned impartial and incorruptible chance. If he opened the one, there came out of it a hungry tiger, the fiercest and most cruel that could be procured, which immediately sprang upon him, and tore him to pieces, as a punishment for his guilt. The moment that the case of the criminal was thus decided, doleful iron bells were clanged, great wails went up from the hired mourners posted on the outer rim of the arena, and the vast audience, with bowed heads and downcast hearts, wended slowly their homeward way, mourning greatly that one so young and fair, or so old and respected, should have merited so dire a fate.

But, if the accused person opened the other door, there came forth from it a lady, the most suitable to his years and station that his majesty could select among his fair subjects; and to this lady he was immediately married, as a reward of his innocence. It mattered not that he might already possess a wife and family, or that his affections might be engaged upon an object of his own selection: the king allowed no such subordinate arrangements to interfere with his great scheme of retribution and reward. The exercises, as in the other instance, took place immediately, and in the arena. Another door opened beneath the king, and a priest, followed by a band of choristers, and dancing maidens blowing joyous airs on golden horns and treading an epithalamic measure, advanced to where the pair stood, side by side; and the wedding was promptly and cheerily solemnized. Then the gay brass bells rang forth their merry peals, the people shouted glad hurrahs, and the innocent man, preceded by children strewing flowers on his path, led his bride to his home.

This was the king's semi-barbaric method of administering justice. Its perfect fairness is obvious. The criminal could not know out of which door would come the lady: he opened either he pleased, without having the slightest idea whether, in the next instant, he was to be devoured or married. On some occasions the tiger came out of one door, and on some out of the other. The decisions of this tribunal were not only fair, they were positively determinate: the accused person was instantly punished if he found himself guilty; and, if innocent, he was rewarded on the spot, whether he liked it or not. There was no escape from the judgments of the king's arena.

The institution was a very popular one. When the people gathered together on one of the great trial days, they never knew whether they were to witness a bloody slaughter or a hilarious wedding. This element of uncertainty lent an interest to the occasion which it could not otherwise have attained. Thus, the masses were entertained and pleased, and the thinking part of the community could bring no charge of unfairness against this plan; for did not the accused person have the whole matter in his own hands?

This semi-barbaric king had a daughter as blooming as his most florid fancies, and with a soul as fervent and imperious as his own. As is usual in such cases, she was the apple of his eye, and was loved by him above all humanity. Among his courtiers was a young man of that fineness of blood and lowness of station common to the conventional heroes of romance who love royal maidens. This royal maiden was well satisfied with her lover, for he was handsome and brave to a degree unsurpassed in all this kingdom; and she loved him with an ardor that had enough of barbarism in it to make it exceedingly warm and strong. This love affair moved on happily for many months, until one day the king happened to discover its existence. He did not hesitate nor waver in regard to his duty in the premises. The youth was immediately cast into prison, and a day was appointed for his trial in the king's arena. This, of course, was an especially important occasion; and his majesty, as well as all the people, was greatly interested in the workings and development of this trial. Never before had such a case occurred; never before had a subject dared to love the daughter of a king. In after-years such things became commonplace enough; but then they were, in no slight degree, novel and startling.

The tiger-cages of the kingdom were searched for the most savage and relentless beasts, from which the fiercest monster might be selected for the arena; and the ranks of maiden youth and beauty throughout the land were carefully surveyed by competent judges, in order that the young man might have a fitting bride in case fate did not determine for him a different destiny. Of course, everybody knew that the deed with which the accused was charged had been done. He had loved the princess, and neither he, she, nor any one else thought of denying the fact; but the king would not think of allowing any fact of this kind to interfere with the workings of the tribunal, in which he took such great delight and satisfaction. No matter how the affair turned out, the youth would be disposed of; and the king would take an æsthetic pleasure in watching the course of events, which would determine whether or not the young man had done wrong in allowing himself to love the princess.

The appointed day arrived. From far and near the people gathered, and thronged the great galleries of the arena; and crowds, unable to gain admittance, massed themselves against its outside walls. The king and his court were in their places, opposite the twin doors,—those fateful portals, so terrible in their similarity.

All was ready. The signal was given. A door beneath the royal party opened, and the lover of the princess walked into the arena. Tall, beautiful, fair, his appearance was greeted with a low hum of admiration and anxiety. Half the audience had not known so grand a youth had lived among them. No wonder the princess loved him! What a terrible thing for him to be there!

As the youth advanced into the arena, he turned, as the custom was, to bow to the king: but he did not think at all of that royal personage; his eyes were fixed upon the princess, who sat to the right of her father. Had it not been for the moiety of barbarism in her nature, it is probable that lady would not have been there; but her intense and fervid soul would not allow her to be absent on an occasion in which she was so terribly interested. From the moment that the decree had gone forth, that her lover should decide his fate in the king's arena, she had thought of nothing, night or day, but this great event and the various subjects connected with it. Possessed of more power, influence, and force of character than any one who had ever before been interested in such a case, she had done what no other person had done,—she had possessed herself of the secret of the doors. She knew in which of the two rooms, that lay behind those doors, stood the cage of the tiger, with its open front, and in which waited the lady. Through these thick doors, heavily curtained with skins on the inside, it was impossible that any noise or suggestion should come from within to the person who should approach to raise the latch of one of them; but gold, and the power of a woman's will, had brought the secret to the princess.

And not only did she know in which room stood the lady ready to emerge, all blushing and radiant, should her door be opened, but she knew who the lady was. It was one of the fairest and loveliest of the damsels of the court who had been selected as the reward of the accused youth, should he be proved innocent of the crime of aspiring to one so far above him; and the princess hated her. Often had she seen, or imagined that she had seen, this fair creature throwing glances of admiration upon the person of her lover, and sometimes she thought these glances were perceived and even returned. Now and then she had seen

them talking together; it was but for a moment or two, but much can
be said in a brief space; it may have been on most unimportant topics,
but how could she know that? The girl was lovely, but she had dared
to raise her eyes to the loved one of the princess; and, with all the intensity of the savage blood transmitted to her through long lines of wholly
barbaric ancestors, she hated the woman who blushed and trembled
behind that silent door.

When her lover turned and looked at her, and his eye met hers as she
sat there paler and whiter than any one in the vast ocean of anxious faces
about her, he saw, by that power of quick perception which is given to
those whose souls are one, that she knew behind which door crouched
the tiger, and behind which stood the lady. He had expected her to know
it. He understood her nature, and his soul was assured that she would
never rest until she had made plain to herself this thing, hidden to all
other lookers-on, even to the king. The only hope for the youth in which
there was any element of certainty was based upon the success of the
princess in discovering this mystery; and the moment he looked upon
her, he saw she had succeeded, as in his soul he knew she would succeed.

Then it was that his quick and anxious glance asked the question:
"Which?" It was as plain to her as if he shouted it from where he stood.
There was not an instant to be lost. The question was asked in a flash;
it must be answered in another.

Her right arm lay on the cushioned parapet before her. She raised her
hand, and made a slight, quick movement toward the right. No one but
her lover saw her. Every eye but his was fixed on the man in the arena.

He turned, and with a firm and rapid step he walked across the empty
space. Every heart stopped beating, every breath was held, every eye was
fixed immovably upon that man. Without the slightest hesitation, he
went to the door on the right, and opened it.

Now, the point of the story is this: Did the tiger come out of that door,
or did the lady?

The more we reflect upon this question, the harder it is to answer. It
involves a study of the human heart which leads us through devious
mazes of passion, out of which it is difficult to find our way. Think of it,
fair reader, not as if the decision of the question depended upon yourself,
but upon that hot-blooded, semi-barbaric princess, her soul at a white
heat beneath the combined fires of despair and jealousy. She had lost
him, but who should have him?

How often, in her waking hours and in her dreams, had she started in
wild horror, and covered her face with her hands as she thought of her
lover opening the door on the other side of which waited the cruel fangs
of the tiger!

But how much oftener had she seen him at the other door! How in her grievous reveries had she gnashed her teeth, and torn her hair, when she saw his start of rapturous delight as he opened the door of the lady! How her soul had burned in agony when she had seen him rush to meet that woman, with her flushing cheek and sparkling eye of triumph; when she had seen him lead her forth, his whole frame kindled with the joy of recovered life; when she had heard the glad shouts from the multitude, and the wild ringing of the happy bells; when she had seen the priest, with his joyous followers, advance to the couple, and make them man and wife before her very eyes; and when she had seen them walk away together upon their path of flowers, followed by the tremendous shouts of the hilarious multitude, in which her one despairing shriek was lost and drowned!

Would it not be better for him to die at once, and go to wait for her in the blessed regions of semi-barbaric futurity?

And yet, that awful tiger, those shrieks, that blood!

Her decision had been indicated in an instant, but it had been made after days and nights of anguished deliberation. She had known she would be asked, she had decided what she would answer, and, without the slightest hesitation, she had moved her hand to the right.

The question of her decision is one not to be lightly considered, and it is not for me to presume to set myself up as the one person able to answer it. And so I leave it with all of you: Which came out of the opened door,—the lady, or the tiger?

12

The Celebrated Jumping Frog of Calaveras County

BY MARK TWAIN

IN compliance with the request of a friend of mine, who wrote me from the East, I called on good-natured, garrulous old Simon Wheeler, and inquired after my friend's friend, *Leonidas W.* Smiley, as requested to do, and I hereunto append the result. I have a lurking suspicion that *Leonidas W.* Smiley is a myth; that my friend never knew such a personage; and that he only conjectured that, if I asked old Wheeler about him, it would remind him of his infamous *Jim* Smiley, and he would go to work and bore me nearly to death with some infernal reminiscence of him as long and tedious as it should be useless to me. If that was the design, it certainly succeeded.

I found Simon Wheeler dozing comfortably by the bar-room stove of the old, dilapidated tavern in the ancient mining camp of Angel's, and I noticed that he was fat and bald-headed, and had an expression of winning gentleness and simplicity upon his tranquil countenace. He roused up and gave me good-day. I told him a friend of mine had commissioned me to make some inquiries about a cherished companion of his boyhood named *Leonidas W.* Smiley—*Rev. Leonidas W.* Smiley— a young minister of the Gospel, who he had heard was at one time a resident of Angel's Camp. I added, that, if Mr. Wheeler could tell me anything about this Rev. Leonidas W. Smiley, I would feel under many obligations to him.

Simon Wheeler backed me into a corner and blockaded me there with his chair, and then sat me down and reeled off the monotonous narrative which follows this paragraph. He never smiled, he never frowned, he never changed his voice from the gentle-flowing key to which he tuned the initial sentence, he never betrayed the slightest suspicion of enthusiasm; but all through the interminable narrative there ran a vein of impressive earnestness and sincerity, which showed me plainly that, so far from his imagining that there was anything ridiculous or funny about his story, he regarded it as a really important matter, and admitted its two heroes as men of transcendent genius in *finesse*. To me, the spectacle of a man drifting serenely along through such a queer yarn without ever smiling, was exquisitely absurd. As I said before, I asked him to tell me what he knew of Rev. Leonidas W. Smiley, and he replied as follows. I let him go on in his own way, and never interrupted him once:

There was a feller here once by the name of *Jim* Smiley, in the winter of '49—or maybe it was the spring of '50—I don't recollect exactly, somehow, though what makes me think it was one or the other is because I remember the big flume wasn't finished when he first came to the camp; but anyway, he was the curiousest man about always betting on anything that turned up you ever see, if he could get anybody to bet on the other side; and if he couldn't, he'd change sides. Any way that suited the other man would suit him—any way just so's he got a bet, *he* was satisfied. But still he was lucky, uncommon lucky—he most always come out winner. He was always ready and laying for a chance; there couldn't be no solit'ry thing mentioned but that feller'd offer to bet on it, and take any side you please, as I was just telling you. If there was a horse-race, you'd find him flush, or you'd find him busted at the end of it; if there was a dog-fight, he'd bet on it; if there was a cat-fight, he'd bet on it; if there was a chicken-fight, he'd bet on it; why, if there was two birds setting on a fence, he would bet you which one would fly first; or if there was a camp meeting, he would be there reg'lar, to bet on Parson Walker, which he judged to be the best exhorter about here, and so he was, too, and a good man. If he even seen a straddle-bug start to go anywheres, he would bet you how long it would take him to get wherever he was going to, and if you took him up, he would foller that straddle-bug to Mexico but what he would find out where he was bound for and how long he was on the road. Lots of the boys here has seen that Smiley, and can tell you about him. Why, it never made no difference to *him*—he would bet on *any*thing—the dangdest feller. Parson Walker's wife laid very sick once, for a good while, and it seemed as if they warn't going to save her; but one morning he came in, and Smiley asked how she was, and he said she was considerable better—thank the Lord for his inf'nit mercy—and coming on so smart that, with the blessing of Prov'dence, she'd get well yet; and Smiley, before he thought, says, "Well, I'll risk two-and-a-half that she don't, anyway."

Thish-yer Smiley had a mare—the boys called her the fifteen-minute nag, but that was only in fun, you know, because, of course, she was faster than that—and he used to win money on that horse, for all she was so slow and always had the asthma, or the distemper, or the consumption, or something of that kind. They used to give her two or three hundred yards start, and then pass her under way; but always at the fag-end of the race she'd get excited and desperate-like, and come cavorting and straddling up, and scattering her legs around limber, sometimes in the air, and sometimes out to one side amongst the fences, and kicking up m-o-r-e dust, and raising m-o-r-e racket with her coughing and sneezing and blowing her nose—and always fetch up at the stand just about a neck ahead, as near as you could cipher it down.

And he had a little small bull pup, that to look at him you'd think he wan't worth a cent but to set around and look ornery and lay for a chance to steal something. But as soon as money was up on him, he was a different dog; his under-jaw'd begin to stick out like the fo'castle of a steamboat, and his teeth would uncover, and shine savage like the furnaces. And a dog might tackle him, and bully-rag him, and bite him, and throw him over his shoulder two or three times, and Andrew Jackson—which was the name of the pup—Andrew Jackson would never let on but what *he* was satisfied, and hadn't expected nothing else—and the bets being doubled and doubled on the other side all the time, till the money was all up; and then all of a sudden he would grab that other dog jest by the j'int of his hind leg and freeze to it—not claw, you understand, but only jest grip and hang on till they throwed up the sponge, if it was a year. Smiley always come out winner on that pup, till he harnessed a dog once that didn't have no hind legs, because they'd been sawed off by a circular saw, and when the thing had gone along far enough, and the money was all up, and he come to make a snatch for his pet holt, he saw in a minute how he'd been imposed on, and how the other dog had him in the door, so to speak, and he 'peared surprised, and then he looked sorter discouraged-like, and didn't try no more to win the fight, and so he got shucked out bad. He give Smiley a look, as much to say his heart was broke and it was *his* fault for putting up a dog that hadn't no hind legs for him to take holt of, which was his main dependence in a fight, and then he limped off a piece and laid down and died. It was a good pup, was that Andrew Jackson, and would have made a name for hisself if he'd lived, for the stuff was in him, and he had genius—I know it, because he hadn't no opportunities to speak of, and it don't stand to reason that a dog could make such a fight as he could under them circumstances, if he hadn't no talent. It always makes me feel sorry when I think of that last fight of his'n, and the way it turned out.

Well, thish-yer Smiley had rat-tarriers, and chicken-cocks, and tom-cats, and all them kind of things, till you couldn't rest, and you couldn't fetch nothing for him to bet on but he'd match you. He ketched a frog one day, and took him home, and said he cal'klated to edercate him; and so he never done nothing for these three months but set in his back yard and learn that frog to jump. And you bet you he *did* learn him, too. He'd give him a little punch behind, and the next minute you'd see that frog whirling in the air like a doughnut—see him turn one summerset, or maybe a couple, if he got a good start, and come down flat-footed and all right, like a cat. He got him up so in the matter of catching flies, and kept him in practice so constant, that he'd nail a fly every time as far as he could see him. Smiley said all a frog wanted was education, and he could do most anything—and I believe him. Why, I've seen him set Dan'l Webster down here on this floor—Dan'l Webster was the name of the frog—and sing out, "Flies, Dan'l, flies!" and quicker'n you could wink, he'd spring straight up, and snake a fly off 'n the counter there, and flop down on the floor again as solid as a gob of mud, and fall to scratching the side of his head with his hind foot as indifferent as if he hadn't no idea he's been doin' any more'n any frog might do. You never see a frog so modest and straight-for'ard as he was, for all he was so gifted. And when it come to fair and square jumping on the dead level, he could get over more ground at one straddle than any animal of his breed you ever see. Jumping on a dead level was his strong suit, you understand; and when it come to that, Smiley would ante up money on him as long as he had a red. Smiley was monstrous proud of his frog, and well he might be, for fellers that had traveled and been everywhere all said he laid over any frog that ever *they* see.

Well, Smiley kept the beast in a little lattice box, and he used to fetch him downtown sometimes and lay for a bet. One day a feller—a stranger in the camp, he was—come across him with his box, and says:

"What might it be that you've got in the box?"

And Smiley says, sorter indifferent like, "It might be a parrot, or it might be a canary, maybe, but it ain't—it's only just a frog."

An' the feller took it, and looked at it careful, and turned it round this way and that, and says, "H'm—so 'tis. Well, what's *he* good for?"

"Well," Smiley says, easy and careless, "He's good enough for *one* thing, I should judge—he can outjump ary frog in Calaveras county."

The feller took the box again, and took another long, particular look, and give it back to Smiley, and says, very deliberate, "Well, I don't see no p'ints about that frog that's any better'n any other frog."

"Maybe you don't," Smiley says. "Maybe you understand frogs, and maybe you don't understand 'em; maybe you've had experience, and maybe you ain't only a amature, as it were. Anyways, I've got *my* opinion, and I'll risk forty dollars that he can outjump any frog in Calaveras county."

And the feller studied a minute, and then says, kinder sad like, "Well, I'm only a stranger here, and I ain't got no frog; but if I had a frog, I'd bet you."

And then Smiley says, "That's all right—that's all right—if you'll hold my box a minute, I'll go and get you a frog." And so the feller took the box, and put up his forty dollars along with Smiley's, and set down to wait.

So he set there a good while thinking and thinking to hisself, and then he got the frog out and prized his mouth open and took a teaspoon and filled him full of quail shot—filled him pretty near up to his chin—and set him on the floor. Smiley he went to the swamp and slopped around in the mud for a long time, and finally he ketched a frog, and fetched him in, and give him to this feller, and says:

"Now, if you're ready, set him alongside of Dan'l, with his forepaws just even with Dan'l, and I'll give the word." Then he says. "One—two—three—jump!" and him and the feller touched up the frogs from behind, and the new frog hopped off, but Dan'l give a heave, and hysted up his shoulders—so—like a Frenchman, but it wasn't no use—he couldn't budge; he was planted as solid as an anvil, and he couldn't no more stir than if he was anchored out. Smiley was a good deal surprised, and he was disgusted too, but he didn't have no idea what the matter was, of course.

The feller took the money and started away; and when he was going out at the door, he sorter jerked his thumb over his shoulder—this way—at Dan'l, and says again, very deliberate, "Well, *I* don't see no p'ints about that frog that's any better'n any other frog."

Smiley he stood scratching his head and looking down at Dan'l a long time, and at last he says, "I do wonder what in the nation that frog throw'd off for—I wonder if there ain't something the matter with him—he 'pears to look mighty baggy, somehow." And he ketched Dan'l by the nap of the neck, and lifted him up and says, "Why, blame my cats, if he don't weigh five pounds!" and turned him upside down, and he belched out a double handful of shot. And then he see how it was, and he was the maddest man—he set the frog down and took out after that feller, but he never ketched him. And—

(Here Simon Wheeler heard his name called from the front yard, and got up to see what was wanted.) And turning to me as he moved away, he said: "Just set where you are, stranger, and rest easy—I ain't going to be gone a second."

But, by your leave, I did not think that a continuation of the history of the enterprising vagabond *Jim* Smiley would be likely to afford me much information concerning the Rev. *Leonidas W*. Smiley, and so I started away.

At the door I met the sociable Wheeler returning, and he buttonholed me and recommenced:

"Well, thish-yer Smiley had a yeller one-eyed cow that didn't have no tail, only jest a short stump like a bannanner, and—"

"Oh, hang Smiley and his afflicted cow!" I muttered, good-naturedly, and bidding the old gentleman good-day, I departed.

13

The Man that Corrupted Hadleyburg

BY MARK TWAIN

I T was many years ago. Hadley-
burg was the most honest and upright town in all the region round
about. It had kept that reputation unsmirched during three generations,
and was prouder of it than of any other of its possessions. It was so proud
of it, and so anxious to insure its perpetuation, that it began to teach the
principles of honest dealing to its babies in the cradle, and made the like
teachings the staple of their culture thenceforward through all the years
devoted to their education. Also, throughout the formative years temptations were kept out of the way of the young people, so that their
honesty could have every chance to harden and solidify, and become a
part of their very bone. The neighboring towns were jealous of this
honorable supremacy, and affected to sneer at Hadleyburg's pride in it
and call it vanity; but all the same they were obliged to acknowledge that
Hadleyburg was in reality an incorruptible town; and if pressed they
would also acknowledge that the mere fact that a young man hailed from
Hadleyburg was all the recommendation he needed when he went forth
from his natal town to seek for responsible employment.

But at last, in the drift of time, Hadleyburg had the ill luck to offend
a passing stranger—possibly without knowing it, certainly without caring, for Hadleyburg was sufficient unto itself, and cared not a rap for
strangers or their opinions. Still, it would have been well to make an
exception in this one's case, for he was a bitter man and revengeful. All
through his wanderings during a whole year he kept his injury in mind,
and gave all his leisure moments to trying to invent a compensating
satisfaction for it. He contrived many plans, and all of them were good,
but none of them was quite sweeping enough; the poorest of them would
hurt a great many individuals, but what he wanted was a plan which
would comprehend the entire town, and not let so much as one person

escape unhurt. At last he had a fortunate idea, and when it fell into his brain it lit up his whole head with an evil joy. He began to form a plan at once, saying to himself, "That is the thing to do—I will corrupt the town."

Six months later he went to Hadleyburg, and arrived in a buggy at the house of the old cashier of the bank about ten at night. He got a sack out of the buggy, shouldered it, and staggered with it through the cottage yard, and knocked at the door. A woman's voice said "Come in," and he entered, and set his sack behind the stove in the parlor, saying politely to the old lady who sat reading the *Missionary Herald* by the lamp:

"Pray keep your seat, madam, I will not disturb you. There—now it is pretty well concealed; one would hardly know it was there. Can I see your husband a moment, madam?"

No, he was gone to Brixton, and might not return before morning.

"Very well, madam, it is no matter. I merely wanted to leave that sack in his care, to be delivered to the rightful owner when he shall be found. I am a stranger; he does not know me; I am merely passing through the town tonight to discharge a matter which has been long in my mind. My errand is now completed, and I go pleased and a little proud, and you will never see me again. There is a paper attached to the sack which will explain everything. Good night, madam."

The old lady was afraid of the mysterious big stranger, and was glad to see him go. But her curiosity was roused, and she went straight to the sack and brought away the paper. It began as follows:

"TO BE PUBLISHED; or, the right man sought out by private inquiry— either will answer. This sack contains gold coin weighing a hundred and sixty pounds four ounces—"

"Mercy on us, and the door not locked!"

Mrs. Richards flew to it all in a tremble and locked it, then pulled down the window-shades and stood frightened, worried, and wondering if there was anything else she could do toward making herself and the money more safe. She listened awhile for burglars, then surrendered to curiosity and went back to the lamp and finished reading the paper:

"I am a foreigner, and am presently going back to my own country, to remain there permanently. I am grateful to America for what I have received at her hands during my long stay under her flag; and to one of her citizens— a citizen of Hadleyburg—I am especially grateful for a great kindness done me a year or two ago. Two great kindnesses, in fact. I will explain. I was a gambler. I say I was. I was a ruined gambler. I arrived in this village at night, hungry and without a penny. I asked for help—in the dark; I was ashamed to beg in the light. I begged of the right man. He gave me twenty dollars—

that is to say, he gave me life, as I considered it. He also gave me fortune; for out of that money I have made myself rich at the gaming-table. And finally, a remark which he made to me has remained with me to this day, and has at last conquered me; and in conquering has saved the remnant of my morals: I shall gamble no more. Now I have no idea who that man was, but I want him found, and I want him to have this money, to give away, throw away, or keep, as he pleases. It is merely my way of testifying my gratitude to him. If I could stay, I would find him myself; but no matter, he will be found. This is an honest town, an incorruptible town, and I know I can trust it without fear. This man can be identified by the remark which he made to me; I feel persuaded that he will remember it.

"And now my plan is this: If you prefer to conduct the inquiry privately, do so. Tell the contents of this present writing to any one who is likely to be the right man. If he shall answer, 'I am the man; the remark I made was so-and-so', apply the test—to wit: open the sack, and in it you will find a sealed envelope containing that remark. If the remark mentioned by the candidate tallies with it, give him the money, and ask no further questions, for he is certainly the right man.

"But if you shall prefer a public inquiry, then publish this present writing in the local paper—with these instructions added, to wit: Thirty days from now, let the candidate appear at the town-hall at eight in the evening (Friday), and hand his remark, in a sealed envelope, to the Rev. Mr. Burgess (if he will be kind enough to act); and let Mr. Burgess there and then destroy the seals of the sack, open it, and see if the remark is correct; if correct, let the money be delivered, with my sincere gratitude, to my benefactor thus identified."

Mrs. Richards sat down, gently quivering with excitement, and was soon lost in thinkings—after this pattern: "What a strange thing it is! . . . And what a fortune for that kind man who set his bread afloat upon the waters! . . . If it had only been my husband that did it!—for we are so poor, so old and poor! . . ." Then, with a sigh—"But it was not my Edward; no, it was not he that gave a stranger twenty dollars. It is a pity, too; I see it now. . . ." Then, with a shudder—"But it is *gambler's* money! the wages of sin: we couldn't take it; we couldn't touch it. I don't like to be near it; it seems a defilement." She moved to a farther chair. . . . "I wish Edward would come, and take it to the bank; a burglar might come at any moment; it is dreadful to be here all alone with it."

At eleven Mr. Richards arrived, and while his wife was saying, "I am *so* glad you've come!" he was saying, "I'm so tired—tired clear out; it is dreadful to be poor, and have to make these dismal journeys at my time of life. Always at the grind, grind, grind, on a salary—another man's slave, and he sitting at home in his slippers, rich and comfortable."

"I am so sorry for you, Edward, you know that; but be comforted: we have our livelihood; we have our good name—"

"Yes, Mary, and that is everything. Don't mind my talk—it's just a moment's irritation and doesn't mean anything. Kiss me—there, it's all gone now, and I am not complaining any more. What have you been getting? What's in the sack?"

Then his wife told him the great secret. It dazed him for a moment; then he said:

"It weighs a hundred and sixty pounds? Why, Mary, it's forty thousand dollars—think of it—a whole fortune! Not ten men in this village are worth that much. Give me the paper."

He skimmed through it and said:

"Isn't it an adventure! Why, it's a romance; it's like the impossible things one reads about in books, and never sees in life." He was well stirred up now; cheerful, even gleeful. He tapped his old wife on the cheek, and said, humorously, "Why, we're rich, Mary, rich; all we've got to do is to bury the money and burn the papers. If the gambler ever comes to inquire, we'll merely look coldly upon him and say: 'What is this nonsense you are talking? We have never heard of you and your sack of gold before;' and then he would look foolish, and—"

"And in the meantime, while you are running on with your jokes, the money is still here, and it is fast getting along toward burglar-time."

"True. Very well, what shall we do—make the inquiry private? No, not that: it would spoil the romance. The public method is better. Think what a noise it will make! And it will make all the other towns jealous; for no stranger would trust such a thing to any town but Hadleyburg, and they know it. It's a great card for us. I must get to the printing-office now, or I shall be too late."

"But stop—stop—don't leave me here alone with it, Edward!"

But he was gone. For only a little while, however. Not far from his own house he met the editor-proprietor of the paper, and gave him the document, and said, "Here is a good thing for you, Cox—put it in."

"It may be too late, Mr. Richards, but I'll see."

At home again he and his wife sat down to talk the charming mystery over; they were in no condition for sleep. The first question was, Who could the citizen have been who gave the stranger the twenty dollars? It seemed a simple one; both answered it in the same breath—

"Barclay Goodson."

"Yes," said Richards, "he could have done it, and it would have been like him, but there's not another in the town."

"Everybody will grant that, Edward—grant it privately, anyway. For six months, now, the village has been its own proper self once more—honest, narrow, self-righteous, and stingy."

"It is what he always called it, to the day of his death—said it right out publicly, too."

"Yes, and he was hated for it."

"Oh, of course; but he didn't care. I reckon he was the best-hated man among us, except the Reverend Burgess."

"Well, Burgess deserves it—he will never get another congregation here. Mean as the town is, it knows how to estimate *him*. Edward, doesn't it seem odd that the stranger should appoint Burgess to deliver the money?"

"Well, yes—it does. That is—that is—"

"Why so much that-*is*-ing? Would *you* select him?"

"Mary, maybe the stranger knows him better than this village does."

"Much *that* would help Burgess!"

The husband seemed perplexed for an answer; the wife kept a steady eye upon him, and waited. Finally Richards said, with the hesitancy of one who is making a statement which is likely to encounter doubt.

"Mary, Burgess is not a bad man."

His wife was certainly surprised.

"Nonsense!" she exclaimed.

"He is not a bad man. I know. The whole of his unpopularity had its foundation in that one thing—the thing that made so much noise."

"That 'one thing,' indeed! As if that 'one thing' wasn't enough, all by itself."

"Plenty. Plenty. Only he wasn't guilty of it."

"How you talk! Not guilty of it! Everybody knows he *was* guilty."

"Mary, I give you my word—he was innocent."

"I can't believe it, and I don't. How do you know?"

"It is a confession. I am ashamed, but I will make it. I was the only man who knew he was innocent. I could have saved him, and—and—well, you know how the town was wrought up—I hadn't the pluck to do it. It would have turned everybody against me. I felt mean, ever so mean; but I didn't dare; I hadn't the manliness to face that."

Mary looked troubled, and for a while was silent. Then she said, stammeringly:

"I—I don't think it would have done for you to—to— One mustn't—er—public opinion—one has to be so careful—so—" It was a difficult road, and she got mired; but after a little she got started again. "It was a great pity, but— Why, we couldn't afford it, Edward—we couldn't indeed. Oh, I wouldn't have had you do it for anything!"

"It would have lost us the good will of so many people, Mary; and then—and then—"

"What troubles me now is, what *he* thinks of us, Edward."

"He? *He* doesn't suspect that I could have saved him."

"Oh," exclaimed the wife, in a tone of relief, "I am glad of that. As long as he doesn't know that you could have saved him, he—he—well, that makes it a great deal better. Why, I might have known he didn't know, because he is always trying to be friendly with us, as little encouragement as we give him. More than once people have twitted me with it. There's the Wilsons, and the Wilcoxes, and the Harknesses, they take a mean pleasure in saying, '*Your friend* Burgess,' because they know it pesters me. I wish he wouldn't persist in liking us so; I can't think why he keeps it up."

"I can explain it. It's another confession. When the thing was new and hot, and the town made a plan to ride him on a rail, my conscience hurt me so that I couldn't stand it, and I went privately and gave him notice, and he got out of the town and stayed out till it was safe to come back."

"Edward! If the town had found it out—"

"*Don't!* It scares me yet, to think of it. I repented of it the minute it was done; and I was even afraid to tell you, lest your face might betray it to somebody. I didn't sleep any that night, for worrying. But after a few days I saw that no one was going to suspect me, and after that I got to feeling glad I did it. And I feel glad yet, Mary—glad through and through."

"So do I, now, for it would have been a dreadful way to treat him. Yes, I'm glad; for really you did owe him that, you know. But, Edward, suppose it should come out yet, some day!"

"It won't."

"Why?"

"Because everybody thinks it was Goodson."

"Of course they would!"

"Certainly. And of course *he* didn't care. They persuaded poor old Sawlsberry to go and charge it on him, and he went blustering over there and did it. Goodson looked him over, like as if he was hunting for a place on him that he could despise the most, then he says, 'So you are the Committee of Inquiry, are you?' Sawlsberry said that was about what he was. 'Hm. Do they require particulars, or do you reckon a kind of a *general* answer will do?' 'If they require particulars, I will come back, Mr. Goodson; I will take the general answer first.' 'Very well, then, tell them to go to hell—I reckon that's general enough. And I'll give you some advice, Sawlsberry; when you come back for the particulars, fetch a basket to carry the relics of yourself home in.'"

"Just like Goodson; it's got all the marks. He had only one vanity: he thought he could give advice better than any other person."

"It settled the business, and saved us, Mary. The subject was dropped."

"Bless you, I'm not doubting *that*."

Then they took up the gold-sack mystery again, with strong interest. Soon the conversation began to suffer breaks—interruptions caused by absorbed thinkings. The breaks grew more and more frequent. At last Richards lost himself wholly in thought. He sat long, gazing vacantly at the floor, and by and by he began to punctuate his thoughts with little nervous movements of his hands that seemed to indicate vexation. Meantime his wife too had relapsed into a thoughtful silence, and her movements were beginning to show a troubled discomfort. Finally Richards got up and strode aimlessly about the room, plowing his hands through his hair, much as a somnambulist might do who was having a bad dream. Then he seemed to arrive at a definte purpose; and without a word he put on his hat and passed quickly out of the house. His wife sat brooding, with a drawn face, and did not seem to be aware that she was alone. Now and then she murmured, "Lead us not into t— . . . but —but—we are so poor, so poor! . . . Lead us not into. . . . Ah, who would be hurt by it?—and no one would ever know. . . . Lead us. . . ." The voice died out in mumblings. After a little she glanced up and muttered in a half-frightened, half-glad way—

"He is gone! But, oh dear, he may be too late—too late. . . . Maybe not—maybe there is still time." She rose and stood thinking, nervously clasping and unclasping her hands. A slight shudder shook her frame, and she said, out of a dry throat, "God forgive me—it's awful to think such things—but . . . Lord, how we are made—how strangely we are made!"

She turned the light low, and slipped stealthily over and kneeled down by the sack and felt of its ridgy sides with her hands, and fondled them lovingly; and there was a gloating light in her poor old eyes. She fell into fits of absence; and came half out of them at times to mutter, "If we had only waited!—oh, if we had only waited a little, and not been in such a hurry!"

Meantime Cox had gone home from his office and told his wife all about the strange thing that had happened, and they had talked it over eagerly, and guessed that the late Goodson was the only man in the town who could have helped a suffering stranger with so noble a sum as twenty dollars. Then there was a pause, and the two became thoughtful and silent. And by and by nervous and fidgety. At last the wife said, as if to herself,

"Nobody knows this secret but the Richardses . . . and us . . . nobody."

The husband came out of his thinkings with a slight start, and gazed wistfully at his wife, whose face was become very pale; then he hesitatingly rose, and glanced furtively at his hat, then at his wife—a sort of mute inquiry. Mrs. Cox swallowed once or twice, with her hand at her throat, then in place of speech she nodded her head. In a moment she was alone, and mumbling to herself.

And now Richards and Cox were hurrying through the deserted streets, from opposite directions. They met, panting, at the foot of the printing-office stairs; by the night-light there they read each other's face. Cox whispered,

"Nobody knows about this but us?"

The whispered answer was,

"Not a soul—on honor, not a soul!"

"If it isn't too late to—"

The men were starting upstairs; at this moment they were overtaken by a boy, and Cox asked,

"Is that you, Johnny?"

"Yes, sir."

"You needn't ship the early mail—nor *any* mail; wait till I tell you."

"It's already gone, sir."

"*Gone?*" It had the sound of an unspeakable disappointment in it.

"Yes, sir. Time-table for Brixton and all the towns beyond changed today, sir—had to get the papers in twenty minutes earlier than common. I had to rush; if I had been two minutes later—"

The men turned and walked slowly away, not waiting to hear the rest. Neither of them spoke during ten minutes; then Cox said, in a vexed tone,

"What possessed you to be in such a hurry, *I* can't make out."

The answer was humble enough:

"I see it now, but somehow I never thought, you know, until it was too late. But the next time—"

"Next time be hanged! It won't come in a thousand years."

Then the friends separated without a good-night, and dragged themselves home with the gait of mortally stricken men. At their homes their wives sprang up with an eager "Well?"—then saw the answer with their eyes and sank down sorrowing, without waiting for it to come in words. In both houses a discussion followed of a heated sort—a new thing; there had been discussions before, but not heated ones, not ungentle ones. The discussions tonight were a sort of seeming plagiarisms of each other. Mrs. Richards said,

"If you had only waited, Edward—if you had only stopped to think; but no, you must run straight to the printing-office and spread it all over the world."

"It *said* publish it."

"That is nothing; it also said do it privately, if you liked. There, now —is that true, or not?"

"Why, yes—yes, it is true; but when I thought what a stir it would make, and what a compliment it was to Hadleyburg that a stranger should trust it so—"

"Oh, certainly, I know all that; but if you had only stopped to think, you would have seen that you *couldn't* find the right man, because he is in his grave, and hasn't left chick nor child nor relation behind him; and as long as the money went to somebody that awfully needed it, and nobody would be hurt by it, and—and—"

She broke down, crying. Her husband tried to think of some comforting thing to say, and presently came out with this:

"But after all, Mary, it must be for the best—it *must* be; we know that. And we must remember that it was so ordered—"

"Ordered! Oh, everything's *ordered*, when a person has to find some way out when he has been stupid. Just the same, it was *ordered* that the money should come to us in this special way, and it was you that must take it on yourself to go meddling with the designs of Providence—and who gave you the right? It was wicked, that is what it was—just blasphemous presumption, and no more becoming to a meek and humble professor of—"

"But, Mary, you know how we have been trained all our lives long, like the whole village, till it is absolutely second nature to us to stop not a single moment to think when there's an honest thing to be done—"

"Oh, I know it, I know it—it's been one everlasting training and training and training in honesty—honesty shielded, from the very cradle, against every possible temptation, and so it's *artificial* honesty, and weak as water when temptation comes, as we have seen this night. God knows I never had shade nor shadow of a doubt of my petrified and indestructible honesty until now—and now, under the very first big and real temptation, I—Edward, it is my belief that this town's honesty is as rotten as mine is; as rotten as yours is. It is a mean town, a hard, stingy town, and hasn't a virtue in the world but this honesty it is so celebrated for and so conceited about; and so help me, I do believe that if ever the day comes that its honesty falls under great temptation, its grand reputation will go to ruin like a house of cards. There, now, I've made confession, and I feel better; I am a humbug, and I've been one all my life, without knowing it. Let no man call me honest again—I will not have it."

"I—well, Mary, I feel a good deal as you do; I certainly do. It seems strange, too, so strange. I never could have believed it—never."

A long silence followed; both were sunk in thought. At last the wife looked up and said,

"I know what you are thinking, Edward."

Richards had the embarrassed look of a person who is caught.

"I am ashamed to confess it, Mary, but—"

"It's no matter, Edward, I was thinking the same question myself."

"I hope so. State it."

"You were thinking, if a body could only guess out *what the remark was* that Goodson made to the stranger."

"It's perfectly true. I feel guilty and ashamed. And you?"

"I'm past it. Let us make a pallet here; we've got to stand watch till the bank vault opens in the morning and admits the sack. . . . Oh dear, oh dear—if we hadn't made the mistake!"

The pallet was made, and Mary said:

"The open sesame—what could it have been? I do wonder what that remark could have been? But come; we will go to bed now."

"And sleep?"

"No, think."

"Yes, think."

By this time the Coxes too had completed their spat and their reconciliation, and were turning in—to think, to think, and toss, and fret, and worry over what the remark could possibly have been which Goodson made to the stranded derelict; that golden remark; that remark worth forty thousand dollars, cash.

The reason that the village telegraph office was open later than usual that night was this: The foreman of Cox's paper was the local representative of the Associated Press. One might say its honorary representative, for it wasn't four times a year that he could furnish thirty words that would be accepted. But this time it was different. His dispatch stating what he had caught got an instant answer:

"Send the whole thing—all the details—twelve hundred words."

A colossal order! The foreman filled the bill; and he was the proudest man in the State. By breakfast-time the next morning the name of Hadleyburg the Incorruptible was on every lip in America, from Montreal to the Gulf, from the glaciers of Alaska to the orange-groves of Florida; and millions and millions of people were discussing the stranger and his money-sack, and wondering if the right man would be found, and hoping some more news about the matter would come soon—right away.

II

Hadleyburg village woke up world-celebrated—astonished—happy—vain. Vain beyond imagination. Its nineteen principal citizens and their wives went about shaking hands with each other, and beaming, and smiling, and congratulating, and saying *this* thing adds a new word to the dictionary—*Hadleyburg*, synonym for *incorruptible*—destined to live in dictionaries forever! And the minor and unimportant citizens and their wives went around acting in much the same way. Everybody ran to the bank to see the gold-sack; and before noon grieved and envious crowds began to flock in from Brixton and all neighboring towns; and that afternoon and next day reporters began to arrive from everywhere to verify the sack and its history and write the whole thing up anew, and make dashing free-hand pictures of the sack, and of Richards's house, and the bank, and the Presbyterian church, and the Baptist church, and the public square, and the town hall where the test would be applied and the money delivered; and damnable portraits of the Richardses, and Pinkerton the banker, and Cox, and the foreman, and Reverend Burgess, and the postmaster—and even of Jack Halliday, who was the loafing, good-natured, no-account, irreverent fisherman, hunter, boys' friend, stray-dogs' friend, typical "Sam Lawson" of the town. The little mean, smirking, oily Pinkerton showed the sack to all comers, and rubbed his sleek palms together pleasantly, and enlarged upon the town's fine old reputation for honesty and upon this wonderful endorsement of it, and hoped and believed that the example would now spread far and wide over the American world, and be epoch-making in the matter of moral regeneration. And so on, and so on.

By the end of a week things had quieted down again; the wild intoxication of pride and joy had sobered to a soft, sweet, silent delight—a sort of deep, nameless, unutterable content. All faces bore a look of peaceful, holy happiness.

Then a change came. It was a gradual change: so gradual that its beginnings were hardly noticed; maybe were not noticed at all, except by Jack Halliday, who always noticed everything; and always made fun of it, too, no matter what it was. He began to throw out chaffing remarks about people not looking quite so happy as they did a day or two ago; and next he claimed that the new aspect was deepening to positive sadness; next, that it was taking on a sick look; and finally he said that everybody was become so moody, thoughtful, and absent-minded that he could rob the meanest man in town of a cent out of the bottom of his breeches pocket and not disturb his reverie.

At this stage—or at about this stage—a saying like this was dropped at bedtime—with a sigh, usually—by the head of each of the nineteen principal households: "Ah, what *could* have been the remark that Goodson made?"

And straightway—with a shudder—came this, from the man's wife: "Oh, *don't!* What horrible thing are you mulling in your mind? Put it away from you, for God's sake!"

But that question was wrung from those men again the next night—and got the same retort. But weaker.

And the third night the men uttered the question yet again—with anguish, and absently. This time—and the following night—the wives fidgeted feebly, and tried to say something. But didn't.

And the night after that they found their tongues and responded—longingly,

"Oh, if we *could* only guess!"

Halliday's comments grew daily more and more sparklingly disagreeable and disparaging. He went diligently about, laughing at the town, individually and in mass. But his laugh was the only one left in the village: it fell upon a hollow and mournful vacancy and emptiness. Not even a smile was findable anywhere. Halliday carried a cigar-box around on a tripod, playing that it was a camera, and halted all passers and aimed the thing and said, "Ready!—now look pleasant, please," but not even this capital joke could surprise the dreary faces into any softening.

So three weeks passed—one week was left. It was Saturday evening—after supper. Instead of the aforetime Saturday-evening flutter and bustle and shopping and larking, the streets were empty and desolate. Richards and his old wife sat apart in their little parlor—miserable and thinking. This was become their evening habit now: the lifelong habit which had preceded it, of reading, knitting, and contented chat, or receiving or paying neighborly calls, was dead and gone and forgotten, ages ago—two or three weeks ago; nobody talked now, nobody read, nobody visited—the whole village sat at home, sighing, worrying, silent. Trying to guess out that remark.

The postman left a letter. Richards glanced listlessly at the superscription and the postmark—unfamiliar, both—and tossed the letter on the table and resumed his might-have-beens and his hopeless dull miseries where he had left them off. Two or three hours later his wife got wearily up and was going away to bed without a good-night—custom now—but she stopped near the letter and eyed it awhile with a dead interest, then broke it open, and began to skim it over. Richards, sitting there with his chair tilted back against the wall and his chin between his knees, heard something fall. It was his wife. He sprang to her side, but she cried out:

"Leave me alone, I am too happy. Read the letter—read it!"

He did. He devoured it, his brain reeling. The letter was from a distant State, and it said:

"I am a stranger to you, but no matter: I have something to tell. I have just arrived home from Mexico, and learned about that episode. Of course you do not know who made that remark, but I know, and I am the only person living who does know. It was GOODSON. I knew him well, many years ago. I passed through your village that very night, and was his guest till the midnight train came along. I overheard him make that remark to the stranger in the dark—it was in Hale Alley. He and I talked of it the rest of the way home, and while smoking in his house. He mentioned many of your villagers in the course of his talk—most of them in a very uncomplimentary way, but two or three favorably; among these latter yourself. I say 'favorably'

—nothing stronger. I remember his saying he did not actually LIKE *any person in the town—not one; but that you—I* THINK *he said you—am almost sure—had done him a very great service once, possibly without knowing the full value of it, and he wished he had a fortune, he would leave it to you when he died, and a curse apiece for the rest of the citizens. Now, then, if it was you that did him that service, you are his legitimate heir, and entitled to the sack of gold. I know that I can trust to your honor and honesty, for in a citizen of Hadleyburg these virtues are an unfailing inheritance, and so I am going to reveal to you the remark, well satisfied that if you are not the right man you will seek and find the right one and see that poor Goodson's debt of gratitude for the service referred to is paid. This is the remark:* 'YOU ARE FAR FROM BEING A BAD MAN: GO, AND REFORM.'*

"HOWARD L. STEPHENSON."

"Oh, Edward, the money is ours, and I am so grateful, *oh*, so grateful —kiss me, dear, it's forever since we kissed—and we needed it so—the money—and now you are free of Pinkerton and his bank, and nobody's slave any more; it seems to me I could fly for joy."

It was a happy half-hour that the couple spent there on the settee caressing each other; it was the old days come again—days that had begun with their courtship and lasted without a break till the stranger brought the deadly money. By and by the wife said:

"Oh, Edward, how lucky it was you did him that grand service, poor Goodson! I never liked him, but I love him now. And it was fine and beautiful of you never to mention it or brag about it." Then, with a touch of reproach, "But you ought to have told *me*, Edward, you ought to have told your wife, you know."

"Well, I—er—well, Mary, you see—"

"Now stop hemming and hawing, and tell me about it, Edward. I always loved you, and now I'm proud of you. Everybody believes there was only one good generous soul in this village, and now it turns out that you—Edward, why don't you tell me?"

"Well—er—er— Why, Mary, I can't!"

"You *can't? Why* can't you?"

"You see, he—well, he—he made me promise I wouldn't."

The wife looked him over, and said, very slowly,

"Made—you—promise? Edward, what do you tell me that for?"

"Mary, do you think I would lie?"

She was troubled and silent for a moment, then she laid her hand within his and said:

"No . . . no. We have wandered far enough from our bearings— God spare us that! In all your life you have never uttered a lie. But now —now that the foundations of things seem to be crumbling from under us, we—we—" She lost her voice for a moment, then said, brokenly,

"Lead us not into temptation. . . . I think you made the promise, Edward. Let it rest so. Let us keep away from that ground. Now—that is all gone by; let us be happy again; it is no time for clouds."

Edward found it something of an effort to comply, for his mind kept wandering—trying to remember what the service was that he had done Goodson.

The couple lay awake the most of the night, Mary happy and busy, Edward busy but not so happy. Mary was planning what she would do with the money. Edward was trying to recall that service. At first his conscience was sore on account of the lie he had told Mary—if it was a lie. After much reflection—suppose it *was* a lie? What then? Was it such a great matter? Aren't we always *acting* lies? Then why not *tell* them? Look at Mary—look what she had done. While he was hurrying off on his honest errand, what was she doing? Lamenting because the papers hadn't been destroyed and the money kept! Is theft better than lying?

That point lost its sting—the lie dropped into the background and left comfort behind it. The next point came to the front: *Had* he rendered that service? Well, here was Goodson's own evidence as reported in Stephenson's letter; there could be no better evidence than that—it was even *proof* that he had rendered it. Of course. So that point was settled. . . . No, not quite. He recalled with a wince that this unknown Mr. Stephenson was just a trifle unsure as to whether the performer of it was Richards or some other—and, oh dear, he had put Richards on his honor! He must himself decide whither that money must go—and Mr. Stephenson was not doubting that if he was the wrong man he would go honorably and find the right one. Oh, it was odious to put a man in such a situation—ah, why couldn't Stephenson have left out that doubt! What did he want to intrude that for?

Further reflection. How did it happen that *Richards's* name remained in Stephenson's mind as indicating the right man, and not some other man's name? That looked good. Yes, that looked very good. In fact, it went on looking better and better, straight along—until by and by it grew into positive *proof.* And then Richards put the matter at once out of his mind, for he had a private instinct that a proof once established is better left so.

He was feeling reasonably comfortable now, but there was still one other detail that kept pushing itself on his notice: of course he had done that service—that was settled; but what *was* that service? He must recall it—he would not go to sleep till he had recalled it; it would make his peace of mind perfect. And so he thought and thought. He thought of a dozen things—possible services, even probable services—but none of them seemed adequate, none of them seemed large enough, none of them seemed worth the money—worth the fortune Goodson had wished he could leave in his will. And besides, he couldn't remember having done them, anyway. Now, then—now, then—what *kind* of a service would it be that would make a man so inordinately grateful? Ah—the saving of his soul! That must be it. Yes, he could remember, now, how he once set himself the task of converting Goodson, and labored at it as much as—he was going to say three months; but upon closer examination it shrunk to a month, then to a week, then to a day, then to nothing. Yes, he remembered now, and with unwelcome vividness, that Goodson had told him to go to thunder and mind his own business—*he* wasn't hankering to follow Hadleyburg to heaven!

So that solution was a failure—he hadn't saved Goodson's soul. Richards was discouraged. Then after a little came another idea: had he saved Goodson's property? No, that wouldn't do—he hadn't any. His life? That is it! Of course. Why, he might have thought of it before. This time he was on the right track, sure. His imagination-mill was hard at work in a minute, now.

Thereafter during a stretch of two exhausting hours he was busy saving Goodson's life. He saved it in all kinds of difficult and perilous ways. In every case he got it saved satisfactorily up to a certain point; then, just as he was beginning to get well persuaded that it had really happened, a troublesome detail would turn up which made the whole thing impossible. As in the matter of drowning, for instance. In that case he had swum out and tugged Goodson ashore in an unconscious state with a great crowd looking on and applauding, but when he had got it all thought out and was just beginning to remember all about it, a whole swarm of disqualifying details arrived on the ground: the town would have known of the circumstance, Mary would have known of it, it would glare like a limelight in his own memory instead of being an inconspicuous service which he had possibly rendered "without knowing its full value." And at this point he remembered that he couldn't swim, anyway.

Ah—*there* was a point which he had been overlooking from the start: it had to be a service which he had rendered "possibly without knowing the full value of it." Why, really, that ought to be an easy hunt—much easier than those others. And sure enough, by and by he found it. Goodson, years and years ago, came near marrying a very sweet and pretty girl, named Nancy Hewitt, but in some way or other the match had been broken off; the girl died, Goodson remained a bachelor, and by and by became a soured one and a frank despiser of the human species. Soon after the girl's death the village found out, or thought it had found out, that she carried a spoonful of Negro blood in her veins. Richards worked at these details a good while, and in the end he thought he remembered things concerning them which must have gotten mislaid in his memory through long neglect. He seemed dimly to remember that it was *he* that found out about the Negro blood; that it was he that told the village; that the village told Goodson where they got it; that he thus saved Goodson from marrying the tainted girl; that he had done him this great service "without knowing the full value of it," in fact without knowing that he *was* doing it; but that Goodson knew the value of it, and what a narrow escape he had had, and so went to his grave grateful to his benefactor and wishing he had a fortune to leave him. It was all clear and simple now, and the more he went over it the more luminous and certain it grew; and at last, when he nestled to sleep satisfied and happy, he remembered the whole thing just as if it had been yesterday. In fact, he dimly remembered Goodson's *telling* him his gratitude once. Meantime Mary had spent six thousand dollars on a new house for herself and a pair of slippers for her pastor, and then had fallen peacefully to rest.

That same Saturday evening the postman had delivered a letter to each of the other principal citizens—nineteen letters in all. No two of the envelopes were alike, and no two of the superscriptions were in the same hand, but the letters inside were just like each other in every detail but one. They were exact copies of the letter received by Richards—handwriting and all—and were all signed by Stephenson, but in place of Richards's name each receiver's own name appeared.

All night long eighteen principal citizens did what their caste-brother Richards was doing at the same time—they put in their energies trying to remember what notable service it was that they had unconsciously done Barclay Goodson. In no case was it a holiday job; still they succeeded.

And while they were at this work, which was difficult, their wives put in the night spending the money, which was easy. During that one night the nineteen wives spent an average of seven thousand dollars each out of the forty thousand in the sack—a hundred and thirty-three thousand altogether.

Next day there was a surprise for Jack Halliday. He noticed that the faces of the nineteen chief citizens and their wives bore that expression of peaceful and holy happiness again. He could not understand it, neither was he able to invent any remarks about it that could damage it or disturb it. And so it was his turn to be dissatisfied with life. His private guesses at the reasons for the happiness failed in all instances, upon examination. When he met Mrs. Wilcox and noticed the placid ecstasy in her face, he said to himself, "Her cat has had kittens"—and went and asked the cook: it was not so; the cook had detected the happiness, but did not know the cause. When Halliday found the duplicate ecstasy in the face of "Shadbelly" Billson (village nickname), he was sure some neighbor of Billson's had broken his leg, but inquiry showed that this had not happened. The subdued ecstasy in Gregory Yates's face could mean but one thing—he was a mother-in-law short: it was another mistake. "And Pinkerton—Pinkerton—he has collected ten cents that he thought he was going to lose." And so on, and so on. In some cases the guesses had to remain in doubt, in the others they proved distinct errors. In the end Halliday said to himself, "Anyway it foots up that there's nineteen Hadleyburg families temporarily in heaven: I don't know how it happened; I only know Providence is off duty today."

An architect and builder from the next State had lately ventured to set up a small business in this unpromising village, and his sign had now been hanging out a week. Not a customer yet; he was a discouraged man, and sorry he had come. But his weather changed suddenly now. First one and then another chief citizen's wife said to him privately:

"Come to my house Monday week—but say nothing about it for the present. We think of building."

He got eleven invitations that day. That night he wrote his daughter and broke off her match with her student. He said she could marry a mile higher than that.

Pinkerton the banker and two or three other well-to-do men planned country-seats—but waited. That kind don't count their chickens until they are hatched.

The Wilsons devised a grand new thing—a fancy-dress ball. They made no actual promises, but told all their acquaintanceship in confidence that they were thinking the matter over and thought they should give it—"and if we do, you will be invited, of course." People were surprised, and said, one to another, "Why, they are crazy, those poor Wilsons, they can't afford it." Several among the nineteen said privately to their husbands, "It is a good idea: we will keep still till their cheap thing is over, then *we* will give one that will make it sick."

The days drifted along, and the bill of future squanderings rose higher and higher, wilder and wilder, more and more foolish and reckless. It began to look as if every member of the nineteen would not only spend his whole forty thousand dollars before receiving-day, but be actually in debt by the time he got the money. In some cases light-headed people did not stop with planning to spend, they really spent—on credit. They bought land, mortgages, farms, speculative stock, fine clothes, horses, and various other things, paid down the bonus, and made themselves liable for the rest—at ten days. Presently the sober second thought came, and Halliday noticed that a ghastly anxiety was beginning to show up in a good many faces. Again he was puzzled, and didn't know what to make of it. "The Wilcox kittens aren't dead, for they weren't born;

nobody's broken a leg; there's no shrinkage in mother-in-laws; *nothing* has happened—it is an unsolvable mystery."

There was another puzzled man, too—the Rev. Mr. Burgess. For days, wherever he went, people seemed to follow him or to be watching out for him; and if he ever found himself in a retired spot, a member of the nineteen would be sure to appear, thrust an envelope privately into his hand, whisper "To be opened at the town hall Friday evening," then vanish away like a guilty thing. He was expecting that there might be one claimant for the sack,—doubtful, however, Goodson being dead,— but it never occurred to him that all this crowd might be claimants. When the great Friday came at last, he found that he had nineteen envelopes.

III

The town hall had never looked finer. The platform at the end of it was backed by a showy draping of flags; at intervals along the walls were festoons of flags; the gallery fronts were clothed in flags; the supporting columns were swathed in flags; all this was to impress the stranger, for he would be there in considerable force, and in a large degree he would be connected with the press. The house was full. The 412 fixed seats were occupied; also the 68 extra chairs which had been packed into the aisles; the steps of the platform were occupied; some distinguished strangers were given seats on the platform; at the horse-shoe of tables which fenced the front and sides of the platform sat a strong force of special correspondents who had come from everywhere. It was the best-dressed house the town had ever produced. There were some tolerably expensive toilets there, and in several cases the ladies who wore them had the look of being unfamiliar with that kind of clothes. At least the town thought they had that look, but the notion could have arisen from the town's knowledge of the fact that these ladies had never inhabited such clothes before.

The gold-sack stood on a little table at the front of the platform where all the house could see it. The bulk of the house gazed at it with a burning interest, a mouth-watering interest, a wistful and pathetic interest; a minority of nineteen couples gazed at it tenderly, lovingly, proprietarily, and the male half of this minority kept saying over to themselves the moving little impromptu speeches of thankfulness for the audience's applause and congratulations which they were presently going to get up and deliver. Every now and then one of these got a piece of paper out of his vest pocket and privately glanced at it to refresh his memory.

Of course there was a buzz of conversation going on—there always is; but at last when the Rev. Mr. Burgess rose and laid his hand on the sack he could hear his microbes gnaw, the place was so still. He related the curious history of the sack, then went on to speak in warm terms of Hadleyburg's old and well-earned reputation for spotless honesty, and of the town's just pride in this reputation. He said that this reputation was a treasure of priceless value; that under Providence its value had now become inestimably enhanced, for the recent episode had spread this fame far and wide, and thus had focused the eyes of the American world upon this village, and made its name for all time, as he hoped and believed, a synonym for commercial incorruptibility. [*Applause.*] "And who is to be the guardian of this noble treasure—the community as a whole? No! The responsibility is individual, not communal. From this day forth each and every one of you is in his own person its special guardian, and individually responsible that no harm shall come to it. Do you—does each of you—accept this great trust? [*Tumultuous assent.*] Then all is well. Transmit it to your children and to your children's children. Today your purity is beyond reproach—see to it that it shall remain so. Today there is not a person in your community who could be beguiled to touch a penny not his own—see to it that you abide in this grace. [*"We will! we will!"*] This is not the place to make comparisons between ourselves and other communities—some of them ungracious toward us; they have their ways, we have ours; let us be content. [*Applause.*] I am done. Under my hand, my friends, rests a stranger's eloquent recognition of what we are; through him the world will always henceforth know what we are. We do not know who he is, but in your name I utter your gratitude, and ask you to raise your voices in endorsement."

The house rose in a body and made the walls quake with the thunders of its thankfulness for the space of a long minute. Then it sat down, and Mr. Burgess took an envelope out of his pocket. The house held its breath while he slit the envelope open and took from it a slip of paper. He read its contents—slowly and impressively—the audience listening with tranced attention to this magic document, each of whose words stood for an ingot of gold:

"*The remark which I made to the distressed stranger was this: "You are very far from being a bad man: go, and reform."*'" Then he continued:

"We shall know in a moment now whether the remark here quoted corresponds with the one concealed in the sack; and if that shall prove to be so—and it undoubtedly will—this sack of gold belongs to a fellow-citizen who will henceforth stand before the nation as the symbol of the special virtue which has made our town famous throughout the land—Mr. Billson!"

The house had gotten itself all ready to burst into the proper tornado of applause; but instead of doing it, it seemed stricken with a paralysis; there was a deep hush for a moment or two, then a wave of whispered murmurs swept the place—of about this tenor: "*Billson!* oh, come, this is *too* thin! Twenty dollars to a stranger—or *anybody—Billson!* tell it to the marines!" And now at this point the house caught its breath all of a sudden in a new access of astonishment, for it discovered that whereas in one part of the hall Deacon Billson was standing up with his head meekly bowed, in another part of it Lawyer Wilson was doing the same. There was a wondering silence now for a while.

Everybody was puzzled, and nineteen couples were surprised and indignant.

Billson and Wilson turned and stared at each other. Billson asked, bitingly,

"Why do *you* rise, Mr. Wilson?"

"Because I have a right to. Perhaps you will be good enough to explain to the house why *you* rise?"

"With great pleasure. Because I wrote that paper."

"It is an impudent falsity! I wrote it myself."

It was Burgess's turn to be paralyzed. He stood looking vacantly at first one of the men and then the other, and did not seem to know what to do. The house was stupefied. Lawyer Wilson spoke up, now, and said,

"I ask the Chair to read the name signed to that paper."

That brought the Chair to itself, and it read out the name,

" 'John Wharton *Billson.*' "

"There!" shouted Billson, "what have you got to say for yourself, now? And what kind of apology are you going to make to me and to this insulted house for the imposture which you have attempted to play here?"

"No apologies are due, sir; and as for the rest of it, I publicly charge you with pilfering my note from Mr. Burgess and substituting a copy of it signed with your own name. There is no other way by which you could have gotten hold of the test-remark; I alone, of living men, possessed the secret of its wording."

There was likely to be a scandalous state of things if this went on; everybody noticed with distress that the short-hand scribes were scribbling like mad; many people were crying "Chair, Chair! Order! Order!" Burgess rapped with his gavel, and said:

"Let us not forget the proprieties due. There has evidently been a mistake somewhere, but surely that is all. If Mr. Wilson gave me an envelope—and I remember now that he did—I still have it."

He took one out of his pocket, opened it, glanced at it, looked surprised and worried, and stood silent a few moments. Then he waved his hand in a wandering and mechanical way, and made an effort or two to say something, then gave it up, despondently. Several voices cried out:

"Read it! read it! What is it?"

So he began in a dazed and sleep-walker fashion:

"*The remark which I made to the unhappy stranger was this: "You are far from being a bad man.* [The house gazed at him, marveling.] *Go, and reform."* [*Murmurs:* "Amazing! What can this mean?"] This one," said the Chair, "is signed Thurlow G. Wilson."

"There!" cried Wilson, "I reckon that settles it! I knew perfectly well my note was purloined."

"Purloined!" retorted Billson. "I'll let you know that neither you nor any man of your kidney must venture to—"

The Chair. "Order, gentlemen, order! Take your seats, both of you, please."

They obeyed, shaking their heads and grumbling angrily. The house was profoundly puzzled; it did not know what to do with this curious emergency. Presently Thompson got up. Thompson was the hatter. He would have liked to be a Nineteener; but such was not for him: his stock of hats was not considerable enough for the position. He said:

"Mr. Chairman, if I may be permitted to make a suggestion, can both of these gentlemen be right? I put it to you, sir, can both have happened to say the very same words to the stranger? It seems to me—"

The tanner got up and interrupted him. The tanner was a disgruntled man; he believed himself entitled to be a Nineteener, but he couldn't get recognition. It made him a little unpleasant in his ways and speech. Said he:

"Sho, *that's* not the point! *That* could happen—twice in a hundred years—but not the other thing. *Neither* of them gave the twenty dollars!"

[*A ripple of applause.*]

Billson. "I did!"

Wilson. "I did!"

Then each accused the other of pilfering.

The Chair. "Order! Sit down, if you please—both of you. Neither of the notes has been out of my possession at any moment."

A Voice. "Good—that settles *that!*"

The Tanner. "Mr. Chairman, one thing is now plain: one of these men has been eavesdropping under the other one's bed, and filching family secrets. If it is not unparliamentary to suggest it, I will remark that both are equal to it. [*The Chair.* "Order! Order!"] I withdraw the remark, sir, and will confine myself to suggesting that *if* one of them has overheard the other reveal the test-remark to his wife, we shall catch him now."

A Voice. "How?"

The Tanner. "Easily. The two have not quoted the remark in exactly the same words. You would have noticed that, if there hadn't been a considerable stretch of time and an exciting quarrel inserted between the two readings."

A Voice. "Name the difference."

The Tanner. "The word *very* is in Billson's note, and not in the other.

Many Voices. "That's so—he's right!"

The Tanner. "And so, if the Chair will examine the test-remark in the sack, we shall know which of these two frauds—[*The Chair.* "Order!"] —which of these two adventurers—[*The Chair.* "Order! Order!"]— which of these two gentlemen—[*laughter and applause*]—is entitled to wear the belt as being the first dishonest blatherskite ever bred in this town—which he has dishonored, and which will be a sultry place for him from now out!" [*Vigorous applause.*]

Many Voices. "Open it!—open the sack!"

Mr. Burgess made a slit in the sack, slid his hand in and brought out an envelope. In it were a couple of folded notes. He said:

"One of these is marked, 'Not to be examined until all written communications which have been addressed to the Chair—if any—shall have been read.' The other is marked '*The Test.*' Allow me. It is worded—to wit:

" 'I do not require that the first half of the remark which was made to me by my benefactor shall be quoted with exactness, for it was not striking, and could be forgotten; but its closing fifteen words are quite striking, and I think easily rememberable; unless *these* shall be accurately reproduced, let the applicant be regarded as an impostor. My benefactor began by saying he seldom gave advice to anyone, but that it always bore the hall-mark of high value when he did give it. Then he said this—and it has never faded from my memory: *"You are far from being a bad man—"* ' "

Fifty Voices. "That settles it—the money's Wilson's! Wilson! Wilson! Speech! Speech!"

People jumped up and crowded around Wilson, wringing his hand and congratulating fervently—meantime the Chair was hammering with the gavel and shouting:

"Order, gentlemen! Order! Order! Let me finish reading, please." When quiet was restored, the reading was resumed—as follows:

" ' *"Go, and reform—or, mark my words—some day, for your sins, you will die and go to hell or Hadleyburg*—TRY AND MAKE IT THE FORMER.*"* ' "

A ghastly silence followed. First an angry cloud began to settle darkly upon the faces of the citizenship; after a pause the cloud began to rise, and a tickled expression tried to take its place; tried so hard that it was only kept under with great and painful difficulty; the reporters, the Brixtonites, and other strangers bent their heads down and shielded their faces with their hands, and managed to hold in by main strength and heroic courtesy. At this most inopportune time burst upon the stillness the roar of a solitary voice—Jack Halliday's:

"*That's* got the hall-mark on it!"

Then the house let go, strangers and all. Even Mr. Burgess's gravity broke down presently, then the audience considered itself officially absolved from all restraint, and it made the most of its privilege. It was a good long laugh, and a tempestuously wholehearted one, but it ceased at last—long enough for Mr. Burgess to try to resume, and for the people to get their eyes partially wiped; then it broke out again; and afterward yet again; then at last Burgess was able to get out these serious words:

"It is useless to try to disguise the fact—we find ourselves in the presence of a matter of grave import. It involves the honor of your town, it strikes at the town's good name. The difference of a single word between the test-remarks offered by Mr. Wilson and Mr. Billson was itself a serious thing, since it indicated that one or the other of these gentlemen had committed a theft—"

The two men were sitting limp, nerveless, crushed; but at these words both were electrified into movement, and started to get up—

"Sit down!" said the Chair, sharply, and they obeyed. "That, as I have said, was a serious thing. And it was—but for only one of them. But the matter has become graver; for the honor of *both* is now in formidable peril. Shall I go even further, and say in inextricable peril? *Both* left out the crucial fifteen words." He paused. During several moments he allowed the pervading stillness to gather and deepen its impressive effects, then added: "There would seem to be but one way whereby this could happen. I ask these gentlemen—Was there *collusion?—agreement?*"

A low murmur sifted through the house; its import was, "He's got them both."

Billson was not used to emergencies; he sat in a helpless collapse. But Wilson was a lawyer. He struggled to his feet, pale and worried, and said:

"I ask the indulgence of the house while I explain this most painful matter. I am sorry to say what I am about to say, since it must inflict irreparable injury upon Mr. Billson, whom I have always esteemed and respected until now, and in whose invulnerability to temptation I entirely believed—as did you all. But for the preservation of my own honor I must speak—and with frankness. I confess with shame—and I now beseech your pardon for it—that I said to the ruined stranger all of the words contained in the test-remark, including the disparaging fifteen.

[*Sensation.*] When the late publication was made I recalled them, and I resolved to claim the sack of coin, for by every right I was entitled to it. Now I will ask you to consider this point, and weigh it well: that stranger's gratitude to me that night knew no bounds; he said himself that he could find no words for it that were adequate, and that if he should ever be able he would repay me a thousand fold. Now, then, I ask you this: Could I expect—could I believe—could I even remotely imagine—that, feeling as he did, he would do so ungrateful a thing as to add those quite unnecessary fifteen words to his test?—set a trap for me?—expose me as a slanderer of my own town before my own people assembled in a public hall? It was preposterous; it was impossible. His test would contain only the kindly opening clause of my remark. Of that I had no shadow of doubt. You would have thought as I did. You would not have expected a base betrayal from one whom you had befriended and against whom you had committed no offense. And so, with perfect confidence, perfect trust, I wrote on a piece of paper the opening words—ending with 'Go, and reform,'—and signed it. When I was about to put it in an envelope I was called into my back office, and without thinking I left the paper lying open on my desk." He stopped, turned his head slowly toward Billson, waited a moment, then added: "I ask you to note this: when I returned, a little later, Mr. Billson was retiring by my street door." [*Sensation.*]

In a moment Billson was on his feet and shouting:

"It's a lie! It's an infamous lie!"

The Chair. "Be seated, sir! Mr. Wilson has the floor."

Billson's friends pulled him into his seat and quieted him, and Wilson went on:

"Those are the simple facts. My note was now lying in a different place on the table from where I had left it. I noticed that, but attached no importance to it, thinking a draught had blown it there. That Mr. Billson would read a private paper was a thing which could not occur to me; he was an honorable man, and he would be above that. If you will allow me to say it, I think his extra word '*very*' stands explained; it is attributable to a defect of memory. I was the only man in the world who could furnish here any detail of the test-remark—by *honorable* means. I have finished."

There is nothing in the world like a persuasive speech to fuddle the mental apparatus and upset the convictions and debauch the emotions of an audience not practiced in the tricks and delusions of oratory. Wilson sat down victorious. The house submerged him in tides of approving applause; friends swarmed to him and shook him by the hand and congratulated him, and Billson was shouted down and not allowed to say a word. The Chair hammered and hammered with its gavel, and kept shouting,

"But let us proceed, gentlemen, let us proceed!"

At last there was a measurable degree of quiet, and the hatter said:

"But what is there to proceed with, sir, but to deliver the money?"

Voices. "That's it! That's it! Come forward, Wilson!"

The Hatter. "I move three cheers for Mr. Wilson, Symbol of the special virtue which—"

The cheers burst forth before he could finish; and in the midst of them—and in the midst of the clamor of the gavel also—some enthusiasts mounted Wilson on a big friend's shoulder and were going to fetch him in triumph to the platform. The Chair's voice now rose above the noise—

"Order! To your places! You forget that there is still a document to be read." When quiet had been restored he took up the document, and was going to read it, but laid it down again, saying, "I forgot; this is not to be read until all written communications received by me have first been read." He took an envelope out of his pocket, removed its enclosure, glanced at it—seemed astonished—held it out and gazed at it—stared at it.

Twenty or thirty voices cried out:

"What is it? Read it! read it!"

And he did—slowly, and wondering:

" 'The remark which I made to the stranger—[*Voices.* "Hello! how's this?"]—was this: "You are far from being a bad man. [*Voices.* "Great Scott!"] Go, and reform." ' [*Voice.* "Oh, saw my leg off!"] Signed by Mr. Pinkerton the banker."

The pandemonium of delight which turned itself loose now was of a sort to make the judicious weep. Those whose withers were unwrung laughed till the tears ran down; the reporters, in throes of laughter, set down disordered pot-hooks which would never in the world be decipherable; and a sleeping dog jumped up, scared out of its wits. and barked itself crazy at the turmoil. All manner of cries were scattered through the din: "We're getting rich—*two* Symbols of Incorruptibility! —without counting Billson!" "*Three!*—count Shadbelly in—we can't have too many!" "All right—Billson's elected!" "Alas, poor Wilson— victim of *two* thieves!"

A Powerful Voice. "Silence! The Chair's fished up something more out of its pocket."

Voices. "Hurrah! Is it something fresh? Read it! read! read!"

The Chair [*reading.*] " 'The remark which I made,' etc.: 'You are far from being a bad man. Go,' etc. Signed, 'Gregory Yates.' "

Tornado of Voices. "Four Symbols!" " 'Rah for Yates!" "Fish again!"

The house was in a roaring humor now, and ready to get all the fun out of the occasion that might be in it. Several Nineteeners, looking pale and distressed, got up and began to work their way toward the aisles, but a score of shouts went up:

"The doors, the doors—close the doors; no Incorruptible shall leave this place! Sit down, everybody!"

The mandate was obeyed.

"Fish again! Read! read!"

The Chair fished again, and once more the familiar words began to fall from its lips—" 'You are far from being a bad man—' "

"Name! name! What's his name?"

" 'L. Ingoldsby Sargent' "

"Five elected! Pile up the Symbols! Go on, go on!"

" 'You are far from being a bad—' "

"Name! name!"

" 'Nicholas Whitworth.' "

"Hooray! hooray! it's a symbolical day!"

Somebody wailed in, and began to sing this rhyme (leaving out "it's") to the lovely "Mikado" tune of "When a man's afraid, a beautiful maid—"; the audience joined in, with joy; then, just in time, somebody contributed another line—

"And don't you this forget—"

The house roared it out. A third line was at once furnished—

"Corruptibles far from Hadleyburg are—"

The house roared that one too. As the last note died, Jack Halliday's voice rose high and clear, freighted with a final line—

"But the Symbols are here, you bet!"

That was sung, with booming enthusiasm. Then the happy house started in at the beginning and sang the four lines through twice, with immense swing and dash, and finished up with a crashing three-times-three and a tiger for "Hadleyburg the Incorruptible and all Symbols of it which we shall find worthy to receive the hall-mark tonight."

Then the shoutings at the Chair began again, all over the place:

"Go on! go on! Read! read some more! Read all you've got!"

"That's it—go on! We are winning eternal celebrity!"

A dozen men got up now and began to protest. They said that this farce was the work of some abandoned joker, and was an insult to the whole community. Without a doubt these signatures were all forgeries--

"Sit down! sit down! Shut up! You are confessing. We'll find *your* names in the lot."

"Mr. Chairman, how many of those envelopes have you got?"

The Chair counted.

"Together with those that have been already examined, there are nineteen."

A storm of derisive applause broke out.

"Perhaps they all contain the secret. I move that you open them all and read every signature that is attached to a note of that sort—and read also the first eight words of the note."

"Second the motion!"

It was put and carried—uproariously. Then poor old Richards got up, and his wife rose and stood at his side. Her head was bent down, so that none might see that she was crying. Her husband gave her his arm, and so supporting her, he began to speak in a quavering voice:

"My friends, you have known us two—Mary and me—all our lives, and I think you have liked us and respected us—"

The Chair interrupted him:

"Allow me. It is quite true—that which you are saying, Mr. Richards: this town *does* know you two; it *does* like you; it *does* respect you; more—it honors you and *loves* you—"

Halliday's voice rang out:

"That's the hall-marked truth, too! If the Chair is right, let the house speak up and say it. Rise! Now, then—hip! hip! hip!—all together!"

The house rose in mass, faced toward the old couple eagerly, filled the air with a snowstorm of waving handkerchiefs, and delivered the cheers with all its affectionate heart.

The Chair then continued:

"What I was going to say is this: We know your good heart, Mr. Richards, but this is not a time for the exercise of charity toward offenders. [*Shouts of "Right! right!"*] I see your generous purpose in your face, but I cannot allow you to plead for these men—"

"But I was going to—"

"Please take your seat, Mr. Richards. We must examine the rest of these notes—simple fairness to the men who have already been exposed requires this. As soon as that has been done—I give you my word for this—you shall be heard."

Many Voices. "Right!—the Chair is right—no interruption can be permitted at this stage! Go on!—the names! the names!—according to the terms of the motion!"

The old couple sat reluctantly down, and the husband whispered to the wife, "It is pitifully hard to have to wait; the shame will be greater than ever when they find we were only going to plead for *ourselves*."

Straightway the jollity broke loose again with the reading of the names.

" 'You are far from being a bad man—' Signature, 'Robert J. Titmarsh.'

" 'You are far from being a bad man—' Signature, 'Eliphalet Weeks.'

" 'You are far from being a bad man—' Signature, 'Oscar B. Wilder.' "

At this point the house lit upon the idea of taking the eight words out of the Chairman's hands. He was not unthankful for that. Thenceforward he held up each note in its turn, and waited. The house droned out the eight words in a massed and measured and musical deep volume of sound (with a daringly close resemblance to a well-known church chant)—" 'You are f-a-r from being a b-a-a-a-d man.' " Then the Chair said, "Signature, 'Archibald Wilcox.' " And so on, and so on, name after name, and everybody had an increasingly and gloriously good time except the wretched Nineteen. Now and then, when a particularly shining name was called, the house made the Chair wait while it chanted the whole of the test-remark from the beginning to the closing words, "And go to hell or Hadleyburg—try and make it the for-or-m-e-r!" and in these special cases they added a grand and agonized and imposing "A-a-a-a-*men!*"

The list dwindled, dwindled, dwindled, poor old Richards keeping tally of the count, wincing when a name resembling his own was pronounced, and waiting in miserable suspense for the time to come when it would be his humiliating privilege to rise with Mary and finish his plea, which he was intending to word thus: ". . . for until now we have never done any wrong thing, but have gone our humble way unreproached. We are very poor, we are old, and have no chick nor child to help us; we were sorely tempted, and we fell. It was my purpose when I got up before to make a confession and beg that my name might not be read out in this public place, for it seemed to us that we could not bear it; but I was prevented. It was just; it was our place to suffer with the rest. It has been hard for us. It is the first time we have ever heard our name fall from any one's lips—sullied. Be merciful—for the sake of the better days; make our shame as light to bear as in your charity you can." At this point in his reverie Mary nudged him, perceiving that his mind was absent. The house was chanting, "You are f-a-r," etc.

"Be ready," Mary whispered. "Your name comes now; he has read eighteen."

The chant ended.

"Next! next! next!" came volleying from all over the house.

Burgess put his hand into his pocket. The old couple, trembling, began to rise. Burgess fumbled a moment, then said,

"I find I have read them all."

Faint with joy and surprise, the couple sank into their seats, and Mary whispered,

"Oh, bless God, we are saved!—he has lost ours—I wouldn't give this for a hundred of those sacks!"

The house burst out with its "Mikado" travesty, and sang it three times with ever-increasing enthusiasm, rising to its feet when it reached for the third time the closing line—

"But the Symbols are here, you bet!"

and finishing up with cheers and a tiger for "Hadleyburg purity and our eighteen immortal representatives of it."

Then Wingate, the saddler, got up and proposed cheers "for the cleanest man in town, the one solitary important citizen in it who didn't try to steal that money—Edward Richards."

They were given with great and moving heartiness; then somebody proposed that Richards be elected sole guardian and Symbol of the now Sacred Hadleyburg Tradition, with power and right to stand up and look the whole sarcastic world in the face.

Passed, by acclamation; then they sang the "Mikado" again, and ended it with,

"And there's *one* Symbol left, you bet!"

There was a pause; then—

A Voice. "Now, then, who's to get the sack?"

The Tanner (with bitter sarcasm). "That's easy. The money has to be divided among the eighteen Incorruptibles. They gave the suffering stranger twenty dollars apiece—and that remark—each in his turn— it took twenty-two minutes for the procession to move past. Staked the stranger—total contribution, $360. All they want is just the loan back —and interest—forty thousand dollars altogether."

Many Voices [derisively.] "That's it! Divvy! divvy! Be kind to the poor—don't keep them waiting!"

The Chair. "Order! I now offer the stranger's remaining document. It says: 'If no claimant shall appear [*grand chorus of groans*], I desire that you open the sack and count out the money to the principal citizens of your town, they to take it in trust [*cries of "Oh! Oh! Oh!"*], and use it in such ways as to them shall seem best for the propagation and preservation of your community's noble reputation for incorruptible honesty [*more cries*]—a reputation to which their names and their efforts will add a new and far-reaching luster.' [*Enthusiastic outburst of sarcastic applause.*] That seems to be all. No—here is a postscript:

"'P. S.—CITIZENS OF HADLEYBURG: There *is* no test-remark—nobody made one. [*Great sensation.*] There wasn't any pauper stranger, nor any twenty-dollar contribution, nor any accompanying benediction and compliment—these are all inventions. [*General buzz and hum of aston-ishment and delight.*] Allow me to tell my story—it will take but a word or two. I passed through your town at a certain time, and re-ceived a deep offense which I had not earned. Any other man would have been content to kill one or two of you and call it square, but to me that would have been a trivial revenge, and inadequate; for the dead do not *suffer*. Besides, I could not kill you all—and, anyway, mad as I am, even that would not have satisfied me. I wanted to damage every man in the place, and every woman—and not in their bodies or in their estate, but in their vanity—the place where feeble and foolish people are most vulnerable. So I disguised myself and came back and studied you. You were easy game. You had an old and lofty reputation for honesty, and naturally you were proud of it—it was your treasure of treasures, the very apple of your eye. As soon as I found out that you carefully and vigilantly kept yourselves and your children *out of tempta-tion,* I knew how to proceed. Why, you simple creatures, the weakest of all weak things is a virtue which has not been tested in the fire. I laid a plan, and gathered a list of names. My project was to corrupt Hadleyburg the Incorruptible. My idea was to make liars and thieves of nearly half a hundred smirchless men and women who had never in their lives uttered a lie or stolen a penny. I was afraid of Goodson. He was neither born nor reared in Hadleyburg. I was afraid that if I started to operate my scheme by getting my letter laid before you, you would say to yourselves, "Goodson is the only man among us who would give away twenty dollars to a poor devil"—and then you might not bite at my bait. But Heaven took Goodson; then I knew I was safe, and I set my trap and baited it. It may be that I shall not catch all the men to whom I mailed the pretended test secret, but I shall catch the most of them, if I know Hadleyburg nature. [*Voices.* "Right—he got every last one of them."] I believe they will even steal ostensible *gamble*-money, rather than miss, poor, tempted, and mistrained fellows. I am hoping to eternally and everlastingly squelch your vanity and give Hadleyburg a new renown—one that will *stick*—and spread far. If I have succeeded, open the sack and summon the Committee on Propagation and Preser-vation of the Hadleyburg Reputation.'"

A Cyclone of Voices. "Open it! Open it! The Eighteen to the front! Committee on Propagation of the Tradition! Forward—the Incorrupt-ibles!"

The Chair ripped the sack wide, and gathered up a handful of bright, broad, yellow coins, shook them together, then examined them—

"Friends, they are only gilded disks of lead!"

There was a crashing outbreak of delight over this news, and when the noise had subsided, the tanner called out:

"By right of apparent seniority in this business, Mr. Wilson is Chairman of the Committee on Propagation of the Tradition. I suggest that he step forward on behalf of his pals, and receive in trust the money."

A Hundred Voices. "Wilson! Wilson! Wilson! Speech! Speech!"

Wilson [*in a voice trembling with anger.*] "You will allow me to say, and without apologies for my language, *damn* the money!"

A Voice. "Oh, and him a Baptist!"

A Voice. "Seventeen Symbols left! Step up, gentlemen, and assume your trust!"

There was a pause—no response.

The Saddler. "Mr. Chairman, we've got *one* clean man left, anyway, out of the late aristocracy; and he needs money, and deserves it. I move that you appoint Jack Halliday to get up there and auction off that sack of gilt twenty-dollar pieces, and give the result to the right man—the man whom Hadleyburg delights to honor—Edward Richards."

This was received with great enthusiasm, the dog taking a hand again; the saddler started the bids at a dollar, the Brixton folk and Barnum's representative fought hard for it, the people cheered every jump that the bids made, the excitement climbed moment by moment higher and higher, the bidders got on their mettle and grew steadily more and more daring, more and more determined, the jumps went from a dollar up to five, then to ten, then to twenty, then fifty, then to a hundred, then—

At the beginning of the auction Richards whispered in distress to his wife: "Oh, Mary, can we allow it? It—it—you see, it is an honor-reward, a testimonial to purity of character, and—and—can we allow it? Hadn't I better get up and—Oh, Mary, what ought we to do?—what do you think we— [*Halliday's voice. "Fifteen I'm bid!—fifteen for the sack!— twenty!—ah, thanks!—thirty—thanks again! Thirty, thirty, thirty!—do I hear forty?—forty it is! Keep the ball rolling, gentlemen, keep it rolling!—fifty!—thanks, noble Roman! going at fifty, fifty, fifty!—seventy! —ninety!—splendid!—a hundred!—pile it up, pile it up!—hundred and twenty—forty!—just in time!—hundred and fifty!—*TWO hundred!— superb! Do I hear two h—thanks!—two hundred and fifty!—"*]

"It is another temptation, Edward—I'm all in a tremble—but, oh, we've escaped *one* temptation, and that ought to warn us to— [*"Six did I hear? —thanks!—six fifty, six f—*SEVEN *hundred!"*] And yet Edward, when you think—nobody susp—[*"Eight hundred dollars!—hurrah!—make it*

*nine!—Mr. Parsons, did I hear you say—thanks—nine!—this noble sack
of virgin lead going at only nine hundred dollars, gilding and all—come!
do I hear—a thousand!—gratefully yours!—did some one say eleven?—
a sack which is going to be the most celebrated in the whole Uni—"*]
Oh, Edward" (beginning to sob), "we are *so* poor!—but—but—do as
you think best—do as you think best."

Edward fell—that is, he sat still; sat with a conscience which was not
satisfied, but which was overpowered by circumstances.

Meantime a stranger, who looked like an amateur detective gotten
up as an impossible English earl, had been watching the evening's proceedings with manifest interest, and with a contented expression in his
face; and he had been privately commenting to himself. He was now
soliloquizing somewhat like this: "None of the Eighteen are bidding;
that is not satisfactory; I must change that— the dramatic unities require it; they must buy the sack they tried to steal; they must pay a
heavy price, too—some of them are rich. And another thing, when I
make a mistake in Hadleyburg nature the man that puts that error upon
me is entitled to a high honorarium, and some one must pay it. This
poor old Richards has brought my judgment to shame; he is an honest
man:—I don't understand it, but I acknowledge it. Yes, he saw my
deuces *and* with a straight flush, and by rights the pot is his. And it shall
be a jack-pot, too, if I can manage it. He disappointed me, but let that
pass."

He was watching the bidding. At a thousand, the market broke; the
prices tumbled swiftly. He waited—and still watched. One competitor
dropped out; then another, and another. He put in a bid or two, now.
When the bids had sunk to ten dollars, he added a five; some one raised
him a three; he waited a moment, then flung in a fifty-dollar jump, and
the sack was his—at $1,282. The house broke out in cheers—then stopped;
for he was on his feet, and had lifted his hand. He began to speak.

"I desire to say a word, and ask a favor. I am a speculator in rarities,
and I have dealings with persons interested in numismatics all over the
world. I can make a profit on this purchase, just as it stands; but there
is a way, if I can get your approval, whereby I can make every one of
these leaden twenty-dollar pieces worth its face in gold, and perhaps
more. Grant me that approval, and I will give part of my gains to your
Mr. Richards, whose invulnerable probity you have so justly and cordially recognized tonight; his share shall be ten thousand dollars, and
I will hand him the money tomorrow. [*Great applause from the house.*
But the "invulnerable probity" made the Richardses blush prettily;
however, it went for modesty, and did no harm.] If you will pass my
proposition by a good majority—I would like a two-thirds vote—I will
regard that as the town's consent, and that is all I ask. Rarities are always

helped by any device which will rouse curiosity and compel remark. Now if I may have your permission to stamp upon the faces of each of these ostensible coins the names of the eighteen gentlemen who—"

Nine-tenths of the audience were on their feet in a moment—dog and all—and the proposition was carried with a whirlwind of approving applause and laughter.

They sat down, and all the Symbols except "Dr." Clay Harkness got up, violently protesting against the proposed outrage, and threatening to—

"I beg you not to threaten me," said the stranger, calmly. "I know my legal rights, and am not accustomed to being frightened at bluster." [*Applause.*] He sat down. "Dr." Harkness saw an opportunity here. He was one of the two very rich men of the place, and Pinkerton was the other. Harkness was proprietor of a mint; that is to say, a popular patent medicine. He was running for the Legislature on one ticket, and Pinkerton on the other. It was a close race and a hot one, and getting hotter every day. Both had strong appetites for money; each had bought a great tract of land, with a purpose; there was going to be a new railway, and each wanted to be in the Legislature and help locate the route to his own advantage; a single vote might make the decision, and with it two or three fortunes. The stake was large, and Harkness was a daring speculator. He was sitting close to the stranger. He leaned over while one or another of the other Symbols was entertaining the house with protests and appeals, and asked, in a whisper,

"What is your price for the sack?"

"Forty thousand dollars."

"I'll give you twenty."

"No."

"Twenty-five."

"No."

"Say thirty."

"The price is forty thousand dollars; not a penny less."

"All right, I'll give it. I will come to the hotel at ten in the morning. I don't want it known; will see you privately."

"Very good." Then the stranger got up and said to the house:

"I find it late. The speeches of these gentlemen are not without merit, not without interest, not without grace; yet if I may be excused I will take my leave. I thank you for the great favor which you have shown me in granting my petition. I ask the Chair to keep the sack for me until tomorrow, and to hand these three five-hundred-dollar notes to Mr. Richards." They were passed up to the Chair. "At nine I will call for the sack, and at eleven will deliver the rest of the ten thousand to Mr. Richards in person, at his home. Good night."

Then he slipped out, and left the audience making a vast noise, which was composed of a mixture of cheers, the "Mikado" song, dog-disapproval, and the chant, "You are f-a-r from being a b-a-a-d man—a-a-a a-men!"

IV

At home the Richardses had to endure congratulations and compliments until midnight. Then they were left to themselves. They looked a little sad, and they sat silent and thinking. Finally Mary sighed and said,

"Do you think we are to blame, Edward—*much* to blame?" and her eyes wandered to the accusing triplet of big bank notes lying on the table, where the congratulators had been gloating over them and reverently fingering them. Edward did not answer at once; then he brought out a sigh and said, hesitatingly:

"We—we couldn't help it, Mary. It—well, it was ordered. *All* things are."

Mary glanced up and looked at him steadily, but he didn't return the look. Presently she said:

"I thought congratulations and praises always tasted good. But—it seems to me, now—Edward?"

"Well?"

"Are you going to stay in the bank?"

"N-no."

"Resign?"

"In the morning—by note."

"It does seem best."

Richards bowed his head in his hands and muttered:

"Before, I was not afraid to let oceans of people's money pour through my hands, but—Mary, I am so tired, so tired—"

"We will go to bed."

At nine in the morning the stranger called for the sack and took it to the hotel in a cab. At ten Harkness had a talk with him privately. The stranger asked for and got five checks on a metropolitan bank—drawn to "Bearer,"—four for $1,500 each, and one for $34,000. He put one of the former in his pocketbook, and the remainder, representing $38,500, he put in an envelope, and with these he added a note, which he wrote after Harkness was gone. At eleven he called at the Richards house and knocked. Mrs. Richards peeped through the shutters, then went and received the envelope, and the stranger disappeared without a word. She came back flushed and a little unsteady on her legs, and gasped out:

"I am sure I recognized him! Last night it seemed to me that maybe I had seen him somewhere before."

"He is the man that brought the sack here?"

"I am almost sure of it."

"Then he is the ostensible Stephenson, too, and sold every important citizen in this town with his bogus secret. Now if he has sent checks instead of money, we are sold, too, after we thought we had escaped. I was beginning to feel fairly comfortable once more, after my night's rest, but the look of that envelope makes me sick. It isn't fat enough; $8,500 in even the largest bank notes makes more bulk than that."

"Edward, why do you object to checks?"

"Checks signed by Stephenson! I am resigned to take the $8,500 if it could come in bank notes—for it does seem that it was so ordered, Mary—but I have never had much courage, and I have not the pluck to try to market a check signed with that disastrous name. It would be a trap. That man tried to catch me; we escaped somehow or other; and now he is trying a new way. If it is checks—"

"Oh, Edward, it is *too* bad!" and she held up the checks and began to cry.

"Put them in the fire! quick! we mustn't be tempted. It is a trick to make the world laugh at *us,* along with the rest, and— Give them to *me,* since you can't do it!" He snatched them and tried to hold his grip till he could get to the stove; but he was human, he was a cashier, and he stopped a moment to make sure of the signature. Then he came near to fainting.

"Fan me, Mary, fan me! They are the same as gold!"

"Oh, how lovely, Edward! Why?"

"Signed by Harkness. What can the mystery of that be, Mary?"

"Edward, do you think—"

"Look here—look at this! Fifteen—fifteen—fifteen—thirty-four. Thirty-eight thousand five hundred! Mary, the sack isn't worth twelve dollars, and Harkness—apparently—has paid about par for it."

"And does it all come to us, do you think—instead of the ten thousand?"

"Why, it looks like it. And the checks are made to 'Bearer,' too."

"Is that good, Edward? What is it for?"

"A hint to collect them at some distant bank, I reckon. Perhaps Harkness doesn't want the matter known. What is that—a note?"

"Yes. It was with the checks."

It was in the "Stephenson" handwriting, but there was no signature. It said:

"I am a disappointed man. Your honesty is beyond the reach of temptation. I had a different idea about it, but I wronged you in that, and I beg pardon, and do it sincerely. I honor you—and that is sincere too. This town is not worthy to kiss the hem of your garment. Dear sir, I made a square bet

with myself that there were nineteen debauchable men in your self-righteous community. I have lost. Take the whole pot, you are entitled to it."

Richards drew a deep sigh, and said:

"It seems written with fire—it burns so. Mary—I am miserable again."

"I, too. Ah, dear, I wish—"

"To think, Mary—he *believes* in me."

"Oh, don't, Edward—I can't bear it."

"If those beautiful words were deserved, Mary—and God knows I believed I deserved them once—I think I could give the forty thousand dollars for them. And I would put that paper away, as representing more than gold and jewels, and keep it always. But now— We could not live in the shadow of its accusing presence, Mary."

He put it in the fire.

A messenger arrived and delivered an envelope.

Richards took from it a note and read it; it was from Burgess.

"You saved me, in a difficult time. I saved you last night. It was at cost of a lie, but I made the sacrifice freely, and out of a grateful heart. None in this village knows so well as I know how brave and good and noble you are. At bottom you cannot respect me, knowing as you do of that matter of which I am accused, and by the general voice condemned; but I beg that you will at least believe that I am a grateful man; it will help me to bear my burden.

[*Signed*] "BURGESS."

"Saved, once more. And on such terms!" He put the note in the fire. "I—I wish I were dead, Mary, I wish I were out of it all."

"Oh, these are bitter, bitter days, Edward. The stabs, through their very generosity, are so deep—and they come so fast!"

Three days before the election each of two thousand voters suddenly found himself in possession of a prized memento—one of the renowned bogus double-eagles. Around one of its faces was stamped these words: "THE REMARK I MADE TO THE POOR STRANGER WAS—" Around the other face was stamped these: "GO, AND REFORM. [SIGNED] PINKERTON." Thus the entire remaining refuse of the renowned joke was emptied upon a single head, and with calamitous effect. It revived the recent vast laugh and concentrated it upon Pinkerton; and Harkness's election was a walk-over.

Within twenty-four hours after the Richardses had received their checks their consciences were quieting down, discouraged; the old couple were learning to reconcile themselves to the sin which they had committed. But they were to learn, now, that a sin takes on new and real terrors when there seems a chance that it is going to be found out. This gives it a fresh and most substantial and important aspect. At church the morning sermon was of the usual pattern; it was the same old things said in the same old way; they had heard them a thousand times and found them innocuous, next to meaningless, and easy to sleep under; but now it was different: the sermon seemed to bristle with accusations; it seemed aimed straight and specially at people who were concealing deadly sins. After church they got away from the mob of congratulators as soon as they could, and hurried homeward, chilled to the bone at they did not know what—vague, shadowy, indefinite fears. And by chance they caught a glimpse of Mr. Burgess as he turned a corner. He paid no attention to their nod of recognition! He hadn't seen it; but they did not know that. What could his conduct mean? It might mean—it might mean—oh, a dozen dreadful things. Was it possible that he knew that Richards could have cleared him of guilt in that bygone time, and had been silently waiting for a chance to even up accounts? At home, in their distress they got to imagining that their servant might have been in the next room listening when Richards revealed the secret to his wife that he knew of Burgess's innocence; next, Richards began to imagine that he had heard the swish of a gown in there at that time; next, he was sure he *had* heard it. They would call Sarah in, on a pretext, and watch her face: if she had been betraying them to Mr. Burgess, it would show in her manner. They asked her some questions—questions which were so random and incoherent and seemingly purposeless that the girl felt sure that the old people's minds had been affected by their sudden good fortune; the sharp and watchful gaze which they bent upon her frightened her, and that completed the business. She blushed, she became nervous and confused, and to the old people these were plain signs of guilt—guilt of some fearful sort or other—without doubt she was a spy and a traitor. When they were alone again they began to piece many unrelated things together and get horrible results out of the combination. When things had got about to the worst, Richards was delivered of a sudden gasp, and his wife asked,

"Oh, what is it?—what is it?"

"The note—Burgess's note! Its language was sarcastic, I see it now." He quoted: "'At bottom you cannot respect me, *knowing,* as you do, of *that matter* of which I am accused'—oh, it is perfectly plain, now, God help me! He knows that I know! You see the ingenuity of the phrasing. It was a trap—and like a fool, I walked into it. And Mary—?"

"Oh, it is dreadful—I know what you are going to say—he didn't return your transcript of the pretended test-remark."

"No—kept it to destroy us with. Mary, he has exposed us to some already. I know it—I know it well. I saw it in a dozen faces after church. Ah, he wouldn't answer our nod of recognition—*he* knew what he had been doing!"

In the night the doctor was called. The news went around in the morning that the old couple were rather seriously ill—prostrated by the exhausting excitement growing out of their great windfall, the congratulations, and the late hours, the doctor said. The town was sincerely distressed; for these old people were about all it had left to be proud of, now.

Two days later the news was worse. The old couple were delirious, and were doing strange things. By witness of the nurses, Richards had exhibited checks—for $8,500? No—for an amazing sum—$38,500! What could be the explanation of this gigantic piece of luck?

The following day the nurses had more news—and wonderful. They had concluded to hide the checks, lest harm come to them; but when they searched they were gone from under the patient's pillow—vanished away. The patient said:

"Let the pillow alone; what do you want?"

"We thought it best that the checks—"

"You will never see them again—they are destroyed. They came from Satan. I saw the hell-brand on them, and I knew they were sent to betray me to sin." Then he fell to gabbling strange and dreadful things which were not clearly understandable, and which the doctor admonished them to keep to themselves.

Richards was right; the checks were never seen again.

A nurse must have talked in her sleep, for within two days the forbidden gabblings were the property of the town; and they were of a surprising sort. They seemed to indicate that Richards had been a claimant for the sack himself, and that Burgess had concealed that fact and then maliciously betrayed it.

Burgess was taxed with this and stoutly denied it. And he said it was not fair to attach weight to the chatter of a sick old man who was out of his mind. Still, suspicion was in the air, and there was much talk.

After a day or two it was reported that Mrs. Richards's delirious deliveries were getting to be duplicates of her husband's. Suspicion flamed up into conviction, now, and the town's pride in the purity of its one undiscredited important citizen began to dim down and flicker toward extinction.

Six days passed, then came more news. The old couple were dying. Richards's mind cleared in his latest hour, and he sent for Burgess. Burgess said:

"Let the room be cleared. I think he wishes to say something in privacy."

"No!" said Richards: "I want witnesses. I want you all to hear my confession, so that I may die a man, and not a dog. I was clean—artificially —like the rest; and like the rest I fell when temptation came. I signed a lie, and claimed the miserable sack. Mr. Burgess remembered that I had done him a service, and in gratitude (and ignorance) he suppressed my claim and saved me. You know the thing that was charged against Burgess years ago. My testimony, and mine alone, could have cleared him, and I was a coward, and left him to suffer disgrace—"

"No—no—Mr. Richards, you—"

"My servant betrayed my secret to him—"

"No one has betrayed anything to me—"

—"and then he did a natural and justifiable thing, he repented of the saving kindness which he had done me, and he *exposed* me—as I deserved—"

"Never!—I make oath—"

"Out of my heart I forgive him."

Burgess's impassioned protestations fell upon deaf ears; the dying man passed away without knowing that once more he had done poor Burgess a wrong. The old wife died that night.

The last of the sacred Nineteen had fallen a prey to the fiendish sack; the town was stripped of the last rag of its ancient glory. Its mourning was not showy, but it was deep.

By act of the Legislature—upon prayer and petition—Hadleyburg was allowed to change its name to (never mind what—I will not give it away), and leave one word out of the motto that for many generations had graced the town's official seal.

It is an honest town once more, and the man will have to rise early that catches it napping again.

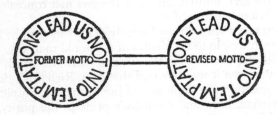

14

Marjorie Daw

BY THOMAS BAILEY ALDRICH

I

DR. DILLON TO EDWARD DELANEY, ESQ., AT THE PINES,
NEAR RYE, N. H.

August 8, 187–.

MY DEAR SIR: I am happy to assure you that your anxiety is without reason. Flemming will be confined to the sofa for three or four weeks, and will have to be careful at first how he uses his leg. A fracture of this kind is always a tedious affair. Fortunately, the bone was very skilfully set by the surgeon who chanced to be in the drug-store where Flemming was brought after his fall, and I apprehend no permanent inconvenience from the accident. *Flemming is doing perfectly well physically;* but I must confess that the irritable and morbid state of mind into which he has fallen causes me a great deal of uneasiness. He is the last man in the world who ought to break his leg. You know how impetuous our friend is ordinarily, what a soul of restlessness and energy, never content unless he is rushing at some object, like a sportive bull at a red shawl; but amiable withal. He is no longer amiable. His temper has become something frightful. Miss Fanny Flemming came up from Newport, where the family are staying for the summer, to nurse him; but he packed her off the next morning in tears. He has a complete set of Balzac's works, twenty-seven volumes, piled up near his sofa, to throw at Watkins whenever that exemplary serving-man appears with his meals. Yesterday I very innocently brought Flemming a small basket of lemons. You know it was a strip of lemon-peel on the curbstone that caused our friend's mischance. Well, he no sooner set his eyes upon these lemons than he fell into such a rage as I cannot adequately describe. This is only one of his moods, and the least distressing. At other times he sits with bowed head regarding his splintered limb, silent, sullen, despairing. When this fit is on him—and it sometimes lasts all day—nothing can distract his melancholy. He refuses to eat, does not even read the newspapers; books, except as projectiles for Watkins, have no charms for him. His state is truly pitiable.

Now, if he were a poor man, with a family depending on his daily labor, this irritability and despondency would be natural enough. But in a young fellow of twenty-four, with plenty of money and seemingly not a care in the world, the thing is monstrous. If he continues to give way to his vagaries in this manner, he will end by bringing on an inflammation of the fibula. It was the fibula he broke. I am at my wits' end to know what to prescribe for him. I have anæsthetics and lotions, to make people sleep and to soothe pain; but I've no medicine that will make a man have a little common sense. That is beyond my skill, but maybe it is not beyond yours. You are Flemming's intimate friend, his *fidus Achates*. Write to him, write to him frequently, distract his mind, cheer him up, and prevent him from becoming a confirmed case of melancholia. Perhaps he has some important plans disarranged by his present confinement. If he has you will know, and will know how to advise him judiciously. I trust your father finds the change beneficial? I am, my dear sir, with great respect, etc.

II

EDWARD DELANEY TO JOHN FLEMMING, WEST 38TH STREET, NEW YORK.

August 9, —.

MY DEAR JACK: I had a line from Dillon this morning, and was rejoiced to learn that your hurt is not so bad as reported. Like a certain personage, you are not so black and blue as you are painted. Dillon will put you on your pins again in two or three weeks, if you will only have patience and follow his counsels. Did you get my note of last Wednesday? I was greatly troubled when I heard of the accident.

I can imagine how tranquil and saintly you are with your leg in a trough! It is deuced awkward, to be sure, just as we had promised ourselves a glorious month together at the seaside; but we must make the best of it. It is unfortunate, too, that my father's health renders it impossible for me to leave him. I think he has much improved; the sea air is his native element; but he still needs my arm to lean upon in his walks, and requires someone more careful than a servant to look after him. I cannot come to you, dear Jack, but I have hours of unemployed time on hand, and I will write you a whole post-office full of letters if that will divert you. Heaven knows, I haven't anything to write about. It isn't as if we were living at one of the beach houses; then I could do you some character studies, and fill your imagination with groups of sea-goddesses, with their (or somebody else's) raven and blond manes hanging down their shoulders. You should have Aphrodite in morning wrapper, in evening costume, and in her prettiest bathing suit. But we are far from all that here. We have rooms in a farmhouse, on a crossroad, two miles from the hotels, and lead the quietest of lives.

I wish I were a novelist. This old house, with its sanded floors and high wainscots, and its narrow windows looking out upon a cluster of pines that turn themselves into Æolian-harps every time the wind blows, would be the place in which to write a summer romance. It should be a story with the odors of the forest and the breath of the sea in it. It should be a novel like one of that Russian fellow's,—what's his name?—Tourguénieff, Turguenef, Turgenif, Toorguniff, Turgénjew—nobody knows how to spell him. Yet I wonder if even a Liza or an Alexandra Paulovna could stir the heart of a man who has constant twinges in his leg. I wonder if one of our own Yankee girls of the best type, haughty and *spirituelle,* would be of any comfort to you in your present deplorable condition. If I thought so, I would hasten down to the Surf House and catch one for you; or, better still, I would find you one over the way.

Picture to yourself a large white house just across the road, nearly opposite our cottage. It is not a house, but a mansion, built, perhaps, in the colonial period, with rambling extensions, and gambrel roof, and a wide piazza on three sides—a self-possessed, high-bred piece of architecture, with its nose in the air. It stands back from the road, and has an obsequious retinue of fringed elms and oaks and weeping willows. Sometimes in the morning, and oftener in the afternoon, when the sun has withdrawn from that part of the mansion, a young woman appears on the piazza with some mysterious Penelope web of embroidery in her hand, or a book. There is a hammock over there—of pineapple fiber, it looks from here. A hammock is very becoming when one is eighteen, and has golden hair, and dark eyes, and an emerald-colored illusion dress looped up after the fashion of a Dresden china shepherdess, and is *chaussée* like a belle of the time of Louis Quatorze. All this splendor goes into that hammock, and sways there like a pond-lily in the golden afternoon. The window of my bedroom looks down on that piazza—and so do I.

But enough of this nonsense, which ill becomes a sedate young attorney taking his vacation with an invalid father. Drop me a line, dear Jack, and tell me how you really are. State your case. Write me a long, quiet letter. If you are violent or abusive, I'll take the law to you.

III

JOHN FLEMMING TO EDWARD DELANEY

August 11, —.

YOUR letter, dear Ned, was a godsend. Fancy what a fix I am in—I, who never had a day's sickness since I was born. My left leg weighs three tons. It is embalmed in spices and smothered in layers of fine linen, like a mummy. I can't move. I haven't moved for five thousand years. I'm of the time of Pharaoh.

I lie from morning till night on a lounge, staring into the hot street. Everybody is out of town enjoying himself. The brown-stone-front houses across the street resemble a row of particularly ugly coffins set up on end. A green mold is settling on the names of the deceased, carved on the silver door-plates. Sardonic spiders have sewed up the keyholes. All is silence and dust and desolation.—I interrupt this a moment, to take a shy at Watkins with the second volume of César Birotteau. Missed him! I think I could bring him down with a copy of Sainte-Beuve or the Dictionnaire Universel, if I had it. These small Balzac books somehow don't quite fit my hand; but I shall fetch him yet. I've an idea Watkins is tapping the old gentleman's Château Yquem. Duplicate key of the wine-cellar. Hibernian soirées in the front basement. Young Cheops upstairs, snug in his cerements. Watkins glides into my chamber, with that colorless, hypocritical face of his drawn out long like an accordion; but I know he grins all the way downstairs, and is glad I have broken my leg. Was not my evil star in the very zenith when I ran up to town to attend that dinner at Delmonico's? I didn't come up altogether for that. It was partly to buy Frank Livingstone's roan mare Margot. And now I shall not be able to sit in the saddle these two months. I'll send the mare down to you at The Pines—is that the name of the place?

Old Dillon fancies that I have something on my mind. He drives me wild with lemons. Lemons for a mind diseased! Nonsense. I am only as restless as the devil under this confinement—a thing I'm not used to. Take a man who has never had so much as a headache or a toothache in his life, strap one of his legs in a section of water-spout, keep him in a room in the city for weeks, with the hot weather turned on, and then expect him to smile and purr and be happy! It is preposterous. I can't be cheerful or calm.

Your letter is the first consoling thing I have had since my disaster, ten days ago. It really cheered me up for half an hour. Send me a screed, Ned, as often as you can, if you love me. Anything will do. Write me more about that little girl in the hammock. That was very pretty, all that about the Dresden china shepherdess and the pond-lily; the imagery a little mixed, perhaps, but very pretty. I didn't suppose you had so much sentimental furniture in your upper story. It shows how one may be familiar for years with the reception-room of his neighbor, and never suspect what is directly under his mansard. I supposed your loft stuffed with dry legal parchments, mortgages and affidavits; you take down a package of manuscript, and lo! there are lyrics and sonnets and can-zonettas. You really have a graphic descriptive touch, Edward Delaney, and I suspect you of anonymous love-tales in the magazines.

I shall be a bear until I hear from you again. Tell me all about your pretty *inconnue* across the road. What is her name? Who is she? Who's her father? Where's her mother? Who's her lover? You cannot imagine how this will occupy me. The more trifling the better. My imprisonment has weakened me intellectually to such a degree that I find your epistolary gifts quite considerable. I am passing into my second child-hood. In a week or two I shall take to India-rubber rings and prongs of coral. A silver cup, with an appropriate inscription, would be a delicate attention on your part. In the meantime, write!

IV

EDWARD DELANEY TO JOHN FLEMMING

August 12, —.

THE sick pasha shall be amused. *Bismillah!* He wills it so. If the story-teller becomes prolix and tedious—the bow-string and the sack, and two Nubians to drop him into the Piscataqua! But, truly, Jack, I have a hard task. There is literally nothing here—except the little girl over the way. She is swinging in the hammock at this moment. It is to me compensa-tion for many of the ills of life to see her now and then put out a small kid boot, which fits like a glove, and set herself going. Who is she, and what is her name? Her name is Daw. Only daughter of Mr. Richard W. Daw, ex-colonel and banker. Mother dead. One brother at Harvard, elder brother killed at the battle of Fair Oaks, nine years ago. Old, rich family, the Daws. This is the homestead, where father and daughter pass eight months of the twelve; the rest of the year in Baltimore and Wash-ington. The New England winter too many for the old gentleman. The daughter is called Marjorie—Marjorie Daw. Sounds odd at first, doesn't it? But after you say it over to yourself half a dozen times, you like it. There's a pleasing quaintness to it, something prim and violet-like. Must be a nice sort of girl to be called Marjorie Daw.

I had mine host of The Pines in the witness-box last night, and drew the foregoing testimony from him. He has charge of Mr. Daw's vegetable garden, and has known the family these thirty years. Of course I shall make the acquaintance of my neighbors before many days. It will be next to impossible for me not to meet Mr. Daw or Miss Daw in some of my walks. The young lady has a favorite path to the sea beach. I shall intercept her some morning, and touch my hat to her. Then the princess will bend her fair head to me with courteous surprise not unmixed with haughtiness. Will snub me, in fact. All this for thy sake, O Pasha of the Snapt Axle-tree! . . . How oddly things fall out! Ten minutes ago I was called down to the parlor—you know the kind of parlors in farmhouses on the coast, a sort of amphibious parlor, with seashells on the mantelpiece and spruce branches in the chimneyplace—where I found my father and Mr. Daw doing the antique polite to each other. He had come to pay his respects to his new neighbors. Mr. Daw is a tall, slim gentleman of about fifty-five, with a florid face and snow-white mustache and sidewhiskers. Looks like Mr. Dombey, or as Mr. Dombey would have looked if he had served a few years in the British Army Mr. Daw was a colonel in the late war, commanding the regiment in which his son was a lieutenant. Plucky old boy, backbone of New Hampshire granite. Before taking his leave, the colonel delivered himself of an invitation as if he were issuing a general order. Miss Daw has a few friends coming, at 4 P. M., to play croquet on the lawn (parade-ground) and have tea (cold rations) on the piazza. Will we honor them with our company? (or be sent to the guardhouse.) My father declines on the plea of ill-health. My father's son bows with as much suavity as he knows, and accepts.

In my next I shall have something to tell you. I shall have seen the little beauty face to face. I have a presentiment, Jack, that this Daw is a *rara avis!* Keep up your spirits, my boy, until I write you another letter— and send me along word how's your leg.

V

EDWARD DELANEY TO JOHN FLEMMING

August 13, —.

The party, my dear Jack, was as dreary as possible. A lieutenant of the navy, the rector of the Episcopal church at Stillwater, and a society swell from Nahant. The lieutenant looked as if he had swallowed a couple of his buttons, and found the bullion rather indigestible; the rector was a pensive youth, of the daffydowndilly sort; and the swell from Nahant was a very weak tidal wave indeed. The women were much better, as they always are; the two Miss Kingsburys of Philadelphia, staying at the Sea-shell House, two bright and engaging girls. But Marjorie Daw!

The company broke up soon after tea, and I remained to smoke a cigar with the colonel on the piazza. It was like seeing a picture to see Miss Marjorie hovering around the old soldier, and doing a hundred gracious little things for him. She brought the cigars and lighted the tapers with her own delicate fingers, in the most enchanting fashion. As we sat there, she came and went in the summer twilight, and seemed, with her white dress and pale gold hair, like some lovely phantom that had sprung into existence out of the smoke-wreaths. If she had melted into air, like the statue of Galatea in the play, I should have been more sorry than surprised.

It was easy to perceive that the old colonel worshipped her, and she him. I think the relation between an elderly father and a daughter just blooming into womanhood the most beautiful possible. There is in it a subtle sentiment that cannot exist in the case of mother and daughter, or that of son and mother. But this is getting into deep water.

I sat with the Daws until half past ten, and saw the moon rise on the sea. The ocean, that had stretched motionless and black against the horizon, was changed by magic into a broken field of glittering ice, interspersed with marvelous silvery fjords. In the far distance the Isles of Shoals loomed up like a group of huge bergs drifting down on us. The Polar regions in a June thaw! It was exceedingly fine. What did we talk about? We talked about the weather—and *you!* The weather has been disagreeable for several days past—and so have you. I glided from one topic to the other very naturally. I told my friends of your accident; how it had frustrated all our summer plans, and what our plans were. I played quite a spirited solo on the fibula. Then I described you; or, rather, I didn't. I spoke of your amiability, of your patience under this severe affliction; of your touching gratitude when Dillon brings you little presents of fruit; of your tenderness to your sister Fanny, whom you would not allow to stay in town to nurse you, and how you heroically sent her back to Newport, preferring to remain alone with Mary, the cook, and your man Watkins, to whom, by the way, you were devotedly attached. If you had been there, Jack, you wouldn't have known yourself. I should have excelled as a criminal lawyer, if I had not turned my attention to a different branch of jurisprudence.

Miss Marjorie asked all manner of leading questions concerning you. It did not occur to me then, but it struck me forcibly afterwards, that she evinced a singular interest in the conversation. When I got back to my room, I recalled how eagerly she leaned forward, with her full, snowy throat in strong moonlight, listening to what I said. Positively, I think I made her like you!

Miss Daw is a girl whom you would like immensely, I can tell you that. A beauty without affectation, a high and tender nature—if one can read the soul in the face. And the old colonel is a noble character, too.

I am glad the Daws are such pleasant people. The Pines is an isolated spot, and my resources are few. I fear I should have found life here somewhat monotonous before long. with no other society than that of my excellent sire. It is true, I might have made a target of the defenseless invalid; but I haven't a taste for artillery, *moi*.

VI

JOHN FLEMMING TO EDWARD DELANEY

August 17, —.

For a man who hasn't a taste for artillery, it occurs to me, my friend, you are keeping up a pretty lively fire on my inner works. But go on. Cynicism is a small brass field-piece that eventually bursts and kills the artilleryman.

You may abuse me as much as you like, and I'll not complain; for I don't know what I should do without your letters. They are curing me. I haven't hurled anything at Watkins since last Sunday, partly because I have grown more amiable under your teaching, and partly because Watkins captured my ammunition one night, and carried it off to the library. He is rapidly losing the habit he had acquired of dodging whenever I rub my ear, or make any slight motion with my right arm. He is still suggestive of the wine-cellar, however. You may break, you may shatter Watkins, if you will, but the scent of the Roederer will hang round him still.

Ned, that Miss Daw must be a charming person. I should certainly like her. I like her already. When you spoke in your first letter of seeing a young girl swinging in a hammock under your chamber window, I was somehow strangely drawn to her. I cannot account for it in the least. What you have subsequently written of Miss Daw has strengthened the impression. You seem to be describing a woman I have known in some previous state of existence, or dreamed of in this. Upon my word, if you were to send me her photograph, I believe I should recognize her at a glance. Her manner, that listening attitude, her traits of character, as you indicate them, the light hair and the dark eyes—they are all familiar things to me. Asked a lot of questions, did she? Curious about me? That is strange.

You would laugh in your sleeve, you wretched old cynic, if you knew how I lie awake nights, with my gas turned down to a star, thinking of The Pines and the house across the road. How cool it must be down there! I long for the salt smell in the air. I picture the colonel smoking his cheroot on the piazza. I send you and Miss Daw off on afternoon rambles along the beach. Sometimes I let you stroll with her under the elms in the moonlight, for you are great friends by this time, I take it, and see each other every day. I know your ways and your manners! Then I fall into a truculent mood, and would like to destroy somebody. Have you noticed anything in the shape of a lover hanging around the colonial

Lares and Penates? Does that lieutenant of the horse marines or that young Stillwater parson visit the house much? Not that I am pining for news of them, but any gossip of the kind would be in order. I wonder, Ned, you don't fall in love with Miss Daw. I am ripe to do it myself. Speaking of photographs, couldn't you manage to slip one of her *cartes-de-visite* from her album—she must have an album, you know—and send it to me? I will return it before it could be missed. That's a good fellow! Did the mare arrive safe and sound? It will be a capital animal this autumn for Central Park.

O—my leg? I forgot about my leg. It's better.

VII

EDWARD DELANEY TO JOHN FLEMMING

August 20, —.

You are correct in your surmises. I am on the most friendly terms with our neighbors. The colonel and my father smoke their afternoon cigar together in our sitting-room or on the piazza opposite, and I pass an hour or two of the day or the evening with the daughter. I am more and more struck by the beauty, modesty, and intelligence of Miss Daw.

You ask me why I do not fall in love with her. I will be frank, Jack: I have thought of that. She is young, rich, accomplished, uniting in herself more attractions, mental and personal, than I can recall in any girl of my acquaintance; but she lacks the something that would be necessary to inspire in me that kind of interest. Possessing this unknown quantity, a woman neither beautiful nor wealthy nor very young could bring me to her feet. But not Miss Daw. If we were shipwrecked together on an uninhabited island—let me suggest a tropical island, for it costs no more to be picturesque—I would build her a bamboo hut, I would fetch her breadfruit and cocoanuts, I would fry yams for her, I would lure the ingenuous turtle and make her nourishing soups, but I wouldn't make love to her—not under eighteen months. I would like to have her for a sister, that I might shield her and counsel her, and spend half my income on thread-laces and camel's-hair shawls. (We are off the island now.) If such were not my feeling, there would still be an obstacle to my loving Miss Daw. A greater misfortune could scarcely befall me than to love her. Flemming, I am about to make a revelation that will astonish you. I may be all wrong in my premises and consequently in my conclusions; but you shall judge.

That night when I returned to my room after the croquet party at the Daws', and was thinking over the trivial events of the evening, I was suddenly impressed by the air of eager attention with which Miss Daw had followed my account of your accident. I think I mentioned this to

you. Well, the next morning, as I went to mail my letter, I overtook Miss
Daw on the road to Rye, where the post-office is, and accompanied her
thither and back, an hour's walk. The conversation again turned on you,
and again I remarked that inexplicable look of interest which had lighted
up her face the previous evening. Since then, I have seen Miss Daw perhaps ten times, perhaps oftener, and on each occasion I found that when I
was not speaking of you or your sister, or some person or place associated
with you, I was not holding her attention. She would be absent-minded,
her eyes would wander away from me to the sea, or to some distant object
in the landscape; her fingers would play with the leaves of a book in a
way that convinced me she was not listening. At these moments if I
abruptly changed the theme—I did it several times as an experiment—
and dropped some remark about my friend Flemming, then the somber
blue eyes would come back to me instantly.

Now, is not this the oddest thing in the world? No, not the oddest.
The effect which you tell me was produced on you by my casual mention
of an unknown girl swinging in a hammock is certainly as strange. You
can conjecture how that passage in your letter of Friday startled me. Is
it possible, then, that two people who have never met, and who are
hundreds of miles apart, can exert a magnetic influence on each other?
I have read of such psychological phenomena, but never credited them.
I leave the solution of the problem to you. As for myself, all other things
being favorable, it would be impossible for me to fall in love with a
woman who listens to me only when I am talking of my friend!

I am not aware that any one is paying marked attention to my fair
neighbor. The lieutenant of the navy—he is stationed at Rivermouth—
sometimes drops in of an evening, and sometimes the rector from Stillwater; the lieutenant the oftener. He was there last night. I would not
be surprised if he had an eye to the heiress; but he is not formidable.
Mistress Daw carries a neat little spear of irony, and the honest lieutenant seems to have a particular facility for impaling himself on the
point of it. He is not dangerous, I should say; though I have known a
woman to satirize a man for years, and marry him after all. Decidedly,
the lowly rector is not dangerous; yet, again, who has not seen Cloth of
Frieze victorious in the lists where Cloth of Gold went down?

As to the photograph. There is an exquisite ivorytype of Marjorie, in
passe-partout, on the drawing-room mantelpiece. It would be missed at
once, if taken. I would do anything reasonable for you, Jack; but I've no
burning desire to be hauled up before the local justice of the peace, on a
charge of petty larceny.

P. S.—Enclosed is a spray of mignonette, which i advise you to treat
tenderly. Yes, we talked of you again last night, as usual. It is becoming
a little dreary for me.

VIII

EDWARD DELANEY TO JOHN FLEMMING

August 22, —.

YOUR letter in reply to my last has occupied my thoughts all the morning. I do not know what to think. Do you mean to say that you are seriously half in love with a woman whom you have never seen—with a shadow, a chimera? for what else can Miss Daw be to you? I do not understand it at all. I understand neither you nor her. You are a couple of ethereal beings moving in finer air than I can breathe with my commonplace lungs. Such delicacy of sentiment is something I admire without comprehending. I am bewildered. I am of the earth earthy, and I find myself in the incongruous position of having to do with mere souls, with natures so finely tempered that I run some risk of shattering them in my awkwardness. I am as Caliban among the spirits!

Reflecting on your letter, I am not sure it is wise in me to continue this correspondence. But no, Jack; I do wrong to doubt the good sense that forms the basis of your character. You are deeply interested in Miss Daw; you feel that she is a person whom you may perhaps greatly admire when you know her: at the same time you bear in mind that the chances are ten to five that, when you do come to know her, she will fall far short of your ideal, and you will not care for her in the least. Look at it in this sensible light, and I will hold back nothing from you.

Yesterday afternoon my father and myself rode over to Rivermouth with the Daws. A heavy rain in the morning had cooled the atmosphere and laid the dust. To Rivermouth is a drive of eight miles, along a winding road lined all the way with wild barberry-bushes. I never saw anything more brilliant than these bushes, the green of the foliage and the pink of the coral berries intensified by the rain. The colonel drove, with my father in front, Miss Daw and I on the back seat. I resolved that for the first five miles your name should not pass my lips. I was amused by the artful attempts she made, at the start, to break through my reticence. Then a silence fell upon her; and then she became suddenly gay. That keenness which I enjoyed so much when it was exercised on the lieutenant was not so satisfactory directed against myself. Miss Daw has great sweetness of disposition, but she can be disagreeable. She is like the young lady in the rhyme, with the curl on her forehead,

> "When she is good,
> She is very, very good,
> And when she is bad, she is horrid!"

I kept to my resolution, however; but on the return home I relented, and talked of your mare! Miss Daw is going to try a side-saddle on Margot some morning. The animal is a trifle too light for my weight. By the by, I nearly forgot to say Miss Daw sat for a picture yesterday to a River-mouth artist. If the negative turns out well, I am to have a copy. So our ends will be accomplished without crime. I wish, though, I could send you the ivorytype in the drawing-room; it is cleverly colored, and would give you an idea of her hair and eyes, which of course the other will not.

No, Jack, the spray of mignonette did not come from me. A man of twenty-eight doesn't enclose flowers in his letters—to another man. But don't attach too much significance to the circumstance. She gives sprays of mignonette to the rector, sprays to the lieutenant. She has even given a rose from her bosom to your slave. It is her jocund nature to scatter flowers, like Spring.

If my letters sometimes read disjointedly, you must understand that I never finish one at a sitting, but write at intervals, when the mood is on me.

The mood is not on me now.

IX

EDWARD DELANEY TO JOHN FLEMMING

August 23, —.

I HAVE just returned from the strangest interview with Marjorie. She has all but confessed to me her interest in you. But with what modesty and dignity! Her words elude my pen as I attempt to put them on paper; and, indeed, it was not so much what she said as her manner; and that I cannot reproduce. Perhaps it was of a piece with the strangeness of this whole business. That she should tacitly acknowledge to a third party the love she feels for a man she has never beheld! But I have lost, through your aid, the faculty of being surprised. I accept things as people do in dreams. Now that I am again in my room, it all appears like an illusion—the black masses of Rembrandtish shadow under the trees, the fireflies whirling in Pyrrhic dances among the shrubbery, the sea over there, Marjorie sitting on the hammock!

It is past midnight, and I am too sleepy to write more.

Thursday Morning.

My father has suddenly taken it into his head to spend a few days at the Shoals. In the meanwhile you will not hear from me. I see Marjorie walking in the garden with the colonel. I wish I could speak to her alone, but shall probably not have an opportunity before we leave.

X

EDWARD DELANEY TO JOHN FLEMMING

August 28, —.

You were passing into your second childhood, were you? Your intellect was so reduced that my epistolary gifts seemed quite considerable to you, did they? I rise superior to the sarcasm in your favor of the 11th instant, when I notice that five days' silence on my part is sufficient to throw you into the depths of despondency.

We returned only this morning from Appledore, that enchanted island —at four dollars per day. I find on my desk three letters from you! Evidently there is no lingering doubt in *your* mind as to the pleasure I derive from your correspondence. These letters are undated, but in what I take to be the latest are two passages that require my consideration. You will pardon my candor, dear Flemming, but the conviction forces itself upon me that as your leg grows stronger your head becomes weaker. You ask my advice on a certain point. I will give it. In my opinion you could do nothing more unwise than to address a note to Miss Daw, thanking her for the flower. It would, I am sure, offend her delicacy beyond pardon. She knows you only through me; you are to her an abstraction, a figure in a dream—a dream from which the faintest shock would awaken her. Of course, if you enclose a note to me and insist on its delivery, I shall deliver it; but I advise you not to do so.

You say you are able, with the aid of a cane, to walk about your chamber, and that you purpose to come to The Pines the instant Dillon thinks you strong enough to stand the journey. Again I advise you not to. Do you not see that, every hour you remain away, Marjorie's glamor deepens, and your influence over her increases? You will ruin everything by precipitancy. Wait until you are entirely recovered; in any case, do not come without giving me warning. I fear the effect of your abrupt advent here—under the circumstances.

Miss Daw was evidently glad to see us back again, and gave me both hands in the frankest way. She stopped at the door a moment, this afternoon, in the carriage; she had been over to Rivermouth for her pictures. Unluckily the photographer had spilt some acid on the plate, and she was obliged to give him another sitting. I have an intuition that something is troubling Marjorie. She had an abstracted air not usual with her. However, it may be only my fancy. . . . I end this, leaving several things unsaid, to accompany my father on one of those long walks which are now his chief medicine—and mine!

XI

EDWARD DELANEY TO JOHN FLEMMING

August 29, —.

I WRITE in great haste to tell you what has taken place here since my letter of last night. I am in the utmost perplexity. Only one thing is plain—*you* must not dream of coming to The Pines. Marjorie has told her father everything! I saw her for a few minutes, an hour ago, in the garden; and, as near as I could gather from her confused statement, the facts are these: Lieutenant Bradly—that's the naval officer stationed at Rivermouth—has been paying court to Miss Daw for some time past, but not so much to her liking as to that of the colonel, who it seems is an old friend of the young gentleman's father. Yesterday (I knew she was in some trouble when she drove up to our gate) the colonel spoke to Marjorie of Bradly—urged his suit, I infer. Marjorie expressed her dislike for the lieutenant with characteristic frankness, and finally confessed to her father—well, I really do not know what she confessed. It must have been the vaguest of confessions, and must have sufficiently puzzled the colonel. At any rate, it exasperated him. I suppose I am implicated in the matter, and that the colonel feels bitterly toward me. I do not see why: I have carried no messages between you and Miss Daw; I have behaved with the greatest discretion. I can find no flaw anywhere in my proceeding. I do not see that anybody has done anything—except the colonel himself.

It is probable, nevertheless, that the friendly relations between the two houses will be broken off. "A plague o' both your houses," say you. I will keep you informed, as well as I can, of what occurs over the way. We shall remain here until the second week in September. Stay where you are, or, at all events, do not dream of joining me. . . . Colonel Daw is sitting on the piazza looking rather wicked. I have not seen Marjorie since I parted with her in the garden.

XII

EDWARD DELANEY TO THOMAS DILLON, M. D.,
MADISON SQUARE, NEW YORK.

August 30, —.

MY DEAR DOCTOR: If you have any influence over Flemming, I beg of you to exert it to prevent his coming to this place at present. There are circumstances, which I will explain to you before long, that make it of the first importance that he should not come into this neighborhood. His appearance here, I speak advisedly, would be disastrous to him. In urging him to remain in New York, or to go to some inland resort, you will be doing him and me a real service. Of course you will not mention my name in this connection. You know me well enough, my dear doctor, to be assured that, in begging your secret co-operation, I have reasons that will meet your entire approval when they are made plain to you. We shall return to town on the 15th of next month, and my first duty will be to present myself at your hospitable door and satisfy your curiosity, if I have excited it. My father, I am glad to state, has so greatly improved that he can no longer be regarded as an invalid. With great esteem, I am, etc., etc.

XIII

EDWARD DELANEY TO JOHN FLEMMING

August 31, —.

YOUR letter, announcing your mad determination to come here, has just reached me. I beseech you to reflect a moment. The step would be fatal to your interests and hers. You would furnish just cause for irritation to R. W. D.; and, though he loves Marjorie tenderly, he is capable of going to any lengths if opposed. You would not like, I am convinced, to be the means of causing him to treat *her* with severity. That would be the result of your presence at The Pines at this juncture. I am annoyed to be obliged to point out these things to you. We are on very delicate ground, Jack; the situation is critical, and the slightest mistake in a move would cost us the game. If you consider it worth the winning, be patient. Trust a little to my sagacity. Wait and see what happens. Moreover, I understand from Dillon that you are in no condition to take so long a journey. He thinks the air of the coast would be the worst thing possible for you; that you ought to go inland, if anywhere. Be advised by me. Be advised by Dillon.

XIV

TELEGRAMS

September 1, —.

1.—TO EDWARD DELANEY

Letter received. Dillon be hanged. I think I ought to be on the ground.

J. F.

2.—TO JOHN FLEMMING

Stay where you are. You would only complicate matters. Do not move until you hear from me.

E. D.

3.—TO EDWARD DELANEY

My being at The Pines could be kept secret. I must see her.

J. F.

4.— TO JOHN FLEMMING

Do not think of it. It would be useless. R. W. D. has locked M. in her room. You would not be able to effect an interview.

E. D.

5.—TO EDWARD DELANEY

Locked her in her room. Good God. That settles the question. I shall leave by the twelve-fifteen express.

J. F.

XV

THE ARRIVAL

ON THE second of September, 187—, as the down express due at 3.40 left the station at Hampton, a young man, leaning on the shoulder of a servant, whom he addressed as Watkins, stepped from the platform into a hack, and requested to be driven to "The Pines." On arriving at the gate of a modest farmhouse, a few miles from the station, the young man descended with difficulty from the carriage, and, casting a hasty glance across the road, seemed much impressed by some peculiarity in the landscape. Again leaning on the shoulder of the person Watkins, he walked to the door of the farmhouse and inquired for Mr. Edward Delaney. He was informed by the aged man who answered his knock, that Mr. Edward Delaney had gone to Boston the day before, but that Mr. Jonas Delaney was within. This information did not appear satisfactory to the stranger, who inquired if Mr. Edward Delaney had left any message for Mr. John Flemming. There *was* a letter for Mr. Flemming, if he were that person. After a brief absence the aged man reappeared with a letter.

XVI

EDWARD DELANEY TO JOHN FLEMMING

September 1, —.

I AM horror-stricken at what I have done! When I began this correspondence I had no other purpose than to relieve the tedium of your sickchamber. Dillon told me to cheer you up. I tried to. I thought you entered into the spirit of the thing. I had no idea, until within a few days, that you were taking matters *au sérieux.*

What can I say? I am in sackcloth and ashes. I am a pariah, a dog of an outcast. I tried to make a little romance to interest you, something soothing and idyllic, and, by Jove! I have done it only too well! My father doesn't know a word of this, so don't jar the old gentleman any more than you can help. I fly from the wrath to come—when you arrive! For O, dear Jack, there isn't any colonial mansion on the other side of the road, there isn't any piazza, there isn't any hammock—there isn't any Marjorie Daw!!

Editha

BY WILLIAM DEAN HOWELLS

T HE air was thick with the war feeling, like the electricity of a storm which has not yet burst. Editha sat looking out into the hot spring afternoon, with her lips parted, and panting with the intensity of the question whether she could let him go. She had decided that she could not let him stay, when she saw him at the end of the still leafless avenue, making slowly up towards the house, with his head down and his figure relaxed. She ran impatiently out on the veranda, to the edge of the steps, and imperatively demanded greater haste of him with her will before she called aloud to him: "George!"

He had quickened his pace in mystical response to her mystical urgence, before he could have heard her; now he looked up and answered, "Well?"

"Oh, how united we are!" she exulted, and then she swooped down the steps to him. "What is it?" she cried.

"It's war," he said, and he pulled her up to him and kissed her.

She kissed him back intensely, but irrelevantly, as to their passion, and uttered from deep in her throat, "How glorious!"

"It's war," he repeated, without consenting to her sense of it; and she did not know just what to think at first. She never knew what to think of him; that made his mystery, his charm. All through their courtship, which was contemporaneous with the growth of the war feeling, she had been puzzled by his want of seriousness about it. He seemed to despise it even more than he abhorred it. She could have understood his abhorring any sort of bloodshed; that would have been a survival of his old life when he thought he would be a minister, and before he changed and took up the law. But making light of a cause so high and noble seemed to show a want of earnestness at the core of his being. Not but that she felt herself able to cope with a congenital defect of that sort, and make his love for her save him from himself. Now perhaps the miracle was already wrought in him. In the presence of the tremendous fact that he announced, all triviality seemed to have gone out of him; she began to feel that. He sank down on the top step, and wiped his forehead with his handkerchief, while she poured out upon him her question of the origin and authenticity of his news.

All the while, in her duplex emotioning, she was aware that now at the very beginning she must put a guard upon herself against urging him, by any word or act, to take the part that her whole soul willed him to take, for the completion of her ideal of him. He was very nearly perfect as he was, and he must be allowed to perfect himself. But he was peculiar, and he might very well be reasoned out of his peculiarity. Before her reasoning went her emotioning: her nature pulling upon his nature, her womanhood upon his manhood, without her knowing the means she was using to the end she was willing. She had always supposed that the man who won her would have done something to win her; she did not know what, but something. George Gearson had simply asked her for her love, on the way home from a concert, and she gave her love to him, without, as it were, thinking. But now, it flashed upon her, if he could do something worthy to *have* won her—be a hero, *her* hero—it would be even better than if he had done it before asking her; it would be grander. Besides, she had believed in the war from the beginning.

"But don't you see, dearest," she said, "that it wouldn't have come to this if it hadn't been in the order of Providence? And I call any war glorious that is for the liberation of people who have been struggling for years against the cruelest oppression. Don't you think so, too?"

"I suppose so," he returned, languidly. "But war! Is it glorious to break the peace of the world?"

"That ignoble peace! It was no peace at all, with that crime and shame at our very gates." She was conscious of parroting the current phrases of the newspapers, but it was no time to pick and choose her words. She must sacrifice anything to the high ideal she had for him, and after a good deal of rapid argument she ended with the climax: "But now it doesn't matter about the how or why. Since the war has come, all that is gone. There are no two sides any more. There is nothing now but our country."

He sat with his eyes closed and his head leant back against the veranda, and he remarked, with a vague smile, as if musing aloud, "Our country —right or wrong."

"Yes, right or wrong!" she returned, fervidly. "I'll go and get you some lemonade." She rose rustling, and whisked away; when she came back with two tall glasses of clouded liquid on a tray, and the ice clucking in them, he still sat as she had left him, and she said, as if there had been no interruption: "But there is no question of wrong in this case. I call it a sacred war. A war for liberty and humanity, if ever there was one. And I know you will see it just as I do, yet."

He took half the lemonade at a gulp, and he answered as he set the glass down: "I know you always have the highest ideal. When I differ from you I ought to doubt myself."

A generous sob rose in Editha's throat for the humility of a man, so very nearly perfect, who was willing to put himself below her.

Besides, she felt, more subliminally, that he was never so near slipping through her fingers as when he took that meek way.

"You shall not say that! Only, for once I happen to be right." She seized his hand in her two hands, and poured her soul from her eyes into his. "Don't you think so?" she entreated him.

He released his hand and drank the rest of his lemonade, and she added, "Have mine, too," but he shook his head in answering, "I've no business to think so, unless I act so, too."

Her heart stopped a beat before it pulsed on with leaps that she felt in her neck. She had noticed that strange thing in men: they seemed to feel bound to do what they believed, and not think a thing was finished when they said it, as girls did. She knew what was in his mind, but she pretended not, and she said, "Oh, I am not sure," and then faltered.

He went on as if to himself, without apparently heeding her: "There's only one way of proving one's faith in a thing like this."

She could not say that she understood, but she did understand.

He went on again. "If I believed—if I felt as you do about the war— Do you wish me to feel as you do?"

Now she was really not sure; so she said: "George, I don't know what you mean."

He seemed to muse away from her as before. "There is a sort of fascination in it. I suppose that at the bottom of his heart every man would like at times to have his courage tested, to see how he would act."

"How can you talk in that ghastly way?"

"It *is* rather morbid. Still, that's what it comes to, unless you're swept away by ambition or driven by conviction. I haven't the conviction or the ambition, and the other thing is what it comes to with me. I ought to have been a preacher, after all; then I couldn't have asked it of myself, as I must, now I'm a lawyer. And you believe it's a holy war, Editha?" he suddenly addressed her. "Oh, I know you do! But you wish me to believe so, too?"

She hardly knew whether he was mocking or not, in the ironical way he always had with her plainer mind. But the only thing was to be outspoken with him.

"George, I wish you to believe whatever you think is true, at any and every cost. If I've tried to talk you into anything, I take it all back."

"Oh, I know that, Editha. I know how sincere you are, and how—I wish I had your undoubting spirit! I'll think it over; I'd like to believe as you do. But I don't, now; I don't, indeed. It isn't this war alone; though this seems peculiarly wanton and needless; but it's every war—so stupid; it makes me sick. Why shouldn't this thing have been settled reasonably?"

"Because," she said, very throatily again, "God meant it to be war."

"You think it was God? Yes, I suppose that is what people will say."

"Do you suppose it would have been war if God hadn't meant it?"

"I don't know. Sometimes it seems as if God had put this world into men's keeping to work it as they pleased."

"Now, George, that is blasphemy."

"Well, I won't blaspheme. I'll try to believe in your pocket Providence," he said, and then he rose to go.

"Why don't you stay to dinner?" Dinner at Balcom's Works was at one o'clock.

"I'll come back to supper, if you'll let me. Perhaps I shall bring you a convert."

"Well, you may come back, on that condition."

"All right. If I don't come, you'll understand."

He went away without kissing her, and she felt it a suspension of their engagement. It all interested her intensely; she was undergoing a tremendous experience, and she was being equal to it. While she stood looking after him, her mother came out through one of the long windows onto the veranda, with a catlike softness and vagueness.

"Why didn't he stay to dinner?"

"Because—because—war has been declared," Editha pronounced, without turning.

Her mother said, "Oh, my!" and then said nothing more until she had sat down in one of the large Shaker chairs and rocked herself for some time. Then she closed whatever tacit passage of thought there had been in her mind with the spoken words: "Well, I hope *he* won't go."

"And *I* hope he *will*," the girl said, and confronted her mother with a stormy exaltation that would have frightened any creature less unimpressionable than a cat.

Her mother rocked herself again for an interval of cogitation. What she arrived at in speech was: "Well, I guess you've done a wicked thing, Editha Balcom."

The girl said, as she passed indoors through the same window her mother had come out by: "I haven't done anything—yet."

In her room, she put together all her letters and gifts from Gearson, down to the withered petals of the first flower he had offered, with that timidity of his veiled in that irony of his. In the heart of the packet she enshrined her engagement ring which she had restored to the pretty box 'ie had brought it her in. Then she sat down, if not calmly yet strongly, and wrote:

"George:—I understood when you left me. But I think we had better emphasize your meaning that if we cannot be one in everything we had better be one in nothing. So I am sending these things for your keeping till you have made up your mind.

"I shall always love you, and therefore I shall never marry anyone else. But the man I marry must love his country first of all, and be able to say to me,

> "'I could not love thee, dear, so much,
> Loved I not honor more.'

"There is no honor above America with me. In this great hour there is no other honor.

"Your heart will make my words clear to you. I had never expected to say so much, but it has come upon me that I must say the utmost.
Editha."

She thought she had worded her letter well, worded it in a way that could not be bettered; all had been implied and nothing expressed.

She had it ready to send with the packet she had tied with red, white, and blue ribbon, when it occurred to her that she was not just to him, that she was not giving him a fair chance. He said he would go and think it over, and she was not waiting. She was pushing, threatening, compelling. That was not a woman's part. She must leave him free, free, free. She could not accept for her country or herself a forced sacrifice.

In writing her letter she had satisfied the impulse from which it sprang; she could well afford to wait till he had thought it over. She put the packet and the letter by, and rested serene in the consciousness of having done what was laid upon her by her love itself to do, and yet used patience, mercy, justice.

She had her reward. Gearson did not come to tea, but she had given him till morning, when, late at night there came up from the village the sound of a fife and drum, with a tumult of voices, in shouting, singing, and laughing. The noise drew nearer and nearer; it reached the street end of the avenue; there it silenced itself, and one voice, the voice she knew best, rose over the silence. It fell; the air was filled with cheers; the fife and drum struck up, with the shouting, singing, and laughing again, but now retreating; and a single figure came hurrying up the avenue.

She ran down to meet her lover and clung to him. He was very gay, and he put his arm round her with a boisterous laugh. "Well, you must call me Captain now; or Cap, if you prefer; that's what the boys call me. Yes, we've had a meeting at the town hall, and everybody has volunteered; and they selected me for captain, and I'm going to the war, the big war, the glorious war, the holy war ordained by the pocket Providence that blesses butchery. Come along: let's tell the whole family about it. Call them from their downy beds, father, mother, Aunt Hitty, and all the folks!"

But when they mounted the veranda steps he did not wait for a larger audience; he poured the story out upon Editha alone.

"There was a lot of speaking, and then some of the fools set up a shout for me. It was all going one way, and I thought it would be a good joke to sprinkle a little cold water on them. But you can't do that with a crowd that adores you. The first thing I knew I was sprinkling hell-fire on them. 'Cry havoc, and let slip the dogs of war.' That was the style. Now that it had come to the fight, there were no two parties; there was one country, and the thing was to fight to a finish as quick as possible. I suggested volunteering then and there, and I wrote my name first of all on the roster. Then they elected me—that's all. I wish I had some ice-water."

She left him walking up and down the veranda, while she ran for the ice-pitcher and a goblet, and when she came back he was still walking up and down, shouting the story he had told her to her father and mother, who had come out more sketchily dressed than they commonly were by day. He drank goblet after goblet of the ice-water without noticing who was giving it, and kept on talking, and laughing through his talk wildly. "It's astonishing," he said, "how well the worse reason looks when you try to make it appear the better. Why, I believe I was the first convert to the war in that crowd tonight! I never thought I should like to kill a man; but now I shouldn't care; and the smokeless powder lets you see the man drop that you kill. It's all for the country! What a thing it is to have a country that *can't* be wrong, but if it is, is right, anyway."

Editha had a great, vital thought, an inspiration. She set down the ice-pitcher on the veranda floor, and ran upstairs and got the letter she had written him. When at last he noisily bade her father and mother, "Well, good-night. I forgot I woke you up: I shan't want any sleep myself," she followed him down the avenue to the gate. There, after the whirling words that seemed to fly away from her thoughts and refuse to serve them, she made a last effort to solemnize the moment that seemed so crazy, and pressed the letter she had written upon him.

"What's this?" he said. "Want me to mail it?"

"No, no. It's for you. I wrote it after you went this morning. Keep it— keep it—and read it sometime—" She thought, and then her inspiration came: "Read it if ever you doubt what you've done, or fear that I regret your having done it. Read it after you've started."

They strained each other in embraces that seemed as ineffective as their words, and he kissed her face with quick, hot breaths that were so unlike him, that made her feel as if she had lost her old lover and found a stranger in his place. The stranger said: "What a gorgeous flower you are, with your red hair, and your blue eyes that look black now, and your face with the color painted out by the white moonshine! Let me hold you under the chin, to see whether I love blood, you tiger-lily!" Then he laughed Gearson's laugh, and released her, scared and giddy. Within her wilfulness she had been frightened by a sense of subtler force in him, and mystically mastered as she had never been before.

She ran all the way back to the house, and mounted the steps panting. Her mother and father were talking of the great affair. Her mother said: "Wa'n't Mr. Gearson in rather of an excited state of mind? Didn't you think he acted curious?"

"Well, not for a man who'd just been elected captain and had set 'em up for the whole of Company A," her father chuckled back.

"What in the world do you mean, Mr. Balcom? Oh! There's Editha!" She offered to follow the girl indoors.

"Don't come, mother!" Editha called, vanishing.

Mrs. Balcom remained to reproach her husband. "I don't see much of anything to laugh at."

"Well, it's catching. Caught it from Gearson. I guess it won't be much of a war, and I guess Gearson don't think so, either. The other fellows will back down as soon as they see we mean it. I wouldn't lose any sleep over it. I'm going back to bed, myself."

Gearson came again next afternoon, looking pale and rather sick, but quite himself, even to his languid irony. "I guess I'd better tell you, Editha, that I consecrated myself to your god of battles last night by pouring too many libations to him down my own throat. But I'm all right now. One has to carry off the excitement, somehow."

"Promise me," she commanded, "that you'll never touch it again!"

"What! Not let the cannikin clink? Not let the soldier drink? Well, I promise."

"You don't belong to yourself now; you don't even belong to *me*.

You belong to your country, and you have a sacred charge to keep yourself strong and well for your country's sake. I have been thinking, thinking all night and all day long."

"You look as if you had been crying a little, too," he said, with his queer smile.

"That's all past. I've been thinking, and worshipping *you*. Don't you suppose I know all that you've been through, to come to this? I've followed you every step from your old theories and opinions."

"Well, you've had a long row to hoe."

"And I know you've done this from the highest motives—"

"Oh, there won't be much pettifogging to do till this cruel war is—"

"And you haven't simply done it for my sake. I couldn't respect you if you had."

"Well, then we'll say I haven't. A man that hasn't got his own respect intact wants the respect of all the other people he can corner. But we won't go into that. I'm in for the thing now, and we've got to face our future. My idea is that this isn't going to be a very protracted struggle; we shall just scare the enemy to death before it comes to a fight at all. But we must provide for contingencies, Editha. If anything happens to me—"

"Oh, George!" She clung to him, sobbing.

"I don't want you to feel foolishly bound to my memory. I should hate that, wherever I happened to be."

"I am yours, for time and eternity—time and eternity." She liked the words; they satisfied her famine for phrases.

"Well, say eternity; that's all right; but time's another thing; and I'm talking about time. But there is something! My mother! If anything happens—"

She winced, and he laughed. "You're not the bold soldier-girl of yesterday!" Then he sobered. "If anything happens, I want you to help my mother out. She won't like my doing this thing. She brought me up to think war a fool thing as well as a bad thing. My father was in the Civil War; all through it; lost his arm in it." She thrilled with the sense of the arm round her; what if that should be lost? He laughed as if divining her: "Oh, it doesn't run in the family, as far as I know!" Then he added, gravely: "He came home with misgivings about war, and they grew on him. I guess he and mother agreed between them that I was to be brought up in his final mind about it; but that was before my time. I only knew him from my mother's report of him and his opinions; I don't know whether they were hers first; but they were hers last. This will be a blow to her. I shall have to write and tell her—"

He stopped, and she asked: "Would you like me to write, too, George?"

"I don't believe that would do. No, I'll do the writing. She'll understand a little if I say that I thought the way to minimize it was to make war on the largest possible scale at once—that I felt I must have been helping on the war somehow if I hadn't helped keep it from coming, and I knew I hadn't; when it came, I had no right to stay out of it."

Whether his sophistries satisfied him or not, they satisfied her. She clung to his breast, and whispered, with closed eyes and quivering lips: "Yes, yes, yes!"

"But if anything should happen, you might go to her and see what you could do for her. You know? It's rather far off; she can't leave her chair—"

"Oh, I'll go, if it's the ends of the earth! But nothing will happen! Nothing *can*! I—"

She felt herself lifted with his rising, and Gearson was saying, with his arm still round her, to her father: "Well, we're off at once, Mr. Balcom. We're to be formally accepted at the capital, and then bunched up with the rest somehow, and sent into camp somewhere, and go to the front as soon as possible. We all want to be in the van, of course; we're the first company to report to the Governor. I came to tell Editha, but I hadn't got round to it."

She saw him again for a moment at the capital, in the station, just before the train started southward with his regiment. He looked well, in his uniform, and very soldierly, but somehow girlish, too, with his clean-shaven face and slim figure. The manly eyes and the strong voice satisfied her, and his preoccupation with some unexpected details of duty flattered her. Other girls were weeping and bemoaning themselves, but she felt a sort of noble distinction in the abstraction, the almost unconsciousness, with which they parted. Only at the last moment he said: "Don't forget my mother. It mayn't be such a walk-over as I supposed," and he laughed at the notion.

He waved his hand to her as the train moved off—she knew it among a score of hands that were waved to other girls from the platform of the car, for it held a letter which she knew was hers. Then he went inside the car to read it, doubtless, and she did not see him again. But she felt safe for him through the strength of what she called her love. What she called her God, always speaking the name in a deep voice and with the implication of a mutual understanding, would watch over him and keep him and bring him back to her. If with an empty sleeve, then he should have three arms instead of two, for both of hers should be his for life. She did not see, though, why she should always be thinking of the arm his father had lost.

There were not many letters from him, but they were such as she could have wished, and she put her whole strength into making hers such as she imagined he could have wished, glorifying and supporting him. She wrote to his mother glorifying him as their hero, but the brief answer she got was merely to the effect that Mrs. Gearson was not well enough to write herself, and thanking her for her letter by the hand of someone who called herself "Yrs truly, Mrs. W. J. Andrews."

Editha determined not to be hurt, but to write again quite as if the answer had been all she expected. Before it seemed as if she could have written, there came news of the first skirmish, and in the list of the killed, which was telegraphed as a trifling loss on our side, was Gearson's name. There was a frantic time of trying to make out that it might be, must be, some other Gearson; but the name and the company and the regiment and the State were too definitely given.

Then there was a lapse into depths out of which it seemed as if she never could rise again; then a lift into clouds far above all grief, black clouds, that blotted out the sun, but where she soared with him, with George—George! She had the fever that she expected of herself, but she did not die in it; she was not even delirious, and it did not last long. When she was well enough to leave her bed, her one thought was of George's mother, of his strangely worded wish that she should go to her and see what she could do for her. In the exaltation of the duty laid upon her—it buoyed her up instead of burdening her—she rapidly recovered.

Her father went with her on the long railroad journey from Northern New York to Western Iowa; he had business out at Davenport, and he said he could just as well go then as any other time; and he went with her to the little country town where George's mother lived in a little house on the edge of the illimitable cornfields, under trees pushed to a top of the rolling prairie. George's father had settled there after the Civil War, as so many other old soldiers had done; but they were Eastern people, and Editha fancied touches of the East in the June rose overhanging the front door, and the garden with early summer flowers stretching from the gate of the paling fence.

It was very low inside the house, and so dim, with the closed blinds, that they could scarcely see one another: Editha tall and black in her crapes which filled the air with the smell of their dyes; her father standing decorously apart with his hat on his forearm, as at funerals; a woman rested in a deep armchair, and the woman who had let the strangers in stood behind the chair.

The seated woman turned her head round and up, and asked the woman behind her chair: "*Who* did you say?"

Editha, if she had done what she expected of herself, would have gone down on her knees at the feet of the seated figure and said, "I am George's Editha," for answer.

But instead of her own voice she heard that other woman's voice, saying: "Well, I don't know as I *did* get the name just right. I guess I'll have to make a little more light in here," and she went and pushed two of the shutters ajar.

"Then Editha's father said, in his public will-now-address-a-few-remarks tone: "My name is Balcom, ma'am—Junius H. Balcom, of Balcom's Works, New York; my daughter—"

"Oh!" the seated woman broke in, with a powerful voice, the voice that always surprised Editha from Gearson's slender frame. "Let me see you. Stand round where the light can strike on your face," and Editha dumbly obeyed. "So, you're Editha Balcom," she sighed.

"Yes," Editha said, more like a culprit than a comforter.

"What did you come for?" Mrs. Gearson asked.

Editha's face quivered and her knees shook. "I came—because—because George—" She could go no further.

"Yes," the mother said, "he told me he had asked you to come if he got killed. You didn't expect that, I suppose, when you sent him."

"I would rather have died myself than done it!" Editha said, with more truth in her deep voice than she ordinarily found in it. "I tried to leave him free—"

"Yes, that letter of yours, that came back with his other things, left him free."

Editha saw now where George's irony came from.

"It was not to be read before—unless—until—I told him so," she faltered.

"Of course, he wouldn't read a letter of yours, under the circumstances, till he thought you wanted him to. Been sick?" the woman abruptly demanded.

"Very sick," Editha said, with self-pity.

"Daughter's life," her father interposed, "was almost despaired of, at one time."

Mrs. Gearson gave him no heed. "I suppose you would have been glad to die, such a brave person as you! I don't believe *he* was glad to die. He was always a timid boy, that way; he was afraid of a good many things; but if he was afraid he did what he made up his mind to. I suppose he made up his mind to go, but I knew what it cost him by what it cost me when I heard of it. I had been through *one* war before. When you sent him you didn't expect he would get killed."

The voice seemed to compassionate Editha, and it was time. "No," she huskily murmured.

"No, girls don't; women don't, when they give their men up to their country. They think they'll come marching back, somehow, just as gay as they went, or if it's an empty sleeve, or even an empty pantaloon, it's all the more glory, and they're so much the prouder of them, poor things!"

The tears began to run down Editha's face; she had not wept till then; but it was now such a relief to be understood that the tears came.

"No, you didn't expect him to get killed," Mrs. Gearson repeated, in a voice which was startlingly like George's again. "You just expected him to kill someone else, some of those foreigners, that weren't there because they had any say about it, but because they had to be there, poor wretches —conscripts, or whatever they call 'em. You thought it would be all right for my George, *your* George, to kill the sons of those miserable mothers and the husbands of those girls that you would never see the faces of." The woman lifted her powerful voice in a psalmlike note. "I thank my God he didn't live to do it! I thank my God they killed him first, and that he ain't livin' with their blood on his hands!" She dropped her eyes, which she had raised with her voice, and glared at Editha. "What you got that black on for?" She lifted herself by her powerful arms so high that her helpless body seemed to hang limp its full length. "Take it off, take it off, before I tear it from your back!"

The lady who was passing the summer near Balcom's Works was sketching Editha's beauty, which lent itself wonderfully to the effects of a colorist. It had come to that confidence which is rather apt to grow between artist and sitter, and Editha had told her everything.

"To think of your having such a tragedy in your life!" the lady said. She added: "I suppose there are people who feel that way about war But when you consider the good this war has done—how much it has done for the country! I can't understand such people, for my part. And when you had come all the way out there to console her—got up out of a sickbed! Well!"

"I think," Editha said, magnanimously, "she wasn't quite in her right mind; and so did papa."

"Yes," the lady said, looking at Editha's lips in nature and then at her lips in art, and giving an empirical touch to them in the picture. "But how dreadful of her! How perfectly—excuse me—how *vulgar!*"

A light broke upon Editha in the darkness which she felt had been without a gleam of brightness for weeks and months. The mystery that had bewildered her was solved by the word; and from that moment she rose from groveling in shame and self-pity, and began to live again in the ideal.

16

The Outcasts of Poker Flat

BY FRANCIS BRET HARTE

AS Mr. John Oakhurst, gambler, stepped into the main street of Poker Flat on the morning of the twenty-third of November, 1850, he was conscious of a change in its moral atmosphere since the preceding night. Two or three men, conversing earnestly together, ceased as he approached, and exchanged significant glances. There was a Sabbath lull in the air, which, in a settlement unused to Sabbath influences, looked ominous.

Mr. Oakhurst's calm, handsome face betrayed small concern of these indications. Whether he was conscious of any predisposing cause, was another question. "I reckon they're after somebody," he reflected; "likely it's me." He returned to his pocket the handkerchief with which he had been whipping away the red dust of Poker Flat from his neat boots, and quietly discharged his mind of any further conjecture.

In point of fact, Poker Flat was "after somebody." It had lately suffered the loss of several thousand dollars, two valuable horses, and a prominent citizen. It was experiencing a spasm of virtuous reaction, quite as lawless and ungovernable as any of the acts that had provoked it. A secret committee had determined to rid the town of all improper persons. This was done permanently in regard of two men who were then hanging from the boughs of a sycamore in the gulch, and temporarily in the banishment of certain other objectionable characters. I regret to say that some of these were ladies. It is but due to the sex, however, to state that their impropriety was professional, and it was only in such easily established standards of evil that Poker Flat ventured to sit in judgment.

Mr. Oakhurst was right in supposing that he was included in this category. A few of the committee had urged hanging him as a possible

THE OUTCASTS OF POKER FLAT 329

example, and a sure method of reimbursing themselves from his pockets of the sums he had won from them. "It's agin justice," said Jim Wheeler, "to let this yer young man from Roaring Camp—an entire stranger—carry away our money." But a crude sentiment of equity residing in the breasts of those who had been fortunate enough to win from Mr. Oakhurst overruled this narrower local prejudice.

Mr. Oakhurst received his sentence with philosophic calmness, none the less coolly that he was aware of the hesitation of his judges. He was too much of a gambler not to accept Fate. With him life was at best an uncertain game, and he recognized the usual percentage in favor of the dealer.

A body of armed men accompanied the deported wickedness of Poker Flat to the outskirts of the settlement. Besides Mr. Oakhurst, who was known to be a coolly desperate man, and for those intimidation the armed escort was intended, the expatriated party consisted of a young woman familiarly known as "The Duchess"; another, who had gained the infelicitous title of "Mother Shipton"; and "Uncle Billy," a suspected sluice-robber and confirmed drunkard. The cavalcade provoked no comments from the spectators, nor was any word uttered by the escort. Only, when the gulch which marked the uttermost limit of Poker Flat was reached, the leader spoke briefly and to the point. The exiles were forbidden to return at the peril of their lives.

As the escort disappeared, their pent-up feelings found vent in a few hysterical tears from the Duchess, some bad language from Mother Shipton, and a Parthian volley of expletives from Uncle Billy. The philosophic Oakhurst alone remained still. He listened calmly to Mother Shipton's desire to cut somebody's heart out, to the repeated statements of the Duchess that she would die on the road, and to the alarming oaths that seemed to be bumped out of Uncle Billy as he rode forward. With the easy good humor characteristic of his class, he insisted upon exchanging his own riding-horse, Five Spot, for the sorry mule which the Duchess rode. But even this act did not draw the party into any closer sympathy. The young woman readjusted her somewhat draggled plumes with a feeble, faded coquetry; Mother Shipton eyed the possessor of Five Spot with malevolence, and Uncle Billy included the whole party in one sweeping anathema.

The road to Sandy Bar—a camp that, not having as yet experienced the regenerating influences of Poker Flat, consequently seemed to offer some invitation to the emigrants—lay over a steep mountain range. It was distant a day's severe journey. In that advanced season, the party soon passed out of the moist, temperate regions of the foothills into the dry, cold, bracing air of the Sierras. The trail was narrow and difficult.

At noon the Duchess, rolling out of her saddle upon the ground, declared her intention of going no farther, and the party halted.

The spot was singularly wild and impressive. A wooded amphitheater, surrounded on three sides by precipitous cliffs of naked granite, sloped gently toward the crest of another precipice that overlooked the valley. It was undoubtedly the most suitable spot for a camp, had camping been advisable. But Mr. Oakhurst knew that scarcely half the journey to Sandy Bar was accomplished, and the party were not equipped or provisioned for delay. This fact he pointed out to his companions curtly, with a philosophic commentary on the folly of "throwing up their hand before the game was played out." But they were furnished with liquor, which in this emergency stood them in place of food, fuel, rest, and prescience. In spite of his remonstrances, it was not long before they were more or less under its influence. Uncle Billy passed rapidly from a bellicose state into one of stupor, the Duchess became maudlin, and Mother Shipton snored. Mr. Oakhurst alone remained erect, leaning against a rock, calmly surveying them.

Mr. Oakhurst did not drink. It interfered with a profession which required coolness, impassiveness, and presence of mind, and, in his own language, he "couldn't afford it." As he gazed at his recumbent fellow-exiles, the loneliness begotten of his pariah-trade, his habits of life, his very vices, for the first time seriously oppressed him. He bestirred himself in dusting his black clothes, washing his hands and face, and other acts characteristic of his studiously neat habits, and for a moment forgot his annoyance. The thought of deserting his weaker and more pitiable companions never perhaps occurred to him. Yet he could not help feeling the want of that excitement which, singularly enough, was most conducive to that calm equanimity for which he was notorious. He looked at the gloomy walls that rose a thousand feet sheer above the circling pines around him; at the sky, ominously clouded; at the valley below, already deepening into shadow. And, doing so, suddenly he heard his own name called.

A horseman slowly ascended the trail. In the fresh, open face of the new-comer Mr. Oakhurst recognized Tom Simson, otherwise known as "The Innocent" of Sandy Bar. He had met him some months before over a "little game," and had, with perfect equanimity, won the entire fortune—amounting to some forty dollars—of that guileless youth. After the game was finished, Mr. Oakhurst drew the youthful speculator behind the door and thus addressed him: "Tommy, you're a good little man, but you can't gamble worth a cent. Don't try it over again." He then handed him his money back, pushed him gently from the room, and so made a devoted slave of Tom Simson.

There was a remembrance of this in his boyish and enthusiastic greeting of Mr. Oakhurst. He had started, he said, to go to Poker Flat to seek his fortune. "Alone?" No, not exactly alone; in fact—a giggle—he had run away with Piney Woods. Didn't Mr. Oakhurst remember Piney? She that used to wait on the table at the Temperance House? They had been engaged a long time, but old Jake Woods had objected, and so they had run away, and were going to Poker Flat to be married, and here they were. And they were tired out, and how lucky it was they had found a place to camp and company. All this the Innocent delivered rapidly, while Piney—a stout, comely damsel of fifteen—emerged from behind the pine-tree, where she had been blushing unseen, and rode to the side of her lover.

Mr. Oakhurst seldom troubled himself with sentiment, still less with propriety; but he had a vague idea that the situation was not felicitous. He retained, however, his presence of mind sufficiently to kick Uncle Billy, who was about to say something, and Uncle Billy was sober enough to recognize in Mr. Oakhurst's kick a superior power that would not bear trifling. He then endeavored to dissuade Tom Simson from delaying further, but in vain. He even pointed out the fact that there was no provision, nor means of making a camp. But, unluckily, the Innocent met this objection by assuring the party that he was provided with an extra mule loaded with provisions, and by the discovery of a rude attempt at a log-house near the trail. "Piney can stay with Mrs. Oakhurst," said the Innocent, pointing to the Duchess, "and I can shift for myself."

Nothing but Mr. Oakhurst's admonishing foot saved Uncle Billy from bursting into a roar of laughter. As it was, he felt compelled to retire up the canyon until he could recover his gravity. There he confided the joke to the tall pine trees, with many slaps of his leg, contortions of his face, and the usual profanity. But when he returned to the party, he found them seated by a fire—for the air had grown strangely chill and the sky overcast—in apparently amicable conversation. Piney was actually talking in an impulsive, girlish fashion to the Duchess, who was listening with an interest and animation she had not shown for many days. The Innocent was holding forth, apparently with equal effect, to Mr. Oakhurst and Mother Shipton, who was actually relaxing into amiability. "Is this yer a d—d picnic?" said Uncle Billy, with inward scorn, as he surveyed the sylvan group, the glancing fire-light, and the tethered animals in the foreground. Suddenly an idea mingled with the alcoholic fumes that disturbed his brain. It was apparently of a jocular nature, for he felt impelled to slap his leg again and cram his fist into his mouth.

As the shadows crept slowly up the mountain, a slight breeze rocked the tops of the pine-trees, and moaned through their long and gloomy aisles. The ruined cabin, patched and covered with pine boughs, was set apart for the ladies. As the lovers parted, they unaffectedly exchanged a kiss, so honest and sincere that it might have been heard above the swaying pines. The frail Duchess and the malevolent Mother Shipton were probably too stunned to remark upon this last evidence of simplicity, and so turned without a word to the hut. The fire was replenished, the men lay down before the door, and in a few minutes were asleep.

Mr. Oakhurst was a light sleeper. Toward morning he awoke benumbed and cold. As he stirred the dying fire, the wind, which was now blowing strongly, brought to his cheek that which caused the blood to leave it—snow!

He started to his feet with the intention of awakening the sleepers, for there was no time to lose. But turning to where Uncle Billy had been lying, he found him gone. A suspicion leaped to his brain and a curse to his lips. He ran to the spot where the mules had been tethered; they were no longer there. The tracks were already rapidly disappearing in the snow.

The momentary excitement brought Mr. Oakhurst back to the fire with his usual calm. He did not waken the sleepers. The Innocent slumbered peacefully, with a smile on his good humored, freckled face; the virgin Piney slept beside her frailer sisters as sweetly as though attended by celestial guardians, and Mr. Oakhurst, drawing his blanket over his shoulders, stroked his mustachios and waited for the dawn. It came slowly in the whirling mist of snowflakes, that dazzled and confused the eye. What could be seen of the landscape appeared magically changed. He looked over the valley, and summed up the present and future in two words—"Snowed in!"

A careful inventory of the provisions, which, fortunately for the party, had been stored within the hut, and so escaped the felonious fingers of Uncle Billy, disclosed the fact that with care and prudence they might last ten days longer. "That is," said Mr. Oakhurst, *sotto voce* to the Innocent, "if you're willing to board us. If you ain't—and perhaps you'd better not—you can wait till Uncle Billy gets back with provisions." For some occult reason, Mr. Oakhurst, could not bring himself to disclose Uncle Billy's rascality, and so offered the hypothesis that he had wandered from the camp and had accidentally stampeded the animals. He dropped a warning to the Duchess and Mother Shipton, who of course knew the facts of their associate's defection. "They'll find out the truth about us *all*, when they find out anything," he added, significantly, "and there's no good frightening them now."

Tom Simson not only put all his worldly store at the disposal of Mr. Oakhurst, but seemed to enjoy the prospect of their enforced seclusion. "We'll have a good camp for a week, and then the snow'll melt, and we'll all go back together." The cheerful gayety of the young man and Mr. Oakhurst's calm infected the others. The Innocent, with the aid of pine boughs, extemporized a thatch for the roofless cabin, and the Duchess directed Piney in the rearrangement of the interior with a taste and tact that opened the blue eyes of that provincial maiden to their fullest extent.

"I reckon now you're used to fine things at Poker Flat," said Piney. The Duchess turned away sharply to conceal something that reddened her cheek through its professional tint, and Mother Shipton requested Piney not to "chatter." But when Mr. Oakhurst returned from a weary search for the trail, he heard the sound of happy laughter echoed from the rocks. He stopped in some alarm, and his thoughts first naturally reverted to the whisky, which he had prudently *cached*. "And yet it don't somehow sound like whisky," said the gambler. It was not until he caught sight of the blazing fire through the still blinding storm, and the group around it, that he settled to the conviction that it was "square fun."

Whether Mr. Oakhurst had *cached* his cards with the whisky as something debarred the free access of the community, I cannot say. It was certain that, in Mother Shipton's words, he "didn't say cards once" during the evening. Haply the time was beguiled by an accordion, produced somewhat ostentatiously by Tom Simson, from his pack. Notwithstanding some difficulties attending the manipulation of this instrument, Piney Woods managed to pluck several reluctant melodies from its keys, to an accompaniment by the Innocent on a pair of bone castinets. But the crowning festivity of the evening was reached in a rude camp-meeting hymn, which the lovers, joining hands, sang with great earnestness and vociferation. I fear that a certain defiant tone and Covenanter's swing to its chorus, rather than any devotional quality, caused it speedily to infect the others, who at last joined in the refrain:

> I'm proud to live in the service of the Lord,
> And I'm bound to die in His army.

The pines rocked, the storm eddied and whirled above the miserable group, and the flames of their altar leaped heavenward, as if in token of the vow.

At midnight the storm abated, the rolling clouds parted, and the stars glittered keenly above the sleeping camp. Mr. Oakhurst, whose professional habits had enabled him to live on the smallest possible amount of sleep, in dividing the watch with Tom Simson, somehow managed to take upon himself the greater part of that duty. He excused himself to the Innocent, by saying that he had "often been a week without sleep." "Doing what?" asked Tom. "Poker!" replied Oakhurst, sententiously, "when a man gets a streak of luck—nigger-luck—he don't get tired. The luck gives in first. Luck," continued the gambler, reflectively, "is a mighty queer thing. All you know about it for certain is that it's bound to change. And it's finding out when it's going to change that makes you. We've had a streak of bad luck since we left Poker Flat—you come along, and slap you get into it, too. If you can hold your cards right along you're all right. For," added the gambler, with cheerful irrelevance,

> "I'm proud to live in the service of the Lord,
> And I'm bound to die in His army."

The third day came, and the sun, looking through the white-curtained valley, saw the outcasts divide their slowly decreasing store of provisions for the morning meal. It was one of the peculiarities of that mountain climate that its rays diffused a kindly warmth over the wintry landscape, as if in regretful commiseration of the past. But it revealed drift on drift of snow piled high around the hut; a hopeless, uncharted, trackless sea of white lying below the rocky shores to which the castaways still clung. Through the marvelously clear air, the smoke of the pastoral village of Poker Flat rose miles away. Mother Shipton saw it, and from a remote pinnacle of her rocky fastness, hurled in that direction a final malediction. It was her last vituperative attempt, and perhaps for that reason was invested with a certain degree of sublimity. It did her good, she privately informed the Duchess. "Just to go out there and cuss, and see." She then set herself to the task of amusing "the child," as she and the Duchess were pleased to call Piney. Piney was no chicken, but it was a soothing and ingenious theory of the pair thus to account for the fact that she didn't swear and wasn't improper.

When night crept up again through the gorges, the reedy notes of the accordion rose and fell in fitful spasms and long-drawn gasps by the flickering camp-fire. But music failed to fill entirely the aching void left by insufficient food, and a new diversion was proposed by Piney—storytelling. Neither Mr. Oakhurst nor his female companions caring to relate their personal experiences, this plan would have failed, too, but for the Innocent. Some months before he had chanced upon a stray copy of Mr. Pope's ingenious translation of the Iliad. He now proposed to narrate the principal incidents of that poem—having thoroughly mastered the argument and fairly forgotten the words—in the current vernacular of Sandy Bar. And so for the rest of that night the Homeric demigods again walked the earth. Trojan bully and wily Greek wrestled in the winds, and the great pines in the canyon seemed to bow to the wrath of the son of Peleus. Mr. Oakhurst listened with quiet satisfaction. Most especially was he interested in the fate of "Ash-heels," as the Innocent persisted in denominating the "swift-footed Achilles."

So with small food and much of Homer and the accordion, a week passed over the heads of the outcasts. The sun again forsook them, and again from leaden skies the snowflakes were sifted over the land. Day by day closer around them drew the snowy circle, until at last they looked from their prison over drifted walls of dazzling white, that towered twenty feet above their heads. It became more and more difficult to replenish their fires, even from the fallen trees beside them, now half-hidden in the drifts. And yet no one complained. The lovers turned from the dreary prospect and looked into each other's eyes, and were happy. Mr. Oakhurst settled himself coolly to the losing game before him. The Duchess, more cheerful than she had been, assumed the care of Piney. Only Mother Shipton—once the strongest of the party— seemed to sicken and fade. At midnight on the tenth day she called Oakhurst to her side. "I'm going," she said, in a voice of querulous weakness, "but don't say anything about it. Don't waken the kids. Take the bundle from under my head and open it." Mr. Oakhurst did so. It contained Mother Shipton's rations for the last week, untouched. "Give 'em to the child," she said, pointing to the sleeping Piney. "You've starved yourself," said the gambler. "That's what they call it," said the woman, querulously, as she lay down again, and, turning her face to the wall, passed quietly away.

The accordion and the bones were put aside that day, and Homer was forgotten. When the body of Mother Shipton had been committed to the snow, Mr. Oakhurst took the Innocent aside, and showed him a pair of snowshoes, which he had fashioned from the old pack-saddle. "There's one chance in a hundred to save her yet," he said, pointing to Piney; "but it's there," he added, pointing toward Poker Flat. "If you can reach there in two days she's safe." "And you?" asked Tom Simson. "I'll stay here," was the curt reply.

The lovers parted with a long embrace. "You are not going, too?" said the Duchess, as she saw Mr. Oakhurst apparently waiting to accompany him. "As far as the canyon," he replied. He turned suddenly, and kissed the Duchess, leaving her pallid face aflame, and her trembling limbs rigid with amazement.

Night came, but not Mr. Oakhurst. It brought the storm again and the whirling snow. Then the Duchess, feeding the fire, found that some one had quietly piled beside the hut enough fuel to last a few days longer. The tears rose to her eyes, but she hid them from Piney.

The women slept but little. In the morning, looking into each other's faces, they read their fate. Neither spoke; but Piney, accepting the position of the stronger, drew near and placed her arm around the Duchess's waist. They kept this attitude for the rest of the day. That night the storm reached its greatest fury, and, rending asunder the protecting pines, invaded the very hut.

Toward morning they found themselves unable to feed the fire, which gradually died away. As the embers slowly blackened, the Duchess crept closer to Piney, and broke the silence of many hours: "Piney, can you pray?" "No, dear," said Piney, simply. The Duchess without knowing exactly why, felt relieved, and, putting her head upon Piney's shoulder, spoke no more. And so reclining, the younger and purer pillowing the head of her soiled sister upon her virgin breast, they fell asleep.

The wind lulled as if it feared to waken them. Feathery drifts of snow, shaken from the long pine boughs, flew like white-winged birds, and settled about them as they slept. The moon through the rifted clouds looked down upon what had been the camp. But all human stain, all trace of earthly travail, was hidden beneath the spotless mantle mercifully flung from above.

They slept all that day and the next, nor did they waken when voices and footsteps broke the silence of the camp. And when pitying fingers brushed the snow from their wan faces, you could scarcely have told from the equal peace that dwelt upon them, which was she that had sinned. Even the Law of Poker Flat recognized this, and turned away, leaving them still locked in each other's arms.

But at the head of the gulch, on one of the largest pine trees, they found the deuce of clubs pinned to the bark with a bowie knife. It bore the following, written in pencil, in a firm hand:

†

BENEATH THIS TREE

LIES THE BODY

OF

JOHN OAKHURST,

WHO STRUCK A STREAK OF BAD LUCK

ON THE 23D OF NOVEMBER, 1850,

AND

HANDED IN HIS CHECKS

ON THE 7TH OF DECEMBER, 1850.

†

And pulseless and cold, with a Derringer by his side and a bullet in his heart, though still calm as in life, beneath the snow lay he who was at once the strongest and yet the weakest of the outcasts of Poker Flat.

17

An Occurrence at Owl Creek Bridge

BY AMBROSE BIERCE

A MAN stood upon a railroad bridge in northern Alabama, looking down into the swift water twenty feet below. The man's hands were behind his back, the wrists bound with a cord. A rope closely encircled his neck. It was attached to a stout cross-timber above his head and the slack fell to the level of his knees. Some loose boards laid upon the sleepers supporting the metals of the railway supplied a footing for him and his executioners—two private soldiers of the Federal army, directed by a sergeant who in civil life may have been a deputy sheriff. At a short remove upon the same temporary platform was an officer in the uniform of his rank, armed. He was a captain. A sentinel at each end of the bridge stood with his rifle in the position known as "support," that is to say, vertical in front of the left shoulder, the hammer resting on the forearm thrown straight across the chest—a formal and unnatural position, enforcing an erect carriage of the body. It did not appear to be the duty of these two men to know what was occurring at the center of the bridge; they merely blockaded the two ends of the foot planking that traversed it.

Beyond one of the sentinels nobody was in sight; the railroad ran straight away into a forest for a hundred yards, then, curving, was lost to view. Doubtless there was an outpost farther along. The other bank of the stream was open ground—a gentle acclivity topped with a stockade of vertical tree trunks, loopholed for rifles, with a single embrasure through which protruded the muzzle of a brass cannon commanding the bridge. Midway of the slope between the bridge and fort were the spectators—a single company of infantry in line, at "parade rest," the butts of the rifles on the ground, the barrels inclining slightly backward against the right shoulder, the hands crossed upon the stock. A lieu-

tenant stood at the right of the line, the point of his sword upon the
ground, his left hand resting upon his right. Excepting the group of
four at the center of the bridge, not a man moved. The company faced
the bridge, staring stonily, motionless. The sentinels, facing the banks
of the stream, might have been statues to adorn the bridge. The captain
stood with folded arms, silent, observing the work of his subordinates,
but making no sign. Death is a dignitary who when he comes announced
is to be received with formal manifestations of respect, even by those
most familiar with him. In the code of military etiquette silence and
fixity are forms of deference.

The man who was engaged in being hanged was apparently about
thirty-five years of age. He was a civilian, if one might judge from his
habit, which was that of a planter. His features were good—a straight
nose, firm mouth, broad forehead, from which his long, dark hair was
combed straight back, falling behind his ears to the collar of his well-
fitting frock coat. He wore a mustache and pointed beard, but no whiskers; his eyes were large and dark gray, and had a kindly expression
which one would hardly have expected in one whose neck was in the
hemp. Evidently this was no vulgar assassin. The liberal military code
makes provision for hanging many kinds of persons, and gentlemen are
not excluded.

The preparations being complete, the two private soldiers stepped
aside and each drew away the plank upon which he had been standing.
The sergeant turned to the captain, saluted and placed himself immediately behind that officer, who in turn moved apart one pace. These
movements left the condemned man and the sergeant standing on the
two ends of the same plank, which spanned three of the cross-ties of the
bridge. The end upon which the civilian stood almost, but not quite,
reached a fourth. This plank had been held in place by the weight of
the captain; it was now held by that of the sergeant. At a signal from
the former the latter would step aside, the plank would tilt and the
condemned man go down between two ties. The arrangement commended itself to his judgment as simple and effective. His face had not
been covered nor his eyes bandaged. He looked a moment at his "un-
steadfast footing," then let his gaze wander to the swirling water of the
stream racing madly beneath his feet. A piece of dancing driftwood
caught his attention and his eyes followed it down the current. How
slowly it appeared to move! What a sluggish stream!

He closed his eyes in order to fix his last thoughts upon his wife and
children. The water, touched to gold by the early sun, the brooding
mists under the banks at some distance down the stream, the fort, the
soldiers, the piece of drift—all had distracted him. And now he became
conscious of a new disturbance. Striking through the thought of his

dear ones was a sound which he could neither ignore nor understand, a sharp, distinct, metallic percussion like the stroke of a blacksmith's hammer upon the anvil; it had the same ringing quality. He wondered what it was, and whether immeasurably distant or near by—it seemed both. Its recurrence was regular, but as slow as the tolling of a death knell. He awaited each stroke with impatience and—he knew not why —apprehension. The intervals of silence grew progressively longer; the delays became maddening. With their greater infrequency the sounds increased in strength and sharpness. They hurt his ear like the thrust of a knife; he feared he would shriek. What he heard was the ticking of his watch.

He unclosed his eyes and saw again the water below him. "If I could free my hands," he thought, "I might throw off the noose and spring into the stream. By diving I could evade the bullets and, swimming vigorously, reach the bank, take to the woods and get away home. My home, thank God, is as yet outside their lines; my wife and little ones are still beyond the invader's farthest advance."

As these thoughts, which have here to be set down in words, were flashed into the doomed man's brain rather than evolved from it the captain nodded to the sergeant. The sergeant stepped aside.

II

Peyton Farquhar was a well-to-do planter, of an old and highly respected Alabama family. Being a slave owner and like other slave owners a politician he was naturally an original secessionist and ardently devoted to the Southern cause. Circumstances of an imperious nature, which it is unnecessary to relate here, had prevented him from taking service with the gallant army that had fought the disastrous campaigns ending with the fall of Corinth, and he chafed under the inglorious restraint, longing for the release of his energies, the larger life of the soldier, the opportunity for distinction. That opportunity, he felt, would come, as it comes to all in war time. Meanwhile he did what he could. No service was too humble for him to perform in aid of the South, no adventure too perilous for him to undertake if consistent with the character of a civilian who was at heart a soldier, and who in good faith and without too much qualification assented to at least a part of the frankly villainous dictum that all is fair in love and war.

One evening while Farquhar and his wife were sitting on a rustic bench near the entrance to his grounds, a gray-clad soldier rode up to the gate and asked for a drink of water. Mrs. Farquhar was only too happy to serve him with her own white hands. While she was fetching the water her husband approached the dusty horseman and inquired eagerly for news from the front.

"The Yanks are repairing the railroads," said the man, "and are getting ready for another advance. They have reached the Owl Creek bridge, put it in order and built a stockade on the north bank. The commandant has issued an order, which is posted everywhere, declaring that any civilian caught interfering with the railroad, its bridges, tunnels or trains will be summarily hanged. I saw the order."

"How far is it to the Owl Creek bridge?" Farquhar asked.

"About thirty miles."

"Is there no force on this side the creek?"

"Only a picket post half a mile out, on the railroad, and a single sentinel at this end of the bridge."

"Suppose a man—a civilian and student of hanging—should elude the picket post and perhaps get the better of the sentinel," said Farquhar, smiling, "what could he accomplish?"

The soldier reflected. "I was there a month ago," he replied. "I observed that the flood of last winter had lodged a great quantity of driftwood against the wooden pier at this end of the bridge. It is now dry and would burn like tow."

The lady had now brought the water, which the soldier drank. He thanked her ceremoniously, bowed to her husband and rode away. An hour later, after nightfall, he repassed the plantation, going northward in the direction from which he had come. He was a Federal scout.

III

As Peyton Farquhar fell straight downward through the bridge he lost consciousness and was as one already dead. From this state he was awakened—ages later, it seemed to him—by the pain of a sharp pressure upon his throat, followed by a sense of suffocation. Keen, poignant agonies seemed to shoot from his neck downward through every fiber of his body and limbs. These pains appeared to flash along well-defined lines of ramification and to beat with an inconceivably rapid periodicity. They seemed like streams of pulsating fire heating him to an intolerable temperature. As to his head, he was conscious of nothing but a feeling of fulness—of congestion. These sensations were unaccompanied by thought. The intellectual part of his nature was already effaced; he had power only to feel, and feeling was torment. He was conscious of motion. Encompassed in a luminous cloud, of which he was now merely the fiery heart, without material substance, he swung through unthinkable arcs of oscillation, like a vast pendulum. Then all at once, with terrible suddenness, the light about him shot upward with the noise of a loud plash; a frightful roaring was in his ears, and all was cold and dark. The power of thought was restored; he knew that the rope had broken and he had fallen into the stream. There was no additional strangulation; the noose about his neck was already suffocating him and kept the water from his lungs. To die of hanging at the bottom of a river!—the idea seemed to him ludicrous. He opened his eyes in the darkness and saw above him a gleam of light, but how distant, how inaccessible! He was still sinking, for the light became fainter and fainter until it was a mere glimmer. Then it began to grow and brighten, and he knew that he was rising toward the surface—knew it with reluctance, for he was now very comfortable. "To be hanged and drowned," he thought, "that is not so bad; but I do not wish to be shot. No; I will not be shot; that is not fair."

He was not conscious of an effort, but a sharp pain in his wrist apprised him that he was trying to free his hands. He gave the struggle his attention, as an idler might observe the feat of a juggler, without interest in the outcome. What splendid effort!—what magnificent, what superhuman strength! Ah, that was a fine endeavor! Bravo! The cord fell away; his arms parted and floated upward, the hands dimly seen on each side in the growing light. He watched them with a new interest as first one and then the other pounced upon the noose at his neck. They tore it away and thrust it fiercely aside, its undulations resembling those of a water snake. "Put it back, put it back!" He thought he shouted these words to his hands, for the undoing of the noose had been succeeded by the direst pang that he had yet experienced. His neck ached horribly; his brain was on fire; his heart, which had been fluttering faintly, gave a great leap, trying to force itself out at his mouth. His whole body was racked and wrenched with an insupportable anguish! But his disobedient hands gave no heed to the command. They beat the water vigorously with quick, downward strokes, forcing him to the surface. He felt his head emerge; his eyes were blinded by the sunlight; his chest expanded convulsively, and with a supreme and crowning agony his lungs engulfed a great draught of air, which instantly he expelled in a shriek!

He was now in full possession of his physical senses. They were, indeed, preternaturally keen and alert. Something in the awful disturbance of his organic system had so exalted and refined them that they made record of things never before perceived. He felt the ripples upon his face and heard their separate sounds as they struck. He looked at the forest on the bank of the stream, saw the individual trees, the leaves and the veining of each leaf—saw the very insects upon them: the locusts, the brilliant-bodied flies, the gray spiders stretching their webs from twig to twig. He noted the prismatic colors in all the dewdrops upon a million blades of grass. The humming of the gnats that danced above the eddies of the stream, the beating of the dragon flies' wings, the strokes of the water-spiders' legs, like oars which had lifted their boat—all these made audible music. A fish slid along beneath his eyes and he heard the rush of its body parting the water.

He had come to the surface facing down the stream; in a moment the visible world seemed to wheel slowly round, himself the pivotal point, and he saw the bridge, the fort, the soldiers upon the bridge, the captain, the sergeant, the two privates, his executioners. They were in silhouette against the blue sky. They shouted and gesticulated, pointing at him. The captain had drawn his pistol, but did not fire; the others were unarmed. Their movements were grotesque and horrible, their forms gigantic.

Suddenly he heard a sharp report and something struck the water smartly within a few inches of his head, spattering his face with spray. He heard a second report, and saw one of the sentinels with his rifle at his shoulder, a light cloud of blue smoke rising from the muzzle. The man in the water saw the eye of the man on the bridge gazing into his own through the sights of the rifle. He observed that it was a gray eye and remembered having read that gray eyes were keenest, and that all famous marksmen had them. Nevertheless, this one had missed.

A counter-swirl had caught Farquhar and turned him half round; he was again looking into the forest on the bank opposite the fort. The sound of a clear, high voice in a monotonous singsong now rang out behind him and came across the water with a distinctness that pierced and subdued all other sounds, even the beating of the ripples in his ears. Although no soldier, he had frequented camps enough to know the dread significance of that deliberate, drawling, aspirated chant; the lieutenant on shore was taking a part in the morning's work. How coldly and pitilessly—with what an even, calm intonation, presaging, and enforcing tranquillity in the men—with what accurately measured intervals fell those cruel words:

"Attention, company! . . . Shoulder arms! . . . Ready! . . . Aim! . . . Fire!"

Farquhar dived—dived as deeply as he could. The water roared in his ears like the voice of Niagara, yet he heard the dulled thunder of the volley and, rising again toward the surface, met shining bits of metal, singularly flattened, oscillating slowly downward. Some of them touched him on the face and hands, then fell away, continuing their descent. One lodged between his collar and neck; it was uncomfortably warm and he snatched it out.

As he rose to the surface, gasping for breath, he saw that he had been a long time under water; he was perceptibly farther down stream—nearer to safety. The soldiers had almost finished reloading; the metal ramrods flashed all at once in the sunshine as they were drawn from the barrels, turned in the air, and thrust into their sockets. The two sentinels fired again, independently and ineffectually.

The hunted man saw all this over his shoulder; he was now swimming vigorously with the current. His brain was as energetic as his arms and legs; he thought with the rapidity of lightning.

"The officer," he reasoned, "will not make that martinet's error a second time. It is as easy to dodge a volley as a single shot. He has probably already given the command to fire at will. God help me, I cannot dodge them all!"

An appalling plash within two yards of him was followed by a loud, rushing sound, *diminuendo,* which seemed to travel back through the air to the fort and died in an explosion which stirred the very river to its deeps! A rising sheet of water curved over him, fell down upon him, blinded him, strangled him! The cannon had taken a hand in the game. As he shook his head free from the commotion of the smitten water he heard the deflected shot humming through the air ahead, and in an instant it was cracking and smashing the branches in the forest beyond.

"They will not do that again," he thought; "the next time they will use a charge of grape. I must keep my eye upon the gun; the smoke will apprise me—the report arrives too late; it lags behind the missile. That is a good gun."

Suddenly he felt himself whirled round and round—spinning like a top. The water, the banks, the forests, the now distant bridge, fort and men—all were commingled and blurred. Objects were represented by their colors only; circular horizontal streaks of color—that was all he saw. He had been caught in a vortex and was being whirled on with a velocity of advance and gyration that made him giddy and sick. In a few moments he was flung upon the gravel at the foot of the left bank of the stream—the southern bank—and behind a projecting point which concealed him from his enemies. The sudden arrest of his motion, the abrasion of one of his hands on the gravel, restored him, and he wept with delight. He dug his fingers into the sand, threw it over himself in handfuls and audibly blessed it. It looked like diamonds, rubies, emeralds; he could think of nothing beautiful which it did not resemble. The trees upon the bank were giant garden plants; he noted a definite order in their arrangement, inhaled the fragrance of their blooms. A strange, roseate light shone through the spaces among their trunks and the wind made in their branches the music of Æolian harps. He had no wish to perfect his escape—was content to remain in that enchanting spot until retaken.

A whiz and rattle of grapeshot among the branches high above his head roused him from his dream. The baffled cannoneer had fired him a random farewell. He sprang to his feet, rushed up the sloping bank, and plunged into the forest.

All that day he traveled, laying his course by the rounding sun. The forest seemed interminable; nowhere did he discover a break in it, not even a woodman's road. He had not known that he lived in so wild a region. There was something uncanny in the revelation.

By nightfall he was fatigued, footsore, famishing. The thought of his wife and children urged him on. At last he found a road which led him in what he knew to be the right direction. It was as wide and straight as a city street, yet it seemed untraveled. No fields bordered it, no dwelling anywhere. Not so much as the barking of a dog suggested human habitation. The black bodies of the trees formed a straight wall on both sides, terminating on the horizon in a point, like a diagram in a lesson in perspective. Overhead, as he looked up through this rift in the wood, shone great golden stars looking unfamiliar and grouped in strange constellations. He was sure they were arranged in some order which had a secret and malign significance. The wood on either side was full of singular noises, among which—once, twice, and again—he distinctly heard whispers in an unknown tongue.

His neck was in pain and lifting his hand to it found it horribly swollen. He knew that it had a circle of black where the rope had bruised it. His eyes felt congested; he could no longer close them. His tongue was swollen with thirst; he relieved its fever by thrusting it forward from between his teeth into the cold air. How softly the turf had carpeted the untraveled avenue—he could no longer feel the roadway beneath his feet!

Doubtless, despite his suffering, he had fallen asleep while walking, for now he sees another scene—perhaps he has merely recovered from a delirium. He stands at the gate of his own home. All is as he left it, and all bright and beautiful in the morning sunshine. He must have traveled the entire night. As he pushes open the gate and passes up the wide white walk, he sees a flutter of female garments; his wife, looking fresh and cool and sweet, steps down from the veranda to meet him. At the bottom of the steps she stands waiting, with a smile of ineffable joy, an attitude of matchless grace and dignity. Ah, how beautiful she is! He springs forward with extended arms. As he is about to clasp her he feels a stunning blow upon the back of the neck; a blinding white light blazes all about him with a sound like the shock of a cannon—then all is darkness and silence!

Peyton Farquhar was dead; his body, with a broken neck, swung gently from side to side beneath the timbers of the Owl Creek bridge.

The Boarded Window

BY AMBROSE BIERCE

IN 1830, only a few miles away from what is now the great city of Cincinnati, lay an immense and almost unbroken forest. The whole region was sparsely settled by people of the frontier—restless souls who no sooner had hewn fairly habitable homes out of the wilderness and attained to that degree of prosperity which today we should call indigence, than, impelled by some mysterious impulse of their nature, they abandoned all and pushed farther westward, to encounter new perils and privations in the effort to regain the meager comforts which they had voluntarily renounced. Many of them had already forsaken that region for the remoter settlements, but among those remaining was one who had been of those first arriving. He lived alone in a house of logs surrounded on all sides by the great forest, of whose gloom and silence he seemed a part, for no one had ever known him to smile nor speak a needless word. His simple wants were supplied by the sale or barter of skins of wild animals in the river town, for not a thing did he grow upon the land which, if needful, he might have claimed by right of undisturbed possession. There were evidences of "improvement"—a few acres of ground immediately about the house had once been cleared of its trees, the decayed stumps of which were half concealed by the new growth that had been suffered to repair the ravage wrought by the ax. Apparently the man's zeal for agriculture had burned with a failing flame, expiring in penitential ashes.

The little log house, with its chimney of sticks, its roof of warping clapboards weighted with traversing poles and its "chinking" of clay, had a single door and, directly opposite, a window. The latter, however, was boarded up—nobody could remember a time when it was not. And none knew why it was so closed; certainly not because of the occupant's dislike of light and air, for on those rare occasions when a hunter had passed that lonely spot the recluse had commonly been seen sunning himself on his doorstep if heaven had provided sunshine for his need. I fancy there are few persons living today who ever knew the secret of that window, but I am one, as you shall see.

The man's name was said to be Murlock. He was apparently seventy years old, actually about fifty. Something besides years had had a hand in his aging. His hair and long, full beard were white, his gray, luster-less eyes sunken, his face singularly seamed with wrinkles which appeared to belong to two intersecting systems. In figure he was tall and spare, with a stoop of the shoulders—a burden bearer. I never saw him; these particulars I learned from my grandfather, from whom also I got the man's story when I was a lad. He had known him when living near by in that early day.

One day Murlock was found in his cabin, dead. It was not a time and place for coroners and newspapers, and I suppose it was agreed that he had died from natural causes or I should have been told, and should remember. I know only that with what was probably a sense of the fitness of things the body was buried near the cabin, alongside the grave of his wife, who had preceded him by so many years that local tradition had retained hardly a hint of her existence. That closes the final chapter of this true story—excepting, indeed, the circumstance that many years afterward, in company with an equally intrepid spirit, I penetrated to the place and ventured near enough to the ruined cabin to throw a stone against it, and ran away to avoid the ghost which every well-informed boy thereabout knew haunted the spot. But there is an earlier chapter—that supplied by my grandfather.

When Murlock built his cabin and began laying sturdily about with his ax to hew out a farm—the rifle, meanwhile, his means of support —he was young, strong and full of hope. In that eastern country whence he came he had married, as was the fashion, a young woman in all ways worthy of his honest devotion, who shared the dangers and privations of his lot with a willing spirit and light heart. There is no known record of her name; of her charms of mind and person tradition is silent and the doubter is at liberty to entertain his doubt; but God forbid that I should share it! Of their affection and happiness there is abundant assurance in every added day of the man's widowed life; for what but the magnetism of a blessed memory could have chained that venturesome spirit to a lot like that?

One day Murlock returned from gunning in a distant part of the forest to find his wife prostrate with fever, and delirious. There was no physician within miles, no neighbor; nor was she in a condition to be left, to summon help. So he set about the task of nursing her back to health, but at the end of the third day she fell into unconsciousness and so passed away, apparently, with never a gleam of returning reason.

From what we know of a nature like his we may venture to sketch in some of the details of the outline picture drawn by my grandfather. When convinced that she was dead, Murlock had sense enough to remember that the dead must be prepared for burial. In performance of this sacred duty he blundered now and again, did certain things incorrectly, and others which he did correctly were done over and over. His occasional failures to accomplish some simple and ordinary act filled him with astonishment, like that of a drunken man who wonders at the suspension of familiar natural laws. He was surprised, too, that he did not weep—surprised and a little ashamed; surely it is unkind not to weep for the dead. "Tomorrow," he said aloud, "I shall have to make the coffin and dig the grave; and then I shall miss her, when she is no longer in sight; but now—she is dead, of course, but it is all right—it *must* be all right, somehow. Things cannot be so bad as they seem."

He stood over the body in the fading light, adjusting the hair and putting the finishing touches to the simple toilet, doing all mechanically, with soulless care. And still through his consciousness ran an undersense of conviction that all was right—that he should have her again as before, and everything explained. He had had no experience in grief; his capacity had not been enlarged by use. His heart could not contain it all, nor his imagination rightly conceive it. He did not know he was so hard struck; *that* knowledge would come later, and never go. Grief is an artist of powers as various as the instruments upon which he plays his dirges for the dead, evoking from some the sharpest, shrillest notes, from others the low, grave chords that throb recurrent like the slow beating of a distant drum. Some natures it startles; some it stupefies. To one it comes like the stroke of an arrow, stinging all the sensibilities to a keener life; to another as the blow of a bludgeon, which in crushing benumbs. We may conceive Murlock to have been that way affected, for (and here we are upon surer ground than that of conjecture) no sooner had he finished his pious work than, sinking into a chair by the side of the table upon which the body lay, and noting how white the profile showed in the deepening gloom, he laid his arms upon the table's edge, and dropped his face into them, tearless yet and unutterably weary. At that moment came in through the open window a long, wailing sound like the cry of a lost child in the far deeps of the darkening woods! But the man did not move. Again, and nearer than before, sounded that unearthly cry upon his failing sense. Perhaps it was a wild beast; perhaps it was a dream. For Murlock was asleep.

Some hours later, as it afterward appeared, this unfaithful watcher awoke and lifting his head from his arms intently listened—he knew not why. There in the black darkness by the side of the dead, recalling all without a shock, he strained his eyes to see—he knew not what. His senses were all alert, his breath was suspended, his blood had stilled its tides as if to assist the silence. Who—what had waked him, and where was it?

Suddenly the table shook beneath his arms, and at the same moment he heard, or fancied that he heard, a light, soft step—another—sounds as of bare feet upon the floor!

He was terrified beyond the power to cry out or move. Perforce he waited—waited there in the darkness through seeming centuries of such dread as one may know, yet live to tell. He tried vainly to speak the dead woman's name, vainly to stretch forth his hand across the table to learn if she were there. His throat was powerless, his arms and hands were like lead. Then occurred something most frightful. Some heavy body seemed hurled against the table with an impetus that pushed it against his breast so sharply as nearly to overthrow him, and at the same instant he heard and felt the fall of something upon the floor with so violent a thump that the whole house was shaken by the impact. A scuffling ensued, and a confusion of sounds impossible to describe. Murlock had risen to his feet. Fear had by excess forfeited control of his faculties. He flung his hands upon the table. Nothing was there!

There is a point at which terror may turn to madness; and madness incites to action. With no definite intent, from no motive but the wayward impulse of a madman, Murlock sprang to the wall, with a little groping seized his loaded rifle, and without aim discharged it. By the flash which lit up the room with a vivid illumination, he saw an enormous panther dragging the dead woman toward the window, its teeth fixed in her throat! Then there were darkness blacker than before, and silence; and when he returned to consciousness the sun was high and the wood vocal with songs of birds.

The body lay near the window, where the beast had left it when frightened away by the flash and report of the rifle. The clothing was deranged, the long hair in disorder, the limbs lay anyhow. From the throat, dreadfully lacerated, had issued a pool of blood not yet entirely coagulated. The ribbon with which he had bound the wrists was broken; the hands were tightly clenched. Between the teeth was a fragment of the animal's ear.

19

The Real Thing

BY HENRY JAMES

WHEN the porter's wife (she used to answer the house-bell) announced "A gentleman—with a lady, sir," I had, as I often had in those days, for the wish was father to the thought, an immediate vision of sitters. Sitters my visitors in this case proved to be; but not in the sense I should have preferred. However, there was nothing at first to indicate that they might not have come for a portrait. The gentleman, a man of fifty, very high and very straight, with a mustache slightly grizzled and a dark gray walking-coat admirably fitted, both of which I noted professionally—I don't mean as a barber or yet as a tailor—would have struck me as a celebrity if celebrities often were striking. It was a truth of which I had for some time been conscious that a figure with a good deal of frontage was, as one might say, almost never a public institution. A glance at the lady helped to remind me of this paradoxical law: she also looked too distinguished to be a "personality." Moreover one would scarcely come across two variations together.

Neither of the pair spoke immediately—they only prolonged the preliminary gaze which suggested that each wished to give the other a chance. They were visibly shy; they stood there letting me take them in—which, as I afterwards perceived, was the most practical thing they could have done. In this way their embarrassment served their cause. I had seen people painfully reluctant to mention that they desired anything so gross as to be represented on canvas; but the scruples of my new friends appeared almost insurmountable. Yet the gentleman might have said "I should like a portrait of my wife," and the lady might have said "I should like a portrait of my husband." Perhaps they were not husband and wife—this naturally would make the matter more delicate. Perhaps they wished to be done together—in which case they ought to have brought a third person to break the news.

"We come from Mr. Rivet," the lady said at last, with a dim smile which had the effect of a moist sponge passed over a "sunk" piece of painting, as well as of a vague allusion to vanished beauty. She was as tall and straight, in her degree, as her companion, and with ten years less to carry. She looked as sad as a woman could look whose face was not charged with expression; that is her tinted oval mask showed friction as an exposed surface shows it. The hand of time had played over her freely, but only to simplify. She was slim and stiff, and so well-dressed, in dark blue cloth, with lappets and pockets and buttons, that it was clear she employed the same tailor as her husband. The couple had an indefinable air of prosperous thrift—they evidently got a good deal of luxury for their money. If I was to be one of their luxuries it would behove me to consider my terms.

"Ah, Claude Rivet recommended me?" I inquired; and I added that it was very kind of him, though I could reflect that, as he only painted landscape, this was not a sacrifice.

The lady looked very hard at the gentleman, and the gentleman looked round the room. Then staring at the floor a moment and stroking his mustache, he rested his pleasant eyes on me with the remark: "He said you were the right one."

"I try to be, when people want to sit."

"Yes, we should like to," said the lady anxiously.

"Do you mean together?"

My visitors exchanged a glance. "If you could do anything with *me,* I suppose it would be double," the gentleman stammered.

"Oh yes, there's naturally a higher charge for two figures than for one."

"We should like to make it pay," the husband confessed.

"That's very good of you," I returned, appreciating so unwonted a sympathy—for I supposed he meant pay the artist.

A sense of strangeness seemed to dawn on the lady. "We mean for the illustrations—Mr. Rivet said you might put one in."

"Put one in—an illustration?" I was equally confused.

"Sketch her off, you know," said the gentleman, coloring.

It was only then that I understood the service Claude Rivet had rendered me; he had told them that I worked in black and white, for magazines, for story books, for sketches of contemporary life, and consequently had frequent employment for models. These things were true, but it was not less true (I may confess it now—whether because the aspiration was to lead to everything or to nothing I leave the reader to guess) that I couldn't get the honors, to say nothing of the emoluments, of a great painter of portraits out of my head. My "illustrations" were my pot-boilers; I looked to a different branch of art (far and away the most interesting it had always seemed to me) to perpetuate my fame. There was no shame in looking to it also to make my fortune; but that fortune was by so much further from being made from the moment my visitors wished to be "done" for nothing. I was disappointed; for in the pictorial sense I had immediately *seen* them. I had seized their type—I had already settled what I would do with it. Something that wouldn't absolutely have pleased them, I afterwards reflected.

"Ah, you're—you're—a—?" I began, as soon as I had mastered my surprise. I couldn't bring out the dingy word "models"; it seemed to fit the case so little.

"We haven't had much practice," said the lady.

"We've got to *do* something, and we've thought that an artist in your line might perhaps make something of us," her husband threw off. He further mentioned that they didn't know many artists and that they had gone first, on the off-chance (he painted views of course, but sometimes put in figures—perhaps I remembered), to Mr. Rivet, whom they had met a few years before at a place in Norfolk where he was sketching.

"We used to sketch a little ourselves," the lady hinted.

"It's very awkward, but we absolutely *must* do something," her husband went on.

"Of course, we're not so *very* young," she admitted, with a wan smile.

With the remark that I might as well know something more about them, the husband had handed me a card extracted from a neat new pocketbook (their appurtenances were all of the freshest) and inscribed with the words "Major Monarch." Impressive as these words were they didn't carry my knowledge much further; but my visitor presently added: "I've left the army, and we've had the misfortune to lose our money. In fact our means are dreadfully small."

"It's an awful bore," said Mrs. Monarch.

They evidently wished to be discreet—to take care not to swagger because they were gentlefolks. I perceived they would have been willing to recognize this as something of a drawback, at the same time that I guessed at an underlying sense—their consolation in adversity—that they *had* their points. They certainly had; but these advantages struck me as preponderantly social; such for instance as would help to make a drawing-room look well. However, a drawing-room was always, or ought to be, a picture.

In consequence of his wife's allusion to their age Major Monarch observed: "Naturally, it's more for the figure that we thought of going in. We can still hold ourselves up." On the instant I saw that the figure was indeed their strong point. His "naturally" didn't sound vain, but it lighted up the question. "*She* has got the best," he continued, nodding at his wife, with a pleasant after-dinner absence of circumlocution. I could only reply, as if we were in fact sitting over our wine, that this didn't prevent his own from being very good; which led him in turn to rejoin: "We thought that if you ever have to do people like us, we might be something like it. *She,* particularly—for a lady in a book, you know."

I was so amused by them that, to get more of it, I did my best to take their point of view; and though it was an embarrassment to find myself appraising physically, as if they were animals on hire or useful blacks, a pair whom I should have expected to meet only in one of the relations in which criticism is tacit, I looked at Mrs. Monarch judicially enough to be able to exclaim, after a moment, with conviction: "Oh, yes, a lady in a book!" She was singularly like a bad illustration.

"We'll stand up, if you like," said the Major; and he raised himself before me with a really grand air.

I could take his measure at a glance—he was six feet two and a perfect gentleman. It would have paid any club in process of formation and in want of a stamp to engage him at a salary to stand in the principal window. What struck me immediately was that in coming to me they had rather missed their vocation; they could surely have been turned to better account for advertising purposes. I couldn't, of course, see the thing in detail, but I could see them make someone's fortune—I don't mean their own. There was something in them for a waistcoat maker, an hotel keeper or a soap vendor. I could imagine "We always use it" pinned on their bosoms with the greatest effect; I had a vision of the promptitude with which they would launch a table d'hôte.

Mrs. Monarch sat still, not from pride but from shyness, and presently her husband said to her: "Get up my dear and show how smart you are." She obeyed, but she had no need to get up to show it. She walked to the end of the studio, and then she came back blushing, with her fluttered eyes on her husband. I was reminded of an incident I had accidentally had a glimpse of in Paris—being with a friend there, a dramatist about to produce a play—when an actress came to him to ask to be intrusted with a part. She went through her paces before him, walked up and down as Mrs. Monarch was doing. Mrs. Monarch did it quite as well, but I abstained from applauding. It was very odd to see such people apply for such poor pay. She looked as if she had ten thousand a year. Her husband had used the word that described her: she was, in the London current jargon, essentially and typically "smart." Her figure was, in the same order of ideas, conspicuously and irreproachably "good." For a woman of her age her waist was surprisingly small; her elbow moreover had the orthodox crook. She held her head at a conventional angle; but why did she come to *me*? She ought to have tried on jackets at a big shop. I feared my visitors were not only destitute, but "artistic"—which would be a great complication. When she sat down again I thanked her, observing that what a draughtsman most valued in his model was the faculty of keeping quiet.

"Oh, *she* can keep quiet," said Major Monarch. Then he added, jocosely: "I've always kept her quiet."

"I'm not a nasty fidget, am I?" Mrs. Monarch appealed to her husband.

He addressed his answer to me. "Perhaps it isn't out of place to mention—because we ought to be quite business-like, oughtn't we?—that when I married her she was known as the Beautiful Statue."

"Oh, dear!" said Mrs. Monarch, ruefully.

"Of course I should want a certain amount of expression," I rejoined.

"Of *course*!" they both exclaimed.

"And then I suppose you know that you'll get awfully tired."

"Oh, we *never* get tired!" they eagerly cried.

"Have you had any kind of practice?"

They hesitated—they looked at each other. "We've been photographed, *immensely*," said Mrs. Monarch.

"She means the fellows have asked us," added the Major.

"I see—because you're so good-looking."

"I don't know what they thought, but they were always after us."

"We always got our photographs for nothing," smiled Mrs. Monarch.

"We might have brought some, my dear," her husband remarked.

"I'm not sure we have any left. We've given quantities away," she explained to me.

"With our autographs and that sort of thing," said the Major.

"Are they to be got in the shops?" I inquired, as a harmless pleasantry.

"Oh, yes; *hers*—they used to be."

"Not now," said Mrs. Monarch, with her eyes on the floor.

II

I could fancy the "sort of thing" they put on the presentation-copies of their photographs, and I was sure they wrote a beautiful hand. It was odd how quickly I was sure of everything that concerned them. If they were now so poor as to have to earn shillings and pence, they never had had much of a margin. Their good looks had been their capital. and they had good-humoredly made the most of the career that this resource marked out for them. It was in their faces, the blankness, the deep intellectual repose of the twenty years of country house visiting which had given them pleasant intonations. I could see the sunny drawing-rooms, sprinkled with periodicals she didn't read, in which Mrs. Monarch had continuously sat; I could see the wet shrubberies in which she had

walked, equipped to admiration for either exercise. I could see the rich
covers the Major had helped to shoot and the wonderful garments in
which, late at night, he repaired to the smoking room to talk about
them. I could imagine their leggings and waterproofs, their knowing
tweeds and rugs, their rolls of sticks and cases of tackle and neat um-
brellas; and I could evoke the exact appearance of their servants and the
compact variety of their luggage on the platforms of country stations.

They gave small tips, but they were liked; they didn't do anything
themselves, but they were welcome. They looked so well everywhere;
they gratified the general relish for stature, complexion and "form."
They knew it without fatuity or vulgarity, and they respected themselves in consequence. They were not superficial; they were thorough
and kept themselves up—it had been their line. People with such a
taste for activity had to have some line. I could feel how, even in a dull
house, they could have been counted upon for cheerfulness. At present
something had happened—it didn't matter what, their little income had
grown less, it had grown least—and they had to do something for pocket
money. Their friends liked them, but didn't like to support them. There
was something about them that represented credit—their clothes, their
manners, their type; but if credit is a large empty pocket in which an
occasional chink reverberates, the chink at least must be audible. What
they wanted of me was to help make it so. Fortunately they had no children—I soon divined that. They would also perhaps wish our relations
to be kept secret: this was why it was "for the figure"—the reproduction
of the face would betray them.

I liked them—they were so simple; and I had no objection to them
if they would suit. But, somehow, with all their perfections I didn't easily
believe in them. After all they were amateurs, and the ruling passion of
my life was the detestation of the amateur. Combined with this was
another perversity—an innate preference for the represented subject over
the real one: the defect of the real one was so apt to be a lack of representation. I liked things that appeared; then one was sure. Whether they
were or not was a subordinate and almost always a profitless question.
There were other considerations, the first of which was that I already had
two or three people in use, notably a young person with big feet, in alpaca, from Kilburn, who for a couple of years had come to me regularly
for my illustrations and with whom I was still—perhaps ignobly—satisfied. I frankly explained to my visitors how the case stood; but they had
taken more precautions than I supposed. They had reasoned out their
opportunity, for Claude Rivet had told them of the projected *édition de
luxe* of one of the writers of our day—the rarest of the novelists—who,
long neglected by the multitudinous vulgar and dearly prized by the attentive (need I mention Philip Vincent?) had had the happy fortune of

seeing, late in life, the dawn and then the full light of a higher criticism
—an estimate in which, on the part of the public, there was something
really of expiation. The edition in question, planned by a publisher of
taste, was practically an act of high reparation; the woodcuts with which
it was to be enriched were the homage of English art to one of the most
independent representatives of English letters. Major and Mrs. Monarch
confessed to me that they had hoped I might be able to work *them* into
my share of the enterprise. They knew I was to do the first of the books,
"Rutland Ramsay," but I had to make clear to them that my participation
in the rest of the affair—this first book was to be a test—was to depend
on the satisfaction I should give. If this should be limited my employers
would drop me without a scruple. It was therefore a crisis for me, and
naturally I was making special preparations, looking about for new
people, if they should be necessary, and securing the best types. I admitted however that I should like to settle down to two or three good
models who would do for everything.

"Should we have often to—a—put on special clothes?" Mrs. Monarch
timidly demanded.

"Dear, yes—that's half the business."

"And should we be expected to supply our own costumes?"

"Oh, no; I've got a lot of things. A painter's models put on—or put off
—anything he likes."

"And do you mean—a—the same?"

"The same?"

Mrs. Monarch looked at her husband again.

"Oh, she was just wondering," he explained, "if the costumes are in
general use." I had to confess that they were, and I mentioned further
that some of them (I had a lot of genuine, greasy last-century things)
had served their time, a hundred years ago, on living, world-stained men
and women. "We'll put on anything that *fits*," said the Major.

"Oh, I arrange that—they fit in the pictures."

"I'm afraid I should do better for the modern books. I would come
as you like," said Mrs. Monarch.

"She has got a lot of clothes at home: they might do for contemporary
life," her husband continued.

"Oh, I can fancy scenes in which you'd be quite natural." And indeed
I could see the slipshod rearrangements of stale properties—the stories
I tried to produce pictures for without the exasperation of reading them
—whose sandy tracts the good lady might help to people. But I had to
return to the fact that for this sort of work—the daily mechanical grind
—I was already equipped; the people I was working with were fully
adequate.

"We only thought we might be more like *some* characters," said **Mrs.** Monarch mildly, getting up.

Her husband also rose; he stood looking at me with a dim wistfulness that was touching in so fine a man. "Wouldn't it be rather a pull sometimes to have—a—to have—?" He hung fire; he wanted me to help him by phrasing what he meant. But I couldn't—I didn't know. So he brought it out, awkwardly: "The *real* thing; a gentleman, you know, or a lady." I was quite ready to give a general assent—I admitted that there was a great deal in that. This encouraged Major Monarch to say, following up his appeal with an unacted gulp: "It's awfully hard—we've tried everything." The gulp was communicative; it proved too much for his wife. Before I knew it Mrs. Monarch had dropped again upon a divan and burst into tears. Her husband sat down beside her, holding one of her hands; whereupon she quickly dried her eyes with the other, while I felt embarrassed as she looked up at me. "There isn't a confounded job I haven't applied for—waited for—prayed for. You can fancy we'd be pretty bad first. Secretaryships and that sort of thing? You might as well ask for a peerage. I'd be *anything*—I'm strong; a messenger or a coalheaver. I'd put on a gold-laced cap and open carriage doors in front of the haberdasher's; I'd hang about a station, to carry portmanteaus; I'd be a postman. But they won't *look* at you; there are thousands, as good as yourself, already on the ground. *Gentlemen,* poor beggars, who have drunk their wine, who have kept their hunters!"

I was as reassuring as I knew how to be, and my visitors were presently on their feet again while, for the experiment, we agreed on an hour. We were discussing it when the door opened and Miss Churm came in with a wet umbrella. Miss Churm had to take the omnibus to Maida Vale and then walk half a mile. She looked a trifle blowsy and slightly splashed. I scarcely ever saw her come in without thinking afresh how odd it was that, being so little in herself, she should yet be so much in others. She was a meager little Miss Churm, but she was an ample heroine of romance. She was only a freckled cockney, but she could represent everything, from a fine lady to a shepherdess; she had the faculty, as she might have had a fine voice or long hair. She couldn't spell, and she loved beer, but she had two or three "points," and practice, and a knack, and mother-wit, and a kind of whimsical sensibility, and a love of the theater, and seven sisters, and not an ounce of respect, especially for the *h*. The first thing my visitors saw was that her umbrella was wet, and in their spotless perfection they visibly winced at it. The rain had come on since their arrival.

"I'm all in a soak; there *was* a mess of people in the 'bus. I wish you lived near a stytion," said Miss Churm. I requested her to get ready as quickly as possible, and she passed into the room in which she always changed her dress. But before going out she asked me what she was to get into this time.

"It's the Russian princess, don't you know?" I answered; "the one with the 'golden eyes,' in black velvet, for the long thing in the *Cheapside.*

"Golden eyes? I *say!*" cried Miss Churm, while my companions watched her with intensity as she withdrew. She always arranged herself, when she was late, before I could turn round; and I kept my visitors a little, on purpose, so they might get an idea, from seeing her, what would be expected of themselves. I mentioned that she was quite my notion of an excellent model—she was really very clever.

"Do you think she looks like a Russian princess?" Major Monarch asked, with lurking alarm.

"When I make her, yes."

"Oh, if you have to *make* her—!" he reasoned, acutely.

"That's the most you can ask. There are so many that are not makeable."

"Well now, *here's* a lady"—and with a persuasive smile he passed his arm into his wife's—"who's already made!"

"Oh, I'm not a Russian princess," Mrs. Monarch protested, a little coldly. I could see that she had known some and didn't like them. There, immediately, was a complication of a kind that I never had to fear with Miss Churm.

This young lady came back in black velvet—the gown was rather rusty and very low on her lean shoulders—and with a Japanese fan in her red hands. I reminded her that in the scene I was doing she had to look over someone's head. "I forget whose it is; but it doesn't matter. Just look over a head."

"I'd rather look over a stove," said Miss Churm; and she took her station near the fire. She fell into position, settled herself into a tall attitude, gave a certain backward inclination to her head and a certain forward droop to her fan, and looked, at least to my prejudiced sense, distinguished and charming, foreign and dangerous. We left her looking so, while I went downstairs with Major and Mrs. Monarch.

"I think I could come about as near it as that," said Mrs. Monarch.

"Oh, you think she's shabby, but you must allow for the alchemy of art."

However, they went off with an evident increase of comfort, founded on their demonstrable advantage in being the real thing. I could fancy them shuddering over Miss Churm. She was very droll about them when I went back, for I told her what they wanted.

"Well, if *she* can sit I'll tyke to bookkeeping," said my model.

"She's very lady-like," I replied, as an innocent form of aggravation. "So much the worse for *you*. That means she can't turn round." "She'll do for the fashionable novels." "Oh yes, she'll *do* for them!" my model humorously declared. "Ain't they bad enough without her?" I had often sociably denounced them to Miss Churm.

III

It was for the elucidation of a mystery in one of these works that I first tried Mrs. Monarch. Her husband came with her, to be useful if necessary—it was sufficiently clear that as a general thing he would prefer to come with her. At first I wondered if this were for "propriety's" sake —if he were going to be jealous and meddling. The idea was too tiresome, and if it had been confirmed it would speedily have brought our acquaintance to a close. But I soon saw there was nothing in it and that if he accompanied Mrs. Monarch it was (in addition to the chance of being wanted) simply because he had nothing else to do. When she was away from him his occupation was gone—she never *had* been away from him. I judged, rightly, that in their awkward situation their close union was their main comfort and that this union had no weak spot. It was a real marriage, an encouragement to the hesitating, a nut for pessimists to crack. Their address was humble (I remember afterwards thinking it had been the only thing about them that was really professional), and I could fancy the lamentable lodgings in which the Major would have been left alone. He could bear them with his wife—he couldn't bear them without her.

He had too much tact to try and make himself agreeable when he couldn't be useful; so he simply sat and waited, when I was too absorbed in my work to talk. But I liked to make him talk—it made my work, when it didn't interrupt it, less sordid, less special. To listen to him was to combine the excitement of going out with the economy of staying at home. There was only one hindrance: that I seemed not to know any of the people he and his wife had known. I think he wondered extremely, during the term of our intercourse, whom the deuce I *did* know. He hadn't a stray sixpence of an idea to fumble for; so we didn't spin it very fine—we confined ourselves to questions of leather and even of liquor (saddlers and breeches makers and how to get good claret cheap), and matters like "good trains" and the habits of small game. His lore on these last subjects was astonishing, he managed to interweave the station-master with the ornithologist. When he couldn't talk about greater things he could talk cheerfully about smaller, and since I couldn't accompany him into reminiscences of the fashionable world he could lower the conversation without a visible effort to my level.

So earnest a desire to please was touching in a man who could so easily have knocked one down. He looked after the fire and had an opinion on the draught of the stove, without my asking him, and I could see that he thought many of my arrangements not half clever enough. I remember telling him that if I were only rich I would offer him a salary to come and teach me how to live. Sometimes he gave a random sigh, of which the essence was: "Give me even such a bare old barrack as *this,* and I'd do something with it!" When I wanted to use him he came alone; which was an illustration of the superior courage of women. His wife could bear her solitary second floor, and she was in general more discreet; showing by various small reserves that she was alive to the propriety of keeping our relations markedly professional—not letting them slide into sociability. She wished it to remain clear that she and the Major were employed, not cultivated, and if she approved of me as a superior, who could be kept in his place, she never thought me quite good enough for an equal.

She sat with great intensity, giving the whole of her mind to it, and was capable of remaining for an hour almost as motionless as if she were before a photographer's lens. I could see she had been photographed often, but somehow the very habit that made her good for that purpose unfitted her for mine. At first I was extremely pleased with her ladylike air, and it was a satisfaction, on coming to follow her lines, to see how good they were and how far they could lead the pencil. But after a few times I began to find her too insurmountably stiff; do what I would with it my drawing looked like a photograph or a copy of a photograph. Her figure had no variety of expression—she herself had no sense of variety. You may say that this was my business, was only a question of placing her. I placed her in every conceivable position, but she managed to obliterate their differences. She was always a lady certainly, and into the bargain was always the same lady. She was the real thing, but always the same thing. There were moments when I was oppressed by the serenity of her confidence that she *was* the real thing. All her dealings with me and all her husband's were an implication that this was lucky for *me.* Meanwhile I found myself trying to invent types that approached her own, instead of making her own transform itself—in the clever way that was not impossible, for instance, to poor Miss Churm. Arrange as I would and take the precautions I would, she always, in my pictures, came out too tall—landing me in the dilemma of having represented a fascinating woman as seven feet high, which, out of respect perhaps to my own very much scantier inches, was far from my idea of such a personage.

The case was worse with the Major—nothing I could do would keep *him* down, so that he became useful only for the representation of brawny giants. I adored variety and range, I cherished human accidents, the illustrative note; I wanted to characterize closely, and the thing in the world I most hated was the danger of being ridden by a type. I had quarrelled with some of my friends about it—I had parted company with them for maintaining that one *had* to be, and that if the type was beautiful (witness Raphael and Leonardo), the servitude was only a gain. I was neither Leonardo nor Raphael; I might only be a presumptuous young modern searcher, but I held that everything was to be sacrificed sooner than character. When they averred that the haunting type in question could easily *be* character, I retorted, perhaps superficially: "Whose?" It couldn't be everybody's—it might end in being nobody's.

After I had drawn Mrs. Monarch a dozen times I perceived more clearly than before that the value of such a model as Miss Churm resided precisely in the fact that she had no positive stamp, combined, of course, with the other fact that what she did have was a curious and inexplicable talent for imitation. Her usual appearance was like a curtain which she could draw up at request for a capital performance. This performance was simply suggestive; but it was a word to the wise—it was vivid and pretty. Sometimes, even, I thought it, though she was plain herself, too insipidly pretty; I made it a reproach to her that the figures drawn from her were monotonously (*bêtement,* as we used to say) graceful. Nothing made her more angry: it was so much her pride to feel that she could sit for characters that had nothing in common with each other. She would accuse me at such moments of taking away her "reputytion."

It suffered a certain shrinkage, this queer quantity, from the repeated visits of my new friends. Miss Churm was greatly in demand, never in want of employment, so I had no scruple in putting her off occasionally, to try them more at my ease. It was certainly amusing at first to do the real thing—it was amusing to do Major Monarch's trousers. They *were* the real thing, even if he did come out colossal. It was amusing to do his wife's back hair (it was so mathematically neat) and the particular "smart" tension of her tight stays. She lent herself especially to positions in which the face was somewhat averted or blurred; she abounded in ladylike back views and *profils perdus.* When she stood erect she took naturally one of the attitudes in which court painters represent queens and princesses; so that I found myself wondering whether, to draw out this accomplishment, I couldn't get the editor of the *Cheapside* to publish a really royal romance, "A Tale of Buckingham Palace." Sometimes, however, the real thing and the make-believe came into contact; by which I mean that Miss Churm, keeping an appointment or coming to make one on days when I had much work in hand, encountered her invidious rivals. The encounter was not on their part, for they noticed her no more than if she had been the housemaid; not from intentional loftiness, but simply because, as yet, professionally, they didn't know how to fraternize, as I could guess that they would have liked—or at least that the Major would. They couldn't talk about the omnibus— they always walked; and they didn't know what else to try—she wasn't interested in good trains or cheap claret. Besides, they must have felt— in the air—that she was amused at them, secretly derisive of their ever knowing how. She was not a person to conceal her scepticism if she had had a chance to show it. On the other hand Mrs. Monarch didn't think her tidy; for why else did she take pains to say to me (it was going out of the way, for Mrs. Monarch), that she didn't like dirty women?

One day when my young lady happened to be present with my other sitters (she even dropped in, when it was convenient, for a chat), I asked her to be so good as to lend a hand in getting tea—a service with which she was familiar and which was one of a class that, living as I did in a small way, with slender domestic resources, I often appealed to my models to render. They liked to lay hands on my property, to break the sitting, and sometimes the china—I made them feel Bohemian. The next time I saw Miss Churm after this incident she surprised me greatly by making a scene about it—she accused me of having wished to humiliate her. She had not resented the outrage at the time, but had seemed obliged and amused, enjoying the comedy of asking Mrs. Monarch, who sat vague and silent, whether she would have cream and sugar, and putting an exaggerated simper into the question. She had tried intonations—as if she too wished to pass for the real thing; till I was afraid my other visitors would take offense.

Oh, *they* were determined not to do this; and their touching patience was the measure of their great need. They would sit by the hour, uncomplaining, till I was ready to use them; they would come back on the chance of being wanted and would walk away cheerfully if they were not. I used to go to the door with them to see in what magnificent order they retreated. I tried to find other employment for them—I introduced them to several artists. But they didn't "take," for reasons I could appreciate, and I became conscious, rather anxiously, that after such disappointments they fell back upon me with a heavier weight. They did me the honor to think that it was I who was most *their* form. They were not picturesque enough for the painters, and in those days there were not so many serious workers in black and white. Besides, they had an eye to the great job I had mentioned to them—they had secretly set their hearts on supplying the right essence for my pictorial vindication of our fine novelist. They knew that for this undertaking I should want no costume effects, none of the frippery of past ages—that it was a case in which everything would be contemporary and satirical and. presumably, genteel. If I could work them into it their future would be assured, for the labor would of course be long and the occupation steady.

One day Mrs. Monarch came without her husband—she explained his absence by his having had to go to the City. While she sat there in her usual anxious stiffness there came, at the door, a knock which I immediately recognized as the subdued appeal of a model out of work. It was followed by the entrance of a young man whom I easily perceived to be a foreigner and who proved in fact an Italian acquainted with no English word but my name, which he uttered in a way that made it seem to include all others. I had not then visited his country, nor was I proficient in his tongue; but as he was not so meanly constituted— what Italian is?—as to depend only on that member for expression he conveyed to me, in familiar but graceful mimicry, that he was in search of exactly the employment in which the lady before me was engaged. I was not struck with him at first, and while I continued to draw I emitted rough sounds of discouragement and dismissal. He stood his ground, however, not importunately, but with a dumb, dog-like fidelity in his eyes which amounted to innocent impudence—the manner of a devoted servant (he might have been in the house for years) unjustly suspected. Suddenly I saw that this very attitude and expression made a picture, whereupon I told him to sit down and wait till I should be free. There was another picture in the way he obeyed me, and I observed as I worked that there were others still in the way he looked wonderingly, with his head thrown back, about the high studio. He might have been crossing himself in St. Peter's. Before I finished I said to myself: "The fellow's a bankrupt orange-monger, but he's a treasure."

When Mrs. Monarch withdrew he passed across the room like a flash to open the door for her, standing there with the rapt, pure gaze of the young Dante spellbound by the young Beatrice. As I never insisted, in such situations, on the blankness of the British domestic, I reflected that he had the making of a servant (and I needed one, but couldn't pay him to be only that), as well as of a model; in short I made up my mind to adopt my bright adventurer if he would agree to officiate in the double capacity. He jumped at my offer, and in the event my rashness (for I had known nothing about him) was not brought home to me. He proved a sympathetic though desultory ministrant, and had in a wonderful degree the *sentiment de la pose*. It was uncultivated, instinctive; a part of the happy instinct which had guided him to my door and helped him to spell out my name on the card nailed to it. He had had no other introduction to me than a guess, from the shape of my high north window, seen outside, that my place was a studio and that as a studio it would contain an artist. He had wandered to England in search of fortune, like other itinerants, and had embarked, with a partner and a small green handcart, on the sale of penny ices. The ices had melted away and the partner had dissolved in their train. My young man wore tight yellow trousers with reddish stripes and his name was Oronte. He was sallow but fair, and when I put him into some old clothes of my own he looked like an Englishman. He was as good as Miss Churm, who could look, when required, like an Italian.

IV

I thought Mrs. Monarch's face slightly convulsed when, on her coming back with her husband, she found Oronte installed. It was strange to have to recognize in a scrap of a lazzarone a competitor to her magnificent Major. It was she who scented danger first, for the Major was anecdotically unconscious. But Oronte gave us tea, with a hundred eager confusions (he had never seen such a queer process), and I think she thought better of me for having at last an "establishment." They saw a couple of drawings that I had made of the establishment, and Mrs. Monarch hinted that it never would have struck her that he had sat for them. "Now the drawings you make from *us,* they look exactly like us," she reminded me, smiling in triumph; and I recognized that this was indeed just their defect. When I drew the Monarchs I couldn't, somehow, get away from them—get into the character I wanted to represent; and I had not the least desire my model should be discoverable in my picture. Miss Churm never was, and Mrs. Monarch thought I hid her, very properly, because she was vulgar; whereas if she was lost it was only as the dead who go to heaven are lost—in the gain of an angel the more.

By this time I had got a certain start with "Rutland Ramsay," the first novel in the great projected series; that is I had produced a dozen drawings, several with the help of the Major and his wife, and I had sent them in for approval. My understanding with the publishers, as I have already hinted, had been that I was to be left to do my work, in this particular case, as I liked, with the whole book committed to me; but my connection with the rest of the series was only contingent. There were moments when, frankly, it *was* a comfort to have the real thing under one's hand; for there were characters in "Rutland Ramsay" that were very much like it. There were people presumably as straight as the Major and women of as good a fashion as Mrs. Monarch. There was a great deal of country-house life—treated, it is true, in a fine, fanciful, ironical, generalized way—and there was a considerable implication of knickerbockers and kilts. There were certain things I had to settle at the outset; such things for instance as the exact appearance of the hero, the particular bloom of the heroine. The author of course gave me a lead, but there was a margin for interpretation. I took the Monarchs into my confidence, I told them frankly what I was about, I mentioned my embarrassments and alternatives. "Oh, take *him!*" Mrs. Monarch murmured sweetly, looking at her husband; and "What could you want better than my wife?" the Major inquired, with the comfortable candor that now prevailed between us.

I was not obliged to answer these remarks—I was only obliged to place my sitters. I was not easy in mind, and I postponed, a little timidly perhaps, the solution of the question. The book was a large canvas, the other figures were numerous, and I worked off at first some of the episodes in which the hero and the heroine were not concerned. When once I had set *them* up I should have to stick to them—I couldn't make my young man seven feet high in one place and five feet nine in another. I inclined on the whole to the latter measurement, though the Major more than once reminded me that *he* looked about as young as anyone. It was indeed quite possible to arrange him, for the figure, so that it would have been difficult to detect his age. After the spontaneous Oronte had been with me a month, and after I had given him to understand several different times that his native exuberance would presently constitute an insurmountable barrier to our further intercourse, I waked to a sense of his heroic capacity. He was only five feet seven, but the remaining inches were latent. I tried him almost secretly at first, for I was really rather afraid of the judgment my other models would pass on such a choice. If they regarded Miss Churm as little better than a snare, what would they think of the representation by a person so little the real thing as an Italian street vendor of a protagonist formed by a public school?

If I went a little in fear of them it was not because they bullied me, because they had got an oppressive foothold, but because in their really pathetic decorum and mysteriously permanent newness they counted on me so intensely. I was therefore very glad when Jack Hawley came home: he was always of such good counsel. He painted badly himself, but there was no one like him for putting his finger on the place. He had been absent from England for a year; he had been somewhere—I don't remember where—to get a fresh eye. I was in a good deal of dread of any such organ, but we were old friends; he had been away for months and a sense of emptiness was creeping into my life. I hadn't dodged a missile for a year.

He came back with a fresh eye, but with the same old black velvet blouse, and the first evening he spent in my studio we smoked cigarettes till the small hours. He had done no work himself, he had only got the eye; so the field was clear for the production of my little things. He wanted to see what I had done for the *Cheapside,* but he was disappointed in the exhibition. That at least seemed the meaning of two or three comprehensive groans which, as he lounged on my big divan, on a folded leg, looking at my latest drawings, issued from his lips with the smoke of the cigarette.

"What's the matter with you?" I asked.

"What's the matter with *you*?"

"Nothing save that I'm mystified."

"You are indeed. You're quite off the hinge. What's the meaning of this new fad?" And he tossed me, with visible irreverence, a drawing in which I happened to have depicted both my majestic models. I asked if he didn't think it good, and he replied that it struck him as execrable, given the sort of thing I had always represented myself to him as wishing to arrive at; but I let that pass, I was so anxious to see exactly what he meant. The two figures in the picture looked colossal, but I supposed this was *not* what he meant, inasmuch as, for aught he knew to the contrary, I might have been trying for that. I maintained that I was working exactly in the same way as when he last had done me the honor to commend me. "Well, there's a big hole somewhere," he answered; "wait a bit and I'll discover it." I depended upon him to do so: where else was the fresh eye? But he produced at last nothing more luminous than "I don't know—I don't like your types." This was lame, for a critic who had never consented to discuss with me anything but the question of execution, the direction of strokes and the mystery of values.

"In the drawings you've been looking at I think my types are very handsome."

"Oh, they won't do!"

"I've had a couple of new models."

"I see you have. *They* won't do."

"Are you very sure of that?"

"Absolutely—they're stupid."

"You mean *I* am—for I ought to get round that."

"You *can't*—with such people. Who are they?"

I told him, as far as was necessary, and he declared, heartlessly: *"Ce sont des gens qu'il faut mettre à la porte."*

"You've never seen them; they're awfully good," I compassionately objected.

"Not seen them? Why, all this recent work of yours drops to pieces with them. It's all I want to see of them."

"No one else has said anything against it—the *Cheapside* people are pleased."

"Everyone else is an ass, and the *Cheapside* people the biggest asses of all. Come, don't pretend, at this time of day, to have pretty illusions about the public, especially about publishers and editors. It's not for *such* animals you work—it's for those who know, *coloro che sanno;* so keep

straight for *me* if you can't keep straight for yourself. There's a certain
sort of thing you tried for from the first—and a very good thing it is.
But this twaddle isn't *in* it." When I talked with Hawley later
about "Rutland Ramsay" and its possible successors he declared that I
must get back into my boat again or I would go to the bottom. His
voice in short was the voice of warning.

I noted the warning, but I didn't turn my friends out of doors. They
bored me a good deal; but the very fact that they bored me admonished
me not to sacrifice them—if there was anything to be done with them
—simply to irritation. As I look back at this phase they seem to me to
have pervaded my life not a little. I have a vision of them as most of the
time in my studio, seated, against the wall, on an old velvet bench to be
out of the way, and looking like a pair of patient courtiers in a royal
ante-chamber. I am convinced that during the coldest weeks of the
winter they held their ground because it saved them fire. Their newness
was losing its gloss, and it was impossible not to feel that they were
objects of charity. Whenever Miss Churm arrived they went away, and
after I was fairly launched in "Rutland Ramsay" Miss Churm arrived
pretty often. They managed to express to me tacitly that they supposed
I wanted her for the low life of the book, and I let them suppose it,
since they had attempted to study the work—it was lying about the
studio—without discovering that it dealt only with the highest circles.
They had dipped into the most brilliant of our novelists without de-
ciphering many passages. I still took an hour from them, now and again,
in spite of Jack Hawley's warning: it would be time enough to dismiss
them, if dismissal should be necessary, when the rigor of the season was
over. Hawley had made their acquaintance—he had met them at my
fireside—and thought them a ridiculous pair. Learning that he was a
painter they tried to approach him, to show him too that they were
the real thing; but he looked at them, across the big room, as if they
were miles away: they were a compendium of everything that he most
objected to in the social system of his country. Such people as that, all
convention and patent leather, with ejaculations that stopped conversation, had no business in a studio. A studio was a place to learn to see, and
how could you see through a pair of feather beds?

The main inconvenience I suffered at their hands was that, at first,
I was shy of letting them discover how my artful little servant had begun
to sit to me for "Rutland Ramsay." They knew that I had been odd
enough (they were prepared by this time to allow oddity to artists) to
pick a foreign vagabond out of the streets, when I might have had a person with whiskers and credentials; but it was some time before they
learned how high I rated his accomplishments. They found him in an
attitude more than once, but they never doubted I was doing him as an

organ grinder. There were several things they never guessed, and one of them was that for a striking scene in the novel, in which a footman briefly figured, it occurred to me to make use of Major Monarch as the menial. I kept putting this off, I didn't like to ask him to don the livery—besides the difficulty of finding a livery to fit him. At last, one day late in the winter, when I was at work on the despised Oronte (he caught one's idea in an instant), and was in the glow of feeling that I was going very straight, they came in, the Major and his wife, with their society laugh about nothing (there was less and less to laugh at), like country callers—they always reminded me of that—who have walked across the park after church and are presently persuaded to stay to luncheon. Luncheon was over, but they could stay to tea—I knew they wanted it. The fit was on me, however, and I couldn't let my ardor cool and my work wait, with the fading daylight, while my model prepared it. So I asked Mrs. Monarch if she would mind laying it out—a request which, for an instant, brought all the blood to her face. Her eyes were on her husband's for a second, and some mute telegraphy passed between them. Their folly was over the next instant; his cheerful shrewdness put an end to it. So far from pitying their wounded pride, I must add, I was moved to give it as complete a lesson as I could. They bustled about together and got out the cups and saucers and made the kettle boil. I know they felt as if they were waiting on my servant, and when the tea was prepared I said: "He'll have a cup, please—he's tired." Mrs. Monarch brought him one where he stood, and he took it from her as if he had been a gentleman at a party, squeezing a crush-hat with an elbow.

Then it came over me that she had made a great effort for me—made it with a kind of nobleness—and that I owed her a compensation. Each time I saw her after this I wondered what the compensation could be. I couldn't go on doing the wrong thing to oblige them. Oh, it *was* the wrong thing, the stamp of the work for which they sat—Hawley was not the only person to say it now. I sent in a large number of the drawings I had made for "Rutland Ramsay," and I received a warning that was more to the point than Hawley's. The artistic adviser of the house for which I was working was of opinion that many of my illustrations were not what had been looked for. Most of these illustrations were the subjects in which the Monarchs had figured. Without going into the question of what *had* been looked for, I saw at this rate I shouldn't get the other books to do. I hurled myself in despair upon Miss Churm, I put her through all her paces. I not only adopted Oronte publicly as my hero, but one morning when the Major looked in to see if I didn't require him to finish a figure for the *Cheapside,* for which he had begun to sit the week before, I told him that I had changed my mind—I would do the drawing from my man. At this my visitor turned pale and stood looking at me. "Is *he* your idea of an English gentleman?" he asked.

I was disappointed, I was nervous, I wanted to get on with my work; so I replied with irritation: "Oh, my dear Major—I can't be ruined for *you!*"

He stood another moment; then, without a word, he quitted the studio. I drew a long breath when he was gone, for I said to myself that I shouldn't see him again. I had not told him definitely that I was in danger of having my work rejected, but I was vexed at his not having felt the catastrophe in the air, read with me the moral of our fruitless collaboration, the lesson that, in the deceptive atmosphere of art, even the highest respectability may fail of being plastic.

I didn't owe my friends money, but I did see them again. They reappeared together, three days later, and under the circumstances there was something tragic in the fact. It was a proof to me that they could find nothing else in life to do. They had threshed the matter out in a dismal conference—they had digested the bad news that they were not in for the series. If they were not useful to me even for the *Cheapside* their function seemed difficult to determine, and I could only judge at first that they had come, forgivingly, decorously, to take a last leave. This made me rejoice in secret that I had little leisure for a scene; for I had placed both my other models in position together and I was pegging away at a drawing from which I hoped to derive glory. It had been suggested by the passage in which Rutland Ramsay, drawing up a chair to Artemisia's piano-stool, says extraordinary things to her while she ostensibly fingers out a difficult piece of music. I had done Miss Churm at the piano before—it was an attitude in which she knew how to take on an absolutely poetic grace. I wished the two figures to "compose" together, intensely, and my little Italian had entered perfectly into my conception. The pair were vividly before me, the piano had been pulled out; it was a charming picture of blended youth and murmured love, which I had only to catch and keep. My visitors stood and looked at it, and I was friendly to them over my shoulder.

They made no response, but I was used to silent company and went on with my work, only a little disconcerted (even though exhilarated by the sense that *this* was at least the ideal thing), at not having got rid of them after all. Presently I heard Mrs. Monarch's sweet voice beside, or rather above me: "I wish her hair was a little better done." I looked up and she was staring with a strange fixedness at Miss Churm, whose back was turned to her. "Do you mind my just touching it?" she went on—a question which made me spring up for an instant, as with the instinctive fear that she might do the young lady a harm. But she quieted me with a glance I shall never forget—I confess I should like to have been able to paint *that*—and went for a moment to my model. She spoke to her softly, laying a hand upon her shoulder and bending over her; and as the girl, understanding, gratefully assented, she disposed her rough curls, with a few quick passes, in such a way as to make Miss Churm's head twice as charming. It was one of the most heroic personal services I have ever seen rendered. Then Mrs. Monarch turned away with a low sigh and, looking about her as if for something to do, stooped to the floor with a noble humility and picked up a dirty rag that had dropped out of my paint box.

The Major meanwhile had also been looking for something to do and, wandering to the other end of the studio, saw before him my breakfast things, neglected, unremoved. "I say, can't I be useful *here*?" he called out to me with an irrepressible quaver. I assented with a laugh that I fear was awkward and for the next ten minutes, while I worked, I heard the light clatter of china and the tinkle of spoons and glass. Mrs. Monarch assisted her husband—they washed up my crockery, they put it away. They wandered off into my little scullery, and I afterwards found that they had cleaned my knives and that my slender stock of plate had an unprecedented surface. When it came over me, the latent eloquence of what they were doing, I confess that my drawing was blurred for a moment—the picture swam. They had accepted their failure, but they couldn't accept their fate. They had bowed their heads in bewilderment to the perverse and cruel law in virtue of which the real thing could be so much less precious than the unreal; but they didn't want to starve. If my servants were my models, my models might be my servants. They would reverse the parts—the others would sit for the ladies and gentlemen, and *they* would do the work. They would still be in the studio—it was an intense dumb appeal to me not to turn them out. "Take us on," they wanted to say—"we'll do *anything*."

When all this hung before me the *afflatus* vanished—my pencil dropped from my hand. My sitting was spoiled and I got rid of my sitters, who were also evidently rather mystified and awestruck. Then, alone with the Major and his wife, I had a most uncomfortable moment. He put their prayer into a single sentence: "I say, you know—just let *us* do for you, can't you?" I couldn't—it was dreadful to see them emptying my slops; but I pretended I could, to oblige them, for about a week. Then I gave them a sum of money to go away; and I never saw them again. I obtained the remaining books, but my friend Hawley repeats that Major and Mrs. Monarch did me a permanent harm, got me into a second-rate trick. If it be true I am content to have paid the price—for the memory.

20

The Author of Beltraffio

BY HENRY JAMES

MUCH as I wished to see him I had kept my letter of introduction three weeks in my pocket-book. I was nervous and timid about meeting him—conscious of youth and ignorance, convinced that he was tormented by strangers, and especially by my country-people, and not exempt from the suspicion that he had the irritability as well as the dignity of genius. Moreover, the pleasure, if it should occur—for I could scarcely believe it was near at hand—would be so great that I wished to think of it in advance, to feel it there against my breast, not to mix it with satisfactions more superficial and usual. In the little game of new sensations that I was playing with my ingenuous mind I wished to keep my visit to the author of "Beltraffio" as a trump-card. It was three years after the publication of that fascinating work, which I had read over five times and which now, with my riper judgment, I admire on the whole as much as ever. This will give you about the date of my first visit—of any duration—to England; for you will not have forgotten the commotion, I may even say the scandal, produced by Mark Ambient's masterpiece. It was the most complete presentation that had yet been made of the gospel of art; it was a kind of aesthetic war cry. People had endeavored to sail nearer to "truth" in the cut of their sleeves and the shape of their sideboards; but there had not as yet been, among English novels, such an example of beauty of execution and "intimate" importance of theme. Nothing had been done in that line from the point of view of art for art. That served me as a fond formula, I may mention, when I was twenty-five; how much it still serves I won't take upon myself to say—especially as the discerning reader will be able to judge for himself. I had been in England, briefly, a twelve-month before the time to which I began by alluding, and had then learned that

Mr. Ambient was in distant lands—was making a considerable tour in the East; so that there was nothing to do but to keep my letter till I should be in London again. It was of little use to me to hear that his wife had not left England and was, with her little boy, their only child, spending the period of her husband's absence—a good many months—at a small place they had down in Surrey. They had a house in London, but actually in the occupation of other persons. All this I had picked up, and also that Mrs. Ambient was charming—my friend the American poet, from whom I had my introduction, had never seen her, his relations with the great man confined to the exchange of letters; but she wasn't, after all, though she had lived so near the rose, the author of "Beltraffio," and I didn't go down into Surrey to call on her. I went to the Continent, spent the following winter in Italy and returned to London in May. My visit to Italy had opened my eyes to a good many things, but to nothing more than the beauty of certain pages in the works of Mark Ambient. I carried his productions about in my trunk—they are not, as you know, very numerous, but he had preluded to "Beltraffio" by some exquisite things—and I used to read them over in the evening at the inn. I used profoundly to reason that the man who drew those characters and wrote that style understood what he saw and knew what he was doing. This is my sole ground for mentioning my winter in Italy. He had been there much in former years—he was saturated with what painters call the "feeling" of that classic land. He expressed the charm of the old hill-cities of Tuscany, the look of certain lonely grass-grown places which, in the past, had echoed with life; he understood the great artists; he understood the spirit of the Renaissance; he understood everything. The scene of one of his earlier novels was laid in Rome, the scene of another in Florence, and I had moved through these cities in company with the figures he set so firmly on their feet. This is why I was now so much happier even than before in the prospect of making his acquaintance.

At last, when I had dallied with my privilege long enough, I dispatched to him the missive of the American poet. He had already gone out of town; he shrank from the rigor of the London "season," and it was his habit to migrate on the first of June. Moreover I had heard he was this year hard at work on a new book, into which some of his impressions of the East were to be wrought, so that he desired nothing so much as quiet days. That knowledge, however, didn't prevent me—*cet âge est sans pitié*—from sending with my friend's letter a note of my own, in which I asked his leave to come down and see him for an hour or two on some day to be named by himself. My proposal was accompanied with a very frank expression of my sentiments, and the effect of the entire appeal was to elicit from the great man the kindest possible invitation. He would be delighted to see me, especially if I should turn up on the following Saturday and would remain till the Monday morning. We would take a walk over the Surrey commons, and I could tell him all about the other great man, the one in America. He indicated to me the best train, and it may be imagined whether on the Saturday afternoon I was punctual at Waterloo. He carried his benevolence to the point of coming to meet me at the little station at which I was to alight, and my heart beat very fast as I saw his handsome face, surmounted with a soft wide-awake and which I knew by a photograph long since enshrined on my mantel shelf, scanning the carriage windows as the train rolled up. He recognized me as infallibly as I had recognized himself; he appeared to know by instinct how a young American of critical pretensions, rash youth, would look when much divided between eagerness and modesty. He took me by the hand and smiled at me and said: "You must be—a—*you,* I think!" and asked if I should mind going on foot to his house, which would take but a few minutes. I remember feeling it a piece of extraordinary affability that he should give directions about the conveyance of my bag; I remember feeling altogether very happy and rosy, in fact quite transported, when he laid his hand on my shoulder as we came out of the station.

I surveyed him, askance, as we walked together; I had already, I had indeed instantly, seen him as all delightful. His face is so well known that I needn't describe it; he looked to me at once an English gentleman and a man of genius, and I thought that a happy combination. There was a brush of the Bohemian in his fineness; you would easily have guessed his belonging to the artist guild. He was addicted to velvet jackets, to cigarettes, to loose shirt-collars, to looking a little disheveled. His features, which were firm but not perfectly regular, are fairly enough represented in his portraits; but no portrait I have seen gives any idea of his expression. There were innumerable things in it, and they chased each other in and out of his face. I have seen people who were grave and gay in quick alternation; but Mark Ambient was grave and gay at one and the same moment. There were other strange oppositions and contradictions in his slightly faded and fatigued countenance. He affected me somehow as at once fresh and stale, at once anxious and indifferent. He had evidently had an active past, which inspired one with curiosity; yet what was that compared to his obvious future? He was just enough above middle height to be spoken of as tall, and rather lean and long in the flank. He had the friendliest frankest manner possible, and yet I could see it cost him something. It cost him small spasms of the self-consciousness that is an Englishman's last and dearest treasure—the thing he pays his way through life by sacrificing small pieces of even as the gallant but moneyless adventurer in "Quentin Durward" broke off links of his brave gold chain. He had been thirty-eight years old at the time "Beltraffio" was published. He asked me about his friend in America, about the length of my stay in England, about the last news in London and the people I had seen there; and I remember looking for the signs of genius in the very form of his questions and thinking I found it. I liked his voice as if I were somehow myself having the use of it.

There was genius in his house too, I thought, when we got there; there was imagination in the carpets and curtains, in the pictures and books, in the garden behind it. where certain old brown walls were muffled in creepers that appeared to me to have been copied from a masterpiece of one of the pre-Raphaelites. That was the way many things struck me at that time, in England—as reproductions of something that existed primarily in art or literature. It was not the picture, the poem, the fictive page, that seemed to me a copy; these things were the originals, and the life of happy and distinguished people was fashioned in their image. Mark Ambient called his house a cottage, and I saw afterwards he was right; for if it hadn't been a cottage it must have been a villa, and a villa, in England at least, was not a place in which one could fancy him at home. But it was, to my vision, a cottage glorified and translated; it was a palace of art, on a slightly reduced scale—and might besides have been the dearest haunt of the old English *genius loci*. It nestled under a cluster of magnificent beeches, it had little creaking lattices that opened out of, or into, pendent mats of ivy, and gables, and old red tiles, as well as a general aspect of being painted in water-colors and inhabited by people whose lives would go on in chapters and volumes. The lawn seemed to me of extraordinary extent, the garden walls of incalculable height, the whole air of the place delightfully still, private, proper to itself. "My wife must be somewhere about," Mark Ambient said as we went in. "We shall find her perhaps—we've about an hour before dinner. She may be in the garden. I'll show you my little place."

We passed through the house and into the grounds, as I should have called them, which extended into the rear. They covered scarce three or four acres, but, like the house, were very old and crooked and full of traces of long habitation, with inequalities of level and little flights of steps—mossy and cracked were these—which connected the different parts with each other. The limits of the place, cleverly dissimulated, were muffled in the great verdurous screens. They formed, as I remember, a thick loose curtain at the further end, in one of the folds of which, as it were, we presently made out from afar a little group. "Ah, there she is!" said Mark Ambient; "and she has got the boy." He noted that last fact in a slightly different tone from any in which he yet had spoken. I wasn't fully aware of this at the time, but it lingered in my ear and I afterwards understood it.

"Is it your son?" I enquired, feeling the question not to be brilliant.

"Yes, my only child. He's always in his mother's pocket. She coddles him too much." It came back to me afterwards too—the sound of these critical words. They weren't petulant; they expressed rather a sudden coldness, a mechanical submission. We went a few steps further, and then he stopped short and called the boy, beckoning to him repeatedly.

"Dolcino, come and see your daddy!" There was something in the way he stood still and waited that made me think he did it for a purpose. Mrs. Ambient had her arm round the child's waist, and he was leaning against her knee; but though he moved at his father's call she gave no sign of releasing him. A lady, apparently a neighbor, was seated near her, and before them was a garden-table on which a tea-service had been placed.

Mark Ambient called again, and Dolcino struggled in the maternal embrace; but, too tightly held, he after two or three fruitless efforts jerked about and buried his head deep in his mother's lap. There was a certain awkwardness in the scene; I thought it odd Mrs. Ambient should pay so little attention to her husband. But I wouldn't for the world have betrayed my thought and, to conceal it, I began loudly to rejoice in the prospect of our having tea in the garden. "Ah, she won't let him come!" said my host with a sigh; and we went our way till we reached the two ladies. He mentioned my name to his wife, and I noticed that he addressed her as "My dear," very genially, without a trace of resentment at her detention of the child. The quickness of the transition made me vaguely ask myself if he were perchance henpecked—a shocking surmise which I instantly dismissed. Mrs. Ambient was quite such a wife as I should have expected him to have; slim and fair, with a long neck and pretty eyes and an air of good breeding. She shone with a certain coldness and practised in intercourse a certain bland detachment, but she was clothed in gentleness as in one of those vaporous redundant scarves that muffle the heroines of Gainsborough and Romney. She had also a vague air of race, justified by my afterwards learning that she was "connected with aristocracy." I have seen poets married to women of whom it was difficult to conceive that they should gratify the poetic fancy—women with dull faces and glutinous minds, who were none the less, however, excellent wives. But there was no obvious disparity in Mark Ambient's union. My hostess—so far as she could be called so—delicate and quiet, in a white dress, with her beautiful child at her side, was worthy of the author of a work so distinguished as "Beltraffio." Round her neck she wore a black velvet ribbon, of which the long ends, tied behind, hung down her back, and to which, in front, was attached a miniature portrait of her little boy. Her smooth shining hair was confined in a net. She gave me an adequate greeting and Dolcino—I thought this small name of endearment delightful—took advantage of her getting up to slip away from her and go to his father, who seized him in silence and held him high for a long moment, kissing him several times.

I had lost no time in observing that the child, not more than seven years old, was extraordinarily beautiful. He had the face of an angel—the eyes, the hair, the smile of innocence, the more than mortal bloom. There was something that deeply touched, that almost alarmed, in his beauty, composed, one would have said, of elements too fine and pure for the breath of this world. When I spoke to him and he came and held out his hand and smiled at me I felt a sudden strange pity for him—quite as if he had been an orphan or a changeling or stamped with some social stigma. It was impossible to be in fact more exempt from these misfortunes, and yet, as one kissed him, it was hard to keep from murmuring all tenderly "Poor little devil!" though why one should have applied this epithet to a living cherub is more than I can say. Afterwards indeed I knew a trifle better; I grasped the truth of his being too fair to live, wondering at same time that his parents shouldn't have guessed it and have been in proportionate grief and despair. For myself I had no doubt of his evanescence, having already more than once caught in the fact the particular infant charm that's as good as a death warrant.

The lady who had been sitting with Mrs. Ambient was a jolly ruddy personage in velveteen and limp feathers, whom I guessed to be the vicar's wife—our hostess didn't introduce me—and who immediately began to talk to Ambient about chrysanthemums. This was a safe subject, and yet there was a certain surprise for me in seeing the author of "Beltraffio" even in such superficial communion with the Church of England. His writings implied so much detachment from that institution, expressed a view of life so profane, as it were, so independent and so little likely in general to be thought edifying, that I should have expected to find him an object of horror to vicars and their ladies—of horror repaid on his own part by any amount of effortless derision. This proved how little I knew as yet of the English people and their extraordinary talent for keeping up their forms, as well as of some of the mysteries of Mark Ambient's hearth and home. I found afterwards that he had, in his study, between nervous laughs and free cigar-puffs, some wonderful comparisons for his clerical neighbors; but meanwhile the chrysanthemums were a source of harmony, as he and the vicaress were equally attached to them, and I was surprised at the knowledge they exhibited of this interesting plant. The lady's visit, however, had presumably been long, and she presently rose for departure and kissed Mrs.

Ambient. Mark started to walk with her to the gate of the grounds, holding Dolcino by the hand.

"Stay with me, darling," Mrs. Ambient said to the boy, who had surrendered himself to his father.

Mark paid no attention to the summons, but Dolcino turned and looked at her in shy appeal. "Can't I go with papa?"

"Not when I ask you to stay with me."

"But please don't ask me, mamma," said the child in his small clear new voice.

"I must ask you when I want you. Come to me, dearest." And Mrs. Ambient, who had seated herself again, held out her long slender slightly too osseous hands.

Her husband stopped, his back turned to her, but without releasing the child. He was still talking to the vicaress, but this good lady, I think, had lost the thread of her attention. She looked at Mrs. Ambient and at Dolcino, and then looked at me, smiling in a highly amused cheerful manner and almost to a grimace.

"Papa," said the child, "mamma wants me not to go with you."

"He's very tired—he has run about all day. He ought to be quiet till he goes to bed. Otherwise he won't sleep." These declarations fell successively and very distinctly from Mrs. Ambient's lips.

Her husband, still without turning round, bent over the boy and looked at him in silence. The vicaress gave a genial irrelevant laugh and observed that he was a precious little pet. "Let him choose," said Mark Ambient. "My dear little boy, will you go with me or will you stay with your mother?"

"Oh, it's a shame!" cried the vicar's lady with increased hilarity.

"Papa, I don't think I can choose," the child answered, making his voice very low and confidential. "But I've been a great deal with mamma today," he then added.

"And very little with papa! My dear fellow, I think you *have* chosen!" On which Mark Ambient walked off with his son, accompanied by re-echoing but inarticulate comments from my fellow visitor.

His wife had seated herself again, and her fixed eyes, bent on the ground, expressed for a few moments so much mute agitation that anything I could think of to say would be but a false note. Yet she none the less quickly recovered herself, to express the sufficiently civil hope that I didn't mind having had to walk from the station. I reassured her on this point, and she went on: "We've got a thing that might have gone for you, but my husband wouldn't order it." After which and another longish pause, broken only by my plea that the pleasure of a walk with our friend would have been quite what I would have chosen, she found for a reply: "I believe the Americans walk very little."

"Yes, we always run," I laughingly allowed.

She looked at me seriously, yet with an absence in her pretty eyes. "I suppose your distances are so great."

"Yes, but we break our marches! I can't tell you the pleasure to me of finding myself here," I added. "I've the greatest admiration for Mr. Ambient."

"He'll like that. He likes being admired."

"He must have a very happy life then. He has many worshippers."

"Oh, yes, I've seen some of them," she dropped, looking away, very far from me, rather as if such a vision were before her at the moment. It seemed to indicate, her tone, that the sight was scarcely edifying, and I guessed her quickly enough to be in no great intellectual sympathy with the author of "Beltraffio." I thought the fact strange, but somehow, in the glow of my own enthusiasm, didn't think it important; it only made me wish rather to emphasize that homage.

"For me, you know," I returned—doubtless with a due *suffisance*—"he's quite the greatest of living writers."

"Of course I can't judge. Of course he's very clever," she said with a patient cheer.

"He's nothing less than supreme, Mrs. Ambient! There are pages in each of his books of a perfection classing them with the greatest things. Accordingly, for me to see him in this familiar way, in his habit as he lives, and apparently to find the man as delightful as the artist—well, I can't tell you how much too good to be true it seems and how great a privilege I think it." I knew I was gushing, but I couldn't help it, and what I said was a good deal less than what I felt. I was by no means sure I should dare to say even so much as this to the master himself, and there was a kind of rapture in speaking it out to his wife which was not affected by the fact that, as a wife, she appeared peculiar. She listened to me with her face grave again and her lips a little compressed, listened as if in no doubt, of course, that her husband was remarkable, but as if at the same time she had heard it frequently enough and couldn't treat it as stirring news. There was even in her manner a suggestion that I was so young as to expose myself to being called forward—an imputation and a word I had always loathed; as well as a hinted reminder that people usually got over their early extravagance. "I assure you that for me this is a red-letter day," I added.

She didn't take this up, but after a pause, looking round her, said abruptly and a trifle dryly: "We're very much afraid about the fruit this year."

My eyes wandered to the mossy mottled garden walls, where plum trees and pears, flattened and fastened upon the rusty bricks, looked like crucified figures with many arms. "Doesn't it promise well?"

"No, the trees look very dull. We had such late frosts."

Then there was another pause. She addressed her attention to the opposite end of the grounds, kept it for her husband's return with the child. "Is Mr. Ambient fond of gardening?" it occurred to me to ask, irresistibly impelled as I felt myself, moreover, to bring the conversation constantly back to him.

"He's very fond of plums," said his wife.

"Ah, well, then I hope your crop will be better than you fear. It's a lovely old place," I continued. "The whole impression's that of certain places he has described. Your house is like one of his pictures."

She seemed a bit frigidly amused at my glow. "It's a pleasant little place. There are hundreds like it."

"Oh, it has his *tone*," I laughed, but sounding my epithet and insisting on my point the more sharply that my companion appeared to see in my appreciation of her simple establishment a mark of mean experience.

It was clear I insisted too much. "His tone?" she repeated with a harder look at me and a slightly heightened color.

"Surely he has a tone, Mrs. Ambient."

"Oh, yes, he has indeed! But I don't in the least consider that I'm living in one of his books at all. I shouldn't care for that in the least," she went on with a smile that had in some degree the effect of converting her really sharp protest into an insincere joke. "I'm afraid I'm not very literary. And I'm not artistic," she stated.

"I'm very sure you're not ignorant, not stupid," I ventured to reply, with the accompaniment of feeling immediately afterwards that I had been both familiar and patronizing. My only consolation was in the sense that she had begun it, had fairly dragged me into it. She had thrust forward her limitations.

"Well, whatever I am I'm very different from my husband. If you like him you won't like me. You needn't say anything. Your liking me isn't 'n the least necessary!"

"Don't defy me!" I could but honorably make answer.

She looked as if she hadn't heard me, which was the best thing she could do; and we sat some time without further speech. Mrs. Ambient had evidently the enviable English quality of being able to be mute without unrest. But at last she spoke—she asked me if there seemed many people in town. I gave her what satisfaction I could on this point, and we talked a little of London and of some of its characteristics at that time of the year. At the end of this I came back irrepressibly to Mark.

"Doesn't he like to be there now? I suppose he doesn't find the proper quiet for his work. I should think his things had been written for the most part in a very still place. They suggest a great stillness following on a kind of tumult. Don't you think so?" I labored on. "I suppose London's a tremendous place to collect impressions, but a refuge like this, in the country, must be better for working them up. Does he get many of his impressions in London, should you say?" I proceeded from point to point in this malign enquiry simply because my hostess, who probably thought me an odious chattering person, gave me time; for when I paused—I've not represented my pauses—she simply continued to let her eyes wander while her long fair fingers played with the medallion on her neck. When I stopped altogether, however, she was obliged to say something and what she said was that she hadn't the least idea where her husband got his impressions. This made me think her, for a moment, positively disagreeable; delicate and proper and rather aristocratically fine as she sat there. But I must either have lost that view a moment later or been goaded by it to further aggression, for I remember asking her if our great man were in a good vein of work and when we might look for the appearance of the book on which he was engaged. I've every reason now to know that she found me insufferable.

She gave a strange small laugh as she said: "I'm afraid you think I know much more about my husband's work than I do. I haven't the least idea what he's doing," she then added in a slightly different, that is a more explanatory, tone and as if from a glimpse of the enormity of her confession. "I don't read what he writes."

She didn't succeed, and wouldn't even had she tried much harder, in making this seem to me anything less than monstrous. I stared at her and I think I blushed. "Don't you admire his genius? Don't you admire 'Beltraffio'?"

She waited, and I wondered what she could possibly say. She didn't speak, I could see, the first words that rose to her lips; she repeated what she had said a few minutes before. "Oh, of course he's very clever!" And with this she got up; our two absentees had reappeared.

II

Mrs. Ambient left me and went to meet them; she stopped and had a few words with her husband that I didn't hear and that ended in her taking the child by the hand and returning with him to the house. Her husband joined me in a moment, looking, I thought, the least bit conscious and constrained, and said that if I would come in with him he would show me my room. In looking back upon these first moments of my visit I find it important to avoid the error of appearing to have at all fully measured his situation from the first or made out the signs of things mastered only afterwards. This later knowledge throws a backward light and makes me forget that, at least on the occasion of my present reference—I mean that first afternoon—Mark Ambient struck me as only enviable. Allowing for this he must yet have failed of much expression as we walked back to the house, though I remember well the answer he made to a remark of mine on his small son.

"That's an extraordinary little boy of yours. I've never seen such a child."

"Why," he asked while we went, "do you call him extraordinary?"

"He's so beautiful, so fascinating. He's like some perfect little work of art."

He turned quickly in the passage, grasping my arm. "Oh, don't call him that, or you'll—you'll—!" But in his hesitation he broke off suddenly, laughing at my surprise. Immediately afterwards, however, he added: "You'll make his little future very difficult."

I declared that I wouldn't for the world take any liberties with his little future—it seemed to me to hang by threads of such delicacy. I should only be highly interested in watching it.

"You Americans are very keen," he commented on this. "You notice more things than we do."

"Ah, if you want visitors who aren't struck with you," I cried, "you shouldn't have asked me down here!"

He showed me my room, a little bower of chintz, with open windows where the light was green, and before he left me said irrelevantly: "As for my small son, you know, we shall probably kill him between us before we've done with him!" And he made this assertion as if he really believed it, without any appearance of jest, his fine near-sighted expressive eyes looking straight into mine.

"Do you mean by spoiling him?"

"No, by fighting for him!"

"You had better give him to me to keep for you," I said. "Let me remove the apple of discord!"

It was my extravagance of course, but he had the air of being perfectly serious. "It would be quite the best thing we could do. I should be all ready to do it."

"I'm greatly obliged to you for your confidence."

But he lingered with his hands in his pockets. I felt as if within a few moments I had, morally speaking, taken several steps nearer to him. He looked weary, just as he faced me then, looked preoccupied and as if there were something one might do for him. I was terribly conscious of the limits of my young ability, but I wondered what such a service might be, feeling at bottom nevertheless that the only thing I could do for him was to like him. I suppose he guessed this and was grateful for what was in my mind, since he went on presently: "I haven't the advantage of being an American, but I also notice a little, and I've an idea that"—here he smiled and laid his hand on my shoulder—"even counting out your nationality you're not destitute of intelligence. I've only known you half an hour, but—!" For which again he pulled up. "You're very young, after all."

"But you may treat me as if I could understand you!" I said; and before he left me to dress for dinner he had virtually given me a promise that he would.

When I went down into the drawing-room—I was very punctual—I found that neither my hostess nor my host had appeared. A lady rose from a sofa, however, and inclined her head as I rather surprisedly gazed at her. "I dare say you don't know me," she said with the modern laugh. "I'm Mark Ambient's sister." Whereupon I shook hands with her, saluting her very low. Her laugh was modern—by which I mean that it consisted of the vocal agitation serving between people who meet in drawing-rooms as the solvent of social disparities, the medium of transitions; but her appearance was—what shall I call it?—medieval. She was pale and angular, her long thin face inhabited by sad dark eyes and her black hair intertwined with golden fillets and curious clasps. She wore a faded velvet robe which clung to her when she moved and was "cut," as to the neck and sleeves, like the garments of old Italians. She suggested a symbolic picture, something akin even to Dürer's Melancholia, and was so perfect an image of a type which I, in my ignorance, supposed to be extinct, that while she rose before me I was almost as much startled as if I had seen a ghost. I afterwards concluded that Miss Ambient wasn't incapable of deriving pleasure from this weird effect, and I now believe that reflection concerned in her having sunk again to her seat with her long lean but not ungraceful arms locked together in an archaic manner on her knees and her mournful eyes addressing me a message of intentness which foreshadowed what I was subsequently to suffer. She was a singular fatuous artificial creature, and I was never more than half to penetrate her motives and mysteries. Of one thing I'm sure at least: that they were considerably less insuperable than her appearance announced. Miss Ambient was a restless romantic disappointed spinster, consumed with the love of Michael-Angelesque attitudes and mystical robes; but I'm now convinced she hadn't in her nature those depths of unutterable thought which, when you first knew her, seemed to look out from her eyes and to prompt her complicated gestures. Those features in especial had a misleading eloquence; they lingered on you with a far-off dimness, an air of obstructed sympathy, which was certainly not always a key to the spirit of their owner; so that, of a truth, a young lady could scarce have been so dejected and disillusioned without having committed a crime for which she was consumed with remorse, or having parted with a hope that she couldn't sanely have entertained. She had, I believe, the usual allowance of rather vain motives; she wished to be looked at, she wished to be married, she wished to be thought original.

It costs me a pang to speak in this irreverent manner of one of Ambient's name, but I shall have still less gracious things to say before I've finished my anecdote, and moreover—I confess it—I owe the young lady a bit of a grudge. Putting aside the curious cast of her face, she had no natural aptitude for an artistic development, had little real intelligence. But her affectations rubbed off on her brother's renown, and as there were plenty of people who darkly disapproved of him they could easily point to his sister as a person formed by his influence. It was quite possible to regard her as a warning, and she had almost compromised him with the world at large. He was the original and she the inevitable imitation. I suppose him scarce aware of the impression she mainly produced, beyond having a general idea that she made up very well as a Rossetti; he was used to her and was sorry for her, wishing she would marry and observing how she didn't. Doubtless I take her too seriously, for she did me no harm, though I'm bound to allow that I can only half-account for her. She wasn't so mystical as she looked, but was a strange indirect uncomfortable embarrassing woman. My story gives the reader at best so very small a knot to untie that I needn't hope to excite his curiosity by delaying to remark that Mrs. Ambient hated her sister-in-law. This I learned but later on, when other matters came to my knowledge. I mention it, however, at once, for I shall perhaps not seem to count too much on having beguiled him if I say he must promptly have guessed it. Mrs. Ambient, a person of conscience, put the best face on her kinswoman, who spent a month with her twice a year; but it took no great insight to recognize the very different personal paste of the two ladies, and that the usual feminine hypocrisies would cost them on either side much more than the usual effort. Mrs. Ambient, smooth-haired, thin-lipped, perpetually fresh, must have regarded her crumpled and disheveled visitor as an equivocal joke; she herself so the opposite of a Rossetti, she herself a Reynolds or a Lawrence, with no more far-fetched note in her composition than a cold ladylike candor and a well-starched muslin dress.

It was in a garment and with an expression of this kind that she made her entrance after I had exchanged a few words with Miss Ambient. Her husband presently followed her and, there being no other company, we went to dinner. The impressions I received at that repast are present to me still. The elements of oddity in the air hovered, as it were, without descending—to any immediate check of my delight. This came mainly of course from Ambient's talk, the easiest and richest I had ever heard. I mayn't say today whether he laid himself out to dazzle a rather juvenile pilgrim from over the sea; but that matters little—it seemed so natural to him to shine. His spoken wit or wisdom, or whatever, had thus a charm almost beyond his written; that is if the high finish of his printed prose be really, as some people have maintained, a fault. There was such a kindness in him, however, that I've no doubt it gave him ideas for me, or about me, to see me sit as open-mouthed as I now figure myself. Not so the two ladies, who not only were very nearly dumb from beginning to end of the meal, but who hadn't even the air of being struck with such an exhibition of fancy and taste. Mrs. Ambient, detached and inscrutable, met neither my eye nor her husband's; she attended to her dinner, watched her servants, arranged the puckers in her dress, exchanged at wide intervals a remark with her sister-in-law and, while she slowly rubbed her lean white hands between the courses, looked out of the window at the first signs of evening—the long June day allowing us to dine without candles. Miss Ambient appeared to give little direct heed to anything said by her brother; but on the other hand she was much engaged in watching its effect upon me. Her "die-away" pupils continued to attach themselves to my countenance, and it was only her air of belonging to another century that kept them from being importunate. She seemed to look at me across the ages, and the interval of time diminished for me the inconvenience. It was as if she knew in a general way that he must be talking very well, but she herself was so at home among such allusions that she had no need to pick them up and was at liberty to see what would become of the exposure of a candid young American to a high aesthetic temperature.

The temperature was aesthetic certainly, but it was less so than I could have desired, for I failed of any great success in making our friend abound about himself. I tried to put him on the ground of his own genius, but he slipped through my fingers every time and shifted the saddle to one or other of his contemporaries. He talked about Balzac and Browning, about what was being done in foreign countries, about his recent tour in the East and the extraordinary forms of life to be observed in that part of the world. I felt he had reasons for holding off from a direct profession of literary faith, a full consistency or sincerity, and therefore dealt instead with certain social topics, treating them with extraordinary humor and with a due play of that power of ironic evocation in which his books abound. He had a deal to say about London as London appears to the observer who has the courage of some of his conclusions during the high-pressure time—from April to July—of its gregarious life. He flashed his faculty of playing with the caught image and liberating the wistful idea over the whole scheme of manners or conception of intercourse of his compatriots, among whom there were evidently not a few types for which he had little love. London in short was grotesque to him, and he made capital sport of it; his only allusion that I can remember to his own work was his saying that he meant some day to do an immense and general, a kind of epic, social satire. Miss

Ambient's perpetual gaze seemed to put to me: "Do you perceive how artistic, how very strange and interesting, we are? Frankly now is it possible to be *more* artistic, *more* strange and interesting, than this? You surely won't deny that we're remarkable." I was irritated by her use of the plural pronoun, for she had no right to pair herself with her brother; and moreover of course I couldn't see my way to—at all genially —include Mrs. Ambient. Yet there was no doubt they were, taken together, unprecedented enough, and, with all allowances, I had never been left, or condemned, to draw so many rich inferences.

After the ladies had retired my host took me into his study to smoke, where I appealingly brought him round, or so tried, to some disclosure of fond ideals. I was bent on proving I was worthy to listen to him, on repaying him for what he had said to me before dinner, by showing him how perfectly I understood. He liked to talk; he liked to defend his convictions and his honor (not that I attacked them); he liked a little perhaps—it was a pardonable weakness—to bewilder the youthful mind even while wishing to win it over. My ingenuous sympathy received at any rate a shock from three or four of his professions—he made me occasionally gasp and stare. He couldn't help forgetting, or rather couldn't know, how little, in another and dryer clime, I had ever sat in the school in which he was master; and he promoted me as at a jump to a sense of its penetralia. My trepidations, however, were delightful; they were just what I had hoped for, and their only fault was that they passed away too quickly; since I found that for the main points I was essentially, I was quite constitutionally, on Mark Ambient's "side." This was the taken stand of the artist to whom every manifestation of human energy was a thrilling spectacle and who felt forever the desire to resolve his experience of life into a literary form. On that high head of the passion for form—the attempt at perfection, the quest for which was to his mind the real search for the Holy Grail—he said the most interesting, the most inspiring things. He mixed with them a thousand illustrations from his own life, from other lives he had known, from history and fiction, and above all from the annals of the time that was dear to him beyond all periods, the Italian cinque-cento. It came to me thus that in his books he had uttered but half his thought, and that what he had kept back—from motives I deplored when I made them out later—was the finer, and braver part. It was his fate to make a great many still more "prepared" people than me not inconsiderably wince; but there was no grain of bravado in his ripest things (I've always maintained it, though often contradicted), and at bottom the poor fellow, disinterested to his finger-tips and regarding imperfection not only as an aesthetic but quite also as a social crime, had an extreme dread of scandal. There are critics who regret that having gone so far he didn't go further; but I regret

nothing—putting aside two or three of the motives I just mentioned—
since he arrived at a noble rarity and I don't see how you can go beyond
that. The hours I spent in his study—this first one and the few that
followed it; they were not after all so numerous—seem to glow, as I look
back on them, with a tone that is partly that of the brown old room,
rich, under the shaded candle-light where we sat and smoked, with the
dusky delicate bindings of valuable books; partly that of his voice, of
which I still catch the echo, charged with the fancies and figures that
came at his command. When we went back to the drawing-room we
found Miss Ambient alone in possession and prompt to mention that
her sister-in-law had a quarter of an hour before been called by the nurse
to see the child, who appeared rather unwell—a little feverish.

"Feverish! how in the world comes he to be feverish?" Ambient asked.
"He was perfectly right this afternoon."

"Beatrice says you walked him about too much—you almost killed
him."

"Beatrice must be very happy—she has an opportunity to triumph!"
said my friend with a bright bitterness which was all I could have
wished it.

"Surely not if the child's ill," I ventured to remark by way of pleading
for Mrs. Ambient.

"My dear fellow, you aren't married—you don't know the nature of
wives!" my host returned with spirit.

I tried to match it. "Possibly not; but I know the nature of mothers."

"Beatrice is perfect as a mother," sighed Miss Ambient quite tremendously and with her fingers interlaced on her embroidered knees.

"I shall go up and see my boy," her brother went on. "Do you suppose
he's asleep?"

"Beatrice won't let you see him, dear"—as to which our young lady
looked at me, though addressing our companion.

"Do you call that being perfect as a mother?" Ambient asked.

"Yes, from her point of view."

'Damn her point of view!" cried the author of "Beltraffio." And he
left the room; after which we heard him ascend the stairs.

I sat there for some ten minutes with Miss Ambient, and we naturally
had some exchange of remarks, which began, I think, by my asking her
what the point of view of her sister-in-law could be.

"Oh, it's so very odd. But we're so very odd altogether. Don't you find
us awfully unlike others of our class?—which indeed mostly, in England, is awful. We've lived so much abroad. I adore 'abroad.' Have you
people like us in America?"

"You're not all alike, you interesting three—or, counting Dolcino, four—surely, surely: so that I don't think I understand your question. We've no one like your brother—I may go so far as that."

"You've probably more persons like his wife," Miss Ambient desolately smiled.

"I can tell you that better when you've told me about her point of view."

"Oh, yes—oh, yes. Well," said my entertainer, "she doesn't like his ideas. She doesn't like them for the child. She thinks them undesirable."

Being quite fresh from the contemplation of some of Mark Ambient's *arcana* I was particularly in a position to appreciate this announcement. But the effect of it was to make me, after staring a moment, burst into laughter which I instantly checked when I remembered the indisposed child above and the possibility of parents nervously or fussily anxious.

"What has that infant to do with ideas?" I asked. "Surely he can't tell one from another. Has he read his father's novels?"

"He's very precocious and very sensitive, and his mother thinks she can't begin to guard him too early." Miss Ambient's head drooped a little to one side and her eyes fixed themselves on futurity. Then of a sudden came a strange alteration; her face lighted to an effect more joyless than any gloom, to that indeed of a conscious insincere grimace, and she added: "When one has children what one writes becomes a great responsibility."

"Children are terrible critics," I prosaically answered. "I'm really glad I haven't any."

"Do you also write then? And in the same style as my brother? And do you like that style? And do people appreciate it in America? I don't write, but I think I feel." To these and various other enquiries and observations my young lady treated me till we heard her brother's step in the hall again and Mark Ambient reappeared. He was so flushed and grave that I supposed he had seen something symptomatic in the condition of his child. His sister apparently had another idea; she gazed at him from afar—as if he had been a burning ship on the horizon—and simply murmured "Poor old Mark!"

"I hope you're not anxious," I as promptly pronounced.

"No, but I'm disappointed. She won't let me in. She has locked the door, and I'm afraid to make a noise." I dare say there might have been a touch of the ridiculous in such a confession, but I liked my new friend so much that it took nothing for me from his dignity. "She tells me— from behind the door—that she'll let me know if he's worse."

"It's very good of her," said Miss Ambient with a hollow sound.

I had exchanged a glance with Mark in which it's possible he read that my pity for him was untinged with contempt, though I scarce know why he should have cared; and as his sister soon afterward got up and took her bedroom candlestick he proposed we should go back to his study. We sat there till after midnight; he put himself into his slippers and an old velvet jacket, he lighted an ancient pipe, but he talked considerably less than before. There were longish pauses in our communion, but they only made me feel we had advanced in intimacy. They helped me further to understand my friend's personal situation and to imagine it by no means the happiest possible. When his face was quiet it was vaguely troubled, showing, to my increase of interest—if that was all that was wanted!—that for him too life was the same struggle it had been for so many another man of genius. At last I prepared to leave him, and then, to my ineffable joy, he gave me some of the sheets of his forthcoming book—which, though unfinished, he had indulged in the luxury, so dear to writers of deliberation, of having "set up," from chapter to chapter, as he advanced. These early pages, the *prémices,* in the language of letters, of that new fruit of his imagination, I should take to my room and look over at my leisure. I was in the act of leaving him when the door of the study noiselessly opened and Mrs. Ambient stood before us. She observed us a moment, her candle in her hand, and then said to her husband that as she supposed he hadn't gone to bed she had come down to let him know Dolcino was more quiet and would probably be better in the morning. Mark Ambient made no reply; he simply slipped past her in the doorway, as if for fear she might seize him in his passage, and bounded upstairs to judge for himself of his child's condition. She looked so frankly discomfited that I for a moment believed her about to give him chase. But she resigned herself with a sigh and her eyes turned, ruefully and without a ray, to the lamplit room where various books at which I had been looking were pulled out of their places on the shelves and the fumes of tobacco hung in mid-air. I bade her good-night and then, without intention, by a kind of fatality, a perversity that had already made me address her overmuch on that question of her husband's powers, I alluded to the precious proof-sheets with which Ambient had entrusted me and which I nursed there under my arm. "They're the opening chapters of his new book," I said. "Fancy my satisfaction at being allowed to carry them to my room!"

She turned away, leaving me to take my candlestick from the table in the hall; but before we separated, thinking it apparently a good occasion to let me know once for all—since I was beginning, it would seem, to be quite "thick" with my host—that there was no fitness in my appealing to her for sympathy in such a case; before we separated, I say, she remarked to me with her quick fine well-bred inveterate curtness: "I dare say you attribute to me ideas I haven't got. I don't take that sort of interest in my husband's proof-sheets. I consider his writings most objectionable!"

III

I had an odd colloquy the next morning with Miss Ambient, whom I found strolling in the garden before breakfast. The whole place looked as fresh and trim, amid the twitter of the birds, as if, an hour before, the housemaids had been turned into it with their dust-pans and feather-brushes. I almost hesitated to light a cigarette and was doubly startled when, in the act of doing so, I suddenly saw the sister of my host, who had, at the best, something of the weirdness of an apparition, stand before me. She might have been posing for her photograph. Her sad-colored robe arranged itself in serpentine folds at her feet; her hands locked themselves listlessly together in front; her chin rested on a *cinque-cento* ruff. The first thing I did after bidding her good-morning was to ask her for news of her little nephew—to express the hope she had heard he was better. She was able to gratify this trust—she spoke as if we might expect to see him during the day. We walked through the shrubberies together and she gave me further light on her brother's household, which offered me an opportunity to repeat to her what his wife had so startled and distressed me with the night before. *Was* it the sorry truth that she thought his productions objectionable?

"She doesn't usually come out with that so soon!" Miss Ambient returned in answer to my breathlessness.

"Poor lady," I pleaded, "she saw I'm a fanatic."

"Yes, she won't like you for that. But you mustn't mind, if the rest of us like you! Beatrice thinks a work of art ought to have a 'purpose.' But she's a charming woman—don't you think her charming? I find in her quite the grand air."

"She's very beautiful," I produced with an effort; while I reflected that though it was apparently true that Mark Ambient was mismated it was also perceptible that his sister was perfidious. She assured me her brother and his wife had no other difference but this one—that she thought his writings immoral and his influence pernicious. It was a fixed idea; she was afraid of these things for the child. I answered that it was in all conscience enough, the trifle of a woman's regarding her husband's mind as a well of corruption, and she seemed much struck with the novelty of my remark. "But there hasn't been any of the sort of trouble that there so often is among married people," she said. "I suppose you can judge for yourself that Beatrice isn't at all—well, whatever they call it when a woman kicks over! And poor Mark doesn't make love to other people either. You might think he would, but I assure you he doesn't. All the same of course, from her point of view, you know, she has a dread of my brother's influence on the child—on the formation of his character, his 'ideals,' poor little brat, his principles. It's as if it were a subtle poison or a contagion—something that would rub off on his tender sensibility when his father kisses him or holds him on his knee. If she could she'd prevent Mark from even so much as touching him. Everyone knows it—visitors see it for themselves; so there's no harm in my telling you. Isn't it excessively odd? It comes from Beatrice's being so religious and so tremendously moral—so *à cheval* on fifty thousand *riguardi*. And then of course we mustn't forget," my companion added, a little unexpectedly, to this polyglot proposition, "that some of Mark's ideas are—well, really—rather impossible, don't you know?"

I reflected as we went into the house, where we found Ambient unfolding *The Observer* at the breakfast-table, that none of them were probably quite so "impossible, don't you know?" as his sister. Mrs. Ambient, a little "the worse," as was mentioned, for her ministrations, during the night to Dolcino, didn't appear at breakfast. Her husband described her however as hoping to go to church. I afterwards learnt that she did go, but nothing naturally was less on the cards than that we should accompany her. It was while the church-bell droned near at hand that the author of "Beltraffio" led me forth for the ramble he had spoken of in his note. I shall attempt here no record of where we went or of what we saw. We kept to the fields and copses and commons, and breathed the same sweet air as the nibbling donkeys and the browsing sheep, whose woolliness seemed to me, in those early days of acquaintance with English objects, but part of the general texture of the small dense landscape, which looked as if the harvest were gathered by the shears and with all nature bleating and braying for the violence. Everything was full of expression for Mark Ambient's visitor—from the big bandy-legged geese whose whiteness was a "note" amid all the tones of green as they wandered beside a neat little oval pool, the foreground of a thatched and whitewashed inn, with a grassy approach and a pictorial sign—from these humble wayside animals to the crests of high woods which let a gable or a pinnacle peep here and there and looked even at a distance like trees of good company, conscious of an individual profile. I admired the hedge-rows, I plucked the faint-hued heather, and I was forever stopping to say how charming I thought the threadlike foot-paths across the fields, which wandered in a diagonal of finer grain from one smooth stile to another. Mark Ambient was abundantly good-natured and was as much struck, dear man, with some of my observations as I was with the literary allusions of the landscape. We sat and smoked on stiles, broaching paradoxes in the decent English air; we took short cuts across a park or two where the bracken was deep and my companion nodded to the old woman at the gate; we skirted rank coverts which rustled here and there as we passed, and we stretched ourselves at last on a heathery hillside where if the sun wasn't too hot neither was the earth too cold, and where the country lay beneath us in a rich blue mist. Of course I had already told him what I thought of his new novel, having the previous night read every word of the opening chapters before I went to bed.

"I'm not without hope of being able to make it decent enough," he said as I went back to the subject while we turned up our heels to the sky. "At least the people who dislike my stuff—and there are plenty of them, I believe—will dislike this thing (if it does turn out well) most." This was the first time I had heard him allude to the people who couldn't read him—a class so generally conceived to sit heavy on the consciousness of the man of letters. A being organized for literature as Mark Ambient was must certainly have had the normal proportion of sensitiveness, of irritability; the artistic *ego,* capable in some cases of such monstrous development, must have been in his composition sufficiently erect and active. I won't therefore go so far as to say that he never thought of his detractors or that he had any illusions with regard to the number of his admirers—he could never so far have deceived himself as to believe he was popular, but I at least then judged (and had occasion to be sure later on) that stupidity ruffled him visibly but little, that he had an air of thinking it quite natural he should leave many simple folk, tasting of him, as simple as ever he found them, and that he very seldom talked about the newspapers, which, by the way, were always even abnormally vulgar about him. Of course he may have thought them over—the newspapers—night and day; the only point I make is that he didn't show it; while at the same time he didn't strike one as a man actively on his guard. I may add that, touching his hope of making the work on which he was then engaged the best of his books, it was only partly carried out. That place belongs incontestably to "Beltraffio," in spite of the beauty of certain parts of its successor. I quite believe, however, that he had at the moment of which I speak no sense of having declined; he was in love with his idea, which was indeed magnificent, and though for him, as I suppose for every sane artist, the act of execution had in it as much torment as joy, he saw his result grow like the crescent of the young moon and promise to fill the disk. "I want to be truer than I've ever been," he said, settling himself on his back with his hands clasped behind his head; "I want to give the impression of life itself. No, you may say what you will, I've always arranged things too much, always smoothed them down and rounded them off and tucked them in—done everything to them that life doesn't do. I've been a slave to the old superstitions."

"You a slave, my dear Mark Ambient? You've the freest imagination of our day!"

"All the more shame to me to have done some of the things I have!

The reconciliation of the two women in 'Natalina,' for instance, which could never really have taken place. That sort of thing's ignoble—I blush when I think of it! This new affair must be a golden vessel, filled with the purest distillation of the actual; and oh, how it worries me, the shaping of the vase, the hammering of the metal! I have to hammer it so fine, so smooth; I don't do more than an inch or two a day. And all the while I have to be so careful not to let a drop of the liquor escape! When I see the kind of things Life herself, the brazen hussy, does, I despair of ever catching her peculiar trick. She has an impudence, Life! If one risked a fiftieth part of the effects she risks! It takes ever so long to believe it. You don't know yet, my dear youth. It isn't till one has been watching her some forty years that one finds out half of what she's up to! Therefore one's earlier things must inevitably contain a mass of rot. And with what one sees, on one side, with its tongue in its cheek, defying one to be real enough, and on the other the *bonnes gens* rolling up their eyes at one's cynicism, the situation has elements of the ludicrous which the poor reproducer himself is doubtless in a position to appreciate better than any one else. Of course one mustn't worry about the *bonnes gens*," Mark Ambient went on while my thoughts reverted to his lady-like wife as interpreted by his remarkable sister.

"To sink your shaft deep and polish the plate through which people look into it—that's what your work consists of," I remember ingeniously observing.

"Ah, polishing one's plate—that's the torment of execution!" he exclaimed, jerking himself up and sitting forward. "The effort to arrive at a surface, if you think anything of that decent sort necessary—some people don't, happily for them! My dear fellow, if you could see the surface I dream of as compared with the one with which I've to content myself. Life's really too short for art—one hasn't time to make one's shell ideally hard. Firm and bright, firm and bright is very well to say—the devilish thing has a way sometimes of being bright, and even of being hard, as mere tough frozen pudding is hard, without being firm. When I rap it with my knuckles it doesn't give the right sound. There are horrible sandy stretches where I've taken the wrong turn because I couldn't for the life of me find the right. If you knew what a dunce I am sometimes! Such things figure to me now base pimples and ulcers on the brow of beauty!"

"They're very bad, very bad," I said as gravely as I could.

"Very bad? They're the highest social offense I know; it ought—it absolutely ought; I'm quite serious—to be capital. If I knew I should be publicly thrashed else I'd manage to find the true word. The people who can't—some of them don't so much as know it when they see it—

would shut their inkstands, and we shouldn't be deluged by this flood of rubbish!"

I shall not attempt to repeat everything that passed between us, nor to explain just how it was that, every moment I spent in his company, Mark Ambient revealed to me more and more the consistency of his creative spirit, the spirit in him that felt all life as plastic material. I could but envy him the force of that passion, and it was at any rate through the receipt of this impression that by the time we returned I had gained the sense of intimacy with him that I have noted. Before we got up for the homeward stretch he alluded to his wife's having once —or perhaps more than once—asked him whether he should like Dolcino to read "Beltraffio." He must have been unaware at the moment of all that this conveyed to me—as well doubtless of my extreme curiosity to hear what he had replied. He had said how much he hoped Dolcino would read *all* his works—when he was twenty; he should like him to know what his father had done. Before twenty it would be useless; he wouldn't understand them.

"And meanwhile do you propose to hide them—to lock them up in a drawer?" Mrs. Ambient had proceeded.

"Oh, no—we must simply tell him they're not intended for small boys. If you bring him up properly after that he won't touch them."

To this Mrs. Ambient had made answer that it might be very awkward when he was about fifteen, say; and I asked her husband if it were his opinion in general then that young people shouldn't read novels.

"Good ones—certainly not!" said my companion. I suppose I had had other views, for I remember saying that for myself I wasn't sure it was bad for them if the novels were "good" to the right intensity of goodness. "Bad for *them.* I don't say so much!" my companion returned. "But very bad, I'm afraid for the poor dear old novel itself." That oblique accidental allusion to his wife's attitude was followed by a greater breadth of reference as we walked home. "The difference between us is simply the opposition between two distinct ways of looking at the world, which have never succeeded in getting on together, or in making any kind of common household, since the beginning of time. They've borne all sorts of names, and my wife would tell you it's the difference between Christian and Pagan. I may be a pagan, but I don't like the name; it sounds sectarian. She thinks me at any rate no better than an ancient Greek. It's the difference between making the most of life and making the least, so that you'll get another better one in some other time and place. Will it be a sin to make the most of that one too, I wonder; and shall we have to be bribed off in the future state as well as in the present? Perhaps I care too much for beauty—I don't know, I doubt if a poor devil *can*; I delight in it, I adore it, I think of it continually, I try to produce it, to reproduce it. My wife holds that we shouldn't cultivate or enjoy it without extraordinary precautions and reserves. She's always afraid of it, always on her guard. I don't know what it can ever have done to her, what grudge it owes her or what resentment rides. And she's so pretty too herself! Don't you think she's lovely? She was at any rate when we married. At that time I wasn't aware of that difference I speak of—I thought it all came to the same thing; in the end, as they say. Well, perhaps it will in the end. I don't know what the end will be. Moreover I care for seeing things as they are; that's the way I try to show them in any professed picture. But you mustn't talk to Mrs. Ambient about things as they are. She has a mortal dread of things as they are."

"She's afraid of them for Dolcino," I said; surprised a moment afterwards at being in a position—thanks to Miss Ambient—to be so explanatory; and surprised even now that Mark shouldn't have shown visibly that he wondered what the deuce I knew about it. But he didn't; he simply declared with a tenderness that touched: "Ah, nothing shall ever hurt *him*!"

He told me more about his wife before we arrived at the gate of home, and if he be judged to have aired overmuch his grievance I'm afraid I must admit that he had some of the foibles as well as the gifts of the artistic temperament; adding, however, instantly that hitherto, to the best of my belief, he had rarely let this particular cat out of the bag. "She thinks me immoral—that's the long and short of it," he said as we paused outside a moment and his hand rested on one of the bars of his gate; while his conscious expressive perceptive eyes—the eyes of a foreigner, I had begun to account them, much more than of the usual Englishman—viewing me now evidently as quite a familiar friend, took part in the declaration. "It's very strange when one thinks it all over, and there's a grand comicality in it that I should like to bring out. She's a very nice woman, extraordinarily well-behaved, upright and clever and with a tremendous lot of good sense about a good many matters. Yet her conception of a novel—she has explained it to me once or twice, and she doesn't do it badly as exposition—is a thing so false that it makes me blush. It's a thing so hollow, so dishonest, so lying, in which life is so blinked and blinded, so dodged and disfigured, that it makes my ears burn. It's two different ways of looking at the whole affair," he repeated, pushing open the gate. "And they're irreconcilable!" he added with a sigh. We went forward to the house, but on the walk, halfway to the door, he stopped and said to me: "If you're going into this kind of thing there's a fact you should know beforehand; it may save you some disappointment. There's a hatred of art, there's a hatred of literature—I mean of the genuine kinds. Oh, the shams—*those* they'll swallow by the bucket!" I looked up at the charming house, with its genial color and crookedness, and I answered with a smile that those evil passions might exist, but that I should never have expected to find them there. "Ah, it doesn't matter after all," he a bit nervously laughed; which I was glad to hear, for I was reproaching myself with having worked him up.

If I had, it soon passed off, for at luncheon he was delightful; strangely delightful considering that the difference between himself and his wife was, as he had said, irreconcilable. He had the art, by his manner, by his smile, by his natural amenity, of reducing the importance of it in the common concerns of life; and Mrs. Ambient, I must add, lent herself to this transaction with a very good grace. I watched her at table for further illustrations of that fixed idea of which Miss Ambient had spoken to me; for in the light of the united revelations of her sister-in-law and her husband she had come to seem to me almost a sinister personage. Yet the signs of a somber fanaticism were not more immediately striking in her than before; it was only after a while that her air of incorruptible conformity, her tapering monosyllabic correctness, began to affect me as in themselves a cold thin flame. Certainly, at first, she resembled a woman with as few passions as possible; but if she had a passion at all it would indeed be that of Philistinism. She might have been (for there are guardian-spirits, I suppose, of all great principles) the very angel of the pink of propriety—putting the pink for a principle. though I'd rather put some dismal cold blue. Mark Ambient, apparently, ten years before, had simply and quite inevitably taken her for an angel, without asking himself of what. He had been right in calling my attention to her beauty. In looking for some explanation of his original surrender to her I saw more than before that she was, physically speaking, a wonderfully cultivated human plant—that he might well have owed her a brief poetic inspiration. It was impossible to be more propped and pencilled, more delicately tinted and petalled.

If I had had it in my heart to think my host a little of a hypocrite for appearing to forget at table everything he had said to me in our walk, I should instantly have cancelled such a judgment on reflecting that the good news his wife was able to give him about their little boy was ground enough for any optimistic reaction. It may have come partly too from a certain compunction at having breathed to me at all harshly on the cool fair lady who sat there—a desire to prove himself not after all so mismated. Dolcino continued to be much better, and it had been promised him he should come downstairs after his dinner. As soon as we had risen from our own meal Mark slipped away, evidently for the purpose of going to his child; and no sooner had I observed this than I became aware his wife had simultaneously vanished.

It happened that Miss Ambient and I, both at the same moment, saw the tail of her dress whisk out of a doorway; an incident that led the young lady to smile at me as if I now knew all the secrets of the Ambients. I passed with her into the garden and we sat down on a dear old bench that rested against the west wall of the house. It was a perfect spot for the middle period of a Sunday in June, and its felicity seemed to come partly from an antique sun-dial which, rising in front of us and forming the center of a small intricate parterre, measured the moments ever so slowly and made them safe for leisure and talk. The garden bloomed in the suffused afternoon, the tall beeches stood still for an example, and, behind and above us, a rose-tree of many seasons, clinging to the faded grain of the brick, expressed the whole character of the scene in a familiar exquisite smell. It struck me as a place to offer genius favor and sanction—not to bristle with challenges and checks. Miss Ambient asked me if I had enjoyed my walk with her brother and whether we had talked of many things.

"Well, of most things," I freely allowed, though I remembered we hadn't talked of Miss Ambient.

"And don't you think some of his theories are very peculiar?"

"Oh, I guess I agree with them all." I was very particular, for Miss Ambient's entertainment, to guess.

"Do you think art's everything?" she put to me in a moment.

"In art, of course I do!"

"And do you think beauty's everything?"

"Everything's a big word, which I think we should use as little as possible. But how can we not want beauty?"

"Ah, there you are!" she sighed, though I didn't quite know what she meant by it. "Of course it's difficult for a woman to judge how far to go," she went on. "I adore everything that gives a charm to life. I'm intensely sensitive to form. But sometimes I draw back—don't you see what I mean?—I don't quite see where I shall be landed. I only want to be quiet, after all," Miss Ambient continued as if she had long been baffled of this modest desire. "And one must be good, at any rate, must not one?" she pursued with a dubious quaver—an intimation apparently that what I might say one way or the other would settle it for her. It was difficult for me to be very original in reply, and I'm afraid I repaid her confidence with an unblushing platitude. I remember moreover attaching to it an enquiry, equally destitute of freshness and still more wanting perhaps in tact, as to whether she didn't mean to go to church, since that was an obvious way of being good. She made answer that she had performed this duty in the morning, and that for her, of Sunday afternoons, supreme virtue consisted in answering the week's letters. Then suddenly and without transition she brought out: "It's quite a

mistake about Dolcino's being better. I've seen him and he's not at all
right."

I wondered, and somehow I think I scarcely believed. "Surely his
mother would know, wouldn't she?"

She appeared for a moment to be counting the leaves on one of the
great beeches. "As regards most matters one can easily say what, in a
given situation, my sister-in-law will, or would, do. But in the present
case there are strange elements at work."

"Strange elements? Do you mean in the constitution of the child?"

"No, I mean in my sister-in-law's feelings."

"Elements of affection of course; elements of anxiety," I concurred.
"But why do you call them strange?"

She repeated my words. "Elements of affection, elements of anxiety.
She's very anxious."

Miss Ambient put me indescribably ill at ease; she almost scared me,
and I wished she would go and write her letters. "His father will have
seen him now," I said, "and if he's not satisfied he will send for the
doctor."

"The doctor ought to have been here this morning," she promptly
returned. "He lives only two miles away."

I reflected that all this was very possibly but a part of the general
tragedy of Miss Ambient's view of things; yet I asked her why she
hadn't urged that view on her sister-in-law. She answered me with a
smile of extraordinary significance and observed that I must have very
little idea of her "peculiar" relations with Beatrice; but I must do her
the justice that she reinforced this a little by the plea that any distinguishable alarm of Mark's was ground enough for a difference of his
wife's. He was always nervous about the child, and as they were pre-
destined by nature to take opposite views, the only thing for the mother
was to cultivate a false optimism. In Mark's absence and that of his
betrayed fear she would have been less easy. I remembered what he had
said about their dealings with their son—that between them they'd
probably put an end to him; but I didn't repeat this to Miss Ambient;
the less so that just then her brother emerged from the house, carrying
the boy in his arms. Close behind him moved his wife, grave and
pale; the little sick face was turned over Ambient's shoulder and toward
the mother. We rose to receive the group, and as they came near us
Dolcino twisted himself about. His enchanting eyes showed me a smile
of recognition, in which, for the moment, I should have taken a due
degree of comfort. Miss Ambient, however, received another impression,
and I make haste to say that her quick sensibility, which visibly went
out to the child, argues that in spite of her affectations she might have

been of some human use. "It won't do at all—it won't do at all," she said to me under her breath. "I shall speak to Mark about the doctor."

Her small nephew was rather white, but the main difference I saw in him was that he was even more beautiful than the day before. He had been dressed in his festal garments—a velvet suit and a crimson sash—and he looked like a little invalid prince too young to know condescension and smiling familiarly on his subjects.

"Put him down, Mark, he's not a bit at his ease," Mrs. Ambient said.

"Should you like to stand on your feet, my boy?" his father asked.

He made a motion that quickly responded. "Oh, yes; I'm remarkably well."

Mark placed him on the ground; he had shining pointed shoes with enormous bows. "Are you happy now, Mr. Ambient?"

"Oh, yes, I'm particularly happy," Dolcino replied. But the words were scarce out of his mouth when his mother caught him up and, in a moment, holding him on her knees, took her place on the bench where Miss Ambient and I had been sitting. This young lady said something to her brother, in consequence of which the two wandered away into the garden together.

IV

I remained with Mrs. Ambient, but as a servant had brought out a couple of chairs I wasn't obliged to seat myself beside her. Our conversation failed of ease, and I, for my part, felt there would be a shade of hypocrisy in my now trying to make myself agreeable to the partner of my friend's existence. I didn't dislike her—I rather admired her; but I was aware that I differed from her inexpressibly. Then I suspected, what I afterwards definitely knew and have already intimated, that the poor lady felt small taste for her husband's so undisguised disciple; and this of course was not encouraging. She thought me an obtrusive and designing, even perhaps a depraved, young man whom a perverse Providence had dropped upon their quiet lawn to flatter his worst tendencies. She did me the honor to say to Miss Ambient, who repeated the speech, that she didn't know when she had seen their companion take such a fancy to a visitor; and she measured apparently my evil influence by Mark's appreciation of my society. I had a consciousness, not oppressive but quite sufficient, of all this; though I must say that if it chilled my flow of small-talk it yet didn't prevent my thinking the beautiful mother and beautiful child, interlaced there against their background of roses, a picture such as I doubtless shouldn't soon see again. I was free, I supposed, to go into the house and write letters, to sit in the drawing-room, to repair to my own apartment and take a nap; but the only use I made of my freedom was to linger still in my chair and say to myself that the light hand of Sir Joshua might have painted Mark Ambient's wife and son. I found myself looking perpetually at the latter small mortal, who looked constantly back at me, and that was enough to detain me. With these vaguely amused eyes he smiled, and I felt it an absolute impossibility to abandon a child with such an expression. His attention never strayed; it attached itself to my face as if among all the small incipient things of his nature throbbed a desire to say something to me. If I could have taken him on my own knee he perhaps would have managed to say it; but it would have been a critical matter to ask his mother to give him up, and it has remained a constant regret for me that on that strange Sunday afternoon I didn't even for a moment hold Dolcino in my arms. He had said he felt remarkably well and was especially happy; but though peace may have been with him as he pillowed his charming head on his mother's breast, dropping his little crimson silk legs from her lap, I somehow didn't think security was. He made no attempt to walk about; he was content to swing his legs softly and strike one as languid and angelic.

Mark returned to us with his sister; and Miss Ambient, repeating her mention of the claims of her correspondence, passed into the house. Mark came and stood in front of his wife, looking down at the child, who immediately took hold of his hand and kept it while he stayed. "I think Mackintosh ought to see him," he said; "I think I'll walk over and fetch him."

"That's Gwendolen's idea, I suppose," Mrs. Ambient replied very sweetly.

"It's not such an out-of-the-way idea when one's child's ill," he returned.

"I'm not ill, papa; I'm much better now," sounded in the boy's silver pipe.

"Is that the truth, or are you only saying it to be agreeable? You've a great idea of being agreeable, you know."

The child seemed to meditate on this distinction, this imputation, for a moment; then his exaggerated eyes, which had wandered, caught my own as I watched him. "Do you think me agreeable?" he inquired with the candor of his age and with a look that made his father turn round to me laughing and ask, without saying it, "Isn't he adorable?"

"Then why don't you hop about, if you feel so lusty?" Ambient went on while his son swung his hand.

"Because mamma's holding me close!"

"Oh, yes; I know how mamma holds you when I come near!" cried Mark with a grimace at his wife.

She turned her charming eyes up to him without deprecation or concession. "You can go for Mackintosh if you like. I think myself it would be better. You ought to drive."

"She says that to get me away," he put to me with a gayety that I thought a little false; after which he started for the doctor's.

I remained there with Mrs. Ambient, though even our exchange of twaddle had run very thin. The boy's little fixed white face seemed, as before, to plead with me to stay, and after a while it produced still another effect, a very curious one, which I shall find it difficult to express. Of course I expose myself to the charge of an attempt to justify by a strained logic after the fact a step which may have been on my part but the fruit of a native want of discretion; and indeed the traceable consequences of that perversity were too lamentable to leave me any desire to trifle with the question. All I can say is that I acted in perfect good faith and that Dolcino's friendly little gaze gradually kindled the spark of my inspiration. What helped it to glow were the other influences— the silent suggestive garden-nook, the perfect opportunity (if it was not an opportunity for that it was an opportunity for nothing) and the plea I speak of, which issued from the child's eyes and seemed to make him say: "The mother who bore me and who presses me here to her bosom—sympathetic little organism that I am—has really the kind of sensibility she has been represented to you as lacking, if you only look for it patiently and respectfully. How is it conceivable she shouldn't have it? How is it possible that *I* should have so much of it—for I'm quite full of it, dear strange gentleman—if it weren't also in some degree in her? I'm my great father's child, but I'm also my beautiful mother's, and I'm sorry for the difference between them!" So it shaped itself before me, the vision of reconciling Mrs. Ambient with her husband, of putting an end to their ugly difference. The project was absurd of course, for had I not had his word for it—spoken with all the bitterness of experience—that the gulf dividing them was well-nigh bottomless? Nevertheless, a quarter of an hour after Mark had left us, I observed to my hostess that I couldn't get over what she had told me the night before about her thinking her husband's compositions "objectionable." I had been so very sorry to hear it, had thought of it constantly and wondered whether it mightn't be possible to make her change her mind. She gave me a great cold stare, meant apparently as an admonition to me to mind my business. I wish I had taken this mute counsel, but I didn't take it. I went on to remark that it seemed an immense pity so much that was interesting should be lost on her.

"Nothing's lost upon me," she said in a tone that didn't make the contradiction less. "I know they're very interesting."

"Don't you like papa's books?" Dolcino asked, addressing his mother

but still looking at me. Then he added to me: "Won't you read them
to me, American gentleman?"

"I'd rather tell you some stories of my own," I said. "I know some that
are awfully good."

"When will you tell them? Tomorrow?"

"Tomorrow with pleasure, if that suits you."

His mother took this in silence. Her husband, during our walk, had
asked me to remain another day; my promise to her son was an implication that I had consented, and it wasn't possible the news could please
her. This ought doubtless to have made me more careful as to what I
said next, but all I can plead is that it didn't. I soon mentioned that just
after leaving her the evening before, and after hearing her apply to her
husband's writings the epithet already quoted, I had on going up to
my room sat down to the perusal of those sheets of his new book that
he had been so good as to lend me. I had sat entranced till nearly three
in the morning—I had read them twice over. "You say you haven't
looked at them. I think it's such a pity you shouldn't. Do let me beg you
to take them up. They're so very remarkable. I'm sure they'll convert
you. They place him in—really—such a dazzling light. All that's best in
him is there. I've no doubt it's a great liberty, by saying all this; but pardon me, and *do* read them!"

"Do read them, mamma!" the boy again sweetly shrilled. "Do read
them!"

She bent her head and closed his lips with a kiss. "Of course I know
he has worked immensely over them," she said; after which she made
no remark, but attached her eyes thoughtfully to the ground. The tone
of these last words was such as to leave me no spirit for further pressure,
and after hinting at a fear that her husband mightn't have caught the
doctor I got up and took a turn about the grounds. When I came back
ten minutes later she was still in her place watching her boy, who had
fallen asleep in her lap. As I drew near she put her finger to her lips
and a short time afterwards rose, holding him; it being now best, she
said, that she should take him upstairs. I offered to carry him and opened
my arms for the purpose; but she thanked me and turned away with
the child still in her embrace, his head on her shoulder. "I'm very
strong," was her last word as she passed into the house, her slim flexible
figure bent backward with the filial weight. So I never laid a longing
hand on Dolcino.

I betook myself to Ambient's study, delighted to have a quiet hour to
look over his books by myself. The windows were open to the garden;
the sunny stillness, the mild light of the English summer, filled the room
without quite chasing away the rich dusky tone that was a part of its
charm and that abode in the serried shelves where old morocco exhaled

the fragrance of curious learning, as well as in the brighter intervals where prints and medals and miniatures were suspended on a surface of faded stuff. The place had both color and quiet; I thought it a perfect room for work and went so far as to say to myself that, if it were mine to sit and scribble in, there was no knowing but I might learn to write as well as the author of "Beltraffio." This distinguished man still didn't reappear, and I rummaged freely among his treasures. At last I took down a book that detained me a while and seated myself in a fine old leather chair by the window to turn it over. I had been occupied in this way for half an hour—a good part of the afternoon had waned—when I became conscious of another presence in the room and, looking up from my quarto, saw that Mrs. Ambient, having pushed open the door quite again in the same noiseless way marking or disguising her entrance the night before, had advanced across the threshold. On seeing me she stopped; she had not, I think, expected to find me. But her hesitation was only of a moment; she came straight to her husband's writing-table as if she were looking for something. I got up and asked her if I could help her. She glanced about an instant and then put her hand upon a roll of papers which I recognized, as I had placed it on that spot at the early hour of my descent from my room.

"Is this the new book?" she asked, holding it up.

"The very sheets," I smiled; "with precious annotations."

"I mean to take your advice"—and she tucked the little bundle under her arm. I congratulated her cordially and ventured to make of my triumph, as I presumed to call it, a subject of pleasantry. But she was perfectly grave and turned away from me, as she had presented herself, without relaxing her rigor; after which I settled down to my quarto again with the reflection that Mrs. Ambient was truly an eccentric. My triumph too suddenly seemed to me rather vain. A woman who couldn't unbend at a moment exquisitely indicated would never understand Mark Ambient. He came back to us at last in person, having brought the doctor with him. "He was away from home," Mark said, "and I went after him to where he was supposed to be. He had left the place, and I followed him to two or three others, which accounts for my delay." He was now with Mrs. Ambient, looking at the child, and was to see Mark again before leaving the house. My host noticed at the end of two minutes that the proof-sheets of his new book had been removed from the table; and when I told him, in reply to his question as to what I knew about them, that Mrs. Ambient had carried them off to read he turned almost pale with surprise. "What has suddenly made her so curious?" he cried; and I was obliged to tell him that I was at the bottom of the mystery. I had had it on my conscience to assure her that she really ought to know of what her husband was capable. "Of what I'm capable? *Elle ne s'en doute que trop!*" said Ambient with a laugh; but he took my meddling very good-naturedly and contented himself with adding that he was really much afraid she would burn up the sheets, his emendations and all, of which latter he had no duplicate. The doctor paid a long visit in the nursery, and before he came down I retired to my own quarters, where I remained till dinner-time. On entering the drawing-room at this hour I found Miss Ambient in possession, as she had been the evening before.

"I was right about Dolcino," she said, as soon as she saw me, with an air of triumph that struck me as the climax of perversity. "He's really very ill."

"Very ill! Why, when I last saw him, at four o'clock, he was in fairly good form."

"There has been a change for the worse, very sudden and rapid, and when the doctor got here he found diphtheritic symptoms. He ought to have been called, as I knew, in the morning, and the child oughtn't to have been brought into the garden."

"My dear lady, he was very happy there," I protested with horror.

"He would be very happy anywhere. I've no doubt he's very happy now, with his poor little temperature—!" She dropped her voice as her brother came in, and Mark let us know that as a matter of course Mrs. Ambient wouldn't appear. It was true the boy had developed diphtheritic symptoms, but he was quiet for the present and his mother earnestly watching him. She was a perfect nurse, Mark said, and Mackintosh would come back at ten. Our dinner wasn't very gay—with my host worried and absent; and his sister annoyed me by her constant tacit assumption, conveyed in the very way she nibbled her bread and sipped her wine, of having "told me so." I had had no disposition to deny anything she might have told me, and I couldn't see that her satisfaction in being justified by the event relieved her little nephew's condition. The truth is that, as the sequel was to prove, Miss Ambient had some of the qualities of the sibyl and had therefore perhaps a right to the sibylline contortions. Her brother was so preoccupied that I felt my presence an indiscretion and was sorry I had promised to remain over the morrow. I put it to Mark that clearly I had best leave them in the morning; to which he replied that, on the contrary, if he was to pass the next days in the fidgets my company would distract his attention. The fidgets had already begun for him, poor fellow; and as we sat in his study with our cigars after dinner he wandered to the door whenever he heard the sound of the doctor's wheels. Miss Ambient, who shared this apartment with us, gave me at such moments significant glances; she had before rejoining us gone upstairs to ask about the child. His mother and his nurse gave a fair report, but Miss Ambient found his fever high and his symptoms very grave. The doctor came at ten o'clock, and I went to bed after hearing from Mark that he saw no present cause for alarm. He had made every provision for the night and was to return early in the morning.

I quitted my room as eight struck the next day and when I came downstairs saw, through the open door of the house, Mrs. Ambient standing at the front gate of the grounds in colloquy with Mackintosh. She wore a white dressing-gown, but her shining hair was carefully tucked away in its net, and in the morning freshness, after a night of watching, she looked as much "the type of the lady" as her sister-in-law had described her. Her appearance, I suppose, ought to have reassured me; but I was still nervous and uneasy, so that I shrank from meeting her with the necessary challenge. None the less, however, was I impatient to learn how the new day found him; and as Mrs. Ambient hadn't seen me I passed into the grounds by a roundabout way and, stopping at a further gate, hailed the doctor just as he was driving off. Mrs. Ambient had returned to the house before he got into his cart.

"Pardon me, but as a friend of the family I should like very much to hear about the little boy."

The stout sharp circumspect man looked at me from head to foot and then said: "I'm sorry to say I haven't seen him."

"Haven't seen him?"

"Mrs. Ambient came down to meet me as I alighted, and told me he was sleeping so soundly, after a restless night, that she didn't wish him disturbed. I assured her I wouldn't disturb him, but she said he was quite safe now and she could look after him herself."

"Thank you very much. Are you coming back?"

"No sir; I'll be hanged if I come back!" cried the honest practitioner in high resentment. And the horse started as he settled beside his man.

I wandered back into the garden, and five minutes later Miss Ambient came forth from the house to greet me. She explained that breakfast wouldn't be served for some time and that she desired a moment herself with the doctor. I let her know that the good vexed man had come and departed, and I repeated to her what he had told me about his dismissal. This made Miss Ambient very serious, very serious indeed, and she sank onto a bench, with dilated eyes, hugging her elbows with crossed arms. She indulged in many strange signs, she confessed herself immensely distressed, and she finally told me what her own last news of her nephew had been. She had sat up very late—after me, after Mark—and before going to bed had knocked at the door of the child's room, opened to her by the nurse. This good woman had admitted her and she had found him quiet, but flushed and "unnatural," with his mother sitting by his bed. "She held his hand in one of hers," said Miss Ambient, "and in the other—what do you think?—the proof-sheets of Mark's new book! She was reading them there intently; did you ever hear of anything so extraordinary? Such a very odd time to be reading an author whom she never could abide!" In her agitation Miss Ambient was guilty of this vulgarism of speech, and I was so impressed by her narrative that only in recalling her words later did I notice the lapse. Mrs. Ambient had looked up from her reading with her finger on her lips—I recognized the gesture she had addressed me in the afternoon—and, though the nurse was about to go to rest, had not encouraged her sister-in-law to relieve her of any part of her vigil. But certainly at that time the boy's state was far from reassuring—his poor little breathing so painful; and what change could have taken place in him in those few hours that would justify Beatrice in denying Mackintosh access? This was the moral of Miss Ambient's anecdote, the moral for herself at least. The moral for me, rather, was that it *was* a very singular time for Mrs. Ambient to be going into a novelist she had never appreciated and who had simply happened to be recommended to her by a young American she disliked. I thought of her sitting there in the sick-chamber in the still hours of the night and after the nurse had left her, turning and turning those pages of genius and wrestling with their magical influence.

I must be sparing of the minor facts and the later emotions of this sojourn—it lasted but a few hours longer—and devote but three words to my subsequent relations with Ambient. They lasted five years—till his death—and were full of interest, of satisfaction and, I may add, of sadness. The main thing to be said of these years is that I had a secret from him which I guarded to the end. I believe he never suspected it, though of this I'm not absolutely sure. If he had so much as an inkling the line he had taken, the line of absolute negation of the matter to himself, shows an immense effort of the will. I may at last lay bare my secret, giving it for what it is worth; now that the main sufferer has gone, that he has begun to be alluded to as one of the famous early dead and that his wife had ceased to survive him; now too that Miss Ambient, whom I also saw at intervals during the time that followed, has, with her embroideries and her attitudes, her necromantic glances and strange intuitions, retired to a Sisterhood, where, as I am told, she is deeply immured and quite lost to the world.

Mark came in to breakfast after this lady and I had for some time been seated there. He shook hands with me in silence, kissed my companion, opened his letters and newspapers and pretended to drink his coffee. But I took these movements for mechanical and was little surprised when he suddenly pushed away everything that was before him and, with his head in his hands and his elbows on the table, sat staring strangely at the cloth.

"What's the matter, *caro fratello mio*?" Miss Ambient quavered, peeping from behind the urn.

He answered nothing, but got up with a certain violence and strode to the window. We rose to our feet, his relative and I, by a common impulse, exchanging a glance of some alarm; and he continued to stare into the garden. "In heaven's name what has got possession of Beatrice?" he cried at last, turning round on us a ravaged face. He looked from one of us to the other—the appeal was addressed to us alike.

Miss Ambient gave a shrug. "My poor Mark, Beatrice is always—Beatrice!"

"She has locked herself up with the boy—bolted and barred the door. She refuses to let me come near him!" he went on.

"She refused to let Mackintosh see him an hour ago!" Miss Ambient promptly returned.

"Refused to let Mackintosh see him? By heaven I'll smash in the door!" And Mark brought his fist down upon the sideboard, which he had now approached, so that all the breakfast-service rang.

I begged Miss Ambient to go up and try to have speech of her sister-in-law, and I drew Mark out into the garden. "You're exceedingly nervous, and Mrs. Ambient's probably right," I there undertook to plead. "Women know; women should be supreme in such a situation. Trust a mother—a devoted mother, my dear friend!" With such words as these I tried to soothe and comfort him, and, marvelous to relate, I succeeded, with the help of many cigarettes, in making him walk about the garden and talk, or suffer me at least to do so for near an hour. When about that time had elapsed his sister reappeared, reaching us rapidly and with a convulsed face while she held her hand to her heart.

"Go for the doctor, Mark—go for the doctor this moment!"

"Is he dying? Has she killed him?" my poor friend cried, flinging away his cigarette.

"I don't know what she has done! But she's frightened, and now she wants the doctor."

"He told me he'd be hanged if he came back!" I felt myself obliged to mention.

"Precisely—therefore Mark himself must go for him, and not a messenger. You must see him and tell him it's to save your child. The trap has been ordered—it's ready."

"To save him? I'll save him, please God!" Ambient cried, bounding with his great strides across the lawn.

As soon as he had gone I felt I ought to have volunteered in his place, and I said as much to Miss Ambient; but she checked me by grasping my arm while we heard the wheels of the dog-cart rattle away from the gate. "He's off—he's off—and now I can think! To get him away—while I think—while I think!"

"While you think of what, Miss Ambient?"

"Of the unspeakable thing that has happened under this roof!"

Her manner was habitually that of such a prophetess of ill that I at first allowed for some great extravagance. But I looked at her hard, and the next thing felt myself turn white. "Dolcino *is* dying then—he's dead?"

"It's too late to save him. His mother has let him die! I tell you that because you're sympathetic, because you've imagination," Miss Ambient was good enough to add, interrupting my expression of horror. "That's why you had the idea of making her read Mark's new book!"

"What has that to do with it? I don't understand you. Your accusation's monstrous."

"I see it all—I'm not stupid," she went on, heedless of my emphasis. "It was the book that finished her—it was that decided her!"

"Decided her? Do you mean she has murdered her child?" I demanded, trembling at my own words.

"She sacrified him; she determined to do nothing to make him live. Why else did she lock herself in, why else did she turn away the doctor? The book gave her a horror; she determined to rescue him—to prevent him from every being touched. He had a crisis at two o'clock in the morning. I know that from the nurse, who had left her then, but whom, for a short time, she called back. The darling got much worse, but she insisted on the nurse's going back to bed, and after that she was alone with him for hours."

"I listened with a dread that stayed my credence, while she stood there with her tearless glare. "Do you pretend then she has no pity, that she's cruel and insane?"

"She held him in her arms, she pressed him to her breast, not to see him; but she gave him no remedies; she did nothing the doctor ordered. Everything's there untouched. She has had the honesty not even to throw the drugs away!"

I dropped upon the nearest bench, overcome with my dismay—quite as much at Miss Ambient's horrible insistence and distinctness as at the monstrous meaning of her words. Yet they came amazingly straight, and if they did have a sense I saw myself too woefully figure in it. Had I been then a proximate cause—? "You're a very strange woman and you say incredible things," I could only reply.

She had one of her tragic headshakes. "You think it necessary to protest, but you're really quite ready to believe me. You've received an impression of my sister-in-law—you've guessed of what she's capable."

I don't feel bound to say what concession on this score I made to Miss

Ambient, who went on to relate to me that within the last half-hour Beatrice had had a revulsion, that she was tremendously frightened at what she had done; that her fright itself betrayed her; and that she would now give heaven and earth to save the child. "Let us hope she will!" I said, looking at my watch and trying to time poor Ambient; whereupon my companion repeated all portentously "Let us hope so!" When I asked her if she herself could do nothing, and whether she oughtn't to be with her sister-in-law, she replied: "You had better go and judge! She's like a wounded tigress!"

I never saw Mrs. Ambient till six months after this, and therefore can't pretend to have verified the comparison. At the latter period she was again the type of the perfect lady. "She'll treat him better after this," I remember her sister-in-law's saying in response to some quick outburst, on my part, of compassion for her brother. Though I had been in the house but thirty-six hours this young lady had treated me with extraordinary confidence, and there was therefore a certain demand I might, as such an intimate, make of her. I extracted from her a pledge that she'd never say to her brother what she had just said to me, that she'd let him form his own theory of his wife's conduct. She agreed with me that there was misery enough in the house without her contributing a new anguish, and that Mrs. Ambient's proceedings might be explained, to her husband's mind, by the extravagance of a jealous devotion. Poor Mark came back with the doctor much sooner than we could have hoped, but we knew five minutes afterwards that it was all too late. His sole, his adored little son was more exquisitely beautiful in death than he had been in life. Mrs. Ambient's grief was frantic; she lost her head and said strange things. As for Mark's—but I won't speak of that. *Basta, basta,* as he used to say. Miss Ambient kept her secret—I've already had occasion to say that she had her good points—but it rankled in her conscience like a guilty participation and, I imagine, had something to do with her ultimately retiring from the world. And, apropos of consciences, the reader is now in a position to judge of my compunction for my effort to convert my cold hostess. I ought to mention that the death of her child in some degree converted her. When the new book came out (it was long delayed) she read it over as a whole, and her husband told me that during the few supreme weeks before her death—she failed rapidly after losing her son, sank into a consumption and faded away at Mentone—she even dipped into the black "Beltraffio."

21

Brer Rabbit, Brer Fox, and the Tar Baby

(AN UNCLE REMUS STORY)

BY JOEL CHANDLER HARRIS

ONE evening recently, the lady whom Uncle Remus calls "Miss Sally" missed her little seven-year-old boy. Making search for him through the house and through the yard, she heard the sound of voices in the old man's cabin, and, looking through the window, saw the child sitting by Uncle Remus. His head rested against the old man's arm, and he was gazing with an expression of the most intense interest into the rough, weather-beaten face, that beamed so kindly upon him. This is what "Miss Sally" heard:

"Bimeby, one day, arter Brer Fox bin doin' all dat he could fer ter ketch Brer Rabbit, en Brer Rabbit bin doin' all he could fer to keep 'im fum it, Brer Fox say to hisse'f dat he'd put up a game on Brer Rabbit, en he ain't mo'n got de wuds out'n his mouf twel Brer Rabbit come a lopin' up de big road, lookin' des ez plump, en ez fat, en ez sassy ez a Moggin hoss in a barley-patch.

" 'Hol' on dar, Brer Rabbit,' sez Brer Fox, sezee.

" 'I ain't got time, Brer Fox,' sez Brer Rabbit, sezee, sorter mendin' his licks.

" 'I wanter have some confab wid you, Brer Rabbit,' sez Brer Fox, sezee.

" 'All right, Brer Fox, but you better holler fum whar you stan'. I'm monstus full er fleas dis mawnin',' sez Brer Rabbit, sezee.

" 'I seed Brer B'ar yistiddy,' sez Brer Fox, sezee, 'en he sorter rake me over de coals kaze you en me ain't make frens en live naberly, en I told 'im dat I'd see you.'

"Den Brer Rabbit scratch one year wid his off hinefoot sorter jub'usly, en den he ups en sez, sezee:

"'All a settin', Brer Fox. Spose'n you drap roun' ter-morrer en take dinner wid me. We ain't got no great doin's at our house, but I speck de old 'oman en de chilluns kin sorter scramble roun' en git up sump'n fer ter stay yo' stummuck.'

"'I'm 'gree'ble, Brer Rabbit,' sez Brer Fox, sezee.

"'Den I'll 'pen' on you,' sez Brer Rabbit, sezee.

"Nex' day, Mr. Rabbit an' Miss Rabbit got up soon, 'fo' day, en raided on a gyarden like Miss Sally's out dar, en got some cabbiges, en some roas'n years, en some sparrer-grass, en dey fix up a smashin' dinner. Bimeby one er de little Rabbits, playin' out in de backyard, come runnin' in hollerin', 'Oh, ma! oh, ma! I seed Mr. Fox a comin'!' En den Brer Rabbit he tuck de chilluns by der years en make um set down, en den him and Miss Rabbit sorter dally roun' waitin' for Brer Fox. En dey keep on waitin', but no Brer Fox ain't come. Atter 'while Brer Rabbit goes to de do', easy like, en peep out, en dar, stickin' fum behime de cornder, wuz de tip-een' er Brer Fox tail. Den Brer Rabbit shot de do' en sot down, en put his paws behime his years en begin fer ter sing:

> "'De Place wharbouts you spill de grease,
>   Right dar youer boun' ter slide,
> An' whar you fine a bunch er ha'r,
>   You'll sholy fine de hide.'

"Nex' day, Brer Fox sont word by Mr. Mink, en skuze hisse'f kaze he wuz too sick fer ter come, en he ax Brer Rabbit fer to come en take dinner wid him, en Brer Rabbit say he wuz gree'ble.

"Bimeby, w'en de shadders wuz at der shortes', Brer Rabbit he sorter brush up en santer down ter Brer Fox's house, en w'en he got dar, he hear somebody groanin', en he look in de do' en dar he see Brer Fox settin' up in a rockin' cheer all wrop up wid flannil, en he look mighty weak. Brer Rabbit look all 'roun', he did, but he ain't see no dinner. De dish-pan wuz settin' on de table, en close by wuz a kyarvin' knife.

"'Look like you gwineter have chicken fer dinner, Brer Fox,' sez Brer Rabbit, sezee.

"'Yes, Brer Rabbit, deyer nice, en fresh, en tender,' sez Brer Fox, sezee.

"Den Brer Rabbit sorter pull his mustarsh, en say: 'You ain't got no calamus root, is you, Brer Fox? I done got so now dat I can't eat no chicken 'ceppin she's seasoned up wid calamus root.' En wid dat Brer Rabbit lipt out er de do' and dodge 'mong de bushes, en sot dar watchin' fer Brer Fox; en he ain't watch long, nudder, kaze Brer Fox flung off de flannil en crope out er de house en got whar he could cloze in on Brer Rabbit, en bimeby Brer Rabbit holler out: 'Oh, Brer Fox! I'll des put yo' calamus root out yer on dish yer stump. Better come git it while hit's fresh,' and wid dat Brer Rabbit gallop off home. En Brer Fox ain't never kotch 'im yet, en w'at's mo', honey, he ain't gwineter."

"Didn't the fox *never* catch the rabbit, Uncle Remus?" asked the little boy the next evening.

"He come mighty nigh it' honey, sho's you born—Brer Fox did. One day atter Brer Rabbit fool 'im wid dat calamus root, Brer Fox went ter wuk en got 'im some tar, en mix it wid some turkentime, en fix up a contrapshun wat he call a Tar-Baby, en he tuck dish yer Tar-Baby en he sot 'er in de big road, en den he lay off in de bushes fer to see wat de news wuz gwineter be. En he didn't hatter wait long, nudder, kaze bimeby here come Brer Rabbit pacin' down de road—lippity-clippity, clippity-lippity—dez ez sassy ez a jay-bird. Brer Fox, he lay low. Brer Rabbit come prancin' 'long twel he spy de Tar-Baby, en den he fotch up on his behime legs like he wuz 'stonished. De Tar-Baby, she sot dar, she did, en Brer Fox, he lay low.

" 'Mawnin'!' sez Brer Rabbit, sezee—'nice wedder dis mawnin',' sezee.

"Tar-Baby ain't sayin' nothin', en Brer Fox, he lay low.

" 'How duz yo' sym'tums seem ter segashuate?' sez Brer Rabbit, sezee.

"Brer Fox, he wink his eye slow, en lay low, en de Tar-Baby, she ain't sayin' nothin'.

" 'How you come on, den? Is you deaf?' sez Brer Rabbit, sezee. 'Kaze if you is, I kin holler louder,' sezee.

"Tar-Baby stay still, en Brer Fox, he lay low.

" 'Youer stuck up, dat's w'at you is,' says Brer Rabbit, sezee, 'en I'm gwineter kyore you, dat's w'at I'm a gwineter do,' sezee.

"Brer Fox, he sorter chuckle in his stummuck, he did, but Tar-Baby ain't sayin' nothin'.

" 'I'm gwineter larn you howter talk ter 'specttubble fokes ef hit's de las' ack,' sez Brer Rabbit, sezee. 'Ef you don't take off dat hat en tell me howdy, I'm gwineter bus' you wide open,' sezee.

"Tar-Baby stay still, en Brer Fox, he lay low.

"Brer Rabbit keep on axin' 'im, en de Tar-Baby, she keep on sayin' nothin', twel present'y Brer Rabbit draw back wid his fis', he did, en blip he tuck 'er side er de head. Right dar's whar he broke his merlasses jug. His fis' stuck, en he can't pull loose. De tar hilt 'im. But Tar-Baby, she stay still, en Brer Fox, he lay low.

" 'Ef you don't lemme loose, I'll knock you agin,' sez Brer Rabbit, sezee, en wid dat he fotch 'er a wipe wid de udder han', en dat stuck. Tar-Baby, she ain't sayin' nothin', en Brer Fox, he lay low.

" 'Tu'n me loose, fo' I kick de natal stuffin' outen you,' sez Brer Rabbit, sezee, but de Tar-Baby, she ain't sayin' nothin'. She des hilt on, en den Brer Rabbit lose de use er his feet in de same way. Brer Fox, he lay low. Den Brer Rabbit squall out dat ef de Tar-Baby don't tu'n 'im loose he butt'er cranksided. En den he butted, en his head got stuck. Den Brer Fox, he sa'ntered fort', lookin' des ez innercent ez one er yo' mammy's mockin'-birds.

" 'Howdy, Brer Rabbit,' sez Brer Fox, sezee. 'You look sorter stuck up dis mawnin',' sezee, en den he rolled on de groun', en laughed en laughed twel he couldn't laugh no mo'. 'I speck you'll take dinner wid me dis time, Brer Rabbit. I done laid in some calamus root, en I ain't gwineter take no skuse,' sez Brer Fox, sezee."

Here Uncle Remus paused, and drew a two-pound yam out of the ashes.

"Did the fox eat the rabbit?" asked the little boy to whom the story had been told.

"Dat's all de fur de tale goes," replied the old man. "He mout, en den agin he moutent. Some say Jedge B'ar come 'long en loosed 'im—some say he didn't. I hear Miss Sally callin'. You better run 'long."

22

The Courting of Sister Wisby

BY SARAH ORNE JEWETT

ALL the morning there had been an increasing temptation to take an outdoor holiday, and early in the afternoon the temptation outgrew my power of resistance. A far away pasture on the long southwestern slope of a high hill was persistently present to my mind, yet there seemed to be no particular reason why I should think of it. I was not sure that I wanted anything from the pasture, and there was no sign, except the temptation, that the pasture wanted anything of me. But I was on the farther side of as many as three fences before I stopped to think again where I was going, and why.

There is no use in trying to tell another person about that afternoon unless he distinctly remembers weather exactly like it. No number of details concerning an Arctic ice blockade will give a single shiver to a child of the tropics. This was one of those perfect New England days in late summer, when the spirit of autumn takes a first stealthy flight, like a spy, through the ripening countryside, and, with feigned sympathy for those who droop with August heat, puts her cool cloak of bracing air about leaf and flower and human shoulders. Every living thing grows suddenly cheerful and strong; it is only when you catch sight of a horror-stricken little maple in swampy soil—a little maple that has second-sight and fore-knowledge of coming disaster to her race—only then does a distrust of autumn's friendliness dim your joyful satisfaction.

In the midwinter there is always a day when one has the first foretaste of spring; in late August there is a morning when the air is for the first time autumn-like. Perhaps it is a hint to the squirrels to get in their first supplies for the winter hoards, or a reminder that summer will soon end, and everybody had better make the most of it. We are always looking forward to the passing and ending of winter, but when summer is here it seems as if summer must always last. As I went across the fields that day, I found myself half lamenting that the world must fade again, even that the best of her budding and bloom was only a preparation for another springtime, for an awakening beyond the coming winter's sleep.

The sun was slightly veiled; there was a chattering group of birds, which had gathered for a conference about their early migration. Yet, oddly enough, I heard the voice of a belated bobolink, and presently saw him rise from the grass and hover leisurely, while he sang a brief tune. He was much behind time if he were still a housekeeper; but as for the other birds who listened, they cared only for their own notes. An old crow went sagging by, and gave a croak at his despised neighbor, just as a black reviewer croaked at Keats—so hard it is to be just to one's contemporaries. The bobolink was indeed singing out of season, and it was impossible to say whether he really belonged most to this summer or to the next. He might have been delayed on his northward journey; at any rate, he had a light heart now, to judge from his song, and I wished that I could ask him a few questions—how he liked being the last man among the bobolinks, and where he had taken singing lessons in the South.

Presently I left the lower fields, and took a path that led higher, where I could look beyond the village to the northern country mountainward. Here the sweet fern grew thick and fragrant, and I also found myself heedlessly treading on pennyroyal. Nearby, in a field corner, I long ago made a most comfortable seat by putting a stray piece of board and bit of rail across the angle of the fences. I have spent many a delightful hour there, in the shade and shelter of a young pitch pine and a wild cherry tree, with a lovely outlook toward the village, just far enough away beyond the green slopes and tall elms of the lower meadows. But that day I still had the feeling of being outward bound, and did not turn aside nor linger. The high pasture land grew more and more enticing.

I stopped to pick some blackberries that twinkled at me like beads among their dry vines, and two or three yellowbirds fluttered up from the leaves of a thistle and then came back again, as if they had complacently discovered that I was only an overgrown yellowbird, in strange disguise but perfectly harmless. They made me feel as if I were an intruder, though they did not offer to peck at me, and we parted company very soon. It was good to stand at last on the great shoulder of the hill. The wind was coming in from the sea, there was a fine fragrance from the pines, and the air grew sweeter every moment. I took new pleasure in the thought that in a piece of wild pasture land like this one may get closest to Nature, and subsist upon what she gives of her own free will. There have been no drudging, heavy-shod ploughmen to overturn the soil, and vex it into yielding artificial crops. Here one has to take just what Nature is pleased to give, whether one is a yellowbird or a human being. It is very good entertainment for a summer wayfarer, and I am asking my reader now to share the winter provision which I harvested that day. Let us hope that the small birds are also faring well after their fashion, but I give them an anxious thought while the snow goes hurrying in long waves across the buried fields, this windy winter night.

I next went farther down the hill, and got a drink of fresh cool water from the brook, and pulled a tender sheaf of sweet flag beside it. The mossy old fence just beyond was the last barrier between me and the pasture which had sent an invisible messenger earlier in the day, but I saw that somebody else had come first to the rendezvous: there was a brown gingham cape-bonnet and a sprigged shoulder-shawl bobbing up and down, a little way off among the junipers. I had taken such uncommon pleasure in being alone that I instantly felt a sense of disappointment; then a warm glow of pleasant satisfaction rebuked my selfishness. This could be no one but dear old Mrs. Goodsoe, the friend of my childhood and fond dependence of my maturer years. I had not seen her for many weeks, but here she was, out on one of her famous campaigns for herbs, or perhaps just returning from a blueberrying expedition. I approached with care, so as not to startle the gingham bonnet; but she heard the rustle of the bushes against my dress, and looked up quickly, as she knelt, bending over the turf. In that position she was hardly taller than the luxuriant junipers themselves.

"I'm a-gittin' in my mulleins," she said briskly, "an' I've been thinking o' you these twenty times since I come out o' the house. I begun to believe you must ha' forgot me at last."

"I have been away from home," I explained. "Why don't you get in your pennyroyal too? There's a great plantation of it beyond the next fence but one."

"Pennyr'yal!" repeated the dear little old woman, with an air of compassion for inferior knowledge; "'tain't the right time, darlin'. Pennyr'yal's too rank now. But for mulleins this day is prime. I've got a dreadful graspin' fit for 'em this year; seems if I must be goin' to need 'em extry. I feel like the squirrels must when they know a hard winter's comin'." And Mrs. Goodsoe bent over her work again, while I stood by and watched her carefully cut the best full-grown leaves with a clumsy pair of scissors, which might have served through at least half a century of herb-gathering. They were fastened to her apron strings by a long piece of list.

"I'm going to take my jack-knife and help you," I suggested, with some fear of refusal. "I just passed a flourishing family of six or seven heads that must have been growing on purpose for you."

"Now be keerful, dear heart," was the anxious response; "choose 'em well. There's odds in mulleins same's there is in angels. Take a plant that's all run up to stalk, and there ain't but little goodness in the leaves. This one I'm at now must ha' been stepped on by some creatur and blighted of its bloom, and the leaves is han'some! When I was small I used to have a notion that Adam an' Eve must ha' took mulleins fer their winter wear. Ain't they just like flannel, for all the world? I've had experience, and I know there's plenty of sickness might be saved to folks if they'd quit horse-radish and such fiery, exasperating things, and use mullein drarves in proper season. Now I shall spread these an' dry 'em nice on my spare floor in the garrit, an' come to steam 'em for use along in the winter there'll be the valley of the whole summer's goodness in 'em, sartin." And she snipped away with the dull scissors while I listened respectfully, and took great pains to have my part of the harvest present a good appearance.

"This is most too dry a head," she added presently, a little out of breath. "There! I can tell you there's win'rows o' young doctors, bilin' over with book-larnin', that is truly ignorant of what to do for the sick, or how to p'int out those paths that well people foller toward sickness. Book-fools I call 'em, them young men, an' some on 'em never'll live to know much better, if they git to be Methuselahs. In my time every middle-aged woman who had brought up a family had some proper ideas of dealin' with complaints. I won't say but there was some fools amongst *them,* but I'd rather take my chances, unless they'd forsook herbs and gone to dealin' with patent stuff. Now my mother really did sense the use of herbs and roots. I never see anybody that come up to her. She was a meek-looking woman, but very understandin', mother was."

"Then that's where you learned so much yourself, Mrs. Goodsoe," I ventured to say.

"Bless your heart, I don't hold a candle to her; 'tis but little I can recall of what she used to say. No, her larnin' died with her," said my friend, in a self-deprecating tone. "Why, there was as many as twenty kinds of roots alone that she used to keep by her, that I forgot the use of; an' I'm sure I shouldn't know where to find the most of 'em, any. There was an herb"—*airb* she called it—"an herb called Pennsylvany; and she used to think everything of nobleliver-wort, but I never could seem to get the right effects from it, as she could. Though I don't know as she ever really did use masterwort where somethin' else wouldn't ha' served. She had a cousin married out in Pennsylvany that used to take pains to get it to her every year or two, and so she felt 'twas important to have it. Some set more by such things as come from a distance, but I rec'lect mother always used to maintain that folks was meant to be doctored with the stuff that grew right about 'em; 'twas sufficient, an' so ordered. That was before the whole population took to livin' on wheels, the way they do now. 'Twas never my idee that we was meant to know what's goin' on all over the world to once. There's goin' to be some sort of a set-back one o' these days, with these telegraphs an 'things, an' letters comin' every hand's turn, and folks leavin' their proper work to answer 'em. I may not live to see it. 'Twas allowed to be difficult for folks to git about in old times, or to git word across the country, and they stood in their lot an' place, and weren't all just alike, either, same as pine-spills."

We were kneeling side by side now, as if in penitence for the march of progress, but we laughed as we turned to look at each other.

"Do you think it did much good when everybody brewed a cracked quart mug of herb-tea?" I asked, walking away on my knees to a new mullein.

"I've always lifted my voice against the practice, far's I could," declared Mrs. Goodsoe; an' I won't deal out none o' the herbs I save for no such nonsense. There was three houses along our road—I call no names—where you couldn't go into the livin' room without findin' a mess o' herb-tea drorin' on the stove or side o' the fireplace, winter or summer, sick or well. One was thoroughwut, one would be camomile, and the other, like as not, yellow dock; but they all used to put in a little new rum to git out the goodness, or keep it from spilin'." (Mrs. Goodsoe favored me with a knowing smile.) "Land, how mother used to laugh! But, poor creatures, they had to work hard, and I guess it never done 'em a mite o' harm; they was all good herbs. I wish you could hear the quawkin' there used to be when they was indulged with a real case o' sickness. Everybody would collect from far an' near; you'd see 'em coming along the road and across the pastures then; everybody clamorin' that nothin' would do no kind o' good but her choice o' teas or drarves to the feet. I wonder there was a babe lived to grow up in the whole lower part o' the town; an' if nothin' else 'peared to ail 'em, word was passed about that 'twas likely Mis' So-and-So's last young one was goin' to be foolish. Land, how they'd gather! I know one day the doctor come to Widder Peck's and the house was crammed so't he could scercely git inside the door; and he says, just as polite, 'Do send for some of the neighbors!' as if there wa'n't a soul to turn to, right or left. You'd ought to seen 'em begin to scatter."

"But don't you think the cars and telegraphs have given people more to interest them, Mrs. Goodsoe? Don't you believe people's lives were narrower then, and more taken up with little things?" I asked, unwisely, being a product of modern times.

"Not one mite, dear," said my companion stoutly. "There was as big thoughts then as there is now; these times was born o' them. The difference is in folks themselves; but now, instead o' doin' their own house-keepin' and watchin' their own neighbors—though that was carried to excess—they git word that a niece's child is ailin' the other side o' Massachusetts, and they drop everything and git on their best clothes, and off they jiggit in the cars. 'Tis a bad sign when folks wear out their best clothes faster 'n they do their everyday ones. The other side o' Massachusetts has got to look after itself by rights. An' besides that, Sunday-keepin's all gone out o' fashion. Some lays it to one thing an' some another, but some o' them old ministers that folks are all a-sighin' for did preach a lot o' stoff that wa'n't nothin' but chaff; 'twa'n't the word o' God out o' either Old Testament or New. But everybody went to meetin' and heard it, and come home, and was set to fightin' with their next door neighbor over it. Now I'm a believer, and I try to live a Christian life, but I'd as soon hear a surveyor's book read out, figgers an' all, as try to get any simple truth out o' most sermons. It's them as is most to blame."

"What was the matter that day at Widow Peck's?" I hastened to ask, for I knew by experience that the good, clear minded soul beside me was apt to grow unduly vexed and distressed when she contemplated the state of religious teaching.

"Why, there wa'n't nothin' the matter, only a gal o' Miss Peck's had met with a dis'pintment and had gone into screechin' fits. 'Twas a rovin' creatur that had come along hayin' time, and he'd gone off an' forsook her betwixt two days; nobody ever knew what become of him. Them Pecks was 'Good Lord, anybody!' kind o' gals, an took up with whoever they could get. One of 'em married Heron, the Irishman; they lived in that little house that was burnt this summer, over on the edge o' the plains. He was a good-hearted creatur, with a laughin' eye and a clever word for everybody. He was the first Irishman that ever came this way, and we was all for gettin' a look at him, when he first used to go by. Mother's folks was what they call Scotch-Irish, though; there was an old race of 'em settled about here. They could foretell events, some on 'em, and had second-sight. I know folks used to say mother's grandmother had them gifts, but mother was never free to speak about it to us. She remembered her well, too."

"I suppose that you mean old Jim Heron, who was such a famous fiddler?" I asked with great interest, for I am always delighted to know more about that rustic hero, parochial Orpheus that he must have been!

"Now, dear heart, I suppose you don't remember him, do you?"

replied Mrs. Goodsoe, earnestly. "Fiddle! He'd about break your heart with them tunes of his, or else set your heels flyin' up the floor in a jig, though you was minister o' the First Parish and all wound up for a funeral prayer. I tell ye there win't no tunes sounds like them used to. It used to seem to me summer nights when I was comin' along the plains road, and he set by the window playin', as if there was a bewitched human creatur in that old red fiddle o' his. He could make it sound just like a woman's voice tellin' somethin' over and over, as if folks could help her out o' her sorrows if she could only make 'em understand. I've set by the stone wall and cried as if my heart was broke, and dear knows it wa'n't in them days. How he would twirl off them jigs and dance tunes! He used to make somethin' han'some out of 'em in fall an' winter, playin' at huskins and dancin' parties; but he was unstiddy by spells, as he got along in years, and never knew what it was to be forehanded. Everybody felt bad when he died; you couldn't help likin' the creatur. He'd got the gift—that's all you could say about it.

"There was a Mis' Jerry Foss, that lived over by the brook bridge, on the plains road, that had lost her husband early, and was left with three child'n. She set the world by 'em, and was a real pleasant, ambitious little woman, and was workin' on as best she could with that little farm, when there come a rage o' scarlet fever, and her boy and two girls was swept off and laid dead within the same week. Everyone o' the neighbors did what they could, but she'd had no sleep since they was taken sick, and after the funeral she set there just like a piece o' marble, and would only shake her head when you spoke to her. They all thought her reason would go; and 'twould certain, if she couldn't have shed tears. An' one o' the neighbors—'twas like mother's sense, but it might have been somebody else—spoke o' Jim Heron. Mother an' one or two o' the women that knew her best was in the house with her. 'T was right in the edge o' the woods and some of us younger ones was over by the wall on the other side of the road where there was a couple of old willows—I remember just how the brook damp felt— and we kept quiet's we could, and some other folks come along down the road, and stood waitin' on the little bridge, hopin' somebody'd come out, I suppose, and they'd git news. Everybody was wrought up, and felt a good deal for her, you know. By an' by Jim Heron come stealin' right out o' the shadows an' set down on the doorstep, an' 'twas a good while before we heard a sound; then, oh, dear me! 'twas what the whole neighborhood felt for that mother all spoke in the notes, an' they told me afterwards that Mis' Foss's face changed in a minute, and she come right over an' got into my mother's lap—she was a little woman—an' laid her head down, and there she cried herself into a blessed sleep.

After awhile one o' the other women stole out an' told the folks, and we all went home. He only played that one tune.

"But there!" resumed Mrs. Goodsoe, after a silence, during which my eyes were filled with tears. "His wife always complained that the fiddle made her nervous. She never 'peared to think nothin' o' poor Heron after she'd once got him."

"That's often the way," I said, with harsh cynicism, though I had no guilty person in my mind at the moment; and we went straying off, not very far apart, up through the pasture. Mrs. Goodsoe cautioned me that we must not get so far off that we could not get back the same day. The sunshine began to feel very hot on our backs, and we both turned toward the shade. We had already collected a large bundle of mullein leaves, which were carefully laid into a clean, calico apron, held together by the four corners, and proudly carried by me, though my companion regarded them with anxious eyes. We sat down together at the edge of the pine woods, and Mrs. Goodsoe proceeded to fan herself with her limp cape-bonnet.

"I declare, how hot it is! The east wind's all gone again," she said. "It felt so cool this forenoon that I overburdened myself with as thick a petticoat as any I've got. I'm despri't afeared of having a chill, now that I ain't so young as once. I hate to be housed up."

"It's only August, after all," I assured her unnecessarily, confirming my statement by taking two peaches out of my pocket, and laying them side by side on the brown pine needles between us.

"Dear sakes alive!" exclaimed the old lady, with evident pleasure. "Where did you get them, now? Doesn't anything taste twice better out-o'-doors? I ain't had such a peach for years. Do le's keep the stones, an' I'll plant 'em; it only takes four years for a peach pit to come to bearing, an' I guess I'm good for four years, 'thout I meet with some accident."

I could not help agreeing, or taking a fond look at the thin little figure, and her wrinkled brown face and kind, twinkling eyes. She looked as if she had properly dried herself, by mistake, with some of her mullein leaves, and was likely to keep her goodness, and to last the longer in consequence. There never was a truer, simple-hearted soul made out of the old-fashioned country dust than Mrs. Goodsoe. I thought, as I looked away from her across the wide country, that nobody was left in any of the farmhouses so original, so full of rural wisdom and reminiscence, so really able and dependable, as she. And nobody had made better use of her time in a world foolish enough to sometimes undervalue medicinal herbs.

When we had eaten our peaches we still sat under the pines, and I was not without pride when I had poked about in the ground with a little twig, and displayed to my crony a long fine root, bright yellow to the eye, and a wholesome bitter to the taste.

"Yis, dear, goldthread," she assented indulgently. "Seems to me there's more of it than anything except grass an' hard-tack. Good for canker, but no better than two or three other things I can call to mind; but I always lay in a good wisp of it, for old times' sake. Now, I want to know why you should ha' bit it, and took away all the taste o' your nice peach? I was just thinkin' what a han'some entertainment we've had. I've got so I 'sociate certain things with certain folks, and goldthread was some-thin' Lizy Wisby couldn't keep house without, no ways whatever. I believe she took so much it kind o' puckered her disposition."

"Lizy Wisby?" I repeated inquiringly.

"You knew her, if ever, by the name of Mis' Deacon Brimblecom," answered my friend, as if this were only a brief preface to further infor-mation, so I waited with respectful expectation. Mrs. Goodsoe had grown tired out in the sun, and a good story would be an excuse for sufficient rest. It was a most lovely place where we sat, halfway up the long hillside; for my part, I was perfectly contented and happy. "You've often heard of Deacon Brimblecom?" she asked, as if a great deal de-pended upon his being properly introduced.

"I remember him," said I. "They called him Deacon Brimfull, you know, and he used to go about with a witch-hazel branch to show people where to dig wells."

"That's the one," said Mrs. Goodsoe, laughing. "I didn't know's you could go so far back. I'm always divided between whether you can remember everything I can, or are only a babe in arms."

"I have a dim recollection of there being something strange about their marriage," I suggested, after a pause, which began to appear dangerous. I was so much afraid the subject would be changed.

"I can tell you all about it," I was quickly answered. "Deacon Brimblecom was very pious accordin' to his lights in his early years. He lived way back in the country then, and there come a rovin' preacher along, and set everybody up that way all by the ears. I've heard the old folks talk it over, but I forget most of his doctrine, except some of his followers was persuaded they could dwell among the angels while yet on airth, and this Deacon Brimfull, as you call him, felt sure he was called by the voice of a spirit bride. So he left a good, deservin' wife he had, an' four children, and built him a new house over to the other side of the land he'd had from his father. They didn't take much pains with the buildin', because they expected to be translated before long, and then the spirit brides and them folks was goin' to appear and divide up the airth amongst 'em, and the world's folks and on-believers was goin' to serve 'em or be sent to torments. They had meetin's about in the schoolhouses, an' all sorts o' goin's on; some on 'em went crazy, but the deacon held on to what wits he had, an' by an' by the spirit bride didn't turn out to be much of a housekeeper, an' he had always been used to good livin', so he sneaked home ag'in. One o' mother's sisters married up to Ash Hill, where it all took place; that's how I come to have the particulars."

"Then how did he come to find his Eliza Wisby?" I inquired. "Do tell me the whole story; you've got mullein leaves enough."

"There's all yisterday's at home, if I haven't," replied Mrs. Goodsoe. "The way he come a-courtin' o' Sister Wisby was this: she went a-courtin' o' him.

"There was a spell he lived to home, and then his poor wife died, and he had a spirit bride in good earnest, an' the child'n was placed about with his folks and hers, for they was both out o' good families; and I don't know what come over him, but he had another pious fit that looked for all the world like the real thing. He hadn't no family cares, and he lived with his brother's folks, and turned his land in with theirs. He used to travel to every meetin' an' conference that was within reach of his old sorrel hoss's feeble legs; he j'ined the Christian Baptists that was just in their early prime, and he was a great exhorter, and got to be called deacon, though I guess he wa'n't deacon, 'less it was for a spare hand when deacon times was scercer'n usual. An' one time there was a four-days' protracted meetin' to the church in the lower part of the town. 'Twas a real solemn time; somethin' more'n usual was goin' forward, an' they collected from the whole country round. Women folks liked it, an' the men too; it give 'em a change, an' they was quartered round free, same as conference folks now. Some on 'em, for a joke, sent Silas Brimblecom up to Lizy Wisby's, though she'd give out she couldn't accommodate nobody, because of expectin' her cousin's folks. Everybody knew 'twas a lie; she was amazin' close considerin' she had plenty to do with. There was a streak that wa'n't just right somewheres in Lizy's wits, I always thought. She was very kind in case o' sickness, I'll say that for her.

"You know where the house is, over there on what they call Windy Hill? There the deacon went, all unsuspectin', and 'stead o' Lizy's resentin' of him she put in her own hoss, and they come back together to evenin' meetin'. She was prominent among the sect herself, an' he bawled and talked, and she bawled and talked, an' took up more'n the time allotted in the exercises, just as if they was showin' off to each what they was able to do at expoundin'. Everybody was laughin' at 'em after the meetin' broke up, and that next day an' the next, an' all through, they was constant, and seemed to be havin' a beautiful occasion. Lizy had always give out she scorned the men, but when she got a chance at a particular one 'twas altogether different, and the deacon seemed to please her somehow or 'nother, and—There! you don't want to listen to this old stuff that's past an' gone?"

"Oh, yes, I do," said I.

"I run on like a clock that's onset her striking hand," said Mrs. Goodsoe mildly. "Sometimes my kitchen timepiece goes on half the forenoon, and I says to myself the day before yesterday I would let it be a warnin', and keep it in mind for a check on my own speech. The next news that was heard was that the deacon an' Lizy—well, opinions differed which of 'em had spoke first, but them fools settled it before the protracted meetin' was over, and give away their hearts before he started for home. They considered 'twould be wise, though, considerin' their short acquaintance, to take one another on trial a spell; 'twas Lizy's notion, and she asked him why he wouldn't come over and stop with her till spring, and then, if both continued to like, they could git married any time 'twas convenient. Lizy, she come and talked it over with mother, and mother disliked to offend her, but she spoke pretty plain; and Lizy felt hurt, an' thought they was showin' excellent judgment, so much harm come from hasty unions and folks comin' to a realizin' sense of each other's failin's when 'twas too late.

"So one day our folks saw Deacon Brimfull a-ridin' by with a gre't coopful of hens in the back o' his wagon, and bundles o' stuff tied to top and hitched to the exes underneath; and he riz a hymn just as he passed the house, and was speedin' the old sorrel with a willer switch. 'Twas most Thanksgivin' time, an' sooner'n she expected him. New Year's was the time she set; but he thought he'd come while the roads was fit for wheels. They was out to meetin' together Thanksgivin' Day, an' that used to be a gre't season for marryin'; so the young folks nudged each other, and some on 'em ventured to speak to the couple as they come down the aisle. Lizy carried it off real well; she wa'n't afraid o' what nobody said or thought, and so home they went. They'd got out her yaller sleigh and her hoss; she never would ride after the deacon's poor old creatur, and I believe it died long o' the winter from stiffenin' up.

"Yes," said Mrs. Goodsoe, emphatically, after we had silently considered the situation for a short space of time, "yes, there was consider'ble talk, now I tell you! The raskil boys pestered 'em just about to death for a while. They used to collect up there an' rap on the winders, and they'd turn out all the deacon's hens 'long at nine o'clock o' night, and chase 'em all over the dingle; an' one night they even lugged the pig right out o' the sty, and shoved it into the back entry, an' run for their lives. They'd stuffed its mouth full o' somethin', so it couldn't squeal till it got there. There wa'n't a sign o' nobody to be seen when Lizy hasted out with the light, and she an' the deacon had to persuade the creatur back as best they could; 'twas a cold night, and they said it took 'em till towards mornin'. You see the deacon was just the kind of a man that a hog wouldn't budge for; it takes a masterful man to deal with a hog. Well, there was no end to the works nor the talk, but Lizy left 'em pretty much alone. She did 'pear kind of dignified about it, I must say!"

"And then, were they married in the spring?"

"I was tryin' to remember whether it was just before Fast Day or just after," responded my friend, with a careful look at the sun, which was nearer the west than either of us had noticed. "I think likely 'twas along in the last o' April, anyway some of us looked out o' the window one Monday mornin' early, and says, 'For goodness' sake! Lizy's sent the deacon home again!' His old sorrel havin' passed away, he was ridin' in Ezry Welsh's hoss-cart, with his hen-coop and more bundles than he had when he come, and looked as meechin' as ever you see. Ezry was drivin', an' he let a glance fly swiftly round to see if any of us was lookin' out; an' then I declare if he didn't have the malice to turn right in towards the barn, where he see my oldest brother, Joshuay, an' says he real natural, 'Joshuay, just step out with your wrench. I believe I hear my kingbolt rattlin' kind o' loose.' Brother, he went out an' took in the sitooation, an' the deacon bowed kind of stiff. Joshuay was so full o' laugh, and Ezry Welsh, that they couldn't look one another in the face. There wa'n't nothing ailed the kingbolt, you know, an' when Josh riz up he says, 'Goin' up country for a spell, Mr. Brimblecom?'

" 'I be,' says the deacon, lookin' dreadful mortified and cast down.

" 'Ain't things turned out well with you an' Sister Wisby?' says Joshuay. 'You had ought to remember that the woman is the weaker vessel.'

" 'Hang her, let her carry less sail, then!' the deacon bu'st out, and he stood right up an' shook his fist there by the hen-coop, he was so mad; an' Ezry's hoss was a young creatur, an' started up and set the deacon right over backwards into the chips. We didn't know but he'd broke his neck; but when he see the women folks runnin' out he jumped up quick as a cat, an' clim into the cart, an' off they went. Ezry said he told him that he couldn't git along with Lizy, she was so fractious in thundery weather; if there was a rumble in the daytime she must go right to bed an' screech, and 'twas night she must git right up an' go an' call him out of a sound sleep. But everybody knew he'd never gone home unless she'd sent him.

"Somehow they made it up ag'in, him an' Lizy, and she had him back. She's been countin' all along on not havin' to hire nobidy to work about the gardin' an' so on, an' she said she wa'n't goin' to let him have a whole winter's board for nothin'. So the old hens was moved back, and they was married right off fair an' square, an' I don't know but they got along well as most folks. He brought his youngest girl down to live with 'em after a while, an' she was a real treasure to Lizy; everybody spoke well o' Phœbe Brimblecom. The deacon got over his pious fit, and there was consider'ble work in him if you kept right after him. He was an amazin' cider-drinker, and he airnt the name you know him by in his latter days. Lizy never trusted him with nothin', but she kep' him well. She left everything she owned to Phœbe, when she died, 'cept somethin' to satisfy the law. There, they're all gone now; seems to me sometimes, when I get thinkin', as if I'd lived a thousand years!"

I laughed, but I found Mrs. Goodsoe's thoughts had taken a serious turn.

"There, I come by some old graves down here in the lower edge of the pasture," she said as we rose to go. "I couldn't help thinking how I should like to be laid right out in the pasture ground, when my time comes; it looked sort o' comfortable, and I have ranged these slopes so many summers. Seems as if I could see right up through the turf and tell when the weather was pleasant, and get the goodness o' the sweet fern. Now, dear, just hand me my apernful o' mulleins out o' the shade. I hope you won't come to need none this winter, but I'll dry some special for you."

"I'm going by the road," said I, "or else by the path across the meadows, so I will walk as far as the house with you. Aren't you pleased with my company?" for she demurred at my going the least bit out of the way.

So we strolled towards the little gray house, with our plunder of mullein leaves slung on a stick which we carried between us. Of course I went in to make a call, as if I had not seen my hostess before; she is the last maker of muster-gingerbread, and before I came away I was kindly measured for a pair of mittens.

"You'll be sure to come an' see them two peach trees after I get 'em well growin'?" Mrs. Goodsoe called after me when I had said good-by; and was almost out of hearing down the road.

23

The Boy Who Drew Cats

BY LAFCADIO HEARN

A LONG, long time ago, in a small country village in Japan, there lived a poor farmer and his wife, who were very good people. They had a number of children, and found it very hard to feed them all. The elder son was strong enough when only fourteen years old to help his father; and the little girls learned to help their mother almost as soon as they could walk.

But the youngest child, a little boy, did not seem to be fit for hard work. He was very clever,—cleverer than all his brothers and sisters; but he was quite weak and small, and people said he could never grow very big. So his parents thought it would be better for him to become a priest than to become a farmer. They took him with them to the village-temple one day, and asked the good old priest who lived there if he would have their little boy for his acolyte, and teach him all that a priest ought to know.

The old man spoke kindly to the lad, and asked him some hard questions. So clever were the answers that the priest agreed to take the little fellow into the temple as an acolyte, and to educate him for the priesthood.

The boy learned quickly what the old priest taught him, and was very obedient in most things. But he had one fault. He liked to draw cats during study-hours, and to draw cats even where cats ought not to have been drawn at all.

Whenever he found himself alone, he drew cats. He drew them on the margins of the priest's books, and on all the screens of the temple, and on the walls, and on the pillars. Several times the priest told him this was not right; but he did not stop drawing cats. He drew them because he could not really help it. He had what is called "the genius of an *artist,*" and just for that reason he was not quite fit to be an acolyte;—a good acolyte should study books.

One day after he had drawn some very clever pictures of cats upon a paper screen, the old priest said to him severely: "My boy, you must go away from this temple at once. You will never make a good priest, but perhaps you will become a great artist. Now let me give you a last piece of advice, and be sure you never forget it. *Avoid large places at night;—keep to small!*"

The boy did not know what the priest meant by saying, *"Avoid large places;—keep to small."* He thought and thought, while he was tying up his little bundle of clothes to go away; but he could not understand those words, and he was afraid to speak to the priest any more, except to say good-by.

He left the temple very sorrowfully, and began to wonder what he should do. If he went straight home he felt sure his father would punish him for having been disobedient to the priest: so he was afraid to go home. All at once he remembered that at the next village, twelve miles away, there was a very big temple. He had heard there were several priests at that temple; and he made up his mind to go to them and ask them to take him for their acolyte.

Now that big temple was closed up but the boy did not know this fact. The reason it had been closed up was that a goblin had frightened the priests away, and had taken possession of the place. Some brave warriors had afterward gone to the temple at night to kill the goblin; but they had never been seen alive again. Nobody had ever told these things to the boy;—so he walked all the way to the village hoping to be kindly treated by the priests.

When he got to the village it was already dark, and all the people were in bed; but he saw the big temple on a hill at the other end of the principal street, and he saw there was a light in the temple. People who tell the story say the goblin used to make that light, in order to tempt lonely travelers to ask for shelter. The boy went at once to the temple, and knocked. There was no sound inside. He knocked and knocked again; but still nobody came. At last he pushed gently at the door, and was quite glad to find that it had not been fastened. So he went in, and saw a lamp burning,—but no priest.

He thought some priest would be sure to come very soon, and he sat down and waited. Then he noticed that everything in the temple was gray with dust, and thickly spun over with cobwebs. So he thought to himself that the priests would certainly like to have an acolyte, to keep the place clean. He wondered why they had allowed everything to get so dusty. What most pleased him, however, were some big white screens, good to paint cats upon. Though he was tired, he looked at once for a writing box, and found one, and ground some ink, and began to paint cats.

He painted a great many cats upon the screens; and then he began to feel very, very sleepy. He was just on the point of lying down to sleep beside one of the screens, when he suddenly remembered the words, *"Avoid large places;—keep to small!"*

The temple was very large; he was all alone; and as he thought of these words—though he could not quite understand them—he began to feel for the first time a little afraid; and he resolved to look for a *small place* in which to sleep. He found a little cabinet, with a sliding door, and went into it, and shut himself up. Then he lay down and fell fast asleep.

Very late in the night he was awakened by a most terrible noise— a noise of fighting and screaming. It was so dreadful that he was afraid even to look through a chink of the little cabinet; he lay very still, holding his breath for fright.

The light that had been in the temple went out; but the awful sounds continued, and became more awful, and all the temple shook. After a long time silence came; but the boy was still afraid to move. He did not move until the light of the morning sun shone into the cabinet through the chinks of the little door.

Then he got out of his hiding place very cautiously, and looked about. The first thing he saw was that all the floor of the temple was covered with blood. And then he saw, lying dead in the middle of it, an enormous, monstrous rat—a goblin-rat—bigger than a cow!

But who or what could have killed it? There was no man or other creature to be seen. Suddenly the boy observed that the mouths of all the cats he had drawn the night before, were red and wet with blood. Then he knew that the goblin had been killed by the cats which he had drawn. And then also, for the first time, he understood why the wise old priest had said to him, *"Avoid large places at night;—keep to small."*

Afterward that boy became a very famous artist. Some of the cats which he drew are still shown to travelers in Japan.

24

The Pearls of Loreto

BY GERTRUDE ATHERTON

WITHIN memory of the most gnarled and coffee-colored Montereño never had there been so exciting a race day. All essential conditions seemed to have held counsel and agreed to combine. Not a wreath of fog floated across the bay to dim the sparkling air. Every horse, every vaquero, was alert and physically perfect. The rains were over; the dust was not gathered. Pio Pico, Governor of the Californias, was in Monterey on one of his brief infrequent visits. Clad in black velvet, covered with jewels and ropes of gold, he sat on his big chestnut horse at the upper end of the field, with General Castro, Doña Modeste Castro, and other prominent Montereños, his interest so keen that more than once the official dignity relaxed, and he shouted "Brava!" with the rest.

And what a brilliant sight it was! The flowers had faded on the hills, for June was upon them; but gayer than the hills had been was the race field of Monterey. Caballeros, with silver on their wide gray hats and on their saddles of embossed leather, gold and silver embroidery on their velvet serapes, crimson sashes about their slender waists, silver spurs and buckskin botas, stood tensely in their stirrups as the racers flew by, or, during the short intervals, pressed each other with eager wagers. There was little money in that time. The golden skeleton within the sleeping body of California had not yet been laid bare. But ranchos were lost and won; thousands of cattle would pass to other hands at the next rodeo; many a superbly caparisoned steed would rear and plunge between the spurs of a new master.

And caballeros were not the only living pictures of that memorable day of a time forever gone. Beautiful women in silken fluttering gowns, bright flowers holding the mantilla from flushed awakened faces, sat their impatient horses as easily as a gull rides a wave. The sun beat down, making dark cheeks pink and white cheeks darker, but those great eyes, strong with their own fires, never faltered. The old women in attendance grumbled vague remonstrances at all things, from the heat to intercepted coquetries. But their charges gave the good dueñas little heed. They shouted until their little throats were hoarse, smashed their fans, beat the sides of their mounts with their tender hands, in imitation of the vaqueros.

"It is the gayest, the happiest, the most careless life in the world," thought Pio Pico, shutting his teeth, as he looked about him "But how long will it last? Curse the Americans! They are coming."

But the bright hot spark that convulsed assembled Monterey shot from no ordinary condition. A stranger was there, a guest of General Castro, Don Vicente de la Vega y Arillaga, of Los Angeles. Not that a stranger was matter for comment in Monterey, capital of California, but this stranger had brought with him horses which threatened to disgrace the famous winners of the North. Two races had been won already by the black Southern beasts.

"Dios de mi alma!" cried the girls, one to the other, "their coats are blacker than our hair! Their nostrils pulse like a heart on fire! Their eyes flash like water in the sun! Ay! the handsome stranger, will he roll us in the dust? Ay! our golden horses, with the tails and manes of silver —how beautiful is the contrast with the vaqueros in their black and silver, their soft white linen! The shame! the shame!—if they are put to shame! Poor Guido! Will he lose this day, when he has won so many? But the stranger is so handsome! Dios de mi vida! his eyes are like dark blue stars. And he is so cold! He alone—he seems not to care. Madre de Dios! Madre de Dios! he wins again! No! no! no! Yes! Ay! yi! yi! B-r-a-v-o!"

Guido Cabañares dug his spurs into his horse and dashed to the head of the field, where Don Vincente sat at the left of General Castro. He was followed hotly by several friends, sympathetic and indignant. As he rode, he tore off his serape and flung it to the ground; even his silk riding clothes sat heavily upon his fury. Don Vicente smiled, and rode forward to meet him.

"At your service, señor," he said, lifting his sombrero.

"Take your mustangs back to Los Angeles!" cried Don Guido, beside himself with rage, the politeness and dignity of his race routed by passion. "Why do you bring your hideous brutes here to shame me in the eyes of Monterey? Why—"

"Yes! Why? Why?" demanded his friends, surrounding De la Vega. "This is not the humiliation of a man, but of the North by the accursed

South! You even would take our capital from us! Los Angeles, the capital of the Californias!"

"What have politics to do with horse racing?" asked De la Vega, coldly. "Other strangers have brought their horses to your field, I suppose."

"Yes, but they have not won. They have not been from the South."

By this time almost every caballero on the field was wheeling about De la Vega. Some felt with Cabañares, others rejoiced in his defeat, but all resented the victory of the South over the North.

"Will you run again?" demanded Cabañares.

"Certainly. Do you think of putting your knife into my neck?"

Cabañares drew back, somewhat abashed, the indifference of the other sputtering like water on his passion.

"It is not a matter for blood," he said sulkily; "but the head is hot and words are quick when horses run neck to neck. And, by the Mother of God, you shall not have the last race. My best horse has not run. Viva El Rayo!"

"Viva El Rayo!" shouted the caballeros.

"And let the race be between you two alone," cried one. "The North or the South! Los Angeles or Monterey! It will be the race of our life."

"The North or the South!" cried the caballeros, wheeling and galloping across the field to the doñas. "Twenty leagues to a real for Guido Cabañares."

"What a pity that Ysabel is not here!" said Doña Modeste Castro to Pio Pico. "How those green eyes of hers would flash today!"

"She would not come," said the Governor. "She said she was tired of the race."

"Of whom do you speak?" asked De la Vega, who had rejoined them.

"Of Ysabel Herrera, La Favorita of Monterey," answered Pio Pico. "The most beautiful woman in the Californias, since Chonita Iturbi y Moncada, my Vicente. It is at her uncle's that I stay. You have heard me speak of my old friend; and surely you have heard of her."

"Ay!" said De la Vega. "I have heard of her."

"Viva El Rayo!"

"Ay, the ugly brute!"

"What name? Vitriolo? Mother of God! Diablo or Demonio would suit him better. He looks as if he had been bred in hell. He will not stand the quirto; and El Rayo is more lightly built. We shall beat by a dozen lengths."

The two vaqueros who were to ride the horses had stripped to their soft linen shirts and black velvet trousers, cast aside their sombreros, and bound their heads with tightly knotted handkerchiefs. Their spurs were fastened to bare brown heels; the cruel quirto was in the hand of each; they rode barebacked, winding their wiry legs in and out of a horsehair rope encircling the body of the animal. As they slowly passed the crowd on their way to the starting point at the lower end of the field, and listened to the rattling fire of wagers and comments, they looked defiant, and alive to the importance of the coming event.

El Rayo shone like burnished copper, his silver mane and tail glittering as if powdered with diamond dust. He was long and graceful of body, thin of flank, slender of leg. With arched neck and flashing eyes, he walked with the pride of one who was aware of the admiration he excited.

Vitriolo was black and powerful. His long neck fitted into well-placed shoulders. He had great depth of girth, immense length from shoulder points to hips, big cannon-bones, and elastic pasterns. There was neither amiability nor pride in his mien; rather a sullen sense of brute power, such as may have belonged to the knights of the Middle Ages. Now and again he curled his lips away from the bit and laid his ears back as if he intended to eat of the elegant Beau Brummel stepping so daintily beside him. Of the antagonistic crowd he took not the slightest notice.

"The race begins! Holy heaven!" The murmur rose to a shout—a deep hoarse shout strangely crossed and recrossed by long silver notes; a thrilling volume of sound rising above a sea of flashing eyes and parted lips and a vivid moving mass of color.

Twice the horses scored, and were sent back. The third time they bounded by the starting post neck and neck, nose to nose. José Abrigo, treasurer of Monterey, dashed his sombrero, heavy with silver eagles, to the ground, and the race was begun.

Almost at once the black began to gain. Inch by inch he fought his way to the front, and the roar with which the crowd had greeted the start dropped into the silence of apprehension.

El Rayo was not easily to be shaken off. A third of the distance had been covered, and his nose was abreast of Vitriolo's flank. The vaqueros sat as if carved from sun-baked clay, as lightly as if hollowed, watching each other warily out of the corners of their eyes.

The black continued to gain. Halfway from home light was visible between the two horses. The pace became terrific, the excitement so intense that not a sound was heard but that of racing hoofs. The horses swept onward like projectiles, the same smoothness, the same suggestion of eternal flight. The bodies were extended until the tense muscles rose under the satin coats. Vitriolo's eyes flashed viciously; El Rayo's strained with determination. Vitriolo's nostrils were as red as angry craters; El Rayo's fluttered like paper in the wind.

Three-quarters of the race was run, and the rider of Vitriolo could tell by the sound of the hoof beats behind him that he had a good lead of at least two lengths over the Northern champion. A smile curled the corners of his heavy lips; the race was his already.

Suddenly El Rayo's vaquero raised his hand, and down came the maddening quirto, first on one side, then on the other. The spurs dug; the blood spurted. The crowd burst into a howl of delight as their favorite responded. Startled by the sound, Vitriolo's rider darted a glance over his shoulder, and saw El Rayo bearing down upon him like a thunderbolt, regaining the ground that he had lost, not by inches, but by feet. Two hundred paces from the finish he was at the black's flanks; one hundred and fifty, he was at his girth; one hundred, and the horses were neck and neck; and still the quirto whirred down on El Rayo's heaving flanks, the spurs dug deeper into his quivering flesh.

The vaquero of Vitriolo sat like an image, using neither whip nor spur, his teeth set, his eyes rolling from the goal ahead to the rider at his side.

The breathless intensity of the spectators had burst. They had begun to click their teeth, to mutter hoarsely, then to shout, to gesticulate, to shake their fists in each other's face, to push and scramble for a better view.

"Holy God!" cried Pio Pico, carried out of himself, "the South is lost! Vitriolo the magnificent! Ah, who would have thought? The black by the gold! Ay! What! No! Holy Mary! Holy God!—"

Six strides more and the race is over. With the bark of a coyote the vaquero of the South leans forward over Vitriolo's neck. The big black responds like a creature of reason. Down comes the quirto once —only once. He fairly lifts his horse ahead and shoots into victory, winner by a neck. The South has vanquished the North.

The crowd yelled and shouted until it was exhausted. But even Cabañares made no further demonstration toward De la Vega. Not only was he weary and depressed, but the victory had been nobly won.

It grew late, and they rode to the town, caballeros pushing as close to doñas as they dared, dueñas in close attendance, one theme on the lips of all. Anger gave place to respect; moreover, De la Vega was the guest of General Castro, the best-beloved man in California. They were willing to extend the hand of friendship; but he rode last, between the General and Doña Modeste, and seemed to care as little for their good will as for their ill.

Pio Pico rode ahead, and as the cavalcade entered the town he broke from it and ascended the hill to carry the news to Ysabel Herrera.

Monterey, rising to her pine-spiked hills, swept like a crescent moon about the sapphire bay. The surf roared and fought the white sand hills of the distant horn; on that nearest the town stood the fort, grim and rude, but pulsating with military life, and alert for American on-slaught. In the valley the red-tiled white adobe houses studded a little city which was a series of corners radiating from a central irregular street. A few mansions were on the hillside to the right, brush crowded sand banks on the left; the perfect curve of hills, thick with pine woods and dense green undergrowth, rose high above and around all, a ram-part of splendid symmetry.

"Ay! Ysabel! Ysabel!" cried the young people, as they swept down the broad street. "Bring her to us, Excellency. Tell her she shall not know until she comes down. We will tell her. Ay! poor Guido!"

The Governor turned and waved his hand, then continued the ascent of the hill, toward a long low house which showed no sign of life.

He alighted and glanced into a room opening upon the corridor which traversed the front. The room was large and dimly lighted by deeply set windows. The floor was bare, the furniture of horsehair; saints and family portraits adorned the white walls; on a chair lay a guitar; it was a typical California sala of that day. The ships brought few luxuries, beyond raiment and jewels, to even the wealthy of that isolated country.

"Ysabel," called the Governor, "where art thou? Come down to the town and hear the fortune of the races. Alvarado Street streams like a comet. Why should the Star of Monterey withhold her light?"

A girl rose from a sofa and came slowly forward to the corridor. Discontent marred her face as she gave her hand to the Governor to kiss, and looked down upon the brilliant town. The Señorita Doña Ysabel Herrera was poor. Were it not for her uncle she would not have where to lay her stately head—and she was La Favorita of Monterey, the proudest beauty in California! Her father had gambled away his last acre, his horse, his saddle, the serape off his back; then sent his motherless girl to his brother, and buried himself in Mexico. Don Antonio took the child to his heart, and sent for a widowed cousin to be her dueña. He bought her beautiful garments from the ships that touched the port, but had no inclination to gratify her famous longing to hang ropes of pearls in her soft black hair, to wind them about her white neck, and band them above her green resplendent eyes.

"Unbend thy brows," said Pio Pico. "Wrinkles were not made for youth."

Ysabel moved her brows apart, but the clouds still lay in her eyes.

"Thou dost not ask of the races, O thou indifferent one! What is the trouble, my Ysabel? Will no one bring the pearls? The loveliest girl in all the Californias has said, 'I will wed no man who does not bring me a lapful of pearls,' and no one has filled the front of that pretty flowered gown. But have reason, niña. Remember that our Alta Cali-

fornia has no pearls on its shores, and that even the pearl fisheries of the
terrible lower country are almost worn out. Will nothing less content
thee?"

"No, señor."

"Dios de mi alma! Thou hast ambition. No woman has had more
offered her than thou. But thou art worthy of the most that man could
give. Had I not a wife myself, I believe I should throw my jewels and
my ugly old head at thy little feet."

Ysabel glanced with some envy at the magnificent jewels with which
the Governor of the Californias was hung, but did not covet the owner
An uglier man than Pio Pico rarely had entered this world. The upper
lip of his enormous mouth dipped at the middle; the broad thick under-
lip hung down with its own weight. The nose was big and coarse, although there was a certain spirited suggestion in the cavernous nostrils.
Intelligence and reflectiveness were also in his little eyes, and they were
far apart. A small white mustache grew above his mouth; about his
chin, from ear to ear, was a short stubby beard, whiter by contrast with
his copper-colored skin. He looked much like an intellectual bear.

And Ysabel? In truth, she had reason for her pride. Her black hair,
unblemished by gloss or tinge of blue, fell waving to her feet. California,
haughty, passionate, restless, pleasure-loving, looked from her dark
green eyes; the soft black lashes dropped quickly when they became too
expressive. Her full mouth was deeply red, but only a faint pink lay in
her white cheeks; the nose curved at bridge and nostrils. About her low
shoulders she held a blue reboso, the finger-tips of each slim hand
resting on the opposite elbow. She held her head a little back, and Pio
Pico laughed as he looked at her.

"Dios!" he said, "but thou might be an Estenega or an Iturbi y Moncada. Surely that lofty head better suits old Spain than the republic of
Mexico. Draw the reboso about thy head now, and let us go down. They
expect thee."

She lifted the scarf above her hair, and walked down the steep rutted
hill with the Governor, her flowered gown floating with a silken rustle
about her. In a few moments she was listening to the tale of the races.

"Ay Ysabel! Dios de mi alma! What a day! A young señor from Los
Angeles won the race—almost all the races—the Señor Don Vicente de
la Vega y Arillaga. He has never been here, before. His horses! Madre
de Dios! They ran like hares. Poor Guido! Válgame Dios! Even thou
wouldst have been moved to pity. But he is so handsome! Look! Look!
He comes now, side by side with General Castro. Dios! his serape is as
stiff with gold as the vestments of the padre."

Ysabel looked up as a man rode past. His bold profile and thin face were passionate and severe; his dark blue eyes were full of power. Such a face was rare among the languid shallow men of her race.

"He rides with General Castro," whispered Benicia Ortega. "He stays with him. We shall see him at the ball tonight."

As Don Vicente passed Ysabel their eyes met for a moment. His opened suddenly with a bold eager flash, his arched nostrils twitching. The color left her face, and her eyes dropped heavily.

Love needed no kindling in the heart of the Californian.

II

The people of Monterey danced every night of their lives, and went nowhere so promptly as to the great sala of Doña Modeste Castro, their leader of fashion, whose gowns were made for her in the city of Mexico.

Ysabel envied her bitterly. Not because the Doña Modeste's skin was whiter than her own, for it could not be, nor her eyes greener, for they were not; but because her jewels were richer than Pio Pico's, and upon all grand occasions a string of wonderful pearls gleamed in her storm-black hair. But one feminine compensation had Ysabel: she was taller; Doña Modeste's slight elegant figure lacked Ysabel's graceful inches, and perhaps she too felt a pang sometimes as the girl undulated above her like a snake about to strike.

At the fashionable hour of ten Monterey was gathered for the dance. All the men except the officers wore black velvet or broadcloth coats and white trousers. All the women wore white, the waist long and pointed, the skirt full. Ysabel's gown was of embroidered crêpe. Her hair was coiled about her head, and held by a tortoise comb framed with a narrow band of gold. Pio Pico, splendid with stars and crescents and rings and pins, led her in, and with his unique ugliness enhanced her beauty.

She glanced eagerly about the room whilst replying absently to the caballeros who surrounded her. Don Vicente de la Vega was not there. The thick circle about her parted, and General Castro bent over her hand, begging the honor of the contradanza. She sighed, and for the moment forgot the Southerner who had flashed and gone like the beginning of a dream. Here was a man—the only man of her knowledge whom she could have loved, and who would have found her those pearls. Californians had so little ambition! Then she gave a light audacious laugh. Governor Pico was shaking hands cordially with General Castro, the man he hated best in California.

No two men could have contrasted more sharply than José Castro and Pio Pico—with the exception of Alvarado the most famous men of their country. The gold trimmings of the general's uniform were his only jewels. His hair and beard—the latter worn *à la Basca,* a narrow

strip curving from upper lip to ear—were as black as Pio Pico's once
had been. The handsomest man in California, he had less consciousness
than the least of the caballeros. His deep gray eyes were luminous with
enthusiasm; his nose was sharp and bold; his firm sensitive mouth was
cut above a resolute chin. He looked what he was, the ardent patriot of
a doomed cause.

"Señorita," he said, as he led Ysabel out to the sweet monotonous
music of the contradanza, "did you see the caballero who rode with me
today?"

A red light rose to Ysabel's cheek. "Which one, commandante? Many
rode with you."

"I mean him who rode at my right, the winner of the races, Vicente,
son of my old friend Juan Bautista de la Vega y Arillaga, of Los Angeles."

"It may be. I think I saw a strange face."

"He saw yours, Doña Ysabel, and is looking upon you now from
the corridor without, although the fog is heavy about him. Cannot you
see him—that dark shadow by the pillar?"

Ysabel never went through the graceful evolutions of the contradanza
as she did that night. Her supple slender body curved and swayed and
glided; her round arms were like lazy snakes uncoiling; her exquisitely
poised head moved in perfect concord with her undulating hips. Her
eyes grew brighter, her lips redder. The young men who stood near
gave as loud a vent to their admiration as if she had been dancing El
Son alone on the floor. But the man without made no sign.

After the dance was over, General Castro led her to her dueña, and
handing her a guitar, begged a song.

She began a light love-ballad, singing with the grace and style of her
Spanish blood; a little mocking thing, but with a wild break now and
again. As she sang, she fixed her eyes coquettishly on the adoring face
of Guido Cabañares, who stood beside her, but saw every movement
of the form beyond the window. Don Guido kept his ardent eyes
riveted upon her but detected no wandering in her glances. His lips
trembled as he listened, and once he brushed the tears from his eyes.
She gave him a little cynical smile, then broke her song in two. The
man in the corridor had vaulted through the window.

Ysabel, clinching her hands the better to control her jumping nerves,
turned quickly to Cabañares, who had pressed behind her, and was
pouring words into her ear.

"Ysabel! Ysabel! hast thou no pity? Dost thou not see that I am fit
to set the world on fire for love of thee? The very water boils as I
drink it—"

She interrupted him with a scornful laugh, the sharper that her voice might not tremble. "Bring me my pearls. What is love worth when it will not grant one little desire?"

He groaned. "I have found a vein of gold on my rancho. I can pick the little shining pieces out with my fingers. I will have them beaten into a saddle for thee—"

But she had turned her back flat upon him, and was making a deep courtesy to the man whom General Castro presented.

"I appreciate the honor of your acquaintance," she murmured mechanically.

"At your feet, señorita," said Don Vicente.

The art of making conversation had not been cultivated among the Californians, and Ysabel plied her large fan with slow grace, at a loss for further remark, and wondering if her heart would suffocate her. But Don Vicente had the gift of words.

"Señorita," he said, "I have stood in the chilling fog and felt the warmth of your lovely voice at my heart. The emotions I felt my poor tongue cannot translate. They swarm in my head like a hive of puzzled bees; but perhaps they look through my eyes," and he fixed his powerful and penetrating gaze on Ysabel's green depths.

A waltz began, and he took her in his arms without asking her indulgence, and regardless of the indignation of the mob of men about her. Ysabel, whose being was filled with tumult, lay passive as he held her closer than man had ever dared before.

"I love you," he said, in his harsh voice. "I wish you for my wife. At once. When I saw you today standing with a hundred other beautiful women, I said: 'She is the fairest of them all. I shall have her.' And I read the future in"—he suddenly dropped the formal "you"—"in thine eyes, cariña. Thy soul sprang to mine. Thy heart is locked in my heart closer, closer than my arms are holding thee now."

The strength of his embrace was violent for a moment; but Ysabel might have been cut from marble. Her body had lost its swaying grace; it was almost rigid. She did not lift her eyes. But De la Vega was not discouraged.

The music finished, and Ysabel was at once surrounded by a determined retinue. This intruding Southerner was welcome to the honors of the race field, but the Star of Monterey was not for him. He smiled as he saw the menace of their eyes.

"I would have her," he thought, "if they were a regiment of Castros —which they are not." But he had not armed himself against diplomacy.

"Señor Don Vicente de la Vega y Arillaga," said Don Guido Cabañares, who had been selected as spokesman, "perhaps you have not learned during your brief visit to our capital that the Señorita Doña Ysabel Herrera, La Favorita of Alta California, has sworn by the Holy

Virgin, by the blessed Junipero Serra, that she will wed no man who does not bring her a lapful of pearls. Can you find those pearls on the sands of the South, Don Vicente? For, by the holy cross of God, you cannot have her without them!"

For a moment De la Vega was disconcerted.

"Is this true?" he demanded, turning to Ysabel.

"What, señor?" she asked vaguely. She had not listened to the words of her protesting admirer.

A sneer bent his mouth. "That you have put a price upon yourself? That the man who ardently wishes to be your husband, who has even won your love, must first hang you with pearls like—" He stopped suddenly, the blood burning his dark face, his eyes opening with an expression of horrified hope. "Tell me! Tell me!" he exclaimed. "Is this true?"

For the first time since she had spoken with him Ysabel was herself. She crossed her arms and tapped her elbows with her pointed fingers.

"Yes," she said, "it is true." She raised her eyes to his and regarded him steadily. They looked like green pools frozen in a marble wall.

The harp, the flute, the guitar, combined again, and once more he swung her from a furious circle. But he was safe; General Castro had joined it. He waltzed her down the long room, through one adjoining, then into another, and, indifferent to the iron conventions of his race, closed the door behind them. They were in the sleeping room of Doña Modeste. The bed with its rich satin coverlet, the bare floor, the simple furniture, were in semi-darkness; only on the altar in the corner were candles burning. Above it hung paintings of saints, finely executed by Mexican hands; an ebony cross spread its black arms against the white wall; the candles flared to a golden Christ. He caught her hands and led her over to the altar.

"Listen to me," he said. "I will bring you those pearls. You shall have such pearls as no queen in Europe possesses. Swear to me here, with your hands on this altar, that you will wed me when I return, no matter how or where I find those pearls."

He was holding her hands between the candelabra. She looked at him with eyes of passionate surrender; the man had conquered worldly ambitions. But he answered her before she had time to speak.

"You love me, and would withdraw the conditions. But I am ready to do a daring and a terrible act. Furthermore, I wish to show you that I can succeed where all other men have failed. I ask only two things now. First, make me the vow I wish."

"I swear it," she said.

"Now," he said, his voice sinking to a harsh but caressing whisper, "give me one kiss for courage and hope."

She leaned slowly forward, the blood pulsing in her lips; but she had been brought up behind grated windows, and she drew back. "No," she said, "not now."

For a moment he looked rebellious; then he laid his hands on her shoulders and pressed her to her knees. He knelt behind her, and together they told a rosary for his safe return.

He left her there and went to his room. From his saddle-bag he took a long letter from an intimate friend, one of the younger Franciscan priests of the Mission of Santa Barbara, where he had been educated. He sought this paragraph:—

"Thou knowest, of course, my Vicente, of the pearl fisheries of Baja California. It is whispered—between ourselves, indeed, it is quite true —that a short while ago the Indian divers discovered an extravagantly rich bed of pearls. Instead of reporting to any of the companies, they have hung them all upon our Most Sacred Lady of Loreto, in the Mission of Loreto; and there, by the grace of God, they will remain. They are worth the ransom of a king, my Vicente, and the Church has come to her own again."

III

The fog lay thick on the bay at dawn next morning. The white waves hid the blue, muffled the roar of the surf. Now and again a whale threw a volume of spray high in the air, a geyser from a phantom sea. Above the white sands straggled the white town, ghostly, prophetic.

De la Vega, a dark sombrero pulled over his eyes, a dark serape enveloping his tall figure, rode, unattended and watchful, out of the town. Not until he reached the narrow road through the brush forest beyond did he give his horse rein. The indolence of the Californian was no longer in his carriage; it looked alert and muscular; recklessness accentuated the sternness of his face.

As he rode, the fog receded slowly. He left the chaparral and rode by green marshes cut with sloughs and stained with vivid patches of orange. The frogs in the tules chanted their hoarse matins. Through brush-covered plains once more, with sparsely wooded hills in the distance, and again the tules, the marsh, the patches of orange. He rode through a field of mustard; the pale yellow petals brushed his dark face, the delicate green leaves won his eyes from the hot glare of the ascending sun, the slender stalks, rebounding, smote his horse's flanks. He climbed hills to avoid the wide marshes, and descended into willow groves and fields of daisies. Before noon he was in the San Juan Mountains, thick with sturdy oaks, bending their heads before the madroño, that belle of the forest, with her robes of scarlet and her crown of bronze. The yellow lilies clung to her skirts, and the buckeye flung his flowers at her feet. The last redwoods were there, piercing the blue air with their thin inflexible arms, gray as a dusty band of friars. Out by the willows, whereunder crept the sluggish river, then between the hills curving about the valley of San Juan Bautista.

At no time is California so beautiful as in the month of June. De la Vega's wild spirit and savage purpose were dormant for the moment as he rode down the valley toward the mission. The hills were like gold, like mammoth fawns veiled with violet mist, like rich tan velvet. Afar, bare blue steeps were pink in their chasms, brown on their spurs. The dark yellow fields were as if thick with gold-dust; the pale mustard was a waving yellow sea. Not a tree marred the smooth hills. The earth sent forth a perfume of its own. Below the plateau from which rose the white walls of the mission was a wide field of bright green corn rising against the blue sky.

The padres in their brown hooded robes came out upon the long corridor of the mission and welcomed the traveler. Their lands had gone from them, their mission was crumbling, but the spirit of hospitality lingered there still. They laid meat and fruit and drink on a table beneath the arches, then sat about him and asked him eagerly for news of the day. Was it true that the United States of America was at war with Mexico, or about to be? True that their beloved flag might fall, and the stars and stripes of an insolent invader rise above the fort of Monterey?

De la Vega recounted the meager and conflicting rumors which had reached California, but, not being a prophet, could not tell them that they would be the first to see the red-white-and-blue fluttering on the mountain before them. He refused to rest more than an hour, but mounted the fresh horse the padres gave him and went his way, riding hard and relentlessly, like all Californians.

He sped onward, through the long hot day, leaving the hills for the marshes and a long stretch of ugly country, traversing the beautiful San Antonio Valley in the night, reaching the Mission of San Miguel at dawn, resting there for a few hours. That night he slept at a hospitable ranch house in the park-like valley of Paso des Robles, a grim silent figure amongst gay-hearted people who delighted to welcome him. The early morning found him among the chrome hills; and at the Mission of San Luis Obsipo the good padres gave him breakfast. The little valley, round as a well, its bare hills red and brown, gray and pink, violet and black, from fire, sloping steeply from a dizzy height, impressed him with a sense of being prisoned in an enchanted vale where no message of the outer world could come, and he hastened on his way.

Absorbed as he was, he felt the beauty he fled past. A line of golden hills lay against sharp blue peaks. A towering mass of gray rocks had been cut and lashed by wind and water, earthquake and fire, into the semblance of a massive castle, still warlike in its ruin. He slept for a few hours that night in the Mission of Santa Ynes, and was high in the Santa Barbara Mountains at the next noon. For brief whiles he forgot his journey's purpose as his horse climbed slowly up the steep trails, knocking the loose stones down a thousand feet and more upon a roof of tree tops which looked stunted brush. Those gigantic masses of immense stones, each wearing a semblance to the face of man or beast; those awful chasms and stupendous heights, densely wooded, bare, and many-hued, rising above, beyond, peak upon peak, cutting through the visible atmosphere—was there no end? He turned in his saddle and looked over low peaks and cañons, rivers and abysms, black peaks smiting the fiery blue, far, far, to the dim azure mountains on the horizon.

"Mother of God!" he thought. "No wonder California still shakes! I would I could have stood upon a star and beheld the awful throes of this country's birth." And then his horse reared between the sharp spurs and galloped on.

He avoided the Mission of Santa Barbara, resting at a rancho outside the town. In the morning, supplied as usual with a fresh horse, he fled onward, with the ocean at his right, its splendid roar in his ears. The cliffs towered high above him; he saw no man's face for hours together; but his thoughts companioned him, savage and sinister shapes whirling about the figure of a woman. On, on, sleeping at ranchos or missions, meeting hospitality everywhere, avoiding Los Angeles, keeping close to the ponderous ocean, he left civilization behind him at last, and with an Indian guide entered upon that desert of mountain tops, Baja California.

Rapid traveling was not possible here. There were no valleys worthy the name. The sharp peaks, multiplying mile after mile, were like teeth of gigantic rakes, black and bare. A wilderness of mountain tops, desolate as eternity, arid, parched, baked by the awful heat, the silence never broken by the cry of a bird, a hut rarely breaking the barren monotony, only an infrequent spring to save from death. It was almost impossible to get food or fresh horses. Many a night De la Vega and his stoical guide slept beneath a cactus, or in the mocking bed of a creek. The mustangs he managed to lasso were almost unridable, and would have bucked to death any but a Californian. Sometimes he lived on cactus fruit and the dried meat he had brought with him; occasionally he shot a rabbit. Again he had but the flesh of the rattlesnake roasted over coals. But honey-dew was on the leaves.

He avoided the beaten trail, and cut his way through naked bushes spiked with thorns, and through groves of cacti miles in length. When the thick fog rolled up from the ocean he had to sit inactive on the rocks,

or lose his way. A furious storm dashed him against a boulder, breaking his mustang's leg; then a torrent, rising like a tidal wave, thundered
down the gulch, and catching him on its crest, flung him upon a tree of
thorns. When dawn came he found his guide dead. He cursed his luck,
and went on.

Lassoing another mustang, he pushed on, having a general idea of the
direction he should take. It was a week before he reached Loreto, a
week of loneliness, hunger, thirst, and torrid monotony. A week, too,
of thought and bitterness of spirit. In spite of his love, which never
cooled, and his courage, which never quailed, Nature, in her guise of
foul and crooked hag, mocked at earthly happiness, at human hope, at
youth and passion.

If he had not spent his life in the saddle, he would have been worn
out when he finally reached Loreto, late one night. As it was, he slept
in a hut until the following afternoon. Then he took a long swim in the
bay, and, later, sauntered through the town.

The forlorn little city was hardly more than a collection of Indians'
huts about a church in a sandy waste. No longer the capital, even the
barracks were toppling. When De la Vega entered the mission, not a
white man but the padre and his assistant was in it; the building was
thronged with Indian worshippers. The mission, although the first
built in California, was in a fair state of preservation. The Stations in
their battered frames were mellow and distinct. The gold still gleamed
in the vestments of the padre.

For a few moments De la Vega dared not raise his eyes to the Lady
of Loreto, standing aloft in the dull blaze of adamantine candles. When
he did, he rose suddenly from his knees and left the mission. The pearls
were there.

It took him but a short time to gain the confidence of the priest and
the little population. He offered no explanation for his coming, beyond
the curiosity of the traveler. The padre gave him a room in the mission,
and spent every hour he could spare with the brilliant stranger. At night
he thanked God for the sudden oasis in his life's desolation. The Indians
soon grew accustomed to the lonely figure wandering about the sand
plains, or kneeling for hours together before the altar in the church.
And whom their padre trusted was to them as sacred and impersonal
as the wooden saints of their religion.

IV

The midnight stars watched over the mission. Framed by the cross-
shaped window sunk deep in the adobe wall above the entrance, a mass
of them assumed the form of the crucifix, throwing a golden trail full
upon the Lady of Loreto, proud in her shining pearls. The long narrow

body of the church seemed to have swallowed the shadows of the ages, and to yawn for more.

De la Vega, booted and spurred, his serape folded about him, his sombrero on his head, opened the sacristy door and entered the church. In one hand he held a sack; in the other, a candle sputtering in a bottle. He walked deliberately to the foot of the altar. In spite of his intrepid spirit, he stood appalled for a moment as he saw the dim radiance enveloping the Lady of Loreto. He scowled over his shoulder at the menacing emblem of redemption and crossed himself. But had it been the finger of God, the face of Ysabel would have shone between. He extinguished his candle, and swinging himself to the top of the altar plucked the pearls from the Virgin's gown and dropped them into the sack. His hand trembled a little, but he held his will between his teeth.

How quiet it was! The waves flung themselves upon the shore with the sullen wrath of impotence. A sea gull screamed now and again, an exclamation point in the silence above the waters. Suddenly De la Vega shook from head to foot, and snatched the knife from his belt. A faint creaking echoed through the hollow church. He strained his ears, holding his breath until his chest collapsed with the shock of outrushing air. But the sound was not repeated, and he concluded that it had been but a vibration of his nerves. He glanced to the window above the doors. The stars in it were no longer visible; they had melted into bars of flame. The sweat stood cold on his face, but he went on with his work.

A rope of pearls, cunningly strung together with strands of seaweed, was wound about the Virgin's right arm. De la Vega was too nervous to uncoil it; he held the sack beneath, and severed the strands with his knife. As he finished, and was about to stoop and cut loose the pearls from the hem of the Virgin's gown, he uttered a hoarse cry and stood rigid. A cowled head, with thin lips drawn over yellow teeth, furious eyes burning deep in withered sockets, projected on its long neck from the Virgin's right and confronted him. The body was unseen.

"Thief!" cried the priest. "Dog! Thou wouldst rob the Church? Accursed! accursed!"

There was not one moment for hesitation, one alternative. Before the priest could complete his malediction, De la Vega's knife had flashed through the fire of the cross. The priest leaped, screeching, then rolled over and down, and rebounded from the railing of the sanctuary.

v

Ysabel sat in the low window-seat of her bedroom, pretending to draw the threads of a cambric handkerchief. But her fingers twitched, and her eyes looked oftener down the hill than upon the delicate work which required such attention. She wore a black gown flowered with yellow roses, and a slender ivory cross at her throat. Her hair hung in two loose braids, sweeping the floor. She was very pale, and her pallor was not due to the nightly entertainments of Monterey.

Her dueña sat beside her. The old woman was the color of strong coffee; but she, too, looked as if she had not slept, and her straight old lips curved tenderly whenever she raised her eyes to the girl's face.

There was no carpet on the floor of the bedroom of La Favorita of Monterey, the heiress of Don Antonio Herrera, and the little bedstead in the corner was of iron, although a heavy satin coverlet trimmed with lace was on it. A few saints looked down from the walls; the furniture was of native wood, square and ugly; but it was almost hidden under fine linen elaborately worked with the deshalados of Spain.

The supper hour was over, and the light grew dim. Ysabel tossed the handkerchief into Doña Juana's lap, and stared through the grating. Against the faded sky a huge cloud, shaped like a fire-breathing dragon, was heavily outlined. The smoky shadows gathered in the woods. The hoarse boom of the surf came from the beach; the bay was uneasy, and the tide was high: the earth had quaked in the morning, and a wind storm fought the ocean. The gay bright laughter of women floated up from the town. Monterey had taken her siesta, enjoyed her supper, and was ready to dance through the night once more.

"He is dead," said Ysabel.

"True," said the old woman.

"He would have come back to me before this."

"True."

"He was so strong and so different, mamita."

"I never forget his eyes. Very bold eyes."

"They could be soft, macheppa."

"True. It is time thou dressed for the ball at the Custom-house, niñita."

Ysabel leaned forward, her lips parting. A man was coming up the hill. He was gaunt; he was burnt almost black. Something bulged beneath his serape.

Doña Juana found herself suddenly in the middle of the room. Ysabel darted through the only door, locking it behind her. The indignant dueña also recognized the man, and her position. She trotted to the door and thumped angrily on the panel; sympathetic she was, but she never could so far forget herself as to permit a young girl to talk with a man unattended.

"Thou shalt not go to the ball tonight," she cried shrilly. "Thou shalt be locked in the dark room. Thou shalt be sent to the rancho. Open! open! thou wicked one. Madre de Dios! I will beat thee with my own hands."

But she was a prisoner, and Ysabel paid no attention to her threats.

The girl was in the sala, and the doors were open. As De la Vega crossed the corridor and entered the room she sank upon a chair, covering her face with her hands.

He strode over to her, and flinging his serape from his shoulder opened the mouth of a sack and poured its contents into her lap. Pearls of all sizes and shapes—pearls black and pearls white, pearls pink and pearls faintly blue, pearls like globes and pearls like pears, pearls as big as the lobe of Pio Pico's ear, pearls as dainty as bubbles of frost—a lapful of gleaming luminous pearls, the like of which caballero had never brought to doña before.

For a moment Ysabel forgot her love and her lover. The dream of a lifetime was reality. She was the child who had cried for the moon and seen it tossed into her lap.

She ran her slim white fingers through the jewels. She took up handfuls and let them run slowly back to her lap. She pressed them to her face; she kissed them with little rapturous cries. She laid them against her breast and watched them chase each other down her black gown. Then at last she raised her head and met the fierce sneering eyes of De la Vega.

"So it is as I might have known. It was only the pearls you wanted. It might have been an Indian slave who brought them to you."

She took the sack from his hand and poured back the pearls. Then she laid the sack on the floor and stood up. She was no longer pale, and her eyes shone brilliantly in the darkening room.

"Yes," she said; "I forgot for a moment. But during many terrible weeks, señor, my tears have not been for the pearls."

The sudden light that was De la Vega's chiefest charm sprang to his eyes. He took her hands and kissed them passionately.

"That sack of pearls would be a poor reward for one tear. But thou hast shed them for me? Say that again. Mi alma! mi alma!"

"I never thought of the pearls—at least not often. At last, not at all. I have been very unhappy, señor. Ay!" The maiden reserve which had been knit like steel about her plastic years burst wide. "Thou art ill! What has happened to thee? Ay, Dios! what it is to be a woman and to suffer! Thou wilt die! Oh, Mother of God!"

"I shall not die. Kiss me, Ysabel. Surely it is time now."

But she drew back and shook her head.

He exclaimed impatiently, but would not release her hand. "Thou meanest that, Ysabel?"

"We shall be married soon—wait."

"I had hoped you would grant me that. For when I tell you where I got those pearls you may drive me from you in spite of your promise —drive me from you with the curse of the devout woman on your lips.

I might invent some excuse to persuade you to fly with me from California tonight, and you would never know. But I am a man—a Spaniard —and a De la Vega. I shall not lie to you."

She looked at him with wide eyes, not understanding, and he went on, his face savage again, his voice harsh. He told her the whole story of that night in the mission. He omitted nothing—the menacing cross, the sacrilegious theft, the deliberate murder; the pictures were painted with blood and fire. She did not interrupt him with cry or gasp, but her expression changed many times. Horror held her eyes for a time, then slowly retreated, and his own fierce pride looked back at him. She lifted her head when he had finished, her throat throbbing, her nostrils twitching.

"Thou hast done that—for me?"

"Ay, Ysabel!"

"Thou hast murdered thy immortal soul—for me?"

"Ysabel!"

"Thou lovest me like that! O God, in what likeness hast thou made me? In whatsoever image it may have been, I thank Thee—and repudiate Thee!"

She took the cross from her throat and broke it in two pieces with her strong white fingers.

"Thou art lost, eternally damned: but I will go down to hell with thee." And she threw herself upon him and kissed him on the mouth.

For a moment he forget the lesson thrust into his brain by the hideous fingers of the desert. He was almost happy. He put his hands about her warm face after a time. "We must go tonight," he said. "I went to General Castro's to change my clothes, and learned that a ship sails for the United States tonight. We will go on that. I dare not delay twenty-four hours. It may be that they are upon my heels now. How can we meet?"

Her thoughts had traveled faster than his words, and she answered at once: "There is a ball at the Custom-house tonight. I will go. You will have a boat below the rocks. You know that the Custom-house is on the rocks at the end of the town, near the fort. No? It will be easier for me to slip from the ball-room than from this house. Only tell me where you will meet me."

"The ship sails at midnight. I too will go to the ball; for with me you can escape more easily. Have you a maid you can trust?"

"My Luisa is faithful."

"Then tell her to be on the beach between the rocks of the Custom-house and the Fort with what you must take with you."

Again he kissed her many times, but softly. "Wear thy pearls tonight. I wish to see thy triumphant hour in Monterey."

"Yes," she said, "I shall wear the pearls."

VI

The corridor of the Custom-house had been enclosed to protect the musicians and supper table from the wind and fog. The store-room had been cleared, the floor scrubbed, the walls hung with the colors of Mexico. All in honor of Pio Pico, again in brief exile from his beloved Los Angeles. The Governor, blazing with diamonds, stood at the upper end of the room by Doña Modeste Castro's side. About them were Castro and other prominent men of Monterey, all talking of the rumored war between the United States and Mexico and prophesying various results. Neither Pico nor Castro looked amiable. The Governor had arrived in the morning to find that the General had allowed pasquinades representing his Excellency in no complimentary light to disfigure the streets of Monterey. Castro, when taken to task, had replied haughtily that it was the Governor's place to look after his own dignity; he, the Commandante-General of the army of the Californias, had more important matters to attend to. The result had been a furious war of words, ending in a lame peace.

"Tell us, Excellency," said José Abrigo, "what will be the outcome?"

"The Americans can have us if they wish," said Pio Pico, bitterly. "We cannot prevent."

"Never!" cried Castro. "What? We cannot protect ourselves against the invasion of bandoleros? Do you forget what blood stings the veins of the Californian? A Spaniard stand with folded arms and see his country plucked from him! Oh, sacrilege! They will never have our Californias while a Californian lives to cut them down!"

"Bravo! bravo!" cried many voices.

"I tell you—" began Pio Pico, but Doña Modeste interrupted him. "No more talk of war tonight," she said peremptorily. "Where is Ysabel?"

"She sent me word by Doña Juana that she could not make herself ready in time to come with me, but would follow with my good friend, Don Antonio, who of course had to wait for her. Her gown was not finished, I believe. I think she had done something naughty, and Doña Juana had tried to punish her, but had not succeeded. The old lady looked very sad. Ah, here is Doña Ysabel now!"

"How lovely she is!" said Doña Modeste. "I think—What! what!—"

"Dios de mi Alma!" exclaimed Pio Pico, "where did she get those pearls?"

The crowd near the door had parted, and Ysabel entered on the arm of her uncle. Don Antonio's form was bent, and she looked taller by contrast. His thin sharp profile was outlined against her white neck, bared for the first time to the eyes of Monterey. Her shawl had just been laid aside, and he was near-sighted and did not notice the pearls.

She had sewn them all over the front of her white silk gown. She had wound them in the black coils of her hair. They wreathed her neck and roped her arms. Never had she looked so beautiful. Her great green eyes were as radiant as spring. Her lips were redder than blood. A pink flame burned in her oval cheeks. Her head moved like a Californian lily on its stalk. No Montereño would ever forget her.

"El Son!" cried the young men, with one accord. Her magnificent beauty extinguished every other woman in the room. She must not hide her light in the contradanza. She must madden all eyes at once.

Ysabel bent her head and glided to the middle of the room. The other women moved back, their white gowns like a snowbank against the garish walls. The thin sweet music of the instruments rose above the boom of the tide. Ysabel lifted her dress with curving arms, displaying arched feet clad in flesh-colored stockings and white slippers, and danced El Son.

Her little feet tapped time to the music; she whirled her body with utmost grace, holding her head so motionless that she could have balanced a glass of water upon it. She was inspired that night; and when, in the midst of the dance, De la Vega entered the room, a sort of madness possessed her. She invented new figures. She glided back and forth, bending and swaying and doubling until to the eyes of her bewildered admirers the outlines of her lovely body were gone. Even the women shouted their approval, and the men went wild. They pulled their pockets inside out and flung handfuls of gold at her feet. Those who had only silver cursed their fate, but snatched the watches from their pockets, the rings from their fingers, and hurled them at her with shouts and cheers. They tore the lace ruffles from their shirts; they rushed to the next room and ripped the silver eagles from their hats. Even Pio Pico flung one of his golden ropes at her feet, a hot blaze in his old ugly face, as he cried:—

"Brava! brava! thou Star of Monterey!"

Guido Cabañares, desperate at having nothing more to sacrifice to his idol, sprang upon a chair, and was about to tear down the Mexican flag, when the music stopped with a crash, as if musicians and instruments had been overturned, and a figure leaped into the room.

The women uttered a loud cry and crossed themselves. Even the men fell back. Ysabel's swaying body trembled and became rigid. De la Vega, who had watched her with folded arms, too entranced to offer her anything but the love that shook him, turned livid to his throat. A friar, his hood fallen back from his stubbled head, his brown habit stiff with dirt, smelling, reeling with fatigue, stood amongst them. His eyes were deep in his ashen face. They rolled about the room until they met De la Vega's.

General Castro came hastily forward. "What does this mean?" he asked. "What do you wish?"

The friar raised his arm, and pointed his shaking finger at De la Vega.

"Kill him!" he said, in a loud hoarse whisper. "He has desecrated the Mother of God!"

Every caballero in the room turned upon De la Vega with furious satisfaction. Ysabel had quickened their blood, and they were willing to cool it in vengeance on the man of whom they still were jealous, and whom they suspected of having brought the wondrous pearls which covered their Favorita tonight.

"What? What?" they cried eagerly. "Has he done this thing?"

"He has robbed the Church. He has stripped the Blessed Virgin of her jewels. He—has—murdered—a—priest of the Holy Catholic Church."

Horror stayed them for a moment, and then they rushed at De la Vega. "He does not deny it!" they cried. "Is it true? Is it true?" and they surged about him hot with menace.

"It is quite true," said De la Vega, coldly. "I plundered the shrine of Loreto and murdered its priest."

The women panted and gasped; for a moment even the men were stunned, and in that moment an ominous sound mingled with the roar of the surf. Before the respite was over, Ysabel had reached his side.

"He did it for me!" she cried, in her clear triumphant voice. "For me! And although you kill us both, I am the proudest woman in all the Californias, and I love him."

"Good!" cried Castro, and he placed himself before them. "Stand back, every one of you. What? are you barbarians, Indians, that you would do violence to a guest in your town? What if he has committed a crime? Is he not one of you, then, that you offer him blood instead of protection? Where is your pride of caste? your *hospitality*? Oh, perfidy! Fall back, and leave the guest of your capital to those who are compelled to judge him."

The caballeros shrank back, sullen but abashed. He had touched the quick of their pride.

"Never mind!" cried the friar. "You cannot protect him from *that*. Listen!"

Had the bay risen about the Custom-house?

"What is that?" demanded Castro, sharply.

"The poor of Monterey; those who love their Cross better than the aristocrats love their caste. They know."

De la Vega caught Ysabel in his arms and dashed across the room and corridor. His knife cut a long rift in the canvas, and in a moment they stood upon the rocks. The shrieking crowd was on the other side of the Custom-house.

"Marcos!" he called to his boatman, "Marcos!"

No answer came but the waves tugging at the rocks not two feet below them. He could see nothing. The fog was thick as night.

"He is not here, Ysabel. We must swim. Anything but to be torn to pieces by those wild cats. Are you afraid?"

"No," she said.

He folded her closely with one arm, and felt with his foot for the edge of the rocks. A wild roar came from behind. A dozen pistols were fired into the air. De la Vega reeled suddenly. "I am shot, Ysabel," he said, his knees bending. "Not in this world, my love!"

She wound her arms about him, and dragging him to the brow of the rocks, hurled herself outward, carrying him with her. The waves tossed them on high, flung them against the rocks and ground them there, playing with them like a lion with its victim, then buried them.

The Return of a Private

BY HAMLIN GARLAND

THE nearer the train drew toward La Crosse, the soberer the little group of "vets" became. On the long way from New Orleans they had beguiled tedium with jokes and friendly chaff; or with planning with elaborate detail what they were going to do now, after the war. A long journey, slowly, irregularly, yet persistently pushing northward. When they entered on Wisconsin territory they gave a cheer, and another when they reached Madison, but after that they sank into a dumb expectancy. Comrades dropped off at one or two points beyond, until there were only four or five left who were bound for La Crosse County.

Three of them were gaunt and brown, the fourth was gaunt and pale, with signs of fever and ague upon him. One had a great scar down his temple, one limped, and they all had unnaturally large, bright eyes, showing emaciation. There were no bands greeting them at the station, no banks of gayly dressed ladies waving handkerchiefs and shouting "Bravo!" as they came in on the caboose of a freight train into the towns that had cheered and blared at them on their way to war. As they looked out or stepped upon the platform for a moment, while the train stood at the station, the loafers looked at them indifferently. Their blue coats, dusty and grimy, were too familiar now to excite notice, much less a friendly word. They were the last of the army to return, and the loafers were surfeited with such sights.

The train jogged forward so slowly that it seemed likely to be midnight before they should reach La Crosse. The little squad grumbled and swore, but it was no use; the train would not hurry, and, as a matter of fact, it was nearly two o'clock when the engine whistled "down brakes."

All of the group were farmers, living in districts several miles out of the town and all were poor.

"Now, boys," said Private Smith, he of the fever and ague, "we are landed in La Crosse in the night. We've got to stay somewhere till mornin'. Now I ain't got no two dollars to waste on a hotel. I've got a wife and children, so I'm goin' to roost on a bench and take the cost of a bed out of my hide."

"Same here," put in one of the other men. "Hide'll grow on again, dollars'll come hard. It's goin' to be mighty hot skirmishin' to find a dollar these days."

"Don't think they'll be a deputation of citizens waitin' to 'scort us to a hotel, eh?" said another. His sarcasm was too obvious to require an answer.

Smith went on, "Then at daybreak we'll start for home—at least, I will."

"Well, I'll be dummed if I'll take two dollars out o' *my* hide," one of the younger men said. "I'm goin' to a hotel, ef I don't never lay up a cent."

"That'll do f'r you," said Smith; "but if you had a wife an' three young uns dependin' on yeh—"

"Which I ain't, thank the Lord! and don't intend havin' while the court knows itself."

The station was deserted, chill and dark, as they came into it at exactly a quarter to two in the morning. Lit by the oil lamps that flared a dull red light over the dingy benches, the waiting room was not an inviting place. The younger man went off to look up a hotel, while the rest remained and prepared to camp down on the floor and benches. Smith was attended to tenderly by the other men, who spread their blankets on the bench for him, and, by robbing themselves, made quite a comfortable bed, though the narrowness of the bench made his sleeping precarious.

It was chill, though August, and the two men, sitting with bowed heads, grew stiff with cold and weariness, and were forced to rise now and again and walk about to warm their stiffened limbs. It did not occur to them, probably, to contrast their coming home with their going forth, or with the coming home of the generals, colonels, or even captains—but to Private Smith, at any rate, there came a sickness at heart almost deadly as he lay there on his hard bed and went over his situation.

In the deep of the night, lying on a board in the town where he had enlisted three years ago, all elation and enthusiasm gone out of him, he faced the fact that with the joy of home-coming was already mingled the bitter juice of care. He saw himself sick, worn out, taking up the work on his half-cleared farm, the inevitable mortgage standing ready with open jaw to swallow half his earnings. He had given three years of his life for a mere pittance of pay, and now—!

Morning dawned at last, slowly, with a pale yellow dome of light rising silently above the bluffs, which stand like some huge storm-devastated castle, just east of the city. Out to the left the great river swept on its massive yet silent way to the south. Bluejays called across the water from hillside to hillside through the clear, beautiful air, and hawks began to skim the tops of the hills. The older men were astir early, but Private Smith had fallen at last into a sleep, and they went out without waking him. He lay on his knapsack, his gaunt face turned toward the ceiling, his hands clasped on his breast, with a curious pathetic effect of weakness and appeal.

An engine switching near woke him at last, and he slowly sat up and stared about. He looked out of the window and saw that the sun was lightening the hills across the river. He rose and brushed his hair as well as he could, folded his blankets up, and went out to find his companions. They stood gazing silently at the river and at the hills.

"Looks natcher'l, don't it?" they said, as he came out.

"That's what it does," he replied. "An' it looks good. D'yeh see that peak?" He pointed at a beautiful symmetrical peak, rising like a slightly truncated cone, so high that it seemed the very highest of them all. It was touched by that morning sun and it glowed like a beacon, and a light scarf of gray morning fog was rolling up its shadowed side.

"My farm's just beyond that. Now, if I can only ketch a ride, we'll be home by dinner-time."

"I'm talkin' about breakfast," said one of the others.

"I guess it's one more meal o' hardtack f'r me," said Smith.

They foraged around, and finally found a restaurant with a sleepy old German behind the counter, and procured some coffee, which they drank to wash down their hardtack.

"Time'll come," said Smith, holding up a piece by the corner, "when this'll be a curiosity."

"I hope to God it will! I bet I've chawed hardtack enough to shingle every house in the coolly. I've chawed it when my lampers was down, and when they wasn't. I've took it dry, soaked, and mashed. I've had it wormy, musty, sour, and blue-moldy. I've had it in little bits and big bits; 'fore coffee an' after coffee. I'm ready f'r a change. I'd like t' git holt jest about now o' some of the hot biscuits my wife c'n make when she lays herself out f'r company."

"Well, if you set there gabblin', you'll never *see* yer wife."

"Come on," said Private Smith. "Wait a moment, boys; le's take suthin'. It's on me." He led them to the rusty tin dipper which hung on a nail beside the wooden water-pail, and they grinned and drank. Then shouldering their blankets and muskets, which they were "takin' home to the boys," they struck out on their last march.

"They called that coffee Jayvy," grumbled one of them, "but it never went by the road where government Jayvy resides. I reckon I know coffee from peas."

They kept together on the road along the turnpike, and up the winding road by the river, which they followed for some miles. The river was very lovely, curving down along its sandy beds, pausing now and then under broad basswood trees, or running in dark, swift, silent currents under tangles of wild grape vines, and drooping alders, and haw trees. At one of these lovely spots the three vets sat down on the thick green sward to rest, "on Smith's account." The leaves of the trees were as fresh and green as in June, the jays called cheery greetings to them, and kingfishers darted to and fro with swooping, noiseless flight.

"I tell yeh, boys, this knocks the swamps of Loueesiana into kingdom come."

"You bet. All they c'n raise down there is snakes, niggers, and p'rticler hell."

"An' fightin' men," put in the older man.

"An' fightin' men. If I had a good hook an' line I'd sneak a pick'rel out o' that pond. Say, remember that time I shot that alligator—"

"I guess we'd better be crawlin' along," interrupted Smith, rising and shouldering his knapsack, with considerable effort, which he tried to hide.

"Say, Smith, lemme give you a lift on that."

"I guess I c'n manage," said Smith grimly.

"Course. But, yo' see, I may not have a chance right off to pay yeh back for the times you've carried my gun and hull caboodle. Say, now, gimme that gun, anyway."

"All right, if yeh feel like it, Jim." Smith replied, and they trudged along doggedly in the sun, which was getting higher and hotter each half-mile.

"Ain't it queer there ain't no teams comin' along," said Smith, after a long silence.

"Well, no, seein's it's Sunday."

"By jinks, that's a fact. It is Sunday. I'll git home in time f'r dinner, sure!" he exulted. "She don't hev dinner usially till about one on Sundays." And he fell into a muse, in which he smiled.

"Well, I'll git home jest about six o'clock, jest about when the boys are milkin' the cows," said old Jim Cranby. "I'll step into the barn, an' then I'll say, 'Heah! why ain't this milkin' done before this time o' day?' An' then won't they yell!" he added, slapping his thigh in great glee.

Smith went on. "I'll jest go up the path. Old Rover'll come down the road to meet me. He won't bark—he'll know me—an' he'll come down waggin' his tail an' showin' his teeth. That's his way of laughin'. An' so I'll walk up to the kitchen door, an' I'll say, '*Dinner* f'r a hungry man!' An' then she'll jump up, an'—"

He couldn't go on. His voice choked at the thought of it. Saunders, the third man, hardly uttered a word, but walked silently behind the others. He had lost his wife the first year he was in the army. She died of pneumonia, caught in the autumn rains while working in the fields in his place.

They plodded along till at last they came to a parting of the ways. To the right the road continued up the main valley; to the left it went over the big ridge.

"Well, boys," began Smith, as they grounded their muskets and looked away up the valley, "here's where we shake hands. We've marched together a good many miles, an' now I s'pose we're done."

"Yes, I don't think we'll do any more of it f'r a while. I don't want to, I know."

"I hope I'll see yeh once in a while, boys, to talk over old times."

"Of course," said Saunders, whose voice trembled a little, too. "It ain't *exactly* like dyin'." They all found it hard to look at each other.

"But we'd ought'r go home with you," said Cranby. "You'll never climb that ridge with all them things on yer back."

"Oh, I'm all right! Don't worry about me. Every step takes me nearer home, yeh see. Well, good-by, boys."

They shook hands. "Good-by. Good luck!"

"Same to you. Lemme know how you find things at home."

"Good-by."

"Good-by."

He turned once before they passed out of sight, and waved his cap, and they did the same, and all yelled. Then all marched away with their long, steady, loping, veteran step. The solitary climber in blue walked on for a time, with his mind filled with the kindness of his comrades, and musing upon the many wonderful days they had had together in camp and field.

He thought of his chum, Billy Tripp. Poor Billy! A "minie" ball fell into his breast one day, fell wailing like a cat, and tore a great ragged hole in his heart. He looked forward to a sad scene with Billy's mother and sweetheart. They would want to know all about it. He tried to recall all that Billy had said, and the particulars of it, but there was little to remember, just that wild wailing sound high in the air, a dull slap, a short, quick, expulsive groan, and the boy lay with his face in the dirt in the plowed field they were marching across.

That was all. But all the scenes he had since been through had not dimmed the horror, the terror of that moment, when his boy comrade fell, with only a breath between a laugh and a death-groan. Poor handsome Billy! Worth millions of dollars was his young life.

These somber recollections gave way at length to more cheerful feelings as he began to approach his home coolly. The fields and houses grew familiar, and in one or two he was greeted by people seated in the doorways. But he was in no mood to talk, and pushed on steadily, though he stopped and accepted a drink of milk once at the well-side of a neighbor.

The sun was burning hot on that slope, and his step grew slower, in spite of his iron resolution. He sat down several times to rest. Slowly he crawled up the rough, reddish-brown road, which wound along the hillside, under great trees, through dense groves of jack oaks, with tree-tops far below him on his left hand, and the hills far above him on his right. He crawled along like some minute, wingless variety of fly.

He ate some hardtack, sauced with wild berries, when he reached the summit of the ridge, and sat there for some time, looked down into his home coolly.

Somber, pathetic figure! His wide, round, gray eyes gazing down into the beautiful valley, seeing and not seeing, the splendid cloud-shadows sweeping over the western hills and across the green and yellow wheat far below. His head dropped forward on his palm, his shoulders took on a tired stoop, his cheek-bones showed painfully. An observer might have said, "He is looking down upon his own grave."

II

Sunday comes in a Western wheat harvest with such sweet and sudden relaxation to man and beast that it would be holy for that reason, if for no other, and Sundays are usually fair in harvest-time. As one goes out into the field in the hot morning sunshine, with no sound abroad save the crickets and the indescribably pleasant silken rustling of the ripened grain, the reaper and the very sheaves in the stubble seem to be resting, dreaming.

Around the house, in the shade of the trees, the men sit, smoking, dozing, or reading the papers, while the women, never resting, move about at the housework. The men eat on Sundays about the same as on other days, and breakfast is no sooner over and out of the way than dinner begins.

But at the Smith farm there were no men dozing or reading. Mrs. Smith was alone with her three children, Mary, nine, Tommy, six, and little Ted, just past four. Her farm, rented to a neighbor, lay at the head of a coolly or narrow gully, made at some far-off post-glacial period by the vast and angry floods of water which gullied these tremendous furrows in the level prairie—furrows so deep that undisturbed portions of the original level rose like hills on either side, rose to quite considerable mountains.

The chickens wakened her as usual that Sabbath morning from dreams of her absent husband, from whom she had not heard for weeks. The shadows drifted over the hills, down the slopes, across the wheat, and up the opposite wall in leisurely way, as if, being Sunday, they could take it easy also. The fowls clustered about the housewife as she went out into the yard. Fuzzy little chickens swarmed out from the coops, where their clucking and perpetually disgruntled mothers tramped about, petulantly thrusting their heads through the spaces between the slats.

A cow called in a deep, musical bass, and a calf answered from a little pen near by, and a pig scurried guiltily out of the cabbages. Seeing all this, seeing the pig in the cabbages, the tangle of grass in the garden, the broken fence which she had mended again and again—the little woman, hardly more than a girl, sat down and cried. The bright Sabbath morning was only a mockery without him!

A few years ago they had bought this farm, paying part, mortgaging the rest in the usual way. Edward Smith was a man of terrible energy. He worked "nights and Sundays," as the saying goes, to clear the farm of its brush and of its insatiate mortgage! In the midst of his Herculean struggle came the call for volunteers, and with the grim and unselfish devotion to his country which made the Eagle Brigade able to "whip its weight in wildcats," he threw down his scythe and grub-axe, turned his cattle loose, and became a blue-coated cog in a vast machine for killing men, and not thistles. While the millionaire sent his money to England for safekeeping, this man, with his girl wife and three babies, left them on a mortgaged farm, and went away to fight for an idea. It was foolish but it was sublime for all that.

That was three years before, and the young wife, sitting on the well curb on this bright Sabbath harvest morning, was righteously rebellious. It seemed to her that she had borne her share of the country's sorrow. Two brothers had been killed, the renter in whose hands her husband had left the farm had proved a villain; one year the farm had been without crops, and now the over-ripe grain was waiting the tardy hand of the neighbor who had rented it, and who was cutting his own grain first.

About six weeks before, she had received a letter saying, "We'll be discharged in a little while." But no other word had come from him. She had seen by the papers that his army was being discharged, and from day to day other soldiers slowly percolated in blue streams back into the state and country, but still her hero did not return.

Each week she had told the children that he was coming, and she had watched the road so long that it had become unconscious; and as she stood at the well, or by the kitchen door, her eyes were fixed unthinkingly on the road that wound down the coolly.

Nothing wears on the human soul like waiting. If the stranded mariner, searching the sun-bright seas, could once give up hope of a ship, that horrible grinding on his brain would cease. It was this waiting, hoping, on the edge of despair, that gave Emma Smith no rest.

Neighbors said, with kind intentions: "He's sick, maybe, an' can't start north just yet. He'll come along one o' these days."

"Why don't he write?" was her question, which silenced them all. This Sunday morning it seemed to her as if she could not stand it longer. The house seemed intolerably lonely. So she dressed the little ones in their best calico dresses and home-made jackets, and, closing up the house, set off down the coolly to old Mother Gray's.

"Old Widder Gray" lived at the "mouth of the coolly." She was a widow woman with a large family of stalwart boys and laughing girls. She was the visible incarnation of hospitality and optimistic poverty. With Western open-heartedness she fed every mouth that asked food of her, and worked herself to death as cheerfully as her girls danced in the neighborhood harvest dances.

She waddled down the path to meet Mrs. Smith with a broad smile on her face.

"Oh, you little dears! Come right to your granny. Gimme a kiss! Come right in, Mis' Smith. How are yeh, anyway? Nice mornin', ain't it? Come in an' set down. Everything's in a clutter, but that won't scare you any."

She led the way into the best room, a sunny, square room, carpeted with a faded and patched rag carpet, and papered with white and green-striped wall-paper, where a few faded effigies of dead members of the family hung in variously sized oval walnut frames. The house resounded with singing, laughter, whistling, tramping of heavy boots, and riotous scufflings. Half-grown boys came to the door and crooked their fingers at the children, who ran out, and were soon heard in the midst of the fun.

"Don't s'pose you've heard from Ed?" Mrs. Smith shook her head. "He'll turn up some day, when you ain't lookin' for 'm." The good old soul had said that so many times that poor Mrs. Smith derived no comfort from it any longer.

"Liz heard from Al the other day. He's comin' some day this week. Anyhow, they expect him."

"Did he say anything of—"

"No, he didn't," Mrs. Gray admitted. "But then it was only a short letter, anyhow. Al ain't much for writin', anyhow. But come out and see my new cheese. I tell yeh, I don't believe I ever had better luck in my life. If Ed should come, I want you should take him up a piece of this cheese."

It was beyond human nature to resist the influence of that noisy, hearty, loving household, and in the midst of the singing and laughing the wife forgot her anxiety, for the time at least, and laughed and sang with the rest.

About eleven o'clock a wagon-load more drove up to the door, and Bill Gray, the widow's oldest son, and his whole family from Sand Lake Cooly piled out amid a good-natured uproar. Every one talked at once, except Bill, who sat in the wagon with his wrists on his knees, a straw in his mouth, and an amused twinkle in his blue eyes.

"Ain't heard nothin' o' Ed, I s'pose?" he asked in a kind of bellow. Mrs. Smith shook her head. Bill, with a delicacy very striking in such a great giant, rolled his quid in his mouth, and said:

"Didn't know but you had. I hear two or three of the Sand Lake boys are comin'. Left New Orleans some time this week. Didn't write nothin' about Ed, but no news is good news in such cases, mother always says."

"Well, go put out yer team," said Mrs. Gray, "an' go'n bring me in some taters, an', Sim, you go see if you c'n find some corn. Sadie, you put on the water to bile. Come now, hustle yer boots, all o' yeh. If I feed this yer crowd, we've got to have some raw materials. If y' think I'm goin' to feed yeh on pie—you're jest mightily mistaken."

The children went off into the fields, the girls put dinner on to boil, and then went to change their dresses and fix their hair. "Somebody might come," they said.

"Land sakes, I *hope* not! I don't know where in time I'd set 'em, 'less they'd eat at the second table," Mrs Gray laughed, in pretended dismay.

The two older boys, who had served their time in the army, lay out on the grass before the house, and whittled and talked desultorily about the war and the crops, and planned buying a threshing-machine. The older girls and Mrs. Smith helped enlarge the table and put on the dishes, talking all the time in that cheery, incoherent, and meaningful way a group of such women have—a conversation to be taken for its spirit rather than for its letter, though Mrs. Gray at last got the ear of them all and dissertated at length on girls.

"Girls in love ain't no use in the whole blessed week," she said. "Sundays they're a-lookin, down the road, expectin' he'll come. Sunday afternoons they can't think o' nothin' else, 'cause he's *here*. Monday mornin's they're sleepy and kind o' dreamy and slimpsy, and good f' nothin' on Tuesday and Wednesday. Thursday they git absent-minded, an' begin to look off toward Sunday again, an' mope aroun' and let the dishwater git cold, right under their noses. Friday they break dishes, an' go off in the best room an' snivel, an' look out o' the winder. Saturdays they have queer spurts o' workin' like all p'ssessed, an' spurts o' frizzin' their hair. An' Sunday they begin it all over again."

The girls giggled and blushed all through this tirade from their mother, their broad faces and powerful frames anything but suggestive of lackadaisical sentiment. But Mrs. Smith said:

"Now, Mrs. Gray, I hadn't ought to stay to dinner. You've got—"

"Now you set right down! If any of them girls' beaux comes, they'll have to take what's left, that's all. They ain't s'posed to have much appetite, nohow. No, you're goin' to stay if they starve, an' they ain't no danger o' that."

At one o'clock the long table was piled with boiled potatoes, cords of boiled corn on the cob, squash and pumpkin pies, hot biscuits, sweet pickles, bread and butter, and honey. Then one of the girls took down a conch-shell from a nail, and going to the door, blew a long, fine, free blast, that showed there was no weakness of lungs in her ample chest.

Then the children came out of the forest of corn, out of the creek, out of the loft of the barn, and out of the garden.

"They come to their feed f'r all the world jest like the pigs when y' holler 'poo-ee!' See 'em scoot!" laughed Mrs. Gray, every wrinkle on her face shining with delight.

The men shut up their jack-knives, and surrounded the horse-trough to souse their faces in the cold, hard water, and in a few moments the table was filled with a merry crowd, and a row of wistful-eyed youngsters circled the kitchen wall, where they stood first on one leg and then on the other, in impatient hunger.

"Now pitch in, Mrs. Smith," said Mrs. Gray, presiding over the table. "You know these men critters. They'll eat every grain of it, if yeh give 'em a chance. I swan, they're made o' India-rubber, their stomachs is, I know it."

"Haf to eat to work," said Bill, gnawing a cob with a swift, circular motion that rivalled a corn-sheller in results.

"More like workin' to eat," put in one of the girls, with a giggle. "More eat 'n work with *you*."

"You needn't say anything, Net. Anyone that'll eat seven ears—"

"I didn't no such thing. You piled your cobs on my plate."

"That'll do to tell Ed Varney. It won't go down here where we know yeh."

"Good land! Eat all yeh want! They's plenty more in the fiel's, but I can't afford to give you young uns tea. The tea is for us women-folks, and 'specially f'r Mis' Smith an' Bill's wife. We're a-goin' to tell fortunes by it."

One by one the men filled up and shoved back, and one by one the children slipped into their places, and by two o'clock the women alone remained around the débris-covered table, sipping their tea and telling fortunes.

As they got well down to the grounds in the cup, they shook them with a circular motion in the hand, and then turned them bottom-side up quickly in the saucer, then twirled them three or four times one way, and three or four times the other, during a breathless pause. Then Mrs. Gray lifted the cup, and, gazing into it with profound gravity, pronounced the impending fate.

It must be admitted that, to a critical observer, she had abundant preparation for hitting close to the mark, as when she told the girls that "somebody was comin'." "It's a man," she went on gravely. "He is cross-eyed—"

"Oh, you hush!" cried Nettie.

"He has red hair, and is death on b'iled corn and hot biscuit."

The others shrieked with delight.

"But he's goin' to get the mitten, that red-headed feller is, for I see another feller comin' up behind him."

"Oh, lemme see, lemme see!" cried Nettie.

"Keep off," said the priestess, with a lofty gesture. "His hair is black. He don't eat so much, and he works more."

The girls exploded in a shriek of laughter, and pounded their sister on the back.

At last came Mrs. Smith's turn, and she was trembling with excitement as Mrs. Gray again composed her jolly face to what she considered a proper solemnity of expression.

"Somebody is comin' to *you*," she said, after a long pause. "He's got a musket on his back. He's a soldier. He's almost here. See?"

She pointed at two little tea-stems, which really formed a faint suggestion of a man with a musket on his back. He had climbed nearly to the edge of the cup. Mrs. Smith grew pale with excitement. She trembled so she could hardly hold the cup in her hand as she gazed into it.

"It's Ed," cried the old woman. "He's on the way home. Heavens an' earth! There he is now!" She turned and waved her hand out toward the road. They rushed to the door to look where she pointed.

A man in a blue coat, with a musket on his back, was toiling slowly up the hill on the sun-bright, dusty road, toiling slowly, with bent head half hidden by a heavy knapsack. So tired it seemed that walking was indeed a process of falling. So eager to get home he would not stop, would not look aside, but plodded on, amid the cries of the locusts, the welcome of the crickets, and the rustle of the yellow wheat. Getting back to God's country, and his wife and babies!

Laughing, crying, trying to call him and the children at the same time, the little wife, almost hysterical, snatched her hat and ran out into the yard. But the soldier had disappeared over the hill into the hollow beyond, and, by the time she had found the children, he was too far away for her voice to reach him. And, besides, she was not sure it was her husband, for he had not turned his head at their shouts. This seemed so strange. Why didn't he stop to rest at his old neighbor's house? Tortured by hope and doubt, she hurried up the coolly as fast as she could push the baby wagon, the blue-coated figure just ahead pushing steadily, silently forward up the coolly.

When the excited, panting little group came in sight of the gate they saw the blue-coated figure standing, leaning upon the rough rail fence, his chin on his palms, gazing at the empty house. His knapsack, canteen, blankets, and musket lay upon the dusty grass at his feet.

He was like a man lost in a dream. His wide, hungry eyes devoured the scene. The rough lawn, the little unpainted house, the field of clear yellow wheat behind it, down across which streamed the sun, now almost ready to touch the high hill to the west, the crickets crying merrily, a cat on the fence near by, dreaming, unmindful of the stranger in blue—

How peaceful it all was. O God! How far removed from all camps, hospitals, battle lines. A little cabin in a Wisconsin coolly, but it was majestic in its peace. How did he ever leave it for those years of tramping, thirsting, killing?

Trembling, weak with emotion, her eyes on the silent figure, Mrs. Smith hurried up to the fence. Her feet made no noise in the dust and grass, and they were close upon him before he knew of them. The oldest boy ran a little ahead. He will never forget that figure, that face. It will always remain as something epic, that return of the private. He fixed his eyes on the pale face covered with a ragged beard.

"Who *are* you, sir?" asked the wife, or, rather, started to ask, for he turned, stood a moment, and then cried:

"Emma!"

"Edward!"

The children stood in a curious row to see their mother kiss this bearded, strange man, the elder girl sobbing sympathetically with her mother. Illness had left the soldier partly deaf, and this added to the strangeness of his manner.

But the youngest child stood away, even after the girl had recognized her father and kissed him. The man turned then to the baby, and said in a curiously unpaternal tone:

"Come here, my little man; don't you know me?" But the baby backed away under the fence and stood peering at him critically.

"My little man!" What meaning in those words! This baby seemed like some other woman's child, and not the infant he had left in his wife's arms. The war had come between him and his baby—he was only a strange man to him, with big eyes; a soldier, with mother hanging to his arm, and talking in a loud voice.

"And this is Tom," the private said, drawing the oldest boy to him. "*He'll* come and see me. *He* knows his poor old pap when he comes home from the war."

The mother heard the pain and reproach in his voice and hastened to apologize.

"You've changed so, Ed. He can't know yeh. This is papa, Teddy; come and kiss him—Tom and Mary do. Come, won't you?" But Teddy still peered through the fence with solemn eyes, well out of reach. He resembled a half-wild kitten that hesitates, studying the tones of one's voice.

"I'll fix him," said the soldier, and sat down to undo his knapsack, out of which he drew three enormous and very red apples. After giving one to each of the older children, he said:

"*Now* I guess he'll come. Eh, my little man? Now come see your pap."

Teddy crept slowly under the fence, assisted by the over-zealous Tommy, and a moment later was kicking and squalling in his father's arms. Then they entered the house, into the sitting room, poor, bare, art-forsaken little room, too, with its rag carpet, its square clock, and its two or three chromos and pictures from *Harper's Weekly* pinned about.

"Emma, I'm all tired out," said Private Smith, as he flung himself down on the carpet as he used to do, while his wife brought a pillow to put under his head, and the children stood about munching their apples.

"Tommy, you run and get me a pan of chips, and Mary, you get the tea-kettle on, and I'll go and make some biscuit."

And the soldier talked. Question after question he poured forth about the crops, the cattle, the renter, the neighbor. He slipped his heavy government brogan shoes off his poor, tired, blistered feet, and lay out with utter, sweet relaxation. He was a free man again, no longer a soldier under command. At supper he stopped once, listened and smiled. "That's old Spot. I know her voice. I s'pose that's her calf out there in the pen. I can't milk her tonight, though. I'm too tired. But I tell you, I'd like a drink o' her milk. What's become of old Rove?"

"He died last winter. Poisoned, I guess." There was a moment of sadness for them all. It was some time before the husband spoke again, in a voice that trembled a little.

"Poor old feller! He'd 'a' known me half a mile away. I expected him to come down the hill to meet me. It 'ud 'a' been more like comin' home if I could 'a' seen him comin' down the road an' waggin' his tail, an' laughin' that way he had. I tell yeh, it kind o' took hold o' me to see the blinds down an' the house shut up."

"But, yeh see, we—we expected you'd write again 'fore you started. And then we thought we'd see you if you *did* come," she hastened to explain.

"Well, I ain't worth a cent on writin'. Besides, it's just as well yeh didn't know when I was comin'. I tell you, it sounds good to hear them chickens out there, an' turkeys, an' the crickets. Do you know they don't have just the same kind o' crickets down South? Who's Sam hired t' help cut yer grain?"

"The Ramsey boys."

"Looks like a good crop; but I'm afraid I won't do much gettin' it cut. This cussed fever an' ague has got me down pretty low. I don't know when I'll get rid of it. I'll bet I've took twenty-five pounds of quinine if I've taken a bit. Gimme another biscuit. I tell yeh, they taste good, Emma. I ain't had anything like it—say, if you'd 'a' hear'd me braggin' to th' boys about your butter 'n' biscuits I'll bet your ears 'ud a' burnt."

The private's wife colored with pleasure. "Oh, you're always a-braggin' about your things. Everybody makes good butter."

"Yes; old lady Snyder, for instance."

"Oh, well, she ain't to be mentioned. She's Dutch."

"Or old Mis' Snively. One more cup o' tea, Mary. That's my girl! I'm feeling better already. I just b'lieve the matter with me is, I'm *starved*."

This was a delicious hour, one long to be remembered. They were like lovers again. But their tenderness, like that of a typical American family, found utterance in tones, rather than in words. He was praising her when praising her biscuit, and she knew it. They grew soberer when he showed where he had been struck, one ball burning the back of his hand, one cutting away a lock of hair from his temple, and one passing through the calf of his leg. The wife shuddered to think how near she had come to being a soldier's widow. Her waiting no longer seemed hard. This sweet, glorious hour effaced it all.

Then they rose, and all went out into the garden and down to the barn. He stood beside her while she milked old Spot. They began to plan fields and crops for next year.

His farm was weedy and encumbered, a rascally renter had run away with his machinery (departing between two days), his children needed clothing, the years were coming upon him, he was sick and emaciated, but his heroic soul did not quail. With the same courage with which he had faced his Southern march he entered upon a still more hazardous future.

Oh, that mystic hour! The pale man with big eyes standing there by the well, with his young wife by his side. The vast moon swinging above the eastern peaks, the cattle winding down the pasture slopes with jangling bells, the crickets singing, the stars blooming out sweet and far and serene; the katydids rhythmically calling, the little turkeys crying querulously, as they settle to roost in the poplar tree near the open gate. The voices at the well drop lower, the little ones nestle in their father's arms at last, and Teddy falls asleep there.

The common soldier of the American volunteer army had returned. His war with the South was over, and his fight, his daily running fight with Nature and against the injustice of his fellow-men, was begun again.

26

A New England Nun

BY MARY E. WILKINS

IT was late in the afternoon, and the light was waning. There was a difference in the look of the tree shadows out in the yard. Somewhere in the distance cows were lowing and a little bell was tinkling; now and then a farm-wagon tilted by, and the dust flew; some blue-shirted laborers with shovels over their shoulders plodded past; little swarms of flies were dancing up and down before the people's faces in the soft air. There seemed to be a gentle stir arising over everything for the mere sake of subsidence—a very premonition of rest and hush and night.

This soft diurnal commotion was over Louisa Ellis also. She had been peacefully sewing at her sitting-room window all the afternoon. Now she quilted her needle carefully into her work, which she folded precisely, and laid in a basket with her thimble and thread and scissors. Louisa Ellis could not remember that ever in her life she had mislaid one of these little feminine appurtenances, which had become, from long use and constant association, a very part of her personality.

Louisa tied a green apron round her waist, and got out a flat straw hat with a green ribbon. Then she went into the garden with a little blue crockery bowl, to pick some currants for her tea. After the currants were picked she sat on the back doorstep and stemmed them, collecting the stems carefully in her apron, and afterward throwing them into the hen-coop. She looked sharply at the grass beside the step to see if any had fallen there.

Louisa was slow and still in her movements; it took her a long time to prepare her tea; but when ready it was set forth with as much grace as if she had been a veritable guest to her own self. The little square table stood exactly in the center of the kitchen, and was covered with a starched linen cloth whose border pattern of flowers glistened. Louisa had a damask napkin on her tea-tray, where were arranged a cut-glass tumbler full of teaspoons, a silver cream-pitcher, a china sugar-bowl, and one pink china cup and saucer. Louisa used china every day— something which none of her neighbors did. They whispered about it among themselves. Their daily tables were laid with common crockery, their sets of best china stayed in the parlor closet, and Louisa Ellis was no richer nor better bred than they. Still she would use the china. She had for her supper a glass dish full of sugared currants, a plate of little cakes, and one of light white biscuits. Also a leaf or two of lettuce, which she cut up daintily. Louisa was very fond of lettuce, which she raised to perfection in her little garden. She ate quite heartily, though in a delicate, pecking way; it seemed almost surprising that any considerable bulk of the food should vanish.

After tea she filled a plate with nicely baked thin corn-cakes, and carried them out into the backyard.

"Caesar!" she called. "Caesar! Caesar!"

There was a little rush, and the clank of a chain, and a large yellow-and-white dog appeared at the door of his tiny hut, which was half hidden among the tall grasses and flowers. Louisa patted him and gave him the corn-cakes. Then she returned to the house and washed the tea-things, polishing the china carefully. The twilight had deepened; the chorus of the frogs floated in at the open window wonderfully loud and shrill, and once in a while a long sharp drone from a tree-toad pierced it. Louisa took off her green gingham apron, disclosing a shorter one of pink-and-white print. She lighted her lamp, and sat down again with her sewing.

In about half an hour Joe Dagget came. She heard his heavy step on the walk, and rose and took off her pink-and-white apron. Under that was still another—white linen with a little cambric edging on the bottom; that was Louisa's company apron: She never wore it without her calico sewing-apron over it unless she had a guest. She had barely folded the pink-and-white one with methodical haste and laid it in a table-drawer when the door opened and Joe Dagget entered.

He seemed to fill up the whole room. A little yellow canary that had been asleep in his green cage at the south window woke up and fluttered wildly, beating his little yellow wings against the wires. He always did so when Joe Dagget came into the room.

"Good-evening," said Louisa. She extended her hand with a kind of solemn cordiality.

"Good-evening, Louisa," returned the man, in a loud voice.

She placed a chair for him, and they sat facing each other, with the table between them. He sat bolt-upright, toeing out his heavy feet squarely, glancing with a good-humored uneasiness around the room. She sat gently erect, folding her slender hands in her white-linen lap.

"Been a pleasant day," remarked Dagget.

"Real pleasant," Louisa assented, softly. "Have you been haying?" she asked, after a little while.

"Yes, I've been haying all day, down in the ten-acre lot. Pretty hot work."

"It must be."

"Yes, it's pretty hot work in the sun."

"Is your mother well today?"

"Yes, mother's pretty well."

"I suppose Lily Dyer's with her now?"

Dagget colored. "Yes, she's with her," he answered, slowly.

He was not very young, but there was a boyish look about his large face. Louisa was not quite as old as he, her face was fairer and smoother, but she gave people the impression of being older.

"I suppose she's a good deal of help to your mother," she said, further.

"I guess she is; I don't know how mother'd get along without her," said Dagget, with a sort of embarrassed warmth.

"She looks like a real capable girl. She's pretty-looking too," remarked Louisa.

"Yes, she is pretty fair-looking."

Presently Dagget began fingering the books on the table. There was a square red autograph album, and a Young Lady's Gift-Book which had belonged to Louisa's mother. He took them up one after the other and opened them; then laid them down again, the album on the Gift-Book.

Louisa kept eying them with mild uneasiness. Finally she rose and changed the position of the books, putting the album underneath. That was the way they had been arranged in the first place.

Dagget gave an awkward little laugh. "Now what difference did it make which book was on top?" said he.

Louisa looked at him with a deprecating smile. "I always keep them that way," murmured she.

"You do beat everything," said Dagget, trying to laugh again. His large face was flushed.

He remained about an hour longer, then rose to take leave. Going out, he stumbled over a rug, and, trying to recover himself, hit Louisa's work-basket on the table, and knocked it on the floor.

He looked at Louisa, then at the rolling spools; he ducked himself awkwardly toward them, but she stopped him. "Never mind," said she; "I'll pick them up after you're gone."

She spoke with a mild stiffness. Either she was a little disturbed, or his nervousness affected her, and made her seem constrained in her effort to reassure him.

When Joe Dagget was outside he drew in the sweet evening air with a sigh, and felt much as an innocent and perfectly well-intentioned bear might after his exit from a china shop.

Louisa, on her part, felt much as the kind-hearted, long-suffering owner of the china shop might have done after the exit of the bear.

She tied on the pink, then the green apron, picked up all the scattered treasures and replaced them in her work-basket, and straightened the rug. Then she set the lamp on the floor, and began sharply examining the carpet. She even rubbed her fingers over it, and looked at them.

"He's tracked in a good deal of dust," she murmured. "I thought he must have."

Louisa got a dustpan and brush, and swept Joe Dagget's track carefully.

If he could have known it, it would have increased his perplexity and uneasiness, although it would not have disturbed his loyalty in the least. He came twice a week to see Louisa Ellis, and every time, sitting there in her delicately sweet room, he felt as if surrounded by a hedge of lace. He was afraid to stir lest he should put a clumsy foot or hand through the fairy web, and he had always the consciousness that Louisa was watching fearfully lest he should.

Still the lace and Louisa commanded perforce his perfect respect and patience and loyalty. They were to be married in a month, after a singular courtship which had lasted for a matter of fifteen years. For fourteen out of the fifteen years the two had not once seen each other, and they had seldom exchanged letters. Joe had been all those years in Australia, where he had gone to make his fortune, and where he had stayed until he made it. He would have stayed fifty years if it had taken so long, and come home feeble and tottering, or never come home at all, to marry Louisa.

But the fortune had been made in the fourteen years, and he had come home now to marry the woman who had been patiently and unquestioningly waiting for him all that time.

Shortly after they were engaged he had announced to Louisa his determination to strike out into new fields, and secure a competency before they should be married. She had listened and assented with the sweet serenity which never failed her, not even when her lover set forth on that long and uncertain journey. Joe, buoyed up as he was by his sturdy determination, broke down a little at the last, but Louisa kissed him with a mild blush, and said good-by.

"It won't be for long," poor Joe had said, huskily; but it was for fourteen years.

In that length of time much had happened. Louisa's mother and brother had died, and she was all alone in the world. But greatest happening of all—a subtle happening which both were too simple to understand—Louisa's feet had turned into a path, smooth maybe under a calm, serene sky, but so straight and unswerving that it could only meet a check at her grave, and so narrow that there was no room for anyone at her side.

Louisa's first emotion when Joe Dagget came home (he had not apprised her of his coming) was consternation, although she would not admit it to herself, and he never dreamed of it. Fifteen years ago she had been in love with him—at least she considered herself to be. Just at that time, gently acquiescing with and falling into the natural drift of girlhood, she had seen marriage ahead as a reasonable feature and a probable desirability of life. She had listened with calm docility to her mother's views upon the subject. Her mother was remarkable for her cool sense and sweet, even temperament. She talked wisely to her daughter when Joe Dagget presented himself, and Louisa accepted him with no hesitation. He was the first lover she had ever had.

She had been faithful to him all these years. She had never dreamed of the possibility of marrying anyone else. Her life, especially for the last seven years, had been full of a pleasant peace, she had never felt discontented nor impatient over her lover's absence; still she had always looked forward to his return and their marriage as the inevitable conclusion of things. However, she had fallen into a way of placing it so far in the future that it was almost equal to placing it over the boundaries of another life.

When Joe came she had been expecting him, and expecting to be married for fourteen years, but she was as much surprised and taken aback as if she had never thought of it.

Joe's consternation came later. He eyed Louisa with an instant confirmation of his old admiration. She had changed but little. She still kept her pretty manner and soft grace, and was, he considered, every whit as attractive as ever. As for himself, his stent was done; he had turned his face away from fortune-seeking, and the old winds of romance whistled as loud and sweet as ever through his ears. All the song which he had been wont to hear in them was Louisa; he had for a long time a loyal belief that he heard it still, but finally it seemed to him that although the winds sang always that one song, it had another name. But for Louisa the wind had never more than murmured; now it had gone down, and everything was still. She listened for a little while with half-wistful attention; then she turned quietly away and went to work on her wedding-clothes.

Joe had made some extensive and quite magnificent alterations in his house. It was the old homestead; the newly married couple would live there, for Joe could not desert his mother, who refused to leave her old home. So Louisa must leave hers. Every morning, rising and going about among her neat maidenly possessions, she felt as one looking her last upon the faces of dear friends. It was true that in a measure she could take them with her, but, robbed of their old environments, they would appear in such new guises that they would almost cease to be themselves. Then there were some peculiar features of her happy solitary life which she would probably be obliged to relinquish altogether. Sterner tasks than these graceful but half-needless ones would probably devolve upon her. There would be a large house to care for; there would be company to entertain; there would be Joe's rigorous and feeble old mother to wait upon; and it would be contrary to all thrifty village traditions for her to keep more than one servant. Louisa had a little still, and she used to occupy herself pleasantly in summer weather with distilling the sweet and aromatic essences from roses and peppermint and spearmint. By-and-by her still must be laid away. Her store of essences was already considerable, and there would be no time for her to distil for the mere pleasure of it. Then Joe's mother would think it foolishness; she had already hinted her opinion in the matter. Louisa dearly loved to sew a linen seam, not always for use, but for the simple, mild pleasure which she took in it. She would have been loath to confess how more than once she had ripped a seam for the mere delight of sewing it together again. Sitting at her window during long sweet afternoons, drawing her needle gently through the dainty fabric, she was peace itself. But there was small chance of such foolish comfort in the future. Joe's mother, domineering, shrewd old matron that she was even in her old age, and very likely even Joe himself, with his honest masculine rudeness, would laugh and frown down all these pretty but senseless old-maiden ways.

Louisa had almost the enthusiasm of an artist over the mere order and cleanliness of her solitary home. She had throbs of genuine triumph at the sight of the window-panes which she had polished until they shone like jewels. She gloated gently over her orderly bureau-drawers, with their exquisitely folded contents redolent with lavender and sweet clover and very purity. Could she be sure of the endurance of even this? She had visions, so startling that she half repudiated them as indelicate, of coarse masculine belongings strewn about in endless litter; of dust and disorder arising necessarily from a coarse masculine presence in the midst of all this delicate harmony.

Among her forebodings of disturbance, not the least was with regard to Caesar. Caesar was a veritable hermit of a dog. For the greater part of his life he had dwelt in his secluded hut, shut out from the society

of his kind and all innocent canine joys. Never had Caesar since his
early youth watched at a woodchuck's hole; never had he known the
delights of a stray bone at a neighbor's kitchen door. And it was all on
account of a sin committed when hardly out of his puppyhood. No one
knew the possible depth of remorse of which this mild-visaged, altogether innocent-looking old dog might be capable; but whether or not
he had encountered remorse, he had encountered a full measure of
righteous retribution. Old Caesar seldom lifted up his voice in a growl
or a bark; he was fat and sleepy; there were yellow rings which looked
like spectacles around his dim old eyes; but there was a neighbor who
bore on his hand the imprint of several of Caesar's sharp, white, youthful teeth, and for that he had lived at the end of a chain, all alone in
a little hut, for fourteen years. The neighbor, who was choleric and
smarting with the pain of his wound, had demanded either Caesar's
death or complete ostracism. So Louisa's brother, to whom the dog had
belonged, had built him his little kennel and tied him up. It was now
fourteen years since, in a flood of youthful spirits, he had inflicted that
memorable bite, and with the exception of short excursions, always at
the end of the chain, under the strict guardianship of his master or
Louisa, the old dog had remained a close prisoner. It is doubtful if, with
his limited ambition, he took much pride in the fact, but it is certain
that he was possessed of considerable cheap fame. He was regarded by
all the children in the village and by many adults as a very monster of
ferocity. St. George's dragon could hardly have surpassed in evil repute
Louisa Ellis's old yellow dog. Mothers charged their children with solemn emphasis not to go too near to him, and the children listened and
believed greedily, with a fascinated appetite for terror, and ran by
Louisa's house stealthily, with many sidelong and backward glances at
the terrible dog. If perchance he sounded a hoarse bark, there was a panic.
Wayfarers chancing into Louisa's yard eyed him with respect, and
inquired if the chain were stout. Caesar at large might have seemed a
very ordinary dog, and excited no comment whatever; chained, his
reputation overshadowed him, so that he lost his own proper outlines
and looked darkly vague and enormous. Joe Dagget, however, with his
good-humored sense and shrewdness, saw him as he was. He strode
valiantly up to him and patted him on the head, in spite of Louisa's
soft clamor of warning, and even attempted to set him loose. Louisa
grew so alarmed that he desisted, but kept announcing his opinion in
the matter quite forcibly at intervals. "There ain't a better-natured dog
in town," he would say, "and it's downright cruel to keep him tied up
there. Some day I'm going to take him out."

Louisa had very little hope that he would not, one of these days, when
their interests and possessions should be more completely fused in one.

She pictured to herself Caesar on the rampage through the quiet and unguarded village. She saw innocent children bleeding in his path. She was herself very fond of the old dog, because he had belonged to her dead brother, and he was always very gentle with her; still she had great faith in his ferocity. She always warned people not to go too near him. She fed him on ascetic fare of corn-mush and cakes, and never fired his dangerous temper with heating and sanguinary diet of flesh and bones. Louisa looked at the old dog munching his simple fare, and thought of her approaching marriage and trembled. Still no anticipation of disorder and confusion in lieu of sweet peace and harmony, no forebodings of Caesar on the rampage, no wild fluttering of her little yellow canary, were sufficient to turn her a hair's breath. Joe Dagget had been fond of her and working for her all these years. It was not for her, whatever came to pass, to prove untrue and break his heart. She put the exquisite little stitches into her wedding-garments, and the time went on until it was only a week before her wedding-day. It was a Tuesday evening, and the wedding was to be a week from Wednesday.

There was a full moon that night. About nine o'clock Louisa strolled down the road a little way. There were harvest-fields on either hand, bordered by low stone walls. Luxuriant clumps of bushes grew beside the wall, and trees—wild cherry and old apple trees—at intervals. Presently Louisa sat down on the wall and looked about her with mildly sorrowful reflectiveness. Tall shrubs of blueberry and meadow-sweet, all woven together and tangled with blackberry vines and horsebriers, shut her in on either side. She had a little clear space between them. Opposite her, on the other side of the road, was a spreading tree; the moon shone between its boughs, and the leaves twinkled like silver. The road was bespread with a beautiful shifting dapple of silver and shadow; the air was full of a mysterious sweetness. "I wonder if it's wild grapes?" murmured Louisa. She sat there some time. She was just thinking of rising, when she heard footsteps and low voices, and remained quiet. It was a lonely place, and she felt a little timid. She thought she would keep still in the shadow and let the persons, whoever they might be, pass her.

But just before they reached her the voices ceased, and the footsteps. She understood that their owners had also found seats upon the stone wall. She was wondering if she could not steal away unobserved, when the voice broke the stillness. It was Joe Dagget's. She sat still and listened.

The voice was announced by a loud sigh, which was as familiar as itself. "Well," said Dagget, "you've made up your mind, then, I suppose?"

"Yes," returned another voice; "I'm going day after tomorrow."

"That's Lily Dyer," thought Louisa to herself. The voice embodied itself in her mind. She saw a girl tall and full-figured, with a firm, fair face, looking fairer and firmer in the moonlight, her strong yellow hair braided in a close knot. A girl full of a calm rustic strength and bloom, with a masterful way which might have beseemed a princess. Lily Dyer was a favorite with the village folk; she had just the qualities to arouse the admiration. She was good and handsome and smart. Louisa had often heard her praises sounded.

"Well," said Joe Dagget, "I ain't got a word to say."

"I don't know what you could say," returned Lily Dyer.

"Not a word to say," repeated Joe, drawing out the words heavily. Then there was a silence. "I ain't sorry," he began at last, "that that happened yesterday—that we kind of let on how we felt to each other. I guess it's just as well we knew. Of course, I can't do anything any different. I'm going right on an' get married next week. I ain't going back on a woman that's waited for me fourteen years, an' break her heart."

"If you should jilt her tomorrow, I wouldn't have you," spoke up the girl, with sudden vehemence.

"Well, I ain't going to give you the chance," said he; "but I don't believe you would, either."

"You'd see I wouldn't. Honor's honor, an' right's right. An' I'd never think anything of any man that went against 'em for me or any other girl; you'd find that out, Joe Dagget."

"Well, you'll find out fast enough that I ain't going against 'em for you or any other girl," returned he. Their voices sounded almost as if they were angry with each other. Louisa was listening eagerly.

"I'm sorry you feel as if you must go away," said Joe, "but I don't know but it's best."

"Of course it's best. I hope you and I have got common-sense."

"Well, I suppose you're right." Suddenly Joe's voice got an undertone of tenderness. "Say, Lily," said he, "I'll get along well enough myself, but I can't bear to think— You don't suppose you're going to fret much over it?"

"I guess you'll find out I sha'n't fret much over a married man."

"Well, I hope you won't—I hope you won't, Lily. God knows I do. And—I hope—one of these days—you'll—come across somebody else—"

"I don't see any reason why I shouldn't." Suddenly her tone changed. She spoke in a sweet, clear voice, so loud that she could have been heard across the street. "No, Joe Dagget," said she, "I'll never marry any other man as long as I live. I've got good sense, an' I ain't going to break my heart nor make a fool of myself; but I'm never going to be married, you can be sure of that. I ain't that sort of a girl to feel this way twice."

Louisa heard an exclamation and a soft commotion behind the bushes; then Lily spoke again—the voice sounded as if she had risen. "This must be put a stop to," said she. "We've stayed here long enough. I'm going home."

Louisa sat there in a daze, listening to their retreating steps. After a while she got up and slunk softly home herself. The next day she did her housework methodically; that was as much a matter of course as breathing; but she did not sew on her wedding-clothes. She sat at her window and meditated. In the evening Joe came. Louisa Ellis had never known that she had any diplomacy in her, but when she came to look for it that night she found it, although meek of its kind, among her little feminine weapons. Even now she could hardly believe that she had heard aright, and that she would not do Joe a terrible injury should she break her troth-plight. She wanted to sound him without betraying too soon her own inclinations in the matter. She did it successfully, and they finally came to an understanding; but it was a difficult thing, for he was as afraid of betraying himself as she.

She never mentioned Lily Dyer. She simply said that while she had no cause of complaint against him, she had lived so long in one way that she shrank from making a change.

"Well, I never shrank, Louisa," said Dagget. "I'm going to be honest enough to say that I think maybe it's better this way; but if you'd wanted to keep on, I'd have stuck to you till my dying day. I hope you know that."

"Yes, I do," said she.

That night she and Joe parted more tenderly than they had done for a long time. Standing in the door, holding each other's hands, a last great wave of regretful memory swept over them.

"Well, this ain't the way we've thought it was all going to end, is it, Louisa?" said Joe.

She shook her head. There was a little quiver on her placid face.

"You let me know if there's ever anything I can do for you," said he. "I ain't ever going to forget you, Louisa." Then he kissed her, and went down the path. Louisa, all alone by herself that night, wept a little, she hardly knew why; but the next morning, on waking, she felt like a queen who, after fearing lest her domain be wrested away from her, sees it firmly insured in her possession.

Now the tall weeds and grasses might cluster around Caesar's little hermit hut, the snow might fall on its roof year in and year out, but he never would go on a rampage through the unguarded village. Now the little canary might turn itself into a peaceful yellow ball night after night, and have no need to wake and flutter with wild terror against its bars. Louisa could sew linen seams, and distil roses, and dust and polish and fold away in lavender, as long as she listed. That afternoon she sat with her needlework at the window, and felt fairly steeped in peace. Lily Dyer, tall and erect and blooming, went past; but she felt no qualm. If Louisa Ellis had sold her birthright she did not know it, the taste of the pottage was so delicious, and had been her sole satisfaction for so long. Serenity and placid narrowness had become to her as the birthright itself. She gazed ahead through a long reach of future days strung together like pearls in a rosary, every one like the others, and all smooth and flawless and innocent, and her heart went up in thankfulness. Outside was the fervid summer afternoon; the air was filled with the sounds of the busy harvest of men and birds and bees; there were halloos, metallic clatterings, sweet calls, and long hummings. Louisa sat, prayerfully numbering her days, like an uncloistered nun.

27

The Mission of Jane

BY EDITH WHARTON

L ETHBURY, surveying his wife across the dinner table, found his transient glance arrested by an indefinable change in her appearance.

"How smart you look! Is that a new gown?" he asked.

Her answering look seemed to deprecate his charging her with the extravagance of wasting a new gown on him, and he now perceived that the change lay deeper than any accident of dress. At the same time, he noticed that she betrayed her consciousness of it by a delicate, almost frightened blush. It was one of the compensations of Mrs. Lethbury's protracted childishness that she still blushed as prettily as at eighteen. Her body had been privileged not to outstrip her mind, and the two, as it seemed to Lethbury, were destined to travel together through an eternity of girlishness.

"I don't know what you mean," she said.

Since she never did, he always wondered at her bringing this out as a fresh grievance against him; but his wonder was unresentful, and he said good-humoredly: "You sparkle so that I thought you had on your diamonds."

She sighed and blushed again.

"It must be," he continued, "that you've been to a dressmaker's opening. You're absolutely brimming with illicit enjoyment."

She stared again, this time at the adjective. His adjectives always embarrassed her: their unintelligibleness savored of impropriety.

"In short," he summed up, "you've been doing something that you're thoroughly ashamed of."

To his surprise she retorted: "I don't see why I should be ashamed of it!"

Lethbury leaned back with a smile of enjoyment. When there was nothing better going he always liked to listen to her explanations.

"Well—?" he said.

She was becoming breathless and ejaculatory. "Of course you'll laugh —you laugh at everything!"

"That rather blunts the point of my derision, doesn't it?" he interjected; but she pushed on without noticing:

"It's so easy to laugh at things."

"Ah," murmured Lethbury with relish, "that's Aunt Sophronia's, isn't it?"

Most of his wife's opinions were heirlooms, and he took a quaint pleasure in tracing their descent. She was proud of their age, and saw no reason for discarding them while they were still serviceable. Some, of course, were so fine that she kept them for state occasions, like her great-grandmother's Crown Derby; but from the lady known as Aunt Sophronia she had inherited a stout set of everyday prejudices that were practically as good as new; whereas her husband's, as she noticed, were always having to be replaced. In the early days she had fancied there might be a certain satisfaction in taxing him with the fact; but she had long since been silenced by the reply: "My dear, I'm not a rich man, but I never use an opinion twice if I can help it."

She was reduced, therefore, to dwelling on his moral deficiencies; and one of the most obvious of these was his refusal to take things seriously. On this occasion, however, some ulterior purpose kept her from taking up his taunt.

"I'm not in the least ashamed!" she repeated, with the air of shaking a banner to the wind; but the domestic atmosphere being calm, the banner drooped unheroically.

"That," said Lethbury judicially, "encourages me to infer that you ought to be, and that, consequently, you've been giving yourself the unusual pleasure of doing something I shouldn't approve of."

She met this with an almost solemn directness. "No," she said. "You won't approve of it. I've allowed for that."

"Ah," he exclaimed, setting down his liquor-glass. "You've worked out the whole problem, eh?"

"I believe so."

"That's uncommonly interesting. And what is it?"

She looked at him quietly. "A baby."

If it was seldom given her to surprise him, she had attained the distinction for once.

"A baby?"

"Yes."

"A--human baby?"

"Of course!" she cried, with the virtuous resentment of the woman who has never allowed dogs in the house.

Lethbury's puzzled stare broke into a fresh smile. "A baby I shan't approve of? Well, in the abstract I don't think much of them, I admit. Is this an abstract baby?"

Again she frowned at the adjective; but she had reached a pitch of exaltation at which such obstacles could not deter her.

"It's the loveliest baby—" she murmured.

"Ah, then it's concrete. It exists. In this harsh world it draws its breath in pain—"

"It's the healthiest child I ever saw!" she indignantly corrected.

"You've seen it, then?"

Again the accusing blush suffused her. "Yes—I've seen it."

"And to whom does the paragon belong?"

And here indeed she confounded him. "To me—I hope," she declared.

He pushed his chair back with an articulate murmur. "To *you*—?"

"To *us*," she corrected.

"Good Lord!" he said. If there had been the least hint of hallucination in her transparent gaze—but no; it was as clear, as shallow, as easily fathomable as when he had first suffered the sharp surprise of striking bottom in it.

It occurred to him that perhaps she was trying to be funny: he knew that there is nothing more cryptic than the humor of the unhumorous

"Is it a joke?" he faltered.

"Oh, I hope not. I want it so much to be a reality—"

He paused to smile at the limitations of a world in which jokes were not realities, and continued gently: "But since it is one already—"

"To us, I mean: to you and me. I want—" her voice wavered, and her eyes with it. "I have always wanted so dreadfully . . . it has been such a disappointment . . . not to . . ."

"I see," said Lethbury slowly.

But he had not seen before. It seemed curious now that he had never thought of her taking it in that way, had never surmised any hidden depths beneath her outspread obviousness. He felt as though he had touched a secret spring in her mind.

There was a moment's silence, moist and tremulous on her part, awkward and slightly irritated on his.

"You've been lonely, I suppose?" he began. It was odd, having suddenly to reckon with the stranger who gazed at him out of her trivial eyes.

"At times," she said.

"I'm sorry."

"It was not your fault. A man has so many occupations; and women who are clever—or very handsome—I suppose that's an occupation too. Sometimes I've felt that when dinner was ordered I had nothing to do till the next day."

"Oh," he groaned.

"It wasn't your fault," she insisted. "I never told you—but when I chose that rose-bud paper for the front-room upstairs, I always thought—"

"Well—?"

"It would be such a pretty paper—for a baby—to wake up in. That was years ago, of course; but it was rather an expensive paper . . . and it hasn't faded in the least . . ." she broke off incoherently.

"It hasn't faded?"

"No—and so I thought . . . as we don't use the room for anything . . . now that Aunt Sophronia is dead . . . I thought I might . . . you might . . . oh, Julian, if you could only have seen it just waking up in its crib!"

"Seen what—where? You haven't got a baby upstairs?"

"Oh, no—not yet," she said, with her rare laugh—the girlish bubbling of merriment that had seemed one of her chief graces in the early days. It occurred to him that he had not given her enough things to laugh about lately. But then she needed such very elementary things: she was as difficult to amuse as a savage. He concluded that he was not sufficiently simple.

"Alice," he said almost solemnly, "what *do* you mean?"

She hesitated a moment: he saw her gather her courage for a supreme effort. Then she said slowly, gravely, as though she were pronouncing a sacramental phrase:

"I'm so lonely without a little child—and I thought perhaps you'd let me adopt one . . . It's at the hospital . . . its mother is dead . . . and I could . . . pet it, and dress it, and do things for it . . . and it's such a good baby . . . you can ask any of the nurses . . . it would never, never bother you by crying . . ."

II

Lethbury accompanied his wife to the hospital in a mood of chastened wonder. It did not occur to him to oppose her wish. He knew, of course, that he would have to bear the brunt of the situation: the jokes at the club, the enquiries, the explanations. He saw himself in the comic role of the adopted father and welcomed it as an expiation. For in his rapid reconstruction of the past he found himself cutting a shabbier figure than he cared to admit. He had always been intolerant of stupid people, and it was his punishment to be convicted of stupidity. As his mind traversed the years between his marriage and this unexpected assumption of paternity, he saw, in the light of an overheated imagination, many signs of unwonted crassness. It was not that he had ceased to think his wife stupid: she *was* stupid, limited, inflexible; but there was a pathos in the struggles of her swaddled mind, in its blind reachings toward the primal emotions. He had always thought she would have been happier with a child; but he had thought it mechanically, because it had so often been thought before, because it was in the nature of things to think it of every woman, because his wife was so eminently one of a species that she fitted into all the generalizations of the sex. But he had regarded this generalization as merely typical of the triumph of tradition over experience. Maternity was no doubt the supreme function of primitive woman, the one end to which her whole organism tended; but the law of increasing complexity had operated in both sexes, and he had not seriously supposed that, outside the world of Christmas fiction and anecdotic art, such truisms had any special hold on the feminine imagination. Now he saw that the arts in question were kept alive by the vitality of the sentiments they appealed to.

Lethbury was in fact going through a rapid process of readjustment. His marriage had been a failure, but he had preserved toward his wife the exact fidelity of act that is sometimes supposed to excuse any divagation of feeling; so that, for years, the tie between them had consisted mainly in his abstaining from making love to other women. The abstention had not always been easy, for the world is surprisingly well-stocked with the kind of women one ought to have married but did not; and Lethbury had not escaped the solicitation of such alternatives. His immunity had been purchased at the cost of taking refuge in the somewhat rarefied atmosphere of his perceptions; and his world being thus limited, he had given unusual care to its details, compensating himself for the narrowness of his horizon by the minute finish of his foreground. It was a world of fine shadings and the nicest proportions, where impulse seldom set a blundering foot, and the feast of reason was undisturbed by an intemperate flow of soul. To such a banquet his wife naturally remained uninvited. The diet would have disagreed with her, and she would probably have objected to the other guests. But Lethbury, miscalculating her needs, had hitherto supposed that he had made ample provision for them, and was consequently at liberty to enjoy his own fare without any reproach of mendicancy at his gates. Now he beheld her pressing a starved face against the windows of his life, and in his imaginative reaction he invested her with a pathos borrowed from the sense of his own shortcomings.

In the hospital the imaginative process continued with increasing force. He looked at his wife with new eyes. Formerly she had been to him a mere bundle of negations, a labyrinth of dead walls and bolted doors. There was nothing behind the walls, and the doors led no whither: he had sounded and listened often enough to be sure of that. Now he felt like a traveler who, exploring some ancient ruin, comes on an inner cell, intact amid the general dilapidation, and painted with images which reveal the forgotten uses of the building.

His wife stood by a white crib in one of the wards. In the crib lay a child, a year old, the nurse affirmed, but to Lethbury's eye a mere dateless fragment of humanity projected against a background of conjecture. Over this anonymous particle of life Mrs. Lethbury leaned, such ecstasy reflected in her face as strikes up, in Correggio's *Night-piece,* from the child's body to the mother's countenance. It was a light that irradiated and dazzled her. She looked up at an enquiry of Lethbury's, but as their glances met he perceived that she no longer saw him, that he had become as invisible to her as she had long been to him. He had to transfer his question to the nurse.

"What is the child's name?" he asked.

"We call her Jane," said the nurse.

III

Lethbury, at first, had resisted the idea of a legal adoption; but when he found that his wife could not be brought to regard the child as hers till it had been made so by process of law, he promptly withdrew his objection. On one point only he remained inflexible; and that was the changing of the waif's name. Mrs. Lethbury, almost at once, had expressed a wish to rechristen it: she fluctuated between Muriel and Gladys, deferring the moment of decision like a lady wavering between two bonnets. But Lethbury was unyielding. In the general surrender of his prejudices this one alone held out.

"But Jane is so dreadful," Mrs. Lethbury protested.

"Well, we don't know that *she* won't be dreadful. She may grow up a Jane."

His wife exclaimed reproachfully. "The nurse says she's the loveliest—"

"Don't they always say that?" asked Lethbury patiently. He was prepared to be inexhaustibly patient now that he had reached a firm foothold of opposition.

"It's cruel to call her Jane," Mrs. Lethbury pleaded.

"It's ridiculous to call her Muriel."

"The nurse is *sure* she must be a lady's child."

Lethbury winced: he had tried, all along, to keep his mind off the question of antecedents.

"Well, let her prove it," he said, with a rising sense of exasperation. He wondered how he could ever have allowed himself to be drawn into such a ridiculous business; for the first time he felt the full irony of it.

He had visions of coming home in the afternoon to a house smelling of linseed and paregoric, and of being greeted by a chronic howl as he went upstairs to dress for dinner. He had never been a club man, but he saw himself becoming one now.

The worst of his anticipations were unfulfilled. The baby was surprisingly well and surprisingly quiet. Such infantile remedies as she absorbed were not potent enough to be perceived beyond the nursery; and when Lethbury could be induced to enter that sanctuary, there was nothing to jar his nerves in the mild pink presence of his adopted daughter. Jars there were, indeed: they were probably inevitable in the disturbed routine of the household; but they occurred between Mrs. Lethbury and the nurses, and Jane contributed to them only a placid stare which might have served as a rebuke to the combatants.

In the reaction from his first impulse of atonement, Lethbury noted with sharpened perceptions the effect of the change on his wife's character. He saw already the error of supposing that it could work any transformation in her. It simply magnified her existing qualities. She was like a dried sponge put in water: she expanded, but she did not change her shape. From the standpoint of scientific observation it was curious to see how her stored instincts responded to the pseudo-maternal call. She overflowed with the petty maxims of the occasion. One felt in her the epitome, the consummation, of centuries of animal maternity, so that this little woman, who screamed at a mouse and was nervous about burglars, came to typify the cave mother rending her prey for her young.

It was less easy to regard philosophically the practical effects of her borrowed motherhood. Lethbury found with surprise that she was becoming assertive and definite. She no longer represented the negative side of his life; she showed, indeed, a tendency to inconvenient affirmations. She had gradually expanded her assumption of motherhood till it included his own share in the relation, and he suddenly found himself regarded as the father of Jane. This was a contingency he had not forseen, and it took all his philosophy to accept it; but there were moments of compensation. For Mrs. Lethbury was undoubtedly happy for the first time in years; and the thought that he had tardily contributed to this end reconciled him to the irony of the means.

At first he was inclined to reproach himself for still viewing the situation from the outside, for remaining a spectator instead of a participant. He had been allured, for a moment, by the vision of several hands meeting over a cradle, as the whole body of domestic fiction bears witness to their doing; and the fact that no such conjunction took place he could explain only on the ground that it was a borrowed cradle. He did not dislike the little girl. She still remained to him a hypothetical presence, a query rather than a fact; but her nearness was not unpleasant, and there were moments when her tentative utterances, her groping steps, seemed to loosen the dry accretions enveloping his inner self. But even at such moments—moments which he invited and caressed—she did not bring him nearer to his wife. He now perceived that he had made a certain place in his life for Mrs. Lethbury, and that she no longer fitted into it. It was too late to enlarge the space, and so she overflowed and encroached. Lethbury struggled against the sense of submergence. He let down barrier after barrier, yielding privacy after privacy; but his wife's personality continued to dilate. She was no longer herself alone: she was herself and Jane. Gradually, in a monstrous fusion of identity, she became herself, himself and Jane; and instead of trying to adapt her to a spare crevice of his character, he found himself carelessly squeezed into the smallest compartment of the domestic economy.

IV

He continued to tell himself that he was satisfied if his wife was happy; and it was not till the child's tenth year that he felt a doubt of her happiness.

Jane had been a preternaturally good child. During the eight years of her adoption she had caused her foster parents no anxiety beyond those connected with the usual succession of youthful diseases. But her unknown progenitors had given her a robust constitution, and she passed unperturbed through measles, chicken pox and whooping cough. If there was any suffering it was endured vicariously by Mrs. Lethbury, whose temperature rose and fell with the patient's, and who could not hear Jane sneeze without visions of a marble angel weeping over a broken column. But though Jane's prompt recoveries continued to belie such premonitions, though her existence continued to move forward on an even keel of good health and good conduct, Mrs. Lethbury's satisfaction showed no corresponding advance. Lethbury, at first, was disposed to add her disappointment to the long list of feminine inconsistencies with which the sententious observer of life builds up his favorable induction; but circumstances presently led him to take a kindlier view of the case.

Hitherto his wife had regarded him as a negligible factor in Jane's evolution. Beyond providing for his adopted daughter, and effacing himself before her, he was not expected to contribute to her well-being. But as time passed he appeared to his wife in a new light. It was he who was to educate Jane. In matters of the intellect, Mrs. Lethbury was the first to declare her deficiencies—to proclaim them, even, with a certain virtuous superiority. She said she did not pretend to be clever, and there was no denying the truth of the assertion. Now, however, she seemed less ready, not to own her limitations, but to glory in them. Confronted with the problem of Jane's instruction she stood in awe of the child.

"I have always been stupid, you know," she said to Lethbury with a new humility, "and I'm afraid I shan't know what is best for Jane. I'm sure she has a wonderfully good mind, and I should reproach myself if I didn't give her every opportunity." She looked at him helplessly. "You must tell me what ought to be done."

Lethbury was not unwilling to oblige her. Somewhere in his mental lumber room there rusted a theory of education such as usually lingers among the impedimenta of the childless. He brought this out, refurbished it, and applied it to Jane. At first he thought his wife had not overrated the quality of the child's mind. Jane seemed extraordinarily intelligent. Her precocious definiteness of mind was encouraging to her inexperienced preceptor. She had no difficulty in fixing her attention, and he felt that every fact he imparted was being etched in metal. He helped his wife to engage the best teachers, and for a while continued to take an ex-official interest in his adopted daughter's studies. But gradually his interest waned. Jane's ideas did not increase with her acquisitions. Her young mind remained a mere receptacle for facts: a kind of cold storage from which anything which had been put there could be taken out at a moment's notice, intact but congealed. She developed, moreover, an inordinate pride in the capacity of her mental storehouse, and a tendency to pelt her public with its contents. She was overheard to jeer at her nurse for not knowing when the Saxon Heptarchy had fallen, and she alternately dazzled and depressed Mrs. Lethbury by the wealth of her chronological allusions. She showed no interest in the significance of the facts she amassed: she simply collected dates as another child might have collected stamps or marbles. To her foster mother she seemed a prodigy of wisdom; but Lethbury saw, with a secret movement of sympathy, how the aptitudes in which Mrs. Lethbury gloried were slowly estranging her from her child.

"She is getting too clever for me," his wife said to him, after one of Jane's historical flights, "but I am so glad that she will be a companion to you."

Lethbury groaned in spirit. He did not look forward to Jane's companionship. She was still a good little girl; but there was something automatic and formal in her goodness, as though it were a kind of moral calisthenics which she went through for the sake of showing her agility. An early consciousness of virtue had moreover constituted her the natural guardian and adviser of her elders. Before she was fifteen she had set about reforming the household. She took Mrs. Lethbury in hand first; then she extended her efforts to the servants, with consequences more disastrous to the domestic harmony; and lastly she applied herself to Lethbury. She proved to him by statistics that he smoked too much, and that it was injurious to the optic nerve to read in bed. She took him to task for not going to church more regularly, and pointed out to him the evils of desultory reading. She suggested that a regular course of study encourages mental concentration, and hinted that inconsecutiveness of thought is a sign of approaching age.

To her adopted mother her suggestions were equally pertinent. She instructed Mrs. Lethbury in an improved way of making beef stock, and called her attention to the unhygienic qualities of carpets. She poured out distracting facts about bacilli and vegetable mold, and demonstrated that curtains and picture frames are a hotbed of animal organisms. She learned by heart the nutritive ingredients of the principal articles of diet, and revolutionized the cuisine by an attempt to establish a scientific average between starch and phosphates. Four cooks left during this experiment, and Lethbury fell into the habit of dining at his club.

Once or twice, at the outset, he had tried to check Jane's ardor; but his efforts resulted only in hurting his wife's feelings. Jane remained impervious, and Mrs. Lethbury resented any attempt to protect her from her daughter. Lethbury saw that she was consoled for the sense of her own inferiority by the thought of what Jane's intellectual companionship must be to him; and he tried to keep up the illusion by enduring with what grace he might the blighting edification of Jane's discourse.

V

As Jane grew up he sometimes avenged himself by wondering if his wife was still sorry that they had not called her Muriel. Jane was not ugly; she developed, indeed, a kind of categorical prettiness which might have been a projection of her mind. She had a creditable collection of features, but one had to take an inventory of them to find out that she was good-looking. The fusing grace had been omitted.

Mrs. Lethbury took a touching pride in her daughter's first steps in the world. She expected Jane to take by her complexion those whom she did not capture by her learning. But Jane's rosy freshness did not work any perceptible ravages. Whether the young men guessed the axioms on her lips and detected the encyclopedia in her eye, or whether they simply found no intrinsic interest in these features, certain it is, that, in spite of her mother's heroic efforts, and of incessant calls on Lethbury's purse, Jane, at the end of her first season, had dropped hopelessly out of the running. A few duller girls found her interesting, and one or two young men came to the house with the object of meeting other young women; but she was rapidly becoming one of the social supernumeraries who are asked out only because they are on people's lists.

The blow was bitter to Mrs. Lethbury; but she consoled herself with the idea that Jane had failed because she was too clever. Jane probably shared this conviction; at all events she betrayed no consciousness of failure. She had developed a pronounced taste for society, and went out, unweariedly and obstinately, winter after winter, while Mrs. Lethbury toiled in her wake, showering attentions on oblivious hostesses. To Lethbury there was something at once tragic and exasperating in the sight of their two figures, the one conciliatory, the other dogged, both pursuing with unabated zeal the elusive prize of popularity. He even began to feel a personal stake in the pursuit, not as it concerned Jane but as it affected his wife. He saw that the latter was the victim of Jane's disappointment: that Jane was not above the crude satisfaction of "taking it out" of her mother. Experience checked the impulse to come to his wife's defense; and when his resentment was at its height, Jane disarmed him by giving up the struggle.

Nothing was said to mark her capitulation; but Lethbury noticed that the visiting ceased and that the dressmaker's bills diminished. At the same time Mrs. Lethbury made it known that Jane had taken up charities; and before long Jane's conversation confirmed this announcement. At first Lethbury congratulated himself on the change; but Jane's domesticity soon began to weigh on him. During the day she was sometimes absent on errands of mercy; but in the evening she was always there. At first she and Mrs. Lethbury sat in the drawing-room together, and Lethbury smoked in the library; but presently Jane formed the habit of joining him there, and he began to suspect that he was included among the objects of her philanthropy.

Mrs. Lethbury confirmed the suspicion. "Jane has grown very serious-minded lately," she said. "She imagines that she used to neglect you and she is trying to make up for it. Don't discourage her," she added innocently.

Such a plea delivered Lethbury helpless to his daughter's ministrations; and he found himself measuring the hours he spent with her by the amount of relief they must be affording her mother. There were even moments when he read a furtive gratitude in Mrs. Lethbury's eye.

But Lethbury was no hero, and he had nearly reached the limit of vicarious endurance when something wonderful happened. They never quite knew afterwards how it had come about, or who first perceived it; but Mrs. Lethbury one day gave tremulous voice to their discovery.

"Of course," she said, "he comes here because of Elise." The young lady in question, a friend of Jane's, was possessed of attractions which had already been found to explain the presence of masculine visitors.

Lethbury risked a denial. "I don't think he does," he declared.

"But Elise is thought very pretty," Mrs. Lethbury insisted.

"I can't help that," said Lethbury doggedly.

He saw a faint light in his wife's eyes, but she remarked carelessly: "Mr. Budd would be a very good match for Elise."

Lethbury could hardly repress a chuckle: he was so exquisitely aware that she was trying to propitiate the gods.

For a few weeks neither said a word; then Mrs. Lethbury once more reverted to the subject.

"It is a month since Elise went abroad," she said.

"Is it?"

"And Mr. Budd seems to come here just as often—"

"Ah," said Lethbury with heroic indifference; and his wife hastily changed the subject.

Mr. Winstanley Budd was a young man who suffered from an excess of manner. Politeness gushed from him in the driest season. He was always performing feats of drawing-room chivalry, and the approach of the most unobtrusive female threw him into attitudes which endangered the furniture. His features, being of the cherubic order, did not lend themselves to this role; but there were moments when he appeared to dominate them, to force them into compliance with an aquiline ideal. The range of Mr. Budd's social benevolence made its object hard to distinguish. He spread his cloak so indiscriminately that one could not always interpret the gesture, and Jane's impassive manner had the effect of increasing his demonstrations: she threw him into paroxysms of politeness.

At first he filled the house with his amenities; but gradually it became apparent that his most dazzling effects were directed exclusively to Jane. Lethbury and his wife held their breath and looked away from each other. They pretended not to notice the frequency of Mr. Budd's visits, they struggled against an imprudent inclination to leave the young people too much alone. Their conclusions were the result of indirect observation, for neither of them dared to be caught watching Mr. Budd: they behaved like naturalists on the trail of a rare butterfly.

In his efforts not to notice Mr. Budd, Lethbury centered his attentions on Jane; and Jane, at this crucial moment, wrung from him a reluctant admiration. While her parents went about dissembling their emotions, she seemed to have none to conceal. She betrayed neither eagerness nor surprise; so complete was her unconcern that there were moments when Lethbury feared it was obtuseness, when he could hardly help whispering to her that now was the moment to lower the net.

Meanwhile the velocity of Mr. Budd's gyrations increased with the ardor of courtship: his politeness became incandescent, and Jane found herself the center of a pyrotechnical display culminating in the "set piece" of an offer of marriage.

Mrs. Lethbury imparted the news to her husband one evening after their daughter had gone to bed. The announcement was made and received with an air of detachment, as though both feared to be betrayed into unseemly exultation; but Lethbury, as his wife ended, could not repress the inquiry, "Have they decided on a day?"

Mrs. Lethbury's superior command of her features enabled her to look shocked. "What can you be thinking of? He only offered himself at five!"

"Of course—of course—" stammered Lethbury—"but nowadays people marry after such short engagements—"

"Engagement!" said his wife solemnly. "There is no engagement."

Lethbury dropped his cigar. "What on earth do you mean?"

"Jane is thinking it over."

"Thinking it over?"

"She has asked for a month before deciding."

Lethbury sank back with a gasp. Was it genius or was it madness? He felt incompetent to decide; and Mrs. Lethbury's next words showed that she shared his difficulty.

"Of course I don't want to hurry Jane—"

"Of course not," he acquiesced.

"But I pointed out to her that a young man of Mr. Budd's impulsive temperament might—might be easily discouraged—"

"Yes; and what did she say?"

"She said that if she was worth winning she was worth waiting for."

VI

The period of Mr. Budd's probation could scarcely have cost him as much mental anguish as it caused his would-be parents-in-law.

Mrs. Lethbury, by various ruses, tried to shorten the ordeal, but Jane remained inexorable; and each morning Lethbury came down to breakfast with the certainty of finding a letter of withdrawal from her discouraged suitor.

When at length the decisive day came, and Mrs. Lethbury, at its close, stole into the library with an air of chastened joy, they stood for a moment without speaking; then Mrs. Lethbury paid a fitting tribute to the proprieties by faltering out: "It will be dreadful to have to give her up—"

Lethbury could not repress a warning gesture; but even as it escaped him he realized that his wife's grief was genuine.

"Of course, of course," he said, vainly sounding his own emotional

shallows for an answering regret. And yet it was his wife who had
suffered most from Jane!

He had fancied that these sufferings would be effaced by the milder
atmosphere of their last weeks together; but felicity did not soften
Jane. Not for a moment did she relax her dominion: she simply widened
it to include a new subject. Mr. Budd found himself under orders with
the others; and a new fear assailed Lethbury as he saw Jane assume
pre-nuptial control of her betrothed. Lethbury had never felt any
strong personal interest in Mr. Budd; but as Jane's prospective husband
the young man excited his sympathy. To his surprise he found that Mrs.
Lethbury shared the feeling.

"I'm afraid he may find Jane a little exacting," she said, after an
evening dedicated to a stormy discussion of the wedding arrangements.
"She really ought to make some concessions. If he *wants* to be married
in a black frock coat instead of a dark gray one—" She paused and looked
doubtfully at Lethbury.

"What can I do about it?" he said.

"You might explain to him—tell him that Jane isn't always—"

Lethbury made an impatient gesture. "What are you afraid of? His
finding her out or his not finding her out?"

Mrs. Lethbury flushed. "You put it so dreadfully!"

Her husband mused for a moment; then he said with an air of cheerful hypocrisy: "After all, Budd is old enough to take care of himself."

But the next day Mrs. Lethbury surprised him. Late in the afternoon
she entered the library, so breathless and inarticulate that he scented a
catastrophe.

"I've done it!" she cried.

"Done what?"

"Told him." She nodded toward the door. "He's just gone. Jane is
out, and I had a chance to talk to him alone."

Lethbury pushed a chair forward and she sank into it.

"What did you tell him? That she is *not* always—"

Mrs. Lethbury lifted a tragic eye. "No; I told him that she always
is—"

"Always *is*—?"

"Yes."

There was a pause. Lethbury made a call on his hoarded philosophy.
He saw Jane suddenly reinstated in her evening seat by the library
fire; but an answering chord in him thrilled at his wife's heroism.

"Well—what did he say?"

Mrs. Lethbury's agitation deepened. It was clear that the blow had
fallen.

"He . . . he said . . . that we . . . had never understood Jane . . ."

or appreciated her . . ." The final syllables were lost in her handkerchief, and she left him marveling at the mechanism of woman.

After that, Lethbury faced the future with an undaunted eye. They had done their duty—at least his wife had done hers—and they were reaping the usual harvest of ingratitude with a zest seldom accorded to such reaping. There was a marked change in Mr. Budd's manner, and his increasing coldness sent a genial glow through Lethbury's system. It was easy to bear with Jane in the light of Mr. Budd's disapproval.

There was a good deal to be borne in the last days, and the brunt of it fell on Mrs. Lethbury. Jane marked her transition to the married state by a seasonable but incongruous display of nerves. She became sentimental, hysterical and reluctant. She quarrelled with her betrothed and threatened to return the ring. Mrs. Lethbury had to intervene, and Lethbury felt the hovering sword of destiny. But the blow was suspended. Mr. Budd's chivalry was proof against all his bride's caprices and his devotion throve on her cruelty. Lethbury feared that he was too faithful, too enduring, and longed to urge him to vary his tactics. Jane presently reappeared with the ring on her finger, and consented to try on the wedding dress; but her uncertainties, her reactions, were prolonged till the final day.

When it dawned, Lethbury was still in an ecstasy of apprehension. Feeling reasonably sure of the principal actors he had centered his fears on incidental possibilities. The clergyman might have a stroke, or the church might burn down, or there might be something wrong with the license. He did all that was humanly possible to avert such contingencies, but there remained that incalculable factor known as the hand of God. Lethbury seemed to feel it groping for him.

At the altar it almost had him by the nape. Mr. Budd was late; and for five immeasurable minutes Lethbury and Jane faced a churchful of conjecture. Then the bridegroom appeared, flushed but chivalrous, and explaining to his father-in-law under cover of the ritual that he had torn his glove and had to go back for another.

"You'll be losing the ring next," muttered Lethbury; but Mr. Budd produced this article punctually, and a moment or two later was bearing its wearer captive down the aisle.

At the wedding breakfast Lethbury caught his wife's eye fixed on him in mild disapproval, and understood that his hilarity was exceeding the bounds of fitness. He pulled himself together and tried to subdue his tone; but his jubilation bubbled over like a champagne glass perpetually refilled. The deeper his draughts the higher it rose.

It was at the brim when, in the wake of the dispersing guests, Jane came down in her traveling dress and fell on her mother's neck.

"I can't leave you!" she wailed, and Lethbury felt as suddenly sobered as a man under a douche. But if the bride was reluctant her captor was relentless. Never had Mr. Budd been more dominant, more aquiline. Lethbury's last fears were dissipated as the young man snatched Jane from her mother's bosom and bore her off to the brougham.

The brougham rolled away, the last milliner's girl forsook her post by the awning, the red carpet was folded up, and the house door closed. Lethbury stood alone in the hall with his wife. As he turned toward her, he noticed the look of tired heroism in her eyes, the deepened lines of her face. They reflected his own symptoms too accurately not to appeal to him. The nervous tension had been horrible. He went up to her, and an answering impulse made her lay a hand on his arm. He held it there a moment.

"Let us go off and have a jolly little dinner at a restaurant," he proposed.

There had been a time when such a suggestion would have surprised her to the verge of disapproval; but now she agreed to it at once.

"Oh, that would be so nice," she murmured with a great sigh of relief and assuagement.

Jane had fulfilled her mission after all: she had drawn them together at last.

28

The Furnished Room

BY O. HENRY

Restless, shifting, fugacious as time itself is a certain vast bulk of the population of the red brick district of the lower West Side. Homeless, they have a hundred homes. They flit from furnished room to furnished room, transients forever—transients in abode, transients in heart and mind. They sing "Home, Sweet Home" in ragtime; they carry their *lares et penates* in a bandbox; their vine is entwined about a picture hat; a rubber plant is their fig tree.

Hence the houses of this district, having had a thousand dwellers, should have a thousand tales to tell, mostly dull ones, no doubt; but it would be strange if there could not be found a ghost or two in the wake of all these vagrant guests.

One evening after dark a young man prowled among these crumbling red mansions, ringing their bells. At the twelfth he rested his lean hand-baggage upon the step and wiped the dust from his hatband and forehead. The bell sounded faint and far away in some remote, hollow depths.

To the door of this, the twelfth house whose bell he had rung, came a housekeeper who made him think of an unwholesome, surfeited worm that had eaten its nut to a hollow shell and now sought to fill the vacancy with edible lodgers.

He asked if there was a room to let.

"Come in," said the housekeeper. Her voice came from her throat; her throat seemed lined with fur. "I have the third-floor-back, vacant since a week back. Should you wish to look at it?"

The young man followed her up the stairs. A faint light trom no particular source mitigated the shadows of the halls. They trod noiselessly upon a stair carpet that its own loom would have forsworn. It seemed to have become vegetable; to have degenerated in that rank, sunless air to lush lichen or spreading moss that grew in patches to the staircase and was viscid under the foot like organic matter. At each turn of the stairs were vacant niches in the wall. Perhaps plants had once been set within them. If so they had died in that foul and tainted air. It may be that statues of the saints had stood there, but it was not difficult to conceive that imps and devils had dragged them forth in the darkness and down to the unholy depths of some furnished pit below.

"This is the room," said the housekeeper, from her furry throat. "It's a nice room. It ain't often vacant. I had some most elegant people in it last summer—no trouble at all, and paid in advance to the minute. The water's at the end of the hall. Sprowls and Mooney kept it three months. They done a vaudeville sketch. Miss B'retta Sprowls—you may have heard of her—oh, that was just the stage names—right there over the dresser is where the marriage certificate hung, framed. The gas is here, and you see there is plenty of closet room. It's a room everybody likes. It never stays idle long."

"Do you have many theatrical people rooming here?" asked the young man.

"They comes and goes. A good proportion of my lodgers is connected with the theaters. Yes, sir, this is the theatrical district. Actor people never stays long anywhere. I get my share. Yes, they comes and they goes."

He engaged the room, paying for a week in advance. He was tired, he said, and would take possession at once. He counted out the money. The room had been made ready, she said, even to towels and water. As the housekeeper moved away he put, for the thousandth time, the question that he carried at the end of his tongue.

"A young girl—Miss Vashner—Miss Eloise Vashner—do you remember such a one among your lodgers? She would be singing on the stage, most likely. A fair girl, of medium height and slender, with reddish, gold hair and dark mole near her left eyebrow."

"No, I don't remember the name. Them stage people has names they change as often as their rooms. They comes and they goes. No, I don't call that one to mind."

No. Always no. Five months of ceaseless interrogation and the inevitable negative. So much time spent by days in questioning managers, agents, schools and choruses; by night among the audiences of theaters from all-star casts down to music halls so low that he dreaded to find what he most hoped for. He who had loved her best had tried to find her. He was sure that since her disappearance from home this great, water-girt city held her somewhere, but it was like a monstrous quicksand, shifting its particles constantly, with no foundation, its upper granules of today buried tomorrow in ooze and slime.

The furnished room received its latest guest with a first glow of pseudo-hospitality, a hectic, haggard, perfunctory welcome like the specious smile of a demirep. The sophistical comfort came in reflected gleams from the decayed furniture, the ragged brocade upholstery of a couch and two chairs, a foot-wide cheap pier glass between the two windows, from one or two gilt picture frames and a brass bedstead in a corner.

The guest reclined, inert, upon a chair, while the room, confused in speech as though it were an apartment in Babel, tried to discourse to him of its divers tenantry.

A polychromatic rug like some brilliant-flowered rectangular, tropical islet lay surrounded by a billowy sea of soiled matting. Upon the gay-papered wall were those pictures that pursue the homeless one from house to house—The Huguenot Lovers, The First Quarrel, The Wedding Breakfast, Psyche at the Fountain. The mantel's chastely severe outline was ingloriously veiled behind some pert drapery drawn rakishly askew like the sashes of the Amazonian ballet. Upon it was some desolate flotsam cast aside by the room's marooned when a lucky sail had borne them to a fresh port—a trifling vase or two, pictures of actresses, a medicine bottle, some stray cards out of a deck.

One by one, as the characters of a cryptograph became explicit, the little signs left by the furnished room's procession of guests developed a significance. The threadbare space in the rug in front of the dresser told that lovely woman had marched in the throng. The tiny fingerprints on the wall spoke of little prisoners trying to feel their way to sun and air. A splattered stain, raying like the shadow of a bursting bomb, witnessed where a hurled glass or bottle had splintered with its contents against the wall. Across the pier glass had been scrawled with a diamond in staggering letters the name "Marie." It seemed that the succession of dwellers in the furnished room had turned in fury—perhaps tempted beyond forebearance by its garish coldness—and wreaked upon it their passions. The furniture was chipped and bruised; the couch, distorted by bursting springs, seemed a horrible monster that had been slain during the stress of some grotesque convulsion. Some more potent upheaval had cloven a great slice from the marble mantel. Each plank in the floor owned its particular cant and shriek as from a separate and individual agony. It seemed incredible that all this malice and injury had been wrought upon the room by those who had called it for a time their home; and yet it may have been the cheated home instinct surviving blindly, the resentful rage at false household gods that had kindled their wrath. A hut that is our own we can sweep and adorn and cherish.

The young tenant in the chair allowed these thoughts to file, soft-shod, through his mind, while there drifted into the room furnished sounds and furnished scents. He heard in one room a tittering and incontinent, slack laughter; in others the monologue of a scold, the rattling of dice, a lullaby, and one crying dully; above him a banjo tinkled with spirit. Doors banged somewhere; the elevated trains roared intermittently; a cat yowled miserably upon a back fence. And he breathed the breath of the house—a dank savor rather than a smell—a cold, musty effluvium as from underground vaults mingled with the reeking exhalations of linoleum and mildewed and rotten woodwork.

Then suddenly, as he rested there, the room was filled with the strong, sweet odor of mignonette. It came as upon a single buffet of wind with such sureness and fragrance and emphasis that it almost seemed a living visitant. And the man cried aloud: "What, dear?" as if he had been called, and sprang up and faced about. The rich odor clung to him and wrapped him around. He reached out his arms for it, all his senses for the time confused and commingled. How could one be peremptorily called by an odor? Surely it must have been a sound. But, was it not the sound that had touched, that had caressed him?

"She has been in this room," he cried, and he sprang to wrest from it a token, for he knew he would recognize the smallest thing that had belonged to her or that she had touched. This enveloping scent of mignonette, the odor that she had loved and made her own—whence came it?

The room had been but carelessly set in order. Scattered upon the flimsy dresser scarf were half a dozen hairpins—those discreet, indistinguishable friends of womankind, feminine of gender, infinite mood and uncommunicative of tense. These he ignored, conscious of their triumphant lack of identity. Ransacking the drawers of the dresser he came upon a discarded, tiny, ragged handkerchief. He pressed it to his face. It was racy and insolent with heliotrope; he hurled it to the floor. In another drawer he found odd buttons, a theater program, a pawnbroker's card, two lost marshmallows, a book on the divination of dreams. In the last was a woman's black satin hair bow, which halted him, poised between ice and fire. But the black satin hair bow also is femininity's demure, impersonal common ornament and tells no tales.

And then he traversed the room like a hound on the scent, skimming the walls, considering the corners of the bulging matting on his hands and knees, rummaging mantel and tables, the curtains and hangings, the drunken cabinet in the corner, for a visible sign, unable to perceive that she was there beside, around, against, within, above him, clinging to him, wooing him, calling him so poignantly through the finer senses that even his grosser ones became cognizant of the call. Once again he answered loudly: "Yes, dear!" and turned, wild-eyed, to gaze on vacancy, for he could not yet discern form and color and love and outstretched arms in the odor of mignonette. Oh, God! whence that odor, and since when have odors had a voice to call? Thus he groped.

He burrowed in crevices and corners, and found corks and cigarettes. These he passed in passive contempt. But once he found in a fold of the matting a half-smoked cigar, and this he ground beneath his heel with a green and trenchant oath. He sifted the room from end to end. He found dreary and ignoble small records of many a peripatetic tenant; but of her whom he sought, and who may have lodged there, and whose spirit seemed to hover there, he found no trace.

And then he thought of the housekeeper.

He ran from the haunted room downstairs and to a door that showed a crack of light. She came out to his knock. He smothered his excitement as best he could.

"Will you tell me, madam," he besought her, "who occupied the room I have before I came?"

"Yes, sir. I can tell you again. 'Twas Sprowls and Mooney, as I said. Miss B'retta Sprowls it was in the theaters, but Missis Mooney she was. My house is well known for respectability. The marriage certificate hung, framed, on a nail over—"

"What kind of a lady was Miss Sprowls—in looks, I mean?"

"Why, black-haired, sir, short, and stout, with a comical face. They left a week ago Tuesday."

"And before they occupied it?"

"Why, there was a single gentleman connected with the draying business. He left owing me a week. Before him was Missis Crowder and her two children, that stayed four months; and back of them was old Mr. Doyle, whose sons paid for him. He kept the room six months. That goes back a year, sir, and further I do not remember."

He thanked her and crept back to his room. The room was dead. The essence that had vivified it was gone. The perfume of mignonette had departed. In its place was the old, stale odor of moldy house furniture, of atmosphere in storage.

The ebbing of his hope drained his faith. He sat staring at the yellow, singing gaslight. Soon he walked to the bed and began to tear the sheets into strips. With the blade of his knife he drove them tightly into every crevice around windows and door. When all was snug and taut he turned out the light, turned the gas full on again and laid himself gratefully upon the bed.

It was Mrs. McCool's night to go with the can for beer. So she fetched it and sat with Mrs. Purdy in one of those subterranean retreats where housekeepers foregather and the worm dieth seldom.

"I rented out my third-floor-back this evening," said Mrs. Purdy, across a fine circle of foam. "A young man took it. He went up to bed two hours ago."

"Now, did ye, Mrs. Purdy, ma'am?" said Mrs. McCool, with intense admiration. "You do be a wonder for rentin' rooms of that kind. And did ye tell him, then?" she concluded in a husky whisper laden with mystery.

"Rooms," said Mrs. Purdy, in her furriest tones, "are furnished for to rent. I did not tell him, Mrs. McCool."

" 'Tis right ye are, ma'am; 'tis by renting rooms we kape alive. Ye have the rale sense for business, ma'am. There be many people will rayjict the rentin' of a room if they be tould a suicide has been after dyin' in the bed of it."

"As you say, we has our living to be making," remarked Mrs. Purdy.

"Yis, ma'am; 'tis true. 'Tis just one wake ago this day I helped ye lay out the third-floor-back. A pretty slip of a colleen she was to be killin' herself wid the gas—a swate little face she had, Mrs. Purdy, ma'am."

"She'd a-been called handsome, as you say," said Mrs. Purdy, assenting but critical, "but for that mole she had a-growin' by her left eyebrow. Do fill up your glass again, Mrs. McCool."

29

A Blackjack Bargainer

BY O. HENRY

THE most disreputable thing in Yancey Goree's law office was Goree himself, sprawled in his creaky old armchair. The rickety little office, built of red brick, was set flush with the street—the main street of the town of Bethel.

Bethel rested upon the foothills of the Blue Ridge. Above it the mountains were piled to the sky. Far below it the turbid Catawba gleamed yellow along its disconsolate valley.

The June day was at its sultriest hour. Bethel dozed in the tepid shade. Trade was not. It was so still that Goree, reclining in his chair, distinctly heard the clicking of the chips in the grand-jury room, where the "court-house gang" was playing poker. From the open back door of the office a well-worn path meandered across the grassy lot to the court-house. The treading out of that path had cost Goree all he ever had—first, inheritance of a few thousand dollars, next, the old family home, and, latterly, the last shreds of his self-respect and manhood. The "gang" had cleaned him out. The broken gambler had turned drunkard and parasite; he had lived to see this day come when the men who had stripped him denied him a seat at the game. His word was no longer to be taken. The daily bout at cards had arranged itself accordingly, and to him was assigned the ignoble part of the onlooker. The sheriff, the county clerk, a sportive deputy, a gay attorney, and a chalk-faced man hailing "from the valley," sat at table, and the sheared one was thus tacitly advised to go and grow more wool.

Soon wearying of his ostracism, Goree had departed for his office, muttering to himself as he unsteadily traversed the unlucky pathway. After a drink of corn whisky from a demijohn under the table, he had flung himself into the chair, staring, in a sort of maudlin apathy, out at the mountains immersed in the summer haze. The little white patch he saw away up on the side of Blackjack was Laurel, the village near which he had been born and bred. There, also, was the birthplace of the feud between the Gorees and the Coltranes. Now no direct heir of the Gorees survived except this plucked and singed bird of misfortune. To the Coltranes, also, but one male supporter was left—Colonel Abner Coltrane, a man of substance and standing, a member of the State Legislature, and a contemporary with Goree's father. The feud had been a typical one of the region; it had left a red record of hate, wrong, and slaughter.

But Yancey Goree was not thinking of feuds. His befuddled brain was hopelessly attacking the problem of the future maintenance of himself and his favorite follies. Of late, old friends of the family had seen to it that he had whereof to eat and a place to sleep, but whisky they would not buy for him, and he must have whisky. His law business was extinct; no case had been intrusted to him in two years. He had been a borrower and a sponge, and it seemed that if he fell no lower it would be from lack of opportunity. One more chance—he was saying to himself —if he had one more stake at the game, he thought he could win; but he had nothing left to sell, and his credit was more than exhausted.

He could not help smiling, even in his misery, as he thought of the man to whom, six months before, he had sold the old Goree homestead. There had come from "back yan' " in the mountains two of the strangest creatures, a man named Pike Garvey and his wife. "Back yan'," with a wave of the hand toward the hills, was understood among the mountaineers to designate the remotest fastnesses, the unplumbed gorges, the haunts of lawbreakers, the wolf's den, and the boudoir of the bear. In the cabin far up on Blackjack's shoulder, in the wildest part of these retreats, this odd couple had lived for twenty years. They had neither dog nor children to mitigate the heavy silence of the hills. Pike Garvey was little known in the settlements, but all who had dealt with him pronounced him "crazy as a loon." He acknowledged no occupation save that of a squirrel hunter, but he "moonshined" occasionally by way of diversion. Once the "revenues" had dragged him from his lair, fighting silently and desperately like a terrier, and he had been sent to state's prison for two years. Released, he popped back into his hole like an angry weasel.

Fortune, passing over many anxious wooers, made a freakish flight into Blackjack's bosky pockets to smile upon Pike and his faithful partner.

One day a party of spectacled, knickerbockered, and altogether absurd prospectors invaded the vicinity of the Garveys' cabin. Pike lifted his squirrel rifle off the hook and took a shot at them at long range on the chance of their being revenues. Happily he missed, and the unconscious agents of good luck drew nearer, disclosing their innocence of anything resembling law or justice. Later on, they offered the Garveys an enormous quantity of ready, green, crisp money for their thirty-acre patch of cleared land, mentioning, as an excuse for such a mad action, some irrelevant and inadequate nonsense about a bed of mica underlying the said property.

When the Garveys became possessed of so many dollars that they faltered in computing them, the deficiencies of life on Blackjack began to grow prominent. Pike began to talk of new shoes, a hogshead of tobacco to set in the corner, a new lock to his rifle; and, leading Martella to a certain spot on the mountainside, he pointed out to her how a small cannon—doubtless a thing not beyond the scope of their fortune in price —might be planted so as to command and defend the sole accessible trail to the cabin, to the confusion of revenues and meddling strangers forever.

But Adam reckoned without his Eve. These things represented to him the applied power of wealth, but there slumbered in his dingy cabin an ambition that soared far above his primitive wants. Somewhere in Mrs. Garvey's bosom still survived a spot of femininity unstarved by twenty years of Blackjack. For so long a time the sounds in her ears had been the scaly-barks dropping in the woods at noon, and the wolves singing among the rocks at night, and it was enough to have purged her vanities. She had grown fat and sad and yellow and dull. But when the means came, she felt a rekindled desire to assume the perquisites of her sex— to sit at tea tables; to buy inutile things; to whitewash the hideous veracity of life with a little form and ceremony. So she coldly vetoed Pike's proposed system of fortifications, and announced that they would descend upon the world, and gyrate socially.

And thus, at length, it was decided, and the thing done. The village of Laurel was their compromise between Mrs. Garvey's preference for one of the large valley towns and Pike's hankering for primeval solitudes. Laurel yielded a halting round of feeble social distractions comportable with Martella's ambitions, and was not entirely without recommendation to Pike, its contiguity to the mountains presenting advantages for sudden retreat in case fashionable society should make it advisable.

Their descent upon Laurel had been coincident with Yancey Goree's feverish desire to convert property into cash, and they bought the old Goree homestead, paying four thousand dollars ready money into the spendthrift's shaking hand.

Thus it happened that while the disreputable last of the Gorees sprawled in his disreputable office, at the end of his row, spurned by the cronies whom he had gorged, strangers dwelt in the halls of his fathers.

A cloud of dust was rolling slowly up the parched street, with something traveling in the midst of it. A little breeze wafted the cloud to one side, and a new, brightly painted carryall, drawn by a slothful gray horse, became visible. The vehicle deflected from the middle of the street as it neared Goree's office, and stopped in the gutter directly in front of his door.

On the front seat sat a gaunt, tall man, dressed in black broadcloth, his rigid hands incarcerated in yellow kid gloves. On the back seat was a lady who triumphed over the June heat. Her stout form was armored in a skin-tight silk dress of the description known as "changeable," being a gorgeous combination of shifting hues. She sat erect, waving a much-ornamented fan, with her eyes fixed stonily far down the street. However Martella Garvey's heart might be rejoicing at the pleasures of her new life, Blackjack had done his work with her exterior. He had carved her countenance to the image of emptiness and inanity; had imbued her with the stolidity of his crags and the reserve of his hushed interiors. She always seemed to hear, whatever her surroundings were, the scaly-barks falling and pattering down the mountainside. She could always hear the awful silence of Blackjack sounding through the stillest of nights.

Goree watched this solemn equipage, as it drove to his door, with only faint interest; but when the lank driver wrapped the reins about his whip, and awkwardly descended, and stepped into the office, he rose unsteadily to receive him, recognizing Pike Garvey, the new, the transformed, the recently civilized.

The mountaineer took the chair Goree offered him. They who cast doubts upon Garvey's soundness of mind had a strong witness in the man's countenance. His face was too long, a dull saffron in hue, and immobile as a statue's. Pale-blue, unwinking round eyes without lashes added to the singularity of his gruesome visage. Goree was at a loss to account for the visit.

"Everything all right at Laurel, Mr. Garvey?" he inquired.

"Everything all right, sir, and mighty pleased is Missis Garvey and me with the property. Missis Garvey likes yo' old place, and she likes the neighborhood. Society is what she 'lows she wants, and she is gettin' of it. The Rogerses, the Hapgoods, the Pratts, and the Troys hev been to see Missis Garvey, and she hev et meals to most of thar houses. The best folks hev axed her to differ'nt kinds of doin's. I cyan't say, Mr. Goree, that sech things suits me—fur me, give me them thar." Garvey's huge yellow-gloved hand flourished in the direction of the mountains. "That's whar I b'long, 'mongst the wild honey bees and the b'ars. But that ain't what I come fur to say, Mr. Goree. Thar's somethin' you got what me and Missis Garvey wants to buy."

"Buy!" echoed Goree. "From me?" Then he laughed harshly. "I reckon you are mistaken about that. I sold out to you, as you yourself expressed it, 'lock, stock, and barrel.' There isn't even a ramrod left to sell."

"You've got it; and we 'uns want it. 'Take the money,' says Missis Garvey, 'and buy it fa'r and squar'.' "

Goree shook his head. "The cupboard's bare," he said.

"We've riz," pursued the mountaineer, undeflected from his object, "a heap. We was pore as possums, and now we could hev folks to dinner every day. We been reco'nized, Missis Garvey says, by the best society. But there's somethin' we need we ain't got. She says it ought to been put in the 'ventory ov the sale, but it 'tain't thar. 'Take the money, then,' she says, 'and buy it fa'r and squar'.' "

"Out with it," said Goree, his racked nerves growing impatient.

Garvey threw his slouch hat upon the table, and leaned forward, fixing his unblinking eyes upon Goree's.

"There's a old feud," he said, distinctly and slowly, " 'tween you 'uns and the Coltranes."

Goree frowned ominously. To speak of his feud to a feudist is a serious breach of the mountain etiquette. The man from "back yan'" knew it as well as the lawyer did.

"Na offense," he went on, "but purely in the way of business. Missis Garvey hev studied all about feuds. Most of the quality folks in the mountains hev 'em. The Settles and the Goforths, the Rankins and the Boyds, the Silers and the Galloways, hev all been cyarin' on feuds f'om twenty to a hundred year. The last man to drap was when yo' uncle, Jedge Paisley Goree, 'journed co't and shot Len Coltrane f'om the bench. Missis Garvey and me, we come f'om the po' white trash. Nobody wouldn't pick a feud with we'uns, no mo'n with a fam'ly of tree toads. Quality people everywhar, says Missis Garvey, has feuds. We 'uns ain't quality, but we're buyin' into it as fur as we can. 'Take the money, then,' says Missis Garvey, 'and buy Mr. Goree's feud, fa'r and squar'.' "

The squirrel hunter straightened a leg half across the room, drew a roll of bills from his pocket, and threw them on the table.

"Thar's two hundred dollars, Mr. Goree; what you would call a fa'r price for a feud that's been 'lowed to run down like yourn hev. Thar's only you left to cyar' on yo' side of it, and you'd make mighty po' killin'. I'll take it off yo' hands, and it'll set me and Missis Garvey up among the quality. Thar's the money."

The little roll of currency on the table slowly untwisted itself, writhing and jumping as its folds relaxed. In the silence that followed Garvey's last speech the rattling of the poker chips in the court-house could be plainly heard. Goree knew that the sheriff had just won a pot, for the subdued whoop with which he always greeted a victory floated across the square upon the crinkly heat waves. Beads of moisture stood on Goree's brow. Stooping, he drew the wicker-covered demijohn from under the table, and filled a tumbler from it.

"A little corn liquor, Mr. Garvey? Of course you are joking about— what you spoke of? Opens quite a new market, doesn't it? Feuds, prime, two-fifty to three. Feuds, slightly damaged—two hundred, I believe you said, Mr. Garvey?"

Goree laughed self-consciously.

The mountaineer took the glass Goree handed him, and drank the whisky without a tremor of the lids of his staring eyes. The lawyer applauded the feat by a look of envious admiration. He poured his own drink, and took it like a drunkard, by gulps, and with shudders at the smell and taste.

"Two hundred," repeated Garvey. "Thar's the money."

A sudden passion flared up in Goree's brain. He struck the table with his fist. One of the bills flipped over and touched his hand. He flinched as if something had stung him.

"Do you come to me," he shouted, "seriously with such a ridiculous, insulting, darned-fool proposition?"

"It's fa'r and squar'," said the squirrel hunter, but he reached out his hand as if to take back the money; and then Goree knew that his own flurry of rage had not been from pride or resentment, but from anger at himself, knowing that he would set foot in the deeper depths that were being opened to him. He turned in an instant from an outraged gentleman to an anxious chafferer recommending his goods.

"Don't be in a hurry, Garvey," he said, his face crimson and his speech thick. "I accept your p-p-proposition, though it's dirt cheap at two hundred. A t-trade's all right when both p-purchaser and b-buyer are s-satisfied. Shall I w-wrap it up for you, Mr. Garvey?"

Garvey rose, and shook out his broadcloth. "Missis Garvey will be pleased. You air out of it, and it stands Coltrane and Garvey. Just a scrap ov writin', Mr. Goree, you bein' a lawyer, to show we traded."

Goree seized a sheet of paper and a pen. The money was clutched in his moist hand. Everything else suddenly seemed to grow trivial and light.

"Bill of sale, by all means. 'Right, title, and interest in and to' . . . 'forever warrant and—' No, Garvey, we'll have to leave out that 'defend'," said Goree with a loud laugh. "You'll have to defend this title yourself."

The mountaineer received the amazing screed that the lawyer handed him, folded it with immense labor, and placed it carefully in his pocket.

Goree was standing near the window. "Step here," he said, raising his finger, "and I'll show you your recently purchased enemy. There he goes, down the other side of the street."

The mountaineer crooked his long frame to look through the window in the direction indicated by the other. Colonel Abner Coltrane, an erect, portly gentleman of about fifty wearing the inevitable long, double-breasted frock coat of the Southern lawmaker, and an old high silk hat, was passing on the opposite sidewalk. As Garvey looked, Goree glanced at his face. If there be such a thing as a yellow wolf, here was its counterpart. Garvey snarled as his unhuman eyes followed the moving figure, disclosing long amber-colored fangs.

"Is that him? Why, that's the man who sent me to the pen'tentiary once!"

"He used to be district attorney," said Goree, carelessly. "And, by the way, he's a first-class shot."

"I kin hit a squirrel's eye at a hundred yard," said Garvey. "So that thar's Coltrane! I made a better trade than I was thinkin'. I'll take keer ov this feud, Mr. Goree, better'n you ever did!"

He moved toward the door, but lingered there, betraying a slight perplexity.

"Anything else today?" inquired Goree with frothy sarcasm. "Any family traditions, ancestral ghosts, or skeletons in the closet? Prices as low as the lowest."

"Thar was another thing," replied the unmoved squirrel hunter, "that Missis Garvey was thinkin' of. 'Tain't so much in my line as t'other, but she wanted partic'lar that I should inquire, and ef you was willin', 'pay fur it,' she says, 'fa'r and squar'.' Thar's a buryin' groun', as you know, Mr. Goree, in the yard of yo' old place, under the cedars. Them that lies thar is yo folks what was killed by the Coltranes. The monuments has the names on 'em. Missis Garvey says a fam'ly buryin' groun' is a sho' sign of quality. She says ef we git the feud, thar's somethin' else ought to go with it. The names on them monuments is 'Goree,' but they can be changed to ourn by——"

"Go! Go!" screamed Goree, his face turning purple. He stretched out both hands toward the mountaineer, his fingers hooked and shaking. "Go, you ghoul! Even a Ch-Chinaman protects the g-graves of his ancestors—go!"

The squirrel hunter slouched out of the door to his carryall. While he was climbing over the wheel Goree was collecting, with feverish celerity, the money that had fallen from his hand to the floor. As the vehicle slowly turned about, the sheep, with a coat of newly grown wool, was hurrying, in indecent haste, along the path to the court-house.

At three o'clock in the morning they brought him back to his office, shorn and unconscious. The sheriff, the sportive deputy, the county clerk, and the gay attorney carried him, the chalk-faced man "from the valley" acting as escort.

"On the table," said one of them, and they deposited him there among the litter of his unprofitable books and papers.

"Yance thinks a lot of a pair of deuces when he's liquored up," sighed the sheriff, reflectively.

"Too much," said the gay attorney. "A man has no business to play poker who drinks as much as he does. I wonder how much he dropped tonight."

"Close to two hundred. What I wonder is whar he got it. Yance ain't had a cent fur over a month, I know."

"Struck a client, maybe. Well, let's get home before daylight. He'll be all right when he wakes up, except for a sort of beehive about the cranium."

The gang slipped away through the early morning twilight. The next eye to gaze upon the miserable Goree was the orb of day. He peered through the uncurtained window, first deluging the sleeper in a flood of faint gold, but soon pouring upon the mottled red of his flesh a searching, white, summer heat. Goree stirred, half unconsciously, among the table's débris, and turned his face from the window. His movement dislodged a heavy law book, which crashed upon the floor. Opening his eyes, he saw, bending over him, a man in a black frock coat. Looking higher, he discovered a well-worn silk hat, and beneath it the kindly, smooth face of Colonel Abner Coltrane.

A little uncertain of the outcome, the colonel waited for the other to make some sign of recognition. Not in twenty years had male members of these two families faced each other in peace. Goree's eyelids puckered as he strained his blurred sight toward this visitor, and then he smiled serenely.

"Have you brought Stella and Lucy over to play?" he said, calmly.

"Do you know me, Yancey?" asked Coltrane.

"Of course I do. You brought me a whip with a whistle in the end."

So he had—twenty-four years ago; when Yancey's father was his best friend.

Goree's eyes wandered about the room. The colonel understood. "Lie still, and I'll bring you some," said he. There was a pump in the yard at the rear, and Goree closed his eyes, listening with rapture to the click of its handle and the bubbling of the falling stream. Coltrane brought a pitcher of the cool water, and held it for him to drink. Presently Goree sat up—a most forlorn object, his summer suit of flax soiled and crumpled, his discreditable head tousled and unsteady. He tried to wave one of his hands toward the colonel.

"Ex-excuse—everything, will you?" he said. "I must have drunk too much whisky last night, and gone to bed on the table." His brows knitted into a puzzled frown.

"Out with the boys a while?" asked Coltrane, kindly.

"No, I went nowhere. I haven't had a dollar to spend in the last two months. Struck the demijohn too often, I reckon, as usual."

Colonel Coltrane touched him on the shoulder.

"A little while ago, Yancey," he began, "you asked me if I had brought Stella and Lucy over to play. You weren't quite awake then, and must have been dreaming you were a boy again. You are awake now, and I want you to listen to me. I have come from Stella and Lucy to their old playmate, and to my old friend's son. They know that I am going to bring you home with me, and you will find them as ready with a welcome as they were in the old days. I want you to come to my house and stay until you are yourself again, and as much longer as you will. We heard of your being down in the world, and in the midst of temptation, and we agreed that you should come over and play at our house once more. Will you come, my boy? Will you drop our old family trouble and come with me?"

"Trouble!" said Goree, opening his eyes wide. "There was never any trouble between us that I know of. I'm sure we've always been the best friends. But, good Lord, Colonel, how could I go to your home as I am—a drunken wretch, a miserable, degraded spendthrift and gambler——"

He lurched from the table to his armchair, and began to weep maudlin tears, mingled with genuine drops of remorse and shame. Coltrane talked to him persistently and reasonably, reminding him of the simple mountain pleasures of which he had once been so fond, and insisting upon the genuineness of the invitation.

Finally he landed Goree by telling him he was counting upon his help in the engineering and transportation of a large amount of felled timber from a high mountainside to a waterway. He knew that Goree had once invented a device for this purpose—a series of slides and chutes—upon which he had justly prided himself. In an instant the poor fellow, delighted at the idea of his being of use to anyone, had paper spread upon the table, and was drawing rapid but pitifully shaky lines in demonstration of what he could and would do.

The man was sickened of the husks; his prodigal heart was turning again toward the mountains. His mind was yet strangely clogged, and his thoughts and memories were returning to his brain one by one, like

carrier pigeons over a stormy sea. But Coltrane was satisfied with the
progress he had made.

Bethel received the surprise of its existence that afternoon when a Coltrane and a Goree rode amicably together through the town. Side by
side they rode, out from the dusty streets and gaping townspeople, down
across the creek bridge, and up toward the mountain. The prodigal had
brushed and washed and combed himself to a more decent figure, but
he was unsteady in the saddle, and he seemed to be deep in the contemplation of some vexing problem. Coltrane left him in his mood,
relying upon the influence of changed surroundings to restore his
equilibrium.

Once Goree was seized with a shaking fit, and almost came to a collapse. He had to dismount and rest at the side of the road. The colonel,
foreseeing such a condition, had provided a small flask of whisky for
the journey but when it was offered to him Goree refused it almost with
violence, declaring he would never touch it again. By and by he was
recovered, and went quietly enough for a mile or two. Then he pulled
up his horse suddenly, and said:

"I lost two hundred dollars last night, playing poker. Now, where did
I get that money?"

"Take it easy, Yancey. The mountain air will soon clear it up. We'll
go fishing, first thing, at the Pinnacle Falls. The trout are jumping there
like bullfrogs. We'll take Stella and Lucy along, and have a picnic on
Eagle Rock. Have you forgotten how a hickory-cured-ham sandwich
tastes, Yancey, to a hungry fisherman?"

Evidently the colonel did not believe the story of his lost wealth; so
Goree retired again into brooding silence.

By late afternoon they had traveled ten of the twelve miles between
Bethel and Laurel. Half a mile this side of Laurel lay the old Goree
place; a mile or two beyond the village lived the Coltranes. The road
was now steep and laborious, but the compensations were many. The
tilted aisles of the forest were opulent with leaf and bird and bloom.
The tonic air put to shame the pharmacopæia. The glades were dark
with mossy shade, and bright with shy rivulets winking from the ferns
and laurels. On the lower side they viewed, framed in the near foliage,
exquisite sketches of the far valley swooning in its opal haze.

Coltrane was pleased to see that his companion was yielding to the
spell of the hills and woods. For now they had but to skirt the base of
Painter's Cliff; to cross Elder Branch and mount the hill beyond, and
Goree would have to face the squandered home of his fathers. Every
rock he passed, every tree, every foot of the roadway, was familiar to
him. Though he had forgotten the woods, they thrilled him like the
music of *Home, Sweet Home.*

They rounded the cliff, descended into Elder Branch, and paused there to let the horses drink and splash in the swift water. On the right was a rail fence that cornered there, and followed the road and stream. Inclosed by it was the old apple orchard of the home place; the house was yet concealed by the brow of the steep hill. Inside and along the fence, pokeberries, elders, sassafras, and sumac grew high and dense. At a rustle of their branches, both Goree and Coltrane glanced up, and saw, a long, yellow, wolfish face above the fence, staring at them with pale, unwinking eyes. The head quickly disappeared; there was a violent swaying of the bushes, and an ungainly figure ran up through the apple orchard in the direction of the house, zigzagging among the trees.

"That's Garvey," said Coltrane; "the man you sold out to. There's no doubt but he's considerably cracked. I had to send him up for moon-shining once, several years ago, in spite of the fact that I believed him irresponsible. Why, what's the matter, Yancey?"

Goree was wiping his forehead, and his face had lost its color. "Do I look queer, too?" he asked, trying to smile. "I'm just remembering a few more things." Some of the alcohol had evaporated from his brain. "I recollect now where I got that two hundred dollars."

"Don't think of it," said Coltrane, cheerfully. "Later on we'll figure it all out together."

They rode out of the branch, and when they reached the foot of the hill Goree stopped again.

"Did you ever suspect I was a very vain kind of fellow, Colonel?" he asked. "Sort of foolish proud about appearances?"

The colonel's eyes refused to wander to the soiled, sagging suit of flax and the faded slouch hat.

"It seems to me," he replied, mystified, but humoring him, "I remember a young buck about twenty, with the tightest coat, the sleekest hair, and the prancingest saddle horse in the Blue Ridge."

"Right you are," said Goree, eagerly. "And it's in me yet, though it don't show. Oh, I'm as vain as a turkey gobbler, and as proud as Lucifer. I'm going to ask you to indulge this weakness of mine in a little matter?"

"Speak out, Yancey. We'll create you Duke of Laurel and Baron of Blue Ridge, if you choose; and you shall have a feather out of Stella's peacock's tail to wear in your hat."

"I'm in earnest. In a few minutes we'll pass the house up there on the hill where I was born, and where my people have lived for nearly a century. Strangers live there now—and look at me! I am about to show myself to them ragged and poverty-stricken, a wastrel and a beggar. Colonel Coltrane, I'm ashamed to do it. I want you to let me wear your coat and hat until we are out of sight beyond. I know you think it a foolish pride, but I want to make as good a showing as I can when I pass the old place."

"Now, what does this mean?" said Coltrane to himself, as he compared his companion's sane looks and quiet demeanor with his strange request. But he was already unbuttoning the coat, assenting readily, as if the fancy were in no wise to be considered strange.

The coat and hat fitted Goree well. He buttoned the former about him with a look of satisfaction and dignity. He and Coltrane were nearly the same size—rather tall, portly, and erect. Twenty-five years were between them, but in appearance they might have been brothers. Goree looked older than his age; his face was puffy and lined; the colonel had the smooth, fresh complexion of a temperate liver. He put on Goree's disreputable old flax coat and faded slouch hat.

"Now," said Goree, taking up the reins, "I'm all right. I want you to ride about ten feet in the rear as we go by, Colonel, so that they can get a good look at me. They'll see I'm no back number yet, by any means. I guess I'll show up pretty well to them once more, anyhow. Let's ride on."

He set out up the hill at a smart trot, the colonel following, as he had been requested.

Goree sat straight in the saddle, with head erect, but his eyes were turned to the right, sharply scanning every shrub and fence and hiding-place in the old homestead yard. Once he muttered to himself, "Will the crazy fool try it, or did I dream half of it?"

It was when he came opposite the little family burying ground that he saw what he had been looking for—a puff of white smoke, coming from the thick cedars in one corner. He toppled so slowly to the left that Coltrane had time to urge his horse to that side, and catch him with one arm.

The squirrel hunter had not overpraised his aim. He had sent the bullet where he intended, and where Goree had expected that it would pass—through the breast of Colonel Abner Coltrane's black frock coat.

Goree leaned heavily against Coltrane, but he did not fall. The horses kept pace, side by side, and the colonel's arm kept him steady. The little white houses of Laurel shone through the trees, half a mile away. Goree reached out one hand and groped until it rested upon Coltrane's fingers, which held his bridle.

"Good friend," he said, and that was all.

Thus did Yancey Goree, as he rode past his old home, make, considering all things, the best showing that was in his power.

30

A Municipal Report

BY O. HENRY

The cities are full of pride,
Challenging each to each—
This from her mountainside,
That from her burthened beach.

R. KIPLING

Fancy a novel about Chicago or Buffalo, let us say, or Nashville, Ten-
nessee! There are just three big cities in the United States that are "story
cities"—New York, of course, New Orleans, and, best of the lot, San
Francisco.—FRANK NORRIS.

E AST is East, and West is San
Francisco, according to Californians. Californians are a race of people;
they are not merely inhabitants of a State. They are the Southerners of
the West. Now, Chicagoans are no less loyal to their city; but when you
ask them why, they stammer and speak of lake fish and the new Odd
Fellows Building. But Californians go into detail.

Of course they have, in the climate, an argument that is good for half
an hour while you are thinking of your coal bills and heavy underwear.
But as soon as they come to mistake your silence for conviction, madness
comes upon them, and they picture the city of the Golden Gate as the
Bagdad of the New World. So far, as a matter of opinion, no refutation
is necessary. But dear cousins all (from Adam and Eve descended),
it is a rash one who will lay his finger on the map and say: "In this town
there can be no romance—what could happen here?" Yes, it is a bold
and a rash deed to challenge in one sentence history, romance, and
Rand and McNally.

NASHVILLE.—A city, port of delivery, and the capital of the State of Tennessee, is on the Cumberland River and on the N. C. & St. L. and the L. & N. railroads. This city is regarded as the most important educational center in the South.

I stepped off the train at 8 P. M. Having searched thesaurus in vain for adjectives, I must, as a substitution, hie me to comparison in the form of a recipe.

Take of London fog 30 parts; malaria 10 parts; gas leaks 20 parts; dewdrops gathered in a brick yard at sunrise, 25 parts; odor of honeysuckle 15 parts. Mix.

The mixture will give you an approximate conception of a Nashville drizzle. It is not so fragrant as a moth-ball nor as thick as pea-soup; but 'tis enough—'twill serve.

I went to a hotel in a tumbril. It required strong self-suppression for me to keep from climbing to the top of it and giving an imitation of Sidney Carton. The vehicle was drawn by beasts of a bygone era and driven by something dark and emancipated.

I was sleepy and tired, so when I got to the hotel I hurriedly paid it the fifty cents it demanded (with approximate lagniappe, I assure you). I knew its habits; and I did not want to hear it prate about its old "marster" or anything that happened "befo' de wah."

The hotel was one of the kind described as "renovated." That means $20,000 worth of new marble pillars, tiling, electric lights and brass cuspidors in the lobby, and a new L. & N. time table and a lithograph of Lookout Mountain in each one of the great rooms above. The management was without reproach, the attention full of exquisite Southern courtesy, the service was as slow as the progress of a snail and as good-humored as Rip Van Winkle. The food was worth traveling a thousand miles for. There is no other hotel in the world where you can get such chicken livers *en brochette*.

At dinner I asked a Negro waiter if there was anything doing in town. He pondered gravely for a minute, and then replied: "Well, boss, I don't really reckon there's anything at all doin' after sundown."

Sundown had been accomplished; it had been drowned in the drizzle long before. So that spectacle was denied me. But I went forth upon the streets in the drizzle to see what might be here.

It is built on undulating grounds; and the streets are lighted by electricity at a cost of $32,470 per annum.

As I left the hotel there was a race riot. Down upon me charged a company of freedmen, or Arabs, or Zulus, armed with—no, I saw with relief that they were not rifles, but whips. And I saw dimly a caravan of black, clumsy vehicles; and at the reassuring shouts, "Kyar you any-where in the town, boss, fuh fifty cents," I reasoned that I was merely a "fare" instead of a victim.

I walked through long streets, all leading uphill. I wondered how those streets ever came down again. Perhaps they didn't until they were "graded." On a few of the "main streets" I saw lights in stores here and there; saw street cars go by conveying worthy burghers hither and yon; saw people pass engaged in the art of conversation, and heard a burst of semi-lively laughter issuing from a soda-water and ice-cream parlor. The streets other than "main" seemed to have enticed upon their borders houses consecrated to peace and domesticity. In many of them lights shone behind discreetly drawn window shades, in a few pianos tinkled orderly and irreproachable music. There was, indeed, little "doing." I wished I had come before sundown. So I returned to my hotel.

In November, 1864, the Confederate General Hood advanced against Nashville, where he shut up a National force under General Thomas. The latter then sallied forth and defeated the Confederates in a terrible conflict.

All my life I have heard of, admired, and witnessed the fine marks-manship of the South in its peaceful conflicts in the tobacco-chewing regions. But in my hotel a surprise awaited me. There were twelve bright, new, imposing, capacious brass cuspidors in the great lobby, tall enough to be called urns and so wide-mouthed that the crack pitcher of a lady baseball team should have been able to throw a ball into one of them at five paces distant. But, although a terrible battle had raged and was still raging, the enemy had not suffered. Bright, new, imposing, capacious, untouched, they stood. But, shades of Jefferson Brick! the tile floor—the beautiful tile floor! I could not avoid thinking of the battle of Nashville, and trying to draw, as is my foolish habit, some deductions about hereditary marksmanship.

Here I first saw Major (by misplaced courtesy) Wentworth Caswell. I knew him for a type the moment my eyes suffered from the sight of him. A rat has no geographical habitat. My old friend, A. Tennyson, said, as he so well said almost everything:

> Prophet, curse me the blabbing lip,
> And curse me the British vermin, the rat.

Let us regard the word "British" as interchangeable *ad lib*. A rat is a rat.

This man was hunting about the hotel lobby like a starved dog that had forgotten where he had buried a bone. He had a face of great acreage, red, pulpy, and with a kind of sleepy massiveness like that of Buddha. He possessed one single virtue—he was very smoothly shaven. The mark of the beast is not indelible upon a man until he goes about with a stubble. I think that if he had not used his razor that day I would have repulsed his advances, and the criminal calendar of the world would have been spared the addition of one murder.

I happened to be standing within five feet of a cuspidor when Major Caswell opened fire upon it. I had been observant enough to perceive that the attacking force was using Gatlings instead of squirrel rifles, so I sidestepped so promptly that the major seized the opportunity to apologize to a noncombatant. He had the blabbing lip. In four minutes he had become my friend and had dragged me to the bar.

I desire to interpolate here that I am a Southerner. But I am not one by profession or trade. I eschew the string tie, the slouch hat, the Prince Albert, the number of bales of cotton destroyed by Sherman, and plug chewing. When the orchestra plays "Dixie" I do not cheer. I slide a little lower on the leather-cornered seat and, well, order another Würzburger and wish that Longstreet had—but what's the use?

Major Caswell banged the bar with his fist, and the first gun at Fort Sumter re-echoed. When he fired the last one at Appomattox I began to hope. But then he began on family trees, and demonstrated that Adam was only a third cousin of a collateral branch of the Caswell family. Genealogy disposed of, he took up, to my distaste, his private family matters. He spoke of his wife, traced her descent back to Eve, and profanely denied any possible rumor that she may have had relations in the land of Nod.

By this time I began to suspect that he was trying to obscure by noise the fact that he had ordered the drinks, on the chance that I would be bewildered into paying for them. But when they were down he crashed a silver dollar loudly upon the bar. Then, of course, another serving was obligatory. And when I had paid for that I took leave of him brusquely; for I wanted no more of him. But before I had obtained my release he had prated loudly of an income that his wife received, and showed a handful of silver money.

When I got my key at the desk the clerk said to me courteously: "If that man Caswell has annoyed you, and if you would like to make a complaint, we will have him ejected. He is a nuisance, a loafer, and without any known means of support, although he seems to have some money most the time. But we don't seem to be able to hit upon any means of throwing him out legally."

"Why, no," said I, after some reflection; "I don't see my way clear to making a complaint. But I would like to place myself on record as asserting that I do not care for his company. Your town," I continued, "seems to be a quiet one. What manner of entertainment, adventure, or excitement have you to offer to the stranger within your gates?"

"Well, sir," said the clerk, "there will be a show here next Thursday. It is—I'll look it up and have the announcement sent up to your room with ice water. Good night."

After I went up to my room I looked out the window. It was only about ten o'clock, but I looked upon a silent town. The drizzle continued, spangled with dim lights, as far apart as currants in a cake sold at the Ladies' Exchange.

"A quiet place," I said to myself, as my first shoe struck the ceiling of the occupant of the room beneath mine. "Nothing of the life here that gives color and good variety to the cities in the East and West. Just a good, ordinary, humdrum, business town."

Nashville occupies a foremost place among the manufacturing centers of the country. It is the fifth boot and shoe market in the United States, the largest candy and cracker manufacturing city in the South, and does an enormous wholesale dry goods, grocery, and drug business.

I must tell you how I came to be in Nashville, and I assure you the digression brings as much tedium to me as it does to you. I was traveling elsewhere on my own business, but I had a commission from a Northern literary magazine to stop over there and establish a personal connection between the publication and one of its contributors, Azalea Adair.

Adair (there was no clue to the personality except the handwriting) had sent in some essays (lost art!) and poems that had made the editors swear approvingly over their one o'clock luncheon. So they had commissioned me to round up said Adair and corner by contract his or her output at two cents a word before some other publisher offered her ten or twenty.

At nine o'clock the next morning, after my chicken livers *en brochette* (try them if you can find that hotel), I strayed out into the drizzle, which was still on for an unlimited run. At the first corner I came upon Uncle Cæsar. He was a stalwart Negro, older than the pyramids, with gray wool and a face that reminded me of Brutus, and a second afterwards of the late King Cettiwayo. He wore the most remarkable coat that I ever had seen or expect to see. It reached to his ankles and had once been a Confederate gray in colors. But rain and sun and age had so variegated it that Joseph's coat, beside it, would have faded to a pale monochrome. I must linger with that coat, for it has to do with the story—the story that is so long in coming, because you can hardly expect anything to happen in Nashville.

Once it must have been the military coat of an officer. The cape of it had vanished, but all adown its front it had been frogged and tasseled magnificently. But now the frogs and tassels were gone. In their stead had been patiently stitched (I surmised by some surviving "black mammy") new frogs made of cunningly twisted common hempen twine. This twine was frayed and disheveled. It must have been added to the coat as a substitute for vanished splendors, with tasteless but painstaking devotion, for it followed faithfully the curves of the long-missing frogs. And, to complete the comedy and pathos of the garment, all its buttons were gone save one. The second button from the top alone remained. The coat was fastened by other twine strings tied through the buttonholes and other holes rudely pierced in the opposite side. There was never such a weird garment so fantastically bedecked and of so many mottled hues. The lone button was the size of a half-dollar, made of yellow horn and sewed on with coarse twine.

This Negro stood by a carriage so old that Ham himself might have started a hack line with it after he left the ark with the two animals hitched to it. As I approached he threw open the door, drew out a feather duster, waved it without using it, and said in deep, rumbling tones:

"Step right in, suh; ain't a speck of dust in it—jus' got back from a funeral, suh."

I inferred that on such gala occasions carriages were given an extra cleaning. I looked up and down the street and perceived that there was little choice among the vehicles for hire that lined the curb. I looked in my memorandum book for the address of Azalea Adair.

"I want to go to 861 Jessamine Street," I said, and was about to step into the hack. But for an instant the thick, long, gorilla-like arm of the Negro barred me. On his massive and saturnine face a look of sudden suspicion and enmity flashed for a moment. Then, with quickly returning conviction, he asked, blandishingly: "What are you gwine there for, boss?"

"What is that to you?" I asked, a little sharply.

"Nothin', suh, jus' nothin'. Only it's a lonesome kind of part of town and few folks ever has business out there. Step right in. The seats is clean—jes' got back from a funeral, suh."

A mile and a half it must have been to our journey's end. I could hear nothing but the fearful rattle of the ancient hack over the uneven brick paving; I could smell nothing but the drizzle, now further flavored with coal smoke and something like a mixture of tar and oleander blossoms. All I could see through the streaming windows were two rows of dim houses.

The city has an area of 10 square miles; 181 miles of streets, of which

137 miles are paved; a system of waterworks that cost $2,000,000, with 77 miles of mains.

Eight-sixty-one Jessamine Street was a decayed mansion. Thirty yards back from the street it stood, outmerged in a splendid grove of trees and untrimmed shrubbery. A row of box bushes overflowed and almost hid the paling fence from sight; the gate was kept closed by a rope noose that encircled the gate post and the first paling of the gate. But when you got inside you saw that 861 was a shell, a shadow, a ghost of former grandeur and excellence. But in the story, I have not yet got inside.

When the hack had ceased from rattling and the weary quadrupeds came to a rest I handed my jehu his fifty cents with an additional quarter, feeling a glow of conscious generosity as I did so. He refused it.

"It's two dollars, suh," he said.

"How's that?" I asked. "I plainly heard you call out at the hotel. 'Fifty cents to any part of the town.' "

"It's two dollars, suh," he repeated obstinately. "It's a long ways from the hotel."

"It is within the city limits and well within them," I argued. "Don't think that you have picked up a greenhorn Yankee. Do you see those hills over there?" I went on, pointing toward the east (I could not see them, myself, for the drizzle); "well, I was born and raised on their other side. You old fool nigger, can't you tell people from other people when you see 'em?"

The grim face of King Cettiwayo softened. "Is you from the South, suh? I reckon it was them shoes of yourn fooled me. They is somethin' sharp in the toes for a Southern gen"'man to wear."

"Then the charge is fifty cents, I suppose?" said I, inexorably.

His former expression, a mingling of cupidity and hostility, returned remained ten seconds, and vanished.

"Boss," he said, "fifty cents is right; but I *needs* two dollars, suh; I'm *obleeged* to have two dollars. I ain't *demandin'* it now, suh; after I knows whar you's from; I'm jus' sayin' that I *has* to have two dollars tonight and business is mighty po'."

Peace and confidence settled upon his heavy features. He had been luckier than he had hoped. Instead of having picked up a greenhorn, ignorant of rates, he had come upon an inheritance.

"You confounded old rascal," I said, reaching down to my pocket, "you ought to be turned over to the police."

For the first time I saw him smile. He knew; *he knew;* HE KNEW.

I gave him two one-dollar bills. As I handed them over I noticed that one of them had seen parlous times. Its upper right-hand corner was

missing, and it had been torn through in the middle, but joined again.
A strip of blue tissue paper, pasted over the split, preserved its nego-
tiability.

Enough of the African bandit for the present: I left him happy, lifted
the rope, and opened the creaky gate.

The house, as I said, was a shell. A paint brush had not touched it in
twenty years. I could not see why a strong wind should not have bowled
it over like a house of cards until I looked again at the trees that hugged
it close—the trees that saw the battle of Nashville and still drew their
protecting branches around it against storm and enemy and cold.

Azalea Adair, fifty years old, white-haired, a descendant of the cava-
liers, as thin and frail as the house she lived in, robed in the cheapest
and cleanest dress I ever saw, with an air as simple as a queen's, received me.

The reception room seemed a mile square, because there was nothing
in it except some rows of books, on unpainted white-pine bookshelves,
a cracked marble-topped table, a rag rug, a hairless horsehair sofa, and
two or three chairs. Yes, there was a picture on the wall, a colored crayon
drawing of a cluster of pansies. I looked around for the portrait of
Andrew Jackson and the pine cone hanging basket but they were not
there.

Azalea Adair and I had conversation, a little of which will be repeated
to you. She was a product of the old South, gently nurtured in the
sheltered life. Her learning was not broad, but was deep and of splendid
originality in its somewhat narrow scope. She had been educated at
home, and her knowledge of the world was derived from inference
and by inspiration. Of such is the precious, small group of essayists
made. While she talked to me I kept brushing my fingers, trying, unconsciously, to rid them guiltily of the absent dust from the half-calf
backs of Lamb, Chaucer, Hazlitt, Marcus Aurelius, Montaigne, and
Hood. She was exquisite, she was a valuable discovery. Nearly everybody nowadays knows too much—oh, so much too much—of real life.

I could perceive clearly that Azalea Adair was very poor. A house and
a dress she had, not much else, I fancied. So, divided between my duty
to the magazine and my loyalty to the poets and essayists who fought
Thomas in the valley of the Cumberland, I listened to her voice which
was like a harpsichord's, and found that I could not speak of contracts.
In the presence of the nine Muses and the three Graces one hesitated to
lower the topic to two cents. There would have to be another colloquy
after I had regained my commercialism. But I spoke of my mission, and
three o'clock of the next afternoon was set for the discussion of the
business proposition.

"Your town," I said, as I began to make ready to depart (which is the time for smooth generalities) "seems to be a quiet, sedate place. A home town, I should say, where few things out of the ordinary ever happen."

It carries on an extensive trade in stoves and hollow ware with the West and South, and its flouring mills have a daily capacity of more than 2,000 barrels.

Azalea Adair seemed to reflect.

"I have never thought of it that way," she said, with a kind of sincere intensity that seemed to belong to her. "Isn't it in the still, quiet places that things do happen? I fancy that when God began to create the earth on the first Monday morning one could have leaned out one's window and heard the drops of mud splashing from His trowel as He built up the everlasting hills. What did the noisiest project in the world—I mean the building of the tower of Babel—result in finally? A page and a half of Esperanto in the *North American Review*."

"Of course," said I, platitudinously, "human nature is the same everywhere; but there is more color—er—more drama and movement and—er—romance in some cities than in others."

"On the surface," said Azalea Adair. "I have traveled many times around the world in a golden airship wafted on two wings—print and dreams. I have seen (on one of my imaginary tours) the Sultan of Turkey bowstring with his own hands one of his wives who had uncovered her face in public. I have seen a man in Nashville tear up his theater tickets because his wife was going out with her face covered—with rice powder. In San Francisco's Chinatown I saw the slave girl Sing Yee dipped slowly, inch by inch, in boiling almond oil to make her swear she would never see her American lover again. She gave in when the boiling oil had reached three inches above her knee. At a euchre party in East Nashville the other night I saw Kitty Morgan cut dead by seven of her schoolmates and lifelong friends because she had married a house painter. The boiling oil was sizzling as high as her heart; but I wish you could have seen the fine little smile that she carried from table to table. Oh, yes, it is a humdrum town. Just a few miles of red brick houses and mud and stores and lumber yards."

Someone had knocked hollowly at the back of the house. Azalea Adair breathed a soft apology and went to investigate the sound. She came back in three minutes with brightened eyes, a faint flush on her cheeks, and ten years lifted from her shoulders.

"You must have a cup of tea before you go," she said, "and a sugar cake."

She reached and shook a little iron bell. In shuffled a small Negro girl about twelve, barefoot, not very tidy, glowering at me with thumb in mouth and bulging eyes.

Azalea Adair opened a tiny, worn purse and drew out a dollar bill, a dollar bill with the upper right-hand corner missing, torn in two pieces and pasted together again with a strip of blue tissue paper. It was one of those bills I had given the piratical Negro—there was no doubt of it.

"Go up to Mr. Baker's store on the corner, Impy," she said, handing the girl the dollar bill, "and get a quarter of a pound of tea—the kind he always sends me—and ten cents' worth of sugar cakes. Now, hurry. The supply of tea in the house happens to be exhausted," she explained to me.

Impy left by the back way. Before the scrape of her hard, bare feet had died away on the back porch, a wild shriek—I was sure it was hers—filled the hollow house. Then the deep, gruff tones of an angry man's voice mingled with the girl's further squeals and unintelligible words.

Azalea Adair rose without surprise or emotion and disappeared. For two minutes I heard the hoarse rumble of the man's voice; then something like an oath and a slight scuffle, and she returned calmly to her chair.

"This is a roomy house," she said, "and I have a tenant for part of it. I am sorry to have to rescind my invitation to tea. It is impossible to get the kind I always use at the store. Perhaps tomorrow Mr. Baker will be able to supply me."

I was sure that Impy had not had time to leave the house. I inquired concerning street-car lines and took my leave. After I was well on my way I remembered that I had not learned Azalea Adair's name. But tomorrow would do.

That same day I started in on the course of iniquity that this uneventful city forced upon me. I was in the town only two days, but in that time I managed to lie shamelessly by telegraph, and to be an accomplice —after the fact, if that is the correct legal term—to a murder.

As I rounded the corner nearest my hotel the Afrite coachman of the polychromatic, nonpareil coat seized me, swung open the dungeony door of his peripatetic sarcophagus, flirted his feather duster and began his ritual: "Step right in, boss. Carriage is clean—jus' got back from a funeral. Fifty cents to any——"

And then he knew me and grinned broadly. " 'Scuse me, boss; you is de gen'l'man what rid out with me dis mawnin'. Thank you kindly, suh."

"I am going out to 861 again tomorrow afternoon at three," said I, "and if you will be here, I'll let you drive me. So you know Miss Adair?" I concluded, thinking of my dollar bill.

"I belonged to her father, Judge Adair, suh," he replied.

"I judge that she is pretty poor," I said. "She hasn't much money to speak of, has she?"

For an instant I looked again at the fierce countenance of King Cettiwayo, and then he changed back to an extortionate old Negro hack driver.

"She ain't gwine to starve, suh," he said, slowly. "She has reso'ces, suh; she has reso'ces."

"I shall pay you fifty cents for the trip," said I.

"Dat is puffeckly correct, suh," he answered, humbly. "I jus' *had* to have dat two dollars dis mawnin', boss."

I went to the hotel and lied by electricity. I wired the magazine: "A. Adair holds out for eight cents a word."

The answer that came back was: "Give it to her quick, you duffer."

Just before dinner "Major" Wentworth Caswell bore down upon me with the greetings of a long-lost friend. I have seen few men whom I have so instantaneously hated, and of whom it was so difficult to be rid. I was standing at the bar when he invaded me; therefore I could not wave the white ribbon in his face. I would have paid gladly for the drinks, hoping thereby, to escape another; but he was one of those despicable, roaring, advertising bibbers who must have brass bands and fireworks attend upon every cent that they waste in their follies.

With an air of producing millions he drew two one-dollar bills from a pocket and dashed one of them upon the bar. I looked once more at the dollar bill with the upper right-hand corner missing, torn through the middle, and patched with a strip of blue tissue paper. It was my dollar bill again. It could have been no other.

I went up to my room. The drizzle and the monotony of a dreary, eventless Southern town had made me tired and listless. I remember that just before I went to bed I mentally disposed of the mysterious dollar bill (which might have formed the clue to a tremendously fine detective story of San Francisco) by saying to myself sleepily: "Seems as if a lot of people here own stock in the Hack-Driver's Trust. Pays dividends promptly, too. Wonder if——" Then I fell asleep.

King Cettiwayo was at his post the next day, and rattled my bones over the stones out to 861. He was to wait and rattle me back again when I was ready.

Azalea Adair looked paler and cleaner and frailer than she had looked on the day before. After she had signed the contract at eight cents per word she grew still paler and began to slip out of her chair. Without much trouble I managed to get her up on the antediluvian horsehair sofa and then I ran out to the sidewalk and yelled to the coffee-colored Pirate to bring a doctor. With a wisdom that I had not suspected in him, he abandoned his team and struck off up the street afoot, realizing the value of speed. In ten minutes he returned with a grave, gray-haired, and capable man of medicine. In a few words (worth much less than eight cents each) I explained to him my presence in the hollow house of mystery. He bowed with stately understanding, and turned to the old Negro.

"Uncle Cæsar," he said, calmly, "run up to my house and ask Miss Lucy to give you a cream pitcher full of fresh milk and half a tumbler of port wine. And hurry back. Don't drive—run. I want you to get back some time this week."

It occurred to me that Dr. Merriman also felt a distrust as to the speeding powers of the land-pirate's steeds. After Uncle Cæsar was gone, lumberingly, but swiftly, up the street, the doctor looked me over with great politeness and as much careful calculation until he had decided that I might do.

"It is only a case of insufficient nutrition," he said. "In other words, the result of poverty, pride, and starvation. Mrs. Caswell has many devoted friends who would be glad to aid her, but she will accept nothing except from that old Negro, Uncle Cæsar, who was once owned by her family."

"Mrs. Caswell!" said I, in surprise. And then I looked at the contract and saw that she had signed it "Azalea Adair Caswell."

"I thought she was Miss Adair," I said.

"Married to a drunken, worthless loafer, sir," said the doctor. "It is said that he robs her even of the small sums that her old servant contributes toward her support."

When the milk and wine had been brought the doctor soon revived Azalea Adair. She sat up and talked of the beauty of the autumn leaves that were then in season and their height of color. She referred lightly to her fainting seizure as the outcome of an old palpitation of the heart. Impy fanned her as she lay on the sofa. The doctor was due elsewhere, and I followed him to the door. I told him that it was within my power and intentions to make a reasonable advance of money to Azalea Adair on future contributions to the magazine, and he seemed pleased.

"By the way," he said, "perhaps you would like to know that you have had royalty for a coachman. Old Cæsar's grandfather was a king in Congo. Cæsar himself has royal ways, as you may have observed."

As the doctor was moving off I heard Uncle Cæsar's voice inside: "Did he git bofe of dem two dollars from you, Mis' Zalea?"

"Yes, Cæsar," I heard Azalea Adair answer, weakly. And then I went in and concluded business negotiations with our contributor. I assumed the responsibility of advancing fifty dollars, putting it as a necessary formality in binding our bargain. And then Uncle Cæsar drove me back to the hotel.

Here ends all of the story as far as I can testify as a witness. The rest must be only bare statements of facts.

At about six o'clock I went out for a stroll. Uncle Cæsar was at his corner. He threw open the door of his carriage, flourished his duster, and began his depressing formula: "Step right in, suh. Fifty cents to anywhere in the city—hack's puffickly clean, suh—jus' got back from a funeral——"

And then he recognized me. I think his eyesight was getting bad. His coat had taken on a few more faded shades of color, the twine strings were more frayed and ragged, the last remaining button—the button of yellow horn—was gone. A motley descendant of kings was Uncle Cæsar!

About two hours later I saw an excited crowd besieging the front of the drug store. In a desert where nothing happens this was manna; so I wedged my way inside. On an extemporized couch of empty boxes and chairs was stretched the mortal corporeality of Major Wentworth Caswell. A doctor was testing him for the mortal ingredient. His decision was that it was conspicuous by its absence.

The erstwhile Major had been found dead on a dark street and brought by curious and ennuied citizens to the drug store. The late human being had been engaged in terrific battle—the details showed that. Loafer and reprobate though he had been, he had been also a warrior. But he had lost. His hands were yet clinched so tightly that his fingers would not be opened. The gentle citizens who had known him stood about and searched their vocabularies to find some good words, if it were possible to speak of him. One kind-looking man said, after much thought: "When 'Cas' was about fo'teen he was one of the best spellers in the school."

While I stood there the fingers of the right hand of "the man that was," which hung down the side of a white pine box, relaxed, and dropped something at my feet. I covered it with one foot quietly, and a little later on I picked it up and pocketed it. I reasoned that in his last struggle his hand must have seized that object unwittingly and held it in a death grip.

At the hotel that night the main topic of conversation, with the possible exceptions of politics and prohibition, was the demise of Major Caswell. I heard one man say to a group of listeners:

"In my opinion, gentlemen, Caswell was murdered by some of these no-account niggers for his money. He had fifty dollars this afternoon which he showed to several gentlemen in the hotel. When he was found the money was not on his person."

I left the city the next morning at nine, and as the train was crossing the bridge over the Cumberland River I took out of my pocket a yellow horn overcoat button the size of a fifty-cent piece, with frayed ends of coarse twine hanging from it, and cast it out of the window into the slow, muddy waters below.

I wonder what's doing in Buffalo!

31

The Bar Sinister

BY RICHARD HARDING DAVIS

Preface

WHEN this story first appeared, the writer received letters of two kinds, one asking a question and the other making a statement. The question was, whether there was any foundation of truth in the story; the statement challenged him to say that there was. The letters seemed to show that a large proportion of readers prefer their dose of fiction with a sweetening of fact. This is written to furnish that condiment, and to answer the question and the statement.

In the dog world, the original of the bull-terrier in the story is known as Edgewood Cold Steel and to his intimates as "Kid." His father was Lord Minto, a thoroughbred bull-terrier, well known in Canada, but the story of Kid's life is that his mother was a black-and-tan named Vic. She was a lady of doubtful pedigree. Among her offspring by Lord Minto, so I have been often informed by many Canadian dog-fanciers, breeders, and exhibitors, was the only white puppy, Kid, in a litter of black-and-tans. He made his first appearance in the show world in 1900 in Toronto, where, under the judging of Mr. Charles H. Mason, he was easily first. During that year, when he came to our kennels, and in the two years following, he carried off many blue ribbons and cups at nearly every first-class show in the country. The other dog, "Jimmy Jocks," who in the book was his friend and mentor, was in real life his friend and companion, Woodcote Jumbo, or "Jaggers," an aristocratic son of a long line of English champions. He has gone to that place where some day all good dogs must go.

In this autobiography I have tried to describe Kid as he really is, and this year, when he again strives for blue ribbons, I trust, should the gentle reader see him at any of the bench-shows, he will give him a friendly pat and make his acquaintance. He will find his advances met with a polite and gentle courtesy.

THE AUTHOR

THE Master was walking most unsteady, his legs tripping each other. After the fifth or sixth round, my legs often go the same way.

But even when the Master's legs bend and twist a bit, you mustn't think he can't reach you. Indeed, that is the time he kicks most frequent. So I kept behind him in the shadow, or ran in the middle of the street. He stopped at many public houses with swinging doors, those doors that are cut so high from the sidewalk that you can look in under them, and see if the Master is inside. At night, when I peep beneath them, the man at the counter will see me first and say, "Here's the Kid, Jerry, come to take you home. Get a move on you"; and the Master will stumble out and follow me. It's lucky for us I'm so white, for, no matter how dark the night, he can always see me ahead, just out of reach of his boot. At night the Master certainly does see most amazing. Sometimes he sees two or four of me, and walks in a circle, so that I have to take him by the leg of his trousers and lead him into the right road. One night, when he was very nasty-tempered and I was coaxing him along, two men passed us, and one of them says, "Look at that brute!" and the other asks, "Which?" and they both laugh. The Master he cursed them good and proper.

But this night, whenever we stopped at a public house, the Master's pals left it and went on with us to the next. They spoke quite civil to me, and when the Master tried a flying kick, they gives him a shove. "Do you want us to lose our money?" says the pals.

I had had nothing to eat for a day and a night, and just before we set out the Master gives me a wash under the hydrant. Whenever I am locked up until all the slop-pans in our alley are empty, and made to take a bath, and the Master's pals speak civil and feel my ribs, I know something is going to happen. And that night, when every time they see a policeman under a lamp-post, they dodged across the street, and when at the last one of them picked me up and hid me under his jacket, I began to tremble; for I knew what it meant. It meant that I was to fight again for the Master.

I don't fight because I like fighting. I fight because if I didn't the other dog would find my throat, and the Master would lose his stakes, and I would be very sorry for him, and ashamed. Dogs can pass me and I can pass dogs, and I'd never pick a fight with none of them. When I see two dogs standing on their hind legs in the streets, clawing each other's ears, and snapping for each other's windpipes, or howling and swearing and rolling in the mud, I feel sorry they should act so, and pretend not to notice. If he'd let me, I'd like to pass the time of day with every dog I meet. But there's something about me that no nice dog can abide. When I trot up to nice dogs, nodding and grinning, to make friends, they always tell me to be off. "Go to the devil!" they bark at me. "Get out!" And when I walk away they shout "Mongrel!" and "Gutter-dog!" and sometimes, after my back is turned, they rush me. I could kill most of them with three shakes, breaking the backbone of the little ones and squeezing the throat of the big ones. But what's the good? They *are* nice dogs; that's why I try to make up to them: and, though it's not for them to say it, I *am* a street dog, and if I try to push into the company of my betters, I suppose it's their right to teach me my place.

Of course they don't know I'm the best fighting bull-terrier of my weight in Montreal. That's why it wouldn't be fair for me to take notice of what they shout. They don't know that if I once locked my jaws on them I'd carry away whatever I touched. The night I fought Kelley's White Rat, I wouldn't loosen up until the Master made a noose in my leash and strangled me; and, as for that Ottawa dog, if the handlers hadn't thrown red pepper down my nose I *never* would have let go of him. I don't think the handlers treated me quite right that time, but maybe they didn't know the Ottawa dog was dead. I did.

I learned my fighting from my mother when I was very young. We slept in a lumber-yard on the river-front, and by day hunted for food along the wharves. When we got it, the other tramp-dogs would try to take it off us, and then it was wonderful to see mother fly at them and drive them away. All I know of fighting I learned from mother, watching her picking the ash-heaps for me when I was too little to fight for myself. No one ever was so good to me as mother. When it snowed and the ice was in the St. Lawrence, she used to hunt alone, and bring me back new bones, and she'd sit and laugh to see me trying to swallow 'em whole. I was just a puppy then; my teeth was falling out. When I was able to fight we kept the whole river-range to ourselves. I had the genuine long "punishing" jaw, so mother said, and there wasn't a man or a dog that dared worry us. Those were happy days, those were; and we lived well, share and share alike, and when we wanted a bit of fun, we chased the fat old wharf-rats! My, how they would squeal!

Then the trouble came. It was no trouble to me. I was too young to care then. But mother took it so to heart that she grew ailing, and wouldn't go abroad with me by day. It was the same old scandal that they're always bringing up against me. I was so young then that I didn't know. I couldn't see any difference between mother—and other mothers.

But one day a pack of curs we drove off snarled back some new names at her, and mother dropped her head and ran, just as though they had whipped us. After that she wouldn't go out with me except in the dark, and one day she went away and never came back, and, though I hunted for her in every court and alley and back street of Montreal, I never found her.

One night, a month after mother ran away, I asked Guardian, the old blind mastiff, whose Master is the night watchman on our slip, what it all meant. And he told me.

"Every dog in Montreal knows," he says, "except you; and every Master knows. So I think it's time you knew."

Then he tells me that my father, who had treated mother so bad, was a great and noble gentleman from London. "Your father had twenty-two registered ancestors, had your father," old Guardian says, "and in him was the best bull-terrier blood of England, the most ancientest, the most royal; the winning 'blue-ribbon' blood, that breeds champions. He had sleepy pink eyes and thin pink lips, and he was as white all over as his own white teeth, and under his white skin you could see his muscles, hard and smooth, like the links of a steel chain. When your father stood still, and tipped his nose in the air, it was just as though he was saying, 'Oh, yes, you common dogs and men, you may well stare. It must be a rare treat for you colonials to see real English royalty.' He certainly was pleased with hisself, was your father. He looked just as proud and haughty as one of them stone dogs in Victoria Park—them as is cut out of white marble. And you're like him," says the old mastiff—"by that, of course, meaning you're white, same as him. That's the only likeness. But, you see, the trouble is, Kid—well, you see, Kid, the trouble is—your mother—"

"That will do," I said, for then I understood without his telling me, and I got up and walked away, holding my head and tail high in the air.

But I was, oh, so miserable, and I wanted to see mother that very minute, and tell her that I didn't care.

Mother is what I am, a street dog; there's no royal blood in mother's veins, nor is she like that father of mine, nor—and that's the worst—she's not even like me. For while I, when I'm washed for a fight, am as white as clean snow, she—and this is our trouble—she, my mother, is a black-and-tan.

When mother hid herself from me, I was twelve months old and able to take care of myself, and as, after mother left me, the wharves were never the same, I moved uptown and met the Master. Before he came, lots of other men-folks had tried to make up to me, and to whistle me home. But they either tried patting me or coaxing me with a piece of meat; so I didn't take to 'em. But one day the Master pulled me out of a street fight by the hind legs, and kicked me good.

"You want to fight, do you?" says he. "I'll give you all the *fighting* you want!" he says, and he kicks me again. So I knew he was my Master, and I followed him home. Since that day I've pulled off many fights for him, and they've brought dogs from all over the province to have a go at me; but up to that night none, under thirty pounds, had ever downed me.

But that night, so soon as they carried me into the ring, I saw the dog was overweight, and that I was no match for him. It was asking too much of a puppy. The Master should have known I couldn't do it. Not that I mean to blame the Master, for when sober, which he sometimes was,—though not, as you might say, his habit,—he was most kind to me, and let me out to find food, if I could get it, and only kicked me when I didn't pick him up at night and lead him home.

But kicks will stiffen the muscles, and starving a dog so as to get him ugly tempered for a fight may make him nasty, but it's weakening to his insides, and it causes the legs to wobble.

The ring was in a hall back of a public house. There was a red-hot whitewashed stove in one corner, and the ring in the other. I lay in the Master's lap, wrapped in my blanket, and, spite of the stove, shivering awful; but I always shiver before a fight: I can't help gettin' excited. While the men-folks were a-flashing their money and taking their last drink at the bar, a little Irish groom in gaiters came up to me and gave me the back of his hand to smell, and scratched me behind the ears.

"You poor little pup," says he; "you haven't no show," he says. "That brute in the tap-room he'll eat your heart out."

"That's what *you* think," says the Master, snarling. "I'll lay you a quid the Kid chews him up."

The groom he shook his head, but kept looking at me so sorry-like that I begun to get a bit sad myself. He seemed like he couldn't bear to leave off a-patting of me, and he says, speaking low just like he would to a man-folk, "Well, good luck to you, little pup," which I thought so civil of him that I reached up and licked his hand. I don't do that to many men. And the Master he knew I didn't, and took on dreadful.

"What 'ave you got on the back of your hand?" says he, jumping up.

"Soap!" says the groom, quick as a rat. "That's more than you've got on yours. Do you want to smell of it?" and he sticks his fist under the Master's nose. But the pals pushed in between 'em.

"He tried to poison the Kid!" shouts the Master.

"Oh, one fight at a time," says the referee. "Get into the ring, Jerry. We're waiting." So we went into the ring.

I could never just remember what did happen in that ring. He give me no time to spring. He fell on me like a horse. I couldn't keep my feet against him, and though, as I saw, he could get his hold when he liked, he wanted to chew me over a bit first. I was wondering if they'd be able to pry him off me, when, in the third round, he took his hold; and I begun to drown, just as I did when I fell into the river off the Red C slip. He closed deeper and deeper on my throat, and everything went black and red and bursting; and then, when I were sure I were dead, the handlers pulled him off, and the Master give me a kick that brought me to. But I couldn't move none, or even wink, both eyes being shut with lumps.

"He's a cur!" yells the Master, "a sneaking, cowardly cur! He lost the fight for me," says he, "because he's a —— —— —— cowardly cur." And he kicks me again in the lower ribs, so that I go sliding across the sawdust. "There's gratitude fer yer," yells the Master. "I've fed that dog, and nussed that dog and housed him like a prince; and now he puts his tail between his legs and sells me out, he does. He's a coward! I've done with him, I am. I'd sell him for a pipeful of tobacco." He picked me up by the tail, and swung me for the men-folks to see. "Does any gentleman here want to buy a dog," he says, "to make into sausage meat?" he says. "That's all he's good for."

Then I heard the little Irish groom say, "I'll give you ten bob for the dog."

And another voice says, "Ah, don't you do it; the dog's same as dead —mebbe he is dead."

"Ten shillings!" says the Master, and his voice sobers a bit; "make it two pounds and he's yours."

But the pals rushed in again.

"Don't you be a fool, Jerry," they say. "You'll be sorry for this when you're sober. The Kid's worth a fiver."

One of my eyes was not so swelled up as the other, and as I hung by my tail, I opened it, and saw one of the pals take the groom by the shoulder.

"You ought to give 'im five pounds for that dog, mate," he says; "that's no ordinary dog. That dog's got good blood in him, that dog has. Why, his father—that very dog's father—"

I thought he never would go on. He waited like he wanted to be sure the groom was listening.

"That very dog's father," says the pal," is Regent Royal, son of Champion Regent Monarch, champion bull-terrier of England for four years."

I was sore, and torn, and chewed most awful, but what the pal said sounded so fine that I wanted to wag my tail, only couldn't, owing to my hanging from it.

But the Master calls out: "Yes, his father was Regent Royal; who's saying he wasn't? but the pup's a cowardly cur, that's what his pup is. And why? I'll tell you why: because his mother was a black-and-tan street dog, that's why!"

I don't see how I got the strength, but, some way, I threw myself out of the Master's grip and fell at his feet, and turned over and fastened all my teeth in his ankle, just across the bone.

When I woke, after the pals had kicked me off him, I was in the smoking car of a railroad train, lying in the lap of the little groom, and he was rubbing my open wounds with a greasy yellow stuff, exquisite to the smell and most agreeable to lick off.

II

"Well, what's your name—Nolan? Well, Nolan, these references are satisfactory," said the young gentleman my new Master called "Mr. Wyndham, sir." "I'll take you on as second man. You can begin today."

My new Master shuffled his feet and put his finger to his forehead. "Thank you, sir," says he. Then he choked like he had swallowed a fish bone. "I have a little dawg, sir," says he.

"You can't keep him," says "Mr. Wyndham, sir," very short.

" 'E's only a puppy, sir," says my new Master; " 'e wouldn't go outside the stables, sir."

"It's not that," says "Mr. Wyndham, sir." "I have a large kennel of very fine dogs; they're the best of their breed in America. I don't allow strange dogs on the premises."

The Master shakes his head, and motions me with his cap, and I crept out from behind the door. "I'm sorry, sir," says the Master. "Then I can't take the place. I can't get along without the dawg, sir."

"Mr. Wyndham, sir," looked at me that fierce that I guessed he was going to whip me, so I turned over on my back and begged with my legs and tail.

"Why, you beat him!" says "Mr. Wyndham, sir," very stern.

"No fear!" the Master says, getting very red. "The party I bought him off taught him that. He never learnt that from me!" He picked me up in his arms, and to show "Mr. Wyndham, sir," how well I loved the Master, I bit his chin and hands.

"Mr. Wyndham, sir," turned over the letters the Master had given him. "Well, these references certainly are very strong," he says. "I guess I'll let the dog stay. Only see you keep him away from the kennels —or you'll both go."

"Thank you, sir," says the Master, grinning like a cat when she's safe behind the area railing.

"He's not a bad bull-terrier," says "Mr. Wyndham, sir," feeling my head. "Not that I know much about the smooth-coated breeds. My dogs are St. Bernards." He stopped patting me and held up my nose. "What's the matter with his ears?" he says. "They're chewed to pieces. Is this a fighting dog?" he asks, quick and rough like.

I could have laughed. If he hadn't been holding my nose, I certainly would have had a good grin at him. Me the best under thirty pounds in the Province of Quebec, and him asking if I was a fighting dog! I ran to the Master and hung down my head modest like, waiting for him to tell my list of battles; but the Master he coughs in his cap most painful. "Fightin' dawg, sir!" he cries. "Lor' bless you, sir, the Kid don't know the word. 'E's just a puppy, sir, same as you see; a pet dog, so to speak. 'E's a regular old lady's lap dog, the Kid is."

"Well, you keep him away from my St. Bernards," says "Mr. Wyndham, sir," "or they might make a mouthful of him."

"Yes, sir; that they might," says the Master. But when we gets outside he slaps his knee and laughs inside hisself, and winks at me most sociable.

The Master's new home was in the country, in a province they called Long Island. There was a high stone wall about his home with big iron gates to it, same as Godfrey's brewery; and there was a house with five red roofs; and the stables, where I lived, was cleaner than the aërated bakery shop. And then there was the kennels; but they was like nothing else in this world that ever I see. For the first days I couldn't sleep of nights for fear some one would catch me lying in such a cleaned-up place, and would chase me out of it; and when I did fall to sleep I'd dream I was back in the old Master's attic, shivering under the rusty stove, which never had no coals in it, with the Master flat on his back on the cold floor, with his clothes on. And I'd wake up scared and whimpering, and find myself on the new Master's cot with his hand on the quilt beside me; and I'd see the glow of the big stove, and hear the high quality horses below stairs stamping in their straw-lined boxes, and I'd snoop the sweet smell of hay and harness soap and go to sleep again.

The stables was my jail, so the Master said, but I don't ask no better home than that jail.

"Now, Kid," says he, sitting on the top of a bucket upside down, "you've got to understand this. When I whistle it means you're not to go out of this 'ere yard. These stables is your jail. If you leave 'em I'll have to leave 'em too, and over the seas, in the County Mayo, an old mother will 'ave to leave her bit of a cottage. For two pounds I must be sending her every month, or she'll have naught to eat, nor no thatch over 'er head. I can't lose my place, Kid, so see you don't lose it for me. You must keep away from the kennels," says he; "they're not for the likes of you. The kennels are for the quality. I wouldn't take a litter of them woolly dogs for one wag of your tail, Kid, but for all that they are your betters, same as the gentry up in the big house are my betters. I know my place and keep away from the gentry, and you keep away from the champions."

So I never goes out of the stables. All day I just lay in the sun on the stone flags, licking my jaws, and watching the grooms wash down the carriages, and the only care I had was to see they didn't get gay and turn the hose on me. There wasn't even a single rat to plague me. Such stables I never did see.

"Nolan," says the head groom, "some day that dog of yours will give you the slip. You can't keep a street dog tied up all his life. It's against his natur'." The head groom is a nice old gentleman, but he doesn't know everything. Just as though I'd been a street dog because I liked it! As if I'd rather poke for my vittels in ash heaps than have 'em handed me in a wash-basin, and would sooner bite and fight than be polite and sociable. If I'd had mother there I couldn't have asked for nothing more. But I'd think of her snooping in the gutters, or freezing of nights under the bridges, or, what's worst of all, running through the hot streets with her tongue down, so wild and crazy for a drink that the people would shout "mad dog" at her and stone her. Water's so good that I don't blame the men-folks for locking it up inside their houses; but when the hot days come, I think they might remember that those are the dog days, and leave a little water outside in a trough, like they do for the horses. Then we wouldn't go mad, and the policemen wouldn't shoot us. I had so much of everything I wanted that it made me think a lot of the days when I hadn't nothing, and if I could have given what I had to mother, as she used to share with me, I'd have been the happiest dog in the land. Not that I wasn't happy then, and most grateful to the Master, too, and if I'd only minded him, the trouble wouldn't have come again.

But one day the coachman says that the little lady they called Miss Dorothy had come back from school, and that same morning she runs over to the stables to pat her ponies, and she sees me.

"Oh, what a nice little, white little dog!" said she. "Whose little dog are you?" says she.

"That's my dog, miss," says the Master. " 'Is name is Kid." And I ran up to her most polite, and licks her fingers, for I never see so pretty and kind a lady.

"You must come with me and call on my new puppies," says she, picking me up in her arms and starting off with me.

"Oh, but please, miss," cries Nolan, "Mr. Wyndham give orders that the Kid's not to go to the kennels."

"That'll be all right," says the little lady; "they're my kennels too. And the puppies will like to play with him."

You wouldn't believe me if I was to tell you of the style of them quality dogs. If I hadn't seen it myself I wouldn't have believed it neither. The Viceroy of Canada don't live no better. There was forty of them, but each one had his own house and a yard—most exclusive— and a cot and a drinking basin all to hisself. They had servants standing round waiting to feed 'em when they was hungry, and valets to wash 'em; and they had their hair combed and brushed like the grooms must when they go out on the box. Even the puppies had overcoats with their names on 'em in blue letters, and the name of each of those they called champions was painted up fine over his front door just like it was a public house or a veterinary's. They were the biggest St. Bernards I ever did see. I could have walked under them if they'd have let me. But they were very proud and haughty dogs, and looked only once at me, and then sniffed in the air. The little lady's own dog was an old gentleman bull dog. He'd come along with us, and when he notices how taken aback I was with all I see, 'e turned quite kind and affable and showed me about.

"Jimmy Jocks," Miss Dorothy called him, but, owing to his weight, he walked most dignified and slow, waddling like a duck, as you might say, and looked much too proud and handsome for such a silly name.

"That's the runway, and that's the trophy house," says he to me, "and that over there is the hospital, where you have to go if you get distemper, and the vet gives you beastly medicine."

"And which of these is your 'ouse, sir?" asks I, wishing to be respectful. But he looked that hurt and haughty. "I don't live in the kennels," says he, most contemptuous. "I am a house dog. I sleep in Miss Dorothy's room. And at lunch I'm let in with the family, if the visitors don't mind. They 'most always do, but they're too polite to say so. Besides," says he, smiling most condescending, "visitors are always afraid of me. It's because I'm so ugly," says he. "I suppose," says he, screwing up his wrinkles and speaking very slow and impressive, "I suppose I'm the ugliest bull dog in America"; and as he seemed to be so pleased to think hisself so, I said, "Yes, sir; you certainly are the ugliest ever I see," at which he nodded his head most approving.

"But I couldn't hurt 'em, as you say," he goes on, though I hadn't said nothing like that, being too polite. "I'm too old," he says; "I haven't any teeth. The last time one of those grizzly bears," said he, glaring at the big St. Bernards, "took a hold of me, he nearly was my death," says he. I thought his eyes would pop out of his head, he seemed so wrought up about it. "He rolled me around in the dirt, he did," says Jimmy Jocks, "an' I couldn't get up. It was low," says Jimmy Jocks, making a face like he had a bad taste in his mouth. "Low, that's what I call it—bad form, you understand, young man, not done in my set—and—and low." He growled 'way down in his stomach, and puffed hisself out, panting and blowing like he had been on a run.

"I'm not a street fighter," he says, scowling at a St. Bernard marked "Champion." "And when my rheumatism is not troubling me," he says, "I endeavor to be civil to all dogs, so long as they are gentlemen."

"Yes, sir," said I, for even to me he had been most affable.

At this we had come to a little house off by itself, and Jimmy Jocks invites me in. "This is their trophy room," he says, "where they keep their prizes. Mine," he says, rather grand-like, "are on the sideboard." Not knowing what a sideboard might be, I said, "Indeed, sir, that must be very gratifying." But he only wrinkled up his chops as much as to say, "It is my right."

The trophy room was as wonderful as any public house I ever see. On the walls was pictures of nothing but beautiful St. Bernard dogs, and rows and rows of blue and red and yellow ribbons; and when I asked Jimmy Jocks why they was so many more of blue than of the others, he laughs and says, "Because these kennels always win." And there was many shining cups on the shelves, which Jimmy Jocks told me were prizes won by the champions.

"Now, sir, might I ask you, sir," says I, "wot is a champion?"

At that he panted and breathed so hard I thought he would bust hisself. "My dear young friend!" says he, "wherever have you been educated? A champion is a—a champion," he says. "He must win nine blue ribbons in the 'open' class. You follow me—that is—against all comers. Then he has the title before his name, and they put his photograph in the sporting papers. You know, of course, that *I* am a champion," says he. "I am Champion Woodstock Wizard III, and the two other Woodstock Wizards, my father and uncle, were both champions."

"But I thought your name was Jimmy Jocks," I said.

He laughs right out at that.

"That's my kennel name, not my registered name," he says. "Why, certainly you know that every dog has two names. Now, for instance, what's your registered name and number?" says he.

"I've got only one name," I says. "Just Kid."

Woodstock Wizard puffs at that and wrinkles up his forehead and pops out his eyes.

"Who are your people?" says he. "Where is your home?"

"At the stable, sir," I said. "My Master is the second groom."

At that Woodstock Wizard III looks at me for quite a bit without winking, and stares all around the room over my head.

"Oh, well," says he at last, "you're a very civil young dog," says he, "and I blame no one for what he can't help," which I thought most fair and liberal. "And I have known many bull-terriers that were champions," says he, "though as a rule they mostly run with fire engines and to fighting. For me, I wouldn't care to run through the streets after a hose cart, nor to fight," says he: "but each to his taste."

I could not help thinking that if Woodstock Wizard III tried to follow a fire engine he would die of apoplexy, and seeing he'd lost his teeth, it was lucky he had no taste for fighting; but, after his being so condescending, I didn't say nothing.

"Anyway," says he, "every smooth-coated dog is better than any hairy old camel like those St. Bernards, and if ever you're hungry down at the stables, young man, come up to the house and I'll give you a bone. I can't eat them myself, but I bury them around the garden from force of habit and in case a friend should drop in. Ah, I see my mistress coming," he says, "and I bid you good day. I regret," he says, "that our different social position prevents our meeting frequent, for you're a worthy young dog with a proper respect for your betters, and in this country there's precious few of them have that." Then he waddles off, leaving me alone and very sad, for he was the first dog in many days that had spoke to me. But since he showed, seeing that I was a stable dog, he didn't want my company, I waited for him to get well away. It was not a cheerful place to wait, the trophy house. The pictures of the champions seemed to scowl at me, and ask what right such as I had even to admire them, and the blue and gold ribbons and the silver cups made me very miserable. I had never won no blue ribbons or silver cups, only stakes for the old Master to spend in the publics; and I hadn't won them for being a beautiful high quality dog, but just for fighting—which, of course, as Woodstock Wizard III says, is low. So I started for the stables, with my head down and my tail between my legs, feeling sorry I had ever left the Master. But I had more reason to be sorry before I got back to him.

The trophy house was quite a bit from the kennels, and as I left it I see Miss Dorothy and Woodstock Wizard III walking back toward them, and, also, that a big St. Bernard, his name was Champion Red Elfberg, had broke his chain and was running their way. When he reaches old Jimmy Jocks he lets out a roar like a grain steamer in a fog, and he makes three leaps for him. Old Jimmy Jocks was about a fourth his size; but he plants his feet and curves his back, and his hair goes up around his neck like a collar. But he never had no show at no time, for the grizzly bear, as Jimmy Jocks had called him, lights on old Jimmy's back and tries to break it, and old Jimmy Jocks snaps his gums and claws the grass, panting and groaning awful. But he can't do nothing, and the grizzly bear just rolls him under him, biting and tearing cruel. The odds was all that Woodstock Wizard III was going to be killed; I had fought enough to see that: but not knowing the rules of the game among champions, I didn't like to interfere between two gentlemen who might be settling a private affair, and, as it were, take it as presuming of me. So I stood by, though I was shaking terrible, and holding myself in like I was on a leash. But at that Woodstock Wizard III, who was underneath, sees me through the dust, and calls very faint, "Help, you!" he says. "Take him in the hind leg," he says. "He's murdering me," he says. And then the little Miss Dorothy, who was crying, and calling to the kennel men, catches at the Red Elfberg's hind legs to pull him off, and the brute, keeping his front pats well in Jimmy's stomach, turns his big head and snaps at her. So that was all I asked for, thank you. I went up under him. It was really nothing. He stood so high that I had only to take off about three feet from him and come in from the side, and my long "punishing jaw," as mother was always talking about, locked on his woolly throat, and my back teeth met. I couldn't shake him, but I shook myself, and every time I shook myself there was thirty pounds of weight tore at his windpipes. I couldn't see nothing for his long hair, but I heard Jimmy Jocks puffing and blowing on one side, and munching the brute's leg with his old gums. Jimmy was an old sport that day, was Jimmy, or Woodstock Wizard III, as I should say. When the Red Elfberg was out and down I had to run, or those kennel men would have had my life. They chased me right into the stables; and from under the hay I watched the head groom take down a carriage whip and order them to the right about. Luckily Master and the young grooms were out, or that day there'd have been fighting for everybody.

Well, it nearly did for me and the Master. "Mr. Wyndham, sir," comes raging to the stables. I'd half killed his best prize-winner, he says, and had oughter be shot, and he gives the Master his notice. But Miss Dorothy she follows him, and says it was his Red Elfberg what began the fight, and that I'd saved Jimmy's life, and that old Jimmy Jocks was worth more to her than all the St. Bernards in the Swiss mountains—wherever they may be. And that I was her champion, anyway. Then she cried over me most beautiful, and over Jimmy Jocks, too, who was that tied up in bandages he couldn't even waddle. So when he heard that side of it, "Mr. Wyndham, sir," told us that if Nolan put me on a chain we could stay. So it came out all right for everybody but me. I was glad the Master kept his place, but I'd never worn a chain before, and it disheartened me. But that was the least of it. For the quality dogs couldn't forgive my whipping their champion, and they came to the fence between the kennels and the stables, and laughed through the bars, barking most cruel words at me. I couldn't understand how they found it out, but they knew. After the fight Jimmy Jocks was most condescending to me, and he said the grooms had boasted to the kennel men that I was a son of Regent Royal, and that when the kennel men asked who was my mother they had had to tell them that too. Perhaps that was the way of it, but, however, the scandal got out, and every one of the quality dogs knew that I was a street dog and the son of a black-and-tan.

"These misalliances will occur," said Jimmy Jocks, in his old-fashioned way; "but no well-bred dog," says he, looking most scornful at the St. Bernards, who were howling behind the palings, "would refer to your misfortune before you, certainly not cast it in your face. I myself remember your father's father, when he made his début at the Crystal Palace. He took four blue ribbons and three specials."

But no sooner than Jimmy would leave me the St. Bernards would take to howling again, insulting mother and insulting me. And when I tore at my chain, they, seeing they were safe, would howl the more. It was never the same after that; the laughs and the jeers cut into my heart, and the chain bore heavy on my spirit. I was so sad that sometimes I wished I was back in the gutter again, where no one was better than me, and some nights I wished I was dead. If it hadn't been for the Master being so kind, and that it would have looked like I was blaming mother, I would have twisted my leash and hanged myself.

About a month after my fight, the word was passed through the kennels that the New York Show was coming, and such goings on as followed I never did see. If each of them had been matched to fight for a thousand pounds and the gate, they couldn't have trained more conscientious. But perhaps that's just my envy. The kennel men rubbed 'em and scrubbed 'em, and trims their hair and curls and combs it, and some dogs they fatted and some they starved. No one talked of nothing but the Show, and the chances "our kennels" had against the other kennels, and if this one of our champions would win over that one, and whether them as hoped to be champions had better show in the "open" or the "limit" class, and whether this dog would beat his own dad, or whether his little puppy sister couldn't beat the two of 'em. Even the grooms had their money up, and day or night you heard nothing but praises of "our" dogs, until I, being so far out of it, couldn't have felt meaner if I had been running the streets with a can to my tail. I knew shows were not for such as me, and so all day I lay stretched at the end of my chain, pretending I was asleep, and only too glad that they had something so important to think of that they could leave me alone.

But one day, before the Show opened, Miss Dorothy came to the stables with "Mr. Wyndham, sir," and seeing me chained up and so miserable, she takes me in her arms.

"You poor little tyke!" says she. "It's cruel to tie him up so; he's eating his heart out, Nolan," she says. "I don't know nothing about bull-terriers," says she, "but I think Kid's got good points," says she, "and you ought to show him. Jimmy Jocks has three legs on the Rensselaer Cup now, and I'm going to show him this time, so that he can get the fourth; and, if you wish, I'll enter your dog too. How would you like that, Kid?" says she. "How would you like to see the most beautiful dogs in the world? Maybe you'd meet a pal or two," says she. "It would cheer you up, wouldn't it, Kid?" says she. But I was so upset I could only wag my tail most violent. "He says it would!" says she, though, being that excited, I hadn't said nothing.

So "Mr. Wyndham, sir," laughs, and takes out a piece of blue paper and sits down at the head groom's table.

"What's the name of the father of your dog, Nolan?" says he. And Nolan says: "The man I got him off told me he was a son of Champion Regent Royal, sir. But it don't seem likely, does it?" says Nolan.

"It does not!" says "Mr. Wyndham, sir," short like.

"Aren't you sure, Nolan?" says Miss Dorothy.

"No, miss," says the Master.

"Sire unknown," says "Mr. Wyndham, sir," and writes it down.

"Date of birth?" asks "Mr. Wyndham, sir."

"I—I—unknown, sir," says Nolan. And "Mr. Wyndham, sir," writes it down.

"Breeder?" says "Mr. Wyndham, sir."

"Unknown," says Nolan, getting very red around the jaws, and I drops my head and tail. And "Mr. Wyndham, sir," writes that down.

"Mother's name?" says "Mr. Wyndham, sir."

"She was a—unknown," says the Master. And I licks his hand.

"Dam unknown," says "Mr. Wyndham, sir," and writes it down. Then he takes the paper and reads out loud: " 'Sire unknown, dam unknown, breeder unknown, date of birth unknown.' You'd better call him the 'Great Unknown,' " says he. "Who's paying his entrance fee?"

"I am," says Miss Dorothy.

Two weeks after we all got on a train for New York, Jimmy Jocks and me following Nolan in the smoking car, and twenty-two of the St. Bernards in boxes and crates and on chains and leashes. Such a barking and howling I never did hear; and when they sees me going, too, they laughs fit to kill.

"Wot is this—a circus?" says the railroad man.

But I had no heart in it. I hated to go. I knew I was no "show" dog, even though Miss Dorothy and the Master did their best to keep me from shaming them. For before we set out Miss Dorothy brings a man from town who scrubbed and rubbed me, and sandpapered my tail, which hurt most awful, and shaved my ears with the Master's razor, so they could 'most see clear through 'em, and sprinkles me over with pipe clay, till I shines like a Tommy's cross-belts.

"Upon my word!" says Jimmy Jocks when he first sees me. "Wot a swell you are! You're the image of your grand-dad when he made his début at the Crystal Palace. He took four firsts and three specials." But I knew he was only trying to throw heart into me. They might scrub, and they might rub, and they might pipe-clay, but they couldn't pipe-clay the insides of me, and they was black-and-tan.

Then we came to a garden, which it was not, but the biggest hall in the world. Inside there was lines of benches a few miles long, and on them sat every dog in America. If all the dog-snatchers in Montreal had worked night and day for a year, they couldn't have caught so many dogs. And they was all shouting and barking and howling so vicious that my heart stopped beating. For at first I thought they was all enraged at my presuming to intrude. But after I got in my place they kept at it just the same, barking at every dog as he come in: daring him to fight, and ordering him out, and asking him what breed of dog he thought he was, anyway. Jimmy Jocks was chained just behind me, and he said he never see so fine a show. "That's a hot class you're in, my lad," he says, looking over into my street, where there were thirty bull-terriers. They was all as white as cream, and each so beautiful that if I could have broke my chain I would have run all the way home and hid myself under the horse-trough.

All night long they talked and sang, and passed greetings with old pals, and the homesick puppies howled dismal. Them that couldn't sleep wouldn't let no others sleep, and all the electric lights burned in the roof, and in my eyes. I could hear Jimmy Jocks snoring peaceful, but I could only doze by jerks, and when I dozed I dreamed horrible. All the dogs in the hall seemed coming at me for daring to intrude, with their jaws red and open, and their eyes blazing like the lights in the roof. "You're a street dog! Get out, you street dog!" they yells. And as they drives me out, the pipe clay drops off me, and they laugh and shriek; and when I looks down I see that I have turned into a black-and-tan.

They was most awful dreams, and next morning, when Miss Dorothy comes and gives me water in a pan, I begs and begs her to take me home; but she can't understand. "How well Kid is!" she says. And when I jumps into the Master's arm and pulls to break my chain, he says, "If he knew all as he had against him, miss, he wouldn't be so gay." And from a book they reads out the names of the beautiful high-bred terriers which I have got to meet. And I can't make 'em understand that I only want to run away and hide myself where no one will see me.

Then suddenly men comes hurrying down our street and begins to brush the beautiful bull-terriers; and the Master rubs me with a towel so excited that his hands tremble awful, and Miss Dorothy tweaks my ears between her gloves, so that the blood runs to 'em, and they turn pink and stand up straight and sharp.

"Now, then, Nolan," says she, her voice shaking just like his fingers, "keep his head up—and never let the judge lose sight of him." When I hears that my legs breaks under me, for I knows all about judges. Twice the old Master goes up before the judge for fighting me with other dogs, and the judge promises him if he ever does it again he'll chain him up in jail. I knew he'd find me out. A judge can't be fooled by no pipe clay. He can see right through you, and he reads your insides.

The judging-ring, which is where the judge holds out, was so like a fighting-pit that when I come in it, and finds six other dogs there, I springs into position, so that when they lets us go I can defend myself. But the Master smooths down my hair and whispers, "Hold 'ard, Kid, hold 'ard. This ain't a fight," says he. "Look your prettiest," he whispers. "Please, Kid, look your prettiest"; and he pulls my leash so tight that I can't touch my pats to the sawdust, and my nose goes up in the air. There was millions of people a-watching us from the railings, and three of our kennel men, too, making fun of the Master and me, and Miss Dorothy with her chin just reaching to the rail, and her eyes so big that I thought she was a-going to cry. It was awful to think that when the judge stood up and exposed me, all those people, and Miss Dorothy, would be there to see me driven from the Show.

The judge he was a fierce-looking man with specs on his nose, and a red beard. When I first come in he didn't see me, owing to my being too quick for him and dodging behind the Master. But when the Master drags me round and I pulls at the sawdust to keep back, the judge looks at us careless-like, and then stops and glares through his specs, and I knew it was all up with me.

"Are there any more?" asks the judge to the gentleman at the gate, but never taking his specs from me.

The man at the gate looks in his book. "Seven in the novice class," says he. "They're all here. You can go ahead," and he shuts the gate.

The judge he doesn't hesitate a moment. He just waves his hand toward the corner of the ring. "Take him away," he says to the Master, "over there, and keep him away"; and he turns and looks most solemn at the six beautiful bull-terriers. I don't know how I crawled to that corner. I wanted to scratch under the sawdust and dig myself a grave. The kennel men they slapped the rail with their hands and laughed at the Master like they would fall over. They pointed at me in the corner, and their sides just shaked. But little Miss Dorothy she presses her lips tight against the rail, and I see tears rolling from her eyes. The Master he hangs his head like he had been whipped. I felt most sorry for him than all. He was so red, and he was letting on not to see the kennel men, and blinking his eyes. If the judge had ordered me right out it wouldn't have disgraced us so, but it was keeping me there while he was judging the high-bred dogs that hurt so hard. With all those people staring, too. And his doing it so quick, without no doubt nor questions. You can't fool the judges. They see inside you.

But he couldn't make up his mind about them high-bred dogs. He scowls at 'em, and he glares at 'em, first with his head on the one side and then on the other. And he feels of 'em, and orders 'em to run about. And Nolan leans against the rails, with his head hung down, and pats me. And Miss Dorothy comes over beside him, but don't say nothing, only wipes her eye with her finger. A man on the other side of the rail he says to the Master, "The judge don't like your dog?"

"No," says the Master.

"Have you ever shown him before?" says the man.

"No," says the Master, "and I'll never show him again. He's my dog," says the Master, "and he suits me! And I don't care what no judges think." And when he says them kind words, I licks his hand most grateful.

The judge had two of the six dogs on a little platform in the middle of the ring, and he had chased the four other dogs into the corners, where they was licking their chops, and letting on they didn't care, same as Nolan was.

The two dogs on the platform was so beautiful that the judge hisself couldn't tell which was the best of 'em, even when he stoops down and holds their heads together. But at last he gives a sigh, and brushes the sawdust off his knees, and goes to the table in the ring, where there was a man keeping score, and heaps and heaps of blue and gold and red and yellow ribbons. And the judge picks up a bunch of 'em and walks to the two gentlemen who was holding the beautiful dogs, and he says to each, "What's his number?" and he hands each gentleman a ribbon. And then he turned sharp and comes straight at the Master.

"What's his number?" says the judge. And Master was so scared that he couldn't make no answer.

But Miss Dorothy claps her hands and cries out like she was laughing, "Three twenty-six," and the judge writes it down and shoves Master the blue ribbon.

I bit the Master, and I jumps and bit Miss Dorothy, and I waggled so hard that the Master couldn't hold me. When I get to the gate Miss Dorothy snatches me up and kisses me between the ears, right before millions of people, and they both hold me so tight that I didn't know which of them was carrying of me. But one thing I knew, for I listened hard, as it was the judge hisself as said it.

"Did you see that puppy I gave first to?" says the judge to the gentleman at the gate.

"I did. He was a bit out of his class," says the gate gentleman.

"He certainly was!" says the judge, and they both laughed.

But I didn't care. They couldn't hurt me then, not with Nolan holding the blue ribbon and Miss Dorothy hugging my ears, and the kennel men sneaking away, each looking like he'd been caught with his nose under the lid of the slop-can.

We sat down together, and we all three just talked as fast as we could. They was so pleased that I couldn't help feeling proud myself, and I barked and leaped about so gay that all the bull-terriers in our street stretched on their chains and howled at me.

"Just look at him!" says one of those I had beat. "What's he giving hisself airs about?"

"Because he's got one blue ribbon!" says another of 'em. "Why, when I was a puppy I used to eat 'em, and if that judge could ever learn to know a toy from a mastiff, I'd have had this one."

But Jimmy Jocks he leaned over from his bench and says, "Well done, Kid. Didn't I tell you so?" What he 'ad told me was that I might get a "commended," but I didn't remind him.

"Didn't I tell you," says Jimmy Jocks, "that I saw your grandfather make his début at the Crystal—"

"Yes, sir, you did, sir," says I, for I have no love for the men of my family.

A gentleman with a showing-leash around his neck comes up just then and looks at me very critical. "Nice dog you've got, Miss Wyndham," says he; "would you care to sell him?"

"He's not my dog," says Miss Dorothy, holding me tight. "I wish he were."

"He's not for sale, sir," says the Master, and I was *that* glad.

"Oh, he's yours, is he?" says the gentleman, looking hard at Nolan. "Well, I'll give you a hundred dollars for him," says he, careless-like.

"Thank you, sir; he's not for sale," says Nolan, but his eyes get very big. The gentleman he walked away; but I watches him, and he talks to a man in a golf-cap, and by and by the man comes along our street, looking at all the dogs, and stops in front of me.

"This your dog?" says he to Nolan. "Pity he's so leggy," says he. "If he had a good tail, and a longer stop, and his ears were set higher, he'd be a good dog. As he is, I'll give you fifty dollars for him."

But, before the Master could speak, Miss Dorothy laughs and says: "You're Mr. Polk's kennel man, I believe. Well, you tell Mr. Polk from me that the dog's not for sale now any more than he was five minutes ago, and that when he is, he'll have to bid against me for him."

The man looks foolish at that, but he turns to Nolan quick-like. "I'll give you three hundred for him," he says.

"Oh, indeed!" whispers Miss Dorothy, like she was talking to herself. "That's it, is it?" And she turns and looks at me just as though she had never seen me before. Nolan he was a-gaping, too, with his mouth open. But he holds me tight.

"He's not for sale," he growls, like he was frightened; and the man looks black and walks away.

"Why, Nolan!" cried Miss Dorothy, "Mr. Polk knows more about bull-terriers than any amateur in America. What can he mean? Why, Kid is no more than a puppy! Three hundred dollars for a puppy!"

"And he ain't no thoroughbred, neither!" cries the Master. "He's 'Unknown,' ain't he? Kid can't help it, of course, but his mother, miss—"

I dropped my head. I couldn't bear he should tell Miss Dorothy. I couldn't bear she should know I had stolen my blue ribbon.

But the Master never told, for at that a gentleman runs up, calling, "Three twenty-six, three twenty-six!" And Miss Dorothy says, "Here he is; what is it?"

"The Winners' class," says the gentleman. "Hurry, please; the judge is waiting for him."

Nolan tries to get me off the chain on to a showing-leash, but he shakes so, he only chokes me. "What is it, miss?" he says. "What is it?"

"The Winners' class," says Miss Dorothy. "The judge wants him with the winners of the other classes—to decide which is the best. It's only a form," says she. "He has the champions against him now."

"Yes," says the gentleman, as he hurries us to the ring. "I'm afraid it's only a form for your dog, but the judge wants all the winners, puppy class even."

We had got to the gate, and the gentleman there was writing down my number.

"Who won the open?" asks Miss Dorothy.

"Oh, who would?" laughs the gentleman. "The old champion, of course. He's won for three years now. There he is. Isn't he wonderful?" says he; and he points to a dog that's standing proud and haughty on the platform in the middle of the ring.

I never see so beautiful a dog—so fine and clean and noble, so white like he had rolled hisself in flour, holding his nose up and his eyes shut, same as though no one was worth looking at. Aside of him we other dogs, even though we had a blue ribbon apiece, seemed like lumps of mud. He was a royal gentleman, a king, he was. His master didn't have to hold his head with no leash. He held it hisself, standing as still as an iron dog on a lawn, like he knew all the people was looking at him. And so they was, and no one around the ring pointed at no other dog but him.

"Oh, what a picture!" cried Miss Dorothy. "He's like a marble figure by a great artist—one who loved dogs. Who is he?" says she, looking in her book. "I don't keep up with terriers."

"Oh, you know him," says the gentleman. "He is the champion of champions, Regent Royal."

The Master's face went red.

"And this is Regent Royal's son," cries he, and he pulls me quick into the ring, and plants me on the platform next my father.

I trembled so that I near fell. My legs twisted like a leash. But my father he never looked at me. He only smiled the same sleepy smile, and he still kept his eyes half shut, like as no one, no, not even his own son, was worth his lookin' at.

The judge he didn't let me stay beside my father, but, one by one, he placed the other dogs next to him and measured and felt and pulled at them. And each one he put down, but he never put my father down. And then he comes over and picks me up and sets me back on the platform, shoulder to shoulder with the Champion Regent Royal, and goes down on his knees, and looks into our eyes.

The gentleman with my father he laughs, and says to the judge, "Thinking of keeping us here all day, John?" But the judge he doesn't hear him, and goes behind us and runs his hand down my side, and holds back my ears, and takes my jaws between his fingers. The crowd around the ring is very deep now, and nobody says nothing. The gentleman at the score-table, he is leaning forward, with his elbows on his knees and his eyes very wide, and the gentleman at the gate is whispering quick to Miss Dorothy, who has turned white. I stood as stiff as stone. I didn't even breathe. But out of the corner of my eye I could see my father licking his pink chops, and yawning just a little, like he was bored.

The judge he had stopped looking fierce and was looking solemn. Something inside him seemed a-troubling him awful. The more he stares at us now, the more solemn he gets, and when he touches us he does it gentle, like he was patting us. For a long time he kneels in the sawdust, looking at my father and at me, and no one around the ring says nothing to nobody.

Then the judge takes a breath and touches me sudden. "It's his," he says. But he lays his hand just as quick on my father. "I'm sorry," says he.

The gentleman holding my father cries:

"Do you mean to tell me—"

And the judge he answers, "I mean the other is the better dog." He takes my father's head between his hands and looks down at him most sorrowful. "The king is dead," says he. "Long live the king! Good-by, Regent," he says.

The crowd around the railings clapped their hands, and some laughed scornful, and every one talks fast, and I start for the gate, so dizzy that I can't see my way. But my father pushes in front of me, walking very daintily, and smiling sleepy, same as he had just been waked, with his head high, and his eyes shut, looking at nobody.

So that is how I "came by my inheritance," as Miss Dorothy calls it; and just for that, though I couldn't feel where I was any different, the crowd follows me to my bench, and pats me, and coos at me, like I was a baby in a baby-carriage. And the handlers have to hold 'em back so that the gentlemen from the papers can make pictures of me, and Nolan walks me up and down so proud, and the men shake their heads and says, "He certainly is the true type, he is!" And the pretty ladies ask Miss Dorothy, who sits beside me letting me lick her gloves to show the crowd what friends we is, "Aren't you afraid he'll bite you?" And Jimmy Jock calls to me, "Didn't I tell you so? I always knew you were one of us. Blood will out, Kid; blood will out. I saw your grandfather," says he, "make his début at the Crystal Palace. But he was never the dog you are!"

After that, if I could have asked for it, there was nothing I couldn't get. You might have thought I was a snow-dog, and they was afeard I'd melt. If I wet my pats, Nolan gave me a hot bath and chained me to the stove; if I couldn't eat my food, being stuffed full by the cook,— for I am a house-dog now, and let in to lunch, whether there is visitors or not,—Nolan would run to bring the vet. It was all tommy rot, as Jimmy says, but meant most kind. I couldn't scratch myself comfortable, without Nolan giving me nasty drinks, and rubbing me outside till it burnt awful; and I wasn't let to eat bones for fear of spoiling my "beautiful" mouth, what mother used to call my "punishing jaw"; and my food was cooked special on a gas-stove; and Miss Dorothy gives me an overcoat, cut very stylish like the champions', to wear when we goes out carriage-driving.

After the next Show, where I takes three blue ribbons, four silver cups, two medals, and brings home forty-five dollars for Nolan, they gives me a "registered" name, same as Jimmy's. Miss Dorothy wanted to call me

"Regent Heir Apparent"; but I was *that* glad when Nolan says, "No; Kid don't owe nothing to his father, only to you and hisself. So, if you please, miss, we'll call him Wyndham Kid." And so they did, and you can see it on my overcoat in blue letters, and painted top of my kennel. It was all too hard to understand. For days I just sat and wondered if I was really me, and how it all come about, and why everybody was so kind. But oh, it was so good they was, for if they hadn't been I'd never have got the thing I most wished after. But, because they was kind, and not liking to deny me nothing, they gave it me, and it was more to me than anything in the world.

It came about one day when we was out driving. We was in the cart they calls the dog-cart because it's the one Miss Dorothy keeps to take Jimmy and me for an airing. Nolan was up behind, and me, in my new overcoat, was sitting beside Miss Dorothy. I was admiring the view, and thinking how good it was to have a horse pull you about so that you needn't get yourself splashed and have to be washed, when I hears a dog calling loud for help, and I pricks up my ears and looks over the horse's head. And I sees something that makes me tremble down to my toes. In the road before us three big dogs was chasing a little old lady-dog. She had a string to her tail, where some boys had tied a can, and she was dirty with mud and ashes, and torn most awful. She was too far done up to get away, and too old to help herself, but she was making a fight for her life, snapping her old gums savage, and dying game. All this I see in a wink, and then the three dogs pinned her down, and I can't stand it no longer, and clears the wheel and lands in the road on my head. It was my stylish overcoat done that, and I cursed it proper, but I gets my pats again quick, and makes a rush for the fighting. Behind me I hear Miss Dorothy cry: "They'll kill that old dog. Wait, take my whip. Beat them off her! The Kid can take care of himself"; and I hear Nolan fall into the road, and the horse come to a stop. The old lady-dog was down, and the three was eating her vicious; but as I come up, scattering the pebbles, she hears, and thinking it's one more of them, she lifts her head, and my heart breaks open like some one had sunk his teeth in it. For, under the ashes and the dirt and the blood, I can see who it is, and I know that my mother has come back to me.

I gives a yell that throws them three dogs off their legs.

"Mother!" I cries. "I'm the Kid," I cries. "I'm coming to you. Mother, I'm coming!"

And I shoots over her at the throat of the big dog, and the other two they sinks their teeth into that stylish overcoat and tears it off me, and that sets me free, and I lets them have it. I never had so fine a fight as that! What with mother being there to see, and not having been let to mix up in no fights since I become a prize-winner, it just naturally did me good, and it wasn't three shakes before I had 'em yelping. Quick as a wink, mother she jumps in to help me, and I just laughed to see her. It was so like old times. And Nolan he made me laugh, too. He was like a hen on a bank, shaking the butt of his whip, but not daring to cut in for fear of hitting me.

"Stop it, Kid," he says, "stop it. Do you want to be all torn up?" says he. "Think of the Boston show," says he. "Think of Chicago. Think of Danbury. Don't you never want to be a champion?" How was I to think of all them places when I had three dogs to cut up at the same time? But in a minute two of 'em begs for mercy, and mother and me lets 'em run away. The big one he ain't able to run away. Then mother and me we dances and jumps, and barks and laughs, and bites each other and rolls each other in the road. There never was two dogs so happy as we. And Nolan he whistles and calls and begs me to come to him; but I just laugh and play larks with mother.

"Now, you come with me," says I, "to my new home, and never try to run away again." And I shows her our house with the five red roofs, set on the top of the hill. But mother trembles awful, and says: "They'd never let me in such a place. Does the Viceroy live there, Kid?" says she. And I laugh at her. "No; I do," I says. "And if they won't let you live there, too, you and me will go back to the streets together, for we must never be parted no more." So we trots up the hill side by side, with Nolan trying to catch me, and Miss Dorothy laughing at him from the cart.

"The Kid's made friends with the poor old dog," says she. "Maybe he knew her long ago when he ran the streets himself. Put her in here beside me, and see if he doesn't follow."

So when I hears that I tells mother to go with Nolan and sit in the cart; but she says no—that she'd soil the pretty lady's frock; but I tells her to do as I say, and so Nolan lifts her, trembling still, into the cart, and I runs alongside, barking joyful.

When we drives into the stables I takes mother to my kennel, and tells her to go inside it and make herself at home. "Oh, but he won't let me!" says she.

"Who won't let you?" says I, keeping my eye on Nolan, and growling a bit nasty, just to show I was meaning to have my way.

"Why, Wyndham Kid," says she, looking up at the name on my kennel.

"But I'm Wyndham Kid!" says I.

"You!" cries mother. "You! Is my little Kid the great Wyndham Kid the dogs all talk about?" And at that, she being very old, and sick, and nervous, as mothers are, just drops down in the straw and weeps bitter.

Well, there ain't much more than that to tell. Miss Dorothy she settled it.

"If the Kid wants the poor old thing in the stables," says she, "let her stay.

"You see," says she, "she's a black-and-tan, and his mother was a black-and-tan, and maybe that's what makes Kid feel so friendly toward her," says she.

"Indeed, for me," says Nolan, "she can have the best there is. I'd never drive out no dog that asks for a crust nor a shelter," he says. "But what will Mr. Wynham do?"

"He'll do what I say," says Miss Dorothy, "and if I say she's to stay, she will stay, and I say—she's to stay!"

And so mother and Nolan and me found a home. Mother was scared at first—not being used to kind people; but she was so gentle and loving that the grooms got fonder of her than of me, and tried to make me jealous by patting of her and giving her the pick of the vittles. But that was the wrong way to hurt my feelings. That's all, I think. Mother is so happy here that I tell her we ought to call it the Happy Hunting Grounds, because no one hunts you, and there is nothing to hunt; it just all comes to you. And so we live in peace, mother sleeping all day in the sun, or behind the stove in the head groom's office, being fed twice a day regular by Nolan, and all the day by the other grooms most irregular. And as for me, I go hurrying around the country to the bench-shows, winning money and cups for Nolan, and taking the blue ribbons away from father.

32

Effie Whittlesy

BY GEORGE ADE

MRS. WALLACE assisted her husband to remove his overcoat and put her warm palms against his red and wind-beaten cheeks.

"I have good news," said she.

"Another bargain sale?"

"Pshaw, no! A new girl, and I really believe she's a jewel. She isn't young or good-looking, and when I asked her if she wanted any nights off she said she wouldn't go out after dark for anything in the world. What do you think of that?"

"That's too good to be true."

"No, it isn't. Wait and see her. She came here from the intelligence office about two o'clock and said she was willing to 'lick right in.' You wouldn't know the kitchen. She has it as clean as a pin."

"What nationality?"

"None—that is, she's a home product. She's from the country—and *green!* But she's a good soul, I'm sure. As soon as I looked at her, I just felt sure that we could trust her."

"Well, I hope so. If she is all that you say, why, for goodness sake give her any pay she wants—put lace curtains in her room and subscribe for all the story papers on the market."

"Bless you, I don't believe she'd read them. Every time I've looked into the kitchen she's been working like a Trojan and singing 'Beulah Land.' "

"Oh, she sings, does she? I knew there'd be some drawback."

"You won't mind that. We can keep the doors closed."

The dinner-table was set in tempting cleanliness. Mrs. Wallace surveyed the arrangement of glass and silver and gave a nod of approval and relief. Then she touched the bell and in a moment the new servant entered.

She was a tall woman who had said her last farewell to girlhood.

Then a very strange thing happened.

Mr. Wallace turned to look at the new girl and his eyes enlarged. He gazed at her as if fascinated either by cap or freckles. An expression of wonderment came to his face and he said, "Well, by George!"

The girl had come very near the table when she took the first overt glance at him. Why did the tureen sway in her hands? She smiled in a frightened way and hurriedly set the tureen on the table.

Mr. Wallace was not long undecided, but during that moment of hesitancy the panorama of his life was rolled backward. He had been reared in the democracy of a small community, and the democratic spirit came uppermost.

"This isn't Effie Whittlesy?" said he.

"For the land's sake!" she exclaimed, backing away, and this was a virtual confession.

"You don't know me."

"Well, if it ain't Ed Wallace!"

Would that words were ample to tell how Mrs. Wallace settled back in her chair blinking first at her husband and then at the new girl, vainly trying to understand what it meant.

She saw Mr. Wallace reach awkwardly across the table and shake hands with the new girl and then she found voice to gasp, "Of all things!"

Mr. Wallace was confused and without a policy. He was wavering between his formal duty as an employer and his natural regard for an old friend. Anyway, it occurred to him that an explanation would be timely.

"This is Effie Whittlesy from Brainerd," said he. "I used to go to school with her. She's been at our house often. I haven't seen her for—I didn't know you were in Chicago," turning to Effie.

"Well, Ed Wallace, you could knock me down with a feather," said Effie, who still stood in a flustered attitude a few paces back from the table. "I had no more idee when I heard the name Wallace that it'd be you, though knowin', of course, you was up here. Wallace is such a common name I never give it a second thought. But the minute I seen you—law! I knew who it was, well enough."

"I thought you were still at Brainerd," said Mr. Wallace, after a pause.

"I left there a year ago November, and come to visit Mort's people. I s'pose you know that Mort has a position with the street-car company. He's doin' *so* well. I didn't want to be no burden on him, so I started out on my own hook, seein' that there was no use of goin' back to Brainerd to slave for two dollars a week. I had a good place with Mr. Sanders, the railroad man on the North Side, but I left becuz they wanted me to serve liquor. I'd about as soon handle a toad as a bottle of beer. Liquor was the ruination of Jesse. He's gone to the dogs—been off with a circus somewheres for two years."

"The family's all broken up, eh!" asked Mr. Wallace.

"Gone to the four winds since mother died. Of course you know that Lora married Huntford Thomas and is livin' on the old Murphy place. They're doin' about as well as you could expect, with Huntford as lazy as he is."

"Yes? That's good," said Mr. Wallace.

Was this an old settlers' reunion or a quiet family dinner? The soup had been waiting.

Mrs. Wallace came into the breach.

"That will be all for the present, Effie," said she.

Effie gave a startled "Oh!" and vanished into the kitchen.

"It means," said Mr. Wallace, "that we were children together, made mud pies in the same puddle and sat next to each other in the old school-house at Brainerd. She is a Whittlesy. Everybody in Brainerd knew the Whittlesys. Large family, all poor as church mice, but sociable—and freckled. Effie's a good girl."

"Effie! *Effie!* And she called you Ed!"

"My dear, there are no misters in Brainerd. Why shouldn't she call me Ed! She never heard me called anything else."

"She'll have to call you something else here. You tell her so."

"Now, don't ask me to put on any airs with one of the Whittlesys, because they know me from away back. Effie has seen me licked at school. She has been at our house, almost like one of the family, when mother was sick and needed another girl. If my memory serves me right, I've taken her to singing-school and exhibitions. So I'm in no position to lord it over, and I wouldn't do it any way. I'd hate to have her go back to Brainerd and report that she met me here in Chicago and I was too stuck up to remember old times and requested her to address me as 'Mister Wallace.' Now, you never lived in a small town."

"No, I never enjoyed that privilege," said Mrs. Wallace, dryly.

"Well, it is a privilege in some respects, but it carries certain penalties with it, too. It's a very poor schooling for a fellow who wants to be a snob."

"I would call it snobbishness to correct a servant who addresses me by my first name. 'Ed' indeed! Why, I never dared to call you that."

"No, you never lived in Brainerd."

"And you say you used to take her to singing-school?"

"Yes, ma'am—twenty years ago, in Brainerd. You're not surprised, are you? You knew when you married me that I was a child of the soil, who worked his way through college and came to the city in a suit of store clothes. I'll admit that my past does not exactly qualify me for the Four Hundred, but it will be great if I ever get into politics."

"I don't object to your having a past, but I was just thinking how pleasant it will be when we give a dinner-party to have her come in and address you as 'Ed.'"

Mr. Wallace patted the tablecloth cheerily with both hands and laughed.

"I really don't believe you'd care," said Mrs. Wallace.

"Effie isn't going to demoralize the household," he said, consolingly. "Down in Brainerd we may be a little slack on the by-laws of etiquette, but we can learn in time."

Mrs. Wallace touched the bell and Effie returned.

As she brought in the second course, Mr. Wallace deliberately en-couraged her by an amiable smile, and she asked, "Do you get the Brainerd papers?"

"Yes—every week."

"There's been a good deal of sickness down there this winter. Lora wrote to me that your uncle Joe had been kind o' poorly."

"I think he's up and around again."

"That's good."

And she edged back to the kitchen.

With the change for dessert she ventured to say: "Mort was wonderin' about you the other day. He said he hadn't saw you for a long time. My! You've got a nice house here."

After dinner Mrs. Wallace published her edict. Effie would have to go. Mr. Wallace positively forbade the "strong talking-to" which his wife advocated. He said it was better that Effie should go, but she must be sent away gently and diplomatically.

Effie was "doing up" the dishes when Mr. Wallace lounged into the kitchen and began a roundabout talk. His wife, seated in the front room, heard the prolonged murmur. Ed and Effie were going over the family histories of Brainerd and recalling incidents that may have re-lated to mud pies or school exhibitions.

Mrs. Wallace had been a Twombley, of Baltimore, and no Twombley, with relatives in Virginia, could humiliate herself into rivalry with a kitchen girl, or dream of such a thing, so why should Mrs. Wallace be uneasy and constantly wonder what Ed and Effie were talking about?

Mrs. Wallace was faint from loss of pride. The night before they had dined with the Gages. Mr. Wallace, a picture of distinction in his eve-ning clothes, had shown himself the bright light of the seven who sat at the table. She had been proud of him. Twenty-four hours later a servant emerges from the kitchen and hails him as "Ed"!

The low talk in the kitchen continued. Mrs. Wallace had a feverish longing to tiptoe down that way and listen, or else go into the kitchen, sweepingly, and with a few succinct commands, set Miss Whittlesy back into her menial station. But she knew that Mr. Wallace would misinterpret any such move and probably taunt her with joking references to her "jealousy," so she forbore.

Mr. Wallace, with an unlighted cigar in his mouth (Effie had forbidden him to smoke in the kitchen), leaned in the doorway and waited to give the conversation a turn.

At last he said: "Effie, why don't you go down and visit Lora for a month or so? She'd be glad to see you."

"I know, Ed, but I ain't a Rockefeller to lay off work a month at a time an' go around visitin' my relations. I'd like to well enough—but—"

"Oh pshaw! I can get you a ticket to Brainerd tomorrow and it won't cost you anything down there."

"No, it ain't Chicago, that's a fact. A dollar goes a good ways down there. But what'll your wife do? She told me today she'd had an awful time gettin' any help."

"Well—to tell you the truth, Effie, you see—you're an old friend of mine and I don't like the idea of your being here in my house as a—well, as a hired girl."

"No, I guess I'm a servant now. I used to be a hird girl when I worked for your ma, but now I'm a servant. I don't see as it makes any difference what you call me, as long as the work's the same."

"You understand what I mean, don't you? Any time you come here to my house I want you to come as an old acquaintance—a visitor, not a servant."

"Ed Wallace, don't be foolish. I'd as soon work for you as anyone, and a good deal sooner."

"I know, but I wouldn't like to see my wife giving orders to an old friend, as you are. You understand, don't you?"

"I don't know. I'll quit if you say so."

"Tut! tut! I'll get you that ticket and you can start for Brainerd tomorrow. Promise me, now."

"I'll go, and tickled enough, if that's the way you look at it."

"And if you come back, I can get you a dozen places to work."

Next evening Effie departed by carriage, although protesting against the luxury.

"Ed Wallace," said she, pausing in the hallway, "they never will believe me when I tell it in Brainerd."

"Give them my best and tell them I'm about the same as ever."

"I'll do that. Good-by."

"Good-by."

Mrs. Wallace, watching from the window, saw Effie disappear into the carriage.

"Thank goodness," said she.

"Yes," said Mr. Wallace, to whom the whole episode had been like a cheering beverage, "I've invited her to call when she comes back."

"To call—here?"

"Most assuredly. I told her you'd be delighted to see her at any time."

"The idea! Did you invite her, really?"

"Of course I did! And I'm reasonably certain that she'll come."

"What shall I do?"

"I think you can manage it, even if you never did live in Brainerd."

Then the revulsion came and Mrs. Wallace, with a return of pride in her husband, said she would try.

33

"Little Gentleman"

BY BOOTH TARKINGTON

THE midsummer sun was stinging hot outside the little barber-shop next to the corner drug store and Penrod, undergoing a toilette preliminary to his very slowly approaching twelfth birthday, was adhesive enough to retain upon his face much hair as it fell from the shears. There is a mystery here: the tonsorial processes are not unagreeable to manhood; in truth, they are soothing; but the hairs detached from a boy's head get into his eyes, his ears, his nose, his mouth, and down his neck, and he does everywhere itch excruciatingly. Wherefore he blinks, winks, weeps, twitches, condenses his countenance, and squirms; and perchance the barber's scissors clip more than intended—belike an outlying flange of ear.

"Um—muh—*ow!*" said Penrod, this thing having happened.

"D' I touch y' up a little?" inquired the barber, smiling falsely.

"Ooh—*uh!*" The boy in the chair offered inarticulate protest, as the wound was rubbed with alum.

"*That* don't hurt!" said the barber. "You *will* get it, though, if you don't sit stiller," he continued, nipping in the bud any attempt on the part of his patient to think that he already had "it."

"Pfuff!" said Penrod, meaning no disrespect, but endeavoring to dislodge a temporary mustache from his lip.

"You ought to see how still that little Georgie Bassett sits," the barber went on, reprovingly. "I hear everybody says he's the best boy in town."

"Pfuff! *Phirr!*" There was a touch of intentional contempt in this.

"I haven't heard nobody around the neighborhood makin' no such remarks," added the barber, "about nobody of the name of Penrod Schofield."

"Well," said Penrod, clearing his mouth after a struggle, "who wants 'em to? Ouch!"

"I hear they call Georgie Bassett the 'little gentleman,'" ventured the barber, provocatively, meeting with instant success.

"They better not call *me* that," returned Penrod truculently. "I'd like to hear anybody try. Just once, that's all! I bet they'd never try it ag—— *Ouch!*"

"Why? What'd you do to 'em?"

"It's all right what I'd *do!* I bet they wouldn't want to call me that again long as they lived!"

"What'd you do if it was a little girl? You wouldn't hit her, would you?"

"Well, I'd—— Ouch!"

"You wouldn't hit a little girl, would you?" the barber persisted, gathering into his powerful fingers a mop of hair from the top of Penrod's head and pulling that suffering head into an unnatural position. "Doesn't the Bible say it ain't never right to hit the weak sex?"

"Ow! *Say*, look *out!*"

"So you'd go and punch a pore, weak, little girl, would you?" said the barber, reprovingly.

"Well, who said I'd hit her?" demanded the chivalrous Penrod. "I bet I'd *fix* her though, all right. She'd see!"

"You wouldn't call her names, would you?"

"No, I wouldn't! What hurt is it to call anybody names?"

"Is that *so!*" exclaimed the barber. "Then you was intending what I heard you hollering at Fisher's grocery delivery wagon driver fer a favor, the other day when I was goin' by your house, was you? I reckon I better tell him, because he says to me after*werds* if he ever lays eyes on you when you ain't in your own yard, he's goin' to do a whole lot o' things you ain't goin' to like! Yessir, that's what he says to *me!*"

"He better catch me first, I guess, before he talks so much."

"Well," resumed the barber, "that ain't sayin' what you'd do if a young lady ever walked up and called you a little gentleman. *I* want to hear what you'd do to her. I guess I know, though—come to think of it."

"What?" demanded Penrod.

"You'd sick that pore ole dog of yours on her cat if she had one, I expect," guessed the barber derisively.

"No, I would not!"

"Well, what *would* you do?"

"I'd do enough. Don't worry about that!"

"Well, suppose it was a boy, then: what'd you do if a boy came up to you and says, 'Hello, little gentleman'?"

"He'd be lucky," said Penrod, with a sinister frown, "if he got home alive."

"Suppose it was a boy twice your size?"

"Just let him try," said Penrod ominously. "You just let him try. He'd never see daylight again; that's all!"

The barber dug ten active fingers into the helpless scalp before him and did his best to displace it, while the anguished Penrod, becoming instantly a seething crucible of emotion, misdirected his natural resentment into maddened brooding upon what he would do to a boy "twice his size" who should dare to call him "little gentleman." The barber shook him as his father had never shaken him; the barber buffeted him, rocked him frantically to and fro; the barber seemed to be trying to wring his neck; and Penrod saw himself in staggering zigzag pictures, destroying large, screaming, fragmentary boys who had insulted him.

The torture stopped suddenly; and clenched, weeping eyes began to see again, while the barber applied cooling lotions which made Penrod smell like a colored housemaid's ideal.

"Now what," asked the barber, combing the reeking locks gently, "what would it make you so mad fer, to have somebody call you a little gentleman? It's a kind of compliment, as it were, you might say. What would you want to hit anybody fer *that* fer?"

To the mind of Penrod, this question was without meaning or reasonableness. It was within neither his power nor his desire to analyze the process by which the phrase had become offensive to him, and was now rapidly assuming the proportions of an outrage. He knew only that his gorge rose at the thought of it.

"You just let 'em try it!" he said threateningly, as he slid down from the chair. And as he went out of the door, after further conversation on the same subject, he called back those warning words once more: "Just let 'em try it! Just once—that's all *I* ask 'em to. They'll find out what they *get!*"

The barber chuckled. Then a fly lit on the barber's nose and he slapped at it, and the slap missed the fly but did not miss the nose. The barber was irritated. At this moment his birdlike eye gleamed a gleam as it fell upon customers approaching: the prettiest little girl in the world, leading by the hand her baby brother, Mitchy-Mitch, coming to have Mitchy-Mitch's hair clipped, against the heat.

It was a hot day and idle, with little to feed the mind—and the barber was a mischievous man with an irritated nose. He did his worst.

Meanwhile, the brooding Penrod pursued his homeward way; no great distance, but long enough for several one-sided conflicts with malign insulters made of thin air. "You better *not* call me that!" he muttered. "You just try it, and you'll get what other people got when *they* tried it. You better not ack fresh with *me!* Oh, you *will,* will you?" He delivered a vicious kick full upon the shins of an iron fence-post, which suffered little, though Penrod instantly regretted his indiscretion. "Oof!" he grunted, hopping; and went on after bestowing a look of awful hostility upon the fence-post. "I guess you'll know better next time," he said, in parting, to this antagonist. "You just let me catch you around here again and I'll——" His voice sank to inarticulate but ominous murmurings. He was in a dangerous mood.

Nearing home, however, his belligerent spirit was diverted to happier interests by the discovery that some workmen had left a caldron of tar in the cross-street, close by his father's stable. He tested it, but found it inedible. Also, as a substitute for professional chewing-gum it was unsatisfactory, being insufficiently boiled down and too thin, though of a pleasant, lukewarm temperature. But it had an excess of one quality— it was sticky. It was the stickiest tar Penrod had ever used for any purposes whatsoever, and nothing upon which he wiped his hands served to rid them of it; neither his polka-dotted shirt waist nor his knickerbockers; neither the fence, nor even Duke, who came unthinkingly wagging out to greet him, and retired wiser.

Nevertheless, tar is tar. Much can be done with it, no matter what its condition; so Penrod lingered by the caldron, though from a neighboring yard could be heard the voices of comrades, including that of Sam Williams. On the ground about the caldron were scattered chips and sticks and bits of wood to the number of a great multitude. Penrod mixed quantities of this refuse into the tar, and interested himself in seeing how much of it he could keep moving in slow swirls upon the ebon surface.

Other surprises were arranged for the absent workmen. The caldron was almost full, and the surface of the tar near the rim. Penrod endeavored to ascertain how many pebbles and brickbats, dropped in, would cause an overflow. Laboring heartily to this end, he had almost accomplished it, when he received the suggestion for an experiment on a much larger scale. Embedded at the corner of a grass-plot across the street was a whitewashed stone, the size of a small watermelon and serving no purpose whatever save the questionable one of decoration. It was easily pried up with a stick; though getting it to the caldron tested the full strength of the ardent laborer. Instructed to perform such a task, he would have sincerely maintained its impossibility; but now, as it was unbidden, and promised rather destructive results, he set about it with unconquerable energy, feeling certain that he would be rewarded with a mighty splash. Perspiring, grunting vehemently, his back aching and all muscles strained, he progressed in short stages until the big stone lay at the base of the caldron. He rested a moment, panting, then lifted the stone, and was bending his shoulders for the heave that would lift it over the rim, when a sweet, taunting voice, close behind him, startled him cruelly.

"How do you do, *little gentleman!*"

Penrod squawked, dropped the stone, and shouted, "Shut up, you dern fool!" purely from instinct, even before his about-face made him aware who had so spitefully addressed him.

It was Marjorie Jones. Always dainty, and prettily dressed, she was in speckless and starchy white today, and a refreshing picture she made, with the new-shorn and powerfully scented Mitchy-Mitch clinging to her hand. They had stolen up behind the toiler, and now stood laughing together in sweet merriment. Since the passing of Penrod's Rupe Collins period he had experienced some severe qualms at the recollection of his last meeting with Marjorie and his Apache behavior; in truth, his heart instantly became as wax at sight of her, and he would have offered her fair speech; but, alas! in Marjorie's wonderful eyes there shone a consciousness of new powers of his undoing, and she denied him opportunity.

"Oh, *oh!*" she cried, mocking his pained outcry. "What a way for a *little gentleman* to talk! Little gentleman don't say wicked——"

"Marjorie!" Penrod, enraged and dismayed, felt himself stung beyond all endurance. Insult from her was bitterer to endure than from any other. "Don't you call me that again!"

"Why not, *little gentleman?*"

He stamped his foot. "You better stop!"

Marjorie sent into his furious face her lovely, spiteful laughter.

"Little gentleman, little gentleman, little gentleman!" she said deliberately. "How's the little gentleman this afternoon? Hello, little gentleman!"

Penrod, quite beside himself, danced eccentrically. "Dry up!" he howled. "Dry up, dry up, dry up, dry *up!*"

Mitchy-Mitch shouted with delight and applied a finger to the side of the caldron—a finger immediately snatched away and wiped upon a handkerchief by his fastidious sister.

" 'Ittle gellamun!" said Mitchy-Mitch.

"You better look out!" Penrod whirled upon this small offender with grim satisfaction. Here was at least something male that could without dishonor be held responsible. "You say that again, and I'll give you the worst——"

"You will *not!*" snapped Marjorie, instantly vitriolic. "He'll say just whatever he wants to, and he'll say it just as *much* as he wants to. Say it again, Mitchy-Mitch!"

" 'Ittle gellamun!" said Mitchy-Mitch promptly.

"Ow-*yah!*" Penrod's tone-production was becoming affected by his mental condition. "You say that again, and I'll——"

"Go on, Mitchy-Mitch," cried Marjorie. "He can't do a thing. He don't *dare!* Say it some more, Mitchy-Mitch—say it a whole lot!"

Mitchy-Mitch, his small, fat face shining with confidence in his immunity, complied.

" 'Ittle gellamun!" he squeaked malevolently. " 'Ittle gellamun! 'Ittle gellamun! 'Ittle gellamun!"

The desperate Penrod bent over the whitewashed rock, lifted it, and then—outdoing Porthos, John Ridd, and Ursus in one miraculous burst of strength—heaved it into the air.

Marjorie screamed.

But it was too late. The big stone descended into the precise midst of the caldron and Penrod got his mighty splash. It was far, far beyond his expectations.

Spontaneously there were grand and awful effects—volcanic spectacles of nightmare and eruption. A black sheet of eccentric shape rose out of the caldron and descended upon the three children, who had no time to evade it.

After it fell, Mitchy-Mitch, who stood nearest the caldron, was the thickest, though there was enough for all. Br'er Rabbit would have fled from any of them.

When Marjorie and Mitchy-Mitch got their breath, they used it vocally; and seldom have more penetrating sounds issued from human throats. Coincidentally, Marjorie, quite berserk, laid hands upon the largest stick within reach and fell upon Penrod with blind fury. He had the presence of mind to flee, and they went round and round the caldron, while Mitchy-Mitch feebly endeavored to follow—his appearance, in this pursuit, being pathetically like that of a bug fished out of an ink-well, alive but discouraged.

Attracted by the riot, Samuel Williams made his appearance, vaulting a fence, and was immediately followed by Maurice Levy and Georgie Bassett. They stared incredulously at the extraordinary spectacle before them.

"Little GEN-TIL-MUN!" shrieked Marjorie, with a wild stroke that landed full upon Penrod's tarry cap.

"*Oooch!*" bleated Penrod.

"It's Penrod!" shouted Sam Williams, recognizing him by the voice. For an instant he had been in some doubt.

"Penrod Schofield!" exclaimed Georgie Bassett. "What does this mean?" That was Georgie's style, and had helped to win him his title.

Marjorie leaned, panting, upon her stick. "I cu-called—uh—him—

oh!" she sobbed—"I called him a lul-little—oh—gentleman! And oh—
lul-look!—oh! lul-look at my du-dress! Lul-look at Mu-mitchy—oh—
Mitch—oh!"

Unexpectedly, she smote again—with results—and then, seizing the
indistinguishable hand of Mitchy-Mitch, she ran wailing homeward
down the street.

"'Little gentleman'?" said Georgie Bassett, with some evidences of
disturbed complacency. "Why that's what they call *me!*"

"Yes, and you *are* one, too!" shouted the maddened Penrod. "But you
better not let anybody call *me* that! I've stood enough around here for
one day, and you can't run over *me,* Georgie Bassett. Just you put that in
your gizzard and smoke it!"

"Anybody has a perfect right," said Georgie, with dignity, "to call a
person a little gentleman. There's lots of names nobody ought to call,
but this one's a *nice*——"

"You better look out!"

Unavenged bruises were distributed all over Penrod, both upon his
body and upon his spirit. Driven by subtle forces, he had dipped his
hands in catastrophe and disaster: it was not for a Georgie Bassett to
beard him. Penrod was about to run amuck.

"I haven't called you a little gentleman, yet," said Georgie. "I only
said it. Anybody's got a right to *say* it."

"Not around *me!* You just try it again and——"

"I shall say it," returned Georgie, "all I please. Anybody in this town
has a right to *say* 'little gentleman'——"

Bellowing insanely, Penrod plunged his right hand into the caldron,
rushed upon Georgie and made awful work of his hair and features.

Alas, it was but the beginning! Sam Williams and Maurice Levy
screamed with delight, and, simultaneously infected, danced about the
struggling pair, shouting frantically:

"Little gentleman! Little gentleman! Sick him, Georgie! Sick him,
little gentleman! Little gentleman! Little gentleman!"

The infuriated outlaw turned upon them with blows and more tar,
which gave Georgie Bassett his opportunity and later seriously impaired
the purity of his fame. Feeling himself hopelessly tarred, he dipped
both hands repeatedly into the caldron and applied his gatherings to
Penrod. It was bringing coals to Newcastle, but it helped to assuage the
just wrath of Georgie.

The four boys gave a fine imitation of the Laocoön group complicated
by an extra figure—frantic splutterings and chokings, strange cries and
stranger words issued from this tangle; hands dipped lavishly into the
inexhaustible reservoir of tar, with more and more picturesque results.
The caldron had been elevated upon bricks and was not perfectly

balanced; and under a heavy impact of the struggling group it lurched and went partly over, pouring forth a Stygian tide which formed a deep pool in the gutter.

It was the fate of Master Roderick Bitts, that exclusive and immaculate person, to make his appearance upon the chaotic scene at this juncture. All in the cool of a white "sailor suit," he turned aside from the path of duty—which led straight to the house of a maiden aunt—and paused to hop with joy upon the sidewalk. A repeated epithet continuously half panted, half squawked, somewhere in the nest of gladiators, caught his ear, and he took it up excitedly, not knowing why.

"Little gentleman!" shouted Roderick, jumping up and down in childish glee. "Little gentleman! Little gentleman! Lit——"

A frightful figure tore itself free from the group, encircled this innocent bystander with a black arm, and hurled him headlong. Full length and flat on his face went Roderick into the Stygian pool. The frightful figure was Penrod. Instantly, the pack flung themselves upon him again, and, carrying them with him, he went over upon Roderick, who from that instant was as active a belligerent as any there.

Thus began the Great Tar Fight, the origin of which proved, afterward, so difficult for parents to trace, owing to the opposing accounts of the combatants. Marjorie said Penrod began it; Penrod said Mitchy-Mitch began it; Sam William said Georgie Bassett began it; Georgie and Maurice Levy said Penrod began it; Roderick Bitts, who had not recognized his first assailant, said Sam Williams began it.

Nobody thought of accusing the barber. But the barber did not begin it; it was the fly on the barber's nose that began it—though, of course, something else began the fly. Somehow, we never manage to hang the real offender.

The end came only with the arrival of Penrod's mother, who had been having a painful conversation by telephone with Mrs. Jones, the mother of Marjorie, and came forth to seek an errant son. It is a mystery how she was able to pick out her own, for by the time she got there his voice was too hoarse to be recognizable.

Mr. Schofield's version of things was that Penrod was insane. "He's a stark, raving lunatic!" declared the father, descending to the library from a before-dinner interview with the outlaw, that evening. "I'd send him to military school, but I don't believe they'd take him. Do you know *why* he says all that awfulness happened?"

"When Margaret and I were trying to scrub him," responded Mrs. Schofield wearily, "he said 'everybody' had been calling him names."

"'Names!'" snorted her husband. "'Little gentleman!' *That's* the vile epithet they called him! And because of it he wrecks the peace of six homes!"

"*Sh!* Yes; he told us about it," said Mrs. Schofield, moaning. "He told us several hundred times, I should guess, though I didn't count. He's got it fixed in his head, and we couldn't get it out. All we could do was to put him in the closet. He'd have gone out again after those boys if we hadn't. I don't know *what* to make of him!"

"He's a mystery to *me!*" said her husband. "And he refuses to explain why he objects to being called 'little gentleman.' Says he'd do the same thing—and worse—if anybody dared to call him that again. He said if the President of the United States called him that he'd try to whip him. How long did you have him locked up in the closet?"

"*Sh!*" said Mrs. Schofield warningly. "About two hours; but I don't think it softened his spirit at all, because when I took him to the barber's to get his hair clipped again, on account of the tar in it Sammy Williams and Maurice Levy were there for the same reason, and they just *whispered* 'little gentleman,' so low you could hardly hear them—and Penrod began fighting with them right before me, and it was really all the barber and I could do to drag him away from them. The barber was very kind about it, but Penrod——"

"I tell you he's a lunatic!" Mr. Schofield would have said the same thing of a Frenchman infuriated by the epithet "camel." The philosophy of insult needs expounding.

"*Sh!*" said Mrs. Schofield. "It does seem a kind of frenzy."

"Why on earth should any sane person mind being called——"

"*Sh!*" said Mrs. Schofield. "It's beyond *me!*"

"What are you *sh*-ing me for?" demanded Mr. Schofield explosively.

"*Sh!*" said Mrs. Schofield. "It's Mr. Kinosling, the new rector of Saint Joseph's."

"Where?"

"*Sh!* On the front porch with Margaret; he's going to stay for dinner. I do hope——"

"Bachelor, isn't he?"

"Yes."

"*Our* old minister was speaking of him the other day," said Mr. Schofield, "and he didn't seem so terribly impressed."

"*Sh!* Yes; about thirty, and of course *so* superior to most of Margaret's friends—boys home from college. She thinks she likes young Robert Williams, I know—but he laughs so much! Of course there isn't any comparison. Mr. Kinosling talks so intellectually; it's a good thing for Margaret to hear that kind of thing, for a change—and, of course, he's very spiritual. He seems very much interested in her." She paused to muse. "I think Margaret likes him; he's so different, too. It's the third time he's dropped in this week, and I——"

"Well," said Mr. Schofield grimly, "if you and Margaret want him to come again, you'd better not let him see Penrod."

"But he's asked to see him; he seems interested in meeting all the family. And Penrod nearly always behaves fairly well at table." She paused, and then put to her husband a question referring to his interview with Penrod upstairs. "Did you—did you—do it?"

"No," he answered gloomily. "No, I didn't, but——" He was interrupted by a violent crash of china and metal in the kitchen, a shriek from Della, and the outrageous voice of Penrod. The well-informed Della, ill-inspired to set up for a wit, had ventured to address the scion of the house roguishly as "little gentleman," and Penrod, by means of the rapid elevation of his right foot, had removed from her supporting hands a laden tray. Both parents started for the kitchen, Mr. Schofield completing his interrupted sentence on the way.

"But I will, now!"

The rite thus promised was hastily but accurately performed in that apartment most distant from the front porch; and, twenty minutes later, Penrod descended to dinner. The Rev. Mr. Kinosling had asked for the pleasure of meeting him, and it had been decided that the only course possible was to cover up the scandal for the present, and to offer an undisturbed and smiling family surface to the gaze of the visitor.

Scorched but not bowed, the smoldering Penrod was led forward for the social formulæ simultaneously with the somewhat bleak departure of Robert Williams, who took his guitar with him, this time, and went in forlorn unconsciousness of the powerful forces already set in secret motion to be his allies.

The punishment just undergone had but made the haughty and unyielding soul of Penrod more stalwart in revolt; he was unconquered. Every time the one intolerable insult had been offered him, his resentment had become the hotter, his vengeance the more instant and furious. And, still burning with outrage, but upheld by the conviction of right, he was determined to continue to the last drop of his blood the defense of his honor, whenever it should be assailed, no matter how mighty or august the powers that attacked it. In all ways, he was a very sore boy.

During the brief ceremony of presentation, his usually inscrutable countenance wore an expression interpreted by his father as one of insane obstinacy, while Mrs. Schofield found it an incentive to inward prayer. The fine graciousness of Mr. Kinosling, however, was unimpaired by the glare of virulent suspicion given him by this little brother: Mr. Kinosling mistook it for a natural curiosity concerning one who might possibly become, in time, a member of the family. He patted Penrod upon the head, which was, for many reasons, in no condition to be patted with any pleasure to the patter. Penrod felt himself in the presence of a new enemy.

"How do you do, my little lad," said Mr. Kinosling. "I trust we shall become fast friends."

To the ear of his little lad, it seemed he said, "A trost we shall bickhome fawst fraınds." Mr. Kinosling's pronunciation was, in fact, slightly precious; and the little lad, simply mistaking it for some cryptic form of mockery of himself, assumed a manner and expression which argued so ill for the proposed friendship that Mrs. Schofield hastily interposed the suggestion of dinner, and the small procession went in to the dining-room.

"It has been a delicious day," said Mr. Kinosling, presently; "warm but balmy." With a benevolent smile he addressed Penrod, who sat opposite him. "I suppose, little gentleman, you have been indulging in the usual outdoor sports of vacation?"

Penrod laid down his fork and glared, open-mouthed at Mr. Kinosling.

"You'll have another slice of breast of the chicken?" Mr. Schofield inquired, loudly and quickly.

"A lovely day!" exclaimed Margaret, with equal promptitude and emphasis. "Lovely, oh, lovely! Lovely!"

"Beautiful, beautiful, beautiful!" said Mrs. Schofield, and after a glance at Penrod which confirmed her impression that he intended to say something, she continued, "Yes, beautiful, beautiful, beautiful, beautiful, beautiful, beautiful!"

Penrod closed his mouth and sank back in his chair—and his relatives took breath.

Mr. Kinosling looked pleased. This responsive family, with its ready enthusiasm, made the kind of audience he liked. He passed a delicate white hand gracefully over his tall, pale forehead, and smiled indulgently.

"Youth relaxes in summer," he said. "Boyhood is the age of relaxation; one is playful, light, free, unfettered. One runs and leaps and enjoys one's self with one's companions. It is good for the little lads to play with their friends; they jostle, push, and wrestle, and simulate little, happy struggles with one another in harmless conflict. The young muscles are toughening. It is good. Boyish chivalry develops, enlarges, expands. The young learn quickly, intuitively, spontaneously. They perceive the obligations of *noblesse oblige*. They begin to comprehend the necessity of caste and its requirements. They learn what birth means —ah,—that is, they learn what it means to be well born. They learn courtesy in their games; they learn politeness, consideration for one another in their pastimes, amusements, lighter occupations. I make it my pleasure to join them often, for I sympathize with them in all their wholesome joys as well as in their little bothers and perplexities. I understand them, you see; and let me tell you it is no easy matter to understand the little lads and lassies." He sent to each listener his beaming glance, and, permitting it to come to rest upon Penrod, inquired: "And what do you say to that, little gentleman?"

Mr. Schofield uttered a stentorian cough. "More? You'd better have some more chicken! More! Do!"

"More chicken!" urged Margaret simultaneously. "Do please! Please! More! Do! More!"

"Beautiful, beautiful," began Mrs. Schofield. "Beautiful, beautiful, beautiful, beautiful——"

It is not known in what light Mr. Kinosling viewed the expression of Penrod's face. Perhaps he mistook it for awe; perhaps he received no impression at all of its extraordinary quality. He was a rather self-engrossed young man, just then engaged in a double occupation, for he not only talked, but supplied from his own consciousness a critical though favorable auditor as well, which of course kept him quite busy. Besides, it is oftener than is suspected the case that extremely peculiar expressions upon the countenances of boys are entirely overlooked, and suggest nothing to the minds of people staring straight at them. Certainly Penrod's expression—which, to the perception of his family, was perfectly horrible—caused not the faintest perturbation in the breast of Mr. Kinosling.

Mr. Kinosling waived the chicken, and continued to talk. "Yes, I think I may claim to understand boys," he said, smiling thoughtfully. "One has been a boy one's self. Ah, it is not all playtime! I hope our young scholar here does not overwork himself at his Latin, at his classics, as I did, so that at the age of eight years I was compelled to wear glasses. He must be careful not to strain the little eyes at his scholar's tasks, not to let the little shoulders grow round over his scholar's desk. Youth is golden; we should keep it golden, bright, glistening. Youth should frolic, should be sprightly; it should play its cricket, its tennis, its handball. It should run and leap; it should laugh, should ring madrigals and glees, carol with the lark, ring out in chanties, folk songs, ballads, roundelays——"

He talked on. At any instant Mr. Schofield held himself ready to cough vehemently and shout, "More chicken," to drown out Penrod in case the fatal words again fell from those eloquent lips; and Mrs. Schofield and Margaret kept themselves prepared at all times to assist him. So passed a threatening meal, which Mrs. Schofield hurried, by every means with decency, to its conclusion. She felt that somehow they would all be safer out in the dark of the front porch, and led the way thither as soon as possible.

"No cigar, I thank you." Mr. Kinosling, establishing himself in a wicker chair beside Margaret, waved away her father's proffer. "I do not smoke. I have never tasted tobacco in any form." Mrs. Schofield was confirmed in her opinion that this would be an ideal son-in-law. Mr. Schofield was not so sure.

"No," said Mr. Kinosling. "No tobacco for me. No cigar, no pipe, no cigarette, no cheroot. For me, a book—a volume of poems, perhaps. Verses, rhymes, lines metrical and cadenced—those are my dissipation. Tennyson by preference: 'Maud,' or 'Idylls of the King'—poetry of the sound Victorian days; there is none later. Or Longfellow will rest me in a tired hour. Yes; for me, a book, a volume in the hand, held lightly between the fingers."

Mr. Kinosling looked pleasantly at his fingers as he spoke, waving his hand in a curving gesture which brought it into the light of a window faintly illuminated from the interior of the house. Then he passed those graceful fingers over his hair, and turned toward Penrod, who was perched upon the railing in a dark corner.

"The evening is touched with a slight coolness," said Mr. Kinosling. "Perhaps I may request the little gentleman——"

"B'gr-r-*ruff!*" coughed Mr. Schofield. "You'd better change your mind about a cigar."

"No, I thank you. I was about to request the lit——"

"*Do* try one," Margaret urged. "I'm sure papa's are nice ones. Do try——"

"No, I thank you. I remarked a slight coolness in the air, and my hat is in the hallway. I was about to request——"

"I'll get it for you," said Penrod suddenly.

"If you will be so good," said Mr. Kinosling. "It is a black bowler hat, little gentleman, and placed upon a table in the hall."

"I know where it is." Penrod entered the door, and a feeling of relief, mutually experienced, carried from one to another of his three relatives their interchanged congratulations that he had recovered his sanity.

"'The day is done, and the darkness,'" began Mr. Kinosling—and recited that poem entire. He followed it with "The Children's Hour," and after a pause, at the close, to allow his listeners time for a little reflection upon his rendition, he passed his hand over his head, and called, in the direction of the doorway:

"I believe I will take my hat now, little gentleman."

"Here it is," said Penrod, unexpectedly climbing over the porch railing, in the other direction. His mother and father and Margaret had supposed him to be standing in the hallway out of deference, and because he thought it tactful not to interrupt the recitations. All of them remembered, later, that this supposed thoughtfulness on his part struck them as unnatural.

"Very good, little gentleman!" said Mr. Kinosling, and being somewhat chilled, placed the hat firmly upon his head, pulling it down as far as it would go. It had a pleasant warmth, which he noticed at once. The next instant, he noticed something else, a peculiar sensation of the scalp—a sensation which he was quite unable to define. He lifted his hand to take the hat off, and entered upon a strange experience: his hat seemed to have decided to remain where it was.

"Do you like Tennyson as much as Longfellow, Mr. Kinosling?" inquired Margaret.

"I—ah—I cannot say," he returned absently. "I—ah—each has his own—ugh! flavor and savor, each his—ah—ah——"

Struck by a strangeness in his tone, she peered at him curiously through the dusk. His outlines were indistinct, but she made out that his arms were uplifted in a singular gesture. He seemed to be wrenching at his head.

"Is—is anything the matter?" she asked anxiously. "Mr. Kinosling, are you ill?"

"Not at—ugh!—all," he replied in the same odd tone. "I—ah—I believe—*ugh!*"

He dropped his hands from his hat, and rose. His manner was slightly agitated. "I fear I may have taken a trifling—ah—cold. I should—ah— perhaps be—ah—better at home. I will—ah—say good night."

At the steps, he instinctively lifted his hand to remove his hat, but did not do so, and, saying "Good night," again in a frigid voice, departed with visible stiffness from that house, to return no more.

"Well, of all——!" cried Mrs. Schofield, astounded. "What was the matter? He just went—like that!" She made a flurried gesture. "In heaven's name, Margaret, what *did* you say to him?"

"*I!*" exclaimed Margaret indignantly. "Nothing! He just *went!*"

"Why, he didn't even take off his hat when he said good night!" said Mrs. Schofield.

Margaret, who had crossed to the doorway, caught the ghost of a whisper behind her, where stood Penrod.

"*You bet he didn't!*"

He knew not that he was overheard.

A frightful suspicion flashed through Margaret's mind—a suspicion that Mr. Kinosling's hat would have to be either boiled off or shaved off. With growing horror she recalled Penrod's long absence when he went to bring the hat.

"Penrod," she cried, "let me see your hands!"

She had toiled at those hands herself late that afternoon, nearly scalding her own, but at last achieving a lily purity.

"Let me see your hands!"

She seized them.

Again they were tarred!

34

A Deal in Wheat

BY FRANK NORRIS

I. THE BEAR—WHEAT AT SIXTY-TWO

AS Sam Lewiston backed the horse into the shafts of his buckboard and began hitching the tugs to the whiffletree, his wife came out from the kitchen door of the house and drew near, and stood for some time at the horse's head, her arms folded and her apron rolled around them. For a long moment neither spoke. They had talked over the situation so long and so comprehensively the night before that there seemed to be nothing more to say.

The time was late in the summer, the place a ranch in South-Western Kansas, and Lewiston and his wife were two of a vast population of farmers, wheat growers, who at that moment were passing through a crisis—a crisis that at any moment might culminate in tragedy. Wheat was down to sixty-six.

At length Emma Lewiston spoke.

"Well," she hazarded, looking vaguely out across the ranch toward the horizon, leagues distant; "well, Sam, there's always that offer of brother Joe's. We can quit—and go to Chicago—if the worst comes."

"And give up!" exclaimed Lewiston, running the lines through the torets. "Leave the ranch! Give up! After all these years!"

His wife made no reply for the moment. Lewiston climbed into the buckboard and gathered up the lines. "Well, here goes for the last try, Emmie," he said. "Good-by, girl. Maybe things will look better in town today."

"Maybe," she said gravely. She kissed her husband good-by and stood for some time looking after the buckboard traveling toward the town in a moving pillar of dust.

"I don't know," she murmured at length; "I don't know just how we're going to make out."

When he reached town, Lewiston tied the horse to the iron railing in front of the Odd-Fellows Hall, the ground floor of which was occupied by the post-office, and went across the street and up the stairway of a building of brick and granite—quite the most pretentious structure of the town—and knocked at a door upon the first landing. The door was furnished with a pane of frosted glass, on which, in gold letters, was inscribed, "Bridges & Co., Grain Dealers."

Bridges himself, a middle-aged man who wore a velvet skull-cap and who was smoking a Pittsburgh stogy, met the farmer at the counter and the two exchanged perfunctory greetings.

"Well," said Lewiston, tentatively, after a while.

"Well, Lewiston," said the other, "I can't take that wheat of yours at any better than sixty-two."

"Sixty-*two*!"

"It's the Chicago price that does it, Lewiston. Truslow is bearing the stuff for all he's worth. It's Truslow and the bear clique that stick the knife into us. The price broke again this morning. We've just got a wire."

"Good heavens," murmured Lewiston, looking vaguely from side to side. "That—that ruins me. I *can't* carry my grain any longer—what with storage charges and—and—Bridges, I don't see just how I'm going to make out. Sixty-two cents a bushel! Why, man, what with this and with that it's cost me nearly a dollar a bushel to raise that wheat, and now Truslow—"

He turned away abruptly with a quick gesture of infinite discouragement.

He went down the stairs, and making his way to where his buckboard was hitched, got in, and, with eyes vacant, the reins slipping and sliding in his limp, half-open hands, drove slowly back to the ranch. His wife had seen him coming, and met him as he drew up before the barn.

"Well?" she demanded.

"Emmie," he said as he got out of the buckboard, laying his arm across her shoulder, "Emmie, I guess we'll take up with Joe's offer. We'll go to Chicago. We're cleaned out!"

II. THE BULL—WHEAT AT A DOLLAR-TEN

. . . .—*and said Party of the Second Part further covenants and agrees to merchandise such wheat in foreign ports, it being understood and agreed between the Party of the First Part and the Party of the Second Part that the wheat hereinbefore mentioned is released and sold to the*

Party of the Second Part for export purposes only, and not for consumption or distribution within the boundaries of the United States of America or of Canada.

"Now, Mr. Gates, if you will sign for Mr. Truslow I guess that'll be all," remarked Hornung when he had finished reading.

Hornung affixed his signature to the two documents and passed them over to Gates, who signed for his principal and client, Truslow—or, as he has been called ever since he had gone into the fight against Hornung's corner—the Great Bear. Hornung's secretary was called in and witnessed the signatures, and Gates thrust the contract into his Gladstone bag and stood up, smoothing his hat.

"You will deliver the warehouse receipts for the grain," began Gates.

"I'll send a messenger to Truslow's office before noon," interrupted Hornung. "You can pay by certified check through the Illinois Trust people."

When the other had taken himself off, Hornung sat for some mo ments gazing abstractedly toward his office windows, thinking over the whole matter. He had just agreed to release to Truslow, at the rate of one dollar and ten cents per bushel, one hundred thousand out of the two million and odd bushels of wheat that he, Hornung, controlled, or actually owned. And for the moment he was wondering if, after all, he had done wisely in not goring the Great Bear to actual financial death. He had made him pay one hundred thousand dollars. Truslow was good for this amount. Would it not have been better to have put a prohibitive figure on the grain and forced the bear into bankruptcy? True, Hornung would then be without his enemy's money, but Truslow would have been eliminated from the situation, and that—so Hornung told himself—was always a consummation most devoutly, strenuously, and diligently to be striven for. Truslow once dead was dead, but the Bear was never more dangerous than when desperate.

"But so long as he can't get *wheat*," muttered Hornung at the end of his reflections, "he can't hurt me. And he can't get it. That I *know*."

For Hornung controlled the situation. So far back as the February of that year an "unknown bull" had been making his presence felt on the floor of the Board of Trade. By the middle of March the commercial reports of the daily press had begun to speak of "the powerful bull clique"; a few weeks later that legendary condition of affairs implied and epitomized in the magic words "Dollar Wheat" had been attained, and by the first of April, when the price had been boosted to one dollar and ten cents a bushel, Hornung had disclosed his hand, and in place of mere rumors, the definite and authoritative news that May wheat had been cornered in the Chicago pit went flashing around the world from Liverpool to Odessa and from Duluth to Buenos Aires.

It was—so the veteran operators were persuaded—Truslow himself who had made Hornung's corner possible. The Great Bear had for once overreached himself, and, believing himself all-powerful, had hammered the price just the fatal fraction too far down. Wheat had gone to sixty-two—for the time, and under the circumstances, an abnormal price. When the reaction came it was tremendous. Hornung saw his chance, seized it, and in a few months had turned the tables, had cornered the product, and virtually driven the bear clique out of the pit.

On the same day that the delivery of the hundred thousand bushels was made to Truslow, Hornung met his broker at his lunch club.

"Well," said the latter, "I see you let go that line of stuff to Truslow."

Hornung nodded; but the broker added:

"Remember, I was against it from the very beginning. I know we've cleared up over a hundred thou'. I would have fifty times preferred to have lost twice that and *smashed Truslow dead*. Bet you what you like he makes us pay for it somehow."

"Huh!" grunted his principal. "How about insurance, and warehouse charges, and carrying expenses on that lot? Guess we'd have had to pay those, too, if we'd held on."

But the other put up his chin, unwilling to be persuaded. "I won't sleep easy," he declared, "till Truslow is busted."

III. THE PIT

Just as Going mounted the steps on the edge of the pit the great gong struck, a roar of a hundred voices developed with the swiftness of successive explosions, the rush of a hundred men surging downward to the center of the pit filled the air with the stamp and grind of feet, a hundred hands in eager, strenuous gestures tossed upward from out the brown of the crowd, the official reporter in his cage on the margin of the pit leaned far forward with straining ear to catch the opening bid, and another day of battle was begun.

Since the sale of the hundred thousand bushels of wheat to Truslow, the "Hornung crowd" had steadily shouldered the price higher until on this particular morning it stood at one dollar and a half. That was Hornung's price. No one else had any grain to sell.

But not ten minutes after the opening, Going was surprised out of all countenance to hear shouted from the other side of the pit these words:

"Sell May at one-fifty."

Going was for the moment touching elbows with Kimbark on one side and with Merriam on the other, all three belonging to the "Hornung crowd." Their answering challenge of "Sold" was as the voice of one man. They did not pause to reflect upon the strangeness of the circumstance. (That was for afterward.) Their response to the offer was as unconscious as reflex action and almost as rapid, and before the pit was well aware of what had happened the transaction of one thousand bushels was down upon Going's trading-card and fifteen hundred dollars had changed hands. But here was a marvel—the whole available supply of wheat cornered, Hornung master of the situation, invincible, unassailable; yet behold a man willing to sell, a bear bold enough to raise his head.

"That was Kennedy, wasn't it, who made that offer?" asked Kimbark, as Going noted down the trade—"Kennedy, that new man?"

"Yes; who do you suppose he's selling for; who's willing to go short at this stage of the game?"

"Maybe he ain't short."

"Short! Great heavens, man, where'd he get the stuff?"

"Blamed if I know. We can account for every handful of May. Steady! Oh, there he goes again.

"Sell a thousand May at one-fifty," vociferated the bear-broker, throwing out his hand, one finger raised to indicate the number of "contracts" offered. This time it was evident that he was attacking the Hornung crowd deliberately, for, ignoring the jam of traders that swept toward him, he looked across the pit to where Going and Kimbark were shouting *"Sold! Sold!"* and nodded his head.

A second time Going made memoranda of the trade, and either the Hornung holdings were increased by two thousands bushels of May wheat or the Hornung bank account swelled by at least three thousand dollars of some unknown short's money.

Of late—so sure was the bull crowd of its position—no one had even thought of glancing at the inspection sheet on the bulletin board. But now one of Going's messengers hurried up to him with the announcement that this sheet showed receipts at Chicago for that morning of twenty-five thousand bushels, and not credited to Hornung. Someone had got hold of a line of wheat overlooked by the "clique" and was dumping it upon them.

Wire the Chief, said Going over his shoulder to Merriam. This one struggled out of the crowd, and on a telegraph blank scribbled:

"Strong bear movement—New man—Kennedy—Selling in lots of five contracts—Chicago receipts twenty-five thousand."

The message was despatched, and in a few moments the answer came back, laconic, of military terseness:

"Support the market."

And Going obeyed, Merriam and Kimbark following, the new broker fairly throwing the wheat at them in thousand-bushel lots.

"Sell May at 'fifty; sell May; sell May." A moment's indecision, an instant's hesitation, the first faint suggestion of weakness, and the market would have broken under them. But for the better part of four hours they stood their ground, taking all that was offered, in constant communication with the Chief, and from time to time stimulated and steadied by his brief, unvarying command:

"Support the market."

At the close of the session they had brought in the twenty-five thousand bushels of May. Hornung's position was as stable as a rock, and the price closed even with the opening figure—one dollar and a half.

But the morning's work was the talk of all La Salle Street. Who was back of the raid? What was the meaning of this unexpected selling? For weeks the pit trading had been merely nominal. Truslow, the Great Bear, from whom the most serious attack might have been expected, had gone to his country seat at Geneva Lake, in Wisconsin, declaring himself to be out of the market entirely. He went bass-fishing every day.

IV.   THE BELT LINE

On a certain day toward the middle of the month, at a time when the mysterious Bear had unloaded some eighty thousand bushels upon Hornung, a conference was held in the library of Hornung's home. His broker attended it, and also a clean-faced, bright-eyed individual whose name of Cyrus Ryder might have been found upon the pay-roll of a rather well-known detective agency. For upward of half an hour after the conference began the detective spoke, the other two listening attentively, gravely.

"Then, last of all," concluded Ryder, "I made out I was a hobo, and began stealing rides on the Belt Line Railroad. Know that road? It just circles Chicago. Truslow owns it. Yes? Well, then I began to catch on. I noticed that cars of certain numbers—thirty-one nought thirty-four, thirty-two one ninety—well, the numbers don't matter, but anyhow, these cars were always switched onto the sidings by Mr. Truslow's main elevator D soon as they came in. The wheat was shunted in, and they were pulled out again. Well, I spotted one car and stole a ride on her. Say, look here, *that car went right around the city on the Belt, and came back to D again, and the same wheat in her all the time.* The grain was re-inspected—it was raw, I tell you—and the warehouse receipts made out just as though the stuff had come in from Kansas or Iowa.

"The same wheat all the time!" interrupted Hornung.

"The same wheat—your wheat, that you sold to Truslow."

"Great snakes!" ejaculated Hornung's broker. "Truslow never took it abroad at all."

"Took it abroad! Say, he's just been running it around Chicago, like the supers in 'Shenandoah,' round an' round, so you'd think it was a new lot, an' selling it back to you again."

"No wonder we couldn't account for so much wheat."

"Bought it from us at one-ten, and made us buy it back—our own wheat—at one-fifty."

Hornung and his broker looked at each other in silence for a moment. Then all at once Hornung struck the arm of his chair with his fist and exploded in a roar of laughter. The broker stared for one bewildered moment, then followed his example.

"Sold! Sold!" shouted Hornung almost gleefully. "Upon my soul it's as good as a Gilbert and Sullivan show. And we— Oh, Lord! Billy, shake on it, and hats off to my distinguished friend, Truslow. He'll be President some day. Hey! What? Prosecute him? Not I."

"He's done us out of a neat hatful of dollars for all that," observed the broker, suddenly grave.

"Billy, it's worth the price."

"Well, tell you what. We were going to boost the price to one seventy-five next week, and make that our settlement figure."

"Can't do it now. Can't afford it."

"No. Here; we'll let out a big link; we'll put wheat at two dollars, and let it go at that."

"Two it is, then," said the broker.

V. THE BREAD LINE

The street was very dark and absolutely deserted. It was a district on the "South Side," not far from the Chicago River, given up largely to wholesale stores, and after nightfall was empty of all life. The echoes slept but lightly hereabouts, and the slightest footfall, the faintest noise, woke them upon the instant and sent them clamoring up and down the length of the pavement between the iron-shuttered fronts. The only light visible came from the side door of a certain "Vienna" bakery, where at one o'clock in the morning loaves of bread were given away to any who should ask. Every evening about nine o'clock the outcasts began to gather about the side door. The stragglers came in rapidly, and the line—the "bread line," as it was called—began to form. By midnight it was usually some hundred yards in length, stretching almost the entire length of the block.

Toward ten in the evening, his collar turned up against the fine drizzle that pervaded the air, his hands in his pockets, his elbows gripping his sides, Sam Lewiston came up and silently took his place at the end of the line.

Unable to conduct his farm upon a paying basis at the time when Truslow, the "Great Bear," had sent the price of grain down to sixty-two cents a bushel, Lewiston had turned over the entire property to his creditors, and, leaving Kansas for good, had abandoned farming, and had left his wife at her sister's boarding house in Topeka with the understanding that she was to join him in Chicago as soon as he had found a steady job Then he had come to Chicago and had turned workman. His brother Joe conducted a small hat factory on Archer Avenue, and for a time he found there a meager employment. But difficulties had occurred, times were bad, the hat factory was involved in debts, the repealing of a certain import duty on manufactured felt overcrowded the home market with cheap Belgian and French products, and in the end his brother had assigned and gone to Milwaukee.

Thrown out of work, Lewiston drifted aimlessly about Chicago, from pillar to post, working a little, earning here a dollar, there a dime, but always sinking, sinking, till at last the ooze of the lowest bottom dragged at his feet and the rush of the great ebb went over him and engulfed him and shut him out from the light, and a park bench became his home and the "bread line" his chief makeshift of subsistence.

He stood now in the enfolding drizzle, sodden, stupefied with fatigue. Before and behind stretched the line. There was no talking. There was no sound. The street was empty. It was so still that the passing of a cable-car in the adjoining thoroughfare grated like prolonged rolling explosions, beginning and ending at immeasurable distances. The drizzle descended incessantly. After a long time midnight struck.

There was something ominous and gravely impressive in this interminable line of dark figures, close-pressed, soundless; a crowd, yet absolutely still; a close-packed, silent file, waiting, waiting in the vast deserted night-ridden street; waiting without a word, without a movement, there under the night and under the slow-moving mists of rain.

Few in the crowd were professional beggars. Most of them were workmen, long since out of work, forced into idleness by long-continued "hard times," by ill luck, by sickness. To them the "bread line" was a godsend. At least they could not starve. Between jobs here in the end was something to hold them up—a small platform, as it were, above the sweep of black water, where for a moment they might pause and take breath before the plunge.

The period of waiting on this night of rain seemed endless to those silent, hungry men; but at length there was a stir. The line moved. The side door opened. Ah, at last! They were going to hand out the bread.

But instead of the usual white aproned undercook with his crowded hampers there now appeared in the doorway a new man—a young fellow who looked like a bookkeeper's assistant. He bore in his hand a placard, which he tacked to the outside of the door. Then he disappeared within the bakery, locking the door after him.

A shudder of poignant despair, an unformed, inarticulate sense of calamity, seemed to run from end to end of the line. What had happened? Those in the rear, unable to read the placard, surged forward, a sense of bitter disappointment clutching at their hearts.

The line broke up, disintegrated into a shapeless throng—a throng that crowded forward and collected in front of the shut door whereon the placard was affixed. Lewiston, with the others, pushed forward. On the placard he read these words:

"Owing to the fact that the price of grain has been increased to two dollars a bushel, there will be no distribution of bread from this bakery until further notice."

Lewiston turned away, dumb, bewildered. Till morning he walked the streets, going on without purpose, without direction. But now at last his luck had turned. Overnight the wheel of his fortunes had creaked and swung upon its axis, and before noon he had found a job in the street-cleaning brigade. In the course of time he rose to be first shift boss, then deputy inspector, then inspector, promoted to the dignity of driving in a red wagon with rubber tires and drawing a salary instead of mere wages. The wife was sent for and a new start made.

But Lewiston never forgot. Dimly he began to see the significance of things. Caught once in the cogs and wheels of a great and terrible engine, he had seen—none better—its workings. Of all the men who had vainly stood in the "bread line" on that rainy night in early summer, he, perhaps, had been the only one who had struggled up to the surface again. How many others had gone down in the great ebb? Grim question; he dared not think how many.

He had seen the two ends of a great wheat operation—a battle between Bear and Bull. The stories (subsequently published in the city's press) of Truslow's countermove in selling Hornung his own wheat, supplied the unseen section. The farmer—he who raised the wheat—was ruined upon one hand; the working man—he who consumed it—was ruined upon the other. But between the two, the great operators, who never saw the wheat they traded in, bought and sold the world's food, gambled in the nourishment of entire nations, practiced their tricks, their chicanery and oblique shifty "deals," were reconciled in their differences, and went on through their appointed way, jovial, contented, enthroned, and unassailable.

35

The Open Boat

A TALE INTENDED TO BE AFTER THE FACT.
BEING THE EXPERIENCE OF FOUR MEN FROM THE SUNK
STEAMER "COMMODORE"

BY STEPHEN CRANE

NONE of them knew the color of the sky. Their eyes glanced level, and were fastened upon the waves that swept toward them. These waves were of the hue of slate, save for the tops, which were of foaming white, and all of the men knew the colors of the sea. The horizon narrowed and widened, and dipped and rose, and at all times its edge was jagged with waves that seemed thrust up in points like rocks. Many a man ought to have a bath-tub larger than the boat which here rode upon the sea. These waves were most wrongfully and barbarously abrupt and tall, and each froth top was a problem in small boat navigation.

The cook squatted in the bottom and looked with both eyes at the six inches of gunwale which separated him from the ocean. His sleeves were rolled over his fat forearms, and two flaps of his unbuttoned vest dangled as he bent to bail out the boat. Often he said: "Gawd! That was a narrow clip." As he remarked it he invariably gazed eastward over the broken sea.

The oiler, steering with one of the two oars in the boat, sometimes raised himself suddenly to keep clear of water that swirled in over the stern. It was a thin little oar and it seemed often ready to snap.

The correspondent, pulling at the other oar, watched the waves and wondered why he was there.

The injured captain, lying in the bow, was at this time buried in that profound dejection and indifference which comes, temporarily at least, to even the bravest and most enduring when, willy-nilly, the firm fails, the army loses, the ship goes down. The mind of the master of a vessel is rooted deep in the timbers of her, though he commanded for a day or a decade, and this captain had on him the stern impression of a scene in the grays of dawn of seven turned faces, and later a stump of a top mast with a white ball on it that slashed to and fro at the waves, went low and lower, and down. Thereafter there was something strange in his voice. Although steady, it was deep with mourning, and of a quality beyond oration or tears.

"Keep 'er a little more south, Billie," said he.

" 'A little more south,' sir," said the oiler in the stern.

A seat in this boat was not unlike a seat upon a bucking broncho, and by the same token, a broncho is not much smaller. The craft pranced and reared, and plunged like an animal. As each wave came, and she rose for it, she seemed like a horse making at a fence outrageously high. The manner of her scramble over these walls of water is a mystic thing, and, moreover, at the top of them were ordinarily these problems in white water, the foam racing down from the summit of each wave, requiring a new leap, and a leap from the air. Then, after scornfully bumping a crest, she would slide, and race, and splash down a long incline, and arrive bobbing and nodding in front of the next menace.

A singular disadvantage of the sea lies in the fact that after successfully surmounting one wave you discover that there is another behind it just as important and just as nervously anxious to do something effective in the way of swamping boats. In a ten-foot dingey one can get an idea of the resources of the sea in the line of waves that is not probable to the average experience which is never at sea in a dingey. As each slatey wall of water approached, it shut all else from the view of the men in the boat, and it was not difficult to imagine that this particular wave was the final outburst of the ocean, the last effort of the grim water. There was a terrible grace in the move of the waves, and they came in silence, save for the snarling of the crests.

In the wan light, the faces of the men must have been gray. Their eyes must have glinted in strange ways as they gazed steadily astern. Viewed from a balcony, the whole thing would doubtless have been weirdly picturesque. But the men in the boat had no time to see it, and if they had had leisure there were other things to occupy their minds. The sun swung steadily up the sky, and they knew it was broad day because the color of the sea changed from slate to emerald green, streaked with amber lights, and the foam was like tumbling snow. The process of the breaking day was unknown to them. They were aware only of this effect upon the color of the waves that rolled toward them.

In disjointed sentences the cook and the correspondent argued as to the difference between a life-saving station and a house of refuge. The cook had said: "There's a house of refuge just north of the Mosquito Inlet Light, and as soon as they see us, they'll come off in their boat and pick us up."

"As soon as who see us?" said the correspondent.

"The crew," said the cook.

"Houses of refuge don't have crews," said the correspondent. "As I understand them, they are only places where clothes and grub are stored for the benefit of shipwrecked people. They don't carry crews."

"Oh, yes, they do," said the cook.

"No, they don't," said the correspondent.

"Well, we're not there yet, anyhow," said the oiler, in the stern.

"Well," said the cook, "perhaps it's not a house of refuge that I'm thinking of as being near Mosquito Inlet Light. Perhaps it's a life-saving station."

"We're not there yet," said the oiler, in the stern.

II

As the boat bounced from the top of each wave, the wind tore through the hair of the hatless men, and as the craft plopped her stern down again the spray splashed past them. The crest of each of these waves was a hill, from the top of which the men surveyed, for a moment, a broad tumultuous expanse, shining and wind-riven. It was probably splendid. It was probably glorious, this play of the free sea, wild with lights of emerald and white and amber.

"Bully good thing it's an on-shore wind," said the cook. "If not, where would we be? Wouldn't have a show."

"That's right," said the correspondent.

The busy oiler nodded his assent.

Then the captain, in the bow, chuckled in a way that expressed humor, contempt, tragedy, all in one. "Do you think we've got much of a show now, boys?" said he.

Whereupon the three were silent, save for a trifle of hemming and hawing. To express any particular optimism at this time they felt to be childish and stupid, but they all doubtless possessed this sense of the situation in their mind. A young man thinks doggedly at such times. On the other hand, the ethics of their condition was decidedly against any open suggestion of hopelessness. So they were silent.

"Oh, well," said the captain, soothing his children, "We'll get ashore all right."

But there was that in his tone which made them think, so the oiler quoth: "Yes! If this wind holds!"

The cook was bailing: "Yes! If we don't catch hell in the surf."

Canton flannel gulls flew near and far. Sometimes they sat down on the sea, near patches of brown seaweed that rolled on the waves with a movement like carpets on a line in a gale. The birds sat comfortably in groups, and they were envied by some in the dingey, for the wrath of the sea was no more to them than it was to a covey of prairie chickens a thousand miles inland. Often they came very close and stared at the men with black bead-like eyes. At these times they were uncanny and sinister in their unblinking scrutiny, and the men hooted angrily at them, telling them to be gone. One came, and evidently decided to alight on the top of the captain's head. The bird flew parallel to the boat and did not circle, but made short sidelong jumps in the air in chicken fashion. His black eyes were wistfully fixed upon the captain's head. "Ugly brute," said the oiler to the bird. "You look as if you were made with a jack-knife." The cook and the correspondent swore darkly at the creature. The captain naturally wished to knock it away with the end of the heavy painter; but he did not dare do it, because anything resembling an emphatic gesture would have capsized this freighted boat, and so with his open hand, the captain gently and carefully waved the gull away. After it had been discouraged from the pursuit the captain breathed easier on account of his hair, and others breathed easier because the bird struck their minds at this time as being somehow gruesome and ominous.

In the meantime the oiler and the correspondent rowed. And also they rowed.

They sat together in the same seat, and each rowed an oar. Then the oiler took both oars; then the correspondent took both oars; then the oiler; then the correspondent. They rowed and they rowed. The very ticklish part of the business was when the time came for the reclining one in the stern to take his turn at the oars. By the very last star of truth, it is easier to steal eggs from under a hen than it was to change seats in the dingey. First the man in the stern slid his hand along the thwart and moved with care, as if he were of Sèvres. Then the man in the rowing seat slid his hand along the other thwart. It was all done with the most extraordinary care. As the two sidled past each other, the whole party kept watchful eyes on the coming wave, and the captain cried: "Look out now! Steady there!"

The brown mats of seaweed that appeared from time to time were like islands, bits of earth. They were traveling, apparently, neither one way nor the other. They were, to all intents, stationary. They informed the men in the boat that it was making progress slowly toward the land.

The captain, rearing cautiously in the bow, after the dingey soared on a great swell, said that he had seen the lighthouse at Mosquito Inlet.

Presently the cook remarked that he had seen it. The correspondent was at the oars then, and for some reason he too wished to look at the lighthouse, but his back was toward the far shore and the waves were important, and for some time he could not seize an opportunity to turn his head. But at last there came a wave more gentle than the others, and when at the crest of it he swiftly scoured the western horizon.

"See it?" said the captain.

"No," said the correspondent slowly, "I didn't see anything."

"Look again," said the captain. He pointed. "It's exactly in that direction."

At the top of another wave, the correspondent did as he was bid, and this time his eyes chanced on a small still thing on the edge of the swaying horizon. It was precisely like the point of a pin. It took an anxious eye to find a lighthouse so tiny.

"Think we'll make it, captain?"

"If this wind holds and the boat don't swamp, we can't do much else," said the captain.

The little boat, lifted by each towering sea, and splashed viciously by the crests, made progress that in the absence of seaweed was not apparent to those in her. She seemed just a wee thing wallowing, miraculously top up, at the mercy of five oceans. Occasionally, a great spread of water, like white flames, swarmed into her.

"Bail her, cook," said the captain serenely.

"All right, captain," said the cheerful cook.

III

It would be difficult to describe the subtle brotherhood of men that was here established on the seas. No one said that it was so. No one mentioned it. But it dwelt in the boat, and each man felt it warm him. They were a captain, an oiler, a cook and a correspondent, and they were friends, friends in a more curiously iron-bound degree than may be common. The hurt captain, lying against the water jar in the bow, spoke always in a low voice and calmly, but he could never command a more ready and swiftly obedient crew than the motley three of the dingey. It was more than a mere recognition of what was best for the common safety. There was surely in it a quality that was personal and heartfelt. And after this devotion to the commander of the boat there was this comradeship that the correspondent, for instance, who had been taught to be cynical of men, knew even at the time was the best experience of his life. But no one said that it was so. No one mentioned it.

"I wish we had a sail," remarked the captain. "We might try my overcoat on the end of an oar and give you two boys a chance to rest." So the cook and the correspondent held the mast and spread wide the overcoat. The oiler steered, and the little boat made good way with her new rig. Sometimes the oiler had to scull sharply to keep a sea from breaking into the boat, but otherwise sailing was a success.

Meanwhile the lighthouse had been growing slowly larger. It had now almost assumed color, and appeared like a little gray shadow on the sky. The man at the oars could not be prevented from turning his head rather often to try for a glimpse of this little gray shadow.

At last, from the top of each wave the men in the tossing boat could see land. Even as the lighthouse was an upright shadow on the sky, this land seemed but a long black shadow on the sea. It certainly was thinner than paper. "We must be about opposite New Smyrna," said the cook, who had coasted this shore often in schooners. "Captain, by the way, I believe they abandoned that life-saving station there about a year ago."

"Did they?" said the captain.

The wind slowly died away. The cook and the correspondent were not now obliged to slave in order to hold high the oar. But the waves continued their old impetuous swooping at the dingey, and the little craft, no longer under way, struggled woundily over them. The oiler or the correspondent took the oars again.

Shipwrecks are à propos of nothing. If men could only train for them and have them occur when the men had reached pink condition, there would be less drowning at sea. Of the four in the dingey none had slept any time worth mentioning for two days and two nights previous to embarking in the dingey, and in the excitement of clambering about the deck of a foundering ship they had also forgotten to eat heartily.

For these reasons, and for others, neither the oiler nor the correspondent was fond of rowing at this time. The correspondent wondered ingenuously how in the name of all that was sane could there be people who thought it amusing to row a boat. It was not an amusement; it was a diabolical punishment, and even a genius of mental aberrations could never conclude that it was anything but a horror to the muscles and a crime against the back. He mentioned to the boat in general how the amusement of rowing struck him, and the weary-faced oiler smiled in full sympathy. Previously to the foundering, by the way, the oiler had worked double-watch in the engine-room of the ship.

"Take her easy, now, boys," said the captain. "Don't spend yourselves. If we have to run a surf you'll need all your strength, because we'll sure have to swim for it. Take your time."

Slowly the land arose from the sea. From a black line it became a line of black and a line of white, trees and sand. Finally, the captain said that he could make out a house on the shore. "That's the house of refuge, sure," said the cook. "They'll see us before long, and come out after us."

The distant lighthouse reared high. "The keeper ought to be able to make us out now, if he's looking through a glass," said the captain. "He'll notify the life-saving people."

"None of those other boats could have got ashore to give word of the wreck," said the oiler, in a low voice. "Else the lifeboat would be out hunting us."

Slowly and beautifully the land loomed out of the sea. The wind came again. It had veered from the northeast to the southeast. Finally, a new sound struck the ears of the men in the boat. It was the low thunder of the surf on the shore. "We'll never be able to make the light-house now," said the captain. "Swing her head a little more north, Billie," said he.

" 'A little more north,' sir," said the oiler.

Whereupon the little boat turned her nose once more down the wind, and all but the oarsman watched the shore grow. Under the influence of this expansion doubt and direful apprehension was leaving the minds of the men. The management of the boat was still most absorbing, but it could not prevent a quiet cheerfulness. In an hour, perhaps, they would be ashore.

Their backbones had become thoroughly used to balancing in the boat, and they now rode this wild colt of a dingey like circus men. The correspondent thought that he had been drenched to the skin, but happening to feel in the top pocket of his coat, he found therein eight cigars. Four of them were soaked with sea water; four were perfectly scatheless. After a search, somebody produced three dry matches, and thereupon the four waifs rode impudently in their little boat, and with an assurance of an impending rescue shining in their eyes, puffed at the big cigars and judged well and ill of all men. Everybody took a drink of water.

IV

"Cook," remarked the captain, "there don't seem to be any signs of life about your house of refuge."

"No," replied the cook. "Funny they don't see us!"

A broad stretch of lowly coast lay before the eyes of the men. It was of dunes topped with dark vegetation. The roar of the surf was plain, and sometimes they could see the white lip of a wave as it spun up the beach. A tiny house was blocked out black upon the sky. Southward, the slim lighthouse lifted its little gray length.

Tide, wind, and waves were swinging the dingey northward. "Funny they don't see us," said the men.

The surf's roar was here dulled, but its tone was, nevertheless, thunderous and mighty. As the boat swam over the great rollers, the men sat listening to this roar. "We'll swamp sure," said everybody.

It is fair to say here that there was not a life-saving station within twenty miles in either direction, but the men did not know this fact, and in consequence they made dark and opprobrious remarks concerning the eyesight of the nation's life-savers. Four scowling men sat in the dingey and surpassed records in the invention of epithets.

"Funny they don't see us."

The lightheartedness of a former time had completely faded. To their sharpened minds it was easy to conjure pictures of all kinds of incompetency and blindness and, indeed, cowardice. There was the shore of the populous land, and it was bitter and bitter to them that from it came no sign.

"Well," said the captain, ultimately, "I suppose we'll have to make a try for ourselves. If we stay out here too long, we'll none of us have strength left to swim after the boat swamps."

And so the oiler, who was at the oars, turned the boat straight for the shore. There was a sudden tightening of muscle. There was some thinking.

"If we don't all get ashore——" said the captain. "If we don't all get ashore, I suppose you fellows know where to send news of my finish?"

They then briefly exchanged some addresses and admonitions. As for the reflections of the men, there was a great deal of rage in them. Perchance they might be formulated thus: "If I am going to be drowned—if I am going to be drowned—if I am going to be drowned, why, in the name of the seven mad gods who rule the sea, was I allowed to come thus far and contemplate sand and trees? Was I brought here merely to have my nose dragged away as I was about to nibble the sacred cheese of life? It is preposterous. If this old ninny woman, Fate, cannot do better than this, she should be deprived of the management of men's fortunes. She is an old hen who knows not her intention. If she has decided to drown me, why did she not do it in the beginning and save me all this trouble? The whole affair is absurd. . . . But no, she cannot mean to drown me. She dare not drown me. She cannot drown me. Not after all this work." Afterward the man might have had an impulse to shake his fist at the clouds: "Just you drown me, now, and then hear what I call you!"

The billows that came at this time were more formidable. They seemed always just about to break and roll over the little boat in a turmoil of foam. There was a preparatory and long growl in the speech of them. No mind unused to the sea would have concluded that the dingey could ascend these sheer heights in time. The shore was still afar. The oiler was a wily surfman. "Boys," he said swiftly, "she won't live three minutes more, and we're too far out to swim. Shall I take her to sea again, captain?"

"Yes! Go ahead!" said the captain.

This oiler, by a series of quick miracles, and fast and steady oarsmanship, turned the boat in the middle of the surf and took her safely to sea again.

There was a considerable silence as the boat bumped over the furrowed sea to deeper water. Then somebody in gloom spoke. "Well, anyhow, they must have seen us from the shore by now."

The gulls went in slanting flight up the wind toward the gray desolate east. A squall, marked by dingy clouds, and clouds brick red, like smoke from a burning building, appeared from the southeast.

"What do you think of those life-saving people? Ain't they peaches?"

"Funny they haven't seen us."

"Maybe they think we're out here for sport! Maybe they think we're fishin'. Maybe they think we're damned fools."

It was a long afternoon. A changed tide tried to force them southward, but the wind and wave said northward. Far ahead, where coastline, sea, and sky formed their mighty angle, there were little dots which seemed to indicate a city on the shore.

"St. Augustine?"

The captain shook his head. "Too near Mosquito Inlet."

And the oiler rowed, and then the correspondent rowed. Then the oiler rowed. It was a weary business. The human back can become the seat of more aches and pains than are registered in books for the composite anatomy of a regiment. It is a limited area, but it can become the theater of innumerable muscular conflicts, tangles, wrenches, knots, and other comforts.

"Did you ever like to row, Billie?" asked the correspondent.

"No," said the oiler. "Hang it!"

When one exchanged the rowing seat for a place in the bottom of the boat, he suffered a bodily depression that caused him to be careless of everything save an obligation to wiggle one finger. There was cold sea water swashing to and fro in the boat, and he lay in it. His head, pillowed on a thwart, was within an inch of the swirl of a wave crest, and sometimes a particularly obstreperous sea came in-board and drenched him once more. But these matters did not annoy him. It is almost certain that if the boat had capsized he would have tumbled comfortably out upon the ocean as if he felt sure that it was a great soft mattress.

"Look! There's a man on the shore!"

"Where?"

"There! See 'im? See 'im?"

"Yes, sure! He's walking along."

"Now he's stopped. Look! He's facing us!"

"He's waving at us!"

"So he is! By thunder!"

"Ah, now we're all right! Now we're all right! There'll be a boat out here for us in half an hour."

"He's going on. He's running. He's going up to that house there."

The remote beach seemed lower than the sea, and it required a searching glance to discern the little black figure. The captain saw a floating stick and they rowed to it. A bath towel was by some weird chance in the boat, and, tying this on the stick, the captain waved it. The oarsman did not dare turn his head, so he was obliged to ask questions.

"What's he doing now?"

"He's standing still again. He's looking, I think. . . . There he goes again. Toward the house. . . . Now he's stopped again."

"Is he waving at us?"

"No, not now! he was, though."

"Look! There comes another man!"

"He's running."

"Look at him go, would you."

"Why, he's on a bicycle. Now he's met the other man. They're both waving at us. Look!"

"There comes something up the beach."

"What the devil is that thing?"

"Why it looks like a boat."

"Why, certainly it's a boat."

"No, it's on wheels."

"Yes, so it is. Well, that must be the life-boat. They drag them along shore on a wagon."

"That's the life-boat, sure."

"No, by——, it's—it's an omnibus."

"I tell you it's a life-boat."

"It is not! It's an omnibus. I can see it plain. See? One of these big hotel omnibuses."

"By thunder, you're right. It's an omnibus, sure as fate. What do you suppose they are doing with an omnibus? Maybe they are going around collecting the life-crew, hey?"

"That's it, likely. Look! There's a fellow waving a little black flag. He's standing on the steps of the omnibus. There come those other two fellows. Now they're all talking together. Look at the fellow with the flag. Maybe he ain't waving it."

"That ain't a flag, is it? That's his coat. Why, certainly, that's his coat."

"So it is. It's his coat. He's taken it off and is waving it around his head. But would you look at him swing it."

"Oh, say, there isn't any life-saving station there. That's just a winter resort hotel omnibus that has brought over some of the boarders to see us drown."

"What's that idiot with the coat mean? What's he signaling, anyhow?"

"It looks as if he were trying to tell us to go north. There must be a life-saving station up there."

"No! He thinks we're fishing. Just giving us a merry hand. See? Ah, there, Willie!"

"Well, I wish I could make something out of those signals. What do you suppose he means?"

"He don't mean anything. He's just playing."

"Well, if he'd just signal us to try the surf again, or to go to sea and wait, or go north, or go south, or go to hell—there would be some reason in it. But look at him. He just stands there and keeps his coat revolving like a wheel. The ass!"

"There come more people."

"Now there's quite a mob. Look! Isn't that a boat?"

"Where? Oh, I see where you mean. No, that's no boat."

"That fellow is still waving his coat."

"He must think we like to see him do that. Why don't he quit it? It don't mean anything."

"I don't know. I think he is trying to make us go north. It must be that there's a life-saving station there somewhere."

"Say, he ain't tired yet. Look at 'im wave."

"Wonder how long he can keep that up. He's been revolving his coat ever since he caught sight of us. He's an idiot. Why aren't they getting men to bring a boat out? A fishing boat—one of those big yawls—could come out here all right. Why don't he do something?"

"Oh, it's all right, now."

"They'll have a boat out here for us in less than no time, now that they've seen us."

A faint yellow tone came into the sky over the low land. The shadows on the sea slowly deepened. The wind bore coldness with it, and the men began to shiver.

"Holy smoke!" said one, allowing his voice to express his impious mood, "if we keep on monkeying out here! If we've got to flounder out here all night!"

"Oh, we'll never have to stay here all night! Don't you worry. They've seen us now, and it won't be long before they'll come chasing out after us."

The shore grew dusky. The man waving a coat blended gradually into this gloom, and it swallowed in the same manner the omnibus and the group of people. The spray, when it dashed uproariously over the side, made the voyagers shrink and swear like men who were being branded.

"I'd like to catch the chump who waved the coat. I feel like soaking him one, just for luck."

"Why? What did he do?"

"Oh, nothing, but then he seemed so damned cheerful."

In the meantime the oiler rowed, and then the correspondent rowed, and then the oiler rowed. Gray-faced and bowed forward, they mechanically, turn by turn, plied the leaden oars. The form of the lighthouse had vanished from the southern horizon, but finally a pale star appeared, just lifting from the sea. The streaked saffron in the west passed before the all-merging darkness, and the sea to the east was black. The land had vanished, and was expressed only by the low and drear thunder of the surf.

"If I am going to be drowned—if I am going to be drowned—if I am going to be drowned, why, in the name of the seven mad gods who rule the sea, was I allowed to come thus far and contemplate sand and trees? Was I brought here merely to have my nose dragged away as I was about to nibble the sacred cheese of life?"

The patient captain, drooped over the water jar, was sometimes obliged to speak to the oarsman.

"Keep her head up! Keep her head up!"

" 'Keep her head up,' sir." The voices were weary and low.

This was surely a quiet evening. All save the oarsman lay heavily and listlessly in the boat's bottom. As for him, his eyes were just capable of noting the tall black waves that swept forward in a most sinister silence, save for an occasional subdued growl of a crest.

The cook's head was on a thwart, and he looked without interest at the water under his nose. He was deep in other scenes. Finally he spoke. "Billie," he murmured, dreamily, "what kind of pie do you like best?"

V

"Pie," said the oiler and the correspondent, agitatedly. "Don't talk about those things, blast you!"

"Well," said the cook, "I was just thinking about ham sandwiches, and——"

A night on the sea in an open boat is a long night. As darkness settled finally, the shine of the light, lifting from the sea in the south, changed to full gold. On the northern horizon a new light appeared, a small bluish gleam on the edge of the waters. These two lights were the furniture of the world. Otherwise there was nothing but waves.

Two men huddled in the stern, and distances were so magnificent in the dingey that the rower was enabled to keep his feet partly warmed by thrusting them under his companions. Their legs indeed extended far under the rowing seat until they touched the feet of the captain forward. Sometimes, despite the efforts of the tired oarsman, a wave came piling into the boat, an icy wave of the night, and the chilling water soaked them anew. They would twist their bodies for a moment and groan, and sleep the dead sleep once more, while the water in the boat gurgled about them as the craft rocked.

The plan of the oiler and the correspondent was for one to row until he lost the ability, and then arouse the other from his sea water couch in the bottom of the boat.

The oiler plied the oars until his head drooped forward, and the overpowering sleep blinded him. And he rowed yet afterward. Then he touched a man in the bottom of the boat and called his name. "Will you spell me for a little while?" he said, meekly.

"Sure, Billie," said the correspondent, awakening and dragging himself to a sitting position. They exchanged places carefully, and the oiler, cuddling down in the sea water at the cook's side, seemed to go to sleep instantly.

The particular violence of the sea had ceased. The waves came without snarling. The obligation of the man at the oars was to keep the boat headed so that the tilt of the rollers would not capsize her, and to preserve her from filling when the crests rushed past. The black waves were silent and hard to be seen in the darkness. Often one was almost upon the boat before the oarsman was aware.

In a low voice the correspondent addressed the captain. He was not sure that the captain was awake, although this iron man seemed to be always awake. "Captain, shall I keep her making for that light north, sir?"

The same steady voice answered him. "Yes. Keep it about two points off the port bow."

The cook had tied a life belt around himself in order to get even the warmth which this clumsy cork contrivance could donate, and he seemed almost stove-like when a rower, whose teeth invariably chattered wildly as soon as he ceased his labor, dropped down to sleep.

The correspondent, as he rowed, looked down at the two men sleeping under foot. The cook's arm was around the oiler's shoulders, and, with their fragmentary clothing and haggard faces, they were the babes of the sea, a grotesque rendering of the old babes in the wood.

Later he must have grown stupid at his work, for suddenly there was a growling of water, and a crest came with a roar and a swash into the boat, and it was a wonder that it did not set the cook afloat in his life belt. The cook continued to sleep, but the oiler sat up, blinking his eyes and shaking with the new cold.

"Oh, I'm awful sorry, Billie," said the correspondent contritely.

"That's all right, old boy," said the oiler, and lay down again and was asleep.

Presently it seemed that even the captain dozed, and the correspondent thought that he was the one man afloat on all the oceans. The wind had a voice as it came over the waves, and it was sadder than the end.

There was a long, loud swishing astern of the boat, and a gleaming trail of phosphorescence, like blue flame, was furrowed on the black waters. It might have been made by a monstrous knife.

Then there came a stillness, while the correspondent breathed with the open mouth and looked at the sea.

Suddenly there was another swish and another long flash of bluish light, and this time it was alongside the boat, and might almost have been reached with an oar. The correspondent saw an enormous fin speed like a shadow through the water, hurling the crystalline spray and leaving the long glowing trail.

The correspondent looked over his shoulder at the captain. His face was hidden, and he seemed to be asleep. He looked at the babes of the sea. They certainly were asleep. So, being bereft of sympathy, he leaned a little way to one side and swore softly into the sea.

But the thing did not then leave the vicinity of the boat. Ahead or astern, on one side or the other, at intervals long or short, fled the long sparkling streak, and there was to be heard the whirroo of the dark fin. The speed and power of the thing was greatly to be admired. It cut the water like a gigantic and keen projectile.

The presence of this biding thing did not affect the man with the same horror that it would if he had been a picnicker. He simply looked at the sea dully and swore in an undertone.

Nevertheless, it is true that he did not wish to be alone. He wished one of his companions to awaken by chance and keep him company with it. But the captain hung motionless over the water jar, and the oiler and the cook in the bottom of the boat were plunged in slumber.

VI

"If I am going to be drowned—if I am going to be drowned—if I am going to be drowned, why, in the name of the seven mad gods who rule the sea, was I allowed to come thus far and contemplate sand and trees?"

During this dismal night, it may be remarked that a man would conclude that it was really the intention of the seven mad gods to drown him, despite the abominable injustice of it. For it was certainly an abominable injustice to drown a man who had worked so hard, so hard. The man felt it would be a crime most unnatural. Other people had drowned at sea since galleys swarmed with painted sails, but still——

When it occurs to a man that nature does not regard him as important, and that she feels she would not maim the universe by disposing of him, he at first wishes to throw bricks at the temple, and he hates deeply the fact that there are no bricks and no temples. Any visible expression of nature would surely be pelleted with his jeers.

Then, if there be no tangible thing to hoot he feels, perhaps, the desire to confront a personification and indulge in pleas, bowed to one knee, and with hands supplicant, saying: "Yes, but I love myself."

A high cold star on a winter's night is the word he feels that she says to him. Thereafter he knows the pathos of his situation.

The men in the dingey had not discussed these matters, but each had, no doubt, reflected upon them in silence and according to his mind. There was seldom any expression upon their faces save the general one of complete weariness. Speech was devoted to the business of the boat.

To chime the notes of his emotion, a verse mysteriously entered the correspondent's head. He had even forgotten that he had forgotten this. verse, but it suddenly was in his mind.

"A soldier of the Legion lay dying in Algiers,
There was a lack of woman's nursing, there was dearth of woman's tears;
But a comrade stood beside him, and he took that comrade's hand,
And he said: 'I shall never see my own, my native land.' "

In his childhood, the correspondent had been made acquainted with the fact that a soldier of the Legion lay dying in Algiers, but he had never regarded the fact as important. Myriads of his school fellows had informed him of the soldier's plight, but the dinning had naturally ended by making him perfectly indifferent. He had never considered it his affair that a soldier of the Legion lay dying in Algiers, nor had it appeared to him as a matter for sorrow. It was less to him than the breaking of a pencil's point.

Now, however, it quaintly came to him as a human, living thing. It was no longer merely a picture of a few throes in the breast of a poet, meanwhile drinking tea and warming his feet at the grate; it was an actuality—stern, mournful, and fine.

The correspondent plainly saw the soldier. He lay on the sand with his feet out straight and still. While his pale left hand was upon his chest in an attempt to thwart the going of his life, the blood came between his fingers. In the far Algerian distance, a city of low square forms was set against a sky that was faint with the last sunset hues. The correspondent, plying the oars and dreaming of the slow and slower movements of the lips of the soldier, was moved by a profound and perfectly impersonal comprehension. He was sorry for the soldier of the Legion who lay dying in Algiers.

The thing which had followed the boat and waited, had evidently grown bored at the delay. There was no longer to be heard the slash of the cut water, and there was no longer the flame of the long trail. The light in the north still glimmered, but it was apparently no nearer to the boat. Sometimes the boom of the surf rang in the correspondent's ears, and he turned the craft seaward then and rowed harder. Southward, someone had evidently built a watch fire on the beach. It was too low and too far to be seen, but it made a shimmering, roseate reflection upon the bluff back of it, and this could be discerned from the boat. The wind came stronger, and sometimes a wave suddenly raged out like a mountain cat, and there was to be seen the sheen and sparkle of a broken crest.

The captain, in the bow, moved on his water jar and sat erect. "Pretty long night," he observed to the correspondent. He looked at the shore. "Those life-saving people take their time."

"Did you see that shark playing around?"

"Yes, I saw him. He was a big fellow, all right."

"Wish I had known you were awake."

Later the correspondent spoke into the bottom of the boat.

"Billie!" There was a slow and gradual disentanglement. "Billie, will you spell me?"

"Sure," said the oiler.

As soon as the correspondent touched the cold comfortable sea water in the bottom of the boat, and had huddled close to the cook's life belt he was deep in sleep, despite the fact that his teeth played all the popular airs. This sleep was so good to him that it was but a moment before he heard a voice call his name in a tone that demonstrated the last stages of exhaustion. "Will you spell me?"

"Sure, Billie."

The light in the north had mysteriously vanished, but the correspondent took his course from the wide-awake captain.

Later in the night they took the boat farther out to sea, and the captain directed the cook to take one oar at the stern and keep the boat facing the seas. He was to call out if he should hear the thunder of the surf. This plan enabled the oiler and the correspondent to get respite together. "We'll give those boys a chance to get into shape again," said the captain. They curled down and, after a few preliminary chatterings and trembles, slept once more the dead sleep. Neither knew they had bequeathed to the cook the company of another shark, or perhaps the same shark.

As the boat caroused on the waves, spray occasionally bumped over the side and gave them a fresh soaking, but this had no power to break their repose. The ominous slash of the wind and the water affected them as it would have affected mummies.

"Boys," said the cook, with the notes of every reluctance in his voice, "she's drifted in pretty close. I guess one of you had better take her to sea again." The correspondent, aroused, heard the crash of the toppled crests.

As he was rowing, the captain gave him some whisky and water, and this steadied the chills out of him. "If I ever get ashore and anybody shows me even a photograph of an oar——"

At last there was a short conversation.

"Billie. . . . Billie, will you spell me?"

"Sure," said the oiler.

VII

When the correspondent again opened his eyes, the sea and the sky were each of the gray hue of the dawning. Later, carmine and gold was painted upon the waters. The morning appeared finally, in its splendor, with a sky of pure blue, and the sunlight flamed on the tips of the waves.

On the distant dunes were set many little black cottages, and a tall white windmill reared above them. No man, nor dog, nor bicycle appeared on the beach. The cottages might have formed a deserted village.

The voyagers scanned the shore. A conference was held in the boat. "Well," said the captain, "if no help is coming we might better try a run through the surf right away. If we stay out here much longer we will be too weak to do anything for ourselves at all." The others silently acquiesced in this reasoning. The boat was headed for the beach. The correspondent wondered if none ever ascended the tall wind tower, and if then they never looked seaward. This tower was a giant, standing with its back to the plight of the ants. It represented in a degree, to the correspondent, the serenity of nature amid the struggles of the individual—nature in the wind, and nature in the vision of men. She did not seem cruel to him then, nor beneficent, nor treacherous, nor wise. But she was indifferent, flatly indifferent. It is, perhaps, plausible that a man in this situation, impressed with the unconcern of the universe, should see the innumerable flaws of his life, and have them taste wickedly in his mind and wish for another chance. A distinction between right and wrong seems absurdly clear to him, then, in this new ignorance of the grave edge, and he understands that if he were given another opportunity he would mend his conduct and his words, and be better and brighter during an introduction or at a tea.

"Now, boys," said the captain, "she is going to swamp, sure. All we can do is to work her in as far as possible, and then when she swamps, pile out and scramble for the beach. Keep cool now, and don't jump until she swamps sure."

The oiler took the oars. Over his shoulders he scanned the surf. "Captain," he said, "I think I'd better bring her about and keep her head-on to the seas and back her in."

"All right, Billie," said the captain. "Back her in." The oiler swung the boat then and, seated in the stern, the cook and the correspondent were obliged to look over their shoulders to contemplate the lonely and indifferent shore.

The monstrous in-shore rollers heaved the boat high until the men were again enabled to see the white sheets of water scudding up the slanted beach. "We won't get in very close," said the captain. Each time a man could wrest his attention from the rollers, he turned his glance toward the shore, and in the expression of the eyes during this contem- plation there was a singular quality. The correspondent, observing the others, knew that they were not afraid, but the full meaning of their glances was shrouded.

As for himself, he was too tired to grapple fundamentally with the fact. He tried to coerce his mind into thinking of it, but the mind was dominated at this time by the muscles, and the muscles said they did not care. It merely occurred to him that if he should drown it would be a shame.

There were no hurried words, no pallor, no plain agitation. The men simply looked at the shore. "Now, remember to get well clear of the boat when you jump," said the captain.

Seaward the crest of a roller suddenly fell with a thunderous crash, and the long white comber came roaring down upon the boat.

"Steady now," said the captain. The men were silent. They turned their eyes from the shore to the comber and waited. The boat slid up the incline, leaped at the furious top, bounced over it, and swung down the long back of the wave. Some water had been shipped and the cook bailed it out.

But the next crashed also. The tumbling, boiling flood of white water caught the boat and whirled it almost perpendicular. Water swarmed in from all sides. The correspondent had his hands on the gunwale at this time, and when the water entered at that place he swiftly withdrew his fingers, as if he objected to wetting them.

The little boat, drunken with this weight of water, reeled and snug- gled deeper into the sea.

"Bail her out, cook! Bail her out," said the captain.

"All right, captain," said the cook.

"Now, boys, the next one will do for us, sure," said the oiler. "Mind to jump clear of the boat."

The third wave moved forward, huge, furious, implacable. It fairly swallowed the dingey, and almost simultaneously the men tumbled into the sea. A piece of life belt had lain in the bottom of the boat, and as the correspondent went overboard he held this to his chest with his left hand.

The January water was icy, and he reflected immediately that it was colder than he had expected to find it on the coast of Florida. This appeared to his dazed mind as a fact important enough to be noted at the time. The coldness of the water was sad; it was tragic. This fact was somehow so mixed and confused with his opinion of his own situation that it seemed almost a proper reason for tears. The water was cold.

When he came to the surface he was conscious of little but the noisy water. Afterward he saw his companions in the sea. The oiler was ahead in the race. He was swimming strongly and rapidly. Off to the correspondent's left, the cook's great white and corked back bulged out of the water, and in the rear the captain was hanging with his one good hand to the keel of the overturned dingey.

There is a certain immovable quality to a shore, and the correspondent wondered at it amid the confusion of the sea.

It seemed also very attractive, but the correspondent knew that it was a long journey, and he paddled leisurely. The piece of life preserver lay under him, and sometimes he whirled down the incline of a wave as if he were on a hand-sled.

But finally he arrived at a place in the sea where travel was beset with difficulty. He did not pause swimming to inquire what manner of current had caught him, but there his progress ceased. The shore was set before him like a bit of scenery on a stage, and he looked at it and understood with his eyes each detail of it.

As the cook passed, much farther to the left, the captain was calling to him, "Turn over on your back, cook! Turn over on your back and use the oar."

"All right, sir." The cook turned on his back, and, paddling with an oar, went ahead as if he were a canoe.

Presently the boat also passed to the left of the correspondent with the captain clinging with one hand to the keel. He would have appeared like a man raising himself to look over a board fence, if it were not for the extraordinary gymnastics of the boat. The correspondent marveled that the captain could still hold to it.

They passed on, nearer to shore—the oiler, the cook, the captain—and following them went the water jar, bouncing gayly over the seas.

The correspondent remained in the grip of this strange new enemy—

a current. The shore, with its white slope of sand and its green bluff, topped with little silent cottages, was spread like a picture before him. It was very near to him then, but he was impressed as one who in a gallery looks at a scene from Brittany or Holland.

He thought: "I am going to drown? Can it be possible? Can it be possible? Can it be possible?" Perhaps an individual must consider his own death to be the final phenomenon of nature.

But later a wave perhaps whirled him out of this small, deadly current, for he found suddenly that he could again make progress toward the shore. Later still, he was aware that the captain, clinging with one hand to the keel of the dingey, had his face turned away from the shore and toward him, and was calling his name. "Come to the boat! Come to the boat!"

In his struggle to reach the captain and the boat, he reflected that when one gets properly wearied, drowning must really be a comfortable arrangement, a cessation of hostilities accompanied by a large degree of relief, and he was glad of it, for the main thing in his mind for some months had been horror of the temporary agony. He did not wish to be hurt.

Presently he saw a man running along the shore. He was undressing with most remarkable speed. Coat, trousers, shirt, everything flew magically off him.

"Come to the boat," called the captain.

"All right, captain." As the correspondent paddled, he saw the captain let himself down to bottom and leave the boat. Then the correspondent performed his one little marvel of the voyage. A large wave caught him and flung him with ease and supreme speed completely over the boat and far beyond it. It struck him even then as an event in gymnastics, and a true miracle of the sea. An overturned boat in the surf is not a plaything to a swimming man.

The correspondent arrived in water that reached only to his waist, but his condition did not enable him to stand for more than a moment. Each wave knocked him into a heap, and the undertow pulled at him.

Then he saw the man who had been running and undressing, and undressing and running, come bounding into the water. He dragged the ashore the cook, and then waded towards the captain, but the captain waved him away, and sent him to the correspondent. He was naked, naked as a tree in winter, but a halo was about his head, and he shone like a saint. He gave a strong pull, and a long drag, and a bully heave at the correspondent's hand. The correspondent, schooled in the minor formulæ, said: "Thanks, old man." But suddenly the man cried: "What's that?" He pointed a swift finger. The correspondent said: "Go."

In the shallows, face downward, lay the oiler. His forehead touched sand that was periodically, between each wave, clear of the sea.

The correspondent did not know all that transpired afterward. When he achieved safe ground he fell, striking the sand with each particular part of his body. It was as if he had dropped from a roof, but the thud was grateful to him.

It seems that instantly the beach was populated with men with blankets, clothes, and flasks, and women with coffee pots and all the remedies sacred to their minds. The welcome of the land to the men from the sea was warm and generous, but a still and dripping shape was carried slowly up the beach, and the land's welcome for it could only be the different and sinister hospitality of the grave.

When it came night, the white waves paced to and fro in the moonlight, and the wind brought the sound of the sea's great voice to the men on shore, and they felt that they could then be interpreters.

36

The Lost Phoebe

BY THEODORE DREISER

THEY lived together in a part of the country which was not so prosperous as it had once been, about three miles from one of those towns that, instead of increasing in population, is steadily decreasing. The territory was not very thickly settled; perhaps a house every other mile or so, with large areas of corn- and wheatland and fallow fields that at odd seasons had been sown to timothy and clover. Their particular house was part log and part frame, the log portion being the old original home of Henry's grandfather. The new portion, of now rain-beaten, time-worn slabs, through which the wind squeaked in the chinks at times, and which several overshadowing elms and a butternut tree made picturesque and reminiscently pathetic, but a little damp, was erected by Henry when he was twenty-one and just married.

That was forty-eight years before. The furniture inside, like the house outside, was old and mildewy and reminiscent of an earlier day. You have seen the what-not of cherry wood, perhaps, with spiral legs and fluted top. It was there. The old-fashioned four-poster bed, with its ball-like protuberances and deep curving incisions, was there also, a sadly alienated descendant of an early Jacobean ancestor. The bureau of cherry was also high and wide and solidly built, but faded-looking, and with a musty odor. The rag carpet that underlay all these sturdy examples of enduring furniture was a weak, faded, lead and pink colored affair woven by Phœbe Ann's own hands, when she was fifteen years younger than she was when she died. The creaky wooden loom on which it had been done now stood like a dusty, bony skeleton, along with a broken rocking-chair, a worm-eaten clothes press—Heavens knows how old—a lime-stained bench that had once been used to keep flowers on outside the door, and other decrepit factors of household utility, in an east room that was a lean-to against this so-called main portion. All sorts of other broken-down furniture were about this place; an antiquated clothes-horse, cracked in two of its ribs; a broken mirror in an old cherry frame, which had fallen from a nail and cracked itself three days before their youngest son, Jerry, died; an extension hat-rack, which once had had porcelain knobs on the ends of its pegs; and a sewing machine, long since outdone in its clumsy mechanism by rivals of a newer generation.

The orchard to the east of the house was full of gnarled old apple trees, worm eaten as to trunks and branches, and fully ornamented with green and white lichens, so that it had a sad, greenish-white, silvery effect in moonlight. The low outhouses, which had once housed chickens, a horse or two, a cow, and several pigs, were covered with patches of moss as to their roof, and the sides had been free of paint for so long that they were blackish-gray as to color, and a little spongy. The picket fence in front, with its gate squeaky and askew, and the side fences of the stake-and-rider type were in an equally run-down condition. As a matter of fact, they had aged synchronously with the persons who lived here, old Henry Reifsneider and his wife Phœbe Ann.

They had lived here, these two, ever since their marriage, forty-eight years before, and Henry had lived here before that from his childhood up. His father and mother, well along in years when he was a boy, had invited him to bring his wife here when he had first fallen in love and decided to marry; and he had done so. His father and mother were the companions of himself and his wife for ten years after they were married, when both died; and then Henry and Phœbe were left with their five children growing lustily apace. But all sorts of things had happened since then. Of the seven children, all told, that had been born to them, three had died; one girl had gone to Kansas; one boy had gone to Sioux Falls, never even to be heard of after; another boy had gone to Washington; and the last girl lived five counties away in the same State, but was so burdened with cares of her own that she rarely gave them a thought. Time and a commonplace home life that had never been attractive had weaned them thoroughly, so that, wherever they were, they gave little thought as to how it might be with their father and mother.

Old Henry Reifsneider and his wife Phœbe were a loving couple. You perhaps know how it is with simple natures that fasten themselves like lichens on the stones of circumstance and weather their days to a crumbling conclusion. The great world sounds widely, but it has no call for them. They have no soaring intellect. The orchard, the meadow, the cornfield, the pig-pen, and the chicken-lot measure the range of their human activities. When the wheat is headed it is reaped and threshed; when the corn is browned and frosted it is cut and shocked; when the timothy is in full head it is cut, and the hay-cock erected. After that comes winter, with the hauling of grain to market, the sawing and splitting of wood, the simple chores of fire-building, meal-getting, occasional repairing, and visiting. Beyond these and the changes of weather —the snows, the rains, and the fair days—there are no immediate, significant things. All the rest of life is a far-off, clamorous phantasmagoria, flickering like Northern lights in the night, and sounding as faintly as cow-bells tinkling in the distance.

Old Henry and his wife Phœbe were as fond of each other as it is possible for two old people to be who have nothing else in this life to be fond of. He was a thin old man, seventy when she died, a queer, crotchety person with coarse gray-black hair and beard, quite straggly and unkempt. He looked at you out of dull, fishy, watery eyes that had deep-brown crow's-feet at the sides. His clothes, like the clothes of many farmers, were aged and angular and baggy, standing out at the pockets, not fitting about the neck, protuberant and worn at elbow and knee. Phœbe Ann was thin and shapeless, a very umbrella of a woman, clad in shabby black, and with a black bonnet for her best wear. As time had passed, and they had only themselves to look after, their movements had become slower and slower, their activities fewer and fewer. The annual keep of pigs had been reduced from five to one grunting porker, and the single horse which Henry now retained was a sleepy animal, not over-nourished and not very clean. The chickens, of which formerly there was a large flock, had almost disappeared, owing to ferrets, foxes, and the lack of proper care, which produces disease. The former healthy garden was now a straggling memory of itself, and the vines and flower-beds that formerly ornamented the windows and dooryard had now become choking thickets. A will had been made which divided the small tax-eaten property equally among the remaining four, so that it was really of no interest to any of them. Yet these two lived together in peace and sympathy, only that now and then old Henry would become unduly cranky, complaining almost invariably that something had been neglected or mislaid which was of no importance at all.

"Phœbe, where's my corn knife? You ain't never minded to let my things alone no more."

"Now you hush, Henry," his wife would caution him in a cracked and squeaky voice. "If you don't, I'll leave yuh. I'll git up and walk out of here some day, and then where would y' be? Y' ain't got anybody but me to look after yuh, so yuh just behave yourself. Your corn knife's on the mantel where it's allus been unless you've gone an' put it summers else."

Old Henry, who knew his wife would never leave him under any circumstances, used to speculate at times as to what he would do if she were to die. That was the one leaving that he really feared. As he climbed on the chair at night to wind the old, long-pendulumed, double-weighted clock, or went finally to the front and the back door to see that they were safely shut in, it was a comfort to know that Phœbe was there, properly ensconced on her side of the bed, and that if he stirred restlessly in the night, she would be there to ask what he wanted.

"Now, Henry, do lie still! You're as restless as a chicken."

"Well, I can't sleep, Phœbe."

"Well, yuh needn't roll so, anyhow. Yuh kin let me sleep."

This usually reduced him to a state of somnolent ease. If she wanted a pail of water, it was a grumbling pleasure for him to get it; and if she did rise first to build the fires, he saw that the wood was cut and placed within easy reach. They divided this simple world nicely between them.

As the years had gone on, however, fewer and fewer people had called. They were well-known for a distance of as much as ten square miles as old Mr. and Mrs. Reifsneider, honest, moderately Christian, but too old to be really interesting any longer. The writing of letters had become an almost impossible burden too difficult to continue or even negotiate via others, although an occasional letter still did arrive from the daughter in Pemberton County. Now and then some old friend stopped with a pie or cake or a roasted chicken or duck, or merely to see that they were well; but even these kindly minded visits were no longer frequent.

One day in the early spring of her sixty-fourth year Mrs. Reifsneider took sick, and from a low fever passed into some indefinable ailment which, because of her age, was no longer curable. Old Henry drove to Swinnerton, the neighboring town, and procured a doctor. Some friends called, and the immediate care of her was taken off his hands. Then one chill spring night she died, and old Henry, in a fog of sorrow and uncertainty, followed her body to the nearest graveyard, an unattractive space with a few pines growing in it. Although he might have gone to the daughter in Pemberton or sent for her, it was really too much trouble and he was too weary and fixed. It was suggested to him at once by one friend and another that he come to stay with them awhile, but he did not see fit. He was so old and so fixed in his notions and so accustomed to the exact surroundings he had known all his days, that he could not think of leaving. He wanted to remain near where they had put his Phœbe; and the fact that he would have to live alone did not trouble him in the least. The living children were notified and the care of him offered if he would leave, but he would not.

"I kin make a shift for myself," he continually announced to old Dr. Morrow, who had attended his wife in this case. "I kin cook a little.

and, besides, it don't take much more'n coffee an' bread in the mornin's to satisfy me. I'll get along now well enough. Yuh just let me be." And after many pleadings and proffers of advice, with supplies of coffee and bacon and baked bread duly offered and accepted, he was left to himself. For a while he sat idly outside his door brooding in the spring sun. He tried to revive his interest in farming, and to keep himself busy and free from thought by looking after the fields, which of late had been much neglected. It was a gloomy thing to come in of an evening, however, or in the afternoon, and find no shadow of Phœbe where everything suggested her. By degrees he put a few of her things away. At night he sat beside his lamp and read in the papers that were left him occasionally or in a Bible that he had neglected for years, but he could get little solace from these things. Mostly he held his hand over his mouth and looked at the floor as he sat and thought of what had become of her, and how soon he himself would die. He made a great business of making his coffee in the morning and frying himself a little bacon at night; but his appetite was gone. The shell in which he had been housed so long seemed vacant, and its shadows were suggestive of immedicable griefs. So he lived quite dolefully for five long months, and then a change began.

It was one night, after he had looked after the front and the back door, wound the clock, blown out the light, and gone through all the selfsame motions that he had indulged in for years, that he went to bed not so much to sleep as to think. It was a moonlight night. The green-lichen-covered orchard just outside and to be seen from his bed where he now lay was a silvery affair, sweetly spectral. The moon shone through the east windows, throwing the pattern of the panes on the wooden floor, and making the old furniture, to which he was accustomed, stand out dimly in the room. As usual he had been thinking of Phœbe and the years when they had been young together, and of the children who had gone, and the poor shift he was making of his present days. The house was coming to be in a very bad state indeed. The bed-clothes were in disorder and not clean, for he made a wretched shift of washing. It was a terror to him. The roof leaked, causing things, some of them, to remain damp for weeks at a time, but he was getting into that brooding state where he would accept anything rather than exert himself. He preferred to pace slowly to and fro or to sit and think.

By twelve o'clock of this particular night he was asleep, however, and by two had waked again. The moon by this time had shifted to a position on the western side of the house, and it now shone in through the windows of the living-room and those of the kitchen beyond. A certain combination of furniture—a chair near a table with his coat on it, the half-open kitchen door casting a shadow, and the position of a lamp near a paper—gave him an exact representation of Phœbe leaning over the table as he had often seen her do in life. It gave him a great start. Could it be she—or her ghost? He had scarcely ever believed in spirits; and still—. He looked at her fixedly in the feeble half-light, his old hair tingling oddly at the roots, and then sat up. The figure did not move. He put his thin legs out of the bed and sat looking at her, wondering if this could really be Phœbe. They had talked of ghosts often in their lifetime, of apparitions and omens; but they had never agreed that such things could be. It had never been a part of his wife's creed that she could have a spirit that could return to walk the earth. Her after-world was quite a different affair, a vague heaven, no less, from which the righteous did not trouble to return. Yet here she was now, bending over the table in her black skirt and gray shawl, her pale profile outlined against the moonlight.

"Phœbe," he called, thrilling from head to toe, and putting out one bony hand, "have yuh come back?"

The figure did not stir, and he arose and walked uncertainly to the door, looking at it fixedly the while. As he drew near, however, the apparition resolved itself into its primal content—his old coat over the high backed chair, the lamp by the paper, the half-open door.

"Well," he said to himself, his mouth open, "I thought shore I saw her." And he ran his hand strangely and vaguely through his hair, the while his nervous tension relaxed. Vanished as it had, it gave him the idea that she might return.

Another night, because of this first illusion, and because his mind was now constantly on her and he was old, he looked out of the window that was nearest his bed and commanded a hen-coop and pig-pen and a part of the wagon-shed, and there, a faint mist exuding from the damp of the ground, he thought he saw her again. It was one of those little wisps of mist, one of those faint exhalations of the earth that rise in a cool night after a warm day, and flicker like small white cypresses of fog before they disappear. In life it had been a custom of hers to cross this lot from her kitchen door to the pig-pen to throw in any scrap that was left from her cooking, and here she was again. He sat up and watched it strangely, doubtfully, because of his previous experience, but inclined, because of the nervous titillation that passed over his body, to believe that spirits really were, and that Phœbe, who would be concerned because of his lonely state, must be thinking about him, and hence returning. What other way would she have? How otherwise could she express herself? It would be within the province of her charity so to do, and like her loving interest in him. He quivered and watched it eagerly; but, a faint breath of air stirring, it wound away toward the fence and disappeared.

A third night, as he was actually dreaming, some ten days later, she came to his bedside and put her hand on his head.

"Poor Henry!" she said. "It's too bad."

He roused out of his sleep, actually to see her, he thought, moving from his bedroom into the one living room, her figure a shadowy mass of black. The weak straining of his eyes caused little points of light to flicker about the outlines of her form. He arose, greatly astonished, walked the floor in the cool room, convinced that Phœbe was coming back to him. If he only thought sufficiently, if he made it perfectly clear by his feeling that he needed her greatly, she would come back, this kindly wife, and tell him what to do. She would perhaps be with him much of the time, in the night, anyhow; and that would make him less lonely, this state more endurable.

In age and with the feeble it is not such a far cry from the subtleties of illusion to actual hallucination, and in due time this transition was made for Henry. Night after night he waited, expecting her return. Once in his weird mood he thought he saw a pale light moving about the room, and another time he thought he saw her walking in the orchard after dark. It was one morning when the details of his lonely state were virtually unendurable that he woke with the thought that she was not dead. How he had arrived at this conclusion it is hard to say. His mind had gone. In its place was a fixed illusion. He and Phœbe had had a senseless quarrel. He had reproached her for not leaving his pipe where he was accustomed to find it, and she had left. It was an aberrated fulfillment of her old jesting threat that if he did not behave himself she would leave him.

"I guess I could find yuh ag'in," he had always said. But her cackling threat had always been:

"Yuh'll not find me if I ever leave yuh. I guess I kin git some place where yuh can't find me."

This morning when he arose he did not think to build the fire in the customary way or to grind his coffee and cut his bread, as was his wont, but solely to meditate as to where he should search for her and how he should induce her to come back. Recently the one horse had been dispensed with because he found it cumbersome and beyond his needs. He took down his soft crush hat after he had dressed himself, a new glint of interest and determination in his eye, and taking his black crook cane from behind the door, where he had always placed it, started out briskly to look for her among the nearest neighbors. His old shoes clumped soundly in the dust as he walked, and his gray-black locks, now grown rather long, straggled out in a dramatic fringe or halo from under his hat. His short coat stirred busily as he walked, and his hands and face were peaked and pale.

"Why, hello, Henry! Where're yuh goin' this mornin'?" inquired Farmer Dodge, who, hauling a load of wheat to market, encountered him on the public road. He had not seen the aged farmer in months, not since his wife's death, and he wondered now, seeing him looking so spry.

"Yuh ain't seen Phœbe, have yuh?" inquired the old man, looking up quizzically.

"Phœbe who?" inquired Farmer Dodge, not for the moment connecting the name with Henry's dead wife.

"Why, my wife Phœbe, o' course. Who do yuh s'pose I mean?" He stared up with a pathetic sharpness of glance from under his shaggy, gray eyebrows.

"Wall, I'll swan, Henry, yuh ain't jokin', are yuh?" said the solid Dodge, a pursy man, with a smooth, hard, red face. "It can't be your wife yuh're talkin' about. She's dead."

"Dead! Shucks!" retorted the demented Reifsneider. "She left me early this mornin', while I was sleepin'. She allus got up to build the fire, but she's gone now. We had a little spat last night, an' I guess that's the reason. But I guess I kin find her. She's gone over to Matilda Race's, that's where she's gone."

He started briskly up the road, leaving the amazed Dodge to stare in wonder after him.

"Well, I'll be switched!" he said aloud to himself. "He's clean out'n his head. That poor old feller's been livin' down there till he's gone outen his mind. I'll have to notify the authorities." And he flicked his whip with great enthusiasm. "Geddap!" he said, and was off.

Reifsneider met no one else in this poorly populated region until he reached the whitewashed fence of Matilda Race and her husband three miles away. He had passed several other houses en route, but these not being within the range of his illusion were not considered. His wife, who had known Matilda well, must be here. He opened the picket-gate which guarded the walk, and stamped briskly up to the door.

"Why, Mr. Reifsneider," exclaimed old Matilda herself, a stout woman, looking out of the door in answer to his knock, "what brings yuh here this mornin'?"

"Is Phœbe here?" he demanded eagerly.

"Phœbe who? What Phœbe?" replied Mrs. Race, curious as to this sudden development of energy on his part.

"Why, my Phœbe, o' course. My wife Phœbe. Who do yuh s'pose? Ain't she here now?"

"Lawsy me!" exclaimed Mrs. Race, opening her mouth. Yuh pore man! So you're clean out'n your mind now. Yuh come right in and sit down. I'll git yuh a cup o' coffee. O' course your wife ain't here; but yuh come in an' sit down. I'll find her fer yuh after a while. I know where she is."

The old farmer's eyes softened, and he entered. He was so thin and pale a specimen, pantalooned and patriarchal, that he aroused Mrs. Race's extremest sympathy as he took off his hat and laid it on his knees, quite softly and mildly.

"We had a quarrel last night, an' she left me," he volunteered.

"Laws! laws!" sighed Mrs. Race, there being no one present with whom to share her astonishment as she went to her kitchen. "The pore man! Now somebody's just got to look after him. He can't be allowed to run around the country this way lookin' for his dead wife. It's turrible."

She boiled him a pot of coffee and brought in some of her new-baked bread and fresh butter. She set out some of her best jam and put a couple of eggs to boil, lying whole-heartedly the while.

"Now yuh stay right there, Uncle Henry, till Jake comes in, an' I'll send him to look for Phœbe. I think it's more'n likely she's over to Swinnerton with some o' her friends. Anyhow, we'll find out. Now yuh just drink this coffee an' eat this bread. Yuh must be tired. Yuh've had a long walk this mornin'." Her idea was to take counsel with Jake, "her man," and perhaps have him notify the authorities.

She bustled about, meditating on the uncertainties of life, while old Reifsneider thrummed on the rim of his hat with his pale fingers and later ate abstractedly of what she offered. His mind was on his wife, however, and since she was not here, or did not appear, it wandered vaguely away to a family by the name of Murray, miles away in another direction. He decided after a time that he would not wait for Jack Race to hunt his wife but would seek her for himself. He must be on, and urge her to come back.

"Well, I'll be goin'," he said, getting up and looking strangely about him. "I guess she didn't come here after all. She went over to the Murrays, I guess. I'll not wait any longer, Mis' Race. There's a lot to do over to the house today." And out he marched in the face of her protests taking to the dusty road again in the warm spring sun, his cane striking the earth as he went.

It was two hours later that this pale figure of a man appeared in the Murrays' doorway, dusty, perspiring, eager. He had tramped all of five miles, and it was noon. An amazed husband and wife of sixty heard his strange query, and realized also that he was mad. They begged him to stay to dinner, intending to notify the authorities later and see what could be done; but though he stayed to partake of a little something, he did not stay long, and was off again to another distant farmhouse, his idea of many things to do and his need of Phœbe impelling him. So it went for that day and the next and the next, the circle of his inquiry ever widening.

The process by which a character assumes the significance of being peculiar, his antics weird, yet harmless, in such a community is often involute and pathetic. This day, as has been said, saw Reifsneider at other doors, eagerly asking his unnatural question, and leaving a trail of amazement, sympathy, and pity in his wake. Although the authorities were informed—the county sheriff, no less—it was not deemed advisable to take him into custody; for when those who knew old Henry, and had for so long, reflected on the condition of the county insane asylum, a place which, because of the poverty of the district, was of staggering aberration and sickening environment, it was decided to let him remain at large; for, strange to relate, it was found on investigation that at night he returned peaceably enough to his lonesome domicile there to discover whether his wife had returned, and to brood in loneliness until the morning. Who would lock up a thin, eager, seeking old man with iron-gray hair and an attitude of kindly, innocent inquiry, particularly when he was well known for a past of only kindly servitude and reliability? Those who had known him best rather agreed that he should be allowed to roam at large. He could do no harm. There were many who were willing to help him as to food, old clothes, the odds and ends of his daily life—at least at first. His figure after a time became not so much a commonplace as an accepted curiosity, and the replies, "Why, no, Henry; I ain't see her," or "No, Henry; she ain't been here today," more customary.

For several years thereafter then he was an odd figure in the sun and rain, on dusty roads and muddy ones, encountered occasionally in strange and unexpected places, pursuing his endless search. Undernourishment, after a time, although the neighbors and those who knew his history gladly contributed from their store, affected his body; for he walked much and ate little. The longer he roamed the public highway in this manner, the deeper became his strange hallucination; and finding it harder and harder to return from his more and more distant pilgrimages, he finally began taking a few utensils with him from his home, making a small package of them, in order that he might not be compelled to return. In an old tin coffee-pot of large size he placed a small tin cup, a knife, fork, and spoon, some salt and pepper, and to the outside of it, by a string forced through a pierced hole, he fastened a plate, which could be released, and which was his woodland table. It was no trouble for him to secure the little food that he needed, and with a strange, almost religious dignity, he had no hesitation in asking for that much. By degrees his hair became longer and longer, his once black hat became an earthen brown, and his clothes threadbare and dusty.

For all of three years he walked, and none knew how wide were his perambulations, nor how he survived the storms and cold. They could not see him, with homely rural understanding and forethought, sheltering himself in haycocks, or by the sides of cattle, whose warm bodies protected him from the cold, and whose dull understandings were not opposed to his harmless presence. Overhanging rocks and trees kept him at times from the rain, and a friendly hay-loft or corn-crib was not above his humble consideration.

The involute progression of hallucination is strange. From asking at doors and being constantly rebuffed or denied, he finally came to the conclusion that although his Phœbe might not be in any of the houses at the doors of which he inquired, she might nevertheless be within the sound of his voice. And so, from patient inquiry, he began to call sad, occasional cries, that ever and anon waked the quiet landscapes and ragged hill regions, and set to echoing his thin "O-o-o Phœbe! O-o-o Phœbe!" It had a pathetic, albeit insane, ring, and many a farmer or plowboy came to know it even from afar and say, "There goes old Reifsneider."

Another thing that puzzled him greatly after a time and after many hundreds of inquiries was, when he no longer had any particular door-yard in view and no special inquiry to make, which way to go. These cross-roads, which occasionally led in four or even six directions, came after a time to puzzle him. But to solve this knotty problem, which became more and more of a puzzle, there came to his aid another hallucination. Phœbe's spirit or some power of the air or wind or nature would tell him. If he stood at the center of the parting of the ways, closed his eyes, turned thrice about, and called "O-o-o Phœbe!" twice, and then threw his cane straight before him, that would surely indicate which way to go, for Phœbe, or one of these mystic powers would surely govern its direction and fall! In whichever direction it went, even though, as was not infrequently the case, it took him back along the path he had already come, or across fields, he was not so far gone in his mind but that he gave himself ample time to search before he called again. Also the hallucination seemed to persist that at some time he would surely find her. There were hours when his feet were sore, and his limbs weary, when he would stop in the heat to wipe his seamed brow, or in the cold to beat his arms. Sometimes, after throwing away his cane, and finding it indicating the direction from which he had just come, he would shake his head wearily and philosophically, as if contemplating the unbelievable or an untoward fate, and then start briskly off. His strange figure came finally to be known in the farthest reaches of three or four counties. Old Reifsneider was a pathetic character. His fame was wide.

Near a little town called Watersville, in Green County, perhaps four miles from that minor center of human activity, there was a place or precipice locally known as the Red Cliff, a sheer wall of red sandstone, perhaps a hundred feet high, which raised its sharp face for half a mile or more above the fruitful cornfields and orchards that lay beneath, and which was surmounted by a thick grove of trees. The slope that slowly led up to it from the opposite side was covered by a rank growth of beech, hickory, and ash, through which threaded a number of wagon-tracks crossing at various angles. In fair weather it had become old Reifsneider's habit, so inured was he by now to the open, to make his bed in some such patch of trees as this, to fry his bacon or boil his eggs at the foot of some tree, before laying himself down for the night. Occasionally, so light and inconsequential was his sleep, he would walk at night. More often, the moonlight or some sudden wind stirring in the trees or a reconnoitering animal arousing him, he would sit up and think, or pursue his quest in the moonlight or the dark, a strange, unnatural, half wild, half savage-looking but utterly harmless creature, calling at lonely road crossings, staring at dark and shuttered houses, and wondering where, where Phœbe could really be.

That particular lull that comes in the systole-diastole of this earthly ball at two o'clock in the morning invariably aroused him, and though he might not go any farther he would sit up and contemplate the darkness or the stars, wondering. Sometimes in the strange processes of his mind he would fancy that he saw moving among the trees the figure of his lost wife, and then he would get up to follow, taking his utensils, always on a string, and his cane. If she seemed to evade him too easily he would run, or plead, or, suddenly losing track of the fancied figure, stand awed or disappointed, grieving for the moment over the almost insurmountable difficulties of his search.

It was in the seventh year of these hopeless peregrinations, in the dawn of a similar springtime to that in which his wife had died, that he came at last one night to the vicinity of this selfsame patch that crowned the rise to the Red Cliff. His far-flung cane, used as a divining-rod at the last cross-roads, had brought him hither. He had walked many, many miles. It was after ten o'clock at night, and he was very weary. Long wandering and little eating had left him but a shadow of his former self. It was a question now not so much of physical strength but of spiritual endurance which kept him up. He had scarcely eaten this day, and now, exhausted, he set himself down in the dark to rest and possibly to sleep.

Curiously on this occasion a strange suggestion of the presence of his wife surrounded him. It would not be long now, he counseled with himself, although the long months had brought him nothing, until he should see her. talk to her. He fell asleep after a time, his head on hi knees. At midnight the moon began to rise, and at two in the morning, his wakeful hour, was a large silver disk shining through the trees to the east. He opened his eyes when the radiance became strong, making a silver pattern at his feet and lighting the woods with strange lusters and silvery, shadowy forms. As usual, his old notion that his wife must be near occurred to him on this occasion, and he looked about him with a speculative, anticipatory eye. What was it that moved in the distant shadows along the path by which he had entered—a pale, flickering will-o'-the-wisp that bobbed gracefully among the trees and riveted his expectant gaze? Moonlight and shadows combined to give it a strange form and a stranger reality, this fluttering of bog-fire or dancing of wandering fireflies. Was it truly his lost Phœbe? By a circuitous route it passed about him, and in his fevered state he fancied that he could see the very eyes of her, not as she was when he last saw her in the black dress and shawl, but now a strangely younger Phœbe, gayer, sweeter, the one whom he had known years before as a girl. Old Reifsneider got up. He had been expecting and dreaming of this hour all these years, and now as he saw the feeble light dancing lightly before him he peered at it questioningly, one thin hand in his gray hair.

Of a sudden there came to him now for the first time in many years the full charm of her girlish figure as he had known it in boyhood, the pleasing, sympathetic smile, the brown hair, the blue sash she had once worn about her waist at a picnic, her gay, graceful movements. He walked around the base of the tree, straining with his eyes, forgetting for once his cane and utensils, and following eagerly after. On she moved before him, a will-o'-the-wisp of the spring, a little flame above her head, and it seemed as though among the small saplings of ash and beech and the thick trunks of hickory and elm that she signaled with a young, a lightsome hand.

"Oh, Phœbe! Phœbe!" he called. "Have yuh really come? Have yuh really answered me?" And hurrying faster, he fell once, scrambling lamely to his feet, only to see the light in the distance dancing illusively on. On and on he hurried until he was fairly running, brushing his ragged arms against the trees striking his hands and face against impeding twigs. His hat was gone, his lungs were breathless, his reason quite astray, when coming to the edge of the cliff he saw her below among a silvery bed of apple trees now blooming in the spring.

"Oh, Phœbe!" he called. "Oh, Phœbe! Oh, no, don't leave me!" And feeling the lure of a world where love was young and Phœbe, as this vision presented her, a delightful epitome of their quondam youth, he gave a gay cry of "Oh, wait, Phœbe!" and leaped.

Some farmer-boys, reconnoitering this region of bounty and prospect some few days afterward, found first the tin utensils tied together under the tree where he had left them, and then later at the foot of the cliff, pale, broken, but elate, a molded smile of peace and delight upon his lips, his body. His old hat was discovered lying under some low-growing saplings, the twigs of which had held it back. No one of all the simple population knew how eagerly and joyously he had found his lost mate.

37

Big Dan Reilly

BY HARVEY O'HIGGINS

*"He is a chip, a hand specimen, from the basement struc-
ture upon which American politics rest."*

H. G. WELLS, 'The Future in America'

CALL it "Headquarters." That is
the way the politicians always refer to it, although it is a club. And
imagine the politicians sitting in their puffy leather chairs around the
reception room of the club that night, looking out on the street lights of
Fifth Avenue, under oil portraits of their worthy predecessors, with
brass cuspidors at their feet and brass match safes at their elbows. And
imagine them raising a cloud of cigar smoke and a private mutter of
political conversation, and an occasional quiet chuckle or an amused
cough that represented laughter—a red-faced, hoarse cough, with one
eyebrow up and a fat hand over the mouth.

"Some of the best men in New York were there," Gatecliff boasted,
in his account of what happened. "Some of *the* best. Millionaires. Heads
of corporations."

He named names that it would be almost blasphemous to repeat in
print.

At the far end of the room, the descending stairs made a railed landing
like a balcony. Big Dan Reilly was in the habit of coming down those
stairs to hold his reception on the floor of the room, nodding and shaking hands and talking here and there freely, unless the matter was so
confidential that it was necessary to withdraw to a corner table. And
everybody always preserved an appearance of taking part in some social
function that was genially informal, perhaps because Dan Reilly's

power was outside the law and any consultation with him might well make itself look as innocent as possible.

This night he appeared, as expected, on the stairs; and they all rose as usual to greet him still chatting, as if their rising were automatic and absent-minded, although it was neither. He descended as far as the landing and stood with his hands in his pockets, looking down sullenly at the men who turned to him in surprise as he waited.

He was dressed in black. Ordinarily he wore clothes that had an air of the race track and the betting ring. His big, good-natured, florid, round face looked heavy, sulky, lowering. He said, "I'll see *you*," and pointed insolently to a man below him.

Silence. Amazed silence.

He looked from face to face. "And I'll see *you*."

This man flushed, examined his cigar, put it between his biting teeth, and smoked with narrowed eyes, thoughtfully.

"And *you*."

A nervous clearing of some embarrassed throat.

"And *you*."

He picked out a half dozen. "The rest o' you," he said, "can go home." And they went home.

"We *went* home!" Gatecliff cried. "We *went home!* But"—and he marked his point with a spiteful forefinger—"it ended Big Dan as the boss of the organization. He never got a chance to speak that way to a group of gentlemen again."

II

From one point of view, the scene ought to be historic. It ought to be painted by the artist who did that museum picture of the French king's confessor, a barefooted monk, descending the grand staircase of the palace while all the silken courtiers bowed and smirked before him. (Dan Reilly, of the Bowery and the underworld, saying contemptuously to the nobility and ruling class of New York, "The rest o' you can go home!")

From another point of view, it is almost as scandalous as anything you will find in the secret memoirs of the French king's court. Gatecliff was there as the confidential adviser of a "traction magnate" who wished to procure for his company a monopoly right in certain city streets in order to operate a public utility; and the magnate was discreetly offering Big Dan and the other leaders of the organization some million dollars' worth of stock in the company, in return for the franchise. (It is impossible to be more explicit without incurring a libel suit.) Moreover, all the other millionaires were there for similar reasons. Big Dan controlled the votes that made it necessary for the "best men" in New York to do business with him. It was illegal, corrupt, poisonous—but there it was. They had to do it, or somebody else would. They put a good face on it— a polite, conventional face—and Big Dan had hitherto looked at that face grimly, but with every appearance of being deceived by it. Now, incredibly, he had reached out his great, brutal hand and smacked it.

Why?

III

The answer is simple. It merely involves an explanation of Big Dan's character and his point of view, the story of his life, a picture of the moral and political background of his career, and an account of his relations with his mother, with Gatecliff, and with Gatecliff's sister Mary.

A man suddenly says a decisive word and makes a final gesture. Behind his impulse to say that word and make that gesture there is a lifetime of growth, experience, emotion. All his past—all that he has known and thought and seen and suffered up to that moment—all has a part in the motive of his action. And all his future comes influenced out of it.

Dan Reilly's moment on the balcony was such a moment. It is not impossible to find its vague beginnings in events that occurred even before his birth. For example:

Some weeks before he was born his father was killed in the "infamous draft riots" of the summer of 1863. His father was the Hugh Reilly, the "Red" Reilly, who led the riots in his district because of the clause in the Conscription Act by which a man could buy exemption for three hundred dollars. Red Reilly could not understand why only the poor in pocket should be forced to die for their country. He died learning it. He was in arrears with his rent at the time—as he was at all times—and the landlord evicted the widow of the traitor, in a burst of patriotism, as soon as he heard what had happened to Reilly.

Red Reilly's unborn son heard it later. He heard it as the story of his father's revolt against those governing classes who had passed a draft law providing for their own exemption. And I believe it is not too far fetched to see him as Red Reilly's son unconsciously carrying on his father's quarrel, when he stood on the stairs at Headquarters and said to later beneficiaries of legislative privilege, "The rest o' you can go home."

And whether that is far fetched or not, this much is certain: the circumstances of his birth strongly determined the psychology of his great dramatic moment.

With his mother evicted as the widow of a delinquent traitor, he might have been born in the gutter if she had not been given shelter by a woman more unfortunate even than she. Consequently, he was born

"amid the most depraved surroundings"—in a tenement that stood in
the back yard of a Grove Street house that was itself sufficiently depraved,
although it kept up an appearance of red-brick respectability with a rare
old Colonial door and a notable fanlight.

The shack behind it was a clapboarded wooden building that had been
a wagon factory, and then a livery stable, before it became unfit for the
use of valuable animals. It was occupied by a number of unpitied outcasts who lived there, practically rent free, by the grace of the woman
who kept the Grove Street house. There were no chimneys in the building. Stovepipes protruded through some of the broken window panes;
but there was no stove in the room in which the future ruler of New
York was born; its regular occupant kept herself warm with alcohol. It
was a room that had been part of the paint shop of the wagon factory,
and in one corner the drip of innumerable cart wheels had deposited a
ridge, a hummock, a rounded stalagmite, of hardened paint. The head
of Mrs. Reilly's mattress took advantage of that mound to make a pillow.

Dan was born on a cool August evening, after a day's rain, by the light
of a blessed candle that had been borrowed from a neighbor. He was a
twelve-pound baby, as lusty as a young porker, and his arrival was as
much an event as if he had been born in a convent. The thwarted
maternal instincts of his neighbors received him with gratified excitement. They carried him up- and downstairs wrapped in an old white-
silk petticoat, exhibiting him from room to room. As a man-child, he
had the rank of a young heir among his slaves.

"There y' are!" as one of them said, admiringly. "Many's the gurl'll
break her heart fer *you,* yuh little Turk!"

The occupants of the Grove Street house lavished gifts on him and
invalid comforts on his mother. For two months they cared for her while
she was too ill to help herself. They brought her sewing to do when she
grew strong enough to resent charity. She said good-by to them regret-
fully when she was well enough to move on to more comfortable
surroundings. And she parted from them with a gratitude that she never
forgot or allowed her son to forget.

Once when the police were making a vice crusade ostentatiously, she
told him the story of his birth and said, "Danny, if y' iver do anything
to make life harder fer the likes o' *thim,* yeh're no son o' mine."

He did a great deal to make life harder for the likes of them, as any
ruler makes life harder for his subjects; there were hundreds of them in
his home district, and they had to pay his henchmen for the protection
they received. But he protected them from other exploitation and from
the sort of hardship and persecution that his mother besought him to
spare them. "The king of the underworld," "his saloons their known
resorts," he accepted them on their own terms as part of his constituency.

He represented them in politics as well as he represented anybody. And he was still representing them when he stood on the balcony at Head-quarters and looked down on those men, who, he knew, despised him secretly as much as they despised his constituents.

IV

Most determinative of all, he stood there as his mother's son.

When she left the Grove Street tenement she carried him to a room in Hudson Street, and settled down to do scrubbing and washing and sewing to support him. She was a frail young woman, from the north of Ireland, thrifty and ambitious. She had married Red Reilly against everyone's advice but his, and she had emigrated to America with him to escape the commiseration of the prejudiced. She was without relatives in New York, and almost without friends. Alone, in silence, like a prisoner digging a tunnel secretly, she set to work to escape from poverty.

And she failed because of a characteristic which, in Big Dan Reilly, made his political fortune. She was insanely charitable. Anyone who asked her for help could have it from her. She would give away her money, her food, her clothes, her bedding. It was as if, having suffered the extreme of shipwreck and been rescued by the charity of the most needy, she was unable thereafter to refuse anyone a share in whatever little she had. She was never able to get ahead. There was never anything for tomorrow in her purse or her larder. And it was this quality in Big Dan that afterward made it possible for him to hold his followers together by what the newspapers called "the cohesive power of public plunder." More of that later.

By the time he was six years old he was selling newspapers and blacking shoes, in order to help her. But only after school hours. She made him go to school faithfully. And even as a shoeblack he showed some organizing ability, for he got the monopoly right to shine the shoes of the policemen in the station house of his precinct, and he did the work so well that he obtained the same work in another precinct and took an assistant. He sold newspapers in City Hall Park long enough to make friends in a press room, where he took the job of helping to carry papers from the presses to the delivery carts, at a salary of a dollar and a half a week.

"When I got to be ten years old," he said once, in a speech on the Bowery, "I got a teacher in school to let me go at two o'clock, an' then I was able to serve that newspaper all to myself. I passed the grammar department o' my school, an' I was one o' seven boys to go to the Free Academy, in Twenty-third Street, I think it was. Free as it was, it wasn't free enough for me to go there. I had to go an' commence the struggle o' life."

And there again, I think, spoke the son of Red Reilly, in revolt against the class that could afford leisure for education, and acutely conscious of the fact that their organs of publicity spoke of him as having "the manners and speech of the typical 'tough.'"

However, to get down to Gatecliff and his sister and the immediate personal motives behind that scene at Headquarters—

V

Big Dan, as a boy, was so large for his age that he arrived at long pants a year earlier than the others of his generation; and this made him inevitably notable among his contemporaries. He was handy with his fists, as they all were, and his size gave him a natural superiority in street fighting, which was their chief recreation. He was kindly and good-natured, so that he did not tyrannize over his companions, but fought the older bullies who would have tyrannized over them. It was so that he first championed young Buttony Gatecliff against oppression, and won the devotion of Buttony's sister.

They called him "Buttony" because he wore his knickerbockers buttoned to his roundabout. He was the timid son of a conciliatory grocer, Amos Gatecliff, who kept a shop on Hudson Street, and he was persecuted by all the little bruisers of the neighborhood, who had learned that they could blackmail him for sweets from his father's shelves by waylaying him on the streets and torturing him with threats of violence unless he brought them tribute. His life had become a continual terror. He had either to steal at home or be hunted like defenseless virtue abroad. His only protector was his sister Mary, who escorted him whenever she could.

She was escorting him home from school one winter afternoon when he was set upon by three of his tormentors. One held her, and the others took Buttony and rubbed his face in the snow and crammed it down his collar and filled his mittens with it and stifled his outcries while they exacted promises of future bribes. Fate brought Danny Reilly on the scene. Mary Gatecliff knew him by sight; she had seen him in her father's shop buying an occasional twist of "orange pekoe" as a present for his mother. She cried out to him.

In an instant he was sprawling on the pavement, with the largest bully under him and the other two on his back. She caught Buttony to her and prevented him from running away while she stood, loyal but terrified into helplessness, watching Big Dan do battle for her. That battle was a primitive affair, bloody and furious. It was not fought according to any Queensberry rules. Dan terrified one opponent into flight by trying to bite the nose off him. He kicked another in the knee-cap and all but broke his leg. The third did not wait his turn. He popped into a basement like a rat into its hole, and escaped by some back exit.

Dan picked up his cap, grinning, brushed the snow off himself, and asked her, "Which way 're yuh goin'?"

As they went she confided all Buttony's troubles to him, and he listened with a touch of that social superiority which he had always felt for the Gatecliffs. They were shopkeepers. They were ingratiatingly polite to customers. They were English, and they had English traditions of class subservience which no young Irishman of Dan's temperament could understand. He walked beside her like a sworded D'Artagnan beside the wife of Bonacieux, the mercer of *The Three Musketeers.*

He said to her at parting, "If any o' them kids ever picks on Buttony again, you come an' tell *me.*"

She was a pale and intense little hero worshiper with black hair and large dark eyes. She raised those eyes to him in a most submissive admiration. "Thanks," she murmured, from her heart.

Thereafter Buttony was safe under Dan's protection and the protection of his gang. The word was passed around that Mary was Dan's "girl" and that any boy who gave Buttony any cause to complain of him might as well prepare to meet his day of judgment.

The gang was merely a group of a dozen boys who played and fought together as boys of a neighborhood always do. They called themselves the Hylos, for no reason that anyone remembers. Dan had found a clubroom for them in a vacant coal cellar; he had found it by merely breaking in a cellar door. They held nightly meetings there, by candlelight, with the cellar windows covered, playing cards, shooting craps, and feasting on apples, bread, bologna, pails of jam, bottles of catsup, tins of salmon or whatever else they had been able to gather during the evening. And they gathered these things as boys rob orchards, in an adventurous spirit of young deviltry.

One of them was a butcher's son, and it was his duty to steal his father's sausage. He afterward became the president of a packing company, and he always spoke of Big Dan with real affection. Another was the son of a baker, and he filched rolls and cakes. The rest went in twos and threes to make organized raids on pushcart peddlers and the goods displayed in front of food shops. Big Dan laid out the tactics of their raids and attended to the police. He would walk up to the officer on the beat and engage him in conversation. "Purty good shine, eh?" he might say, pointing to his patron's shoes, boyish and innocent, with no sign of shrewdness in his big smile. And while the officer was being "jollied" the other Hylos would grab their loot and run. Their organized mischief annoyed the precinct for a whole winter before the police discovered that their station shoeblack was the leader of the gang.

—even though he once saved his confederates by accidentally tripping up an officer when the pursuit broke out prematurely.

They would occasionally "roll a rummy"; that is to say, if they met a drunken man in a quiet spot they would relieve him of any money that he had, on the pragmatic theory that they might as well have it as the first crook he met. One or two of them snatched purses, although this was forbidden by their leader except in cases where it was evident that the owner of the purse could well afford to lose it. They took part in election campaigns, pestering the cart-tail orators of the opposing party, pelting the illuminated wagons that carried "transparencies" through the streets, marching uninvited in torchlight processions, and raiding the bonfires on election nights to obtain fuel for their own rejoicings. In all these undertakings they acted like a "gang of young ruffians." But they had no idea that they were a gang of young ruffians. They thought they were merely a mutual amusement club for social recreation and innocent adventure.

They had no more idea that their street activities were criminal than they had that their pranks in the parish church were impious. Several of them, including Big Dan, were altar boys and acolytes. They relieved the tedium of religious services by carrying their candles so as to drip hot grease on the heads of the boys in front of them, by putting bent pins on sanctuary benches and tying knots in the arms of the soutanes. They did these things while carefully maintaining the devout expressions of young cherubs in a heavenly choir, and their victims kept the same pious faces while they retaliated and defended themselves. No boy thought of appealing to the priests for protection any more than he would have thought of running to the police for aid in a street fight; it was against the code and social usage. And if the priests knew what was going on behind their backs, they ignored it—as the police usually did.

Buttony came into the Hylos under Dan's wing, and he was endured there for Dan's sake, but with no enthusiasm. The others did not like him. Smoking made him sick. He had no natural gift for profanity and he was unpleasantly ingratiating and self-conscious in its use. He was not of their religion, which made him an outlander. He stole with a **tremblingly** defiant air, as if he expected to be struck by lightning. And, of course, it was he who was caught.

He was arrested one night for trying to snatch a purse in emulation of a more expert associate. He was taken to the station house and locked up. As soon as Big Dan heard of it he went to the station on the general pretext of his interest in police boots, and he was caught trying to pick the lock of Buttony's cell. He was locked up, himself. Buttony, despairing of rescue, confessed the secrets of the Hylo gang to the police captain.

Plain clothes men gathered in the other boys. By midnight all the Hylos were behind bars, and the station house was besieged by their parents, their relatives, and their friends, all of whom were eloquent with the conviction of their own respectability and the prisoners' innocence.

The captain of the precinct at the time was that Joe Mehlin who afterward became Superintendent of Police and a power in opposition to Big Dan—a pompadoured, red-haired disciplinarian with light-blue eyes that looked peculiarly cold in the setting of his sandy complexion. He was resolved to be revenged on the Hylos for the trouble they had given him. He was especially set on punishing Big Dan because he had found it impossible to break the boy down, to make him penitent, to make him cower.

"You got us all wrong, Cap," Dan kept saying, cheerfully, unawed. "We ain't crooks—none of us. It's a frame-up on the kid. He's no dip. An' he's so scared he don't know what he's talkin' about. He'd say anythin'."

And the captain would reply: "All right, Reilly. Then I'll send you all up. You can't make a fool o' me. You'll get five years fer this."

The other boys took their tone from Dan. His attempt to rescue Buttony had been the final act of daring that had made a melodramatic hero of him. They stood behind him solidly. It was all or none. And by morning the accumulated political influence of the whole neighborhood, its Assemblyman, its priests, and its Senator was settling down in a menacing pressure on the police captain.

He stood out so long that his final collapse was all the more humiliating to him, and he consoled himself by giving Big Dan a brutal measure of the third degree before he released the boy.

"Listen here, Cap," Reilly said, when he had reached the safety of the station-house door, "I'll get yuh fer this some day, an' I'll get yuh good."

Of course, he kept his promise. Among the people whom he represents it is a point of honor to avenge an injury as faithfully as to reward a friend. It is the whole duty of a moral life to be "no quitter" and "no ingrate."

And poor Buttony was forever damned in the eyes of the district by being both a quitter and an ingrate. He had confessed, and he had betrayed his friends. He tried to regain his standing in the world by recanting his confession everywhere. He told his parents that it was false, that he had been frightened into it. And Dan assisted him, at home, by assuring Mary Gatecliff that they were all innocent, particularly Buttony. She believed him; she accepted his attempt to rescue her brother as a deed of romantic faithfulness that had been done for her as much as for Buttony; and she rewarded Dan by letting him kiss her.

Her parents were less easily convinced. They saved Buttony from immediate purgatory at the hands of the Hylos by moving uptown to take him away from evil associates. Big Dan, after a touching farewell! to Mary, remained to enjoy his laurels.

To tell the truth, he was relieved to have her go. She was older than he, and he had begun to find her too intense and humorless in her fixed idea of his devotion to her. He had not the temperament needed to make a humble cavalier. He forgot her, for the time.

Buttony had learned that you cannot break the law without risking punishment. Big Dan had learned that you can escape punishment if you have influence enough to control the police. Buttony went to the Free Academy to be educated in the ethics of respectability; he studied law at Columbia; he became an agent of the Citizens' League; and he turned against his memories of his boyhood escapades with all the fervor of a convert repenting of his sins. Big Dan continued to take his education from the streets.

VI

And here we approach the real heart of his mystery. When the Hylos were forced to dissolve, by the continued intrusion of the police, Dan and his older followers were absorbed by the James Phelan Athletic Association—which was athletic in the way that the Y. M. C. A. is athletic, and political as the Y. M. C. A. is religious. Its two glories were Jimmy Phelan, the district leader, and Kid McCann, the champion lightweight. Its membership included the politicians, the ward heelers, the pugilists, the gamblers, the professional crooks, the young sports, the political aspirants, and all the doubtful light and leading of the district. In its rooms and on the streets, after working hours, Big Dan became familiar with every form of common vice. Yet he practiced none of them. Why?

He had promised his mother that he would not use either tobacco or alcohol until he was twenty-one, but why did he keep the promise? He had directed the Hylos in all their boyish raids and depredations, but why did he never join in their petty thieving? The young bloods of the Phelan Association put him in the way of becoming a prize fighter and trained him for the ring. Why did he never take to that ambition? Why did he continue working in the press room on Park Row until he was elected Assemblyman from his district? What was the secret of his strength of will that carried him to one ambition and not to another, that kept him above weaknesses which he never seemed to condemn, that made him the king of the underworld—as it had made him the leader of the Hylos—but preserved him from being, in the professional sense of the word, a "crook"?

Well, Big Dan, even as a child, had a bodily superiority that made him admired and complimented, and I believe it was this first sense of physical importance that formed the backbone of his personality. His early leadership among his companions must have confirmed his innate conviction of natural eminence. Certainly he developed a sort of instinct of aristocracy that showed in his mother, too, in her inordinate alms-giving. As the head of the Hylos, he refrained from the thieving as the foreman of a work gang refrains from work. When Buttony was arrested and Dan went to release him, it was from an obvious impulse of *noblesse oblige*. His promise that he would not smoke or drink he kept, as a boy, because he was fond of his mother; and he kept it, as he grew older, because his habits of abstinence were habits of which he became proud, since they were *his* habits, and different from the prevailing habits around him. Moreover, in his experience of life, drunkenness was a form of weakness of which the predatory took advantage—as the Hylos rolled a rummy—and all those in his circle who pandered to vice exploited similar weaknesses. Big Dan had no intention of allowing himself to be exploited, and some obscure sense of responsibility for the weak prevented him from becoming an exploiter of them. He accepted training as a pugilist until he was expert enough to make anyone respect his blows, but he went no farther; he balked at being the fighting cock of a group of prize-ring promoters. He became one of the stalwarts who did the "strong-arm" work about the polls, prevented members of the opposing party from casting their votes, and supplied the consequent vacancy with a loyal impersonator when a rival voter had been carried home. Among his people, this sort of activity is regarded as good exercise for a growing lad, and Big Dan took plenty of it. But he did not himself impersonate; he was too conspicuous, physically. When he became ward captain he did not, himself, buy votes; he received the money and disbursed it to his craftier lieutenants. And his sense of superiority and of responsibility slowly promoted him to a leadership and an authority which his amiable good nature kept beneficent and popular.

His mother aided him throughout. Her pride in him was colossal; she may have helped to lay the foundations of his nature with that pride. She trusted him and leaned on him even in his school days; and it may have been this that made him responsible. She was a wise judge of character; she knew the affairs of the whole neighborhood; and her gossip was an education to him. When she gave anything out of her charity, she always said, "This is from Danny, now," and Danny got the credit of it. When he became captain of his ward, she acted as his chief of staff and busied herself all day "lookin' to his finces" as she called it, while he was away at his work. She reported to him at supper, while he ate her cooking, and he would say, grinning: "If *you* ain't the crafty one! Would yuh like to run fer the Presidency? Tip me the wink an' I'll speak to Phelan."

"You an' yer Phelan," she would reply. "I c'u'd get it from *him* quicker than yeh c'u'd, yerself."

"That's true enough, y' ol' ward heeler," he would admit. And it was.

Their intercourse was conducted in this disrespectful tone of rough banter that served to disguise the shamefacedness of an idolatrous love.

She had been prematurely gray as a young woman. Now she was white haired. Dan called her "Granny" to tease her, and she had become "Granny" affectionately to the whole ward. They came to her for every sort of advice and assistance. They came to her with their quarrels, and she listened to both sides and sympathized with both, but joined neither. It was her private boast that she had never had a quarrel in her life. She had an inexhaustible tolerance, and I do not believe she ever passed an adverse moral judgment on anybody who was not rich. "Poor people has to make a livin'," she would say, in forgiveness of all her neighbors' notorious delinquencies; and yet she was a devout churchgoer and prayed for Danny morning, noon, and night.

She was popular with the mothers, who are the real heads of the families in the tenements. The men are too often stupefied by hard labor and alcoholic recreation. They are less ambitious than their wives; they have a weaker sense of responsibility to their children; they do not endure poverty so hardily; they die younger. "Granny" Reilly was the confidante and adviser, the visiting nurse and Lady Bountiful, of every mother, wife, and widow in the neighborhood; and they were all "for her" and for her son. It was her influence as much as anything that elected him to the legislature.

VII

That happened in 1887, when he was twenty-four years old. And one of the first results of it was to bring Mary Gatecliff back into his life. She wrote, congratulating him on his election, formally. He went to call on her, because he was an awkward letter writer and he had self-confidence enough to go anywhere. He did not hesitate even when he found the Gatecliffs living on West Twenty-third Street in one of the houses of London Terrace that still maintained the tradition of the row's earlier magnificence.

Gatecliff had become a wholesale grocer, with a string of retail shops; his wife had developed formal manners and a complete loss of hearing; Buttony had married a daughter of money and moved still farther uptown; and Mary Gatecliff was not at all the youngster who had kissed Dan good-by in the hallway on Hudson Street. She had been to a finishing school. She was meditatively quiet, a solitary reader, silent and observant. It seemed impossible that she could ever have any but a feel, ing of kindly superiority for Big Dan. She probably thought that she had written to him out of such a feeling.

But Dan had once roused in her a tumultuous emotion, and he was the only man who had. That, I think, is the explanation of the affair that followed—one of those mysterious love affairs that are the despair of parents and the scandal of friends. Her intelligence had been educated out of all sympathy with him, but there was something else in her that had not. Her emotions responded to their old stimulus at sight of him, and she was struck with a flush and thrill that startled her. His voice shook her; she did not know why. He was aware of it. He had a compelling tone of confident familiarity, and he took her hand, smiling at her. He called her "Mary" cheerfully, and talked to her about her former neighbors and old times, with laughter. He seemed genuinely big hearted, human, rough, and winning. He was humorous about himself and his mother and his political "spiels" and his career. "She's so pop'lar," he said, "that they've elected *me*. I tell her she'll have to gi' me her proxy so's I c'n vote." And while Mary Gatecliff was critical of his slurred speech and his "Bowery mannerisms," she forgave them because, in the back of her mind, she was thinking that they could be easily corrected.

She parted from him with a girlish friendliness of manner that would have seemed impossible to her a few hours earlier. She hurried to bed and then lay awake, excited, far into the night, with her reason apparently cool about him, but her emotions deeply stirred.

And it was not many days before her reason took the tone of her emotion. She believed that Abraham Lincoln might have been such a young politician as Dan if Lincoln had been less melancholy. Dan was of the people, uneducated, a poor boy; but she knew that most of the leaders of the nation had been that. She began to feel that what he most needed was a friend with high ideals and the culture of a better class to influence and guide him.

She wrote him again, sending him a book of which she had spoken to him. Her father saw him on his second visit, but her father's business had given him a great respect for the financial virtue of political influence, and he was pleasant to the young Assemblyman. Her mother saw him; but her mother, being deaf, talked unceasingly to cover her infirmity. She seemed rather more than pleasant. Dan was used to having people pleasant to him; it did not impress him. Mary talked to him of his plans and his ambitions, with an encouraging interest. He was not unused to young feminine interest, either. He jollied her as he jollied his mother; and because he was leaving for Albany next day he put his arm around her at parting, and kissed her good-by as he might have kissed his mother.

She wrote him in Albany, a letter that accepted her surrender to his caress as if it had been the last surrender of love. He was deeply moved by it. It was the sort of letter that only an intense and idealistic girl can write when all her barriers are broken down. Dan replied clumsily, jocularly, but in terms which he had never before been able to use to anyone but his mother.

VIII

He arrived at the legislature like a fraternity athlete entering a college where friends have preceded him. It was a legislature that was acclaimed by the newspapers of the day the "most corrupt, discreditable, unprincipled, and venal that ever assembled in the capital of any civilized community." Big Dan and his friends were as little worried by that criticism as if they were the class of '87 being scolded by their teachers. He attended committee meetings and debates as a college "sport" attends lectures. He had nothing but good-natured contempt for Buttony Gatecliff—now Harold A. Gatecliff, agent of the Citizens' League—whom he found lobbying in support of various reform measures. In Dan's eyes Gatecliff had become a studious and spectacled prig, and after one unpleasant interview they agreed to go their separate ways. It never occurred to Dan that Buttony might be dangerous. And he did not mention Mary to him. That, he thought, was no affair of Buttony's.

The legislators were "doing business on a basis of from five dollars upward." Some of the upstate members were quoted at one hundred dollars each. Big Dan organized a "union to maintain prices" among the New York and Brooklyn members, and they got as high as five hundred dollars each for their votes. They helped to pass a bill to free insurance companies from back taxes of $700,000 and future taxes of $200,000 a year. Big Dan voted for it gayly. He voted to expend a million and a half for patent ballot boxes, to the sole profit of the firm that made them and the members who voted for them. For his constituency he obtained a free public bath and permission for newspaper vendors to erect news stands "within the stoop line" on New York City streets. He helped to introduce a number of "strike bills"—which are bills threatening to penalize corporations that are rich enough and timid enough to pay for immunity. He made his mark as a humorist at committee meetings. His union to maintain prices became known as "the Black Horse Cavalry," and he led it as ably as he had led the Hylos. He had more money than his mother could give away; he bought her an old red-brick house in the Greenwich Village quarter; and he financed his first saloon, with one of his boyhood friends as its proprietor. His political influence protected it from the police. Altogether, his first year in the legislature was happy and profitable in a boyish and innocent sort of way—"innocent" in *his* eyes, that is.

His affair with Mary Gatecliff ran along less happily for her than for him, since she found herself committed to a man who remained obviously more free than she. His affection had no vows. It did not even find words for itself. And it masked its sincerity in boyish grins and clumsy playfulness. She trembled when he kissed her, suffocated by the beating of her heart; and then she wept, when he was gone, because she could neither resist him nor apparently make him respect the weakness that yielded to him. She denied her feeling for him to her father. She could not, in self-respect, admit the humiliating terms of it. "We're just friends," she said.

Love, to her, was something abstract and transcendental, of the nature of a religion, exacting in its worship and rather solemn. To Dan it was a merely human relation. He took her affection as he took his mother's. He repaid it—as he repaid his mother's—with rough kindliness when he was with her and devoted thoughts when he was away. And he left the unconsidered future to develop itself and their relations, sure of himself and his success.

IX

So he came to the crisis and the turning point in his career. Imagine him a burly twenty-six, rubicund and round-faced, well dressed, prosperous, known to everybody in his district and liked by them all. His passage down his native street was a triumphal progress. The policeman on the beat saluted him. The loafers on the saloon corners stopped him to borrow money. The street children pointed him out and followed him. The shopkeepers shook hands with him. He was buttonholed and solicited by constituents and office seekers, and he released himself with a broad smile and a pat on the shoulder and such promises as he knew he could keep. He smiled at the girls, with his hat on the back of his head. He touched the brim of it with a wave of the hand when their mothers greeted him. He joked with the priest. A universal favorite, as kindly as a prince who wishes to be popular, he walked with the sun on his face and a prosperous future before him. And he never looked back at the past that followed him—an invisible figure, which he thought nobody saw, because he never looked at it himself—until suddenly that figure stepped up beside him, took his arm firmly, and walked him into a future that was a sinister counterfeit of all he had expected.

There was to be a centennial celebration in New York City in 1889, and in April of that year a bill was introduced at Albany to give the city police the power to arrest suspected criminals at sight, so as to protect the centennial crowds from pickpockets and street walkers and hold-up men. Big Dan opposed the bill on the legitimate grounds that no man or woman should be arrested unless upon specific charges. He fought the bill in committee. He fought it on the floor of the house. He rallied his Black Horse Cavalry against it, traded influence to defeat it, and "swapped" votes.

Unfortunately, Inspector Mehlin was behind the bill, and so was the Citizens' League. Mehlin called in the newspaper men and gave them an interview in which he described Big Dan as "the associate of thieves and criminals," "a political crook, prize fighter, and strong-arm man," "opposed to the bill because all the criminals were his friends and if the bill went through it would hurt his saloon business." And the secretary of the Citizens' League followed with a sketch of Big Dan's life, supplied by Gatecliff: "Born amid the most depraved surroundings . . . the leader of a gang of young ruffians known to the police as the Hylo gang . . . his manners and speech those of the typical 'tough' . . . the companion of thieves and prostitutes . . . his saloons their known resorts . . . perhaps the most dangerous man that New York City ever sent to Albany . . . the recognized leader of that group of piratical Assemblymen known as 'the Black Horse Cavalry' . . . the king of the underworld . . . a political brigand holding his followers together by the cohesive power of public plunder," etc., etc.

Big Dan woke next morning to find himself infamous. In vain he denied the statements on the floor of the house. He was not convincing. He would not desert his friends, Barney This and Fitzey That, thieves and burglars, whom Mehlin had named. He admitted that he knew them, but denied that his friendship was guilty. He could not deny his leadership of the Black Horse. Not to their faces. He spoke lamely and confusedly. He defeated the bill, but he did not clear himself. He could not. Mehlin had made too picturesque and colorful a figure of him. The Albany correspondents took it up. The editorial writers enlarged on it. And Dan's place in the social system was forever fixed.

He did not realize it. It was years before he realized it.

Mary Gatecliff saw her brother, learned the truth, about the Hylos and about the legislature, and wrote to Dan: "It is terrible. There is nothing I can say. Do not come again. I could not trust myself to speak to you." And when he called she would not see him; and when he wrote she did not answer.

That cut him to the vitals. He could not picture any circumstances in which he would have turned his back on Mary before her enemies. It put her in a class with her brother; they had a "yellow streak."

Dan's criminal associates had not. They rallied to him. They elected him vice-president of the Phelan Association, and made speeches to him as "the man who never went back on a friend." The underworld had found a champion; they crowded to his saloon. The neighbors came to assure his mother that whatever the lying police and the newspapers might say, they knew that Danny was a good boy. Most significant of all, Cass Harley came.

And with Cass Harley, Dan's future took him by the arm. Harley was then a corporation lawyer, lobbyist, and "fixer." The Black Horse Cavalry had been worrying him and his clients. He came to make peace. He came to offer Dan an alliance with the financial powers upon whom, as a piratical Assemblyman, Dan had been preying.

"We need a leader in the legislature, Dan," he said. "The boys won't follow Cassidy. You and your friends had us blocked a half dozen times last session, and it's going to be worse now. We need you and we can take care of you."

Dan asked, only, "Can you get Mehlin fer me?"

"Yes," Harley promised, "we can get Mehlin. And we can stop most of this newspaper stuff."

"I don't care about the papers," Dan said. "They can't hurt me down here. But I want Mehlin's scalp. He lied about me."

"We all know that," Harley assured him, although he was there because he believed what Mehlin had said. "Tell me, can we help your organizations in any way? Need any campaign contributions?"

"I'll see y' about that later." Dan rose heavily, to end the interview. "Get Mehlin first."

Harley nodded. "It may take me a little time. I'll begin right away."

He "got" Mehlin. He got him so painfully that Mehlin came to Dan, in an attempt to save himself, and apologized and begged for his place. That simply made him a "quitter." Dan went down into his change pocket and drew out some silver.

"Mehlin," he said, "you once ga' me a quarter more'n I'd earned blackin' boots. It was the only decent thing y' ever did. Take it, an' get out before I throw y' out. We're quits."

Here was Reilly's first conspicuous public display of power. It marked him as an autocrat to the underworld. It brought a thousand willing agents to his service. And with these adherents at one end of the social system and Cass Harley and his clients at the other, he was supported by a combination of influence that was invincible. He was made the political boss of his district. He was no longer "Big Dan"; he was "the Big One." When Jimmy Phelan died, the Phelan Association became the Dan Reilly Association, with Granny Reilly as the empress dowager behind the throne. Under her direction as much as Dan's, it developed into a political association for the distribution of discriminating alms. An official chaplain attended marriages, christenings, and funerals to leave flowers "from Big Dan." A dispossess-man went to court every morning for lists of evicted tenants and gave them aid. A recognized place finder occupied himself getting work for voters from every business man and corporation in New York that could be reached by the Big One; and with Cass Harley to assist, there were few that could not be reached. But, unlike any of his predecessors in such a situation, Reilly did not sell out to the powers whom Harley served. He did not even lose himself among the higher-ups. He stuck to his district. He spoke of sacred Headquarters as "the dead man's rest," and kept away from it. He poured great sums of money through the Dan Reilly Association into the needy purses of his constituents, and took from them, in return, their votes. Thanks to his mother, he had made, unconsciously, an important discovery in the science of democratic government—a discovery that put him at last on the balcony at Headquarters. It was this:

Among business men, farmers, manufacturers, and such, a voter marks his ballot in support of the party that gives him either a policy or a tariff to protect his livelihood. But there are no farmers or manufacturers or accumulations of invested capital among the tenement dwellers. When those people vote for the party that assures their livelihood, they vote for the party that gives them jobs. Big Dan's political machine became an organization that gave the workingman, the poor, the unemployed, and the petty criminal work or money or protection in exchange for their votes. Reilly became the Hanna of his party, locally.

He was soon dictating to Cass Harley; and Harley, angered, assisted the newspapers and the Citizens' League in an attempt to destroy him. They made the Big One a social outlaw, as picturesque as Robin Hood; but he polled an overwhelming vote in his district, dictated terms to Harley's clients, and ended Harley's political career. Then he reached for the principal backers of the Citizens' League and forced them to drop Gatecliff, who as its secretary, had directed the publicity against him. He even fought the party Boss and defeated him in a characteristic activity.

The Boss was interested in horse breeding and racing; his henchmen introduced a bill at Albany to suppress pool rooms because pool rooms hurt the race tracks by making it unnecessary to go to the races in order to bet; and Reilly, leading the pool room forces, proposed another bill making all betting illegal, whether on the tracks or in the pool rooms. The reformers flocked to Reilly's support. The Boss, in order to get Big Dan to withdraw his bill, had to withdraw his own. He never forgave Big Dan and was never asked to. "What do I care fer Headquarters," Reilly laughed. "I can carry my distric' whether I'm in th' organization er not." He carried it when a reform wave engulfed the party in every other district of the city, and it was he who served notice on the Boss that his abdication was expected as a consequence of that defeat.

He was now at the point where he should have been able to assume the crown of his career. And he could not touch it. Mehlin and Gatecliff and Cass Harley and the Citizens' League had done their work too well. The rival leaders at Headquarters could not oppose his power, but they did not conceal from him the obvious fact that to put a man of his reputation on the party throne would mean the public ruin of the party. The reform wave was still running high.

"Better fake up a stool pigeon, Dan," they advised him, "an' work behind him till this blows over. We know it ain't true, what they say of yuh. But the public don't know it."

In the secret silences of his thought he blamed it all on Gatecliff, and whatever business or undertaking Gatecliff entered on he contrived to blight it, mysteriously. Mary Gatecliff tried to see him. She wrote to ask for an interview. He did not answer. She persisted with a letter begging him not to ruin her brother. He muttered, "What do you two think yuh've done to *me?*" and threw the letter into the waste basket.

When Mary married the head of the traction company, he watched for Buttony to appear in the company's affairs; and when Gatecliff showed as a confidential legal adviser to the president of the concern, Dan set a new trap in the shape of a traction franchise with which he intended to "gold brick" them. Gatecliff, persecuted as he had been in his youth, was willing again to pay tribute. He undertook negotiations with Headquarters, and Dan handed him over to a lieutenant. The price was agreed upon, but the company offered stock, and Dan would not move except for half the amount of ready money paid in advance. He planned to accept that bribe and then secretly to manipulate the legislature to refuse the franchise. The traction heads had to take his word as his bond. He had never broken his word in the past, and everybody knew it.

X

It was toward the end of these negotiations that he came to his dramatic moment on the Headquarters stairs.

He came there in black because he had been to the funeral of his mother. He came there feeling suddenly empty, bitter, resentful—empty of all ambition to remain in control at Headquarters, now that his mother was no longer alive to be proud of his power; bitter because of the public obloquy under which both he and his mother had suffered; and resentful toward those best men of the community who dreaded him, despised him, and waited on him. As he had walked down the aisle of the church, behind his mother's coffin, he had seen Mary Gatecliff in a pew, and she had looked at him with sympathy, with pity, with a pleading reproach. He had said to himself, "Her husband made her come, to jolly me along." But he knew better. Her eyes were the strained eyes of a victim of disillusion, looking at a fellow sufferer in unhappiness, and mutely asking him, in the face of death, why they had so maimed each other's lives.

The look accused him and accused herself. It forgave him and asked forgiveness. And with that look in his memory he paused on the railed landing of the stairs and saw her brother and her husband below him, waiting hopefully for the word from him that would spring the fall of his trap. He despised them. He was ashamed of himself and of them. He wanted to insult them contemptuously while he saved them. And he wanted to slap their whole respected world in the face. And he slapped it. "The rest o' yuh can go home."

XI

It was his last official act at Headquarters. "I'm sick," he told the man who was to succeed him. "An' I'm through here. That deal with Gatecliff and his bunch, that's off. If anyone wants to see me, tell 'em to go to hell."

He retired to one of his Bowery lairs and took to his bed. The painted woman who was nursing him persuaded him to drink some hot toddy, to put him to sleep. It went to his head and he talked of his mother.

"I had a funny feelin' up there at the cemet'ry," he said. "They buried her on the side of a hill. An' the sun was shinin'. An' they dug the grave like a box, cuttin' it down straight on the sides an' makin' the corners square, *you* know, like a box. An' the shell just fitted into it like it was made fer it. An' there was somethin' about the look o' that grave, an' the way it was made, that all of a sudden made me feel contented about havin' her in it—somethin', *you* know, consolin'. An' when they lowered her into it the shell fitted so tight that the air came up slow, an' when she settled down in it it made a sort o' sigh, like you're happy." He began to weep. "I never knew a grave c'u'd be like that. It—it looked comfor'ble."

"Now," the woman said, impatiently, "you ain't goin' to talk about graves bein' comfortable. You ain't as sick as all that. You got nothin' but a cold."

And Big Dan, like a great child, motherless, rolled over and covered his face with the pillow and sobbed.

XII

One of the frankest of our foreign critics wrote of Dan at the height of his power: "He is a living proof that the workingman believes he has the same right to vote for work that the business man has to vote for trade. He indicates that in a democracy where all are politically free the wage slave will sell his political freedom to ameliorate the conditions of his economic servitude. He signifies that poverty can organize and follow its leader and plunder property unabashed by all the moral fulminations of its victim. He means that no reform movement can permanently defeat his kind until the reformers recognize that the voter on the lower East Side has the same right to sell his vote for a wage as the voter on the upper West Side has to sell his vote for an income."

And all of that may be true, but I think if this social philosopher had seen Dan blubbering into a pillow, he might have understood that the Big One was what he was because he had never been anything but an overgrown boy, with merely boyish ideals of loyalty to his gang, with a boy's immature sense of responsibility to society, with all a boy's unsocialized ego instincts, and a boy's dependence on affection, and a boy's hatred for his censors, and a boy's revolt against his punishment.

38

The Good Anna

BY GERTRUDE STEIN

THE tradesmen of Bridgepoint learned to dread the sound of "Miss Mathilda", for with that name the good Anna always conquered.

The strictest of the one-price stores found that they could give things for a little less, when the good Anna had fully said that "Miss Mathilda" could not pay so much and that she could buy it cheaper "by Lindheims."

Lindheims was Anna's favorite store, for there they had bargain days, when flour and sugar were sold for a quarter of a cent less for a pound, and there the heads of the departments were all her friends and always managed to give her the bargain prices, even on other days.

Anna led an arduous and troubled life.

Anna managed the whole little house for Miss Mathilda. It was a funny little house, one of a whole row of all the same kind that made a close pile like a row of dominos that a child knocks over, for they were built along a street which at this point came down a steep hill. They were funny little houses, two stories high, with red brick fronts and long white steps.

This one little house was always very full with Miss Mathilda, an under servant, stray dogs and cats and Anna's voice that scolded, managed, and grumbled all day long.

"Sallie! Can't I leave you alone a minute but you must run to the door to see the butcher boy come down the street and there is Miss Mathilda calling for her shoes. Can I do everything while you go around always thinking about nothing at all? If I ain't after you every minute you would be forgetting all the time, and I take all this pains, and when you come to me you was as ragged as a buzzard and as dirty as a dog. Go and find Miss Mathilda her shoes where you put them this morning."

"Peter!",—her voice rose higher,—"Peter!",—Peter was the youngest and the favorite dog,—"Peter, if you don't leave Baby alone,"—Baby was an old, blind terrier that Anna had loved for many years,—"Peter, if you don't leave Baby alone, I take a rawhide to you, you bad dog."

The good Anna had high ideals for canine chastity and discipline. The three regular dogs, the three that always lived with Anna, Peter and old Baby, and the fluffy little Rags, who was always jumping up into the air just to show that he was happy, together with the transients, the many stray ones that Anna always kept until she found them homes, were all under strict orders never to be bad one with the other.

A sad disgrace did once happen in the family. A little transient terrier for whom Anna had found a home suddenly produced a crop of pups. The new owners were certain that this Foxy had known no dog since she was in their care. The good Anna held to it stoutly that her Peter and her Rags were guiltless, and she made her statement with so much heat that Foxy's owners were at last convinced that these results were due to their neglect.

"You bad dog," Anna said to Peter that night, "you bad dog."

"Peter was the father of those pups," the good Anna explained to Miss Mathilda, "and they look just like him too, and poor little Foxy, they were so big that she could hardly have them, but Miss Mathilda, I would never let those people know that Peter was so bad."

Periods of evil thinking came very regularly to Peter and to Rags and to the visitors within their gates. At such times Anna would be very busy and scold hard, and then too she always took great care to seclude the bad dogs from each other whenever she had to leave the house. Sometimes just to see how good it was that she had made them, Anna would leave the room a little while and leave them all together, and then she would suddenly come back. Back would slink all the wicked-minded dogs at the sound of her hand upon the knob, and then they would sit desolate in their corners like a lot of disappointed children whose stolen sugar has been take from them.

Innocent blind old Baby was the only one who preserved the dignity becoming in a dog.

You see that Anna led an arduous and troubled life.

The good Anna was a small, spare, German woman, at this time about forty years of age. Her face was worn, her cheeks were thin, her mouth drawn and firm, and her light-blue eyes were very bright. Sometimes they were full of lightning and sometimes full of humor, but they were always sharp and clear.

Her voice was a pleasant one, when she told the histories of bad Peter and of Baby and of little Rags. Her voice was a high and piercing one when she called to the teamsters and to the other wicked men, what she wanted that should come to them, when she saw them beat a horse or kick a dog. She did not belong to any society that could stop them and she told them so most frankly, but her strained voice and her glittering eyes, and her queer piercing German English first made them afraid and then ashamed. They all knew too, that all the policemen on the beat were her friends. These always respected and obeyed Miss Annie, as they called her, and promptly attended to all of her complaints.

For five years Anna managed the little house for Miss Mathilda. In these five years there were four different under servants.

The one that came first was a pretty, cheerful Irish girl. Anna took her with a doubting mind. Lizzie was an obedient, happy servant, and Anna began to have a little faith. This was not for long. The pretty, cheerful Lizzie disappeared one day without her notice and with all her baggage and returned no more.

This pretty, cheerful Lizzie was succeeded by a melancholy Molly.

Molly was born in America, of German parents. All her people had been long dead or gone away. Molly had always been alone. She was a tall, dark, sallow, thin-haired creature, and she was always troubled with a cough, and she had a bad temper, and always said ugly dreadful swear words.

Anna found all this very hard to bear, but she kept Molly a long time out of kindness. The kitchen was constantly a battle-ground. Anna scolded and Molly swore strange oaths, and then Miss Mathilda would shut her door hard to show that she could hear it all.

At last Anna had to give it up. "Please, Miss Mathilda, won't you speak to Molly," Anna said, "I can't do a thing with her. I scold her, and she don't seem to hear and then she swears so that she scares me. She loves you, Miss Mathilda, and you scold her please once."

"But Anna," cried poor Miss Mathilda, "I don't want to," and that large, cheerful, but faint-hearted woman looked all aghast at such a prospect. "But you must, please, Miss Mathilda!" Anna said.

Miss Mathilda never wanted to do any scolding. "But you must, please, Miss Mathilda," Anna said.

Miss Mathilda every day put off the scolding, hoping always that Anna would learn to manage Molly better. It never did get better and at last Miss Mathilda saw that the scolding simply had to be.

It was agreed between the good Anna and her Miss Mathilda that Anna should be away when Molly would be scolded. The next evening that it was Anna's evening out, Miss Mathilda faced her task and went down into the kitchen.

Molly was sitting in the little kitchen leaning her elbows on the table. She was a tall, thin, sallow girl, aged twenty-three, by nature slatternly and careless but trained by Anna into superficial neatness. Her drab striped cotton dress and gray-black checked apron increased the length and sadness of her melancholy figure. "Oh, Lord!" groaned Miss Mathilda to herself as she approached her.

"Molly, I want to speak to you about your behavior to Anna!" Here Molly dropped her head still lower on her arms and began to cry.

"Oh! Oh!" groaned Miss Mathilda.

"It's all Miss Annie's fault, all of it," Molly said at last, in a trembling voice, "I do my best."

"I know Anna is often hard to please," began Miss Mathilda, with a twinge of mischief, and then she sobered herself to her task, "but you must remember, Molly, she means it for your good and she is really very kind to you."

"I don't want her kindness," Molly cried, "I wish you would tell me what to do, Miss Mathilda, and then I would be all right. I hate Miss Annie."

"This will never do, Molly," Miss Mathilda said sternly, in her deepest. firmest tones, "Anna is the head of the kitchen and you must either obey her or leave."

"I don't want to leave you," whimpered melancholy Molly. "Well, Molly, then try and do better," answered Miss Mathilda, keeping a good stern front, and backing quickly from the kitchen.

"Oh! Oh!" groaned Miss Mathilda, as she went back up the stairs.

Miss Mathilda's attempt to make peace between the constantly contending women in the kitchen had no real effect. They were very soon as bitter as before.

At last it was decided that Molly was to go away. Molly went away to work in a factory in the town, and she went to live with an old woman in the slums, a very bad old woman, Anna said.

Anna was never easy in her mind about the fate of Molly. Sometimes she would see or hear of her. Molly was not well, her cough was worse, and the old woman really was a bad one.

After a year of this unwholesome life, Molly was completely broken down. Anna then again took her in charge. She brought her from her work and from the woman where she lived, and put her in a hospital to stay till she was well. She found a place for her as nursemaid to a little girl out in the country, and Molly was at last established and content.

Molly had had, at first, no regular successor. In a few months its was going to be the summer and Miss Mathilda would be gone away, and old Katy would do very well to come in every day and help Anna with her work.

Old Katy was a heavy, ugly, short and rough old German woman, with a strange distorted German-English all her own. Anna was worn out now with her attempt to make the younger generation do all that it should and rough old Katy never answered back, and never wanted her own way. No scolding or abuse could make its mark on her uncouth and aged peasant hide. She said her "Yes, Miss Annie," when an answer had to come, and that was always all that she could say.

"Old Katy is just a rough old woman, Miss Mathilda," Anna said, "but I think I keep her here with me. She can work and she don't give me trouble like I had with Molly all the time."

Anna always had a humorous sense from this old Katy's twisted peasant English, from the roughness on her tongue of buzzing s's and from the queer ways of her brutish servile humor. Anna could not let old Katy serve at table—old Katy was too coarsely made from natural earth for that—and so Anna had all this to do herself and that she never liked, but even then this simple rough old creature was pleasanter to her than any of the upstart young.

Life went on very smoothly now in these few months before the summer came. Miss Mathilda every summer went away across the ocean to be gone for several months. When she went away this summer old Katy was so sorry, and on the day that Miss Mathilda went, old Katy cried hard for many hours. An earthy, uncouth, servile peasant creature old Katy surely was. She stood there on the white stone steps of the little red brick house, with her bony, square dull head with its thin, tanned, toughened skin and its sparse and kinky grizzled hair, and her strong, squat figure a little overmade on the right side, clothed in her blue striped cotton dress, all clean and always washed but rough and harsh to see—and she stayed there on the steps till Anna brought her in, blubbering, her apron to her face, and making queer guttural broken moans.

When Miss Mathilda early in the fall came to her house again old Katy was not there.

"I never thought old Katy would act so, Miss Mathilda," Anna said, "when she was so sorry when you went away, and I gave her full wages all the summer, but they are all alike, Miss Mathilda, there isn't one of them that's fit to trust. You know how Katy said she liked you, Miss Mathilda, and went on about it when you went away and then she was so good and worked all right until the middle of the summer, when I got sick, and then she went away and let me all alone and took a place out in the country, where they gave her some more money. She didn't say a word, Miss Mathilda, she just went off and left me there alone when I was sick after that awful hot summer that we had, and after all we done for her when she had no place to go, and all summer I gave her better things to eat than I had for myself. Miss Mathilda, there isn't one of them has any sense of what's the right way for a girl to do, not one of them."

Old Katy was never heard from any more.

No under servant was decided upon now for several months. Many came and many went, and none of them would do. At last Anna heard of Sallie.

Sallie was the oldest girl in a family of eleven, and Sallie was just sixteen years old. From Sallie down they came always little and littler in her family, and all of them were always out at work excepting only the few littlest of them all.

Sallie was a pretty blonde and smiling German girl, and stupid and a little silly. The littler they came in her family the brighter they all were. The brightest of them all was a little girl of ten. She did a good day's work washing dishes for a man and wife in a saloon, and she earned a fair day's wage, and then there was one littler still. She only worked for half the day. She did the housework for a bachelor doctor. She did it all, all of the housework and received each week her eight cents for her wage. Anna was always indignant when she told that story.

"I think he ought to give her ten cents, Miss Mathilda, any way. Eight cents is so mean when she does all his work and she is such a bright little thing too, not stupid like our Sallie. Sallie would never learn to do a thing if I didn't scold her all the time, but Sallie is a good girl, and I take care and she will do all right."

Sallie was a good, obedient German child. She never answered Anna back, no more did Peter, old Baby and little Rags and so though always Anna's voice was sharply raised in strong rebuke and worn expostulation, they were a happy family all there together in the kitchen.

Anna was a mother now to Sallie, a good incessant German mother who watched and scolded hard to keep the girl from any evil step. Sallie's temptations and transgressions were much like those of naughty Peter and jolly little Rags, and Anna took the same way to keep all three from doing what was bad.

Sallie's chief badness, besides forgetting all the time and never washing her hands clean to serve at table, was the butcher boy.

He was an unattractive youth enough, that butcher boy. Suspicion began to close in around Sallie that she spent the evenings when Anna was away, in company with this bad boy.

"Sallie is such a pretty girl, Miss Mathilda," Anna said, "and she is so dumb and silly, and she puts on that red waist, and she crinkles up her hair with irons so I have to laugh, and then I tell her if she only washed her hands clean it would be better than all that fixing all the time, but you can't do a thing with the young girls nowadays, Miss Mathilda. Sallie is a good girl but I got to watch her all the time."

Suspicion closed in around Sallie more and more, that she spent

Anna's evenings out with this boy sitting in the kitchen. One early morning Anna's voice was sharply raised.

"Sallie, this ain't the same banana that I brought home yesterday, for Miss Mathilda, for her breakfast, and you was out early in the street this morning, what was you doing there?"

"Nothing, Miss Annie, I just went out to see, that's all and that's the same banana, 'deed it is, Miss Annie."

"Sallie, how can you say so and after all I do for you, and Miss Mathilda is so good to you. I never brought home no bananas yesterday with specks on it like that. I know better, it was that boy was here last night and ate it while I was away, and you was out to get another this morning. I don't want no lying, Sallie."

Sallie was stout in her defense but then she gave it up and she said it was the boy who snatched it as he ran away at the sound of Anna's key opening the outside door. "But I will never let him in again, Miss Annie, 'deed I won't," said Sallie.

And now it was all peaceful for some weeks and then Sallie with fatuous simplicity began on certain evenings to resume her bright red waist, her bits of jewels and her crinkly hair.

One pleasant evening in the early spring, Miss Mathilda was standing on the steps beside the open door, feeling cheerful in the pleasant, gentle night. Anna came down the street, returning from her evening out. "Don't shut the door, please, Miss Mathilda," Anna said in a low voice, "I don't want Sallie to know I'm home."

Anna went softly through the house and reached the kitchen door. At the sound of her hand upon the knob there was a wild scramble and a bang, and then Sallie sitting there alone when Anna came into the room, but, alas, the butcher boy forgot his overcoat in his escape.

You see that Anna led an arduous and troubled life.

Anna had her troubles, too, with Miss Mathilda. "And I slave and slave to save the money and you go out and spend it all on foolishness," the good Anna would complain when her mistress, a large and careless woman, would come home with a bit of porcelain, a new etching and sometimes even an oil painting on her arm.

"But Anna," argued Miss Mathilda, "if you didn't save this money, don't you see I could not buy these things," and then Anna would soften and look pleased until she learned the price, and then wringing her hands, "Oh, Miss Mathilda, Miss Mathilda," she would cry, "and you gave all that money out for that, when you need a dress to go out in so bad." "Well, perhaps I will get one for myself next year, Anna," Miss Mathilda would cheerfully concede. "If we live till then, Miss Mathilda, I see that you do," Anna would then answer darkly.

Anna had great pride in the knowledge and possessions of her cherished Miss Mathilda, but she did not like her careless way of wearing always her old clothes. "You can't go out to dinner in that dress, Miss Mathilda," she would say, standing firmly before the outside door, "You got to go and put on your new dress you always look so nice in." "But Anna, there isn't time." "Yes there is, I go up and help you fix it, please, Miss Mathilda, you can't go out to dinner in that dress and next year if we live till then, I make you get a new hat, too. It's a shame, Miss Mathilda, to go out like that."

The poor mistress sighed and had to yield. It suited her cheerful, lazy temper to be always without care but sometimes it was a burden to endure, for so often she had it all to do again unless she made a rapid dash out of the door before Anna had a chance to see.

Life was very easy always for this large and lazy Miss Mathilda, with the good Anna to watch and care for her and all her clothes and goods. But, alas, this world of ours is after all much what it should be and cheerful Miss Mathilda had her troubles too with Anna.

It was pleasant that everything for one was done, but annoying often that what one wanted most just then, one could not have when one had foolishly demanded and not suggested one's desire. And then Miss Mathilda loved to go out on joyous, country tramps when, stretching free and far with cheerful comrades, over rolling hills and cornfields, glorious in the setting sun, and dogwood white and shining underneath the moon and clear stars over head, and brilliant air and tingling blood, it was hard to have to think of Anna's anger at the late return, though Miss Mathilda had begged that there might be no hot supper cooked that night. And then when all the happy crew of Miss Mathilda and her friends, tired with fullness of good health and burning winds and glowing sunshine in the eyes, stiffened and justly worn and wholly ripe for pleasant food and gentle content, were all come together to the little house—it was hard for all that tired crew who loved the good things Anna made to eat, to come to the closed door and wonder there if it was Anna's evening in or out, and then the others must wait shivering on their tired feet, while Miss Mathilda softened Anna's heart, or if Anna was well out, boldly ordered youthful Sallie to feed all the hungry lot.

Such things were sometimes hard to bear and often grievously did Miss Mathilda feel herself a rebel with the cheerful Lizzies, the melancholy Mollies, the rough old Katies and the stupid Sallies.

Miss Mathilda had other troubles too, with the good Anna. Miss Mathilda had to save her Anna from the many friends, who in the kindly fashion of the poor, used up her savings and then gave her promises in place of payments.

The good Anna had many curious friends that she had found in the twenty years that she had lived in Bridgepoint, and Miss Mathilda would often have to save her from them all.

II. THE LIFE OF THE GOOD ANNA

Anna Federner, this good Anna, was of solid lower middle-class South German stock.

When she was seventeen years old she went to service in a bourgeois family, in the large city near her native town, but she did not stay there long. One day her mistress offered her maid—that was Anna—to a friend, to see her home. Anna felt herself to be a servant, not a maid, and so she promptly left the place.

Anna had always a firm old world sense of what was the right way for a girl to do.

No argument could bring her to sit an evening in the empty parlor, although the smell of paint when they were fixing up the kitchen made her very sick, and tired as she always was, she never would sit down during the long talks she held with Miss Mathilda. A girl was a girl and should act always like a girl, both as to giving all respect and as to what she had to eat.

A little time after she left this service, Anna and her mother made the voyage to America. They came second-class, but it was for them a long and dreary journey. The mother was already ill with consumption. They landed in a pleasant town in the far South and there the mother slowly died.

Anna was now alone and she made her way to Bridgepoint where an older half brother was already settled. This brother was a heavy, lumbering, good-natured German man, full of the infirmity that comes of excess of body.

He was a baker and married and fairly well to do.

Anna liked her brother well enough but was never in any way dependent on him.

When she arrived in Bridgepoint, she took service with Miss Mary Wadsmith.

Miss Mary Wadsmith was a large, fair, helpless woman, burdened with the care of two young children. They had been left her by her brother and his wife who had died within a few months of each other.

Anna soon had the household altogether in her charge.

Anna found her place with large, abundant women, for such were always lazy, careless or all helpless, and so the burden of their lives could fall on Anna, and give her just content. Anna's superiors must be always these large helpless women, or be men, for none others could give themselves to be made so comfortable and free.

Anna had no strong natural feeling to love children, as she had to love cats and dogs, and a large mistress. She never became deeply fond of Edgar and Jane Wadsmith. She naturally preferred the boy, for boys love always better to be done for and made comfortable and full of eating, while in the little girl she had to meet the feminine, the subtle opposition, showing so early always in a young girl's nature.

For the summer, the Wadsmiths had a pleasant house out in the country, and the winter months they spent in hotel apartments in the city.

Gradually it came to Anna to take the whole direction of their movements, to make all the decisions as to their journeyings to and fro, and for the arranging of the places where they were to live.

Anna had been with Miss Mary for three years, when little Jane began to raise her strength in opposition. Jane was a neat, pleasant little girl, pretty and sweet with a young girl's charm, and with two blonde braids carefully plaited down her back.

Miss Mary, like her Anna, had no strong natural feeling to love children, but she was fond of these two young ones of her blood, and yielded docilely to the stronger power in the really pleasing little girl. Anna always preferred the rougher handling of the boy, while Miss Mary found the gentle force and the sweet domination of the girl to please her better.

In a spring when all the preparations for the moving had been made, Miss Mary and Jane went together to the country home, and Anna, after finishing up the city matters, was to follow them in a few days with Edgar, whose vacation had not yet begun.

Many times during the preparations for this summer, Jane had met Anna with sharp resistance, in opposition to her ways. It was simple for little Jane to give unpleasant orders, not from herself but from Miss Mary, large, docile, helpless Miss Mary Wadsmith who could never think out any orders to give Anna from herself.

Anna's eyes grew slowly sharper, harder, and her lower teeth thrust a little forward and pressing strongly up, framed always more slowly the "Yes, Miss Jane," to the quick, "Oh, Anna! Miss Mary says she wants you to do it so!"

On the day of their migration, Miss Mary had been already put into the carriage. "Oh, Anna!" cried little Jane running back into the house, "Miss Mary says that you are to bring along the blue dressings out of her room and mine." Anna's body stiffened, "We never use them in the summer, Miss Jane," she said thickly. "Yes, Anna, but Miss Mary thinks it would be nice, and she told me to tell you not to forget, goodby!" and the little girl skipped lightly down the steps into the carriage and they drove away.

Anna stood still on the steps, her eyes hard and sharp and shining, and her body and her face stiff with resentment. And then she went into the house, giving the door a shattering slam.

Anna was very hard to live with in those next three days. Even Baby, the new puppy, the pride of Anna's heart, a present from her friend the widow, Mrs. Lehntman—even this pretty little black-and-tan felt the heat of Anna's scorching flame. And Edgar, who had looked forward to those days, to be for him filled full of freedom and of things to eat —he could not rest a moment in Anna's bitter sight.

On the third day, Anna and Edgar went to the Wadsmith country home. The blue dressings out of the two rooms remained behind.

All the way, Edgar sat in front with the colored man and drove. It was an early spring day in the South. The fields and woods were heavy from the soaking rains. The horses dragged the carriage slowly over the long road, sticky with brown clay and rough with masses of stones thrown here and there to be broken and trodden into place by passing teams. Over and through the soaking earth was the feathery new spring growth of little flowers, of young leaves and of ferns. The tree tops were all bright with reds and yellows, with brilliant gleaming whites and gorgeous greens. All the lower air was full of the damp haze rising from heavy soaking water on the earth, mingled with a warm and pleasant smell from the blue smoke of the spring fires in all the open fields. And above all this was the clear, upper air, and the songs of birds and the joy of sunshine and of lengthening days.

The languor and the stir, the warmth and weight and the strong feel of life from the deep centers of the earth that come always with the early, soaking spring, when it is not answered with an active fervent joy, give always anger, irritation and unrest.

To Anna alone there in the carriage, drawing always nearer to the struggle with her mistress, the warmth, the slowness, the jolting over stones, the steaming from the horses, the cries of men and animals and birds, and the new life all round about were simply maddening. "Baby! if you don't lie still, I think I kill you. I can't stand it any more like this."

At this time Anna, about twenty-seven years of age, was not yet all thin and worn. The sharp bony edges and corners of her head and face were still rounded out with flesh, but already the temper and the humor showed sharply in her clean blue eyes, and the thinning was begun about the lower jaw, that was so often strained with the upward pressure of resolve.

Today, alone there in the carriage, she was all stiff and yet all trembling with the sore effort of decision and revolt.

As the carriage turned into the Wadsmith gate, little Jane ran out to see. She just looked at Anna's face; she did not say a word about blue dressings.

Anna got down from the carriage with little Baby in her arms. She took out all the goods that she had brought and the carriage drove away. Anna left everything on the porch, and went in to where Miss Mary Wadsmith was sitting by the fire.

Miss Mary was sitting in a large armchair by the fire. All the nooks and crannies of the chair were filled full of her soft and spreading body. She was dressed in a black satin morning gown, the sleeves, great monster things, were heavy with the mass of her soft flesh. She sat there always, large, helpless, gentle. She had a fair, soft, regular, good-looking face, with pleasant, empty, gray-blue eyes, and heavy sleepy lids.

Behind Miss Mary was the little Jane, nervous and jerky with excite- ment as she saw Anna come into the room.

"Miss Mary," Anna began. She had stopped just within the door, her body and her face stiff with repression, her teeth closed hard and the white lights flashing sharply in the pale, clean blue of her eyes. Her bearing was full of the strange coquetry of anger and of fear, the stiff- ness, the bridling, the suggestive movement underneath the rigidness of forced control, all the queer ways the passions have to show them- selves all one.

"Miss Mary," the words came slowly with thick utterance and with jerks, but always firm and strong. "Miss Mary, I can't stand it any more like this. When you tell me anything to do, I do it. I do everything I can and you know I work myself sick for you. The blue dressings in your room makes too much work to have for summer. Miss Jane don't know what work is. If you want to do things like that I go away."

Anna stopped still. Her words had not the strength of meaning they were meant to have, but the power in the mood of Anna's soul fright- ened and awed Miss Mary through and through.

Like in all large and helpless women, Miss Mary's heart beat weakly in the soft and helpless mass it had to govern. Little Jane's excitements had already tried her strength. Now she grew pale and fainted quite away.

"Miss Mary!" cried Anna running to her mistress and supporting all her helpless weight back in the chair. Little Jane, distracted, flew about as Anna ordered, bringing smelling salts and brandy and vinegar and water and chafing poor Miss Mary's wrists.

Miss Mary slowly opened her mild eyes. Anna sent the weeping little Jane out of the room. She herself managed to get Miss Mary quiet on the couch.

There was never a word more said about blue dressings.

Anna had conquered, and a few days later little Jane gave her a green parrot to make peace.

For six more years little Jane and Anna lived in the same house. They were careful and respectful to each other to the end.

Anna liked the parrot very well. She was fond of cats too and of horses, but best of all animals she loved the dog and best of all dogs, little Baby, the first gift from her friend, the widow Mrs. Lehntman.

The widow Mrs. Lehntman was the romance in Anna's life.

Anna met her first at the house of her half brother, the baker, who had known the late Mr. Lehntman, a small grocer, very well.

Mrs. Lehntman had been for many years a midwife. Since her husband's death she had herself and two young children to support.

Mrs. Lehntman was a good-looking woman. She had a plump well-rounded body, clear olive skin, bright dark eyes and crisp black curling hair. She was pleasant, magnetic, efficient and good. She was very attractive, very generous and very amiable.

She was a few years older than our good Anna, who was soon entirely subdued by her magnetic, sympathetic charm.

Mrs. Lehntman in her work loved best to deliver young girls who were in trouble. She would take these into her own house and care for them in secret, till they could guiltlessly go home or back to work, and then slowly pay her the money for their care. And so through this new friend Anna led a wider and more entertaining life, and often she used up her savings in helping Mrs. Lehntman through those times when she was giving very much more than she got.

It was through Mrs. Lehntman that Anna met Dr. Shonjen who employed her when at last it had to be that she must go away from her Miss Mary Wadsmith.

During the last years with her Miss Mary, Anna's health was very bad, as indeed it always was from that time on until the end of her strong life.

Anna was a medium-sized, thin, hard-working, worrying woman.

She had always had bad headaches and now they came more often and more wearing.

Her face grew thin, more bony and more worn, her skin stained itself pale yellow, as it does with working sickly women, and the clear blue of her eyes went pale.

Her back troubled her a good deal, too. She was always tired at her work and her temper grew more difficult and fretful.

Miss Mary Wadsmith often tried to make Anna see a little to herself, and get a doctor, and the little Jane, now blossoming into a pretty, sweet young woman, did her best to make Anna do things for her good. Anna was stubborn always to Miss Jane, and fearful of interference in her ways. Miss Mary Wadsmith's mild advice she easily could always turn aside.

Mrs. Lehntman was the only one who had any power over Anna. She induced her to let Dr. Shonjen take her in his care.

No one but a Dr. Shonjen could have brought a good and German Anna first to stop her work and then submit herself to operation, but he knew so well how to deal with German and poor people. Cheery, jovial, hearty, full of jokes that made much fun and yet were full of simple common sense and reasoning courage, he could persuade even a good Anna to do things that were for her own good.

Edgar had now been for some years away from home, first at a school and then at work to prepare himself to be a civil engineer. Miss Mary and Jane promised to take a trip for all the time that Anna was away and so there would be no need for Anna's work, nor for a new girl to take Anna's place.

Anna's mind was thus a little set at rest. She gave herself to Mrs. Lehntman and the doctor to do what they thought best to make her well and strong.

Anna endured the operation very well, and was patient, almost docile, in the slow recovery of her working strength. But when she was once more at work for her Miss Mary Wadsmith, all the good effect of these several months of rest were soon worked and worried well away.

For all the rest of her strong working life Anna was never really well. She had bad headaches all the time and she was always thin and worn.

She worked away her appetite, her health and strength, and always for the sake of those who begged her not to work so hard. To her thinking, in her stubborn, faithful, German soul, this was the right way for a girl to do.

Anna's life with Miss Mary Wadsmith was now drawing to an end.

Miss Jane, now altogether a young lady, had come out into the world. Soon she would become engaged and then be married, and then perhaps Miss Mary Wadsmith would make her home with her.

In such a household Anna was certain that she would never take a place. Miss Jane was always careful and respectful and very good to Anna, but never could Anna be a girl in a household where Miss Jane would be the head. This much was very certain in her mind, and so these last two years with her Miss Mary were not as happy as before.

The change came very soon.

Miss Jane became engaged and in a few months was to marry a man from out of town, from Curden, an hour's railway ride from Bridgepoint.

Poor Miss Mary Wadsmith did not know the strong resolve Anna had made to live apart from her when this new household should be formed. Anna found it very hard to speak to her Miss Mary of this change.

The preparations for the wedding went on day and night.

Anna worked and sewed hard to make it all go well.

Miss Mary was much fluttered, but content and happy with Anna to make everything so easy for them all.

Anna worked so all the time to drown her sorrow and her conscience too, for somehow it was not right to leave Miss Mary so. But what else could she do? She could not live as her Miss Mary's girl, in a house where Miss Jane would be the head.

The wedding day grew always nearer. At last it came and passed.

The young people went on their wedding trip, and Anna and Miss Mary were left behind to pack up all the things.

Even yet poor Anna had not had the strength to tell Miss Mary her resolve, but now it had to be.

Anna every spare minute ran to her friend Mrs. Lehntman for comfort and advice. She begged her friend to be with her when she told the news to Miss Mary.

Perhaps if Mrs. Lehntman had not been in Bridgepoint, Anna would have tried to live in the new house. Mrs. Lehntman did not urge her to this thing nor even give her this advice, but feeling for Mrs. Lehntman as she did made even faithful Anna not quite so strong in her dependence on Miss Mary's need as she would otherwise have been.

Remember, Mrs. Lehntman was the romance in Anna's life.

All the packing was now done and in a few days Miss Mary was to go to the new house, where the young people were ready for her coming.

At last Anna had to speak.

Mrs. Lehntman agreed to go with her and help to make the matter clear to poor Miss Mary.

The two women came together to Miss Mary Wadsmith sitting placid by the fire in the empty living room. Miss Mary had seen Mrs. Lehntman many times before, and so her coming in with Anna raised no suspicion in her mind.

It was very hard for the two women to begin.

It must be very gently done, this telling to Miss Mary of the change. She must not be shocked by suddenness or with excitement.

Anna was all stiff, and inside all a-quiver with shame, anxiety and grief. Even courageous Mrs. Lehntman, efficient, impulsive and complacent as she was and not deeply concerned in the event, felt awkward, abashed and almost guilty in that large, mild, helpless presence. And at her side to make her feel the power of it all, was the intense conviction of poor Anna, struggling to be unfeeling, self-righteous and suppressed,

"Miss Mary"—with Anna when things had to come they came always sharp and short—"Miss Mary, Mrs. Lehntman has come here with me, so I can tell you about not staying with you there in Curden. Of course I go help you to get settled and then I think I come back and stay right here in Bridgepoint. You know my brother he is here and all his family, and I think it would be not right to go away from them so far, and you know you don't want me now so much, Miss Mary, when you are all together there in Curden."

Miss Mary Wadsmith was puzzled. She did not understand what Anna meant by what she said.

"Why, Anna, of course you can come to see your brother whenever you like to, and I will always pay your fare. I thought you understood all about that, and we will be very glad to have your nieces come to stay with you as often as they like. There will always be room enough in a big house like Mr. Goldthwaite's."

It was now for Mrs. Lehntman to begin her work.

"Miss Wadsmith does not understand just what you mean, Anna," she began. "Miss Wadsmith, Anna feels how good and kind you are, and she talks about it all the time, and what you do for her in every way you can, and she is very grateful and never would want to go away from you, only she thinks it would be better now that Mrs. Goldthwaite has this big new house and will want to manage it in her own way, she thinks perhaps it would be better if Mrs. Goldthwaite had all new servants with her to begin with, and not a girl like Anna who knew her when she was a little girl. That is what Anna feels about it now, and she asked me and I said to her that I thought it would be better for you all and you knew she liked you so much and that you were so good to her, and you would understand how she thought it would be better in the new house if she stayed on here in Bridgepoint, anyway for a little while until Mrs. Goldthwaite was used to her new house. Isn't that it, Anna, that you wanted Miss Wadsmith to know?"

"Oh Anna," Miss Mary Wadsmith said it slowly and in a grieved tone of surprise that was very hard for the good Anna to endure, "Oh Anna, I didn't think that you would ever want to leave me after all these years."

"Miss Mary!" it came in one tense jerky burst, "Miss Mary, it's only working under Miss Jane now would make me leave you so. I knew how good you are and I work myself sick for you and for Mr. Edgar and for Miss Jane too, only Miss Jane she will want everything different from like the way we always did, and you know, Miss Mary, I can't have Miss Jane watching at me all the time, and every minute something new. Miss Mary, it would be very bad and Miss Jane don't really want me to come with you to the new house, I know that all the time. Please, Miss Mary, don't feel bad about it or think I ever want to go away from you if I could do things right for you the way they ought to be."

Poor Miss Mary. Struggling was not a thing for her to do. Anna would surely yield if she would struggle, but struggling was too much work and too much worry for peaceful Miss Mary to endure. If Anna would do so she must. Poor Miss Mary Wadsmith sighed, looked wistfully at Anna and then gave it up.

"You must do as you think best, Anna," she said at last letting all of her soft self sink back into the chair. "I am very sorry and so I am sure will be Miss Jane when she hears what you have thought it best to do. It was very good of Mrs. Lehntman to come with you and I am sure she does it for your good. I suppose you want to go out a little now. Come back in an hour, Anna, and help me go to bed." Miss Mary closed her eyes and rested still and placid by the fire.

The two women went away.

This was the end of Anna's service with Miss Mary Wadsmith, and soon her new life taking care of Dr. Shonjen was begun.

Keeping house for a jovial bachelor doctor gave new elements of understanding to Anna's maiden German mind. Her habits were as firm fixed as before, but it always was with Anna that things that had been done once with her enjoyment and consent could always happen any time again, such as her getting up at any hour of the night to make a supper and cook hot chops and chicken fry for Dr. Shonjen and his bachelor friends.

Anna loved to work for men, for they could eat so much and with such joy. And when they were warm and full, they were content, and let her do whatever she thought best. Not that Anna's conscience ever slept, for neither with interference or without would she strain less to keep on saving every cent and working every hour of the day. But truly she loved it best when she could scold. Now it was not only other girls and the colored man, and dogs, and cats, and horses and her parrot, but her cheery master, jolly Dr. Shonjen, whom she could guide and constantly rebuke to his own good.

The doctor really loved her scoldings as she loved his wickedness and his merry joking ways.

These days were happy days with Anna.

Her freakish humor now first showed itself, her sense of fun in the queer ways that people had, that made her later find delight in brutish servile Katy, in Sallie's silly ways and in the badness of Peter and Rags. She loved to make sport with the skeletons the doctor had, to make them move and make strange noises till the Negro boy shook in his shoes and his eyes rolled white in his agony of fear.

Then Anna would tell these histories to her doctor. Her worn, thin, lined, determined face would form for itself new and humorous creases, and her pale blue eyes would kindle with humor and with joy as her doctor burst into his hearty laugh. And the good Anna full of the coquetry of pleasing would bridle with her angular, thin, spinster body, straining her stories and herself to please.

These early days with jovial Dr. Shonjen were very happy days with the good Anna.

All of Anna's spare hours in these early days she spent with her friend, the widow Mrs. Lehntman. Mrs. Lehntman lived with her two children in a small house in the same part of the town as Dr. Shonjen. The older of these two children was a girl named Julia and was now about thirteen years of age. This Julia Lehntman was an unattractive girl enough, harsh featured, dull and stubborn as had been her heavy German father. Mrs. Lehntman did not trouble much with her, but gave her always all she wanted that she had, and let the girl do as she liked. This was not from indifference or dislike on the part of Mrs. Lehntman, it was just her usual way.

Her second child was a boy, two years younger than his sister, a bright, pleasant, cheery fellow, who, too, did what he liked with his money and his time. All this was so with Mrs. Lehntman because she had so much in her head and in her house that clamored for her concentration and her time.

This slackness and neglect in the running of the house, and the indifference in this mother for the training of her young was very hard for our good Anna to endure. Of course she did her best to scold, to save for Mrs. Lehntman, and to put things in their place the way they ought to be.

Even in the early days when Anna was first won by the glamour of Mrs. Lehntman's brilliancy and charm, she had been uneasy in Mrs. Lehntman's house with a need of putting things to rights. Now that the two children growing up were of more importance in the house, and now that long acquaintance had brushed the dazzle out of Anna's eyes, she began to struggle to make things go here as she thought was right.

She watched and scolded hard these days to make young Julia do the way she should. Not that Julia Lehntman was pleasant in the good Anna's sight, but it must never be that a young girl growing up should have no one to make her learn to do things right.

The boy was easier to scold, for scoldings never sank in very deep, and indeed he liked them very well, for they brought with them new things to eat, and lively teasing, and good jokes.

Julia, the girl, grew very sullen with it all, and very often won hei point, for after all Miss Annie was no relative of hers and had no business coming there and making trouble all the time. Appealing to the mother was no use. It was wonderful how Mrs. Lehntman could listen and not hear, could answer and yet not decide, could say and do what she was asked and yet leave things as they were before.

One day it got almost too bad for even Anna's friendship to bear out.

"Well, Julia, is your mamma out?" Anna asked, one Sunday summer afternoon, as she came into the Lehntman house.

Anna looked very well this day. She was always careful in her dress and sparing of new clothes. She made herself always fulfill her own ideal of how a girl should look when she took her Sundays out. Anna knew so well the kind of ugliness appropriate to each rank in life.

It was interesting to see how when she bought things for Miss Wadsmith and later for her cherished Miss Mathilda and always entirely from her own taste and often as cheaply as she bought things for her friends or for herself, that on the one hand she chose the things having the right air for a member of the upper class, and for the others always the things having the awkward ugliness that we call Dutch. She knew the best thing in each kind, and she never in the course of her strong life compromised her sense of what was the right thing for a girl to wear.

On this bright summer Sunday afternoon she came to the Lehntmans', much dressed up in her new, brick red, silk waist trimmed with broad black beaded braid, a dark cloth skirt and a new stiff, shiny, black straw hat, trimmed with colored ribbons and a bird. She had on new gloves, and a feather boa about her neck.

Her spare, thin, awkward body and her worn, pale yellow face though lit up now with the pleasant summer sun made a queer discord with the brightness of her clothes.

She came to the Lehntman house, where she had not been for several days, and opening the door that is always left unlatched in the houses of the lower middle class in the pleasant cities of the South, she found Julia in the family sitting room alone.

"Well, Julia, where is your mamma?" Anna asked. "Ma is out but come in, Miss Annie, and look at our new brother." "What you talk so foolish for, Julia," said Anna sitting down. "I ain't talkin' foolish, Miss Annie. Didn't you know mamma has just adopted a cute, nice little baby boy?" "You talk so crazy, Julia, you ought to know better than to say such things." Julia turned sullen. "All right, Miss Annie, you don't need to believe what I say, but the little baby is in the kitchen and ma will tell you herself when she comes in."

It sounded most fantastic, but Julia had an air of truth and Mrs. Lehntman was capable of doing stranger things. Anna was disturbed.

"What you mean, Julia," she said. "I don't mean nothin', Miss Annie, you don't believe the baby is in there, well you can go and see it for yourself."

Anna went into the kitchen. A baby was there all right enough, and a lusty little boy he seemed. He was very tight asleep in a basket that stood in the corner by the open door.

"You mean your mamma is just letting him stay here a little while," Anna said to Julia who had followed her into the kitchen to see Miss Annie get real mad. "No, that ain't it, Miss Annie. The mother was that girl, Lily that came from Bishop's place out in the country, and she don't want no children, and ma liked the little boy so much, she said she'd keep him here and adopt him for her own child."

Anna, for once, was fairly dumb with astonishment and rage. The front door slammed.

"There's ma now," cried Julia in an uneasy triumph, for she was not quite certain in her mind which side of the question she was on, "There's ma now, and you can ask her for yourself if I ain't told you true."

Mrs. Lehntman came into the kitchen where they were. She was bland, impersonal and pleasant, as it was her wont to be. Still today, through this her usual manner that gave her such success in her practice as a midwife, there shone an uneasy consciousness of guilt, for like all who had to do with the good Anna, Mrs. Lehntman dreaded her firm character, her vigorous judgments and the bitter fervor of her tongue.

It had been plain to see in the six years these women were together, how Anna gradually had come to lead. Not really lead, of course, for Mrs. Lehntman never could be led, she was so very devious in her ways; but Anna had come to have direction whenever she could learn what Mrs. Lehntman meant to do before the deed was done. Now it was hard to tell which would win out. Mrs. Lehntman had her unhearing mind and her happy way of giving a pleasant well-diffused attention, and then she had it on her side that, after all, this thing was already done.

Anna was, as usual, determined for the right. She was stiff and pale with her anger and her fear, and nervous, and all a-tremble as was her usual way when a bitter fight was near.

Mrs. Lehntman was easy and pleasant as she came into the room. Anna was stiff and silent and very white.

"We haven't seen you for a long time, Anna," Mrs. Lehntman cordially began. "I was just gettin' worried thinking you was sick. My! but it's a hot day today. Come into the sittin' room, Anna, and Julia will make us some ice tea."

Anna followed Mrs. Lehntman into the other room in a stiff silence, and when there she did not, as invited, take a chair.

As always with Anna when a thing had to come it came very short and sharp. She found it hard to breathe just now, and every word came with a jerk.

"Mrs. Lehntman, it ain't true what Julia said about your taking that Lily's boy to keep. I told Julia when she told me she was crazy to talk so."

Anna's real excitements stopped her breath, and made her words come sharp and with a jerk. Mrs. Lehntman's feelings spread her breath, and made her words come slow, but more pleasant and more easy even than before.

"Why, Anna," she began, "don't you see Lily couldn't keep her boy, for she is working at the Bishop's now, and he is such a cute dear little chap, and you know how fond I am of little fellers, and I thought it would be nice for Julia and for Willie to have a little brother. You know Julia always loves to play with babies, and I have to be away so much, and Willie he is running in the streets every minute all the time, and you see a baby would be sort of nice company for Julia, and you know you are always saying, Anna, Julia should not be on the streets so much and the baby will be so good to keep her in."

Anna was every minute paler with indignation and with heat.

"Mrs. Lehntman, I don't see what business it is for you to take another baby for your own, when you can't do what's right by Julia and Willie you got here already. There's Julia, nobody tells her a thing when I ain't here, and who is going to tell her now how to do things for that baby? She ain't got no sense what's the right way to do with children, and you out all the time, and you ain't got no time for your own neither, and now you want to be takin' up with strangers. I know you was careless, Mrs. Lehntman, but I didn't think that you could do this so. No, Mrs. Lehntman, it ain't your duty to take up with no others, when you got two children of your own, that got to get along just any way they can, and you know you ain't got any too much money all the time, and you are all so careless here and spend it all the time, and Julia and Willie growin' big. It ain't right, Mrs. Lehntman, to do so."

This was as bad as it could be. Anna had never spoken her mind so to her friend before. Now it was too harsh for Mrs. Lehntman to allow, herself to really hear. If she really took the meaning in these words she could never ask Anna to come into her house again, and she liked Anna very well, and was used to depend on her savings and her strength. And then too Mrs. Lehntman could not really take in harsh ideas. She was too well diffused to catch the feel of any sharp firm edge.

Now she managed to understand all this in a way that made it easy for her to say, "Why, Anna, I think you feel too bad about seeing what the children are doing every minute in the day. Julia and Willie are real good, and they play with all the nicest children in the square. If you had some, all your own, Anna, you'd see it don't do no harm to let them do a little as they like, and Julia likes this baby so, and sweet dear little boy, it would be so kind of bad to send him to a 'sylum now, you know it would, Anna, when you like children so yourself, and are so good to my Willie all the time. No indeed, Anna, it's easy enough to say I should send this poor, cute little boy to a 'sylum when I could keep him here so nice, but you know, Anna, you wouldn't like to do it yourself, now you really know you wouldn't, Anna, though you talk to me so hard.—My, it's hot today, what you doin' with that ice tea in there Julia, when Miss Annie is waiting all this time for her drink?"

Julia brought in the ice tea. She was so excited with the talk she had been hearing from the kitchen, that she slopped it on the plate out of the glasses a good deal. But she was safe, for Anna felt this trouble so deep down that she did not even see those awkward, bony hands, adorned today with a new ring, those stupid, foolish hands that always did things the wrong way.

"Here, Miss Annie," Julia said, "Here, Miss Annie, is your glass of tea, I know you like it good and strong."

"No, Julia, I don't want no ice tea here. Your mamma ain't able to afford now using her money upon ice tea for her friends. It ain't right she should now any more. I go out to see Mrs. Drehten. She does all she can, and she is sick now working so hard taking care of her own children. I go there now. Good-by, Mrs. Lehntman, I hope you don't get no bad luck doin' what it ain't right for you to do."

"My, Miss Annie is real mad now," Julia said, as the house shook, as the good Anna shut the outside door with a concentrated shattering slam.

It was some months now that Anna had been intimate with Mrs. Drehten.

Mrs. Drehten had had a tumor and had to come to Dr. Shonjen to be treated. During the course of her visits there, she and Anna had learned to like each other very well. There was no fever in this friendship, it was just the interchange of two hard-working, worrying women, the one large and motherly, with the pleasant, patient, soft, worn, tolerant face, that comes with a German husband to obey, and seven solid girls and boys to bear and rear, and the other was our good Anna with her spinster body, her firm jaw, her humorous, light, clean eyes and her lined, worn, thin, pale yellow face.

Mrs. Drehten lived a patient, homely, hard-working life. Her husband an honest, decent man enough, was a brewer, and somewhat given to over-drinking, and so he was often surly and stingy and unpleasant.

The family of seven children was made up of four stalwart, cheery, filial sons, and three hard-working obedient simple daughters.

It was a family life the good Anna very much approved and also she was much liked by them all. With a German woman's feeling for the masterhood in men, she was docile to the surly father and rarely rubbed him the wrong way. To the large, worn, patient, sickly mother she was a sympathetic listener, wise in counsel and most efficient in her help. The young ones, too, liked her very well. The sons teased her all the time and roared with boisterous pleasure when she gave them back sharp hits. The girls were all so good that her scoldings here were only in the shape of good advice, sweetened with new trimmings for their hats, and ribbons, and sometimes on their birthdays, bits of jewels.

It was here that Anna came for comfort after her grievous stroke at her friend the widow, Mrs. Lehntman. Not that Anna would tell Mrs. Drehten of this trouble. She could never lay bare the wound that came to her through this idealized affection. Her affair with Mrs. Lehntman was too sacred and too grievous ever to be told. But here in this large household, in busy movement and variety in strife, she could silence the uneasiness and pain of her own wound.

The Drehtens lived out in the country in one of the wooden, ugly houses that lie in groups outside of our large cities.

The father and the sons all had their work here making beer, and the mother and her girls scoured and sewed and cooked.

On Sundays they were all washed very clean, and smelling of kitchen soap. The sons, in their Sunday clothes, loafed around the house or in the village, and on special days went on picnics with their girls. The daughters in their awkward, colored finery went to church most of the day and then walking with their friends.

They always came together for their supper, where Anna always was most welcome, the jolly Sunday evening supper that German people love. Here Anna and the boys gave it to each other in sharp hits and hearty boisterous laughter, the girls made things for them to eat, and waited on them all, the mother loved all her children all the time, and the father joined in with his occasional unpleasant word that made a bitter feeling but which they had all learned to pass as if it were not said.

It was to the comfort of this house that Anna came that Sunday summer afternoon, after she had left Mrs. Lehntman and her careless ways.

The Drehten house was open all about. No one was there but Mrs. Drehten resting in her rocking chair, out in the pleasant, scented, summer air.

Anna had had a hot walk from the cars.

She went into the kitchen for a cooling drink, and then came out and sat down on the steps near Mrs. Drehten.

Anna's anger had changed. A sadness had come to her. Now with the patient, friendly, gentle mother talk of Mrs. Drehten, this sadness changed to resignation and to rest.

As the evening came on the young ones dropped in one by one. Soon the merry Sunday evening supper was begun.

It had not been all comfort for our Anna, these months of knowing Mrs. Drehten. It had made trouble for her with the family of her half brother, the fat baker.

Her half brother, the fat baker, was a queer kind of a man. He was a huge, unwieldy creature, all puffed out all over, and no longer able to walk much, with his enormous body and the big swollen, bursted veins in his great legs. He did not try to walk much now. He sat around his place, leaning on his great thick stick, and watching his workmen at their work.

On holidays, and sometimes of a Sunday, he went out in his bakery wagon. He went then to each customer he had and gave them each a large, sweet, raisined loaf of caky bread. At every house with many groans and gasps he would descend his heavy weight out of the wagon, his good-featured, black-haired, flat, good-natured face shining with oily perspiration, with pride in labor and with generous kindness. Up each stoop he hobbled with the help of his big stick, and into the nearest chair in the kitchen or in the parlor, as the fashion of the house demanded, and there he sat and puffed, and then presented to the mistress or the cook the raisined German loaf his boy supplied him.

Anna had never been a customer of his. She had always lived in another part of town, but he never left her out in these bakery progresses of his, and always with his own hand he gave her her festive loaf.

Anna liked her half brother well enough. She never knew him really well, for he rarely talked at all and least of all to women, but he seemed to her honest, and good and kind, and he never tried to interfere in Anna's ways. And then Anna liked the loaves of raisined bread, for in the summer she and the second girl could live on them, and not be buying bread with the household money all the time.

But things were not so simple with our Anna, with the other members of her half brother's house.

Her half brother's family was made up of himself, his wife, and their two daughters.

Anna never liked her brother's wife.

The youngest of the two daughters was named after her aunt Anna.

Anna never liked her half brother's wife. This woman had been very good to Anna, never interfering in her ways, always glad to see her and to make her visits pleasant, but she had not found favor in our good Anna's sight.

Anna had, too, no real affection for her nieces. She never scolded them or tried to guide them for their good. Anna never criticized or interfered in the running of her half brother's house.

Mrs. Federner was a good-looking, prosperous woman, a little harsh and cold within her soul perhaps, but trying always to be pleasant, good and kind. Her daughters were well-trained, quiet, obedient, well-dressed girls, and yet our good Anna loved them not, nor their mother, nor any of their ways.

It was in this house that Anna had first met her friend, the widow, Mrs. Lehntman.

The Federners had never seemed to feel it wrong in Anna, her devotion to this friend and her care of her and of her children. Mrs. Lehntman and Anna and her feelings were all somehow too big for their attack. But Mrs. Federner had the mind and tongue that blacken things. Not really to blacken black, of course, but just to roughen and to rub on a little smut. She could somehow make even the face of the Almighty seem pimply and a little coarse, and so she always did this with her friends, though not with the intent to interfere.

This was really true with Mrs. Lehntman that Mrs. Federner did not mean to interfere, but Anna's friendship with the Drehtens was a very different matter.

Why should Mrs. Drehten, that poor common working wife of a man who worked for others in a brewery and who always drank too much, and was not like a thrifty, decent German man, why should that Mrs. Drehten and her ugly, awkward daughters be getting presents from her husband's sister all the time, and her husband always so good to Anna, and one of the girls having her name too, and those Drehtens all strangers to her and never going to come to any good? It was not right for Anna to do so.

Mrs. Federner knew better than to say such things straight out to her husband's fiery, stubborn sister, but she lost no chance to let Anna feel and see what they all thought.

It was easy to blacken all the Drehtens, their poverty, the husband's drinking, the four big sons carrying on and always lazy, the awkward, ugly daughters dressing up with Anna's help and trying to look so fine, and the poor, weak, hard-working sickly mother, so easy to degrade with large dosings of contemptuous pity.

Anna could not do much with these attacks for Mrs. Federner always ended with, "And you so good to them, Anna, all the time. I don't see now they could get along at all if you didn't help them all the time, but you are so good, Anna, and got such a feeling heart, just like your brother, that you give anything away you got to anybody that will ask you for it, and that's shameless enough to take it when they ain't no relatives of yours. Poor Mrs. Drehten, she is a good woman. Poor thing, it must be awful hard for her to have to take things from strangers all the time, and her husband spending it on drink. I was saying to Mrs. Lehntman, Anna, only yesterday, how I never was so sorry for anyone as Mrs. Drehten, and how good it was for you to help them all the time."

All this meant a gold watch and chain to her goddaughter for her birthday, the next month, and a new silk umbrella for the elder sister. Poor Anna, and she did not love them very much, these relatives of hers, and they were the only kin she had.

Mrs. Lehntman never joined in, in these attacks. Mrs. Lehntman was diffuse and careless in her ways, but she never worked such things for her own ends, and she was too sure of Anna to be jealous of her other friends.

All this time Anna was leading her happy life with Dr. Shonjen. She had every day her busy time. She cooked and saved and sewed and scrubbed and scolded. And every night she had her happy time, in seeing her doctor like the fine things she bought so cheap and cooked so good for him to eat. And then he would listen and laugh so loud, as she told him stories of what had happened on that day.

The doctor, too, liked it better all the time and several times in these five years he had of his own motion raised her wages.

Anna was content with what she had and grateful for all her doctor did for her.

So Anna's serving and her giving life went on, each with its varied pleasures and its pains.

The adopting of the little boy did not put an end to Anna's friendship for the widow Mrs. Lehntman. Neither the good Anna nor the careless Mrs. Lehntman would give each other up excepting for the gravest cause.

Mrs. Lehntman was the only romance Anna ever knew. A certain magnetic brilliancy in person and in manner made Mrs. Lehntman a woman other women loved. Then, too, she was generous and good and honest, though she was so careless always in her ways. And then she trusted Anna and liked her better than any of her other friends, and Anna always felt this very much.

No, Anna could not give up Mrs. Lehntman, and soon she was busier than before making Julia do things right for little Johnny.

And now new schemes were working strong in Mrs. Lehntman's head, and Anna must listen to her plans and help her make them work.

Mrs. Lehntman always loved best in her work to deliver young girls who were in trouble. She would keep these in her house until they could go to their homes or to their work, and slowly pay her back the money for their care.

Anna had always helped her friend to do this thing, for like all the good women of the decent poor, she felt it hard that girls should not be helped, not girls that were really bad of course, these she condemned and hated in her heart and with her tongue, but honest, decent, good, hard-working, foolish girls who were in trouble.

For such as these Anna always liked to give her money and her strength.

Now Mrs. Lehntman thought that it would pay to take a big house for herself to take in girls and to do everything in a big way.

Anna did not like this plan.

Anna was never daring in her ways. Save and you will have the money you have saved, was all that she could know.

Not that the good Anna had it so.

She saved and saved and always saved, and then here and there, to this friend and to that, to one in her trouble and to the other in her joy, in sickness, death, and weddings, or to make young people happy, it always went, the hard-earned money she had saved.

Anna could not clearly see how Mrs. Lehntman could make a big house pay. In the small house where she had these girls, it did not pay, and in a big house there was so much more that she would spend.

Such things were hard for the good Anna to very clearly see. One day she came into the Lehntman house. "Anna," Mrs. Lehntman said, "you know that nice big house on the next corner that we saw to rent. I took it for a year just yesterday. I paid a little down you know so I could have it sure all right and now you fix it up just like you want. I let you do just what you like with it."

Anna knew that it was now too late. However, "But, Mrs. Lehntman you said you would not take another house, you said so just last week. Oh, Mrs. Lehntman, I didn't think that you would do this so!"

Anna knew so well it was too late.

"I know, Anna, but it was such a good house, just right you know and someone else was there to see, and you know you said it suited very well, and if I didn't take it the others said they would, and I wanted to ask you, only there wasn't time, and really, Anna, I don't need much help, it will go so well I know. I just need a little to begin and to fix up with and that's all Anna that I need, and I know it will go awful well. You wait, Anna, and you'll see, and I let you fix it up just like you want, and you will make it look so nice, you got such sense in all these things. It will be a good place. You see, Anna, if I ain't right in what I say."

Of course Anna gave the money for this thing though she could not believe that it was best. No, it was very bad. Mrs. Lehntman could never make it pay and it would cost so much to keep. But what could our poor Anna do? Remember, Mrs. Lehntman was the only romance Anna ever knew.

Anna's strength in her control of what was done in Mrs. Lehntman's house was not now what it had been before that Lily's little Johnny came. That thing had been for Anna a defeat. There had been no fighting to a finish but Mrs. Lehntman had very surely won.

Mrs. Lehntman needed Anna just as much as Anna needed Mrs. Lehntman, but Mrs. Lehntman was more ready to risk Anna's loss, and so the good Anna grew always weaker in her power to control.

In friendship, power always has its downward curve. One's strength to manage rises always higher until there comes a time one does not win, and though one may not really lose, still from the time that victory is not sure, one's power slowly ceases to be strong. It is only in a close tie, such as marriage, that influence can mount and grow always stronger with the years and never meet with a decline. It can only happen so when there is no way to escape.

Friendship goes by favor. There is always danger of a break or of a stronger power coming in between. Influence can only be a steady march when one can surely never break away.

Anna wanted Mrs. Lehntman very much and Mrs. Lehntman needed Anna, but there were always other ways to do and if Anna had once given up she might do so again, so why should Mrs. Lehntman have real fear?

No, while the good Anna did not come to open fight she had been stronger. Now Mrs. Lehntman could always hold out longer. She knew too that Anna had a feeling heart. Anna could never stop doing all she could for anyone that really needed help. Poor Anna had no power to say no.

And then, too, Mrs. Lehntman was the only romance Anna ever knew. Romance is the ideal in one's life and it is very lonely living with it lost.

So the good Anna gave all her savings for this place, although she knew that this was not the right way for her friend to do.

For some time now they were all very busy fixing up the house. It swallowed all Anna's savings fixing up this house, for when Anna once began to make it nice, she could not leave it be until it was as good as for the purpose it should be.

Somehow it was Anna now that really took the interest in the house. Mrs. Lehntman, now the thing was done, seemed very lifeless, without interest in the house, uneasy in her mind and restless in her ways, and more diffuse even than before in her attention. She was good and kind to all the people in her house, and let them do whatever they thought best.

Anna did not fail to see that Mrs. Lehntman had something on her mind that was all new. What was it that disturbed Mrs. Lehntman so? She kept on saying it was all in Anna's head. She had no trouble now at all. Everybody was so good and it was all so nice in the new house. But surely there was something here that was all wrong.

Anna heard a good deal of all this from her half brother's wife, the hard-speaking Mrs. Federner.

Through the fog of dust and work and furnishing in the new house, and through the disturbed mind of Mrs. Lehntman, and with the dark hints of Mrs. Federner, there loomed up to Anna's sight a man, a new doctor that Mrs. Lehntman knew.

Anna had never met the man but she heard of him very often now. Not from her friend, the widow Mrs. Lehntman. Anna knew that Mrs. Lehntman made of him a mystery that Anna had not the strength just then to vigorously break down.

Mrs. Federner gave always dark suggestions and unpleasant hints. Even good Mrs. Drehten talked of it.

Mrs. Lehntman never spoke of the new doctor more than she could help. This was most mysterious and unpleasant and very hard for our good Anna to endure.

Anna's troubles came all of them at once.

Here in Mrs. Lehntman's house loomed up dismal and forbidding, a mysterious, perhaps an evil man. In Dr. Shonjen's house were beginning signs of interest in the doctor in a woman.

This, too, Mrs. Federner often told to the poor Anna. The doctor surely would be married soon, he liked so much now to go to Mr. Weingartner's house where there was a daughter who loved Doctor, everybody knew.

In these days the living room in her half brother's house was Anna's torture chamber. And worst of all there was so much reason for her half sister's words. The doctor certainly did look like marriage and Mrs. Lehntman acted very queer.

Poor Anna. Dark were these days and much she had to suffer.

The doctor's trouble came to a head the first. It was true Doctor **was** engaged and to be married soon. He told Anna so himself.

What was the good Anna now to do? Dr. Shonjen wanted her of course to stay. Anna was so sad with all these troubles. She knew here in the doctor's house it would be bad when he was married, but she had not the strength now to be firm and go away. She said at last that she would try and stay.

Doctor got married now very soon. Anna made the house all beautiful and clean and she really hoped that she might stay. But this was not for long.

Mrs. Shonjen was a proud, unpleasant woman. She wanted constant service and attention and never even a thank you to a servant. Soon all Doctor's old people went away. Anna went to Doctor and explained. She told him what all the servants thought of his new wife. Anna bade him a sad farewell and went away.

Anna was now most uncertain what to do. She could go to Curden to her Miss Mary Wadsmith who always wrote how much she needed Anna, but Anna still dreaded Miss Jane's interfering ways. Then too, she could not yet go away from Bridgepoint and from Mrs. Lehntman, unpleasant as it always was now over there.

Through one of Doctor's friends Anna heard of Miss Mathilda. Anna was very doubtful about working for a Miss Mathilda. She did not think it would be good working for a woman any more. She had found it very good with Miss Mary but she did not think that many women would be so.

Most women were interfering in their ways.

Anna heard that Miss Mathilda was a great big woman, not so big perhaps as her Miss Mary, still she was big, and the good Anna liked them better so. She did not like them thin and small and active and always looking in and always prying.

Anna could not make up her mind what was the best thing now for her to do. She could sew and this way make a living, but she did not like such business very well.

Mrs. Lehntman urged the place with Miss Mathilda. She was sure Anna would find it better so. The good Anna did not know.

"Well, Anna," Mrs. Lehntman said, "I tell you what we do. I go with you to that woman that tells fortunes, perhaps she tell us something that will show us what is the best way for you now to do."

It was very bad to go to a woman who tells fortunes. Anna was of strong South German Catholic religion and the German priests in the churches always said that it was very bad to do things so. But what else now could the good Anna do? She was so mixed and bothered in her mind, and troubled with this life that was all wrong, though she did try so hard to do the best she knew. "All right, Mrs. Lehntman," Anna said at last, "I think I go there now with you."

This woman who told fortunes was a medium. She had a house in the lower quarter of the town. Mrs. Lehntman and the good Anna went to her.

The medium opened the door for them herself. She was a loose-made, dusty, dowdy woman with a persuading, conscious and embracing manner and very greasy hair.

The woman let them come into the house.

The street door opened straight into the parlor, as is the way in the small houses of the South. The parlor had a thick and flowered carpet on the floor. The room was full of dirty things all made by hand. Some hung upon the wall, some were on the seats and over backs of chairs and some on tables and on those what-nots that poor people love. And everywhere were little things that break. Many of these little things were broken and the place was stuffy and not clean.

No medium uses her parlor for her work. It is always in her eating room that she has her trances.

The eating room in all these houses is the living room in winter. It has a round table in the center covered with a decorated woolen cloth, that has soaked in the grease of many dinners, for though it should be always taken off, it is easier to spread the cloth upon it than change it for the blanket deadener that one owns. The upholstered chairs are dark and worn, and dirty. The carpet has grown dingy with the food that's fallen from the table, the dirt that's scraped from off the shoes, and the dust that settles with the ages. The somber greenish colored paper on the walls has been smoked a dismal dirty gray, and all pervading is the smell of soup made out of onions and fat chunks of meat.

The medium brought Mrs. Lehntman and our Anna into this eating room, after she had found out what it was they wanted. They all three sat around the table and then the medium went into her trance.

The medium first closed her eyes and then they opened very wide and lifeless. She took a number of deep breaths, choked several times and swallowed very hard. She waved her hand back every now and then, and she began to speak in a monotonous slow, even tone.

"I see—I see—don't crowd so on me,—I see—I see—too many forms —don't crowd so on me—I see—I see—you are thinking of something —you don't know whether you want to do it now. I see—I see—don't crowd so on me—I see—I see—you are not sure,—I see—I see—a house with trees around it—it is dark—it is evening—I see—I see—you go in the house—I see—I see you come out—it will be all right—you go and do it—do what you are not certain about—it will come out all right— it is best and you should do it now."

She stopped, she made deep gulps, her eyes rolled back into her head, she swallowed hard and then she was her former dingy and bland self again.

"Did you get what you wanted that the spirit should tell you?" the woman asked. Mrs. Lehntman answered yes, it was just what her friend had wanted so bad to know. Anna was uneasy in this house with super-stition, with fear of her good priest, and with disgust at all the dirt and grease, but she was most content for now she knew what it was best for her to do.

Anna paid the woman for her work and then they came away.

"There, Anna, didn't I tell you how it would all be? You see the spirit says so too. You must take the place with Miss Mathilda, that is what I told you was the best thing for you to do. We go out and see her where she lives tonight. Ain't you glad, Anna, that I took you to this place, so you know now what you will do?"

Mrs. Lehntman and Anna went that evening to see Miss Mathilda. Miss Mathilda was staying with a friend who lived in a house that did have trees about. Miss Mathilda was not there herself to talk with Anna.

If it had not been that it was evening, and so dark, and that this house had trees all round about, and that Anna found herself going in and coming out just as the woman that day said that she would do, had it not all been just as the medium said, the good Anna would never have taken the place with Miss Mathilda.

Anna did not see Miss Mathilda and she did not like the friend who acted in her place.

This friend was a dark, sweet, gentle little mother woman, very easy to be pleased in her own work and very good to servants, but she felt that acting for her young friend, the careless Miss Mathilda, she must be very careful to examine well and see that all was right and that Anna would surely do the best she knew. She asked Anna all about her ways and her intentions and how much she would spend, and how often she went out and whether she could wash and cook and sew.

The good Anna set her teeth fast to endure and would hardly answer anything at all. Mrs. Lehntman made it all go fairly well.

The good Anna was all worked up with her resentment, and Mis Mathilda's friend did not think that she would do.

However, Miss Mathilda was willing to begin and as for Anna, she knew that the medium said it must be so. Mrs. Lehntman, too, was sure, and said she knew that this was the best thing for Anna now to do. So Anna sent word at last to Miss Mathilda, that if she wanted her, she would try if it would do.

So Anna began a new life taking care of Miss Mathilda.

Anna fixed up the little red brick house where Miss Mathilda was going to live and made it very pleasant, clean and nice. She brought over her dog, Baby, and her parrot. She hired Lizzie for a second girl to be with her and soon they were all content. All except the parrot, for Miss Mathilda did not like its scream. Baby was all right but not the parrot. But then Anna never really loved the parrot, and so she gave it to the Drehten girls to keep.

Before Anna could really rest content with Miss Mathilda, she had to tell her good German priest what it was that she had done, and how very bad it was that she had been and how she would never do so again.

Anna really did believe with all her might. It was her fortune never to live with people who had any faith, but then that never worried Anna. She prayed for them always as she should, and she was very sure that they were good. The doctor loved to tease her with his doubts and Miss Mathilda liked to do so too, but with the tolerant spirit of her church, Anna never thought that such things were bad for them to do.

Anna found it hard to always know just why it was that things went wrong. Sometimes her glasses broke and then she knew that she had not done her duty by the church, just in the way that she should do.

Sometimes she was so hard at work that she would not go to mass. Something always happened then. Anna's temper grew irritable and her ways uncertain and distraught. Everybody suffered and then her glasses broke. That was always very bad because they cost so much to fix. Still in a way it always ended Anna's troubles, because she knew then that all this was because she had been bad. As long as she could scold it might be just the bad ways of all the thoughtless careless world, but when her glasses broke that made it clear. That meant that it was she herself who had been bad.

No, it was no use for Anna not to do the way she should, for things always then went wrong and finally cost money to make whole, and this was the hardest thing for the good Anna to endure.

Anna almost always did her duty. She made confession and her mission whenever it was right. Of course she did not tell the father when she deceived people for their good, or when she wanted them to give something for a little less.

When Anna told such histories to her doctor and later to her cherished Miss Mathilda, her eyes were always full of humor and enjoyment as she explained that she had said it so, and now she would not have to tell the father for she had not really made a sin.

But going to a fortune teller Anna knew was really bad. That had to be told to the father just as it was and penance had then to be done.

Anna did this and now her new life was well begun, making Miss Mathilda and the rest do just the way they should.

Yes, taking care of Miss Mathilda were the happiest days of all the good Anna's strong hard-working life.

With Miss Mathilda Anna did it all. The clothes, the house, the hats, what she should wear and when and what was always best for her to do. There was nothing Miss Mathilda would not let Anna manage, and only be too glad if she would do.

Anna scolded and cooked and sewed and saved so well, that Miss Mathilda had so much to spend, that it kept Anna still busier scolding all the time about the things she bought, that made so much work for Anna and the other girl to do. But for all the scolding, Anna was proud almost to bursting of her cherished Miss Mathilda with all her knowledge and her great possessions, and the good Anna was always telling of it all to everybody that she knew.

Yes, these were the happiest days of all her life with Anna, even though with her friends there were great sorrows. But these sorrows did not hurt the good Anna now, as they had done in the years that went before.

Miss Mathilda was not a romance in the good Anna's life, but Anna gave her so much strong affection that it almost filled her life as full.

It was well for the good Anna that her life with Miss Mathilda was so happy, for now in these days, Mrs. Lehntman went altogether bad. The doctor she had learned to know, was too certainly an evil as well as a mysterious man, and he had power over the widow and midwife, Mrs. Lehntman.

Anna never saw Mrs. Lehntman at all now any more.

Mrs. Lehntman had borrowed some more money and had given Anna a note then for it all, and after that Anna never saw her any more. Anna now stopped altogether going to the Lehntmans'. Julia, the tall, gawky, good, blonde, stupid daughter, came often to see Anna, but she could tell little of her mother.

It certainly did look very much as if Mrs. Lehntman had now gone altogether bad. This was a great grief to the good Anna, but not so great a grief as it would have been had not Miss Mathilda meant so much to her now.

Mrs. Lehntman went from bad to worse. The doctor, the mysterious and evil man, got into trouble doing things that were not right to do.

Mrs. Lehntman was mixed up in this affair.

It was just as bad as it could be, but they managed, both the doctor and Mrs. Lehntman, finally to come out safe.

Everybody was so sorry about Mrs. Lehntman. She had been really a good woman before she met this doctor, and even now she certainly had not been really bad.

For several years now Anna never even saw her friend.

But Anna always found new people to befriend, people who, in the kindly fashion of the poor, used up her savings and then gave promises in place of payments. Anna never really thought that these people would be good, but when they did not do the way they should, and when they did not pay her back the money she had loaned, and never seemed the better for her care, then Anna would grow bitter with the world.

No, none of them had any sense of what was the right way for them to do. So Anna would repeat in her despair.

The poor are generous with their things. They give always what they have, but with them to give or to receive brings with it no feeling that they owe the giver for the gift.

Even a thrifty German Anna was ready to give all that she had saved, and so not be sure that she would have enough to take care of herself if she fell sick, or for old age, when she could not work. Save and you will have the money you have saved was true only for the day of saving, even for a thrifty German Anna. There was no certain way to have it for old age, for the taking care of what is saved can never be relied on, for it must always be in strangers' hands in a bank or in investments by a friend.

And so when any day one might need life and help from others of the working poor, there was no way a woman who had a little saved could say them no.

So the good Anna gave her all to friends and strangers, to children, dogs and cats, to anything that asked or seemed to need her care.

It was in this way that Anna came to help the barber and his wife who lived around the corner, and who somehow could never make ends meet. They worked hard, were thrifty, had no vices, but the barber was one of them who never can make money. Whoever owed him money did not pay. Whenever he had a chance at a good job he fell sick and could not take it. It was never his own fault that he had trouble, but he never seemed to make things come out right.

His wife was a blonde, thin, pale, German little woman, who bore her children very hard, and worked too soon, and then till she was sick. She too always had things that went wrong.

They both needed constant help and patience, and the good Anna gave both to them all the time.

Another woman who needed help from the good Anna, was one who was in trouble from being good to others.

This woman's husband's brother, who was very good, worked in a shop where there was a Bohemian, who was getting sick with a consumption. This man got so much worse he could not do his work, but he was not so sick that he could stay in a hospital. So this woman had him living there with her. He was not a nice man, nor was he thankful for all the woman did for him. He was cross to her two children and made a great mess always in her house. The doctor said he must have many things to eat, and the woman and the brother of the husband got them for him.

There was no friendship, no affection, no liking even for the man this woman cared for, no claim of common country or kin, but in the kindly fashion of the poor this woman gave her all and made her house a nasty place, and for a man who was not even grateful for the gift.

Then, of course, the woman herself got into trouble. Her husband's brother was now married. Her husband lost his job. She did not have the money for the rent. It was the good Anna's savings that were handy.

So it went on. Sometimes a little girl, sometimes a big one was in trouble and Anna heard of them and helped them to find places.

Stray dogs and cats Anna always kept until she found them homes. She was always careful to learn whether these people would be good to animals.

Out of the whole collection of stray creatures, it was the young Peter and the jolly little Rags, Anna could not find it in her heart to part with. These became part of the household of the good Anna's Miss Mathilda.

Peter was a very useless creature, a foolish, silly, cherished, coward male. It was wild to see him rush up and down in the back yard, barking and bouncing at the wall, when there was some dog out beyond, but when the very littlest one there was got inside of the fence and only looked at Peter, Peter would retire to his Anna and blot himself out between her skirts.

When Peter was left downstairs alone, he howled. "I am all alone," he wailed, and then the good Anna would have to come and fetch him up. Once when Anna stayed a few nights in a house not far away, she had to carry Peter all the way, for Peter was afraid when he found himself on the street outside his house. Peter was a good-sized creature and he sat there and he howled, and the good Anna carried him all the way in her own arms. He was a coward was this Peter, but he had kindly, gentle eyes and a pretty collie head, and his fur was very thick and white and nice when he was washed. And then Peter never strayed away, and he looked out of his nice eyes and he liked it when you rubbed him down, and he forgot you when you went away, and he barked whenever there was any noise.

When he was a little pup he had one night been put into the yard and that was all of his origin she knew. The good Anna loved him well and spoiled him as a good German mother always does her son.

Little Rags was very different in his nature. He was a lively creature made out of ends of things, all fluffy and dust color, and he was always bounding up into the air and darting all about over and then under silly Peter and often straight into solemn fat, blind, sleepy Baby, and then in a wild rush after some stray cat.

Rags was a pleasant, jolly little fellow. The good Anna liked him very well, but never with her strength as she loved her good-looking coward, foolish young man, Peter.

Baby was the dog of her past life and she held Anna with old ties of past affection. Peter was the spoiled, good-looking young man, of her

middle age, and Rags was always something of a toy. She liked him but
he never struck in very deep. Rags had strayed in somehow one day
and then when no home for him was quickly found, he had just stayed
right there.

It was a very happy family there all together in the kitchen, the good
Anna and Sallie and old Baby and young Peter and the jolly little Rags.

The parrot had passed out of Anna's life. She had really never loved
the parrot and now she hardly thought to ask for him, even when she
visited the Drehtens.

Mrs. Drehten was the friend Anna always went to, for her Sundays.
She did not get advice from Mrs. Drehten as she used to from the
widow, Mrs. Lehntman, for Mrs. Drehten was a mild, worn, unaggres-
sive nature that never cared to influence or to lead. But they could
mourn together for the world these two worn, working German women,
for its sadness and its wicked ways of doing. Mrs. Drehten knew so
well what one could suffer.

Things did not go well in these days with the Drehtens. The
children were all good, but the father with his temper and his spending
kept everything from being what it should.

Poor Mrs. Drehten still had trouble with her tumor. She could hardly
do any work now any more. Mrs. Drehten was a large, worn, patient
German woman, with a soft face, lined, yellow brown in color and the
look that comes from a German husband to obey, and many solid girls
and boys to bear and rear, and from being always on one's feet and
never having any troubles cured.

Mrs. Drehten was always getting worse, and now the doctor thought
it would be best to take the tumor out.

It was no longer Dr. Shonjen who treated Mrs. Drehten. They all
went now to a good old German doctor they all knew.

"You see, Miss Mathilda," Anna said, "All the old German patients
don't go no more now to Doctor. I stayed with him just so long as I could
stand it, but now he is moved away up town too far for poor people,
and his wife, she holds her head up so and always is spending so much
money just for show, and so he can't take right care of us poor people
any more. Poor man, he has got always to be thinking about making
money now. I am awful sorry about Doctor, Miss Mathilda, but he
neglected Mrs. Drehten shameful when she had her trouble, so now
I never see him any more. Doctor Herman is a good, plain, German
doctor and he would never do things so, and Miss Mathilda, Mrs.
Drehten is coming in tomorrow to see you before she goes to the hospital for her operation. She could not go comfortable till she had seen
you first to see what you would say."

All Anna's friends reverenced the good Anna's cherished Miss Mathilda. How could they not do so and still remain friends with the good Anna? Miss Mathilda rarely really saw them but they were always sending flowers and words of admiration through her Anna. Every now and then Anna would bring one of them to Miss Mathilda for advice.

It is wonderful how poor people love to take advice from people who are friendly and above them, from people who read in books and who are good.

Miss Mathilda saw Mrs. Drehten and told her she was glad that she was going to the hospital for operation for that surely would be best, and so good Mrs. Drehten's mind was set at rest.

Mrs. Drehten's tumor came out very well. Mrs. Drehten was afterwards never really well, but she could do her work a little better, and be on her feet and yet not get so tired.

And so Anna's life went on, taking care of Miss Mathilda and all her clothes and goods, and being good to every one that asked or seemed to need her help.

Now, slowly, Anna began to make it up with Mrs. Lehntman. They could never be as they had been before. Mrs. Lehntman could never be again the romance in the good Anna's life, but they could be friends again, and Anna could help all the Lehntmans in their need. This slowly came about.

Mrs. Lehntman had now left the evil and mysterious man who had been the cause of all her trouble. She had given up, too, the new big house that she had taken. Since her trouble her practice had been very quiet. Still she managed to do fairly well. She began to talk of paying the good Anna. This, however, had not gotten very far.

Anna saw Mrs. Lehntman a good deal now. Mrs. Lehntman's crisp, black, curly hair had gotten streaked with gray. Her dark, full, good-looking face had lost its firm outline, gone flabby and a little worn. She had grown stouter and her clothes did not look very nice. She was as bland as ever in her ways, and as diffuse as always in her attention, but through it all there was uneasiness and fear and uncertainty lest some danger might be near.

She never said a word of her past life to the good Anna, but it was very plain to see that her experience had not left her easy, nor yet altogether free.

It had been hard for this good woman, for Mrs. Lehntman was really a good woman, it had been a very hard thing for this German woman to do what everybody knew and thought was wrong. Mrs. Lehntman was strong and she had courage, but it had been very hard to bear. Even the good Anna did not speak to her with freedom. There always remained a mystery and a depression in Mrs Lehntman's affair.

And now the blonde, foolish, awkward daughter, Julia was in trouble. During the years the mother gave her no attention, Julia kept company with a young fellow who was a clerk somewhere in a store down in the city. He was a decent, dull young fellow, who did not make much money and could never save it, for he had an old mother he supported. He and Julia had been keeping company for several years and now it was needful that they should be married. But then how could they marry? He did not make enough to start them and to keep on supporting his old mother too. Julia was not used to working much and she said, and she was stubborn, that she would not live with Charley's dirty, cross, old mother. Mrs. Lehntman had no money. She was just beginning to get on her feet. It was of course, the good Anna's savings that were handy.

However, it paid Anna to bring about this marriage, paid her in scoldings and in managing the dull, long, awkward Julia, and her good, patient, stupid Charley. Anna loved to buy things cheap, and fix up a new place.

Julia and Charley were soon married and things went pretty well with them. Anna did not approve their slack, expensive ways of doing.

"No, Miss Mathilda," she would say, "The young people nowadays have no sense for saving and putting money by so they will have something to use when they need it. There's Julia and her Charley. I went in there the other day, Miss Mathilda, and they had a new table with a marble top and on it they had a grand new plush album. 'Where you get that album?' I asked Julia. 'Oh, Charley he gave it to me for my birthday,' she said, and I asked her if it was paid for and she said not all yet but it would be soon. Now I ask you what business have they, Miss Mathilda, when they ain't paid for anything they got already, what business have they to be buying new things for her birthdays. Julia she don't do no work, she just sits around and thinks how she can spend the money, and Charley he never puts one cent by. I never see anything like the people nowadays, Miss Mathilda, they don't seem to have any sense of being careful about money. Julia and Charley when they have any children they won't have nothing to bring them up with right. I said that to Julia, Miss Mathilda, when she showed me those silly things that Charley bought her, and she just said in her silly, giggling way, perhaps they won't have any children. I told her she ought to be ashamed of talking so, but I don't know, Miss Mathilda, the young people nowadays have no sense at all of what's the right way for them to do, and perhaps it's better if they don't have any children, and then Miss Mathilda you know there is Mrs. Lehntman. You know she regular adopted little Johnny just so she could pay out some more money just as if she didn't have trouble enough taking care of her own children. No, Miss Mathilda, I never see how people can do things so. People don't seem to have no sense of right or wrong or anything these days, Miss Mathilde; they are just careless and thinking always of themselves and how they can always have a happy time. No, Miss Mathilda, I don't see how people can go on and do things so."

The good Anna could not understand the careless and bad ways of all the world and always she grew bitter with it all. No, not one of them had any sense of what was the right way for them to do.

Anna's past life was now drawing to an end. Her old blind dog, Baby, was sick and like to die. Baby had been the first gift from her friend the widow, Mrs. Lehntman, in the old days when Anna had been with Miss Mary Wadsmith, and when these two women had first come together.

Through all the years of change, Baby had stayed with the good Anna, growing old and fat and blind and lazy. Baby had been active and a ratter when she was young, but that was so long ago it was forgotten, and for many years now Baby had wanted only her warm basket and her dinner.

Anna in her active life found need of others, of Peter and the funny little Rags, but always Baby was the eldest and held her with the ties of old affection. Anna was harsh when the young ones tried to keep poor Baby out and use her basket. Baby had been blind now for some years as dogs get, when they are no longer active. She got weak and fat and breathless and she could not even stand long any more. Anna had always to see that she got her dinner and that the young active ones did not deprive her.

Baby did not die with a real sickness. She just got older and more blind and coughed and then more quiet, and then slowly one bright summer's day she died.

There is nothing more dreary than old age in animals. Somehow it is all wrong that they should have gray hair and withered skin, and blind old eyes, and decayed and useless teeth. An old man or an old woman almost always has some tie that seems to bind them to the younger, realer life. They have children or the remembrance of old duties, but a dog that's old and so cut off from all its world of struggle, is like a dreary, deathless Struldbrug, the dreary dragger on of death through life.

And so one day old Baby died. It was dreary, more than sad, for the good Anna. She did not want the poor old beast to linger with its weary age, and blind old eyes and dismal shaking cough, but this death left Anna very empty. She had the foolish young man Peter, and the jolly little Rags for comfort, but Baby had been the only one that could remember.

The good Anna wanted a real graveyard for her Baby, but this could not be in a Christian country, and so Anna all alone took her old friend done up in decent wrappings and put her into the ground in some quiet place that Anna knew of.

The good Anna did not weep for poor old Baby. Nay, she had not time even to feel lonely, for with the good Anna it was sorrow upon sorrow. She was now no longer to keep house for Miss Mathilda.

When Anna had first come to Miss Mathilda she had known that it might only be for a few years, for Miss Mathilda was given to much wandering and often changed her home, and found new places where she went to live. The good Anna did not then think much about this, for when she first went to Miss Mathilda she had not thought that she would like it and so he had not worried about staying. Then in those happy years that they had been together, Anna had made herself forget it. This last year when she knew that it was coming she had tried hard to think it would not happen.

"We won't talk about it now, Miss Mathilda, perhaps we all be dead by then," she would say when Miss Mathilda tried to talk it over. Or, "If we live till then, Miss Mathilda, perhaps you will be staying on right here."

No, the good Anna could not talk as if this thing were real, it was too weary to be once more left with strangers.

Both the good Anna and her cherished Miss Mathilda tried hard to think that this would not really happen. Anna made missions and all kinds of things to keep her Miss Mathilda and Miss Mathilda thought out all the ways to see if the good Anna could not go with her, but neither the missions nor the plans had much success. Miss Mathilda would go, and she was going far away to a new country where Anna could not live, for she would be too lonesome.

There was nothing that these two could do but part. Perhaps we all be dead by then, the good Anna would repeat, but even that did not really happen. If we all live till then, Miss Mathilda, came out truer. They all did live till then, all except poor old blind Baby, and they simply had to part.

Poor Anna and poor Miss Mathilda. They could not look at each other that last day. Anna could not keep herself busy working. She just went in and out and sometimes scolded.

Anna could not make up her mind what she should do now for her future. She said that she would for a while keep this little red brick house that they had lived in. Perhaps she might just take in a few boarders. She did not know, she would write about it later and tell it all to Miss Mathilda.

The dreary day dragged out and then all was ready and Miss Mathilda left to take her train. Anna stood strained and pale and dry eyed on the white stone steps of the little red brick house that they had lived in.

The last thing Miss Mathilda heard was the good Anna bidding foolish Peter say good-by and be sure to remember Miss Mathilda.

III. THE DEATH OF GOOD ANNA

Everyone who had known of Miss Mathilda wanted the good Anna now to take a place with them, for they all knew how well Anna could take care of people and all their clothes and goods. Anna too could always go to Curden to Miss Mary Wadsmith, but none of all these ways seemed very good to Anna.

It was not now any longer that she wanted to stay near Mrs. Lehntman. There was no one now that made anything important, but Anna was certain that she did not want to take a place where she would be under some new people. No one could ever be for Anna as had been her cherished Miss Mathilda. No one could ever again so freely let her do it all. It would be better Anna thought in her strong strained weary body, it would be better just to keep on there in the little red brick house that was all furnished, and make a living taking in some boarders. Miss Mathilda had let her have the things, so it would not cost any money to begin. She could perhaps manage to live on so. She could do all the work and do everything as she thought best, and she was too weary with the changes to do more than she just had to, to keep living. So she stayed on in the house where they had lived, and she found some men, she would not take in women, who took her rooms and who were her boarders.

Things soon with Anna began to be less dreary. She was very popular with her few boarders. They loved her scoldings and the good things she made for them to eat. They made good jokes and laughed loud and always did whatever Anna wanted, and soon the good Anna got so that she liked it very well. Not that she did not always long for Miss Mathilda. She hoped and waited and was very certain that some time, in one year or in another Miss Mathilda would come back, and then of course would want her, and then she could take all good care of her again.

Anna kept all Miss Mathilda's things in the best order. The boarders were well scolded if they ever made a scratch on Miss Mathilda's table.

Some of the boarders were hearty good South German fellows and Anna always made them go to mass. One boarder was a lusty German student who was studying in Bridgepoint to be a doctor. He was Anna's special favorite and she scolded him as she used to her old doctor so that he always would be good. Then, too, this cheery fellow always sang when he was washing, and that was what Miss Mathilda always used to do. Anna's heart grew warm again with this young fellow who seemed to bring back to her everything she needed.

And so Anna's life in these days was not all unhappy. She worked and scolded, she had her stray dogs and cats and people, who all asked and seemed to need her care, and she had hearty German fellows who loved her scoldings and ate so much of the good things that she knew so well the way to make.

No, the good Anna's life in these days was not all unhappy. She did not see her old friends much, she was too busy, but once in a great while she took a Sunday afternoon and went to see good Mrs. Drehten.

The only trouble was that Anna hardly made a living. She charged so little for her board and gave her people such good things to eat, that she could only just make both ends meet. The good German priest to whom she always told her troubles tried to make her have the boarders pay a little higher, and Miss Mathilda always in her letters urged her to this thing, but the good Anna somehow could not do it. Her boarders were nice men but she knew they did not have much money, and then she could not raise on those who had been with her and she could not ask the new ones to pay higher, when those who were already there were paying just what they had paid before. So Anna let it go just as she had begun it. She worked and worked all day and thought all night how she could save, and with all the work she just managed to keep living. She could not make enough to lay any money by.

Anna got so little money that she had all the work to do herself. She could not pay even the little Sallie enough to keep her with her.

Not having little Sallie nor having anyone else working with her, made it very hard for Anna ever to go out, for she never thought that it was right to leave a house all empty. Once in a great while of a Sunday, Sallie who was now working in a factory would come and stay in the house for the good Anna, who would then go out and spend the afternoon with Mrs. Drehten.

No, Anna did not see her old friends much any more. She went sometimes to see her half brother and his wife and her nieces, and they always came to her on her birthdays to give presents, and her half brother never left her out of his festive raisined-bread-giving progresses. But these relatives of hers had never meant very much to the good Anna. Anna always did her duty by them all, and she liked her half brother very well and the loaves of raisined bread that he supplied her were most welcome now, and Anna always gave her goddaughter and her sister handsome presents, but no one in this family had ever made a way inside to Anna's feelings.

Mrs. Lehntman she saw very rarely. It is hard to build up new on an old friendship when in that friendship there has been bitter disillusion. They did their best, both these women, to be friends, but they were never able to again touch one another nearly. There were too many things between them that they could not speak of, things that had never been explained nor yet forgiven. The good Anna still did her best for foolish Julia and still every now and then saw Mrs. Lehntman, but this family had now lost all its real hold on Anna.

Mrs. Drehten was now the best friend that Anna knew. Here there was never any more than the mingling of their sorrows. They talked over all the time the best way for Mrs. Drehten now to do; poor Mrs. Drehten who with her chief trouble, her bad husband, had really now no way that she could do. She just had to work and to be patient and to love her children and be very quiet. She always had a soothing mother influence on the good Anna who with her irritable, strained, worn-out body would come and sit by Mrs. Drehten and talk all her troubles over.

Of all the friends that the good Anna had had in these twenty years in Bridgepoint, the good father and patient Mrs. Drehten were the only ones that were now near to Anna and with whom she could talk her troubles over.

Anna worked, and thought, and saved, and scolded, and took care of all the boarders, and of Peter and of Rags, and all the others. There was never any end to Anna's effort and she grew always more tired, more pale yellow, and in her face more thin and worn and worried. Sometimes she went farther in not being well, and then she went to see Dr. Herman who had operated on good Mrs. Drehten.

The things that Anna really needed were to rest sometimes and eat more so that she could get stronger, but these were the last things that Anna could bring herself to do. Anna could never take a rest. She must work hard through the summer as well as through the winter, else she could never make both ends meet. The doctor gave her medicines to make her stronger but these did not seem to do much good.

Anna grew always more tired, her headaches came oftener and harder, and she was now almost always feeling very sick. She could not sleep much in the night. The dogs with their noises disturbed her and everything in her body seemed to pain her.

The doctor and the good father tried often to make her give herself more care. Mrs. Drehten told her that she surely would not get well unless for a little while she would stop working. Anna would then promise to take care, to rest in bed a little longer and to eat more so that she would get stronger, but really how could Anna eat when she always did the cooking and was so tired of it all, before it was half ready for the table?

Anna's only friendship now was with good Mrs. Drehten who was too gentle and too patient to make a stubborn faithful German Anna ever do the way she should, in the things that were for her own good.

Anna grew worse all through this second winter. When the summer came the doctor said that she simply could not live on so. He said she must go to his hospital and there he would operate upon her. She would then be well and strong and able to work hard all next winter.

Anna for some time would not listen. She could not do this, for she had her house all furnished and she simply could not let it go. At last a woman came and said she would take care of Anna's boarders and then Anna said that she was prepared to go.

Anna went to the hospital for her operation. Mrs. Drehten was herself not well but she came into the city, so that some friend would be with the good Anna. Together, then, they went to this place where the doctor had done so well by Mrs. Drehten.

In a few days they had Anna ready. Then they did the operation, and then the good Anna with her strong, strained, worn-out body died.

Mrs. Drehten sent word of her death to Miss Mathilda.

"Dear Miss Mathilda," wrote Mrs. Drehten, "Miss Annie died in the hospital yesterday after a hard operation. She was talking about you and Doctor and Miss Mary Wadsmith all the time. She said she hoped you would take Peter and the little Rags to keep when you came back to America to live. I will keep them for you here, Miss Mathilda. Miss Annie died easy, Miss Mathilda, and sent you her love."

39

Paul's Case

BY WILLA CATHER

I T was Paul's afternoon to appear before the faculty of the Pittsburgh High School to account for his various misdemeanors. He had been suspended a week ago, and his father had called at the Principal's office and confessed his perplexity about his son. Paul entered the faculty room suave and smiling. His clothes were a trifle outgrown, and the tan velvet on the collar of his open overcoat was frayed and worn; but for all that there was something of the dandy about him, and he wore an opal pin in his neatly knotted black four-in-hand, and a red carnation in his buttonhole. This latter adornment the faculty somehow felt was not properly significant of the contrite spirit befitting a boy under the ban of suspension.

Paul was tall for his age and very thin, with high, cramped shoulders and a narrow chest. His eyes were remarkable for a certain hysterical brilliancy, and he continually used them in a conscious, theatrical sort of way, peculiarly offensive in a boy. The pupils were abnormally large, as though he were addicted to belladonna, but there was a glassy glitter about them which that drug does not produce.

When questioned by the Principal as to why he was there, Paul stated, politely enough, that he wanted to come back to school. This was a lie, but Paul was quite accustomed to lying; found it, indeed, indispensable for overcoming friction. His teachers were asked to state their respective charges against him, which they did with such a rancor and aggrieved-ness as evinced that this was not a usual case. Disorder and impertinence were among the offenses named, yet each of his instructors felt that it was scarcely possible to put into words the real cause of the trouble, which lay in a sort of hysterically defiant manner of the boy's; in the contempt which they all knew he felt for them, and which he seemingly made not the least effort to conceal. Once, when he had been making a synopsis of a paragraph at the blackboard, his English teacher had stepped to his side and attempted to guide his hand. Paul had started back with a shudder and thrust his hands violently behind him. The astonished woman could scarcely have been more hurt and embarrassed had he struck at her. The insult was so involuntary and definitely personal as to be unforgettable. In one way and another, he had made all his teachers, men and women alike, conscious of the same feeling of physical aversion. In one class he habitually sat with his hand shading his eyes; in another he always looked out of the window during the recitation; in another he made a running commentary on the lecture, with humorous intent.

His teachers felt this afternoon that his whole attitude was symbolized by his shrug and his flippantly red carnation flower, and they fell upon him without mercy, his English teacher leading the pack. He stood through it smiling, his pale lips parted over his white teeth. (His lips were continually twitching, and he had a habit of raising his eyebrows that was contemptuous and irritating to the last degree.) Older boys than Paul had broken down and shed tears under that ordeal, but his set smile did not once desert him, and his only sign of discomfort was the nervous trembling of the fingers that toyed with the buttons of his overcoat, and an occasional jerking of the other hand which held his hat. Paul was always smiling, always glancing about him, seeming to feel that people might be watching him and trying to detect something. This conscious expression, since it was as far as possible from boyish mirthfulness, was usually attributed to insolence or "smartness."

As the inquisition proceeded, one of his instructors repeated an impertinent remark of the boy's, and the Principal asked him whether he thought that a courteous speech to make to a woman. Paul shrugged his shoulders slightly and his eyebrows twitched.

"I don't know," he replied. "I didn't mean to be polite or impolite, either. I guess it's a sort of way I have, of saying things regardless."

The Principal asked him whether he didn't think that a way it would be well to get rid of. Paul grinned and said he guessed so. When he was told that he could go, he bowed gracefully and went out. His bow was like a repetition of the scandalous red carnation.

His teachers were in despair, and his drawing master voiced the feeling of them all when he declared there was something about the boy which none of them understood. He added: "I don't really believe that smile of his comes altogether from insolence; there's something sort of haunted about it. The boy is not strong, for one thing. There is something wrong about the fellow."

The drawing master had come to realize that, in looking at Paul, one saw only his white teeth and the forced animation of his eyes. One warm afternoon the boy had gone to sleep at his drawing board, and his master had noted with amazement what a white, blue-veined face it was; drawn and wrinkled like an old man's about the eyes, the lips twitching even in his sleep.

His teachers left the building dissatisfied and unhappy; humiliated to have felt so vindictive toward a mere boy, to have uttered this feeling in cutting terms, and to have set each other on, as it were, in the gruesome game of intemperate reproach. One of them remembered having seen a miserable street cat set at bay by a ring of tormentors.

As for Paul, he ran down the hill whistling the Soldiers' Chorus from *Faust,* looking wildly behind him now and then to see whether some of his teachers were not there to witness his light-heartedness. As it was now late in the afternoon and Paul was on duty that evening as usher at Carnegie Hall, he decided that he would not go home to supper.

When he reached the concert hall the doors were not yet open. It was chilly outside, and he decided to go up into the picture gallery—always deserted at this hour—where there were some of Raffelli's gay studies of Paris streets and an airy blue Venetian scene or two that always exhilarated him. He was delighted to find no one in the gallery but the old guard, who sat in the corner, a newspaper on his knee, a black patch over one eye and the other closed. Paul possessed himself of the place and walked confidently up and down, whistling under his breath. After a while he sat down before a blue Rico and lost himself. When he bethought him to look at his watch, it was after seven o'clock, and he rose with a start and ran downstairs, making a face at Augustus Cæsar, peering out from the cast-room, and an evil gesture at the Venus of Milo as he passed her on the stairway.

When Paul reached the ushers' dressing-room half a dozen boys were there already, and he began excitedly to tumble into his uniform. It was one of the few that at all approached fitting, and Paul thought it very becoming—though he knew the tight, straight coat accentuated his narrow chest, about which he was exceedingly sensitive. He was always excited while he dressed, twanging all over to the tuning of the strings and the preliminary flourishes of the horns in the music-room; but tonight he seemed quite beside himself, and he teased and plagued the boys until, telling him that he was crazy, they put him down on the floor and sat on him.

Somewhat calmed by his suppression, Paul dashed out to the front of the house to seat the early comers. He was a model usher. Gracious and smiling he ran up and down the aisles. Nothing was too much trouble for him; he carried messages and brought programs as though it were his greatest pleasure in life, and all the people in his section thought him a charming boy, feeling that he remembered and admired them. As the house filled, he grew more and more vivacious and animated, and the color came to his cheeks and lips. It was very much as though this were a great reception and Paul were the host. Just as the musicians came out to take their places, his English teacher arrived with checks for the seats which a prominent manufacturer had taken for the season. She betrayed some embarrassment when she handed Paul the tickets, and a *hauteur* which subsequently made her feel very foolish. Paul was startled for a moment, and had the feeling of wanting to put her out; what business had she here among all these fine people and gay colors? He looked her over and decided that she was not appropriately dressed and must be a fool to sit downstairs in such togs. The tickets had probably been sent her out of kindness, he reflected, as he put down a seat for her, and she had about as much right to sit there as he had.

When the symphony began Paul sank into one of the rear seats with a long sigh of relief, and lost himself as he had done before the Rico. It was not that symphonies, as such, meant anything in particular to Paul, but the first sigh of the instruments seemed to free some hilarious spirit within him; something that struggled there like the Genius in the bottle found by the Arab fisherman. He felt a sudden zest of life; the lights danced before his eyes and the concert hall blazed into unimaginable splendor. When the soprano soloist came on, Paul forgot even the nastiness of his teacher's being there, and gave himself up to the peculiar intoxication such personages always had for him. The soloist chanced to be a German woman, by no means in her first youth, and the mother of many children; but she wore a satin gown and a tiara, and she had that indefinable air of achievement, that world-shine upon her, which always blinded Paul to any possible defects.

After a concert was over, Paul was often irritable and wretched until he got to sleep,—and tonight he was even more than usually restless. He had the feeling of not being able to let down; of its being impossible to give up this delicious excitement which was the only thing that could be called living at all. During the last number he withdrew and, after hastily changing his clothes in the dressing-room, slipped out to the side door where the singer's carriage stood. Here he began pacing rapidly up and down the walk, waiting to see her come out.

Over yonder the Schenley, in its vacant stretch, loomed big and square through the fine rain, the windows of its twelve stories glowing like those of a lighted cardboard house under a Christmas tree. All the actors and singers of any importance stayed there when they were in the city, and a number of the big manufacturers of the place lived there in the winter. Paul had often hung about the hotel, watching the people go in and out, longing to enter and leave schoolmasters and dull care behind him forever.

At last the singer came out, accompanied by the conductor, who helped her into her carriage and closed the door with a cordial *auf wiedersehen*, —which set Paul to wondering whether she were not an old sweetheart of his. Paul followed the carriage over to the hotel, walking so rapidly as not to be far from the entrance when the singer alighted and disappeared behind the swinging glass doors which were opened by a Negro in a tall hat and a long coat. In the moment that the door was ajar, it seemed to Paul that he, too, entered. He seemed to feel himself go after her up the steps, into the warm, lighted building, into an exotic, a tropical world of shiny, glistening surfaces and basking ease. He reflected upon the mysterious dishes that were brought into the dining-room, the green bottles in buckets of ice, as he had seen them in the supper party pictures of the Sunday supplement. A quick gust of wind brought the rain down with sudden vehemence, and Paul was startled to find that he was still outside in the slush of the gravel driveway; that his boots were letting in the water and his scanty overcoat was clinging wet about him; that the lights in front of the concert hall were out, and that the rain was driving in sheets between him and the orange glow of the windows above him. There it was, what he wanted—tangibly before him, like the fairy world of a Christmas pantomime; as the rain beat in his face, Paul wondered whether he were destined always to shiver in the black night outside, looking up at it.

He turned and walked reluctantly toward the car tracks. The end had to come some time; his father in his night-clothes at the top of the stairs, explanations that did not explain, hastily improvised fictions that were forever tripping him up, his upstairs room and its horrible yellow wall paper, the creaking bureau with the greasy plush collar-box, and over his painted wooden bed the pictures of George Washington and John Calvin, and the framed motto, "Feed my Lambs," which had been worked in red worsted by his mother, whom Paul could not remember.

Half an hour later, Paul alighted from the Negley Avenue car and went slowly down one of the side streets off the main thoroughfare. It was a highly respectable street, where all the houses were exactly alike, and where business men of moderate means begot and reared large families of children, all of whom went to Sabbath-school and learned the shorter catechism, and were interested in arithmetic; all of whom were as exactly alike as their homes, and of a piece with the monotony in which they lived. Paul never went up Cordelia Street without a shudder of loathing. His home was next the house of the Cumberland minister. He approached it tonight with the nerveless sense of defeat, the hopeless feeling of sinking back forever into ugliness and commonness that he had always had when he came home. The moment he turned into Cordelia Street he felt the waters close above his head.

After each of these orgies of living, he experienced all the physical depression which follows a debauch; the loathing of respectable beds, of common food, of a house permeated by kitchen odors; a shuddering repulsion for the flavorless, colorless mass of everyday existence; a morbid desire for cool things and soft lights and fresh flowers.

The nearer he approached the house, the more absolutely unequal Paul felt to the sight of it all; his ugly sleeping chamber; the cold bathroom with the grimy zinc tub, the cracked mirror, the dripping spiggots; his father, at the top of the stairs, his hairy legs sticking out from his nightshirt, his feet thrust into carpet slippers. He was so much later than usual that there would certainly be inquiries and reproaches. Paul stopped short before the door. He felt that he could not be accosted by his father tonight; that he could not toss again on that miserable bed. He would not go in. He would tell his father that he had no car fare, and it was raining so hard he had gone home with one of the boys and stayed all night.

Meanwhile, he was wet and cold. He went around to the back of the house and tried one of the basement windows, found it open, raised it cautiously, and scrambled down the cellar wall to the floor. There he stood, holding his breath, terrified by the noise he had made; but the floor above him was silent, and there was no creak on the stairs. He found a soap-box, and carried it over to the soft ring of light that streamed from the furnace door, and sat down. He was horribly afraid of rats, so he did not try to sleep, but sat looking distrustfully at the dark, still terrified lest he might have awakened his father. In such reactions, after one of the experiences which made days and nights out of the dreary blanks of the calendar, when his senses were deadened, Paul's head was always singularly clear. Suppose his father had heard him getting in at the window and had come down and shot him for a burglar? Then, again, suppose his father had come down, pistol in hand, and he had cried out in time to save himself, and his father had been horrified to think how nearly he had killed him? Then, again, suppose a day should come when his father would remember that night, and wish there had been no warning cry to stay his hand? With this last supposition Paul entertained himself until daybreak.

The following Sunday was fine; the sodden November chill was broken by the last flash of autumnal summer. In the morning Paul had to go to church and Sabbath-school, as always. On seasonable Sunday afternoons the burghers of Cordelia Street usually sat out on their front "stoops," and talked to their neighbors on the next stoop, or called to those across the street in neighborly fashion. The men sat placidly on gay cushions placed upon the steps that led down to the sidewalk, while the women, in their Sunday "waists," sat in rockers on the cramped porches, pretending to be greatly at their ease. The children played in the streets; there were so many of them that the place resembled the recreation grounds of a kindergarten. The men on the steps—all in their shirt sleeves, their vests unbuttoned—sat with their legs well apart, their stomachs comfortably protruding, and talked of the prices of things, or told anecdotes of the sagacity of their various chiefs and overlords. They occasionally looked over the multitude of squabbling children, listened affectionately to their high-pitched, nasal voices, smiling to see their own proclivities reproduced in their offspring, and interspersed their legends of the iron kings with remarks about their sons' progress at school, their grades in arithmetic, and the amounts they had saved in their toy banks. On this last Sunday of November, Paul sat all the afternoon on the lowest step of his "stoop," staring into the street, while his sisters, in their rockers, were talking to the minister's daughters next door about how many shirtwaists they had made in the last week, and how many waffles someone had eaten at the last church supper. When the weather was warm, and his father was in a particularly jovial frame of mind, the girls made lemonade, which was always brought out in a red-glass pitcher, ornamented with forget-me-nots in blue enamel. This the girls thought very fine, and the neighbors joked about the suspicious color of the pitcher.

Today Paul's father, on the top step, was talking to a young man who shifted a restless baby from knee to knee. He happened to be the young man who was daily held up to Paul as a model, and after whom it was his father's dearest hope that he would pattern. This young man was of a ruddy complexion, with a compressed, red mouth, and faded, near-sighted eyes, over which he wore thick spectacles, with gold bows that curved about his ears. He was clerk to one of the magnates of a great steel corporation, and was looked upon in Cordelia Street as a young man with a future. There was a story that, some five years ago—he was now barely twenty-six—he had been a trifle 'dissipated,' but in order to curb his appetites and save the loss of time and strength that a sowing of wild oats might have entailed, he had taken his chief's advice, oft reiterated to his employees, and at twenty-one had married the first woman whom he could persuade to share his fortunes. She happened to be an angular school mistress, much older than he, who also wore thick glasses, and who had now borne him four children, all near-sighted, like herself.

The young man was relating how his chief, now cruising in the Mediterranean, kept in touch with all the details of the business, arranging his office hours on his yacht just as though he were at home, and "knocking off work enough to keep two stenographers busy." His father told, in turn, the plan his corporation was considering, of putting in an electric railway plant at Cairo. Paul snapped his teeth; he had an awful apprehension that they might spoil it all before he got there. Yet he rather liked to hear these legends of the iron kings, that were told and retold on Sundays and holidays; these stories of palaces in Venice, yachts on the Mediterranean, and high play at Monte Carlo appealed to his fancy, and he was interested in the triumphs of cash boys who had become famous, though he had no mind for the cash-boy stage.

After supper was over, and he had helped to dry the dishes, Paul nervously asked his father whether he could go to George's to get some help in his geometry, and still more nervously asked for car fare. This latter request he had to repeat, as his father, on principle, did not like to hear requests for money, whether much or little. He asked Paul whether he could not go to some boy who lived nearer, and told him that he ought not to leave his school work until Sunday; but he gave him the dime. He was not a poor man, but he had a worthy ambition to come up in the world. His only reason for allowing Paul to usher was that he thought a boy ought to be earning a little.

Paul bounded upstairs, scrubbed the greasy odor of the dishwater from his hands with the ill-smelling soap he hated, and then shook over his fingers a few drops of violet water from the bottle he kept hidden in his drawer. He left the house with his geometry conspicuously under his arm, and the moment he got out of Cordelia Street and boarded a downtown car, he shook off the lethargy of two deadening days, and began to live again.

The leading juvenile of the permanent stock company which played at one of the downtown theaters was an acquaintance of Paul's, and the boy had been invited to drop in at the Sunday night rehearsals whenever he could. For more than a year Paul had spent every available moment loitering about Charley Edwards's dressing-room. He had won a place among Edwards's following not only because the young actor, who could not afford to employ a dresser, often found him useful, but because he recognized in Paul something akin to what churchmen term "vocation."

It was at the theater and at Carnegie Hall that Paul really lived; the rest was but a sleep and a forgetting. This was Paul's fairy tale, and it had for him all the allurement of a secret love. The moment he inhaled the gassy, painty, dusty odor behind the scenes, he breathed like a prisoner set free, and felt within him the possibility of doing or saying splendid, brilliant things. The moment the cracked orchestra beat out the overture from *Martha,* or jerked at the serenade from *Rigoletto,* all stupid and ugly things slid from him, and his senses were deliciously, yet delicately fired.

Perhaps it was because, in Paul's world, the natural nearly always wore the guise of ugliness, that a certain element of artificiality seemed to him necessary in beauty. Perhaps it was because his experience of life elsewhere was so full of Sabbath-school picnics, petty economies, wholesome advice as to how to succeed in life, and the unescapable odors of cooking, that he found this existence so alluring, these smartly-clad men and women so attractive, that he was so moved by these starry apple orchards that bloomed perennially under the limelight.

It would be difficult to put it strongly enough how convincingly the stage entrance of that theater was for Paul the actual portal of Romance. Certainly none of the company ever suspected it, least of all Charley Edwards. It was very like the old stories that used to float about London of fabulously rich Jews, who had subterranean halls, with palms, and fountains, and soft lamps and richly apparelled women who never saw the disenchanting light of London day. So, in the midst of that smoke-palled city, enamored of figures and grimy toil, Paul had his secret temple, his wishing-carpet, his bit of blue-and-white Mediterranean shore bathed in perpetual sunshine.

Several of Paul's teachers had a theory that his imagination had been perverted by garish fiction; but the truth was, he scarcely ever read at all. The books at home were not such as would either tempt or corrupt a youthful mind, and as for reading the novels that some of his friends urged upon him—well, he got what he wanted much more quickly from music; any sort of music, from an orchestra to a barrel organ. He needed only the spark, the indescribable thrill that made his imagination master of his senses, and he could make plots and pictures enough of his own. It was equally true that he was not stage-struck—not, at any rate, in the usual acceptation of that expression. He had no desire to become an actor, any more than he had to become a musician. He felt no necessity to do any of these things; what he wanted was to see, to be in the atmosphere, float on the wave of it, to be carried out, blue league after blue league, away from everything.

After a night behind the scenes, Paul found the school-room more than ever repulsive; the bare floors and naked walls; the prosy men who never wore frock coats, or violets in their buttonholes; the women with their dull gowns, shrill voices, and pitiful seriousness about prepositions that govern the dative. He could not bear to have the other pupils think, for a moment, that he took these people seriously; he must convey to them that he considered it all trivial, and was there only by way of a joke, anyway. He had autograph pictures of all the members of the stock company which he showed his classmates, telling them the most incredible stories of his familiarity with these people, of his acquaintance with the soloists who came to Carnegie Hall, his suppers with them and the flowers he sent them. When these stories lost their effect, and his audience grew listless, he would bid all the boys good-by, announcing that he was going to travel for a while; going to Naples, to California, to Egypt. Then, next Monday, he would slip back, conscious and nervously smiling; his sister was ill, and he would have to defer his voyage until spring.

Matters went steadily worse with Paul at school. In the itch to let his instructors know how heartily he despised them, and how thoroughly he was appreciated elsewhere, he mentioned once or twice that he had no time to fool with theorems; adding—with a twitch of the eyebrows and a touch of that nervous bravado which so perplexed them—that he was helping the people down at the stock company; they were old friends of his.

The upshot of the matter was, that the Principal went to Paul's father, and Paul was taken out of school and put to work. The manager at Carnegie Hall was told to get another usher in his stead; the door-keeper at the theater was warned not to admit him to the house; and Charley Edwards remorsefully promised the boy's father not to see him again.

The members of the stock company were vastly amused when some of Paul's stories reached them—especially the women. They were hard-working women, most of them supporting indolent husbands or brothers, and they laughed rather bitterly at having stirred the boy to such fervid and florid inventions. They agreed with the faculty and with his father, that Paul's was a bad case.

The east-bound train was plowing through a January snowstorm; the dull dawn was beginning to show gray when the engine whistled a mile out of Newark. Paul started up from the seat where he had lain curled in uneasy slumber, rubbed the breath-misted window glass with his hand, and peered out. The snow was whirling in curling eddies above the white bottom lands, and the drifts lay already deep in the fields and along the fences, while here and there the long dead grass and dried weed stalks protruded black above it. Lights shone from the scattered houses, and a gang of laborers who stood beside the track waved their lanterns.

Paul had slept very little, and he felt grimy and uncomfortable. He had made the all-night journey in a day coach because he was afraid if he took a Pullman he might be seen by some Pittsburgh business man who had noticed him in Denny & Carson's office. When the whistle woke him, he clutched quickly at his breast pocket, glancing about him with an uncertain smile. But the little, clay-bespattered Italians were still sleeping, the slatternly women across the aisle were in open-mouthed oblivion, and even the crumby, crying babies were for the nonce stilled. Paul settled back to struggle with his impatience as best he could.

When he arrived at the Jersey City station, he hurried through his breakfast, manifestly ill at ease and keeping a sharp eye about him. After he reached the Twenty-third Street station, he consulted a cabman, and had himself driven to a men's furnishing establishment which was just opening for the day. He spent upward of two hours there, buying with endless reconsidering and great care. His new street suit he put on in the fitting-room; the frock coat and dress clothes he had bundled into the cab with his new shirts. Then he drove to a hatter's and a shoe house. His next errand was at Tiffany's, where he selected silver-mounted brushes and a scarf-pin. He would not wait to have his silver marked, he said. Lastly, he stopped at a trunk shop on Broadway, and had his purchases packed into various traveling bags.

It was a little after one o'clock when he drove up to the Waldorf, and, after settling with the cabman, went into the office. He registered from Washington; said his mother and father had been abroad, and that he had come down to await the arrival of their steamer. He told his story plausibly and had no trouble, since he offered to pay for them in advance, in engaging his rooms; a sleeping-room, sitting room and bath.

Not once, but a hundred times Paul had planned this entry into New York. He had gone over every detail of it with Charley Edwards, and in his scrap book at home there were pages of description about New York hotels, cut from the Sunday papers.

When he was shown to his sitting room on the eighth floor, he saw at a glance that everything was as it should be; there was but one detail in his mental picture that the place did not realize, so he rang for the bell boy and sent him down for flowers. He moved about nervously until the boy returned, putting away his new linen and fingering it delightedly as he did so. When the flowers came, he put them hastily into water, and then tumbled into a hot bath. Presently he came out of his white bath-room, resplendent in his new silk underwear, and playing with the tassels of his red robe. The snow was whirling so fiercely outside his windows that he could scarcely see across the street; but within, the air was deliciously soft and fragrant. He put the violets and jonquils on the tabouret beside the couch, and threw himself down with a long sigh, covering himself with a Roman blanket. He was thoroughly tired; he had been in such haste, he had stood up to such a strain, covered so much ground in the last twenty-four hours, that he wanted to think how it had all come about. Lulled by the sound of the wind, the warm air, and the cool fragrance of the flowers, he sank into deep, drowsy retrospection.

It had been wonderfully simple; when they had shut him out of the theater and concert hall, when they had taken away his bone, the whole thing was virtually determined. The rest was a mere matter of opportunity. The only thing that at all surprised him was his own courage— for he realized well enough that he had always been tormented by fear, a sort of apprehensive dread that, of late years, as the meshes of the lies he had told closed about him, had been pulling the muscles of his body tighter and tighter. Until now, he could not remember a time when he had not been dreading something. Even when he was a little boy, it was always there—behind him, or before, or on either side. There had always been the shadowed corner, the dark place into which he dared not look, but from which something seemed always to be watching him—and Paul had done things that were not pretty to watch, he knew.

But now he had a curious sense of relief, as though he had at last thrown down the gauntlet to the thing in the corner.

Yet it was but a day since he had been sulking in the traces; but yesterday afternoon that he had been sent to the bank with Denny & Carson's deposit, as usual—but this time he was instructed to leave the book to be balanced. There was above two thousand dollars in checks, and nearly a thousand in the bank notes which he had taken from the book and quietly transferred to his pocket. At the bank he had made out a new deposit slip. His nerves had been steady enough to permit of his returning to the office, where he had finished his work and asked for a full day's holiday tomorrow, Saturday, giving a perfectly reasonable pretext. The bank book, he knew, would not be returned before Monday or Tuesday, and his father would be out of town for the next week. From the time he slipped the bank notes into his pocket until he boarded the night train for New York, he had not known a moment's hesitation.

How astonishingly easy it had all been; here he was, the thing done; and this time there would be no awakening, no figure at the top of the stairs. He watched the snowflakes whirling by his window until he fell asleep.

When he awoke, it was four o'clock in the afternoon. He bounded up with a start; one of his precious days gone already! He spent nearly an hour in dressing, watching every stage of his toilet carefully in the mirror. Everything was quite perfect; he was exactly the kind of boy he had always wanted to be.

When he went downstairs, Paul took a carriage and drove up Fifth avenue toward the Park. The snow had somewhat abated; carriages and tradesmen's wagons were hurrying soundlessly to and fro in the winter twilight; boys in woolen mufflers were shoveling off the doorsteps; the avenue stages made fine spots of color against the white street. Here and there on the corners whole flower gardens blooming behind glass windows, against which the snow flakes stuck and melted; violets, roses,

carnations, lilies of the valley—somehow vastly more lovely and alluring that they blossomed thus unnaturally in the snow. The Park itself
was a wonderful stage winter-piece.

When he returned, the pause of the twilight had ceased, and the tune
of the streets had changed. The snow was falling faster, lights streamed
from the hotels that reared their many stories fearlessly up into the
storm, defying the raging Atlantic winds. A long, black stream of carriages poured down the avenue, intersected here and there by other
streams, tending horizontally. There were a score of cabs about the
entrance of his hotel, and his driver had to wait. Boys in livery were
running in and out of the awning stretched across the sidewalk, up and
down the red velvet carpet laid from the door to the street. Above, about,
within it all, was the rumble and roar, the hurry and toss of thousands
of human beings as hot for pleasure as himself, and on every side of
him towered the glaring affirmation of the omnipotence of wealth.

The boy set his teeth and drew his shoulders together in a spasm of
realization; the plot of all dramas, the text of all romances, the nerve-
stuff of all sensations was whirling about him like the snowflakes.
He burnt like a faggot in a tempest.

When Paul came down to dinner, the music of the orchestra floated
up the elevator shaft to greet him. As he stepped into the thronged
corridor, he sank back into one of the chairs against the wall to get his
breath. The lights, the chatter, the perfumes, the bewildering medley of
color—he had, for a moment, the feeling of not being able to stand it. But
only for a moment; these were his own people, he told himself. He went
slowly about the corridors, through the writing-rooms, smoking-rooms,
reception-rooms, as though he were exploring the chambers of an enchanted palace, built and peopled for him alone.

When he reached the dining room he sat down at a table near a
window. The flowers, the white linen, the many-colored wine glasses,
the gay toilettes of the women, the low popping of corks, the undulating
repetitions of the *Blue Danube* from the orchestra, all flooded Paul's
dream with bewildering radiance. When the roseate tinge of his champagne was added—that cold, precious, bubbling stuff that creamed and
foamed in his glass—Paul wondered that there were honest men in the
world at all. This was what all the world was fighting for, he reflected;
this was what all the struggle was about. He doubted the reality of his
past. Had he ever known a place called Cordelia Street, a place where
fagged-looking business men boarded the early car? Mere rivets in a
machine they seemed to Paul,—sickening men, with combings of children's hair always hanging to their coats, and the smell of cooking in
their clothes. Cordelia Street—Ah, that belonged to another time and
country! Had he not always been thus, had he not sat here night after

night, from as far back as he could remember, looking pensively over just such shimmering textures, and slowly twirling the stem of a glass like this one between his thumb and middle finger? He rather thought he had.

He was not in the least abashed or lonely. He had no especial desire to meet or to know any of these people; all he demanded was the right to look on and conjecture, to watch the pageant. The mere stage properties were all he contended for. Nor was he lonely later in the evening, in his loge at the Opera. He was entirely rid of his nervous misgivings, of his forced aggressiveness, of the imperative desire to show himself different from his surroundings. He felt now that his surroundings explained him. Nobody questioned the purple; he had only to wear it passively. He had only to glance down at his dress coat to reassure himself that here it would be impossible for anyone to humiliate him.

He found it hard to leave his beautiful sitting room to go to bed that night, and sat long watching the raging storm from his turret window. When he went to sleep, it was with the lights turned on in his bedroom; partly because of his old timidity, and partly so that, if he should wake in the night, there would be no wretched moment of doubt, no horrible suspicion of yellow wall-paper, or of Washington and Calvin above his bed.

On Sunday morning the city was practically snow-bound. Paul breakfasted late, and in the afternoon he fell in with a wild San Francisco boy, a freshman at Yale, who said he had run down for a "little flyer" over Sunday. The young man offered to show Paul the night side of the town, and the two boys went off together after dinner, not returning to the hotel until seven o'clock the next morning. They had started out in the confiding warmth of a champagne friendship, but their parting in the elevator was singularly cool. The freshman pulled himself together to make his train, and Paul went to bed. He awoke at two o'clock in the afternoon, very thirsty and dizzy, and rang for ice water, coffee, and the Pittsburgh papers.

On the part of the hotel management, Paul excited no suspicion. There was this to be said for him, that he wore his spoils with dignity and in no way made himself conspicuous. His chief greediness lay in his ears and eyes, and his excesses were not offensive ones. His dearest pleasures were the gray winter twilights in his sitting room; his quiet enjoyment of his flowers, his clothes, his wide divan, his cigarette and his sense of power. He could not remember a time when he had felt so at peace with himself. The mere release from the necessity of petty lying, lying every day and every day, restored his self-respect. He had never lied for pleasure, even at school; but to make himself noticed and admired, to assert his difference from other Cordelia Street boys; and

he felt a good deal more manly, more honest, even, now that he had
no need for boastful pretensions, now that he could, as his actor friends
used to say, "dress the part." It was characteristic that remorse did not
occur to him. His golden days went by without a shadow, and he made
each as perfect as he could.

On the eighth day after his arrival in New York, he found the whole
affair exploited in the Pittsburgh papers, exploited with a wealth of
detail which indicated that local news of a sensational nature was at a
low ebb. The firm of Denny & Carson announced that the boy's father
had refunded the full amount of his theft, and that they had no intention of prosecuting. The Cumberland minister had been interviewed,
and expressed his hope of yet reclaiming the motherless lad, and Paul's
Sabbath-school teacher declared that she would spare no effort to that
end. The rumor had reached Pittsburgh that the boy had been seen in a
New York hotel, and his father had gone East to find him and bring
him home.

Paul had just come in to dress for dinner; he sank into a chair, weak
in the knees, and clasped his head in his hands. It was to be worse than
jail, even; the tepid waters of Cordelia Street were to close over him
finally and forever. The gray monotony stretched before him in hopeless, unrelieved years; Sabbath-school, Young People's Meeting, the
yellow-papered room, the damp dish-towels; it all rushed back upon
him with sickening vividness. He had the old feeling that the orchestra
had suddenly stopped, the sinking sensation that the play was over. The
sweat broke out on his face, and he sprang to his feet, looked about him
with his white, conscious smile, and winked at himself in the mirror.
With something of the childish belief in miracles with which he had
so often gone to class, all his lessons unlearned, Paul dressed and dashed
whistling down the corridor to the elevator.

He had no sooner entered the dining room and caught the measure
of the music, than his remembrance was lightened by his old elastic
power of claiming the moment, mounting with it, and finding it all
sufficient. The glare and glitter about him, the mere scenic accessories
had again, and for the last time, their old potency. He would show
himself that he was game, he would finish the thing splendidly. He
doubted, more than ever, the existence of Cordelia Street, and for the
first time he drank his wine recklessly. Was he not, after all, one of
these fortunate beings? Was he not still himself, and in his own place?
He drummed a nervous accompaniment to the music and looked about
him, telling himself over and over that it had paid.

He reflected drowsily, to the swell of the violin and the chill sweetness
of his wine, that he might have done it more wisely. He might have
caught an outbound steamer and been well out of their clutches before

now. But the other side of the world had seemed too far away and too uncertain then; he could not have waited for it; his need had been too sharp. If he had to choose over again, he would do the same thing tomorrow. He looked affectionately about the dining room, now gilded with a soft mist. Ah, it had paid indeed!

Paul was awakened next morning by a painful throbbing in his head and feet. He had thrown himself across the bed without undressing, and had slept with his shoes on. His limbs and hands were lead heavy, and his tongue and throat were parched. There came upon him one of those fateful attacks of clear-headedness that never occurred except when he was physically exhausted and his nerves hung loose. He lay still and closed his eyes and let the tide of realities wash over him.

His father was in New York; "stopping at some joint or other," he told himself. The memory of successive summers on the front stoop fell upon him like a weight of black water. He had not a hundred dollars left; and he knew now, more than ever, that money was everything, the wall that stood between all he loathed and all he wanted. The thing was winding itself up; he had thought of that on his first glorious day in New York, and had even provided a way to snap the thread. It lay on his dressing-table now; he had got it out last night when he came blindly up from dinner,—but the shiny metal hurt his eyes, and he disliked the look of it, anyway.

He rose and moved about with a painful effort, succumbing now and again to attacks of nausea. It was the old depression exaggerated; all the world had become Cordelia Street. Yet somehow he was not afraid of anything, was absolutely calm; perhaps because he had looked into the dark corner at last, and knew. It was bad enough, what he saw there; but somehow not so bad as his long fear of it had been. He saw everything clearly now. He had a feeling that he had made the best of it, that he had lived the sort of life he was meant to live, and for half an hour he sat staring at the revolver. But he told himself that was not the way, so he went downstairs and took a cab to the ferry.

When Paul arrived at Newark, he got off the train and took another cab, directing the driver to follow the Pennsylvania tracks out of the town. The snow lay heavy on the roadways and had drifted deep in the open fields. Only here and there the dead grass or dried weed stalks projected, singularly black, above it. Once well into the country, Paul dismissed the carriage and walked, floundering along the tracks, his mind a medley of irrelevant things. He seemed to hold in his brain an actual picture of everything he had seen that morning. He remembered every feature of both his drivers, the toothless old woman from whom he had bought the red flowers in his coat, the agent from whom he had got his ticket. and all of his fellow-passengers on the ferry. His mind, unable to cope with vital matters near at hand, worked feverishly and deftly at sorting and grouping these images. They made for him a part of the ugliness of the world, of the ache in his head, and the bitter burning on his tongue. He stooped and put a handful of snow into his mouth as he walked, but that, too, seemed hot. When he reached a little hillside, where the tracks ran through a cut some twenty feet below him, he stopped and sat down.

The carnations in his coat were drooping with the cold, he noticed; all their red glory over. It occurred to him that all the flowers he had seen in the show windows that first night must have gone the same way, long before this. It was only one splendid breath they had, in spite of their brave mockery at the winter outside the glass. It was a losing game in the end, it seemed, this revolt against the homilies by which the world is run. Paul took one of the blossoms carefully from his coat and scooped a little hole in the snow, where he covered it up. Then he dozed a while, from his weak condition, seeming insensible to the cold.

The sound of an approaching train woke him, and he started to his feet, remembering only his resolution, and afraid lest he should be too late. He stood watching the approaching locomotive, his teeth chattering, his lips drawn away from them in a frightened smile; once or twice he glanced nervously sidewise, as though he were being watched. When the right moment came, he jumped. As he fell, the folly of his haste occurred to him with merciless clearness, the vastness of what he had left undone. There flashed through his brain, clearer than ever before, the blue of Adriatic water, the yellow of Algerian sands.

He felt something strike his chest,—his body was being thrown swiftly through the air, on and on, immeasurably far and fast, while his limbs gently relaxed. Then, because the picture-making mechanism was crushed, the disturbing visions flashed into black, and Paul dropped back into the immense design of things.

40

To Build a Fire

BY JACK LONDON

DAY had broken cold and gray, exceedingly cold and gray, when the man turned aside from the main Yukon trail and climbed the high earth-bank, where a dim and little-traveled trail led eastward through the fat spruce timberland. It was a steep bank, and he paused for breath at the top, excusing the act to himself by looking at his watch. It was nine o'clock. There was no sun nor hint of sun, though there was not a cloud in the sky. It was a clear day, and yet there seemed an intangible pall over the face of things, a subtle gloom that made the day dark, and that was due to the absence of sun. This fact did not worry the man. He was used to the lack of sun. It had been days since he had seen the sun, and he knew that a few more days must pass before that cheerful orb, due south, would just peep above the sky-line and dip immediately from view.

The man flung a look back along the way he had come. The Yukon lay a mile wide and hidden under three feet of ice. On top of this ice were as many feet of snow. It was all pure white, rolling in gentle, undulations where the ice-jams of the freeze-up had formed. North and south, as far as his eye could see, it was unbroken white, save for a dark hairline that curved and twisted from around the spruce-covered island to the south, and that curved and twisted away into the north, where it disappeared behind another spruce-covered island. This dark hair-line was the trail—the main trail—that led south five hundred miles to the Chilcoot Pass, Dyea, and salt water; and that led north seventy miles to Dawson, and still on to the north a thousand miles to Nulato, and finally to St. Michael on Bering Sea, a thousand miles and half a thousand more.

But all this—the mysterious, far-reaching hair-line trail, the absence of

sun from the sky, the tremendous cold, and the strangeness and weirdness of it all—made no impression on the man. It was not because he
was long used to it. He was a newcomer in the land, a *chechaquo,* and
this was his first winter. The trouble with him was that he was without
imagination. He was quick and alert in the things of life, but only in
the things, and not in the significances. Fifty degrees below zero meant
eighty-odd degrees of frost. Such fact impressed him as being cold and
uncomfortable, and that was all. It did not lead him to meditate upon
his frailty as a creature of temperature, and upon man's frailty in general, able only to live within certain narrow limits of heat and cold; and
from there on it did not lead him to the conjectural field of immortality
and man's place in the universe. Fifty degrees below zero stood for a
bite of frost that hurt and that must be guarded against by the use of
mittens, ear-flaps, warm moccasins, and thick socks. Fifty degrees below
zero was to him just precisely fifty degrees below zero. That there should
be anything more to it than that was a thought that never entered his
head.

As he turned to go on, he spat speculatively. There was a sharp, explosive crackle that startled him. He spat again. And again, in the air,
before it could fall to the snow, the spittle crackled. He knew that at
fifty below spittle crackled on the snow, but this spittle had crackled in
the air. Undoubtedly it was colder than fifty below—how much colder
he did not know. But the temperature did not matter. He was bound for
the old claim on the left fork of Henderson Creek, where the boys were
already. They had come over across the divide from the Indian Creek
country, while he had come the roundabout way to take a look at the
possibilities of getting out logs in the spring from the islands in the
Yukon. He would be in to camp by six o'clock; a bit after dark, it was
true, but the boys would be there, a fire would be going, and a hot supper
would be ready. As for lunch, he pressed his hand against the protruding bundle under his jacket. It was also under his shirt, wrapped up in
a handkerchief and lying against the naked skin. It was the only way to
keep the biscuits from freezing. He smiled agreeably to himself as he
thought of those biscuits, each cut open and sopped in bacon grease, and
each enclosing a generous slice of fried bacon.

He plunged in among the big spruce trees. The trail was faint. A foot
of snow had fallen since the last sled had passed over, and he was glad
he was without a sled, traveling light. In fact, he carried nothing but the
lunch wrapped in the handkerchief. He was surprised, however, at the
cold. It certainly was cold, he concluded, as he rubbed his numb nose
and cheek-bones with his mittened hand. He was a warm-whiskered
man, but the hair on his face did not protect the high cheek-bones and
the eager nose that thrust itself aggressively into the frosty air.

At the man's heels trotted a dog, a big native husky, the proper wolf-dog, gray-coated and without any visible or temperamental difference from its brother, the wild wolf. The animal was depressed by the tremendous cold. It knew that it was no time for traveling. Its instinct told it a truer tale than was told to the man by the man's judgment. In reality, it was not merely colder than fifty below zero; it was colder than sixty below, than seventy below. It was seventy-five below zero. Since the freezing point is thirty-two above zero, it meant that one hundred and seven degrees of frost obtained. The dog did not know anything about thermometers. Possibly in its brain there was no sharp consciousness of a condition of very cold such as was in the man's brain. But the brute had its instinct. It experienced a vague but menacing apprehension that subdued it and made it slink along at the man's heels, and that made it question eagerly every unwonted movement of the man as if expecting him to go into camp or to seek shelter somewhere and build a fire. The dog had learned fire, and it wanted fire, or else to burrow under the snow and cuddle its warmth away from the air.

The frozen moisture of its breathing had settled on its fur in a fine powder of frost, and especially were its jowls, muzzle, and eyelashes whitened by its crystalled breath. The man's red beard and mustache were likewise frosted, but more solidly, the deposit taking the form of ice and increasing with every warm, moist breath he exhaled. Also, the man was chewing tobacco, and the muzzle of ice held his lips so rigidly that he was unable to clear his chin when he expelled the juice. The result was that a crystal beard of the color and solidity of amber was increasing its length on his chin. If he fell down it would shatter itself, like glass, into brittle fragments. But he did not mind the appendage. It was the penalty all tobacco-chewers paid in that country, and he had been out before in two cold snaps. They had not been so cold as this, he knew, but by the spirit thermometer at Sixty Mile he knew they had been registered at fifty below and at fifty-five.

He held on through the level stretch of woods for several miles, crossed a wide flat of nigger-heads, and dropped down a bank to the frozen bed of a small stream. This was Henderson Creek, and he knew he was ten miles from the forks. He looked at his watch. It was ten o'clock. He was making four miles an hour, and he calculated that he would arrive at the forks at half-past twelve. He decided to celebrate that event by eating his lunch there.

The dog dropped in again at his heels, with a tail drooping discouragement, as the man swung along the creek-bed. The furrow of the old sled-trail was plainly visible, but a dozen inches of snow covered the marks of the last runners. In a month no man had come up or down that silent creek. The man held steadily on. He was not much given to thinking, and just then particularly he had nothing to think about save that he would eat lunch at the forks and that at six o'clock he would be in camp with the boys. There was nobody to talk to; and, had there been, speech would have been impossible because of the ice-muzzle on his mouth. So he continued monotonously to chew tobacco and to increase the length of his amber beard.

Once in a while the thought reiterated itself that it was very cold and that he had never experienced such cold. As he walked along he rubbed his cheek-bones and nose with the back of his mittened hand. He did this automatically, now and again changing hands. But rub as he would, the instant he stopped his cheek-bones went numb, and the following instant the end of his nose went numb. He was sure to frost his cheeks; he knew that, and experienced a pang of regret that he had not devised a nose-strap of the sort Bud wore in cold snaps. Such a strap passed across the cheeks, as well, and saved them. But it didn't matter much, after all. What were frosted cheeks? A bit painful, that was all; they were never serious.

Empty as the man's mind was of thoughts, he was keenly observant, and he noticed the changes in the creek, the curves and bends and timber-jams, and always he sharply noted where he placed his feet. Once, coming around a bend, he shied abruptly, like a startled horse, curved away from the place where he had been walking, and retreated several paces back along the trail. The creek he knew was frozen clear to the bottom,—no creek could contain water in that arctic winter,—but he knew also that there were springs that bubbled out from the hillsides and ran along under the snow and on top the ice of the creek. He knew that the coldest snaps never froze these springs, and he knew likewise their danger. They were traps. They hid pools of water under the snow that might be three inches deep, or three feet. Sometimes a skin of ice half an inch thick covered them, and in turn was covered by the snow. Sometimes there were alternate layers of water and ice-skin, so that when one broke through he kept on breaking through for a while, sometimes wetting himself to the waist.

That was why he had shied in such panic. He had felt the give under his feet and heard the crackle of a snow-hidden ice-skin. And to get his feet wet in such a temperature meant trouble and danger. At the very least it meant delay, for he would be forced to stop and build a fire, and under its protection to bare his feet while he dried his socks and moc- casins. He stood and studied the creek-bed and its banks, and decided that the flow of water came from the right. He reflected a while, rubbing his nose and cheeks, then skirted to the left, stepping gingerly and test- ing the footing for each step. Once clear of the danger, he took a fresh chew of tobacco and swung along at his four-mile gait.

In the course of the next two hours he came upon several similar traps. Usually the snow above the hidden pools had a sunken, candied appearance that advertised the danger. Once again, however, he had a close call; and once, suspecting danger, he compelled the dog to go on in front. The dog did not want to go. It hung back until the man shoved it forward, and then it went quickly across the white, unbroken surface. Suddenly it broke through, floundered to one side, and got away to firmer footing. It had wet its forefeet and legs, and almost immediately the water that clung to it turned to ice. It made quick efforts to lick the ice off its legs, then dropped down in the snow and began to bite out the ice that had formed between the toes. This was a matter of instinct. To permit the ice to remain would mean sore feet. It did not know this. It merely obeyed the mysterious prompting that arose from the deep crypts of its being. But the man knew, having achieved a judgment on the subject, and he removed the mitten from his right hand and helped tear out the ice-particles. He did not expose his fingers more than a minute, and was astonished at the swift numbness that smote them. It certainly was cold. He pulled on the mitten hastily, and beat the hand savagely across his chest.

At twelve o'clock the day was at its brightest. Yet the sun was too far south on its winter journey to clear the horizon. The bulge of the earth intervened between it and Henderson Creek, where the man walked under a clear sky at noon and cast no shadow. At half-past twelve, to the minute, he arrived at the forks of the creek. He was pleased at the speed he had made. If he kept it up, he would certainly be with the boys by six. He unbuttoned his jacket and shirt and drew forth his lunch. The action consumed no more than a quarter of a minute, yet in that brief moment the numbness laid hold of the exposed fingers. He did not put the mitten on, but, instead, struck the fingers a dozen sharp smashes against his leg. Then he sat down on a snow-covered log to eat. The sting that followed upon the striking of his fingers against his leg ceased so quickly that he was startled. He had had no chance to take a bite of biscuit. He struck the fingers repeatedly and returned them to the mitten, baring the other hand for the purpose of eating. He tried to take a mouthful, but the ice-muzzle prevented. He had forgotten to build a fire and thaw out. He chuckled at his foolishness, and as he chuckled he noted the numbness creeping into the exposed fingers. Also, he noted that the stinging which had first come to his toes when he sat down was already passing away. He wondered whether the toes were warm or numb. He moved them inside the moccasins and decided that they were numb.

He pulled the mitten on hurriedly and stood up. He was a bit frightened. He stamped up and down until the stinging returned into the feet.

It certainly was cold, was his thought. That man from Sulphur Creek had spoken the truth when telling how cold it sometimes got in the country. And he had laughed at him at the time! That showed one must not be too sure of things. There was no mistake about it, it *was* cold. He strode up and down, stamping his feet and threshing his arms, until reassured by the returning warmth. Then he got out matches and proceeded to make a fire. From the undergrowth, where high water of the previous spring had lodged a supply of seasoned twigs, he got his firewood. Working carefully from a small beginning, he soon had a roaring fire, over which he thawed the ice from his face and in the protection of which he ate his biscuits. For the moment the cold of space was outwitted. The dog took satisfaction in the fire, stretching out close enough for warmth and far enough away to escape being singed.

When the man had finished, he filled his pipe and took his comfortable time over a smoke. Then he pulled on his mittens, settled the earflaps of his cap firmly about his ears, and took the creek trail up the left fork. The dog was disappointed and yearned back toward the fire. This man did not know cold. Possibly all the generations of his ancestry had been ignorant of cold, of real cold, of cold one hundred and seven degrees below freezing point. But the dog knew; all its ancestry knew, and it had inherited the knowledge. And it knew that it was not good to walk abroad in such fearful cold. It was the time to lie snug in a hole in the snow and wait for a curtain of cloud to be drawn across the face of outer space whence this cold came. On the other hand, there was no keen intimacy between the dog and the man. The one was the toil-slave of the other, and the only caresses it had ever received were the caresses of the whiplash and of harsh and menacing throat-sounds that threatened the whiplash. So the dog made no effort to communicate its apprehension to the man. It was not concerned in the welfare of the man; it was for its own sake that it yearned back toward the fire. But the man whistled, and spoke to it with the sound of whiplashes, and the dog swung in at the man's heel and followed after.

The man took a chew of tobacco and proceeded to start a new amber beard. Also, his moist breath quickly powdered with white his mustache, eyebrows, and lashes. There did not seem to be so many springs on the left fork of the Henderson, and for half an hour the man saw no signs of any. And then it happened. At a place where there were no signs, where the soft, unbroken snow seemed to advertise solidity beneath, the man broke through. It was not deep. He wet himself halfway to the knees before he floundered out to the firm crust.

He was angry, and cursed his luck aloud. He had hoped to get into camp with the boys at six o'clock, and this would delay him an hour, for

he would have to build a fire and dry out his foot-gear. This was imperative at that low temperature—he knew that much; and he turned aside
to the bank, which he climbed. On top, tangled in the underbrush about
the trunks of several small spruce trees, was a high-water deposit of dry
firewood—sticks and twigs, principally, but also larger portions of
seasoned branches and fine, dry, last-year's grasses. He threw down
several large pieces on top of the snow. This served for a foundation
and prevented the young flame from drowning itself in the snow it
otherwise would melt. The flame he got by touching a match to a
small shred of birch bark that he took from his pocket. This burned
even more readily than paper. Placing it on the foundation, he fed the
young flame with wisps of dry grass and with the tiniest dry twigs.

He worked slowly and carefully, keenly aware of his danger. Gradually, as the flame grew stronger, he increased the size of the twigs with
which he fed it. He squatted in the snow, pulling the twigs out from
their entanglement in the brush and feeding directly to the flame. He
knew there must be no failure. When it is seventy-five below zero, a
man must not fail in his first attempt to build a fire—that is, if his feet
are wet. If his feet are dry, and he fails, he can run along the trail for
half a mile and restore his circulation. But the circulation of wet and
freezing feet cannot be restored by running when it is seventy-five
below. No matter how fast he runs, the wet feet will freeze the harder.

All this the man knew. The old-timer on Sulphur Creek had told
him about it the previous fall, and now he was appreciating the advice.
Already all sensation had gone out of his feet. To build the fire he had
been forced to remove his mittens, and the fingers had quickly gone
numb. His pace of four miles an hour had kept his heart pumping
blood to the surface of his body and to all the extremities. But the instant
he stopped, the action of the pump eased down. The cold of space smote
the unprotected tip of the planet, and he, being on that unprotected tip,
received the full force of the blow. The blood of his body recoiled before
it. The blood was alive, like the dog, and like the dog it wanted to hide
away and cover itself up from the fearful cold. So long as he walked
four miles an hour, he pumped that blood, willy-nilly, to the surface;
but now it ebbed away and sank down into the recesses of his body. The
extremities were the first to feel its absence. His wet feet froze the faster,
and his exposed fingers numbed the faster, though they had not yet
begun to freeze. Nose and cheeks were already freezing, while the skin
of all his body chilled as it lost its blood.

But he was safe. Toes and nose and cheeks would be only touched by
the frost, for the fire was beginning to burn with strength. He was feeding it with twigs the size of his finger. In another minute he would be
able to feed it with branches the size of his wrist, and then he could

remove his wet foot-gear, and, while it dried, he could keep his naked feet warm by the fire, rubbing them at first, of course, with snow. The fire was a success. He was safe. He remembered the advice of the old-timer on Sulphur Creek, and smiled. The old-timer had been very serious in laying down the law that no man must travel alone in the Klondike after fifty below. Well, here he was; he had had the accident; he was alone; and he had saved himself. Those old-timers were rather womanish, some of them, he thought. All a man had to do was to keep his head, and he was all right. Any man who was a man could travel alone. But it was surprising, the rapidity with which his cheeks and nose were freezing. And he had not thought his fingers could go lifeless in so short a time. Lifeless they were, for he could scarcely make them move together to grip a twig, and they seemed remote from his body and from him. When he touched a twig, he had to look and see whether or not he had hold of it. The wires were pretty well down between him and his finger-ends.

All of which counted for little. There was the fire, snapping and crackling and promising life with every dancing flame. He started to untie his moccasins. They were coated with ice; the thick German socks were like sheaths of iron halfway to the knees; and the moccasin strings were like rods of steel all twisted and knotted as by some conflagration. For a moment he tugged with his numb fingers, then, realizing the folly of it, he drew his sheath-knife.

But before he could cut the strings, it happened. It was his own fault or, rather, his mistake. He should not have built the fire under the spruce tree. He should have built it in the open. But it had been easier to pull the twigs from the brush and drop them directly on the fire. Now the tree under which he had done this carried a weight of snow on its boughs. No wind had blown for weeks, and each bough was fully freighted. Each time he had pulled a twig he had communicated a slight agitation to the tree—an imperceptible agitation, so far as he was concerned, but an agitation sufficient to bring about the disaster. High up in the tree one bough capsized its load of snow. This fell on the boughs beneath, capsizing them. This process continued, spreading out and involving the whole tree. It grew like an avalanche, and it descended without warning upon the man and the fire, and the fire was blotted out! Where it had burned was a mantle of fresh and disordered snow.

The man was shocked. It was as though he had just heard his own sentence of death. For a moment he sat and stared at the spot where the fire had been. Then he grew very calm. Perhaps the old-timer on Sulphur Creek was right. If he had only had a trail-mate he would have been in no danger now. The trail-mate could have built the fire. Well, it was up to him to build the fire over again, and this second time there must be no failure. Even if he succeeded, he would most likely lose some toes. His feet must be badly frozen by now, and there would be some time before the second fire was ready.

Such were his thoughts, but he did not sit and think them. He was busy all the time they were passing through his mind. He made a new foundation for a fire, this time in the open, where no treacherous tree could blot it out. Next, he gathered dry grasses and tiny twigs from the high-water flotsam. He could not bring his fingers together to pull them out, but he was able to gather them by the handful. In this way he got many rotten twigs and bits of green moss that were undesirable, but it was the best he could do. He worked methodically, even collecting an armful of the larger branches to be used later when the fire gathered strength. And all the while the dog sat and watched him, a certain yearning wistfulness in its eyes, for it looked upon him as the fire-provider, and the fire was slow in coming.

When all was ready, the man reached in his pocket for a second piece of birch bark. He knew the bark was there, and, though he could not feel it with his fingers, he could hear its crisp rustling as he fumbled for it. Try as he would, he could not clutch hold of it. And all the time, in his consciousness, was the knowledge that each instant his feet were freezing. This thought tended to put him in a panic, but he fought against it and kept calm. He pulled on his mittens with his teeth, and threshed his arms back and forth, beating his hands with all his might against his sides. He did this sitting down, and he stood up to do it; and all the while the dog sat in the snow, its wolf-brush of a tail curled around warmly over its forefeet, its sharp wolf-ears pricked forward intently as it watched the man. And the man, as he beat and threshed with his arms and hands, felt a great surge of envy as he regarded the creature that was warm and secure in its natural covering.

After a time he was aware of the first far-away signals of sensation in his beaten fingers. The faint tingling grew stronger till it evolved into a stinging ache that was excruciating, but which the man hailed with satisfaction. He stripped the mitten from his right hand and fetched forth the birch bark. The exposed fingers were quickly going numb again. Next he brought out his bunch of sulphur matches. But the tremendous cold had already driven the life out of his fingers. In his effort to separate one match from the others, the whole bunch fell in the snow. He tried to pick it out of the snow, but failed. The dead fingers could neither touch nor clutch. He was very careful. He drove the thought of his freezing feet, and nose, and cheeks, out of his mind, devoting his whole soul to the matches. He watched, using the sense of vision in place of that of touch, and when he saw his fingers on each side the bunch, he closed them—that is, he willed to close them, for the wires were down, and the fingers did not obey. He pulled the mitten on the right hand, and beat it fiercely against his knee. Then, with both mittened hands, he scooped the bunch of matches, along with much snow, into his lap. Yet he was no better off.

After some manipulation he managed to get the bunch between the heels of his mittened hands. In this fashion he carried it to his mouth. The ice crackled and snapped when by a violent effort he opened his mouth. He drew the lower jaw in, curled the upper lip out of the way, and scraped the bunch with his upper teeth in order to separate a match. He succeeded in getting one, which he dropped on his lap. He was no better off. He could not pick it up. Then he devised a way. He picked it up in his teeth and scratched it on his leg. Twenty times he scratched before he succeeded in lighting it. As it flamed he held it with his teeth to the birch bark. But the burning brimstone went up his nostrils and into his lungs, causing him to cough spasmodically. The match fell into the snow and went out.

The old-timer on Sulphur Creek was right, he thought in the moment of controlled despair that ensued: after fifty below, a man should travel with a partner. He beat his hands, but failed in exciting any sensation. Suddenly he bared both hands, removing the mittens with his teeth. He caught the whole bunch between the heels of his hands. His arm-muscles not being frozen enabled him to press the hand-heels tightly against the matches. Then he scratched the bunch along his leg. It flared into flame, seventy sulphur matches at once! There was no wind to blow them out. He kept his head to one side to escape the strangling fumes, and held the blazing bunch to the birch bark. As he so held it, he became aware of sensation in his hand. His flesh was burning. He could smell it. Deep down below the surface he could feel it. The sensation developed into pain that grew acute. And still he endured it, holding the flame of the matches clumsily to the bark that would not light readily because his own burning hands were in the way, absorbing most of the flame.

At last, when he could endure no more, he jerked his hands apart. The blazing matches fell sizzling into the snow, but the birch bark was alight. He began laying dry grasses and the tiniest twigs on the flame. He could not pick and choose, for he had to lift the fuel between the heels of his hands. Small pieces of rotten wood and green moss clung to the twigs, and he bit them off as well as he could with his teeth. He cherished the flame carefully and awkwardly. It meant life, and it must not perish. The withdrawal of blood from the surface of his body now made him begin to shiver, and he grew more awkward. A large piece of green moss fell squarely on the little fire. He tried to poke it out with his fingers, but his shivering frame made him poke too far, and he disrupted the nucleus of the little fire, the burning grasses and tiny twigs separating and scattering. He tried to poke them together again, but in spite of the tenseness of the effort, his shivering got away with him, and the twigs were hopelessly scattered. Each twig gushed a puff of smoke and went out. The fire-provider had failed. As he looked apathetically about him, his eyes chanced on the dog, sitting across the ruins of the fire from him, in the snow, making restless, hunching movements, slightly lifting one forefoot and then the other, shifting its weight back and forth on them with wistful eagerness.

The sight of the dog put a wild idea into his head. He remembered the tale of the man, caught in a blizzard, who killed a steer and crawled inside the carcass, and so was saved. He would kill the dog and bury his hands in the warm body until the numbness went out of them. Then he could build another fire. He spoke to the dog, calling it to him; but in his voice was a strange note of fear that frightened the animal, who had never known the man to speak in such way before. Something was the matter, and its suspicious nature sensed danger—it knew not what danger, but somewhere, somehow, in its brain arose an apprehension of the man. It flattened its ears down at the sound of the man's voice, and its restless, hunching movements and the liftings and shiftings of its forefeet became more pronounced; but it would not come to the man. He got on his hands and knees and crawled toward the dog. This unusual posture again excited suspicion, and the animal sidled mincingly away.

The man sat up in the snow for a moment and struggled for calmness. Then he pulled on his mittens, by means of his teeth, and got upon his feet. He glanced down at first in order to assure himself that he was really standing up, for the absence of sensation in his feet left him unrelated to the earth. His erect position in itself started to drive the webs of suspicion from the dog's mind; and when he spoke peremptorily, with the sound of whiplashes in his voice, the dog rendered its customary allegiance and came to him. As it came within reaching distance, the man lost his control. His arms flashed out to the dog, and he experienced genuine surprise when he discovered that his hands could not clutch, that there was neither bend nor feeling in the fingers. He had forgotten for the moment that they were frozen and that they were freezing more and more. All this happened quickly, and before the animal could get away, he encircled its body with his arms. He sat down in the snow, and in this fashion held the dog, while it snarled and whined and struggled.

But it was all he could do, hold its body encircled in his arms and sit there. He realized that he could not kill the dog. There was no way to do it. With his helpless hands he could neither draw nor hold his sheath-knife nor throttle the animal. He released it, and it plunged wildly away, with tail between its legs, and still snarling. It halted forty feet away and surveyed him curiously, with ears sharply pricked forward. The man looked down at his hands in order to locate them, and found them hanging on the ends of his arms. It struck him as curious that one should have to use his eyes in order to find out where his hands were. He began threshing his arms back and forth, beating the mittened hands against his sides. He did this for five minutes, violently, and his heart pumped enough blood up to the surface to put a stop to his shivering. But no sensation was aroused in the hands. He had an impression that they hung like weights on the ends of his arms, but when he tried to run the impression down, he could not find it.

A certain fear of death, dull and oppressive, came to him. This fear quickly became poignant as he realized that it was no longer a mere matter of freezing his fingers and toes, or of losing his hands and feet, but that it was a matter of life and death with the chances against him. This threw him into a panic, and he turned and ran up the creek-bed along the old, dim trail. The dog joined in behind and kept up with him. He ran blindly, without intention, in fear such as he had never known in his life. Slowly, as he plowed and floundered through the snow, he began to see things again,—the banks of the creek, the old timber-jams, the leafless aspens, and the sky. The running made him feel better. He did not shiver. Maybe, if he ran on, his feet would thaw out; and, anyway, if he ran far enough, he would reach camp and the boys. Without doubt he would lose some fingers and toes and some of his face; but the boys would take care of him, and save the rest of him when he got there. And at the same time there was another thought in his mind that said he would never get to the camp and the boys; that it was too many miles away, that the freezing had too great a start on him, and that he would soon be stiff and dead. This thought he kept in the background and refused to consider. Sometimes it pushed itself forward and demanded to be heard, but he thrust it back and strove to think of other things.

It struck him as curious that he could run at all on feet so frozen that he could not feel them when they struck the earth and took the weight of his body. He seemed to himself to skim along above the surface, and to have no connection with the earth. Somewhere he had once seen a winged Mercury, and he wondered if Mercury felt as he felt when skimming over the earth.

His theory of running until he reached camp and the boys had one flaw in it: he lacked the endurance. Several times he stumbled, and finally he tottered, crumpled up, and fell. When he tried to rise, he failed. He must sit and rest, he decided, and next time he would merely

walk and keep on going. As he sat and regained his breath, he noted
that he was feeling quite warm and comfortable. He was not shivering,
and it even seemed that a warm glow had come to his chest and trunk.
And yet, when he touched his nose or cheeks, there was no sensation.
Running would not thaw them out. Nor would it thaw out his hands
and feet. Then the thought came to him that the frozen portions of his
body must be extending. He tried to keep this thought down, to forget
it, to think of something else; he was aware of the panicky feeling that
it caused, and he was afraid of the panic. But the thought asserted itself,
and persisted, until it produced a vision of his body totally frozen. This
was too much, and he made another wild run along the trail. Once he
slowed down to a walk, but the thought of the freezing extending itself
made him run again.

And all the time the dog ran with him, at his heels. When he fell
down a second time, it curled its tail over its forefeet and sat in front
of him, facing him, curiously eager and intent. The warmth and security of the animal angered him, and he cursed it till it flattened down
its ears appeasingly. This time the shivering came more quickly upon
the man. He was losing in his battle with the frost. It was creeping into
his body from all sides. The thought of it drove him on, but he ran no
more than a hundred feet, when he staggered and pitched headlong. It
was his last panic. When he had recovered his breath and control, he
sat up and entertained in his mind the conception of meeting death with
dignity. However, the conception did not come to him in such terms.
His idea of it was that he had been making a fool of himself, running
around like a chicken with its head cut off—such was the simile that
occurred to him. Well, he was bound to freeze anyway, and he might
as well take it decently. With this new-found peace of mind came the
first glimmerings of drowsiness. A good idea, he thought, to sleep off
to death. It was like taking an anæsthetic. Freezing was not so bad as
people thought. There were lots worse ways to die.

He pictured the boys finding his body next day. Suddenly he found
himself with them, coming along the trail and looking for himself. And,
still with them, he came around a turn in the trail and found himself
lying in the snow. He did not belong with himself any more, for even
then he was out of himself, standing with the boys and looking at himself in the snow. It certainly was cold, was his thought. When he got
back to the States he could tell the folks what real cold was. He drifted
on from this to a vision of the old-timer on Sulphur Creek. He could
see him quite clearly, warm and comfortable, and smoking a pipe.

"You were right, old hoss; you were right," the man mumbled to the
old-timer of Sulphur Creek.

Then the man drowsed off into what seemed to him the most comfortable and satisfying sleep he had ever known. The dog sat facing him and waiting. The brief day drew to a close in a long, slow twilight. There were no signs of a fire to be made, and, besides, never in the dog's experience had it known a man to sit like that in the snow and make no fire. As the twilight drew on, its eager yearning for the fire mastered it, and with a great lifting and shifting of forefeet, it whined softly, then flattened its ears down in anticipation of being chidden by the man. But the man remained silent. Later, the dog whined loudly. And still later it crept close to the man and caught the scent of death. This made the animal bristle and back away. A little longer it delayed, howling under the stars that leaped and danced and shone brightly in the cold sky. Then it turned and trotted up the trail in the direction of the camp it knew, where were the other food-providers and fire-providers.

41

I'm a Fool

BY SHERWOOD ANDERSON

IT was a hard jolt for me, one of the most bitterest I ever had to face. And it all came about through my own foolishness too. Even yet, sometimes, I want to cry or swear or kick myself. Perhaps, even now, after all this time, there will be a kind of satisfaction in making myself look cheap by telling of it.

It began at three o'clock one October afternoon as I sat in the grandstand at the fall trotting and pacing meet at Sandusky, Ohio.

To tell the truth, I felt a little foolish that I should be sitting in the grandstand at all. During the summer before I had left my home town with Harry Whitehead and, with a nigger named Burt, had taken a job as swipe with one of the two horses Harry was campaigning through the fall race meets that year. Mother cried and my sister Mildred, who wanted to get a job as school teacher in our town that fall, stormed and scolded about the house all during the week before I left. They both thought it something disgraceful that one of our family should take a place as a swipe with race horses. I've an idea Mildred thought my taking the place would stand in the way of her getting the job she'd been working so long for.

But after all I had to work and there was no other work to be got. A big lumbering fellow of nineteen couldn't just hang around the house and I had got too big to mow people's lawns and sell newspapers. Little chaps who could get next to people's sympathies by their sizes were always getting jobs away from me. There was one fellow who kept saying to everyone who wanted a lawn mowed or a cistern cleaned that he was saving money to work his way through college, and I used to lie awake nights thinking up ways to injure him without being found out. I kept thinking of wagons running over him and bricks falling on his head as he walked along the street. But never mind him.

I got the place with Harry and I liked Burt fine. We got along splendid together. He was a big nigger with a lazy sprawling body and soft kind eyes, and when it came to a fight he could hit like Jack Johnson. He had Bucephalus, a big black pacing stallion that could do 2.09 or 2.10 if he had to, and I had a little gelding named Doctor Fritz that never lost a race all fall when Harry wanted him to win.

We set out from home late in July in a box car with the two horses, and after that, until late November, we kept moving along to the race meets and the fairs. It was a peachy time for me, I'll say that. Sometimes, now, I think that boys who are raised regular in houses, and never have a fine nigger like Burt for best friend, and go to high school and college, and never steal anything or get drunk a little, or learn to swear from fellows who know how, or come walking up in front of a grandstand in their shirt sleeves and with dirty horsey pants on when the races are going on and the grandstand is full of people all dressed up— What's the use talking about it? Such fellows don't know nothing at all. They've never had no opportunity.

But I did. Burt taught me how to rub down a horse and put the bandages on after a race and steam a horse out and a lot of valuable things for any man to know. He could wrap a bandage on a horse's leg so smooth that if it had been the same color you would think it was his skin, and I guess he'd have been a big driver, too, and got to the top like Murphy and Walter Cox and the others if he hadn't been black.

Gee whizz, it was fun. You got to a county seat town maybe, say, on a Saturday or Sunday, and the fair began the next Tuesday and lasted until Friday afternoon. Doctor Fritz would be, say, in the 2.25 trot on Tuesday afternoon and on Thursday afternoon Bucephalus would knock 'em cold in the "free-for-all" pace. It left you a lot of time to hang around and listen to horse talk, and see Burt knock some yap cold that got too gay, and you'd find out about horses and men and pick up a lot of stuff you could use all the rest of your life if you had some sense and salted down what you heard and felt and saw.

And then at the end of the week when the race meet was over, and Harry had run home to tend up to his livery stable business, you and Burt hitched the two horses to carts and drove slow and steady across country to the place for the next meeting so as not to overheat the horses, etc., etc., you know.

Gee whizz, gosh amighty, the nice hickorynut and beechnut and oaks and other kinds of trees along the roads, all brown and red, and the good smells, and Burt singing a song that was called Deep River, and the country girls at the windows of houses and everything. You can stick your colleges up your nose for all me. I guess I know where I got my education.

Why, one of those little burgs of towns you come to on the way, say now, on a Saturday afternoon, and Burt says, "let's lay up here." And you did.

And you took the horses to a livery stable and fed them and you got your good clothes out of a box and put them on.

And the town was full of farmers gaping, because they could see you were race horse people, and the kids maybe never see a nigger before and was afraid and run away when the two of us walked down their main street.

And that was before prohibition and all that foolishness, and so you went into a saloon, the two of you, and all the yaps come and stood around, and there was always someone pretended he was horsey and knew things and spoke up and began asking questions, and all you did was to lie and lie all you could about what horses you had, and I said I owned them, and then some fellow said, "Will you have a drink of whisky?" and Burt knocked his eye out the way he could say, offhand like, "Oh, well, all, all right, I'm agreeable to a little nip. I'll split a quart with you." Gee whizz.

But that isn't what I want to tell my story about. We got home late in November and I promised mother I'd quit the race horses for good. There's a lot of things you've got to promise a mother because she don't know any better.

And so, there not being any work in our town any more than when I left there to go to the races, I went off to Sandusky and got a pretty good place taking care of the horses for a man who owned a teaming and delivery and storage business there. It was a pretty good place with good eats and a day off each week and sleeping on a cot in the big barn, and mostly just shoveling in hay and oats to a lot of big good-enough skates of horses that couldn't have trotted a race with a toad. I wasn't dissatisfied and I could send money home.

And then, as I started to tell you, the fall races come to Sandusky and I got the day off and I went. I left the job at noon and had on my good clothes and my new brown derby hat I'd just bought the Saturday before, and a stand-up collar.

First of all I went downtown and walked about with the dudes. I've always thought to myself, "put up a good front," and so I did it. I had forty dollars in my pocket and so I went into the West House, a big hotel, and walked up to the cigar stand. "Give me three twenty-five cent cigars," I said. There was a lot of horse men and strangers and dressed-up people from other towns standing around in the lobby and in the bar, and I mingled amongst them. In the bar there was a fellow with a cane and a Windsor tie on, that it made me sick to look at him. I like a man to be a man and dress up, but not to go put on that kind of airs. So I pushed him aside, kind of rough, and had me a drink of whisky. And then he looked at me as though he thought he'd get gay, but he changed his mind and didn't say anything. And then I had another drink of whisky, just to show him something, and went out and had a hack out to the races all to myself, and when I got there I bought myself the best seat I could get up in the grandstand, but didn't go in for any of these boxes. That's putting on too many airs.

And so there I was, sitting up in the grandstand as gay as you please and looking down on the swipes coming out with their horses and with their dirty horsey pants on and the horse blankets swung over their shoulders same as I had been doing all the year before. I liked one thing about the same as the other, sitting up there and feeling grand and being down there and looking up at the yaps and feeling grander and more important too. One thing's about as good as another if you take it just right. I've often said that.

Well, right in front of me, in the grandstand that day, there was a fellow with a couple of girls and they was about my age. The young fellow was a nice guy all right. He was the kind maybe that goes to college and then comes to be a lawyer or maybe a newspaper editor or something like that, but he wasn't stuck on himself. There are some of that kind are all right and he was one of the ones.

He had his sister with him and another girl and the sister looked around over his shoulder, accidental at first, not intending to start anything—she wasn't that kind—and her eyes and mine happened to meet.

You know how it is. Gee, she was a peach. She had on a soft dress, kind of a blue stuff, and it looked carelessly made, but was well sewed and made and everything. I knew that much. I blushed when she looked right at me and so did she. She was the nicest girl I've ever seen in my life. She wasn't stuck on herself and she could talk proper grammar without being like a school teacher or something like that. What I mean is, she was O.K. I think maybe her father was well-to-do, but not rich to make her chesty because she was his daughter, as some are. Maybe he owned a drug store or a dry goods store in their home town, or something like that. She never told me and I never asked.

My own people are all O.K. too, when you come to that. My grandfather was Welsh and over in the old country, in Wales, he was—but never mind that.

The first heat of the first race come off and the young fellow setting there with the two girls left them and went down to make a bet. I knew what he was up to, but he didn't talk big and noisy and let everyone around know he was a sport, as some do. He wasn't that kind. Well, he come back and I heard him tell the two girls what horse he'd bet on, and when the heat was trotted they all half got to their feet and acted in the excited, sweaty way people do when they've got money down on a race, and the horse they bet on is up there pretty close at the end, and they think maybe he'll come on with a rush, but he never does because he hasn't got the old juice in him, come right down to it.

And, then, pretty soon, the horses came out for the 2.18 pace and there was a horse in it I knew. He was a horse Bob French had in his string, but Bob didn't own him. He was a horse owned by a Mr. Mathers down at Marietta, Ohio.

This Mr. Mathers had a lot of money and owned a coal mine or something, and he had a swell place out in the country, and he was stuck on race horses, but was a Presbyterian or something, and I think more than likely his wife was one, too, maybe a stiffer one than himself. So he never raced his horses hisself, and the story round the Ohio race tracks was that when one of his horses got ready to go to the races he turned him over to Bob French and pretended to his wife he was sold.

So Bob had the horses and he did pretty much as he pleased and you can't blame Bob; at least, I never did. Sometimes he was out to win and sometimes he wasn't. I never cared much about that when I was swiping a horse. What I did want to know was that my horse had the speed and could go out in front if you wanted him to.

And, as I'm telling you, there was Bob in this race with one of Mr. Mathers' horses, was named "About Ben Ahem" or something like that, and was fast as a streak. He was a gelding and had a mark of 2.21, but could step in .08 or .09.

Because when Burt and I were out, as I've told you, the year before, there was a nigger Burt knew, worked for Mr. Mathers, and we went out there one day when we didn't have no race on at the Marietta Fair and our boss Harry had gone home.

And so everyone was gone to the fair but just this one nigger, and he took us all through Mr. Mathers' swell house and he and Burt tapped a bottle of wine Mr. Mathers had hid in his bedroom, back in a closet, without his wife knowing, and he showed us this Ahem horse. Burt was always stuck on being a driver, but didn't have much chance to get to the top, being a nigger, and he and the other nigger gulped that whole bottle of wine and Burt got a little lit up.

So the nigger let Burt take this About Ben Ahem and step him a mile in a track Mr. Mathers had all to himself, right there on the farm. And Mr. Mathers had one child, a daughter, kinda sick and not very good-looking, and she came home and we had to hustle and get About Ben Ahem stuck back in the barn.

I'm only telling you to get everything straight. At Sandusky, that afternoon I was at the fair, this young fellow with the two girls was fussed, being with the girls and losing his bet. You know how a fellow is that way. One of them was his girl and the other his sister. I had figured that out.

"Gee whizz," I says to myself, "I'm going to give him the dope."

He was mighty nice when I touched him on the shoulder. He and the girls were nice to me right from the start and clear to the end. I'm not blaming them.

And so he leaned back and I gave him the dope on About Ben Ahem. "Don't bet a cent on this first heat because he'll go like an oxen hitched to a plough, but when the first heat is over go right down and lay on your pile." That's what I told him.

Well, I never saw a fellow treat any one sweller. There was a fat man sitting beside the little girl that had looked at me twice by this time, and I at her, and both blushing, and what did he do but have the nerve to turn and ask the fat man to get up and change places with me so I could set with his crowd.

Gee whizz, amighty. There I was. What a chump I was to go and get gay up there in the West House bar, and just because that dude was standing there with a cane and that kind of a necktie on, to go and get all balled up and drink that whisky, just to show off.

Of course, she would know, me setting right beside her and letting her smell of my breath. I could have kicked myself right down out of that grandstand and all around that race track and made a faster record than most of the skates of horses they had there that year.

Because that girl wasn't any mutt of a girl. What wouldn't I have given right then for a stick of chewing gum to chew, or a lozenger, or some licorice, or most anything. I was glad I had those twenty-five cent cigars in my pocket, and right away I give that fellow one and lit one myself. Then that fat man got up and we changed places and there I was plunked down beside her.

They introduced themselves, and the fellow's best girl he had with him, was named Miss Elinor Woodbury, and her father was a manufacturer of barrels from a place called Tiffin, Ohio. And the fellow himself was named Wilbur Wessen and his sister was Miss Lucy Wessen.

I suppose it was their having such swell names got me off my trolley. A fellow, just because he has been a swipe with a race horse, and works taking care of horses for a man in the teaming, delivery and storage business, isn't any better or worse than anyone else. I've often thought that, and said it, too.

But you know how a fellow is. There's something in that kind of nice clothes, and the kind of nice eyes she had, and the way she looked at me, awhile before, over her brother's shoulder, and me looking back at her, and both of us blushing.

I couldn't show her up for a boob, could I?

I made a fool of myself, that's what I did. I said my name was Walter Mathers from Marietta, Ohio, and then I told all three of them the smashingest lie you ever heard. What I said was that my father owned the horse About Ben Ahem, and that he had let him out to this Bob French for racing purposes, because our family was proud and had never gone into racing that way, in our own name, I mean. Then I had got started, and they were all leaning over and listening, and Miss Lucy Wessen's eyes were shining, and I went the whole hog.

I told about our place down at Marietta, and about the big stables and the grand brick house we had on a hill, up above the Ohio River, but I knew enough not to do it in no bragging way. What I did was to start things and then let them drag the rest out of me. I acted just as reluctant to tell as I could. Our family hasn't got any barrel factory, and, since I've known us, we've always been pretty poor, but not asking anything of anyone at that, and my grandfather, over in Wales—but never mind that.

We set there talking like we had known each other for years and years, and I went and told them that my father had been expecting maybe this Bob French wasn't on the square, and had sent me up to Sandusky on the sly to find out what I could.

And I bluffed it through I had found out all about the 2.18 pace in which About Ben Ahem was to start.

I said he would lose the first heat by pacing like a lame cow and then he would come back and skin 'em alive after that. And to back up what I said I took thirty dollars out of my pocket and handed it to Mr. Wilbur Wessen and asked him would he mind, after the first heat, to go down and place it on About Ben Ahem for whatever odds he could get. What I said was that I didn't want Bob French to see me and none of the swipes.

Sure enough the first heat come off and About Ben Ahem went off his stride, up the back stretch, and looked like a wooden horse or a sick one, and come in to be last. Then this Wilbur Wessen went down to the betting place under the grandstand and there I was with the two girls, and when that Miss Woodbury was looking the other way once, Lucy Wessen kinda, with her shoulder you know, kinda touched me. You know how a woman can do. They get close, but not getting gay either. You know what they do. Gee whizz.

And then they give me a jolt. What they had done when I didn't know, was to get together, and they had decided Wilbur Wessen would bet fifty dollars, and the two girls had gone and put in ten dollars each of their own money, too. I was sick then, but I was sicker later.

About the gelding, About Ben Ahem, and their winning their money

I wasn't worried a lot about that. It come out O.K. Ahem stepped the next three heats like a bushel of spoiled eggs going to market before they could be found out, and Wilbur Wessen had got nine to two for the money. There was something else eating at me.

Because Wilbur come back after he had bet the money, and after that he spent most of his time talking to that Miss Woodbury, and Lucy Wessen and I was left alone together like on a desert island. Gee, if I'd only been on the square or if there had been any way of getting myself on the square. There ain't any Walter Mathers, like I said to her and them, and there hasn't ever been one, but if there was, I bet I'd go to Marietta, Ohio, and shoot him tomorrow.

There I was, big boob that I am. Pretty soon the race was over, and Wilbur had gone down and collected our money, and we had a hack downtown, and he stood us a swell dinner at the West House, and a bottle of champagne beside.

And I was with that girl and she wasn't saying much, and I wasn't saying much either. One thing I know. She wasn't stuck on me because of the lie about my father being rich and all that. There's a way you know. . . . Craps amighty. There's a kind of girl you see just once in your life, and if you don't get busy and make hay then you're gone for good and all and might as well go jump off a bridge. They give you a look from inside of them somewhere, and it ain't no vamping, and what it means is—you want that girl to be your wife, and you want nice things around her like flowers and swell clothes, and you want her to have the kids you're going to have, and you want good music played and no ragtime. Gee whizz.

There's a place over near Sandusky, across a kind of bay, and it's called Cedar Point. And when we had had that dinner we went over to it in a launch, all by ourselves. Wilbur and Miss Lucy and that Miss Woodbury had to catch a ten o'clock train back to Tiffin, Ohio, because when you're out with girls like that you can't get careless and miss any trains and stay out all night like you can with some kinds of Janes.

And Wilbur blowed himself to the launch and it cost him fifteen cold plunks, but I wouldn't ever have knew it if I hadn't listened. He wasn't no tin horn kind of a sport.

Over at the Cedar Point place we didn't stay around where there was a gang of common kind of cattle at all.

There was big dance halls and dining places for yaps, and there was a beach you could walk along and get where it was dark, and we went there.

She didn't talk hardly at all and neither did I, and I was thinking how glad I was my mother was all right, and always made us kids learn to eat with a fork at table and not swill soup and not be noisy and rough like a gang you see around a race track that way.

Then Wilbur and his girl went away up the beach and Lucy and I set down in a dark place where there was some roots of old trees the water had washed up, and after that, the time, till we had to go back in the launch and they had to catch their trains, wasn't nothing at all. It went like winking your eye.

Here's how it was. The place we were setting in was dark, like I said, and there was roots from that old stump sticking up like arms, and there was a watery smell, and the night was like—as if you could put your hand out and feel it—so warm and soft and dark and sweet like an orange.

I most cried and I most swore and I most jumped up and danced, I was so mad and happy and sad.

When Wilbur come back from being alone with his girl, and she saw him coming, Lucy she says, "We got to go to the train now," and she was most crying, too, but she never knew nothing I knew, and she couldn't be so all busted up. And then, before Wilbur and Miss Woodbury got up to where she was, she put her face up and kissed me quick and put her head up against me and she was all quivering and— Gee whizz.

Sometimes I hope I have cancer and die. I guess you know what I mean. We went in the launch across the bay to the train like that, and it was dark too. She whispered and said it was like she and I could get out of the boat and walk on the water, and it sounded foolish, but I knew what she meant.

And then quick, we were right at the depot, and there was a big gang of yaps, the kind that goes to the fairs, and crowded and milling around like cattle, and how could I tell her? "It won't be long because you'll write and I'll write to you." That's all she said.

I got a chance like a hay barn afire. A swell chance I got.

And maybe she would write me, down at Marietta that way, and the letter would come back, and stamped on the front of it by the U.S.A. "there ain't any such guy," or something like that, whatever they stamp on a letter that way.

And me trying to pass myself off for a bigbug and a swell—to her, as decent a little body as God ever made. Craps amighty. A swell chance I got.

And then the train come in and she got on, and Wilbur Wessen come and shook hands with me, and that Miss Woodbury was nice too, and bowed to me and I at her and the train went and I busted out and cried like a kid.

Gee, I could have run after that train and made Dan Patch look like a freight train after a wreck, but socks amighty, what was the use? Did you ever see such a fool?

I'll bet you what—if I had an arm broke right now or a train had run over my foot—I wouldn't go to no doctor at all. I'd go set down and let her hurt and hurt—that's what I'd do.

I'll bet you what—if I hadn't a drunk that booze I'd a never been such a boob as to go tell such a lie—that couldn't never be made straight to a lady like her.

I wish I had that fellow right here that had on a Windsor tie and carried a cane. I'd smash bim for fair. Gosh darn his eyes. He's a big fool—that's what he is.

And if I'm not another you just go find me one and I'll quit working and be a bum and give him my job. I don't care nothing for working and earning money and saving it for no such boob as myself.

42

I Want to Know Why

BY SHERWOOD ANDERSON

WE got up at four in the morning, that first day in the East. On the evening before we had climbed off a freight train at the edge of town, and with the true instinct of Kentucky boys had found our way across town and to the race track and the stables at once. Then we knew we were all right. Hanley Turner right away found a nigger we knew. It was Bildad Johnson who in the winter works at Ed Becker's livery barn in our home town, Beckersville. Bildad is a good cook as almost all our niggers are and of course he, like everyone in our part of Kentucky who is anyone at all, likes the horses. In the spring Bildad begins to scratch around. A nigger from our country can flatter and wheedle anyone into letting him do most anything he wants. Bildad wheedles the stable men and the trainers from the horse farms in our country around Lexington. The trainers come into town in the evening to stand around and talk and maybe get into a poker game. Bildad gets in with them. He is always doing little favors and telling about things to eat, chicken browned in a pan, and how is the best way to cook sweet potatoes and corn bread. It makes your mouth water to hear him. When the racing season comes on and the horses go to the races and there is all the talk on the streets in the evenings about the new colts, and everyone says when they are going over to Lexington or to the spring meeting at Churchhill Downs or to Latonia, and the horsemen that have been down to New Orleans or maybe at the winter meeting at Havana in Cuba come home to spend a week before they start out again, at such a time when everything talked about in Beckersville is just horses and nothing else and the outfits start out and horse racing is in every breath of air you breathe, Bildad shows up with a job as cook for some outfit. Often when I think about it, his always going all season to the races and working in the livery barn in the winter where horses are and where men like to come and talk about horses, I wish I was a nigger. It's a foolish thing to say, but that's the way I am about being around horses, just crazy. I can't help it.

Well, I must tell you about what we did and let you in on what I'm talking about. Four of us boys from Beckersville, all whites and sons of men who live in Beckersville regular, made up our minds we were going to the races, not just to Lexington or Louisville, I don't mean, but to the big Eastern track we were always hearing our Beckersville men talk about, to Saratoga. We were all pretty young then. I was just turned fifteen and I was the oldest of the four. It was my scheme. I admit that and I talked the others into trying it. There was Hanley Turner and Henry Rieback and Tom Tumberton and myself. I had thirty-seven dollars I had earned during the winter working nights and Saturdays in Enoch Myer's grocery. Henry Rieback had eleven dollars and the others, Hanley and Tom, had only a dollar or two each. We fixed it all up and laid low until the Kentucky spring meetings were over and some of our men, the sportiest ones, the ones we envied the most, had cut out—then we cut out too.

I won't tell you the trouble we had beating our way on freights and all. We went through Cleveland and Buffalo and other cities and saw Niagara Falls. We bought things there, souvenirs and spoons and cards and shells with pictures of the falls on them for our sisters and mothers, but thought we had better not send any of the things home. We didn't want to put the folks on our trail and maybe be nabbed.

We got into Saratoga as I said at night and went to the track. Bildad fed us up. He showed us a place to sleep in hay over a shed and promised to keep still. Niggers are all right about things like that. They won't squeal on you. Often a white man you might meet, when you had run away from home like that, might appear to be all right and give you a quarter or a half dollar or something, and then go right and give you away. White men will do that, but not a nigger. You can trust them. They are squarer with kids. I don't know why.

At the Saratoga meeting that year there were a lot of men from home. Dave Williams and Arthur Mulford and Jerry Myers and others. Then there was a lot from Louisville and Lexington Henry Rieback knew but I didn't. They were professional gamblers and Henry Rieback's father is one too. He is what is called a sheet writer and goes away most of the year to tracks. In the winter when he is home in Beckersville he don't stay there much but goes away to cities and deals faro. He is a nice man and generous, is always sending Henry presents, a bicycle and a gold watch and a Boy Scout suit of clothes and things like that.

My own father is a lawyer. He's all right, but don't make much money and can't buy me things and anyway I'm getting so old now I don't expect it. He never said nothing to me against Henry, but Hanley Turner and Tom Tumberton's fathers did. They said to their boys that money so come by is no good and they didn't want their boys brought up to hear gamblers' talk and be thinking about such things and maybe embrace them.

That's all right and I guess the men know what they are talking about, but I don't see what it's got to do with Henry or with horses either. That's what I'm writing this story about. I'm puzzled. I'm getting to be a man and want to think straight and be O.K., and there's something I saw at the race meeting at the Eastern track I can't figure out.

I can't help it, I'm crazy about thoroughbred horses. I've always been that way. When I was ten years old and saw I was going to be big and couldn't be a rider I was so sorry I nearly died. Harry Hellinfinger in Beckersville, whose father is Postmaster, is grown up and too lazy to work, but likes to stand around in the street and get up jokes on boys like sending them to a hardware store for a gimlet to bore square holes and other jokes like that. He played one on me. He told me that if I would eat a half a cigar I would be stunted and not grow any more and maybe could be a rider. I did it. When father wasn't looking I took a cigar out of his pocket and gagged it down some way. It made me awful sick and the doctor had to be sent for and then it did no good. I kept right on growing. It was a joke. When I told what I had done and why, most fathers would have whipped me but mine didn't.

Well, I didn't get stunted and didn't die. It serves Harry Hellinfinger right. Then I made up my mind I would like to be a stable boy, but had to give that up too. Mostly niggers do that work and I knew father wouldn't let me go into it. No use to ask him.

If you've never been crazy about thoroughbreds it's because you've never been around where they are much and don't know any better. They're beautiful. There isn't anything so lovely and clean and full of spunk and honest and everything as some race horses. On the big horse farms that are all around our town Beckersville there are tracks and the horses run in the early morning. More than a thousand times I've got out of bed before daylight and walked two or three miles to the tracks. Mother wouldn't of let me go but father always says, "Let him alone." So I got some bread out of the bread box and some butter and jam, gobbled it and lit out.

At the tracks you sit on the fence with men, whites and niggers, and they chew tobacco and talk, and then the colts are brought out. It's early and the grass is covered with shiny dew and in another field

a man is plowing and they are frying things in a shed where the track
niggers sleep, and you know how a nigger can giggle and laugh and
say things that make you laugh. A white man can't do it and some
niggers can't but a track nigger can every time.

And so the colts are brought out and some are just galloped by
stable boys, but almost every morning on a big track owned by a rich
man who lives maybe in New York, there are always, nearly every
morning, a few colts and some of the old race horses and geldings and
mares that are cut loose.

It brings a lump up into my throat when a horse runs. I don't mean
all horses but some. I can pick them nearly every time. It's in my blood
like in the blood of race track niggers and trainers. Even when they just
go slop-jogging along with a little nigger on their backs I can tell a
winner. If my throat hurts and it's hard for me to swallow, that's him.
He'll run like Sam Hill when you let him out. If he don't win every
time it'll be a wonder and because they've got him in a pocket behind
another or he was pulled or got off bad at the post or something. If I
wanted to be a gambler like Henry Rieback's father I could get rich.
I know I could and Henry says so too. All I would have to do is to wait
till that hurt comes when I see a horse and then bet every cent. That's
what I would do if I wanted to be a gambler, but I don't.

When you're at the tracks in the morning—not the race tracks but
the training tracks around Beckersville—you don't see a horse, the
kind I've been talking about, very often, but it's nice anyway. Any
thoroughbred, that is sired right and out of a good mare and trained by
a man that knows how, can run. If he couldn't what would he be there
for and not pulling a plow?

Well, out of the stables they come and the boys are on their backs and
it's lovely to be there. You hunch down on top of the fence and itch
inside you. Over in the sheds the niggers giggle and sing. Bacon is being
fried and coffee made. Everything smells lovely. Nothing smells better
than coffee and manure and horses and niggers and bacon frying and
pipes being smoked out of doors on a morning like that. It just gets
you, that's what it does.

But about Saratoga. We was there six days and not a soul from home
seen us and everything came off just as we wanted it to, fine weather
and horses and races and all. We beat our way home and Bildad gave
us a basket with fried chicken and bread and other eatables in, and I
had eighteen dollars when we got back to Beckersville. Mother jawed
and cried but Pop didn't say much. I told everything we done except
one thing. I did and saw that alone. That's what I'm writing about. It
got me upset. I think about it at night. Here it is.

At Saratoga we laid up nights in the hay in the shed Bildad had showed us and ate with the niggers early and at night when the race people had all gone away. The men from home stayed mostly in the grandstand and betting field, and didn't come out around the places where the horses are kept except to the paddocks just before a race when the horses are saddled. At Saratoga they don't have paddocks under an open shed as at Lexington and Churchhill Downs and other tracks down in our country, but saddle the horses right out in an open place under trees on a lawn as smooth and nice as Banker Bohon's front yard here in Beckersville. It's lovely. The horses are sweaty and nervous and shine and the men come out and smoke cigars and look at them and the trainers are there and the owners, and your heart thumps so you can hardly breathe.

Then the bugle blows for post and the boys that ride come running out with their silk clothes on and you run to get a place by the fence with the niggers.

I always am wanting to be a trainer or owner, and at the risk of being seen and caught and sent home I went to the paddocks before every race. The other boys didn't but I did.

We got to Saratoga on a Friday and on Wednesday the next week the big Mullford Handicap was to be run. Middlestride was in it and Sunstreak. The weather was fine and the track fast. I couldn't sleep the night before.

What had happened was that both these horses are the kind it makes my throat hurt to see. Middlestride is long and looks awkward and is a gelding. He belongs to Joe Thompson, a little owner from home who only has a half dozen horses. The Mullford Handicap is for a mile and Middlestride can't untrack fast. He goes away slow and is always way back at the half, then he begins to run and if the race is a mile and a quarter he'll just eat up everything and get there.

Sunstreak is different. He is a stallion and nervous and belongs on the biggest farm we've got in our country, the Van Riddle place that belongs to Mr. Van Riddle of New York. Sunstreak is like a girl you think about sometimes but never see. He is hard all over and lovely too. When you look at his head you want to kiss him. He is trained by Jerry Tillford who knows me and has been good to me lots of times, lets me walk into a horse's stall to look at him close and other things. There isn't anything as sweet as that horse. He stands at the post quiet and not letting on, but he is just burning up inside. Then when the barrier goes up he is off like his name, Sunstreak. It makes you ache to see him. It hurts you. He just lays down and runs like a bird dog. There can't anything I ever see run like him except Middlestride when he gets untracked and stretches himself.

Gee! I ached to see that race and those two horses run, ached and dreaded it too. I didn't want to see either of our horses beaten. We had never sent a pair like that to the races before. Old men in Beckersville said so and the niggers said so. It was a fact.

Before the race I went over to the paddocks to see. I looked a last look at Middlestride, who isn't such a much standing in a paddock that way, then I went to see Sunstreak.

It was his day. I knew when I see him. I forgot all about being seen myself and walked right up. All the men from Beckersville were there and no one noticed me except Jerry Tillford. He saw me and something happened. I'll tell you about that.

I was standing looking at that horse and aching. In some way, I can't tell how, I knew just how Sunstreak felt inside. He was quiet and letting the niggers rub his legs and Mr. Van Riddle himself put the saddle on, but he was just a raging torrent inside. He was like the water in the river at Niagara Falls just before it goes plunk down. That horse wasn't thinking about running. He don't have to think about that. He was just thinking about holding himself back till the time for the running came. I knew that. I could just in a way see right inside him. He was going to do some awful running and I knew it. He wasn't bragging or letting on much or prancing or making a fuss, but just waiting. I knew it and Jerry Tillford his trainer knew. I looked up and then that man and I looked into each other's eyes. Something happened to me. I guess I loved the man as much as I did the horse because he knew what I knew. Seemed to me there wasn't anything in the world but that man and the horse and me. I cried and Jerry Tillford had a shine in his eyes. Then I came away to the fence to wait for the race. The horse was better than me, more steadier, and now I know better than Jerry. He was the quietest and he had to do the running.

Sunstreak ran first of course and he busted the world's record for a mile. I've seen that if I never see anything more. Everything came out just as I expected. Middlestride got left at the post and was way back and closed up to be second, just as I knew he would. He'll get a world's record too some day. They can't skin the Beckersville country on horses.

I watched the race calm because I knew what would happen. I was sure. Hanley Turner and Henry Rieback and Tom Tumberton were all more excited than me.

A funny thing had happened to me. I was thinking about Jerry Tillford the trainer and how happy he was all through the race. I liked him that afternoon even more than I ever liked my own father. I almost forgot the horses thinking that way about him. It was because of what I had seen in his eyes as he stood in the paddocks beside Sunstreak before the race started. I knew he had been watching and working with Sunstreak since the horse was a baby colt, had taught him to run and be patient and when to let himself out and not to quit, never. I knew that for him it was like a mother seeing her child do something brave or wonderful. It was the first time I ever felt for a man like that.

After the race that night I cut out from Tom and Hanley and Henry. I wanted to be by myself and I wanted to be near Jerry Tillford if I could work it. Here is what happened.

The track in Saratoga is near the edge of town. It is all polished up and trees around, the evergreen kind, and grass and everything painted and nice. If you go past the track you get to a hard road made of asphalt for automobiles, and if you go along this for a few miles there is a road turns off to a little rummy-looking farm house set in a yard.

That night after the race I went along that road because I had seen Jerry and some other men go that way in an automobile. I didn't expect to find them. I walked for a ways and then sat down by a fence to think. It was the direction they went in. I wanted to be as near Jerry as I could. I felt close to him. Pretty soon I went up the side road—I don't know why—and came to the rummy farm house. I was just lonesome to see Jerry, like wanting to see your father at night when you were a young kid. Just then an automobile came along and turned in. Jerry was in it and Henry Rieback's father, and Arthur Bedford from home, and Dave Williams and two other men I didn't know. They got out of the car and went into the house, all but Henry Rieback's father who quarreled with them and said he wouldn't go. It was only about nine o'clock, but they were all drunk and the rummy-looking farm house was a place for bad women to stay in. That's what it was. I crept up along a fence and looked through a window and saw.

It's what gives me the fantods. I can't make it out. The women in the house were all ugly mean-looking women, not nice to look at or be near. They were homely too, except one who was tall and looked a little like the gelding Middlestride, but not clean like him, but with a hard ugly mouth. She had red hair. I saw everything plain. I got up by an old rose bush by an open window and looked. The women had on loose dresses and sat around in chairs. The men came in and some sat on the women's laps. The place smelled rotten and there was rotten talk, the kind a kid hears around a livery stable in a town like Beckersville in the winter but don't ever expect to hear talked when there are women around. It was rotten. A nigger wouldn't go into such a place.

I looked at Jerry Tillford. I've told you how I had been feeling about him on account of his knowing what was going on inside of Sunstreak in the minute before he went to the post for the race in which he made a world's record.

Jerry bragged in that bad woman house as I know Sunstreak

wouldn't never have bragged. He said that he made that horse, that it was him that won the race and made the record. He lied and bragged like a fool. I never heard such silly talk.

And then, what do you suppose he did! He looked at the woman in there, the one that was lean and hard-mouthed and looked a little like the gelding Middlestride, but not clean like him, and his eyes began to shine just as they did when he looked at me and at Sunstreak in the paddocks at the track in the afternoon. I stood there by the window—gee!—but I wished I hadn't gone away from the tracks, but had stayed with the boys and the niggers and the horses. The tall rotten-looking woman was between us just as Sunstreak was in the paddocks in the afternoon.

Then, all of a sudden, I began to hate that man. I wanted to scream and rush in the room and kill him. I never had such a feeling before. I was so mad clean through that I cried and my fists were doubled up so my finger-nails cut my hands.

And Jerry's eyes kept shining and he waved back and forth, and then he went and kissed that woman and I crept away and went back to the tracks and to bed and didn't sleep hardly any, and then next day I got the other kids to start home with me and never told them anything I seen.

I been thinking about it ever since. I can't make it out. Spring has come again and I'm nearly sixteen and go to the tracks mornings same as always, and I see Sunstreak and Middlestride and a new colt named Strident I'll bet will lay them all out, but no one thinks so but me and two or three niggers.

But things are different. At the tracks the air don't taste as good or smell as good. It's because a man like Jerry Tillford, who knows what he does, could see a horse like Sunstreak run, and kiss a woman like that the same day. I can't make it out. Darn him, what did he want to do like that for? I keep thinking about it and it spoils looking at horses and smelling things and hearing niggers laugh and everything. Sometimes I'm so mad about it I want to fight someone. It gives me the fantods. What did he do it for? I want to know why.

43

The Great Pancake Record

BY OWEN JOHNSON

LITTLE Smeed stood apart, in the obscure shelter of the station, waiting to take his place on the stage which would carry him to the great new boarding school. He was frail and undersized, with a long, pointed nose and vacant eyes that stupidly assisted the wide mouth to make up a famished face. The scarred bag in his hand hung from one clasp, the premature trousers were at half-mast, while pink polka-dots blazed from the cuffs of his nervous sleeves.

By the wheels of the stage "Fire Crackers" Glendenning and "Jock" Hasbrouck, veterans of the Kennedy House, sporting the 'varsity initials on their sweaters and caps, were busily engaged in cross-examining the new boys who clambered timidly to their places on top. Presently, Fire Crackers, perceiving Smeed, hailed him.

"Hello, over there—what's your name?"

"Smeed, sir."

"Smeed what?"

"Johnnie Smeed."

The questioner looked him over with disfavor and said aggressively:

"You're not for the Kennedy?"

"No, sir."

"What house?"

"The Dickinson, sir."

"The Dickinson, eh? That's a good one," said Fire Crackers, with a laugh, and, turning to his companion, he added, "Say, Jock, won't Hickey and the old Turkey be wild when they get this one?"

Little Smeed, uncomprehending of the judgment that had been passed, stowed his bag inside and clambered up to a place on the top.

Jimmy, at the reins, gave a warning shout. The horses, stirred by the whip, churned obediently through the sideways of Trenton.

Lounging on the stage were half a dozen newcomers, six well-assorted types, from the well-groomed stripling of the city to the aggressive, big-limbed animal from the West, all profoundly under the sway of the two old boys who sat on the box with Jimmy and rattled on with quiet superiority. The coach left the outskirts of the city and rolled into the white highway that leads to Lawrenceville. The known world departed for Smeed. He gazed fearfully ahead, waiting the first glimpse of the new continent.

Suddenly Fire Crackers turned and, scanning the embarrassed group, singled out the strong Westerner with an approving glance.

"You're for the Kennedy?"

The boy, stirring uneasily, blurted out:

"Yes, sir."

"What's your name?"

"Tom Walsh."

"How old are you?"

"Eighteen."

"What do you weigh?"

"One hundred and seventy."

"Stripped?"

"What? Oh, no, sir—regular way."

"You've played a good deal of football?"

"Yes, sir."

Hasbrouck took up the questioning with a critical appreciation.

"What position?"

"Guard and tackle."

"You know Bill Stevens?"

"Yes, sir."

"He spoke about you; said you played on the Military Academy. You'll try for the 'varsity?"

"I guess so."

Hasbrouck turned to Fire Crackers in solemn conclave.

"He ought to stand up against Turkey if he knows anything about the game. If we get a good end we ought to give that Dickinson crowd the fight of their lives."

"There's a fellow came from Montclair they say is pretty good," Fire Crackers said, with solicitous gravity. "The line'll be all right if we can get some good halves. That's where the Dickinson has it on us."

Smeed listened in awe to the two statesmen studying out the chances of the Kennedy eleven for the house championship, realizing suddenly that there were new and sacred purposes about his new life of which he had no conception. Then, absorbed by the fantasy of the trip and the strange unfolding world into which he was jogging, he forgot the lords of the Kennedy, forgot his fellows in ignorance, forgot that he didn't play football and was only a stripling, forgot everything but the fascination of the moment when the great school would rise out of the distance and fix itself indelibly in his memory.

"There's the water tower," said Jimmy, extending the whip; "you'll see the school from the top of the hill."

Little Smeed craned forward with a sudden thumping of his heart. In the distance, a mile away, a cluster of brick and tile sprang out of the green, like a herd of red deer surprised in the forest. Groups of boys began to show on the roadside. Strange greetings were flung back and forth.

"Hello-oo, Fire Crackers!"

"How-de-do, Saphead!"

"Oh, there, Jock Hasbrouck!"

"Oh, you Morning Glory!"

"Oh, you Kennedys, we're going to lick you!"

"Yes you are, Dickinson!"

The coach passed down the shaded vault of the village street, turned into the campus, passed the ivy-clad house of the head master and rolled around a circle of well-trimmed lawn, past the long, low Upper House where the Fourth Form gazed at them in senior superiority; past the great brown masses of Memorial Hall and the pointed chapel, around to where the houses were ranged in red, extended bodies. Little Smeed felt an abject sinking of the heart at this sudden exposure to the thousand eyes fastened upon him from the wide esplanade of the Upper, from the steps of Memorial, from house, windows and stoops, from the shade of apple trees and the glistening road.

All at once the stage stopped and Jimmy cried:

"Dickinson!"

At one end of the red-brick building, overrun with cool vines, a group of boys were lolling in flannels and light jerseys. A chorus went up.

"Hello, Fire Crackers!"

"Hello, Jock!"

"Hello, you Hickey boy!"

"Hello, Turkey; see what we've brought you!"

Smeed dropped to the ground amid a sudden hush.

"Fare," said Jimmy aggressively.

Smeed dug into his pocket and tendered the necessary coin. The coach squeaked away, while from the top Fire Crackers' exulting voice returned in insolent exultation:

"Hard luck, Dickinson! Hard luck, you, old Hickey!"

Little Smeed, his hat askew, his collar rolled up, his bag at his feet, stood in the road, alone in the world, miserable and thoroughly frightened. One path led to the silent, hostile group on the steps, another went in safety to the master's entrance. He picked up his bag hastily.

"Hello, you—over there!"

Smeed understood it was a command. He turned submissively and approached with embarrassed steps. Face to face with these superior beings, tanned and muscular, stretched in Olympian attitudes, he realized all at once the hopelessness of his ever daring to associate with such demi-gods. Still he stood, shifting from foot to foot, eying the steps, waiting for the solemn ordeal of examination and classification to be over.

"Well, Hungry—what's your name?"

Smeed comprehended that the future was decided, and that to the grave he would go down as "Hungry" Smeed. With a sigh of relief he answered:

"Smeed—John Smeed."

"Sir!"

"Sir."

"How old?"

"Fifteen."

"Sir!!"

"Sir."

"What do you weigh?"

"One hundred and six—sir!"

A grim silence succeeded this depressing information. Then some one in the back, as a mere matter of form, asked:

"Never played football?"

"No, sir."

"Baseball?"

"No, sir."

"Anything on the track?"

"No, sir."

"Sing?"

"No, sir," said Smeed, humbly.

"Do anything at all?"

Little Smeed glanced at the eaves where the swallows were swaying and then down at the soft couch of green at his feet and answered faintly:

"No, sir—I'm afraid not."

Another silence came, then some one said, in a voice of deepest conviction:

"A dead loss!"

Smeed went sadly into the house.

At the door he lingered long enough to hear the chorus burst out:

"A fine football team we'll have!"

"It's a put-up job!"

"They don't want us to win the championship again—that's it!"

"I say, we ought to kick."

Then, after a little, the same deep voice:

"A dead loss!"

With each succeeding week Hungry Smeed comprehended more fully the enormity of his offense in doing nothing and weighing one hundred and six pounds. He saw the new boys arrive, pass through the fire of christening, give respectable weights and go forth to the gridiron to be whipped into shape by Turkey and the Butcher, who played on the school eleven. Smeed humbly and thankfully went down each afternoon to the practice, carrying the sweaters and shin-guards, like the grateful little beast of burden that he was. He watched his juniors, Spider and Red Dog, rolling in the mud or flung gloriously under an avalanche of bodies; but then, they weighed over one hundred and thirty, while he was still at one hundred and six—a dead loss! The fever of house loyalty invaded him; he even came to look with resentment on the Faculty and to repeat secretly to himself that they never would have unloaded him on the Dickinson if they hadn't been willing to stoop to any methods to prevent the House again securing the championship.

The fact that the Dickinson, in an extraordinary manner, finally won by the closest of margins, consoled Smeed but a little while. There were no more sweaters to carry, or pails of barley water to fetch, or guard to be mounted on the old rail fence, to make certain that the spies from the Davis and Kennedy did not surprise the secret plays which Hickey and Slugger Jones had craftily evolved.

With the long winter months he felt more keenly his obscurity and the hopelessness of ever leaving a mark on the great desert of school life that would bring honor to the Dickinson. He resented even the lack of the mild hazing the other boys received—he was too insignificant to be so honored. He was only a "dead loss," good for nothing but to squeeze through his recitations, to sleep enormously, and to eat like a glutton with a hunger that could never be satisfied, little suspecting the future that lay in this famine of his stomach.

For it was written in the inscrutable fates that Hungry Smeed should leave a name that would go down imperishably to decades of schoolboys, when Dibbles' touchdown against Princeton and Kafer's home run should be only tinkling sounds. So it happened, and the agent of this divine destiny was Hickey.

It so happened that examinations being still in the threatening distance, Hickey's fertile brain was unoccupied with methods of facilitating his scholarly progress by homely inventions that allowed formulas and dates to be concealed in the palm and disappear obligingly up the sleeve on the approach of the Natural Enemy. Moreover, Hickey and Hickey's friends were in straitened circumstances, with all credit gone at the jigger-shop, and the appetite for jiggers in an acute stage of deprivation.

In this keenly sensitive, famished state of his imagination, Hickey suddenly became aware of a fact fraught with possibilities. Hungry Smeed had an appetite distinguished and remarkable even in that company of aching voids.

No sooner had this pregnant idea become his property than Hickey confided his hopes to Doc Macnooder, his chum and partner in plans that were dark and mysterious. Macnooder saw in a flash the glorious and lucrative possibilities. A very short series of tests sufficed to convince the twain that in little Smeed they had a phenomenon who needed only to be properly developed to pass into history.

Accordingly, on a certain muddy morning in March, Hickey and Doc Macnooder, with Smeed in tow, stole into the jigger-shop at an hour in defiance of regulations and fraught with delightful risks of detection.

Al, the watch-dog of the jigger, was tilted back, near a farther window, the parted tow hair falling doglike over his eyes, absorbed in the reading of Spenser's Faerie Queen, an abnormal taste which made him absolutely incomprehensible to the boyish mind. At the sound of the stolen entrance, Al put down the volume and started mechanically to rise. Then, recognizing his visitors, he returned to his chair, saying wearily:

"Nothing doing, Hickey."

"Guess again," said Hickey, cheerily. "We're not asking you to hang us up this time, Al."

"You haven't got any money," said Al, the recorder of allowances; "not unless you stole it."

"Al, we don't come to take your hard-earned money, but to do you good," put in Macnooder impudently. "We're bringing you a little sporting proposition."

"Have you come to pay up that account of yours?" said Al. "If not, run along, you Macnooder; don't waste my time, with your wildcat schemes."

"Al, this is a sporting proposition," took up Hickey.

"Has *he* any money?" said Al, who suddenly remembered that Smeed was not yet under suspicion.

"See here, Al," said Macnooder, "we'll back Smeed to eat the jiggers against you—for the crowd!"

"Where's your money?"

"Here," said Hickey; "this goes up if we lose." He produced a gold watch of Smeed's, and was about to tender it when he withdrew it with a sudden caution. "On the condition, if we win I get it back and you won't hold it up against my account."

"All right. Let's see it."

The watch was given to Al, who looked it over, grunted in approval, and then looked at little Smeed.

"Now, Al," said Macnooder softly, "give us a gambling chance; he's only a runt."

Al considered, and Al was wise. The proposition came often and he never lost. A jigger is unlike any other ice cream; it is dipped from the creamy tin by a cone-shaped scoop called a jigger, which gives it an unusual and peculiar flavor. Since those days the original jigger has been contaminated and made ridiculous by offensive alliances with upstart syrups, meringues and macaroons with absurd titles; but then the boy went to the simple jigger as the sturdy Roman went to the cold waters of the Tiber. A double jigger fills a large soda glass when ten cents has been laid on the counter, and two such glasses quench all desire in the normal appetite.

"If he can eat twelve double jiggers," Al said slowly, "I'll set them up and the jiggers for youse. Otherwise, I'll hold the watch."

At this there was a protest from the backers of the champion, with the result that the limit was reduced to ten.

"Is it a go?" Al said, turning to Smeed, who had waited modestly in the background.

"Sure," he answered, with calm certainty.

"You've got nerve, you have," said Al, with a scornful smile, scooping up the first jiggers and shoving the glass to him. "Then doubles is the record in these parts, young fellow!"

Then little Smeed, methodically, and without apparent pain, ate the ten doubles.

Conover's was not in the catalogue that anxious parents study, but then catalogues are like epitaphs in a cemetery. Next to the jigger-shop, Conover's was quite the most important institution in the school. In a little white Colonial cottage, Conover, veteran of the late war, and Mrs. Conover, still in active service, supplied pancakes and maple syrup on a cash basis, two dollars credit to second-year boys in good repute. Conover's, too, had its traditions. Twenty-six pancakes, large and thick, in one continuous sitting, was the record, five years old, standing to the credit of Guzzler Wilkins, which succeeding classes had attacked in vain. Wily Conover, to stimulate such profitable tests, had solemnly pledged himself to the delivery of free pancakes to all comers during that day on which any boy, at one continuous sitting, unaided, should succeed in swallowing the awful number of thirty-two. Conover was not considered a prodigal.

This deed of heroic accomplishment and public benefaction was the true goal of Hickey's planning. The test of the jigger-shop was but a preliminary trying out. With medical caution, Doc Macnooder refused to permit Smeed to go beyond the ten doubles, holding very wisely that the jigger record could wait for a further day. The amazed Al was sworn to secrecy.

It was Wednesday, and the following Saturday was decided upon for the supreme test at Conover's. Smeed at once was subjected to a graduated system of starvation. Thursday he was hungry, but Friday he was so ravenous that a watch was instituted on all his movements.

The next morning the Dickinson House, let into the secret, accompanied Smeed to Conover's. If there was even a possibility of free pancakes, the House intended to be satisfied before the deluge broke.

Great was the astonishment at Conover's at the arrival of the procession.

"Mr. Conover," said Hickey, in the quality of manager, "we're going after that pancake record."

"Mr. Wilkins' record?" said Conover, seeking vainly the champion in the crowd.

"No—after that record of *yours*," answered Hickey. "Thirty-two pancakes—we're here to get free pancakes today—that's what we're here for."

"So, boys, so," said Conover, smiling pleasantly; "and you want to begin now?"

"Right off the bat."

"Well, where is he?"

"Little Smeed, famished to the point of tears, was thrust forward. Conover, who was expecting something on the lines of a buffalo, smiled confidently.

"So, boys, so," he said, leading the way with alacrity. "I guess we're ready, too."

"Thirty-two pancakes, Conover—and we get 'em free!"

"That's right," answered Conover, secure in his knowledge of boyish capacity. "If that little boy there can eat thirty-two I'll make them all day free to the school. That's what I said, and what I say goes—and that's what I say now."

Hickey and Doc Macnooder whispered the last instructions in Smeed's
ear.

"Cut out the syrup."

"Loosen your belt."

"Eat slowly."

In a low room, with the white rafters impending over his head, beside
a basement window flanked with geraniums, little Smeed sat down to
battle for the honor of the Dickinson and the record of the school.
Directly under his eyes, carved on the wooden table, a name challenged
him, standing out of the numerous initials—Guzzler Wilkins.

"I'll keep count," said Hickey. "Macnooder and Turkey, watch the
pancakes."

"Regulation size, Conover," cried that cautious Red Dog; "no doubling now. All fair and above board."

"All right, Hickey, all right," said Conover, leering wickedly from
the door; "if that little grasshopper can do it, you get the cakes."

"Now, Hungry," said Turkey, clapping Smeed on the shoulder.
"Here is where you get your chance. Remember, Kid, old sport, it's for
the Dickinson."

Smeed heard in ecstasy; it was just the way Turkey talked to the
eleven on the eve of a match. He nodded his head with a grim little
shake and smiled nervously at the thirty-odd Dickinsonians who formed
around him a pit of expectant and hungry boyhood from the floor to
the ceiling.

"All ready!" sang out Turkey, from the doorway.

"Six pancakes!"

"Six it is," replied Hickey, chalking up a monster 6 on the slate that
swung from the rafters. The pancakes placed before the ravenous Smeed
vanished like snow-flakes on a July lawn.

A cheer went up, mingled with cries of caution.

"Not so fast."

"Take your time."

"Don't let them be too hot."

"Not too hot, Hickey!"

Macnooder was instructed to watch carefully over the temperature
as well as the dimensions.

"Ready again," came the cry.

"Ready—how many?"

"Six more."

"Six it is," said Hickey, adding a second figure to the score. "Six and
six are twelve."

The second batch went the way of the first.

"Why, that boy is starving," said Conover, opening his eyes.

"Sure he is," said Hickey. "He's eating 'way back in last week—he hasn't had a thing for ten days."

"Six more," cried Macnooder.

"Six it is," answered Hickey. "Six and twelve is eighteen."

"Eat them one at a time, Hungry."

"No, let him alone."

"He knows best."

"Not too fast, Hungry, not too fast."

"Eighteen for Hungry, eighteen. Hurrah!"

"Thirty-two is a long ways to go," said Conover, gazing apprehensively at the little David who had come so impudently into his domain; "fourteen pancakes is an awful lot."

"Shut up, Conover."

"No trying to influence him there."

"Don't listen to him, Hungry."

"He's only trying to get you nervous."

"Fourteen more, Hungry—fourteen more."

"Ready again," sang out Macnooder.

"Ready here."

"Three pancakes."

"Three it is," responded Hickey. "Eighteen and three is twenty-one." But a storm of protest arose.

"Here, that's not fair!"

"I say, Hickey, don't let them do that."

"I say, Hickey, it's twice as hard that way."

"Oh, go on."

"Sure it is."

"Of course it is."

"Don't you know that you can't drink a glass of beer if you take it with a teaspoon?"

"That's right, Red Dog's right! Six at a time."

"Six at a time!"

A hurried consultation was now held and the reasoning approved. Macnooder was charged with the responsibility of seeing to the number as well as the temperature and dimensions.

Meanwhile Smeed had eaten the pancakes.

"Coming again!"

"All ready here."

"Six pancakes!"

"Six," said Hickey; "twenty-one and six is twenty-seven."

"That'll beat Guzzler Wilkins."

"So it will."

"Five more makes thirty-two."

"Easy, Hungry, easy."

"Hungry's done it; he's done it."

"Twenty-seven and the record!"

"Hurrah!"

At this point Smeed looked about anxiously.

"It's pretty dry," he said, speaking for the first time.

Instantly there was a panic. Smeed was reaching his limit—a groan
went up.

"Oh, Hungry."

"Only five more."

"Give him some water."

"Water, you loon; do you want to end him?"

"Why?"

"Water'll swell up the pancakes, crazy."

"No water, no water."

Hickey approached his man with anxiety.

"What is it, Hungry? Anything wrong?" he said tenderly.

"No, only it's a little dry," said Smeed, unmoved. "I'm all right, but
I'd like just a drop of syrup now."

The syrup was discussed, approved and voted.

"You're sure you're all right," said Hickey.

"Oh, yes."

Conover, in the last ditch, said carefully:

"I don't want no fits around here."

A cry of protest greeted him.

"Well, son, that boy can't stand much more. That's just like the Guzzler. He was taken short and we had to work over him for an hour."

"Conover, shut up!"

"Conover, you're beaten."

"Conover, that's an old game."

"Get out."

"Shut up."

"Fair play."

"Fair play! Fair play!"

A new interruption came from the kitchen. Macnooder claimed that
Mrs. Conover was doubling the size of the cakes. The dish was brought.
There was no doubt about it. The cakes were swollen. Pandemonium
broke loose. Conover capitulated, the cakes were rejected.

"Don't be feazed by that," said Hickey, warningly to Smeed.

"I'm not," said Smeed.

"All ready," came Macnooder's cry.

"Ready here."

"Six pancakes!"

"Regulation size?"

"Regulation."

"Six it is," said Hickey, at the slate. "Six and twenty-seven is thirty-three."

"Wait a moment," sang out the Butcher. "He has only to eat thirty-two."

"That's so—take one off."

"Give him five, Hickey—five only."

"If Hungry says he can eat six," said Hickey, firmly, glancing at his protégé, "he can. We're out for big things. Can you do it, Hungry?"

And Smeed, fired with the heroism of the moment, answered in disdainful simplicity:

"Sure!"

A cheer that brought two Davis House boys running in greeted the disappearance of the thirty-third. Then everything was forgotten in the amazement of the deed.

"Please, I'd like to go on," said Smeed.

"Oh, Hungry, can you do it?"

"Really?"

"You're goin' on?"

"Holy cats!"

"How'll you take them?" said Hickey, anxiously.

"I'll try another six," said Smeed, thoughtfully, "and then we'll see."

Conover, vanquished and convinced, no longer sought to intimidate him with horrid suggestions.

"Mr. Smeed," he said, giving him his hand in admiration, "you go ahead; you make a great record."

"Six more," cried Macnooder.

"Six it is," said Hickey, in an awed voice; "six and thirty-three makes thirty-nine!"

Mrs. Conover and Macnooder, no longer antagonists, came in from the kitchen to watch the great spectacle. Little Smeed alone, calm and unconscious, with the light of a great ambition on his forehead, ate steadily, without vacillation.

"Gee, what a stride!"

"By Jiminy, where does he put it?" said Conover, staring helplessly.

"Holy cats!"

"Thirty-nine—thirty-nine pancakes—gee!!!"

"Hungry," said Hickey, entreatingly, "do you think you could eat another—make it an even forty?"

"Three more," said Smeed, pounding the table with a new authority. This time no voice rose in remonstrance. The clouds had rolled away. They were in the presence of a master.

"Pancakes coming."

"Bring them in!"

"Three more."

"Three it is," said Hickey, faintly. "Thirty-nine and three makes forty-two—forty-two. Gee!"

In profound silence the three pancakes passed regularly from the plate down the throat of little Smeed. Forty-two pancakes!

"Three more," said Smeed.

Doc Macnooder rushed in hysterically.

"Hungry, go the limit—the limit! If anything happens I'll bleed you."

"Shut up, Doc!"

"Get out, you wild man."

Macnooder was sent ignominiously back into the kitchen, with the curses of the Dickinson, and Smeed assured of their unfaltering protection.

"Three more," came the cry from the chastened Macnooder.

"Three it is," said Hickey. "Forty-two and three makes—forty-five."

"Holy cats!"

Still little Smeed, without appreciable abatement of hunger, continued to eat. A sense of impending calamity and alarm began to spread. Forty-five pancakes, and still eating! It might turn into a tragedy.

"Say, bub—say, now," said Hickey, gazing anxiously down into the pointed face, "you've done enough—don't get rash."

"I'll stop when it's time," said Smeed; "bring 'em on now, one at a time."

"Forty-six, forty-seven, forty-eight, forty-nine!"

Suddenly, at the moment when they expected him to go on forever, little Smeed stopped, gazed at his plate, then at the fiftieth pancake, and said:

"That's all."

"Forty-nine pancakes! Then, and only then, did they return to a realization of what had happened. They cheered Smeed, they sang his praises, they cheered again, and then, pounding the table, they cried, in a mighty chorus:

"We want pancakes!"

"Bring us pancakes!"

"Pancakes, pancakes, we want pancakes!"

Twenty minutes later, Red Dog and the Egghead, fed to bursting, rolled out of Conover's, spreading the uproarious news.

"Free pancakes! Free pancakes!"

The nearest houses, the Davis and the Rouse, heard and came with a rush.

Red Dog and the Egghead staggered down into the village and over to the circle of houses, throwing out their arms like returning bacchanalians.

"Free pancakes!"

"Hungry Smeed's broken the record!"

"Pancakes at Conover's—free pancakes!"

The word jumped from house to house, the campus was emptied in a trice. The road became choked with the hungry stream that struggled, fought, laughed and shouted as it stormed to Conover's.

"Free pancakes! Free pancakes!"

"Hurrah for Smeed!"

"Hurrah for Hungry Smeed!!"

44

Porcelain Cups

30 MAY, 1593

BY JAMES BRANCH CABELL

"She was the admirablest lady that ever lived: therefore, Master Doctor, if you will do us that favor, as to let us see that peerless dame, we should think ourselves much beholding unto you."

There was a double wedding some two weeks later in the chapel at Longaville: and each marriage appears to have been happy enough.

The tenth Marquis of Falmouth had begotten sixteen children within seventeen years, at the end of which period his wife unluckily died in producing a final pledge of affection. This child, a daughter, survived, and was christened Cynthia: of her you may hear later.

Meanwhile the Earl and the Countess of Pevensey had propagated more moderately; and Pevensey had played a larger part in public life than was allotted to Falmouth, who did not shine at court. Pevensey, indeed, has his sizable niche in history: his Irish expeditions, in 1575, were once notorious, as well as the circumstances of the Earl's death in that year at Triloch Lenoch. His more famous son, then a boy of eight, succeeded to the title, and somewhat later, as the world knows, to the hazardous position of chief favorite to Queen Elizabeth.

"For Pevensey has the vision of a poet,"—thus Langard quotes the lonely old Queen,—"and to balance it, such mathematics as add two and two correctly, where you others smirk and assure me it sums up to whatever the Queen prefers. I have need of Pevensey: in this parched little age all England has need of Pevensey."

That is as it may have been: at all events, it is with this Lord Pevensey, at the height of his power, that we have now to do.

OF GREATNESS INTIMATELY VIEWED

A H, but they are beyond praise," said Cynthia Allonby, enraptured. "I have never seen the like of them! and certainly you should have presented them to the Queen."

"Her majesty already possesses a cup of that ware," replied Lord Pevensey. "It was one of her New Year's gifts, from Robert Cecil. Hers is, I believe, not quite so fine as either of yours; but then, they tell me, there is not the like of this pair in England, nor indeed on the hither side of Cataia."

He set the two pieces of Chinese pottery upon the shelves in the south corner of the room. These cups were of that sea-green tint called céladon, with a very wonderful glow and radiance. Such oddities were the last vogue at court; and Cynthia could not but speculate as to what monstrous sum Lord Pevensey had paid for this his most recent gift to her.

Now he turned, smiling, a really superb creature in his blue and gold. "I had today another message from the Queen—"

"George," Cynthia said, with fond concern, "it frightens me to see you thus foolhardy, in tempting alike the Queen's anger and the Plague."

"Eh, as goes the Plague, it spares nine out of ten," he answered, lightly. "The Queen, I grant you, is another pair of sleeves, for an irritated Tudor spares nobody."

But Cynthia Allonby kept silence, and did not exactly smile, while she appraised her famous young kinsman. She was flattered by, and a little afraid of, the gay self confidence which led anybody to take such chances. . . . Two weeks ago it was that the terrible painted old Queen had named Lord Pevensey to go straightway into France, where, rumor had it, King Henri was preparing to renounce the Reformed Religion, and making his peace with the Pope: and for two weeks Pevensey had lingered, on one pretense or another, at his house in London, with the Plague creeping about the city like an invisible incalculable flame, and the Queen asking questions at Windsor. Of all the monarchs that had ever reigned in England, Elizabeth Tudor was the least used to having her orders disregarded. Meanwhile Lord Pevensey came every day to the Marquis of Falmouth's lodgings at Deptford: and every day Lord Pevensey pointed out to the Marquis' daughter that Pevensey, whose wife had died in childbirth a year back, did not intend to go into France, for nobody could foretell how long a stay, as a widower. Certainly it was all very flattering. . . .

"Yes, and you would be an excellent match," said Cynthia, aloud, "if that were all. And yet, what must I reasonably expect in marrying, sir, the famous Earl of Pevensey?"

"A great deal of love and petting, my dear. And if there were anything else to which you had a fancy, I would get it for you."

Her glance went to those lovely cups and lingered fondly. "Yes, dear Master Generosity, if it could be purchased or manufactured, you would get it for me—"

"If it exists I will get it for you," he declared.

"I think that it exists. But I am not learned enough to know what it is. George, if I married you I would have money and fine clothes and gilded coaches, and an army of maids and pages, and honor from all men. And you would be kind to me, I know, when you returned from the day's work at Windsor—or Holyrood, or the Louvre. But do you not see that I would always be to you only a rather costly luxury, like those cups, which the Queen's minister could afford to keep for his hours of leisure?"

He answered: "You are all in all to me. You know it. Oh, very well do you know and abuse your power, you adorable and lovely baggage, who have kept me dancing attendance for a fortnight, without ever giving me an honest yes or no." He gesticulated. "Well, but life is plaguily dull in Deptford village; and it amuses you to twist a Queen's adviser around your finger! I see it plainly, you minx, and I acquiesce because it delights me to give you pleasure, even at the cost of some dignity. Yet I may no longer shirk the Queen's business,—no, not even to amuse you, my dear."

"You said you had heard from her—again?"

"I had this morning my orders, under Gloriana's own fair hand, either to depart tomorrow into France or else to come tomorrow to Windsor. I need not say that in the circumstances I consider France the more wholesome."

Now the girl's voice was hurt and wistful. "So, for the thousandth time, is it proven that Queen's business means more to you than I do. Yes, certainly it is just as I said, George."

He observed, unruffled: "My dear, I scent unreason. This is a high matter. If the French King compounds with Rome, it means war for Protestant England. Even you must see that."

She replied, sadly: "Yes, even I! oh, certainly, my lord, even a half-witted child of seventeen can perceive as much as that."

"I was not speaking of half-witted persons, as I remember. Well, it chances that I am honored by the friendship of our gallant Béarnais, and am supposed to have some claim upon him, thanks to my good fortune last year in saving his life from the assassin Barrière. It chances that I may perhaps become, under providence, the instrument of preserving my fellow countrymen from much grief and trumpet-sounding and throat-cutting. Instead of pursuing that chance, two weeks ago—as was my duty,—I have dangled at your apron strings, in the vain hope of softening the most variable and hardest heart in the world. Now, clearly, I have not the right to do that any longer."

She admired the ennobled, the slightly rapt look which, she knew, denoted that George Bulmer was doing his duty as he saw it, even in her disappointment. "No, you have not the right. You are wedded to your statecraft, to your patriotism, to your self-advancement, or christen it what you will. You are wedded, at all events, to your man's business. You have not the time for such trifles as giving a maid that foolish and lovely sort of wooing to which every maid looks forward in her heart of hearts. Indeed, when you married the first time it was a kind of infidelity; and I am certain that poor, dear mouse-like Mary must have felt that often and over again. Why, do you not see, George, even now, that your wife will always come second to your real love?"

"In my heart, dear sophist, you will always come first. But it is not permitted that any loyal gentleman devote every hour of his life to sighing and making sonnets, and to the general solacing of a maid's loneliness in this dull little Deptford. Nor would you, I am sure, desire me to do so."

"I hardly know what I desire," she told him ruefully. "But I know that when you talk of your man's business I am lonely and chilled and far away from you. And I know that I cannot understand more than half your fine high notions about duty and patriotism and serving England and so on," the girl declared: and she flung wide her lovely little hands, in a despairing gesture. "I admire you, sir, when you talk of England. It makes you handsomer—yes, even handsomer!—somehow. But all the while I am remembering that England is just an ordinary island inhabited by a number of ordinary persons, for the most of whom I have no particular feeling one way or the other."

He looked down at her for an instant, with queer tenderness. Then he smiled.

"No, I could not quite make you understand, my dear. But, ah, why fuddle that quaint little brain by trying to understand such matters as lie without your realm? For a woman's kingdom is the home, my dear, and her throne is in the heart of her husband—"

"All this is but another way of saying your lordship would have us cups upon a shelf," she pointed out,—"in readiness for your leisure."

He shrugged, said "Nonsense!" and began more lightly to talk of other matters. Thus and thus he would do in France, such and such trinkets he would fetch back,—"as toys for the most whimsical, the loveliest, and the most obstinate child in all the world," he phrased it. And they would be married, Pevensey declared, in September: nor (he gayly said) did he propose to have any further argument about it. Children should be seen—the proverb was dusty, but it particularly applied to pretty children.

Cynthia let him talk. She was just a little afraid of his self-confidence, and of this tall nobleman's habit of getting what he wanted, in the end: but she dispiritedly felt that Pevensey had failed her. Why, George Bulmer treated her as if she were a silly infant; and his want of her, even in that capacity, was a secondary matter: he was going into France, for all his petting talk, and was leaving her to shift as she best might, until he could spare the time to resume his love-making. . . .

WHAT COMES OF SCRIBBLING

Now, when Pevensey had gone, the room seemed darkened by the withdrawal of so much magnificence. Cynthia watched from the window as the tall Earl rode away, with three handsomely clad retainers. Yes, George was very fine and admirable, no doubt of it: even so, there was relief in the reflection that for a month or two she was rid of him.

Turning, she faced a lean, disheveled man, who stood by the Magdalen tapestry scratching his chin. He had unquiet bright eyes, this out-at-elbows poet whom a marquis' daughter was pleased to patronize, and his red hair was unpardonably tousled. Nor were his manners beyond reproach, for now, without saying anything, he, too, went to the window. He dragged one foot a little as he walked.

"So my lord Pevensey departs! Look how he rides in triumph! like lame Tamburlaine, with Techelles and Usumcasane and Theridamas to attend him, and with the sunset turning the dust raised by their horses' hoofs into a sort of golden haze about them. It is a beautiful world. And truly, Mistress Cyn," the poet said, reflectively, "that Pevensey is a very splendid ephemera. If not a king himself, at least he goes magnificently to settle the affairs of kings. Were modesty not my failing, Mistress Cyn, I would acclaim you as strangely lucky, in being beloved by two fine fellows that have not their like in England."

"Truly, you are not always thus modest, Kit Marlowe—"

"But, Lord, how seriously Pevensey takes it all! and takes himself in particular! Why, there departs from us, in befitting state, a personage whose opinion as to every topic in the world is written legibly in the carriage of those fine shoulders, even when seen from behind and from so considerable a distance. And in not one syllable do any of these opinions differ from the opinions of his great-great-grandfathers. Oho, and hark to Deptford! now all the oafs in the Cornmarket are cheering this bulwark of Protestant England, this rising young hero of a people with no nonsense about them. Yes, it is a very quaint and rather splendid ephemera."

The daughter of a marquis could not quite approve of the way in which this shoemaker's son, howsoever talented, railed at his betters. "Pevensey will be the greatest man in these kingdoms some day. Indeed, Kit Marlowe, there are those who say he is that much already."

"Oh, very probably! Still, I am puzzled by human greatness. A century hence what will he matter, this Pevensey? His ascent and his declension will have been completed, and his foolish battles and treaties will have given place to other foolish battles and treaties, and oblivion will have swallowed this glistening bluebottle, plumes and fine lace and stately ruff and all. Why, he is but an adviser to the queen of half an island, whereas my Tamburlaine was lord of all the golden ancient East: and what does my Tamburlaine matter now, save that he gave Kit Marlowe the subject of a drama? Hah, softly though! for does even that very greatly matter? Who really cares today about what scratches were made upon wax by that old Euripides, the latchet of whose sandals I am not worthy to unloose? No, not quite worthy, as yet!"

And thereupon the shabby fellow sat down in the tall leather-covered chair which Pevensey had just vacated: and this Marlowe nodded his flaming head portentously. "Hoh, look you, I am displeased, Mistress Cyn, I cannot lend my approval to this over-greedy oblivion that gapes for all. No, it is not a satisfying arrangement, that I should teeter insecurely through the void on a gob of mud, and be expected by and by to relinquish even that crazy foothold. Even for Kit Marlowe death lies in wait! and it may be, not anything more after death, not even any lovely words to play with. Yes, and this Marlowe may amount to nothing, after all: and his one chance of amounting to that which he intends may be taken away from him at any moment!"

He touched the breast of a weather-beaten doublet. He gave her that queer twisted sort of smile which the girl could not but find attractive, somehow. He said:

"Why, but this heart thumping here inside me may stop any moment like a broken clock. Here is Euripides writing better than I: and here in my body, under my hand, is the mechanism upon which depend all those masterpieces that are to blot the Athenian from the reckoning, and I have no control of it!"

"Indeed, I fear that you control few things," she told him, "and that least of all do you control your taste for taverns and bad women. Oh, I hear tales of you!" And Cynthia raised a reproving forefinger.

"True tales, no doubt." He shrugged. "Lacking the moon he vainly cried for, the child learns to content himself with a penny whistle."

"Ah, but the moon is far away," the girl said, smiling,—"too far to hear the sound of human crying: and besides, the moon, as I remember it, was never a very amorous goddess—"

"Just so," he answered: "also she was called Cynthia, and she, too, was beautiful."

"Yet is it the heart that cries to me, my poet?" she asked him, softly, "or just the lips?"

"Oh, both of them, most beautiful and inaccessible of goddesses." Then Marlowe leaned toward her, laughing and shaking that disreputable red head. "Still, you are very foolish, in your latest incarnation, to be wasting your rays upon carpet earls who will not outwear a century. Were modesty not my failing, I repeat, I could name somebody who will last longer. Yes, and—if but I lacked that plaguey virtue,—I would advise you to go a-gypsying with that nameless somebody, so that two manikins might snatch their little share of the big things that are eternal, just as the butterfly fares intrepidly and joyously, with the sun for his torchboy, through a universe wherein thought cannot estimate the unimportance of a butterfly, and wherein not even the chaste moon is very important. Yes, certainly I would advise you to have done with this vanity of courts and masques, of satins and fans and fiddles, this dallying with tinsels and bright vapors; and very movingly I would exhort you to seek out Arcadia, traveling hand in hand with that still nameless somebody." And of a sudden the restless man began to sing.

Sang Kit Marlowe:

> "Come live with me and be my love,
> And we will all the pleasures prove
> That hills and valleys, dales and fields,
> Woods or steepy mountain yields.
>
> "And we will sit upon the rocks,
> And see the shepherds feed their flocks
> By shallow rivers, to whose falls
> Melodious birds sing madrigals—"

But the girl shook her small, wise head decisively. "That is all very fine, but, as it happens, there is no such place as this Arcadia, where people can frolic in perpetual sunlight the year round, and find their food and clothing miraculously provided. No, nor can you, I am afraid, give me what all maids really, in their heart of hearts, desire far more than any sugar-candy Arcadia. Oh, as I have so often told you, Kit, I think you love no woman. You love words. And your seraglio is tenanted by very beautiful words, I grant you, though there is no longer any Sestos builded of agate and crystal, either, Kit Marlowe. For, as you may perceive, sir, I have read all that lovely poem you left with me last Thursday—"

She saw how interested he was, saw how he almost smirked. "Aha, so you think it not quite bad, eh, the conclusion of my *Hero and Leander?*"

"It is your best. And your middlemost, my poet, is better than aught else in English," she said, politely, and knowing how much he delighted to hear such remarks.

"Come, I retract my charge of foolishness, for you are plainly a wench of rare discrimination. And yet you say I do not love you! Cynthia, you are beautiful, you are perfect in all things. You are that heavenly Helen of whom I wrote, some persons say, acceptably enough. How strange it was I did not know that Helen was dark-haired and pale! for certainly yours is that immortal loveliness which must be served by poets in life and death."

"And I wonder how much of these ardors," she thought, "is kindled by my praise of his verses?" She bit her lip, and she regarded him with a hint of sadness. She said, aloud: "But I did not, after all, speak to Lord Pevensey concerning the printing of your poem. Instead, I burned your *Hero and Leander.*"

She saw him jump, as under a whiplash. Then he smiled again, in that wry fashion of his.

"I lament the loss to letters, for it was my only copy. But you knew that."

"Yes, Kit, I knew it was your only copy."

"Oho! and for what reason did you burn it, may one ask?"

"I thought you loved it more than you loved me. It was my rival, I thought—" The girl was conscious of remorse commingled with a mounting joy.

"And so you thought a jingle scribbled upon a bit of paper could be your rival with me!"

Then Cynthia no longer doubted, but gave a joyous little sobbing laugh, for the love of her disreputable dear poet was sustaining the stringent testing she had devised. She touched his freckled hand caressingly, and her face was as no man had ever seen it, and her voice, too, caressed him.

"Ah, you have made me the happiest of women, Kit! Kit, I am almost disappointed in you, though, that you do not grieve more for the loss of that beautiful poem."

His smiling did not waver; yet the lean, red-haired man stayed motionless. "Why, but see how lightly I take the destruction of my life-work in this, my masterpiece! For I can assure you it was a masterpiece, the fruit of two years' toil and of much loving repolishment—"

"Ah, but you love me better than such matters, do you not?" she asked him, tenderly. "Kit Marlowe, I adore you! Sweetheart, do you not understand that a woman wants to be loved utterly and entirely? She wants no rivals, not even paper rivals. And so often when you talked of poetry I have felt lonely and chilled and far away from you, and I have been half envious, dear, of your Heroes and Helens and your other good-for-nothing Greek minxes. But now I do not mind them at all. And I will make amends, quite prodigal amends, for my naughty jealousy: and my poet shall write me some more lovely poems, so he shall—"

He said, "You fool!"

And she drew away from him, for this man was no longer smiling.

"You burned my *Hero and Leander!* You! you big-eyed fool! You lisping idiot! you wriggling, cuddling worm! you silken bag of guts! had not even you the wit to perceive it was immortal beauty which would have lived long after you and I were stinking dirt? And you, a half-witted animal, a shining, chattering parrot, lay claws to it!"

Marlowe had risen in a sort of seizure, in a condition which was really quite unreasonable when you considered that only a poem was at stake, even a rather long poem.

And Cynthia began to smile, with tremulous hurt-looking young lips. "So my poet's love is as selfish as Pevensey's love! And I was right, after all."

"Oh, oh!" said Marlowe, "that ever a poet should love a woman! What jokes does the lewd flesh contrive!" Of a sudden he was calmer; and then rage fell away from him like a dropped cloak, and he viewed her as with respectful wonder. "Why, but you sitting there, with goggling innocent bright eyes, are an allegory of all that is most droll and tragic. Yes, and indeed there is no reason to blame you. It is not your fault that every now and then is born a man who serves an idea which is to him the most important thing in the world. It is not your fault that this man perforce inhabits a body to which the most important thing in the world is a woman. Certainly, it is not your fault that this compost makes yet another jumble of his two desires, and persuades himself that the two are somehow allied. The woman inspires, the woman uplifts, the woman strengthens him for his high work, saith he! Well, well, perhaps there are such women, but by land and sea I have encountered none of them."

All this was said while Marlowe shuffled about the room, with bent shoulders, and nodding his tousled red head, and limping as he walked. Now Marlowe turned, futile and shabby-looking, just where a while ago Lord Pevensey had loomed resplendent. Again she saw the poet's queer, twisted, jeering smile.

"What do you care for my ideals? What do you care for the ideals of that tall earl whom for a fortnight you have held from his proper business? or for the ideals of any man alive? Why, not one thread of that dark hair, not one snap of those white little fingers, except when ideals irritate you by distracting a man's attention from Cynthia Allonby. Otherwise, he is welcome enough to play with his incomprehensible toys."

He jerked a thumb toward the shelves behind him.

"Oho, you virtuous pretty ladies! what all you value is such matters as those cups: they please the eye, they are worth sound money, and people envy you the possession of them. So you cherish your shiny mud cups, and you burn my *Hero and Leander*: and I declaim all this dull nonsense over the ashes of my ruined dreams, thinking at bottom of how pretty you are, and of how much I would like to kiss you. That is the real tragedy, the immemorial tragedy, that I should still hanker after you, my Cynthia—"

His voice dwelt tenderly upon her name. His fever-haunted eyes were tender, too, for just a moment. Then he grimaced.

"No, I was wrong,—the tragedy strikes deeper. The root of it is that there is in you and in all your glittering kind no malice, no will to do harm nor to hurt anything. but just a bland and invincible and, upon the whole, a well-meaning stupidity, informing a bright and soft and delicately scented animal. So you work ruin among those men who serve ideals, not foreplanning ruin, not desiring to ruin anything, not even having sufficient wit to perceive the ruin when it is accomplished. You are, when all is done, not even detestable, not even a worthy peg whereon to hang denunciatory sonnets, you shallow-pated pretty creatures whom poets—oh, and in youth all men are poets!—whom poets, now and always are doomed to hanker after to the detriment of their poesy. No, I concede it: you kill without premeditation, and without ever suspecting your hands to be anything but stainless. So in logic I must retract all my harsh words; and I must, without any hint of reproach, endeavor to bid you a somewhat more civil farewell."

She had regarded him, throughout this preposterous and uncalled-for harangue, with sad composure, with a forgiving pity. Now she asked him, very quietly, "Where are you going, Kit?"

"To the Golden Hind, O gentle, patient and unjustly persecuted virgin martyr!" he answered, with an exaggerated bow,—"since that is the part in which you now elect to posture."

"Not to that low, vile place again!"

"But certainly I intend in that tavern to get tipsy as quickly as possible: for then the first woman I see will for the time become the woman whom I desire. and who exists nowhere." And with that the red-haired man departed, limping and singing as he went to look for a trull in Nell Bull's pot-house.

Sang Kit Marlowe:

> *"And I will make her beds of roses*
> *And a thousand fragrant posies;*
> *A cap of flowers, and a kirtle*
> *Embroidered all with leaves of myrtle.*
>
> *"A gown made of the finest wool*
> *Which from our pretty lambs we pull;*
> *Fair-lined slippers for the cold,*
> *With buckles of the purest gold—"*

ECONOMICS OF EGERIA

She sat quite still when Marlowe had gone. "He will get drunk again," she thought despondently. "Well, and why should it matter to me if he does, after all that outrageous ranting? He has been unforgivably insulting—Oh, but none the less, I do not want to have him babbling of the roses and gold of that impossible fairy world which the poor, frantic child really believes in, to some painted woman of the town who will laugh at him. I loathe the thought of her laughing at him—and kissing him! His notions are wild foolishness; but I at least wish they were not foolishness, and that hateful woman will not care one way or the other."

So Cynthia sighed, and to comfort her forlorn condition fetched a hand-mirror from the shelves whereon glowed her green cups. She touched each cup caressingly in passing; and that which she found in the mirror, too, she regarded not unappreciatively, from varying angles. . . . Yes, after all, dark hair and a pale skin had their advantages at a court where pink and yellow women were so much the fashion as to be common. Men remembered you more distinctively. Though nobody cared for men, in view of their unreasonable behavior, and their absolute self-centeredness. . . . Oh, it was pitiable, it was grotesque, she reflected sadly, how Pevensey and Kit Marlowe had both failed her, after so many pretty speeches.

Still, there was a queer pleasure in being wooed by Kit: his insane notions went to one's head like wine. She would send Meg for him again tomorrow. And Pevensey was, of course, the best match imaginable. . . . No, it would be too heartless to dismiss George Bulmer outright. It was unreasonable of him to desert her because a Gascon threatened to go to mass: but, after all, she would probably marry George, in the end. He was really almost unendurably silly, though, about England and freedom and religion and right and wrong and things like that. Yes, it would be tedious to have a husband who often talked to you as though he were addressing a public assemblage. . . . Yet, he was very handsome, particularly in his high-flown and most tedious moments; that year-old son of his was sickly, and would probably die soon, the sweet forlorn little pet, and not be a bother to anybody: and her dear old father would be profoundly delighted by the marriage of his daughter to a man whose wife could have at will a dozen céladon cups, and anything else she chose to ask for. . . .

But now the sun had set, and the room was growing quite dark. So Cynthia stood a-tiptoe, and replaced the mirror upon the shelves, setting it upright behind those wonderful green cups which had anew reminded her of Pevensey's wealth and generosity. She smiled a little, to think of what fun it had been to hold George back, for two whole weeks, from discharging that horrible old Queen's stupid errands.

TREATS PHILOSOPHICALLY OF BREAKAGE

The door opened. Stalwart young Captain Edward Musgrave came with a lighted candle, which he placed carefully upon the table in the room's center.

He said: "They told me you were here. I come from London. I bring news for you."

"You bring no pleasant tidings, I fear—"

"As Lord Pevensey rode through the Strand this afternoon, on his way home, the Plague smote him. That is my sad news. I grieve to bring such news, for your cousin was a worthy gentleman and universally respected."

"Ah," Cynthia said, very quiet, "so Pevensey is dead. But the Plague kills quickly!"

"Yes, yes, that is a comfort, certainly. Yes, he turned quite black in the face, they report, and before his men could reach him had fallen from his horse. It was all over almost instantly. I saw him afterward, hardly a pleasant sight. I came to you as soon as I could. I was vexatiously detained—"

"So George Bulmer is dead, in a London gutter! It seems strange, because he was here, befriended by monarchs, and very strong and handsome and self-confident, hardly two hours ago. Is that his blood upon your sleeve?"

"But of course not! I told you I was vexatiously detained, almost at your gates. Yes, I had the ill luck to blunder into a disgusting business. The two rapscallions tumbled out of a doorway under my horse's very nose, egad! It was a near thing I did not ride them down. So I stopped, naturally. I regretted stopping, afterward, for I was too late to be of help. It was at the Golden Hind, of course. Something really ought to be done about that place. Yes, and that rogue Marler bled all over a new doublet, as you see. And the Deptford constables held me with their foolish interrogatories—"

"So one of the fighting men was named Marlowe! Is he dead, too, dead in another gutter?"

"Marlowe or Marler, or something of the sort—wrote plays and sonnets and such stuff, they tell me. I do not know anything about him,—though, I give you my word, now, those greasy constables treated me as though I were a noted frequenter of pot-houses. That sort of thing is most annoying. No, it was the other two who were fighting. Marler was dead before I got to him. They were all drunk together, and squabbling over the bill for what they had drunk. And so, as I was saying, this other rascal dug a knife into him—"

But now, to Captain Musgrave's discomfort, Cynthia Allonby had begun to weep, heartbrokenly.

So he cleared his throat, and he patted the back of her hand. "It is a great shock to you naturally,—oh, most naturally, and does you great credit. But come now, Pevensey is gone, as we must all go some day, and our tears cannot bring him back, my dear. We can but hope he is better off, poor fellow, and look on it as a mysterious dispensation and that sort of thing, my dear—"

"Oh, Ned, but people are so cruel! People will be saying that it was I who kept poor Cousin George in London these last two weeks, and that but for me he would have been in France long ago! And then the Queen, Ned!—why, that pig-headed old woman will be blaming it on me, that there is nobody to prevent that detestable French King from turning Catholic and dragging England into new wars, and I shall not be able to go to any of the Court dances! nor to the masques!" sobbed Cynthia, "nor anywhere!"

"Now, you talk tender-hearted and angelic nonsense. It is noble of you to feel that way, of course. But Pevensey did not take proper care of himself, and that is all there is to it. Now I have remained in London since the Plague's outbreak. I stayed with my regiment, naturally. We have had a few deaths, of course. People die everywhere. But the Plague has never bothered me. And why has it never bothered me? Simply because I was sensible, took the pains to consult an astrologer, and by his advice wear about my neck, night and day, a bag containing tablets of toad's blood and arsenic. It is an infallible specific for men born in February. No, not for a moment do I wish to speak harshly of the dead, but sensible persons cannot but consider Lord Pevensey's death to have been caused by his own carelessness."

"Now, certainly that is true," the girl said, brightening. "It was really his own carelessness and his dear lovable rashness. And somebody could explain it to the Queen. Besides, I often think that wars are good for the public spirit of a nation, and bring out its true manhood. But then it upset me, too, a little, Ned, to hear about this Marlowe.—for I must tell you that I knew the poor man, very slightly. So I happen to know that today he flung off in a rage, and began drinking, because somebody, almost by pure chance, had burned a packet of his verses—"

Thereupon Captain Musgrave raised heavy eyebrows, and guffawed so heartily that the candle flickered. "To think of the fellow's putting it on that plea! when he could so easily have written some more verses. That is the trouble with these poets, if you ask me: they are not practical even in their ordinary everyday lying. No, no, the truth of it was that the rogue wanted a pretext for making a beast of himself, and seized the first that came to hand. Egad, my dear, it is a daily practice with these poets. They hardly draw a sober breath. Everybody knows that."

Cynthia was looking at him in the half-lit room with very flattering admiration. . . . Seen thus, with her scarlet lips a little parted—disclosing pearls,—and with her naïve dark eyes aglow, she was quite incredibly pretty and caressable. She had almost forgotten until now that this stalwart soldier, too, was in love with her. But now her spirits were rising venturously, and she knew that she liked Ned Musgrave. He had sensible notions; he saw things as they really were, and with him there would never be any nonsense about toplofty ideas. Then, too, her dear old white-haired father would be pleased, because there was a very fair estate. . . .

So Cynthia said: "I believe you are right, Ned. I often wonder how they can be so lacking in self-respect. Oh, I am certain you must be right, for it is just what I felt without being able quite to express it. You will stay for supper with us, of course. Yes, but you must, because it is always a great comfort for me to talk with really sensible persons. I do not wonder that you are not very eager to stay, though, for I am probably a fright, with my eyes red, and with my hair all tumbling down, like an old witch's. Well, let us see what can be done about it, sir! There was a hand-mirror—"

And thus speaking, she tripped, with very much the reputed grace of a fairy, toward the far end of the room, and standing a-tiptoe, groped at the obscure shelves, with a resultant crash of falling china.

"Oh, but my lovely cups!" said Cynthia, in dismay. "I had forgotten they were up there: and now I have smashed both of them, in looking for my mirror, sir, and trying to prettify myself for you. And I had so fancied them, because they had not their like in England."

She looked at the fragments, and then at Musgrave, with wide, innocent hurt eyes. She was really grieved by the loss of her quaint toys. But Musgrave, in his sturdy, common-sense way, only laughed at her seriousness over such kickshaws.

"I am for an honest earthenware tankard myself!" he said, jovially, as the two went in to supper.

45

Wild Oranges

BY JOSEPH HERGESHEIMER

THE ketch drifted into the serene inclosure of the bay as silently as the reflections moving over the mirror-like surface of the water. Beyond a low arm of land that hid the sea the western sky was a single, clear yellow; farther on the left the pale, incalculably old limbs of cypress, their roots bare, were hung with gathering shadows as delicate as their own faint foliage. The stillness was emphasized by the ceaseless murmur of the waves breaking on the far, seaward bars.

John Woolfolk brought the ketch up where he intended to anchor and called to the stooping white-clad figure in the bow: "Let go!" There was an answering splash, a sudden rasp of hawser, the booms swung idle, and the yacht imperceptibly settled into her berth. The wheel turned impotently; and, absent-minded, John Woolfolk locked it. He dropped his long form on a carpet-covered folding chair near by. He was tired. His sailor, Poul Halvard, moved about with a noiseless and swift efficiency; he rolled and cased the jib, and then, with a handful of canvas stops, secured and covered the mainsail and proceeded aft to the jigger. Unlike Woolfolk, Halvard was short—a square figure with a smooth, deep-tanned countenance, colorless and steady, pale blue eyes. His mouth closed so tightly that it appeared immovable, as if it had been carved from some obdurate material that opened for the necessities of neither speech nor sustenance.

Tall John Woolfolk was darkly tanned, too, and had a gray gaze, by turns sharply focused with bright black pupils and blankly introspective. He was garbed in white flannels, with bare ankles and sandals, and an old, collarless silk shirt, with sleeves rolled back on virile arms incongruously tattooed with gauzy green cicadas.

He stayed motionless while Halvard put the yacht in order for the

758

night. The day's passage through twisting inland waterways, the hazard of the tides on shifting flats, the continual concentration on details at once trivial and highly necessary, had been more wearing than the cyclone the ketch had weathered off Barbuda the year before. They had been landbound since dawn; and all day John Woolfolk's instinct had revolted against the fields and wooded points, turning toward the open sea.

Halvard disappeared into the cabin; and, soon after, a faint, hot air, the smell of scorched metal, announced the lighting of the vapor stove, the preparations for supper. Not a breath stirred the surface of the bay. The water, as transparently clear as the hardly darkened air, lay like a great amethyst clasped by its dim corals and the arm of the land. The glossy foliage that, with the exception of a small silver beach, choked the shore might have been stamped from metal. It was, John Woolfolk suddenly thought, amazingly still. The atmosphere, too, was peculiarly heavy, languorous. It was laden with the scents of exotic, flowering trees; he recognized the smooth, heavy odor of oleanders and the clearer sweetness of orange blossoms.

He was idly surprised at the latter; he had not known that orange groves had been planted and survived in Georgia. Woolfolk gazed more attentively at the shore, and made out, in back of the luxuriant tangle, the broad white façade of a dwelling. A pair of marine glasses lay on the deck at his hand; and, adjusting them, he surveyed the face of a distinguished ruin. The windows on the stained wall were broken in—they resembled the empty eyes of the dead; storms had battered loose the neglected roof, leaving a corner open to sun and rain; he could see through the foliage lower down great columns fallen about a sweeping portico.

The house was deserted, he was certain of that—the melancholy wreckage of a vanished and resplendent time. Its small principality, flourishing when commerce and communication had gone by water, was one of the innumerable victims of progress and of the concentration of effort into huge impersonalities. He thought he could trace other even more complete ruins, but his interest waned. He laid the glasses back upon the deck. The choked bubble of boiling water sounded from the cabin, mingled with the irregular sputter of cooking fat and the clinking of plates and silver as Halvard set the table. Without, the light was fading swiftly; the wavering cry of an owl quivered from the cypress across the water, and the western sky changed from paler yellow to green. Woolfolk moved abruptly, and, securing a bucket to the handle of which a short rope had been spliced and finished with an ornamental Turk's-head, he swung it overboard and brought it up half full. In the darkness of the bucket the water shone with a faint phosphoi scence. Then from a basin he lathered his hands with a thick, pinkish paste, washed his face, and started toward the cabin.

He was already in the companionway when, glancing across the still surface of the bay, he saw a swirl moving into view about a small point. He thought at first that it was a fish, but the next moment saw the white, graceful silhouette of an arm. It was a woman swimming. John Woolfolk could now plainly make out the free, solid mass of her hair, the naked, smoothly turning shoulder. She was swimming with deliberate ease, with a long, single overarm stroke; and it was evident that she had not seen the ketch. Woolfolk stood, his gaze level with the cabin top, watching her assured progress. She turned again, moving out from the shore, then suddenly stopped. Now, he realized, she saw him.

The swimmer hung motionless for a breath; then, with a strong, sinuous drive, she whirled about and made swiftly for the point of land. She was visible for a short space, low in the water, her hair wavering in the clear flood, and then disappeared abruptly behind the point, leaving behind—a last vanishing trace of her silent passage—a smooth, subsiding wake on the surface of the bay.

John Woolfolk mechanically descended the three short steps to the cabin. There had been something extraordinary in the woman's brief appearance out of the odorous tangle of the shore, with its ruined habitation. It had caught him unprepared, in a moment of half weary relaxation, and his imagination responded with a faint question to which it had been long unaccustomed. But Halvard, in crisp white, standing behind the steaming supper viands, brought his thoughts again to the day's familiar routine.

The cabin was divided through its forward half by the centerboard casing, and against it a swinging table had been elevated, an immaculate cover laid, and the yacht's china, marked in cobalt with the name *Gar,* placed in a polished and formal order. Halvard's service from the stove to the table was as silent and skillful as his housing of the sails; he replaced the hot dishes with cold, and provided a glass bowl of translucent preserved figs.

Supper at an end, Woolfolk rolled a cigarette from shag that resembled coarse black tea and returned to the deck. Night had fallen on the shore, but the water still held a pale light; in the east the sky was filled with an increasing, cold radiance. It was the moon, rising swiftly above the flat land. The moonlight grew in intensity, casting inky shadows of the spars and cordage across the deck, making the light in the cabin a reddish blur by contrast. The icy flood swept over the land, bringing out with a new emphasis the close, glossy foliage and broken façade—it appeared unreal, portentous. The odors of the flowers, of the orange blossoms, uncoiled in heavy, palpable waves across the water, accompanied by the owl's fluctuating cry. The sense of imminence increased, of a *genius loci* unguessed and troublous, vaguely threatening in the perfumed dark.

II

John Woolfolk had said nothing to Halvard of the woman he had seen swimming in the bay. He was conscious of no particular reason for remaining silent about her; but the thing had become invested with a glamour that, he felt, would be destroyed by commonplace discussion. He had no personal interest in the episode, he was careful to add. Interests of that sort, serving to connect him with the world, with society, with women, had totally disappeared from his life. He rolled and lighted a fresh cigarette, and in the minute orange spurt of the match his mouth was somber and forbidding.

The unexpected appearance on the glassy water had merely started into being a slight, fanciful curiosity. The women of that coast did not commonly swim at dusk in their bays; such simplicity obtained now only in the reaches of the highest civilization. There were, he knew, no hunting camps here, and the local inhabitants were mere sodden squatters. A chart lay in its flat canvas case by the wheel; and, in the crystal flood of the moon, he easily reaffirmed from it his knowledge of the yacht's position. Nothing could be close by but scattered huts and such wreckage as that looming palely above the oleanders.

Yet a woman had unquestionably appeared swimming from behind the point of land off the bow of the *Gar*. The women native to the locality, and the men, too, were fanatical in the avoidance of any unnecessary exterior application of water. His thoughts moved in a monotonous circle, while the enveloping radiance constantly increased. It became as light as a species of unnatural day, where every leaf was clearly revealed but robbed of all color and familiar meaning.

He grew restless, and rose, making his way forward about the narrow deck-space outside the cabin. Halvard was seated on a coil of rope beside the windlass and stood erect as Woolfolk approached. The sailor was smoking a short pipe, and the bowl made a crimson spark in his thick, powerful hand. John Woolfolk fingered the wood surface of the windlass bitts and found it rough and gummy. Halvard said instinctively:

"I'd better start scraping the mahogany tomorrow, it's getting white."

Woolfolk nodded. Halvard was a good man. He had the valuable quality of commonly anticipating spoken desires. He was a Norwegian, out of the Lofoden Islands, where sailors are surpassingly schooled in the Arctic seas. Poul Halvard, so far as Woolfolk could discover, was impervious to cold, to fatigue, to the insidious whispering of mere flesh.

He was a man without temptation, with an untroubled allegiance to a duty that involved an endless, exacting labor; and for those reasons he was austere, withdrawn from the community of more fragile and sympathetic natures. At times his inflexible integrity oppressed John Woolfolk. Halvard, he thought, was a difficult man to live up to.

He turned and absently surveyed the land. His restlessness increased. He felt a strong desire for a larger freedom of space than that offered by the *Gar,* and it occurred to him that he might go ashore in the tender. He moved aft with this idea growing to a determination. In the cabin, on the shelf above the berths built against the sides of the ketch, he found an old blue flannel coat, with crossed squash rackets and a monogram embroidered in yellow on the breast pocket. Slipping it on, he dropped over the stern of the tender.

Halvard came instantly aft, but Woolfolk declined the mutely offered service. The oars made a silken swish in the still bay as he pulled away from the yacht. The latter's riding light, swung on the forestay, hung without a quiver, like a fixed yellow star. He looked once over his shoulder, and then the bow of the tender ran with a soft shock upon the beach. Woolfolk bedded the anchor in the sand and then stood gazing curiously before him.

On his right a thicket of oleanders drenched the air with the perfume of their heavy poisonous flowering, and behind them a rough clearing of saw grass swept up to the débris of the fallen portico. To the left, beyond the black hole of a decaying well, rose the walls of a second brick building, smaller than the dwelling. A few shreds of rotten porch clung to its face; and the moonlight, pouring through a break above, fell in a livid bar across the obscurity of a high single chamber.

Between the crumbling piles there was the faint trace of a footway, and Woolfolk advanced to where, inside a dilapidated sheltering fence, he came upon a dark, compact mass of trees and smelled the increasing sweetness of orange blossoms. He struck the remains of a board path, and progressed with the cold, waxen leaves of the orange trees brushing his face. There was, he saw in the gray brightness, ripe fruit among the branches, and he mechanically picked an orange and then another. They were small but heavy, and had fine skins.

He tore one open and put a section in his mouth. It was at first surprisingly bitter, and he involuntarily flung away what remained in his hand. But after a moment he found that the oranges possessed a pungency and zestful flavor that he had tasted in no others. Then he saw, directly before him, a pale, rectangular light which he recognized as the opened door of a habitation.

III

He advanced more slowly, and a low, irregular house detached itself from the tangled growth pressing upon it from all sides. The doorway, dimly lighted by an invisible lamp from within, was now near by; and John Woolfolk saw a shape cross it, so swiftly furtive that it was gone before he realized that a man had vanished into the hall. There was a second stir on the small covered portico, and the slender, white-clad figure of a woman moved uncertainly forward. He stopped just at the moment in which a low, clear voice demanded: "What do you want?"

The question was directly put, and yet the tone held an inexplicably acute apprehension. The woman's voice bore a delicate, bell-like shiver of fear.

"Nothing," he hastened to assure her. "When I came ashore I thought no one was living here."

"You're from the white boat that sailed in at sunset?"

"Yes," he replied, "and I am returning immediately."

"It was like magic" she continued. "Suddenly, without a sound, you were anchored in the bay." Even this quiet statement bore the shadowy alarm. John Woolfolk realized that it had not been caused by his abrupt appearance; the faint accent of dread was fixed in the illusive form before him.

"I have robbed you, too," he continued in a lighter tone. "Your oranges are in my pocket."

"You won't like them," she returned indirectly; "they've run wild. We can't sell them."

"They have a distinct flavor of their own," he assured her. "I should be glad to have some on the *Gar*."

"All you want."

"My man will get them and pay you."

"Please don't—" She stopped abruptly, as if a sudden consideration had interrupted a liberal courtesy. When she spoke again the apprehension, Woolfolk thought, had increased to palpable fright. "We would charge you very little," she said finally. "Nicholas attends to that."

Silence fell upon them. She stood with her hand resting lightly against an upright support, coldly revealed by the moon. John Woolfolk saw that, although slight, her body was delicately full, and that her shoulders held a droop which somehow resembled the shadow on her voice. She bore an unmistakable refinement of being, strange in that locality of meager humanity. Her speech totally lacked the unintelligible, loose slurring of the natives.

"Won't you sit down," she at last broke the silence. "My father was here when you came up, but he went in. Strangers disturb him."

Woolfolk moved to the portico, elevated above the ground, where he found a momentary place. The woman sank back into a low chair. The stillness gathered about them once more, and he mechanically rolled a cigarette. Her white dress, although simply and rudely made, gained distinction from her free, graceful lines; her feet, in black, heelless slippers, were narrow and sharply cut. He saw that her countenance bore an even pallor on which her eyes made shadows like those on marble.

These details, unremarkable in themselves, were charged with a peculiar intensity. John Woolfolk, who long ago had put such considerations from his existence, was yet clearly conscious of the disturbing quality of her person. She possessed the indefinable property of charm. Such women, he knew, stirred life profoundly, reanimating it with extraordinary efforts and desires. Their mere passage, the pressure of their fingers, were more imperative than the life service of others; the flutter of their breath could be more tryannical than the most poignant memories and vows.

John Woolfolk thought these things in a manner absolutely detached. They touched him at no point. Nevertheless, the faint curiosity stirred within him remained. The house unexpectedly inhabited behind the ruined façade on the water, the magnetic woman with the echo of apprehension in her cultivated voice, the parent, so easily disturbed, even the mere name "Nicholas," all held a marked potentiality of emotion; they were set in an almost hysterical key.

He was suddenly conscious of the odorous pressure of the flowering trees, of the orange blossoms and the oleanders. It was stifling. He felt that he must escape at once, from all the cloying and insidious scents of the earth, to the open and sterile sea. The thick tangle in the colorless light of the moon, the dimmer portico with its enigmatic figure, were a cunning essence of the existence from which he had fled. Life's traps were set with just such treacheries—perfume and mystery and the veiled lure of sex.

He rose with an uncouth abruptness, a meager commonplace, and hurried over the path to the beach, toward the refuge, the release, of the *Gar*.

John Woolfolk woke at dawn. A thin, bluish light filled the cabin; above, Halvard was washing the deck. The latter was vigorously swabbing the cockpit when Woolfolk appeared, but he paused.

"Perhaps," the sailor said, "you will stay here for a day or two. I'd like to unship the propeller, and there's the scraping. It's a good anchorage."

"We're moving on south," Woolfolk replied, stating the determination with which he had retired. Then the full sense of Halvard's words penetrated his waking mind. The propeller, he knew, had not opened properly for a week; and the anchorage was undoubtedly good. This was the last place, before entering the Florida passes, for whatever minor adjustments were necessary.

The matted shore, flushed with the rising sun, was starred with white and deep pink blooms; a ray gilded the blank wall of the deserted mansion. The scent of the orange blossoms was not so insistent as it had been on the previous evening. The land appeared normal; it exhibited none of the disturbing influence of which he had been first conscious. Last night's mood seemed absurd.

"You are quite right," he altered his pronouncement; "we'll put the *Gar* in order here. People are living behind the grove, and there'll be water."

He had, for breakfast, oranges brought down the coast, and he was surprised at their sudden insipidity. They were little better than faintly sweetened water. He turned and in the pocket of his flannel coat found one of those he had picked the night before. It was as keen as a knife; the peculiar aroma had, without doubt, robbed him of all desire for the cultivated oranges of commerce.

Halvard was in the tender, under the stern of the ketch, when it occurred to John Woolfolk that it would be wise to go ashore and establish his assertion of an adequate water supply. He explained this briefly to the sailor, who put him on the small shingle of sand. There he turned to the right, moving idly in a direction away from that he had taken before.

He crossed the corner of the demolished abode, made his way through a press of sere cabbage palmettos, and emerged suddenly on the blinding expanse of the sea. The limpid water lay in a bright rim over corrugated and pitted rock, where shallow ultramarine pools spread gardens of sulphur-yellow and rose anemones. The land curved in upon the left; a ruined landing extended over the placid tide, and, seated there with her back toward him, a woman was fishing.

It was, he saw immediately, the woman of the portico. At the moment of recognition she turned, and after a brief inspection, slowly waved her hand. He approached, crossing the openings in the precarious boarding of the landing, until he stood over her. She said:

"There's an old sheepshead under here I've been after for a year. If you'll be very still you can see him."

She turned her face up to him, and he saw that her cheeks were without trace of color. At the same time he reaffirmed all that he felt before with regard to the potent quality of her being. She had a lustrous mass of warm brown hair twisted into a loose knot that had slid forward over a broad, low brow; a pointed chin; and pale, disturbing lips. But her eyes were her most notable feature—they were widely opened and extraordinary in color; the only similitude that occurred to John

Woolfolk was the gray greenness of olive leaves. In them he felt the same foreboding that had shadowed her voice. The fleet passage of her gaze left an indelible impression of an expectancy that was at once a dread and a strangely youthful candor. She was, he thought, about thirty.

She wore now a russet skirt of thin, coarse texture that, like the dress of the evening, took a slim grace from her fine body, and a white waist, frayed from many washings, open upon her smooth, round throat.

"He's usually by this post," she continued, pointing down through the clear gloom of the water.

Woolfolk lowered himself to a position at her side, his gaze following her direction. There, after a moment, he distinguished the sheepshead, barred in black and white, wavering about the piling. His companion was fishing with a short, heavy rod from which time had dissolved the varnish, an ineffectual brass reel that complained shrilly whenever the lead was raised or lowered, and a thick, freely knotted line.

"You should have a leader," he told her. "The old gentleman can see your line too plainly."

There was a sharp pull, she rapidly turned the handle of the protesting reel, and drew up a gasping, bony fish with extended red wings.

"Another robin!" she cried tragically. "This is getting serious. Dinner," she informed him, "and not sport, is my object."

He looked out to where a channel made a deep blue stain through the paler cerulean of the sea. The tide, he saw from the piling, was low.

"There should be a rockfish in the pass," he pronounced.

"What good if there is?" she returned. "I couldn't possibly throw out there. And if I could, why disturb a rock with this?" She shook the short awkward rod, the knotted line.

He privately acknowledged the palpable truth of her objections, and rose.

"I've some fishing things on the ketch," he said, moving away. He blew shrilly on a whistle from the beach, and Halvard dropped over the *Gar's* side into the tender.

Woolfolk was soon back on the wharf, stripping the canvas cover from the long cane tip of a fishing rod brilliantly wound with green and vermilion, and fitting it into a dark, silver-capped butt. He locked a capacious reel into place, and, drawing a thin line through agate guides, attached a glistening steel leader and chained hook. Then, adding a freely swinging lead, he picked up the small mullet that lay by his companion.

"Does that have to go?" she demanded. "It's such a slim chance, and it is my only mullet."

He ruthlessly sliced a piece from the silvery side; and, rising and switching his reel's gear, he cast. The lead swung far out across the water and fell on the farther side of the channel.

"But that's dazzling!" she exclaimed; "as though you had shot it out of a gun."

He tightened the line, and sat with the rod resting in a leather socket fastened to his belt.

"Now," she stated, "we will watch at the vain sacrifice of an only mullet."

The day was superb, the sky sparkled like a great blue sun; schools of young mangrove snappers swept through the pellucid water. The woman said:

"Where did you come from and where are you going?"

"Cape Cod," he replied; "and I am going to the Guianas."

"Isn't that South America?" she queried. "I've traveled far—on maps. Guiana," she repeated the name softly. For a moment the faint dread in her voice changed to longing. "I think I know all the beautiful names of places on the earth," she continued: "Tarragona and Seriphos and Cambodia."

"Some of them you have seen?"

"None," she answered simply. "I was born here, in the house you know, and I have never been fifty miles away."

This, he told himself, was incredible. The mystery that surrounded her deepened, stirring more strongly his impersonal curiosity.

"You are surprised," she added; "it's mad, but true. There—there is a reason." She stopped abruptly, and neglecting her fishing rod, sat with her hands clasped about slim knees. She gazed at him slowly, and he was impressed once more by the remarkable quality of her eyes, gray-green like olive leaves and strangely young. The momentary interest created in her by romantic and far names faded, gave place to the familiar trace of fear. In the long past he would have responded immediately to the appeal of her pale, magnetic countenance. . . . He had broken all connection with society, with—

There was a sudden, impressive jerk at his line, the rod instantly assumed the shape of a bent bow, and, as he rose, the reel spindle was lost in a gray blur and the line streaked out through the dipping tip. His companion hung breathless at his shoulder.

"He'll take all your line," she lamented as the fish continued his straight, outward course, while Woolfolk kept an even pressure on the rod.

"A hundred yards," he announced as he felt a threaded mark wheel from under his thumb. Then: "A hundred and fifty. I'm afraid it's a shark." As he spoke the fish leaped clear of the water, a spot of molten silver, and fell back in a sparkling blue spray. "It's a rock," he added.

He stopped the run momentarily; the rod bent perilously double, but the fish halted. Woolfolk reeled in smoothly, but another rush followed, as strong as the first. A long, equal struggle ensued, the thin line was drawn as rigid as metal, the rod quivered and arched. Once the rock-fish was close enough to be clearly distinguishable—strongly built, heavy-shouldered, with black stripes drawn from gills to tail. But he was off again with a short, blundering rush.

"If you will hold the rod," Woolfolk directed his companion, "I'll gaff him." She took the rod while he bent over the wharf's side. The fish, on the surface of the water, half turned; and, striking the gaff through a gill, Woolfolk swung him up on the boarding.

"There," he pronounced, "are several dinners. I'll carry him to your kitchen."

"Nicholas would do it, but he's away," she told him; "and my father is not strong enough. That's a leviathan."

John Woolfolk placed a handle through the rockfish's gills, and, carrying it with an obvious effort, he followed her over a narrow, trampled path through the rasped palmettos. They approached the dwelling from behind the orange grove; and, coming suddenly to the porch, surprised an incredibly thin, gray man in the act of lighting a small stone pipe with a reed stem. He was sitting, but, seeing Woolfolk, he started sharply to his feet, and the pipe fell, shattering the bowl.

"My father," the woman pronounced: "Lichfield Stope."

"Millie," he stuttered painfully, "you know—I—strangers—"

John Woolfolk thought, as he presented himself, that he had never before seen such an immaterial living figure. Lichfield Stope was like the shadow of a man draped with unsubstantial, dusty linen. Into his waxen face beat a pale infusion of blood, as if a diluted wine had been poured into a semi-opaque goblet; his sunken lips puffed out and collapsed; his fingers, dust-colored like his garb, opened and shut with a rapid, mechanical rigidity.

"Father," Millie Stope remonstrated, "you must manage yourself better. You know I wouldn't bring anyone to the house who would hurt us. And see—we are fetching you a splendid rockfish."

The older man made a convulsive effort to regain his composure.

"Ah, yes," he muttered; "just so."

The flush receded from his indeterminate countenance. Woolfolk saw that he had a goatee laid like a wasted yellow finger on his chin, and that his hands hung on wrists like twisted copper wires from circular cuffs fastened with large mosaic buttons.

"We are alone here," he proceeded in a fluctuating voice, the voice of a shadow; "the man is away. My daughter—I—" He grew inaudible, although his lips maintained a faint movement.

The fear that lurked illusively in the daughter was in the parent magnified to an appalling panic, an instinctive, acute agony that had crushed everything but a thin, tormented spark of life. He passed his hand over a brow as dry as the spongy limbs of the cypress, brushing a scant lock like dead, bleached moss.

"The fish," he pronounced; "yes . . . acceptable."

"If you will carry it back for me," Millie Stope requested; "we have no ice; I must put it in water." He followed her about a bay window with ornamental fretting that bore the shreds of old, variegated paint. He could see, amid an incongruous wreckage within, a dismantled billiard table, its torn cloth faintly green beneath a film of dust. They turned and arrived at the kitchen door. "There, please." She indicated a bench on the outside wall, and he deposited his burden.

"You have been very nice," she told him, making her phrase less commonplace by a glance of her wide, appealing eyes. "Now, I suppose, you will go on across the world?"

"Not tonight," he replied distantly.

"Perhaps, then, you will come ashore again. We see so few people. My father would be benefited. It was only at first, so suddenly—he was startled."

"There is a great deal to do on the ketch," he replied indirectly, maintaining his retreat from the slightest advance of life. "I came ashore to discover if you had a large water supply and if I might fill my casks."

"Rain water," she informed him; "the cistern is full."

"Then I'll send Halvard to you." He withdrew a step, but paused at the incivility of his leaving.

A sudden weariness had settled over the shoulders of Millie Stope; she appeared young and very white. Woolfolk was acutely conscious of her utter isolation with the shivering figure on the porch, the unmaterialized Nicholas. She had delicate hands.

"Good-by," he said, bowing formally. "And thank you for the fishing."

He whistled sharply for the tender.

IV

Throughout the afternoon, with a triangular scraping iron, he assisted Halvard in removing the whitened varnish from the yacht's mahogany They worked silently, with only the shrill note of the edges drawing across the wood, while the westering sun plunged its diagonal rays far into the transparent depths of the bay. The *Gar* floated motionless on water like a pale evening over purple and silver flowers threaded by fish painted the vermilion and green of parrakeets. Inshore the pallid cypresses seemed, as John Woolfolk watched them, to twist in febrile pain. With the waning of day the land took on its air of unhealthy mystery; the mingled, heavy scents floated out in a sickly tide; the ruined façade glimmered in the half light.

Woolfolk's thoughts turned back to the woman living in the miasma of perfume and secret fear. He heard again her wistful voice pronounce the names of far places, of Tarragona and Seriphos, investing them with the accent of an intense hopeless desire. He thought of the inexplicable place of her birth and of the riven, unsubstantial figure of the man with the blood pulsing into his ocherous face. Some old, profound error or calamity had laid its blight upon him, he was certain; but the most lamentable inheritance was not sufficient to account for the acute apprehension in his daughter's tones. This was different in kind from the spiritual collapse of the aging man. It was actual, he realized that; proceeding—in part at least—from without.

He wondered, scraping with difficulty the underturning of a cathead, if whatever dark tide was centered above her would, perhaps, descend through the oleander-scented night and stifle her in the stagnant dwelling. He had a swift, vividly complete vision of the old man face down upon the floor in a flickering, reddish light.

He smiled in self-contempt at this neurotic fancy; and, straightening his cramped muscles, rolled a cigarette. It might be that the years he had spent virtually alone on the silence of various waters had affected his brain. Halvard's broad, concentrated countenance, the steady, grave gaze and determined mouth, cleared Woolfolk's mind of its phantoms. He moved to the cockpit and from there said:

"That will do for today."

Halvard followed, and commenced once more the familiar, ordered preparations for supper. John Woolfolk, smoking while the sky turned to malachite, became sharply aware of the unthinkable monotony of the universal course, of the centuries wheeling in dull succession into infinity. Life seemed to him no more varied than the wire drum in which squirrels raced nowhere. His own lot, he told himself grimly, was no worse than another. Existence was all of the same drab piece. It had seemed gay enough when he was young, worked with gold and crimson threads, and then—

His thoughts were broken by Halvard's appearance in the companionway, and he descended to his solitary supper in the contracted, still cabin.

Again on deck his sense of the monotony of life trebled. He had been cruising now about the edges of continents for twelve years. For twelve years he had taken no part in the existence of the cities he had passed, as often as possible without stopping, and of the villages gathered invitingly under their canopies of trees. He was—yes, he must be—forty-six. Life was passing away; well, let it . . . worthless.

The growing radiance of the moon glimmered across the water and folded the land in a gossamer veil. The same uneasiness, the inchoate desire to go ashore that had seized upon him the night before, reasserted its influence. The face of Millie Stope floated about him like a magical gardenia in the night of the matted trees. He resisted the pressure longer than before; but in the end he was seated in the tender, pulling toward the beach.

He entered the orange grove and slowly approached the house beyond. Millie Stope advanced with a quick welcome.

"I'm glad," she said simply. "Nicholas is back. The fish weighed—"

"I think I'd better not know," he interrupted. "I might be tempted to mention it in the future, when it would take on the historic suspicion of the fish story."

"But it was imposing," she protested. "Let's go to the sea; it's so limitless in the moonlight."

He followed her over the path to where the remains of the wharf projected into a sea as black, and as solid apparently, as ebony, and across which the moon flung a narrow way like a chalk mark. Millie Stope seated herself on the boarding and he found a place near by. She leaned forward, with her arms propped up and her chin couched on her palms. Her potency increased rather than diminished with association; her skin had a rare texture; her movements, the turn of the wrists, were distinguished. He wondered again at the strangeness of her situation.

She looked about suddenly and surprised his palpable questioning.

"You are puzzled," she pronounced. "Perhaps you are setting me in the middle of romance. Please don't! Nothing you might guess—" She broke off abruptly, returned to her former pose. "And yet," she added presently, "I have a perverse desire to talk about myself. It's perverse because, although you are a little curious, you have no real interest in what I might say. There is something about you like—yes, like the cast-iron dog that used to stand in our lawn. It rusted away, cold to the last and indifferent, although I talked to it by the hour. But I did get a little comfort from its stolid painted eye. Perhaps you'd act in the same way.

"And then," she went on when Woolfolk had somberly failed to comment, "you are going away, you will forget, it can't possibly matter. I must talk, now that I have urged myself this far. After all, you needn't have come back. But where shall I begin? You should know something of the very first. That happened in Virginia. . . . My father didn't go to war," she said, sudden and clear. She turned her face toward him, and he saw that it had lost its flower-like quality; it looked as if it had been carved in stone.

"He lived in a small, intensely loyal town," she continued; "and when Virginia seceded it burned with a single high flame of sacrifice. My father had been always a diffident man; he collected mezzotints and avoided people. So, when the enlistment began, he shrank away from the crowds and hot speeches, and the men went off without him. He lived in complete retirement then, with his prints, in a town of women. It wasn't impossible at first; he discussed the situation with the few old tradesmen that remained, and exchanged bows with the wives and daughters of his friends. But when the dead commenced to be brought in from the front it got worse. Belle Semple—he had always thought her unusually nice and pretty—mocked at him on the street. Then one morning he found an apron tied to the knob of the front door.

"After that he went out only at night. His servants had deserted him, and he lived by himself in a biggish, solemn house. Sometimes the news of losses and deaths would be shouted through his windows; once stones were thrown in, but mostly he was let alone. It must have been frightful in his empty rooms when the South went from bad to worse." She paused, and John Woolfolk could see, even in the obscurity, the slow shudder that passed over her.

When the war was over and what men were left returned—one with hands gone at the wrists, another without legs in a shabby wheelchair—the life of the town started once more, but my father was forever outside of it. Little subscriptions for burials were made up, small schemes for getting the necessities, but he was never asked. Men spoke to him again, even some of the women. That was all.

"I think it was then that a curious, perpetual dread fastened on his mind—a fear of the wind in the night, of breaking twigs or sudden voices. He ordered things to be left on the steps, and he would peer out from under the blind to make sure that the walk was empty before he opened the door.

"You must realize," she said in a sharper voice, "that my father was not a pure coward at first. He was an extremely sensitive man who hated the rude stir of living and who simply asked to be left undisturbed with his portfolios. But life's not like that. The war hunted him out and ruined him; it destroyed his being, just as it destroyed the fortunes of others.

"Then he began to think—it was absolute fancy—that there was a conspiracy in the town to kill him. He sent some of his things away, got together what money he had, and one night left his home secretly on foot. He tramped south for weeks, living for a while in small place after place, until he reached Georgia, and then a town about fifty miles from here—"

She broke off, sitting rigidly erect, looking out over the level black sea with its shifting, chalky line of light, and a long silence followed. The antiphonal crying of the owls sounded over the bubbling swamp, the mephitic perfume hung like a vapor on the shore. John Woolfolk shifted his position.

"My mother told me this," his companion said suddenly. "Father repeated it over and over through the nights after they were married. He slept only in snatches, and would wake with a gasp and his heart almost bursting. I know almost nothing about her, except that she had a brave heart—or she would have gone mad. She was English and had been a governess. They met in the little hotel where they were married. Then father bought this place, and they came here to live."

Woolfolk had a vision of the tenuous figure of Lichfield Stope; he was surprised that such acute agony had left the slightest trace of humanity; yet the other, after forty years of torment, still survived to shudder at a chance footfall, the advent of a casual and harmless stranger.

This, then, was by implication the history of the woman at his side; it disposed of the mystery that had veiled her situation here. It was surprisingly clear, even to the subtle influence that, inherited from her father, had set the shadow of his own obsession upon her voice and eyes. Yet, in the moment that she had been made explicable, he recalled the conviction that the knowledge of an actual menace lurked in her mind; he had seen it in the tension of her body, in the anxiety of fleet backward glances.

The latter, he told himself, might be merely a symptom of mental sickness, a condition natural to the influences under which she had been formed. He tested and rejected that possibility—there could be no doubt of her absolute sanity. It was patent in a hundred details of her carriage, in her mentality as it had been revealed in her restrained, balanced narrative.

There was, too, the element of her mother to be considered. Millie Stope had known very little about her, principally the self-evident fact of the latter's "brave heart." It would have needed that to remain steadfast through the racking recitals of the long, waking darks; to accompany to this desolate and lonely refuge the man who had had an apron tied to his doorknob. In the degree that the daughter had been a prey to the man's fear she would have benefited from the stiffer qualities of the English governess. Life once more assumed its enigmatic mask.

His companion said:

"All that—and I haven't said a word about myself, the real end of my soliloquy. I'm permanently discouraged; I have qualms about boring you. No, I shall never find another listener as satisfactory as the iron dog."

A light glimmered far at sea. "I sit here a great deal," she informed him, "and watch the ships, a thumbprint of blue smoke at day and a spark at night, going up and down their water roads. You are enviable —getting up your anchor, sailing where you like, safe and free." Her voice took on a passionate intensity that surprised him; it was sick with weariness and longing, with sudden revolt from the pervasive apprehension.

"Safe and free," he repeated thinly, as if satirizing the condition implied by those commonplace, assuaging words. He had, in his flight from society, sought simply peace. John Woolfolk now questioned all his implied success. He had found the elemental hush of the sea, the iron aloofness of rocky and uninhabited coasts, but he had never been able to still the dull rebellion within, the legacy of the past. A feeling of complete failure settled over him. His safety and freedom amounted to this—that life had broken him and cast him aside.

A long, hollow wail rose from the land, and Millie Stope moved sharply.

"There's Nicholas," she exclaimed, "blowing on the conch! They don't know where I am; I'd better go in."

A small, evident panic took possession of her; the shiver in her voice swelled.

"No, don't come," she added. "I'll be quicker without you." She made her way over the wharf to the shore, but there paused. "I suppose you'll be going soon?"

"Tomorrow probably," he answered.

On the ketch Halvard had gone below for the night. The yacht swayed slightly to an unseen swell; the riding light moved backward and forward, its ray flickering over the glassy water. John Woolfolk brought his bedding from the cabin and, disposing it on deck, lay with his wakeful dark face set against the far, multitudinous worlds.

v

In the morning Halvard proposed a repainting of the engine.

"The Florida air," he said, "eats metal overnight." And the ketch remained anchored.

Later in the day Woolfolk sounded the water casks cradled in the cockpit, and, when they answered hollow, directed his man with regard to their refilling. They drained a cask. Halvard put it on the tender and pulled in to the beach. There he shouldered the empty container and disappeared among the trees.

Woolfolk was forward, preparing a chain hawser for coral anchorages, when he saw Halvard tramping shortly back over the sand. He entered the tender and, with a vicious shove, rowed with a powerful, vindictive sweep toward the ketch. The cask evidently had been left behind. He made the tender fast and swung aboard with his notable agility.

"There's a damn idiot in that house," he declared, in a surprising departure from his customary detached manner.

"Explain yourself," Woolfolk demanded shortly.

"But I'm going back after him," the sailor stubbornly proceeded. "I'll turn any knife out of his hand." It was evident that he was laboring under an intense growing excitement and anger.

"The only idiot's not on land," Woolfolk told him. "Where's the water cask you took ashore?"

"Broken."

"How?"

"I'll tell you fast enough. There was nobody about when I went up to the house, although there was a chair rocking on the porch as if a person had just left. I knocked at the door; it was open, and I was certain that I heard someone inside, but nobody answered. Then after a bit I went around back. The kitchen was open, too, and no one in sight. I saw the water cistern and thought I'd fill up, when you could say something afterward. I did, and was rolling the cask about the house when this—loggerhead came out of the bushes. He wanted to know what I was getting away with, and I explained, but it didn't suit him. He said I might be telling facts and again I mightn't. I saw there was no use talking, and started rolling the cask again; but he put his foot on it, and I pushed one way and he the other—"

"And between you, you stove in the cask," Woolfolk interrupted.

"That's it," Poul Halvard answered concisely. "Then I got mad, and offered to beat in his face, but he had a knife. I could have broken it out of his grip—I've done it before in a place or two—but I thought I'd better come aboard and report before anything general began."

John Woolfolk was momentarily at a loss to establish the identity of Halvard's assailant.

He soon realized, however, that it must be Nicholas, whom he had never seen, and who had blown such an imperative summons on the conch the night before. Halvard's temper was communicated to him; he moved abruptly to where the tender was fastened.

"Put me ashore," he directed. He would make it clear that his man was not to be interrupted in the execution of his orders, and that his property could not be arbitrarily destroyed.

When the tender ran upon the beach and had been secured, Halvard started to follow him, but Woolfolk waved him back. There was a stir on the portico as he approached, the flitting of an unsubstantial form; but, hastening, John Woolfolk arrested Lichfield Stope in the doorway.

"Morning," he nodded abruptly. "I came to speak to you about a water cask of mine."

The other swayed like a thin, gray column of smoke.

"Ah, yes," he pronounced with difficulty. "Water cask—"

"It was broken here a little while back."

At the suggestion of violence such a pitiable panic fell upon the older man that Woolfolk halted. Lichfield Stope raised his hands as if to ward off the mere impact of the words themselves; his face was stained with the thin red tide of congestion.

"You have a man named Nicholas," Woolfolk proceeded. "I should like to see him."

The other made a gesture as tremulous and indeterminate as his speech and appeared to dissolve into the hall. John Woolfolk stood for a moment undecided and then moved about the house toward the kitchen. There, he thought, he might obtain an explanation of the breaking of the cask. A man was walking about within and came to the door as Woolfolk approached.

The latter told himself that he had never seen a blanker countenance. In profile it showed a narrow brow, a huge, drooping nose, a pinched mouth and insignificant chin. From the front the face of the man in the doorway held the round, unscored cheeks of a fat and sleepy boy. The eyes were mere long glimmers of vision in thick folds of flesh; the mouth, upturned at the corners, lent a fixed, mechanical smile to the whole. It was a countenance on which the passage of time and thoughts had left no mark; its stolidity had been moved by no feeling. His body was heavy and sagging. It possessed, Woolfolk recognized, a considerable unwieldy strength, and was completely covered by a variously spotted and streaked apron.

"Are you Nicholas?" John Woolfolk demanded.

The other nodded.

"Then, I take it, you are the man who broke my water cask."

"It was full of our water," Nicholas replied in a thick voice.

"That," said Woolfolk, "I am not going to argue with you. I came ashore to instruct you to let my man and my property alone."

"Then leave our water be."

John Woolfolk's temper, the instinctive arrogance of men living apart from the necessary submissions of communal life, in positions—however small—of supreme command, flared through his body.

"I told you," he repeated shortly, "that I would not discuss the question of the water. I have no intention of justifying myself to you. Remember—your hands off."

The other said surprisingly: "Don't get me started!" A spasm of emotion made a faint, passing shade on his sodden countenance; his voice held almost a note of appeal.

"Whether you 'start' or not is without the slightest significance," Woolfolk coldly responded.

"Mind," the man went on, "I spoke first."

A steady twitching commenced in a muscle at the flange of his nose. Woolfolk was aware of an increasing tension in the other, that gained a peculiar oppressiveness from the lack of any corresponding outward expression. His heavy, blunt hand fumbled under the maculate apron; his chest heaved with a sudden, tempestuous breathing. "Don't start me," he repeated in a voice so blurred that the words were hardly recognizable. He swallowed convulsively, his emotion mounting to an inchoate passion, when suddenly a change was evident. He made a short, violent effort to regain his self-control, his gaze fastened on a point behind Woolfolk.

The latter turned and saw Millie Stope approaching, her countenance haggard with fear. "What has happened?" she cried breathlessly while yet a little distance away. "Tell me at once—"

"Nothing," Woolfolk promptly replied, appalled by the agony in her voice. "Nicholas and I had a small misunderstanding. A triviality," he added, thinking of the other's hand groping beneath the apron.

VI

On the morning following the breaking of his water cask John Woolfolk saw the slender figure of Millie on the beach. She waved and called, her voice coming thin and clear across the water:

"Are visitors—encouraged?"

He sent Halvard in with the tender, and as they approached, dropped a gangway over the *Gar's* side. She stepped lightly down into the cockpit with a naïve expression of surprise at the yacht's immaculate order. The sails lay precisely housed, the stays, freshly tarred, glistened in the sun, the brasswork and newly varnished mahogany shone, the mathematically coiled ropes rested on a deck as spotless as wood could be scraped.

"Why," she exclaimed, "it couldn't be neater if you were two nice old ladies!"

"I warn you," Woolfolk replied, "Halvard will not regard that particularly as a compliment. He will assure you that the order of a proper yacht is beyond the most ambitious dream of a mere house-keeper."

She laughed as Halvard placed a chair for her. She was, Woolfolk thought, lighter in spirit on the ketch than she had been on shore; there was the faintest imaginable stain on her petal-like cheeks; her eyes, like olive leaves, were almost gay. She sat with her slender knees crossed, her fine arms held with hands clasped behind her head, and clad in a crisply ironed, crude white dress, into the band of which she had thrust a spray of orange blossoms.

John Woolfolk was increasingly conscious of her peculiar charm. Millie Stope, he suddenly realized, was like the wild oranges in the neglected grove at her door. A man brought in contact with her magnetic being charged with appealing and mysterious emotions, in a setting of exotic night and black sea, would find other women, the ordinary concourse of society, insipid—like faintly sweetened water.

She was entirely at home on the ketch, sitting against the im-maculate rim of deck and the sea. He resented that familiarity as an unwarranted intrusion of the world he had left. Other people, women among them, had unavoidably crossed his deck, but they had been patently alien, momentary; but Millie, with her still delight at the yacht's compact comfort, her intuitive comprehension of its various details—the lamps set in gimbals, the china racks and chart cases slung overhead—entered at once into the spirit of the craft that was John Woolfolk's sole place of being.

He was now disturbed by the ease with which she had established herself both in the yacht and in his imagination. He had thought, after so many years, to have destroyed all the bonds which ordinarily connect men with life; but now a mere curiosity had grown into a tangible interest, and the interest showed unmistakable signs of be-coming sympathy.

She smiled at him from her position by the wheel; and he instinc-tively responded with such an unaccustomed, ready warmth that he said abruptly, seeking refuge in occupation:

"Why not reach out to sea? The conditions are perfect."

"Ah, please!" she cried. "Just to take up the anchor would thrill me for months."

A light west wind was blowing; and deliberate, exactly spaced swells, their tops laced with iridescent spray, were sweeping in from a sea like a glassy blue pavement. Woolfolk issued a short order, and the sailor moved forward with his customary smooth swiftness. The sails were shaken loose, the mainsail slowly spread its dazzling expanse to the sun, the jib and jigger were trimmed, and the anchor came up with a short rush.

Millie rose with her arms outspread, her chin high and eyes closed. "Free!" she proclaimed with a slow, deep breath.

The sails filled and the ketch forged ahead. John Woolfolk, at the wheel, glanced at the chart section beside him.

"There's four feet on the bar at low water," he told Halvard. "The tide's at half flood now."

The *Gar* increased her speed, slipping easily out of the bay, gladly, it seemed to Woolfolk, turning toward the sea. The bow rose, and the ketch dipped forward over a spent wave. Millie Stope grasped the wheelbox. "Free!" she said again with shining eyes.

The yacht rose more sharply, hung on a wave's crest and slid lightly downward. Woolfolk, with a sinewy, dark hand directing their course, was intent upon the swelling sails. Once he stopped, tightening a halyard, and the sailor said:

"The main peak won't flatten, sir."

The swells grew larger. The *Gar* climbed their smooth heights and coasted like a feather beyond. Directly before the yacht they were unbroken, but on either side they foamed into a silver quickly reabsorbed in the deeper water within the bar.

Woolfolk turned from his scrutiny of the ketch to his companion, and was surprised to see her, with all the joy evaporated from her countenance, clinging rigidly to the rail. He said to himself, "Seasick." Then he realized that it was not a physical illness that possessed her, but a profound, increasing terror. She endeavored to smile back at his questioning gaze, and said in a small, uncertain voice:

"It's so—so big!"

For a moment he saw in her a clear resemblance to the shrinking figure of Lichfield Stope. It was as though suddenly she had lost her fine profile and become indeterminate, shadowy. The gray web of the old deflection in Virginia extended over her out of the past—of the past that, Woolfolk thought, would not die.

The *Gar* rose higher still, dropped into the deep, watery valley, and the woman's face was drawn and wet, the back of her straining hand was dead white. Without further delay John Woolfolk put the wheel sharply over and told his man, "We're going about." Halvard busied himself with the shaking sails.

"Really—I'd rather you didn't," Millie gasped. "I must learn . . . no longer a child."

But Woolfolk held the ketch on her return course; his companion's panic was growing beyond her control. They passed once more between the broken waves and entered the still bay with its border of flowering earth. There, when the yacht had been anchored, Millie sat gazing silently at the open sea whose bigness had so unexpectedly distressed her. Her face was pinched, her mouth set in a straight, hard line. That, somehow, suggested to Woolfolk the enigmatic governess; it was in contradiction to the rest.

"How strange," she said at last in an insuperably weary voice, "to be forced back to this place that I loathe, by myself, by my own cowardice. It's exactly as if my spirit were chained—then the body could never be free. What is it," she demanded of John Woolfolk, "that lives in our own hearts and betrays our utmost convictions and efforts, and destroys us against all knowledge and desire?"

"It may be called heredity," he replied; "that is its simplest phase. The others extend into the realms of the fantastic."

"It's unjust," she cried bitterly, "to be condemned to die in a pit with all one's instinct in the sky!"

The old plea of injustice quivered for a moment over the water and then died away. John Woolfolk had made the same passionate protest, he had cried it with clenched hands at the withdrawn stars, and the profound inattention of Nature had appalled his agony. A thrill of pity moved him for the suffering woman beside him. Her mouth was still unrelaxed. There was in her the material for a struggle against the invidious past.

In her slender frame the rebellion took on an accent of the heroic. Woolfolk recalled how utterly he had gone down before mischance. But his case had been extreme, he had suffered an unendurable wrong at the hand of Fate. Halvard diverted his thoughts by placing before them a tray of sugared pineapple and symmetrical cakes. Millie, too, lost her tension; she showed a feminine pleasure at the yacht's fine napkins, approved the polish of the glass.

"It's all quite wonderful," she said.

"I have nothing else to care for," Woolfolk told her.

"No place nor people on land?"

"None."

"And you are satisfied?"

"Absolutely," he replied with an unnecessary emphasis. He was, he told himself aggressively; he wanted nothing more from living and had nothing to give. Yet his pity for Millie Stope mounted obscurely, bringing with it thoughts, dim obligations and desires, to which he had declared himself dead.

"I wonder if you are to be envied?" she queried.

A sudden astounding willingness to speak of himself, even of the past, swept over him.

"Hardly," he replied. "All the things that men value were killed for me in an instant, in the flutter of a white skirt."

"Can you talk about it?"

"There's almost nothing to tell; it was so unrelated, so senseless and blind. It can't be dressed into a story, it has no moral—no meaning. Well—it was twelve years ago. I had just been married, and we had gone to a property in the country. After two days I had to go into town, and when I came back Ellen met me in a breaking cart. It was a flag station, buried in maples, with a white road winding back to where we were staying.

"Ellen had trouble in holding the horse when the train left, and the beast shied going from the station. It was Monday, clothes hung from a line in a side yard and a skirt fluttered in a little breeze. The horse reared, the strapped back of the seat broke, and Ellen was thrown—on her head. It killed her."

He fell silent. Millie breathed sharply, and a ripple struck with a faint slap on the yacht's side. Then: "One can't allow that," he continued in a lower voice, as if arguing with himself; "arbitrary, wanton; impossible to accept such conditions—

"She was young," he once more took up the narrative; "a girl in a tennis skirt with a gay scarf about her waist—quite dead in a second. The clothes still fluttered on the line. You see," he ended, "nothing instructive, tragic—only a crude dissonance."

"Then you left everything?"

He failed to answer, and she gazed with a new understanding and interest over the *Gar*. Her attention was attracted to the beach, and, following her gaze, John Woolfolk saw the bulky figure of Nicholas gazing at them from under his palm. A palpable change, a swift shadow, enveloped Millie Stope.

"I must go back," she said uneasily; "there will be dinner, and my father has been alone all morning."

But Woolfolk was certain that, however convincing the reasons she put forward, it was none of these that was taking her so hurriedly ashore. The dread that for the past few hours had almost vanished from her tones, her gaze, had returned multiplied. It was, he realized, the objective fear; her entire being was shrinking as if in anticipation of an imminent calamity, a physical blow.

Woolfolk himself put her on the beach; and, with the tender canted on the sand, steadied her spring. As her hand rested on his arm it gripped him with a sharp force; a response pulsed through his body; and an involuntary color rose in her pale, fine cheeks.

Nicholas, stolidly set with his shoes half buried in the sand, surveyed them without a shade of feeling on his thick countenance. But

Woolfolk saw that the other's fingers were crawling toward his pocket. He realized that the man's dully smiling mask concealed sultry, ungoverned emotions, blind springs of hate.

VII

Again on the ketch the inevitable reaction overtook him. He had spoken of Ellen's death to no one until now, through all the years when he had been a wanderer on the edge of his world, and he bitterly regretted his reference to it. In speaking he had betrayed his resolution of solitude. Life, against all his instinct, his wishes, had reached out and caught him, however lightly, in its tentacles.

The least surrender, he realized, the slightest opening of his interest, would bind him with a multitude of attachments; the octopus that he dreaded, uncoiling arm after arm, would soon hold him again, a helpless victim for the fury Chance.

He had made a disastrous error in following his curiosity, the insistent scent of the wild oranges, to the house where Millie had advanced on the dim portico. His return there had been the inevitable result of the first mistake, and the rest had followed with a fatal ease. Whatever had been the deficiences of the past twelve years he had been free from new complications, fresh treacheries. Now, with hardly a struggle, he was falling back into the old trap.

The wind died away absolutely, and a haze gathered delicately over the sea, thickening through the afternoon, and turned rosy by the declining sun. The shore had faded from sight.

A sudden energy leaped through John Woolfolk and rang out in an abrupt summons to Halvard. "Get up anchor," he commanded.

Poul Halvard, at the mainstay, remarked tentatively: "There's not a capful of wind."

The wide calm, Woolfolk thought, was but a part of a general conspiracy against his liberty, his memories. "Get the anchor up," he repeated harshly. "We'll go under the engine." The sudden jarring of the *Gar's* engine sounded muffled in a shut space like the flushed heart of a shell. The yacht moved forward, with a wake like folded gauze, into a shimmer of formless and pure color.

John Woolfolk sat at the wheel, motionless except for an occasional scant shifting of his hands. He was sailing by compass; the patent log, trailing behind on its long cord, maintained a constant, jerking register on its dial. He had resolutely banished all thought save that of navigation. Halvard was occupied forward, clearing the deck of the accumulations of the anchorage. When he came aft Woolfolk said shortly: "No mess."

The haze deepened and night fell, and the sailor lighted and placed the port and starboard lights. The binnacle lamp threw up a dim, orange radiance on Woolfolk's somber countenance. He continued for three and four and then five hours at the wheel, while the smooth clamor of the engine, a slight quiver of the hull, alone marked their progress through an invisible element.

Once more he had left life behind. This had more the aspect of a flight than at any time previous. It was, obscurely, an unpleasant thought, and he endeavored—unsuccessfully—to put it from him. He was but pursuing the course he had laid out, following his necessary, inflexible determination.

His mind for a moment turned independently back to Millie with her double burden of fear. He had left her without a word, isolated with Nicholas, concealing with a blank smile his enigmatic being, and with her impotent parent.

Well, he was not responsible for her, he had paid for the privilege of immunity; he had but listened to her story, volunteering nothing. John Woolfolk wished, however, that he had said some final, useful word to her before going. He was certain that, looking for the ketch and unexpectedly finding the bay empty, she would suffer a pang, if only of loneliness. In the short while that he had been there she had come to depend on him for companionship, for relief from the insuperable monotony of her surroundings; for, perhaps, still more. He wondered what that more might contain. He thought of Millie at the present moment, probably lying awake, steeped in dread. His flight now assumed the aspect of an act of cowardice, of desertion. He rehearsed wearily the extenuations of his position, but without any palpable relief.

An even more disturbing possibility lodged in his thoughts—he was not certain that he did not wish to be actually back with Millie again. He felt the quick pressure of her fingers on his arm as she jumped from the tender; her magnetic personality hung about him like an aroma. Cloaked in mystery, pale and irresistible, she appealed to him from the edge of the wild oranges.

This, he told himself again, was but the manner in which a ruthless Nature set her lures; it was the deceptive vestment of romance. He held the ketch relentlessly on her course, with—now—all his thoughts, his inclinations, returning to Millie Stope. In a final, desperate rally of his scattering resolution he told himself that he was unfaithful to the tragic memory of Ellen. This last stay broke abruptly, and left him defenseless against the tyranny of his mounting desires. Strangely he felt the sudden pressure of a stirring wind upon his face; and, almost with an oath, he put the wheel sharply over and the *Gar* swung about.

Poul Halvard had been below, by inference asleep; but when the yacht changed her course he immediately appeared on deck. He moved aft, but Woolfolk made no explanation, the sailor put no questions. The wind freshened, grew sustained. Woolfolk said:

"Make sail."

Soon after, the mainsail rose, a ghostly white expanse on the night. John Woolfolk trimmed the jigger, shut off the engine; and, moving through a sudden, vast hush, they retraced their course. The bay was ablaze with sunlight, the morning well advanced, when the ketch floated back to her anchorage under the oleanders.

VIII

Whether he returned or fled, Woolfolk thought, he was enveloped in an atmosphere of defeat. He relinquished the wheel, but remained seated, drooping at his post. The indefatigable Halvard proceeded with the efficient discharge of his narrow, exacting duties. After a short space John Woolfolk descended to the cabin, where, on an unmade berth, he fell immediately asleep.

He woke to a dim interior and twilight gathering outside. He shaved—without conscious purpose—with meticulous care, and put on the blue flannel coat. Later he rowed himself ashore and proceeded directly through the orange grove to the house beyond.

Mille Stope was seated on the portico, and laid a restraining hand on her father's arm as he rose attempting to retreat at Woolfolk's approach. The latter, with a commonplace greeting, resumed his place.

Millie's face was dim and potent in the gloom, and Lichfield Stope more than ever resembled an uneasy ghost. He muttered in indistinct response to a period directed at him by Woolfolk and turned with a low, urgent appeal to his daughter. The latter, with a hopeless gesture, relinquished his arm, and the other vanished.

"You were sailing this morning," Millie commented listlessly.

"I had gone," he said without explanation. Then he added: "But I came back."

A silence threatened them which he resolutely broke: "Do you remember, when you told me about your father, that you wanted really to talk about yourself? Will you do that now?"

"Tonight I haven't the courage."

"I am not idly curious," he persisted.

"Just what are you?"

"I don't know," he admitted frankly. "At the present moment I'm lost, fogged. But, meanwhile, I'd like to give you any assistance in my power. You seem, in a mysterious way, needful of help."

She turned her head sharply in the direction of the open hall and said in a high, clear voice, that yet rang strangely false: "I am quite well cared for by my father and Nicholas." She moved closer to him, dragging her chair across the uneven porch, in the rasp of which she added, quick and low:

"Don't—please."

A mounting exasperation seized him at the secrecy that veiled her, hid her from him, and he answered stiffly: "I am merely intrusive."

She was seated above him, and she leaned forward and swiftly pressed his fingers, loosely clasped about a knee. Her hand was as cold as salt. His irritation vanished before a welling pity. He got now a sharp, recognized happiness from her nearness; his feeling for her increased with the accumulating seconds. After the surrender, the admission, of his return he had grown elemental, sensitized to emotions rather than to processes of intellect. His ardor had the poignancy of the period beyond youth. It had a trace of the consciousness of the fatal waning of life which gave it a depth denied to younger passions. He wished to take Millie Stope at once from all memory of the troublous past, to have her alone in a totally different and thrilling existence.

It was a personal and blind desire, born in the unaccustomed tumult of his newly released feelings.

They sat for a long while, silent or speaking in trivialities, when he proposed a walk to the sea; but she declined in that curiously loud and false tone. It seemed to Woolfolk that, for the moment, she had addressed someone not immediately present; and involuntarily he looked around. The light of the hidden lamp in the hall fell in a pale, unbroken rectangle on the irregular porch. There was not the shifting of a pound's weight audible in the stillness.

Millie breathed unevenly; at times he saw she shivered uncontrollably. At this his feeling mounted beyond all restraint. He said, taking her cold hand: "I didn't tell you why I went last night—it was because I was afraid to stay where you were; I was afraid of the change you were bringing about in my life. That's all over now, I—"

"Isn't it quite late?" she interrupted him uncomfortably. She rose and her agitation visibly increased.

He was about to force her to hear all that he must say, but he stopped at the mute wretchedness of her pallid face. He stood gazing up at her from the rough sod. She clenched her hands, her breast heaved sharply, and she spoke in a level, strained voice:

"It would have been better if you had gone—without coming back. My father is unhappy with anyone about except myself—and Nicholas. You see—he will not stay on the porch nor walk about his grounds. I am not in need of assistance, as you seem to think. And—thank you Good night."

He stood without moving, his head thrown back, regarding her with a searching frown. He listened again, unconsciously, and thought he heard the low creaking of a board from within. It could be nothing but the uneasy peregrination of Lichfield Stope. The sound was repeated, grew louder, and the sagging bulk of Nicholas appeared in the doorway.

The latter stood for a moment, a dark, magnified shape; and then, moving across the portico to the farthest window, closed the shutters. The hinges gave out a rasping grind, as if they had not been turned for months, and there was a faint rattle of falling particles of rusted iron. The man forced shut a second set of shutters with a sudden violence and went slowly back into the house. Millie Stope said once more:

"Good night."

It was evident to Woolfolk that he could gain nothing more at present; and stifling an angry protest, an impatient troop of questions, he turned and strode back to the tender. However, he hadn't the slightest intention of following Millie's indirectly expressed wish for him to leave. He had the odd conviction that at heart she did not want him to go; the evening, he elaborated this feeling, had been all a strange piece of acting. Tomorrow he would tear apart the veil that hid her from him; he would ignore her every protest and force the truth from her.

He lifted the tender's anchor from the sand and pulled sharply across the water to the *Gar*. A reddish, misshapen moon hung in the east, and when he had mounted to his deck it was suddenly obscured by a high, racing scud of cloud; the air had a damper, thicker feel. He instinctively moved to the barometer, which he found depressed. The wind, that had continued steadily since the night before, increased, and there was a corresponding stir among the branches ashore, a slapping of the yacht's cordage against the spars. He turned forward and half absently noted the increasing strain on the hawser disappearing into the dark tide. The anchor was firmly bedded. The pervasive far murmur of the waves on the outer bars grew louder.

The yacht swung lightly over the choppy water, and a strong affection for the ketch that had been his home, his occupation, his solace through the past dreary years expanded his heart. He knew the *Gar's* every capability and mood, and they were all good. She was an exceptional boat. His feeling was acute, for he knew that the yacht had been superseded. It was already an element of the past, of that past in which Ellen lay dead in a tennis skirt, with a bright scarf about her young waist.

He placed his hand on the mainmast, in the manner in which another might drop a palm on the shoulder of a departing faithful companion, and the wind in the rigging vibrated through the wood like a sentient and affectionate response. Then he went resolutely down into the cabin, facing the future.

John Woolfolk woke in the night, listened for a moment to the straining hull and wind shrilling aloft, and then rose and went forward again to examine the mooring. A second hawser now reached into the darkness. Halvard had been on deck and put out another anchor. The wind beat salt and stinging from the sea, utterly dissipating the languorous breath of the land, the odors of the exotic, flowering trees.

IX

In the morning a storm, driving out of the east, enveloped the coast in a frigid, lashing rain. The wind mounted steadily through the middle of the day with an increasing pitch accompanied by the basso of the racing seas. The bay grew opaque and seamed with white scars. After the meridian the rain ceased, but the wind maintained its volume, clamoring beneath a leaden pall.

John Woolfolk, in dripping yellow oilskins, occasionally circled the deck of his ketch. Halvard had everything in a perfection of order. When the rain stopped, the sailor dropped into the tender and with a boat sponge bailed vigorously. Soon after, Woolfolk stepped out upon the beach. He was without any plan but the determination to put aside whatever obstacles held Millie from him. This rapidly crystallized into the resolve to take her with him before another day ended. His feeling for her, increasing to a passionate need, had destroyed the suspension, the deliberate calm of his life, as the storm had dissipated the sunny peace of the coast.

He paused before the ruined façade, weighing her statement that it would have been better if he had not returned; and he wondered how that would affect her willingness, her ability, to see him today. He added the word "ability" instinctively and without explanation. And he decided that, in order to have any satisfactory speech with her, he must come upon her alone, away from the house. Then he could force her to hear to the finish what he wanted to say; in the open they might escape from the inexplicable inhibition that lay upon her expression of feeling, of desire. It would be necessary, at the same time, to avoid the notice of anyone who would warn her of his presence. This precluded his waiting at the familiar place on the rotting wharf.

Three marble steps, awry and moldy, descended to the lawn from a French window in the side of the desolate mansion. They were screened by a tangle of rose-mallow, and there John Woolfolk seated himself—waiting

The wind shrilled about the corner of the house; there was a mournful clatter of shingles from above and the frenzied lashing of boughs. The noise was so great that he failed to hear the slightest indication of the approach of Nicholas until that individual passed directly before him. Nicholas stopped at the inner fringe of the beach and, from a point where he could not be seen from the ketch, stood gazing out at the *Gar* pounding on her long anchor chains. The man remained for an appressively extended period; Woolfolk could see his heavy, drooping shoulders and sunken head; and then the other moved to the left, crossing the rough open behind the oleanders. Woolfolk had a momentary glimpse of a huge nose and rapidly moving lips above an impotent chin.

Nicholas, he realized, remained a complete enigma to him; beyond the conviction that the man was, in some minor way, leaden-witted, he knew nothing.

A brief, watery ray of sunlight fell through a rift in the flying clouds and stained the tossing foliage pale gold; it was followed by a sudden drift of rain, then once more the naked wind. Woolfolk was fast determining to go up to the house and insist upon Millie's hearing him, when unexpectedly she appeared in a somber, fluttering cloak, with her head uncovered and hair blown back from her pale brow. He waited until she had passed him, and then rose, softly calling her name.

She stopped and turned, with a hand pressed to her heart. "I was afraid you'd gone out," she told him. "The sea is like a pack of wolves." Her voice was a low complexity of relief and fear.

"Not alone," he replied; "not without you."

"Madness," she murmured, gathering her wavering cloak about her breast. She swayed, graceful as a reed in the wind, charged with potency. He made an involuntary gesture toward her with his arms; but in a sudden accession of fear she eluded him.

"We must talk," he told her. "There is a great deal that needs explaining, that—I think—I have a right to know, the right of your dependence on something to save you from yourself. There is another right, but only you can give that—"

"Indeed," she interrupted tensely, "you mustn't stand here talking to me."

"I shall allow nothing to interrupt us," he returned decidedly. "I have been long enough in the dark."

"But you don't understand what you will, perhaps, bring on yourself—on me."

"I'm forced to ignore even that last."

She glanced hurriedly about. "Not here then, if you must."

She walked from him, toward the second ruined pile that fronted the bay. The steps to the gaping entrance had rotted away and they were forced to mount an insecure side piece. The interior, as Woolfolk had seen, was composed of one high room, while, above, a narrow, open second story hung like a ledge. On both sides were long counters with mounting sets of shelves behind them.

"This was the store," Millie told him. "It was a great estate."

A dim and moldering fragment of cotton stuff was hanging from a forgotten bolt; above, some tinware was eaten with rust; a scale had crushed in the floor and lay broken on the earth beneath; and a ledger, its leaves a single, sodden film of gray, was still open on a counter. A precarious stair mounted to the flooring above, and Millie Stope made her way upward, followed by Woolfolk.

There, in the double gloom of the clouds and a small dormer window obscured by cobwebs, she sank on a broken box. The decayed walls shook perilously in the blasts of the wind. Below they could see the empty floor, and through the doorway the somber, gleaming greenery without.

All the patient expostulation that John Woolfolk had prepared disappeared in a sudden tyranny of emotion, of hunger for the slender, weary figure before him. Seating himself at her side, he burst into a torrential expression of passionate desire that mounted with the tide of his eager words. He caught her hands, held them in a painful grip, and gazed down into her still, frightened face. He stopped abruptly, was silent for a tempestuous moment, and then baldly repeated the fact of his love.

Millie Stope said:

"I know so little about the love you mean." Her voice trailed to silence; and in a lull of the storm they heard the thin patter of rats on the floor below, the stir of bats among the rafters.

"It's quickly learned," he assured her. "Millie, do you feel any response at all in your heart—the slightest return of my longing?"

"I don't know," she answered, turning toward him a troubled scrutiny. "Perhaps in another surrounding, with things different, I might care for you very much—"

"I am going to take you into that other surrounding," he announced.

She ignored his interruption. "But we shall never have a chance to learn." She silenced his attempted protest with a cool, flexible palm against his mouth. "Life," she continued, "is so dreadfully in the dark. One is lost at the beginning. There are maps to take you safely to the Guianas, but none for souls. Perhaps religions are— Again I don't know. I have found nothing secure—only a whirlpool into which I will not drag others."

"I will drag you out," he asserted.

She smiled at him, in a momentary tenderness, and continued: "When I was young I never doubted that I would conquer life. I pictured myself rising in triumph over circumstance, as a gull leaves the sea. . . . When I was young . . . If I was afraid of the dark then I thought, of course, I would outgrow it; but it has grown deeper than my courage. The night is terrible now." A shiver passed over her.

"You are ill," he insisted, "but you shall be cured."

"Perhaps, a year ago, something might have been done, with assistance; yes—with you. Then, whatever is, hadn't materialized. Why did you delay?" she cried in sudden suffering.

"You'll go with me tonight," he declared stoutly.

"In this?" She indicated the wind beating with the blows of a great fist against the swaying sides of the demolished store. "Have you seen the sea? Do you remember what happened on the day I went with you when it was so beautiful and still?"

John Woolfolk realized, wakened to a renewed mental clearness by the threatening of all that he desired, that—as Millie had intimated—life was too complicated to be solved by a single longing; love was not the all-powerful magician of conventional acceptance; there were other, no less profound, depths.

He resolutely abandoned his mere inchoate wanting, and considered the elements of the position that were known to him. There was, in the first place, that old, lamentable dereliction of Lichfield Stope's, and its aftermath in his daughter. Millie had just recalled to Woolfolk the duration, the activity, of its poison. Here there was no possibility of escape by mere removal; the stain was within; and it must be thoroughly cleansed before she could cope successfully, happily, with life. In this, he was forced to acknowledge, he could help her but little; it was an affair of spirit; and spiritual values—though they might be supported from without—had their growth and decrease strictly in the individual they animated.

Still, he argued, a normal existence, a sense of security, would accomplish a great deal; and that in turn hung upon the elimination of the second, unknown element—the reason for her backward glances, her sudden, loud banalities, yesterday's mechanical repudiation of his offered assistance and the implied wish for him to go. He said gravely:

"I have been impatient, but you came so sharply into my empty existence that I was upset. If you are ill you can cure yourself. Never forget your mother's 'brave heart.' But there is something objective, immediate, threatening you. Tell me what it is, Millie, and together we will overcome and put it away from you forever."

She gazed panic-stricken into the empty gloom below. "No! no!"

she exclaimed, rising. "You don't know. I won't drag you down. You must go away at once, tonight, even in the storm."

"What is it?" he demanded.

She stood rigidly erect with her eyes shut and hands clasped at her sides. Then she slid down upon the box, lifting to him a white mask of fright.

"It's Nicholas," she said, hardly above her breath.

A sudden relief swept over John Woolfolk. In his mind he dismissed as negligible the heavy man fumbling beneath his soiled apron. He wondered how the other could have got such a grip on Millie Stope's imagination.

The mystery that had enveloped her was fast disappearing, leaving them without an obstacle to the happiness he proposed. Woolfolk said curtly:

"Has Nicholas been annoying you?"

She shivered, with clasped straining hands.

"He says he's crazy about me," she told him in a shuddering voice that contracted his heart. "He says that I must—must marry him, or—" Her period trailed abruptly out to silence.

Woolfolk grew animated with determination, an immediate purpose.

"Where would Nicholas be at this hour?" he asked.

She rose hastily, clinging to his arm. "You mustn't," she exclaimed, yet not loudly. "You don't know! He is watching—something frightful would happen."

"Nothing 'frightful,'" he returned tolerantly, preparing to descend. "Only unfortunate for Nicholas."

"You mustn't," she repeated desperately, her sheer weight hanging from her hands clasped about his neck. "Nicholas is not—not human. There's something funny about him. I don't mean funny, I—"

He unclasped her fingers and quietly forced her back to the seat on the box. Then he took a place at her side.

"Now," he asked reasonably, "what is this about Nicholas?"

She glanced down into the desolate cavern of the store; the ghostly remnant of cotton goods fluttered in a draft like a torn and grimy cobweb; the lower floor was palpably bare.

"He came in April," she commenced in a voice without any life. "The woman we had had for years was dead; and when Nicholas asked for work we were glad to take him. He wanted the smallest possible wages and was willing to do everything; he even cooked quite nicely. At first he was jumpy—he had asked if many strangers went by; but then when no one appeared he got easier. . . . He got easier and began to do extra things for me. I thanked him—until I under stood. Then I asked father to send him away, but he was afraid; and, before I could get up my courage to do it, Nicholas spoke—

"He said he was crazy about me, and would I please try and be good to him. He had always wanted to marry, he went on, and live right, but things had gone against him. I told him that he was impertinent and that he would have to go at once; but he cried and begged me not to say that, not to get him 'started.' "

That, John Woolfolk recalled, was precisely what the man had said to him.

"I went back to father and told him why he must send Nicholas off, but father nearly suffocated. He turned almost black. Then I got frightened and locked myself in my room, while Nicholas sat out on the stair and sobbed all night. It was ghastly! In the morning I had to go down, and he went about his duties as usual.

"That evening he spoke again, on the porch, twisting his hands exactly as if he were making bread. He repeated that he wanted me to be nice to him. He said something wrong would happen if I pushed him to it.

"I think if he had threatened to kill me it would have been more possible than his hints and sobs. The thing went along for a month, then six weeks, and nothing more happened. I started again and again to tell them at the store, two miles back in the pines, but I could never get away from Nicholas; he was always at my shoulder, muttering and twisting his hands.

"At last I found something." She hesitated, glancing once more down through the empty gloom, while her fingers swiftly fumbled in the band of her waist.

"I was cleaning his room—it simply had to be done—and had out a bureau drawer, when I saw this underneath. He was not in the house, and I took one look at it, then put the things back as near as possible as they were. I was so frightened that I slipped it in my dress—had no chance to return it."

He took from her unresisting hand a folded rectangle of coarse gray paper; and, opening it, found a small handbill with the crudely reproduced photograph of a man's head with a long drooping nose, sleepy eyes in thick folds of flesh, and a lax under-lip with a fixed, dull smile:

Wanted for Murder!

The authorities of Coweta offer Three Hundred Dollars for the apprehension of the below, Iscah Nicholas, convicted of the murder of Elizabeth Slakto, an aged woman.

General description: Age about forty-eight. Head receding, with large nose and stupid expression. Body corpulent but strong. Nicholas has no trade and works at general utility. He is a homicidal maniac.

WANTED FOR MURDER!

"He told me that his name was Nicholas Brandt," Millie noted in her dull voice.

A new gravity possessed John Woolfolk.

"You must not go back to the house," he decided.

"Wait," she replied. "I was terribly frightened when he went up to his room. When he came down he thanked me for cleaning it. I told him he was mistaken, that I hadn't been in there, but I could see he was suspicious. He cried all the time he was cooking dinner, in a queer choked way; and afterward touched me—on the arm. I swam, but all the water in the bay wouldn't take away the feel of his fingers. Then I saw the boat—you came ashore.

"Nicholas was dreadfully upset, and hid in the pines for a day or more. He told me if I spoke of him it would happen, and if I left it would happen—to father. Then he came back. He said that you were —were in love with me, and that I must send you away. He added that you must go today, for he couldn't stand waiting any more. He said that he wanted to be right, but that things were against him. This morning he got dreadful—if I fooled him he'd get you, and me, too, and then there was always father for something extra special. That, he warned me, would happen if I stayed away for more than an hour." She rose, trembling violently. "Perhaps it's been an hour now. I must go back."

John Woolfolk thought rapidly; his face was grim. If he had brought a pistol from the ketch he would have shot Iscah Nicholas without hesitation. Unarmed, he was reluctant to precipitate a crisis with such serious possibilities. He could secure one from the *Gar*, but even that short lapse of time might prove fatal—to Millie or Lichfield Stope. Millie's story was patently fact in every detail. He thought more rapidly still—desperately.

"I must go back," she repeated, her words lost in a sudden blast of wind under the dilapidated roof.

He saw that she was right.

"Very well," he acquiesced. "Tell him that you saw me, and that I promised to go tonight. Act quietly; say that you have been upset, but that you will give him an answer tomorrow. Then at eight o'clock —it will be dark early tonight—walk out to the wharf. That is all

But it must be done without any hesitation; you must be even cheerful, kinder to him."

He was thinking: She must be out of the way when I meet Nicholas. She must not be subjected to the ordeal that will release her from the dread fast crushing her spirit.

She swayed, and he caught her, held her upright, circled in his steady arms.

"Don't let him hurt us," she gasped. "Oh, don't!"

"Not now," he reassured her. "Nicholas is finished. But you must help by doing exactly as I have told you. You'd better go on. It won't be long, hardly three hours, until freedom."

She laid her cold cheek against his face, while her arms crept round his neck. She said nothing; and he held her to him with a sudden throb of feeling. They stood for a moment in the deepening gloom, bound in a straining embrace, while the rats gnawed in the sagging walls of the store and the storm thrashed without. She reluctantly descended the stair, crossed the broken floor and disappeared through the door.

A sudden unwillingness to have her return alone to the sobbing menace of Iscah Nicholas, the impotent wraith that had been Lichfield Stope, carried him in an impetuous stride to the stair. But there he halted. The plan he had made held, in its simplicity, a larger measure of safety than any immediate, unconsidered course.

John Woolfolk waited until she had had time to enter the orange-grove; then he followed, turning toward the beach.

He found Halvard already at the sand's edge, waiting uneasily with the tender, and they crossed the broken water to where the *Gar's* cabin flung out a remote, peaceful light.

X

The sailor immediately set about his familiar, homely tasks, while Woolfolk made a minute inspection of the ketch's rigging. He descended to supper with an expression of abstraction, and ate mechanically whatever was placed before him. Afterward he rolled a cigarette, which he neglected to light, and sat motionless, chin on breast, in the warm stillness.

Halvard cleared the table and John Woolfolk roused himself. He turned to the shelf that ran above the berths and secured a small, locked tin box. For an hour or more he was engaged alternately writing and carefully reading various papers sealed with vermilion wafers. Then he called Halvard.

"I'll get you to witness these signatures," he said, rising. Poul Halvard hesitated; then, with a furrowed brow, clumsily grasped the pen.

"Here," Woolfolk indicated. The man wrote slowly, linking fortu. itously the unsteady letters of his name. This arduous task accomplished, he immediately rose. John Woolfolk again took his place, turning to address the other, when he saw that one side of Halvard's face was bluish and rapidly swelling.

"What's the matter with your jaw?" he promptly inquired.

Halvard avoided his gaze, obviously reluctant to speak, but Woolfolk's silent interrogation was insistent. Then:

"I met that Nicholas," Halvard admitted; "without a knife."

"Well?" Woolfolk insisted.

"There's something wrong with this cursed place," Halvard said defiantly. "You can laugh, but there's a matter in the air that's not natural. My grandmother could have named it. She heard the ravens that called Tollfsen's death, and read Linga's eyes before she strangulated herself. Anyhow, when you didn't come back I got doubtful and took the tender in. Then I saw Nicholas beating up through the bushes, hiding here and there, and doubling through the grass; so I come on him from the back and—and kicked him, quite sudden.

"He went on his hands, but got up quick for a hulk like himself. Sir, this is hard to believe, but it's Biblical—he didn't take any more notice of the kick than if it had been a flag halyard brushed against him. He said 'Go away,' and waved his foolish hands.

"I closed in, still careful of the knife, with a remark, and got onto his heart. He only coughed and kept telling me in a crying whisper to go away. Nicholas pushed me back—that's how I got this face. What was the use? I might as well have hit a pudding. Even talk didn't move him. In a little it sent me cold." He stopped abruptly, grew sullen; it was evident that he would say no more in that direction. Woolfolk opened another subject:

"Life, Halvard," he said, "is uncertain; perhaps tonight I shall find it absolutely unreliable. What I am getting at is this: if anything happens to me—death, to be accurate—the *Gar* is yours, the ketch and a sum of money. It is secured to you in this box, which you will deliver to my address in Boston. There is another provision that I'll mention merely to give you the opportunity to repeat it verbally from my lips: the bulk of anything I have, in the possibility we are considering, will go to a Miss Stope, the daughter of Lichfield Stope, formerly of Virginia." He stood up. "Halvard," Woolfolk said abruptly, extending his hand, expressing for the first time his repeated thought, "you are a good man. You are the only steady quantity I have ever known. I have paid you for a part of this, but the most is beyond dollars. That I am now acknowledging."

Halvard was cruelly embarrassed. He waited, obviously desiring a chance to retreat, and Woolfolk continued in a different vein:

"I want the canvas division rigged across the cabin and three berths made. Then get the yacht ready to go out at any time."

One thing more remained; and, going deeper into the tin box, John Woolfolk brought out a packet of square envelopes addressed to him in a faded, angular hand. They were all that remained now of his youth, of the past. Not a ghost, not a remembered fragrance nor accent, rose from the delicate paper. They had been the property of a man dead twelve years ago, slain by incomprehensible mischance; and the man in the contracted cabin, vibrating from the elemental and violent forces without, forebore to open them. He burned the packet to a blackish ash on a plate.

It was, he saw from the chronometer, seven o'clock; and he rose charged with tense energy, engaged in activities of a far different order. He unwrapped from many folds of oiled silk a flat, amorphous pistol, uglier in its bleak outline than the familiar weapons of more graceful days; and, sliding into place a filled cartridge clip, he threw a load into the barrel. This he deposited in the pocket of a black wool jacket, closely buttoned about his long, hard body, and went up on deck.

Halvard, in a glistening yellow coat, came close up to him, speaking with the wind whipping the words from his lips. He said: "She's ready, sir."

For a moment Woolfolk made no answer; he stood gazing anxiously into the dark that enveloped and hid Millie Stope from him. There was another darkness about her, thicker than the mere light, like a black cerement dropping over her soul. His eyes narrowed as he replied to the sailor: "Good!"

XI

John Woolfolk peered through the night toward the land.

"Put me ashore beyond the point," he told Halvard; "at a half-sunk wharf on the sea."

The sailor secured the tender, and, dropping into it, held the small boat steady while Woolfolk followed. With a vigorous push they fell away from the *Gar*. Halvard's oars struck the water smartly and forced the tender forward into the beating wind. They made a choppy passage to the rim of the bay, where, turning, they followed the thin, pale glimmer of the broken water on the land's edge. Halvard pulled with short telling strokes, his oarblades stirring into momentary being livid blurs of phosphorescence.

John Woolfolk guided the boat about the point where he had first seen Millie swimming. He recalled how strange her unexpected appearance had seemed. It had, however, been no stranger than the actuality which had driven her into the bay in the effort to cleanse the stain of Iscah Nicholas' touch. Woolfolk's face hardened; he was suddenly conscious of the cold weight in his pocket. He realized that he would kill Nicholas at the first opportunity and without the slightest hesitation.

The tender passed about the point, and he could hear more clearly the sullen clamor of the waves on the seaward bars. The patches of green sky had grown larger, the clouds swept by with the apparent menace of solid, flying objects. The land lay in a low, formless mass on the left. It appeared secretive, a masked place of evil. Its influence reached out and subtly touched John Woolfolk's heart with the premonition of base treacheries. The tormented trees had the sound of Iscah Nicholas sobbing. He must take Millie away immediately; banish its last memory from her mind, its influence from her soul. It was the latter he always feared, which formed his greatest hazard—to tear from her the tendrils of the invidious past.

The vague outline of the ruined wharf swam forward, and the tender slid into the comparative quiet of its partial protection.

"Make fast," Woolfolk directed. "I shall be out of the boat for a while." He hesitated; then: "Miss Stope will be here; and if, after an hour, you hear nothing from me, take her out to the ketch for the night. Insist on her going. If you hear nothing from me still, make the first town and report."

He mouted by a cross pinning to the insecure surface above; and, picking his way to solid earth, waited. He struck a match and, covering the light with his palm, saw that it was ten minutes before eight. Millie, he had thought, would reach the wharf before the hour he had indicated. She would not at any cost be late.

The night was impenetrable. Halvard was as absolutely lost as if he had dropped, with all the world save the bare, wet spot where Woolfolk stood, into a nether region from which floated up great, shuddering gasps of agony. He followed this idea more minutely, picturing the details of such a terrestrial calamity; then he put it from him with an oath. Black thoughts crept insidiously into his mind like rats in a cellar. He had ordinarily a rigidly disciplined brain, an incisive logic, and he was disturbed by the distorted visions that came to him unbidden. He wished, in a momentary panic, instantly suppressed, that he were safely away with Millie in the ketch.

He was becoming hysterical, he told himself with compressed lips—no better than Lichfield Stope. The latter rose grayly in his memory, and fled across the sea, a phantom body pulsing with a veined fire like that stirred from the nocturnal bay. He again consulted his watch, and said aloud, incredulously: "Five minutes past eight." The inchoate crawling of his thoughts changed to an acute, tangible doubt, a mounting dread.

He rehearsed the details of his plan, tried it at every turning. It had seemed to him at the moment of its birth the best—no, the only—thing to do, and it was still without obvious fault. Some trivial happening, an unforeseen need of her father's, had delayed Millie for a minute or two. But the minutes increased and she did not appear. All his conflicting emotions merged into a cold passion of anger. He would kill Nicholas without a word's preliminary. The time drew out, Millie did not materialize, and his anger sank to the realization of appalling possibilities.

He decided that he would wait no longer. In the act of moving forward he thought he heard, rising thinly against the fluctuating wind, a sudden cry. He stopped automatically, listening with every nerve, but there was no repetition of the uncertain sound. As Woolfolk swiftly considered it he was possessed by the feeling that he had not heard the cry with his actual ear but with a deeper, more unaccountable sense. He went forward in a blind rush, feeling with extended hands for the opening in the tangle, groping a stumbling way through the close dark of the matted trees. He fell over an exposed root, blundered into a chill, wet trunk, and finally emerged at the side of the desolate mansion. Here his way led through saw grass, waist high, and the blades cut at him like lithe, vindictive knives. No light showed from the face of the house toward him, and he came abruptly against the bay window of the dismantled billiard room.

A sudden caution arrested him—the sound of his approach might precipitate a catastrophe, and he soundlessly felt his passage about the house to the portico. The steps creaked beneath his careful tread, but the noise was lost in the wind. At first he could see no light; the hall door, he discovered, was closed; then he was aware of a faint glimmer seeping through a drawn window shade on the right. From without he could distinguish nothing. He listened, but not a sound rose. The stillness was more ominous than cries.

John Woolfolk took the pistol from his pocket and, automatically releasing the safety, moved to the door, opening it with his left hand. The hall was unlighted; he could feel the pressure of the darkness above. The dank silence flowed over him like chill water rising above his heart. He turned, and a dim thread of light, showing through the chink of a partly closed doorway, led him swiftly forward. He paused a moment before entering, shrinking from what might be revealed beyond, and then flung the door sharply open.

His pistol was directed at a low-trimmed lamp in a chamber empty of all life. He saw a row of large black portfolios on low supports, a sewing bag spilled of its contents from a chair, a table bore a tin tobacco jar and the empty skin of a plantain. Then his gaze rested upon the floor, on a thin, inanimate body in crumpled alpaca trousers and dark jacket, with a peaked, congested face upturned toward the pale light. It was Lichfield Stope—dead.

Woolfolk bent over him, searching for a mark of violence, for the cause of the other's death. At first he found nothing; then, as he moved the body—its lightness came to him as a shock—he saw that one fragile arm had been twisted and broken; the hand hung like a withered autumn leaf from its circular cuff fastened with the mosaic button. That was all.

He straightened up sharply, with his pistol leveled at the door. But there had been no noise other than that of the wind plucking at the old tin roof, rattling the shrunken frames of the windows. Lichfield Stope had fallen back with his countenance lying on a doubled arm, as if he were attempting to hide from his extinguished gaze the horror of his end. The lamp was of the common glass variety, without shade; and, in a sudden eddy of air, it flickered, threatened to go out, and a thin ribbon of smoke swept up against the chimney and vanished.

On the wall was a wide stipple print of the early nineteenth century— the smooth sward of a village glebe surrounded by the low stone walls of ancient dwellings, with a timbered inn behind broad oaks and a swinging sign. It was—in the print—serenely evening, and long shad- ows slipped out through an ambient glow. Woolfolk, with pistol ele- vated, became suddenly conscious of the withdrawn scene, and for a moment its utter peace held him spellbound. It was another world, for the security, the unattainable repose of which, he longed with a pas- sionate bitterness.

The wind shifted its direction and beat upon the front of the house; a different set of windows rattled, and the blast swept compact and cold up through the blank hall. John Woolfolk cursed his inertia of mind, and once more addressed the profound, tragic mystery that sur- rounded him.

He thought: Nicholas has gone—with Millie. Or perhaps he has left her—in some dark, upper space. A maddening sense of impotence set- tled upon him. If the man had taken Millie out into the night he had no chance of following, finding them. Impenetrable screens of bushes lay on every hand, with, behind them, mile after mile of shrouded pine woods.

His plan had gone terribly amiss, with possibilities which he could not bring himself to face. All that had happened before in his life, and that had seemed so insupportable at the time, faded to insignificance

Shuddering waves of horror swept over him. He raised his hand unsteadily, drew it across his brow, and it came away dripping wet. He was oppressed by the feeling familiar in evil dreams—of gazing with leaden limbs at deliberate, unspeakable acts.

He shook off the numbness of dread. He must act—at once! How? A thousand men could not find Iscah Nicholas in the confused darkness without. To raise the scattered and meager neighborhood would consume an entire day.

The wind agitated a rocking chair in the hall, an erratic creaking responded, and Woolfolk started forward, and stopped as he heard and then identified the noise. This, he told himself, would not do; the hysteria was creeping over him again. He shook his shoulders, wiped his palm and took a fresh grip on the pistol.

Then from above came the heavy, unmistakable fall of a foot. It was not repeated; the silence spread once more, broken only from without. But there was no possibility of mistake, there had been no subtlety in the sound—a slow foot had moved, a heavy body had shifted.

At this actuality a new determination seized him; he was conscious of a feeling that almost resembled joy, an immeasurable relief at the prospect of action and retaliation. He took up the lamp, held it elevated while he advanced to the door with a ready pistol. There, however, he stopped, realizing the mark he would present moving, conveniently illuminated, up the stair. The floor above was totally unknown to him; at any turning he might be surprised, overcome, rendered useless. He had a supreme purpose to perform. He had already, perhaps fatally, erred, and there must be no further misstep.

John Woolfolk realized that he must go upstairs in the dark, or with, at most, in extreme necessity, a fleeting and guarded matchlight. This, too, since he would be entirely without knowledge of his surroundings, would be inconvenient, perhaps impossible. He must try. He put the lamp back upon the table, moving it farther out of the eddy from the door, where it would stay lighted against a possible pressing need. Then he moved from the wan radiance into the night of the hall.

XII

He formed in his mind the general aspect of the house: its width faced the orange grove, the stair mounted on the hall's right, in back of which a door gave to the billiard room; on the left was the chamber of the lamp, and that, he had seen, opened into a room behind, while the kitchen wing, carried to a chamber above, had been obviously added. It was probable that he would find the same general arrangement on the second floor. The hall would be smaller; a space inclosed for a bath; and a means of ascent to the roof.

John Woolfolk mounted the stair quickly and as silently as possible, placing his feet squarely on the body of the steps. At the top the hand-rail disappeared; and, with his back to a plaster wall, he moved until he encountered a closed door. That interior was above the billiard room; it was on the opposite floor he had heard the footfall, and he was certain that no one had crossed the hall or closed a door. He continued, following the dank wall. At places the plaster had fallen, and his fingers encountered the bare skeleton of the house. Farther on he narrowly escaped knocking down a heavily framed picture—another, he thought, of Lichfield Stope's mezzotints—but he caught it, left it hanging crazily awry.

He passed an open door, recognized the bathroom from the flat odor of chlorides, reached an angle of the wall and proceeded with renewed caution. Next he encountered the cold panes of a window and then found the entrance to the room above the kitchen.

He stopped—it was barely possible that the sound he heard had echoed from here. He revolved the wisdom of a match, but—he had progressed very well so far—decided negatively. One aspect of the situation troubled him greatly—the absence of any sound or warning from Millie. It was highly improbable that his entrance to the house had been unnoticed. The contrary was probable—that his sudden appearance had driven Nicholas above.

Woolfolk started forward more hurriedly, urged by his increasing apprehension, when his foot went into the opening of a depressed step and flung him sharply forward. In his instinctive effort to avoid falling the pistol dropped clattering into the darkness. A sudden choked cry sounded beside him, and a heavy, enveloping body fell on his back. This sent him reeling against the wall, where he felt the muscles of an unwieldy arm tighten about his neck.

John Woolfolk threw himself back, when a wrist heavily struck his shoulder and a jarring blow fell upon the wall. The hand, he knew, had held a knife, for he could feel it groping desperately over the plaster, and he put all his strength into an effort to drag his assailant into the middle of the floor.

It was impossible now to recover his pistol, but he would make it difficult for Nicholas to get the knife. The struggle in that way was equalized. He turned in the gripping arms about him and the men were chest to chest. Neither spoke; each fought solely to get the other prostrate, while Nicholas developed a secondary pressure toward the blade buried in the wall. This Woolfolk successfully blocked. In the supreme effort to bring the struggle to a decisive end neither dealt the other minor injuries. There were no blows—nothing but the straining pull of arms, the sudden weight of bodies, the cunning twisting of legs. They fought swiftly, whirling and staggering from place to place.

The hot breath of an invisible gaping mouth beat upon Woolfolk's cheek. He was an exceptionally powerful man. His spare body had been hardened by its years of exposure to the elements, in the constant labor he had expended on the ketch, the long contests with adverse winds and seas, and he had little doubt of his issuing successful from the present crisis. Iscah Nicholas, though his strength was beyond question, was heavy and slow. Yet he was struggling with surprising agility. He was animated by a convulsive energy, a volcanic outburst characteristic of the obsession of monomania.

The strife continued for an astonishing, an absurd, length of time. Woolfolk became infuriated at his inability to bring it to an end, and he expended an even greater effort. Nicholas' arms were about his chest; he was endeavoring by sheer pressure to crush Woolfolk's opposition, when the latter injected a mounting wrath into the conflict. They spun in the open like a grotesque human top, and fell. Woolfolk was momentarily underneath, but he twisted lithely uppermost. He felt a heavy, blunt hand leave his arm and feel, in the dark, for his face. Its purpose was to spoil, and he caught it and savagely bent it down and back; but a cruel forcing of his leg defeated his purpose.

This, he realized, could not go on indefinitely; one or the other would soon weaken. An insidious doubt of his ultimate victory lodged like a burr in his brain. Nicholas' strength was inhuman; it increased rather than waned. He was growing vindictive in a petty way—he tore at Woolfolk's throat, dug the flesh from his lower arm. Thereafter warm and gummy blood made John Woolfolk's grip insecure.

The doubt of his success grew; he fought more desperately. His thoughts, which till now had been clear, logically aloof, were blurred in blind spurts of passion. His mentality gradually deserted him; he reverted to lower and lower types of the human animal; during the accumulating seconds of the strife he swung back through countless centuries to the primitive, snarling brute. His shirt was torn from a shoulder, and he felt the sweating, bare skin of his opponent pressed against him.

The conflict continued without diminishing. He struggled once more to his feet, with Nicholas, and they exchanged battering blows, dealt necessarily at random. Sometimes his arm swept violently through mere space, at others his fist landed with a satisfying shock on the body of his antagonist. The dark was occasionally crossed by flashes before Woolfolk's smitten eyes, but no actual light pierced the profound night of the upper hall. At times their struggle grew audible, smacking blows fell sharply; but there was no other sound except that of the wind tearing at the sashes thundering dully in the loose tin roof, rocking the dwelling.

They fell again, and equally their efforts slackened, their grips became more feeble. Finally, as if by common consent, they rolled apart. A leaden tide of apathy crept over Woolfolk's battered body, folded his aching brain. He listened in a sort of indifferent attention to the tempestuous breathing of Iscah Nicholas. John Woolfolk wondered dully where Millie was. There had been no sign of her since he had fallen down the step and she had cried out. Perhaps she was dead from fright. He considered this possibility in a hazy, detached manner. She would be better dead—if he failed.

He heard, with little interest, a stirring on the floor beside him, and thought with an overwhelming weariness and distaste that the strife was to commence once more. But, curiously, Nicholas moved away from him. Woolfolk was glad; and then he was puzzled for a moment by the sliding of hands over an invisible wall. He slowly realized that the other was groping for the knife he had buried in the plaster. John Woolfolk considered a similar search for the pistol he had dropped; he might even light a match. It was a rather wonderful weapon and would spray lead like a hose of water. He would like exceedingly well to have it in his hand with Nicholas before him.

Then in a sudden mental illumination he realized the extreme peril of the moment; and, lurching to his feet, he again threw himself on the other.

The struggle went on, apparently to infinity; it was less vigorous now; the blows, for the most part, were impotent. Iscah Nicholas never said a word; and fantastic thoughts wheeled through Woolfolk's brain. He lost all sense of the identity of his opponent and became convinced that he was combating an impersonal hulk—the thing that gasped and smeared his face, that strove to end him, was the embodied and evil spirit of the place, a place that even Halvard had seen was damnably wrong. He questioned if such a force could be killed, if a being materialized from the outer dark could be stopped by a pistol of even the latest, most ingenious mechanism.

They fell and rose, and fell. Woolfolk's fingers were twisted in a damp lock of hair; they came away—with the hair. He moved to his knees, and the other followed. For a moment they rested face to face, with arms limply clasped about the opposite shoulders. Then they turned over on the floor; they turned once more, and suddenly the darkness was empty beneath John Woolfolk. He fell down and down, beating his head on a series of sharp edges; while a second, heavy body fell with him by turns under and above.

XIII

He rose with the ludicrous alacrity of a man who had taken a public and awkward misstep. The wan lamplight, diffused from within, made just visible the bulk that had descended with him. It lay without motion, sprawling upon a lower step and the floor. John Woolfolk moved backward from it, his hand behind him, feeling for the entrance to the lighted room. He shifted his feet carefully, for the darkness was wheeling about him in visible black rings streaked with pale orange as he passed into the room.

Here objects, dimensions, became normally placed, recognizable. He saw the mezzotint with its sere and sunny peace, the portfolios on their stands, like grotesque and flattened quadrupeds, and Lichfield Stope on the floor, still hiding his dead face in the crook of his arm.

He saw these things, remembered them, and yet now they had new significance—they oozed a sort of vital horror, they seemed to crawl with a malignant and repulsive life. The entire room was charged with this palpable, sentient evil. John Woolfolk defiantly faced the still, cold inclosure; he was conscious of an unseen scrutiny, of a menace that lived in pictures, moved the fingers of the dead, and that could take actual bulk and pound his heart sore.

He was not afraid of the wrongness that inhabited this muck of house and grove and matted bush. He said this loudly to the prostrate form; then, waiting a little, repeated it. He would smash the print with its fallacious expanse of peace. The broken glass of the smitten picture jingled thinly on the floor. Woolfolk turned suddenly and defeated the purpose of whatever had been stealthily behind him; anyway it had disappeared. He stood in a strained attitude, listening to the aberrations of the wind without, when an actual presence slipped by him, stopping in the middle of the floor.

It was Millie Stope. Her eyes were opened to their widest extent, but they had the peculiar blank fixity of the eyes of the blind. Above them her hair slipped and slid in a loosened knot.

"I had to walk round him," she protested in a low, fluctuating voice, "there was no other way. . . . Right by his head. My skirt—" She broke off and, shuddering, came close to John Woolfolk. "I think we'd better go away," she told him, nodding. "It's quite impossible here, with him in the hall, where you have to pass so close."

Woolfolk drew back from her. She too was a part of the house; she had led him there—a white flame that he had followed into the swamp. And this was no ordinary marsh. It was, he added aloud, "A swamp of souls."

"Then," she replied, "we must leave at once."

A dragging sound rose from the hall. Millie Stope cowered in a voiceless accession of terror; but John Woolfolk, lamp in hand, moved to the door. He was curious to see exactly what was happening. The bulk had risen; a broad back swayed like a pendulum, and a swollen hand gripped the stair rail. The form heaved itself up a step, paused, tottering, and then mounted again. Woolfolk saw at once that the other was going for the knife buried in the wall above. He watched with an impersonal interest the dragging ascent. At the seventh step it ceased; the figure crumpled, slid halfway back to the floor.

"You can't do it," Woolfolk observed critically.

The other sat bowed, with one leg extended stiffly downward, on the stair that mounted from the pale radiance of the lamp into impenetrable darkness. Woolfolk moved back into the room and replaced the lamp on its table. Millie Stope still stood with open, hanging hands, a countenance of expectant dread. Her eyes did not shift from the door as he entered and passed her; her gaze hung starkly on what might emerge from the hall.

A deep loathing of his surroundings swept over John Woolfolk, a sudden revulsion from the dead man on the floor, from the ponderous menace on the stair, the white figure that had brought it all upon him. A mounting horror of the place possessed him, and he turned and incontinently fled. A complete panic enveloped him at his flight, a blind necessity to get away, and he ran heedlessly through the night, with head up and arms extended. His feet struck upon a rotten fragment of board that broke beneath him, he pushed through a tangle of grass, and then his progress was held by soft and dragging sand. A moment later he was halted by a chill flood rising abruptly to his knees. He drew back sharply and fell on the beach, with his heels in the water of the bay.

An insuperable weariness pinned him down, a complete exhaustion of brain and body. A heavy wind struck like a wet cloth on his face. The sky had been swept clear of clouds, and stars sparkled in the pure depths of the night. They were white, with the exception of one that burned with an unsteady yellow ray and seemed close by. This, John Woolfolk thought, was strange. He concentrated a frowning gaze upon it—perhaps in falling into the soiled atmosphere of the earth it had lost its crystal gleam and burned with a turgid light. It was very, very probable.

He continued to watch it, facing the tonic wind, until with a clearing of his mind, a gasp of joyful recognition, he knew that it was the riding light of the *Gar*.

Woolfolk sat very still under the pressure of his renewed sanity. Fact upon fact, memory on memory, returned, and in proper perspective built up again his mentality, his logic, his scattered powers of being. The *Gar* rode uneasily on her anchor chains; the wind was shifting. They must get away!—Halvard, waiting at the wharf—Millie—

He rose hurriedly to his feet—he had deserted Millie; left her, in all her anguish, with her dead parent and Iscah Nicholas. His love for her swept back, infinitely heightened by the knowledge of her suffering. At the same time there returned the familiar fear of a permanent disarrangement in her of chords that were unresponsive to the clumsy expedients of affection and science. She had been subjected to a strain that might well unsettle a relatively strong will; and she had been fragile in the beginning.

She must be a part of no more scenes of violence, he told himself, moving hurriedly through the orange grove; she must be led quietly to the tender—that is, if it were not already too late. His entire effort to preserve her had been a series of blunders, each one of which might well have proved fatal, and now, together, perhaps had.

He mounted to the porch and entered the hall. The light flowed undisturbed from the room on the right; and, in its thin wash, he saw that Iscah Nicholas had disappeared from the lower steps. Immediately, however, and from higher up, he heard a shuffling, and could just make out a form heaving obscurely in the gloom. Nicholas patently was making progress toward the consummation of his one fixed idea; but Woolfolk decided that at present he could best afford to ignore him.

He entered the lighted room, and found Millie seated and gazing in dull wonderment at the figure on the floor.

"I must tell you about my father," she said conversationally. "You know, in Virginia, the women tied an apron to his door because he would not go to war, and for years that preyed on his mind, until he was afraid of the slightest thing. He was without a particle of strength— just to watch the sun cross the sky wearied him, and the smallest disagreement upset him for a week."

She stopped, lost in amazement at what she contemplated, what was to follow.

"Then Nicholas— But that isn't important. I was to meet a man— we were going away together, to some place where it would be peaceful. We were to sail there. He said at eight o'clock. Well, at seven Nicholas was in the kitchen. I got father into his very heaviest coat, and laid out a muffler and his gloves, then sat and waited. I didn't need anything extra, my heart was quite warm. Then father asked why I had changed his coat—if I'd told him, he would have died of fright—he said he was too hot, and he fretted and worried. Nicholas heard him, and he wanted to know why I had put on father's winter coat. He found the muffler and gloves ready and got suspicious.

"He stayed in the hall, crying a little—Nicholas cried right often—while I sat with father and tried to think of some excuse to get away. At last I had to go—for an orange, I said—but Nicholas wouldn't believe it. He pushed me back and told me I was going out to the other.

"'Nicholas,' I said, 'don't be silly; nobody would come away from a boat on a night like this. Besides, he's gone away.' We had that last made up. But he pushed me back again. Then I heard father move behind us, and I thought—he's going to die of fright right now. But father's footsteps came on across the floor and up to my side.

"'Don't do that, Nicholas,' he told him; 'take your hand from my daughter.' He swayed a little, his lips shook, but he stood facing him. It was father!" Her voice died away, and she was silent for a moment, gazing at the vision of that unsuspected and surprising courage. "Of course Nicholas killed him," she added. "He twisted him away and father died. That didn't matter," she told Woolfolk; "but the other was terribly important, anyone can see that."

John Woolfolk listened intently, but there was no sound from without. Then, with every appearance of leisure, he rolled and lighted a cigarette.

"Splendid!" he said of her recital; "and I don't doubt you're right about the important thing." He moved toward her, holding out his hand. 'Splendid! But we must go on—the man is waiting for you."

"It's too late," she responded indifferently. She redirected her thoughts to her parent's enthralling end. "Do you think a man as brave as that should lie on the floor?" she demanded. "A flag," she added obscurely, considering an appropriate covering for the still form.

"No, not on the floor," Woolfolk instantly responded. He bent and, lifting the body of Lichfield Stope, carried it into the hall, where, relieved at the opportunity to dispose of his burden, he left it in an obscure corner.

Iscah Nicholas was stirring again. John Woolfolk waited, gazing up the stair, but the other progressed no more than a step. Then he returned to Millie.

"Come," he said. "No time to lose." He took her arm and exerted a gentle pressure toward the door.

"I explained that it was too late," she reiterated, evading him. "Father really lived, but I died. 'Swamp of souls,'" she added in a lower voice. "Someone said that, and it's true; it happened to me."

"The man waiting for you will be worried," he suggested. "He depends absolutely on your coming."

"Nice man. Something had happened to him too. He caught a rockfish and Nicholas boiled it in milk for our breakfast." At the mention of Iscah Nicholas a slight shiver passed over her. This was what Woolfolk hoped for—a return of her normal revulsion from her surroundings, from the past.

"Nicholas," he said sharply, contradicted by a faint dragging from the stair, "is dead."

"If you could only assure me of that," she replied wistfully. "If I could be certain that he wasn't in the next shadow I'd go gladly. Any other way it would be useless." She laid her hand over her heart. "I must get him out of here— My father did. His lips trembled a little, but he said quite clearly: 'Don't do that. Don't touch my daughter.'"

"Your father was a singularly brave man," he assured her, rebelling against the leaden monotony of speech that had fallen upon them. "Your mother too was brave," he temporized. He could, he decided, wait no longer. She must, if necessary, be carried away forcibly. It was a desperate chance—the least pressure might result in a permanent, jangling discord. Her waist, torn, he saw, upon her pallid shoulder, was an insufficient covering against the wind and night. Looking about he discovered the muffler, laid out for her father, crumpled on the floor; and, with an arm about her, folded it over her throat and breast.

"Now we're away," he declared in a forced lightness.

She resisted him for a moment, and then collapsed into his support. John Woolfolk half led, half carried her into the hall. His gaze searched the obscurity of the stair; it was empty; but from above came the sound of a heavy, dragging step.

XIV

Outside she cowered pitifully from the violent blast of the wind, the boundless, stirred space. They made their way about the corner of the house, leaving behind the pale, glimmering rectangle of the lighted window. In the thicket Woolfolk was forced to proceed more slowly. Millie stumbled weakly over the rough way, apparently at the point of slipping to the ground. He felt a supreme relief when the cool sweep of the sea opened before him and Halvard emerged from the gloom.

He halted for a moment, with his arm about Millie's shoulders, facing his man. Even in the dark he was conscious of Poul Halvard's stalwart being, of his rocklike integrity.

"I was delayed," he said finally, amazed at the inadequacy of his words to express the pressure of the past hours. Had they been two or four? He had been totally unconscious of the passage of actual time. In the dark house behind the orange grove he had lived through tormented ages, descended into depths beyond the measured standard of Greenwich. Halvard said:

"Yes, sir."

The sound of a blundering progress rose from the path behind them, the breaking of branches and the slipping of a heavy tread on the water-soaked ground. John Woolfolk, with an oath, realized that it was Nicholas, still animated by his fixed, murderous idea. Millie Stope recognized the sound, too, for she trembled violently on his arm. He knew that she could support no more violence, and he turned to the dim. square-set figure before him.

"Halvard, it's that fellow Nicholas. He's insane—has a knife. Will you stop him while I get Miss Stope into the tender? She's pretty well through." He laid his hand on the other's shoulder as he started immediately forward. "I shall have to go on, Halvard, if anything unfortunate occurs," he said in a different voice.

The sailor made no reply; but as Woolfolk urged Millie out over the wharf he saw Halvard throw himself upon a dark bulk that broke from the wood.

The tender was made fast fore and aft; and, getting down into the uneasy boat, Woolfolk reached up and lifted Millie bodily to his side. She dropped in a still, white heap on the bottom. He unfastened the painter and stood holding the tender close to the wharf, with his head above its platform, straining his gaze in the direction of the obscure struggle on land.

He could see nothing, and heard only an occasional trampling of the underbrush. It was difficult to remain detached, give no assistance, while Halvard encountered Iscah Nicholas. Yet with Millie in a semi-collapse, and the bare possibility of Nicholas' knifing them both, he felt that this was his only course. Halvard was an unusually powerful, active man, and the other must have suffered from the stress of his long conflict in the hall.

The thing terminated speedily. There was the sound of a heavy fall, a diminishing thrashing in the saw grass, and silence. An indistinguishable form advanced over the wharf, and Woolfolk prepared to shove the tender free. But it was Poul Halvard. He got down, Woolfolk thought, clumsily, and mechanically assumed his place at the oars. Woolfolk sat aft, with an arm about Millie Stope. The sailor said fretfully:

"I stopped him. He was all pumped out. Missed his hand at first—the dark—a scratch."

He rested on the oars, fingering his shoulder. The tender swung dangerously near the corrugated rock of the shore, and Woolfolk sharply directed: "Keep way on her."

"Yes, sir," Halvard replied, once more swinging into his short, efficient stroke. It was, however, less sure than usual; an oar missed its hold and skittered impotently over the water drenching Woolfolk with a brief, cold spray. Again the bow of the tender dipped into the point of land they were rounding, and John Woolfolk spoke more abruptly than before.

He was seriously alarmed about Millie. Her face was apathetic, almost blank, and her arms hung across his knees with no more response than a doll's. He wondered desperately if, as she had said, her spirit had died; if the Millie Stope that had moved him so swiftly and tragically from his long indifference, his aversion to life, had gone, leaving him more hopelessly alone than before. The sudden extinction of Ellen's life had been more supportable than Millie's crouching dumbly at his feet. His arm unconsciously tightened about her, and she gazed up with a momentary, questioning flicker of her wide-opened eyes. He repeated her name in a deep whisper, but her head fell forward loosely, and left him in racking doubt.

Now he could see the shortly swaying riding light of the *Gar*. Halvard was propelling them vigorously but erratically forward. At times he remuttered his declarations about the encounter with Nicholas. The stray words reached Woolfolk:

"Stopped him—the cursed dark—a scratch."

He brought the tender awkwardly alongside the ketch, with a grinding shock, and held the boats together while John Woolfolk shifted Millie to the deck. Woolfolk took her immediately into the cabin; where, lighting a swinging lamp, he placed her on one of the prepared berths and endeavored to wrap her in a blanket. But, in a shuddering access of fear, she rose with outheld palms.

"Nicholas!" she cried shrilly. "There—at the door!"

He sat beside her, restraining her convulsive effort to cower in a far, dark angle of the cabin.

"Nonsense" he told her brusquely. "You are on the *Gar*. You are safe. In an hour you will be in a new world."

"With John Woolfolk?"

"I am John Woolfolk."

"But he—you—left me."

"I am here," he insisted with a tightening of his heart. He rose, animated by an overwhelming necessity to get the ketch under way, to leave at once, forever, the invisible shore of the bay. He gently folded her again in the blanket, but she resisted him. "I'd rather stay up," she said with a sudden lucidity. "It's nice here; I wanted to come before, but he wouldn't let me."

A glimmer of hope swept over him as he mounted swiftly to the deck. "Get up the anchors," he called; "reef down the jigger and put on a handful of jib."

There was no immediate response, and he peered over the obscured

deck in search of Halvard. The man rose slowly from a sitting posture
by the main boom. "Very good, sir," he replied in a forced tone.

He disappeared forward, while Woolfolk, shutting the cabin door
on the confusing illumination within, lighted the binnacle lamp, bent
over the engine, swiftly making connections and adjustments, and
cranked the wheel with a sharp, expert turn. The explosions settled
into a dull, regular succession, and he coupled the propeller and slowly
maneuvered the ketch up over the anchors, reducing the strain on the
hawsers and allowing Halvard to get in the slack. He waited impatiently for the sailor's cry of all clear, and demanded the cause of the
delay.

"The bight slipped," the other called in a muffled, angry voice. "One's
clear now," he added. "Bring her up again." The ketch forged ahead,
but the wait was longer than before. "Caught," Halvard's voice drifted
thinly aft; "coral ledge." Woolfolk held the *Gar* stationary until the
sailor cried weakly: "Anchor's apeak."

They moved imperceptibly through the dark, into the greater force
of the wind beyond the point. The dull roar of the breaking surf ahead
grew louder. Halvard should have had the jib up and been aft at the
jigger, but he failed to appear. John Woolfolk wondered, in a mounting impatience, what was the matter with the man. Finally an obscure
form passed him and hung over the housed sail, stripping its cover and
removing the stops. The sudden thought of a disconcerting possibility
banished Woolfolk's annoyance. "Halvard," he demaded, "did Nicholas
knife you?"

"A scratch," the other stubbornly reiterated. "I'll tie it up later. No
time now—I stopped him permanent."

The jigger, reefed to a mere irregular patch, rose with a jerk, and the
ketch rapidly left the protection of the shore. She dipped sharply and,
flattened over by a violent ball of wind, buried her rail in the black,
swinging water, and there was a small crash of breaking china from
within. The wind appeared to sweep high up in empty space and occasionally descend to deal the yacht a staggering blow. The bar, directly
ahead—as Halvard had earlier pointed out—was now covered with the
smother of a lowering tide. The pass, the other had discovered, too, had
filled. It was charted at four feet, the *Gar* drew a full three, and Woolfolk knew that there must be no error, no uncertainty, in running out.

Halvard was so long in stowing away the jigger shears that Woolfolk turned to make sure that the sailor had not been swept from the
deck. The "scratch," he was certain, was deeper than the other admitted. When they were safely at sea he would insist upon an examination.

The subject of this consideration fell rather than stepped into the cockpit, and stood rocked by the motion of the swells, clinging to the cabin's edge. Woolfolk shifted the engine to its highest speed, and they were driving through the tempestuous dark on to the bar. He was now confronted by the necessity for an immediate decision. Halvard or himself would have to stand forward, clinging precariously to a stay, and repeatedly sound the depth of the shallowing water as they felt their way out to sea. He gazed anxiously at the dark bulk before him, and saw that the sailor had lost his staunchness of outline, his aspect of invincible determination.

"Halvard," he demanded again sharply, "this is no time for pretense. How are you?"

"All right," the other repeated desperately, through clenched teeth. "I've—I've taken knives from men before—on the docks at Stockholm. I missed his hand at first—it was the night."

The cabin door swung open, and a sudden lurch flung Millie Stope against the wheel. Woolfolk caught and held her until the wave rolled by. She was stark with terror, and held abjectly to the rail while the next swell lifted them upward. He attempted to urge her back to the protection of the cabin, but she resisted with such a convulsive determination that he relinquished the effort and enveloped her in his glistening oilskin.

This had consumed a perilous amount of time; and, swiftly decisive, he commanded Halvard to take the wheel. He swung himself to the deck and secured the long sounding pole. He could see ahead on either side the dim white bars forming and dissolving, and called to the man at the wheel:

"Mark the breakers! Fetch her between."

On the bow, leaning out over the surging tide, he drove the sounding pole forward and down, but it floated back free. They were not yet on the bar. The ketch heeled until the black plain of water rose above his knees, driving at him with a deceitful force, sinking back slowly as the yacht straightened buoyantly. He again sounded; the pole struck bottom, and he cried:

"Five."

The infuriated beating of the waves on the obstruction drawn across their path drowned his voice, and he shouted the mark once more. Then after another sounding:

"Four and three."

The yacht fell away dangerously before a heavy diagonal blow; she hung for a moment, rolling like a log, and then slowly regained her way. Woolfolk's apprehension increased. It would, perhaps, have been better if they had delayed, to examine Halvard's injury. The man had insisted that it was of no moment, and John Woolfolk had been driven by a consuming desire to leave the miasmatic shore. He swung the pole forward and cried:

"Four and a half."

The water was shoaling rapidly. The breaking waves on the port and starboard swept by with lightning rapidity. The ketch veered again, shipped a crushing weight of water, and responded more slowly than before to a tardy pressure of the rudder. The greatest peril, John Woolfolk knew, lay directly before them. He realized from the action of the ketch that Halvard was steering uncertainly, and that at any moment the *Gar* might strike and fall off too far for recovery, when she could not live in the pounding surf.

"Four and one," he cried hoarsely. And then immediately after: "Four."

Chance had been against him from the first, he thought, and there flashed through his mind the dark panorama, the accumulating disasters of the night. A negation lay upon his existence that would not be lifted. It had followed him like a sinister shadow for years to this obscure, black smother of water, to the *Gar* reeling crazily forward under an impotent hand. The yacht was behaving heroically; no other ketch could have lived so long, responded so gallantly to a wavering wheel.

"Three and three," he shouted above the combined stridor of wind and sea.

The next minute would see their safe passage or a helpless hulk beating to pieces on the bar, with three human fragments whirling under the crushing masses of water, floating. perhaps, with the dawn into the tranquillity of the bay.

"Three and a half," he cried monotonously.

The *Gar* trembled like a wounded and dull animal. The solid seas were reaching hungrily over Woolfolk's legs. A sudden stolidity possessed him. He thrust the pole out deliberately, skillfully:

"Three and a quarter."

A lower sounding would mean the end. He paused for a moment, his dripping face turned to the far stars; his lips moved in silent, unformulated aspirations—Halvard and himself, in the sea that had been their home; but Millie was so fragile! He made the sounding precisely, between the heaving swells, and marked the pole instantly driven backward by their swinging flight.

"Three and a half." His voice held a new, uncontrollable quiver. He sounded again immediately: "And three-quarters."

They had passed the bar.

XV

A gladness like the white flare of burning powder swept over him, and then he became conscious of other, minor, sensations—his head ached intolerably from the fall down the stair, and a grinding pain shot through his shoulder, lodging in his torn lower arm at the slightest movement. He slipped the sounding pole into its loops on the cabin and hastily made his way aft to the relief of Poul Halvard.

The sailor was nowhere visible; but, in an intermittent, reddish light that faded and swelled as the cabin door swung open and shut, Woolfolk saw a white figure clinging to the wheel—Millie.

Instantly his hands replaced hers on the spokes and, as if with a palpable sigh of relief, the *Gar* steadied to her course. Millie Stope clung to the deck rail, sobbing with exhaustion.

"He's—he's dead!" she exclaimed, between her racking inspirations. She pointed to the floor of the cockpit, and there, sliding grotesquely with the motion of the seaway, was Poul Halvard. An arm was flung out, as if in ward against the ketch's side, but it crumpled, the body hit heavily, a hand seemed to clutch at the boards it had so often and thoroughly swabbed; but without avail. The face momentarily turned upward; it was haggard beyond expression, and bore stamped upon it, in lines that resembled those of old age, the agonized struggle against the inevitable last treachery of life.

"When—" John Woolfolk stopped in sheer, leaden amazement.

"Just when you called 'Three and a quarter.' Before that he had fallen on his knees. He begged me to help him hold the wheel. He said you'd be lost if I didn't. He talked all the time about keeping her head up and up. I helped him. Your voice came back years apart. At the last he was on the floor, holding the bottom of the wheel. He told me to keep it steady, dead ahead. His voice grew so weak that I couldn't hear; and then all at once he slipped away. I—I held on—called to you. But against the wind—"

He braced his knee against the wheel and, leaning out, found the jigger sheet and flattened the reefed sail; he turned to where the jib sheet led after, and then swung the ketch about. The yacht rode smoothly, slipping forward over the long, even ground swell, and he turned with immeasurable emotion to the woman beside him.

The light from the cabin flooded out over her face, and he saw that, miraculously, the fear had gone. Her countenance was drawn with weariness and the hideous strain of the past minutes, but her gaze squarely met the night and sea. Her chin was lifted, its graceful line firm, and her mouth was in repose. She had, as he had recognized she alone must, conquered the legacy of Lichfield Stope; while he, John Woolfolk, and Halvard, had put Nicholas out of her life. She was free.

"If you could go below—" he suggested. "In the morning, with this wind, we'll be at anchor under a fringe of palms, in water like a blue silk counterpane."

"I think I could now, with you," she replied. She pressed her lips, salt and enthralling, against his face, and made her way into the cabin. He locked the wheel momentarily and, following, wrapped her in the blankets, on the new sheets prepared for her coming. Then, putting out the light, he shut the cabin door and returned to the wheel.

The body of Poul Halvard struck his feet and rested there. A good man, born by the sea, who had known its every expression; with a faithful and simple heart, as such men occasionally had.

The diminished wind swept in a clear diapason through the pellucid sky; the resplendent sea reached vast and magnetic to its invisible horizon. A sudden distaste seized John Woolfolk for the dragging death ceremonials of land. Halvard had known the shore mostly as a turbulent and unclean strip that had finally brought about his end.

He leaned forward and found beyond any last doubt that the other was dead; a black, clotted surface adhered to the wound which his pride, his invincible determination, had driven him to deny.

In the space beneath the afterdeck Woolfolk found a spare folded anchor for the tender, a length of rope; and he slowly completed the preparations for his purpose. He lifted the body to the narrow deck outside the rail, and, in a long dip, the waves carried it smoothly and soundlessly away. John Woolfolk said:

" ' . . . Commit his body to the deep, looking for the general resurrection . . . through . . . Christ.' "

Then, upright and motionless at the wheel, with the wan radiance of the binnacle lamp floating up over his hollow cheeks and set gaze, he held the ketch southward through the night.

46

A Jury of Her Peers

BY SUSAN GLASPELL

WHEN Martha Hale opened the storm-door and got a cut of the north wind, she ran back for her big woolen scarf. As she hurriedly wound that round her head her eye made a scandalized sweep of her kitchen. It was no ordinary thing that called her away—it was probably further from ordinary than anything that had ever happened in Dickson County. But what her eye took in was that her kitchen was in no shape for leaving: her bread all ready for mixing, half the flour sifted and half unsifted.

She hated to see things half done; but she had been at that when the team from town stopped to get Mr. Hale, and then the sheriff came running in to say his wife wished Mrs. Hale would come too—adding, with a grin, that he guessed she was getting scary and wanted another woman along. So she had dropped everything right where it was.

"Martha!" now came her husband's impatient voice. "Don't keep folks waiting out here in the cold."

She again opened the storm-door, and this time joined the three men and the one woman waiting for her in the big two-seated buggy.

After she had the robes tucked around her she took another look at the woman who sat beside her on the back seat. She had met Mrs. Peters the year before at the county fair, and the thing she remembered about her was that she didn't seem like a sheriff's wife. She was small and thin and didn't have a strong voice. Mrs. Gorman, sheriff's wife before Gorman went out and Peters came in, had a voice that somehow seemed to be backing up the law with every word. But if Mrs. Peters didn't look like a sheriff's wife, Peters made it up in looking like a sheriff. He was to a dot the kind of man who could get himself elected sheriff—a heavy man with a big voice, who was particularly genial with the law-abiding, as if to make it plain that he knew the difference between criminals and non-criminals. And right there it came into Mrs. Hale's mind, with a stab, that this man who was so pleasant and lively with all of them was going to the Wrights' now as a sheriff.

"The country's not very pleasant this time of year," Mrs. Peters at last ventured, as if she felt they ought to be talking as well as the men.

Mrs. Hale scarcely finished her reply, for they had gone up a little hill and could see the Wright place now, and seeing it did not make her feel like talking. It looked very lonesome this cold March morning. It had always been a lonesome-looking place. It was down in a hollow, and the poplar trees around it were lonesome-looking trees. The men were looking at it and talking about what had happened. The county attorney was bending to one side of the buggy, and kept looking steadily at the place as they drew up to it.

"I'm glad you came with me," Mrs. Peters said nervously, as the two women were about to follow the men in through the kitchen door.

Even after she had her foot on the door-step, her hand on the knob, Martha Hale had a moment of feeling she could not cross that threshold. And the reason it seemed she couldn't cross it now was simply because she hadn't crossed it before. Time and time again it had been in her mind, "I ought to go over and see Minnie Foster"—she still thought of her as Minnie Foster, though for twenty years she had been Mrs. Wright. And then there was always something to do and Minnie Foster would go from her mind. But *now* she could come.

The men went over to the stove. The women stood close together by the door. Young Henderson, the county attorney, turned around and said, "Come up to the fire, ladies."

Mrs. Peters took a step forward, then stopped. "I'm not—cold," she said.

And so the two women stood by the door, at first not even so much as looking around the kitchen.

The men talked for a minute about what a good thing it was the sheriff had sent his deputy out that morning to make a fire for them, and then Sheriff Peters stepped back from the stove, unbuttoned his outer coat, and leaned his hands on the kitchen table in a way that seemed to mark the beginning of official business. "Now, Mr. Hale," he said in a sort of semi-official voice, "before we move things about, you tell Mr. Henderson just what it was you saw when you came here yesterday morning."

The county attorney was looking around the kitchen.

"By the way," he said, "has anything been moved?" He turned to the sheriff. "Are things just as you left them yesterday?"

Peters looked from cupboard to sink; from that to a small worn rocker a little to one side of the kitchen table.

"It's just the same."

"Somebody should have been left here yesterday," said the county attorney.

"Oh—yesterday," returned the sheriff, with a little gesture as of yesterday having been more than he could bear to think of. "When I had to send Frank to Morris Center for that man who went crazy—let me tell you, I had my hands full *yesterday*. I knew you could get back from Omaha by today, George, and as long as I went over everything here myself—"

"Well, Mr. Hale," said the county attorney, in a way of letting what was past and gone go, "tell just what happened when you came here yesterday morning."

Mrs. Hale, still leaning against the door, had that sinking feeling of the mother whose child is about to speak a piece. Lewis often wandered along and got things mixed up in a story. She hoped he would tell this straight and plain, and not say unnecessary things that would just make things harder for Minnie Foster. He didn't begin at once, and she noticed that he looked queer—as if standing in that kitchen and having to tell what he had seen there yesterday morning made him almost sick.

"Yes, Mr. Hale?" the county attorney reminded.

"Harry and I had started to town with a load of potatoes," Mrs. Hale's husband began.

Harry was Mrs. Hale's oldest boy. He wasn't with them now, for the very good reason that those potatoes never got to town yesterday and he was taking them this morning, so he hadn't been home when the sheriff stopped to say he wanted Mr. Hale to come over to the Wright place and tell the county attorney his story there, where he could point it all out. With all Mrs. Hale's other emotions came the fear now that maybe Harry wasn't dressed warm enough—they hadn't any of them realized how that north wind did bite.

"We come along this road," Hale was going on, with a motion of his hand to the road over which they had just come, "and as we got in sight of the house I says to Harry, 'I'm goin' to see if I can't get John Wright to take a telephone.' You see," he explained to Henderson, "unless I can get somebody to go in with me they won't come out this branch road except for a price *I* can't pay. I'd spoke to Wright about it once before; but he put me off, saying folks talked too much anyway, and all he asked was peace and quiet—guess you know about how much he talked himself. But I thought maybe if I went to the house and talked about it before his wife, and said all the women-folks liked the telephones, and that in this lonesome stretch of road it would be a good thing—well, I said to Harry that that was what I was going to say—though I said at the same time that I didn't know as what his wife wanted made much difference to John—"

Now there he was!—saying things he didn't need to say. Mrs. Hale tried to catch her husband's eye, but fortunately the county attorney interrupted with:

"Let's talk about that a little later, Mr. Hale. I do want to talk about that, but I'm anxious now to get along to just what happened when you got here."

When he began this time, it was very deliberately and carefully:

"I didn't see or hear anything. I knocked at the door. And still it was all quiet inside. I knew they must be up—it was past eight o'clock. So I knocked again, louder, and I thought I heard somebody say, 'Come in.' I wasn't sure—I'm not sure yet. But I opened the door—this door," jerking a hand toward the door by which the two women stood, "and there, in that rocker"—pointing to it—"sat Mrs. Wright."

Everyone in the kitchen looked at the rocker. It came into Mrs. Hale's mind that that rocker didn't look in the least like Minnie Foster—the Minnie Foster of twenty years before. It was a dingy red, with wooden rungs up the back, and the middle rung was gone, and the chair sagged to one side.

"How did she—look?" the county attorney was inquiring.

"Well," said Hale, "she looked—queer."

"How do you mean—queer?"

As he asked it he took out a note-book and pencil. Mrs. Hale did not like the sight of that pencil. She kept her eye fixed on her husband, as if to keep him from saying unnecessary things that would go into that note-book and make trouble.

Hale did speak guardedly, as if the pencil had affected him too.

"Well, as if she didn't know what she was going to do next. And kind of—done up."

"How did she seem to feel about your coming?"

"Why, I don't think she minded—one way or other. She didn't pay much attention. I said, 'Ho' do, Mrs. Wright? It's cold, ain't it?' And she said, 'Is it?'—and went on pleatin' at her apron.

"Well, I was surprised. She didn't ask me to come up to the stove, or to sit down, but just set there, not even lookin' at me. And so I said: 'I want to see John.'

"And then she—laughed. I guess you would call it a laugh.

"I thought of Harry and the team outside, so I said, a little sharp, 'Can I see John?' 'No,' says she—kind of dull like. 'Ain't he home?' says I. Then she looked at me. 'Yes,' says she, 'he's home.' 'Then why can't I see him?' I asked her, out of patience with her now. ' 'Cause he's dead,' says she, just as quiet and dull—and fell to pleatin' her apron. 'Dead?' says I, like you do when you can't take in what you've heard.

"She just nodded her head, not getting a bit excited, but rockin' back and forth.

" 'Why—where is he?' says I, not knowing *what* to say.

"She just pointed upstairs—like this"—pointing to the room above.

"I got up, with the idea of going up there myself. By this time I— didn't know what to do. I walked from there to here; then I says: 'Why, what did he die of?'

" 'He died of a rope round his neck,' says she; and just went on pleatin at her apron."

Hale stopped speaking, and stood staring at the rocker, as if he were still seeing the woman who had sat there the morning before. Nobody spoke; it was as if every one were seeing the woman who had sat there the morning before.

"And what did you do then?" the county attorney at last broke the silence.

"I went out and called Harry. I thought I might—need help. I got Harry in, and we went upstairs." His voice fell almost to a whisper. "There he was—lying over the—"

"I think I'd rather have you go into that upstairs," the county attorney interrupted, "where you can point it all out. Just go on now with the rest of the story."

"Well, my first thought was to get that rope off. It looked—"

He stopped, his face twitching.

"But Harry, he went up to him, and he said, 'No, he's dead all right, and we'd better not touch anything.' So we went downstairs.

"She was still sitting that same way. 'Has anybody been notified?' I asked. 'No,' says she, unconcerned.

" 'Who did this, Mrs. Wright?' said Harry. He said it businesslike, and she stopped pleatin' at her apron. 'I don't know,' she says. 'You don't *know*?' says Harry. 'Weren't you sleepin' in the bed with him?' 'Yes,' says she, 'but I was on the inside.' 'Somebody slipped a rope round his neck and strangled him, and, you didn't wake up?' says Harry. 'I didn't wake up,' she said after him.

"We may have looked as if we didn't see how that could be, for after a minute she said, 'I sleep sound.'

"Harry was going to ask her more questions, but I said maybe that weren't our business; maybe we ought to let her tell her story first to the coroner or the sheriff. So Harry went fast as he could over to High Road—the Rivers' place, where there's a telephone."

"And what did she do when she knew you had gone for the coroner?"
The attorney got his pencil in his hand all ready for writing.

"She moved from that chair to this one over here"—Hale pointed to
a small chair in the corner—"and just sat there with her hands held
together and looking down. I got a feeling that I ought to make some
conversation, so I said I had come in to see if John wanted to put in a
telephone; and at that she started to laugh, and then she stopped and
looked at me—scared."

At sound of a moving pencil the man who was telling the story looked
up.

"I dunno—maybe it wasn't scared," he hastened; "I wouldn't like to
say it was. Soon Harry got back, and then Dr. Lloyd came, and you,
Mr. Peters, and so I guess that's all I know that you don't."

He said that last with relief, and moved a little, as if relaxing. Every
one moved a little. The county attorney walked toward the stair door.

"I guess we'll go upstairs first—then out to the barn and around
there."

He paused and looked around the kitchen.

"You're convinced there was nothing important here?" he asked the
sheriff. "Nothing that would—point to any motive?"

The sheriff too looked all around, as if to re-convince himself.

"Nothing here but kitchen things," he said, with a little laugh for
the insignificance of kitchen things.

The county attorney was looking at the cupboard—a peculiar, ungainly structure, half closet and half cupboard, the upper part of it being
built in the wall, and the lower part just the old-fashioned kitchen cupboard. As if its queerness attracted him, he got a chair and opened the
upper part and looked in. After a moment he drew his hand away sticky.

"Here's a nice mess," he said resentfully.

The two women had drawn nearer, and now the sheriff's wife spoke.

"Oh—her fruit," she said, looking to Mrs. Hale for sympathetic understanding. She turned back to the county attorney and explained: "She
worried about that when it turned so cold last night. She said the fire
would go out and her jars might burst."

Mrs. Peters' husband broke into a laugh.

"Well, can you beat the women! Held for murder, and worrying
about her preserves!"

The young attorney set his lips.

"I guess before we're through with her she may have something more
serious than preserves to worry about."

"Oh, well," said Mrs. Hale's husband, with good-natured superiority,
"women are used to worrying over trifles."

The two women moved a little closer together. Neither of them spoke.
The county attorney seemed suddenly to remember his manners—and
think of his future.

"And yet," said he, with the gallantry of a young politician, "for all
their worries, what would we do without the ladies?"

The women did not speak, did not unbend. He went to the sink and
began washing his hands. He turned to wipe them on the roller towel
—whirled it for a cleaner place.

"Dirty towels! Not much of a housekeeper, would you say, ladies?"

He kicked his foot against some dirty pans under the sink.

"There's a great deal of work to be done on a farm," said Mrs. Hale
stiffly.

"To be sure. And yet"—with a little bow to her—"I know there are
some Dickson County farm-houses that do not have such roller towels."
He gave it a pull to expose its full length again.

"Those towels get dirty awful quick. Men's hands aren't always as
clean as they might be."

"Ah, loyal to your sex, I see," he laughed. He stopped and gave her a
keen look. "But you and Mrs. Wright were neighbors. I suppose you
were friends, too."

Martha Hale shook her head.

"I've seen little enough of her of late years. I've not been in this house
—it's more than a year."

"And why was that? You didn't like her?"

"I liked her well enough," she replied with spirit. "Farmers' wives
have their hands full, Mr. Henderson. And then—" She looked around
the kitchen.

"Yes?" he encouraged.

"It never seemed a very cheerful place," said she, more to herself than
to him.

"No," he agreed; "I don't think anyone would call it cheerful. I
shouldn't say she had the home-making instinct."

"Well, I don't know as Wright had, either," she muttered.

"You mean they didn't get on very well?" he was quick to ask.

"No; I don't mean anything," she answered, with decision. As she
turned a little away from him, she added: "But I don't think a place
would be any the cheerfuler for John Wright's bein' in it."

"I'd like to talk to you about that a little later, Mrs. Hale," he said.
"I'm anxious to get the lay of things upstairs now."

He moved toward the stair door, followed by the two men.

"I suppose anything Mrs. Peters does'll be all right?" the sheriff inquired. "She was to take in some clothes for her, you know—and a few
little things. We left in such a hurry yesterday."

The county attorney looked at the two women whom they were leaving alone there among the kitchen things.

"Yes—Mrs. Peters," he said, his glance resting on the woman who was not Mrs. Peters, the big farmer woman who stood behind the sheriff's wife. "Of course Mrs. Peters is one of us," he said, in a manner of entrusting responsibility. "And keep your eye out, Mrs. Peters, for anything that might be of use. No telling; you women might come upon a clue to the motive—and that's the thing we need."

Mr. Hale rubbed his face after the fashion of a showman getting ready for a pleasantry.

"But would the women know a clue if they did come upon it?" he said; and, having delivered himself of this, he followed the others through the stair door.

The women stood motionless and silent, listening to the footsteps, first upon the stairs, then in the room above them.

Then, as if releasing herself from something strange, Mrs. Hale began to arrange the dirty pans under the sink, which the county attorney's disdainful push of the foot had deranged.

"I'd hate to have men comin' into my kitchen," she said testily—"snoopin' round and criticizin'."

"Of course it's no more than their duty," said the sheriff's wife, in her manner of timid acquiescence.

"Duty's all right," replied Mrs. Hale bluffly; "but I guess that deputy sheriff that come out to make the fire might have got a little of this on." She gave the roller towel a pull. "Wish I'd thought of that sooner! Seems mean to talk about her for not having things slicked up, when she had to come away in such a hurry."

She looked around the kitchen. Certainly it was not "slicked up." Her eye was held by a bucket of sugar on a low shelf. The cover was off the wooden bucket, and beside it was a paper bag—half full.

Mrs. Hale moved toward it.

"She was putting this in there," she said to herself—slowly.

She thought of the flour in her kitchen at home—half sifted, half not sifted. She had been interrupted, and had left things half done. What had interrupted Minnie Foster? Why had that work been left half done? She made a move as if to finish it,—unfinished things always bothered her,—and then she glanced around and saw that Mrs. Peters was watching her—and she didn't want Mrs. Peters to get that feeling she had got of work begun and then—for some reason—not finished.

"It's a shame about her fruit," she said, and walked toward the cupboard that the county attorney had opened, and got on the chair, murmuring: "I wonder if it's all gone."

It was a sorry enough looking sight, but "Here's one that's all right," she said at last. She held it toward the light. "This is cherries, too." She looked again. "I declare I believe that's the only one."

With a sigh, she got down from the chair, went to the sink, and wiped off the bottle.

"She'll feel awful bad, after all her hard work in the hot weather. I remember the afternoon I put up my cherries last summer."

She set the bottle on the table, and, with another sigh, started to sit down in the rocker. But she did not sit down. Something kept her from sitting down in that chair. She straightened—stepped back, and, half turned away, stood looking at it, seeing the woman who had sat there "pleatin' at her apron."

The thin voice of the sheriff's wife broke in upon her: "I must be getting those things from the front-room closet." She opened the door into the other room, started in, stepped back. "You coming with me, Mrs. Hale?" she asked nervously. "You—you could help me get them."

They were soon back—the stark coldness of that shut-up room was not a thing to linger in.

"My!" said Mrs. Peters, dropping the things on the table and hurrying to the stove.

Mrs. Hale stood examining the clothes the woman who was being detained in town had said she wanted.

"Wright was close!" she exclaimed, holding up a shabby black skirt that bore the marks of much making over. "I think maybe that's why she kept so much to herself. I s'pose she felt she couldn't do her part; and then, you don't enjoy things when you feel shabby. She used to wear pretty clothes and be lively—when she was Minnie Foster, one of the town girls, singing in the choir. But that—oh, that was twenty years ago."

With a carefulness in which there was something tender, she folded the shabby clothes and piled them at one corner of the table. She looked up at Mrs. Peters, and there was something in the other woman's look that irritated her.

"She don't care," she said to herself. "Much difference it makes to her whether Minnie Foster had pretty clothes when she was a girl."

Then she looked again, and she wasn't so sure; in fact, she hadn't at any time been perfectly sure about Mrs. Peters. She had that shrinking manner, and yet her eyes looked as if they could see a long way into things.

"This all you was to take in?" asked Mrs. Hale.

"No," said the sheriff's wife; "she said she wanted an apron. Funny thing to want," she ventured in her nervous little way, for there's not much to get you dirty in jail, goodness knows. But I suppose just to make her feel more natural. If you're used to wearing an apron—. She said they were in the bottom drawer of this cupboard. Yes—here they are. And then her little shawl that always hung on the stair door."

She took the small gray shawl from behind the door leading upstairs, and stood a minute looking at it.

Suddenly Mrs. Hale took a quick step toward the other woman.

"Mrs. Peters!"

"Yes, Mrs. Hale?"

"Do you think she—did it?"

A frightened look blurred the other thing in Mrs. Peters' eyes.

"Oh, I don't know," she said, in a voice that seemed to shrink away from the subject.

"Well, I don't think she did," affirmed Mrs. Hale stoutly. "Asking for an apron, and her little shawl. Worryin' about her fruit."

"Mr. Peters says—." Footsteps were heard in the room above; she stopped, looked up, then went on in a lowered voice: "Mr. Peters says—it looks bad for her. Mr. Henderson is awful sarcastic in a speech, and he's going to make fun of her saying she didn't—wake up."

For a moment Mrs. Hale had no answer. Then, "Well, I guess John Wright didn't wake up—when they was slippin' that rope under his neck," she muttered.

"No, it's *strange*," breathed Mrs. Peters. "They think it was such a—funny way to kill a man."

She began to laugh; at sound of the laugh, abruptly stopped.

"That's just what Mr. Hale said," said Mrs. Hale, in a resolutely natural voice. "There was a gun in the house. He says that's what he can't understand."

"Mr. Henderson said, coming out, that what was needed for the case was a motive. Something to show anger—or sudden feeling."

"Well, I don't see any signs of anger around here," said Mrs. Hale. "I don't—"

She stopped. It was as if her mind tripped on something. Her eye was caught by a dish-towel in the middle of the kitchen table. Slowly she moved toward the table. One half of it was wiped clean, the other half messy. Her eyes made a slow, almost unwilling turn to the bucket of sugar and the half empty bag beside it. Things begun—and not finished.

After a moment she stepped back, and said, in that manner of releasing herself:

"Wonder how they're finding things upstairs? I hope she had it a little more red up up there. You know,"—she paused, and feeling gathered,—"it seems kind of *sneaking*: locking her up in town and coming out here to get her own house to turn against her!"

"But, Mrs. Hale," said the sheriff's wife, "the law is the law."

"I s'pose 'tis," answered Mrs. Hale shortly.

She turned to the stove, saying something about that fire not being much to brag of. She worked with it a minute, and when she straightened up she said aggressively:

"The law is the law—and a bad stove is a bad stove. How'd you like to cook on this?"—pointing with the poker to the broken lining. She opened the oven door and started to express her opinion of the oven; but she was swept into her own thoughts, thinking of what it would mean, year after year, to have that stove to wrestle with. The thought of Minnie Foster trying to bake in that oven—and the thought of her never going over to see Minnie Foster—.

She was startled by hearing Mrs. Peters say: "A person gets discouraged—and loses heart."

The sheriff's wife had looked from the stove to the sink—to the pail of water which had been carried in from outside. The two women stood there silent, above them the footsteps of the men who were looking for evidence against the woman who had worked in that kitchen. That look of seeing into things, of seeing through a thing to something else, was in the eyes of the sheriff's wife now. When Mrs. Hale next spoke to her, it was gently:

"Better loosen up your things, Mrs. Peters. We'll not feel them when we go out."

Mrs. Peters went to the back of the room to hang up the fur tippet she was wearing. A moment later she exclaimed, "Why, she was piecing a quilt," and held up a large sewing basket piled high with quilt pieces.

Mrs. Hale spread some of the blocks on the table.

"It's log-cabin pattern," she said, putting several of them together "Pretty, isn't it?"

They were so engaged with the quilt that they did not hear the footsteps on the stairs. Just as the stair door opened Mrs. Hale was saying:

"Do you suppose she was going to quilt it or just knot it?"

The sheriff threw up his hands.

"They wonder whether she was going to quilt it or just knot it!"

There was a laugh for the ways of women, a warming of hands over the stove, and then the county attorney said briskly:

"Well, let's go right out to the barn and get that cleared up."

"I don't see as there's anything so strange," Mrs. Hale said resentfully, after the outside door had closed on the three men—"our taking up our time with little things while we're waiting for them to get the evidence. I don't see as it's anything to laugh about."

"Of course they've got awful important things on their minds," said the sheriff's wife apologetically.

They returned to an inspection of the block for the quilt. Mrs. Hale was looking at the fine, even sewing, and preoccupied with thoughts of the woman who had done that sewing, when she heard the sheriff's wife say, in a queer tone:

"Why, look at this one."

She turned to take the block held out to her.

"The sewing," said Mrs. Peters, in a troubled way. "All the rest of them have been so nice and even—but—this one. Why, it looks as if she didn't know what she was about!"

Their eyes met—something flashed to life, passed between them; then, as if with an effort, they seemed to pull away from each other. A moment Mrs. Hale sat there, her hands folded over that sewing which was so unlike all the rest of the sewing. Then she had pulled a knot and drawn the threads.

"Oh, what are you doing, Mrs. Hale?" asked the sheriff's wife, startled.

"Just pulling out a stitch or two that's not sewed very good," said Mrs. Hale mildly.

"I don't think we ought to touch things," Mrs. Peters said, a little helplessly.

"I'll just finish up this end," answered Mrs. Hale, still in that mild, matter-of-fact fashion.

She threaded a needle and started to replace bad sewing with good. For a little while she sewed in silence. Then, in that thin, timid voice, she heard:

"Mrs. Hale!"

"Yes, Mrs. Peters?"

"What do you suppose she was so—nervous about?"

"Oh, I don't know," said Mrs. Hale, as if dismissing a thing not important enough to spend much time on. "I don't know as she was— nervous. I sew awful queer sometimes when I'm just tired."

She cut a thread, and out of the corner of her eye looked up at Mrs. Peters. The small, lean face of the sheriff's wife seemed to have tightened up. Her eyes had that look of peering into something. But next moment she moved, and said in her thin, indecisive way:

"Well, I must get those clothes wrapped. They may be through sooner than we think. I wonder where I could find a piece of paper—and string."

"In that cupboard, maybe," suggested Mrs. Hale, after a glance around.

One piece of the crazy sewing remained unripped. Mrs. Peters' back turned, Martha Hale now scrutinized that piece, compared it with the dainty, accurate sewing of the other blocks. The difference was startling. Holding this block made her feel queer, as if the distracted thoughts of the woman who had perhaps turned to it to try and quiet herself were. communicating themselves to her.

Mrs. Peters' voice roused her.

"Here's a bird-cage," she said. "Did she have a bird, Mrs. Hale?"

"Why, I don't know whether she did or not." She turned to look at the cage Mrs. Peters was holding up. "I've not been here in so long." She sighed. "There was a man round last year selling canaries cheap--but I don't know as she took one. Maybe she did. She used to sing real pretty herself."

Mrs. Peters looked around the kitchen.

"Seems kind of funny to think of a bird here." She half laughed—an attempt to put up a barrier. "But she must have had one—or why would she have a cage? I wonder what happened to it."

"I suppose maybe the cat got it," suggested Mrs. Hale, resuming her sewing.

"No; she didn't have a cat. She's got that feeling some people have about cats—being afraid of them. When they brought her to our house yesterday, my cat got in the room, and she was real upset and asked me to take it out."

"My sister Bessie was like that," laughed Mrs. Hale.

The sheriff's wife did not reply. The silence made Mrs. Hale turn round. Mrs. Peters was examining the bird-cage.

"Look at this door," she said slowly. "It's broke. One hinge has been pulled apart."

Mrs. Hale came nearer.

"Looks as if someone must have been—rough with it."

Again their eyes met—startled, questioning, apprehensive. For a moment neither spoke nor stirred. Then Mrs. Hale, turning away, said brusquely:

"If they're going to find any evidence, I wish they'd be about it. I don't like this place."

"But I'm awful glad you came with me, Mrs. Hale." Mrs. Peters put the bird-cage on the table and sat down. "It would be lonesome for me —sitting here alone."

"Yes, it would, wouldn't it?" agreed Mrs. Hale, a certain determined naturalness in her voice. She had picked up the sewing, but now it dropped in her lap, and she murmured in a different voice: "But I tell you what I *do* wish, Mrs. Peters. I wish I had come over sometimes when she was here. I wish—I had."

"But of course you were awful busy, Mrs. Hale. Your house—and your children."

"I could've come," retorted Mrs. Hale shortly. "I stayed away because it weren't cheerful— and that's why I ought to have come. I"—she looked around—"I've never liked this place. Maybe because it's down in a hollow and you don't see the road. I don't know what it is, but it's a lonesome place, and always was. I wish I had come over to see Minnie Foster sometimes. I can see now—" She did not put it into words.

"Well, you mustn't reproach yourself," counseled Mrs. Peters. "Somehow, we just don't see how it is with other folks till—something comes up."

"Not having children makes less work," mused Mrs. Hale, after a silence, "but it makes a quiet house—and Wright out to work all day—and no company when he did come in. Did you know John Wright, Mrs. Peters?"

"Not to know him. I've seen him in town. They say he was a good man."

"Yes—good," conceded John Wright's neighbor grimly. "He didn't drink, and kept his word as well as most, I guess, and paid his debts. But he was a hard man, Mrs. Peters. Just to pass the time of day with him—." She stopped, shivered a little. "Like a raw wind that gets to the bone." Her eye fell upon the cage on the table before her, and she added, almost bitterly: "I should think she would've wanted a bird!"

Suddenly she leaned forward, looking intently at the cage. "But what do you s'pose went wrong with it?"

"I don't know," returned Mrs. Peters; "unless it got sick and died."

But after she said it she reached over and swung the broken door. Both women watched it as if somehow held by it.

"You didn't know—her?" Mrs. Hale asked, a gentler note in her voice.

"Not till they brought her yesterday," said the sheriff's wife.

"She—come to think of it, she was kind of like a bird herself. Real sweet and pretty, but kind of timid and—fluttery. How—she—did—change."

That held her for a long time. Finally, as if struck with a happy thought and relieved to get back to everyday things, she exclaimed:

"Tell you what, Mrs. Peters, why don't you take the quilt in with you? It might take up her mind."

"Why, I think that's a real nice idea, Mrs. Hale," agreed the sheriff's wife, as if she too were glad to come into the atmosphere of a simple kindness. "There couldn't possibly be any objection to that, could there? Now, just what will I take? I wonder if her patches are in here—and her things."

They turned to the sewing basket.

"Here's some red," said Mrs. Hale, bringing out a roll of cloth. Underneath that was a box. "Here, maybe her scissors are in here—and her things." She held it up. "What a pretty box! I'll warrant that was something she had a long time ago—when she was a girl."

She held it in her hand a moment; then, with a little sigh, opened it.
Instantly her hand went to her nose.

"Why—!"

Mrs. Peters drew nearer—then turned away.

"There's something wrapped up in this piece of silk," faltered Mrs.
Hale.

"This isn't her scissors," said Mrs. Peters, in a shrinking voice.

Her hand not steady, Mrs. Hale raised the piece of silk. "Oh, Mrs.
Peters!" she cried. "It's—"

Mrs. Peters bent closer.

"It's the bird," she whispered.

"But, Mrs. Peters!" cried Mrs. Hale. "*Look* at it! Its *neck*—look at its
neck! It's all—other side *to*."

She held the box away from her.

The sheriff's wife again bent closer.

"Somebody wrung its neck," said she, in a voice that was slow and
deep.

And then again the eyes of the two women met—this time clung
together in a look of dawning comprehension, of growing horror. Mrs
Peters looked from the dead bird to the broken door of the cage. Again
their eyes met. And just then there was a sound at the outside door.

Mrs. Hale slipped the box under the quilt pieces in the basket, and
sank into the chair before it. Mrs. Peters stood holding to the table. The
county attorney and the sheriff came in from outside.

"Well, ladies," said the county attorney, as one turning from serious
things to little pleasantries, "have you decided whether she was going
to quilt it or knot it?"

"We think," began the sheriff's wife in a flurried voice, "that she was
going to—knot it."

He was too preoccupied to notice the change that came in her voice on
that last.

"Well, that's very interesting, I'm sure," he said tolerantly. "He caught
sight of the bird-cage. "Has the bird flown?"

"We think the cat got it," said Mrs. Hale in a voice curiously even.

He was walking up and down, as if thinking something out.

"Is there a cat?" he asked absently.

Mrs. Hale shot a look up at the sheriff's wife.

"Well, not *now*," said Mrs. Peters. "They're superstitious, you know;
they leave."

She sank into her chair.

The county attorney did not heed her. "No sign at all of anyone having come in from the outside," he said to Peters, in the manner of continuing an interrupted conversation. "Their own rope. Now let's go

upstairs again and go over it, piece by piece. It would have to have been someone who knew just the—"

The stair door closed behind them and their voices were lost.

The two women sat motionless, not looking at each other, but as if peering into something and at the same time holding back. When they spoke now it was as if they were afraid of what they were saying, but as if they could not help saying it.

"She liked the bird," said Martha Hale, low and slowly. "She was going to bury it in that pretty box."

"When I was a girl," said Mrs. Peters, under her breath, "my kitten—there was a boy took a hatchet, and before my eyes—before I could get there—" She covered her face an instant. "If they hadn't held me back I would have"—she caught herself, looked upstairs where footsteps were heard, and finished weakly—"hurt him."

Then they sat without speaking or moving.

"I wonder how it would seem," Mrs. Hale at last began, as if feeling her way over strange ground—"never to have had any children around?" Her eyes made a slow sweep of the kitchen, as if seeing what that kitchen had meant through all the years. "No, Wright wouldn't like the bird," she said after that—"a thing that sang. She used to sing. He killed that too." Her voice tightened.

Mrs. Peters moved uneasily.

"Of course we don't know who killed the bird."

"I knew John Wright," was Mrs. Hale's answer.

"It was an awful thing was done in this house that night, Mrs. Hale," said the sheriff's wife. "Killing a man while he slept—slipping a thing round his neck that choked the life out of him."

Mrs. Hale's hand went out to the bird cage.

"His neck. Choked the life out of him."

"We don't *know* who killed him," whispered Mrs. Peters wildly. "We don't *know*."

Mrs. Hale had not moved. "If there had been years and years of—nothing, then a bird to sing to you, it would be awful—still—after the bird was still."

It was as if something within her not herself had spoken, and it found in Mrs. Peters something she did not know as herself.

"I know what stillness is," she said, in a queer, monotonous voice. "When we homesteaded in Dakota, and my first baby died—after he was two years old—and me with no other then—"

Mrs. Hale stirred.

"How soon do you suppose they'll be through looking for the evidence?"

"I know what stillness is," repeated Mrs. Peters, in just that same way.

Then she too pulled back. "The law has got to punish crime, Mrs. Hale,"
she said in her tight little way.

"I wish you'd seen Minnie Foster," was the answer, "when she wore
a white dress with blue ribbons, and stood up there in the choir and
sang."

The picture of that girl, the fact that she had lived neighbor to that
girl for twenty years, and had let her die for lack of life, was suddenly
more than she could bear.

"Oh, I *wish* I'd come over here once in a while!" she cried. "That was
a crime! That was a crime! Who's going to punish that?"

"We mustn't take on," said Mrs. Peters, with a frightened look toward
the stairs.

"I might 'a' *known* she needed help! I tell you, it's *queer*, Mrs. Peters.
We live close together, and we live far apart. We all go through the same
things—it's all just a different kind of the same thing! If it weren't—
why do you and I *understand?* Why do we *know*—what we know this
minute?"

She dashed her hand across her eyes. Then, seeing the jar of fruit on
the table, she reached for it and choked out:

"If I was you I wouldn't *tell* her her fruit was gone! Tell her it *ain't.*
Tell her it's all right—all of it. Here—take this in to prove it to her! She
—she may never know whether it was broke or not."

She turned away.

Mrs. Peters reached out for the bottle of fruit as if she were glad to
take it—as if touching a familiar thing, having something to do, could
keep her from something else. She got up, looked about for something
to wrap the fruit in, took a petticoat from the pile of clothes she had
brought from the front room, and nervously started winding that round
the bottle.

"My!" she began, in a high, false voice, "it's a good thing the men
couldn't hear us! Getting all stirred up over a little thing like a—dead
canary." She hurried over that. "As if that could have anything to do
with—with— My, wouldn't they *laugh?*"

Footsteps were heard on the stairs.

"Maybe they would," muttered Mrs. Hale—"maybe they wouldn't."

"No, Peters," said the county attorney incisively; "it's all perfectly
clear, except the reason for doing it. But you know juries when it comes
to women. If there was some definite thing—something to show. Something to make a story about. A thing that would connect up with this
clumsy way of doing it."

In a covert way Mrs. Hale looked at Mrs. Peters. Mrs. Peters was
looking at her. Quickly they looked away from each other. The outer
door opened and Mr. Hale came in.

"I've got the team round now," he said. "Pretty cold out there."

"I'm going to stay here awhile by myself," the county attorney suddenly announced. "You can send Frank out for me, can't you?" he asked the sheriff. "I want to go over everything. I'm not satisfied we can't do better."

Again, for one brief moment, the two women's eyes found one another.

The sheriff came up to the table.

"Did you want to see what Mrs. Peters was going to take in?"

The county attorney picked up the apron. He laughed.

"Oh, I guess they're not very dangerous things the ladies have picked out."

Mrs. Hale's hand was on the sewing basket in which the box was concealed. She felt that she ought to take her hand off the basket. She did not seem able to. He picked up one of the quilt blocks which she had piled on to cover the box. Her eyes felt like fire. She had a feeling that if he took up the basket she would snatch it from him.

But he did not take it up. With another little laugh, he turned away, saying:

"No; Mrs. Peters doesn't need supervising. For that matter, a sheriff's wife is married to the law. Ever think of it that way, Mrs. Peters?"

Mrs. Peters was standing beside the table. Mrs. Hale shot a look up at her; but she could not see her face. Mrs. Peters had turned away. When she spoke, her voice was muffled.

"Not—just that way," she said.

"Married to the law!" chuckled Mrs. Peters' husband. He moved toward the door into the front room, and said to the county attorney:

"I just want you to come in here a minute, George. We ought to take a look at these windows."

"Oh—windows," said the county attorney scoffingly.

"We'll be right out, Mr. Hale," said the sheriff to the farmer, who was still waiting by the door.

Hale went to look after the horses. The sheriff followed the county attorney into the other room. Again—for one final moment—the two women were alone in that kitchen.

Martha Hale sprang up, her hands tight together, looking at that other woman, with whom it rested. At first she could not see her eyes, for the sheriff's wife had not turned back since she turned away at that suggestion of being married to the law. But now Mrs. Hale made her turn back. Her eyes made her turn back. Slowly, unwillingly, Mrs. Peters turned her head until her eyes met the eyes of the other woman. There was a moment when they held each other in a steady, burning look in which there was no evasion nor flinching. Then Martha Hale's eyes pointed the way to the basket in which was hidden the thing that would make certain the conviction of the other woman—that woman who was not there and yet who had been there with them all through that hour.

For a moment Mrs. Peters did not move. And then she did it. With a rush forward, she threw back the quilt pieces, got the box, tried to put it in her handbag. It was too big. Desperately she opened it, started to take the bird out. But there she broke—she could not touch the bird. She stood there helpless, foolish.

There was the sound of a knob turning in the inner door. Martha Hale snatched the box from the sheriff's wife, and got it in the pocket of her big coat just as the sheriff and the county attorney came back into the kitchen.

"Well, Henry," said the county attorney facetiously, "at least we found out that she was not going to quilt it. She was going to—what is it you call it, ladies?"

Mrs. Hale's hand was against the pocket of her coat.

"We call it—knot it, Mr. Henderson."

47

The Afternoon of a Faun

BY EDNA FERBER

THOUGH he rarely heeded its summons—cagy boy that he was—the telephone rang oftenest for Nick. Because of the many native noises of the place, the telephone had a special bell that was a combination buzz and ring. It sounded above the roar of outgoing cars, the splash of the hose, the sputter and hum of the electric battery in the rear. Nick heard it, unheeding. A voice—Smitty's or Mike's or Elmer's—answering its call. Then, echoing through the gray, vaulted spaces of the big garage: "Nick! Oh, Ni-ick!"

From the other side of the great cement-floored enclosure, or in muffled tones from beneath a car: "Whatcha want?"

"Dame on the wire."

"I ain't in."

The obliging voice again, dutifully repeating the message: "He ain't in. . . . Well, it's hard to say. He might be in in a couple hours and then again he might not be back till late. I guess he's went to Hammond on a job——" (Warming to his task now.) "Say, won't I do? . . . Who's fresh! Aw, say, *lady!*"

You'd think, after repeated rebuffs of this sort, she could not possibly be so lacking in decent pride as to leave her name for Smitty or Mike or Elmer to bandy about. But she invariably did, baffled by Nick's elusiveness. She was likely to be any one of a number. Miss Bauers phoned: Will you tell him, please? (A nasal voice, and haughty, with the hauteur that seeks to conceal secret fright.) Tell him it's important. Miss Ahearn phoned: Will you tell him, please? Just say Miss Ahearn. A-h-e-a-r-n. Miss Olson: Just Gertie. But oftenest Miss Bauers.

Cupid's messenger, wearing grease-grimed overalls and the fatuous grin of the dalliant male, would transmit his communication to the uneager Nick.

" 'S wonder you wouldn't answer the phone onct yourself. Says you was to call Miss Bauers any time you come in between one and six at Hyde Park—wait a min't'—yeh—Hyde Park 6079, and any time after six at——"

"Wha'd she want?"

"Well, how the hell should *I* know! Says call Miss Bauers any time between one and six at Hyde Park 6——"

"Swell chanst. *Swell* chanst!"

Which explains why the calls came oftenest for Nick. He was so indifferent to them. You pictured the patient and persistent Miss Bauers, or the oxlike Miss Olson, or Miss Ahearn, or just Gertie hovering within hearing distance of the telephone listening, listening—while one o'clock deepened to six—for the call that never came; plucking up fresh courage at six until six o'clock dragged on to bedtime. When next they met: "I bet you was there all the time. Pity you wouldn't answer a call when a person leaves their name. You could of give me a ring. I bet you was there all the time."

"Well, maybe I was."

Bewildered, she tried to retaliate with the boomerang of vituperation.

How could she know? How could she know that this slim, slick young garage mechanic was a woodland creature in disguise—a satyr in store clothes—a wild thing who perversely preferred to do his own pursuing? How could Miss Bauers know—she who cashiered in the Green Front Grocery and Market on Fifty-third Street? Or Miss Olson, at the Rialto ticket window? Or the Celtic, emotional Miss Ahearn, the manicure? Or Gertie the goof? They knew nothing of mythology; of pointed ears and pug noses and goat's feet. Nick's ears, to their fond gaze, presented an honest red surface protruding from either side of his head. His feet, in tan laced shoes, were ordinary feet, a little more than ordinarily expert, perhaps, in the convolutions of the dance at Englewood Masonic Hall, which is part of Chicago's vast South Side. No; a faun, to Miss Bauers, Miss Olson, Miss Ahearn, and just Gertie, was one of those things in the Lincoln Park Zoo.

Perhaps, sometimes, they realized, vaguely, that Nick was different. When, for example, they tried—and failed—to picture him looking interestedly at one of those three-piece bedroom sets glistening like pulled taffy in the window of the instalment furniture store, while they, shy yet proprietary, clung to his arm and eyed the price ticket. Now $98.50. You couldn't see Nick interested in bedroom sets, in price tickets, in any of those settled, fixed, everyday things. He was fluid, evasive, like quicksilver, though they did not put it thus.

Miss Bauers, goaded to revolt, would say pettishly: "You're like a mosquito, that's what. Person never knows from one minute to the other where you're at."

"Yeh," Nick would retort. "When you know where a mosquito's at, what do you do to him? Plenty. I ain't looking to be squashed."

Miss Ahearn, whose public position (the Hygienic Barber Shop. Gent's manicure, 50c.) offered unlimited social opportunities, would assume a gay indifference. "They's plenty boys begging to take me out every hour in the day. Swell lads, too. I ain't waiting round for any greasy mechanic like you. Don't think it. Say, lookit your nails! They'd queer you with me, let alone what else all is wrong with you."

In answer Nick would put one hand—one broad, brown, steel-strong hand with its broken discolored nails—on Miss Ahearn's arm, in its flimsy georgette sleeve. Miss Ahearn's eyelids would flutter and close, and a little shiver would run with icy-hot feet all over Miss Ahearn.

Nick was like that.

Nick's real name wasn't Nick at all—or scarcely at all. His last name was Nicholas, and his parents, long before they became his parents, traced their origin to some obscure Czechoslovakian province—long before we became so glib with our Czechoslovakia. His first name was Dewey, knowing which you automatically know the date of his birth. It was a patriotic but unfortunate choice on the part of his parents. The name did not fit him; was too mealy; not debonair enough. Nick. Nicky in tenderer moments (Miss Bauers, Miss Olson, Miss Ahearn, just Gertie, et al.).

His method with women was firm and somewhat stern, but never brutal. He never waited for them if they were late. Any girl who assumed that her value was enhanced in direct proportion to her tardiness in keeping an engagement with Nick found herself standing disconsolate on the corner of Fifty-third and Lake trying to look as if she were merely waiting for the Lake Park car and not peering wistfully up and down the street in search of a slim, graceful, hurrying figure that never came.

It is difficult to convey in words the charm that Nick possessed. Seeing him, you beheld merely a medium-sized young mechanic in reasonably grimed garage clothes when working; and in tight pants, tight coat, silk shirt, long-visored green cap when at leisure. A rather pallid skin due to the nature of his work. Large deft hands, a good deal like the hands of a surgeon, square, blunt-fingered, spatulate. Indeed, as you saw him at work, a wire-netted electric bulb held in one hand, the other plunged deep into the vitals of the car on which he was engaged, you thought of a surgeon performing a major operation. He wore one of those round skullcaps characteristic of his craft (the brimless crown of an old felt hat). He would deftly remove the transmission case and plunge his hand deep into the car's guts, feeling expertly about with his engine-wise fingers as a surgeon feels for liver, stomach, gall bladder, intestines, appendix. When he brought up his hands, all dripping with grease (which is the warm blood of the car), he invariably had put his finger on the sore spot.

All this, of course, could not serve to endear him to the girls. On the contrary, you would have thought that his hands alone, from which he could never quite free the grease and grit, would have caused some feeling of repugnance among the lily-fingered. But they, somehow, seemed always to be finding an excuse to touch him: his tie, his hair, his coat sleeve. They seemed even to derive a vicarious thrill from holding his hat or cap when on an outing. They brushed imaginary bits of lint from his coat lapel. They tried on his seal ring, crying: "Oo, lookit, how big it is for me, even my thumb!" He called this "pawing a guy over"; and the lint ladies he designated as "thread pickers."

No; it can't be classified, this powerful draw he had for them. His conversation furnished no clue. It was commonplace conversation, limited, even dull. When astonished, or impressed, or horrified, or amused, he said: "Ken yuh feature that!" When emphatic or confirmatory, he said: "You *tell* 'em!"

It wasn't his car and the opportunities it furnished for drives, both country and city. That motley piece of mechanism represented such an assemblage of unrelated parts as could only have been made to coordinate under Nick's expert guidance. It was out of commission more than half the time, and could never be relied upon to furnish a holiday. Both Miss Bauers and Miss Ahearn had twelve-cylinder opportunities that should have rendered them forever unfit for travel in Nick's one-lung vehicle of locomotion.

It wasn't money. Though he was generous enough with what he had, Nick couldn't be generous with what he hadn't. And his wage at the garage was $40 a week. Miss Ahearn's silk stockings cost $4.50.

His unconcern should have infuriated them, but it served to pique. He wasn't actually as unconcerned as he appeared, but he had early learned that effort in their direction was unnecessary. Nick had little imagination; a gorgeous selfishness; a tolerantly contemptuous liking for the sex. Naturally, however, his attitude toward them had been somewhat embittered by being obliged to watch their method of driving a car in and out of the Ideal Garage doorway. His own manipulation of the wheel was nothing short of wizardry.

He played the harmonica.

Each Thursday afternoon was Nick's half day off. From twelve until seven-thirty he was free to range the bosky highways of Chicago. When his car—he called it "the bus"—was agreeable, he went awheel in search of amusement. The bus being indisposed, he went afoot. He rarely made plans in advance; usually was accompanied by some successful telephonee. He rather liked to have a silken skirt beside him fluttering and flirting in the breeze as he broke the speed regulations.

On this Thursday afternoon in July he had timed his morning job to a miraculous nicety so that at the stroke of twelve his workaday garments dropped from him magically, as though he were a male (and reversed) Cinderella. There was a wash room and a rough sort of sleeping room containing two cots situated in the second story of the Ideal Garage. Here Nick shed the loose garments of labor for the fashionably tight habiliments of leisure. Private chauffeurs whose employers housed their cars in the Ideal Garage used this nook for a lounge and smoker. Smitty, Mike, Elmer, and Nick snatched stolen siestas there in the rare absences of the manager. Sometimes Nick spent the night there when forced to work overtime. His home life, at best, was a sketchy affair. Here chauffeurs, mechanics, washers lolled at ease exchanging soft-spoken gossip, motor chat, speculation, comment, and occasional verbal obscenity. Each possessed a formidable knowledge of that neighborhood section of Chicago known as Hyde Park. This knowledge was not confined to car costs and such impersonal items, but included meals, scandals, relationships, finances, love affairs, quarrels, peccadillos. Here Nick often played his harmonica, his lips sweeping the metal length of it in throbbing rendition of such sure-fire sentimentality as The Long, Long Trail, or Mammy, while the others talked, joked, kept time with tapping feet or wagging heads.

Today the hot little room was empty except for Nick, shaving before the cracked mirror on the wall, and old Elmer, reading a scrap of yesterday's newspaper as he lounged his noon hour away. Old Elmer was thirty-seven, and Nicky regarded him as an octogenarian. Also, old Elmer's conversation bored Nick to the point of almost sullen resentment. Old Elmer was a family man. His talk was all of his family—the wife, the kids, the flat. A garrulous person, lank, pasty, dish-faced, and amiable. His half day off was invariably spent tinkering about the stuffy little flat—painting, nailing up shelves, mending a broken window shade, puttying a window, playing with his pasty little boy, aged sixteen months, and his pasty little girl, aged three years. Next day he regaled his fellow workers with elaborate recitals of his holiday hours.

"Believe me, that kid's a caution. Sixteen months old, and what does he do yesterday? He unfastens the ketch on the back-porch gate. We got a gate on the back porch, see." (This frequent "see" which interlarded Elmer's verbiage was not used in an interrogatory way, but as a period, and by way of emphasis. His voice did not take the rising inflection as he uttered it.) "What does he do, he opens it. I come home, and the wife says to me: 'Say, you better get busy and fix a new ketch on that gate to the back porch. Little Elmer, first thing I know, he'd got it open today and was crawling out almost.' Say, can you beat that for a kid sixteen months——"

Nick had finished shaving, had donned his clean white soft shirt. His soft collar fitted to a miracle about his strong throat. Nick's sartorial effects were a triumph—on forty a week. "Say, can't you talk about nothing but that kid of yours? I bet he's a bum specimen at that. Runt, like his pa."

Elmer flung down his newspaper in honest indignation as Nick had wickedly meant he should. "Is that so! Why, we was wrastling round— me and him, see—last night on the floor, and what does he do, he raises his mitt and hands me a wallop in the stomick it like to knock the wind out of me. That's all. Sixteen months——"

"Yeh. I suppose this time next year he'll be boxing for money."

Elmer resumed his paper. "What do *you* know." His tone mingled pity with contempt.

Nick took a last critical survey of the cracked mirror's reflection and found it good. "Nothing, only this: you make me sick with your kids and your missus and your place. Say, don't you never have no fun?"

"Fun! Why, say, last Sunday we was out to the beach, and the kid swum out first thing you know——"

"Oh, shut up!" He was dressed now. He slapped his pockets. Harmonica. Cigarettes. Matches. Money. He was off, his long-visored cloth cap pulled jauntily over his eyes.

Elmer, bearing no rancor, flung a last idle query: "Where you going?"

"How should I know? Just bumming around. Bus is outa commission, and I'm outa luck."

He clattered down the stairs, whistling.

Next door for a shine at the Greek bootblack's. Enthroned on the dais, a minion at his feet, he was momentarily monarchial. How's the boy? Good? Same here. Down, his brief reign ended. Out into the bright noon-day glare of Fifty-third Street.

A fried-egg sandwich. Two blocks down and into the white-tiled lunchroom. He took his place in the row perched on stools in front of the white slab, his feet on the railing, his elbows on the counter. Four white-aproned vestals with blotchy skins performed rites over the steaming nickel urns, slid dishes deftly along the slick surface of the white slab, mopped up moisture with a sly gray rag. No nonsense about them. This was the rush hour. Hungry men from the shops and offices and garages of the district were bent on food (not badinage). They ate silently, making a dull business of it. Coffee? What kinda pie do you want? No fooling here. "Hello, Jessie."

As she mopped the slab in front of him you noticed a slight softening of her features, intent so grimly on her task. "What's yours?"

"Bacon-and-egg sandwich. Glass of milk. Piece of pie. Blueberry."

Ordinarily she would not have bothered. But with him: "The blueberry ain't so good today, I noticed. Try the peach?"

"All right." He looked at her. She smiled. Incredibly, the dishes ordered seemed to leap out at her from nowhere. She crashed them down on the glazed white surface in front of him. The bacon-and-egg sandwich was served open-faced, an elaborate confection. Two slices of white bread, side by side. On one reposed a fried egg, hard, golden, delectable, indigestible. On the other three crisp curls of bacon. The ordinary order held two curls only. A dish so rich in calories as to make it food sufficient for a day. Jessie knew nothing of calories, nor did Nick. She placed a double order of butter before him—two yellow pats, moisture-beaded. As she scooped up his milk from the can you saw that the glass was but three-quarters filled. From a deep crock she ladled a smaller scoop and filled the glass to the top. The deep crock held cream. Nick glanced up at her again. Again Jessie smiled. A plain damsel, Jessie, and capable. She went on about her business. What's yours? Coffee with? White or rye? No nonsense about her. And yet: "Pie all right?"

"Yeh. It's good."

She actually blushed.

He finished, swung himself off the stool, nodded to Jessie. She stacked his dishes with one lean, capable hand, mopped the slab with the other, but as she made for the kitchen she flung a glance at him over her shoulder.

"Day off?"

"Yeh."

"Some folks has all the luck."

He grinned. His teeth were strong and white and even. He walked toward the door with his light quick step, paused for a toothpick as he paid his check, was out again into the July sunlight. Her face became dull again.

Well, not one o'clock. Guessed he'd shoot a little pool. He dropped into Moriarty's cigar store. It was called a cigar store because it dealt in magazines, newspapers, soft drinks, golf balls, cigarettes, pool, billiards, chocolates, chewing gum, and cigars. In the rear of the store were four green-topped tables, three for pool and one for billiards. He hung about aimlessly, watching the game at the one occupied table. The players were slim young men like himself, their clothes replicas of his own, their faces lean and somewhat hard. Two of them dropped out. Nick took a cue from the rack, shed his tight coat. They played under a glaring electric light in the heat of the day, yet they seemed cool, aloof, immune from bodily discomfort. It was a strangely silent game and as mirthless as that of the elfin bowlers in Rip Van Winkle. The slim-waisted shirted figures bent plastically over the table in the graceful postures of the game. You heard only the click of the balls, an occasional low-voiced exclamation. A solemn crew, and unemotional.

Now and then: "What's all the shootin' fur?"

"In she goes."

Nick, winner, tired of it in less than an hour. He bought a bottle of some acidulous drink just off the ice and refreshed himself with it, drinking from the bottle's mouth. He was vaguely restless, dissatisfied. Out again into the glare of two o'clock Fifty-third Street. He strolled up a block toward Lake Park Avenue. It was hot. He wished the bus wasn't sick. Might go in swimming, though. He considered this idly. Hurried steps behind him. A familiar perfume wafted to his senses. A voice nasal yet cooing. Miss Bauers. Miss Bauers on pleasure bent, palpably, being attired in the briefest of silks, white-strapped slippers, white silk stockings, scarlet hat. The Green Front Grocery and Market closed for a half day each Thursday afternoon during July and August. Nicky had not availed himself of the knowledge.

"Well, if it ain't Nicky! I just seen you come out of Moriarty's as I was passing." (She had seen him go in an hour before and had waited a patient hour in the drug store across the street.) "What you doing around loose this hour the day, anyway?"

"I'm off 'safternoon."

"Are yuh? So'm I." Nicky said nothing. Miss Bauers shifted from one plump silken leg to the other. "What you doing?"

"Oh, nothing much."

"So'm I. Let's do it together." Miss Bauers employed the direct method.

"Well," said Nick, vaguely. He didn't object particularly. And yet he was conscious of some formless program forming mistily in his mind —a program that did not include the berouged, bepowdered, plump, and silken Miss Bauers.

"I phoned you this morning, Nicky. Twice."

"Yeh?"

"They said you wasn't in."

"Yeh?"

A hard young woman, Miss Bauers, yet simple: powerfully drawn toward this magnetic and careless boy; powerless to forge chains strong enough to hold him. "Well, how about Riverview? I ain't been this summer."

"Oh, that's so darn far. Take all day getting there, pretty near."

"Not driving, it wouldn't."

"I ain't got the bus. Busted."

His apathy was getting on her nerves. "How about a movie, then?" Her feet hurt. It was hot.

His glance went up the street toward the Harper, down the street toward the Hyde Park. The sign above the Harper offered Mother o' Mine. The lettering above the Hyde Park announced Love's Sacrifice.

"Gawd, no," he made decisive answer.

Miss Bauers's frazzled nerves snapped. "You make me sick! Standing there. Nothing don't suit you. Say, I ain't so crazy to go round with you. Cheap guy! Prob'ly you'd like to go over to Wooded Island or something, in Jackson Park, and set on the grass and feed the squirrels. That'd be a treat for me, that would." She laughed a high, scornful tear-near laugh.

"Why—say——" Nick stared at her, and yet she felt he did not see her. A sudden peace came into his face—the peace of a longing fulfilled. He turned his head. A Lake Park Avenue street car was roaring its way toward them. He took a step toward the roadway. "I got to be going."

Fear flashed its flame into Miss Bauers's pale blue eyes. "Going! How do you mean, going? Going where?"

"I got to be going." The car had stopped opposite them. His young face was stern, implacable. Miss Bauers knew she was beaten, but she clung to hope tenaciously, piteously. "I got to see a party, see?"

"You never said anything about it in the first place. Pity you wouldn't say so in the first place. Who you got to see, anyway?" She knew it was useless to ask. She knew she was beating her fists against a stone wall, but she must needs ask notwithstanding: "Who you got to see?"

"I got to see a party. I forgot." He made the car step in two long strides; had swung himself up. "So long!" The car door slammed after him. Miss Bauers, in her unavailing silks, stood disconsolate on the hot street corner.

He swayed on the car platform until Sixty-third Street was reached. There he alighted and stood a moment at the curb surveying idly the populous corner. He purchased a paper bag of hot peanuts from a vender's glittering scarlet and nickel stand, and crossed the street into the pathway that led to Jackson Park, munching as he went. In an open space reserved for games some boys were playing baseball with much hoarse hooting and frenzied action. He drew near to watch. The ball, misdirected, sailed suddenly toward him. He ran backward at its swift approach, leaped high, caught it, and with a long curving swing, so easy as to appear almost effortless, sent it hurtling back. The lad on the pitcher's mound made as if to catch it, changed his mind, dodged, started after it.

The boy at bat called to Nick: "Heh, you! Wanna come on and pitch?"

Nick shook his head and went on.

He wandered leisurely along the gravel path that led to the park golf shelter. The wide porch was crowded with golfers and idlers. A four-some was teed up at the first tee. Nick leaned against a porch pillar waiting for them to drive. That old boy had pretty good practise swing. . . . Stiff, though. . . . Lookit that dame. Je's! I bet she takes fifteen shots before she ever gets on to the green. . . . There, that kid had pretty good drive. Must of been hundred and fifty, anyway. Pretty good for a kid.

Nick, in the course of his kaleidoscopic career, had been a caddie at thirteen in torn shirt and flapping knickers. He had played the smooth, expert, scornful game of the caddie with a natural swing from the lithe waist and a follow-through that was the envy of the muscle-bound men who watched him. He hadn't played in years. The game no longer interested him. He entered the shelter lunchroom. The counters were lined with lean, brown, hungry men and lean, brown, hungry women. They were eating incredible dishes considering that the hour was 3 P. M. and the day a hot one. Corned-beef hash with a poached egg on top; wieners and potato salad; meat pies; hot roast beef sandwiches; steaming cups of coffee in thick white ware; watermelon. Nick slid a leg over a stool as he had done earlier in the afternoon. Here, too, the Hebes were of stern stuff, as they needs must be to serve these ravenous hordes of club swingers who swarmed upon them from dawn to dusk. Their task it was to wait upon the golfing male, which is man at his simplest—reduced to the least common denominator and shorn of all attraction for the female eye and heart. They represented merely hungry mouths, weary muscles, reaching fists. The waitresses served them as a capable attendant serves another woman's child—efficiently and without emotion.

"Blueberry pie à la mode," said Nick—"with strawberry ice cream."

Inured as she was to the horrors of gastronomic miscegenation, the waitress—an old girl—recoiled at this.

"Say, I don't think you'd like that. They don't mix so very good. Why don't you try the peach pie instead with the strawberry ice cream —if you want strawberry?" He looked so young and cool and fresh.

"Blueberry," repeated Nick sternly, and looked her in the eye. The old waitress laughed a little and was surprised to find herself laughing. " 'S for you to say." She brought him the monstrous mixture, and he devoured it to the last chromatic crumb.

"Nothing the matter with that," he remarked as she passed, dish-laden.

She laughed again tolerantly, almost tenderly. "Good thing you're young." Her busy glance lingered a brief moment on his face. He sauntered out.

Now he took the path to the right of the shelter, crossed the road, struck the path again, came to a rustic bridge that humped high in the middle, spanning a cool green stream, willow-bordered. The cool green stream was an emerald chain that threaded its way in a complete circlet about the sylvan spot known as Wooded Island, relic of World's Fair days.

The little island lay, like a thing under enchantment, silent, fragrant, golden, green, exquisite. Squirrels and blackbirds, rabbits and pigeons mingled in Æsopian accord. The air was warm and still, held by the encircling trees and shrubbery. There was not a soul to be seen. At the far north end the two Japanese model houses, survivors of the exposition, gleamed white among the trees.

Nick stood a moment. His eyelids closed, languorously. He stretched his arms out and up deliciously, bringing his stomach in and his chest out. He took off his cap and stuffed it into his pocket. He strolled across the thick cool nap of the grass, deserting the pebble path. At the west edge of the island a sign said: "No One Allowed in the Shrubbery." Ignoring it, Nick parted the branches, stopped and crept, reached the bank that sloped down to the cool green stream, took off his coat, and lay relaxed upon the ground. Above him the tree branches made a pattern against the sky. Little ripples lipped the shore. Scampering velvet-footed things, feathered things, winged things made pleasant stir among the leaves. Nick slept.

He awoke in half an hour refreshed. He lay there, thinking of nothing—a charming gift. He found a stray peanut in his pocket and fed it to a friendly squirrel. His hand encountered the cool metal of his harmonica. He drew out the instrument, placed his coat, folded, under his head, crossed his knees, one leg swinging idly, and began to play rapturously. He was perfectly happy. He played Gimme Love, whose jazz measures are stolen from Mendelssohn's Spring Song. He did not know this. The leaves rustled. He did not turn his head.

"Hello, Pan!" said a voice. A girl came down the slope and seated herself beside him. She was not smiling.

Nick removed the harmonica from his lips and wiped his mouth with the back of his hand. "Hello who?"

"Hello, Pan."

"Wrong number, lady," Nick said, and again applied his lips to the mouth organ. The girl laughed then, throwing back her head. Her throat was long and slim and brown. She clasped her knees with her arms and looked at Nick amusedly. Nick thought she was a kind of homely little thing.

"Pan," she explained, "was a pagan deity. He played pipes in the woods."

"'S all right with me," Nick ventured, bewildered but amiable. He wished she'd go away. But she didn't. She began to take off her shoes and stockings. She went down to the water's edge, then, and paddled her feet. Nick sat up, outraged. "Say, you can't do that."

She glanced back at him over her shoulder. "Oh, yes, I can. It's so hot." She wriggled her toes ecstatically.

The leaves rustled again, briskly, unmistakably this time. A heavy tread. A rough voice. "Say, looka here! Get out of there, you! What the——" A policeman, red-faced, wroth. "You can't do that! Get outa here!"

It was like a movie, Nick thought.

The girl turned her head. "Oh, now, Mr. Elwood," she said.

"Oh, it's you, miss," said the policeman. You would not have believed it was the same policeman. He even giggled. "Thought you was away."

"I was. In fact, I am, really. I just got sick of it and ran away for a day. Drove. Alone. The family'll be wild."

"All the way?" said the policeman, incredulously. "Say, I thought that looked like your car standing out there by the road; but I says no, she ain't in town." He looked sharply at Nick, whose face had an Indian composure, though his feelings were mixed. "Who's this?"

"He's a friend of mine. His name's Pan." She was drying her feet with an inadequate rose-colored handkerchief. She crept crabwise up the bank, and put on her stockings and slippers.

"Why'n't you come out and set on a bench?" suggested the policeman, worriedly.

The girl shook her head. "In Arcadia we don't sit on benches. I should think you'd know that. Go on away, there's a dear. I want to talk to this —to Pan."

He persisted. "What'd your pa say, I'd like to know!" The girl shrugged her shoulders. Nick made as though to rise. He was worried. A nut, that's what. She pressed him down with a hard brown hand.

"Now it's all right. He's going. Old Fuss!" The policeman stood a brief moment longer. Then the foliage rustled again. He was gone. The girl sighed, happily. "Play that thing some more, will you? You're a wiz at it, aren't you?"

"I'm pretty good," said Nick, modestly. Then the outrageousness of her conduct struck him afresh. "Say, who're you, anyway?"

"My name's Berry—short for Bernice. . . . What's yours, Pan?"

"Nick—that is—Nick."

"Ugh, terrible! I'll stick to Pan. What d'you do when you're not Panning?" Then, at the bewilderment in his face: "What's your job?"

"I work in the Ideal Garage. Say, you're pretty nosey, ain't you?"

"Yes, pretty. . . . That accounts for your nails, h'm?" She looked at her own brown paws. " 'Bout as bad as mine. I drove one hundred and fifty miles today."

"Ya-as, you did!"

"I did! Started at six. And I'll probably drive back tonight."

"You're crazy!"

"I know it," she agreed, "and it's wonderful. . . . Can you play the Tommy Toddle?"

"Yeh. It's kind of hard, though, where the runs are. I don't get the runs so very good." He played it. She kept time with head and feet. When he had finished and wiped his lips:

"Elegant!" She took the harmonica from him, wiped it brazenly on the much-abused, rose-colored handkerchief and began to play, her cheeks puffed out, her eyes round with effort. She played the Tommy Toddle, and her runs were perfect. Nick's chagrin was swallowed by his admiration and envy.

"Say, kid, you got more wind than a factory whistle. Who learned you to play?"

She struck her chest with a hard brown fist. "Tennis. . . . Tim taught me."

"Who's Tim?"

"The—a chauffeur."

Nick leaned closer. "Say, do you ever go to the dances at Englewood Masonic Hall?"

"I never have."

" 'Jah like to go some time?"

"I'd love it." She grinned up at him, her teeth flashing white in her brown face.

"It's swell here," he said, dreamily. "Like the woods?"

"Yes."

"Winter, when it's cold and dirty, I think about how it's here summers. It's like you could take it out of your head and look at it whenever you wanted to."

"Endymion."

"Huh?"

"A man said practically the same thing the other day. Name of Keats."

"Yeh?"

"He said: 'A thing of beauty is a joy forever.' "

"That's one way putting it," he agreed, graciously.

Unsmilingly she reached over with one slim forefinger, as if compelled, and touched the blond hairs on Nick's wrist. Just touched them. Nick remained motionless. The girl shivered a little, deliciously. She glanced at him shyly. Her lips were provocative. Thoughtlessly, blindly, Nick suddenly flung an arm about her, kissed her. He kissed her as he had never kissed Miss Bauers—as he had never kissed Miss Ahearn, Miss Olson, or just Gertie. The girl did not scream, or push him away, or slap him, or protest, or giggle as would have the above-mentioned young ladies. She sat breathing rather fast, a tinge of scarlet showing beneath the tan.

"Well, Pan," she said, low-voiced, "you're running true to form, anyway." She eyed him appraisingly. "Your appeal is in your virility, I suppose. Yes."

"My what?"

She rose. "I've got to go."

Panic seized him. "Say, don't drive back tonight, huh? Wherever it is you've got to go. You ain't driving back tonight?"

She made no answer; parted the bushes, was out on the gravel path in the sunlight, a slim, short-skirted, almost childish figure. He followed. They crossed the bridge, left the island, reached the roadway almost in silence. At the side of the road was a roadster. Its hood was the kind that conceals power. Its lamps were two giant eyes rimmed in precious metal. Its line spelled strength. Its body was foreign. Nick's engine-wise eyes saw these things at a glance.

"That your car?"

"Yes."

"Gosh!"

She unlocked it, threw in the clutch, shifted, moved. "Say!" was wrung from Nick helplessly. She waved at him. "Good-by, Pan." He stared, stricken. She was off swiftly, silently; flashed around a corner; was hidden by the trees and shrubs.

He stood a moment. He felt bereaved, cheated. Then a little wave of exaltation shook him. He wanted to talk to someone. "Gosh!" he said again. He glanced at his wrist. Five-thirty. He guessed he'd go home. He guessed he'd go home and get one of Ma's dinners. One of Ma's dinners and talk to Ma. The Sixty-third Street car. He could make it and back in plenty time.

Nick lived in that section of Chicago known as Englewood, which is not so sylvan as it sounds, but appropriate enough for a faun. Not only that; he lived in S. Green Street, Englewood. S. Green Street, near Seventieth, is almost rural with its great elms and poplars, its frame cottages, its back gardens. A neighborhood of thrifty, foreign-born fathers and mothers, many children, tree-lined streets badly paved. Nick turned in at a two-story brown frame cottage. He went around to the back. Ma was in the kitchen.

Nick's presence at the evening meal was an uncertain thing. Sometimes he did not eat at home for a week, excepting only his hurried early breakfast. He rarely spent an evening at home, and when he did used the opportunity for making up lost sleep. Pa never got home from work until after six. Nick liked his dinner early and hot. On his rare visits his mother welcomed him like one of the Gracchi. Mother and son understood each other wordlessly, having much in common. You would not have thought it of her (forty-six bust, forty waist, measureless hips), but Ma was a nymph at heart. Hence Nick.

"Hello, Ma!" She was slamming expertly about the kitchen.

"Hello, yourself," said Ma. Ma had a line of slang gleaned from her numerous brood. It fell strangely from her lips. Ma had never quite lost a tinge of foreign accent, though she had come to America when a girl. A hearty, zestful woman, savoring life with gusto, undiminished by child-bearing and hard work. "Eating home, Dewey?" She alone used his given name.

"Yeh, but I gotta be back by seven-thirty. Got anything ready?"

"Dinner ain't, but I'll get you something. Plenty. Platter ham and eggs and a quick fry. Cherry cobbler's done. I'll fix you some." (Cherry cobbler is shortcake with a soul.)

He ate enormously at the kitchen table, she hovering over him.

"What's the news, Dewey?"

"Ain't none." He ate in silence. Then: "How old was you when you married Pa?"

"Me? Say, I wasn't no more'n a kid. I gotta laugh when I think of it."

"What was Pa earning?"

She laughed a great hearty laugh, dipping a piece of bread sociably in the ham fat on the platter as she stood by the table, just to bear him company.

"Say, earn! If he'd of earned what you was earning now, we'd of thought we was millionaires. Time Etty was born he was pulling down thirteen a week, and we saved on it." She looked at him suddenly, sharply. "Why?"

"Oh, I was just wondering."

"Look what good money he's getting now! If I was you, I wouldn't stick around no old garage for what they give you. You could get a good job in the works with Pa; first thing you know you'd be pulling down big money. You're smart like that with engines. . . . Takes a lot of money nowadays for feller to get married."

"You *tell* 'em," agreed Nick. He looked up at her, having finished eating. His glance was almost tender. "How'd you come to marry Pa, anyway? You and him's so different."

The nymph in Ma leaped to the surface and stayed there a moment, sparkling, laughing, dimpling. "Oh, I dunno. I kept running away and he kept running after. Like that."

He looked up again quickly at that. "Yeh. That's it. Fella don't like to have no girl chasing him all the time. Say, he likes to do the chasing himself. Ain't that the truth?"

"You *tell* 'em!" agreed Ma. A great jovial laugh shook her. Heavy-footed now, but light of heart.

Suddenly: "I'm thinking of going to night school. Learn something. I don't know nothing."

"You do, too, Dewey!"

"Aw, wha'd I know? I never had enough schooling. Wished I had."

"Who's doings was it? You wouldn't stay. Wouldn't go no more than sixth reader and quit. Nothing wouldn't get you to go."

He agreed gloomily. "I know it. I don't know what nothing is. Uh— Arcadia—or—now—vitality or nothing."

"Oh, that comes easy," she encouraged him, "when you begin once."

He reached for her hand gratefully. "You're a swell cook, Ma." He had a sudden burst of generosity, of tenderness. "Soon's the bus is fixed I'll take you joy-riding over to the lake."

Ma always wore a boudoir cap of draggled lace and ribbon for motoring. Nick almost never offered her a ride. She did not expect him to.

She pushed him playfully. "Go on! You got plenty young girls to take riding, not your ma."

"Oh, girls!" he said, scornfully. Then in another tone: "Girls."

He was off. It was almost seven. Pa was late. He caught a car back to Fifty-third Street. Elmer was lounging in the cool doorway of the garage. Nick, in sheer exuberance of spirits, squared off, doubled his fists, and danced about Elmer in a semicircle, working his arms as a prizefighter does, warily. He jabbed at Elmer's jaw playfully.

"What you been doing," inquired that long-suffering gentleman, "makes you feel so good? Where you been?"

"Oh, nowheres. Bumming round. Park."

He turned in the direction of the stairway. Elmer lounged after him. "Oh, say, dame's been calling you for the last hour and a half. Like to busted the phone. Makes me sick."

"Aw, Bauers."

"No, that wasn't the name. Name's Mary or Berry, or something like that. A dozen times, I betcha. Says you was to call her as soon as you come in. Drexel 47—wait a min't'—yeh—that's right—Drexel 473——"

"Swell chanst," said Nick. Suddenly his buoyancy was gone. His shoulders drooped. His cigarette dangled limp. Disappointment curved his lips, burdened his eyes. "*Swell* chanst!"

48

Some Like Them Cold

BY RING LARDNER

N. Y., Aug. 3.

DEAR MISS GILLESPIE: How about our bet now as you bet me I would forget all about you the minute I hit the big town and would never write you a letter. Well girlie it looks like you lose so pay me. Seriously we will call all bets off as I am not the kind that bet on a sure thing and it sure was a sure thing that I would not forget a girlie like you and all that is worrying me is whether it may not be the other way round and you are wondering who this fresh guy is that is writeing you this letter. I bet you are so will try and refreshen your memory.

Well girlie I am the handsome young man that was wondering round the Lasalle st. station Monday and "happened" to sit down beside of a mighty pretty girlie who was waiting to meet her sister from Toledo and the train was late and I am glad of it because if it had not of been that little girlie and I would never of met. So for once I was a lucky guy but still I guess it was time I had some luck as it was certainly tough luck for you and I to both be liveing in Chi all that time and never get together till a half hour before I was leaveing town for good.

Still "better late than never" you know and maybe we can make up for lost time though it looks like we would have to do our makeing up at long distants unless you make good on your threat and come to N. Y. I wish you would do that little thing girlie as it looks like that was the only way we would get a chance to play round together as it looks like they was little or no chance of me comeing back to Chi as my whole future is in the big town. N. Y. is the only spot and specially for a man that expects to make my liveing in the song writeing game as here is the Mecca for that line of work and no matter how good a man may be they don't get no recognition unless they live in N. Y.

Well girlie you asked me to tell you all about my trip. Well I remember you saying that you would give anything to be makeing it yourself

851

but as far as the trip itself was conserned you ought to be thankfull you did not have to make it as you would of sweat your head off. I know I did specially wile going through Ind. Monday P. M. but Monday night was the worst of all trying to sleep and finely I give it up and just layed there with the prespiration rolling off of me though I was laying on top of the covers and nothing on but my underwear.

Yesterday was not so bad as it rained most of the A. M. comeing through N. Y. state and in the P. M. we road along side of the Hudson all P. M. Some river girlie and just looking at it makes a man forget all about the heat and everything else except a certain girlie who I seen for the first time Monday and then only for a half hour but she is the kind of a girlie that a man don't need to see her only once and they would be no danger of forgetting her. There I guess I better lay off that subject or you will think I am a "fresh guy."

Well that is about all to tell you about the trip only they was one amuseing incidence that come off yesterday which I will tell you. Well they was a dame got on the train at Toledo Monday and had the birth opp. mine but I did not see nothing of her that night as I was out smokeing till late and she hit the hay early but yesterday A. M. she come in the dinner and sit at the same table with me and tried to make me and it was so raw that the dinge waiter seen it and give me the wink and of course I paid no tension and I waited till she got through so as they would be no danger of her folling me out but she stopped on the way out to get a tooth pick and when I come out she was out on the platform with it so I tried to brush right by but she spoke up and asked me what time it was and I told her and she said she guessed her watch was slow so I said maybe it just seemed slow on acct. of the company it was in.

I don't know if she got what I was driveing at or not but any way she give up trying to make me and got off at Albany. She was a good looker but I have no time for gals that tries to make strangers on a train.

Well if I don't quit you will think I am writing a book but will expect a long letter in answer to this letter and we will see if you can keep your promise like I have kept mine. Don't dissapoint me girlie as I am all alone in a large city and hearing from you will keep me from getting home sick for old Chi though I never thought so much of the old town till I found out you lived there. Don't think that is kidding girlie as I mean it.

You can address me at this hotel as it looks like I will be here right along as it is on 47th st. right off of old Broadway and handy to everything and am only paying $21 per wk. for my rm. and could of got one for $16 but without bath but am glad to pay the differents as am lost without my bath in the A. M. and sometimes at night too.

Tomorrow I expect to commence fighting the "battle of Broadway" and will let you know how I come out that is if you answer this letter. In the mean wile girlie au reservoir and don't do nothing I would not do.

Your new friend (?)

Chas. F. Lewis.

Chicago, Ill., Aug. 6.

My Dear Mr. Lewis: Well, that certainly was a "surprise party" getting your letter and you are certainly a "wonder man" to keep your word as I am afraid most men of your sex are gay deceivers but maybe you are "different." Any way it sure was a surprise and will gladly pay the bet if you will just tell me what it was we bet. Hope it was not money as I am a "working girl" but if it was not more than a dollar or two will try to dig it up even if I have to "beg, borrow or steal."

Suppose you will think me a "case" to make a bet and then forget what it was, but you must remember, Mr. Man, that I had just met you and was "dazzled." Joking aside I was rather "fussed" and will tell you why. Well, Mr. Lewis, I suppose you see lots of girls like the one you told me about that you saw on the train who tried to "get acquainted" but I want to assure you that I am not one of those kind and sincerely hope you will believe me when I tell you that you was the first man I ever spoke to meeting them like that and my friends and the people who know me would simply faint if they knew I ever spoke to a man without a "proper introduction."

Believe me, Mr. Lewis, I am not that kind and I don't know now why I did it only that you was so "different" looking if you know what I mean and not at all like the kind of men that usually try to force their attentions on every pretty girl they see. Lots of times I act on impulse and let my feelings run away from me and sometimes I do things on the impulse of the moment which I regret them later on, and that is what I did this time, but hope you won't give me cause to regret it and I know you won't as I know you are not that kind of a man a specially after what you told me about the girl on the train. But any way as I say, I was in a "daze" so can't remember what it was we bet, but will try and pay it if it does not "break" me.

Sis's train got in about ten minutes after yours had gone and when she saw me what do you think was the first thing she said? Well, Mr. Lewis, she said: "Why Mibs (That is a pet name some of my friends have given me) what has happened to you? I never seen you have as much color." So I passed it off with some remark about the heat and changed the subject as I certainly was not going to tell her that I had just been talking to a man who I had never met or she would have dropped dead from the shock. Either that or she would not of believed me as it would be hard for a person who knows me well to imagine me doing a thing like that as I have quite a reputation for "squelching" men who try to act fresh. I don't mean anything personal by that, Mr. Lewis, as am a good judge of character and could tell without you telling me that you are not that kind.

Well, Sis and I have been on the "go" ever since she arrived as I took yesterday and today off so I could show her the "sights" though she says she would be perfectly satisfied to just sit in the apartment and listen to me "rattle on." Am afraid I am a great talker, Mr. Lewis, but Sis says it is as good as a show to hear me talk as I tell things in such a different way as I cannot help from seeing the humorous side of everything and she says she never gets tired of listening to me, but of course she is my sister and thinks the world of me, but she really does laugh like she enjoyed my craziness.

Maybe I told you that I have a tiny little apartment which a girl friend of mine and I have together and it is hardly big enough to turn round in, but still it is "home" and I am a great home girl and hardly ever care to go out evenings except occasionally to the theater or dance. But even if our "nest" is small we are proud of it and Sis complimented us on how cozy it is and how "homey" it looks and she said she did not see how we could afford to have everything so nice and Edith (my girl friend) said: "Mibs deserves all the credit for that. I never knew a girl who could make a little money go a long ways like she can." Well, of course she is my best friend and always saying nice things about me, but I do try and I hope I get results. Have always said that good taste and being careful is a whole lot more important than lots of money though it is nice to have it.

You must write and tell me how you are getting along in the "battle of Broadway" (I laughed when I read that) and whether the publishers like your songs though I know they will. Am crazy to hear them and hear you play the piano as I love good jazz music even better than classical, though I suppose it is terrible to say such a thing. But I usually say just what I think though sometimes I wish afterwards I had not of. But still I believe it is better for a girl to be her own self and natural instead of always acting. But am afraid I will never have a chance to hear you play unless you come back to Chi and pay us a visit as my "threat" to come to New York was just a "threat" and I don't see any hope of ever getting there unless some rich New Yorker should fall in love with me and take me there to live. Fine chance for poor little me, eh Mr. Lewis?

Well, I guess I have "rattled on" long enough and you will think I am writing a book unless I quit and besides, Sis has asked me as a special favor to make her a pie for dinner. Maybe you don't know it, Mr. Man-but I am quite famous for my pie and pastry, but I don't suppose a "genius" is interested in common things like that.

Well, be sure and write soon and tell me what N. Y. is like and all about it and don't forget the little girlie who was "bad" and spoke to a strange man in the station and have been blushing over it ever since.

Your friend (?)
Mabelle Gillespie.

N. Y., Aug. 10.

Dear Girlie: I bet you will think I am a fresh guy commencing that way but Miss Gillespie is too cold and a man can not do nothing cold in this kind of weather specially in this man's town which is the hottest place I ever been in and I guess maybe the reason why New Yorkers is so bad is because they think they are all ready in H—— and can not go no worse place no matter how they behave themselves. Honest girlie I certainly envy you being where there is a breeze off the old Lake and Chi may be dirty but I never heard of nobody dying because they was dirty but four people died here yesterday on acct. of the heat and I seen two different women flop right on Broadway and had to be taken away in the ambulance and it could not of been because they was dressed too warm because it would be impossible for the women here to leave off any more cloths.

Well have not had much luck yet in the battle of Broadway as all the heads of the big music publishers is out of town on their vacation and the big boys is the only ones I will do business with as it would be silly for a man with the stuff I have got to waste my time on somebody that is just on the staff and have not got the final say. But I did play a couple of my numbers for the people up to Levy's and Goebel's and they went crazy over them in both places. So it looks like all I have to do is wait for the big boys to get back and then play my numbers for them and I will be all set. What I want is to get taken on the staff of one of the big firms as that gives a man the inside and they will plug your numbers more if you are on the staff. In the mean wile have not got nothing to worry me but am just seeing the sights of the big town as have saved up enough money to play round for a wile and any way a man that can play piano like I can don't never have to worry about starveing. Can certainly make the old music box talk girlie and am always good for a $75 or $100 job.

Well have been here a week now and on the go every minute and I thought I would be lonesome down here but no chance of that as I have been treated fine by the people I have met and have sure met a bunch of them. One of the boys liveing in the hotel is a vaudeville actor and he is a member of the Friars club and took me over there to dinner the other night and some way another the bunch got wise that I could play piano so of course I had to sit down and give them some of my numbers and everybody went crazy over them. One of the boys I met there was Paul Sears the song writer but he just writes the lyrics and has wrote a bunch of hits and when he heard some of my melodies he called me over to one side and said he would like to work with me on some numbers. How is that girlie as he is one of the biggest hit writers in N. Y.

N. Y. has got some mighty pretty girlies and I guess it would not be hard to get acquainted with them and in fact several of them has tried to make me since I been here but I always figure that a girl must be something wrong with her if she tries to make a man that she don't know nothing about so I pass them all up. But I did meet a couple of pips that a man here in the hotel went up on Riverside Drive to see them and insisted on me going along and they got on some way that I could make a piano talk so they was nothing but I must play for them so I sit down and played some of my own stuff and they went crazy over it.

One of the girls wanted I should come up and see her again, and I said I might but I think I better keep away as she acted like she wanted to vamp me and I am not the kind that likes to play round with a gal just for their company and dance with them etc. but when I see the right gal that will be a different thing and she won't have to beg me to come and see her as I will camp right on her trail till she says yes. And it won't be none of these N. Y. fly by nights neither. They are all right to look at but a man would be a sucker to get serious with them as they might take you up and next thing you know you would have a wife on your hands that don't know a dish rag from a waffle iron.

Well girlie will quit and call it a day as it is too hot to write any more and I guess I will turn on the cold water and lay in the tub a wile and then turn in. Don't forget to write to

Your friend,
Chas. F. Lewis.

Chicago, Ill., Aug. 13.

Dear Mr. Man: Hope you won't think me a "silly Billy" for starting my letter that way but "Mr. Lewis" is so formal and "Charles" is too much the other way and any way I would not dare to call a man by their first name after only knowing them only two weeks. Though I may as well confess that Charles is my favorite name for a man and have always been crazy about it as it was my father's name. Poor old dad, he died of cancer three years ago, but left enough insurance so that mother and we girls were well provided for and do not have to do anything to support ourselves though I have been earning my own living for two years to make things easier for mother and also because I simply can't bear to be doing nothing as I feel like a "drone." So I flew away from the "home nest" though mother felt bad about it as I was her favorite and she always said I was such a comfort to her as when I was in the house she never had to worry about how things would go.

But there I go gossiping about my domestic affairs just like you would be interested in them though I don't see how you could be though personly I always like to know all about my friends, but I know men are different so will try and not bore you any longer. Poor Man, I certainly feel sorry for you if New York is as hot as all that. I guess it has been very hot in Chi, too, at least everybody has been complaining about how terrible it is. Suppose you will wonder why I say "I guess" and you will think I ought to know if it is hot. Well, sir, the reason I say "I guess" is because I don't feel the heat like others do or at least I don't let myself feel it. That sounds crazy I know, but don't you think there is a good deal in mental suggestion and not letting yourself feel things? I believe that if a person simply won't allow themselves to be affected by disagreeable things, why such things won't bother them near as much. I know it works with me and that is the reason why I am never cross when things go wrong and "keep smiling" no matter what happens and as far as the heat is concerned, why I just don't let myself feel it and my friends say I don't even look hot no matter if the weather is boiling and Edith, my girl friend, often says that I am like a breeze and it cools her off just to have me come in the room. Poor Edie suffers terribly during the hot weather and says it almost makes her mad at me to see how cool and unruffled I look when everybody else is perspiring and have red faces etc.

I laughed when I read what you said about New York being so hot that people thought it was the "other place." I can appreciate a joke, Mr. Man, and that one did not go "over my head." Am still laughing at some of the things you said in the station though they probably struck me funnier than they would most girls as I always see the funny side and sometimes something is said and I laugh and the others wonder what I am laughing at as they cannot see anything in it themselves, but it is just the way I look at things so of course I cannot explain to them why I laughed and they think I am crazy. But I had rather part with almost anything rather than my sense of humor as it helps me over a great many rough spots.

Sis has gone back home though I would of liked to of kept her here much longer, but she had to go though she said she would of liked nothing better than to stay with me and just listen to me "rattle on." She always says it is just like a show to hear me talk as I always put things in such a funny way and for weeks after she has been visiting me she thinks of some of the things I said and laughs over them. Since she left Edith and I have been pretty quiet though poor Edie wants to be on the "go" all the time and tries to make me go out with her every evening to the pictures and scolds me when I say I had rather stay home and read and calls me a "book worm." Well, it is true that I had rather stay home with a good book than go to some crazy old picture and the last two nights I have been reading myself to sleep with Robert W. Service's poems. Don't you love Service or don't you care for "highbrow" writings?

Personly there is nothing I love more than to just sit and read a good book or sit and listen to somebody play the piano, I mean if they can really play and I really believe I like popular music better than the classical though I suppose that is a terrible thing to confess, but I love all kinds of music but a specially the piano when it is played by somebody who can really play.

Am glad you have not "fallen" for the "ladies" who have tried to make your acquaintance in New York. You are right in thinking there must be something wrong with girls who try to "pick up" strange men as no girl with self respect would do such a thing and when I say that, Mr. Man, I know you will think it is a funny thing for me to say on account of the way our friendship started, but I mean it and I assure you that was the first time I ever done such a thing in my life and would never of thought of doing it had I not known you were the right kind of a man as I flatter myself that I am a good judge of character and can tell pretty well what a person is like by just looking at them and I assure you I had made up my mind what kind of a man you were before I allowed myself to answer your opening remark. Otherwise I am the last girl in the world that would allow myself to speak to a person without being introduced to them.

When you write again you must tell me all about the girl on Riverside Drive and what she looks like and if you went to see her again and all about her. Suppose you will think I am a little old "curiosity shop" for asking all those questions and will wonder why I want to know. Well, sir, I won't tell you why, so there, but I insist on you answering all questions and will scold you if you don't. Maybe you will think that the reason why I am so curious is because I am "jealous" of the lady in question. Well, sir, I won't tell you whether I am or not, but will keep you "guessing." Now, don't you wish you knew?

Must close or you will think I am going to "rattle on" forever or maybe you have all ready become disgusted and torn my letter up. If so all I can say is poor little me—she was a nice little girl and meant well. but the man did not appreciate her.

There! Will stop or you will think I am crazy if you do not all ready.

Yours (?)

Mabelle.

N. Y., *Aug. 20.*

Dear Girlie: Well girlie I suppose you thought I was never going to answer your letter but have been busier than a one armed paper hanger the last week as have been working on a number with Paul Sears who is one of the best lyric writers in N. Y. and has turned out as many hits as Berlin or Davis or any of them. And believe me girlie he has turned out another hit this time that is he and I have done it together. It is all done now and we are just waiting for the best chance to place it but will not place it nowheres unless we get the right kind of a deal but maybe will publish it ourselves.

The song is bound to go over big as Sears has wrote a great lyric and I have give it a great tune or at least every body that has heard it goes crazy over it and it looks like it would go over bigger than any song since Mammy and would not be surprised to see it come out the hit of the year. If it is handled right we will make a bbl. of money and Sears says it is a cinch we will clean up as much as $25000 apiece which is pretty fair for one song but this one is not like the most of them but has got a great lyric and I have wrote a melody that will knock them out of their seats. I only wish you could hear it girlie and hear it the way I play it. I had to play it over and over about 50 times at the Friars last night.

I will copy down the lyric of the chorus so you can see what it is like and get the idea of the song though of course you can't tell much about it unless you hear it played and sang. The title of the song is When They're Like You and here is the chorus:

> "*Some like them hot, some like them cold.*
> *Some like them when they're not too darn old.*
> *Some like them fat, some like them lean.*
> *Some like them only at sweet sixteen.*
> *Some like them dark, some like them light.*
> *Some like them in the park, late at night.*
> *Some like them fickle, some like them true,*
> *But the time I like them is when they're like you.*"

How is that for a lyric and I only wish I could play my melody for you as you would go nuts over it but will send you a copy as soon as the song is published and you can get some of your friends to play it over for you and I know you will like it though it is a different melody when I play it or when somebody else plays it.

Well girlie you will see how busy I have been and am libel to keep right on being busy as we are not going to let the grass grow under our feet but as soon as we have got this number placed we will get busy on another one as a couple like that will put me on Easy st. even if they don't go as big as we expect but even 25 grand is a big bunch of money and if a man could only turn out one hit a year and make that much out of it I would be on Easy st. and no more hammering on the old music box in some cabaret.

Who ever we take the song to we will make them come across with one grand for advance royaltys and that will keep me going till I can turn out another one. So the future looks bright and rosey to yours truly and I am certainly glad I come to the big town though sorry I did not do it a whole lot quicker.

This is a great old town girlie and when you have lived here a wile you wonder how you ever stood for a burg like Chi which is just a hick town along side of this besides being dirty etc. and a man is a sucker to stay there all their life specially a man in my line of work as N. Y. is the Mecca for a man that has got the musical gift. I figure that all the time I spent in Chi was just wasteing my time and never really started to live till I come down here and I have to laugh when I think of the boys out there that is trying to make a liveing in the song writing game and most of them starve to death all their life and the first week I am down here I meet a man like Sears and the next thing you know we have turned out a song that will make us a fortune.

Well girlie you asked me to tell you about the girlie up on the Drive that tried to make me and asked me to come and see her again. Well I can assure you you have no reasons to be jealous in that quarter as I have not been back to see her as I figure it is wasteing my time to play round with a dame like she that wants to go out somewheres every night and if you married her she would want a house on 5th ave. with a dozen servants so I have passed her up as that is not my idea of home.

What I want when I get married is a real home where a man can stay home and work and maybe have a few of his friends in once in a wile and entertain them or go to a good musical show once in a wile and have a wife that is in sympathy with you and not nag at you all the wile but be a real help mate. The girlie up on the Drive would run me ragged and have me in the poor house inside of a year even if I was makeing 25 grand out of one song. Besides she wears a make up that you would have to blast to find out what her face looks like. So I have not been back there and don't intend to see her again so what is the use of me telling you about her. And the only other girlie I have met is a sister of

Paul Sears who I met up to his house wile we was working on the song but she don't hardly count as she has not got no use for the boys but treats them like dirt and Paul says she is the coldest proposition he ever seen.

Well I don't know no more to write and besides have got a date to go out to Paul's place for dinner and play some of my stuff for him so as he can see if he wants to set words to some more of my melodies. Well don't do nothing I would not do and have as good a time as you can in old Chi and will let you know how we come along with the song.

Chas. F. Lewis.

Chicago, Ill., Aug. 23.

Dear Mr. Man: I am thrilled to death over the song and think the words awfully pretty and am crazy to hear the music which I know must be great. It must be wonderful to have the gift of writing songs and then hear people play and sing them and just think of making $25,000 in such a short time. My, how rich you will be and I certainly congratulate you though am afraid when you are rich and famous you will have no time for insignificant little me or will you be an exception and remember your "old" friends even when you are up in the world? I sincerely hope so.

Will look forward to receiving a copy of the song and will you be sure and put your name on it? I am all ready very conceited just to think that I know a man that writes songs and makes all that money.

Seriously I wish you success with your next song and I laughed when I read your remark about being busier than a one armed paper hanger. I don't see how you think up all those comparisons and crazy things to say. The next time one of the girls asks me to go out with them I am going to tell them I can't go because I am busier than a one armed paper hanger and then they will think I made it up and say: "The girl is clever."

Seriously I am glad you did not go back to see the girl on the Drive and am also glad you don't like girls who makes themselves up so much as I think it is disgusting and would rather go round looking like a ghost than put artificial color on my face. Fortunately I have a complexion that does not need "fixing" but even if my coloring was not what it is I would never think of lowering myself to "fix" it. But I must tell you a joke that happened just the other day when Edith and I were out at lunch and there was another girl in the restaurant whom Edie knew and she introduced her to me and I noticed how this girl kept staring at me and finally she begged my pardon and asked if she could ask me a personal question and I said yes and she asked me if my complexion was really "mine." I assured her it was and she said: "Well, I thought so because I did not think anybody could put it on so artistically. I certainly envy you." Edie and I both laughed.

Well, if that girl envies me my complexion, why I envy you living in New York. Chicago is rather dirty though I don't let that part of it bother me as I bathe and change my clothing so often that the dirt does not have time to "settle." Edie often says she cannot see how I always keep so clean looking and says I always look like I had just stepped out of a band box. She also calls me a fish (jokingly) because I spend so much time in the water. But seriously I do love to bathe and never feel so happy as when I have just "cleaned up" and put on fresh clothing.

Edie has just gone out to see a picture and was cross at me because I would not go with her. I told her I was going to write a letter and she wanted to know to whom and I told her and she said: "You write to him so often that a person would almost think you was in love with him." I just laughed and turned it off, but she does says the most embarrassing things and I would be angry if it was anybody but she that said them.

Seriously I had much rather sit here and write letters or read or just sit and dream than go out to some crazy old picture show except once in awhile I do like to go to the theater and see a good play and a specially a musical play if the music is catchy. But as a rule I am contented to just stay home and feel cozy and lots of evenings Edie and I sit here without saying hardly a word to each other though she would love to talk but she knows I had rather be quiet and she often says it is just like living with a deaf and dumb mute to live with me because I make so little noise round the apartment. I guess I was born to be a home body as I so seldom care to go "gadding."

Though I do love to have company once in awhile, just a few congenial friends whom I can talk to and feel at home with and play cards or have some music. My friends love to drop in here, too. as they say Edie and I always give them such nice things to eat. Though poor Edie has not much to do with it, I am afraid, as she hates anything connected with cooking which is one of the things I love best of anything and I often say that when I begin keeping house in my own home I will insist on doing most of my own work as I would take so much more interest in it than a servant, though I would want somebody to help me a little if I could afford it as I often think a woman that does all her own work is liable to get so tired that she loses interest in the bigger things of life like books and music. Though after all what bigger thing is there than home making a specially for a woman?

I am sitting in the dearest old chair that I bought yesterday at a little store on the North Side. That is my one extravagance, buying furniture and things for the house, but I always say it is economy in the long run as I will always have them and have use for them and when I can pick them up at a bargain I would be silly not to. Though heaven knows I will never be "poor" in regards to furniture and rugs and things like that as mother's house in Toledo is full of lovely things which she says she is going to give to Sis and myself as soon as we have real homes of our own. She is going to give me the first choice as I am her favorite. She has the loveliest old things that you could not buy now for love or money including lovely old rugs and a piano which Sis wanted to have a player attachment put on it but I said it would be an insult to the piano so we did not get one. I am funny about things like that, a specially old furniture and feel towards them like people whom I love.

Poor mother, I am afraid she won't live much longer to enjoy her lovely old things as she has been suffering for years from stomach trouble and the doctor says it has been worse lately instead of better and her heart is weak besides. I am going home to see her a few days this fall as it may be the last time. She is very cheerful and always says she is ready to go now as she has had enough joy out of life and all she would like would be to see her girls settled down in their own homes before she goes.

There I go, talking about my domestic affairs again and I will bet you are bored to death though personly I am never bored when my friends tell me about themselves. But I won't "rattle on" any longer, but will say good night and don't forget to write and tell me how you come out with the song and thanks for sending me the words to it. Will you write a song about me some time? I would be thrilled to death! But I am afraid I am not the kind of girl that inspires men to write songs about them, but am just a quiet "mouse" that loves home and am not giddy enough to be the heroine of a song.

Well, Mr. Man, good night and don't wait so long before writing again to

Yours (?)

Mabelle.

N. Y., Sept. 8.

Dear Girlie: Well girlie have not got your last letter with me so cannot answer what was in it as I have forgotten if there was anything I was supposed to answer and besides have only a little time to write as I have a date to go out on a party with the Sears. We are going to the Georgie White show and afterwards somewheres for supper. Sears is the boy who wrote the lyric to my song and it is him and his sister I am going on the party with. The sister is a cold fish that has no use for men but she is show crazy and insists on Paul takeing her to 3 or 4 of them a week.

Paul wants me to give up my room here and come and live with them as they have plenty of room and I am running a little low on money but don't know if I will do it or not as am afraid I would freeze to death in the same house with a girl like the sister as she is ice cold but she don't hang round the house much as she is always takeing trips or going to shows or somewheres.

So far we have not had no luck with the song. All the publishers we have showed it to has went crazy over it but they won't make the right kind of a deal with us and if they don't loosen up and give us a decent royalty rate we are libel to put the song out ourselves and show them up. The man up to Goebel's told us the song was O. K. and he liked it but it was more of a production number than anything else and ought to go in a show like the Follies but they won't be in N. Y. much longer and what we ought to do is hold it till next spring.

Mean wile I am working on some new numbers and also have taken a position with the orchestra at the Wilton and am going to work there starting next week. They pay good money $60 and it will keep me going.

Well girlie that is about all the news. I believe you said your father was sick and hope he is better and also hope you are getting along O. K. and take care of yourself. When you have nothing else to do write to your friend,

Chas. F. Lewis.

Chicago, Ill., Sept. 11.

Dear Mr. Lewis: Your short note reached me yesterday and must say I was puzzled when I read it. It sounded like you was mad at me though I cannot think of any reason why you should be. If there was something I said in my last letter that offended you I wish you would tell me what it was and I will ask your pardon though I cannot remember anything I could of said that you could take offense at. But if there was something, why I assure you, Mr. Lewis, that I did not mean anything by it. I certainly did not intend to offend you in any way.

Perhaps it is nothing I wrote you, but you are worried on account of the publishers not treating you fair in regards to your song and that is why your letter sounded so distant. If that is the case I hope that by this time matters have rectified themselves and the future looks brighter. But any way, Mr. Lewis, don't allow yourself to worry over business cares as they will all come right in the end and I always think it is silly for people to worry themselves sick over temporary troubles, but the best way is to "keep smiling" and look for the "silver lining" in the cloud. That is the way I always do and no matter what happens, I manage to smile and my girl friend, Edie, calls me Sunny because I always look on the bright side.

Remember also, Mr. Lewis, that $60 is a salary that a great many men would like to be getting and are living on less than that and supporting a wife and family on it. I always say that a person can get along on whatever amount they make if they manage things in the right way.

So if it is business troubles, Mr. Lewis, I say don't worry, but look on the bright side. But if it is something I wrote in my last letter that offended you I wish you would tell me what it was so I can apologize as I assure you I meant nothing and would not say anything to hurt you for the world.

Please let me hear from you soon as I will not feel comfortable until I know I am not to blame for the sudden change.

Sincerely,
Mabelle Gillespie.

N. Y., Sept. 24.

Dear Miss Gillespie: Just a few lines to tell you the big news or at least it is big news to me. I am engaged to be married to Paul Sears' sister and we are going to be married early next month and live in Atlantic City where the orchestra I have been playing with has got an engagement in one of the big cabarets.

I know this will be a surprise to you as it was even a surprise to me as I did not think I would ever have the nerve to ask the girlie the big question as she was always so cold and acted like I was just in the way. But she said she supposed she would have to marry somebody some time and she did not dislike me as much as most of the other men her brother brought round and she would marry me with the understanding that she would not have to be a slave and work round the house and also I would have to take her to a show or somewheres every night and if I could not take her myself she would "run wild" alone. Atlantic City will be O. K. for that as a lot of new shows opens down there and she will be able to see them before they get to the big town. As for her being a slave, I would hate to think of marrying a girl and then have them spend their lives in druggery round the house. We are going to live in a hotel till we find something better but will be in no hurry to start house keeping as we will have to buy all new furniture.

Betsy is some doll when she is all fixed up and believe me she knows how to fix herself up. I don't know what she uses but it is weather proof and I have been out in a rain storm with her and we both got drowned but her face stayed on. I would almost think it was real only she tells me different.

Well girlie I may write to you again once in a wile as Betsy says she don't give a damn if I write to all the girls in the world just so I don't make her read the answers but that is all I can think of to say now except good bye and good luck and may the right man come along soon and he will be a lucky man getting a girl that is such a good cook and got all that furniture etc.

But just let me give you a word of advice before I close and that is don't never speak to strange men who you don't know nothing about as they may get you wrong and think you are trying to make them. It just happened that I knew better so you was lucky in my case but the luck might not last.

Your friend,

Chas. F. Lewis.

Chicago, Ill., Sept. 27.

My Dear Mr. Lewis: Thanks for your advice and also thank your fiance for her generosity in allowing you to continue your correspondence with her "rivals," but personly I have no desire to take advantage of that generosity as I have something better to do than read letters from a man like you, a specially as I have a man friend who is not so generous as Miss Sears and would strongly object to my continuing a correspondence with another man. It is at his request I am writing this note to tell you not to expect to hear from me again.

Allow me to congratulate you on your engagement to Miss Sears and I am sure she is to be congratulated too, though if I met the lady I would be tempted to ask her to tell me her secret, namely how she is going to "run wild" on $60.

Sincerely,

Mabelle Gillespie.

49

The Golden Honeymoon

BY RING LARDNER

MOTHER says that when I start talking I never know when to stop. But I tell her the only time I get a chance is when she ain't around, so I have to make the most of it. I guess the fact is neither one of us would be welcome in a Quaker meeting, but as I tell Mother, what did God give us tongues for if He didn't want we should use them? Only she says He didn't give them to us to say the same thing over and over again, like I do, and repeat myself. But I say:

"Well, Mother," I say, "when people is like you and I and been married fifty years, do you expect everything I say will be something you ain't heard me say before? But it may be new to others, as they ain't nobody else lived with me as long as you have."

So she says:

"You can bet they ain't, as they couldn't nobody else stand you that long."

"Well," I tell her, "you look pretty healthy."

"Maybe I do," she will say, "but I looked even healthier before I married you."

You can't get ahead of Mother.

Yes, sir, we was married just fifty years ago the seventeenth day of last December and my daughter and son-in-law was over from Trenton to help us celebrate the Golden Wedding. My son-in-law is John H. Kramer, the real estate man. He made $12,000 one year and is pretty well thought of around Trenton; a good, steady, hard worker. The Rotarians was after him a long time to join, but he kept telling them his home was his club. But Edie finally made him join. That's my daughter.

Well, anyway, they come over to help us celebrate the Golden Wedding and it was pretty crimpy weather and the furnace don't seem to heat up no more like it used to and Mother made the remark that she hoped this winter wouldn't be as cold as the last, referring to the winter previous. So Edie said if she was us, and nothing to keep us home, she certainly wouldn't spend no more winters up here and why didn't we just shut off the water and close up the house and go down to Tampa, Florida? You know we was there four winters ago and stayed five weeks, but it cost us over three hundred and fifty dollars for hotel bill alone. So Mother said we wasn't going no place to be robbed. So my son-in-law spoke up and said that Tampa wasn't the only place in the South, and besides we didn't have to stop at no high price hotel but could rent us a couple rooms and board out somewheres, and he had heard that St. Petersburg, Florida, was *the* spot and if we said the word he would write down there and make inquiries.

Well, to make a long story short, we decided to do it and Edie said it would be our Golden Honeymoon and for a present my son-in-law paid the difference between a section and a compartment so as we could have a compartment and have more privatecy. In a compartment you have an upper and lower berth just like the regular sleeper, but it is a shut in room by itself and got a wash bowl. The car we went in was all compartments and no regular berths at all. It was all compartments.

We went to Trenton the night before and stayed at my daughter and son-in-law and we left Trenton the next afternoon at 3.23 P. M.

This was the twelfth day of January. Mother set facing the front of the train, as it makes her giddy to ride backwards. I set facing her, which does not affect me. We reached North Philadelphia at 4.03 P. M. and we reached West Philadelphia at 4.14, but did not go into Broad Street. We reached Baltimore at 6.30 and Washington, D.C., at 7.25. Our train laid over in Washington two hours till another train come along to pick us up and I got out and strolled up the platform and into the Union Station. When I come back, our car had been switched on to another track, but I remembered the name of it, the La Belle, as I had once visited my aunt out in Oconomowoc, Wisconsin, where there was a lake of that name, so I had no difficulty in getting located. But Mother had nearly fretted herself sick for fear I would be left.

"Well," I said, "I would of followed you on the next train."

"You could of," said Mother, and she pointed out that she had the money.

"Well," I said, "we are in Washington and I could of borrowed from the United States Treasury. I would of pretended I was an Englishman."

Mother caught the point and laughed heartily.

Our train pulled out of Washington at 9.40 P. M. and Mother and I turned in early, I taking the upper. During the night we passed through the green fields of old Virginia, though it was too dark to tell if they was green or what color. When we got up in the morning, we was at Fayetteville, North Carolina. We had breakfast in the dining car and after breakfast I got in conversation with the man in the next compartment to ours. He was from Lebanon, New Hampshire, and a man about eighty years of age. His wife was with him, and two unmarried daughters and I made the remark that I should think the four of them would be crowded in one compartment, but he said they had made the trip every winter for fifteen years and knowed how to keep out of each other's way. He said they was bound for Tarpon Springs.

We reached Charleston, South Carolina, at 12.50 P. M. and arrived at Savannah, Georgia, at 4.20. We reached Jacksonville, Florida, at 8.45 P. M. and had an hour and a quarter to lay over there, but Mother made a fuss about me getting off the train, so we had the darky make up our berths and retired before we left Jacksonville. I didn't sleep good as the train done a lot of hemming and hawing, and Mother never sleeps good on a train as she says she is always worrying that I will fall out. She says she would rather have the upper herself, as then she would not have to worry about me, but I tell her I can't take the risk of having it get out that I allowed my wife to sleep in an upper berth. It would make talk.

We was up in the morning in time to see our friends from New Hampshire get off at Tarpon Springs, which we reached at 6.53 A. M.

Several of our fellow passengers got off at Clearwater and some at Belleair, where the train backs right up to the door of the mammoth hotel. Belleair is the winter headquarters for the golf dudes and everybody that got off there had their bag of sticks, as many as ten and twelve in a bag. Women and all. When I was a young man we called it shinny and only needed one club to play with and about one game of it would of been a-plenty for some of these dudes, the way we played it.

The train pulled into St. Petersburg at 8.20 and when we got off the train you would think they was a riot, what with all the darkies barking for the different hotels.

I said to Mother, I said:

"It is a good thing we have got a place picked out to go to and don't have to choose a hotel, as it would be hard to choose amongst them if every one of them is the best."

She laughed.

We found a jitney and I give him the address of the room my son-in-law had got for us and soon we was there and introduced ourselves to the lady that owns the house, a young widow about forty-eight years of age. She showed us our room, which was light and airy with a comfortable bed and bureau and washstand. It was twelve dollars a week, but the location was good, only three blocks from Williams Park.

St. Pete is what folks calls the town, though they also call it the Sunshine City, as they claim they's no other place in the country where they's fewer days when Old Sol don't smile down on Mother Earth, and one of the newspapers gives away all their copies free every day when the sun don't shine. They claim to of only give them away some sixty-odd times in the last eleven years. Another nickname they have got for the town is "the Poor Man's Palm Beach," but I guess they's men that comes there that could borrow as much from the bank as some of the Willie boys over to the other Palm Beach.

During our stay we paid a visit to the Lewis Tent City, which is the headquarters for the Tin Can Tourists. But may be you ain't heard about them. Well, they are an organization that takes their vacation trips by auto and carries everything with them. That is, they bring along their tents to sleep in and cook in and they don't patronize no hotels or cafeterias, but they have got to be bona fide auto campers or they can't belong to the organization.

They tell me they's over 200,000 members to it and they call themselves the Tin Canners on account of most of their food being put up in tin cans. One couple we seen in the Tent City was a couple from Brady, Texas, named Mr. and Mrs. Pence, which the old man is over eighty years of age and they had come in their auto all the way from home, a distance of 1,641 miles. They took five weeks for the trip, Mr. Pence driving the entire distance.

The Tin Canners hails from every State in the Union and in the summer time they visit places like New England and the Great Lakes region, but in the winter the most of them comes to Florida and scatters all over the State. While we was down there, they was a national convention of them at Gainesville, Florida, and they elected a Fredonia, New York, man as their president. His title is Royal Tin Can Opener of the World. They have got a song wrote up which everybody has got to learn it before they are a member:

> "The tin can forever! Hurrah, boys! Hurrah!
>   Up with the tin can! Down with the foe!
>   We will rally round the campfire, we'll rally once again,
>   Shouting, 'We auto camp forever!'"

That is something like it. And the members has also got to have a tin can fastened on to the front of their machine.

I asked Mother how she would like to travel around that way and she said:

"Fine, but not with an old rattle brain like you driving."

"Well," I said, "I am eight years younger than this Mr. Pence who drove here from Texas."

"Yes," she said, "but he is old enough to not be skittish."

You can't get ahead of Mother.

Well, one of the first things we done in St. Petersburg was to go to the Chamber of Commerce and register our names and where we was from as they's great rivalry amongst the different States in regards to the number of their citizens visiting in town and of course our little State don't stand much of a show, but still every little bit helps, as the fella says. All and all, the man told us, they was eleven thousand names registered, Ohio leading with some fifteen hundred-odd and New York State next with twelve hundred. Then come Michigan, Pennsylvania and so on down, with one man each from Cuba and Nevada.

The first night we was there, they was a meeting of the New York-New Jersey Society at the Congregational Church and a man from Ogdensburg, New York State, made the talk. His subject was Rainbow Chasing. He is a Rotarian and a very convicting speaker, though I forget his name.

Our first business, of course, was to find a place to eat and after trying several places we run on to a cafeteria on Central Avenue that suited us up and down. We eat pretty near all our meals there and it averaged about two dollars per day for the two of us, but the food was well cooked and everything nice and clean. A man don't mind paying the price if things is clean and well cooked.

On the third day of February, which is Mother's birthday, we spread ourselves and eat supper at the Poinsettia Hotel and they charged us seventy-five cents for a sirloin steak that wasn't hardly big enough for one.

I said to Mother: "Well," I said, "I guess it's a good thing every day ain't your birthday or we would be in the poorhouse."

"No," says Mother, "because if every day was my birthday, I would be old enough by this time to of been in my grave long ago."

You can't get ahead of Mother.

In the hotel they had a card-room where they was several men and ladies playing five hundred and this new fangled whist bridge. We also seen a place where they was dancing, so I asked Mother would she like to trip the light fantastic toe and she said no, she was too old to squirm like you have got to do now days. We watched some of the young folks at it awhile till Mother got disgusted and said we would have to see a good movie to take the taste out of our mouth. Mother is a great movie heroyne and we go twice a week here at home.

But I want to tell you about the Park. The second day we was there we visited the Park, which is a good deal like the one in Tampa, only bigger, and they's more fun goes on here every day than you could shake a stick at. In the middle they's a big bandstand and chairs for the folks to set and listen to the concerts, which they give you music for all tastes, from Dixie up to classical pieces like Hearts and Flowers.

Then all around they's places marked off for different sports and games—chess and checkers and dominoes for folks that enjoys those kind of games, and roque and horse-shoes for the nimbler ones. I used to pitch a pretty fair shoe myself, but ain't done much of it in the last twenty years.

Well, anyway, we bought a membership ticket in the club which costs one dollar for the season, and they tell me that up to a couple years ago it was fifty cents, but they had to raise it to keep out the riffraff.

Well, Mother and I put in a great day watching the pitchers and she wanted I should get in the game, but I told her I was all out of practice and would make a fool of myself, though I seen several men pitching who I guess I could take their measure without no practice. However, they was some good pitchers, too, and one boy from Akron, Ohio, who could certainly throw a pretty shoe. They told me it looked like he would win the championship of the United States in the February tournament. We come away a few days before they held that and I never did hear if he win. I forget his name, but he was a clean cut young fella and he has got a brother in Cleveland that's a Rotarian.

Well, we just stood around and watched the different games for two or three days and finally I set down in a checker game with a man named Weaver from Danville, Illinois. He was a pretty fair checker player, but he wasn't no match for me, and I hope that don't sound like bragging. But I always could hold my own on a checker-board and the folks around here will tell you the same thing. I played with this Weaver pretty near all morning for two or three mornings and he beat me one game and the only other time it looked like he had a chance, the noon whistle blowed and we had to quit and go to dinner.

While I was playing checkers, Mother would set and listen to the band, as she loves music, classical or no matter what kind, but anyway she was setting there one day and between selections the woman next to her opened up a conversation. She was a woman about Mother's own age, seventy or seventy-one, and finally she asked Mother's name and Mother told her her name and where she was from and Mother asked her the same question, and who do you think the woman was?

Well, sir, it was the wife of Frank M. Hartsell, the man who was engaged to Mother till I stepped in and cut him out, fifty-two years ago! Yes, sir!

You can imagine Mother's surprise! And Mrs. Hartsell was surprised, too, when Mother told her she had once been friends with her husband.

though Mother didn't say how close friends they had been, or that Mother and I was the cause of Hartsell going out West. But that's what we was. Hartsell left his town a month after the engagement was broke off and ain't never been back since. He had went out to Michigan and become a veterinary, and that is where he had settled down, in Hillsdale, Michigan, and finally married his wife.

Well, Mother screwed up her courage to ask if Frank was still living and Mrs. Hartsell took her over to where they was pitching horse-shoes and there was old Frank, waiting his turn. And he knowed Mother as soon as he seen her, though it was over fifty years. He said he knowed her by her eyes.

"Why, it's Lucy Frost!" he says, and he throwed down his shoes and quit the game.

Then they come over and hunted me up and I will confess I wouldn't of knowed him. Him and I is the same age to the month, but he seems to show it more, some way. He is balder for one thing. And his beard is all white, where mine has still got a streak of brown in it. The very first thing I said to him, I said:

"Well, Frank, that beard of yours makes me feel like I was back north. It looks like a regular blizzard."

"Well," he said, "I guess yourn would be just as white if you had it dry cleaned."

But Mother wouldn't stand that.

"Is that so!" she said to Frank. "Well, Charley ain't had no tobacco in his mouth for over ten years!"

And I ain't!

Well, I excused myself from the checker game and it was pretty close to noon, so we decided to all have dinner together and they was nothing for it only we must try their cafeteria on Third Avenue. It was a little more expensive than ours and not near as good, I thought. I and Mother had about the same dinner we had been having every day and our bill was $1.10. Frank's check was $1.20 for he and his wife. The same meal wouldn't of cost them more than a dollar at our place.

After dinner we made them come up to our house and we all set in the parlor, which the young woman had give us the use of to entertain company. We begun talking over old times and Mother said she was a-scared Mrs. Hartsell would find it tiresome listening to we three talk over old times, but as it turned out they wasn't much chance for nobody else to talk with Mrs. Hartsell in the company. I have heard lots of women that could go it, but Hartsell's wife takes the cake of all the women I ever seen. She told us the family history of everybody in the State of Michigan and bragged for a half hour about her son, who she said is in the drug business in Grand Rapids, and a Rotarian.

When I and Hartsell could get a word in edgeways we joked one another back and forth and I chafed him about being a horse doctor.

"Well, Frank," I said, "you look pretty prosperous, so I suppose they's been plenty of glanders around Hillsdale."

"Well," he said, "I've managed to make more than a fair living. But I've worked pretty hard."

"Yes," I said, "and I suppose you get called out all hours of the night to attend births and so on.'

Mother made me shut up.

Well, I thought they wouldn't never go home and I and Mother was in misery trying to keep awake, as the both of us generally always takes a nap after dinner. Finally they went, after we had made an engagement to meet them in the Park the next morning, and Mrs. Hartsell also invited us to come to their place the next night and play five hundred. But she had forgot that they was a meeting of the Michigan Society that evening, so it was not till two evenings later that we had our first card game.

Hartsell and his wife lived in a house on Third Avenue North and had a private setting room besides their bedroom. Mrs. Hartsell couldn't quit talking about their private setting room like it was something wonderful. We played cards with them, with Mother and Hartsell partners against his wife and I. Mrs. Hartsell is a miserable card player and we certainly got the worst of it.

After the game she brought out a dish of oranges and we had to pretend it was just what we wanted, though oranges down there is like a young man's whiskers; you enjoy them at first, but they get to be a pesky nuisance.

We played cards again the next night at our place with the same partners and I and Mrs. Hartsell was beat again. Mother and Hartsell was full of compliments for each other on what a good team they made, but the both of them knowed well enough where the secret of their success laid. I guess all and all we must of played ten different evenings and they was only one night when Mrs. Hartsell and I come out ahead. And that one night wasn't no fault of hern.

When we had been down there about two weeks, we spent one evening as their guest in the Congregational Church, at a social give by the Michigan Society. A talk was made by a man named Bitting of Detroit, Michigan, on How I was Cured of Story Telling. He is a big man in the Rotarians and give a witty talk.

A woman named Mrs. Oxford rendered some selections which Mrs. Hartsell said was grand opera music, but whatever they was my daughter Edie could of give her cards and spades and not made such a hullabaloo about it neither.

Then they was a ventriloquist from Grand Rapids and a young woman about forty-five years of age that mimicked different kinds of birds. I whispered to Mother that they all sounded like a chicken, but she nudged me to shut up.

After the show we stopped in a drug store and I set up the refreshments and it was pretty close to ten o'clock before we finally turned in. Mother and I would of preferred tending the movies, but Mother said we mustn't offend Mrs. Hartsell, though I asked her had we came to Florida to enjoy ourselves or to just not offend an old chatter-box from Michigan.

I felt sorry for Hartsell one morning. The women folks both had an engagement down to the chiropodist's and I run across Hartsell in the Park and he foolishly offered to play me checkers.

It was him that suggested it, not me, and I guess he repented himself before we had played one game. But he was too stubborn to give up and set there while I beat him game after game and the worst part of it was that a crowd of folks had got in the habit of watching me play and there they all was, looking on, and finally they seen what a fool Frank was making of himself, and they began to chafe him and pass remarks. Like one of them said:

"Who ever told you you was a checker player!"

And:

"You might maybe be good for tiddle-de-winks, but not checkers!"

I almost felt like letting him beat me a couple games. But the crowd would of knowed it was a put up job.

Well, the women folks joined us in the Park and I wasn't going to mention our little game, but Hartsell told about it himself and admitted he wasn't no match for me.

"Well," said Mrs. Hartsell, "checkers ain't much of a game anyway, is it?" She said: "It's more of a children's game, ain't it? At least, I know my boy's children used to play it a good deal."

"Yes, ma'am," I said. "It's a children's game the way your husband plays it, too."

Mother wanted to smooth things over, so she said:

"Maybe they's other games where Frank can beat you."

"Yes," said Mrs. Hartsell, "and I bet he could beat you pitching horse-shoes."

"Well," I said, "I would give him a chance to try, only I ain't pitched a shoe in over sixteen years."

"Well," said Hartsell, "I ain't played checkers in twenty years."

"You ain't never played it," I said.

"Anyway," says Frank, "Lucy and I is your master at five hundred."

Well, I could of told him why that was, but had decency enough to hold my tongue.

It had got so now that he wanted to play cards every night and when I or Mother wanted to go to a movie, any one of us would have to pretend we had a headache and then trust to goodness that they wouldn't see us sneak into the theater. I don't mind playing cards when my partner keeps their mind on the game, but you take a woman like Hartsell's wife and how can they play cards when they have got to stop every couple seconds and brag about their son in Grand Rapids?

Well, the New York-New Jersey Society announced that they was goin' to give a social evening too and I said to Mother, I said:

"Well, that is one evening when we will have an excuse not to play five hundred."

"Yes," she said, "but we will have to ask Frank and his wife to go to the social with us as they asked us to go to the Michigan social."

"Well," I said, "I had rather stay home than drag that chatter-box everywheres we go."

So Mother said:

"You are getting too cranky. Maybe she does talk a little too much but she is good hearted. And Frank is always good company."

So I said:

"I suppose if he is such good company you wished you had of married him."

Mother laughed and said I sounded like I was jealous. Jealous of a cow doctor!

Anyway we had to drag them along to the social and I will say that we give them a much better entertainment than they had given us.

Judge Lane of Paterson made a fine talk on business conditions and a Mrs. Newell of Westfield imitated birds, only you could really tell what they was the way she done it. Two young women from Red Bank sung a choral selection and we clapped them back and they gave us Home to Our Mountains and Mother and Mrs. Hartsell both had tears in their eyes. And Hartsell, too.

Well, some way or another the chairman got wind that I was there and asked me to make a talk and I wasn't even going to get up, but Mother made me, so I got up and said:

"Ladies and gentlemen," I said. "I didn't expect to be called on for a speech on an occasion like this or no other occasion as I do not set myself up as a speech maker, so will have to do the best I can, which I often say is the best anybody can do."

Then I told them the story about Pat and the motorcycle, using the brogue, and it seemed to tickle them and I told them one or two other stories, but altogether I wasn't on my feet more than twenty or twenty-five minutes and you ought to of heard the clapping and hollering when I set down. Even Mrs. Hartsell admitted that I am quite a speech-ifier and said if I ever went to Grand Rapids, Michigan, her son would make me talk to the Rotarians.

When it was over, Hartsell wanted we should go to their house and play cards, but his wife reminded him that it was after 9.30 P. M., rather a late hour to start a card game, but he had went crazy on the subject of cards, probably because he didn't have to play partners with his wife. Anyway, we got rid of them and went home to bed.

It was the next morning, when we met over to the Park, that Mrs. Hartsell made the remark that she wasn't getting no exercise so I suggested that why didn't she take part in the roque game.

She said she had not played a game of roque in twenty years, but if Mother would play she would play. Well, at first Mother wouldn't hear of it, but finally consented, more to please Mrs. Hartsell than anything else.

Well, they had a game with a Mrs. Ryan from Eagle, Nebraska, and a young Mrs. Morse from Rutland, Vermont, who Mother had met down to the chiropodist's. Well, Mother couldn't hit a flea and they all laughed at her and I couldn't help from laughing at her myself and finally she quit and said her back was too lame to stoop over. So they got another lady and kept on playing and soon Mrs. Hartsell was the one everybody was laughing at, as she had a long shot to hit the black ball, and as she made the effort her teeth fell out on to the court. I never seen a woman so flustered in my life. And I never heard so much laughing, only Mrs. Hartsell didn't join in and she was madder than a hornet and wouldn't play no more, so the game broke up.

Mrs. Hartsell went home without speaking to nobody, but Hartsell stayed around and finally he said to me, he said:

"Well, I played you checkers the other day and you beat me bad and now what do you say if you and me play a game of horse-shoes?"

I told him I hadn't pitched a shoe in sixteen years, but Mother said:

"Go ahead and play. You used to be good at it and maybe it will come back to you."

Well, to make a long story short, I give in. I oughtn't to of never tried it, as I hadn't pitched a shoe in sixteen years, and I only done it to humor Hartsell.

Before we started, Mother patted me on the back and told me to do my best, so we started in and I seen right off that I was in for it, as I hadn't pitched a shoe in sixteen years and didn't have my distance. And besides, the plating had wore off the shoes so that they was points right where they stuck into my thumb and I hadn't throwed more than two or three times when my thumb was raw and it pretty near killed me to hang on to the shoe, let alone pitch it.

Well, Hartsell throws the awkwardest shoe I ever seen pitched and to see him pitch you wouldn't think he would ever come nowheres near, but he is also the luckiest pitcher I ever seen and he made some pitches where the shoe lit five and six feet short and then schoonered up and was a ringer. They's no use trying to beat that kind of luck.

They was a pretty fair size crowd watching us and four or five other ladies besides Mother, and it seems like, when Hartsell pitches, he has got to chew and it kept the ladies on the anxious seat as he don't seem to care which way he is facing when he leaves go.

You would think a man as old as him would of learnt more manners.

Well, to make a long story short, I was just beginning to get my distance when I had to give up on account of my thumb, which I showed it to Hartsell and he seen I couldn't go on, as it was raw and bleeding. Even if I could of stood it to go on myself, Mother wouldn't of allowed it after she seen my thumb. So anyway I quit and Hartsell said the score was nineteen to six, but I don't know what it was. Or don't care, neither.

Well, Mother and I went home and I said I hoped we was through with the Hartsells as I was sick and tired of them, but it seemed like she had promised we would go over to their house that evening for another game of their everlasting cards.

Well, my thumb was giving me considerable pain and I felt kind of out of sorts and I guess maybe I forgot myself, but anyway, when we was about through playing Hartsell made the remark that he wouldn't never lose a game of cards if he could always have Mother for a partner.

So I said:

"Well, you had a chance fifty years ago to always have her for a partner, but you wasn't man enough to keep her."

I was sorry the minute I had said it and Hartsell didn't know what to say and for once his wife couldn't say nothing. Mother tried to smooth things over by making the remark that I must of had something stronger than tea or I wouldn't talk so silly. But Mrs. Hartsell had froze up like an iceberg and hardly said good night to us and I bet her and Frank put in a pleasant hour after we was gone.

As we was leaving, Mother said to him: "Never mind Charley's nonsense, Frank. He is just mad because you beat him all hollow pitching horse-shoes and playing cards."

She said that to make up for my slip, but at the same time she certainly riled me. I tried to keep ahold of myself, but as soon as we was out of the house she had to open up the subject and began to scold me for the break I had made.

Well, I wasn't in no mood to be scolded. So I said:

"I guess he is such a wonderful pitcher and card player that you wished you had married him."

"Well," she said, "at least he ain't a baby to give up pitching because his thumb has got a few scratches."

"And how about you," I said, "making a fool of yourself on the roque court and then pretending your back is lame and you can't play no more!"

"Yes," she said, "but when you hurt your thumb I didn't laugh at you, and why did you laugh at me when I sprained my back?"

"Who could help from laughing!" I said.

"Well," she said, "Frank Hartsell didn't laugh."

"Well," I said, "why didn't you marry him?"

"Well," said Mother, "I almost wished I had!"

"And I wished so, too!" I said.

"I'll remember that!" said Mother, and that's the last word she said to me for two days.

We seen the Hartsells the next day in the Park and I was willing to apologize, but they just nodded to us. And a couple days later we heard they had left for Orlando, where they have got relatives.

I wished they had went there in the first place.

Mother and I made it up setting on a bench.

"Listen, Charley," she said. "This is our Golden Honeymoon and we don't want the whole thing spoilt with a silly old quarrel."

"Well," I said, "did you mean that about wishing you had married Hartsell?"

"Of course not," she said, "that is, if you didn't mean that you wished I had, too."

So I said:

"I was just tired and all wrought up. I thank God you chose me instead of him as they's no other woman in the world who I could of lived with all these years."

"How about Mrs. Hartsell?" says Mother.

"Good gracious!" I said. "Imagine being married to a woman that plays five hundred like she does and drops her teeth on the roque court!"

"Well," said Mother, "it wouldn't be no worse than being married to a man that expectorates towards ladies and is such a fool in a checker game."

So I put my arm around her shoulder and she stroked my hand and I guess we got kind of spoony.

They was two days left of our stay in St. Petersburg and the next to the last day Mother introduced me to a Mrs. Kendall from Kingston, Rhode Island, who she had met at the chiropodist's.

Mrs. Kendall made us acquainted with her husband, who is in the grocery business. They have got two sons and five grandchildren and one great-grandchild. One of their sons lives in Providence and is way up in the Elks as well as a Rotarian.

We found them very congenial people and we played cards with them the last two nights we was there. They was both experts and I only wished we had met them sooner instead of running into the Hartsells. But the Kendalls will be there again next winter and we will see more of them, that is, if we decide to make the trip again.

We left the Sunshine City on the eleventh day of February, at 11 A. M. This give us a day trip through Florida and we seen all the country we had passed through at night on the way down.

We reached Jacksonville at 7 P. M. and pulled out of there at 8.10 P. M. We reached Fayetteville, North Carolina, at nine o'clock the following morning, and reached Washington, D. C., at 6.30 P. M., laying over there half an hour.

We reached Trenton at 11.01 P. M. and had wired ahead to my daughter and son-in-law and they met us at the train and we went to their house and they put us up for the night. John would of made us stay up all night, telling about our trip, but Edie said we must be tired and made us go to bed. That's my daughter.

The next day we took our train for home and arrived safe and sound, having been gone just one month and a day.

Here comes Mother, so I guess I better shut up.

50

The Man Who Saw Through Heaven

BY WILBUR DANIEL STEELE

EOPLE have wondered (there being obviously no question of romance involved) how I could ever have allowed myself to be let in for the East African adventure of Mrs. Diana in search of her husband. There were several reasons. To begin with, the time and effort and money weren't mine; they were the property of the wheel of which I was but a cog, the Society through which Diana's life had been insured, along with the rest of that job lot of missionaries. The "letting in" was the firm's. In the second place, the wonderers have not counted on Mrs. Diana's capacity for getting things done for her. Meek and helpless. Yes, but God was on her side. Too meek, too helpless to move mountains herself, if those who happened to be handy didn't move them for her then her God would know the reason why. Having dedicated her all to making straight the Way, why should her neighbor cavil at giving a little? The writer for one, a colonial governor-general for another, railway magnates, insurance managers, *safari* leaders, the ostrich farmer of Ndua, all these and a dozen others in their turns have felt the hundred-ton weight of her thin-lipped meekness—have seen her in metaphor sitting grimly on the doorsteps of their souls.

A third reason lay in my own troubled conscience. Though I did it in innocence, I can never forget that it was I who personally conducted Diana's party to the Observatory on that fatal night in Boston before it sailed. Had it not been for that kindly intentioned "hunch" of mine, the astonished eye of the Reverend Hubert Diana would never have gazed through the floor of Heaven, and he would never have undertaken to measure the Infinite with the foot rule of his mind.

It all started so simply. My boss at the shipping-and-insurance office gave me the word in the morning. "Bunch of missionaries for the *Platonic* tomorrow. They're on our hands in a way. Show 'em the town.'" It wasn't so easy when you think of it: one male and seven females on their way to the heathen; though it was easier in Boston than it might have been in some other towns. The evening looked the simplest. My friend Krum was at the Observatory that semester; there at least I was sure their sensibilities would come to no harm.

On the way out in the street car, seated opposite to Diana and having to make conversation, I talked of Krum and of what I knew of his work with the spiral nebulæ. Having to appear to listen, Diana did so (as all day long) with a vaguely indulgent smile. He really hadn't time for me. That night his life was exalted as it had never been, and would perhaps never be again. Tomorrow's sailing, the actual fact of leaving all to follow Him, held his imagination in thrall. Moreover, he was a bridegroom of three days with his bride beside him, his nerves at once assuaged and thrilled. No, but more. As if a bride were not enough, arrived in Boston, he had found himself surrounded by a very galaxy of womanhood gathered from the four corners; already within hours one felt the chaste tentacles of their feminine dependence curling about the party's unique man; already their contacts with the world of their new lives began to be made through him; already they saw in part through his eyes. I wonder what he would have said if I had told him he was a little drunk.

In the course of the day I think I had got him fairly well. As concerned his Church he was at once an asset and a liability. He believed its dogma as few still did, with a simplicity, "the old-time religion." He was born that kind. Of the stuff of the fanatic, the reason he was not a fanatic was that, curiously impervious to little questionings, he had never been aware that his faith was anywhere attacked. A self-educated man, he had accepted the necessary smattering facts of science with a serene indulgence, as simply so much further proof of what the Creator could do when He put His Hand to it. Nor was he conscious of any conflict between these facts and the fact that there existed a substantial Heaven, geographically up, and a substantial Hot Place, geographically down.

So, for his Church, he was an asset in these days. And so, and for the same reason, he was a liability. The Church must after all keep abreast of the times. For home consumption, with modern congregations, especially urban ones, a certain streak of "healthy" scepticism is no longer amiss in the pulpit; it makes people who read at all more comfortable in their pews. A man like Hubert Diana is more for the cause than a hundred. But what to do with him? Well, such things arrange themselves. There's the Foreign Field. The blacker the heathen the whiter the light they'll want, and the solider the conception of a God the Father enthroned in a Heaven of which the sky above them is the visible floor.

And that, at bottom, was what Hubert Diana believed. Accept as he would with the top of his brain the fact of a spherical earth zooming through space, deep in his heart he knew that the world lay flat from modern Illinois to ancient Palestine, and that the sky above it, blue by day and by night festooned with guiding stars for wise men, was the nether side of a floor on which the resurrected trod.

I shall never forget the expression of his face when he realized he was looking straight through it that night. In the quiet dark of the dome I saw him remove his eye from the eyepiece of the telescope up there on the staging and turn it, in the ray of a hooded bulb, on the demon's keeper, Krum.

"What's that, Mr. Krum? I didn't get you!"

"I say, that particular cluster you're looking at——"

"This star, you mean?"

"You'd have to count awhile to count the stars describing their orbits in that 'star,' Mr. Diana. But what I was saying—have you ever had the wish I used to have as a boy—that you could actually look back into the past? With your own two eyes?"

Diana spoke slowly. He didn't know it, but it had already begun to happen; he was already caught. "I have often wished, Mr. Krum, that I might actually look back into the time of our Lord. Actually. Yes."

Krum grunted. He was young. "We'd have to pick a nearer neighbor than *Messier* 79 then. The event you see when you put your eye to that lens is happening much too far in the past. The lightwaves thrown off by that particular cluster on the day, say, of the Crucifixion —*you* won't live to see them. They've hardly started yet—a mere twenty centuries on their way—leaving them something like eight hundred and thirty centuries yet to come before they reach the earth."

Diana laughed the queerest catch of a laugh. "And—and there— there won't be any earth here, then, to welcome them."

"*What?*" It was Krum's turn to look startled. So for a moment the two faces remained in confrontation, the one, as I say, startled, the other exuding visibly little sea-green globules of sweat. It was Diana that caved in first, his voice hardly louder than a whisper.

"W-w-will there?"

None of us suspected the enormousness of the thing that had happened in Diana's brain. Krum shrugged his shoulders and snapped his fingers. Deliberately. *Snap!* "What's a thousand centuries or so in the cosmic reckoning?" He chuckled. "We're just beginning to get out among 'em with *Messier,* you know. In the print room, Mr. Diana, I can show you photographs of clusters to which, if you cared to go, traveling at the speed of light——"

The voice ran on; but Diana's eye had gone back to the eyepiece, and his affrighted soul had re-entered the big black tube sticking its snout out of the slit in the iron hemisphere. . . . "At the speed of light!" . . . That unsuspected, that wildly chance-found chink in the armor of his philosophy! The body is resurrected and it ascends to Heaven instantaneously. At what speed must it be borne to reach instantaneously that city beyond the ceiling of the sky? At a speed inconceivable, mystical. At, say (as he had often said to himself), *the speed of light.* . . . And now, hunched there in the trap that had caught him, black rods, infernal levers and wheels, he was aware of his own eye passing vividly through unpartitioned emptiness, *eight hundred and fifty centuries at the speed of light!*

"And still beyond these," Krum was heard, "we begin to come into the regions of the spiral nebulæ. We've some interesting photographs in the print room, if you've the time."

The ladies below were tired of waiting. One had "lots of packing to do." The bride said, "Yes, I do think we should be getting along, Hubert, dear; if you're ready——"

The fellow actually jumped. It's lucky he didn't break anything. His face looked greener and dewier than ever amid the contraptions above. "If you—you and the ladies, Cora—wouldn't mind—if Mr.—Mr.—(he'd mislaid my name) would see you back to the hotel——" Meeting silence, he began to expostulate. "I feel that this is a rich experience. I'll follow shortly; I know the way."

In the car going back into the city Mrs. Diana set at rest the flutterings of six hearts. Being unmarried they couldn't understand men as she did. When I think of that face of hers, to which I was destined to grow only too accustomed in the weary, itchy days of the trek into Kavirondoland, with its slightly tilted nose, its irregular pigmentation, its easily inflamed lids, and long moist cheeks, like those of a hunting dog, glorying in weariness, it seems incredible that a light of coyness could have found lodgment there. But that night it did. She sat serene among her virgins.

"You don't know Bert. You wait; he'll get a perfectly wonderful sermon out of all that tonight, Bert will."

Krum was having a grand time with his neophyte. He would have stayed up all night. Immured in the little print room crowded with files and redolent of acids, he conducted his disciple "glassy-eyed" through the dim frontiers of space, holding before him one after another the likenesses of universes sister to our own, islanded in immeasurable vacancy, curled like glimmering crullers on their private Milky Ways.

and hiding in their wombs their myriad "coal-pockets," star-dust fœ-
tuses of which—their quadrillion years accomplished—their litters of
new suns would be born, to bear their planets, to bear their moons in
turn.

"And beyond these?"

Always, after each new feat of distance, it was the same. "And beyond?" Given an ell, Diana surrendered to a pop-eyed lust for nothing
less than light-years. "And still beyond?"

"Who knows?"

"The mind quits. For if there's no end to these nebulæ——"

"But supposing there is?"

"An end? But, Mr. Krum, in the very idea of an ending——"

"An end to what we might call this particular category of magnitudes. Eh?"

"I don't get that."

"Well, take this—take the opal in your ring there. The numbers and
distances inside that stone may conceivably be to themselves as staggering as ours to us in our own system. Come! that's not so far-fetched.
What are we learning about the structure of the atom? A nucleus (call
it a sun) revolved about in eternal orbits by electrons (call them planets,
worlds). Infinitesimal; but after all what are bigness and littleness but
matters of comparison? To eyes on one of those electrons (don't be
too sure there aren't any) its tutelary sun may flame its way across a
heaven a comparative ninety million miles away. Impossible for them
to conceive of a boundary to their billions of atomic systems, molecular
universes. In that category of magnitudes its diameter is infinity; once
it has made the leap into our category and become an opal it is merely
a quarter of an inch. That's right, Mr. Diana, you may well stare at it:
between *now* and *now* ten thousand histories may have come and gone
down there. . . . And just so the diameter of our own cluster of universes, going over into another category, may be——"

"May be a—a ring—a little stone—in a—a—a—ring."

Krum was tickled by the way the man's imagination jumped and
engulfed it.

"Why not? That's as good a guess as the next. A ring, let's say, worn
carelessly on the—well, say the tentacle—of some vast organism—some
inchoate creature hobnobbing with its cloudy kind in another system
of universes—which in turn——"

It is curious that none of them realized next day that they were dealing with a stranger, a changed man. Why he carried on, why he capped
that night of cosmic debauch by shaving, eating an unremarkable
breakfast, packing his terrestrial toothbrush and collars, and going up

the gangplank in tow of his excited convoy to sail away, is beyond explanation—unless it was simply that he was in a daze.

It wasn't until four years later that I was allowed to know what had happened on that ship, and even then the tale was so disjointed, warped, and opinionated, so darkly seen in the mirror of Mrs. Diana's orthodoxy, that I had almost to guess what it was *really* all about.

"When Hubert turned irreligious . . ." That phrase, recurrent on her tongue in the meanderings of the East African quest to which we were by then committed, will serve to measure her understanding. Irreligious! Good Lord! But from that sort of thing I had to reconstruct the drama. Evening after evening beside her camp fire (appended to the Mineral Survey Expedition Toward Uganda through the kindness —actually the worn-down surrender—of the Protectorate government) I lingered a while before joining the merrier engineers, watched with fascination the bumps growing under the mosquitoes on her forehead, and listened to the jargon of her mortified meekness and her scandalized faith.

There had been a fatal circumstance, it seems, at the very outset. If Diana could but have been seasick, as the rest of them were (horribly), all might still have been well. In the misery of desired death, along with the other contents of a heaving midriff, he might have brought up the assorted universes of which he had been led too rashly to partake. But he wasn't. As if his wife's theory was right, as if Satan was looking out for him, he was spared to prowl the swooping decks immune. Four days and nights alone. Time enough to digest and assimilate into his being beyond remedy that lump of whirling magnitudes and to feel himself surrendering with a strange new ecstasy to the drunkenness of liberty.

Such liberty! Given Diana's type, it is hard to imagine it adequately. The abrupt, complete removal of the toils of reward and punishment; the withdrawal of the surveillance of an all-seeing, all-knowing Eye; the windy assurance of being responsible for nothing, important to no one, no longer (as the police say) "wanted"! It must have been beautiful in those few days of its first purity, before it began to be discolored by his contemptuous pity for others, the mask of his inevitable loneliness and his growing fright.

The first any of them knew of it—even his wife—was in mid-voyage, the day the sea went down and the seven who had been sick came up. There seemed an especial Providence in the calming of the waters; it was Sunday morning and Diana had been asked to conduct the services.

He preached on the text: "For of such is the kingdom of Heaven."

"If our concept of God means anything it means a God *all*-mighty,

Creator of *all* that exists, Director of the *infinite,* cherishing in His Heaven the saved souls of *all space and all time."*

Of course; amen. And wasn't it nice to feel like humans again, and real sunshine pouring up through the lounge ports from an ocean suddenly grown kind? . . . But—then—*what* was Diana *saying?*

Mrs. Diana couldn't tell about it coherently even after a lapse of fifty months. Even in a setting as remote from that steamer's lounge as the equatorial bush, the ember-reddened canopy of thorn trees, the meandering camp fires, the chant and tramp somewhere away of Kikuyu porters dancing in honor of an especial largesse of fat zebra meat—even here her memory of that impious outburst was too vivid, too aghast.

"It was Hubert's look! The way he stared at us! As if you'd said he was licking his chops! . . . That *'Heaven'* of his!"

It seems they hadn't waked up to what he was about until he had the dimensions of his sardonic Paradise irreparably drawn in. The final haven of all right souls. Not alone the souls released from this our own tiny earth. In the millions of solar systems we see as stars how many millions of satellites must there be upon which at some time in their histories conditions suited to organic life subsist? Uncounted hordes of wheeling populations! Of men? God's creatures at all events, a portion of them reasoning. Weirdly shaped perhaps, but what of that? And that's only to speak of our own inconsiderable cluster of universes. That's to say nothing of other systems of magnitudes, where God's creatures are to our world what we are to the worlds in the atoms in our finger rings. (He had shaken *his,* here, in their astounded faces.) And all these, all the generations of these enormous and microscopic beings harvested through a time beside which the life span of our earth is as a second in a million centuries: all these brought to rest for an eternity to which time itself is a watch tick—all crowded to rest pellmell, thronged, serried, packed, packed to suffocation in layers unnumbered light-years deep. This must needs be our concept of Heaven if God is the God of the Whole. If, on the other hand——

The other hand was the hand of the second officer, the captain's delegate at divine worship that Sabbath day. He at last had "come to."

I don't know whether it was the same day or the next; Mrs. Diana was too vague. But here's the picture. Seven women huddled in the large stateroom on B-deck, conferring in whispers, aghast, searching one another's eye obliquely even as they bowed their heads in prayer for some light—and of a sudden the putting back of the door and the in-marching of the Reverend Hubert. . . .

As Mrs. Diana tried to tell me, "You understand, don't you, he had just taken a bath? And he hadn't—he had forgotten to——"

Adam-innocent there he stood. Not a stitch. But I don't believe for a minute it was a matter of forgetting. In the high intoxication of his soul release, already crossed (by the second officer) and beginning to show his zealot claws, he needed some gesture stunning enough to witness to his separation, his unique rightness, his contempt of match-flare civilizations and infinitesimal taboos.

But I can imagine that stateroom scene: the gasps, the heads colliding in aversion, and Diana's six weedy feet of birthday suit towering in the shadows, and ready to sink through the deck I'll warrant, now the act was irrevocable, but still grimly carrying it off.

"And if, on the other hand, you ask me to bow down before a God peculiar to this one earth, this one grain of dust lost among the giants of space, watching its sparrows fall, profoundly interested in a speck called Palestine no bigger than the quadrillionth part of one of the atoms in the ring here on my finger——"

Really scared by this time, one of the virgins shrieked. It was altogether too close quarters with a madman.

Mad? Of course there was the presumption: "Crazy as a loon." Even legally it was so adjudged at the *Platonic's* first port of call, Algiers, where, when Diana escaped ashore and wouldn't come back again, he had to be given over to the workings of the French Law. I talked with the magistrate myself some forty months later, when, "let in" for the business as I have told, I stopped there on my way out.

"But what would you?" were his words. "We must live in the world as the world lives, is it not? Sanity? Sanity is what? Is it, for example, an intellectual clarity, a balanced perception of the realities? Naturally, speaking out of court, your friend was of a sanity—of a sanity, sir——" Here the magistrate made with thumb and fingers the gesture only the French can make for a thing that is matchless, a beauty, a transcendent instance of any kind. He himself was Gallic, rational. Then, with a lift of shoulder: "But what would you? We must live in the world that seems."

Diana, impounded in Algiers for deportation, escaped. What after all are the locks and keys of this pinchbeck category of magnitudes? More remarkable still, there in Arab Africa, he succeeded in vanishing from the knowledge and pursuit of men. And of women. His bride, now that their particular mission had fallen through, was left to decide whether to return to America or to go on with two of the company, the Misses Brookhart and Smutts, who were bound for a school in Smyrna. In the end she followed the latter course. It was there, nearly four years later, that I was sent to join her by an exasperated and worn-out Firm.

By that time she knew again where her husband-errant was—or where at least, from time to time in his starry dartings over this our mote of dust, he had been heard of, spoken to, seen.

Could we but have a written history of those years of his apostolic vagabondage, a record of the towns in which he was jailed or from which he was kicked out, of the ports in which he starved, of the ships on which he stowed away, presently to reveal himself in proselyting ardor, denouncing the earthlings, the fatelings, the dupes of bugaboo, meeting scoff with scoff, preaching the new revelation red-eyed, like an angry prophet. Or was it, more simply, like a man afraid?

Was that the secret, after all, of his prodigious restlessness? Had it anything in common with the swarming of those pale worms that flee the Eye of the Infinite around the curves of the stone you pick up in a field? Talk of the man without a country! What of the man without a universe?

It is curious that I never suspected his soul's dilemma until I saw the first of his mud-sculptures in the native village of Ndua in the province of Kasuma in British East. Here it was, our objective attained, we parted company with the government *safari* and shifted the burden of Way-straightening to the shoulders of Major Wyeside, the ostrich farmer of the neighborhood.

While still on the *safari* I had put to Mrs. Diana a question that had bothered me: "Why on earth should your husband ever have chosen this particular neck of the woods to land up in? Why Kavirondoland?"

"It was here we were coming at the time Hubert turned irreligious, to found a mission. It's a coincidence, isn't it?"

And yet I would have sworn Diana hadn't a sense of humor about him anywhere. But perhaps it *wasn't* an ironic act. Perhaps it was simply that, giving up the struggle with a society blinded by "a little learning" and casting about for a virgin field, he had remembered this.

"I supposed he was a missionary," Major Wyeside told us with a flavor of indignation. "I went on that. I let him live here—six or seven months of it—while he was learning the tongue. I was a bit nonplussed, to put it mildly, when I discovered what he was up to."

What things Diana had been up to the Major showed us in one of the huts in the native kraal—a round dozen of them, modeled in mud and baked. Blackened blobs of mud, that's all. Likenesses of nothing under the sun, fortuitous masses sprouting haphazard tentacles, only two among them showing postules that might have been experimental heads. . . . The ostrich farmer saw our faces.

"Rum, eh? Of course I realized the chap was anything but fit. A walking skeleton. Nevertheless, whatever it is about these beasties, there's not a nigger in the village has dared set foot inside this hut since Diana left. You can see for yourselves it's about to crash. There's another like it he left at Suki, above here. Taboo, no end!"

So Diana's "hunch" had been right. He had found his virgin field, indeed, fit soil for his cosmic fright. A religion in the making, here before our eyes.

"This was at the very last before he left," Wyeside explained. "He took to making these mud pies quite of a sudden; the whole lot within a fortnight's time. Before that he had simply talked, harangued. He would sit here in the doorway of an evening with the niggers squatted around and harangue 'em by the hour. I knew something of it through my house-boys. The most amazing rot. All about the stars to begin with, as if these black baboons could half grasp *astronomy!* But that seemed all proper. Then there was talk about a something a hundred times as big and powerful as the world, sun, moon, and stars put together— some perfectly enormous stupendous awful being—but knowing how mixed the boys can get, it still seemed all regular—simply the parson's way of getting at the notion of an Almighty God. But no, they insisted, there wasn't any God. That's the point, they said; there *is no* God. . . . Well, that impressed me as a go. That's when I decided to come down and get the rights of this star-swallowing monstrosity the beggar was feeding my labor on. And here he sat in the doorway with one of these beasties—here it is, this one—waving it furiously in the niggers' be- nighted faces. And do you know what he'd done?—you can see the mark here still on this wabble-leg, this tentacle-business—he had taken off a ring he had and screwed it on just here. His finger ring, my word of honor! And still, if you'll believe it, I didn't realize he was just daft. Not until he spoke to me. 'I find,' he was good enough to enlighten me, 'I find I have to make it somehow concrete.' . . . 'Make what?' . . . 'Our wearer.' 'Our *what, where?*' . . . 'In the following category.' . . . His actual words, honor bright. I was going to have him sent down-country where he could be looked after. He got ahead of me though. He cleared out. When I heard he'd turned up at Suki I ought, I suppose, to have attended to it. But I was having trouble with leopards. And you know how things go."

From there we went to Suki, the Major accompanying. It was as like Ndua as one flea to its brother, a stockade inclosing round houses of mud, wattles, and thatch, and full of naked heathen. The Kavirondo are the nakedest of all African peoples and, it is said, the most moral. It put a great strain on Mrs. Diana; all that whole difficult anxious time, as it were detachedly, I could see her itching to get them into Mother Hubbard and cast-off Iowa pants.

Here too, as the Major had promised, we found a holy of holies, rather a dreadful of dreadfuls, "taboo no end," its shadows cluttered with the hurlothrumbos of Diana's artistry. What puzzled me was their number. Why this appetite for experimentation? There was an un- certainty; one would think its effect on potential converts would be bad. Here, as in Ndua, Diana had contented himself at first with words and skyward gesticulations. Not for so long however. Feeling the need of giving his concept of the cosmic "wearer" a substance much earlier, he had shut himself in with the work, literally—a fever of creation. We counted seventeen of the nameless "blobs," all done, we were told, in the seven days and nights before their maker had again cleared out. The villagers would hardly speak of him; only after spitting to protect themselves, their eyes averted, and in an undertone, would they mention him: "He of the Ring." Thereafter we were to hear of him only as "He of the Ring."

Leaving Suki, Major Wyeside turned us over (thankfully, I warrant) to a native who told us his name was Charlie Kamba. He had spent some years in Nairobi, running for an Indian outfitter, and spoke English remarkably well. It was from him we learned, quite casually, when our modest eight-load *safari* was some miles on its way, that the primary object of our coming was nonexistent. Hubert Diana was dead.

Dead nearly five weeks—a moon and a little—and buried in the mission church at Tara Hill.

Mission church! There was a poser for us. *Mission church?*

Well then, Charlie Kamba gave us to know that he was paraphrasing in a large way suitable to our habits of thought. We wouldn't have understood *his* informant's "wizard house" or "house of the effigy."

I will say for Mrs. Diana that in the course of our halt of lugubrious amazement she shed tears. That some of them were not tears of unrealized relief it would be hardly natural to believe. She had desired loyally to find her husband, but when she should have found him—what? This problem, sturdily ignored so long, was now removed.

Turn back? Never! Now it would seem the necessity for pressing forward was doubled. In the scrub-fringed ravine of our halt the porters resumed their loads, the dust stood up again, the same caravan moved on. But how far it was now from being the same.

From that moment it took on, for me at least, a new character. It wasn't the news especially; the fact that Diana was dead had little to do with it. Perhaps it was simply that the new sense of something aimfully and cumulatively dramatic in our progress had to have a beginning, and that moment would do as well as the next.

Six villages: M'nann, Leika, Leikapo, Shamba, Little Tara, and Tara, culminating in the apotheosis of Tara Hill. Six stops for the night on the road it had cost Diana as many months to cover in his singular pilgrimage to his inevitable goal. Or in his flight to it. Yes, his stampede. Now the pipers at that four-day orgy of liberty on the *Platonic's* decks were at his heels for their pay. Now that his strength was failing, the hosts of loneliness were after him, creeping out of their dreadful magnitudes, the hounds of space. Over all that ground it seemed to me we were following him not by the word of hearsay but, as one follows a wounded animal making for its earth, by the droppings of his blood.

Our progress had taken on a pattern; it built itself with a dramatic artistry; it gathered suspense. As though it were a story at its most breathless places "continued in our next," and I a reader forgetting the road's weariness, the dust, the torment of insects never escaped, the inadequate food, I found myself hardly able to keep from running on ahead to reach the evening's village, to search out the inevitable repository of images left by the white stranger who had come and tarried there awhile and gone again.

More concrete and ever more concrete. The immemorial compromise with the human hunger for a symbol to see with the eyes, touch with the hands. Hierarchy after hierarchy of little mud effigies—one could see the necessity pushing the man. Out of the protoplasmic blobs of Ndua, Suki, even M'nann, at Leikapo Diana's concept of infinity (so pure in that halcyon epoch at sea), of categories nested within categories like Japanese boxes, of an over-creature wearing our cosmos like a trinket, unawares, had become a mass with legs to stand on and a real head. The shards scattered about in the filth of the hut there (as if in violence of despair) were still monstrosities, but with a sudden stride of concession their monstrousness was the monstrousness of lizard and turtle and crocodile. At Shamba there were dozens of huge-footed birds.

It is hard to be sure in retrospect, but I do believe that by the time we reached Little Tara I began to see the thing as a whole—the fœtus, working out slowly, blindly, but surely, its evolution in the womb of fright. At Little Tara there was a change in the character of the exhibits; their numbers had diminished, their size had grown. There was a boar with tusks and a bull the size of a dog with horns, and on a tusk and on a horn an indentation left by a ring.

I don't believe Mrs. Diana got the thing at all. Toward the last she wasn't interested in the huts of relics; at Little Tara she wouldn't go near the place; she was "too tired." It must have been pretty awful, when you think of it, even if all she saw in them was the mud-pie play of a man reverted to a child.

There was another thing at Little Tara quite as momentous as the jump to boar and bull. Here at last a mask had been thrown aside. Here there had been no pretense of proselyting, no astronomical lectures, no doorway harangues. Straightway he had arrived (a fabulous figure already, long heralded), he had commandeered a house and shut himself up in it and there, mysterious, assiduous, he had remained three days and nights, eating nothing, but drinking gallons of the foul water they left in gourds outside his curtain of reeds. No one in the village had ever seen what he had done and left there. Now, candidly, those labors were for himself alone.

Here at last in Tara the moment of that confession had overtaken the fugitive. It was he, ill with fever and dying of nostalgia—not these naked black baboon men seen now as little more than blurs—who had to give the Beast of the Infinite a name and a shape. And more and more, not only a shape, but a *shapeliness*. From the instant when, no longer able to live alone with nothingness, he had given it a likeness in Ndua mud, and perceived that it was intolerable and fled its face, the turtles and distorted crocodiles of Leikapo and the birds of Shamba had become inevitable, and no less inevitable the Little Tara boar and bull. Another thing grows plain in retrospect: the reason why, done to death (as all the way they reported him) he couldn't die. He didn't dare to. Didn't dare to close his eyes.

It was at Little Tara we first heard of him as "Father Witch," a name come back, we were told, from Tara, where he had gone. I had heard it pronounced several times before it suddenly obtruded from the native context as actually two English words. That was what made it queer. It was something they must have picked up by rote, uncomprehending; something then they could have had from no lips but his own. When I repeated it after them with a better accent they pointed up toward the north, saying "Tara! Tara!"—their eagerness mingled with awe.

I shall never forget Tara as we saw it, after our last blistering scramble up a gorge, situated in the clear air on a slope belted with cedars. A mid-African stockade left by some blunder in an honest Colorado landscape, or a newer and bigger Vermont. Here at the top of our journey, black savages, their untidy *shambas,* the very Equator, all these seemed as incongruous as a Gothic cathedral in a Congo marsh. I wonder if Hubert Diana knew whither his instinct was guiding him on the long road of his journey here to die. . . .

He had died and he was buried, not in the village, but about half a mile distant, on the ridge; this we were given to know almost before we had arrived. There was no need to announce ourselves, the word of our coming had outrun us; the populace was at the gates.

"Our Father Witch! Our Father Witch!" They knew what we were after; the funny parrot-wise English stood out from the clack and clatter of their excited speech. "Our Father Witch! Ay! Ay!" With a common eagerness they gesticulated at the hilltop beyond the cedars.

Certainly here was a change. No longer the propitiatory spitting, the averted eyes, the uneasy whispering allusion to him who had passed that way: here in Tara they would shout him from the housetops, with a kind of civic pride.

We learned the reason for this on our way up the hill. It was because they were his chosen, the initiate.

We made the ascent immediately, against the village's advice. It was near evening; the return would be in the dark; it was a bad country for goblins; wouldn't tomorrow morning do? . . . No, it wouldn't do the widow. Her face was set. . . . And so, since we were resolved to go, the village went with us, armed with rattles and drums. Charlie Kamba walked beside us, sifting the information a hundred were eager to give.

These people were proud, he said, because their wizard was more powerful than all the wizards of all the other villages "in the everywhere together." If he cared to he could easily knock down all the other villages in the "everywhere," destroying all the people and all the cattle. If he cared to he could open his mouth and swallow the sky and the stars. But Tara he had chosen. Tara he would protect. He made their mealies to grow and their cattle to multiply.

I protested, "But he is *dead* now!"

Charlie Kamba made signs of deprecation. I discerned that he was far from being clear about the thing himself.

Yes, he temporized, this Father Witch was dead, quite dead. On the other hand he was up there. On the other hand he would never die. He was longer than forever. Yes, quite true, he was dead and buried under the pot.

I gave it up. "How did he die?"

Well, he came to this village of Tara very suffering, very sick. The dead man who walked. His face was very sad. Very eaten. Very frightened. He came to this hill. So he lived here for two full moons, very hot, very eaten, very dead. These men made him a house as he commanded them, also a stockade. In the house he was very quiet, very dead, making magic two full moons. Then he came out and they that were waiting saw him. He had made the magic, and the magic had made him well. His face was kind. He was happy. He was full fed. He was full fed, these men said, without any eating. Yes, they carried up to him very fine food, because they were full of wonder and some fear, but he did not eat any of it. Some water he drank. So, for two days and the night between them, he continued sitting in the gate of the stockade, very happy, very full fed. He told these people very much about their wizard, who is bigger than everywhere and longer than forever and can, if he cares to, swallow the sky and stars. From time to time however, ceasing to talk to these people, he got to his knees and talked in his own strange tongue to Our Father Witch, his eyes held shut. When he had done this just at sunset of the second day he fell forward on his face. So he remained that night. The next day these men took him into the house and buried him under the pot. On the other hand Our Father Witch is longer than forever. He remains there still. . . .

The first thing I saw in the hut's interior was the earthen pot at the northern end, wrong-side-up on the ground. I was glad I had preceded Mrs. Diana. I walked across and sat down on it carelessly, hoping so that her afflicted curiosity might be led astray. It gave me the oddest feeling, though, to think of what was there beneath my nonchalant sitting-portion—aware as I was of the Kavirondo burial of a great man—up to the neck in mother earth, and the rest of him left out in the dark of the pot for the undertakings of the ants. I hoped his widow wouldn't wonder about that inverted vessel of clay.

I needn't have worried. Her attention was arrested otherwheres. I shall not forget the look of her face, caught above me in the red shaft of sundown entering the western door, as she gazed at the last and the largest of the Reverend Hubert Diana's gods. That long, long cheek of hers, buffeted by sorrow, startled now and mortified. Not till that moment, I believe, had she comprehended the steps of mud-images she had been following for what they were, the steps of idolatry.

For my part, I wasn't startled. Even before we started up the hill, knowing that her husband had dared to die here, I could have told her pretty much what she would find.

This overlord of the cosmic categories that he had fashioned (at last) in his own image sat at the other end of the red-streaked house upon a bench—a throne?—of mud. Diana had been no artist. An ovoid two-eyed head, a cylindrical trunk, two arms, two legs, that's all. But indubitably man, man-size. Only one finger of one of the hands had been done with much care. It wore an opal, a two-dollar stone from Mexico, set in a silver ring. This was the hand that was lifted, and over it the head was bent.

I've said Diana was no artist. I'll take back the words. The figure was crudeness itself, but in the relation between that bent head and that lifted hand there was something which was something else. A sense of scrutiny one would have said no genius of mud could ever have conveyed. An attitude of interest centered in that bauble, intense and static, breathless and eternal all in one—penetrating to its bottom atom. to the last electron, to a hill upon it, and to a two-legged mite about to die. Marking (yes, I'll swear to the incredible) the sparrow's fall.

The magic was made. The road that had commenced with the blobs of Ndua—the same that commenced with our hairy ancestors listening to the night-wind in their caves—was run.

And from here Diana, of a sudden happy, of a sudden looked after, "full fed," had walked out——

But no; I couldn't stand that mortified sorrow on the widow's face any longer. She had to be made to see what she wanted to see. I said it aloud:

"From here, Mrs. Diana, your husband walked out——"

"He had sunk to idolatry. *Idolatry!*"

"To the bottom, yes. And come up its whole history again. And from here he walked out into the sunshine to kneel and talk with 'Our Father Which——' "

She got it. She caught it. I wish you could have seen the light going up those long, long cheeks as she got it:

"Our Father which art in Heaven, Hallowed be Thy Name!"

We went down hill in the darkness, protected aginst goblins by a vast rattling of gourds and beating of goat-hide drums.

51

Tact

BY THOMAS BEER

Y OU make me sick," said Mrs.
Egg. She spoke with force. Her three daughters murmured, "Why
mamma!" A squirrel ran up an apple tree that shaded the veranda; a
farm hand turned from weeding the mint bed by the garage. Mrs. Egg
didn't care. Her chins shook fiercely. She ate a wafer, emptied her glass
of iced tea and spread her little hands with their buried rings on the
table.

"You make me sick, girls," she said. "Dammy's been home out of the
Navy precisely seven weeks an' two days, an' a hour hasn't passed but
what one of you've been phonin' me from town about what he has or
ain't done unbecomin' to a boy that's engaged to Edith Sims! I don't
know why you girls expect a boy that was champion heavyweight
wrestler of the Atlantic Fleet an' stands six foot four and a half inches
in his bare feet to get all thrilled over bein' engaged. A person that was
four years in the Navy an' went clean to Japan has naturally been in love
before, and—"

"Mamma!"

Mrs. Egg ate another sugar wafer and continued relentlessly "—ain't
likely to get all worked up over bein' engaged to a sixteen-year-old girl
who can't cook any better than a Cuban, on his own say-so. As for those
spiced guavas he sent home from Cuba in March," she mused, "I thought
they were fierce. As for his takin' Edith Sims out drivin' in overalls and
a shirt, Adam John Egg is the best-lookin' person in this family and you
know it. You three girls are the sent'mentalest women in the state of
Ohio and I don't know how your husbands stand it. My gee! D'you
expect Dammy to chase this girl around heavin' roses at her like a fool
in a movie?" She panted and peered into the iced-tea pitcher, then aimed
an affable bawl at the kitchen door. "Benjamina! I'd be awful obliged

if you'd make up some more iced tea, please. Dammy'll be through pickin' peaches soon and he's usually thirsty about four o'clock."

Her new cook came down the long veranda. The daughters stared at this red-haired girl, taller than their tall selves. Benjamina lifted the vacant pitcher and carried it silently away. Her slim height vanished into the kitchen and the oldest daughter whispered, "Mercy, mamma, she's almost as tall as Dammy!"

"She's just six feet," said Mrs. Egg with deliberate clarity meant to reach Benjamina, "but extremely graceful, I think. My gee! It's perfectly embarrassin' to ask a girl as refined as that to clear the table or dust. She went through high school in Cleveland and can read all the French in the cookbook exactly as if it made sense. It's a pleasure to have such a person in the house."

The second daughter leaned forward and said, "Mamma, that's another thing! I do think it's pretty—untactful of Dammy to take this girl's brother around in the car and introduce him to Edith Sims and her folks as if—"

"I think it was extremely sensible," Mrs. Egg puffed. "Hamish is a very int'restin' boy, and has picked up milkin' remarkably when he's only been here a week, and Dammy's taught him to sem'phore, or whatever that wiggling-your-arms thing is called. And he appreciates Dammy a lot." The plate of sugar wafers was stripped to crumbs. Mrs. Egg turned her flushed face and addressed the unseen: "Benjamina, you might bring some more cookies when the tea's ready, and some of those cup cakes you made this mornin'. Dammy ate five of them at lunch."

Benjamina answered "Yes, Mrs. Egg" in her slow fashion.

"Mamma," said the youngest daughter, "it's all right for you to say that Dammy is absolutely perfect, but the Simses are the most refined people in town, and it does look disgraceful for Dammy not to dress up *a little* when he goes there, and he's got all those beautiful tailor-made clothes from New York."

Mrs. Egg patiently drawled, "Fern, that's an awful uninterestin' remark. Dammy looks exactly like a seal in a aquarium when he's dressed up, his things fit so smooth; but a boy that was four years in the Navy and helps milk a hundred and twenty-seven cows twice a day, besides mendin' all the machinery on the place, is *not* called upon to dress up evenings to go see a girl he's known all his life. He's twenty-one years and nine weeks old, an' capable of managin' his own concerns. . . . Thank you, Benjamina," she told the red-haired girl as the fresh pitcher clinked on the table and the cup cakes gleamed in yellow charm beside it. "I do hate to trouble you on such a hot day."

Benjamina smiled nicely and withdrew. Mrs. Egg ate one of the cup cakes and thought it admirable. She broke out, "My gee! There's another thing! You girls keep actin' as if Dammy wasn't as smart as should be! On the other hand, he drove to Cleveland and looked at the list of persons willin' to work in the country and didn't waste time askin' the agency questions, but went round to Benjamina's flat and ate some choc'late cake. Then he loaded her and Hamish into the car and brought 'em down, all between six in the mornin' and twelve at night. I've had eight days of rest an' comfort since! My gee! Your papa's the second biggest dairyman in this state, but that don't keep me in intell'gent cooks!"

The three young matrons sighed. Mrs. Egg considered them for a moment over her glass, and sniffed, "Mercy! This has been a pleasant afternoon!"

"Mamma," said the first-born, "you can't very well deny that Dammy's awful careless for an engaged man. He ought to've got a ring for Edith Sims when he was home at Christmas and the engagement came off. And—"

Mrs. Egg lost patience. She exclaimed, "Golden Jerusalem! Dammy got engaged at Judge Randolph's party the night before he went back to Brooklyn to his ship! My gee! I never heard such idiotic nonsense! You girls act as if Edith Sims—whose ears are much too big even if she does dress her hair low—was too good for Adam Egg! She's a nice child, an' her folks are nice and all the rest of it! . . . Dammy," she panted as the marvel appeared, "here's the girls!"

Adam came up the veranda with a clothes basket of peaches on his right shoulder. He nodded his black head to his sisters and put the basket noiselessly down. Then he blew smoke from both nostrils of his bronze, small nose and rubbed its bridge with the cigarette. He seldom spoke. Mrs. Egg filled a glass with iced tea and Adam began to absorb this pensively. His sisters cooed and his mother somewhat forgave them. They had sense enough to adore Adam, anyhow. In hours of resolute criticism Mrs. Egg sometimes admitted that Adam's nose was too short. He was otherwise beyond praise. His naked dark shoulders rippled and convulsed as he stooped to gather three cup cakes. A stained undershirt hid some of his terrific chest and his canvas trousers hung beltless on his narrow hips. Mrs. Egg secretly hoped that he would change these garments before he went to call on Edie Sims. The three cup cakes departed through his scarlet mouth into his insatiable system of muscles, and Adam lit his next cigarette. Smoke surged in a tide about his immovable big eyes. He looked at the road beyond the apple trees, then swung and made swift, enigmatic gestures with his awesome arms to young Hamish Saunders, loitering by the garage. Hamish responded with more flappings of his lesser arms and trotted down the grass. A letter carrier approached the delivery box at the gates of the monstrous farm.

"What did you sem'phore to Hamish, lamb?" Mrs. Egg asked.

Adam said "Mail" and sat down on the floor.

He fixed a black stare on the pitcher and Mrs. Egg filled his glass. Muscles rose in ovals and ropes under the hairless polish of his arm as he took the frail tumbler. His hard throat stirred and his short feet wriggled in moccasins of some soiled, soft leather, indicating satisfaction. Mrs. Egg beamed. Benjamina made tea perfectly. She must tactfully tell the girl that Adam liked it. No female could hear that fact without a thrill.

"Package for you," said young Hamish, bounding up the steps. He gave Adam a stamped square box, announced "I signed for it," and retired shyly from the guests to read a post card. He was a burly lad of sixteen, in a shabby darned jersey and some outgrown breeches of Adam's. Mrs. Egg approved of him; he appreciated Adam.

The marvel tore the box to pieces with his lean fingers and got out a flat case of velvet. Two rings glittered in its satin lining. Adam contemplated the diamond of the engagement ring and the band of gold set with tiny brilliants which would forever nail Edith Sims to his perfections. His sisters squealed happily. Mrs. Egg thought how many pounds of Egg's A1 Butter were here consumed in vainglory and sighed gently. But she drawled, "My gee, Dammy! Nobody can poss'bly say you ain't got good taste in jewelry, anyhow," and shot a stare of fierce pride at her daughters. They rose. She knew that the arrival of these gauds would be known in Ilium forthwith. She said "Well, good evenin', girls," and accepted their kisses.

Adam paid no attention to the going of the oldest daughter's motor car; he was staring at the rings, and the blank brown of his forehead was disturbed by some superb and majestic fancy current under the dense smoothness of his jet hair. Hamish Saunders came shyly to peep at the gems and stooped his curly red head. The boy had large gray eyes, like those of his sister, and her hawk nose, which Mrs. Egg thought patrician.

"Hamish, you ain't had any tea yet, lamb. Dammy's left some. Benjamina puts in exactly sugar enough, an' I never heard of mint in iced tea before. It's awful interestin'."

Hamish soberly drank some tea and asked Adam, "Want the motor bike, Mr. Egg?"

Adam nodded. The boy went leaping down the flagged walk to the garage and busily led Adam's red motorcycle back to the veranda steps. Then he gazed with reverence at Adam's shoulders, felt his own right biceps and sadly walked off toward the barns. The herd of the Egg

Dairy Company was an agitation of twinkling horns and multicolored hides in the white-fenced yard. The ten hired men were sponging their hands at the model washstand by the colossal water tower's engine house. Mrs. Egg ate the last cup cake and looked at the town of Ilium, spread in a lizard of trees on the top of a long slope. The motor containing her female offspring was sliding into the main street. The daughters would stop at the Sims house to tell the refined Edith that her engagement ring had come.

Mrs. Egg pursed her lips courageously and said, "Dammy, you might change your duds, dear, before you take Edith her sol'taire. It's kind of a formal occasion, sort of."

The giant pronounced lazily the one syllable "Punk," and turned his face toward his mother. Then he said, "You've got awful pretty hands, mamma."

"Mercy, Dammy," Mrs. Egg panted, flushing. Her prodigiousness shook in the special chair of oak under the blow of this compliment. She tittered, "Well, your papa—I do hope it ain't so hot in Chicago—used to say so before I got stout."

Adam blew a snake of smoke from his left nostril and surprised her with a whole sentence. He drawled, "Was a oiler on the Nevada that sung a song about pale hands, pink tipped like some kind of a flower, mamma."

"Mercy," said Mrs. Egg, "I know that song! A person sang it at the Presbyterian supper in 1910 when the oysters were bad, and some people thought it wasn't correct for a church party, bein' a pretty passionate kind of song. It was awful popular for a while after that . . . Benjamina would know, her papa havin' kept a music store. I'll ask her. Help me up, lamb."

Adam arose and took his mother kindly out of her chair with one motion. Mrs. Egg passed voluminously over the sill into the kitchen and addressed her superior cook.

"There's a sent'mental kind of song that Dammy's interested in which is about some gump lovin' a woman's pale hands beside the shallow Marne or some such place."

Benjamina brushed back her blazing hair with both slender hands and looked at the rosy nails.

"Pale Hands. I think—No, it's the Kashmir love song. It used to be sung a great deal."

Adam said "Thanks" in the doorway.

Then he turned, jamming the jewel case into his pocket, and lounged down the steps. His shoulders gleamed like oiled wood. He picked a handful of peaches from the basket, which would have burdened two mortals, and split one in his terrible fingers. He ate a peach absently and threw the red stone at a roaming chicken, infamously busy in the nasturtiums. Mrs. Egg leaned on the side of the door. A slight nervousness made her reach for the radishes which Benjamina was cleaning. Radishes always stimulated Mrs. Egg. She ate two and hoped that Edith Sims wouldn't happen to look at Adam's back. The undershirt showed both shoulder blades and most of the sentiment "Damn Kaiser Bill" tattooed in pink across Adam. It seemed indecorous at the moment of betrothal, and Mrs. Egg winced.

Then she wondered. Adam took another peach and pressed it in a hand. Its blood welled over his shoulder and smeared the rear of the shirt brilliantly. He scrubbed it thoroughly into the back of his cropped hair and massaged his flat abdomen with a second fruit. After some study he kicked his feet out of the moccasins and doubled down in his fluid manner to rub both insteps with black grease from valves of the motorcycle. Then he signaled contentment by a prolonged pouring of smoke from his mouth, gave his mother a glance as he tucked the cast moccasins into the fork of the apple tree and fled down the driveway with a coughing of his machine's engine, barefoot, unspeakably soiled and magnificently shimmering with peach blood.

"Oh, Lord!" said Mrs. Egg.

Benjamina looked up from the radishes and asked "What did you say?"

Mrs. Egg meditated, eating a radish. Adam had favored Benjamina with some notice in these ten days, and his approval of her cooking was manifest. He had even eaten veal goulash, a dish which he usually declined. The girl was a lady, anyhow. Mrs. Egg exploded.

"Benjamina, Dammy's up to somethin'! His sisters keep tellin' me he ain't tactful, either! My gee! He simply washed himself in peach juice and went off to give Edith Sims her engagement ring! And left his moc'sins in the apple tree where he always used to put his cigarettes when his papa didn't think he was old enough to smoke. But heaven knows, I can't see that anything ever hurt Dammy! He's always been the neatest boy that ever lived, and had all his clothes made when he was in the Navy. It's perfectly true that he ain't dressed respectable once since he got home. Mercy, the other day he went in to see Edith in a half a khaki shirt that he'd been usin' to clean the garage floor with!"

Benjamina pared a radish with a flutter of her white fingers and asked, "How long have they been engaged, Mrs. Egg?"

"He had ten days' liberty, Christmas, and was home. It perfectly upset me, because Dammy hadn't ever paid any attention to the child. They got engaged at a dance Judge Randolph gave. It was extremely sudden," Mrs. Egg pondered, "although the Simses are very refined folks and Edith's a nice girl. . . . A boy who was four years in the Navy naturally ought to know when he's in love or not. But men do fall in love in the most accidental manner, Benjamina! They don't seem to have any intentions of it. My gee! A man who takes to runnin' after a girl for her money is within my comprehensions, or because she's good-lookin'. But what most men marry most women for is beyond me. I'm forty-six years of age," she said, "but I still get surprised at things. I think I'll lie down. . . . Do you man'cure your nails, or are they as pink as that all the time?"

"They're naturally pink," Benjamina said.

"They're awfully pretty," Mrs. Egg yawned, pausing in her advance to the door of the living room. Then it seemed guileful to increase this praise. She added "Dammy was sayin' so," and strolled into the living room, where twenty-five photographs of Adam stood on shelves and tables.

She closed the door and stopped to eat a peppermint out of a glass urn beside the phonograph's cabinet. Excitements worked in her. She brushed a fly from the picture of Adam in wrestling tights and sank on a vast couch. The leather cushions hissed, breathing out air under her descent. She closed her eyes and brooded. . . . If Adam wanted to annoy Edith Sims, he had chosen a means cleverly. The girl was elaborate as to dress and rather haughty about clothes. She had praised a shirt of Judge Randolph's second son before Adam pointedly on Sunday at tea in the veranda. Perturbations and guesses clattered in Mrs. Egg's mind. Then a real clatter in the kitchen roused her.

"I milked three cows," said Hamish Saunders to his sister in a loud and complacent voice.

Benjamina said less loudly but with vigor, "Hamish, you got a post card! I saw you reading it! I told you not to write anyone where we'd gone to. Now—"

Mrs. Egg knew that the boy was wiggling. He said, "Oh, I wrote Tick Matthews. He won't tell Cousin Joe, Benjy."

"He'll tell his mother and she'll tell everyone in the building! I didn't want anyone to know where we'd gone to!"

Mrs. Egg sat up. In a little, the lad spoke with a sound of male determination. He spoke airily. His hands must be jammed into his pockets. He said, "Now Cousin Joe ain't going to come runnin' down here after us, Benjy. You've gone off, so that ought to sort of show him you ain't going to marry him. I was asking Adam if there's any law that a person's guardian can make 'em live with him if they don't want to—"

"You told him!"

"I did not!"

The girl said, "Don't talk so loud, Hamish! Mrs. Egg's taking a nap upstairs. You told him!"

"I didn't tell him a thing! I said there was a guy I knew that had run off from his guardian and—"

Benjamina burst into queer, vexed laughter. She said, "You might as well have told him! The day he came to the flat he asked who else lived there besides us. Cousin Joe's pipes were all over the place. It—"

"Look here! There's a judge in this town, and Mrs. Egg or Adam would tell him we're not children or imbeciles or nothin'! If Cousin Joe came down here lookin' for us—" Presently he said with misery on each syllable, "Don't cry, Benjy. . . . But nothin'll happen. . . . Anyhow, you'll be twenty-one in October and the court'll give you our income, 'stead of payin' it to Cousin Joe. . . . Bet you a dollar it's more than he says it is!" He whistled seven notes of a bugle call and then whimpered, "Quit cryin', Benjy!"

"F-finish these radishes," Benjamina commanded; "I want to go brush my hair."

There was the light sound of her soles on the back stairs. Mrs. Egg lay down again, wishing that the urn of peppermints was within reach. In the kitchen Hamish said "Aw, hell!" and the chair by the table creaked as he slumped into it. He would pare radishes very badly, Mrs. Egg thought.

She now thought of Benjamina with admiration. Adam had seen the girl's name on a list of women willing to take service in the country, at a Cleveland agency. He had gone to interview Benjamina, Mrs. Egg gathered, because a cook on the U. S. S. *Nevada* had been named Saunders and the word looked auspicious. Accident, said Mrs. Egg to herself, was the dominant principle of life. She was much interested. Benjamina had taken proper steps to get away from an unpleasant guardian and should be shielded from any consequences. Certainly a girl who could cook to satisfy Adam wasn't to be given back to some nameless male in Cleveland, in a flat. Mrs. Egg abhorred flats. A man who would coop two children in a flat deserved no consideration. And Adam required gallons of peach butter for winter use. Mrs. Egg arose, stalked openly into the kitchen and addressed Hamish as an equal. She said, "Bub, you're an awful tactful boy, and have sense. Dammy said so himself. Honesty is my policy, an' I may as well say that I could hear all you were talkin' with Benjamina right now. . . . Who is this Cousin Joe you've run off from?"

Hamish cut a radish in two and wretchedly stammered, "H-he's dad's cousin. He's a louse!"

Mrs. Egg drawled, "My gee! That's a awful good description of your relation! Now, I haven't any intention to lose Benjamina when she's the best cook I ever had, an' you're not as bad at milkin' as you might be. If this person comes down here or makes any fuss I'll see to it that he don't get anywheres. So if Benjamina gets frightened you tell her that I'm goin' to look after this."

"Yes'm," said Hamish.

He looked at Mrs. Egg with an awe that was soothing. She beamed and strolled out of the kitchen. Descending the steps one by one, she came to the level walk of the dooryard and marched along it toward the barns. Mr. Egg was taking a holiday with his sister, married to a dyspeptic clergyman in Chicago, and it was her duty to aid Adam by surveying the cows. She entered the barnyard and rounded the corner of the cows' palace into a group of farm hands bent above a trotting of dice on the clay. Adam looked up from this sport and said " 'Lo, mamma," cheerfully.

"My gee," Mrs. Egg faltered, regarding a pile of silver before his knees, "I never saw you win a cent at any game before, Dammy!"

The giant grinned, cast the dice and raked three dollars toward him. His eyes were black lights. He announced "This is my lucky day, mamma!" and all the worshipful youths chuckled as he stood up. He walked over a Swede's stooped back and dragged Mrs. Egg away from her husband's hirelings. Then he lit a cigarette and consumed half its length in an appalling suction. The smoke jetted from his nostrils in a flood. He patted Mrs. Egg's upper chin with a thumb and said, "She gave me the air, mamma!"

"What?"

"She told me to fly my kite! She's off me! She's goin' to marry Jim Randolph. It's all flooie. . . . I'd like a tub of champagne an' five fried hens for supper! Mamma," said Adam, "I ain't engaged to that girl any more!" Therewith he took all the silver from his pocket and sent it in a chiming shower up the roof of the cow barn. His teeth flashed between his parted lips and dimples invaded his brown cheeks. He swung his arms restlessly and his mother thought that he would break into a dance. Adam reflected, "It's hell what happens by accident, mamma. Was a bowl of punch in the lib'ry at that dance of Judge Randolph's Christmas-time that'd knock the teeth out of a horse. Had six cups. Saw this girl's hand hangin' over the banisters when I was headin' for the front door. I kissed it. Mamma, there ain't any way of tellin' a girl in this town that you don't mean anything when you kiss her. They don't understand it."

A devastating admiration of her child made Mrs. Egg's heart cavort. His manners were sublime. He lit another cigarette and stated, "Well, that's all of that." Then, wearied with much speech, he was still.

"Mercy, Dammy! This is an awful relief! Your sisters have been holdin' forth about Edith Sims bein' much more refined than God all afternoon. I was gettin' kind of scared of her. . . . What's that phonograph plate, lamb?"

Adam didn't answer, but ripped the envelope from the grained disk, and Mrs. Egg saw, on the advertising, "Kashmiri Song." But her thoughts had sunk to a profound and cooling peace; there would be no more Edith Sims. She drawled, "Edith's pretty awful sedate, Dammy. I don't think she'd have the sand to run off from—a person she didn't like, or make her own livin'."

The giant flung up his arms and made certain gestures. Hamish Saunders came hurtling from the house for orders. Adam said, "Go get me some clothes, kid—white. And shoes 'n a cake of soap. Then come swimmin'. Put this plate with the rest. Hustle!" He ground his nose with a fist, staring after the boy, then said, "Nice kid, mamma."

"Mercy, yes, Dammy! Dammy, it's pretty ridiculous to have Benjamina and the boy cat in the kitchen, and it takes tact to keep a nice girl like that contented. I think they'd better take their meals with us, sweetheart."

He nodded and strode off among the regular files of apple and pear trees toward the aimless riverlet that watered the farm. Mrs. Egg felt hunger stir in her bulk. She plucked an apple leaf and chewed its fragrant pulp, marching up the walk. Benjamina was soberly chopping the chickens for dinner into convenient bits.

Mrs. Egg applauded her performance, saying, "We'd better have 'em fried, I think. Dammy prefers it. And when you've got time you might go get one of those very big green bottles of pear cider down in the cellar, honey. It's awful explosive stuff and Hamish hadn't better drink any. And lay the table for four, because it's pretty lonely for Dammy eatin' with me steadily. . . . Edith Sims busted their engagement this afternoon, by the way, though it isn't at all important."

"Isn't it?"

Mrs. Egg refreshed herself with a bit of cracker from the table and drawled, "Not a bit, deary. I've never heard of anybody's heart breakin' under the age of thirty over a busted engagement. Dammy's pretty much relieved, though too polite to say so, and Edith'll marry Judge Randolph's second boy, who's a very nice kid and has curly hair, although his teeth stick out some. So it don't seem to matter except to my daughters, who'll want Dammy to go into full mourning and die of sorrow. They're tearful girls, but nice. Let me show you how Dammy likes tomatoes fried when they're done with the chicken."

"Mrs. Egg," said Benjamina, "you're—a remarkable person." The slim, pale fingers twisted themselves against her dull blue frock into the likeness of a frightened white moth. She went on, "You—you never get excited."

"My gee! I haven't any patience with excitement, Benjamina. Things either go right or they go wrong. In either case, it's no good foamin' at the mouth and tryin' to kick the roof off. I'm like Dammy. I prefer to be calm," said Mrs. Egg. "As for scatterin' rays of sunshine like a Sunday-school hymn, most people don't thank anyone to do so—nor me, when I have indigestion."

"I—I feel much calmer since I've been here," Benjamina said. "It was so hot in the flat in Cleveland, and noisy. And it's very kind of you to ask Hamish and me to eat with you and Mr. Egg."

Her hands had become steadfast. She smiled a little.

"It'll be much more sociable, honey," Mrs. Egg reflected. "Even if Dammy don't talk, he likes company, havin' been in the Navy where he had lots. . . . Where's the biscuit flour? There's time to make some before supper."

The kitchen dimmed and Benjamina's tall body dulled into a restful shadow. She moved without noise and her pleasant voice was low. Mrs. Egg devised biscuits in comfort and smelled Adam's cigarettes in the living room. Hamish came to stimulate the making of this meal by getting his large feet in the way, and Mrs. Egg was scolding him tranquilly when the phonograph loosed a series of lazy notes. Then it sang, fervidly, of pale hands that it had loved beside some strange name.

"It's that Kashmir business," said Mrs. Egg. "Open the door, bub, so's we can hear."

The music swelled as the door opened and a circle of smoke died in the kitchen. Mrs. Egg saw Adam as a white pillar in the gloom. The machine sobbed "Where are you now? Where are you now?" with an oily sadness.

"Real touching," Mrs. Egg mentioned.

A crashing of the orchestra intervened. Then the voice cried, "Pale hands, pink tipped, like lotus flowers that—" The words jumbled into sounds. Mrs. Egg hungrily yawned. The tenor wailed, "I would have rather felt you on my throat, crushing out life, than waving me farewell!" and the girl stirred beside the doorway, her hands in motion. The song expired with a thin noise of violins. Adam stopped the plate. An inexplicable silence filled the house, as if this stale old melody had wakened something that listened. Then Adam lit a cigarette.

"Supper near ready, mamma?"

"Pretty near, lamb," said Mrs. Egg.

Supper was pleasant. Hamish talked buoyantly of cows. He was impressed by their stupidity and their artless qualities. Benjamina gazed at the four candles with gray eyes and smiled at nothing. Adam ate fourteen hot biscuits and three mounds of an ice cream that held fresh raspberries. He stared at the ceiling gravely, and his white shirt tightened as he breathed out the first smoke above a cup of coffee.

Then he said, "We'll go to the movies. Get your hat, Miss Saunders."

"But the dishes aren't washed!" Benjamina exclaimed.

"The kid and I'll wash 'em," Adam vouchsafed.

Mrs. Egg yawned, "Go ahead, Benjamina," and watched the girl's hands flutter as she left the green dining room.

Adam blew a ring of smoke, which drooped, dissolving about a candle. He reached across the table for the coffeepot and filled his cup, then looked at Hamish.

"What's she scared of, kid?"

"Cousin Joe," said Hamish presently. "He's—our guardian—wants to marry her. Y'see, we have some money from dad's store. Cousin Joe's a lawyer and the bank pays him the money."

"Lived with him in Cleveland?"

Hamish groaned, "You saw where we lived! Benjy couldn't keep the place lookin' decent. He knocked his pipe out wherever he sat. But Benjy'll be twenty-one in October and the bank'll pay her the money."

"An' this Joe's a sour plum?"

"Well," said Hamish, with the manner of last justice, "he can sing pretty well."

Mrs. Egg was thinking of bed at ten o'clock when the telephone rang and the anguished voice of her youngest daughter came pouring from Ilium:

"Mamma! Dammy's got that girl in a box at the movies!"

"I'm glad," said Mrs. Egg, "that they're sitting in a box. My gee! It's hot as I ever felt it for this time of year, Fern! Benjamina's such a large person that she—"

"Oh, mamma! And it's all over town that Edith Sims is going to marry—"

"I can't pretend that I'm either surprised or sorry, Fern. As for Dammy marryin' a girl he would have had to stoop over a yard to kiss after breakfast, it never seemed a just kind of arrangement to me, although I didn't want to criticize her. The Simses are nice folks—awful refined. Mercy, but don't Dammy look well in white pants?"

"Mamma! You simply haven't any heart!"

"I'll be forty-seven in December, Fern," said Mrs. Egg. "Good night."

She drowsily ascended to her cool bedroom, where a vacuum flask of iced lemonade stood with a package of oatmeal crackers on the bedside table. In the dark she lay listening to the obliging wind that now moved in the ten acres of orchard, and sometimes she chuckled, nibbling a cracker. Finally she slept, and was wakened by Adam's voice.

"Was it a nice picture, Dammy?"

"Fair. Where's that law dictionary dad got last year, mamma?"

"It's in the pantry, under the paraffin for the preserves, sweetheart."

"Thanks," said Adam, and his feet went softly away.

Mrs. Egg resumed her slumbers composedly, and woke on the first clash of milk pails in the barnyard. Day was clear. Adam could get in the rest of the peaches and paint the garage roof without discomfort. She ate a cracker, dressing, and went down the back stairs to find Benjamina grinding coffee in a white gown that set off color in her cheeks.

"Mercy," said Mrs. Egg, "but you're up real early!"

"I don't think it can be very healthy for Mr. Egg and Hamish to wait so long for breakfast," the girl said.

"The men's cook down at the bunk house always has coffee for Dammy. It's a sad time that Dammy can't get himself a meal around here, honey. But it's nice to have breakfast early. I think he's hungrier in the mornin'."

"Isn't he always hungry?"

"Always," Mrs. Egg assured her, beginning to pare chilled peaches; "and he likes your oatmeal, I notice. Bein' Scotch by descent, you understand the stuff. You've been here ten days, and it's remarkable how you've learned what Dammy likes. If he was talkative it wouldn't take so much intelligence. A very good way is to watch his toes. If they move he likes what he's eatin'. My gee! It was easy to tell when he was little and went barefooted. He's too tactful to complain about anything."

"He said, driving down from Cleveland, that he hated talking much," Benjamina murmured.

Adam's black head showed above his blue milking shirt in the barnyard. Mrs. Egg watched the tall girl's gray eyes quicken as she gazed down the wet grass. Morning mist fairly smoked from the turf and the boles of apple trees were moist. Hamish was lugging pails to the dairy valiantly.

"The high school here," said Mrs. Egg, "is very good for the size of the town, and Hamish will be perfectly comfortable in winters. You mustn't be alarmed by my husband when he comes back from Chicago. It's a nervous habit he has of winkin' his left eye. It don't mean a thing. I'll try to get hold of some girl that's reasonably intell'gent to do waitin' on table and dusting, which is not good for your hands."

"It's very nice here," Benjamina said, still looking at the barnyard.

Mrs. Egg decided that she was a beautiful creature. Her color improved breath by breath, and her face had the look of a goddess on a coin. The vast woman ate a peach and inspected this virgin hopefully. Then the pale hands shot to Benjamina's throat and she whirled from the window. Hamish tumbled through the door, his shoes smeared with milk and his mouth dragged into a gash of fright.

"It's Cousin Joe! He's gettin' out of a buggy at the gate!"

"Gracious!" said Mrs. Egg.

She rose and walked into the veranda, smoothing her hair. The man limping up from the white gates was tall and his shoulders seemed broad. He leaned on a cane. He wore a hat made of rough rings of straw. Mrs. Egg greatly disliked him at once, and went down the steps slowly, sideways. Adam was lounging up from the barnyard and some farm hands followed him in a clump of tanned faces. Light made their eyes flash. The woman sighed. There might be a deal of angry talk before she got rid of the lame person in black. He advanced and she awaited him under the apple tree below the steps. When he approached she saw that his hair was dull brown and sleek as he took off his hat.

"Mrs. Egg?"

"I am," said Mrs. Egg.

The man smoothly bowed. He was less than six feet tall, but burly and not pale. His mouth smiled charmingly. He glanced at Adam, smoking on the steps, and twirled the cane in his hand. He said, "My name's Hume. I'm an attorney. I'm the guardian of Benjamina and Hamish Saunders, my cousin's children. They're here, I understand?"

"I understand," Mrs. Egg drawled, "that you ain't much of a guardian, and they're better off here."

Adam's voice came over her shoulder, "They're goin' to stay here."

Cold sweat rose in Mrs. Egg's clenched hands. She turned and saw Adam's nostrils rigid, yellow on his bronze face. She said, "Go in to breakfast, Dammy. I'm talkin' to this person."

Adam might lose his temper. He must go away. She looked at him for a moment, and the farm hands made new shadows on the turf, approaching curiously. Then Adam turned and walked into the kitchen.

"We're wasting time," the man said, always smoothly. "Benjy's my ward and she's going back to Cleveland with me."

"I don't see as that follows, precisely," Mrs. Egg panted.

"The nearest justice would."

"Then you'd better get the nearest justice to say it," said Mrs. Egg, "because Benjamina's perfectly well off here. As for sendin' her back to Cleveland for you to make love at in a flat—my gee!"

She felt herself impolitic and tactless in saying this, but rage had mounted. Her chins were shaking. The man's clothes smelled of pipe smoke. His collar wasn't clean. He was a dog. The kitchen door slammed. She dreaded that Adam might lose his temper and thrash this fellow. The man looked over her head.

"Here," said Adam, "get out the way, mamma, please! Let's settle this! Come ahead, Benj'mina. He can't hurt you." He was leading the girl down the steps by a hand. Smoke welled from his nostrils and his eyes had partly shut. He brought the white girl to face her cousin and said,

"Now! My name's Adam Egg. Benjamina's married to me. Show him your rings, kid."

The farm hands gasped and an Irish lad whooped. Adam undid his brown fingers from the pale hand. The big diamond and the circlet of little stones blazed below the rosy nails. Mrs. Egg put her palm on her mouth and a scream was a pain in her throat. She hadn't seen Adam married! He threw away the cigarette by a red motion of his tongue and drawled, "Go back in the house, kid!"

The man clamped a hand on his cane and said "Without my permission!"

"She's twenty," Adam grunted, his shoulders tremulous under the thin blue shirt, "so what you goin' to do?"

Then nothing happened. Benjamina walked up the steps and stood with an arm about Hamish at the top. A farm hand lit a pipe. Mrs. Egg's heart beat horribly with the pain of having missed Adam's wedding. The man's face was getting green. He was odious, completely. He said, "Their property stays in my control!"

"The hell with their property!"

Nothing happened. The man stood poking his cane into the turf and turning the thick end among grass blades. Hamish came down one step. Then the man backed and whirled up his cane.

Mrs. Egg shrieked "Dammy!" and bruised her lip with her teeth.

The heavy cane seemed to balance a long while against the sun. Adam stood. The thing fell across his right shoulder and broke with a cracking sound. The blue shirt tore and Benjamina screamed. Adam's whole length shook and his lips were gray for a second. He slung out both hands and caught the fellow's throat. He said, "Now! You've 'saulted me with a dangerous weapon, see? Now, get out of here! Here's your witnesses! You hit me! All I've got to do is walk you in to a judge and you'll get a year, see? That's law! Get out of this! I could kill you," he drawled, "an' I will if you ain't out the gates in one minute!"

His shoulders heaved. The shirt split down his back. The man went spinning in a queer rotation along the grass, like some collapsing toy. Adam stood with his hands raised, watching. The figure stumbled twice. Then it lurched toward the white gates in a full run, and the farm hands yelled. Adam dropped his hands and ripped the shirt from his shoulder. A band of scarlet had risen on the bronze of his chest. He said thickly, "Damn if he ain't a husky! Hey, Hamish, get me some iodine, will you?"

Benjamina ran down the steps and dragged the rings from her fingers. She babbled, "Oh! Oh, Adam! What did you let him strike you for? I'm so sorry!" She thrust the rings into one of his palms and cried, "You shouldn't have let him hit you! He's so strong!"

"What was I goin' to say if he said to show any weddin' certificate? If he hit me it was assault, an' I could get rid of him."

Mrs. Egg wailed, "Then you ain't married, Dammy?"

"No."

Adam leaned on the apple tree and stared at Benjamina, turning the rings in his hand. After a moment the girl flushed and walked away into the orchard of rustling boughs. A morning wind made the giant's torn shirt flap. He sent his eyes to the gaping hired men and drawled "What about those cows?"

Feet thudded off on the grass. Hamish came bounding down the steps with a bottle of iodine and a handkerchief.

"My gee, Dammy," said Mrs. Egg, grasping the bottle, "if your sisters have the nerve to say you're tactless after this I'll— Sit down, lamb! Oh, Dammy, how can you think as fast as that?"

Adam lit a cigarette and blew smoke through his nostrils. His face was again blank and undisturbed. He asked "Peaches for breakfast?"

"Anything you want, lamb! Benjamina has oatmeal ready."

He clicked the rings in his hand and his feet wriggled in the moccasins. Then he said "Mamma," strangely.

"Yes, Dammy."

"Mamma, I've put Miss Saunders in a hell of a position, sayin' we're married."

"That's so, Dammy. It'll be all over town in no time."

Adam arose from the grass and examined his mother for a whole minute. His nostrils shook somewhat. He took the engagement ring from one palm and handed it to Hamish, ordering, "Kid, you go take that to your sister and tell her it's with my compliments. I hate talkin'."

The boy's red hair went flashing under the trees. Mrs. Egg watched him halt by his sister, who was wiping her eyes beside a trunk. They conferred. Soon Hamish turned about and began to make swift signs with his arms.

Adam said, "Good enough. . . . I guess I'll call her Ben." He lit his next cigarette and walked up the steps.

Mrs. Egg screamed, "Dammy! Ain't you goin' to go kiss her?"

Adam's eyes opened on his mother in alarm.

He said, "I'm thirsty, mamma. And I've got to get a fresh shirt. Couldn't kiss anybody in this one. It wouldn't be polite."

Then he waved his cigarette to his new love and slammed the kitchen door behind him.

52

Silent Snow, Secret Snow

BY CONRAD AIKEN

JUST why it should have happened, or why it should have happened just when it did, he could not, of course, possibly have said; nor perhaps could it even have occurred to him to ask. The thing was above all a secret, something to be preciously concealed from Mother and Father; and to that very fact it owed an enormous part of its deliciousness. It was like a peculiarly beautiful trinket to be carried unmentioned in one's trouser-pocket—a rare stamp, an old coin, a few tiny gold links found trodden out of shape on the path in the park, a pebble of carnelian, a sea shell distinguishable from all others by an unusual spot or stripe—and, as if it were anyone of these, he carried around with him everywhere a warm and persistent and increasingly beautiful sense of possession. Nor was it only a sense of possession—it was also a sense of protection. It was as if, in some delightful way, his secret gave him a fortress, a wall behind which he could retreat into heavenly seclusion. This was almost the first thing he had noticed about it—apart from the oddness of the thing itself—and it was this that now again, for the fiftieth time, occurred to him, as he sat in the little schoolroom. It was the half hour for geography. Miss Buell was revolving with one finger, slowly, a huge terrestrial globe which had been placed on her desk. The green and yellow continents passed and repassed, questions were asked and answered, and now the little girl in front of him, Deirdre, who had a funny little constellation of freckles on the back of her neck, exactly like the Big Dipper, was standing up and telling Miss Buell that the equator was the line that ran round the middle.

Miss Buell's face, which was old and grayish and kindly, with gray stiff curls beside the cheeks, and eyes that swam very brightly, like little minnows, behind thick glasses, wrinkled itself into a complication of amusements.

"Ah! I see. The earth is wearing a belt, or a sash. Or someone drew a line round it!"

"Oh, no—not that—I mean—"

In the general laughter, he did not share, or only a very little. He was thinking about the Arctic and Antarctic regions, which of course, on the globe, were white. Miss Buell was now telling them about the tropics, the jungles, the steamy heat of equatorial swamps, where the birds and butterflies, and even the snakes, were like living jewels. As he listened to these things, he was already, with a pleasant sense of half-effort, putting his secret between himself and the words. Was it really an effort at all? For effort implied something voluntary, and perhaps even something one did not especially want; whereas this was distinctly pleasant, and came almost of its own accord. All he needed to do was to think of that morning, the first one, and then of all the others—

But it was all so absurdly simple! It had amounted to so little. It was nothing, just an idea—and just why it should have become so wonderful, so permanent, was a mystery—a very pleasant one, to be sure, but also, in an amusing way, foolish. However, without ceasing to listen to Miss Buell, who had now moved up to the north temperate zones, he deliberately invited his memory of the first morning. It was only a moment or two after he had waked up—or perhaps the moment itself. But was there, to be exact, an exact moment? Was one awake all at once? or was it gradual? Anyway, it was after he had stretched a lazy hand up towards the headrail, and yawned, and then relaxed again among his warm covers, all the more grateful on a December morning, that the thing had happened. Suddenly, for no reason, he had thought of the postman, he remembered the postman. Perhaps there was nothing so odd in that. After all, he heard the postman almost every morning in his life—his heavy boots could be heard clumping round the corner at the top of the little cobbled hill-street, and then, progressively nearer, progressively louder, the double knock at each door, the crossings and re-crossings of the street, till finally the clumsy steps came stumbling across to the very door, and the tremendous knock came which shook the house itself.

(Miss Buell was saying "Vast wheat-growing areas in North America and Siberia.")

Dierdre had for the moment placed her left hand across the back of her neck.)

But on this particular morning, the first morning, as he lay there with his eyes closed, he had for some reason *waited* for the postman. He wanted to hear him come round the corner. And that was precisely the joke—he never did. He never came. He never had come—*round the corner*—again. For when at last the steps *were* heard, they had already, he was quite sure, come a little down the hill, to the first house; and even so, the steps were curiously different—they were softer, they had a new secrecy about them, they were muffled and indistinct; and while the rhythm of them was the same, it now said a new thing—it said peace, it said remoteness, it said cold, it said sleep. And he had understood the situation at once—nothing could have seemed simpler—there had been snow in the night, such as all winter he had been longing for; and it was this which had rendered the postman's first footsteps inaudible, and the later ones faint. Of course! How lovely! And even now it must be snowing—it was going to be a snowy day—the long white ragged lines were drifting and sifting across the street, across the faces of the old houses, whispering and hushing, making little triangles of white in the corners between cobblestones, seething a little when the wind blew them over the ground to a drifted corner; and so it would be all day, getting deeper and deeper and silenter and silenter.

(Miss Buell was saying "Land of perpetual snow.")

All this time, of course (while he lay in bed), he had kept his eyes closed, listening to the nearer progress of the postman, the muffled footsteps thumping and slipping on the snow-sheathed cobbles; and all the other sounds—the double knocks, a frosty far-off voice or two, a bell ringing thinly and softly as if under a sheet of ice—had the same slightly abstracted quality, as if removed by one degree from actuality—as if everything in the world had been insulated by snow. But when at last, pleased, he opened his eyes, and turned them towards the window, to see for himself this long-desired and now so clearly imagined miracle—what he saw instead was brilliant sunlight on a roof; and when, astonished, he jumped out of bed and stared down into the street, expecting to see the cobbles obliterated by the snow, he saw nothing but the bare bright cobbles themselves.

Queer, the effect this extraordinary surprise had had upon him—all the following morning he had kept with him a sense as of snow falling about him, a secret screen of new snow between himself and the world. If he had not dreamed such a thing—and how could he have dreamed it while awake?—how else could one explain it? In any case, the delusion had been so vivid as to affect his entire behavior. He could not now remember whether it was on the first or the second morning—or was it even the third?—that his mother had drawn attention to some oddness in his manner.

"But my darling—" she had said at the breakfast table—"what has come over you? You don't seem to be listening. . . ."

And how often that very thing had happened since!

(Miss Buell was now asking if anyone knew the difference between the North Pole and the Magnetic Pole. Deirdre was holding up her flickering brown hand, and he could see the four white dimples that marked the knuckles.)

Perhaps it hadn't been either the second or third morning—or even the fourth or fifth. How could he be sure? How could he be sure just when the delicious *progress* had become clear? Just when it had really *begun?* The intervals weren't very precise. . . . All he now knew was, that at some point or other—perhaps the second day, perhaps the sixth— he had noticed that the presence of the snow was a little more insistent, the sound of it clearer; and, conversely, the sound of the postman's foot-steps more indistinct. Not only could he not hear the steps come round the corner, he could not even hear them at the first house. It was below the first house that he heard them; and then, a few days later, it was below the second house that he heard them; and a few days later again, below the third. Gradually, gradually, the snow was becoming heavier, the sound of its seething louder, the cobblestones more and more muffled. When he found, each morning, on going to the window, after the ritual of listening, that the roofs and cobbles were as bare as ever, it made no difference. This was, after all, only what he had expected. It was even what pleased him, what rewarded him: the thing was his own, belonged to no one else. No one else knew about it, not even his mother and father. There, outside, were the bare cobbles; and here, inside, was the snow. Snow growing heavier each day, muffling the world, hiding the ugly, and deadening increasingly—above all—the steps of the postman.

"But my darling—" she had said at the luncheon table—"what has come over you? You don't seem to listen when people speak to you. That's the third time I've asked you to pass your plate. . . ."

How was one to explain this to Mother? or to Father? There was, of course, nothing to be done about it: nothing. All one could do was to laugh embarrassedly, pretend to be a little ashamed, apologize, and take a sudden and somewhat disingenuous interest in what was being done or said. The cat had stayed out all night. He had a curious swelling on his left cheek—perhaps somebody had kicked him, or a stone had struck him. Mrs. Kempton was or was not coming to tea. The house was going to be house cleaned, or "turned out," on Wednesday instead of Friday. A new lamp was provided for his evening work—perhaps it was eye-strain which accounted for this new and so peculiar vagueness of his— Mother was looking at him with amusement as she said this, but with something else as well. A new lamp? A new lamp. Yes Mother, No Mother, Yes Mother. School is going very well. The geometry is very easy. The history is very dull. The geography is very interesting—par-ticularly when it takes one to the North Pole. Why the North Pole? Oh, well, it would be fun to be an explorer. Another Peary or Scott or

Shackleton. And then abruptly he found his interest in the talk at an end, stared at the pudding on his plate, listened, waited, and began once more—ah how heavenly, too, the first beginnings—to hear or feel—for could he actually hear it?—the silent snow, the secret snow.

(Miss Buell was telling them about the search for the Northwest Passage, about Hendrik Hudson, the Half Moon.)

This had been, indeed, the only distressing feature of the new experience: the fact that it so increasingly had brought him into a kind of mute misunderstanding, or even conflict, with his father and mother. It was as if he were trying to lead a double life. On the one hand he had to be Paul Hasleman, and keep up the appearance of being that person—dress, wash, and answer intelligently when spoken to—; on the other, he had to explore this new world which had been opened to him. Nor could there be the slightest doubt—not the slightest—that the new world was the profounder and more wonderful of the two. It was irresistible. It was miraculous. Its beauty was simply beyond anything—beyond speech as beyond thought—utterly incommunicable. But how, then, between the two worlds, of which he was thus constantly aware, was he to keep a balance? One must get up, one must go to breakfast, one must talk with Mother, go to school, do one's lessons—and, in all this, try not to appear too much of a fool. But if all the while one was also trying to extract the full deliciousness of another and quite separate existence, one which could not easily (if at all) be spoken of—how was one to manage? How was one to explain? Would it be safe to explain? Would it be absurd? Would it merely mean that he would get into some obscure kind of trouble?

These thoughts came and went, came and went, as softly and secretly as the snow; they were not precisely a disturbance, perhaps they were even a pleasure; he liked to have them; their presence was something almost palpable, something he could stroke with his hand, without closing his eyes, and without ceasing to see Miss Buell and the schoolroom and the globe and the freckles on Deirdre's neck; nevertheless he did in a sense cease to see, or to see the obvious external world, and substituted for this vision the vision of snow, the sound of snow, and the slow, almost soundless, approach of the postman. Yesterday, it had been only at the sixth house that the postman had become audible; the snow was much deeper now, it was falling more swiftly and heavily, the sound of its seething was more distinct, more soothing, more persistent. And this morning, it had been—as nearly as he could figure—just above the seventh house—perhaps only a step or two above: at most, he had heard two or three footsteps before the knock had sounded.
. . . And with each such narrowing of the sphere, each nearer approach of the limit at which the postman was first audible, it was odd how

sharply was increased the amount of illusion which had to be carried
into the ordinary business of daily life. Each day, it was harder to get
out of bed, to go to the window, to look out at the—as always—perfectly
empty and snowless street. Each day it was more difficult to go through
the perfunctory motions of greeting Mother and Father at breakfast, to
reply to their questions, to put his books together and go to school. And
at school, how extraordinarily hard to conduct with success simultaneously the public life and the life that was secret. There were times
when he longed—positively ached—to tell everyone about it—to burst
out with it—only to be checked almost at once by a far-off feeling as of
some faint absurdity which was inherent in it—but *was* it absurd?—
and more importantly by a sense of mysterious power in his very
secrecy. Yes: it must be kept secret. That, more and more, became clear.
At whatever cost to himself, whatever pain to others—

(Miss Buell looked straight at him, smiling, and said, "Perhaps we'll
ask Paul. I'm sure Paul will come out of his day-dream long enough to
be able to tell us. Won't you, Paul." He rose slowly from his chair,
resting one hand on the brightly varnished desk, and deliberately
stared through the snow towards the blackboard. It was an effort, but it
was amusing to make it. "Yes," he said slowly, "it was what we now
call the Hudson River. This he thought to be the Northwest Passage.
He was disappointed." He sat down again, and as he did so Deirdre half
turned in her chair and gave him a shy smile, of approval and admiration.)

At whatever pain to others.

This part of it was very puzzling, very puzzling. Mother was very
nice, and so was Father. Yes, that was all true enough. He wanted to
be nice to them, to tell them everything—and yet, was it really wrong
of him to want to have a secret place of his own?

At bedtime, the night before, Mother had said, "If this goes on, my
lad, we'll have to see a doctor, we will! We can't have our boy—" But
what was it she had said? "Live in another world"? "Live so far away"?
The word "far" had been in it, he was sure, and then Mother had taken
up a magazine again and laughed a little, but with an expression which
wasn't mirthful. He had felt sorry for her. . . .

The bell rang for dismissal. The sound came to him through long
curved parallels of falling snow. He saw Deirdre rise, and had himself
risen almost as soon—but not quite as soon—as she.

II

On the walk homeward, which was timeless, it pleased him to see
through the accompaniment, or counterpoint, of snow, the items of
mere externality on his way. There were many kinds of bricks in the

sidewalks, and laid in many kinds of pattern. The garden walls too were various, some of wooden palings, some of plaster, some of stone. Twigs of bushes leaned over the walls; the little hard green winter-buds of lilac, on gray stems, sheathed and fat; other branches very thin and fine and black and dessicated. Dirty sparrows huddled in the bushes, as dull in color as dead fruit left in leafless trees. A single starling creaked on a weather vane. In the gutter, beside a drain, was a scrap of torn and dirty newspaper, caught in a little delta of filth: the word ECZEMA appeared in large capitals, and below it was a letter from Mrs. Amelia D. Cravath, 2100 Pine Street, Fort Worth, Texas, to the effect that after being a sufferer for years she had been cured by Caley's Ointment. In the little delta, beside the fan-shaped and deeply runncled continent of brown mud, wcre lost twigs, descended from their parent trees, dead matches, a rusty horse-chestnut burr, a small concentration of sparkling gravel on the lip of the sewer, a fragment of eggshell, a streak of yellow sawdust which had been wet and was now dry and congealed, a brown pebble, and a broken feather. Further on was a cement sidewalk, ruled into geometrical parallelograms, with a brass inlay at one end commemorating the contractors who had laid it, and, halfway across, an irregular and random series of dog-tracks, immortalized in synthetic stone. He knew these well, and always stepped on them; to cover the little hollows with his own foot had always been a queer pleasure; today he did it once more, but perfunctorily and detachedly, all the while thinking of something else. That was a dog, a long time ago, who had made a mistake and walked on the cement while it was still wet. He had probably wagged his tail, but that hadn't been recorded. Now, Paul Hasleman, aged twelve, on his way home from school, crossed the same river, which in the meantime had frozen into rock. Homeward through the snow, the snow falling in bright sunshine. Homeward?

Then came the gateway with the two posts surmounted by egg-shaped stones which had been cunningly balanced on their ends, as if by Columbus, and mortared in the very act of balance: a source of perpetual wonder. On the brick wall just beyond, the letter H had been stenciled, presumably for some purpose. H? H.

The green hydrant, with a little green-painted chain attached to the brass screw-cap.

The elm tree, with the great gray wound in the bark, kidney-shaped, into which he always put his hand—to feel the cold but living wood. The injury, he had been sure, was due to the gnawings of a tethered horse. But now it deserved only a passing palm, a merely tolerant eye. There were more important things. Miracles. Beyond the thoughts of trees, mere elms. Beyond the thoughts of sidewalks, mere stone, mere brick, mere cement. Beyond the thoughts even of his own shoes, which trod these sidewalks obediently, bearing a burden—far above—of elaborate mystery. He watched them. They were not very well polished; he had neglected them, for a very good reason: they were one of the many parts of the increasing difficulty of the daily return to daily life, the morning struggle. To get up, having at last opened one's eyes, to go to the window, and discover no snow, to wash, to dress, to descend the curving stairs to breakfast—

At whatever pain to others, nevertheless, one must persevere in severance, since the incommunicability of the experience demanded it. It was desirable of course to be kind to Mother and Father, especially as they seemed to be worried, but it was also desirable to be resolute. If they should decide—as appeared likely—to consult the doctor, Doctor Howells, and have Paul inspected, his heart listened to through a kind of dictaphone, his lungs, his stomach—well, that was all right. He would go through with it. He would give them answer for question, too—perhaps such answers as they hadn't expected? No. That would never do. For the secret world must, at all costs, be preserved.

The bird-house in the apple-tree was empty—it was the wrong time of year for wrens. The little round black door had lost its pleasure. The wrens were enjoying other houses, other nests, remoter trees. But this too was a notion which he only vaguely and grazingly entertained—as if, for the moment, he merely touched an edge of it; there was something further on, which was already assuming a sharper importance; something which already teased at the corners of his eyes, teasing also at the corner of his mind. It was funny to think that he so wanted this, so awaited it—and yet found himself enjoying this momentary dalliance with the bird-house, as if for a quite deliberate postponement and enhancement of the approaching pleasure. He was aware of his delay, of his smiling and detached and now almost uncomprehending gaze at the little bird-house; he knew what he was going to look at next: it was his own little cobbled hill-street, his own house, the little river at the bottom of the hill, the grocer's shop with the cardboard man in the window—and now, thinking of all this, he turned his head, still smiling, and looking quickly right and left through the snow-laden sunlight.

And the mist of snow, as he had foreseen, was still on it—a ghost of snow falling in the bright sunlight, softly and steadily floating and turning and pausing, soundlessly meeting the snow that covered, as with a transparent mirage, the bare bright cobbles. He loved it—he stood still and loved it. Its beauty was paralyzing—beyond all words, all experience, all dream. No fairy-story he had ever read could be compared with it—none had ever given him this extraordinary combination of ethereal loveliness with a something else, unnameable, which was just faintly and deliciously terrifying. What was this thing? As he thought of it, he

looked upward toward his own bedroom window, which was open—
and it was as if he looked straight into the room and saw himself lying
half awake in his bed. There he was—at this very instant he was still
perhaps actually there—more truly there than standing here at the edge
of the cobbled hill-street, with one hand lifted to shade his eyes against
the snow-sun. Had he indeed ever left his room, in all this time? since
that very first morning? Was the whole progress still being enacted
there, was it still the same morning, and himself not yet wholly awake?
And even now, had the postman not yet come round the corner? . . .

This idea amused him, and automatically, as he thought of it, he
turned his head and looked toward the top of the hill. There was, of
course, nothing there—nothing and no one. The street was empty and
quiet. And all the more because of its emptiness it occurred to him to
count the houses—a thing which, oddly enough, he hadn't before
thought of doing. Of course, he had known there weren't many—many,
that is, on his own side of the street, which were the ones that figured
in the postman's progress—but nevertheless it came to him as something
of a shock to find that there were precisely *six,* above his own house—
his own house was the seventh.

Six!

Astonished, he looked at his own house—looked at the door, on which
was the number thirteen—and then realized that the whole thing was
exactly and logically and absurdly what he ought to have known. Just
the same, the realization gave him abruptly, and even a little frighten-
ingly, a sense of hurry. He was being hurried—he was being rushed.
For—he knit his brows—he couldn't be mistaken—it was just above the
seventh house, his *own* house, that the postman had first been audible
this very mornnig. But in that case—in that case—did it mean that tomorrow he would hear nothing? The knock he had heard must have
been the knock of their own door. Did it mean—and this was an idea
which gave him a really extraordinary feeling of surprise—that he
would never hear the postman again?—that tomorrow morning the
postman would already have passed the house, in a snow by then so
deep as to render his footsteps completely inaudible? That he would
have made his approach down the snow-filled street so soundlessly, so
secretly, that he, Paul Hasleman, there lying in bed, would not have
waked in time, or, waking, would have heard nothing?

But how could that be? Unless even the knocker should be muffled
in the snow—frozen tight, perhaps? . . . But in that case—

A vague feeling of disappointment came over him; a vague sadness,
as if he felt himself deprived of something which he had long looked
forward to, something much prized. After all this, all this beautiful
progress, the slow delicious advance of the postman through the silent

and secret snow, the knock creeping closer each day, and the footsteps nearer, the audible compass of the world thus daily narrowed, narrowed, narrowed, as the snow soothingly and beautifully encroached and deepened, after all this, was he to be defrauded of the one thing he had so wanted—to be able to count, as it were, the last two or three solemn footsteps, as they finally approached his own door? Was it all going to happen, at the end, so suddenly? or indeed, had it already happened? with no slow and subtle gradations of menace, in which he could luxuriate?

He gazed upward again, toward his own window which flashed in the sun: and this time almost with a feeling that it would be better if he *were* still in bed, in that room; for in that case this must still be the first morning, and there would be six more mornings to come—or, for that matter, seven or eight or nine—how could he be sure?—or even more.

III

After supper, the inquisition began. He stood before the doctor, under the lamp, and submitted silently to the usual thumpings and tappings.

"Now will you please say 'Ah!'?"

"Ah!"

"Now again please, if you don't mind."

"Ah."

"Say it slowly, and hold it if you can—"

"Ah-h-h-h-h-h—"

"Good."

How silly all this was. As if it had anything to do with his throat! Or his heart or lungs!

Relaxing his mouth, of which the corners, after all this absurd stretching, felt uncomfortable, he avoided the doctor's eyes, and stared towards the fireplace, past his mother's feet (in gray slippers) which projected from the green chair, and his father's feet (in brown slippers) which stood neatly side by side on the hearth rug.

"Hm. There is certainly nothing wrong there . . ."

He felt the doctor's eyes fixed upon him, and, as if merely to be polite, returned the look, but with a feeling of justifiable evasiveness.

"Now, young man, tell me,—do you feel all right?"

"Yes, sir, quite all right."

"No headaches? no dizziness?"

"No, I don't think so."

"Let me see. Let's get a book, if you don't mind—yes, thank you, that will do splendidly—and now, Paul, if you'll just read it, holding it as you would normally hold it—"

He took the book and read:

"And another praise have I to tell for this the city our mother, the gift of a great god, a glory of the land most high; the might of horses, the might of young horses, the might of the sea. . . . For thou, son of Cronus, our lord Poseidon, hast throned herein this pride, since in these roads first thou didst show forth the curb that cures the rage of steeds. And the shapely oar, apt to men's hands, hath a wondrous speed on the brine, following the hundred-footed Nereids. . . . O land that art praised above all lands, now is it for thee to make those bright praises seen in deeds."

He stopped, tentatively, and lowered the heavy book.

"No—as I thought—there is certainly no superficial sign of eye-strain."

Silence thronged the room, and he was aware of the focused scrutiny of the three people who confronted him. . . .

"We could have his eyes examined—but I believe it is something else."

"What could it be?" This was his father's voice.

"It's only this curious absent-minded—" This was his mother's voice. In the presence of the doctor, they both seemed irritatingly apologetic.

"I believe it is something else. Now Paul—I would like very much to ask you a question or two. You will answer them, won't you—you know I'm an old, old friend of yours, eh? That's right! . . ."

His back was thumped twice by the doctor's fat fist,—then the doctor was grinning at him with false amiability, while with one finger-nail he was scratching the top button of his waistcoat. Beyond the doctor's shoulder was the fire, the fingers of flame making light prestidigitation against the sooty fireback, the soft sound of their random flutter the only sound.

"I would like to know—is there anything that worries you?"

The doctor was again smiling, his eyelids low against the little black pupils, in each of which was a tiny white bead of light. Why answer him? why answer him at all? "At whatever pain to others"—but it was all a nuisance, this necessity for resistance, this necessity for attention: it was as if one had been stood up on a brilliantly lighted stage, under a great round blaze of spotlight; as if one were merely a trained seal, or a performing dog, or a fish, dipped out of an aquarium and held up by the tail. It would serve them right if he were merely to bark or growl. And meanwhile, to miss these last few precious hours, these hours of which every minute was more beautiful than the last, more menacing—? He still looked, as if from a great distance, at the beads of light in the doctor's eyes, at the fixed false smile, and then, beyond, once more at his mother's slippers, his father's slippers, the soft flutter of the fire. Even here, even amongst these hostile presences, and in this arranged light, he could see the snow, he could hear it—it was in the corners of the room, where the shadow was deepest, under the sofa, behind the half-opened door which led to the dining room. It was gentler here, softer, its seethe the quietest of whispers, as if, in deference to a drawing room, it had quite deliberately put on its "manners"; it kept itself out of sight, obliterated itself, but distinctly with an air of saying, "Ah, but just wait! Wait till we are alone together! Then I will begin to tell you something new! Something white! something cold! something sleepy! something of cease, and peace, and the long bright curve of space! Tell them to go away. Banish them. Refuse to speak. Leave them, go upstairs to your room, turn out the light and get into bed—I will go with you, I will be waiting for you, I will tell you a better story than Little Kay of the Skates, or The Snow Ghost—I will surround your bed, I will close the windows, pile a deep drift against the door, so that none will ever again be able to enter. Speak to them! . . ." It seemed as if the little hissing voice came from a slow white spiral of falling flakes in the corner by the front window—but he could not be sure. He felt himself smiling, then, and said to the doctor, but without looking at him, looking beyond him still—

"Oh, no, I think not—"

"But are you sure, my boy?"

His father's voice came softly and coldly then—the familiar voice of silken warning. . . .

"You needn't answer at once, Paul—remember we're trying to help you—think it over and be quite sure, won't you?"

He felt himself smiling again, at the notion of being quite sure. What a joke! As if he weren't so sure that reassurance was no longer necessary, and all this cross-examination a ridiculous farce, a grotesque parody! What could they know about it? These gross intelligences, these humdrum minds so bound to the usual, the ordinary? Impossible to tell them about it! Why, even now, even now, with the proof so abundant, so formidable, so imminent, so appallingly present here in this very room, could they believe it?—could even his mother believe it? No—it was only too plain that if anything were said about it, the merest hint given, they would be incredulous—they would laugh—they would say "Absurd!"—think things about him which weren't true. . . .

"Why no, I'm not worried—why should I be?"

He looked then straight at the doctor's low-lidded eyes, looked from one of them to the other, from one bead of light to the other, and gave a little laugh.

The doctor seemed to be disconcerted by this. He drew back in his chair, resting a fat white hand on either knee. The smile faded slowly from his face.

Well, Paul!" he said, and paused gravely, "I'm afraid you don't take this quite seriously enough. I think you perhaps don't quite realize—don't quite realize—" He took a deep quick breath, and turned, as if helplessly, at a loss for words, to the others. But Mother and Father were both silent—no help was forthcoming.

"You must surely know, be aware, that you have not been quite your-self, of late? don't you know that? . . ."

It was amusing to watch the doctor's renewed attempt at a smile, a queer disorganized look, as of confidential embarrassment.

"I feel all right, sir," he said, and again gave the little laugh.

"And we're trying to help you." The doctor's tone sharpened.

"Yes sir, I know. But why? I'm all right. I'm just *thinking,* that's all."

His mother made a quick movement forward, resting a hand on the back of the doctor's chair.

"Thinking?" she said. "But my dear, about what?"

This was a direct challenge—and would have to be directly met. But before he met it, he looked again into the corner by the door, as if for reassurance. He smiled again at what he saw, at what he heard. The little spiral was still there, still softly whirling, like the ghost of a white kitten chasing the ghost of a white tail, and making as it did so the faintest of whispers. It was all right! If only he could remain firm, every-thing was going to be all right.

"Oh, about anything, about nothing,—*you* know the way you do!"

"You mean—day-dreaming?"

"Oh, no—thinking!"

"But thinking about *what?*"

"Anything."

He laughed a third time—but this time, happening to glance upward towards his mother's face, he was appalled at the effect his laughter seemed to have upon her. Her mouth had opened in an expression of horror. . . . This was too bad! Unfortunate! He had known it would cause pain, of course—but he hadn't expected it to be quite so bad as this. Perhaps—perhaps if he just gave them a tiny gleaming hint—?

"About the snow," he said.

"What on earth!" This was his father's voice. The brown slippers came a step nearer on the hearth-rug.

"But my dear, what do you mean!" This was his mother's voice.

The doctor merely stared.

"Just *snow,* that's all. I like to think about it."

"Tell us about it, my boy."

"But that's all it is. There's nothing to tell. *You* know what snow is?"

This he said almost angrily, for he felt that they were trying to corner him. He turned sideways so as no longer to face the doctor, and the better to see the inch of blackness between the window-sill and the low

ered curtain,—the cold inch of beckoning and delicious night. At once
he felt better, more assured.

"Mother—can I go to bed, now, please? I've got a headache."

"But I thought you said—"

"It's just come. It's all these questions—! Can I, mother?"

"You can go as soon as the doctor has finished."

"Don't you think this thing ought to be gone into thoroughly, and
now?" This was Father's voice. The brown slippers again came a step
nearer, the voice was the well-known "punishment" voice, resonant and
cruel.

"Oh, what's the use, Norman—"

Quite suddenly, everyone was silent. And without precisely facing
them, nevertheless he was aware that all three of them were watching
him with an extraordinary intensity—staring hard at him—as if he had
done something monstrous, or was himself some kind of monster. He
could hear the soft irregular flutter of the flames; the cluck-click-cluck-
click of the clock; far and faint, two sudden spurts of laughter from the
kitchen, as quickly cut off as begun; a murmur of water in the pipes;
and then, the silence seemed to deepen, to spread out, to become world-
long and worldwide, to become timeless and shapeless, and to center
inevitably and rightly, with a slow and sleepy but enormous concentration of all power, on the beginning of a new sound. What this new sound
was going to be, he knew perfectly well. It might begin with a hiss, but
it would end with a roar—there was no time to lose—he must escape.
It mustn't happen here—

Without another word, he turned and ran up the stairs.

IV

Not a moment too soon. The darkness was coming in long white waves.
A prolonged sibilance filled the night—a great seamless seethe of wild
influence went abruptly across it—a cold low humming shook the windows. He shut the door and flung off his clothes in the dark. The bare
black floor was like a little raft tossed in waves of snow, almost overwhelmed, washed under whitely, up again, smothered in curled billows
of feather. The snow was laughing: it spoke from all sides at once: it
pressed closer to him as he ran and jumped exulting into his bed.

"Listen to us!" it said. "Listen! We have come to tell you the story we
told you about. You remember? Lie down. Shut your eyes, now—you
will no longer see much—in this white darkness who could see, or want
to see? We will take the place of everything. . . . Listen—"

A beautiful varying dance of snow began at the front of the room,
came forward and then retreated, flattened out toward the floor, then
rose fountain-like to the ceiling, swayed, recruited itself from a new

stream of flakes which poured laughing in through the humming window, advanced again, lifted long white arms. It said peace, it said remoteness, it said cold—it said—

But then a gash of horrible light fell brutally across the room from the opening door—the snow drew back hissing—something alien had come into the room—something hostile. This thing rushed at him, clutched at him, shook him—and he was not merely horrified, he was filled with such a loathing as he had never known. What was this? this cruel disturbance? this act of anger and hate? It was as if he had to reach up a hand toward another world for any understanding of it,—an effort of which he was only barely capable. But of that other world he still remembered just enough to know the exorcising words. They tore themselves from his other life suddenly—

"Mother! Mother! Go away! I hate you!"

And with that effort, everything was solved, everything became all right: the seamless hiss advanced once more, the long white wavering lines rose and fell like enormous whispering sea-waves, the whisper becoming louder, the laughter more numerous.

"Listen!" it said. "We'll tell you the last, the most beautiful and secret story—shut your eyes—it is a very small story—a story that gets smaller and smaller—it comes inward instead of opening like a flower—it is a flower becoming a seed—a little cold seed—do you hear? we are leaning closer to you—"

The hiss was now becoming a roar—the whole world was a vast moving screen of snow—but even now it said peace, it said remoteness, it said cold, it said sleep.

53

Big Blonde

BY DOROTHY PARKER

HAZEL MORSE was a large, fair woman of the type that incites some men when they use the word "blonde" to click their tongues and wag their heads roguishly. She prided herself upon her small feet and suffered for her vanity, boxing them in snub-toed, high-heeled slippers of the shortest bearable size. The curious things about her were her hands, strange terminations to the flabby white arms splattered with pale tan spots—long, quivering hands with deep and convex nails. She should not have disfigured them with little jewels.

She was not a woman given to recollections. At her middle thirties, her old days were a blurred and flickering sequence, an imperfect film, dealing with the actions of strangers.

In her twenties, after the deferred death of a hazy widowed mother, she had been employed as a model in a wholesale dress establishment— it was still the day of the big woman, and she was then prettily colored and erect and high-breasted. Her job was not onerous, and she met numbers of men and spent numbers of evenings with them, laughing at their jokes and telling them she loved their neckties. Men liked her, and she took it for granted that the liking of many men was a desirable thing. Popularity seemed to her to be worth all the work that had to be put into its achievement. Men liked you because you were fun, and when they liked you they took you out, and there you were. So, and successfully, she was fun. She was a good sport. Men like a good sport.

No other form of diversion, simpler or more complicated, drew her attention. She never pondered if she might not be better occupied doing something else. Her ideas, or, better, her acceptances, ran right along with those of the other substantially built blondes in whom she found her friends.

When she had been working in the dress establishment some years she met Herbie Morse. He was thin, quick, attractive, with shifting lines about his shiny, brown eyes and a habit of fiercely biting at the skin around his finger nails. He drank largely; she found that entertaining. Her habitual greeting to him was an allusion to his state of the previous night.

"Oh, what a peach you had," she used to say, through her easy laugh. "I thought I'd die, the way you kept asking the waiter to dance with you."

She liked him immediately upon their meeting. She was enormously amused at his fast, slurred sentences, his interpolations of apt phrases from vaudeville acts and comic strips; she thrilled at the feel of his lean arm tucked firm beneath the sleeve of her coat; she wanted to touch the wet, flat surface of his hair. He was as promptly drawn to her. They were married six weeks after they had met.

She was delighted at the idea of being a bride; coquetted with it, played upon it. Other offers of marriage she had had, and not a few of them, but it happened that they were all from stout, serious men who had visited the dress establishment as buyers; men from Des Moines and Houston and Chicago and, in her phrase, even funnier places. There was always something immensely comic to her in the thought of living elsewhere than New York. She could not regard as serious proposals that she share a western residence.

She wanted to be married. She was nearing thirty now, and she did not take the years well. She spread and softened, and her darkening hair turned her to inexpert dabblings with peroxide. There were times when she had little flashes of fear about her job. And she had had a couple of thousand evenings of being a good sport among her male acquaintances. She had come to be more conscientious than spontaneous about it.

Herbie earned enough, and they took a little apartment far uptown. There was a Mission-furnished dining room with a hanging central light globed in liver-colored glass; in the living room were an "overstuffed suite," a Boston fern and a reproduction of the Henner "Magdalene" with the red hair and the blue draperies; the bedroom was in gray enamel and old rose, with Herbie's photograph on Hazel's dressing-table and Hazel's likeness on Herbie's chest of drawers.

She cooked—and she was a good cook—and marketed and chatted with the delivery boys and the colored laundress. She loved the flat, she loved her life, she loved Herbie. In the first months of their marriage, she gave him all the passion she was ever to know.

She had not realized how tired she was. It was a delight, a new game, a holiday, to give up being a good sport. If her head ached or her arches throbbed, she complained piteously, babyishly. If her mood was quiet, she did not talk. If tears came to her eyes, she let them fall.

She fell readily into the habit of tears during the first year of her marriage. Even in her good sport days, she had been known to weep lavishly and disinterestedly on occasion. Her behavior at the theater was a standing joke. She could weep at anything in a play—tiny garments, love both unrequited and mutual, seduction, purity, faithful servitors, wedlock, the triangle.

"There goes Haze," her friends would say, watching her. "She's off again."

Wedded and relaxed, she poured her tears freely. To her who had laughed so much, crying was delicious. All sorrows became her sorrows; she was Tenderness. She would cry long and softly over newspaper accounts of kidnapped babies, deserted wives, unemployed men, strayed cats, heroic dogs. Even when the paper was no longer before her, her mind revolved upon these things and the drops slipped rhythmically over her plump cheeks.

"Honestly," she would say to Herbie, "all the sadness there is in the world when you stop to think about it!"

"Yeah," Herbie would say.

She missed nobody. The old crowd, the people who had brought her and Herbie together, dropped from their lives, lingeringly at first. When she thought of this at all, it was only to consider it fitting. This was marriage. This was peace.

But the thing was that Herbie was not amused.

For a time, he had enjoyed being alone with her. He found the voluntary isolation novel and sweet. Then it palled with a ferocious suddenness. It was as if one night, sitting with her in the steam-heated living room, he would ask no more; and the next night he was through and done with the whole thing.

He became annoyed by her misty melancholies. At first, when he came home to find her softly tired and moody, he kissed her neck and patted her shoulder and begged her to tell her Herbie what was wrong. She loved that. But time slid by, and he found that there was never anything really, personally, the matter.

"Ah, for God's sake," he would say, "Crabbing again. All right, sit here and crab your head off. I'm going out."

And he would slam out of the flat and come back late and drunk.

She was completely bewildered by what happened to their marriage. First they were lovers; and then, it seemed without transition, they were enemies. She never understood it.

There were longer and longer intervals between his leaving his office and his arrival at the apartment. She went through agonies of picturing him run over and bleeding, dead and covered with a sheet. Then she lost her fears for his safety and grew sullen and wounded. When a person wanted to be with a person, he came as soon as possible. She desperately wanted him to want to be with her; her own hours only marked the time till he would come. It was often nearly nine o'clock before he came home to dinner. Always he had had many drinks, and their effect would die in him, leaving him loud and querulous and bristling for affronts.

He was too nervous, he said, to sit and do nothing for an evening. He boasted, probably not in all truth, that he had never read a book in his life.

"What am I expected to do—sit around this dump on my tail all night?" he would ask, rhetorically. And again he would slam out.

She did not know what to do. She could not manage him. She could not meet him.

She fought him furiously. A terrific domesticity had come upon her, and she would bite and scratch to guard it. She wanted what she called "a nice home." She wanted a sober, tender husband, prompt at dinner, punctual at work. She wanted sweet, comforting evenings. The idea of intimacy with other men was terrible to her; the thought that Herbie might be seeking entertainment in other women set her frantic.

It seemed to her that almost everything she read—novels from the drug-store lending library, magazine stories, women's pages in the papers—dealt with wives who lost their husbands' love. She could bear those, at that, better than accounts of neat, companionable marriage and living happily ever after.

She was frightened. Several times when Herbie came home in the evening, he found her determinedly dressed—she had had to alter those of her clothes that were not new, to make them fasten—and rouged.

"Let's go wild tonight, what do you say?" she would hail him. "A person's got lots of time to hang around and do nothing when they're dead."

So they would got out, to chop houses and the less expensive cabarets. But it turned out badly. She could no longer find amusement in watching Herbie drink. She could not laugh at his whimsicalities, she was so tensely counting his indulgences. And she was unable to keep back her remonstrances—"Ah, come on, Herb, you've had enough, haven't you? You'll feel something terrible in the morning."

He would be immediately enraged. All right, crab; crab, crab, crab, crab, that was all she ever did. What a lousy sport *she* was! There would be scenes, and one or the other of them would rise and stalk out in fury.

She could not recall the definite day that she started drinking, herself. There was nothing separate about her days. Like drops upon a window-pane, they ran together and trickled away. She had been married six months; then a year; then three years.

She had never needed to drink, formerly. She could sit for most of a night at a table where the others were imbibing earnestly and never droop in looks or spirits, nor be bored by the doings of those about her. If she took a cocktail, it was so unusual as to cause twenty minutes or so of jocular comment. But now anguish was in her. Frequently, after a quarrel, Herbie would stay out for the night, and she could not learn from him where the time had been spent. Her heart felt tight and sore in her breast, and her mind turned like an electric fan.

She hated the taste of liquor. Gin, plain or in mixtures, made her promptly sick. After experiment, she found that Scotch whisky was best for her. She took it without water, because that was the quickest way to its effect.

Herbie pressed it on her. He was glad to see her drink. They both felt it might restore her high spirits, and their good times together might again be possible.

" 'Atta girl," he would approve her. "Let's see you get boiled, baby."

But it brought them no nearer. When she drank with him, there would be a little while of gayety and then, strangely without beginning, they would be in a wild quarrel. They would wake in the morning not sure what it had all been about, foggy as to what had been said and done, but each deeply injured and bitterly resentful. There would be days of vengeful silence.

There had been a time when they had made up their quarrels, usually in bed. There would be kisses and little names and assurances of fresh starts. . . . "Oh, it's going to be great now, Herb. We'll have swell times. I was a crab. I guess I must have been tired. But everything's going to be swell. You'll see."

Now there were no gentle reconciliations. They resumed friendly relations only in the brief magnanimity caused by liquor, before more liquor drew them into new battles. The scenes became more violent. There were shouted invectives and pushes, and sometimes sharp slaps. Once she had a black eye. Herbie was horrified next day at sight of it. He did not go to work; he followed her about, suggesting remedies and heaping dark blame on himself. But after they had had a few drinks— "to pull themselves together"—she made so many wistful references to her bruise that he shouted at her and rushed out and was gone for two days.

Each time he left the place in a rage, he threatened never to come back. She did not believe him, nor did she consider separation. Somewhere in her head or her heart was the lazy, nebulous hope that things would change and she and Herbie settle suddenly into soothing married life.

Here were her home, her furniture, her husband, her station. She summoned no alternatives.

She could no longer bustle and potter. She had no more vicarious tears; the hot drops she shed were for herself. She walked ceaselessly about the rooms, her thoughts running mechanically round and round Herbie. In those days began the hatred of being alone that she was never to overcome. You could be by yourself when things were all right, but when you were blue you got the howling horrors.

She commenced drinking alone, little, short, drinks all through the day. It was only with Herbie that alcohol made her nervous and quick in offense. Alone, it blurred sharp things for her. She lived in a haze of it. Her life took on a dream-like quality. Nothing was astonishing.

A Mrs. Martin moved into the flat across the hall. She was a great blonde woman of forty, a promise in looks of what Mrs. Morse was to be. They made acquaintance, quickly became inseparable. Mrs. Morse spent her days in the opposite apartment. They drank together, to brace themselves after the drinks of the nights before.

She never confided her troubles about Herbie to Mrs. Martin. The subject was too bewildering to her to find comfort in talk. She let it be assumed that her husband's business kept him much away. It was not regarded as important; husbands, as such, played but shadowy parts in Mrs. Martin's circle.

Mrs. Martin had no visible spouse; you were left to decide for yourself whether he was or was not dead. She had an admirer, Joe, who came to see her almost nightly. Often he brought several friends with him— "The Boys," they were called. The Boys were big, red, good-humored men, perhaps forty-five, perhaps fifty. Mrs. Morse was glad of invitations to join the parties—Herbie was scarcely ever at home at night now. If he did come home, she did not visit Mrs. Martin. An evening alone with Herbie meant inevitably a quarrel, yet she would stay with him. There was always her thin and wordless idea that, maybe, this night, things would begin to be all right.

The Boys brought plenty of liquor along with them whenever they came to Mrs. Martin's. Drinking with them, Mrs. Morse became lively and good-natured and audacious. She was quickly popular. When she had drunk enough to cloud her most recent battle with Herbie, she was excited by their approbation. Crab, was she? Rotten sport, was she? Well, there were some that thought different.

Ed was one of The Boys. He lived in Utica—had "his own business" there, was the awed report—but he came to New York almost every week. He was married. He showed Mrs. Morse the then current photographs of Junior and Sister, and she praised them abundantly and sin-

cerely. Soon it was accepted by the others that Ed was her particular
friend.

He staked her when they all played poker; sat next her and occasionally rubbed his knee against hers during the game. She was rather
lucky. Frequently she went home with a twenty-dollar bill or a ten-
dollar bill or a handful of crumpled dollars. She was glad of them.
Herbie was getting, in her words, something awful about money. To
ask him for it brought an instant row.

"What the hell do you do with it?" he would say. "Shoot it all on
Scotch?"

"I try to run this house half-way decent," she would retort. "Never
thought of that, did you? Oh, no, his lordship couldn't be bothered
with that."

Again, she could not find a definite day, to fix the beginning of Ed's
proprietorship. It became his custom to kiss her on the mouth when he
came in, as well as for farewell, and he gave her little quick kisses of
approval all through the evening. She liked this rather more than she
disliked it. She never thought of his kisses when she was not with him.

He would run his hand lingeringly over her back and shoulders.

"Some dizzy blonde, eh?" he would say. "Some doll."

One afternoon she came home from Mrs. Martin's to find Herbie in
the bedroom. He had been away for several nights, evidently on a prolonged drinking bout. His face was gray, his hands jerked as if they
were on wires. On the bed were two old suitcases, packed high. Only
her photograph remained on his bureau, and the wide doors of his closet
disclosed nothing but coat-hangers.

"I'm blowing," he said. "I'm through with the whole works. I got a
job in Detroit."

She sat down on the edge of the bed. She had drunk much the night
before, and the four Scotches she had had with Mrs. Martin had only
increased her fogginess.

"Good job?" she said.

"Oh, yeah," he said. "Looks all right."

He closed a suitcase with difficulty, swearing at it in whispers.

"There's some dough in the bank," he said. "The bank book's in your
top drawer. You can have the furniture and stuff."

He looked at her, and his forehead twitched.

"God damn it, I'm through, I'm telling you," he cried. "I'm through."

"All right, all right," she said. "I heard you, didn't I?"

She saw him as if he were at one end of a canyon and she at the other.
Her head was beginning to ache bumpingly, and her voice had a dreary,
tiresome tone. She could not have raised it.

"Like a drink before you go?" she asked.

Again he looked at her, and a corner of his mouth jerked up.

"Cockeyed again for a change, aren't you?" he said. "That's nice. Sure, get a couple of shots, will you?"

She went to the pantry, mixed him a stiff highball, poured herself a couple of inches of whisky and drank it. Then she gave herself another portion and brought the glasses into the bedroom. He had strapped both suitcases and had put on his hat and overcoat.

He took his highball.

"Well," he said, and he gave a sudden, uncertain laugh. "Here's mud in your eye."

"Mud in your eye," she said.

They drank. He put down his glass and took up the heavy suitcases.

"Got to get a train around six," he said.

She followed him down the hall. There was a song, a song that Mrs. Martin played doggedly on the phonograph, running loudly through her mind. She had never liked the thing.

> *"Night and daytime,*
> *Always playtime.*
> *Ain't we got fun?"*

At the door he put down the bags and faced her.

"Well," he said. "Well, take care of yourself. You'll be all right, will you?"

"Oh, sure," she said.

He opened the door, then came back to her, holding out his hand.

" 'By, Haze," he said. "Good luck to you."

She took his hand and shook it.

"Pardon my wet glove," she said.

When the door had closed behind him, she went back to the pantry.

She was flushed and lively when she went in to Mrs. Martin's that evening. The Boys were there, Ed among them. He was glad to be in town, frisky and loud and full of jokes. But she spoke quietly to him for a minute.

"Herbie blew today," she said. "Going to live out West."

"That so?" he said. He looked at her and played with the fountain pen clipped to his waistcoat pocket.

"Think he's gone for good, do you?" he asked.

"Yeah," she said. "I know he is. I know. Yeah."

"You going to live on across the hall just the same?" he said. "Know what you're going to do?"

"Gee, I don't know," she said. "I don't give much of a damn."

"Oh, come on, that's no way to talk," he told her. "What you need—
you need a little snifter. How about it?"

"Yeah," she said. "Just straight."

She won forty-three dollars at poker. When the game broke up, Ed
took her back to her apartment.

"Got a little kiss for me?" he asked.

He wrapped her in his big arms and kissed her violently. She was
entirely passive. He held her away and looked at her.

"Little tight, honey?" he asked, anxiously. "Not going to be sick, are
you?"

"Me?" she said. "I'm swell."

II

When Ed left in the morning, he took her photograph with him. He
said he wanted her picture to look at, up in Utica. "You can have that
one on the bureau," she said.

She put Herbie's picture in a drawer, out of her sight. When she could
look at it, she meant to tear it up. She was fairly successful in keeping
her mind from racing around him. Whisky slowed it for her. She was
almost peaceful, in her mist.

She accepted her relationship with Ed without question or enthusiasm. When he was away, she seldom thought definitely of him. He
was good to her; he gave her frequent presents and a regular allowance.
She was even able to save. She did not plan ahead of any day, but her
wants were few, and you might as well put money in the bank as have
it lying around.

When the lease of her apartment neared its end, it was Ed who
suggested moving. His friendship with Mrs. Martin and Joe had become strained over a dispute at poker; a feud was impending.

"Let's get the hell out of here," Ed said. "What I want you to have
is a place near the Grand Central. Make it easier for me."

So she took a little flat in the Forties. A colored maid came in every
day to clean and to make coffee for her—she was "through with that
housekeeping stuff," she said, and Ed, twenty years married to a passionately domestic woman, admired this romantic uselessness and felt
doubly a man of the world in abetting it.

The coffee was all she had until she went out to dinner, but alcohol
kept her fat. Prohibition she regarded only as a basis for jokes. You
could always get all you wanted. She was never noticeably drunk and
seldom nearly sober. It required a larger daily allowance to keep her
misty-minded. Too little, and she was achingly melancholy.

Ed brought her to Jimmy's. He was proud, with the pride of the
transient who would be mistaken for a native, in his knowledge of

small, recent restaurants occupying the lower floors of shabby brownstone houses; places where, upon mentioning the name of an habitué friend, might be obtained strange whisky and fresh gin in many of their ramifications. Jimmy's place was the favorite of his acquaintances.

There, through Ed, Mrs. Morse met many men and women, formed quick friendships. The men often took her out when Ed was in Utica. He was proud of her popularity.

She fell into the habit of going to Jimmy's alone when she had no engagement. She was certain to meet some people she knew, and join them. It was a club for her friends, both men and women.

The women at Jimmy's looked remarkably alike, and this was curious, for, through feuds, removals and opportunities of more profitable contacts, the personnel of the group changed constantly. Yet always the newcomers resembled those whom they replaced. They were all big women and stout, broad of shoulder and abundantly breasted, with faces thickly clothed in soft, high-colored flesh. They laughed loud and often, showing opaque and lusterless teeth like squares of crockery. There was about them the health of the big, yet a slight, unwholesome suggestion of stubborn preservation. They might have been thirty-six or forty-five or anywhere between.

They composed their titles of their own first names with their husbands' surnames—Mrs. Florence Miller, Mrs. Vera Riley, Mrs. Lilian Block. This gave at the same time the solidity of marriage and the glamour of freedom. Yet only one or two were actually divorced. Most of them never referred to their dimmed spouses; some, a shorter time separate, described them in terms of great biological interest. Several were mothers, each of an only child—a boy at school somewhere, or a girl being cared for by a grandmother. Often, well on towards morning, there would be displays of kodak portraits and of tears.

They were comfortable women, cordial and friendly and irrepressibly matronly. Theirs was the quality of ease. Become fatalistic, especially about money matters, they were unworried. Whenever their funds dropped alarmingly, a new donor appeared; this had always happened. The aim of each was to have one man, permanently, to pay all her bills, in return for which she would have immediately given up other admirers and probably would have become exceedingly fond of him; for the affections of all of them were, by now, unexacting, tranquil, and easily arranged. This end, however, grew increasingly difficult yearly. Mrs. Morse was regarded as fortunate.

Ed had a good year, increased her allowance and gave her a sealskin coat. But she had to be careful of her moods with him. He insisted upon gayety. He would not listen to admissions of aches or weariness.

"Hey, listen," he would say, "I got worries of my own, and plenty.

Nobody wants to hear other people's troubles, sweetie. What you got to do, you got to be a sport and forget it. See? Well, slip us a little smile, then. That's my girl."

She never had enough interest to quarrel with him as she had with Herbie, but she wanted the privilege of occasional admitted sadness. It was strange. The other women she saw did not have to fight their moods. There was Mrs. Florence Miller who got regular crying jags, and the men sought only to cheer and comfort her. The others spent whole evenings in grieved recitals of worries and ills; their escorts paid them deep sympathy. But she was instantly undesirable when she was low in spirits. Once, at Jimmy's, when she could not make herself lively, Ed had walked out and left her.

"Why the hell don't you stay home and not go spoiling everybody's evening?" he had roared.

Even her slightest acquaintances seemed irritated if she were not conspicuously light-hearted.

"What's the matter with you, anyway?" they would say. "Be your age, why don't you? Have a little drink and snap out of it."

When her relationship with Ed had continued nearly three years, he moved to Florida to live. He hated leaving her; he gave her a large check and some shares of a sound stock, and his pale eyes were wet when he said good-by. She did not miss him. He came to New York infrequently, perhaps two or three times a year, and hurried directly from the train to see her. She was always pleased to have him come and never sorry to see him go.

Charley, an acquaintance of Ed's that she had met at Jimmy's, had long admired her. He had always made opportunities of touching her and leaning close to talk to her. He asked repeatedly of all their friends if they had ever heard such a fine laugh as she had. After Ed left, Charley became the main figure in her life. She classified him and spoke of him as "not so bad." There was nearly a year of Charley; then she divided her time between him and Sydney, another frequenter of Jimmy's; then Charley slipped away altogether.

Sydney was a little, brightly dressed, clever Jew. She was perhaps nearest contentment with him. He amused her always; her laughter was not forced.

He admired her completely. Her softness and size delighted him. And he thought she was great, he often told her, because she kept gay and lively when she was drunk.

"Once I had a gal," he said, "used to try and throw herself out of the window every time she got a can on. Jee-zuss," he added, feelingly.

Then Sydney married a rich and watchful bride, and then there was Billy. No—after Sydney came Ferd, then Billy. In her haze, she never recalled how men entered her life and left it. There were no surprises. She had no thrill at their advent, nor woe at their departure. She seemed to be always able to attract men. There was never another as rich as Ed, but they were all generous to her, in their means.

Once she had news of Herbie. She met Mrs. Martin dining at Jimmy's, and the old friendship was vigorously renewed. The still admiring Joe, while on a business trip, had seen Herbie. He had settled in Chicago, he looked fine, he was living with some woman—seemed to be crazy about her. Mrs. Morse had been drinking vastly that day. She took the news with mild interest, as one hearing of the sex peccadilloes of somebody whose name is, after a moment's groping, familiar.

"Must be damn near seven years since I saw him," she commented. "Gee. Seven years."

More and more, her days lost their individuality. She never knew dates, nor was sure of the day of the week.

"My God, was that a year ago!" she would exclaim, when an event was recalled in conversation.

She was tired so much of the time. Tired and blue. Almost everything could give her the blues. Those old horses she saw on Sixth Avenue—struggling and slipping along the car-tracks, or standing at the curb, their heads dropped level with their worn knees. The tightly stored tears would squeeze from her eyes as she teetered past on her aching feet in the stubby, champagne-colored slippers.

The thought of death came and stayed with her and lent her a sort of drowsy cheer. It would be nice, nice and restful, to be dead.

There was no settled, shocked moment when she first thought of killing herself; it seemed to her as if the idea had always been with her. She pounced upon all the accounts of suicides in the newspapers. There was an epidemic of self-killings—or maybe it was just that she searched for the stories of them so eagerly that she found many. To read of them roused reassurance in her; she felt a cozy solidarity with the big company of the voluntary dead.

She slept, aided by whisky, till deep into the afternoons, then lay abed, a bottle and glass at her hand, until it was time to dress to go out for dinner. She was beginning to feel toward alcohol a little puzzled distrust, as toward an old friend who has refused a simple favor. Whisky could still soothe her for most of the time, but there were sudden, inexplicable moments when the cloud fell treacherously away from her, and she was sawn by the sorrow and bewilderment and nuisance of all living. She played voluptuously with the thought of cool, sleepy retreat. She had never been troubled by religious belief and no vision of an after-life intimidated her. She dreamed by day of never again putting on tight shoes, of never having to laugh and listen and admire, of never more being a good sport. Never.

But how would you do it? It made her sick to think of jumping from heights. She could not stand a gun. At the theater, if one of the actors drew a revolver, she crammed her fingers into her ears and could not even look at the stage until after the shot had been fired. There was no gas in her flat. She looked long at the bright blue veins in her slim wrists—a cut with a razor blade, and there you'd be. But it would hurt, hurt like hell, and there would be blood to see. Poison—something tasteless and quick and painless—was the thing. But they wouldn't sell it to you in drug-stores, because of the law.

She had few other thoughts.

There was a new man now—Art. He was short and fat and exacting and hard on her patience when he was drunk. But there had been only occasionals for some time before him, and she was glad of a little stability. Too, Art must be away for weeks at a stretch, selling silks, and that was restful. She was convincingly gay with him, though the effort shook her.

"The best sport in the world," he would murmur, deep in her neck. "The best sport in the world."

One night, when he had taken her to Jimmy's, she went into the dressing-room with Mrs. Florence Miller. There, while designing curly mouths on their faces with lip-rouge, they compared experiences of insomnia.

"Honestly," Mrs. Morse said, "I wouldn't close an eye if I didn't go to bed full of Scotch. I lie there and toss and turn and toss and turn. Blue! Does a person get blue lying awake that way!"

"Say, listen, Hazel," Mrs. Miller said, impressively, "I'm telling you I'd be awake for a year if I didn't take veronal. That stuff makes you sleep like a fool."

"Isn't it poison, or something?" Mrs. Morse asked.

"Oh, you take too much and you're out for the count," said Mrs. Miller. "I just take five grains—they come in tablets. I'd be scared to fool around with it. But five grains, and you cork off pretty."

"Can you get it anywhere?" Mrs. Morse felt superbly Machiavellian.

"Get all you want in Jersey," said Mrs. Miller. "They won't give it to you here without you have a doctor's prescription. Finished? We'd better go back and see what the boys are doing."

That night, Art left Mrs. Morse at the door of her apartment; his mother was in town. Mrs. Morse was still sober, and it happened that there was no whisky left in her cupboard. She lay in bed, looking up at the black ceiling.

She rose early, for her, and went to New Jersey. She had never taken the tube, and did not understand it. So she went to the Pennsylvania Station and bought a railroad ticket to Newark. She thought of nothing in particular on the trip out. She looked at the uninspired hats of the women about her and gazed through the smeared window at the flat, gritty scene.

In Newark, in the first drug-store she came to, she asked for a tin of talcum powder, a nail-brush and a box of veronal tablets. The powder and the brush were to make the hypnotic seem also a casual need. The clerk was entirely unconcerned. "We only keep them in bottles," he said, and wrapped up for her a little glass vial containing ten white tablets, stacked one on another.

She went to another drug-store and bought a face-cloth, an orange-wood stick and a bottle of veronal tablets. The clerk was also uninterested.

"Well, I guess I got enough to kill an ox," she thought, and went back to the station.

At home, she put the little vials in the drawer of her dressing-table and stood looking at them with a dreamy tenderness.

"There they are, God bless them," she said, and she kissed her finger-tip and touched each bottle.

The colored maid was busy in the living room.

"Hey, Nettie," Mrs. Morse called. "Be an angel, will you? Run around to Jimmy's and get me a quart of Scotch."

She hummed while she awaited the girl's return.

During the next few days, whisky ministered to her as tenderly as it had done when she first turned to its aid. Alone, she was soothed and vague, at Jimmy's she was the gayest of the groups. Art was delighted with her.

Then, one night, she had an appointment to meet Art at Jimmy's for an early dinner. He was to leave afterward on a business excursion, to be away for a week. Mrs. Morse had been drinking all the afternoon; while she dressed to go out, she felt herself rising pleasurably from drowsiness to high spirits. But as she came out into the street the effects of the whisky deserted her completely, and she was filled with a slow, grinding wretchedness so horrible that she stood swaying on the pavement, unable for a moment to move forward. It was a gray night with spurts of mean, thin snow, and the streets shone with dark ice. As she slowly crossed Sixth Avenue, consciously dragging one foot past the other, a big, scarred horse pulling a rickety express-wagon crashed to his knees before her. The driver swore and screamed and lashed the beast insanely, bringing the whip back over his shoulder for every blow, while the horse struggled to get a footing on the slippery asphalt. A group gathered and watched with interest.

Art was waiting when Mrs. Morse reached Jimmy's.

"What's the matter with you, for God's sake?" was his greeting to her.

"I saw a horse," she said. "Gee, I—a person feels sorry for horses. I—it isn't just horses. Everything's kind of terrible, isn't it? I can't help getting sunk."

"Ah, sunk, me eye," he said. "What's the idea of all the bellyaching? What have you got to be sunk about?"

"I can't help it," she said.

"Ah, help it, me eye," he said. "Pull yourself together, will you? Come on and sit down, and take that face off you."

She drank industriously and she tried hard, but she could not overcome her melancholy. Others joined them and commented on her gloom, and she could do no more for them than smile weakly. She made little dabs at her eyes with her handkerchief, trying to time her movements so they would be unnoticed, but several times Art caught her and scowled and shifted impatiently in his chair.

When it was time for him to go to his train, she said she would leave, too, and go home.

"And not a bad idea, either," he said. "See if you can't sleep yourself out of it. I'll see you Thursday. For God's sake, try and cheer up by then, will you?"

"Yeah," she said. "I will."

In her bedroom, she undressed with a tense speed wholly unlike her usual slow uncertainty. She put on her nightgown, took off her hair-net and passed the comb quickly through her dry, vari-colored hair. Then she took the two little vials from the drawer and carried them into the bathroom. The splintering misery had gone from her, and she felt the quick excitement of one who is about to receive an anticipated gift.

She uncorked the vials, filled a glass with water and stood before the mirror, a tablet between her fingers. Suddenly she bowed graciously to her reflection, and raised the glass to it.

"Well, here's mud in your eye," she said.

The tablets were unpleasant to take, dry and powdery and sticking obstinately half-way down her throat. It took her a long time to swallow all twenty of them. She stood watching her reflection with deep, impersonal interest, studying the movements of the gulping throat. Once more she spoke aloud.

"For God's sake, try and cheer up by Thursday, will you?" she said. "Well, you know what he can do. He and the whole lot of them."

She had no idea how quickly to expect effect from the veronal. When she had taken the last tablet, she stood uncertainly, wondering, still with a courteous, vicarious interest, if death would strike her down then and there. She felt in no way strange, save for a slight stirring of sickness from the effort of swallowing the tablets, nor did her reflected face look at all different. It would not be immediate, then; it might even take on hour or so.

She stretched her arms high and gave a vast yawn.

"Guess I'll go to bed," she said. "Gee, I'm nearly dead."

That struck her as comic, and she turned out the bathroom light and went in and laid herself down in her bed, chuckling softly all the time.

"Gee, I'm nearly dead," she quoted. "That's a hot one!"

III

Nettie, the colored maid, came in late the next afternoon to clean the apartment, and found Mrs. Morse in her bed. But then, that was not unusual. Usually, though, the sounds of cleaning waked her, and she did not like to wake up. Nettie, an agreeable girl, had learned to move softly about her work.

But when she had done the living room and stolen in to tidy the little square bedroom, she could not avoid a tiny clatter as she arranged the objects on the dressing-table. Instinctively, she glanced over her shoulder at the sleeper, and without warning a sickly uneasiness crept over her. She came to the bed and stared down at the woman lying there.

Mrs. Morse lay on her back, one flabby, white arm flung up, the wrist against her forehead. Her stiff hair hung untenderly along her face. The bed covers were pushed down, exposing a deep square of soft neck and a pink nightgown, its fabric worn uneven by many launderings; her great breasts, freed from their tight confiner, sagged beneath her arm-pits. Now and then she made knotted, snoring sounds, and from the corner of her opened mouth to the blurred turn of her jaw ran a lane of crusted spittle.

"Mis' Morse," Nettie called. "Oh, Mis' Morse! It's terrible late."

Mrs. Morse made no move.

"Mis' Morse," said Nettie. "Look, Mis' Morse. How'm I goin' get this bed made?"

Panic sprang upon the girl. She shook the woman's hot shoulder.

"Ah, wake up, will yuh?" she whined. "Ah, please wake up."

Suddenly the girl turned and ran out in the hall to the elevator door, keeping her thumb firm on the black, shiny button until the elderly car and its Negro attendant stood before her. She poured a jumble of words over the boy, and led him back to the apartment. He tiptoed creakingly in to the bedside; first gingerly, then so lustily that he left marks on the soft flesh, he prodded the unconscious woman.

"Hey, there!" he cried, and listened intently, as for an echo.

"Jeez. Out like a light," he commented.

At his interest in the spectacle, Nettie's panic left her. Importance was big in both of them. They talked in quick, unfinished whispers, and it was the boy's suggestion that he fetch the young doctor who lived on the ground floor. Nettie hurried along with him. They looked forward to the limelit moment of breaking their news of something untoward, something pleasurably unpleasant. Mrs. Morse had become the medium of drama. With no ill wish to her, they hoped that her state was serious, that she would not let them down by being awake and normal on their return. A little fear of this determined them to make the most, to the doctor, of her present condition. "Matter of life and death," returned to Nettie from her thin store of reading. She considered startling the doctor with the phrase.

The doctor was in and none too pleased at interruption. He wore a yellow and blue striped dressing-gown, and he was lying on his sofa, laughing with a dark girl, her face scaly with inexpensive powder, who perched on the arm. Half-emptied highball glasses stood beside them, and her coat and hat were neatly hung up with the comfortable implication of a long stay.

Always something, the doctor grumbled. Couldn't let anybody alone after a hard day. But he put some bottles and instruments into a case, changed his dressing-gown for his coat and started out with the Negroes.

"Snap it up there, big boy," the girl called after him. "Don't be all night."

The doctor strode loudly into Mrs. Morse's flat and on to the bedroom, Nettie and the boy right behind him. Mrs. Morse had not moved; her sleep was as deep, but soundless, now. The doctor looked sharply at her, then plunged his thumbs into the lidded pits above her eyeballs and threw his weight upon them. A high, sickened cry broke from Nettie.

"Look like he tryin' to push her right on th'ough the bed," said the boy. He chuckled.

Mrs. Morse gave no sign under the pressure. Abruptly the doctor abandoned it, and with one quick movement swept the covers down to the foot of the bed. With another he flung her nightgown back and lifted the thick, white legs, cross-hatched with blocks of tiny, iris-colored veins. He pinched them repeatedly, with long, cruel nips, back of the knees. She did not awaken.

"What's she been drinking?" he asked Nettie, over his shoulder.

With the certain celerity of one who knows just where to lay hands on a thing, Nettie went into the bathroom, bound for the cupboard where Mrs. Morse kept her whisky. But she stopped at the sight of the two vials, with their red and white labels, lying before the mirror. She brought them to the doctor.

"Oh, for the Lord Almighty's sweet sake!" he said. He dropped Mrs. Morse's legs, and pushed them impatiently across the bed. "What did she want to go taking that tripe for? Rotten yellow trick, that's what a thing like that is. Now we'll have to pump her out, and all that stuff. Nuisance, a thing like that is; that's what it amounts to. Here, George, take me down in the elevator. You wait here, maid. She won't do anything."

"She won' die on me, will she?" cried Nettie.

"No," said the doctor. "God, no. You couldn't kill her with an ax."

IV

After two days, Mrs. Morse came back to consciousness, dazed at first, then with a comprehension that brought with it the slow, saturating wretchedness.

"Oh, Lord, oh, Lord," she moaned, and tears for herself and for life striped her cheeks.

Nettie came in at the sound. For two days she had done the ugly, incessant tasks in the nursing of the unconscious, for two nights she had caught broken bits of sleep on the living-room couch. She looked coldly at the big, blown woman in the bed.

"What you been tryin' to do, Mis' Morse?" she said. "What kine o' work is that, takin' all that stuff?"

"Oh, Lord," moaned Mrs. Morse, again, and she tried to cover her eyes with her arms. But the joints felt stiff and brittle, and she cried out at their ache.

"Tha's no way to ack, takin' them pills," said Nettie. "You can thank you' stars you heah at all. How you feel now?"

"Oh, I feel great," said Mrs. Morse. "Swell, I feel."

Her hot, painful tears fell as if they would never stop.

"Tha's no way to take on, cryin' like that," Nettie said. "After what you done. The doctor, he says he could have you arrested, doin' a thing like that. He was fit to be tied, here."

"Why couldn't he let me alone?" wailed Mrs. Morse. "Why the hell couldn't he have?"

"Tha's terr'ble, Mis' Morse, swearin' an' talkin' like that," said Nettie, "after what people done for you. Here I ain' had no sleep at all for two nights, an' I had to give up goin' out to my other ladies!"

"Oh, I'm sorry, Nettie," she said. "You're a peach. I'm sorry I've given you so much trouble. I couldn't help it. I just got sunk. Didn't you ever feel like doing it? When everything looks just lousy to you?"

"I wouldn' think o' no such thing," declared Nettie. "You got to cheer up. Tha's what you got to do. Everybody's got their troubles."

"Yeah," said Mrs. Morse. "I know."

"Come a pretty picture card for you," Nettie said. "Maybe that will cheer you up."

She handed Mrs. Morse a post-card. Mrs. Morse had to cover one eye with her hand, in order to read the message; her eyes were not yet focusing correctly.

It was from Art. On the back of a view of the Detroit Athletic Club he had written: "Greeting and salutations. Hope you have lost that gloom. Cheer up and don't take any rubber nickels. See you on Thursday."

She dropped the card to the floor. Misery crushed her as if she were between great smooth stones. There passed before her a slow, slow pageant of days spent lying in her flat, of evenings at Jimmy's being a good sport, making herself laugh and coo at Art and other Arts; she saw a long parade of weary horses and shivering beggars and all beaten, driven, stumbling things. Her feet throbbed as if she had crammed them into the stubby champagne-colored slippers. Her heart seemed to swell and harden.

"Nettie," she cried, "for heaven's sake pour me a drink, will you?"

The maid looked doubtful.

"Now you know, Mis' Morse," she said, "you been near daid. I don' know if the doctor he let you drink nothin' yet."

"Oh, never mind him," she said. "You get me one, and bring in the bottle. Take one yourself."

"Well," said Nettie.

She poured them each a drink, deferentially leaving hers in the bathroom to be taken in solitude, and brought Mrs. Morse's glass in to her.

Mrs. Morse looked into the liquor and shuddered back from its odor. Maybe it would help. Maybe, when you had been knocked cold for a few days, your very first drink would give you a lift. Maybe whisky would be her friend again. She prayed without addressing a God, without knowing a God. Oh, please, please, let her be able to get drunk, please keep her always drunk.

She lifted the glass.

"Thanks, Nettie," she said. "Here's mud in your eye."

The maid giggled. "Tha's the way, Mis' Morse," she said. "You cheer up, now."

"Yeah," said Mrs. Morse. "Sure."

54

The Arrow

BY CHRISTOPHER MORLEY

I SUPPOSE the reason why cabin stewards fold them like that, instead of tucking 'em in as bed-clothes are arranged on shore, is that if the ship founders you can get out of your bunk so much quicker. The life preservers are up there, on top of the little wardrobe. The picture of Mr. Boddy-Finch, the resolute-looking man with a mustache, showing how to wear the life waistcoat, is on the panel of the door. Mr. Boddy-Finch's mustache has a glossy twist, probably waxed like that to keep it from getting wet while he's demonstrating his waistcoat. He guarantees that the thing will keep you afloat for forty-eight hours: how can he tell unless he's tried it? Amusing scene, Mr. Boddy-Finch floating competently in the Mersey while a jury of ship owners on the dock cheer him on toward the forty-eighth hour.

So he was thinking as he got into the berth and carefully snugged himself into the clothes that were folded, not tucked. The detective story slid down beside the pillow. No bed companion is so soothing as a book you don't intend to read. He had realized just now that the strangeness had worn off. This was his first voyage. He had supposed, of course, he would be ill, but he had never felt more at home, physically, in his life. The distemper that had burdened him was of another sort; but now it was gone—gone so quietly and completely that he hardly missed it yet. He only knew that some secretive instinct had brought him early to his bunk, not to sleep, but because there, in that narrow solitude, he could examine the queer delicious mood now pervading him.

The steady drum and quiver of a slow ship finding her own comfortable way through heavy sea. The little stateroom, which he had to himself, was well down and amidships; the great double crash and rhythm of the engines was already part of his life. A pounding hum, pounding hum, pounding hum. He invented imitative phrases to accompany that cadence. Oh, lyric love, half piston and half crank! Roofed over by the upper berth, shaded from the lamp by the clicking chintz curtain, this was his lair to spy out on the laws of life. He could see his small snug dwelling sink and sway. Marvellous cradling ease, sweet equation of all forces. He studied the pattern of honest bolts in the white iron ceiling. Surely, with reference to himself, they were rigid: yet he saw them rise and dip and swing. The corridor outside was one long creak. There was a dropping sag of his berth as it caved beneath him, then a climbing push as it rose, pressing under his shoulders. He waited, in curious lightness and thrill, to feel the long slow lift, the hanging pause, the beautiful sinking plunge. The downward slope then gently tilted sideways. His knees pressed hard against the board, he could see his toothbrush glide across the tumbler. He was incredibly happy in an easy bliss. This primitive cycle of movement seemed a part of the secret rhymes of biology. Now he under-stood why sailors often feel ill when they reach the dull, flat solidity of earth.

The lull and ecstasy of the sea is what man was meant for. The whole swinging universe takes you up in its arms, and you know both desire and fulfilment. And down below, from far within, like—oh, like things you believed you'd forgotten—that steady, grumbling hum. The first night he was a bit anxious when she rolled: his entrails yawned when she leaned over so heavily on emptiness. But then he had divined something; it is the things that frighten you that are really worth while. Now, when she canted he did not hold back; he leaned with her, as though eager to come as close as possible to that seethe and hiss along her dripping side. It was the inexpressive faces of stewards and stewardesses that had best fortified him. They stood on duty along the exclaiming passages, priests of this white ritual world. Their sallow sexton faces seemed gravely reassuring the congregation that all was calculated, charted, and planned. They flexed and balanced serenely like vicars turning eastward at the appointed clause. He had barely escaped horrifying one of them, his bedroom steward who came in suddenly—the door was open—while he was doing a private caper of triumph at realizing he wasn't ill. He repeated his silly chant, smiling in the berth:

> "*Wallow in a hollow with a pounding hum,*
> *Pillow on a billow with a pounding hum,*
> *Now the Atlantic*
> *Drives me frantic,*
> *Pounding pounding pounding hum!*"

If you ever tell anyone this story, he said to me—long afterward, when he first talked about it—make it very matter-of-fact. I know that some writers have a way of putting things handsomely, picturesquely, full of ingenious, witty phrases. That's dangerous, because people get a notion that these affairs are only the invention of literary folks.

The first days were very uneasy. He couldn't read, he couldn't bear talking the gay chaff that is legal tender on shipboard, he dreaded the discovery of a mutual friend in Pelham Manor that thrills adjoining deck chairs. He couldn't write, nor imagine concentrating his mind on cards; besides, he was young enough to be alarmed by the warning notice about Professional Gamblers. He'd have enjoyed more deck tennis but the courts were usually occupied by young engineer-officers and a group of girls whose parents, in desperation, were sending them abroad to school. They were rather noisily true to type and carried with them everywhere a toy phonograph, the size of a candy box. This occult machine, busily rotating dark spirals of jazz, was heard intermittently like a pagan refrain. It uttered such cries as Pan might ejaculate under ether. Long after the diligent ship's orchestra had couched themselves it chattered, in dark corners of the deck, against the thunder of yeasty sea. Evidently it was hastening its damsels into a concentric *cul de sac* where they would eventually find themselves blocked. There would, perhaps, be the momentary alleviation of a picture in the Sunday paper ("Among the season's interesting brides") after which they would be irretrievable wives and mothers—with friends in Pelham Manor.

He paced the deck endlessly in windy bright September. Weariness is the only drug for that sea unease. At night the mastheads swung solemnly against clear grainy sky. Even the Dipper seemed swinging. Here and there he paused, in a kind of dream, vacantly studying the log of the day's run, pondering on the chart a shoal called the Virgins, or watching, through a brass-rimmed port, cheerful people gossiping in the lounge. He was too shy and too excited to enter into the innocent pastimes of the voyage. Sometimes he went into the smokeroom for a drink. Brought up in the Prohibition era, acquainted only with raw gin and fusel oils, leprous distilments, he had never before encountered honest ripened Scotch. When that hale benevolent spirit amazed him with its pure warmth, it occurred to him that perhaps there is no reason why the glamor of life should not be taken neat. It need not always be smuggled about in medicine bottles or under false and counterfeit labels. But the smokeroom frightened some essential chastity in his mind. It was full of women smoking and drinking. They wore cheese-colored silk stockings, provokingly obvious, and their eyes were sportively bright. Perhaps they were gamblers even more professional than those referred to in the sign. One evening, when he had a bad cold, the doctor gave him some phenacetin and aspirin tablets to take with hot toddy. That night he lay stewing in his warm cradle, submerged in a heavy ocean of sleep, rolled in a nothingness so perfect it was almost prenatal. So he told the doctor the next morning, and caught a flash from that officer's eyes. Both put the phrase aside where it wouldn't get broken, for private meditation. Being diffident, he did not tell the doctor what jolly dreams had swum through the deep green caverns of his swoon. His mind lay on the bottom like a foundered galleon, its treasures corroding in the strong room, while white mermaids . . . No, they weren't mermaids, he said to himself.

But now I know why the steamship companies arrange so many distractions for their passengers.

As nearly as I can make out, his obscure agitations resolved themselves into a certainty that something was going to happen. But he could put no label on this strange apprehensive sentiment. When you can put your feelings into words, they cease to be dangerous. Now you see, he added, why my bunk was the safest place.

He paused. I think he realized that I didn't see, altogether; and I nearly remarked, in the jocular way an old friend can say things, that if he expected any editor to be interested in this story it was time he got into it something more tangible than phenacetin mermaids. The ladies with cheese-colored stockings had sounded promising. But somehow, with no notion at all of what he was coming to, I wanted him to work it out in his own way. After all, it's only the very cheap kind of stories that have to be told in a hurry.

Evidently it would be wrong to imagine that his disturbance was unhappy. For I get the impression that, little by little, a secret elation possessed him: on that special evening when he retired early to his berth, he was particularly certain that some blissful meaning lay inside this experience. For suddenly, at the heart of that unsteady clamor, he lay infinitely at peace. The dull crash of those huge pistons was an unerring music; the grave plunging of the ship was perfect rest. He lay trembling with happiness, in what he described (rather oddly) as a kind of piety; a physical piety.

I wanted him to make this a little plainer, but he was rather vague. "I felt, more truly than ever before, a loyalty to the physical principles of the universe. I felt like Walt Whitman."

I decided not to pursue this further, but in a determined effort to explain himself he made another odd remark, which I suppose ought to be put in the record. "One day the chief engineer took me down to see the machinery. But before we went below he made me leave my watch in his cabin. He said that if I had it on me when we went by the dynamos their magnetic power was so strong that it would throw my watch into a kind of trance. It would be interesting as a specimen of polarization, he said, but it wouldn't be a timepiece. Well, it was like that with me. There are some instincts that it's better to leave behind when you go in a ship. I felt polarized."

It appears that he felt himself on the verge of great mental illuminations; but, as one turns away from a too brilliant light, he averted himself from the effort of thinking. He took up the detective story, but it lacked its usual soporific virtue. And presently, still wakeful, he slipped on his dressing gown and went for a hot bath. The bathroom, farther down the corridor, would be unoccupied at this hour. On that deck all ports were screwed up, on account of the heavy weather, and it was undeniably stuffy. Several stateroom doors were hooked ajar, for ventilation, and as he passed along . . .

"I should have told you" (he interrupted himself) "about the day we sailed from New York, a marvelous warm autumn noon, the buoys chiming like lunch bells as we slipped down toward Staten Island. I got down to the ship rather early. After seeing my baggage safely in the stateroom and looking at some parcels that had been sent me—you know that little diary, *My Trip Abroad,* that someone always gives you; I'm sorry to have to say its pages are still blank—I sat in the writing room scribbling some postcards. You must realize what an extraordinary adventure all this was for me. My Trip Abroad! With a sense of doing something rather dangerous, I went off the pier to mail my cards. I remember the drowsy Saturday sunlight of that wide cobbly space; taxis driving up; the old Fourteenth Street trolleys rumbling along as usual, and in a few hours I should be far away from it all. It was then, returning across the street, that I noticed the head of some goddess or other carved over the piers. I wondered why, but I didn't dally to speculate. I had a naïve fear that the ship might somehow slide off without me—though there was still nearly an hour to sailing time.

"A friend had come down to see me off, and we palavered about this and that: he was an old traveler and was probably amused at my excitement. The deck was thronged with people saying good-by, and while my friend and I were having our final words, there was a bunch of women near us. My companion may have observed that I was hardly paying attention to our talk. I was noticing a gray dress that had its back turned toward me. It was an exquisitely attractive thing, a sort of cool silky stuff with crisp little pleats. Its plain simplicity made it admirably piquant. Somehow I had a feeling that anyone who would wear so delicious a costume must be interesting. I can't attempt to describe the garment in technical terms, but it was draped just properly flat behind the shoulders and tactfully snug over the hips. What caught my eye especially was a charming frill that went down the middle, accompanied by a file of buttons and ending in a lively little black bow. I only saw the back of this outfit, which included a bell-shaped gray hat and a dark shingled nape. I noted that its wearer was tall and athletic in carriage, but my friend then recaptured my attention. When he had gone the dress had vanished. A visitor, I supposed; it was obviously the summery kind of thing that would be worn, on a warm day, to go down to say good-by to someone who was leaving. But several times, in my various considerings, I had remembered it. I thought particularly of what I called the Spinal Frill and the impudent little twirl of ribbon that ended it. Did or did not anyone who wore that know how enchantingly inciting it was? It must be put there with some intention. But was it the wearer's intention, or only some casual fancy of the dressmaker's? Yet it was there to be admired; and if I had gone to the lady and told her how much I admired it, wouldn't I only have been doing my duty?

"Well, as I started to say, when I went by that partly open door I saw that gray dress hanging in a stateroom. It was on a hanger, its back toward me. It looked rather limp and dejected, but there could be no doubt about the frill and the buttons and the bow.

"I was hurrying, as you do hurry when you go along a public passage in your dressing gown, and it really didn't occur to me until I was comfortably soaking in a deep tub of slanting hot water that I might have noted the number of the room. Then I could probably have found out from the passenger list who she was. But even so, I was glad I hadn't. I didn't want to seem to spy on the gray dress: I admired it too much for that; and also, just in the instant I saw it, it looked so emaciated, so helpless, almost as if it were seasick. I couldn't have taken advantage of it. I dallied in my bath for some time; when I returned, all the doors were shut."

II

The following day there was that subtle change that comes over every Atlantic voyage about three-quarters of the way across. Perhaps it happens at the place where the waves are parted, like hair. For on one side you see them rolling in toward America; on the other they move with equal regularity toward England and France. So obviously there must be a place where they turn back to back. The feeling of Europe being near increased the humility of passengers making their maiden voyage; more than ever they shrank from the masterful condescension of those anxious to explain what an intolerable thrill the first sight of Land's End would be. A certain number of English ladies, who had lain mummified and plaided in their chairs, now began to pace the deck like Britannia's daughters. Even one or two French, hitherto almost buried under the general mass of Anglo-Saxon assertiveness, pricked up and showed a meager brightness. The young women with the phonograph, if they had been listening, might now have learned how to pronounce Cherbourg. Friendships that had been still a trifle green and hard suddenly ripened and even fell squashily overripe. Champagne popped in the dining saloon; the directors of Messrs. Bass prepared to declare another dividend; there was a fancy-dress ball. A homeward-bound English lecturer hoped that the weather would be clear going up the Chops of the Channel; for then, he said, in the afternoon light you will see the rocks of Cornwall shining like opals. But the weather grew darker and wetter; and with every increase of moisture and gale the British passengers grew ruddier and more keen. Even the breakfast kippers seemed stronger, more pungent, as they approached their native waters; the grapefruit correspondingly pulpier and less fluent. It was borne in upon the Americans that they were now a long way from home. Hard-headed business men, whose trans-actions with the smokeroom steward now proved to have had some uses, were showing their wives how to distinguish the half-crown from the florin. It struck them oddly that it might be some time before they would see again the Detroit *Free Press* or the Boston *Transcript.* Thus, in varying manners, came the intuition (which always reaches the American with a peculiar shock) that they were approaching a different world—a world in which they were only too likely to be regarded as spoiled and plunderable children. The young women with the phono-graph, subconsciously resenting this, kept the record going prodigiously.

In a mildly expectant way he had kept an eye open for a possible reappearance of the gray frock; but ratiocination persuaded him it was unlikely. For it was not the kind of dress one would wear for dancing—obviously, it was not an evening gown, for it had no hos-pitable exposures; yet it certainly had looked too flimsy for outdoor appearance in this weather. Perhaps it was a garment too tenuous ever to be worn at all in Britain, he pondered, as the chill increased. Then came the fancy-dress ball, for which he was enlivened by the Scotch and the enthusiasm of his steward, who admired his tentatively suggested costume of bath towels and curtains. A stewardess pinned him together, loudly praising his originality, although she had seen one just like it almost every voyage for twenty years. He found himself dancing with a charming creature who might even, by her build and color, have been the gray unknown. He had intended to be a trifle lofty with her, for he doubted whether she was his intellectual equal; but neither the cocktails nor the movement of the ship were conducive to Platonic demeanor. He decided to try her with a hypothetical question.

"If you had a gray dress with long sleeves and a nice little white collar, on what sort of occasion would you wear it?" he asked.

"When I became a grandmother," she replied promptly.

"There was nothing grandmotherly about it," he insisted. "It had a spinal frill and a velvet bow on the bottom."

She laughed so they had to stop twirling.

"The bottom of what? the skirt?"

"No, at the end of the frill. On the saddle, so to speak—the haunches."

"Haunches!" she cried. "If you were any good as a dancer you'd know they don't have haunches nowadays. D'you see any haunches on me? I'm sorry I didn't get to know you sooner, you're priceless. This music is spinal frill enough for me. Come on, Rudolph, step on it."

So they danced. The second-cabin saloon, tables and chairs removed (she was a one-class ship in her last years), was now called the Italian Garden, a humorous attempt on the part of the steamship architects to persuade passengers they were not at sea. It was used for dancing and Divine Service, two activities so diverse that they canceled out perfectly. The slippery floor swung gravely; every now and then there was a yell and a merry shuffling as a deeper roll tilted the crowd out of step and they slid against stanchions and the potted shrubs that symbolized Italy. The musicians, remembering that to-morrow would be the day to take up their collection, braced themselves on their chairs and played valiantly. Like a drumming undertone came the driving tremor of the hull, pounding hum, pounding hum; the ceaseless onward swing of the old vessel, dancing with them, curtseying stiffly to her partner, smashing her wide wet bows into swathes of white darkness. Then the serio-comic yammer of the tune overcame everything, moving pulse and nerves to its rhythm, repeated again and again until it seemed as though the incessant music must cause some actual catabolism in the blood. You remember the song that was the favorite that year:

> *"When Katie has fits of the vapours*
> *And feels that occasional peeve*
> *That cuts such irrational capers*
> *In the veins of the daughters of Eve,*
> *There's still one elixir*

> *That surely can fix her,*
> *Whatever depressions may vex—*
> *Sitting up late,*
> *Tête-à-tête,*
> *With the so-called Opposite Sex."*

Before quitting, they went on deck for a gust of fresh air. He wondered vaguely why he had not enjoyed more of this sort of frolic during the previous eight days. This, evidently, was what life was intended for: he was as healthily and gladly weary as a woodchopper. Would she expect him to offer a few modest endearments? It seemed almost discourteous not to, when the whole world was so lyric and propitious. But as they rounded the windbreak into the full dark blast of the night, they collided with one of the phonograph urchins, embracing and embraced with some earnest young squire. They hurried by and stood a few moments alone forward of the deckhouse. There was a clean cold scourge of wind, a bitter sparkle of stars among cloudy scud.

"Oh," she exclaimed angrily, "will we never be there? I hate it, hate it, this sensual rolling sea."

She cried an embarrassed good-night and was gone. He remembered the head carved on the piers and guessed now who the goddess was.

The next day was the last. At the Purser's office appeared the notice *Heavy Baggage for Plymouth Must Be Ready for Removal by 6 P. M.* The tender bubble of timelessness was pricked. The heaviest baggage of all, the secret awareness of Immensity, was rolled away from the heart. Again the consoling trivialities of earth resumed their sway; though those not debarking until Cherbourg had a sense of reprieve, as of criminals not to die until a day later. The phonograph wenches, regardless of a whole continent of irregular verbs waiting for them, packed the French grammars they had never opened during the voyage, and unaware of plagiarism, made the customary jokes about the Scilly Islands.

He slept late. When he came on deck in mid-morning he could smell England. The wind was still sharp but ingrained with fragrance, motes of earthen savor. Almost with dismay, as they drew in toward narrower seas, he felt the long plunge of the ship soften to a gentler swing. In the afternoon a fiery sunset broke out in the dèbris of storm they had left astern; the blaze licked along rags of oily cloud, just in time to tinge the first Cornish crags a dull purple. He avoided the English ladies whose voices were rising higher and higher toward their palates, but he forgave them. This was plainly fairyland, and those returning to it might well grow a little crazed. He saw comic luggers with tawny sails, tumbling in the Channel, like pictures from old books: he imagined them manned by gnomes. He was almost indignant at the calm way the liner pushed on into the evening, regardless of these amazements. He would have liked her to go shouting past these darkening headlands, saluting each jeweled lighthouse with a voice of silver steam.

It was late when she stole gently up Plymouth Sound and anchored in quiet blackness. There was Stygian solemnity in that silent unknown waterway: the red wink of a beacon and the far lights of the town only increased the strangeness. After days of roll and swing, the strong deck seemed lifeless underfoot, while some spirit level in his brain was still tilting to and fro. The good fabric of the ship was suddenly alien and sorry; stairways and passages and smells that had grown dearly familiar could be left behind without a pang. It was truly a death, things that had had close intimacy and service now lost their meaning forever. Glaring electric lights were hung outside, brightening the dead water; slowly into this brilliance came a tender, ominous as Charon's ferry. He waited anxiously to hear the voices of its crew, the voices of ghosts, tne voices of another life. It was called *Sir Richard Grenville,* amusing contrast to the last boat whose name he had noticed in New York, the tug *Francis X. McCafferty.* Then, realizing that the *Sir Richard* was coming for him, he broke from his spell, hurrying to join the drill of departing passengers.

"Stand close about, ye Stygian set," he thought, remembering Landor, as they crowded together on the small tender, craning upward. The ship loomed over them like an apartment house, the phonograph girls and others, making a night of it before reaching Cherbourg, chirping valediction and rendezvous. As they moved gently away, a curly puff of flame leaped from the ships funnel. Some accumulation of soot or gases, momentarily ignited, gushed rosy sparks. He never knew whether this was a customary occurrence or an accident, but for an instant it weirdly strengthened the Stygian color of the scene. It was as though the glory of her burning vitals, now not spent in threshing senseless sea, must ease itself by some escape. In the hush that followed the passengers' squeaks of surprise he heard the toy phonograph, poised on the rail, tinning its ultimatum.

Later, just as he was getting into the boat train, he thought he saw, far down the platform a glimpse of the gray dress.

So, by night, he entered into fairyland.

III

What he remembered best of those first days in London was an extraordinary sense of freedom; freedom not merely from external control but also from the uneasy caperings of self. To be in so great a city, unknown and unregarded, was to have the privileged detachment of a god. It was a cleansing and perspective experience, one which few of our gregarious race properly relish. He had no business to transact, no errand to accomplish, no duty to perform. Only to enjoy, to observe, to live in the devotion of the eye. So, in his quiet way, he entered unsuspected into circulation, passing like a well-counterfeited coin. Comedy herself, goddess of that manly island, seemed unaware of him. Occasionally, in the movement of the day, he saw near him others who were evident compatriots, but he felt no impulse to hail and fraternize. The reticence of that vastly incurious city was an excellent sedative. Once he got out his *My Trip Abroad* album to record some impressions, but desisted after a few lines. "I felt too modest to keep a diary," was his explanation.

Except for the left-hand traffic, which cost him some rapid skipping on street crossings, he encountered no phenomena of surprise. London seemed natural, was exactly what it should be. At first the dusky light led him to believe, every morning, that some fierce downpour was impending; but day after day moved through gossamer tissues and gradations of twilight, even glimmered into cool fawn-colored sunshine, without the apparently threatened storm. In the arbored Bloomsbury squares morning lay mild as yellow wine; smoke of burning leaves sifted into the sweet opaque air. Noon softly thickened into evening; evening kept tryst with night.

His conviction of being in fairyland, when I come to put down what he said, seemed to rest on very trifling matters. The little hotel where he stayed was round the corner from a post office, and in an alley thereby were big scarlet vans, with horses, and initialed by the King. These ruddy wagons in the dusk, the reliable shape of policemen's helmets and boots, a bishop in the hotel who fell upon his breakfast haddock as though it were a succulent heresy, the grossness of "small" change, and a black-gowned bar lady in a *bodega* who served glasses of sherry with the air of a duchess—these were some of the details he mentioned. His description of men in the subway, sitting in seats with upholstered arms, smoking pipes and wearing silk hats, was, perhaps, to a New Yorker, more convincing suggestion of sorcery. But apparently the essence of London's gramarye was just that there were no shocking surprises. Fairyland should indeed be where all the incongruous fragments of life might fall into place, and things happen beautifully without indignation or the wrench of comedy. London seemed so reasonable, natural, humane, and polite. If ever you felt any inclination to be lonely or afraid, he said, the mere look of the taxicabs was reassuring. They were so tall and bulky and respectable; they didn't look "fast," their drivers were settled and genteel. He even formed an idea that London fairies, if encountered, would wear very tiny frock coats and feed on the daintiest minuscule sausages; with mustard, of course; and miniature fried fish after the theater.

The region where Shaftesbury Avenue and Charing Cross Road transect in an X, like policemen's braces, was his favorite resort. There was no rectitude in the union of these highways, theirs was a gay liaison that had begotten huge families of promiscuous byways and crooked disorderly stepstreets. One parent absorbed in literature, the other gayly theatrical, the young streets had grown up as best they could. In the innumerable bookshops of Charing Cross Road he spent October afternoons; the public lavatory of Piccadilly Circus was near for washing his hands, always necessary after browsing along second-hand shelves. Then the cafés of Soho were pleasant to retire to, taking with him some volume he had found. No man is lonely while eating spaghetti, for it requires so much attention. He dined early, to visit the pit queues before the theaters opened. There courageous eccentrics sang or juggled or contorted, to coax largesse from the crowd.

It may have been some book he was looking at that sharpened his ear. Outside the bookshop a street piano was grinding, and presently the bathos of the tune, its clapping clanging gusto, became unendurable. It was sad with linked saccharine long drawn out, braying and gulping a fat glutton grief. It had an effect, he said, of sweet spaghetti boiled in tears. It was an air that had been much played on the ship, and for a moment he felt the dingy bookshop float and sway. The verses he had been reading may also have had some effect: poetry, pointed so brutally direct at the personal identity, is only too likely to bring the heart back to itself and its disease of self-consciousness that is never quite cured. The melody ended and began again. It was a tune concocted specially for dusk, for the hour when filing cases are shut and vanity cases opened; for the dusk, dreadful to solitary men; and he fled down Shaftesbury Avenue to escape. But the deboshed refrain pursued him, it lodged in his fertile cortex like a spore and shot jigging tendrils along his marrow. The ship, forgotten in these days of fresh experience, returned to his thought. He felt her, rolling the whole pebbled sky and wrinkled sea like a cloak about her wet shoulders; he saw her, still in a dark harbor, gushing a sudden flight of sparks.

I'll wash my hands and go up to a show, he thought.

A golden filtration was flowing into the cool dusk of Piccadilly Circus. The imprisoned fire had begun to pace angrily to and fro in the wire cages of advertising signs. Rows of sitting silhouettes, carried smoothly forward on the tops of buses, moved across the pale light. Black against the shimmer was the figure of a winged boy, lifted on one foot's tiptoe, gazing downward part in mischief, part in serene calculation. His outstretched bow was lax, his hand still drawn back after loosing the string. The frolic knave, tilted in airy balance, gauged the travel of his dart. His curved wings, tremulous to poise him so, seemed visibly to spread and flatten in the diamond air. Along a slant of shadow, where light was grained with slopes of sunset, sped the unseen flash.

And having, as he thought, washed his hands of the matter; coming blithely upstairs from the basin, he received the skewer full in the breast.

The shock thrust him backward upon another pedestrian. "Careful how you poke that umbrella about," someone said. At first he felt dizzy, and did not know what had happened until a warm tingling drew his attention. The thing had pierced clean through him, a little aside of the middle waistcoat button.

It was prettily opalescent, with tawny gilt feathers. Sparkles from the electric signs played on the slender wand; the feathered butt projected at least eight inches in front of his midriff. Anxiously reaching behind, he felt that an equal length protruded from his back, ending in a barbed head, dreadfully keen.

His first thought was not one of alarm, though he realized that such a perforation might be serious. "Isn't that just my luck," he reflected, "with my new suit on?" For only that morning he had put on his first British tweeds.

The horns of buses and cars, the roar of traffic, seemed very loud: almost like a crash of applause, the great shout of a sport-loving throng acclaiming this champion shot. He stood there, tottering a little, suddenly concentrated full on himself. It was surprising that there was no pain. A hot prickling and trembling, that was all. Indeed he felt unusually alert, and anxious to avoid attracting attention. People might think it somehow ill-mannered to be transfixed like this in such a public place; an American kind of thing to do. He tried to pull out the arrow, both forward and backward, but it would not budge; and tugging at it merely suffused his whole system with eddies of fever. Already several people were looking curiously at him. He hastily gathered his loose overcoat, which had been flapping open when he was hit, over the feathery tail. Unpleasantly conscious of the shaft emerging from his back, and which he could not hide, he set off toward the nearest policeman.

As he crossed the darkening and crowded Circus, edging carefully sideways to avoid spitting anyone with his awkward fixture, it appeared more and more difficult to consult a policeman in this matter. The all-competent, solid, and honorable London bobby seemed the last person to whom one would willingly confess so intimate and absurd a humiliation. And as he was not in pain or weakened, but even strongly exhilarated and feeling a desire to sing, when he stood beside the constable he found it difficult to mention the topic.

Without removing his vigilant gaze from the traffic, the policeman bent a courteous ear down toward him.

"Which bus for Bedford Square?" he found himself asking.

"Number 38, sir." (Or whatever the number was.)

He had intended to remark, as casually as possible, and with his best English lift of intonation, "I say, constable, I've had a little accident, I wonder if you'd help me." But he had a clear vision of the astounded officer halting all the traffic and a morbid crowd gathering to stare while the stalwart fellow placed a huge foot on his chest and hauled out the shaft. He would have to lie down on the pavement, it would be very painful, he might scream. No, it was too public.

"See here, constable," he said nervously, "has anyone been shooting arrows round here?"

Still watching the stream of vehicles, the policeman took his arm in a powerful grasp and held it kindly but firmly until there was a pause. Then he turned and looked at him carefully.

"Not this early in the evening," he said. "Why the pubs is only just open. Later on, I dare say, the air is thick with 'em. Now, you take my advice, get along 'ome to Bedford Square and 'ave some black coffee."

"Well, look here!" he cried angrily. "What do you think of that?" He flung open his overcoat to show the thin pearly shaft and the sparkling feathers.

The bobby gazed unmoved. "Button up your coat," he advised. "Someone'll nip that nice watch chain." He escorted him to a neighboring curb.

"Here's where your bus stops. Now, no more o' your nonsense."

The attentive faces of the throng alarmed the young American into silence. He mounted the omnibus, and sat carefully ajar on the outside of a seat, to prevent the arrow striking anything. But even so, three passengers complained that he was jabbing them, and he was put off before they reached Oxford Street.

IV

Returned to his hotel, he evaded the talkative doorman and gained the privacy of his chamber. He took off his outer garments, though with some difficulty, and studied his casualty. The arrow had caused no laceration or visible injury; it had pierced him as cleanly as a needle would enter a pudding. He was aware of a warm tickling, a quickening excitement threaded through some inmost node of his being. The unreasonable missile had traversed some region more intimate even than heart or brain or anything palpable. It seemed to be lodged in his very identity, in some surprised and tender essence he could only describe as Me. He tried to break off the projecting ends of the dart; but when he wrenched and twisted, it proved strangely flexible though apparently so glassy and brittle. He backed against the window, hooked the barbed point over the sill, and gave a gigantic heave to pull it out. It was immovable, and the effort only left him dizzy and shaken, with flying volleys of anguish that scattered down every frantic nerve. He desisted and sat for a while almost faint while the chair twirled under him and the delicate engine shone and burned and quivered in his vitals. Now it glowed and sparkled with frolic luster until he was almost proud of so singular a stickpin; now it paled and dwindled until he clutched at his breast to see if it were really there.

He was aroused by the dinner gong. Evidently he must make plans to carry on his life with this fantastic inherent. He rang for hot water. When the chambermaid appeared he was standing in his shirt sleeves directly under the light, waiting anxiously to see if she would cry out when she noticed his condition. Chambermaids, he reasoned, are trained to observe anything unusual.

She brought the water, drew the blinds, and turned down the bed without comment. He stood rotating under the lamp so that she could see him from all angles.

"Chambermaid," he said nervously, "I wonder if you would——"

He hesitated, realizing that someone in the hall might overhear. He closed the door. The maid looked surprised, as his previous conduct in the house had given no suggestion of eccentricity.

He wished he knew her name: it woul have made it easier, somehow, to call her Betsy or Maggie.

"My shirt," he said, struggling for an easy familiar tone. "I want you to help me with my shirt."

"It's a pretty pattern, ain't it, sir?" she remarked cheerfully. "Oh, you want it mended, don't you? It's torn, what a pity; you must've caught it on a nail."

"Yes, but how about the back?" he asked, turning. "Is that torn too?"

"Oh, Lor', so it is; a nasty little 'ole."

"Is that all?"

"Well, beg pardon, sir. I b'lieve your undervest's tore too, let me— ouch!"

She gave a squeak.

"What's the matter?" he cried.

"That's not fair!" she exclaimed angrily, rubbing her plump forearm, evidently puzzled whether this was a practical joke or some new method of beginning a flirtation.

His spirits improved at this evidence of the arrow's invisibility. Keeping at a discreet distance, he suggested that she must have pricked herself on some fastening in her dress.

"All I say is, it's taking a liberty to go shoving pins into people that's trying to be 'elpful."

He pacified her by making a generous offer for the repair of his linen.

"You see," he explained, "the doctor says I don't get enough ventilation. He wants me to have a little loophole in the front and back of my clothes—then there'll always be a current of air. Now if you'll do that for me, I mean cut out the holes and hem them, I'll give you a pound."

"It'll be blessed draughty with winders cut in your clo'es," she said. "You ain't seen a London winter. 'Owever, it's your fun'ral, not mine. A quid? I'll embroider them 'oles proper for a quid."

He went down to dinner somewhat fortified. It was the first time he had taken any meal except breakfast in the hotel, and his arrival agitated the head waiter, a small pallid creature troubled by any sudden decision. He had to stand in full publicity while a table was found for him, but none of the diners noticed any oddity in his outline. If they only knew, he thought.

The places against the wall were all occupied; he must take one in the center of the room; and he discovered that when he sat the butt of the arrow exactly encountered the edge of the board, while the point protruded below the top rail of the open chairback. He had to sit far out, reaching his food at arm's length; worse still, this brought him dangerously near an adjoining table, where the Bishop was. The head waiter, perpetually anxious about offending someone or inadvertently making some blunder in sedentary precedences, presently approached to push in his seat for him. The American foresaw the maneuver just in time, and leaped to his feet; the servant, very much startled, apologized, wondering what error had been committed. He managed to frame some explanation about a sudden cramp in his foot, and prevented a second attempt on the chair by saying that a leg of the table was in the way. But the waiter, with the timorous obstinacy of his kind, hung about zealously. Already a number of eyes were on them, keen with that specially recognizable disapproval which human beings exhibit when anyone behaves queerly in a dining room. Even the Bishop, who was doing wonders with some sort of steaming jam roll, looked halfway round.

"It was really damned embarrassing," he told me. "By some accidental recommendation I had fallen into a hotel—or *an* hotel, as they called it—that catered solely to English. A Continental or American visitor was almost unheard of; most of their patrons, as I noted in the register, had such extravagantly British names as Mrs. Elphin-Elphinstone, The Moated Grange, Monk Hopton, Salop. There was even a Lady in the house, for, turning over the mail on the hall table, I had noted a letter delightfully addressed to Nurse Edwards, care of Lady Smithers; you can hardly guess how unco that seemed to me. As for the Bishop, I don't know that he really was one; I call him so because that was the impression he gave me, but he may have been something even more mysterious, such as a Prebendary. Anyhow, in those first days I had been pleasantly aware of having slipped by good hazard into a pure tissue of England. I had been faced by unfamiliar questions, propounded with sacred solemnity, as when that fool waiter would ask if I wanted thick soup or clear; or my coffee black or white; or sweet or savory? But I had successfully disguised my excitements, happy just not to be noticed. Now this was all ended. The villainy of chance had marked me with a stigma sure to make me grotesque, and not even pitiable because it could not be seen. I wondered desperately, as I carefully conveyed my soup in long trajectory toward my mouth, whether a cube of that solid Yorkshire pudding of theirs could be used as a buffer on the point of my arrow, to prevent the waitress from spearing herself. She was an enthusiastic girl and kept rushing toward the narrow space between my chair and the Bishop's with relays of Brussels sprouts or stewed cheese; and each time I had to turn hurriedly and reach for whatever she brought before she could get behind me.

"In this morbid sharpening of my senses, I'm afraid I may have returned a little resentfully the gazes that came my way. The fact is, I was studying the other guests more closely than before. I envied them their perfect adaptation to the scene, their rich normality, their subconscious certainty that what they were doing was regular and right. They could not possibly have guessed that their fresh gobbling voices, their simultaneous use of knife and fork, the actual food they ate and clothes they wore, were all astounding to me: they were happy, bless them, because they were unaware of themselves, just as I had been;

their tender psyche was not spitted like an unchloroformed butterfly. I thought bitterly how mad a man is to come abroad, for it makes him sensible of the strangeness of life instead of merging undissenting into it, which is the only peace. But queerer still: as soon as *my* behavior became indecorously odd, as it now unavoidably was, they seemed more cordial. I suppose that in some way the report had gone round that I was an American; well, as long as my demeanor was indistinct from that of any other well-behaved young man, they were gently disappointed; but when I showed signs of strangeness it satisfied some vague notion in their minds. And in the oblique profile of the Bishop, as I glanced over my shoulder, I could divine the enigmatic radiation of a man who is about to say something. I watched him apprehensively, and when he pushed his chair back, I got hastily to my feet. He seemed surprised at what he can only have thought an excessive courtesy; but he had his cup in his hand and asked me, most charmingly, if he might take coffee at my table.

"I may as well admit that he captivated me at once. I had thought, watching him a few times at breakfast, that there was a certain ludicrous discrepancy between his clean-shaven austerity and the extreme gusto with which he approached his food and his morning *Times*. I could imagine him removing from his mind things in the paper that disagreed with him just as efficiently as he set aside bones in his haddock But, after all, I don't know why a bishop shouldn't enjoy his meals as heartily as anyone else. And here he was, the star boarder, in pure goodness of heart taking pains to be gracious to a young alien. His clear gray eyes were so magnificently direct, it seemed incredible he should not see my gruesome predicament. In pursuit of theological niceties he must have accepted without question many paradoxes just as puzzling as my arrow; but he showed no sign. I yearned to confess my trouble. Who better than a bishop should be able to understand and console my difficulty? But, curiously, I saw in him the same ruddy benign solidity, the same aversion from surprise that had made it difficult to appeal to the policeman. I suspected that he was being kind to me on the tacit understanding that I would behave more or less as he expected me to; and I made a resolute attempt to hide my distress. I tucked my napkin over the hole in my waistcoat and welcomed him as courteously as possible.

"'I trust you won't think I'm intruding,' he said, 'but I heard you were an American going up to Oxford, and as an old Oxonian myself I wanted to wish you luck. I suppose you are a Rhodes Scholar?'

"I assented.

"'I met a most charming Rhodes Scholar once, also from Ohio,' he continued. (I wish you could have heard his genial pronunciation of the word, equally accenting all three syllables.) 'A fine, manly fellow. It has been an excellent thing for the old varsity to have so many young Americans; you seem to bring us a freshness of outlook, vigorous high spirits that we need.

"I feared inwardly that he must be disappointed in me as an example of high spirits.

"'I suppose you have already graduated from some American university,' he said. 'I wonder if it could be Princeton? I had a friendly invitation from there at one time, to lecture in the Divinity School? No? Having taken a degree already makes your men a little more mature in some ways than our undergraduates.'

"I explained that I was twenty-two. I did not insist how considerable an age it then seemed.

"'Which college are you going to at Oxford?' he asked.

"'St. John's.'

"'Ah, quite one of the best. You will be very happy there. Trinity was my shop, but I often used to go to John's for meetings of the Archery Club. Perhaps you didn't know that there's great enthusiasm at St. John's about their historic Archery Club. They have marvelous lunches and then go out in the garden to shoot with bows and arrows. Sometimes, when the lunch has been excessive, it's a bit dangerous, arrows flying round all over the place. But it's quite the leading club at John's; it would be an amusing experience for you if you were elected.'

"I was far too depressed to enter with much enthusiasm into the notion of the Archery Club, or tell him that I would make a singularly appropriate member. I was realizing that, of course, my whole Oxford career, so eagerly anticipated, was completely blighted. Undergraduates, more than any others, are children of conformity, and anyone so cruelly unique must necessarily be a pariah. I mumbled doleful replies while he chatted kindly on. But the arrow fretted me with stealthy fire, and the cleric's amiable regard became rather pebbly. His was an established mind, neatly reticulated into a seemly satisfying world; the slightest whisper of my furious fancies would have pained him unspeakably. The obvious necessity for concealing everything I was really thinking about made me gloomy and solemn.

"'I'm glad you approach your studies in a serious spirit,' he said finally. 'You won't be wasting your time in mere pranks.'

"He finished his coffee and rose. Sunk in private misery, I forgot to rise with him. He turned to pick up his napkin from the next table, and standing so backed directly on my naked barb. It reached him blithely in the postern, honoring him in the breech as Hamlet might have said; that chub elastic region certainly had not been so invaded since he was an urchin at school. At the moment I was absently finishing my savory; when I heard him leap and yell I turned aghast; he, seeing me fork in hand, can only have thought I had wantonly prodded him in sheer overplus of savagery. The head waiter came running; the other guests stared to see the admired prelate distractedly chafing his postremity and glaring excommunication. 'Let me explain,' I cried wildly, ready to confess all and cast myself on his mercy; but the very phrase condemned me. I will not elaborate the dreadful scene. I still remember the face of the head waiter. If it had been Mrs. Elphin-Elphinstone herself who had been impaled, he could not have been more scandalized. There was only one decency possible. I packed, paid my bill, called a taxi, and sought another lodging. It occurred to me, in the cab, that perhaps I should have sent for Nurse Edwards, care of Lady Smithers, and offered to pay for a compress or tourniquet. But a tourniquet would have been awkward."

V

A long and restless night gave ample opportunity for meditation. Sleep was difficult: he had to lie accurately on edge, and could not turn over on the other side without first getting out of bed. If he dozed into peaceful oblivion some uncanny movement would jar the weapon and bring him back to his affliction. There it was, fantastic, inextricable, struck through the very pulse of his consciousness. Besides being infernally uncomfortable, the thing suggested further privations. A life of celibacy, for instance—a thought distasteful to young men. If it had not been for a bottle of brandy in his luggage he would hardly have slept at all; but he discovered that generous potations seemed to dull the point of the shaft and make it smaller. A lukewarm consolation crept into his mind: perhaps everyone else was also concealing some equally embarrassing anguish—a secret that perhaps did not take the same awkward shape, but was just as disturbing.

The following day the arrow baffled him by showing itself strangely variable. As he slunk shamefully from his lodging it seemed as big as a harpoon; he hailed a taxi, to avoid any possible collision, and went to the Express Company. There, after a difficult time standing sideways in the line of people pressing vigorously toward the teller's grill, he managed to cash a check. He was leaving, intending to visit an American doctor, when he was greeted by an old crony who came boisterously forward. He dodged behind a pillar and extended his hand warily. His friend, thinking this a drollery of some sort, laughed gayly and peered round the column. "What's on your chest?" he cried, noting the furtive behavior. The sufferer's hand flew to his wishbone, but the remark was purely accidental, for the encumbrance had now shrunk to such modest size that he could lap his overcoat over the feathery butt and guard the rearward point by covering it with one gloved hand behind his back. Encouraged, he postponed medical consultation and, as his friend would not be shaken off, they lunched together. For a couple of hours, when he privily rummaged in his bosom, he could have sworn there was nothing there. Yet it returned again later, pricking him with impossible suggestions, so that he had to stand apart round less frequented street corners, struggling to master the glittering thing by strong force of will; or else hire a taxi and ride expensively secure until it shrank to manageable dimension.

But, without committing himself in any way, he had learned from his friend one fact which promised to be helpful. At the American Embassy there was a young man employed who was, as the customary tautology has it, a fraternity brother of theirs. This means that the young official was bound, by some juvenile severities of their Greek-letter union, to mutual succor in distress. So in one of the ante-rooms of the Embassy's business office we see the stricken one mysteriously consulting his fellow Hellenist. There was an exchange of passwords as Greek met Greek, though not in any accent approvable by Liddell and Scott; and the visitor displayed, for identification, a generous sheaf of testimonials from Middle-Western pastors and pedagogues. With these muniments Rhodes Scholars are always plentifully provided. The attaché, who, with spats and cutaway and a conviction that no gentleman sallies abroad without a cane, had also put on certain fatigue of the homeland simplicities, glanced hastily through the assurances that his brother was of modest and winning nature, a fine influence in the Christian life of the community, a brilliant scholar, a leader of glee clubs, and a triple-threat halfback. He noticed that, in spite of these resources, the caller looked somewhat haggard, exhaled a faint vapor of cognac, and had a curious habit of standing averted, holding one arm doubled back behind his shoulders. He prepared himself with several irrefutable reasons why the Ambassador was not at liberty.

"See here," said the caller, in whom after several days of wretchedness the sentiment of anger was now uttermost, "is this the place to file a complaint against the British Government?"

The young diplomat was fully aware that complaints against the British, or any other government, were rarely efficacious. And his promotion, slow at best, depended largely on his finesse in preventing the channels of communication from being choked with the assorted woes of American travelers. Accordingly he had framed a polite theorem for the various emergencies of his bureau, to the effect that the United States Government, though undoubtedly a sovereign power, cannot safeguard its citizens against all the miscellaneous vexations of life. This apothegm, though frequently in use, he was always able to uttter as if freshly inspired for the immediate instance. It was ready to his lips, but something in the manner of his inquirer led him to a more comradely candor.

"Why, yes," he said, "if necessary. But I doubt if it'll do much good. And it depends on the nature of the complaint. If it's an income tax——"

"It's no use my trying to explain. You wouldn't believe me. I've been to a doctor and all he can suggest is that it's a case of *hyper-aesthesia sagittaria.* He's delighted about it, but then he doesn't have to live with it."

"You'll pardon me, I'm sure," said the attaché, "but if you can state the nature of the grievance——"

"I've drawn up a document about the whole affair," said the plaintiff, producing a manuscript. "Now, remember, this is entirely confidential except as regards official channels. But it's the only recourse I have. If you'll run your eye over this——"

The clerk read:

WHEREAS —— ——, a citizen of the United States of America, 22 years of age, residing temporarily at 18, Torrington Square, London, desires to make complaint against H. M. Government as follows:

Whereas on the 3rd day of October instant, about the hour of five P. M., the said ——, on his lawful occasions and peaceably pursuing his own concerns, was walking through Piccadilly Circus, when a missile nearest describable as an arrow, projected by person or persons unknown, did so strike and transfix the body and soul of said —— that he has thereafter gone in peril of his life and wits. And whereas the said arrow is not by any ascertainable means removable from the body of the plaintiff, and whereas it has afflicted him grievously in mind, body, and estate, subjecting him to extreme humiliations and necessitating medical treatment for a highly nervous and excited condition and repeated hire of motor taxicabs to prevent embarrassing H. M. subjects on the sidewalks; and whereas the petitioner feels his future career and tranquillity gravely compromised by this affliction, he respectfully submits that it is the plain duty of H. M. Government, acting through the London County Council or any other lawful body, to keep the region of Piccadilly Circus free of such random projectiles and that neglect of such precautions has resulted in a delict upon the person of a citizen of the United States.

Your petitioner therefore prays that damages be awarded commensurate with the offense, and that the American Ambassador in London be instructed to make representations to that end to the officers of H. M. Government.

"But I don't see any arrow," objected the fraternity brother.

"Hush! Not so loud!" said the petitioner, looking round nervously at several other citizens who were waiting their turn to make complaints. He leaned across the counter and whispered hoarsely.

The clerk seemed a little shocked. He read the document again and privately concluded that the Ohio chapters of the Nu Nu Phi ought to be more careful in their elections. But one business of an embassy is to allow Time to anoint its healing lotion upon human abrasions, and he fell back on sound governmental principles.

"Well," he said, "I'll put this through the proper routine. But don't expect questions to be asked about it in Parliament next week. First it'll have to go before some Congressional committee in Washington, I suppose, and when they see the word *arrow* they'll probably refer it to the Bureau of Indian Affairs. Also, it must pass through our legal department here, to be put in correct form."

But he was almost ashamed of his flippancy when he saw the exalted earnestness of the other man.

"Did you ever have a secret so important," asked the caller, "that no one could possibly be told, and yet everyone knew it anyhow?"

"Why, sure; that's what embassies are for, to deny that sort of thing." As he spoke he thought anxiously of his own secrecies: private experiments with a monocle that he had never dared wear publicly, and that it was near closing time and he had an engagement to meet a young lady for tea at Rumpelmayer's.

"Put your hand here," the caller said, opening his overcoat.

The attaché did as directed. He felt a sharp sting and a warm hypodermic sparkle snaked up his arm. For an instant he was giddy, the office behind him with its terraced filing cases seemed to rock and grow dim. He clung to the counter as to the bulwark of a ship. He heard music faintly played, the light chatter of voices, and in a brightness soft as candleshine he saw the face of the damsel at Rumpelmayer's.

He steadied himself, fixing his mind on the tight-lipped engraving of George Washington.

"Really, you know . . . sorcery . . . I'm not sure that this comes under the scope of this office."

The impatience of several ladies waiting attention began to be audible.

"Do what you can," said the plaintiff, and repeated the covenant of their Greek-letter federation. He left, making a wide zigzag to give the other clients a safe offing. The attaché, concealing behind the counter a hasty glance at his wrist watch, assigned two elderly ladies to a confrère and selected the younger one for himself. The only consolation in this job, he reflected, was that perplexity did sometimes descend upon traveling citizens who were really attractive; but even so, not as alluring as the graceful creature who would soon be in St. James's Street, taking her tea and pastry with only one hand.

VI

The plaintiff in Torrington Square was surprised to receive, a few days later, a letter from the American Embassy. It was embossed with the official seal of the United States, which he was startled to observe consisted of an eagle with excessively straddled legs one of which held a cluster of arrows and the other a foliage that he took to be an olive bough. Arrows, he thought ironically, he could supply for himself; the message, written in the attaché's own hand, was evidently intended to be of the nature of the olive branch. It was informal and cordial.

"Your statement," he read, "is having due attention. I have been thinking about the matter and, speaking as a friend and brother in old Nunu, I believe perhaps you take it too seriously. I think that when you get up to Oxford the pleasant surroundings of that peaceful place will soon remedy the condition; in the meantime I suggest that you enjoy some innocent diversion. Nothing is more entertaining than a professional Anglo-American Hands Across the Sea meeting, so I am enclosing a ticket to the annual luncheon of the Atlantic Harmony. You will find this well worth attending, Lord Aliquot is to take the chair and Admiral Stripes, U. S. N., will be one of the speakers. Yours cordially."

The date set for the luncheon was the day before he would leave for Oxford. He decided to go.

The attaché was right: one of those meetings at which the two chief branches of the Anglo-Saxon race convene to confess their mutual esteem is indeed fruitful study for the pensive. The Atlantic Harmony lunched in the ballroom of a huge hotel; behind the high table the banners of both nations were draped and blended; an orchestra in the gallery burst into traditional airs; cocktails began and champagne followed. Dishes sacred to England and America were on the menu, and judging by the notable bulk of most of the ladies, there was no danger of the race perishing of starvation. It was an orgy of friendly sentiment; for the time being the Atlantic Ocean seemed a mere trickle; one had to remind one's self that only the fortunately high rate of steamship fares prevented two mutually infatuated populations from putting their affections to the proof *en masse*. Even a man with a serious gravamen pending against the British Government could not resist the general infection of good will. He waited in the lobby until the crowd had gone in, which made it possible to reach his seat without spiking anyone; and by the time the wine had made a few circulations he was in excellent humor. Contemplating the worthy people who are drawn by irresistible magnetism to affairs of this sort, he began to wonder what was the law forbidding Anglo-American friendship to be endorsed by the young and slender. The ladies were mostly silvery and, in the case of his immediate neighbors, deaf; and the gentlemen solid; but their enthusiasm was terrific. References by Lord Aliquot to the Mother Country, cousins, blood thicker than water, the critical days of 1917, the language of Shakespeare, Magna Charta, Your Great President, were received with instantaneous crashes of applause. Admiral Stripes, forgetting the extreme efficiency of the submarine cables, very nearly made Lord Aliquot a present of the United States Navy. Lord Aliquot, after humorously remarking that he himself had made the supreme sacrifice for Anglo-American union by marrying an American wife, insisted that nothing could go seriously wrong between two nations nurtured in the same sense of fair play and reverence for pure womanhood. His Lordship, an old hand at these affairs, took care to end each paragraph with an obvious bait for applause. This gave him time to be quite sure that the next one would not contain anything regrettable. An American minister, chaplain of the Harmony, offered a prayer for all branches of the English-Speaking Peoples, on whom heavier than elsewhere rests the great burden of human liberty. If any Frenchman had been taken, manacled, into the room, and compelled to listen to the speeches, he would have ended in convulsions. In short, it was one of those occasions, familiar to statesmen, that cannot possibly do any harm and offer a hard-working nonconformist parson a free meal and an opportunity to address the Deity in public. Meanwhile, the Swiss and German waiters scoured about busily, the champagne flowed, and when "Dixie" was played, many who had never seen a cotton field scrambled up and shouted in pure hysteria.

During the halloo that followed "Dixie" he rose and cheered with the rest. Then he saw, sitting opposite across the large round table, a girl who had been hidden from him by a bushy centerpiece of flowers. She was dark, with close-cropped hair; a little absent-looking, as though she did not take this luncheon very seriously; she had a cloak thrown over her shoulders. He was just raising his glass, with a vague intention of toasting the universe at large, when he caught her gaze. They studied each other solemnly, as becomes strangers crossing unexpectedly in so large a waste. Then, in the flush of the moment, he smiled and lifted his glass. She reached for hers, and they drank, look to look. Then, a little embarrassed, he sat down.

But something in her face or gesture fretted him, bothered him as does a cut-off telephone call; he was waiting and wondering. He tried to get another glimpse of her, but the floral piece was impenetrable.

There was no time to lose: one of the neighboring matrons was asking him what was that music which had just been played, and the chairman was already hammering for silence. He stood up again for one more look, and saw that the man on her left, elevated by champagne and the gallant megalomania of the occasion, was still erect and vocal. He also saw how far back she sat from the table. Her hand, stretched out at arm's length, still lingered on the wine glass stem.

He ran round to her side of the table, and seized the joyful gentleman. "Quick!" he said. "They want us to change places. Makes it more sociable!" The other gayly assented, and took his place between the two dowagers; nor did he ever discover their infirmity.

"Aren't you warm with that cloak on?" he asked. "Can I take it off for you?"

Her quick little movement of alarm, drawing the wrap closer round her, showed him he had not made a mistake. But he did not pause to wonder at his certainty. Shy as he had always been, now it was as though he looked at a woman for the first time, and saw not the strange capricious nymph of legend but the appealing creature of warmth and trouble, ridiculous as himself. Perhaps it was the grotesque pangs of the previous days that had tutored him. Terror of other human beings had vanished; his blemish was not shameful but something to be proud of; and his next words were divinely inspired—they were brief but exactly right.

"You darling," he said.

The clapping that followed was probably intended for the Viscount Aliquot, but it came too pat to be ignored.

"And that's the first thing that's been said here that was really worth applause," he added.

She looked at him steadily, something in her eyes that might once have been terror changing into amusement; and then returned her gaze to Lord Aliquot, who seemed very far away, gesticulating at the other end of the great room. "You mustn't talk while people are whispering," she said.

She couldn't possibly have been any different, he thought triumphantly. He had a strong conviction that those dark eyebrows, the delightful soft stubble at the base of her boyish neck, that wistfully shortened upper lip had always been growing and curving like that just intentionally for him. He was waiting hopefully (as was Lord Aliquot) for Lord Aliquot to be interrupted by another round of applause.

"Of course the proper thing to say," he murmured, "would be: Haven't we met before somewhere? But it's more important to know, When are we going to meet again?"

"We haven't parted yet."

"Splendid. But are you going to listen to me or to the speeches?"

"Evidently I can't do both."

"Well, there'll be a National Anthem soon; I can feel it coming. They'll stand up, and we can slip away. Besides, it always embarrasses me to sing 'The Star-Spangled Banner' before strangers. Let's go and have tea somewhere."

"But we haven't finished lunch yet."

"Don't let's waste time. I've got to go to Oxford tomorrow. By the way, if you had a gray dress with a little frill down the back, on what sort of occasions would you wear it?"

"Why, right here; but I can't, it's got a hole in it."

He leaned toward her, to whisper something, and the ends of their arrows touched. There was a clear puff of sparkling brightness, like two highly charged wires making contact. Some weary guests at the speakers' table brisked up and felt their cravats, believing the time for the flashlight pictures had come. Lord Aliquot, taking it for some sort of signal, called the company to their feet for the American Anthem.

"Hurry! if we wait they'll get beyond the words they know, then everyone will spot us beating it."

They reached the door before anyone except Lord Aliquot had got beyond "What so proudly we hailed."

"'What so proudly we hailed,'" he said, as the words pursued them into the lobby. "That suggests taxis. Let's grab one."

VII

"Anthem? Nonsense, we've just had one."

But then they saw the old fellow meant a hansom. There it was, drawn up by the——

"Bet you don't know how they spell curb over here," he said as they climbed in. "They spell it K, E, R, B. You know it's the first time I ever rode in one of these things. Who's that talking to us from the sky?"

They looked up and saw a curious portrait floating upside down above them. It was framed in a little black square, like an old Flemish master—the color of Tudor brick grizzled with lichen. It proved to be the face of the lisping cabby.

"Oh, anywhere where one does drive in London."

"I want to see the Serpentine," she said. "I'm always reading about it."

"Very good, mith." The brick portrait floated a moment genially and then said with bronchial jocularity, "Adam and Eve and the Ther pentine." They laughed—the sudden perfect laughter of those overtaken unawares by the excellence of the merry-making world. The cab tilted, jingled, swayed off, rolling lightly like a canoe.

"Of course this is simply magic. Things just don't happen like this."

he said as they settled themselves. "Are you comfortable? If I put my arm around you, it would prevent the point of yours from punching into the seat. You see, I can sit sort of diagonal, and then if you slide over this way——"

"It gives me a spinal frill when it touches anything," she admitted.

He looked at her amazed.

"Yes, that girl on the ship told me what you said. She was my room-mate."

"Why didn't I ever see your on board?"

"You did, but you didn't look at me."

"I'll make up for it now."

"Besides, I was ill. Not just seasick ill, ill in my mind. Don't let me go in a ship again—it's too elemental."

The tips of the two arrows touched, and again there was a little fizzing flash. Just the thing for lighting cigarettes, they found, and practiced it.

"As a matter of fact I have two arms," he added presently.

"The dusk comes early in London," she said.

"You darling," he repeated, saying it with the accent that can only be uttered in a hansom.

"I think mine's loose," she said. "It seems to waggle a little."

"Mine doesn't bother me a bit as long as we sit like this."

"I thought I was mad."

"So did I. Now I know it. I went to an astrologer, one of those fellows in a dressing gown on Oxford Street. He asked me my birthday, December 21st. He said that I came just between two signs of the Zodiac, Sagittarius and the Goat. I guess I'm both of them at once."

Rocking lightly, tingling like a tray of highballs, the cab jingled. Music came from somewhere—a street piano perhaps—the same old tune, drifting sadly on waves of soft smoky air; a mendicant melody with no visible means of support. They called to the cabby to follow it, they pursued the vagrant chords down unknown ways of dusk, while London behind them muted its rhythm to a pounding hum. At last they found the minstrel, pulled up beside him, and startled him by their new method of lighting cigarettes.

"I'm still not quite sure of the difference between a half-crown and a florin," he said.

"Then give him both."

When they reached the Serpentine it was too dark to appreciate it.

"Let's bruise it with our heel," she said. "I mean, let's go somewhere. Let's go home, wherever that is."

"Where was it we first met?" He searched his memory. "Long ago. Yes, at that hotel. We'll go back there to tea."

"Is it all right to feel a bit queer in a hansom cab? I mean, almost as though you were on board a ship? I guess I'm worried about my arrow. It doesn't seem to fit as well as it did. My precious arrow. . . ."

His also was trembling strangely. Two lonelinesses must always feel disconcerted when they encounter.

"Darling, darling"; and as she came close into his arms with a queer shudder, the two sparkling darts slipped quietly to the back of the seat.

In the palm room of that hotel is a ceiling of painted mythology. While you wait for anyone who may be coming to have tea with you, you can examine a series of episodes gracefully conjectured from the life of a famous family. First there is Aphrodite, rising alluringly from the foam of a blue sea whose crumbling surf is pink with sunrise. Then there is the marriage, if one calls it so, of Aphrodite and Hephæstus— Vulcan, if you prefer, the fellow the Swedes name their matches for. It was a queer marriage for so handsome a goddess when Aphrodite became the first Mrs. Smith; but handsome women so often choose odd-looking men. Then there's their small boy, Eros, with the toy bow and arrows his father made for him, asking Vulcan to sharpen the darts for him; and his father, busy about thunderbolts, replying that the toys are quite sharp enough. In the last scene Eros, grown to a braw laddie, is trying a chance shot at Psyche. You generally have plenty of time to study all four scenes.

In that hour, late for tea and early for dinner, the palm room was comfortably quiet. The hotel, after the fitful fever of the Atlantic Harmony, slept well. The occasional clink of a teaspoon or a thicker waft of cigarette smoke rising through foliage gave the only trace of what various big game lurked in that jungle. An orchestra groaned softly somewhere far away. It was all so extremely hotel-like, they might just as well have still been on board a ship.

"By the way," he said, "you haven't told me how you happened to go to that lunch."

"Why, it was a young man at the Embassy. He gave me a ticket when I went there to complain about Piccadilly Circus. I mean, about arrows flying round like that. It shouldn't be allowed."

It was at this moment that he noticed the ceiling. It interested him so that he stood up and cricked his neck to see it accurately.

"Have you had all the tea you need? I've got an idea. There's an errand we ought to do." He carefully picked up the arrows which he had laid under his chair.

The hansom was outside.

"Why, it's still waiting!" she cried. " 'What so proudly we hailed at the twilight's last gleaming.' "

"He must have come back for us. I guess he knows the symptoms."

"The blessed old thing."

"And for all he knew, he might have had to wait till tomorrow."

She made no reply to this, but skipped lightly in. The charioteer leaned indulgently downward, his head on one side, like a disillusioned old centaur looking kindly upon the pranks of a couple of young demi-gods.

"Well, guvner, which way thith time? 'Ampthtead 'eath?"

"We want to go and look at a statue."

"Lord love a duck, guvner, the gallerieth ith clothed."

"The statue in Piccadilly Circus. What do they call it?"

" 'Im? Why that'th Cupid."

They drew up in a side street and crossed the crowded space on foot. Happy as he was, quit of the infernal pang, once more oblivious of terror, mortal loneliness, and dismay, yet the cicatrix of the arrow was still tender. For an instant, as she pressed close beside him, he realized that none of these exquisite moments could be lived again.

The same bobby was directing the traffic; the same imprisoned fires paced like tigers on the rooftops. The winged boy, tiptoe in jaunty malice, was black against the emerald sky. He pointed to the dainty silhouette of the bow.

"A circus is where one would expect to find sharpshooters," she said.

He climbed past the flower girls, who were arranging their stock of evening boutonnières, and laid the two shining arrows at the base of the frolic statue.

"Here, you dropped something," he said to Eros.

The flower sellers, shrewdest critics of romance in the most romantic city in the world, held out their nosegays. But the two did not see.

"Well, we're only young once," he said.

"But there's two of us. That makes us young twice."

"I suppose at least we ought to know each other's names."

"It's so much nicer not to."

"Much. Let's be just P and Q."

"P for Psyche?"

"And Q for Cupid."

They walked back to where the cab was waiting.

"Do we have to mind them?" she asked.

"What?"

"Our P's and Q's."

"Hop in, you adorable idiot."

"Where to, guvner?"

"Wherever you please."

"Hullo, it's the same hotel. He thinks we're staying here."

"Maybe he's right."

"But we haven't any baggage. Not even our arrows."

"I can fix that."

"Sorry, guvner, but I'm off. The mare'th earned 'er tea. Will you be goin' out agin tonight?"

"What are you going to tell him?" she asked in sudden panic.

"Nothing. I want to hear you do it."

How delicious her voice was:

"You needn't wait."

55

A Cycle of Manhattan

BY THYRA SAMTER WINSLOW

THE Rosenheimers arrived in New York on a day in April. New York, flushed with the first touch of Spring, moved on inscrutably, almost suavely unaware. It was the greatest thing that had ever happened to the Rosenheimers, and even in the light of the profound experiences that were to follow it kept its vast grandeur and separateness, its mysterious and benumbing superiority. Viewed later, in half-tearful retrospect, it took on the character of something unearthly, unmatchable and never quite clear—a violent gallimaufry of strange tongues, humiliating questionings, freezing uncertainties, sudden and paralyzing activities.

The Rosenheimers came by way of the Atlantic Ocean, and if anything remained unclouded in their minds it was a sense of that dour and implacable highway's unfriendliness. They thought of it ever after as an intolerable motion, a penetrating and suffocating smell. They saw it through drenched skylights—now and then as a glimpse of blinding blue on brisk, heaving mornings. They remembered the harsh, unintelligible exactions of officials in curious little blue coats. They dreamed for years of endless nights in damp, smothering bunks. They carried off the taste of strange foods, barbarously served. The Rosenheimers came in the steerage.

There were, at that time, seven of them, if you count Mrs. Feinberg. As Mrs. Feinberg had, for a period of eight years—the age of the oldest Rosenheimer child—been called nothing but Grandma by the family and occasionally Grandma Rosenheimer by outsiders, she was practically a Rosenheimer, too. Grandma was Mrs. Rosenheimer's mother, a decent simple, round-shouldered "sheideled," little old woman, to whom life was a ceaseless washing of dishes, making of beds, caring for children and cooking of meals. She ruled them all, unknowing.

The head of the house of Rosenheimer was, fittingly, named Abraham. This had abbreviated itself, even in Lithuania, to a more intimate Abe. Abe Rosenheimer was thirty-three, sallow, thin-cheeked and bearded, with a slightly aquiline nose. He was already growing bald. He was not tall and he stooped. He was a clothing cutter by trade. Since his marriage, nine years before, he had been saving to bring his family over. Only the rapid increase of its numbers had prevented him coming sooner.

Abraham Rosenheimer was rather a silent man and he looked stern. Although he recognized his inferiority in a superior world, he was not without his ambitions. These looked toward a comfortable home, his own chair with a lamp by it, no scrimping about meat at meals and a little money put by. He had heard stories about fortunes that could be made in America and in his youth they had stirred him. Now he was not much swayed by them. He was fond of his family and he wanted them "well taken care of," but in the world that he knew the rich and the poor were separated by an unscalable barrier. Unless incited temporarily to revolution by fiery acquaintances he was content to hope for a simple living, work not too hard or too long, a little leisure, tranquillity.

He had a comfortable faith which included the belief that, if a man does his best, he'll usually be able to make a living for his family. "Health is the big thing," he would say, and "The Lord will provide." Outside of his prayer-book, he did little reading. It never occurred to him that he might be interested in the outside world. He knew of the existence of none of the arts. His home and his work were all he had ever thought about.

Mrs. Rosenheimer, whose first name was Minnie, was thirty-one. She was a younger and prettier reproduction of her mother, plump and placid, with a mouth inclined to petulancy.

There were four Rosenheimer children. Yetta was eight, Isaac six, Carrie three and little Emanuel had just had his first birthday. Yetta and Carrie were called by their own first names, but Isaac, in America, almost immediately gave way to Ike and little Emanuel became Mannie. They were much alike, dark-haired, dark-eyed, restless, shy, wondering.

The Rosenheimers had several acquaintances in New York, people from the little village near Grodno who had preceded them to America. Most of these now lived in the Ghetto that was arising on the East Side of New York, and Rosenheimer had thought that his family would go there, too, so as to be near familiar faces. He had written several months before, to one Abramson, a sort of a distant cousin, who had been in America for twelve years. As Abramson had promised to meet them, he decided to rely on Abramson's judgment in finding a home in the city.

Abramson was at Ellis Island and greeted the family with vehement embraces. He seemed amazingly well dressed and at home. He wore a large watchchain and no less than four rings. He introduced his wife, whom he had married since coming to America, though she, too, had come from the old country. She wore silk and carried a parasol.

"I've got a house all picked out for you," he explained in familiar Yiddish. "It isn't in the Ghetto, where some of our friends live, but it's cheap, with lots of comforts and near where you can get work, too."

Any house would have suited the Rosenheimers. They were pitifully anxious to get settled, to rid themselves of the foundationless feeling which had taken possession of them. With eager docility, Yetta carrying Mannie and each of the others carrying a portion of the bundles of wearing apparel and feather comforts which formed their luggage, they followed Abramson to a surface car and to their new home. In their foreign clothes and with their bundles they felt almost as uncomfortable as they had been on shipboard.

The Rosenheimers' new home was in MacDougal Street. They looked with awe on the exterior and pronounced it wonderful. Such a fine building! Of red brick it was! There were three stories. The first story was a stable, the big open door. Little Isaac had to be pulled past the restless horses in front of it. The whole family stood for a moment, drinking in the wonders, then followed Abramson up the stairs. On the second floor several families lived in what the Rosenheimers thought was palatial grandeur. Even their own home was elegant. It consisted of two rooms—the third floor front. They could hardly be convinced that they were to have all that space. There was a stove in the second room and gas fixtures in both of them—and there was a bathroom, with running water, in the general hall! The Rosenheimers didn't see that the paper was falling from the walls and that, where it had been gone for some years, the plaster was falling, too. Nor that the floor was roughly uneven.

"Won't it be too expensive?" asked Rosenheimer. Abramson chuckled. Though he himself was but a trimmer by trade, he was pleased with the role of fairy godfather. He liked twirling wonders in the faces of these simple folk. In comparison, he felt himself quite a success, a cosmopolite. Just about Rosenheimer's age, he had small deposits in two savings banks, a three-room apartment, a wife and two American sons, Sam and Morrie. Both were in public school, and both could speak "good English." He patted Rosenheimer on the back jovially.

"You don't need to worry," he said. "A good cutter here in New York don't have to worry. Even a 'greenhorn' makes a living. There's

half a dozen places *you* can choose from. I'll tell you about it, and
where to go, tomorrow. Now, we'll go over to my house and have
something to eat. Then you'll see how you'll be living in a few years.
You can borrow some things from us until you get your own. My
wife will be glad to go with Mrs. Rosenheimer and show her where
to buy."

The Rosenheimers gave signs of satisfaction as they dropped their
bundles and sat down on the empty boxes that stood around, or on
the floor. This was something like it! Here they had a fine home in a
big brick house, a sure chance of Rosenheimer getting a good job,
friends to tell them about things—they had already found their place
in New York! Grandma, trembling with excitement, took Mannie in
her arms and held him up dramatically.

"See, Mannie, see Mannischen—this is fine—this is the way to live!"

II

Things turned out even more miraculously than the Rosenheimers had
dared to hope. After only three days Rosenheimer found a job as a
pants cutter at the fabulous wages he had heard of. He could not only
pay the high rent, twelve dollars a month, he would also have enough
left over for food and clothes, and to furnish the home, if they were
careful. Maybe, after the house was in order, there would even be a
little to put by. Of course it was no use being too happy about it, he
told Mrs. Rosenheimer.

"It looks fine now, but you know you can't always tell. It takes a
whole lot to feed a big family."

Although secretly delighted, he was solemn and rather silent over
his good fortune. Abraham Rosenheimer was a cautious man.

Mrs. Abramson initiated Grandma and Mrs. Rosenheimer into New
York buying. It was fascinating, even more so than buying had been
at home. There were neighborhood shops where Yiddish was spoken,
and already the family was beginning to learn a little English. Mrs.
Rosenheimer listened closely to what people said and the children
picked up words, playing in the street.

The next weeks were orgies of buying. Not that much was bought,
for there wasn't much money and it had to be spent very carefully, but
each article meant exploring, looking and haggling. Grandma took the
lead in buying—didn't Grandma always do such things? Grandma
was only fifty-seven and spry for her age. Didn't she take care of the
children and do more than her share of the housework?

Grandma was supremely happy. She liked to buy and she felt that
merchants couldn't fool her, even in this strange country. A table was
the first thing she purchased. It was almost new and quite large. It was

pine and bare of finish, but after Grandma had scrubbed it and scoured it it looked clean and wholesome. It was quite a nice table and only wobbled a little when you leaned on it heavily, for the legs weren't quite even. One was a little loose and Grandma didn't seem able to fasten it. Assisted by Mrs. Rosenheimer and Yetta, she scrubbed the whole flat, so that it equalled the new table in immaculateness. There were families who liked dirt—Grandma had seen them, even in America—but she was glad she didn't belong to one of them.

Then came chairs, each one picked out with infinite care and much sibilant whispering between Grandma, Mrs. Rosenheimer and Mrs. Abramson. There was a rocker, slat-backed, from which most of the slats were missing, though it still rocked "as good as new." The next chair was leather-covered, though the leather was cut through in places, allowing the horse-hair stuffing to protrude. But, as Mrs. Abramson pointed out, this was an advantage, it showed that the filling wasn't an inferior cotton. There were two straight chairs, one with a leatherette seat, nailed on with bright-colored nails, the other with a wicker seat, quite neatly mended. There was a cot for Grandma and a bed for Mr. and Mrs. Rosenheimer and Emanuel. The other children were well and strong and could sleep on the floor, of course. Hadn't they brought fine soft feathers with them?

All of the furniture was second- or third-hand and the previous owners had not treated it with much care. So Grandma got some boxes to help out, and she and the Rosenheimers worked over them, pulling and driving nails. Finally they had a cupboard which held all of the new dishes—almost new, if you don't mind a few hardly noticeable nicked edges—and decorated with fine pink roses. Some of the boxes were still used as chairs, "to help out." One fine, high one did very nicely as an extra table, with a grand piece of brand-new oilcloth, in a marbled pattern, tacked over it. They had a home now.

Grandma and Mrs. Rosenheimer marketed every day at the stores and markets in the neighborhood. Rosenheimer sometimes complained that they used too much money, but then, he "liked to eat well." The little Rosenheimers grew round and merry.

Grandma and Mr. and Mrs. Rosenheimer, looking at the children and at their two big rooms—all their own and so nicely furnished—could hardly imagine anything finer. Grandma and Rosenheimer were absolutely at peace. But Mrs. Rosenheimer knew that, with more money, there were a lot of things you could buy. She had walked through Washington Square and up Fifth Avenue. She had seen people in fine clothes, people of her own race, too. She didn't have much, after all. Still, most of the time she was content.

Gradually, too, Rosenheimer saw shadows of wealth. He heard

rumors of how fortunes were made overnight—his boss now, a few years before, had been a poor boy . . . Nevertheless, smoking his cigarettes and reading his Yiddish paper after his evening meal, or talking with Abramson or one of the men he had met, he was well satisfied with New York as he had found it.

III

As the months passed, the Rosenheimers drank in, unbelievably fast, the details of the city. Already the children were beginning to speak English, not just odd words, here and there, but whole sentences. Already, too, they were beginning to be ashamed of being "greenhorns" and were planning the time when they could say they had been over for years or had been born here. Little Mannie was beginning to talk and everyone said he spoke English without an accent.

Yetta and Ike started to school. Each day they brought home some startling bit of information that the family received and assimilated without an eye-wink. Although most of the men at the shop spoke Yiddish, Rosenheimer was learning English, too. He even spoke, vaguely, about learning to read it and write it, and he began to look over English papers, now and then, interestedly. Mrs. Rosenheimer also showed faint literary leanings and sometimes asked questions about things.

Ike was always eager to tell everything he had learned. In a sharp little voice he would instruct, didactically, anyone within hearing distance. He rather annoyed Rosenheimer, who was not blinded by the virtues of his eldest son. But he was Mrs. Rosenheimer's favorite. She would sit, hands folded across her ample lap, smiling proudly as he unrolled his fathomless knowledge.

"Listen at that boy! Ain't he wonderful, the way he knows so much?" she would exclaim.

Yetta's learning took the form, principally, of wanting things. Each day, it seemed, she could find out something else she didn't have, that belonged to all American children. And, no matter how penniless Rosenheimer had just declared himself to be, unsmilingly and a bit shamefacedly, he would draw pennies out of the depths of the pocket of his shiny trousers.

Only Grandma showed no desire to learn the ways of the new country. She didn't mind picking up a little English, of course, though she'd got along very nicely all of her life without it. Still, in a new country, it didn't hurt to know something about the language. But as for reading —well, Yiddish was good enough for her, though she didn't mind admitting she didn't read Yiddish easily. Grandma had little use for the printed word.

Each week the Rosenheimers' clothes changed nearer to the prevailing styles of MacDougal Street. Only a few weeks after they arrived Mrs. Rosenheimer, overcome by her new surroundings, bought, daringly, a lace sailor collar, which she fastened around the neck of her old-world costume. As the months passed, even this failed to satisfy. The dress itself finally disappeared, reappearing as a school frock for Yetta, and Mrs. Rosenheimer wore a modest creation of red plaid worsted which Grandma and she had made, huge sleeves, bell skirt and all, after one they had seen in Washington Square on a "society lady."

Just a year after they arrived in America, Mrs. Rosenheimer discarded her *sheidel*. She even tried to persuade Grandma to leave hers off, but Grandma demurred. There were things you couldn't do decently, even in a new country. Mrs. Rosenheimer made the innovation in a spirit of fear, but when no doom overtook her and she found in a few weeks how "stylish" she looked, she never regretted the change. She was wearing curled bangs, good as the next one, before long.

Little Ike had a new suit, bought ready-made, his first bought suit, not long afterwards. The trousers were a bit too long, but surely that was an advantage, for he was growing fast, going on eight. They couldn't call him a "greenhorn" now. He came home, too, with reports of how smart his teacher said he was and of the older boys, unbelievers, whom he had "got ahead of" in school. His shrill voice would grow louder and higher as he would explain to the admiring Mrs. Rosenheimer and Grandma what a fine lad he was getting to be.

Other signs of change now appeared. Scarcely a year had gone by before lace curtains appeared at the two front windows. They were of different patterns, but what of that? They had been cheaper that way, as "samples." By tautly drawn strings, white and stiff they hung, adding a touch of elegance to the abode. Only three months later a couch was added, the former grandeur of its tufted surface not at all dimmed by a few years of wear. Yetta and Carrie slept on it, luxuriously, one at each end. It was a long couch and they were so little.

Then a cupboard for dishes appeared. Grandma bought it from a family that was "selling out." It had glass doors. At least there had been glass doors. One was broken now, but who noticed that? In the corner of the front room, opposite the couch, it looked very "stylish." And not long afterward there was a carpet in the front room, three strips of it, with a red and green pattern. Then, indeed, the Rosenheimers felt that they could, very proudly, "be at home to their friends." They had company, now, families of old friends and new, from the Ghetto and from their own neighborhood. And they visited, *en masse,* in return.

There wasn't much money, of course. Rosenheimer was getting good wages, but children eat a lot and beg for pennies between meals. And shoes! But like many men of his race and disposition, Rosenheimer never contributed quite all of his funds to his household. Nor did he take his women into his confidence. He felt that they could not counsel him wisely, which was probably right, for neither Grandma nor Mrs. Rosenheimer was interested in anything outside of their home and their friends. Besides this, he had a natural secrecy, a dislike of talking things over with his family. So, each week, he made an infinitesimal addition to the savings account he had started. He even considered various investments—he knew of men who were buying the tenements in which they lived on wages no bigger than his, living in the basement and taking care of the house outside of working hours. But he felt that he was still too much the "greenhorn" for such enterprises, so he kept on with his small and secret savings.

IV

In 1897 another member was added to the family. This meant a big expense, a midwife and later a doctor, but Rosenheimer had had a raise by this time—he was, in fact, now a foreman—so the expense was met without difficulty. There was real joy at the arrival of this baby—more than at the coming of any of the previous children. For this was an American baby, and seemed, in some way, to make the whole family more American. The baby was a girl and even the sex seemed satisfactory, though, of course, at every previous addition the Rosenheimers had hoped for a boy.

There was a great discussion, then, about names. Before this, a baby had always been named after some dead ancestor or relative without much ado. It was best to name a child after a relative, but, according to custom, if the name didn't quite suit, you took the initial instead. By some process of reasoning, this was supposed to be naming the child "after" the honored relative. Now the Rosenheimers wanted something grandly American for the new baby. Grandma wanted Dora, after her mother. But Dora didn't sound American enough. Ike suggested Della, but that didn't suit, either. Finally Yetta brought home Dorothy. It was a very stylish name, it seemed, and was finally accepted.

Little Emanuel, aged four, was told that "his nose was out of joint." He cried and felt of it. It seemed quite straight to him. It was. He was a handsome little fellow, and, when Mrs. Rosenheimer took him out with her, folks would stop and ask about him. She was glad when she could answer them in English. And as for Mannie—at four he talked as if no other country than America had ever existed.

Very gradually, Mrs. Rosenheimer grew tired of MacDougal Street. She tried to introduce this dissatisfaction into the rest of the family. Grandma was very happy here. With little shrugs and gestures she decried any further change. Weren't they all getting along finely? Wasn't Rosenheimer near his work? Weren't the children fat and healthy? What could they have better than this—two rooms, running water, gas and everything? Didn't they know people all around them? Rosenheimer was indifferent. Some of his friends, including the Abramsons, had already moved "farther out." Still, he didn't see the use of spending so much money; they were all right where they were. Times were hard; you couldn't tell what might happen. Still, if Minnie had her heart set on it— The children were ready for any change.

Mrs. Rosenheimer, revolving the matter endlessly in her mind, found many reasons for moving. All of her friends, it seemed, had fled from the noise and dirt of MacDougal Street. On first coming to New York she had been disappointed at not living in the Ghetto over on the East Side. Now, when she visited there, she wondered how she had ever liked it. When she moved she wanted something really fine—and where her friends were, too. She had a good many friends outside of the Ghetto now. On arriving in America she hadn't known MacDougal Street was dirty. She knew it now. And the little Italian children in the neighborhood—oh, they were all right, of course, but—not just whom you'd want your children to play with, exactly. Why, every day Ike would come home with terrible things they had said to him. And their home, which had looked so grand, was old and ugly, too, when compared with those of other people. Of course Grandma liked it, but, after all, Grandma was old-fashioned. Mrs. Rosenheimer discovered, almost in one breath, that her mother belonged to a passing generation, and didn't keep up with the times—that she, herself, really had charge of the household.

Out in East Seventy-seventh Street there were some tenements, not at all like those of MacDougal Street nor the Ghetto, but brand-new, just the same as rich people had. Each flat had a regular kitchen with a sink and running water and a fine new gas stove. The front room had a mirror in it that belonged to the house—and—unbelievably but actually true—there was a bathroom for each family. It had a tub in it, painted white, and a washstand—both with running water—and already there was oilcloth, in blue and white, on the bathroom floor. The outer halls had gas in them that burned all night—some sort of a law. Those tenements were elegant—that was the way to live.

Rosenheimer got another raise. There was some sort of an organization of cutters, a threatened strike, and then sudden success. Mrs. Rosenheimer never understood much about it but it meant more money. Now Rosenheimer had no legitimate reason for keeping his family in MacDougal Street.

So he and Mrs. Rosenheimer and Grandma went out to the new

tenements and looked around. Mrs. Rosenheimer acted as spokesman, talking with the woman at the renting office, asking questions, pointing things out. At the end of the afternoon Rosenheimer rented one of the four-room flats in a new tenement building.

On the way home, Mrs. Rosenheimer leaned close to her husband.

"Ain't it grand, the way we are going to live now?" she asked.

"If we can pay for it."

"With you doing so well, how you talk!"

"Good enough, but money, these days—"

"Abe, do you want to do something for me?"

"Go on, something more to spend money on."

"Not a cent, Abe. Only, won't you—shave your beard? Moving to a new neighborhood and all. Not for me, but the neighbors should see what an American father the children have got."

Rosenheimer frowned a bit uneasily. Mrs. Rosenheimer didn't refer to it again, but three days later he came home strangely thin and white-looking—his beard gone. Only a little mustache, soft and mixed with red, remained.

Before the Rosenheimers moved they sold the worst of their furniture to the very man from whom they bought it, five years before, taking only the big bed, the table and the couch. It was Mrs. Rosenheimer who insisted on this.

"Trash we've got, when you compare it to the way others live. We need new things in a fine new flat."

On the day they were moving, Yetta said something. The family were amazed into silence. Yetta was thirteen now, a tall girl, rather plump, with black hair and flashing eyes.

"When we move, let's get rid of some of our name," she said. "I hate it. It's awfully long—Rosenheimer. Nobody ever says it all, anyhow. Let's call ourselves Rosenheim "

"Why, why," muttered her father, finally, "how you talk! Change my name, as if I was a criminal or something."

"Aw," Yetta pouted, she was her father's favorite and she knew it, "this family of greenhorns make me tired. Rosenheimer—if it was longer you'd like it better. Ike Rosenheimer and Carrie Rosenheimer and Yetta Rosenheimer! It's awful. Leaving off two letters would only help a little—and that's too much for you. Since the Abramsons moved they are Abrams, and you know it. And Sam—do you know what? At school they called him MacDougal because he lived here on this street and he liked it better than Sam, so he's calling himself MacDougal Abrams now. And here, you old-timers—"

"She's right, Mamma," said Ike, "our names are awful."

Mannie didn't say anything. He sucked a great red lollypop. At six one doesn't care much about names. Nor did Carrie, who was eight.

There was a letter-box for each family in the entrance hall of the new tenement building and a space for the name of the family just above it. Maybe Rosenheimer had taken the advice of his children. Perhaps he wrote in large letters and couldn't get all of his name in the space made for it. Anyhow, Rosenheim was announced to the world as the occupant of Flat 52.

V

Flat 52 was quite as handsome as Mrs. Rosenheim had dreamed it would be. There were four rooms in it. In the parlor was the famous built-in mirror, with a ledge below it to hold ornaments. And, before long, ornaments there were, three big vases. They were got with coupons from the coffee and tea store at the corner—it was a lucky thing all the Rosenheims liked coffee. There was the couch, too, but best of all was the new table. It was brand-new—no one else had ever used it before. Mrs. Rosenheim bought it in Avenue A and was paying for it weekly out of the household allowance. It was red and shiny and round and each little Rosenheim was warned not to press sticky fingers on it, though it was always full of finger marks.

On the table was a mat of blue plush and on the plush mat was—yes —a book—"Wonders of Natural History." It had been Yetta's birthday present from her father and was quite handsome enough, colored pictures, red binding and all, to grace even this gem of a table. There was a new rug in this room, too, though it was new only to the Rosenheims. There were roses woven right into it and Grandma thought it was the most beautiful thing she had ever seen. She liked to sit and look at it as she rocked.

Yetta, Carrie and Grandma slept in the front room—just the three of them alone in the biggest room. There was a cot, covered with a Turkish spread, for the girls and Grandma slept on the couch—no sleeping on the floor any more for this family. So wonderful was the new home that there was a bedroom devoted exclusively to the rites of sleeping. Mr. and Mrs. Rosenheim and Dorothy occupied it. The third room was the dining room, where Ike and Mannie slept all alone on a cot and weren't afraid. No one slept in the kitchen or bathroom at all. In the dining room there was a whole "set" of furniture, bought from the family that was moving out, a square table and six chairs. It was lucky Mannie and Dorothy were so little they could sit on others' laps.

The dining room with its fine "set," brought the habit of regular meals with it. In MacDougal Street there was a supper-time, of course, but the children weren't always there and the other meals had been rather haphazard, half of the family standing up, likely as not. Now there was a regular breakfast in the morning, everyone sitting down, and early enough for Rosenheim to get to work on time and Yetta and Ike and Carrie to get to school. Lunch was still informal, eaten standing around the kitchen. Supper was a grand meal, everyone sitting down at the same time, the table all set with tablecloth and dishes, as if it were a party.

It was easy to settle down into the pleasant rhythm of East Seventy-seventh Street. There were big new tenements on each side of the street and before long each member of the family made lots of friends.

Rosenheim didn't have as many friends as the others. He didn't care for them. His hours were long and he was getting into the habit of working, sometimes, at night. It takes a lot of money to pay rent—six dollars every week—and buy clothes and food for a family and save a little, too. Rosenheim didn't complain unless his usual solemn face and prediction of hard times can be called complaining. It never occurred to him that he had anything to complain about. Didn't he have a fine home and a lot to eat, a home grander than he ought to spend the money for, even? When he wasn't busy, he and Abrams and a friend of theirs, sometimes a man named Moses, would play cards long hours at a time, talking in loud, seemingly angry voices and smoking long cigarettes. Or, with coat, collar and shoes off, as he always sat in the house, he would read the paper—he could read English quite easily, but he preferred Yiddish. He didn't talk much and the children were taught "not to worry Papa," when he was at home.

Grandma grew to like the new home in time, though it never seemed quite as pleasant as that in MacDougal Street. She did all of the cooking, of course, and could order the children around as much as she wanted to, though they were good children as a rule, when you let them see who was boss. She would exclaim with clasped hands over the grandeur of things and beg her God that the people from her home town might see "how we live like this." She was always busy. She never learned to speak English well, and though at sixty-two she could drive a bargain as well as ever, she didn't feel quite comfortable in the near-by shops as she had in MacDougal Street. Gradually her daughter took over the marketing from her.

The spirit of change had reached Mrs. Rosenheim and she did what she could to grasp it. She tried again to persuade Grandma to take off her *sheidel*.

"See, Grandma, these other people. Ain't you as good as them? It ain't nothing to be ashamed of, a *sheidel*, but here in America we do what others do."

But Grandma kept her *sheidel*. She couldn't yield everything to the customs of the unbelievers. She even muttered things about "forgetting your own people."

Mrs. Rosenheim tried to acquire "elegant English." She was very proud of her children because their language was unsullied by accent. But perhaps because she never liked to read and it never occurred to her that she might study, or because her tongue had lost its flexibility, she was never able to conceal her foreignness. She was becoming a little self-satisfied, too, a bit complacent with her own ways, and this may have hindered her progress. The new language issued forth in a strange, twisted form, the "w's" and "v's" transposed, the intonations of the Yiddish always noticeable. She managed to make nearly all of the ordinary grammatical errors of the native and a few pet ones of her own. Her sentences were full of inversions. Her voice, never very low, became louder and louder and the singing intonations more marked as she grew excited. Rosenheim spoke with an accent, too, which he always retained, but his voice was quite low and he soon overcame the strange sing-song of his native tongue. Then, too, Rosenheim never talked very much.

Mrs. Rosenheim bloomed in East Seventy-seventh Street. Her mother did the cooking and Yetta helped with the housework. Even then, with so many children in the house, there was enough to do, but she spent much time in visiting her neighbors, gossiping about her children, the prices of food, other neighbors. Although her family came first, she began to pay more attention to herself, buying clothes that were not absolutely necessary, cheap things that looked fine to her. She became ambitious, too. She found that there was another life not bounded by the tenements and that "other people," the rich part of the world, were not much different outside of their possession of money. Her humility was wearing away. "We're as good as anybody" came to her mind, and was beginning to fertilize. She didn't want to associate with anyone outside of her own group, but she liked to feel that others were not superior. The children, continuing their acquisitiveness, encouraged their mother.

Yetta had her fourteenth birthday soon after the family moved to East Seventy-seventh Street. She began to mature rather rapidly, arranging her hair in an exaggerated following of the fashion and even purchased and wore a pair of corsets. She had a high color and her flashing eyes made her quite attractive. Her mouth was rather wide. Yetta did not speak with a foreign accent, but her voice was a trifle hoarse and was not well modulated. She had a lot to say about nearly everything and delighted in saying it. The niceties of conversation had not been introduced into the Rosenheim family life and most of the things Yetta thought of occurred when someone else was talking. Her favorite method of attracting attention was to interrupt or talk down, in a louder voice, anyone who had the floor. Ike had this pleasant little habit, too, so between them conversation rose in roaring waves of sound.

Yetta felt that many things about her could be improved. She began to criticize things at home—her clothes; her mother's language, which was too full of errors, too singing to suit her daughter; the actions of the younger children. She never liked to read, but she "loved a good time" and was always with a group of girls and boys, laughing and talking.

Ike was much like Yetta, though a bit more serious, more inclined to argument. He could argue over anything even at twelve. He, too, had definite notions about the upbringing of the younger children and the modernity of the household. He didn't want anyone making fun of the family he belonged to. His own name came in for his disapproval about this time.

He had a fight with a boy named Jim and Jim hit him and called him names. But the cruelest part of Jim's name-calling had been merely to repeat, over and over again, "Ikey Rosenheim, Ikey Rosenheim." For this cruelty Ike had fought Jim and had emerged not entirely victorious, bringing back a black eye and the memory of the derision in the mouth of the enemy.

"I'm going to change my name," Ike announced at supper that night. "I don't care what this family says. You make me sick, naming me Ike. You might have known. This family has terrible names. No wonder people make fun of us. After this I'm—I'm going to be—Harold."

"Oh, no, not Harold," Grandma wailed, with uplifted hands.

"No," Mrs. Rosenheim groaned, "you've got to keep the letter, the 'I.' You were named after your Papa's father."

"There's a lot of good names beginning with 'I,'" Yetta encouraged. So, between them, they found Irving, which seemed satisfactory to everyone. Little Irving, at school, told his teacher that Ike had been a nickname and that the family wanted him called by his own name, now. Jim, not satisfied with Irving Rosenheim as a reproach, had to find something else to fight about.

Carrie and Mannie and Dorothy were still too little to bother about names. They begged for pennies for lollypops on sticks, candy apples, licorice and other delicacies that the neighborhood afforded, satisfied to tag after Mrs. Rosenheim as she did the marketing. They were nice children, though of course Dorothy was a little spoiled—the youngest child and always having her own way about everything.

VI

During the next year something came up in a business way that caused Rosenheim and Abrams to hold long consultations during many evenings. They nodded together over bits of paper on which there were many figures. Mrs. Rosenheim felt that they had "something in their heads" they weren't telling her about, but, being a dutiful wife—and knowing her husband, and how useless it would have been—she didn't press matters. A few weeks later she found out. E. G. Plotski had died suddenly, leaving no near relatives except a wife. Abrams had heard about the case. Mrs. Plotski couldn't keep up the business alone. If she couldn't "sell out," complete, she was going to give it up and sell the machinery. She had some cousins in a far-Western place called, Abrams believed, Iowa, and was desirous of living with them. If Mrs. Plotski "gave up the business" there was a tremendous loss, it seemed to Abrams and Rosenheim—for Plotski already had operators, customers, "good will." And with their knowledge of the pants business . . .

It seemed, indeed, a visitation, as if a whole pants business had descended to them as a direct reward for their long and faithful work. But Mrs. Plotski had friends, not just in a position to buy the business, it seemed, but quite capable of giving advice about selling it. And herein lay the need of much nodding and figuring. Finally it was settled. Abrams and Rosenheim went to their several banks—it's never safe to put all of your savings in one bank, even if it does look like a fine big one—drew out their savings accounts, for of course they had no checking accounts, and, after the usual legalities had been concluded, were the joint partners of The Acme Pants Company, Men's and Boys' Pants.

After they had signed their names, Marcus L. Abrams and Abraham G. Rosenheim, Rosenheim allowed his stern face to relax into a rather sad smile.

"Good, eh, Marcus? Here, I'm only 'over' seven years and I'm partner in a business already. Of course, we can expect hard times, but, a business ain't anything to be ashamed of."

The family saw Rosenheim's new signature and liked it. Irving wrote it above the letter-box. The G stood for nothing in particular, but Rosenheim had no middle name and of course he ought to have one. It was indeed American. The neighborhood did not notice, it was used to changes.

Abrams and Rosenheim worked all day and most of the night. They "went over the books" with great deliberation. They looked into every minute detail of the business, and wrote numerous letters by hand on the old Acme Pants Company letterheads that they found in Plotski's desk. When this paper was used up they ordered more, retaining the cut of the building at the top but substituting their names for the name of the deceased former owner.

They were very happy over their new business, though you would never have known it by their actions. They always wore long faces.

The factory did well. People liked ready-made pants, it seemed. The two men hurried around seeking new trade, satisfied with as small a profit as possible. They bought job lots of woolens from the factories and did numberless other things to reduce expenses. Rosenheim cut the pants and Abrams was not too proud to do his share of the menial labor. Before another year had passed the whole of the third floor loft belonged to the Acme Pants Company.

Mrs. Rosenheim was proud of her husband. It was mighty fine, these days, to speak of "my husband's factory" to those women whose more unfortunate spouses were forced to exist on mere wages handed them by their overlords. But even this, in time, stopped satisfying. What good does it do for your husband to own a factory if you still live in a tenement in East Seventy-seventh Street? Mrs. Rosenheim knew that her husband was working hard and was nearly always worried over money matters, bills to meet, wages to be paid. But, as long as he actually was a manufacturer, and owner of a business, a payer of wages, it was unbelievable that they should live in a tenement. Weren't they as good as anybody? Several months ago the Abrams had moved. Of course, with only two boys the expenses were less, but what of that? And the Moskowskis—now the Mosses—had moved, too. The Rosenheims had been in the tenement three years and now the neighborhood was filling up with terrible people, straight from the Ghetto—or the old country—and bringing foreign habits with them. It was no place to bring up growing American children.

It was Yetta who precipitated the moving. Although he petted and humored Dorothy, it was his oldest child who was Rosenheim's favorite. Now Yetta tried all of her most endearing tricks.

"Papa," she said, "I'm sixteen. I ought to get out of this neighborhood. Ask Mamma. I'm almost a young lady. I want good things—a fine man like you with a factory shouldn't keep his children in the tenements. All of my crowd are gone. I miss them something awful. You don't want me to go with the—the 'greenhorns' who are moving in around here, do you?"

Similar arguments managed to convince Rosenheim. Anyhow, one night he nodded solemnly and consented to move.

"You women will ruin me yet, with all your spending," he said, but Yetta, tall though she was, jumped on his lap and kissed his thin cheek

"None of that," he said, in assumed brusqueness, as he pushed her away. "You make a fool of your old Papa, eh? Well, go along and get your fine flat."

Mrs. Rosenheim and Yetta, accompanied by Mrs. and Miss Graham, a recent and becoming transformation of their old friends, the Grabinskis, went apartment hunting. They decided on the Bronx, new and good enough for any manufacturer's family. They had friends there and there were lots of stores. It was a nice neighborhood, Yetta thought, with lots of young people who wore good clothes. She could have a fine time.

No longer were the Rosenheims satisfied with the first apartment shown them. Yetta and her mother had grown critical. Yetta's ambitions had limitations, of course. She didn't aspire to an elevator apartment or anything like that—but she didn't want a tenement. She wanted a big living room, for she was approaching the beau age and already was going to the theater with MacDougal Abrams and Milton Cohn. They visited dozens of apartments, examining the kitchens and halls, exclaiming over the plumbing. Grandma wanted a big kitchen and she ought to have it, as long as she did most of the cooking. And they had been crowded for years—Yetta didn't want anyone sleeping in the front room, nor even in the dining room. Young girls do get such notions! Mrs. Rosenheim wanted grand decorations in the lower hall.

After much stepclimbing they found their apartment. It was on the fourth floor, rear, of a walk-up apartment, but the rent was forty dollars a month and they dared not pay more. Rosenheim looked dour when the news was broken to him, but, with sad headshaking and remarks about business being bad, he said they might take it.

The entrance hall of the apartment-house was of marble. The letter-boxes were of brass and shining. The stairs leading to the apartment were carpeted. The apartment itself had seven rooms. A few years before the Rosenheims wouldn't have believed an apartment could be so large. Now they all accepted it rather indifferently. Wasn't Rosenheim a factory owner? Didn't some of their friends live just as grandly? The woodwork was shining oak. The floors glittered blondly. Mr. and Mrs. Rosenheim had a bedroom all alone, Grandma shared a tiny cubicle with Dorothy. Yetta and Carrie had their room and there was a room for the boys. All the rooms had new beds of white enameled iron, fantastically twisted and with big brass knobs.

The Rosenheims got rid of most of their old things at a sale before they left East Seventy-seventh Street. Then Mrs. Rosenheim and Yetta bought things suitable for the grandeur of their new home at an instalment house in Sixth Avenue. There was a three-piece parlor set stained to a red imitation of mahogany. The round table had come with them, as had the vases. The dining room boasted a new "set," a round table that pulled apart and had four extra leaves and sat on a huge pedestal, and eight chairs—two with arms, making one for each of them. There were brand-new rugs, one for each room, most of them in patterns of birds and beasts and flowers in bright colorings, though the front room displayed a gay and exciting "Oriental pattern."

One of the startling changes of the new régime was the name above the letter-box. A simple and chaste A. G. Rosen was announced in Irving's most careful writing. Rosenheim explained that, at the factory, everyone called him Rosen for short and it might make it confusing to keep the old name. The family hailed Rosen joyfully. Surely they were real Americans, now.

VII

They were settled only a few months when Yetta begged and got—a piano. Shiningly red, it matched the rest of the living-room furniture. It was an upright, of course, and Yetta draped a pale silk scarf embroidered in gold threads over it, with a vase at either end to hold it in place. Soon she and Carrie were taking lessons from a Mme. Roset of the neighborhood, making half-hours horrible with scales and five-finger exercises.

There were now other forms of art in the household, too. For his birthday the children gave their father enlargements of the photographs of him and their mother. These were "hand-made crayons" in gray, with touches of color on lips and cheeks and framed in wide carved oak, trimmed with gold. They were placed side by side above the piano, which stood slightly diagonally in one corner.

The children were growing up. Yetta felt herself quite a young lady and didn't go to school. There was no use going any more—she wasn't going to be a teacher, was she? She had a lovely handwriting, with fine loops at the ends of the "y's" and "g's." It seemed a shame to spend her days in school when there were so many things to do outside. No one tried to persuade her to keep on going. Her father was slightly of the opinion that too much learning wasn't good for a girl anyhow. Men didn't like "smart" girls and Yetta was growing up. If she wanted to go to school he might have consented, but she didn't. She preferred putting on her best clothes, her hat an exaggerated copy of something she had seen in Broadway and had had made after her description at a neighborhood shop, a cheap fur around her neck, high-heeled shoes. Thus attired, she went walking.

In the morning she had to help a little with the bed-making, dusting and ironing. But in the afternoons she was free. She'd meet some of "the girls" or "the boys" and drink soda, laughing and giggling over things.

She used the latest slang and talked rather loudly. At night there were dances or the crowd would go, in pairs or groups, to the theater, sitting in the gallery, usually, and laughing heartily over the jokes. They were fondest of vaudeville. Yetta was awfully happy when she had enough spending money and a new dress—a bit more exaggerated in style than any of her friends. She couldn't imagine anything finer than the new neighborhood and the new apartment.

Grandma was just a trifle bewildered in the Bronx. She didn't seem to fit in. The children, growing up, were developing unexpected opinions of their own that didn't agree with her ideas. They called her old-fashioned and giggled at her advice. There was plenty to do and Grandma liked housework. But sixty-five isn't young and Grandma had worked hard in her day. Four flights of stairs aren't easy, either, so Grandma didn't go out often. Occasionally, she walked around the neighborhood, not knowing just what to do. Mrs. Rosen did all her own marketing or telephoned for things—there was a telephone in the new apartment. There were a few old friends to go to see, foreign-born women, like herself, and with these she would talk in comfortable Yiddish. But each one lived several blocks away. You didn't talk to strangers in this neighborhood, it seemed, and you could go for weeks and not see anyone you knew. A funny place, America.

Still, there were pleasant things for Grandma—good food and the fun of preparing it, a comfortable home. Mrs. Rosen didn't like to work as well as she used to, so finally she hired a woman who came in, one day a week, to do the washing in the morning and the scrubbing of kitchen and bath in the afternoon. Grandma was quite excited over this innovation. For the first time in her life she could fold her gnarled old hands and watch someone do the work for her.

"They should hear about this back home," she would say. "Abe with a factory and us with seven rooms and a washwoman and all. We've got it lucky, ain't it, Minnie?"

Mrs. Rosen, though annoyed at her mother's simplicity, agreed. Already Mrs. Rosen was planning bigger things. It didn't seem at all impossible to her that some day they might even have a regular servant girl.

Mrs. Rosen was well satisfied, generally. Occasionally she, too, regretted some of the pleasant things that Seventy-seventh Street had meant for her. She had liked the friendly chatter of the neighborhood. Here in the Bronx you had to be "dressed" all the time. In Seventy-seventh Street you could go out in the morning in your house-dress, with a basket, and spend a pleasant hour or so bargaining with the shopkeepers and talking with friends, always meeting little groups you knew. On the steps, in the evening you could call back and forth.

Money was good; she was glad she had it. A servant girl would be fine; it was a lot of work for her and Grandma, cleaning up after five children. But this neighborhood was stylish enough. You knew some of your neighbors here, even if they weren't so friendly. Maybe, after you got better acquainted . . .

It was nice, having a lot of rooms and new clothes and all that. Mrs. Rosen finally met new acquaintances and liked them. She played cards in the afternoons now and a few months later joined a euchre club which met every Tuesday afternoon at the homes of its members in turn. There were "refreshments" after the game, cold meat and potato salad, usually, and the prizes were hand-painted china and "honiton lace" centerpieces. Mrs. Rosen won quite an assortment as the months passed.

Irving was getting to be a big boy. He looked a little like his father, thin, a trifle sallow, with a slightly aquiline nose—but much handsomer, his mother thought. His eyes were not strong and quite early he had to wear glasses. He adopted nose-glasses and before he quite got used to them he had formed the habit of tilting his head up, to keep them from falling off. He had rather a sharp chin and wore his black hair straight back and sleek.

When the family moved to the Bronx he was fourteen, had on a first pair of long trousers, and was in the first year of the high school. He was quick in his studies and would argue with his teachers about anything under discussion. He still liked long dissertations at home and had about decided to be a lawyer. In the years that followed he read quite a little, not so much for the love of reading—he had little of that—but from a desire "to keep up with things," so he could discuss and dissect and argue. He liked the theater as he grew older, but preferred serious dramas.

Carrie was quieter than either Yetta or Irving, but she observed a great deal. She liked to spend money, begging it from her parents. "We're rich, why can't I have more things?" she would say, buying unnecessarily expensive ribbons and purses. She liked to correct the family, too, and, when her mother grew vocal and her voice took on the sing-song of her native tongue, Carrie would say, "Don't talk so loud, Mother. We aren't deaf, you know," or "This is America. We try to speak English here." Mrs. Rosen would check herself rather shamefacedly, instead of "calling the child down," as she felt she should have done. Carrie liked expensive clothes and she liked putting them on and taking long walks with just one girl friend, talking quietly. She thought Yetta's crowd awfully loud. Mannie and Dorothy were good-looking little children, still coaxers of pennies and both rather spoiled.

The Acme Pants Company grew, but in spite of its growth none of the family dared suggest any extravagant changes. Rosen spoke too much about hard times for that. And he did worry, too, for with the enlarging of the business came the borrowing of money and notes to meet. He worked at night for weeks at a time and grew thinner. Outside of his usual solemnity he never complained. He enjoyed the business as much for its own sake as for the things he was able to give his family. It was far more interesting and absorbing to him than they were. Even at home his mind was filled with business detail and in the midst of a meal or a friendly discussion his eyes would grow vacant, he would fumble for a pencil and write something down on an envelope. Spare evenings, he played cards with Abrams or Moss or Hammer or fell asleep over his newspaper—an English one, nearly always, now. He still took off his coat in the house and sometimes his collar and tie. It was Carrie who said to him, "Papa, why do you start undressing as soon as you get home?" He always kept on his shoes and sometimes his collar and tie after that.

He never took much part in the family life. Irving bored him. He was not interested in "women's doings," and could ignore whole evenings of conversation about people and clothes. His business was the one thing he cared to talk about—his family knew nothing about business. What was there left? None of them knew or cared anything about world affairs. It isn't likely Rosen would have been interested if they had. So, unconsciously, he drew apart more and more. He paid bills, with a little grumbling. He handed out money when necessary. He greeted all luxuries with something about "hard times." He accepted all innovations with apparent disregard. He was never cross or disagreeable. Everyone was a little quieter when he was at home. Otherwise it was as if he were not there at all.

VIII

A year later, when she was eighteen, Yetta became, suddenly, Yvette. The crowd she was going with thought Yetta an awful name, old-fashioned and foreign. And certainly there was nothing foreign about her. She had seen Yvette in a book—and, with the right initial and all Yvette Rosen sounded fine. After that she frowned at anyone, even old Grandma, if the old name crept in.

The family became more extravagant as the days passed, though not extraordinarily so. But why not? Even Rosen had to admit, grudgingly, that the factory was growing. Little things—Mrs. Rosen had a fine black silk dress, with revers of green satin, lace covered. She bought Grandma a black silk, too, for days when company came in. And Yvette —how that girl did wear out clothes, to parties nearly every night! And

Irving wanted "his own money" and was put on an allowance, though he always begged his mother for more before the month was half over. Books cost a lot, it seemed, and you can't be a tightwad with a bunch of fellows. And Carrie had a notion that the family was very rich—when she got new things she wanted the best. Even Mannie and Dorothy needed new things frequently.

In 1906 Irving was graduated, at 18, from the high school. It was a big event for the family. All of them, even Grandma, who didn't go out much, attended the graduation exercises. At the hall they chatted about how fine and smart Irving was until Carrie, who could be very petulant at fifteen, "shushed" them all into silence.

On the way home Mrs. Rosen couldn't help calling her husband's attention to his family—weren't they something to be proud of? To think that only a few years before . . .

It was Irving who first spoke dissatisfaction with the Bronx apartment. Irving was to enter Columbia University in the fall and he wanted to be a little nearer his school.

"You don't know how it is," he said, one night at dinner. "Everyone laughs at the Bronx. I went to a vaudeville show with Yvette last week, though Heavens knows why she goes to it, and at the mention of the Bronx everyone laughed. It isn't only that. Here we are in a walk-up apartment, when we could have something better. I'm starting—to—to make friends. I've got to make a place for myself. I'm eighteen. When we were younger it didn't make much difference, now we ought to get out of here."

Carrie agreed with him.

"It certainly is terrible here," she said. "I don't like this high school, either. I want to go to a private school. There are several good ones in Harlem and a real fine one on Riverside Drive that I've heard about. Irving is right. You'd think we were poor, the way we live here—no servants or anything. When I meet new girls I'm ashamed to bring them home. Ada is going to private school, and Beatrice has moved to Long Island. I don't know anyone around here—but trash and poor people."

Even Mannie, at thirteen, was tired of the Bronx and Dorothy, at nine, was ready for any change.

The Bronx suited Yvette. She had her crowd here. Still, there was something in what the others were saying. Harlem sounded more stylish certainly. She had friends there, too, and could get acquainted easily enough.

Mrs. Rosen didn't know. She felt, with Yvette, that things were very nice as they were. The old friendliness of East Seventy-seventh Street would never come back, and she, too, had acquaintances in Harlem. It would cost more to live—but didn't they have the money? There could be a servant and new furniture—the children had been hard on the things that had been so shining four years ago. After all, they were rich people, and the children had to have advantages.

Gradually Rosen, grumblingly, was won over. Couldn't he see how terrible it was—all their money, and still living in the Bronx? How could people know he was a success? Their apartment was old-fashioned—that funny tub and only one bathroom for the whole family. And Grandma ought to have a room for herself—with five children there ought to be a servant girl—what was the use of having money if you couldn't get things with it?

Again there was a series of house-huntings. This time Irving accompanied his mother and Yvette. Irving was very critical. Things others pronounced "grand" he didn't like at all. At eighteen he considered himself quite a man. As a coming lawyer he felt that his surroundings should reflect his own glory. What did his folks know about things? Didn't he go to homes they never entered, the Wissels' and the Durham-Levi's? Irving wanted a home with style to it. He hadn't definite ideas about decoration, but it must look fine and big as you came in. He thought they ought to inquire a little about the neighbors—to find out if they were just the sort one would want to live near. Their present neighbors certainly were awful.

The new apartment was in West 116th Street. The building was large and red, with white stone ornaments. The lower halls were grandly ornamental and a great velvet curtain hung toward the rear. There was an elevator, rather uncertain, with iron grille work in front. That would make it nice for Grandma—she could get out more. The living room had a gas grate and the woodwork was stylishly Mission finished.

Followed the usual buying orgy and this, too, Irving consented to attend. The piano came with them, but there was a new parlor set, great heavy pieces of Mission, square and dark, with leather cushions. A huge Mission davenport was the pièce de résistance. The dining room had a brand new "set"—there might be company to dinner—a big table, twelve chairs and a sideboard with a mirrored back. In the bedrooms there were great brass beds, the posts three inches across, and large mahogany dressers with "swell fronts," curved generously outward.

In the living room, too, there were fine rugs, "real Orientals" this time, about six small ones, oases of red and blue on the light inlaid floor. The family admired the lighting fixtures—a cluster of fourteen lights in the living room, to which they added a fancy lamp with a shade composed of bits of colored glass in a floral pattern; in the dining room a great dome of multi-colored glass hung directly over the table.

Then Mrs. Rosen hired their first maid, though the family referred to her as "the girl." Her name was Marie and she didn't have a very easy life of it. At first Mrs. Rosen and Grandma helped her, but Mrs. Rosen disliked housework increasingly and she didn't want Grandma to work if she didn't. Grandma had always done all the cooking, but as "the girl" learned to prepare the dishes liked by the Rosen family she gradually took over the cooking, too. Then, when "the girl" complained about working too hard a woman was hired for two days each week to do the washing and heavy cleaning.

Grandma wasn't quite as content as she had been, most likely because she wasn't so busy. Grandma couldn't read English at all and Yiddish very little, even if the children would have allowed a Yiddish paper in the house, now, which is doubtful. Grandma had never had the reading habit, nor, for that matter, any habits of leisure. She had thought that life meant service and now there was nothing to do. It was harder for her to go out because she walked very slowly. There were fewer places to go, fewer friends, fewer Yiddish shops. People would stare, embarrassingly, at Grandma's *sheidel* and Grandma hadn't learned to speak English very well. Mrs. Rosen spoke with an accent, but that was different; people could hardly understand Grandma.

There was always lots of company in the house and Grandma liked young people, but there was so little to say to them. Unless she knew them awfully well they couldn't understand her, or Yvette or Irving would frown at her attempts at conversation. Everyone smiled at Grandma and shook hands, but that was all—it was more comfortable to stay in her room, usually. There seemed to be fewer old people than there had been. Fewer seemed to live in Harlem, anyhow. In Mac-Dougal Street and even in East Seventy-seventh Street and the Bronx, Grandma had met old ladies, occasionally, people from her own village, and had had long talks with them, interrupted with nods and shakes of the head and tongue cluckings. Here it was different. She loved her family, of course, but she didn't seem to fit in. Darning stockings wasn't enough. Of course, Grandma was glad the family was doing so nicely—a fine big apartment with an elevator and a servant girl—and she had two new bonnets and her old one not nearly worn out yet—where did she go to wear it?—and her own room and everything she wanted. And Irving bringing her home candy she liked and Yvette singing for her—Grandma knew she ought to be awfully happy. Yet there seemed to be something—missing—

Mrs. Rosen grew to like the new apartment, though at first it had overawed her a little. But before long she belonged to two card clubs—she had known members of both of them when she lived in the Bronx. She even tried to persuade Rosen to learn euchre or bridge so that he could join a club that played in the evening. But Rosen didn't like "ladies' games."

There were some things about the new neighborhood Mrs. Rosen didn't like at all. The neighbors seemed so cold and distant. As if she wanted to know them! Wasn't her husband the owner of a factory— with more money than any of them, more than likely? Yet they minced by her, as if they thought so much of themselves. Well, she could put on airs, too!

That winter Mrs. Rosen went to a beauty parlor for the first time. The women of her set were going, it seemed. It made your hair thicker to have it shampooed and waved, especially when it was starting to get gray. Though it did hurt a little, she grew used to manicures, too, after a while. Mrs. Rosen even considered dieting. But, after a few attempts she gave it up. Just the things she shouldn't eat were the ones she liked best. After all, she was forty-four, though she knew no one would ever guess it, and if at that age you are a little plump who is there to say anything against it? She bought a fur coat that winter, seal, of course, with a great sweep to it and a hat to match, with a curved feather. Now, let one of her neighbors say something! She knew she looked mighty fine—as good as anyone in her crowd. Why shouldn't she? Wasn't her husband a well-known manufacturer?

Rosen wasn't quite as busy as he had been, though the Acme Pants Company was getting along splendidly. But with things in good condition there was time to spare. He could have spent more time with his family had he cared to but it seemed tiresome when he did. Irving annoyed him more than ever with his debates and arguments. In the evening he fell asleep over his paper—he didn't care for other literature except an occasional trade magazine. He still played cards with a few old friends he had made when he first came to America, and who, like himself, had prospered. He kept his coat on in the evenings now, or wore the smoking jacket Carrie had given him. What if their friends came in—he had to look nice for their sakes, didn't he? There was a little room, off the living room, which the family spoke of as "Papa's den." There was a couch here, brought over from the Bronx, and a desk. Under pretense of being busy, Rosen would read in there, until he fell asleep.

IX

The next year there was a great change in the Acme Pants Company. An opportunity came almost over night and he and Abrams, after long discussions—at the factory this time—joined the Rex Pants Company, McKensey and Hamberg, partners, and the four formed the Rex Suit Company, Gentlemen's Ready-Tailored Suits. Ready-tailored suits, it seemed, were more in demand every day. The four had capital enough to swing something good and to introduce a new name. Until then, most ready-made suits were mere trade goods. But a few firms had learned the value of a trade name and advertising, and Rosen and Abrams agreed with McKensey and Hamberg that there was room for one more and great possibilities in the idea. They rented an immense loft building and were soon making and selling a line of ready-made suits under the name of the King Brand. They hired an advertising man, giving him an absurdly high salary, an office of his own, with a stenographer and all of that, and agreed to pay exorbitant rates to magazines just for the privilege of a half or a quarter of a page of blank space on which to advertise their wares. A few months later, tall, exquisite young men, in graceful poses, accompanied by impossibly thin young women or sporty dogs looked at you from the magazines under such captivating captions as "King's Suits for the Kings of America" or "Every Inch a King in a King Brand Suit."

Rosen was interested again. Here, expenses were mounting, though profits might mount, too. Now he could figure again, and plan and talk things over with Abrams. Abrams, however, was Abrams no longer. He was Adams, now. He had signed himself Adams when the new firm was organized. Even Rosen's name had changed—he dropped one more letter. The indefinite Abraham G. had been altered and he blossomed forth as Abraham Lincoln Rose, to the delight of his children.

Irving was going to Columbia. He had joined a debating club and even his mother had to admit that, at this time, he was pretty much of a bore. He even called his father "Governor" on occasions and twirled a cane on holidays. He was "getting in with fine people" and dined at the homes of new friends, bringing back stories of families who didn't interrupt when you were talking and who had servants who knew how to serve meals. He felt he was going to be quite important and he wanted his family to live up to him.

Carrie was going to a private school—the only kind of school suitable for rich girls. It was in Riverside Drive, and she met some mighty fine girls there. Like Irving, she brought home stories showing the heights of other and the degradation of her own family. "—We are such rich people and still we never have anything."

Carrie objected to her name, too, it seemed. "Carrie" was such a cheap name. Nobody would know you were rich with a name like that. She was going to be Carolyn after this. Carolyn Rose was a pretty name, wasn't it?

Carolyn loved to spend money. She had decided that the family was really wealthy, that it was all bluff about hard times and saving. She wanted a gold mesh bag and got it before Yvette even knew there were gold bags in the world. Carolyn had a fur coat as expensive as her mother's, but with a smarter, more girlish cut. She disregarded the stupid idea, made up by someone who didn't have the money, probably, that diamonds were for older people, and persuaded her parents to give her a big diamond ring, set in platinum, for her seventeenth birthday.

Yvette's clothes were always a bit loud, too extreme, even cheap looking. Although she paid big prices for them they were still tawdry. Carolyn's tastes were not quiet, but she managed to look "expensive." Her hair was black and sleek and she knew she had "style." She liked collars a bit higher than anyone else wore, when they wore high, a bit lower when low collars came in. She was no slavish follower of fashion, like Yvette. She added a bit of "elegance" to whatever fashion had dared to ask for. She liked smooth broadcloth suits, much tailored, for day wear, and elaborate chiffon evening gowns. She talked with an "accent" but not the kind her mother had. She said "cahn't" when she could remember it, and thought one ought to have "tone." She had languid airs.

Mannie was growing into a nice child. He was quiet and he started to read when he was just a little fellow. Now you could find him, any time, curled up with a book he'd brought home from school. He didn't care much for out-of-door games. He was the first of the family to have literary leanings, though Dorothy read, too, when she couldn't find anything that pleased her better.

Dorothy was petted and spoiled by the whole family. She got things even before she could think to ask for them. Because there was never anything for her to be cross about the family said she had "a wonderful disposition" though she had a pouting mouth and did not smile very much.

Dorothy was "a little beauty." Although the family kept always with their own race and declared, on all possible occasions, their great pride in it and their aversion to associating with those of other faiths, the thing that delighted them most about Dorothy was, for some unexplainable reason, that everyone said "she looked like a Gentile." Mrs. Rose would repeat to her friends that people had said, "you'd never guess it —just like a Gentile that child looks." Her friends agreed and there was nothing in their minds but cordial congratulation over the fact. Dorothy had lighter hair than the others and gray eyes. She was a slender little thing, quiet, determined, impatient.

"We ought to have an automobile," she said, one day. That was in 1909, before cars had become as much of a necessity as they are now, and Dorothy was only twelve. Two weeks later, after many hugs, her father bought a car, a red one that would hold any five of them. Irving soon learned to drive it and later Carolyn and Dorothy learned, too. Grandma could never be persuaded to enter the car—it didn't look safe to her. Mrs. Rose rode, but it was always sitting stiffly erect with unrelaxed muscles. Rose asked Irving to drive him places, occasionally, when he was in a hurry. He never liked the automobile except as a convenience.

That year Grandma died. She was sick only a few days and didn't complain even then. The doctor came and fussed over her and finally a nurse came, but Grandma persuaded her daughter to send the nurse away. Grandma seemed quite content to die, and though the family was fond of her, her going did not cause any undue emotion. Mrs. Rose wept loudly at the funeral and Rose looked unusually solemn in the weeks that followed. He had been very fond of Grandma and had appreciated the little things she always loved doing for him. But, after all, as Mrs. Rose would say to her husband, "it ain't as if she was a baby at 72. It ain't as though Mamma ain't had everything money could buy these last years. A grand life she's had, nothing to do and her own room and all. Many times she spoke of it. It's good we was able to give it to her. She was a good woman but now she's gone and I can say I ain't got nothing to reproach myself for."

X

In 1910, when Yvette was twenty-four, she became engaged to marry MacDougal Adams. Already MacDougal was sales manager for the Rex Suit Company, and he was doing well. He had grown into a handsome fellow who would be quite fat, one day, if he didn't diet carefully. He was crisply black-haired, ruddy-faced. He made friends easily and was jovial most of the time. He had no subtleties, but Yvette was not the one to notice. She considered him very modern, and liked the way he "caught on to things." Her friends—and the announcement Yvette mailed to the newspapers—spoke of the affair as "a childhood romance," as indeed it was. It pleased the Roses and the Adams, too. They gave a reception at a hall on 125th Street to celebrate the occasion, each of the families inviting special friends, with Dorothy and little Helen Nacker to pass flowers to the guests. There was a band behind artificial palms, and waiters in white aprons passed refreshments. Yvette wore a dress of pink and Carolyn wore yellow. Carolyn didn't think the party fine enough, and Mannie and Dorothy didn't like it much, either. The rest of the family thought it a successful affair.

Mrs. Rose, Yvette and Carolyn spent the following weeks shopping. Yvette had to have a complete trousseau, starting with table linens and ending with silk stockings. Three months later Yvette and MacDougal were married at the Waldorf with Carolyn and Maurice Adams as attendants. Only the most intimate friends were invited to the elaborate banquet which followed, though later there was an "informal reception" with much wine. MacDougal had just bought an automobile—black, though Yvette would have preferred a gayer color—and, after a short Atlantic City honeymoon the young couple took a new and elaborate apartment in Central Park West and settled down, with two maids, to domesticity.

"Ain't it grand, Papa?" Mrs. Rose had said to her husband after their first call on the young couple. And even Rose had to agree that Yvette was getting all that could be expected.

Carolyn was "the young lady of the family," now. She was not as easily satisfied as Yvette had been. She called Yvette's crowd "loudly vulgar," though she was a trifle loud, herself, at times. She raised eyebrows and drew away when fate included her in her sister's parties. She was glad when her sister married—now she could entertain her loud friends in her own home. Maybe Yvette would even tone down a little; she laughed too loudly, and her terrible taste in clothes! Her mother talked loudly, too, except when she tried very hard to remember—and it was terrible the way she shrieked and sing-songed when she grew excited—but at least you could remonstrate with her.

The Harlem apartment didn't suit Carolyn at all. Here she was, out of school, nearly twenty—and living in—Harlem. She had gone to a series of morning lectures at one of the hotels and one of the lectures had been on furniture—it seemed all of the things in the Harlem apartment were entirely wrong. Carolyn knew this was true, too. Hadn't she been to other homes, where people knew things? They were rich and had one maid—and she didn't know how to wait on the table—and the family treated her as if she were one of them. And Irving talked back to his father, rather impudently, even when company was there, and the car with a sight—she was ashamed to use it. The least they could have was a new car and a chauffeur.

Irving agreed with all of Carolyn's criticisms, excepting those which concerned himself. He was twenty-three, why shouldn't he have things nicer? Dorothy, going on fourteen, also found the Harlem house distasteful.

"A terrible neighborhood," said Dorothy, who became Dorothea, that year. "It's too far from school and we do need a new car. I'm ashamed to tell anyone where I live. I want a big room and my own bath, so I can ask girls to stay all night, if I want to."

Rose sighed, said the family would break him and times were hard. Mrs. Rose sighed, too. Still, Harlem wasn't such a friendly neighborhood—the other couldn't be worse. And with only one girl there was too much for her to do. If they had a man to drive the car and a cook, maybe—

Carolyn went house-hunting alone. She said she'd take the others with her "when she found something." Two weeks later she took her mother and Dorothea to see the new apartment. It was a foregone conclusion with Carolyn that they would take it—just the formality of mailing the lease for her father's signature.

The apartment was on Riverside Drive, in a huge building of cream-colored brick. At the door was a Negro uniformed in dark green, and another similarly clad attended the mirrored elevator. The halls had Oriental rugs and were lit and draped with an expensiveness that suited even Carolyn. Of course it was pretty far out on the Drive—but it looked rich—and living on the Drive was rather grand, at that. Mrs. Rose was speechless at first, but later the apartment seemed quite satisfying. She liked the ornateness, the grandeur—it was even finer than Yvette's, than any of her friends. Why shouldn't it be, with Abe a partner in a big factory and all—?

The woodwork of the apartment was white enamel. There were little panels in the living room, waiting to be papered, and the dining room had a white enameled plate rail. The lighting fixtures were of the new "inverted" style, on heavy brass chains ending with carved brass holders of white frosted globes. There were French doors of mahogany leading into the living room and dining room, a huge butler's pantry with numerous shelves, a kitchen with a big hooded range and immense white sink, large bedrooms, four baths.

"If—if your Papa will pay for it," Mrs. Rose admitted weakly.

"Oh, he'll pay," said Carolyn, "why shouldn't he—a rich man like him?"

When the men of the family came to see the apartment Irving pronounced it "immense." Mr. Rose looked at the apartment, saw the library that he could have for his own, the big bedroom and bath—and gave in with unexpectedly little persuasion. After all—his friends were living well—why shouldn't he? He was making money—the family might as well spend it. Didn't the way you live show how well you were doing? Not that he was making so much, of course, but, with Yvette married—if Carolyn wanted the apartment.

Mannie and Dorothea were rather indifferent. Still, Mannie was in prep school and cared most about books—even writing a poem occasionally. He was eighteen. At fourteen, Dorothea didn't care about details as long as they were moving. Her new room was nice and big. Still, they ought to have a new car—Dorothea was quite pouty over the old one.

Carolyn took charge of the furnishings of the new apartment. Mrs.

Rose, with uplifted hands, declared her ignorance of periods "and such nonsense," but begged her daughter not to spend too much money. "You know your Papa. There is a limit even with him."

Irving gave a long-winded dissertation about what to get and told about a fine apartment he had visited, farther down on the Drive—two girls he knew, their father was a criminal lawyer. Carolyn didn't listen very closely. She knew what she wanted.

Accompanied by her most intimate friend, Eloise Morton, daughter of S. G. Morton, the box people (both of Eloise's parents had been born in America), Carolyn visited a number of shops. She called the stores where Yvette traded "middle class," but she was afraid of the decorating shops and called the things in the window "junk."

"You might like that old stuff," she said to Eloise, "but I can't see anything to it. Old chairs, stiff and funny—a hundred dollars apiece and then a fake, probably. A whole room full of that doesn't look like anything. I like things that show their full value, that you can tell cost a lot of money."

Eloise agreed that her friend had the right idea.

Carolyn didn't allow any mere furniture clerk to suggest or dictate to her. Hadn't she seen a lot of fine homes? Didn't she go to every new show in town and look especially at the stage settings? Hadn't she heard a furniture lecture? Who could advise her?

She didn't want her mother with her, she'd "simply spoil things if she started to talk." Carolyn and Eloise, alone, could give an impression of taste, elegance and riches.

Carolyn decided on Adam furniture for the living room. If the ghosts of the brothers Adam groaned a bit Carolyn was too busy to hear. She liked "sets" for the living rooms—didn't everyone have them?—so she chose a great davenport of mahogany with cane sides and back, motifs slightly after some of the Adam designs scattered over the woodwork. The upholstery was rose velour. There were two huge chairs of similar design, one a rocking chair. Other chairs were of cane and mahogany, one a Venetian, one a fireside. There was a great oblong table, too, that Carolyn knew showed good judgment, for it was of "dull antique mahogany." It, too, bore motifs of the house of Adam. There was a floor lamp with a rose shade and two table lamps to match and several pieces of "stylish" painted furniture, factory made. Carolyn looked with scorn on the little rugs that had seemed so fine a few years ago. She chose now an immense Oriental in rose and tan for the living room and a Chinese rug in dark blue to combine with the intricately carved Queen Anne furniture of the dining room.

There were elaborately patterned filet lace curtains throughout the house. Before this Mrs. Rose had always hemmed and hung the curtains. Now Carolyn gave orders for them. The over-drapes and portières were of rose velour, heavily lined, and above the windows were elaborate valances, edged with fringe and wide gold braid. There were blue velour curtains in the dining room.

In the bedrooms Carolyn's imagination had full play. Her parents' room was in mahogany with twin poster beds. Her own room was in ivory, cane inset. Dorothea's was white enameled, painted with blue scenes.

For the walls of the living room, between the paneling, Carolyn chose a scenic paper in gray. On this were to be hung elaborate oil paintings in scalloped gold frames: "A Scene at Twilight," "The Fisherman's Return." In the dining room the paper was in tapestry effect, red and blue fruit and flowers.

The family moved into the new apartment in October, 1911. The moving was simple, for the old furniture was to be sold and professional movers attended to the packing of ornaments and dishes.

Mrs. Rose and Irving were impressed with the effects wrought by Carolyn's taste and her father's money, but it did not take the family long to settle down to the pleasures of life that Riverside Drive opened to them.

XI

Moving to the Drive, the Roses made the final change in their name. Mannie, usually quiet, was the one to propose it.

"Rose is so—so peculiar," said Mannie. "Anyone could tell it had been something else, Rosen or worse. I'm eighteen and go to College this fall. I'm not going to have a name so—so ordinary. Let's change it to Ross. That's not distinctive but it isn't queer or foreign. I'm changing my first name just a little, too. I've never been called Emanuel, anyhow. Mannie isn't a name at all. I'm going to register at College as Manning Ross."

There was no letter-box to announce the change, but the elevator man knew the new occupants of Apartment 31—he wrote the names down with a blurring stub of a pencil to be sure to remember them—were Mr. and Mrs. A. Lincoln Ross, the two Misses Ross and two young men, Irving and Manning.

The family had liked Rose—but there might be something in what Manning said. But no more changes. Mr. Ross put his foot down, this time. He was meeting important men in business, Gentiles, and he didn't want any more monkey-business about names. Ross was all right and Ross it would have to stay. And it did.

Mrs. Ross took great delight in getting her new servants. It made her feel superior and important, driving up to an employment agent and interviewing prospective retainers. She took Carolyn along for advice and counsel—Carolyn went out a lot and knew about such things.

Carolyn would have liked a retinue, but Ross rebelled—expenses were awful and each servant was another mouth to feed. The old "girl" had got married so they finally chose a cook who was not above helping with other things, a waitress who could combine housework with waiting, and a chauffeur. Besides, the washerwoman would still come for two days each week.

Soon after the family was settled, Mr. Ross bought a big limousine, American made, but one that Carolyn thought looked really expensive. The chauffeur was in uniform, of course. He happened to be a young Irish boy and it seemed to Carolyn, sometimes, that he smiled a bit sarcastically and annoyingly as he held the door open for them, especially after her mother had spoken with an accent or her old sing-song.

Mr. Ross didn't object to the new luxuries. It was much more comfortable driving to the office in the limousine than waiting for Irving or one of the girls to take him or depending on less comfortable modes of transportation. He had more room to himself, too. He liked the way the new cook prepared things—he was getting indigestion and had to be careful about what he ate—though he still remembered with real emotion the pot-roasts and fish and stuffed goose that Grandma had delighted to prepare. These new dishes—salads and things like that—everything served separately—you could get used to it—it didn't make much difference—here he was, used to a maid in cap and apron, waiting on table—and Minnie used to it, too, excepting when she forgot and talked to her or reached across the table for things. Still, Minnie meant well, a good woman, rather fat these last years, but a good woman who loved her family—none of this new foolishness some of the women had, he'd noticed—

Mr. Ross didn't pay much attention to women. He never had. He saw what fine girls his daughters were, that was about all. He couldn't have recognized half a dozen of their best friends, whom he saw constantly at his home, if he had passed them on the street.

His business—that was something. Still, even that didn't keep him busy, the way it used to. This new arrangement, the offices and the factory separated—of course it was for the best. He could always go over to the factory when he wanted to, though there wasn't much need —machinery he didn't understand, everything in such order—with a head for every little department, not to mention the big ones. And, with three partners you couldn't say things as if it were your own business. Mr. Ross was fifty-three, but it hadn't been an easy fifty-three years and things had gone along rather rapidly for a while. Not that he was an old man—far from it. Still, things that had passed seemed pleasanter than they had seemed in the passing—and things to come lacked luster.

This wasn't age—certainly not—he felt as well as he had twenty years ago, practically. Give him some real work to do, you'd find out. But there was so little to do, now. You'd go down to the office about ten and dictate a few letters and potter around with things. You'd examine "swatches" and find that an expert had already given them a chemical analysis. You'd go to luncheon and be careful about what you ate. After luncheon, a little sleepily, you'd dictate more letters, if there were any more and see a few men on business, young upstarts, most likely, or Gentiles who wanted something for nothing—or consult with your partners. Then, you'd drive home after a while and read the paper or listen to Carolyn play on the new player piano or talk with Dorothea, though there wasn't much to talk about. Dinner then, and a game with Adams, though he had rheumatism these last years and wasn't the man he had been. Or Moss would drive over. There was a club, even, if you cared to go to it—a lot of strange men who didn't care anything about you—a club—at least they were of your own race—Dorothea was always asking questions about why the family didn't mix with other people—such notions a child gets—

The Rex Suit Company was still progressing. The great factories were outside New York, but the business offices occupied a whole floor of an office building, each partner with his own mahogany furnished office, with its rows of bells and its private stenographers. There was an expert to decide each thing. MacDougal was in the sales department and Maurice, the younger Adams boy, was advertising manager—a big advertising agent had charge of all of the advertising, of course. And what advertising the firm did, too! Double pages in the popular weeklies at thousands of dollars a page. Everyone was familiar with the "Kingly Men." Girls cut them out and mounted them for their rooms. "America's Kings in Kingly Suits" had been familiar enough to get applause at a musical comedy when it was used to introduce two juveniles. "Every Inch a King for the Kings of Creation" and other well-known slogans ran in letters four feet high above the artists's conception of the "Kingly Man" on the billboards.

Each year there was an ornate catalogue of the styles, "for the Prep Youth," "for the College Man," "for the Younger Set," "for the Older Fellow." Hundreds of merchants all over the country displayed King Brand signs and carried King Brand suits. The Rex Company had invented half sizes, adjustable models and the giving with each suit of an extra bit of goods and two extra buttons for mending. There wasn't much you could plan about for the Rex Company. Likely as not, someone else would have thought of it first, anyway.

Mr. Ross was accustomed to meeting men, now. He liked to meet them, in business. He would listen, weigh what they said, learn from them. He never talked much. He always retained his look of severity. He was known as "a crackerjack of a business man," "a man you couldn't put anything over on," but the other partners were good business men, too. There was nothing for Mr. Ross to work for.

Outside of business he had little. His family still seemed apart, yet he would have done anything to have saved them trouble or pain. He liked Yvette because she was frank and lively, but these last years he liked Dorothea, too, though there was nothing against Carolyn, a fine girl, if she did like to spend money. Minnie was all right—the boys would be, too, when they got a little older and settled down.

Mr. Ross didn't mind listening to the mechanical piano or the Victrola at home, but he did not care for other kinds of music. Concerts made him miserable and fidgety. He saw nothing in them and after several for charity and one visit to the opera he refused to partake of music outside of the home. He had never learned to like reading. He was still content with the daily papers and glanced, occasionally, at a weekly devoted to current events. He knew nothing about art and said so. He didn't want to be bothered with "such notions." Drama of all kinds bored him and even musical comedies entertained him only for a little while. Usually he got to thinking of business in the midst of things and lost all consciousness of what was going on.

Mr. Ross had no social ambitions, so, with no business worries and no outside interests, his days began to drag unpleasantly. He thought often of other days, of "the other side"; when he had been planning to come to America—he was glad that was over—of MacDougal Street, the hard work he had done there, the long hours, the overtime, the little economies so both ends would meet, then the newer tenement, with things a little easier, the beginnings of the factory—those had been real days—staying awake planning to meet bills, figuring to the dollar how to get money to pay the "help" and have enough left for living expenses, then Harlem and now Riverside. It was good to have planned and worked. Still, now he was used to his comforts. He liked space and quiet and the car—but, with nothing to do—

Mrs. Ross had long since relaxed her anxiety over her husband. He had never talked business and he seemed just like always, willing to listen to her stories of how she had spent the day. Mrs. Ross was quite content with the Drive. The aloofness of the neighbors, that had been disagreeable to her in Harlem, became one of her own characteristics now. She became more and more aware of her own importance. She had disliked the way "outsiders" and Gentiles had treated her, years before. Now, her last vestige of humbleness gone, she felt herself more than "as good as anyone." Wasn't she Mrs. A. Lincoln Ross, wife of

Ross of the Rex Suit Company, a real figure in New York? Didn't she get her picture in the paper when she gave money to charity? Didn't people treat her with respect as soon as they found out who she was? She was frankly fat, but she didn't mind. She had expensive dress-makers and tailors and she thought the results of her toilet satisfactory. After all, she was nearly fifty.

Her voice had toned down, during the years, as had Yvette's. When talking with those she considered important, she even tried to put an elegant swing into her sentences. Usually, though, her voice was ac-cented, ordinary, uninteresting. She still made errors and sometimes quite a lot of sing-song crept in.

In the morning Mrs. Ross attended to her household affairs, giving directions to the servants, ordering her own provisions over the tele-phone, even planning meals. She looked into the ice-box to see what provisions remained, rubbed fingers across furniture for dust, examined linens. She was a good housekeeper. In the afternoon, with Yvette, whom she found most congenial, or an acquaintance, she went for a drive or shopped. She dropped most of her old friends who had not progressed and she had no sentimental regrets concerning them. A few earlier friends she kept up with, asking them for luncheon or for a drive, with a hint of patronage. Through her daughters she met other women of her own age and circumstances. To these she tried to be pleasant, using her best language and manners. She had no intimacies with these women.

During the second year of the family's residence on the Drive, Mrs. Ross was asked to belong to several committees of important charitable organizations. She joined these gladly and gave generous sums. She liked the society of her own race. She did not feel at home with "out-siders" nor know what to say to them—she felt that they were constantly criticizing her. She had decided social ambitions, however, and wanted Mr. Ross to join a well-known club composed of members of his people. She was proud to know women who, a few years ago, or even now, were she less wealthy, would have ignored her. To the arts she was as indifferent as her husband.

XII

Irving was a lawyer now. He had a nice office in one of the newer buildings devoted to professional men, but not much practice. His father found it just as convenient to give him some of the smaller business of the firm as to increase his allowance. When anything im-portant came up Mr. Ross agreed with his partners that it was best to let a better-established lawyer handle the case.

Irving—who became Irwin about this time—could have joined a

large firm as a junior member, but he preferred independence. He didn't like to work hard or long and he had heard of the tasks performed by the younger members of big firms. He liked to waste time, browsing around book-stores, walking through the lobbies of hotels, calling on friends. He had a large acquaintance with women and had as many dinner invitations as he could accept. Wasn't he a great catch, a young lawyer with a rich father? And good company.

At twenty-five, Irwin still loved an argument. Although never a great reader, he liked to pose as one, quoting well-known authorities, reading and talking about authors unknown to his hearers. His hair was always immaculately sleeked, though it had just a perceptible wave. He had his favorite manicurist at one of the larger hotels. He smoked an expensive brand of cigarettes, carrying them in an elaborate silver and gold case and fitting each one carefully into an extremely long amber cigarette holder before smoking it. He used affected gestures, pounding on a table to emphasize a point he was making. He still wore nose-glasses, now large lensed and tortoise rimmed, and from habit he held his head too high.

Irwin was proud of his acquaintance with half a dozen actresses of minor importance. These he took to teas, dinners and suppers, talking later as if the engagement had had special significance. He was careful about his acquaintance with other women, choosing those that were, to him, of social importance. He had the same distrust his parents had for those outside of his own race. He never attended services at a synagogue, but to him religion and race were intermingled and he did not attempt to differentiate between them. Since boyhood he had suffered from prejudice far more than his sisters. He was proud to associate with "outsiders," liked to think he looked and spoke and acted like one of them. But he would never have married a Gentile.

Carolyn was now the liveliest member of the Riverside Drive household. She didn't think much of race and creed. She envied other women in some things, but she thought herself all that was desirable and attractive. She liked best the people of her own race, but she preferred them with American or English accents, appearance and accomplishments. She liked to associate only with people of great wealth. Always gowned a bit ahead of fashion, perfectly groomed, silky, smooth, crisp, she went to the theater, evenings and matinées, to luncheons and to parties, giggling and laughing, quite moderately, of course, and had a gay time. She loved musical comedy and after-theater suppers. She didn't care for the opera, but even the most serious drama could give her something to giggle about afterwards. Her hair and eyes were dark with something of the Orient about them, but her skin was fairer and clearer than her mother's or Yvette's, her round little nose was always white with powder and her eyebrows narrow and smooth, her lips and cheeks pinkly attractive.

You could see Carolyn almost any fair afternoon on the Avenue with Eloise or Helen or Mary Louise, stopping in at one little shop for a bit of lingerie, at another for flowers. They spent money with no thought of its value. Most of them could not remember poverty. Those who could found spending the best method of forgetting. Occasionally they met several of "the boys" for tea. When they didn't they bought tea for themselves at Maillard's, usually, or the Plaza. There was always a car waiting and they wore low pumps or slippers and the thinnest of stockings even when the snow was on the ground.

Carolyn "went with" Jack Morton, Eloise's brother. She had met Eloise at the Riverside Drive School. Jack was at Harvard, then, but he was graduated a year later and was "catching on" nicely in his father's box factory. The Mortons thought the Rosses a step below them socially, for the Mortons were a little farther removed from "the old country." Outside of that, they liked Carolyn. So no one was surprised, when, in 1914, when Carolyn was twenty-three, she announced her engagement to Jack. The Rosses thought Carolyn had "done well," as indeed she had, for Jack Morton was a likeable fellow, full of practical jokes and fond of poker playing, but on the whole quite a desirable husband.

Ross gave his daughter a diamond lavaliere for an engagement present, and as Carolyn picked it out herself it was quite glittering. He promised her the furniture for her new apartment as a wedding present. The Mortons gave Carolyn a small car, green, with cushions to match, which she pronounced "a young wonder." They had an engagement "at home" and were married a few months later at one of the newer hotels. Carolyn hoped that it was quite evident to the friends of both families that they were both very wealthy.

The young couple took a three weeks' trip to Florida—Jack couldn't stay away from the business longer than that. Then they went to the Astor, but Carolyn wanted to entertain her friends and a hotel does keep you cooped up so. She and Jack finally decided on a small apartment in a high-priced new building in Park Avenue. They had only one maid to start with for they both preferred eating at restaurants. With the car you could eat at a different place and go to a show or some place every night.

Without Carolyn the Riverside Drive apartment seemed quiet. Manning went to Harvard for a year, dissatisfied with the unexclusiveness of Columbia.

Dorothea liked school, too, and was now taking a few harmless courses which gave her something to do, though they didn't satisfy her.

Nothing quite pleased Dorothea. She hadn't been satisfied with Carolyn's school—girls of only one creed went there, so narrow. Dorothea said that school was a joke. She had chosen a more expensive school, patronized by daughters of rich men generally. Her new study courses were at Columbia and with private teachers. Mr. Ross didn't like them.

"It isn't as if she had to be a teacher," he said. "A girl can have too much book-learning."

But Dorothea went. She had always been different. Her clothes, for one thing. Couldn't she have had anything she wanted? Look at Carolyn—always dressed like a picture—the family had to admit that, themselves. Even Yvette, though she liked bright colors, was a good dresser. It wasn't as if Dorothea was economical. She spent as much as Carolyn did. Carolyn wore things that "looked expensive," rich broadcloth, elaborate furs—Dorothea preferred rough tweeds. She paid extraordinary sums for little suits that Mrs. Ross thought looked as if she'd got them for twenty dollars in Third Avenue. They were of mixed weaves, in grey or tan, and she wore big tailored collars over her coats, not mannish-looking or freakish, just plain. She paid fifty dollars for her little round velour hats. She wore heavy gloves and shoes, even when she went out with Carolyn, sleek in white gloves, thin pumps and furs. Dorothea paid huge prices for plain little evening frocks which she bought at exclusive little places. Even then she was not satisfied.

Dorothea wore a perpetual little pout—something had always just gone wrong. She spent her time wondering what to do, dipping in "courses" on a variety of subjects, at settlement work, "going with people she didn't have to associate with," her mother thought. Clad in a trim-fitting habit she rode whole mornings in Central Park. She exhibited funny little Belgian Griffins at shows. She went to benefits and tournaments. Yet she was always a trifle "put out," a bit bored. Things weren't ever good enough, or quite what she had expected.

For her twentieth birthday Dorothea asked for and received a new car, a good-looking foreign-made roadster. About time the family had more than one car! She didn't want a chauffeur. Hadn't she been driving as long as she could remember, learning on the old red one? She liked driving the car best of all.

The family, the family's friends, what any one said or did—all displeased Dorothea. She made sport of Irwin's pet affectations to his face, to her mother's horror. She called Yvette's things "impossible" and made fun of Carolyn's diamonds. She treated her mother as a person of no consequence, never asking her opinion about things. Although she had nothing in common with her father, she made a great fuss over him and he grew to like her better than any other member of his family. She took him out in her car, though he didn't quite enjoy the rides, expecting to be tipped over at every corner. Dorothea drove perfectly, with the recklessness of a racer.

Dorothea went with "outsiders." She seemed as much at home with members of other races as with her own. She'd bring in unexpected guests, making the family feel ill at ease. While guests were there she'd bring up bits of family history the rest were trying their hardest to keep out of sight.

"Dad," she'd say, "here's some one that wants to meet you. He's heard a lot about you. . . . Can you believe that less than twenty-five years ago Dad came to America with no money at all?" then, with a little gesture and a smile, "and now look at him." She'd throw an arm around her father, who, ill at ease, would greet the stranger.

If Mr. Ross had been unsuccessful, he would have looked like any of a thousand of his race whom you can see leaving the shops any evening at the closing hour. But his wealth haloed him. It was impossible to separate him from his money. Thin, stoop-shouldered, solemn, quiet and accented of speech, he stood for success. To Dorothea her father was immensely important. She was the first who had ever made much of him. It embarrassed him—he was a simple old fellow in many ways—but he liked it.

Mrs. Ross thought Dorothea didn't appreciate her.

"It's always her Dad, her Dad," she'd say, "never a word about how I worked when she was small or all I do for her—just Dad this, Dad that —and Irwin don't like it—that you're always bringing up old times, about Papa being a cutter. The other night when that fine Miss Tannenheim was here, you said it, when you was talking to that big blond fellow you brought in. . . ."

"You're a dear, Mother," Dorothea would give her mother the tiniest touch of a kiss on her broad cheek, "but Irv's a mess and he knows it. The Tannenheim person is a cheap old thing with a mean eye and she'll marry him some day, if he isn't watching."

"Dad," said Dorothea, one day, "let's move. You can't guess how sick I am of Riverside Drive."

"What's the matter? Haven't you got things nice here?"

"Nice—on the Drive?"

"We're always moving, it seems. Only four years ago . . ."

"I know, Dad. That's just it. A man of your position ought to have a home. Apartments are nothing. This one is simply awful. Riverside Drive is fearfully ordinary, vulgar—don't you think so? Such a cheap collection of the newly rich. Dad, you ought to have your own home in town, anyhow, and something permanent in the country."

XIII

The idea of a home appealed to Mr. Ross. He felt, now, that he had always wanted a real home. Dorothea called for him in the car and they explored the streets east of Fifth Avenue. Finally, without consulting the rest of the family, Ross bought a five-story house in East Sixty-fifth Street, just off Fifth Avenue.

"Mother will think this is terrible," Dorothea said as she kissed him, "but you and I like it, don't we? I know it cost an awful lot, Dad, but you can see it's really an investment. After it's made over a bit inside it will do for a family home for years. Imagine you—after all you've done—not having a family home."

Ross really liked the house. It seemed almost—homelike. The rest of the family were not pleased. The married daughters—of course it was not their affair—but, they wondered if it was just the right thing. Of course nice people lived in houses, but none of their friends.

"That's why we bought it," said Dorothea.

Irwin "guessed it was all right." Manning was indifferent.

Mrs. Ross held up bejeweled hands and wailed.

"Oh, Dorothea, just as I'm beginning to get into things and can ask people here to a fine apartment on the Drive—an address I can be proud of—and here you buy an old house—I thought a young girl like you would want things swell—here we've got servants and all—"

"Don't you worry," said Dorothea, "it will be 'swell' enough—awful word. And as for servants—"

The family moved to the East Sixty-fifth Street house a few months later. Dorothea didn't run around after furniture as those of her family who had chosen furniture before her had done. She turned the whole house over to Miss Lessing, in Madison Avenue. Miss Lessing's corps of exquisitely minded young men came in, looked around, made sketches, brought drapery material and wood finishes, all of which Dorothea examined critically.

"At last we'll have some place we can ask our friends," she said.

The house in East Sixty-fifth Street was rather nice. It was done in English things, mostly, painted walls and rather soft taffetas. There were some big easy chairs that could be pulled around, comfortably, in front of the fireplace. Perhaps because of its seeming simplicity and the plainness of the walls and carpets Mr. Ross liked it more than any home he had ever had. He felt it belonged to him. Mrs. Ross never liked it.

"It's too plain," she said, "nothing to it. No one would believe how much it cost you, Papa. Mrs. Sinsheimer has got an apartment on Park Avenue, just a block from Carolyn. Fourteen rooms. She had a deco-

1ator, too, but he got different things than this—gold furniture. It looks like something. We had a fine place on Riverside Drive and Dorothea drags us here, where there ain't even lights enough to see by, at night."

Still, Mrs. Ross found out, from what people said, that there must be something desirable about the new home. She even acquired a bit of the patter Dorothea used, pointing, with something like pride, to "a real Chippendale escritoire, one of the nicest examples in America," and "some Wedgwood plaques, three, from an original set of four, you know," and "of course, we are getting old and it's nice we can have a home where we can gather the sort of things we like, as a background."

Irwin didn't "think much of the place, myself," but it was a good idea, the old folks having a home . . . he was glad he didn't have to be ashamed of it, though, for his part . . . now, that country place Dorothea was talking about . . .

Yes, Dorothea had been talking about a country place. After they were settled in the new home, she continued to talk. They had five servants now—they wouldn't even need two sets—Dad could see how it took that many to run any kind of a house—and they could just shut up the town house in Spring and open it in Fall. All the family could be there, too, Yvette and the new baby, and Carolyn and their husbands . . . "a real family together. Dad, a permanent family like ours ought to have a decent country place."

The country place was on Long Island, finally. Dorothea picked it out and put the decorations in the hands of the same firm of decorators, who did rather startling things with colored wicker, chintz and tiled floors.

It was near a famous country club and Dorothea knew, as did the rest of them, that none of the men of her family could ever be admitted. It didn't seem fair to her, of course, and yet . . . Dad was a great one —there oughtn't to be any place Dad couldn't get into. But Dad didn't care. Though, from things he said, Dorothea knew he had felt things . . . expected them. He hadn't even hoped this much of life. Irwin didn't like being left out of things . . . and yet, Dorothea, looking at Irwin, hearing him argue in his rather nasal tone, gesturing with his long amber cigarette holder, couldn't blame members of the club, exactly. . . . It wasn't because of Irwin's race . . . maybe the members, themselves, weren't so wonderful . . . and yet there were her two brothers-in-law, one rather fat, both slow-minded, card-playing, a bit loud and blatant, always bringing money into the conversation . . . Yvette, loud, laughing, so heavy, mentally, Carolyn, with her cheap talk of money and spending . . . her mother . . . it wasn't fair to criticize her, her mother'd had a hard time of it when she was young, and yet . . .

Dorothea knew that, somehow, the men she liked didn't belong to her race. Hamilton Fournier, now . . . of course, if she'd marry him, there would be an awful talk, lots of crying and going on about religion . . . that sort of thing. She could hear her mother . . . she remembered when Freda Moss married,—"He'll throw it up to you." Yet, if you are proud of your race . . . doesn't that . . . can you have a thing "thrown up to you" that you are proud of? It was a big problem, too big for Dorothea. She felt that she'd always had everything she wanted . . . she could keep on having . . .

The family settled down comfortably in the new home, Manning with them. He was going to school in town, now.

Mrs. Ross was getting to like the new home better . . . it wasn't Riverside Drive, of course, but people didn't look down on her here. She was even getting in with Mrs. Rosenblatt—now that she lived near her. That crowd—she didn't have their education, but what of it, she was richer than most of them. Who were they, to be so exclusive? Maybe, by next year, if she donated to their Orphans' Nursery Fund . . .

Mr. Ross's indigestion seemed a little worse. The doctor came to see him several times each week and he had to be more careful with his diet. There seemed to be less to do at the office. He could retire, of course, but that would take away the only interesting thing he had—the few hours at the office. He even tried outdoor exercise, but after one attempt, he gave up golf as impossible. He gave to organized charities rather liberally and was even appointed on a committee which he never attended—he knew it was his money they wanted. He would sit, as he had always sat in the evening, falling asleep over his paper, or, bundled up beyond the necessity of the weather, he would climb into the car and spend a few hours with an old friend, or someone would come to see him, playing cards, as always. But a few of the old friends had died, another had moved away . . . there had never been many of them. He was just an old man, and lonesome, with nothing interesting to do or think about. . . .

XIV

Manning stopped school the year after the family moved into their new home. He had had a year at Harvard and a year or so at art school. Now, at twenty-two, he felt that he was a sculptor. His father was disappointed—Manning had started out a nice boy—it did seem that one of the boys . . .

But Manning shrugged sensitive shoulders at anything as crude as the clothing business, even wholesale. His soul was not in such things. And Mr. Ross had to admit that the position of model was about the only one in the establishment that Manning could have filled. Manning went in, rather heavily, for the arts that the rest of the family had neglected. Of course Dorothea read, but Manning thought she skimmed too lightly over real literature. And Irwin—an impossible, material fellow.

Manning wore his hair a trifle long. He talked knowingly of Byzantine enamels and the School of Troyes. He knew Della Robbia and the Della-Cruscans. There was nothing he didn't know about French ivories. He knew how champlevé enameling differed from other methods . . . there were few mysteries for Manning. His personal contributions to Wanty consisted of fantastic heads, influenced slightly by the French of the Fourteenth Century, in bas-relief—very flat relief, of course.

Manning's friends felt they formed a real part of New York's "new serious Bohemia." They ate in "unexploited" Greenwich Village restaurants, never complaining about the poorly cooked food, sitting for hours at the bare, painted tables, talking eagerly in the dim candle or lamp light. They expressed disgust when "uptowners" discovered their retreats and sometimes moved elsewhere. You could find them every Saturday and Sunday night in parties of from four to ten, at the Brevoort, sometimes with pretty girls who didn't listen to what they were saying, sometimes with homely little "artistic" ones, hung with soiled embroidered smocks, who listened too eagerly, talking of life and art, revolution and undiscovered genius.

There was no question that Manning's father should continue his allowance—there is no money in sincere art these days. Manning knew that even his father must recognize that. Manning spent his summer with the family on Long Island—it was hot in town. But, when one's family is of the bourgeoisie, it does draw one's energy so. In the autumn Manning decided he must have a real studio, some place he could work and expand, going to "the town house" for week-ends. Having one's family uptown was quite all right, of course—but you couldn't expect an artist to live with them.

Mr. Ross agreed to the studio. He was getting accustomed to Dorothea's friends, unbelievers though they were. He found he could not accept the artistic friends that Manning thought so delightful.

Manning found his studio, finally. The rent was terrific, of course, but the building had been rebuilt at great expense and was absolutely desirable in location, construction, everything. He furnished it himself in Italian and Spanish Renaissance things. Rather nice! When it was furnished—though they probably couldn't "get it" he'd let the family see it.

One Sunday, after a family reunion dinner, Manning announced that his studio was done. If the family liked they might all run down that way—a sort of informal reception . . . of course, they probably couldn't understand it all. . . .

It was in the Village, of course, but not "of" it. Did they think the Village was slumming? Uptown people did. But that's where you'd find real thought, people who accomplished things. . . .

"Why, my new studio has real atmosphere"—Manning ran his fingers through his hair as he spoke. "It's in a wonderful old building, magnificent lines and the architect left them all—it's just inside he's remodeled. I've the third floor front, two magnificent rooms, a huge fireplace, some lovely Italian things . . . and the view from the window is so quaint and artistic . . . of course you may not understand it . . . this family . . . it's just a block from Washington Square."

"Why, that's where . . ." began Mrs. Ross.

Irwin silenced her.

"Don't begin old times, Mamma. Most of us haven't as long memories as you," he said.

"Come on, now that we're all here, let's go down," Manning went on, "I want you to see something really artistic. A friend of mine, DuBroil —I think you've met him—did me a stunning name plate in copper, just my name, Manning Cuyler Ross. I'm so glad I took Cuyler for a middle name last year. And there is just the single word, 'masks.' I thought it was—rather good. And I've a stunning bit of tapestry on the south wall. Come on—you've got your cars here, we'd better get started—"

It was a pleasant drive. The three cars drew up, almost at once, in front of Manning's studio, as he, in the front car, pointed it out to them.

They made quite a party as they turned out in front of the building —a prosperous American family—Mr. and Mrs. Lincoln Ross, well-dressed, commanding, in their fifties, which isn't old, these days; MacDougal Adams, plump, pompous; Yvette Ross Adams, in handsome furs and silks; Jack Morton, sleek, black-haired; his always exquisitely gowned wife, Carolyn Ross Morton; Irwin Ross, in a well-fitting cutaway, eyebrows raised inquiringly, chatting alertly; Dorothea Ross, attractive and girlish in rough tan homespun, and Manning Cuyler Ross, their host, pleasantly artistic.

"Here's the place," said Manning. "No elevator, real Bohemia, three flights up, uncarpeted stairs. Come on, Mother."

Mrs. Ross was strangely pale, and on the faces of Yvette and Irwin and MacDougal Adams there were curious shadows. The rest, save for Mr. Ross, were too young to remember. As for him he broke, for the first time in years, into a broad smile. Manning went rattling on.

"This," he proclaimed, "is the way to live! None of your middle-class fripperies. Plain living, high thinking—this is the life!"

They came to the studio at last, and all stood about in silence while Manning explained its charms—the clear light, the plain old woodwork, the lovely view of the square, the remote, old-world atmosphere. In the midst of his oratory Mr. Ross sidled up to Mamma Ross and reached stealthily for her hand.

"Do you remember, Minnie," he whispered, "this room—this old place—those old days—"

"Hush," said Mamma Ross, "the children will hear you."

56

Maria Concepción

BY KATHERINE ANNE PORTER

MARIA CONCEPCION walked carefully, keeping to the middle of the white dusty road, where the maguey thorns and the treacherous curved spines of organ cactus had not gathered so profusely. She would have enjoyed resting for a moment in the dark shade by the roadside, but she had no time to waste drawing cactus needles from her feet. Juan and his chief would be waiting for their food in the damp trenches of the buried city.

She carried about a dozen living fowls slung over her right shoulder, their feet fastened together. Half of them fell upon the flat of her back, the balance dangled uneasily over her breast. They wriggled their benumbed and swollen legs against her neck, they twisted their stupefied eyes and peered into her face inquiringly. She did not see them or think of them. Her left arm was tired with the weight of the food basket, and she was hungry after her long morning's work.

Her straight back outlined itself strongly under her clean bright blue cotton rebozo. Instinctive serenity softened her black eyes, shaped like almonds, set far apart, and tilted a bit endwise. She walked with the free, natural, guarded ease of the primitive woman carrying an unborn child. The shape of her body was easy, the swelling life was not a distortion, but the right inevitable proportions of a woman. She was entirely contented. Her husband was at work and she was on her way to market to sell her fowls.

Her small house sat half-way up a shallow hill, under a clump of pepper-trees, a wall of organ cactus enclosing it on the side nearest to the road. Now she came down into the valley, divided by the narrow spring, and crossed a bridge of loose stones near the hut where María Rosa the beekeeper lived with her old godmother, Lupe the medicine woman. María Concepción had no faith in the charred owl bones, the singed rabbit fur, the cat entrails, the messes and ointments sold by Lupe to the ailing of the village. She was a good Christian, and drank simple herb teas for headache and stomach ache, or bought her remedies bottled, with printed directions that she could not read, at the drugstore near the city market, where she went almost daily. But she often bought a jar of honey from young María Rosa, a pretty, shy child only fifteen years old.

María Concepción and her husband, Juan Villegas, were each a little past their eighteenth year. She had a good reputation with the neighbors as an energetic religious woman who could drive a bargain to the end. It was commonly known that if she wished to buy a new rebozo for herself or a shirt for Juan, she could bring out a sack of hard silver coins for the purpose.

She had paid for the license, nearly a year ago, the potent bit of stamped paper which permits people to be married in the church. She had given money to the priest before she and Juan walked together up to the altar the Monday after Holy Week. It had been the adventure of the villagers to go, three Sundays one after another, to hear the banns called by the priest for Juan de Dios Villegas and María Concepción Manríquez, who were actually getting married in the church, instead of behind it, which was the usual custom, less expensive, and as binding as any other ceremony. But María Concepción was always as proud as if she owned a hacienda.

She paused on the bridge and dabbled her feet in the water, her eyes resting themselves from the sun-rays in a fixed gaze to the far-off mountains, deeply blue under their hanging drift of clouds. It came to her that she would like a fresh crust of honey. The delicious aroma of bees, their slow thrilling hum, awakened a pleasant desire for a flake of sweetness in her mouth.

"If I do not eat it now, I shall mark my child," she thought, peering through the crevices in the thick hedge of cactus that sheered up nakedly, like bared knife blades set protectingly around the small clearing. The place was so silent she doubted if María Rosa and Lupe were at home.

The leaning jacal of dried rush-withes and corn sheaves, bound to tall saplings thrust into the earth, roofed with yellowed maguey leaves flattened and overlapping like shingles, hunched drowsy and fragrant in the warmth of noonday. The hives, similarly made, were scattered towards the back of the clearing, like small mounds of clean vegetable refuse. Over each mound there hung a dusty golden shimmer of bees.

A light gay scream of laughter rose from behind the hut; a man's short laugh joined in. "Ah, hahahaha!" went the voices together high and low, like a song.

"So María Rosa has a man!" María Concepción stopped short, smiling, shifted her burden slightly, and bent forward shading her eyes to see more clearly through the spaces of the hedge.

María Rosa ran, dodging between beehives, parting two stunted jasmine bushes as she came, lifting her knees in swift leaps, looking over her shoulder and laughing in a quivering, excited way. A heavy jar, swung to her wrist by the handle, knocked against her thighs as she ran. Her toes pushed up sudden spurts of dust, her half-raveled braids showered around her shoulders in long crinkled wisps.

Juan Villegas ran after her, also laughing strangely, his teeth set, both rows gleaming behind the small soft black beard growing sparsely on his lips, his chin, leaving his brown cheeks girl-smooth. When he seized her, he clenched so hard her chemise gave way and ripped from her shoulder. She stopped laughing at this, pushed him away and stood silent, trying to pull up the torn sleeve with one hand. Her pointed chin and dark red mouth moved in an uncertain way, as if she wished to laugh again; her long black lashes flickered with the quick-moving lights in her hidden eyes.

María Concepción did not stir nor breathe for some seconds. Her forehead was cold, and yet boiling water seemed to be pouring slowly along her spine. An unaccountable pain was in her knees, as if they were broken. She was afraid Juan and María Rosa would feel her eyes fixed upon them and would find her there, unable to move, spying upon them. But they did not pass beyond the enclosure, nor even glance towards the gap in the wall opening upon the road.

Juan lifted one of María Rosa's loosened braids and slapped her neck with it playfully. She smiled softly, consentingly. Together they moved back through the hives of honey-comb. María Rosa balanced her jar on one hip and swung her long full petticoats with every step. Juan flourished his wide hat back and forth, walking proudly as a game-cock.

María Concepción came out of the heavy cloud which enwrapped her head and bound her throat, and found herself walking onward, keeping the road without knowing it, feeling her way delicately, her ears strumming as if all María Rosa's bees had hived in them. Her careful sense of duty kept her moving toward the buried city where Juan's chief, the American archeologist, was taking his midday rest, waiting for his food.

Juan and María Rosa! She burned all over now, as if a layer of tiny fig-cactus bristles, as cruel as spun glass, had crawled under her skin. She wished to sit down quietly and wait for her death, but not until she had cut the throats of her man and that girl who were laughing and kissing under the cornstalks. Once when she was a young girl she had come back from market to find her jacal burned to a pile of ash and her few silver coins gone. A dark empty feeling had filled her; she kept moving about the place, not believing her eyes, expecting it all to take shape again before her. But it was gone, and though she knew an enemy had done it, she could not find out who it was, and could only curse and threaten the air. Now here was a worse thing, but she knew her enemy. María Rosa, that sinful girl, shameless! She heard herself saying a harsh, true word about María Rosa, saying it aloud as if she expected someone to agree with her: "Yes, she is a whore! She has no right to live."

At this moment the gray untidy head of Givens appeared over the edges of the newest trench he had caused to be dug in his field of excavations. The long deep crevasses, in which a man might stand without being seen, lay crisscrossed like orderly gashes of a giant scalpel. Nearly all of the men of the community worked for Givens, helping him to uncover the lost city of their ancestors. They worked all the year through and prospered, digging every day for those small clay heads and bits of pottery and fragments of painted walls for which there was no good use on earth, being all broken and encrusted with clay. They themselves could make better ones, perfectly stout and new, which they took to town and peddled to foreigners for real money. But the unearthly delight of the chief in finding these wornout things was an endless puzzle. He would fairly roar for joy at times, waving a shattered pot or a human skull above his head, shouting for his photographer to come and make a picture of this!

Now he emerged, and his young enthusiast's eyes welcomed María Concepción from his old-man face, covered with hard wrinkles and burned to the color of red earth. "I hope you've brought me a nice fat one." He selected a fowl from the bunch dangling nearest him as María Concepción, wordless, leaned over the trench. "Dress it for me, there's a good girl. I'll broil it."

María Concepción took the fowl by the head, and silently, swiftly drew her knife across its throat, twisting the head off with the casual firmness she might use with the top of a beet.

"Good God, woman, you do have nerve," said Givens, watching her. "I can't do that. It gives me the creeps."

"My home country is Guadalajara," explained María Concepción, without bravado, as she picked and gutted the fowl.

She stood and regarded Givens condescendingly, that diverting white man who had no woman of his own to cook for him, and moreover appeared not to feel any loss of dignity in preparing his own food. He squatted now, eyes squinted, nose wrinkled to avoid the smoke, turning the roasting fowl busily on a stick. A mysterious man, undoubtedly rich, and Juan's chief, therefore to be respected, to be placated.

"The tortillas are fresh and hot, señor," she murmured gently. "With your permission I will now go to market."

"Yes, yes, run along; bring me another of these tomorrow." Givens turned his head to look at her again. Her grand manner sometimes reminded him of royalty in exile. He noticed her unnatural paleness. "The sun is too hot, eh?" he asked.

"Yes, sir. Pardon me, but Juan will be here soon?"

"He ought to be here now. Leave his food. The others will eat it."

She moved away; the blue of her rebozo became a dancing spot in the heat waves that rose from the gray-red soil. Givens liked his Indians best when he could feel a fatherly indulgence for their primitive childish ways. He told comic stories of Juan's escapades, of how often he had saved him, in the past five years, from going to jail, and even from being shot, for his varied and always unexpected misdeeds.

"I am never a minute too soon to get him out of one pickle or another," he would say. "Well, he's a good worker, and I know how to manage him."

After Juan was married, he used to twit him, with exactly the right shade of condescension, on his many infidelities to María Concepción. "She'll catch you yet, and God help you!" he was fond of saying, and Juan would laugh with immense pleasure.

It did not occur to María Concepción to tell Juan she had found him out. During the day her anger against him died, and her anger against María Rosa grew. She kept saying to herself, "When I was a young girl like María Rosa, if a man had caught hold of me so, I would have broken my jar over his head." She forgot completely that she had not resisted even so much as María Rosa, on the day that Juan had first taken hold of her. Besides she had married him afterwards in the church, and that was a very different thing.

Juan did not come home that night, but went away to war and María Rosa went with him. Juan had a rifle at his shoulder and two pistols at his belt. María Rosa wore a rifle also, slung on her back along with the blankets and the cooking pots. They joined the nearest detachment of troops in the field, and María Rosa marched ahead with the battalion of experienced women of war, which went over the crops like locusts, gathering provisions for the army. She cooked with them, and ate with them what was left after the men had eaten. After battles she went out on the field with the others to salvage clothing and ammunition and guns from the slain before they should begin to swell in the heat. Sometimes they would encounter the women from the other army, and a second battle as grim as the first would take place.

There was no particular scandal in the village. People shrugged, grinned. It was far better that they were gone. The neighbors went around saying that María Rosa was safer in the army than she would be in the same village with María Concepción.

María Concepción did not weep when Juan left her; and when the baby was born, and died within four days, she did not weep. "She is mere stone," said old Lupe, who went over and offered charms to preserve the baby.

"May you rot in hell with your charms," said María Concepción.

If she had not gone so regularly to church, lighting candles before the saints, kneeling with her arms spread in the form of a cross for hours at a time, and receiving holy communion every month, there might have been talk of her being devil-possessed, her face was so changed and blind-looking. But this was impossible when, after all, she had been married by the priest. It must be, they reasoned, that she was being punished for her pride. They decided that this was the true cause for everything: she was altogether too proud. So they pitied her.

During the year that Juan and María Rosa were gone María Concepción sold her fowls and looked after her garden and her sack of hard coins grew. Lupe had no talent for bees, and the hives did not prosper. She began to blame María Rosa for running away, and to praise María Concepción for her behavior. She used to see María Concepción at the market or at church, and she always said that no one could tell by looking at her now that she was a woman who had such a heavy grief.

"I pray God everything goes well with María Concepción from this out," she would say, "for she has had her share of trouble."

When some idle person repeated this to the deserted woman, she went down to Lupe's house and stood within the clearing and called to the medicine woman, who sat in her doorway stirring a mess of her infallible cure for sores: "Keep your prayers to yourself, Lupe, or offer them for others who need them. I will ask God for what I want in this world."

"And will you get it, you think, María Concepción?" asked Lupe, tittering cruelly and smelling the wooden mixing spoon. "Did you pray for what you have now?"

Afterward everyone noticed that María Concepción went oftener to church, and even seldomer to the village to talk with the other women as they sat along the curb, nursing their babies and eating fruit, at the end of the market-day.

"She is wrong to take us for enemies," said old Soledad, who was a thinker and a peace-maker. "All women have these troubles. Well, we should suffer together."

But María Concepción lived alone. She was gaunt, as if something were gnawing her away inside, her eyes were sunken, and she would not speak a word if she could help it. She worked harder than ever, and her butchering knife was scarcely ever out of her hand.

Juan and María Rosa, disgusted with military life, came home one day without asking permission of anyone. The field of war had unrolled itself, a long scroll of vexations, until the end had frayed out within twenty miles of Juan's village. So he and María Rosa, now lean as a wolf, burdened with a child daily expected, set out with no farewells to the regiment and walked home.

They arrived one morning about daybreak. Juan was picked up on sight by a group of military police from the small barracks on the edge of town, and taken to prison, where the officer in charge told him with impersonal cheerfulness that he would add one to a catch of ten waiting to be shot as deserters the next morning.

María Rosa, screaming and falling on her face in the road, was taken under the armpits by two guards and helped briskly to her jacal, now sadly run down. She was received with professional importance by Lupe, who helped the baby to be born at once.

Limping with foot soreness, a layer of dust concealing his fine new clothes got mysteriously from somewhere, Juan appeared before the captain at the barracks. The captain recognized him as head digger for his good friend Givens, and dispatched a note to Givens saying: "I am holding the person of Juan Villegas awaiting your further disposition."

When Givens showed up Juan was delivered to him with the urgent request that nothing be made public about so humane and sensible an operation on the part of military authority.

Juan walked out of the rather stifling atmosphere of the drumhead court, a definite air of swagger about him. His hat, of unreasonable dimensions and embroidered with silver thread, hung over one eyebrow, secured at the back by a cord of silver dripping with bright blue tassels. His shirt was of a checkerboard pattern in green and black, his white cotton trousers were bound by a belt of yellow leather tooled in red. His feet were bare, full of stone bruises, and sadly ragged as to toenails. He removed his cigarette from the corner of his full-lipped wide mouth. He removed the splendid hat. His black dusty hair, pressed moistly to his forehead, sprang up suddenly in a cloudly thatch on his crown. He bowed to the officer, who appeared to be gazing at a vacuum. He swung his arm wide in a free circle upsoaring towards the prison window, where forlorn heads poked over the window sill, hot eyes following after the lucky departing one. Two or three of the heads nodded, and a half dozen hands were flipped at him in an effort to imitate his own casual and heady manner.

Juan kept up this insufferable pantomime until they rounded the first clump of fig-cactus. Then he seized Givens' hand and burst into oratory. "Blessed be the day your servant Juan Villegas first came under your eyes. From this day my life is yours without condition, ten thousand thanks with all my heart!"

"For God's sake stop playing the fool," said Givens irritably. "Some day I'm going to be five minutes too late."

"Well, it is nothing much to be shot, my chief—certainly you know I was not afraid—but to be shot in a drove of deserters, against a cold wall, just in the moment of my home-coming, by order of that . . ."

Glittering epithets tumbled over one another like explosions of a rocket. All the scandalous analogies from the animal and vegetable worlds were applied in a vivid, unique and personal way to the life, loves, and family history of the officer who had just set him free. When he had quite cursed himself dry, and his nerves were soothed, he added: "With your permission, my chief!"

"What will María Concepción say to all this?" asked Givens. "You are very informal, Juan, for a man who was married in the church."

Juan put on his hat.

"Oh, María Concepción! That's nothing. Look, my chief, to be married in the church is a great misfortune for a man. After that he is not himself any more. How can that woman complain when I do not drink even at fiestas enough to be really drunk? I do not beat her; never, never. We were always at peace. I say to her, Come here, and she comes straight. I say, Go there, and she goes quickly. Yet sometimes I looked at her and thought, Now I am married to that woman in the church, and I felt a sinking inside, as if something were lying heavy on my stomach. With María Rosa it is all different. She is not silent; she talks. When she talks too much, I slap her and say, Silence, thou simpleton! and she weeps. She is just a girl with whom I do as I please. You know how she used to keep those clean little bees in their hives? She is like their honey to me. I swear it. I would not harm María Concepción because I am married to her in the church; but also, my chief, I will not leave María Rosa, because she pleases me more than any other woman."

"Let me tell you, Juan, things haven't been going as well as you think. You be careful. Some day María Concepción will just take your head off with that carving knife of hers. You keep that in mind."

Juan's expression was the proper blend of masculine triumph and sentimental melancholy. It was pleasant to see himself in the rôle of hero to two such desirable women. He had just escaped from the threat of a disagreeable end. His clothes were new and handsome, and they had cost him just nothing. María Rosa had collected them for him here and there after battles. He was walking in the early sunshine, smelling the good smells of ripening cactus-figs, peaches, and melons, of pungent berries dangling from the pepper-trees, and the smoke of his cigarette under his nose. He was on his way to civilian life with his patient chief. His situation was ineffably perfect, and he swallowed it whole.

"My chief," he addressed Givens handsomely, as one man of the world to another, "women are good things, but not at this moment. With your permission, I will now go to the village and eat. My God, *how* I shall eat! Tomorrow morning very early I will come to the buried city and work like seven men. Let us forget María Concepción and María Rosa. Each one in her place. I will manage them when the times comes."

News of Juan's adventure soon got abroad, and Juan found many friends about him during the morning. They frankly commended his way of leaving the army. It was in itself the act of a hero. The new hero ate a great deal and drank somewhat, the occasion being better than a feast-day. It was almost noon before he returned to visit María Rosa.

He found her sitting on a clean straw mat, rubbing fat on her three-hour-old son. Before this felicitous vision Juan's emotions so twisted him that he returned to the village and invited every man in the "Death and Resurrection" pulque shop to drink with him.

Having thus taken leave of his balance, he started back to María Rosa, and found himself unaccountably in his own house, attempting to beat María Concepción by way of reëstablishing himself in his legal household.

María Concepción, knowing all the events of that unhappy day, was not in a yielding mood, and refused to be beaten. She did not scream nor implore; she stood her ground and resisted; she even struck at him. Juan, amazed, hardly knowing what he did, stepped back and gazed at her inquiringly through a leisurely whirling film which seemed to have lodged behind his eyes. Certainly he had not even thought of touching her. Oh, well, no harm done. He gave up, turned away, half-asleep on his feet. He dropped amiably in a shadowed corner and began to snore.

María Concepción, seeing that he was quiet, began to bind the legs of her fowls. It was market-day and she was late. She fumbled and tangled the bits of cord in her haste, and set off across the plowed fields instead of taking the accustomed road. She ran with a crazy panic in her head, her stumbling legs. Now and then she would stop and look about her, trying to place herself, then go on a few steps, until she realized that she was not going towards the market.

At once she came to her senses completely, recognized the thing that troubled her so terribly, was certain of what she wanted. She sat down quietly under a sheltering thorny bush and gave herself over to her long devouring sorrow. The thing which had for so long squeezed her whole body into a tight dumb knot of suffering suddenly broke with shocking violence. She jerked with the involuntary recoil of one who receives a blow, and the sweat poured from her skin as if the wounds of her whole life were shedding their salt ichor. Drawing her rebozo over her head, she bowed her forehead on her updrawn knees, and sat there in deadly silence and immobility. From time to time she lifted her head where the sweat formed steadily and poured down her face, drenching the front of her chemise, and her mouth had the shape of crying, but there were no tears and no sound. All her being was a dark confused memory of grief burning in her at night, of deadly baffled anger eating at her by day, until her very tongue tasted bitter, and her feet were as heavy as if she were mired in the muddy roads during the time of rains.

After a great while she stood up and threw the rebozo off her face, and set out walking again.

Juan awakened slowly, with long yawns and grumblings, alternated with short relapses into sleep full of visions and clamors. A blur of orange light seared his eyeballs when he tried to unseal his lids. There came from somewhere a low voice weeping without tears, saying meaningless phrases over and over. He began to listen. He tugged at the leash of his stupor, he strained to grasp those words which terrified him even though he could not quite hear them. Then he came awake with frightening suddenness, sitting up and staring at the long sharpened streak of light piercing the corn-husk walls from the level disappearing sun.

María Concepción stood in the doorway, looming colossally tall to his betrayed eyes. She was talking quickly, and calling his name. Then he saw her clearly.

"God's name!" said Juan, frozen to the marrow, "here I am facing my death!" for the long knife she wore habitually at her belt was in her hand. But instead, she threw it away, clear from her, and got down on her knees, crawling toward him as he had seen her crawl many times toward the shrine at Guadalupe Villa. He watched her approach with such horror that the hair of his head seemed to be lifting itself away from him. Falling forward upon her face, she huddled over him, lips moving in a ghostly whisper. Her words became clear, and Juan understood them all.

For a second he could not move nor speak. Then he took her head between both his hands, and supported her in this way, saying swiftly, anxiously reassuring, almost in a babble:

"Oh, thou poor creature! Oh, madwoman! Oh, my María Concepción, unfortunate! Listen. . . . Don't be afraid. Listen to me! I will hide thee away, I thy own man will protect thee! Quiet! Not a sound!"

Trying to collect himself, he held her and cursed under his breath for a few moments in the gathering darkness. María Concepción bent over, face almost on the ground, her feet folded under her, as if she would hide behind him. For the first time in his life Juan was aware of danger. This was danger. María Concepción would be dragged away between two gendarmes, with him following helpless and unarmed, to spend the rest of her days in Belén Prison, maybe. Danger! The night swarmed with threats. He stood up and dragged her up with him. She was silent and perfectly rigid, holding to him with resistless strength, her hands stiffened on his arms.

"Get me the knife," he told her in a whisper. She obeyed, her feet slipping along the hard earth floor, her shoulders straight, her arms close to her side. He lighted a candle. María Concepción held the knife out to him. It was stained and dark even to the handle with drying blood.

He frowned at her harshly, noting the same stains on her chemise and hands.

"Take off thy clothes and wash thy hands," he ordered. He washed the knife carefully, and threw the water wide of the doorway. She watched him and did likewise with the bowl in which she had bathed.

"Light the brasero and cook food for me," he told her in the same peremptory tone. He took her garments and went out. When he returned, she was wearing an old soiled dress, and was fanning the fire in the charcoal burner. Seating himself cross-legged near her, he stared at her as at a creature unknown to him, who bewildered him utterly, for whom there was no possible explanation. She did not turn her head, but kept silent and still, except for the movements of her strong hands fanning the blaze which cast sparks and small jets of white smoke, flaring and dying rhythmically with the motion of the fan, lighting her face and darkening it by turns.

Juan's voice barely disturbed the silence: "Listen to me carefully, and tell me the truth, and when the gendarmes come here for us, thou shalt have nothing to fear. But there will be something for us to settle between us afterward."

The light from the charcoal burner shone in her eyes; a yellow phosphorescence glimmered behind the dark iris.

"For me everything is settled now," she answered, in a tone so tender, so grave, so heavy with suffering, that Juan felt his vitals contract. He wished to repent openly, not as a man, but as a very small child. He could not fathom her, nor himself, nor the mysterious fortunes of life grown so instantly confused where all had seemed so gay and simple. He felt too that she had become invaluable, a woman without equal among a million women, and he could not tell why. He drew an enormous sigh that rattled in his chest.

"Yes, yes, it is all settled. I shall not go away again. We must stay here together."

Whispering, he questioned her and she answered whispering, and he instructed her over and over until she had her lesson by heart. The hostile darkness of the night encroached upon them, flowing over the narrow threshold, invading their hearts. It brought with it sighs and murmurs, the pad of secretive feet in the near-by road, the sharp staccato whimper of wind through the cactus leaves. All these familiar, once friendly cadences were now invested with sinister terrors; a dread, formless and uncontrollable, took hold of them both.

"Light another candle," said Juan, loudly, in too resolute, too sharp a tone. "Let us eat now."

They sat facing each other and ate from the same dish, after their old habit. Neither tasted what they ate. With food half-way to his mouth, Juan listened. The sound of voices rose, spread, widened at the turn of the road along the cactus wall. A spray of lantern light shot through the hedge, a single voice slashed the blackness, ripped the fragile layer of silence suspended above the hut.

"Juan Villegas!"

"Pass, friends!" Juan roared back cheerfully.

They stood in the doorway, simple cautious gendarmes from the village, mixed-bloods themselves with Indian sympathies, well known to all the community. They flashed their lanterns almost apologetically upon the pleasant, harmless scene of a man eating supper with his wife.

"Pardon, brother," said the leader. "Someone has killed the woman María Rosa, and we must question her neighbors and friends." He paused, and added with an attempt at severity, "Naturally!"

"Naturally," agreed Juan. "You know that I was a good friend of María Rosa. This is bad news."

They all went away together, the men walking in a group, María Concepción following a few steps in the rear, near Juan. No one spoke.

The two points of candlelight at María Rosa's head fluttered uneasily; the shadows shifted and dodged on the stained darkened walls. To María Concepción everything in the smothering enclosing room shared an evil restlessness. The watchful faces of those called as witnesses, the faces of old friends, were made alien by the look of speculation in their eyes. The ridges of the rose-colored rebozo thrown over the body varied continually, as though the thing it covered was not perfectly in repose. Her eyes swerved over the body in the open painted coffin, from the candle tips at the head to the feet, jutting up thinly, the small scarred soles protruding, freshly washed, a mass of crooked, half-healed wounds, thorn-pricks and cuts of sharp stones. Her gaze went back to the candle flame, to Juan's eyes warning her, to the gendarmes talking among themselves. Her eyes would not be controlled.

With a leap that shook her her gaze settled upon the face of María Rosa. Instantly her blood ran smoothly again: there was nothing to fear.

Even the restless light could not give a look of life to that fixed countenance. She was dead. María Concepción felt her muscles give way
softly; her heart began beating steadily without effort. She knew no more
rancor against that pitiable thing, lying indifferently in its blue coffin
under the fine silk rebozo. The mouth drooped sharply at the corners in
a grimace of weeping arrested half-way. The brows were distressed; the
dead flesh could not cast off the shape of its last terror. It was all finished.
María Rosa had eaten too much honey and had had too much love. Now
she must sit in hell, crying over her sins and her hard death forever and
ever.

Old Lupe's cackling voice arose. She had spent the morning helping
María Rosa, and it had been hard work. The child had spat blood the
moment it was born, a bad sign. She thought then that bad luck would
come to the house. Well, about sunset she was in the yard at the back of
the house grinding tomatoes and peppers. She had left mother and babe
asleep. She heard a strange noise in the house, a choking and smothered
calling, like someone wailing in sleep. Well, such a thing is only natural.
But there followed a light, quick, thudding sound—

"Like the blows of a fist?" interrupted an officer.

"No, not at all like such a thing."

"How do you know?"

"I am well acquainted with that sound, friends," retorted Lupe. "This
was something else."

She was at a loss to describe it exactly. A moment later, there came the
sound of pebbles rolling and slipping under feet; then she knew someone
had been there and was running away.

"Why did you wait so long before going to see?"

"I am old and hard in the joints," said Lupe. "I cannot run after people.
I walked as fast as I could to the cactus hedge, for it is only by this way
that anyone can enter. There was no one in the road, sir, no one. Three
cows, and a dog driving them; nothing else. When I got to María Rosa,
she was lying all tangled up, and from her neck to her middle she was
full of knife-holes. It was a sight to move the Blessed Image Himself!
Her eyes were—"

"Never mind. Who came oftenest to her house before she went away?
Did you know her enemies?"

Lupe's face congealed, closed. Her spongy skin drew into a network of
secretive wrinkles. She turned withdrawn and expressionless eyes upon
the gendarmes.

"I am an old woman. I do not see well. I cannot hurry on my feet. I
know no enemy of María Rosa. I did not see anyone leave the clearing."

"You did not hear splashing in the spring near the bridge?"

"No, sir."

"Why, then, do our dogs follow a scent there and lose it?"

"God only knows, my friend. I am an old wo—"

"Yes. How did the footfalls sound?"

"Like the tread of an evil spirit!" Lupe broke forth in a swelling oracular tone that startled them. The Indians stirred uneasily, glanced at the dead, then at Lupe. They half expected her to produce the evil spirit among them at once.

The gendarme began to lose his temper.

"No, poor unfortunate; I mean, were they heavy or light? The foot-steps of a man or of a woman? Was the person shod or barefoot?"

A glance at the listening circle assured Lupe of their thrilled attention. She enjoyed the dangerous importance of her situation. She could have ruined that María Concepción with a word, but it was even sweeter to make fools of these gendarmes who went about spying on honest people. She raised her voice again. What she had not seen she could not describe, thank God! No one could harm her because her knees were stiff and she could not run even to seize a murderer. As for knowing the difference between footfalls, shod or bare, man or woman, nay, between devil and human, who ever heard of such madness?

"My eyes are not ears, gentlemen," she ended grandly, "but upon my heart I swear those footsteps fell as the tread of the spirit of evil!"

"Imbecile!" yapped the leader in a shrill voice. "Take her away, one of you! Now, Juan Villegas, tell me—"

Juan told his story patiently, several times over. He had returned to his wife that day. She had gone to market as usual. He had helped her prepare her fowls. She had returned about mid-afternoon, they had talked, she had cooked, they had eaten, nothing was amiss. Then the gendarmes came with the news about María Rosa. That was all. Yes, María Rosa had run away with him, but there had been no bad blood between him and his wife on this account, nor between his wife and María Rosa. Everybody knew that his wife was a quiet woman.

María Concepción heard her own voice answering without a break. It was true at first she was troubled when her husband went away, but after that she had not worried about him. It was the way of men, she believed. She was a church-married woman and knew her place. Well, he had come home at last. She had gone to market, but had come back early, because now she had her man to cook for. That was all.

Other voices broke in. A toothless old man said: "She is a woman of good reputation among us, and María Rosa was not." A smiling young mother, Anita, baby at breast, said: "If no one thinks so, how can you accuse her? It was the loss of her child and not of her husband that changed her so." Another: "María Rosa had a strange life, apart from us. How do we know who might have come from another place to do her evil?" And old Soledad spoke up boldly: "When I saw María Concepción in the market today, I said, 'Good luck to you, María Concepción, this is a happy day for you!' " and she gave María Concepción a long easy stare, and the smile of a born wise-woman.

María Concepción suddenly felt herself guarded, surrounded, upborne by her faithful friends. They were around her, speaking for her, defending her, the forces of life were ranged invincibly with her against the beaten dead. María Rosa had thrown away her share of strength in them, she lay forfeited among them. María Concepción looked from one to the other of the circling, intent faces. Their eyes gave back reassurance, understanding, a secret and mighty sympathy.

The gendarmes were at a loss. They, too, felt that sheltering wall cast impenetrably around her. They were certain she had done it, and yet they could not accuse her. Nobody could be accused; there was not a shred of true evidence. They shrugged their shoulders and snapped their fingers and shuffled their feet. Well, then, good night to everybody. Many pardons for having intruded. Good health!

A small bundle lying against the wall at the head of the coffin squirmed like an eel. A wail, a mere sliver of sound, issued. María Concepción took the son of María Rosa in her arms.

"He is mine," she said clearly, "I will take him with me."

No one assented in words, but an approving nod, a bare breath of complete agreement, stirred among them as they made way for her.

María Concepción, carrying the child, followed Juan from the clearing. The hut was left with its lighted candles and a crowd of old women who would sit up all night, drinking coffee and smoking and telling ghost stories.

Juan's exaltation had burned out. There was not an ember of excitement left in him. He was tired. The perilous adventure was over. María Rosa had vanished, to come no more forever. Their days of marching, of eating, of quarreling and making love between battles, were all over. Tomorrow he would go back to dull and endless labor, he must descend into the trenches of the buried city as María Rosa must go into her grave. He felt his veins fill up with bitterness, with black unendurable melancholy. Oh, Jesus! what bad luck overtakes a man!

Well, there was no way out of it now. For the moment he craved only to sleep. He was so drowsy he could scarcely guide his feet. The occasional light touch of the woman at his elbow was as unreal, as ghostly as the brushing of a leaf against his face. He did not know why he had fought to save her, and now he forgot her. There was nothing in him except a vast blind hurt like a covered wound.

He entered the jacal, and without waiting to light a candle, threw off his clothing, sitting just within the door. He moved with lagging, half-awake hands, to strip his body of its heavy finery. With a long groaning sigh of relief he fell straight back on the floor, almost instantly asleep, his arms flung up and outward.

María Concepción, a small clay jar in her hand, approached the gentle little mother goat tethered to a sapling, which gave and yielded as she pulled at the rope's end after the farthest reaches of grass about her. The kid, tied up a few feet away, rose bleating, its feathery fleece shivering in the fresh wind. Sitting on her heels, holding his tether, she allowed him to suckle a few moments. Afterward—all her movements very deliberate and even—she drew a supply of milk for the child.

She sat against the wall of her house, near the doorway. The child, fed and asleep, was cradled in the hollow of her crossed legs. The silence overfilled the world, the skies flowed down evenly to the rim of the valley, the stealthy moon crept slantwise to the shelter of the mountains. She felt soft and warm all over; she dreamed that the newly born child was her own, and she was resting deliciously.

María Concepción could hear Juan's breathing. The sound vapored from the low doorway, calmly; the house seemed to be resting after a burdensome day. She breathed, too, very slowly and quietly, each inspiration saturating her with repose. The child's light, faint breath was a mere shadowy moth of sound in the silver air. The night, the earth under her, seemed to swell and recede together with a limitless, unhurried, benign breathing. She drooped and closed her eyes, feeling the slow rise and fall within her own body. She did not know what it was, but it eased her all through. Even as she was falling asleep, head bowed over the child, she was still aware of a strange, wakeful happiness.

57

The Secret Life of Walter Mitty

BY JAMES THURBER

WE'RE going through!" The Commander's voice was like thin ice breaking. He wore his full-dress uniform, with the heavily braided white cap pulled down rakishly over one cold gray eye. "We can't make it, sir. It's spoiling for a hurricane, if you ask me." "I'm not asking you, Lieutenant Berg," said the Commander. "Throw on the power light! Rev her up to 8,500! We're going through!" The pounding of the cylinders increased: ta-pocketa-pocketa-pocketa-*pocketa-pocketa*. The Commander stared at the ice forming on the pilot window. He walked over and twisted a row of complicated dials. "Switch on No. 8 auxiliary!" he shouted. "Switch on No. 8 auxiliary!" repeated Lieutenant Berg. "Full strength in No. 3 turret!" shouted the Commander. "Full strength in No. 3 turret!" The crew, bending to their various tasks in the huge, hurtling eight-engined Navy hydroplane, looked at each other and grinned. "The Old Man'll get us through," they said to one another. "The Old Man ain't afraid of Hell!" . . .

"Not so fast! You're driving too fast!" said Mrs. Mitty. "What are you driving so fast for?"

"Hmm?" said Walter Mitty. He looked at his wife, in the seat beside him, with shocked astonishment. She seemed grossly unfamiliar, like a strange woman who had yelled at him in a crowd. "You were up to fifty-five," she said. "You know I don't like to go more than forty. You were up to fifty-five." Walter Mitty drove on toward Waterbury in silence, the roaring of the SN202 through the worst storm in twenty years of Navy flying fading in the remote, intimate airways of his mind. "You're tensed up again," said Mrs. Mitty. "It's one of your days. I wish you'd let Dr. Renshaw look you over."

Walter Mitty stopped the car in front of the building where his wife went to have her hair done. "Remember to get those overshoes while I'm having my hair done," she said. "I don't need overshoes," said Mitty. She put her mirror back into her bag. "We've been all through that," she said, getting out of the car. "You're not a young man any longer." He raced the engine a little. "Why don't you wear your gloves? Have you lost your gloves?" Walter Mitty reached in a pocket and brought out the gloves. He put them on, but after she had turned and gone into the building and he had driven on to a red light, he took them off again. "Pick it up, brother!" snapped a cop as the light changed, and Mitty hastily pulled on his gloves and lurched ahead. He drove around the streets aimlessly for a time, and then he drove past the hospital on his way to the parking lot.

. . . "It's the millionaire banker, Wellington McMillan," said the pretty nurse. "Yes?" said Walter Mitty, removing his gloves slowly. "Who has the case?" "Dr. Renshaw and Dr. Benbow, but there are two specialists here, Dr. Remington from New York and Mr. Pritchard-Mitford from London. He flew over." A door opened down a long, cool corridor and Dr. Renshaw came out. He looked distraught and haggard. "Hello, Mitty," he said. "We're having the devil's own time with McMillan, the millionaire banker and close personal friend of Roosevelt. Obstreosis of the ductal tract. Tertiary. Wish you'd take a look at him." "Glad to," said Mitty.

In the operating room there were whispered introductions: "Dr. Remington, Dr. Mitty. Mr. Pritchard-Mitford, Dr. Mitty." "I've read your book on streptothricosis," said Pritchard-Mitford, shaking hands. "A brilliant performance, sir." "Thank you," said Walter Mitty. "Didn't know you were in the States, Mitty," grumbled Remington. "Coals to Newcastle, bringing Mitford and me up here for a tertiary." "You are very kind," said Mitty. A huge, complicated machine, connected to the operating table, with many tubes and wires, began at this moment to go pocketa-pocketa-pocketa. "The new anesthetizer is giving way!" shouted an interne. "There is no one in the East who knows how to fix it!" "Quiet, man!" said Mitty, in a low, cool voice. He sprang to the machine, which was now going pocketa-pocketa-queep-pocketa-queep. He began fingering delicately a row of glistening dials. "Give me a fountain pen!" he snapped. Someone handed him a fountain pen. He pulled a faulty piston out of the machine and inserted the pen in its place. "That will hold for ten minutes," he said. "Get on with the operation." A nurse hurried over and whispered to Renshaw, and Mitty saw the man turn pale. "Coreopsis has set in," said Renshaw nervously. "If you would take over, Mitty?" Mitty looked at him and at the craven figure of Benbow, who drank, and at the grave, uncertain faces of the two great specialists. "If you wish," he said. They slipped a white gown on him; he adjusted a mask and drew on thin gloves; nurses handed him shining . . .

"Back it up, Mac! Look out for that Buick!" Walter Mitty jammed on the brakes. "Wrong lane, Mac," said the parking-lot attendant, looking at Mitty closely. "Gee. Yeh," muttered Mitty. He began cautiously to back out of the lane marked "Exit Only." "Leave her sit there," said the attendant. "I'll put her away." Mitty got out of the car. "Hey, better leave the key." "Oh," said Mitty, handing the man the ignition key. The attendant vaulted into the car, backed it up with insolent skill, and put it where it belonged.

They're so damn cocky, thought Walter Mitty, walking along Main Street; they think they know everything. Once he had tried to take his chains off, outside New Milford, and he had got them wound around the axles. A man had had to come out in a wrecking car and unwind them, a young, grinning garageman. Since then Mrs. Mitty always made him drive to a garage to have the chains taken off. The next time, he thought, I'll wear my right arm in a sling; they won't grin at me then. I'll have my right arm in a sling and they'll see I couldn't possibly take the chains off myself. He kicked at the slush on the sidewalk. "Overshoes," he said to himself, and he began looking for a shoe store.

When he came out into the street again, with the overshoes in a box under his arm, Walter Mitty began to wonder what the other thing was his wife had told him to get. She had told him twice, before they set out from their house for Waterbury. In a way he hated these weekly trips to town—he was always getting something wrong. Kleenex, he thought, Squibb's, razor blades? No. Toothpaste, toothbrush, bicarbonate, carborundum, initiative and referendum? He gave it up. But she would remember it. "Where's the what's-its-name?" she would ask. "Don't tell me you forgot the what's-its-name." A newsboy went by shouting something about the Waterbury trial.

. . . "Perhaps this will refresh your memory." The District Attorney suddenly thrust a heavy automatic at the quiet figure on the witness stand. "Have you ever seen this before?" Walter Mitty took the gun and examined it expertly. "This is my Webley-Vickers 50.80," he said calmly. An excited buzz ran around the courtroom. The judge rapped for order. "You are a crack shot with any sort of firearms, I believe?" said the District Attorney, insinuatingly. "Objection!" shouted Mitty's attorney. "We have shown that the defendant could not have fired the shot. We have shown that he wore his right arm in a sling on the night of the fourteenth of July." Walter Mitty raised his hand briefly and the bickering attorneys were stilled. "With any known make of gun," he said evenly, "I could have killed Gregory Fitzhurst at three hundred feet *with my left hand."* Pandemonium broke loose in the courtroom. A woman's scream rose above the bedlam and suddenly a lovely, dark-haired girl was in Walter Mitty's arms. The District Attorney struck at her savagely. Without rising from his chair, Mitty let the man have it on the point of the chin. "You miserable cur!" . . .

"Puppy biscuit," said Walter Mitty. He stopped walking and the buildings of Waterbury rose up out of the misty courtroom and surrounded him again. A woman who was passing laughed. "He said 'Puppy biscuit,'" she said to her companion. "That man said 'Puppy biscuit' to himself." Walter Mitty hurried on. He went into an A. & P., not the first one he came to but a smaller one farther up the street. "I want some biscuit for small, young dogs," he said to the clerk. "Any special brand, sir?" The greatest pistol shot in the world thought a moment. "It says 'Puppies Bark for It' on the box," said Walter Mitty.

His wife would be through at the hairdresser's in fifteen minutes, Mitty saw in looking at his watch, unless they had trouble drying it; sometimes they had trouble drying it. She didn't like to get to the hotel first; she would want him to be there waiting for her as usual. He found a big leather chair in the lobby, facing a window, and he put the overshoes and the puppy biscuit on the floor beside it. He picked up an old copy of *Liberty* and sank down into the chair. "Can Germany Conquer the World Through the Air?" Walter Mitty looked at the pictures of bombing planes and of ruined streets.

. . . "The cannonading has got the wind up in young Raleigh, sir," said the sergeant. Captain Mitty looked up at him through tousled hair. "Get him to bed," he said wearily. "With the others. I'll fly alone." "But you can't, sir," said the sergeant anxiously. "It takes two men to handle that bomber and the Archies are pounding hell out of the air. Von Richtman's circus is between here and Saulier." "Somebody's got to get that ammunition dump," said Mitty. "I'm going over. Spot of brandy?" He poured a drink for the sergeant and one for himself. War thundered and whined around the dugout and battered at the door. There was a rending of wood and splinters flew through the room. "A bit of a near thing," said Captain Mitty carelessly. "The box barrage is closing in," said the sergeant. "We only live once, Sergeant," said Mitty, with his faint, fleeting smile. "Or do we?" He poured another brandy and tossed it off. "I never see a man could hold his brandy like you, sir," said the sergeant. "Begging your pardon, sir." Captain Mitty stood up and strapped on his huge Webley-Vickers automatic. "It's forty kilometers through hell, sir," said the sergeant. Mitty finished one last brandy. "After all," he said softly, "what isn't?" The pounding of the cannon increased; there was the rat-tat-tatting of machine guns, and from somewhere came the menacing pocketa-pocketa-pocketa of the new flame-throwers. Walter Mitty walked to the door of the dugout humming "Auprès de Ma Blonde." He turned and waved to the sergeant. "Cheerio!" he said. . . .

Something struck his shoulder. "I've been looking all over this hotel for you," said Mrs. Mitty. "Why do you have to hide in this old chair? How did you expect me to find you?" "Things close in," said Walter Mitty vaguely. "What?" Mrs. Mitty said. "Did you get the what's-its-name? The puppy biscuit? What's in that box?" "Overshoes," said Mitty. "Couldn't you have put them on in the store?" "I was thinking," said Walter Mitty. "Does it ever occur to you that I am sometimes thinking?" She looked at him. "I'm going to take your temperature when I get you home," she said.

They went out through the revolving doors that made a faintly derisive whistling sound when you pushed them. It was two blocks to the parking lot. At the drugstore on the corner she said, "Wait here for me. I forgot something. I won't be a minute." She was more than a minute. Walter Mitty lighted a cigarette. It began to rain, rain with sleet in it. He stood up against the wall of the drugstore, smoking. . . . He put his shoulders back and his heels together. "To hell with the handkerchief," said Walter Mitty scornfully. He took one last drag on his cigarette and snapped it away. Then, with that faint, fleeting smile playing about his lips, he faced the firing squad; erect and motionless, proud and disdainful, Walter Mitty the Undefeated, inscrutable to the last.

58

The Rich Boy

BY F. SCOTT FITZGERALD

BEGIN with an individual, and before you know it you find that you have created a type; begin with a type, and you find that you have created—nothing. That is because we are all queer fish, queerer behind our faces and voices than we want any one to know or than we know ourselves. When I hear a man proclaiming himself an "average, honest, open fellow," I feel pretty sure that he has some definite and perhaps terrible abnormality which he has agreed to conceal—and his protestation of being average and honest and open is his way of reminding himself of his misprision.

There are no types, no plurals. There is a rich boy, and this is his and not his brothers' story. All my life I have lived among his brothers but this one has been my friend. Besides, if I wrote about his brothers I should have to begin by attacking all the lies that the poor have told about the rich and the rich have told about themselves—such a wild structure they have erected that when we pick up a book about the rich, some instinct prepares us for unreality. Even the intelligent and impassioned reporters of life have made the country of the rich as unreal as fairy-land.

Let me tell you about the very rich. They are different from you and me. They possess and enjoy early, and it does something to them, makes them soft where we are hard, and cynical where we are trustful, in a way that, unless you were born rich, it is very difficult to understand. They think, deep in their hearts, that they are better than we are because we had to discover the compensations and refuges of life for ourselves. Even when they enter deep into our world or sink below us, they still think that they are better than we are. They are different. The only way I can describe young Anson Hunter is to approach him as if he were a foreigner and cling stubbornly to my point of view. If

I accept his for a moment I am lost—I have nothing to show but a preposterous movie.

II

Anson was the eldest of six children who would some day divide a fortune of fifteen million dollars, and he reached the age of reason—is it seven?—at the beginning of the century when daring young women were already gliding along Fifth Avenue in electric "mobiles." In those days he and his brother had an English governess who spoke the language very clearly and crisply and well, so that the two boys grew to speak as she did—their words and sentences were all crisp and clear and not run together as ours are. They didn't talk exactly like English children but acquired an accent that is peculiar to fashionable people in the city of New York.

In the summer the six children were moved from the house on 71st Street to a big estate in Northern Connecticut. It was not a fashionable locality—Anson's father wanted to delay as long as possible his children's knowledge of that side of life. He was a man somewhat superior to his class, which composed New York society, and to his period, which was the snobbish and formalized vulgarity of the Gilded Age, and he wanted his sons to learn habits of concentration and have sound constitutions and grow up into right-living and successful men. He and his wife kept an eye on them as well as they were able until the two older boys went away to school, but in huge establishments this is difficult—it was much simpler in the series of small and medium-sized houses in which my own youth was spent—I was never far out of the reach of my mother's voice, of the sense of her presence, her approval or disapproval.

Anson's first sense of his superiority came to him when he realized the half-grudging American deference that was paid to him in the Connecticut village. The parents of the boys he played with always inquired after his father and mother, and were vaguely excited when their own children were asked to the Hunters' house. He accepted this as the natural state of things, and a sort of impatience with all groups of which he was not the center—in money, in position, in authority—remained with him for the rest of his life. He disdained to struggle with other boys for precedence—he expected it to be given him freely, and when it wasn't he withdrew into his family. His family was sufficient, for in the East money is still a somewhat feudal thing, a clan-forming thing. In the snobbish West, money separates families to form "sets."

At eighteen, when he went to New Haven, Anson was tall and thick-set, with a clear complexion and a healthy color from the ordered life he had led in school. His hair was yellow and grew in a funny way on his head, his nose was beaked—these two things kept him from being handsome—but he had a confident charm and a certain brusque style, and the upper-class men who passed him on the street knew without being told that he was a rich boy and had gone to one of the best schools. Nevertheless, his very superiority kept him from being a success in college—the independence was mistaken for egotism, and the refusal to accept Yale standards with the proper awe seemed to belittle all those who had. So, long before he graduated, he began to shift the center of his life to New York.

He was at home in New York—there was his own house with "the kind of servants you can't get any more"—and his own family, of which, because of his good humor and a certain ability to make things go, he was rapidly becoming the center, and the débutante parties, and the correct manly world of the men's clubs, and the occasional wild spree with the gallant girls whom New Haven only knew from the fifth row. His aspirations were conventional enough—they included even the irreproachable shadow he would some day marry, but they differed from the aspirations of the majority of young men in that there was no mist over them, none of that quality which is variously known as "idealism" or "illusion." Anson accepted without reservation the world of high finance and high extravagance, of divorce and dissipation, of snobbery and of privilege. Most of our lives end as a compromise—it was as a compromise that his life began.

He and I first met in the late summer of 1917 when he was just out of Yale, and, like the rest of us, was swept up into the systematized hysteria of the war. In the blue-green uniform of the naval aviation he came down to Pensacola, where the hotel orchestras played "I'm Sorry, Dear," and we young officers danced with the girls. Everyone liked him, and though he ran with the drinkers and wasn't an especially good pilot, even the instructors treated him with a certain respect. He was always having long talks with them in his confident, logical voice—talks which ended by his getting himself, or, more frequently, another young officer, out of some impending trouble. He was convivial, bawdy, robustly avid for pleasure, and we were all surprised when he fell in love with a conservative and rather proper girl.

Her name was Paula Legendre, a dark, serious beauty from somewhere in California. Her family kept a winter residence just outside of town, and in spite of her primness she was enormously popular; there is a large class of men whose egotism can't endure humor in a woman. But Anson wasn't that sort, and I couldn't understand the attraction of her "sincerity"—that was the thing to say about her—for his keen and somewhat sardonic mind.

Nevertheless, they fell in love—and on her terms. He no longer joined the twilight gathering at the De Sota bar, and whenever they were seen together they were engaged in a long, serious dialogue, which must have gone on several weeks. Long afterward he told me that it was not about anything in particular but was composed on both sides of immature and even meaningless statements—the emotional content that gradually came to fill it grew up not out of the words but out of its enormous seriousness. It was a sort of hypnosis. Often it was interrupted, giving way to that emasculated humor we call fun; when they were alone it was resumed again, solemn, low-keyed, and pitched so as to give each other a sense of unity in feeling and thought. They came to resent any interruptions of it, to be unresponsive to facetiousness about life, even to the mild cynicism of their contemporaries. They were only happy when the dialogue was going on, and its seriousness bathed them like the amber glow of an open fire. Toward the end there came an interruption they did not resent—it began to be interrupted by passion.

Oddly enough, Anson was as engrossed in the dialogue as she was and as profoundly affected by it, yet at the same time aware that on his side much was insincere, and on hers much was merely simple. At first, too, he despised her emotional simplicity as well, but with his love her nature deepened and blossomed, and he could despise it no longer. He felt that if he could enter into Paula's warm safe life he would be happy. The long preparation of the dialogue removed any constraint— he taught her some of what he had learned from more adventurous women, and she responded with a rapt holy intensity. One evening after a dance they agreed to marry, and he wrote a long letter about her to his mother. The next day Paula told him that she was rich, that she had a personal fortune of nearly a million dollars.

III

It was exactly as if they could say "Neither of us has anything: we shall be poor together"—just as delightful that they should be rich instead. It gave them the same communion of adventure. Yet when Anson got leave in April, and Paula and her mother accompanied him North, she was impressed with the standing of his family in New York and with the scale on which they lived. Alone with Anson for the first time in the rooms where he had played as a boy, she was filled with a comfortable emotion, as though she were pre-eminently safe and taken care of. The pictures of Anson in a skull cap at his first school, of Anson on horseback with the sweetheart of a mysterious forgotten summer, of Anson in a gay group of ushers and bridesmaids at a wedding, made her jealous of his life apart from her in the past, and so completely did his authoritative person seem to sum up and typify these possessions of his that she was inspired with the idea of being married immediately and returning to Pensacola as his wife.

But an immediate marriage wasn't discussed—even the engagement was to be secret until after the war. When she realized that only two days of his leave remained, her dissatisfaction crystallized in the intention of making him as unwilling to wait as she was. They were driving to the country for dinner and she determined to force the issue that night.

Now a cousin of Paula's was staying with them at the Ritz, a severe, bitter girl who loved Paula but was somewhat jealous of her impressive engagement, and as Paula was late in dressing, the cousin, who wasn't going to the party, received Anson in the parlor of the suite.

Anson had met friends at five o'clock and drunk freely and indiscreetly with them for an hour. He left the Yale Club at a proper time, and his mother's chauffeur drove him to the Ritz, but his usual capacity was not in evidence, and the impact of the steam-heated sitting-room made him suddenly dizzy. He knew it, and he was both amused and sorry.

Paula's cousin was twenty-five, but she was exceptionally naïve, and at first failed to realize what was up. She had never met Anson before, and she was surprised when he mumbled strange information and nearly fell off his chair, but until Paula appeared it didn't occur to her that what she had taken for the odor of a dry-cleaned uniform was really whisky. But Paula understood as soon as she appeared; her only thought was to get Anson away before her mother saw him, and at the look in her eyes the cousin understood too.

When Paula and Anson descended to the limousine they found two men inside, both asleep; they were the men with whom he had been drinking at the Yale Club, and they were also going to the party. He had entirely forgotten their presence in the car. On the way to Hempstead they awoke and sang. Some of the songs were rough, and though Paula tried to reconcile herself to the fact that Anson had few verbal inhibitions, her lips tightened with shame and distaste.

Back at the hotel the cousin, confused and agitated, considered the incident, and then walked into Mrs. Legendre's bedroom, saying: "Isn't he funny?"

"Who is funny?"

"Why—Mr. Hunter. He seemed so funny."

Mrs. Legendre looked at her sharply.

"How is he funny?"

"Why, he said he was French. I didn't know he was French."

"That's absurd. You must have misunderstood." She smiled: "It was a joke."

The cousin shook her head stubbornly.

"No. He said he was brought up in France. He said he couldn't speak any English, and that's why he couldn't talk to me. And he couldn't!"

Mrs. Legendre looked away with impatience just as the cousin added thoughtfully, "Perhaps it was because he was so drunk," and walked out of the room.

This curious report was true. Anson, finding his voice thick and un-controllable, had taken the unusual refuge of announcing that he spoke no English. Years afterwards he used to tell that part of the story, and he invariably communicated the uproarious laughter which the memory aroused in him.

Five times in the next hour Mrs. Legendre tried to get Hempstead on the phone. When she succeeded, there was a ten-minute delay before she heard Paula's voice on the wire.

"Cousin Jo told me Anson was intoxicated."

"Oh, no. . . ."

"Oh, yes. Cousin Jo says he was intoxicated. He told her he was French, and fell off his chair and behaved as if he was very intoxicated. I don't want you to come home with him."

"Mother, he's all right! Please don't worry about——"

"But I do worry. I think it's dreadful. I want you to promise me not to come home with him."

"I'll take care of it, mother. . . ."

"I don't want you to come home with him."

"All right, mother. Good-by."

"Be sure now, Paula. Ask some one to bring you."

Deliberately Paula took the receiver from her ear and hung it up. Her face was flushed with helpless annoyance. Anson was stretched asleep out in a bedroom upstairs, while the dinner-party below was proceeding lamely toward conclusion.

The hour's drive had sobered him somewhat—his arrival was merely hilarious—and Paula hoped that the evening was not spoiled, after all, but two imprudent cocktails before dinner completed the disaster. He talked boisterously and somewhat offensively to the party at large for fifteen minutes, and then slid silently under the table; like a man in an old print—but, unlike an old print, it was rather horrible without being at all quaint. None of the young girls present remarked upon the incident—it seemed to merit only silence. His uncle and two other men carried him up-stairs, and it was just after this that Paula was called to the phone.

An hour later Anson awoke in a fog of nervous agony, through which he perceived after a moment the figure of his uncle Robert standing by the door.

". . . I said are you better?"

"What?"

"Do you feel better, old man?"

"Terrible," said Anson.

"I'm going to try you on another bromo-seltzer. If you can hold it down, it'll do you good to sleep."

With an effort Anson slid his legs from the bed and stood up.

"I'm all right," he said dully.

"Take it easy."

"I thin' if you gave me a glassbrandy I could go down-stairs."

"Oh, no——"

"Yes, that's the only thin'. I'm all right now. . . . I suppose I'm in Dutch dow' there."

"They know you're a little under the weather," said his uncle deprecatingly. "But don't worry about it. Schuyler didn't even get here. He passed away in the locker-room over at the Links."

Indifferent to any opinion, except Paula's, Anson was nevertheless determined to save the débris of the evening, but when after a cold bath he made his appearance most of the party had already left. Paula got up immediately to go home.

In the limousine the old serious dialogue began. She had known that he drank, she admitted, but she had never expected anything like this —it seemed to her that perhaps they were not suited to each other, after all. Their ideas about life were too different, and so forth. When she finished speaking, Anson spoke in turn, very soberly. Then Paula said she'd have to think it over; she wouldn't decide tonight; she was not angry but she was terribly sorry. Nor would she let him come into the hotel with her, but just before she got out of the car she leaned and kissed him unhappily on the cheek.

The next afternoon Anson had a long talk with Mrs. Legendre while Paula sat listening in silence. It was agreed that Paula was to brood over the incident for a proper period and then, if mother and daughter thought it best, they would follow Anson to Pensacola. On his part he apologized with sincerity and dignity—that was all; with every card in her hand Mrs. Legendre was unable to establish any advantage over him. He made no promises, showed no humility, only delivered a few serious comments on life which brought him off with rather a moral superiority at the end. When they came South three weeks later, neither Anson in his satisfaction nor Paula in her relief at the reunion realized that the psychological moment had passed forever.

IV

He dominated and attracted her, and at the same time filled her with anxiety. Confused by his mixture of solidity and self-indulgence, of sentiment and cynicism—incongruities which her gentle mind was unable to resolve—Paula grew to think of him as two alternating personalities. When she saw him alone, or at a formal party, or with his casual inferiors, she felt a tremendous pride in his strong, attractive presence, the paternal, understanding stature of his mind. In other company she became uneasy when what had been a fine imperviousness to mere gentility showed its other face. The other face was gross, humorous, reckless of everything but pleasure. It startled her mind temporarily away from him, even led her into a short covert experiment with an old beau, but it was no use—after four months of Anson's enveloping vitality there was an anæmic pallor in all other men.

In July he was ordered abroad, and their tenderness and desire reached a crescendo. Paula considered a last-minute marriage—decided against it only because there were always cocktails on his breath now, but the parting itself made her physically ill with grief. After his departure she wrote him long letters of regret for the days of love they had missed by waiting. In August Anson's plane slipped down into the North Sea. He was pulled onto a destroyer after a night in the water and sent to hospital with pneumonia; the armistice was signed before he was finally sent home.

Then, with every opportunity given back to them, with no material obstacle to overcome, the secret weavings of their temperaments came between them, drying up their kisses and their tears, making their voices less loud to one another, muffling the intimate chatter of their hearts until the old communication was only possible by letters, from far away. One afternoon a society reporter waited for two hours in the Hunters' house for a confirmation of their engagement. Anson denied it; nevertheless an early issue carried the report as a leading paragraph —they were "constantly seen together at Southampton, Hot Springs, and Tuxedo Park." But the serious dialogue had turned a corner into a long-sustained quarrel, and the affair was almost played out. Anson got drunk flagrantly and missed an engagement with her, whereupon Paula made certain behavioristic demands. His despair was helpless before his pride and his knowledge of himself: the engagement was definitely broken.

"Dearest," said their letters now, "Dearest, Dearest, when I wake up in the middle of the night and realize that after all it was not to be, I feel that I want to die. I can't go on living any more. Perhaps when we meet this summer we may talk things over and decide differently—we were so excited and sad that day, and I don't feel that I can live all my life without you. You speak of other people. Don't you know there are no other people for me, but only you. . . ."

But as Paula drifted here and there around the East she would sometimes mention her gayeties to make him wonder. Anson was too acute to wonder. When he saw a man's name in her letters he felt more sure of her and a little disdainful—he was always superior to such things. But he still hoped that they would some day marry.

Meanwhile he plunged vigorously into all the movement and glitter of post-bellum New York, entering a brokerage house, joining half a dozen clubs, dancing late, and moving in three worlds—his own world, the world of young Yale graduates, and that section of the half-world which rests one end on Broadway. But there was always a thorough and infractible eight hours devoted to his work in Wall Street, where the combination of his influential family connection, his sharp intelligence, and his abundance of sheer physical energy brought him almost immediately forward. He had one of those invaluable minds with partitions in it; sometimes he appeared at his office refreshed by less than an hour's sleep, but such occurrences were rare. So early as 1920 his income in salary and commissions exceeded twelve thousand dollars.

As the Yale tradition slipped into the past he became more and more of a popular figure among his classmates in New York, more popular than he had ever been in college. He lived in a great house, and had the means of introducing young men into other great houses. Moreover, his life already seemed secure, while theirs, for the most part, had arrived again at precarious beginnings. They commenced to turn to him for amusement and escape, and Anson responded readily, taking pleasure in helping people and arranging their affairs.

There were no men in Paula's letters now, but a note of tenderness ran through them that had not been there before. From several sources he heard that she had "a heavy beau," Lowell Thayer, a Bostonian of wealth and position, and though he was sure she still loved him, it made him uneasy to think that he might lose her, after all. Save for one unsatisfactory day she had not been in New York for almost five months, and as the rumors multiplied he became increasingly anxious to see her. In February he took his vacation and went down to Florida.

Palm Beach sprawled plump and opulent between the sparkling sapphire of Lake Worth, flawed here and there by house-boats at anchor, and the great turquoise bar of the Atlantic Ocean. The huge bulks of the Breakers and the Royal Poinciana rose as twin paunches from the bright level of the sand, and around them clustered the Dancing Glade, Bradley's House of Chance, and a dozen modistes and milliners with goods at triple prices from New York. Upon the trellised veranda of the Breakers two hundred women stepped right, stepped left, wheeled, and slid in that then celebrated calisthenic known as the double-shuffle, while in half-time to the music two thousand bracelets clicked up and down on two hundred arms.

At the Everglades Club after dark Paula and Lowell Thayer and Anson and a casual fourth played bridge with hot cards. It seemed to Anson that her kind, serious face was wan and tired—she had been around now for four, five, years. He had known her for three.

"Two spades."

"Cigarette? . . . Oh, I beg your pardon. By me."

"By."

"I'll double three spades."

There were a dozen tables of bridge in the room, which was filling up with smoke. Anson's eyes met Paula's, held them persistently even when Thayer's glance fell between them. . . .

"What was bid?" he asked abstractedly.

"Rose of Washington Square."

sang the young people in the corners:

"I'm withering there
In basement air——"

The smoke banked like fog, and the opening of a door filled the room with blown swirls of ectoplasm. Little Bright Eyes streaked past the tables seeking Mr. Conan Doyle among the Englishmen who were posing as Englishmen about the lobby.

"You could cut it with a knife."

". . . cut it with a knife."

". . . a knife."

At the end of the rubber Paula suddenly got up and spoke to Anson in a tense, low voice. With scarcely a glance at Lowell Thayer, they walked out the door and descended a long flight of stone steps—in a moment they were walking hand in hand along the moonlit beach.

"Darling, darling. . . ." They embraced recklessly, passionately, in a shadow. . . . Then Paula drew back her face to let his lips say what she wanted to hear—she could feel the words forming as they kissed again. . . . Again she broke away, listening, but as he pulled her close once more she realized that he had said nothing—only *"Darling! Darling!"* in that deep, sad whisper that always made her cry. Humbly, obediently, her emotions yielded to him and the tears streamed down her face, but her heart kept on crying: "Ask me—oh, Anson, dearest, ask me!"

"Paula. . . . *Paula!*"

The words wrung her heart like hands, and Anson, feeling her tremble, knew that emotion was enough. He need say no more, commit
their destinies to no practical enigma. Why should he, when he might
hold her so, biding his own time, for another year—forever? He was
considering them both, her more than himself. For a moment, when
she said suddenly that she must go back to her hotel, he hesitated,
thinking, first, "This is the moment, after all," and then: "No, let it
wait—she is mine. . . ."

He had forgotten that Paula too was worn away inside with the
strain of three years. Her mood passed forever in the night.

He went back to New York next morning filled with a certain restless dissatisfaction. Late in April, without warning, he received a tele-
gram from Bar Harbor in which Paula told him that she was engaged
to Lowell Thayer, and that they would be married immediately in
Boston. What he never really believed could happen had happened at
last.

Anson filled himself with whisky that morning, and going to the
office, carried on his work without a break—rather with a fear of what
would happen if he stopped. In the evening he went out as usual, saying nothing of what had occurred; he was cordial, humorous, unab-
stracted. But one thing he could not help—for three days, in any place,
in any company, he would suddenly bend his head into his hands and
cry like a child.

V

In 1922 when Anson went abroad with the junior partner to investigate
some London loans, the journey intimated that he was to be taken
into the firm. He was twenty-seven now, a little heavy without being
definitely stout, and with a manner older than his years. Old people
and young people liked him and trusted him, and mothers felt safe
when their daughters were in his charge, for he had a way, when he
came into a room, of putting himself on a footing with the oldest and
most conservative people there. "You and I," he seemed to say, "we're
solid. We understand."

He had an instinctive and rather charitable knowledge of the weaknesses of men and women, and, like a priest, it made him the more concerned for the maintenance of outward forms. It was typical of him
that every Sunday morning he taught in a fashionable Episcopal Sunday-school—even though a cold shower and a quick change into a cut-
away coat were all that separated him from the wild night before.

After his father's death he was the practical head of his family, and,
in effect, guided the destinies of the younger children. Through a com-

plication his authority did not extend to his father's estate, which was administered by his Uncle Robert, who was the horsy member of the family, a good-natured, hard-drinking member of that set which centers about Wheatley Hills.

Uncle Robert and his wife, Edna, had been great friends of Anson's youth, and the former was disappointed when his nephew's superiority failed to take a horsy form. He backed him for a city club which was the most difficult in America to enter—one could only join if one's family had "helped to build up New York" (or, in other words, were rich before 1880)—and when Anson, after his election, neglected it for the Yale Club, Uncle Robert gave him a little talk on the subject. But when on top of that Anson declined to enter Robert Hunter's own conservative and somewhat neglected brokerage house, his manner grew cooler. Like a primary teacher who has taught all he knew, he slipped out of Anson's life.

There were so many friends in Anson's life—scarcely one for whom he had not done some unusual kindness and scarcely one whom he did not occasionally embarrass by his bursts of rough conversation or his habit of getting drunk whenever and however he liked. It annoyed him when anyone else blundered in that regard—about his own lapses he was always humorous. Odd things happened to him and he told them with infectio is laughter.

I was working in New York that spring, and I used to lunch with him at the Yale Club, which my university was sharing until the completion of our own. I had read of Paula's marriage, and one afternoon, when I asked him about her, something moved him to tell me the story. After that he frequently invited me to family dinners at his house and behaved as though there was a special relation between us, as though with his confidence a little of that consuming memory had passed into me.

I found that despite the trusting mothers, his attitude toward girls was not indiscriminately protective. It was up to the girl—if she showed an inclination toward looseness, she must take care of herself, even with him.

"Life," he would explain sometimes, "has made a cynic of me."

By life he meant Paula. Sometimes, especially when he was drinking, it became a little twisted in his mind, and he thought that she had callously thrown him over.

This "cynicism," or rather his realization that naturally fast girls were not worth sparing, led to his affair with Dolly Karger. It wasn't his only affair in those years, but it came nearest to touching him deeply, and it had a profound effect upon his attitude toward life.

Dolly was the daughter of a notorious "publicist" who had married into society. She herself grew up into the Junior League, came out at the Plaza, and went to the Assembly; and only a few old families like the Hunters could question whether or not she "belonged," for her picture was often in the papers, and she had more enviable attention than many girls who undoubtedly did. She was dark-haired, with carmine lips and a high, lovely color, which she concealed under pinkish-gray powder all through the first year out, because high color was unfashionable—Victorian-pale was the thing to be. She wore black, severe suits and stood with her hands in her pockets, leaning a little forward, with a humorous restraint on her face. She danced exquisitely—better than anything she liked to dance—better than anything except making love. Since she was ten she had always been in love, and, usually, with some boy who didn't respond to her. Those who did—and there were many—bored her after a brief encounter, but for her failures she reserved the warmest spot in her heart. When she met them she would always try once more—sometimes she succeeded, more often she failed.

It never occurred to this gypsy of the unattainable that there was a certain resemblance in those who refused to love her—they shared a hard intuition that saw through to her weakness, not a weakness of emotion but a weakness of rudder. Anson perceived this when he first met her, less than a month after Paula's marriage. He was drinking rather heavily, and he pretended for a week that he was falling in love with her. Then he dropped her abruptly and forgot—immediately he took up the commanding position in her heart.

Like so many girls of that day Dolly was slackly and indiscreetly wild. The unconventionality of a slightly older generation had been simply one facet of a post-war movement to discredit obsolete manners—Dolly's was both older and shabbier, and she saw in Anson the two extremes which the emotionally shiftless woman seeks, an abandon to indulgence alternating with a protective strength. In his character she felt both the sybarite and the solid rock, and these two satisfied every need of her nature.

She felt that it was going to be difficult, but she mistook the reason --she thought that Anson and his family expected a more spectacular marriage, but she guessed immediately that her advantage lay in his tendency to drink.

They met at the large débutante dances, but as her infatuation increased they managed to be more and more together. Like most mothers, Mrs. Karger believed that Anson was exceptionally reliable, so she allowed Dolly to go with him to distant country clubs and suburban houses without inquiring closely into their activities or questioning her explanations when they came in late. At first these explanations might have been accurate, but Dolly's worldly ideas of capturing

Anson were soon engulfed in the rising sweep of her emotion. Kisses 'n the back of taxis and motor-cars were no longer enough; they did a curious thing:

They dropped out of their world for a while and made another world just beneath it where Anson's tippling and Dolly's irregular hours would be less noticed and commented on. It was composed, this world, of varying elements—several of Anson's Yale friends and their wives, two or three young brokers and bond salesmen and a handful of un-attached men, fresh from college, with money and a propensity to dis-sipation. What this world lacked in spaciousness and scale it made up for by allowing them a liberty that it scarcely permitted itself. More-over, it centered around them and permitted Dolly the pleasure of a faint condescension—a pleasure which Anson, whose whole life was a con-descension from the certitudes of his childhood, was unable to share.

He was not in love with her, and in the long feverish winter of their affair he frequently told her so. In the spring he was weary—he wanted to renew his life at some other source—moreover, he saw that either he must break with her now or accept the responsibility of a definite seduction. Her family's encouraging attitude precipitated his decision—one evening when Mr. Karger knocked discreetly at the library door to announce that he had left a bottle of old brandy in the dining room, Anson felt that life was hemming him in. That night he wrote her a short letter in which he told her that he was going on his vacation, and that in view of all the circumstances they had better meet no more.

It was June. His family had closed up the house and gone to the country, so he was living temporarily at the Yale Club. I had heard about his affair with Dolly as it developed—accounts salted with hu-mor, for he despised unstable women, and granted them no place in the social edifice in which he believed—and when he told me that night that he was definitely breaking with her I was glad. I had seen Dolly here and there, and each time with a feeling of pity at the hope-lessness of her struggle, and of shame at knowing so much about her that I had no right to know. She was what is known as "a pretty little thing," but there was a certain recklessness which rather fascinated me. Her dedication to the goddess of waste would have been less ob-vious had she been less spirited—she would most certainly throw her-self away, but I was glad when I heard that the sacrifice would not be consummated in my sight.

Anson was going to leave the letter of farewell at her house next morning. It was one of the few houses left open in the Fifth Avenue district, and he knew that the Kargers, acting upon erroneous informa-tion from Dolly, had foregone a trip abroad to give their daughter her

chance. As he stepped out the door of the Yale Club into Madison Avenue the postman passed him, and he followed back inside. The first lette
that caught his eye was in Dolly's hand.

He knew what it would be—a lonely and tragic monologue, full ot
the reproaches he knew, the invoked memories, the "I wonder if's"—all
the immemorial intimacies that he had communicated to Paula Legendre in what seemed another age. Thumbing over some bills, he
brought it on top again and opened it. To his surprise it was a short,
somewhat formal note, which said that Dolly would be unable to go to
the country with him for the week-end, because Perry Hull from Chicago had unexpectedly come to town. It added that Anson had brought
this on himself: "—if I felt that you loved me as I love you I would go
with you at any time, any place, but Perry is *so* nice, and he so much
wants me to marry him——"

Anson smiled contemptuously—he had had experience with such
decoy epistles. Moreover, he knew how Dolly had labored over this
plan, probably sent for the faithful Perry and calculated the time of his
arrival—even labored over the note so that it would make him jealous
without driving him away. Like most compromises, it had neither force
nor vitality but only a timorous despair.

Suddenly he was angry. He sat down in the lobby and read it again.
Then he went to the phone, called Dolly and told her in his clear, compelling voice that he had received her note and would call for her at
five o'clock as they had previously planned. Scarcely waiting for the
pretended uncertainty of her "Perhaps I can see you for an hour," he
hung up the receiver and went down to his office. On the way he tore
his own letter into bits and dropped it in the street.

He was not jealous—she meant nothing to him—but at her pathetic
ruse everything stubborn and self-indulgent in him came to the surface.
It was a presumption from a mental inferior and it could not be overlooked. If she wanted to know to whom she belonged she would see.

He was on the door-step at quarter past five. Dolly was dressed for
the street, and he listened in silence to the paragraph of "I can only see
you for an hour," which she had begun on the phone.

"Put on your hat, Dolly," he said, "we'll take a walk."

They strolled up Madison Avenue and over to Fifth while Anson's
shirt dampened upon his portly body in the deep heat. He talked little,
scolding her, making no love to her, but before they had walked six
blocks she was his again, apologizing for the note, offering not to see
Perry at all as an atonement, offering anything. She thought that he
had come because he was beginning to love her.

"I'm hot," he said when they reached 71st Street. "This is a winter suit. If I stop by the house and change, would you mind waiting for me down-stairs? I'll only be a minute."

She was happy; the intimacy of his being hot, of any physical fact about him, thrilled her. When they came to the iron-grated door and Anson took out his key she experienced a sort of delight.

Down-stairs it was dark, and after he ascended in the lift Dolly raised a curtain and looked out through opaque lace at the houses over the way. She heard the lift machinery stop, and with the notion of teasing him pressed the button that brought it down. Then on what was more than an impulse she got into it and sent it up to what she guessed was his floor.

"Anson," she called, laughing a little.

"Just a minute," he answered from his bedroom . . . then after a brief delay: "Now you can come in."

He had changed and was buttoning his vest. "This is my room," he said lightly. "How do you like it?"

She caught sight of Paula's picture on the wall and stared at it in fascination, just as Paula had stared at the pictures of Anson's childish sweethearts five years before. She knew something about Paula—sometimes she tortured herself with fragments of the story.

Suddenly she came close to Anson, raising her arms. They embraced. Outside the area window a soft artificial twilight already hovered, though the sun was still bright on a back roof across the way. In half an hour the room would be quite dark. The uncalculated opportunity overwhelmed them, made them both breathless, and they clung more closely. It was eminent, inevitable. Still holding one another, they raised their heads—their eyes fell together upon Paula's picture, staring down at them from the wall.

Suddenly Anson dropped his arms, and sitting down at his desk tried the drawer with a bunch of keys.

"Like a drink?" he asked in a gruff voice.

"No, Anson."

He poured himself half a tumbler of whisky, swallowed it, and then opened the door into the hall.

"Come on," he said.

Dolly hesitated.

"Anson—I'm going to the country with you tonight, after all. You understand that, don't you?"

"Of course," he answered brusquely.

In Dolly's car they rode on to Long Island, closer in their emotions than they had ever been before. They knew what would happen—not with Paula's face to remind them that something was lacking, but when they were alone in the still, hot Long Island night they did not care.

The estate in Port Washington where they were to spend the week-end belonged to a cousin of Anson's who had married a Montana copper operator. An interminable drive began at the lodge and twisted under imported poplar saplings toward a huge, pink, Spanish house. Anson had often visited there before.

After dinner they danced at the Linx Club. About midnight Anson assured himself that his cousins would not leave before two—then he explained that Dolly was tired; he would take her home and return to the dance later. Trembling a little with excitement, they got into a borrowed car together and drove to Port Washington. As they reached the lodge he stopped and spoke to the night watchman.

"When are you making a round, Carl?"

"Right away."

"Then you'll be here till everybody's in?"

"Yes, sir."

"All right. Listen: if any automobile, no matter whose it is, turns in at this gate, I want you to phone the house immediately." He put a five-dollar bill into Carl's hand. "Is that clear?"

"Yes, Mr. Anson." Being of the Old World, he neither winked nor smiled. Yet Dolly sat with her face turned slightly away.

Anson had a key. Once inside he poured a drink for both of them—Dolly left hers untouched—then he ascertained definitely the location of the phone, and found that it was within easy hearing distance of their rooms, both of which were on the first floor.

Five minutes later he knocked at the door of Dolly's room.

"Anson?" He went in, closing the door behind him. She was in bed, leaning up anxiously with elbows on the pillow; sitting beside her he took her in his arms.

"Anson, darling."

He didn't answer.

"Anson. . . . Anson! I love you. . . . Say you love me. Say it now—can't you say it now? Even if you don't mean it?"

He did not listen. Over her head he perceived that the picture of Paula was hanging here upon this wall.

He got up and went close to it. The frame gleamed faintly with thrice-reflected moonlight—within was a blurred shadow of a face that he saw he did not know. Almost sobbing, he turned around and stared with abomination at the little figure on the bed.

"This is all foolishness," he said thickly. "I don't know what I was thinking about. I don't love you and you'd better wait for somebody that loves you. I don't love you a bit, can't you understand?"

His voice broke, and he went hurriedly out. Back in the salon he was pouring himself a drink with uneasy fingers, when the front door opened suddenly, and his cousin came in.

"Why, Anson, I hear Dolly's sick," she began solicitously. "I hear she's sick. . . ."

"It was nothing," he interrupted, raising his voice so that it would carry into Dolly's room. "She was a little tired. She went to bed."

For a long time afterward Anson believed that a protective God sometimes interfered in human affairs. But Dolly Karger, lying awake and staring at the ceiling, never again believed in anything at all.

VI

When Dolly married during the following autumn, Anson was in London on business. Like Paula's marriage, it was sudden, but it affected him in a different way. At first he felt that it was funny, and had an inclination to laugh when he thought of it. Later it depressed him—it made him feel old.

There was something repetitive about it—why, Paula and Dolly had belonged to different generations. He had a foretaste of the sensation of a man of forty who hears that the daughter of an old flame has married. He wired congratulations and, as was not the case with Paula, they were sincere—he had never really hoped that Paula would be happy.

When he returned to New York, he was made a partner in the firm, and, as his responsibilities increased, he had less time on his hands. The refusal of a life-insurance company to issue him a policy made such an impression on him that he stopped drinking for a year, and claimed that he felt better physically, though I think he missed the convivial recounting of those Celliniesque adventures which, in his early twenties, had played such a part of his life. But he never abandoned the Yale Club. He was a figure there, a personality, and the tendency of his class, who were now seven years out of college, to drift away to more sober haunts was checked by his presence.

His day was never too full nor his mind too weary to give any sort of aid to anyone who asked it. What had been done at first through pride and superiority had become a habit and a passion. And there was always something—a younger brother in trouble at New Haven, a quarrel to be patched up between a friend and his wife, a position to be found for this man, an investment for that. But his specialty was the solving of problems for young married people. Young married people fascinated him and their apartments were almost sacred to him—he knew the story of their love affair, advised them where to live and how, and remembered their babies' names. Toward young wives his attitude was circumspect: he never abused the trust which their husbands—

strangely enough in view of his unconcealed irregularities—invariably reposed in him.

He came to take a vicarious pleasure in happy marriages, and to be inspired to an almost equally pleasant melancholy by those that went astray. Not a season passed that he did not witness the collapse of an affair that perhaps he himself had fathered. When Paula was divorced and almost immediately remarried to another Bostonian, he talked about her to me all one afternoon. He would never love any one as he had loved Paula, but he insisted that he no longer cared.

"I'll never marry," he came to say; "I've seen too much of it, and I know a happy marriage is a very rare thing. Besides, I'm too old."

But he did believe in marriage. Like all men who spring from a happy and successful marriage, he believed in it passionately—nothing he had seen would change his belief, his cynicism dissolved upon it like air. But he did really believe he was too old. At twenty-eight he began to accept with equanimity the prospect of marrying without romantic love; he resolutely chose a New York girl of his own class, pretty, intelligent, congenial, above reproach—and set about falling in love with her. The things he had said to Paula with sincerity, to other girls with grace, he could no longer say at all without smiling, or with the force necessary to convince.

"When I'm forty," he told his friends, "I'll be ripe. I'll fall for some chorus girl like the rest."

Nevertheless, he persisted in his attempt. His mother wanted to see him married, and he could now well afford it—he had a seat on the Stock Exchange, and his earned income came to twenty-five thousand a year. The idea was agreeable: when his friends—he spent most of his time with the set he and Dolly had evolved—closed themselves in behind domestic doors at night, he no longer rejoiced in his freedom. He even wondered if he should have married Dolly. Not even Paula had loved him more, and he was learning the rarity, in a single life, of encountering true emotion.

Just as this mood began to creep over him a disquieting story reached his ear. His aunt Edna, a woman just this side of forty, was carrying on an open intrigue with a dissolute, hard-drinking young man named Cary Sloane. Everyone knew of it except Anson's Uncle Robert, who for fifteen years had talked long in clubs and taken his wife for granted.

Anson heard the story again and again with increasing annoyance. Something of his old feeling for his uncle came back to him, a feeling that was more than personal, a reversion toward that family solidarity on which he had based his pride. His intuition singled out the essential point of the affair, which was that his uncle shouldn't be hurt. It was his first experiment in unsolicited meddling, but with his knowledge of

Edna's character he felt that he could handle the matter better than a district judge or his uncle.

His uncle was in Hot Springs. Anson traced down the sources of the scandal so that there should be no possibility of mistake and then he called Edna and asked her to lunch with him at the Plaza next day. Something in his tone must have frightened her, for she was reluctant, but he insisted, putting off the date until she had no excuse for refusing.

She met him at the appointed time in the Plaza lobby, a lovely, faded, gray-eyed blonde in a coat of Russian sable. Five great rings, cold with diamonds and emeralds, sparkled on her slender hands. It occurred to Anson that it was his father's intelligence and not his uncle's that had earned the fur and the stones, the rich brilliance that buoyed up her passing beauty.

Though Edna scented his hostility, she was unprepared for the directness of his approach.

"Edna, I'm astonished at the way you've been acting," he said in a strong, frank voice. "At first I couldn't believe it."

"Believe what?" she demanded sharply.

"You needn't pretend with me, Edna. I'm talking about Cary Sloane. Aside from any other consideration, I didn't think you could treat Uncle Robert——"

"Now look here, Anson——" she began angrily, but his peremptory voice broke through hers:

"——and your children in such a way. You've been married eighteen years, and you're old enough to know better."

"You can't talk to me like that! You——"

"Yes, I can. Uncle Robert has always been my best friend." He was tremendously moved. He felt a real distress about his uncle, about his three young cousins.

Edna stood up, leaving her crab-flake cocktail untasted.

"This is the silliest thing——"

"Very well, if you won't listen to me I'll go to Uncle Robert and tell him the whole story—he's bound to hear it sooner or later. And afterward I'll go to old Moses Sloane."

Edna faltered back into her chair.

"Don't talk so loud," she begged him. Her eyes blurred with tears. "You have no idea how your voice carries. You might have chosen a less public place to make all these crazy accusations."

He didn't answer.

"Oh, you never liked me, I know," she went on. "You're just taking advantage of some silly gossip to try and break up the only interesting friendship I've ever had. What did I ever do to make you hate me so?"

Still Anson waited. There would be the appeal to his chivalry, then to his pity, finally to his superior sophistication—when he had shouldered his way through all these there would be admissions, and he could come to grips with her. By being silent, by being impervious, by returning constantly to his main weapon, which was his own true emotion, he bullied her into frantic despair as the luncheon hour slipped away. At two o'clock she took out a mirror and a handkerchief, shined away the marks of her tears and powdered the slight hollows where they had lain. She had agreed to meet him at her own house at five.

When he arrived she was stretched on a *chaise-longue* which was covered with cretonne for the summer, and the tears he had called up at luncheon seemed still to be standing in her eyes. Then he was aware of Cary Sloane's dark anxious presence upon the cold hearth.

"What's this idea of yours?" broke out Sloane immediately. "I understand you invited Edna to lunch and then threatened her on the basis of some cheap scandal."

Anson sat down.

"I have no reason to think it's only scandal."

"I hear you're going to take it to Robert Hunter, and to my father."

Anson nodded.

"Either you break it off—or I will," he said.

"What God damned business is it of yours, Hunter?"

"Don't lose your temper, Cary," said Edna nervously. "It's only a question of showing him how absurd——"

"For one thing, it's my name that's being handed around," interrupted Anson. "That's all that concerns you, Cary."

"Edna isn't a member of your family."

"She most certainly is!" His anger mounted. "Why—she owes this house and the rings on her fingers to my father's brains. When Uncle Robert married her she didn't have a penny."

They all looked at the rings as if they had a significant bearing on the situation. Edna made a gesture to take them from her hand.

"I guess they're not the only rings in the world," said Sloane.

"Oh, this is absurd," cried Edna. "Anson, will you listen to me? I've found out how the silly story started. It was a maid I discharged who went right to the Chilicheffs—all these Russians pump things out of their servants and then put a false meaning on them." She brought down her fist angrily on the table: "And after Tom lent them the limousine for a whole month when we were South last winter——"

"Do you see?" demanded Sloane eagerly. "This maid got hold of the wrong end of the thing. She knew that Edna and I were friends, and she carried it to the Chilicheffs. In Russia they assume that if a man and a woman——"

He enlarged the theme to a disquisition upon social relations in the Caucasus.

"If that's the case it better be explained to Uncle Robert," said Anson dryly, "so that when the rumors do reach him he'll know they're not true."

Adopting the method he had followed with Edna at luncheon he let them explain it all away. He knew that they were guilty and that presently they would cross the line from explanation into justification and convict themselves more definitely than he could ever do. By seven they had taken the desperate step of telling him the truth—Robert Hunter's neglect, Edna's empty life, the casual dalliance that had flamed up into passion—but like so many true stories it had the misfortune of being old, and its enfeebled body beat helplessly against the armor of Anson's will. The threat to go to Sloane's father sealed their helplessness, for the latter, a retired cotton broker out of Alabama, was a notorious fundamentalist who controlled his son by a rigid allowance and the promise that at his next vagary the allowance would stop forever.

They dined at a small French restaurant, and the discussion continued —at one time Sloane resorted to physical threats, a little later they were both imploring him to give them time. But Anson was obdurate. He saw that Edna was breaking up, and that her spirit must not be refreshed by any renewal of their passion.

At two o'clock in a small night-club on 53rd Street, Edna's nerves suddenly collapsed, and she cried to go home. Sloane had been drinking heavily all evening, and he was faintly maudlin, leaning on the table and weeping a little with his face in his hands. Quickly Anson gave them his terms. Sloane was to leave town for six months, and he must be gone within forty-eight hours. When he returned there was to be no resumption of the affair, but at the end of a year Edna might, if she wished, tell Robert Hunter that she wanted a divorce and go about it in the usual way.

He paused, gaining confidence from their faces for his final word.

"Or there's another thing you can do," he said slowly, "if Edna wants to leave her children, there's nothing I can do to prevent your running off together."

"I want to go home!" cried Edna again. "Oh, haven't you done enough to us for one day?"

Outside it was dark, save for a blurred glow from Sixth Avenue down the street. In that light those two who had been lovers looked for the last time into each other's tragic faces, realizing that between them there was not enough youth and strength to avert their eternal parting. Sloane walked suddenly off down the street and Anson tapped a dozing taxi-driver on the arm

It was almost four; there was a patient flow of cleaning water along the ghostly pavement of Fifth Avenue, and the shadows of two night women flitted over the dark façade of St. Thomas's church. Then the desolate shrubbery of Central Park where Anson had often played as a child, and the mounting numbers, significant as names, of the marching streets. This was his city, he thought, where his name had flourished through five generations. No change could alter the permanence of its place here, for change itself was the essential substratum by which he and those of his name identified themselves with the spirit of New York. Resourcefulness and a powerful will—for his threats in weaker hands would have been less than nothing—had beaten the gathering dust from his uncle's name, from the name of his family, from even this shivering figure that sat beside him in the car.

Cary Sloane's body was found next morning on the lower shelf of a pillar of Queensboro Bridge. In the darkness and in his excitement he had thought that it was the water flowing black beneath him, but in less than a second it made no possible difference—unless he had planned to think one last thought of Edna, and call out her name as he struggled feebly in the water.

VII

Anson never blamed himself for his part in this affair—the situation which brought it about had not been of his making. But the just suffer with the unjust, and he found that his oldest and somehow his most precious friendship was over. He never knew what distorted story Edna told, but he was welcome in his uncle's house no longer.

Just before Christmas Mrs. Hunter retired to a select Episcopal heaven, and Anson became the responsible head of his family. An unmarried aunt who had lived with them for years ran the house, and attempted with helpless inefficiency to chaperone the younger girls. All the children were less self-reliant than Anson, more conventional both in their virtues and in their shortcomings. Mrs. Hunter's death had postponed the début of one daughter and the wedding of another. Also it had taken something deeply material from all of them, for with her passing the quiet, expensive superiority of the Hunters came to an end.

For one thing, the estate, considerably diminished by two inheritance taxes and soon to be divided among six children, was not a notable fortune any more. Anson saw a tendency in his youngest sisters to speak rather respectfully of families that hadn't "existed" twenty years ago. His own feeling of precedence was not echoed in them—sometimes they were conventionally snobbish, that was all. For another thing, this was the last summer they would spend on the Connecticut estate; the clamor against it was too loud: "Who wants to waste the best months of the year shut up in that dead old town?" Reluctantly he yielded—the house would go into the market in the fall, and next summer they would rent a smaller place in Westchester County. It was a step down from the expensive simplicity of his father's idea, and, while he sympathized with the revolt, it also annoyed him; during his mother's lifetime he had gone up there at least every other week-end—even in the gayest summers.

Yet he himself was part of this change, and his strong instinct for life had turned him in his twenties from the hollow obsequies of that abortive leisure class. He did not see this clearly—he still felt that there was a norm, a standard of society. But there was no norm, it was doubtful if there had ever been a true norm in New York. The few who still paid and fought to enter a particular set succeeded only to find that as a society it scarcely functioned—or, what was more alarming, that the Bohemia from which they fled sat above them at table.

At twenty-nine Anson's chief concern was his own growing loneliness. He was sure now that he would never marry. The number of weddings at which he had officiated as best man or usher was past all counting— there was a drawer at home that bulged with the official neckties of this or that wedding-party, neckties standing for romances that had not endured a year, for couples who had passed completely from his life. Scarf-pins, gold pencils, cuff-buttons, presents from a generation of grooms had passed through his jewel-box and been lost—and with every ceremony he was less and less able to imagine himself in the groom's place. Under his hearty good-will toward all those marriages there was despair about his own.

And as he neared thirty he became not a little depressed at the inroads that marriage, especially lately, had made upon his friendships. Groups of people had a disconcerting tendency to dissolve and disappear. The men from his own college—and it was upon them he had expended the most time and affection—were the most elusive of all. Most of them were drawn deep into domesticity, two were dead, one lived abroad, one was in Hollywood writing continuities for pictures that Anson went faithfully to see.

Most of them, however, were permanent commuters with an intricate family life centering around some suburban country club, and it was from these that he felt his estrangement most keenly.

In the early days of their married life they had all needed him; he gave them advice about their slim finances, he exorcised their doubts about the advisability of bringing a baby into two rooms and a bath, especially he stood for the great world outside. But now their financial troubles were in the past and the fearfully expected child had evolved into an absorbing family. They were always glad to see old Anson, but they dressed up for him and tried to impress him with their present importance, and kept their troubles to themselves. They needed him no longer.

A few weeks before his thirtieth birthday the last of his early and intimate friends was married. Anson acted in his usual role of best man, gave his usual silver tea-service, and went down to the usual *Homeric* to say good-by. It was a hot Friday afternoon in May, and as he walked from the pier he realized that Saturday closing had begun and he was free until Monday morning.

"Go where?" he asked himself.

The Yale Club, of course; bridge until dinner, then four or five raw cocktails in somebody's room and a pleasant confused evening. He regretted that this afternoon's groom wouldn't be along—they had always been able to cram so much into such nights: they knew how to attach women and how to get rid of them, how much consideration any girl deserved from their intelligent hedonism. A party was an adjusted thing—you took certain girls to certain places and spent just so much on their amusement; you drank a little, not much, more than you ought to drink, and at a certain time in the morning you stood up and said you were going home. You avoided college boys, sponges, future engagements, fights, sentiment, and indiscretions. That was the way it was done. All the rest was dissipation.

In the morning you were never violently sorry—you made no resolutions, but if you had overdone it and your heart was slightly out of order, you went on the wagon for a few days without saying anything about it, and waited until an accumulation of nervous boredom projected you into another party.

The lobby of the Yale Club was unpopulated. In the bar three very young alumni looked up at him, momentarily and without curiosity.

"Hello there, Oscar," he said to the bartender. "Mr. Cahill been around this afternoon?"

"Mr. Cahill's gone to New Haven."

"Oh . . . that so?"

"Gone to the ball game. Lot of men gone up."

Anson looked once again into the lobby, considered for a moment, and then walked out and over to Fifth Avenue. From the broad window of one of his clubs—one that he had scarcely visited in five years—a gray man with watery eyes stared down at him. Anson looked quickly away —that figure sitting in vacant resignation, in supercilious solitude, depressed him. He stopped and, retracing his steps, started over 47th Street toward Teak Warden's apartment. Teak and his wife had once been his most familiar friends—it was a household where he and Dolly Karger had been used to go in the days of their affair. But Teak had taken to drink, and his wife had remarked publicly that Anson was a bad influence on him. The remark reached Anson in an exaggerated form—when it was finally cleared up, the delicate spell of intimacy was broken, never to be renewed.

"Is Mr. Warden at home?" he inquired.

"They've gone to the country."

The fact unexpectedly cut at him. They were gone to the country and he hadn't known. Two years before he would have known the date, the hour, come up at the last moment for a final drink, and planned his first visit to them. Now they had gone without a word.

Anson looked at his watch and considered a week-end with his family, but the only train was a local that would jolt through the aggressive heat for three hours. And tomorrow in the country, and Sunday—he was in no mood for porch-bridge with polite undergraduates, and dancing after dinner at a rural roadhouse, a diminutive of gayety which his father had estimated too well.

"Oh, no," he said to himself. . . . "No."

He was a dignified, impressive young man, rather stout now, but otherwise unmarked by dissipation. He could have been cast for a pillar of something—at times you were sure it was not society, at others nothing else—for the law, for the church. He stood for a few minutes motionless on the sidewalk in front of a 47th Street apartment house; for almost the first time in his life he had nothing whatever to do.

Then he began to walk briskly up Fifth Avenue, as if he had just been reminded of an important engagement there. The necessity of dissimulation is one of the few characteristics that we share with dogs, and I think of Anson on that day as some well-bred specimen who had been disappointed at a familiar back door. He was going to see Nick, once a fashionable bartender in demand at all private dances, and now employed in cooling non-alcoholic champagne among the labyrinthine cellars of the Plaza Hotel.

"Nick," he said, "what's happened to everything?"

"Dead," Nick said.

"Make me a whisky sour." Anson handed a pint bottle over the counter. "Nick, the girls are different; I had a little girl in Brooklyn and she got married last week without letting me know."

"That a fact? Ha-ha-ha," responded Nick diplomatically. "Slipped it over on you."

"Absolutely," said Anson. "And I was out with her the night before."

"Ha-ha-ha," said Nick, "ha-ha-ha!"

"Do you remember the wedding, Nick, in Hot Springs where I had the waiters and the musicians singing 'God save the King'?"

"Now where was that, Mr. Hunter?" Nick concentrated doubtfully. "Seems to me that was——"

"Next time they were back for more, and I began to wonder how much I'd paid them," continued Anson.

"—seems to me that was at Mr. Trenholm's wedding."

"Don't know him," said Anson decisively. He was offended that a strange name should intrude upon his reminiscences; Nick perceived this.

"Naw—aw—" he admitted, "I ought to know that. It was one of *your* crowd—Brakins . . . Baker——"

"Bicker Baker," said Anson responsively. "They put me in a hearse after it was over and covered me up with flowers and drove me away."

"Ha-ha-ha," said Nick. "Ha-ha-ha."

Nick's simulation of the old family servant paled presently and Anson went up-stairs to the lobby. He looked around—his eyes met the glance of an unfamiliar clerk at the desk, then fell upon a flower from the morning's marriage hesitating in the mouth of a brass cuspidor. He went out and walked slowly toward the blood-red sun over Columbus Circle. Suddenly he turned around and, retracing his steps to the Plaza, immured himself in a telephone-booth.

Later he said that he tried to get me three times that afternoon, that he tried everyone who might be in New York—men and girls he had not seen for years, an artist's model of his college days whose faded number was still in his address book—Central told him that even the exchange existed no longer. At length his quest roved into the country, and he held brief disappointing conversations with emphatic butlers and maids. So-and-so was out, riding, swimming, playing golf, sailed to Europe last week. Who shall I say phoned?

It was intolerable that he should pass the evening alone—the private reckonings which one plans for a moment of leisure lose every charm when the solitude is enforced. There were always women of a sort, but the ones he knew had temporarily vanished, and to pass a New York evening in the hired company of a stranger never occurred to him—he would have considered that that was something shameful and secret, the diversion of a traveling salesman in a strange town.

Anson paid the telephone bill—the girl tried unsuccessfully to joke with him about its size—and for the second time that afternoon started to leave the Plaza and go he knew not where. Near the revolving door the figure of a woman, obviously with child, stood sideways to the light —a sheer beige cape fluttered at her shoulders when the door turned and, each time, she looked impatiently toward it as if she were weary of waiting. At the first sight of her a strong nervous thrill of familiarity went over him, but not until he was within five feet of her did he realize that it was Paula.

"Why, Anson Hunter!"

His heart turned over.

"Why, Paula——"

"Why, this is wonderful. I can't believe it, *Anson!*"

She took both his hands, and he saw in the freedom of the gesture that the memory of him had lost poignancy to her. But not to him—he felt that old mood that she evoked in him stealing over his brain, that gentleness with which he had always met her optimism as if afraid to mar its surface.

"We're at Rye for the summer. Pete had to come East on business—you know of course I'm Mrs. Peter Hagerty now—so we brought the children and took a house. You've got to come out and see us."

"Can I?" he asked directly. "When?"

"When you like. Here's Pete." The revolving door functioned, giving up a fine tall man of thirty with a tanned face and a trim mustache. His immaculate fitness made a sharp contrast with Anson's increasing bulk, which was obvious under the faintly tight cut-away coat.

"You oughtn't to be standing," said Hagerty to his wife. "Let's sit down here." He indicated lobby chairs, but Paula hesitated.

"I've got to go right home," she said. "Anson, why don't you—why don't you come out and have dinner with us tonight? We're just getting settled, but if you can stand that——"

Hagerty confirmed the invitation cordially.

"Come out for the night."

Their car waited in front of the hotel, and Paula with a tired gesture sank back against silk cushions in the corner.

"There's so much I want to talk to you about," she said, "it seems hopeless."

"I want to hear about you."

"Well"—she smiled at Hagerty—"that would take a long time too. I have three children—by my first marriage. The oldest is five, then four, then three." She smiled again. "I didn't waste much time having them, did I?"

"Boys?"

"A boy and two girls. Then—oh, a lot of things happened, and I got a divorce in Paris a year ago and married Pete. That's all—except that I'm awfully happy."

In Rye they drove up to a large house near the Beach Club, from which there issued presently three dark, slim children who broke from an English governess and approached them with an esoteric cry. Abstractedly and with difficulty Paula took each one into her arms, a caress which they accepted stiffly, as they had evidently been told not to bump into Mummy. Even against their fresh faces Paula's skin showed scarcely any weariness—for all her physical languor she seemed younger than when he had last seen her at Palm Beach seven years ago.

At dinner she was preoccupied, and afterward, during the homage to the radio, she lay with closed eyes on the sofa, until Anson wondered if his presence at this time were not an intrusion. But at nine o'clock when Hagerty rose and said pleasantly that he was going to leave them by themselves for a while, she began to talk slowly about herself and the past.

"My first baby," she said—"the one we call Darling, the biggest little girl—I wanted to die when I knew I was going to have her, because Lowell was like a stranger to me. It didn't seem as though she could be my own. I wrote you a letter and tore it up. Oh, you were *so* bad to me, Anson."

It was the dialogue again, rising and falling. Anson felt a sudden quickening of memory.

"Weren't you engaged once?" she asked—"a girl named Dolly something?"

"I wasn't ever engaged. I tried to be engaged, but I never loved anybody but you, Paula."

"Oh," she said. Then after a moment: "This baby is the first one I ever really wanted. You see, I'm in love now—at last."

He didn't answer, shocked at the treachery of her remembrance. She must have seen that the "at last" bruised him, for she continued:

"I was infatuated with you, Anson—you could make me do anything you liked. But we wouldn't have been happy. I'm not smart enough for you. I don't like things to be complicated like you do." She paused. "You'll never settle down," she said.

The phrase struck at him from behind—it was an accusation that of all accusations he had never merited.

"I could settle down if women were different," he said. "If I didn't understand so much about them, if women didn't spoil you for other women, if they had only a little pride. If I could go to sleep for a while and wake up into a home that was really mine—why, that's what I'm made for, Paula, that's what women have seen in me and liked in me. It's only that I can't get through the preliminaries any more."

Hagerty came in a little before eleven; after a whisky Paula stood up and announced that she was going to bed. She went over and stood by her husband.

"Where did you go, dearest?" she demanded.

"I had a drink with Ed Saunders."

"I was worried. I thought maybe you'd run away."

She rested her head against his coat.

"He's sweet, isn't he, Anson?" she demanded.

"Absolutely," said Anson, laughing.

She raised her face to her husband.

"Well, I'm ready," she said. She turned to Anson: "Do you want to see our family gymnastic stunt?"

"Yes," he said in an interested voice.

"All right. Here we go!"

Hagerty picked her up easily in his arms.

"This is called the family acrobatic stunt," said Paula. "He carries me up-stairs. Isn't it sweet of him?"

"Yes," said Anson.

Hagerty bent his head slightly until his face touched Paula's.

"And I love him," she said, "I've just been telling you, haven't I, Anson?"

"Yes," he said.

"He's the dearest thing that ever lived in this world; aren't you, darling? . . . Well, good night. Here we go. Isn't he strong?"

"Yes," Anson said.

"You'll find a pair of Pete's pajamas laid out for you. Sweet dreams— see you at breakfast."

"Yes," Anson said.

VIII

The older members of the firm insisted that Anson should go abroad for the summer. He had scarcely had a vacation in seven years, they said. He was stale and needed a change. Anson resisted.

"If I go," he declared, "I won't come back any more."

"That's absurd, old man. You'll be back in three months with all this depression gone. Fit as ever."

"No." He shook his head stubbornly. "If I stop, I won't go back to work. If I stop, that means I've given up—I'm through."

"We'll take a chance on that. Stay six months if you like—we're not afraid you'll leave us. Why, you'd be miserable if you didn't work."

They arranged his passage for him. They liked Anson—everyone liked Anson—and the change that had been coming over him cast a sort of pall over the office. The enthusiasm that had invariably signaled up business, the consideration toward his equals and his inferiors, the lift of his vital presence—within the past four months his intense nervousness had melted down these qualities into the fussy pessimism of a man of forty. On every transaction in which he was involved he acted as a drag and a strain.

"If I go I'll never come back," he said.

Three days before he sailed Paula Legendre Hagerty died in child-birth. I was with him a great deal then, for we were crossing together.

but for the first time in our friendship he told me not a word of how he felt, nor did I see the slightest sign of emotion. His chief preoccupation was with the fact that he was thirty years old—he would turn the conversation to the point where he could remind you of it and then fall silent, as if he assumed that the statement would start a chain of thought sufficient to itself. Like his partners, I was amazed at the change in him, and I was glad when the *Paris* moved off into the wet space between the worlds, leaving his principality behind.

"How about a drink?" he suggested.

We walked into the bar with that defiant feeling that characterizes the day of departure and ordered four Martinis. After one cocktail a change came over him—he suddenly reached across and slapped my knee with the first joviality I had seen him exhibit for months.

"Did you see that girl in the red tam?" he demanded, "the one with the high color who had the two police dogs down to bid her good-by."

"She's pretty," I agreed.

'I looked her up in the purser's office and found out that she's alone. I'm going down to see the steward in a few minutes. We'll have dinner with her tonight."

After a while he left me, and within an hour he was walking up and down the deck with her, talking to her in his strong, clear voice. Her red tam was a bright spot of color against the steel-green sea, and from time to time she looked up with a flashing bob of her head, and smiled with amusement and interest, and anticipation. At dinner we had champagne, and were very joyous—afterward Anson ran the pool with infectious gusto, and several people who had seen me with him asked me his name. He and the girl were talking and laughing together on a lounge in the bar when I went to bed.

I saw less of him on the trip than I had hoped. He wanted to arrange a foursome, but there was no one available, so I saw him only at meals. Sometimes, though, he would have a cocktail in the bar, and he told me about the girl in the red tam, and his adventures with her, making them all bizarre and amusing, as he had a way of doing, and I was glad that he was himself again, or at least the self that I knew, and with which I felt at home. I don't think he was ever happy unless someone was in love with him, responding to him like filings to a magnet, helping him to explain himself, promising him something. What it was I do not know. Perhaps they promised that there would always be women in the world who would spend their brightest, freshest, rarest hours to nurse and protect that superiority he cherished in his heart.

59

The Body of an American

BY JOHN DOS PASSOS

Whereasthe Congressof-
theunitedstates byaconcurrentresolutionadoptedon the4thdayofmarch
lastauthorizedthe Secretaryofwar to cause to be brought to theunited-
statesthe body of an Americanwhowasamemberoftheamericanexpedi-
tionaryforcesineurope wholosthislifeduringtheworldwarandwhoseiden-
tityhasnotbeenestablished for burial inthememorialamphitheatreofthe
nationalcemeteryatarlingtonvirginia

In the tarpaper morgue at Chalons-sur-Marne in the reek of chloride
of lime and the dead, they picked out the pine box that held all that was
left of
enie menie minie moe plenty other pine boxes stacked up there containing what they'd scraped up of Richard Roe
and other person or persons unknown. Only one can go. How did
they pick John Doe?
Make sure he aint a dinge, boys,
make sure he aint a guinea or a kike,
how can you tell a guy's a hunredpercent when all you've got's a
gunnysack full of bones, bronze buttons stamped with the screaming
eagle and a pair of roll puttees?
. . . and the gagging chloride and the puky dirtstench of the yearold
dead . . .

The day withal was too meaningful and tragic for applause. Silence,
tears, songs and prayer, muffled drums and soft music were the instru-
mentalities today of national approbation.

John Doe was born (thudding din of blood in love into the shuddering soar of a man and a woman alone indeed together lurching into

and ninemonths sick drowse waking into scared agony and the pain
and blood and mess of birth). John Doe was born

and raised in Brooklyn, in Memphis, near the lakefront in Cleveland,
Ohio, in the stench of the stockyards in Chi, on Beacon Hill, in an old
brick house in Alexandria Virginia, on Telegraph Hill, in a halftim-
bered Tudor cottage in Portland the city of roses,

in the Lying-In Hospital old Morgan endowed on Stuyvesant Square,
across the railroad tracks, out near the country club, in a shack cabin
tenement apartmenthouse exclusive residential suburb;

scion of one of the best families in the social register, won first prize
in the baby parade at Coronado Beach, was marbles champion of the
Little Rock grammarschools, crack basketballplayer at the Booneville
High, quarterback at the State Reformatory, having saved the sheriff's
kid from drowning in the Little Missouri River was invited to Washington to be photographed shaking hands with the President on the
White House steps;—

though this was a time of mourning, such an assemblage necessarily
has about it a touch of color. In the boxes are seen the court uniforms of
foreign diplomats, the gold braid of our own and foreign fleets and
armies, the black of the conventional morning dress of American statesmen, the varicolored furs and outdoor wrapping garments of mothers
and sisters come to mourn, the drab and blue of soldiers and sailors, the
glitter of musical instruments and the white and black of a vested choir

—busboy harveststiff hogcaller boyscout champeen cornshucker of
Western Kansas bellhop at the United States Hotel at Saratoga Springs
office boy callboy fruiter telephone lineman longshoreman lumberjack
plumber's helper,

worked for an exterminating company in Union City, filled pipes in
an opium joint in Trenton, N. J.

Y.M.C.A. secretary, express agent, truckdriver, fordmechanic, sold
books in Denver Colorado: Madam would you be willing to help a
young man work his way through college?

President Harding, with a reverence seemingly more significant because of his high temporal station, concluded his speech:

We are met today to pay the impersonal tribute;
the name of him whose body lies before us took flight with his im-
perishable soul . . .
as a typical soldier of this representative democracy he fought and died
believing in the indisputable justice of his country's cause . . .

by raising his right hand and asking the thousands within the sound
of his voice to join in the prayer:

Our Father which art in heaven hallowed be thy name . . .

Naked he went into the army;
they weighed you, measured you, looked for flat feet, squeezed your
penis to see if you had clap, looked up your anus to see if you had piles,
counted your teeth, made you cough, listened to your heart and lungs,
made you read the letters on the card, charted your urine and your
intelligence,
gave you a service record for a future (imperishable soul)
and an identification tag stamped with your serial number to hang
around your neck, issued O D regulation equipment, a condiment can
and a copy of the articles of war.
Atten'SHUN suck in your gut you c——r wipe that smile off your
face eyes right wattja tink dis is a choirch-social? For-war-D'ARCH.

John Doe
and Richard Roe and other person or persons unknown
drilled hiked, manual of arms, ate slum, learned to salute, to soldier,
to loaf in the latrines, forbidden to smoke on deck, overseas guard duty,
forty men and eight horses, shortarm inspection and the ping of shrapnel and the shrill bullets combing the air and the sorehead woodpeckers
the machineguns mud cooties gasmasks and the itch.
Say feller tell me how I can get back to my outfit.

John Doe had a head
for twentyodd years intensely the nerves of the eyes the ears the
palate the tongue the fingers the toes the armpits, the nerves warmfeel-
ing under the skin charged the coiled brain with hurt sweet warm cold
mine must dont sayings print headlines:
Thou shalt not the multiplication table long division, Now is the
time for all good men knocks but once at a young man's door, It's a
great life if Ish gebibbel, The first five years'll be the Safety First, Suppose a hun tried to rape your my country right or wrong, Catch 'em
young, What he dont know wont treat 'em rough, Tell 'em nothin, He
got what was coming to him he got his, This is a white man's country,
Kick the bucket, Gone west, If you dont like it you can croaked him
Say buddy cant you tell me how I can get back to my oufit?

Cant help jumpin when them things go off, give me the trots them
things do. I lost my identification tag swimmin in the Marne, rough-
housin with a guy while we was waitin to be deloused, in bed with a
girl named Jeanne (Love moving picture wet French postcard dream

began with saltpeter in the coffee and ended at the propho station);—
Say soldier for chrissake cant you tell me how I can get back to my outfit?

John Doe's
heart pumped blood:
alive thudding silence of blood in your ears
down in the clearing in the Oregon forest where the punkins were punkincolor pouring into the blood through the eyes and the fallcolored trees and the bronze hoopers were hopping through the dry grass, where tiny striped snails hung on the underside of the blades and the flies hummed, wasps droned, bumblebees buzzed, and the woods smelt of wine and mushrooms and apples, homey smell of fall pouring into the blood,
and I dropped the tin hat and the sweaty pack and lay flat with the dogday sun licking my throat and adamsapple and the tight skin over the breastbone.

The shell had his number on it.

The blood ran into the ground.

The service record dropped out of the filing cabinet when the quarter-master sergeant got blotto that time they had to pack up and leave the billets in a hurry.
The identification tag was in the bottom of the Marne.

The blood ran into the ground, the brains oozed out of the cracked skull and were licked up by the trenchrats, the belly swelled and raised a generation of bluebottle flies,
and the incorruptible skeleton,
and the scraps of dried viscera and skin bundled in khaki

they took to Chalons-sur-Marne
and laid it out neat in a pine coffin
and took it home to God's Country on a battleship
and buried it in a sarcophagus in the Memorial Amphitheatre in the Arlington National Cemetery
and draped the Old Glory over it
and the bugler played taps
and Mr. Harding prayed to God and the diplomats and the generals and the admirals and the brass-hats and the politicians and the hand-somely dressed ladies out of the society column of the *Washington Post* stood up solemn
and thought how beautiful sad Old Glory God's Country it was to have the bugler play taps and the three volleys made their ears ring.

Where his chest ought to have been they pinned
the Congressional Medal, the D.S.C., the Medaille Militaire, the Belgian Croix de Guerre, the Italian gold medal, the Vitutea Militara sent by Queen Marie of Rumania, the Czechoslovak war cross, the Virtuti Militari of the Poles, a wreath sent by Hamilton Fish, Jr., of New York, and a little wampum presented by a deputation of Arizona redskins in warpaint and feathers. All the Washingtonians brought flowers.

Woodrow Wilson brought a bouquet of poppies.

60

A Rose for Emily

BY WILLIAM FAULKNER

WHEN Miss Emily Grierson died, our whole town went to her funeral: the men through a sort of respectful affection for a fallen monument, the women mostly out of curiosity to see the inside of her house, which no one save an old man-servant— a combined gardener and cook—had seen in at least ten years.

It was a big, squarish frame house that had once been white, decorated with cupolas and spires and scrolled balconies in the heavily lightsome style of the Seventies, set on what had once been our most select street. But garages and cotton gins had encroached and obliterated even the august names of that neighborhood; only Miss Emily's house was left, lifting its stubborn and coquettish decay above the cotton wagons and the gasoline pumps—an eyesore among eyesores. And now Miss Emily had gone to join the representatives of those august names where they lay in the cedar-bemused cemetery among the ranked and anonymous graves of Union and Confederate soldiers who fell at the battle of Jefferson.

Alive, Miss Emily had been a tradition, a duty, and a care; a sort of hereditary obligation upon the town, dating from that day in 1894 when Colonel Sartoris, the mayor—he who fathered the edict that no Negro woman should appear on the streets without an apron—remitted her taxes, the dispensation dating from the death of her father on into perpetuity. Not that Miss Emily would have accepted charity. Colonel Sartoris invented an involved tale to the effect that Miss Emily's father had loaned money to the town, which the town, as a matter of business, preferred this way of repaying. Only a man of Colonel Sartoris' generation and thought could have invented it, and only a woman could have believed it.

When the next generation, with its more modern ideas, became mayors and aldermen, this arrangement created some little dissatisfaction. On the first of the year they mailed her a tax notice. February came, and there was no reply. They wrote her a formal letter, asking her to call at the sheriff's office at her convenience. A week later the mayor wrote her himself, offering to call or to send his car for her, and received in reply a note on paper of an archaic shape, in a thin, flowing calligraphy in faded ink, to the effect that she no longer went out at all. The tax notice was also enclosed, without comment.

They called a special meeting of the Board of Aldermen. A deputation waited upon her, knocked at the door through which no visitor had passed since she ceased giving china-painting lessons eight or ten years earlier. They were admitted by the old Negro into a dim hall from which a stairway mounted into still more shadow. It smelled of dust and disuse—a close, dank smell. The Negro led them into the parlor. It was furnished in heavy, leather-covered furniture. When the Negro opened the blinds of one window, they could see that the leather was cracked; and when they sat down, a faint dust rose sluggishly about their thighs, spinning with slow motes in the single sun-ray. On a tarnished gilt easel before the fireplace stood a crayon portrait of Miss Emily's father.

They rose when she entered—a small, fat woman in black, with a thin gold chain descending to her waist and vanishing into her belt, leaning on an ebony cane with a tarnished gold head. Her skeleton was small and spare; perhaps that was why what would have been merely plumpness in another was obesity in her. She looked bloated, like a body long submerged in motionless water, and of that pallid hue. Her eyes, lost in the fatty ridges of her face, looked like two small pieces of coal pressed into a lump of dough as they moved from one face to another while the visitors stated their errand.

She did not ask them to sit. She just stood in the door and listened quietly until the spokesman came to a stumbling halt. Then they could hear the invisible watch ticking at the end of the gold chain.

Her voice was dry and cold. "I have no taxes in Jefferson. Colonel Sartoris explained it to me. Perhaps one of you can gain access to the city records and satisfy yourselves."

"But we have. We are the city authorities, Miss Emily. Didn't you get a notice from the sheriff, signed by him?"

"I received a paper, yes," Miss Emily said. "Perhaps he considers himself the sheriff . . . I have no taxes in Jefferson."

"But there is nothing on the books to show that, you see. We must go by the—"

"See Colonel Sartoris. I have no taxes in Jefferson."

"But, Miss Emily—"

"See Colonel Sartoris." (Colonel Sartoris had been dead almost ten years.) "I have no taxes in Jefferson. Tobe!" The Negro appeared. "Show these gentlemen out."

II

So she vanquished them, horse and foot, just as she had vanquished their fathers thirty years before about the smell. That was two years after her father's death and a short time after her sweetheart—the one we believed would marry her—had deserted her. After her father's death she went out very little; after her sweetheart went away, people hardly saw her at all. A few of the ladies had the temerity to call, but were not received, and the only sign of life about the place was the Negro man— a young man then—going in and out with a market basket.

"Just as if a man—any man—could keep a kitchen properly," the ladies said; so they were not surprised when the smell developed. It was another link between the gross, teeming world and the high and mighty Griersons.

A neighbor, a woman, complained to the mayor, Judge Stevens, eighty years old.

"But what will you have me do about it, madam?" he said.

"Why, send her word to stop it," the woman said. "Isn't there a law?"

"I'm sure that won't be necessary," Judge Stevens said. "It's probably just a snake or a rat that nigger of hers killed in the yard. I'll speak to him about it."

The next day he received two more complaints, one from a man who came in diffident deprecation. "We really must do something about it, Judge. I'd be the last one in the world to bother Miss Emily, but we've got to do something." That night the Board of Aldermen met—three graybeards and one younger man, a member of the rising generation.

"It's simple enough," he said. "Send her word to have her place cleaned up. Give her a certain time to do it in, and if she don't . . ."

"Dammit, sir," Judge Stevens said, "will you accuse a lady to her face of smelling bad?"

So the next night, after midnight, four men crossed Miss Emily's lawn and slunk about the house like burglars, sniffing along the base of the brickwork and at the cellar openings while one of them performed a regular sowing motion with his hand out of a sack slung from his shoulder. They broke open the cellar door and sprinkled lime there, and in all the outbuildings. As they recrossed the lawn, a window that had been dark was lighted and Miss Emily sat in it, the light behind her, and her upright torso motionless as that of an idol. They crept quietly across the lawn and into the shadow of the locusts that lined the street. After a week or two the smell went away.

That was when people had begun to feel really sorry for her. People in our town, remembering how Old Lady Wyatt, her great-aunt, had gone completely crazy at last, believed that the Griersons held themselves a little too high for what they really were. None of the young men was quite good enough to Miss Emily and such. We had long thought of them as a tableau: Miss Emily a slender figure in white in the background, her father a spraddled silhouette in the foreground, his back to her and clutching a horse-whip, the two of them framed by the back-flung front door. So when she got to be thirty and was still single, we were not pleased exactly, but vindicated; even with insanity in the family she wouldn't have turned down all of her chances if they had really materialized.

When her father died, it got about that the house was all that was left to her; and in a way, people were glad. At last they could pity Miss Emily. Being left alone, and a pauper, she had become humanized. Now she too would know the old thrill and the old despair of a penny more or less.

The day after his death all the ladies prepared to call at the house and offer condolence and aid, as is our custom. Miss Emily met them at the door, dressed as usual and with no trace of grief on her face. She told them that her father was not dead. She did that for three days, with the ministers calling on her, and the doctors, trying to persuade her to let them dispose of the body. Just as they were about to resort to law and force, she broke down, and they buried her father quickly.

We did not say she was crazy then. We believed she had to do that. We remembered all the young men her father had driven away, and we knew that with nothing left, she would have to cling to that which had robbed her, as people will.

III

She was sick for a long time. When we saw her again, her hair was cut short, making her look like a girl, with a vague resemblance to those angels in colored church windows—sort of tragic and serene.

The town had just let the contracts for paving the sidewalks, and in the summer after her father's death they began the work. The construction company came with niggers and mules and machinery, and a foreman named Homer Barron, a Yankee—a big, dark, ready man, with a big voice and eyes lighter than his face. The little boys would follow in groups to hear him cuss the niggers, and the niggers singing in time to the rise and fall of picks. Pretty soon he knew everybody in town. Whenever you heard a lot of laughing anywhere about the square, Homer Barron would be in the center of the group. Presently we began to see him and Miss Emily on Sunday afternoons driving in the yellow-wheeled buggy and the matched team of bays from the livery stable.

At first we were glad that Miss Emily would have an interest, because the ladies all said, "Of course a Grierson would not think seriously of a Northerner, a day laborer." But there were still others, older people, who said that even grief could not cause a real lady to forget *noblesse oblige*—without calling it *noblesse oblige*. They just said, "Poor Emily. Her kinsfolk should come to her." She had some kin in Alabama; but years ago her father had fallen out with them over the estate of Old Lady Wyatt, the crazy woman, and there was no communication between the two families. They had not even been represented at the funeral.

And as soon as the old people said, "Poor Emily," the whispering began. "Do you suppose it's really so?" they said to one another. "Of course it is. What else could . . ." This behind their hands; rustling of craned silk and satin behind jalousies closed upon the sun of Sunday afternoon as the thin, swift clop-clop-clop of the matched team passed: "Poor Emily."

She carried her head high enough—even when we believed that she was fallen. It was as if she demanded more than ever the recognition of her dignity as the last Grierson; as if it had wanted that touch of earthiness to reaffirm her imperviousness. Like when she bought the rat poison, the arsenic. That was over a year after they had begun to say "Poor Emily," and while the two female cousins were visiting her.

"I want some poison," she said to the druggist. She was over thirty then, still a slight woman, though thinner than usual, with cold, haughty black eyes in a face the flesh of which was strained across the temples and about the eye-sockets as you imagine a lighthouse-keeper's face ought to look. "I want some poison," she said.

"Yes, Miss Emily. What kind? For rats and such? I'd recom—"

"I want the best you have. I don't care what kind."

The druggist named several. "They'll kill anything up to an elephant. But what you want is—"

"Arsenic," Miss Emily said. "Is that a good one?"

"Is . . . arsenic? Yes, ma'am. But what you want—"

"I want arsenic."

The druggist looked down at her. She looked back at him, erect, her face like a strained flag. "Why, of course," the druggist said. "If that's what you want. But the law requires you to tell what you are going to use it for."

Miss Emily just stared at him, her head tilted back in order to look him eye for eye, until he looked away and went and got the arsenic and wrapped it up. The Negro delivery boy brought her the package;

the druggist didn't come back. When she opened the package at home there was written on the box, under the skull and bones: "For rats."

IV

So the next day we all said, "She will kill herself"; and we said it would be the best thing. When she had first begun to be seen with Homer Barron, we had said, "She will marry him." Then we said, "She will persuade him yet," because Homer himself had remarked—he liked men, and it was known that he drank with the younger men in the Elks' Club—that he was not a marrying man. Later we said, "Poor Emily" behind the jalousies as they passed on Sunday afternoon in the glittering buggy, Miss Emily with her head high and Homer Barron with his hat cocked and a cigar in his teeth, reins and whip in a yellow glove.

Then some of the ladies began to say that it was a disgrace to the town and a bad example to the young people. The men did not want to interfere, but at last the ladies forced the Baptist minister—Miss Emily's people were Episcopal—to call upon her. He would never divulge what happened during that interview, but he refused to go back again. The next Sunday they again drove about the streets, and the following day the minister's wife wrote to Miss Emily's relations in Alabama.

So she had blood-kin under her roof again and we sat back to watch developments. At first nothing happened. Then we were sure that they were to be married. We learned that Miss Emily had been to the jeweler's and ordered a man's toilet set in silver, with the letter H. B. on each piece. Two days later we learned that she had bought a complete outfit of men's clothing, including a nightshirt, and we said, "They are married." We were really glad. We were glad because the two female cousins were even more Grierson than Miss Emily had ever been.

So we were not surprised when Homer Barron—the streets had been finished some time since—was gone. We were a little disappointed that there was not a public blowing-off, but we believed that he had gone on to prepare for Miss Emily's coming, or to give her a chance to get rid of the cousins. (By that time it was a cabal, and we were all Miss Emily's allies to help circumvent the cousins.) Sure enough, after another week they departed. And, as we had expected all along, within three days Homer Barron was back in town. A neighbor saw the Negro man admit him at the kitchen door at dusk one evening.

And that was the last we saw of Homer Barron. And of Miss Emily for some time. The Negro man went in and out with the market basket, but the front door remained closed. Now and then we would see her at a window for a moment, as the men did that night when they sprinkled the lime, but for almost six months she did not appear on the streets.

Then we knew that this was to be expected too; as if that quality of her father which had thwarted her woman's life so many times had been too virulent and too furious to die.

When we next saw Miss Emily, she had grown fat and her hair was turning gray. During the next few years it grew grayer and grayer until it attained an even pepper-and-salt iron-gray, when it ceased turning Up to the day of her death at seventy-four it was still that vigorous iron-gray, like the hair of an active man.

From that time on her front door remained closed, save for a period of six or seven years, when she was about forty, during which she gave lessons in china-painting. She fitted up a studio in one of the downstairs rooms, where the daughters and granddaughters of Colonel Sartoris' contemporaries were sent to her with the same regularity and in the same spirit that they were sent to church on Sundays with a twenty-five-cent piece for the collection plate. Meanwhile her taxes had been remitted.

Then the newer generation became the backbone and the spirit of the town, and the painting pupils grew up and fell away and did not send their children to her with boxes of color and tedious brushes and pictures cut from the ladies' magazines. The front door closed upon the last one and remained closed for good. When the town got free postal delivery, Miss Emily alone refused to let them fasten the metal numbers above her door and attach a mailbox to it. She would not listen to them.

Daily, monthly, yearly we watched the Negro grow grayer and more stooped, going in and out with the market basket. Each December we sent her a tax notice, which would be returned by the post office a week later, unclaimed. Now and then we would see her in one of the downstairs windows—she had evidently shut up the top floor of the house—like the carven torso of an idol in a niche, looking or not looking at us, we could never tell which. Thus she passed from generation to generation—dear, inescapable, impervious, tranquil, and perverse.

And so she died. Fell ill in the house filled with dust and shadows, with only a doddering Negro man to wait on her. We did not even know she was sick; we had long since given up trying to get any information from the Negro. He talked to no one, probably not even to her, for his voice had grown harsh and rusty, as if from disuse.

She died in one of the downstairs rooms, in a heavy walnut bed with a curtain, her gray head propped on a pillow yellow and moldy with age and lack of sunlight.

V

The Negro met the first of the ladies at the front door and let them in, with their hushed, sibilant voices and their quick, curious glances, and then he disappeared. He walked right through the house and out the back and was not seen again.

The two female cousins came at once. They held the funeral on the second day, with the town coming to look at Miss Emily beneath a mass of bought flowers, with the crayon face of her father musing profoundly above the bier and the ladies sibilant and macabre; and the very old men—some in their brushed Confederate uniforms—on the porch and the lawn, talking of Miss Emily as if she had been a contemporary of theirs, believing that they had danced with her and courted her perhaps, confusing time with its mathematical progression, as the old do, to whom all the past is not a diminishing road but, instead, a huge meadow which no winter ever quite touches, divided from them now by the narrow bottle-neck of the most recent decade of years.

Already we knew that there was one room in that region above stairs which no one had seen in forty years, and which would have to be forced. They waited until Miss Emily was decently in the ground before they opened it.

The violence of breaking down the door seemed to fill this room with pervading dust. A thin, acrid pall as of the tomb seemed to lie everywhere upon this room decked and furnished as for a bridal: upon the valence curtains of faded rose color, upon the rose-shaded lights, upon the dressing table, upon the delicate array of crystal and the man's toilet things backed with tarnished silver, silver so tarnished that the monogram was obscured. Among them lay a collar and tie, as if they had just been removed, which, lifted, left upon the surface a pale crescent in the dust. Upon a chair hung the suit, carefully folded; beneath it the two mute shoes and the discarded socks.

The man himself lay in the bed.

For a long while we just stood there, looking down at the profound and fleshless grin. The body had apparently once lain in the attitude of an embrace, but now the long sleep that outlasts love, that conquers even the grimace of love, had cuckolded him. What was left of him, rotted beneath what was left of the nightshirt, had become inextricable from the bed in which he lay; and upon him and upon the pillow beside him lay that even coating of the patient and biding dust.

Then we noticed that in the second pillow was the indentation of a head. One of us lifted something from it, and leaning forward, that faint and invisible dust dry and acrid in the nostrils, we saw a long strand of iron-gray hair.

61

The Killers

BY ERNEST HEMINGWAY

THE door of Henry's lunch-room opened and two men came in. They sat down at the counter.

"What's yours?" George asked them.

"I don't know," one of the men said. "What do you want to eat, Al?"

"I don't know," said Al. "I don't know what I want to eat."

Outside it was getting dark. The street-light came on outside the window. The two men at the counter read the menu. From the other end of the counter Nick Adams watched them. He had been talking to George when they came in.

"I'll have a roast pork tenderloin with apple sauce and mashed potatoes," the first man said.

"It isn't ready yet."

"What the hell do you put it on the card for?"

"That's the dinner," George explained. "You can get that at six o'clock."

George looked at the clock on the wall behind the counter.

"It's five o'clock."

"The clock says twenty minutes past five," the second man said.

"It's twenty minutes fast."

"Oh, to hell with the clock," the first man said. "What have you got to eat?"

"I can give you any kind of sandwiches," George said. "You can have ham and eggs, bacon and eggs, liver and bacon, or a steak."

"Give me chicken croquettes with green peas and cream sauce and mashed potatoes."

"That's the dinner."

"Everything we want's the dinner, eh? That's the way you work it."

"I can give you ham and eggs, bacon and eggs, liver——"

"I'll take ham and eggs," the man called Al said. He wore a derby hat and a black overcoat buttoned across the chest. His face was small and white and he had tight lips. He wore a silk muffler and gloves.

"Give me bacon and eggs," said the other man. He was about the same size as Al. Their faces were different, but they were dressed like twins. Both wore overcoats too tight for them. They sat leaning forward, their elbows on the counter.

"Got anything to drink?" Al asked.

"Silver beer, bevo, ginger-ale," George said.

"I mean you got anything to *drink?*"

"Just those I said."

"This is a hot town," said the other. "What do they call it?"

"Summit."

"Ever hear of it?" Al asked his friend.

"No," said the friend.

"What do you do here nights?" Al asked.

"They eat the dinner," his friend said. "They all come here and eat the big dinner."

"That's right," George said.

"So you think that's right?" Al asked George.

"Sure."

"You're a pretty bright boy, aren't you?"

"Sure," said George.

"Well, you're not," said the other little man. "Is he, Al?"

"He's dumb," said Al. He turned to Nick. "What's your name?"

"Adams."

"Another bright boy," Al said. "Ain't he a bright boy, Max?"

"The town's full of bright boys," Max said.

George put the two platters, one of ham and eggs, the other of bacon and eggs, on the counter. He set down two side-dishes of fried potatoes and closed the wicket into the kitchen.

"Which is yours?" he asked Al.

"Don't you remember?"

"Ham and eggs."

"Just a bright boy," Max said. He leaned forward and took the ham and eggs. Both men ate with their gloves on. George watched them eat.

"What are *you* looking at?" Max looked at George.

"Nothing."

"The hell you were. You were looking at me."

"Maybe the boy meant it for a joke, Max," Al said.

George laughed.

"*You* don't have to laugh," Max said to him. "*You* don't have to laugh at all, see?"

"All right," said George.

"So he thinks it's all right." Max turned to Al. "He thinks it's all right. That's a good one."

"Oh, he's a thinker," Al said. They went on eating.

"What's the bright boy's name down the counter?" Al asked Max.

"Hey, bright boy," Max said to Nick. "You go around on the other side of the counter with your boy friend."

"What's the idea?" Nick asked.

"There isn't any idea."

"You better go around, bright boy," Al said. Nick went around behind the counter.

"What's the idea?" George asked.

"None of your damn business," Al said. "Who's out in the kitchen?"

"The nigger."

"What do you mean the nigger?"

"The nigger that cooks."

"Tell him to come in."

"What's the idea?"

"Tell him to come in."

"Where do you think you are?"

"We know damn well where we are," the man called Max said. "Do we look silly?"

"You talk silly," Al said to him. "What the hell do you argue with this kid for? Listen," he said to George, "tell the nigger to come out here."

"What are you going to do to him?"

"Nothing. Use your head, bright boy. What would we do to a nigger?"

George opened the slit that opened back into the kitchen. "Sam," he called. "Come in here a minute."

The door to the kitchen opened and the nigger came in. "What was it?" he asked. The two men at the counter took a look at him.

"All right, nigger. You stand right there," Al said.

Sam, the nigger, standing in his apron, looked at the two men sitting at the counter. "Yes, sir," he said. Al got down from his stool.

"I'm going back to the kitchen with the nigger and bright boy," he said. "Go on back to the kitchen, nigger. You go with him, bright boy." The little man walked after Nick and Sam, the cook, back into the kitchen. The door shut after them. The man called Max sat at the counter opposite George. He didn't look at George but looked in the mirror that ran along back of the counter. Henry's had been made over from a saloon into a lunch-counter.

"Well, bright boy," Max said, looking into the mirror, "why don't you say something?"

"What's it all about?"

"Hey, Al," Max called, "bright boy wants to know what it's all about."

"Why don't you tell him?" Al's voice came from the kitchen.

"What do you think it's all about?"

"I don't know."

"What do you think?"

Max looked into the mirror all the time he was talking.

"I wouldn't say."

"Hey, Al, bright boy says he wouldn't say what he thinks it's all about."

"I can hear you, all right," Al said from the kitchen. He had propped open the slit that dishes passed through into the kitchen with a catsup bottle. "Listen, bright boy," he said from the kitchen to George. "Stand a little further along the bar. You move a little to the left, Max." He was like a photographer arranging for a group picture.

"Talk to me, bright boy," Max said. "What do you think's going to happen?"

George did not say anything.

"I'll tell you," Max said. "We're going to kill a Swede. Do you know a big Swede named Ole Andreson?"

"Yes."

"He comes here to eat every night, don't he?"

"Sometimes he comes here."

"He comes here at six o'clock, don't he?"

"If he comes."

"We know all that, bright boy," Max said. "Talk about something else. Ever go to the movies?"

"Once in a while."

"You ought to go to the movies more. The movies are fine for a bright boy like you."

"What are you going to kill Ole Andreson for? What did he ever do to you?"

"He never had a chance to do anything to us. He never even seen us."

"And he's only going to see us once," Al said from the kitchen.

"What are you going to kill him for, then?" George asked.

"We're killing him for a friend. Just to oblige a friend, bright boy."

"Shut up," said Al from the kitchen. "You talk too goddam much."

"Well, I got to keep bright boy amused. Don't I, bright boy?"

"You talk too damn much," Al said. "The nigger and my bright boy are amused by themselves. I got them tied up like a couple of girl friends in the convent."

"I suppose you were in a convent."

"You never know."

"You were in a kosher convent. That's where you were."

George looked up at the clock.

"If anybody comes in you tell them the cook is off, and if they keep after it, you tell them you'll go back and cook yourself. Do you get that, bright boy?"

"All right," George said. "What you going to do with us afterward?"

"That'll depend," Max said. "That's one of those things you never know at the time."

George looked up at the clock. It was a quarter past six. The door from the street opened. A street-car motorman came in.

"Hello, George," he said. "Can I get supper?"

"Sam's gone out," George said. "He'll be back in about half an hour."

"I'd better go up the street," the motorman said. George looked at the clock. It was twenty minutes past six.

"That was nice, bright boy," Max said. "You're a regular little gentleman."

"He knew I'd blow his head off," Al said from the kitchen.

"No," said Max. "It ain't that. Bright boy is nice. He's a nice boy. I like him."

At six-fifty-five George said: "He's not coming."

Two other people had been in the lunch-room. Once George had gone out to the kitchen and made a ham-and-egg sandwich "to go" that a man wanted to take with him. Inside the kitchen he saw Al, his derby hat tipped back, sitting on a stool beside the wicket with the muzzle of a sawed-off shotgun resting on the ledge. Nick and the cook were back to back in the corner, a towel tied in each of their mouths. George had cooked the sandwich, wrapped it up in oiled paper, put it in a bag, brought it in, and the man had paid for it and gone out.

"Bright boy can do everything," Max said. "He can cook and everything. You'd make some girl a nice wife, bright boy."

"Yes?" George said. "Your friend, Ole Andreson, isn't going to come."

"We'll give him ten minutes," Max said.

Max watched the mirror and the clock. The hands of the clock marked seven o'clock, and then five minutes past seven.

"Come on, Al," said Max. "We better go. He's not coming."

"Better give him five minutes," Al said from the kitchen.

In the five minutes a man came in, and George explained that the cook was sick.

"Why the hell don't you get another cook?" the man asked. "Aren't you running a lunch-counter?" He went out.

"Come on, Al," Max said.

"What about the two bright boys and the nigger?"

"They're all right."

"You think so?"

"Sure. We're through with it."

"I don't like it," said Al. "It's sloppy. You talk too much."

"Oh, what the hell," said Max. "We got to keep amused, haven't we?"

"You talk too much, all the same," Al said. He came out from the kitchen. The cut-off barrels of the shotgun made a slight bulge under the waist of his too tight-fitting overcoat. He straightened his coat with his gloved hands.

"So long, bright boy," he said to George. "You got a lot of luck."

"That's the truth," Max said. "You ought to play the races, bright boy."

The two of them went out the door. George watched them, through the window, pass under the arc-light and cross the street. In their tight overcoats and derby hats they looked like a vaudeville team. George went back through the swinging-door into the kitchen and untied Nick and the cook.

"I don't want any more of that," said Sam, the cook. "I don't want any more of that."

Nick stood up. He had never had a towel in his mouth before.

"Say," he said. "What the hell?" He was trying to swagger it off.

"They were going to kill Ole Andreson," George said. "They were going to shoot him when he came in to eat."

"Ole Andreson?"

"Sure."

The cook felt the corners of his mouth with his thumbs.

"They all gone?" he asked.

"Yeah," said George. "They're gone now."

"I don't like it," said the cook. "I don't like any of it at all."

"Listen," George said to Nick. "You better go see Ole Andreson."

"All right."

"You better not have anything to do with it at all," Sam, the cook, said. "You better stay way out of it."

"Don't go if you don't want to," George said.

"Mixing up in this ain't going to get you anywhere," the cook said "You stay out of it."

"I'll go see him," Nick said to George. "Where does he live?"

The cook turned away.

"Little boys always know what they want to do," he said.

"He lives up at Hirsch's rooming-house," George said to Nick.

"I'll go up there."

Outside the arc-light shone through the bare branches of a tree. Nick walked up the street beside the car-tracks and turned at the next arc-light down a side-street. Three houses up the street was Hirsch's rooming house. Nick walked up the two steps and pushed the bell. A woman came to the door.

"Is Ole Andreson here?"

"Do you want to see him?"

"Yes, if he's in."

Nick followed the woman up a flight of stairs and back to the end of a corridor. She knocked on the door.

"Who is it?"

"It's somebody to see you, Mr. Andreson," the woman said.

"It's Nick Adams."

"Come in."

Nick opened the door and went into the room. Ole Andreson was lying on the bed with all his clothes on. He had been a heavyweight prizefighter and he was too long for the bed. He lay with his head on two pillows. He did not look at Nick.

"What was it?" he asked.

"I was up at Henry's," Nick said, "and two fellows came in and tied up me and the cook, and they said they were going to kill you."

It sounded silly when he said it. Ole Andreson said nothing.

"They put us out in the kitchen," Nick went on. "They were going to shoot you when you came in to supper."

Ole Andreson looked at the wall and did not say anything.

"George thought I better come and tell you about it."

"There isn't anything I can do about it," Ole Andreson said.

"I'll tell you what they were like."

"I don't want to know what they were like," Ole Andreson said. He looked at the wall. "Thanks for coming to tell me about it."

"That's all right."

Nick looked at the big man lying on the bed.

"Don't you want me to go and see the police?"

"No," Ole Andreson said. "That wouldn't do any good."

"Isn't there something I could do?"

"No. There ain't anything to do."

"Maybe it was just a bluff."

"No. It ain't just a bluff."

Ole Andreson rolled over toward the wall.

"The only thing is," he said, talking toward the wall, "I just can't make up my mind to go out. I been in here all day."

"Couldn't you get out of town?"

"No," Ole Andreson said. "I'm through with all that running around."

He looked at the wall.

"There ain't anything to do now."

"Couldn't you fix it up some way?"

"No. I got in wrong." He talked in the same flat voice. "There ain't anything to do. After a while I'll make up my mind to go out."

"I better go back and see George," Nick said.

"So long," said Ole Andreson. He did not look toward Nick. "Thanks for coming around."

Nick went out. As he shut the door he saw Ole Andreson with all his clothes on, lying on the bed looking at the wall.

"He's been in his room all day," the landlady said downstairs. "I guess he don't feel well. I said to him: 'Mr. Andreson, you ought to go out and take a walk on a nice fall day like this,' but he didn't feel like it."

"He doesn't want to go out."

"I'm sorry he don't feel well," the woman said. "He's an awfully nice man. He was in the ring, you know."

"I know it."

"You'd never know it except from the way his face is," the woman said. They stood talking just inside the street door. "He's just as gentle."

"Well, good night, Mrs. Hirsch," Nick said.

"I'm not Mrs. Hirsch," the woman said. "She owns the place. I just look after it for her. I'm Mrs. Bell."

"Well, good night, Mrs. Bell," Nick said.

"Good night," the woman said.

Nick walked up the dark street to the corner under the arc-light, and then along the car-tracks to Henry's eating-house. George was inside, back of the counter.

"Did you see Ole?"

"Yes," said Nick. "He's in his room and he won't go out."

The cook opened the door from the kitchen when he heard Nick's voice.

"I don't even listen to it," he said and shut the door.

"Did you tell him about it?" George asked.

"Sure. I told him but he knows what it's all about."

"What's he going to do?"

"Nothing."

"They'll kill him."

"I guess they will."

"He must have got mixed up in something in Chicago."

"I guess so," said Nick.

"It's a hell of a thing."

"It's an awful thing," Nick said.

They did not say anything. George reached down for a towel and wiped the counter.

"I wonder what he did?" Nick said.

"Double-crossed somebody. That's what they kill them for."

"I'm going to get out of this town," Nick said.

"Yes," said George. "That's a good thing to do."

"I can't stand to think about him waiting in the room and knowing he's going to get it. It's too damned awful."

"Well," said George, "you better not think about it."

The Gambler, the Nun, and the Radio

BY ERNEST HEMINGWAY

T HEY brought them in around midnight and then, all night long, everyone along the corridor heard the Russian.

"Where is he shot?" Mr. Frazer asked the night nurse.

"In the thigh, I think."

"What about the other one?"

"Oh, he's going to die, I'm afraid."

"Where is he shot?"

"Twice in the abdomen. They only found one of the bullets."

They were both beet workers, a Mexican and a Russian, and they were sitting drinking coffee in an all-night restaurant when someone came in the door and started shooting at the Mexican. The Russian crawled under a table and was hit, finally, by a stray shot fired at the Mexican as he lay on the floor with two bullets in his abdomen. That was what the paper said.

The Mexican told the police he had no idea who shot him. He believed it to be an accident.

"An accident that he fired eight shots at you and hit you twice, there?"

"Si, señor," said the Mexican, who was named Cayetano Ruiz.

"An accident that he hit me at all, the cabron," he said to the interpreter.

"What does he say?" asked the detective sergeant, looking across the bed at the interpreter.

"He says it was an accident."

"Tell him to tell the truth, that he is going to die," the detective said.

"Na," said Cayetano. "But tell him that I feel very sick and would prefer not to talk so much."

"He says that he is telling the truth," the interpreter said. Then, speaking confidently, to the detective, "He don't know who shot him. They shot him in the back."

"Yes," said the detective. "I understand that, but why did the bullets all go in the front?"

"Maybe he is spinning around," said the interpreter.

"Listen," said the detective, shaking his finger almost at Cayetano's nose, which projected, waxen yellow, from his dead-man's face in which his eyes were alive as a hawk's. "I don't give a damn who shot you, but I've got to clear this thing up. Don't you want the man who shot you to be punished? Tell him that," he said to the interpreter.

"He says to tell who shot you."

"Mandarlo al carajo," said Cayetano, who was very tired.

"He says he never saw the fellow at all," the interpreter said. "I tell you straight they shot him in the back."

"Ask him who shot the Russian."

"Poor Russian," said Cayetano. "He was on the floor with his head enveloped in his arms. He started to give cries when they shoot him and he is giving cries ever since. Poor Russian."

"He says some fellow that he doesn't know. Maybe the same fellow that shot him."

"Listen," the detective said. "This isn't Chicago. You're not a gangster. You don't have to act like a moving picture. It's all right to tell who shot you. Anybody would tell who shot them. That's all right to do. Suppose you don't tell who he is and he shoots somebody else. Suppose he shoots a woman or a child. You can't let him get away with that. You tell him," he said to Mr. Frazer. "I don't trust that damn interpreter."

"I am very reliable," the interpreter said. Cayetano looked at Mr. Frazer.

"Listen, amigo," said Mr. Frazer. "The policeman says that we are not in Chicago but in Hailey, Montana. You are not a bandit and this has nothing to do with the cinema."

"I believe him," said Cayetano softly. "*Ya lo creo.*"

"One can, with honor, denounce one's assailant. Everyone does it here, he says. He says what happens if after shooting you, this man shoots a woman or a child?"

"I am not married," Cayetano said.

"He says any woman, any child."

"The man is not crazy," Cayetano said.

"He says you should denounce him," Mr. Frazer finished.

"Thank you," Cayetano said. "You are of the great translators. I speak English, but badly. I understand it all right. How did you break your leg?"

"A fall off a horse."

"What bad luck. I am very sorry. Does it hurt much?"

"Not now. At first, yes."

"Listen, amigo," Cayetano began. "I am very weak. You will pardon me. Also I have much pain; enough pain. It is very possible that I die. Please get this policeman out of here because I am very tired." He made as though to roll to one side; then held himself still.

"I told him everything exactly as you said and he said to tell you, truly, that he doesn't know who shot him and that he is very weak and wishes you would question him later on," Mr. Frazer said.

"He'll probably be dead later on."

"That's quite possible."

"That's why I want to question him now."

"Somebody shot him in the back, I tell you," the interpreter said.

"Oh, for Chrisake," the detective sergeant said, and put his notebook in his pocket.

Outside in the corridor the detective sergeant stood with the interpreter beside Mr. Frazer's wheeled chair.

"I suppose you think somebody shot him in the back too?"

"Yes," Frazer said. "Somebody shot him in the back. What's it to you?"

"Don't get sore," the sergeant said. "I wish I could talk spik."

"Why don't you learn?"

"You don't have to get sore. I don't get any fun out of asking that spik questions. If I could talk spik it would be different."

"You don't need to talk Spanish," the interpreter said. "I am a very reliable interpreter."

"Oh, for Chrisake," the sergeant said. "Well, so long. I'll come up and see you."

"Thanks. I'm always in."

"I guess you are all right. That was bad luck all right. Plenty bad luck."

"It's coming along good now since he spliced the bone."

"Yes, but it's a long time. A long, long time."

"Don't let anybody shoot you in the back."

"That's right," he said. "That's right. Well, I'm glad you're not sore."

"So long," said Mr. Frazer.

Mr. Frazer did not see Cayetano again for a long time, but each morning Sister Cecilia brought news of him. He was so uncomplaining she said and he was very bad now. He had peritonitis and they thought he could not live. Poor Cayetano, she said. He had such beautiful hands and such a fine face and he never complains. The odor, now, was really terrific. He would point toward his nose with one finger and smile and shake his head, she said. He felt badly about the odor. It embarrassed him, Sister Cecilia said. Oh, he was such a fine patient. He always smiled. He wouldn't go to confession to Father but he promised to say his prayers, and not a Mexican had been to see him since he had been brought in. The Russian was going out at the end of the week. I could never feel anything about the Russian, Sister Cecilia said. Poor fellow, he suffered too. It was a greased bullet and dirty and the wound infected, but he made so much noise and then I always like the bad ones. That Cayetano, he's a bad one. Oh, he must really be a bad one, a thoroughly bad one, he's so fine and delicately made and he's never done any work with his hands. He's not a beet worker. I know he's not a beet worker. His hands are as smooth and not a callus on them. I know he's a bad one of some sort. I'm going down and pray for him now. Poor Cayetano, he's having a dreadful time and he doesn't make a sound. What did they have to shoot him for? Oh, that poor Cayetano! I'm going right down and pray for him.

She went right down and prayed for him.

In that hospital a radio did not work very well until it was dusk. They said it was because there was so much ore in the ground or something about the mountains, but anyway it did not work well at all until it began to get dark outside; but all night it worked beautifully and when one station stopped you could go farther west and pick up another. The last one that you could get was Seattle, Washington, and due to the difference in time, when they signed off at four o'clock in the morning it was five o'clock in the morning in the hospital; and at six o'clock you could get the morning revelers in Minneapolis. That was on account of the difference in time, too, and Mr. Frazer used to like to think of the morning revelers arriving at the studio and picture how they would look getting off a street car before daylight in the morning carrying their instruments. Maybe that was wrong and they kept their instruments at the place they reveled, but he always pictured them with their instruments. He had never been in Minneapolis and believed he probably would never go there, but he knew what it looked like that early in the morning.

Out of the window of the hospital you could see a field with tumbleweed coming out of the snow, and a bare clay butte. One morning the doctor wanted to show Mr. Frazer two pheasants that were out there in the snow, and pulling the bed toward the window, the reading light fell off the iron bedstead and hit Mr. Frazer on the head. This does not sound so funny now but it was very funny then. Everyone was looking out the window, and the doctor, who was a most excellent doctor, was pointing at the pheasants and pulling the bed toward the window, and then, just as in a comic section, Mr. Frazer was knocked out by the leaded base of the lamp hitting the top of his head. It seemed the antithesis of healing or whatever people were in the hospital for, and everyone thought it was very funny, as a joke on Mr. Frazer and on the doctor. Everything is much simpler in a hospital, including the jokes.

From the other window, if the bed was turned, you could see the town, with a little smoke above it, and the Dawson mountains looking like real mountains with the winter snow on them. Those were the two views since the wheeled chair had proved to be premature. It is really best to be in bed if you are in a hospital; since two views, with time to observe them, from a room the temperature of which you control, are much better than any number of views seen for a few minutes from hot, empty rooms that are waiting for someone else, or just abandoned, which you are wheeled in and out of. If you stay long enough in a room the view, whatever it is, acquires a great value and becomes very important and you would not change it, not even by a different angle. Just as, with the radio, there are certain things that you become fond of, and you welcome them and resent the new things. The best tunes they had that winter were "Sing Something Simple," "Singsong Girl," and "Little White Lies." No other tunes were as satisfactory, Mr. Frazer felt. "Betty Co-ed" was a good tune too, but the parody of the words which came unavoidably into Mr. Frazer's mind, grew so steadily and increasingly obscene that there being no one to appreciate it, he finally abandoned it and let the song go back to football.

About nine o'clock in the morning they would start using the X-ray machine, and then the radio, which, by then, was only getting Hailey, became useless. Many people in Hailey who owned radios protested about the hospital's X-ray machine which ruined their morning reception, but there was never any action taken, although many felt it was a shame the hospital could not use their machine at a time when people were not using their radios.

About the time when it became necessary to turn off the radio Sister Cecilia came in.

"How's Cayetano, Sister Cecilia?" Mr. Frazer asked.

"Oh, he's very bad."

"Is he out of his head?"

"No, but I'm afraid he's going to die."

"How are you?"

"I'm very worried about him, and do you know that absolutely no one has come to see him? He could die just like a dog for all those Mexicans care. They're really dreadful."

"Do you want to come up and hear the game this afternoon?"

"Oh, no," she said. "I'd be too excited. I'll be in the chapel praying."

"We ought to be able to hear it pretty well," Mr. Frazer said. "They're playing out on the coast and the difference in time will bring it late enough so we can get it all right."

"Oh, no. I couldn't do it. The world series nearly finished me. When the Athletics were at bat I was praying right out loud: 'Oh, Lord, direct their batting eyes! Oh, Lord, may he hit one! Oh, Lord, may he hit safely!' Then when they filled the bases in the third game, you remember, it was too much for me. 'Oh, Lord, may he hit it out of the lot! Oh, Lord, may he drive it clean over the fence!' Then you know when the Cardinals would come to bat it was simply dreadful. 'Oh, Lord, may they not see it! Oh, Lord, don't let them even catch a glimpse of it! Oh, Lord, may they fan!' And this game is even worse. It's Notre Dame. Our Lady. No, I'll be in the chapel. For Our Lady. They're playing for Our Lady. I wish you'd write something sometime for Our Lady. You could do it. You know you could do it, Mr. Frazer."

"I don't know anything about her that I could write. It's mostly been written already," Mr. Frazer said. "You wouldn't like the way I write. She wouldn't care for it either."

"You'll write about her sometime," Sister said. "I know you will. You must write about Our Lady."

"You'd better come up and hear the game."

"It would be too much for me. No, I'll be in the chapel doing what I can."

That afternoon they had been playing about five minutes when a probationer came into the room and said, "Sister Cecilia wants to know how the game is going?"

"Tell her they have a touchdown already."

In a little while the probationer came into the room again.

"Tell her they're playing them off their feet," Mr. Frazer said.

A little later he rang the bell for the nurse who was on floor duty. "Would you mind going down to the chapel or sending word down to Sister Cecilia that Notre Dame has them fourteen to nothing at the end of the first quarter and that it's all right? She can stop praying."

In a few minutes Sister Cecilia came into the room. She was very excited. "What does fourteen to nothing mean? I don't know anything about this game. That's a nice safe lead in baseball. But I don't know

anything about football. It may not mean a thing. I'm going right back
down to the chapel and pray until it's finished."

"They have them beaten," Frazer said. "I promise you. Stay and
listen with me."

"No. No. No. No. No. No. No," she said. "I'm going right down to
the chapel to pray."

Mr. Frazer sent down word whenever Notre Dame scored, and
finally, when it had been dark a long time, the final result.

"How's Sister Cecilia?"

"They're all at chapel," she said.

The next morning Sister Cecilia came in. She was very pleased and
confident.

"I knew they couldn't beat Our Lady," she said. "They couldn't.
Cayetano's better too. He's much better. He's going to have visitors. He
can't see them yet, but they are going to come and that will make him
feel better and know he's not forgotten by his own people. I went down
and saw that O'Brien boy at Police Headquarters and told him that he's
got to send some Mexicans up to see poor Cayetano. He's going to send
some this afternoon. Then that poor man will feel better. It's wicked
the way no one has come to see him."

That afternoon about five o'clock three Mexicans came into the room.

"Can one?" asked the biggest one, who had very thick lips and was
quite fat.

"Why not?" Mr. Frazer answered. "Sit down, gentlemen. Will you
take something?"

"Many thanks," said the big one.

"Thanks," said the darkest and smallest one.

"Thanks, no," said the thin one. "It mounts to my head." He tapped
his head.

The nurse brought some glasses. "Please give them the bottle," Frazer
said. "It is from Red Lodge," he explained.

"That of Red Lodge is the best," said the big one. "Much better than
that of Big Timber."

"Clearly," said the smallest one, "and costs more too."

"In Red Lodge it is of all prices," said the big one.

"How many tubes has the radio?" asked the one who did not drink.
"Seven."

"Very beautiful," he said. "What does it cost?"

"I don't know," Mr. Frazer said. "It is rented."

"You gentlemen are friends of Cayetano?"

"No," said the big one. "We are friends of he who wounded him."

"We were sent here by the police," the smallest one said.

"We have a little place," the big one said. "He and I," indicating the one who did not drink. "He has a little place too," indicating the small, dark one. "The police tell us we have to come—so we come."

"I am very happy you have come."

"Equally," said the big one.

"Will you have another little cup?"

"Why not?" said the big one.

"With your permission," said the smallest one.

"Not me," said the thin one. "It mounts to my head."

"It is very good," said the smallest one.

"Why not try some?" Mr. Frazer asked the thin one. "Let a little mount to your head."

"Afterwards comes the headache," said the thin one.

"Could you not send friends of Cayetano to see him?" Frazer asked.

"He has no friends."

"Every man has friends."

"This one, no."

"What does he do?"

"He is a card-player."

"Is he good?"

"I believe it."

"From me," said the smallest one, "he won one hundred and eighty dollars. Now there is no longer one hundred and eighty dollars in the world."

"From me," said the thin one, "he won two hundred and eleven dollars. Fix yourself on that figure."

"I never played with him," said the fat one.

"He must be very rich," Mr. Frazer suggested.

"He is poorer than we," said the little Mexican. "He has no more than the shirt on his back."

"And that shirt is of little value now," Mr. Frazer said. "Perforated as it is."

"Clearly."

"The one who wounded him was a card-player?"

"No, a beet worker. He has had to leave town."

"Fix yourself on this," said the smallest one. "He was the best guitar player ever in this town. The finest."

"What a shame."

"I believe it," said the biggest one. "How he could touch the guitar."

"There are no good guitar players left?"

"Not the shadow of a guitar player."

"There is an accordion player who is worth something," the thin man said.

"There are a few who touch various instruments," the big one said. "You like music?"

"How would I not?"

"We will come one night with music? You think the sister would allow it? She seems very amiable."

"I am sure she would permit it when Cayetano is able to hear it."

"Is she a little crazy?" asked the thin one.

"Who?"

"That sister?"

"No," Mr. Frazer said. "She is a fine woman of great intelligence and sympathy."

"I distrust all priests, monks, and sisters," said the thin one.

"He had bad experiences when a boy," the smallest one said.

"I was acolyte," the thin one said proudly. "Now I believe in nothing. Neither do I go to mass."

"Why? Does it mount to your head?"

"No," said the thin one. "It is alcohol that mounts to my head. Religion is the opium of the poor."

"I thought mariajuana was the opium of the poor," Frazer said.

"Did you ever smoke opium?" the big one asked.

"No."

"Nor I," he said. "It seems it is very bad. One commences and cannot stop. It is a vice."

"Like religion," said the thin one.

"This one," said the smallest Mexican, "is very strong against religion."

"It is necessary to be very strong against something," Mr. Frazer said politely.

"I respect those who have faith even though they are ignorant," the thin one said.

"Good," said Mr. Frazer.

"What can we bring you?" asked the big Mexican. "Do you lack for anything?"

"I would be glad to buy some beer if there is good beer."

"We will bring beer."

"Another copita before you go?"

"It is very good."

"We are robbing you."

"I can't take it. It goes to my head. Then I have a bad headache and sick at the stomach."

"Good-by, gentlemen."

"Good-by and thanks."

They went out and there was supper and then the radio, turned to be as quiet as possible and still be heard, and the stations finally signing off in this order: Denver, Salt Lake City, Los Angeles, and Seattle. Mr. Frazer received no picture of Denver from the radio. He could see Denver from the *Denver Post,* and correct the picture from *The Rocky Mountain News.* Nor did he ever have any feel of Salt Lake City or Los Angeles from what he heard from those places. All he felt about Salt Lake City was that it was clean, but dull, and there were too many ballrooms mentioned in too many big hotels for him to see Los Angeles. He could not feel it for the ballrooms. But Seattle he came to know very well, the taxicab company with the big white cabs (each cab equipped with radio itself) he rode in every night out to the roadhouse on the Canadian side where he followed the course of parties by the musical selections they phoned for. He lived in Seattle from two o'clock on, each night, hearing the pieces that all the different people asked for, and it was as real as Minneapolis, where the revelers left their beds each morning to make that trip down to the studio. Mr. Frazer grew very fond of Seattle, Washington.

The Mexicans came and brought beer but it was not good beer. Mr. Frazer saw them but he did not feel like talking, and when they went he knew they would not come again. His nerves had become tricky and he disliked seeing people while he was in this condition. His nerves went bad at the end of five weeks, and while he was pleased they lasted that long yet he resented being forced to make the same experiment when he already knew the answer. Mr. Frazer had been through this all before. The only thing which was news to him was the radio. He played it all night long, turned so low he could barely hear it, and he was learning to listen to it without thinking.

Sister Cecilia came into the room about ten o'clock in the morning on that day and brought the mail. She was very handsome, and Mr. Frazer liked to see her and to hear her talk, but the mail, supposedly coming from a different world, was more important. However, there was nothing in the mail of any interest.

"You look *so* much better," she said. "You'll be leaving us soon."

"Yes," Mr. Frazer said. "You look very happy this morning."

"Oh, I am. This morning I feel as though I might be a saint."

Mr. Frazer was a little taken aback at this.

"Yes," Sister Cecilia went on. "That's what I want to be. A saint. Ever since I was a little girl I've wanted to be a saint. When I was a girl I thought if I renounced the world and went into the convent I would be a saint. That was what I wanted to be and that was what I thought I had to do to be one. I expected I would be a saint. I was

absolutely sure I would be one. For just a moment I thought I was
one. I was so happy and it seemed so simple and easy. When I awoke
in the morning I expected I would be a saint, but I wasn't. I've never
become one. I want to be one. All I want is to be a saint. That is all I've
ever wanted. And this morning I feel as though I might be one. Oh,
I hope I will get to be one."

"You'll be one. Everybody gets what they want. That's what they
always tell me."

"I don't know now. When I was a girl it seemed so simple. I knew
I would be a saint. Only I believed it took time when I found it did not
happen suddenly. Now it seems almost impossible."

"I'd say you had a good chance."

"Do you really think so? No, I don't want just to be encouraged.
Don't just encourage me. I want to be a saint. I want so to be a saint."

"Of course you'll be a saint," Mr. Frazer said.

"No, probably I won't be. But, oh, if I could only be a saint! I'd be
perfectly happy."

"You're three to one to be a saint."

"No, don't encourage me. But, oh, if I could only be a saint! If I
could only be a saint!"

"How's your friend Cayetano?"

"He's going to get well but he's paralyzed. One of the bullets hit the
big nerve that goes down through his thigh and that leg is paralyzed.
They only found it out when he got well enough so that he could move."

"Maybe the nerve will regenerate."

"I'm praying that it will," Sister Cecilia said. "You ought to see him."

"I don't feel like seeing anybody."

"You know you'd like to see him. They could wheel him in here."

"All right."

They wheeled him in, thin, his skin transparent, his hair black and
needing to be cut, his eyes very laughing, his teeth bad when he smiled.
"Hola, amigo! Que tal?"

"As you see," said Mr. Frazer. "And thou?"

"Alive and with the leg paralyzed."

"Bad," Mr. Frazer said. "But the nerve can regenerate and be as good
as new."

"So they tell me."

"What about the pain?"

"Not now. For a while I was crazy with it in the belly. I thought the
pain alone would kill me."

Sister Cecilia was observing them happily.

"She tells me you never made a sound," Mr. Frazer said.

"So many people in the ward," the Mexican said deprecatingly. "What class of pain do you have?"

"Big enough. Clearly not as bad as yours. When the nurse goes out I cry an hour, two hours. It rests me. My nerves are bad now."

"You have the radio. If I had a private room and a radio I would be crying and yelling all night long."

"I doubt it."

"*Hombre, si.* It's very healthy. But you cannot do it with so many people."

"At least," Mr. Frazer said, "the hands are still good. They tell me you make your living with the hands."

"And the head," he said, tapping his forehead. "But the head isn't worth as much."

"Three of your countrymen were here."

"Sent by the police to see me."

"They brought some beer."

"It probably was bad."

"It was bad."

"Tonight, sent by the police, they come to serenade me." He laughed, then tapped his stomach. "I cannot laugh yet. As musicians they are fatal."

"And the one who shot you?"

"Another fool. I won thirty-eight dollars from him at cards. That is not to kill about."

"The three told me you win much money."

"And am poorer than the birds."

"How?"

"I am a poor idealist. I am the victim of illusions." He laughed, then grinned and tapped his stomach. "I am a professional gambler but I like to gamble. To really gamble. Little gambling is all crooked. For real gambling you need luck. I have no luck."

"Never?"

"Never. I am completely without luck. Look, this cabron who shoots me just now. Can he shoot? No. The first shot he fires into nothing. The second is intercepted by a poor Russian. That would seem to be luck. What happens? He shoots me twice in the belly. He is a lucky man. I have no luck. He could not hit a horse if he were holding the stirrup. All luck."

"I thought he shot you first and the Russian after."

"No, the Russian first, me after. The paper was mistaken."

"Why didn't you shoot him?"

"I never carry a gun. With my luck, if I carried a gun I would be hanged ten times a year. I am a cheap card player, only that." He stopped, then continued. "When I make a sum of money I gamble and when I gamble I lose. I have passed at dice for three thousand dollars and crapped out for the six. With good dice. More than once."

"Why continue?"

"If I live long enough the luck will change. I have bad luck now for fifteen years. If I ever get any good luck I will be rich." He grinned. "I am a good gambler, really I would enjoy being rich."

"Do you have bad luck with all games?"

"With everything and with women." He smiled again, showing his bad teeth.

"Truly?"

"Truly."

"And what is there to do?"

"Continue, slowly, and wait for luck to change."

"But with women?"

"No gambler has luck with women. He is too concentrated. He works nights. When he should be with the woman. No man who works nights can hold a woman if the woman is worth anything."

"You are a philosopher."

"No, hombre. A gambler of the small towns. One small town, then another, then a big town, then start over again."

"Then shot in the belly."

"The first time," he said. "That has only happened once."

"I tire you talking?" Mr. Frazer suggested.

"No," he said. "I must tire you."

"And the leg?"

"I have no great use for the leg. I am all right with the leg or not. I will be able to circulate."

"I wish you luck, truly, and with all my heart," Mr. Frazer said.

"Equally," he said. "And that the pain stops."

"It will not last, certainly. It is passing. It is of no importance."

"That it passes quickly."

"Equally."

That night the Mexicans played the accordion and other instruments in the ward and it was cheerful and the noise of the inhalations and exhalations of the accordion, and of the bells, the traps, and the drum came down the corridor. In that ward there was a rodeo rider who had come out of the chutes on Midnight on a hot dusty afternoon with a big crowd watching, and now, with a broken back, was going to learn to work in leather and to cane chairs when he got well enough to leave the hospital. There was a carpenter who had fallen with a scaffolding and broken both ankles and both wrists. He had lit like a cat without a cat's resiliency. They could fix him up so that he could work again but it would take a long time. There was a boy from a farm, about sixteen years old, with a broken leg that had been badly set and was to be rebroken. There was Cayetano Ruiz, a small-town gambler with a paralyzed leg. Down the corridor Mr. Frazer could hear them all laughing and merry with the music made by the Mexicans who had been sent by the police. The Mexicans were having a good time. They came in, very excited, to see Mr. Frazer and wanted to know if there was anything he wanted them to play, and they came twice more to play at night of their own accord.

The last time they played Mr. Frazer lay in his room with the door open and listened to the noisy, bad music and could not keep from thinking. When they wanted to know what he wished played, he asked for the Cucaracha, which has the sinister lightness and deftness of so many of the tunes men have gone to die to. They played noisily and with emotion. The tune was better than most of such tunes, to Mr. Frazer's mind, but the effect was all the same.

In spite of this introduction of emotion, Mr. Frazer went on thinking. Usually he avoided thinking all he could, except when he was writing, but now he was thinking about those who were playing and what the little one had said.

Religion is the opium of the people. He believed that, that dyspeptic little joint-keeper. Yes, and music is the opium of the people. Old mount-to-the-head hadn't thought of that. And now economics is the opium of the people; along with patriotism the opium of the people in Italy and Germany. What about sexual intercourse; was that an opium of the people? Of some of the people. Of some of the best of the people. But drink was a sovereign opium of the people, oh, an excellent opium. Although some prefer the radio, another opium of the people, a cheap one he had just been using. Along with these went gambling, an opium of the people if there ever was one, one of the oldest. Ambition was another, an opium of the people, along with a belief in any new form of government. What you wanted was the minimum of government, always less government. Liberty, what we believed in, now the name of a McFadden publication. We believed in that although they had not found a new name for it yet. But what was the real one? What was the real, the actual, opium of the people? He knew it very well. It was gone just a little way around the corner in that well-lighted part of his mind that was there after two or more drinks in the evening; that he knew was there (it was not really there of course). What was it? He knew very well. What was it? Of course; bread was the opium of the people. Would he remember that and would it make sense in the daylight? Bread is the opium of the people.

"Listen," Mr. Frazer said to the nurse when she came. "Get that little thin Mexican in here, will you, please?"

"How did you like it?" the Mexican said at the door.

"Very much."

"It is a historic tune," the Mexican said. "It is the tune of the real revolution."

"Listen," said Mr. Frazer. "Why should the people be operated on without an anæsthetic?"

"I do not understand."

"Why are not all the opiums of the people good? What do you want to do with the people?"

"They should be rescued from ignorance."

"Don't talk nonsense. Education is an opium of the people. You ought to know that. You've had a little."

"You do not believe in education?"

"No," said Mr. Frazer. "In knowledge, yes."

"I do not follow you."

"Many times I do not follow myself with pleasure."

"You want to hear the Cucaracha another time?" asked the Mexican worriedly.

"Yes," said Mr. Frazier. "Play the Cucaracha another time. It's better than the radio."

Revolution, Mr. Frazer thought, is no opium. Revolution is a catharsis; an ecstasy which can only be prolonged by tyranny. The opiums are for before and for after. He was thinking well, a little too well.

They would go now in a little while, he thought, and they would take the Cucaracha with them. Then he would have a little spot of the giant killer and play the radio, you could play the radio so that you could hardly hear it.

63

The Red Pony

BY JOHN STEINBECK

I. THE GIFT

AT daybreak Billy Buck emerged from the bunkhouse and stood for a moment on the porch looking up at the sky. He was a broad, bandy-legged little man with a walrus mustache, with square hands, puffed and muscled on the palms. His eyes were a contemplative, watery gray and the hair which protruded from under his Stetson hat was spiky and weathered. Billy was still stuffing his shirt into his blue jeans as he stood on the porch. He unbuckled his belt and tightened it again. The belt showed, by the worn shiny places opposite each hole, the gradual increase of Billy's middle over a period of years. When he had seen to the weather, Billy cleared each nostril by holding its mate closed with his forefinger and blowing fiercely. Then he walked down to the barn, rubbing his hands together. He curried and brushed two saddle horses in the stalls, talking quietly to them all the time; and he had hardly finished when the iron triangle started ringing at the ranch house. Billy stuck the brush and currycomb together and laid them on the rail, and went up to breakfast. His action had been so deliberate and yet so wasteless of time that he came to the house while Mrs. Tiflin was still ringing the triangle. She nodded her gray head to him and withdrew into the kitchen. Billy Buck sat down on the steps, because he was a cow-hand, and it wouldn't be fitting that he should go first into the dining room. He heard Mr. Tiflin in the house, stamping his feet into his boots.

The high jangling note of the triangle put the boy Jody in motion. He was only a little boy, ten years old, with hair like dusty yellow grass and with shy polite gray eyes, and with a mouth that worked when he thought. The triangle picked him up out of sleep. It didn't occur to him to disobey the harsh note. He never had: no one he knew ever had. He brushed the tangled hair out of his eyes and skinned his nightgown off. In a moment he was dressed—blue chambray shirt and overalls. It was late in the summer, so of course there were no shoes to bother with. In the kitchen he waited until his mother got from in front of the sink and went back to the stove. Then he washed himself and brushed back his wet hair with his fingers. His mother turned sharply on him as he left the sink. Jody looked shyly away.

"I've got to cut your hair before long," his mother said. "Breakfast's on the table. Go on in, so Billy can come."

Jody sat at the long table which was covered with white oilcloth washed through to the fabric in some places. The fried eggs lay in rows on their platter. Jody took three eggs on his plate and followed with three thick slices of crisp bacon. He carefully scraped a spot of blood from one of the egg yolks.

Billy Buck clumped in. "That won't hurt you," Billy explained. "That's only a sign the rooster leaves."

Jody's tall stern father came in then and Jody knew from the noise on the floor that he was wearing boots, but he looked under the table anyway, to make sure. His father turned off the oil lamp over the table, for plenty of morning light now came through the windows.

Jody did not ask where his father and Billy Buck were riding that day, but he wished he might go along. His father was a disciplinarian. Jody obeyed him in everything without questions of any kind. Now, Carl Tiflin sat down and reached for the egg platter.

"Got the cows ready to go, Billy?" he asked.

"In the lower corral," Billy said. "I could just as well take them in alone."

"Sure you could. But a man needs company. Besides your throat gets pretty dry." Carl Tiflin was jovial this morning.

Jody's mother put her head in the door. "What time do you think to be back, Carl?"

"I can't tell. I've got to see some men in Salinas. Might be gone till dark."

The eggs and coffee and big biscuits disappeared rapidly. Jody followed the two men out of the house. He watched them mount their horses and drive six old milk cows out of the corral and start over the hill toward Salinas. They were going to sell the old cows to the butcher.

When they had disappeared over the crown of the ridge Jody walked up the hill in back of the house. The dogs trotted around the house corner hunching their shoulders and grinning horribly with pleasure.

Jody patted their heads—Doubletree Mutt with the big thick tail and yellow eyes, and Smasher, the shepherd, who had killed a coyote and lost an ear in doing it. Smasher's one good ear stood up higher than a collie's ear should. Billy Buck said that always happened. After the frenzied greeting the dogs lowered their noses to the ground in a businesslike way and went ahead, looking back now and then to make sure that the boy was coming. They walked up through the chicken yard and saw the quail eating with the chickens. Smasher chased the chickens a little to keep in practice in case there should ever be sheep to herd. Jody continued on through the large vegetable patch where the green corn was higher than his head. The cow-pumpkins were green and small yet. He went on to the sagebrush line where the cold spring ran out of its pipe and fell into a round wooden tub. He leaned over and drank close to the green mossy wood where the water tasted best. Then he turned and looked back on the ranch, on the low, whitewashed house girded with red geraniums, and on the long bunkhouse by the cypress tree where Billy Buck lived alone. Jody could see the great black kettle under the cypress tree. That was where the pigs were scalded. The sun was coming over the ridge now, glaring on the whitewash of the houses and barns, making the wet grass blaze softly. Behind him, in the tall sagebrush, the birds were scampering on the ground, making a great noise among the dry leaves; the squirrels piped shrilly on the side-hills. Jody looked along at the farm buildings. He felt an uncertainty in the air, a feeling of change and of loss and of the gain of new and unfamiliar things. Over the hillside two big black buzzards sailed low to the ground and their shadows slipped smoothly and quickly ahead of them. Some animal had died in the vicinity. Jody knew it. It might be a cow or it might be the remains of a rabbit. The buzzards overlooked nothing. Jody hated them as all decent things hate them, but they could not be hurt because they made away with carrion.

After a while the boy sauntered down hill again. The dogs had long ago given him up and gone into the brush to do things in their own way. Back through the vegetable garden he went, and he paused for a moment to smash a green muskmelon with his heel, but he was not happy about it. It was a bad thing to do, he knew perfectly well. He kicked dirt over the ruined melon to conceal it.

Back at the house his mother bent over his rough hands, inspecting his fingers and nails. It did little good to start him clean to school, for too many things could happen on the way. She sighed over the black cracks on his fingers, and then gave him his books and his lunch and started him on the mile walk to school. She noticed that his mouth was working a good deal this morning.

Jody started his journey. He filled his pockets with little pieces of white quartz that lay in the road, and every so often he took a shot at a bird or at some rabbit that had stayed sunning itself in the road too long. At the crossroads over the bridge he met two friends and the three of them walked to school together, making ridiculous strides and being rather silly. School had just opened two weeks before. There was still a spirit of revolt among the pupils.

It was four o'clock in the afternoon when Jody topped the hill and looked down on the ranch again. He looked for the saddle horses, but the corral was empty. His father was not back yet. He went slowly, then, toward the afternoon chores. At the ranch house, he found his mother sitting on the porch, mending socks.

"There's two doughnuts in the kitchen for you," she said. Jody slid to the kitchen, and returned with half of one of the doughnuts already eaten and his mouth full. His mother asked him what he had learned in school that day, but she didn't listen to his doughnut-muffled answer. She interrupted, "Jody, tonight see you fill the wood-box clear full. Last night you crossed the sticks and it wasn't only about half full. Lay the sticks flat tonight. And Jody, some of the hens are hiding eggs, or else the dogs are eating them. Look about in the grass and see if you can find any nests."

Jody, still eating, went out and did his chores. He saw the quail come down to eat with the chickens when he threw out the grain. For some reason his father was proud to have them come. He never allowed any shooting near the house for fear the quail might go away.

When the wood-box was full, Jody took his twenty-two rifle up to the cold spring at the brush line. He drank again and then aimed the gun at all manner of things, at rocks, at birds on the wing, at the big black pig kettle under the cypress tree, but he didn't shoot, for he had no cartridges and wouldn't have until he was twelve. If his father had seen him aim the rifle in the direction of the house he would have put the cartridges off another year. Jody remembered this and did not point the rifle down the hill again. Two years was enough to wait for cartridges. Nearly all of his father's presents were given with reservations which hampered their value somewhat. It was good discipline.

The supper waited until dark for his father to return. When at last he came in with Billy Buck, Jody could smell the delicious brandy on their breaths. Inwardly he rejoiced, for his father sometimes talked to him when he smelled of brandy, sometimes even told things he had done in the wild days when he was a boy.

After supper, Jody sat by the fireplace and his shy polite eyes sought the room corners, and he waited for his father to tell what it was he contained, for Jody knew he had news of some sort. But he was dis-appointed. His father pointed a stern finger at him.

"You'd better go to bed, Jody. I'm going to need you in the morning."

That wasn't so bad. Jody liked to do things he had to do as long as they weren't routine things. He looked at the floor and his mouth worked out a question before he spoke it. "What are we going to do in the morning, kill a pig?" he asked softly.

"Never you mind. You better get to bed."

When the door was closed behind him, Jody heard his father and Billy Buck chuckling and he knew it was a joke of some kind. And later, when he lay in bed, trying to make words out of the murmurs in the other room, he heard his father protest, "But, Ruth, I didn't give much for him."

Jody heard the hoot-owls hunting mice down by the barn, and he heard a fruit tree limb tap-tapping against the house. A cow was lowing when he went to sleep.

When the triangle sounded in the morning, Jody dressed more quickly even than usual. In the kitchen, while he washed his face and combed back his hair, his mother addressed him irritably. "Don't you go out until you get a good breakfast in you."

He went into the dining room and sat at the long white table. He took a steaming hotcake from the platter, arranged two fried eggs on it, covered them with another hotcake and squashed the whole thing with his fork.

His father and Billy Buck came in. Jody knew from the sound on the floor that both of them were wearing flat-heeled shoes, but he peered under the table to make sure. His father turned off the oil lamp, for the day had arrived, and he looked stern and disciplinary, but Billy Buck didn't look at Jody at all. He avoided the shy questioning eyes of the boy and soaked a whole piece of toast in his coffee.

Carl Tiflin said crossly, "You come with us after breakfast!"

Jody had trouble with his food then, for he felt a kind of doom in the air. After Billy had tilted his saucer and drained the coffee which had slopped into it, and had wiped his hands on his jeans, the two men stood up from the table and went out into the morning light together, and Jody respectfully followed a little behind them. He tried to keep his mind from running ahead, tried to keep it absolutely motionless.

His mother called, "Carl! Don't you let it keep him from school."

They marched past the cypress, where a singletree hung from a limb to butcher the pigs on, and past the black iron kettle, so it was not a pig killing. The sun shone over the hill and threw long, dark shadows of the trees and buildings. They crossed a stubble-field to shortcut to the barn. Jody's father unhooked the door and they went in. They had been walking toward the sun on the way down. The barn was black as night in contrast and warm from the hay and from the beasts. Jody's father moved over toward the one box stall. "Come here!" he ordered. Jody could begin to see things now. He looked into the box stall and then stepped back quickly.

A red pony colt was looking at him out of the stall. Its tense ears were forward and a light of disobedience was in its eyes. Its coat was rough and thick as an airedale's fur and its mane was long and tangled. Jody's throat collapsed in on itself and cut his breath short.

"He needs a good currying," his father said, "and if I ever hear of you not feeding him or leaving his stall dirty, I'll sell him off in a minute."

Jody couldn't bear to look at the pony's eyes any more. He gazed down at his hands for a moment, and he asked very shyly, "Mine?" No one answered him. He put his hand out toward the pony. Its gray nose came close, sniffing loudly, and then the lips drew back and the strong teeth closed on Jody's fingers. The pony shook its head up and down and seemed to laugh with amusement. Jody regarded his bruised fingers. "Well," he said with pride—"Well, I guess he can bite all right." The two men laughed, somewhat in relief. Carl Tiflin went out of the barn and walked up a side-hill to be by himself, for he was embarrassed, but Billy Buck stayed. It was easier to talk to Billy Buck. Jody asked again—"Mine?"

Billy became professional in tone. "Sure! That is, if you look out for him and break him right. I'll show you how. He's just a colt. You can't ride him for some time."

Jody put out his bruised hand again, and this time the red pony let his nose be rubbed. "I ought to have a carrot," Jody said. "Where'd we get him, Billy?"

"Bought him at a sheriff's auction," Billy explained. "A show went broke in Salinas and had debts. The sheriff was selling off their stuff."

The pony stretched out his nose and shook the forelock from his wild eyes. Jody stroked the nose a little. He said softly, "There isn't a —saddle?"

Billy Buck laughed. "I'd forgot. Come along."

In the harness room he lifted down a little saddle of red morocco leather. "It's just a show saddle," Billy Buck said disparagingly. "It isn't practical for the brush, but it was cheap at the sale."

Jody couldn't trust himself to look at the saddle either, and he couldn't speak at all. He brushed the shining red leather with his finger-tips, and after a long time he said, "It'll look prettv on him though."

He thought of the grandest and prettiest things he knew. "If he hasn't a name already, I think I'll call him Gabilan Mountains," he said.

Billy Buck knew how he felt. "It's a pretty long name. Why don't you just call him Gabilan? That means hawk. That would be a fine name for him." Billy felt glad. "If you will collect tail hair, I might be able to make a hair rope for you sometime. You could use it for a hackamore."

Jody wanted to go back to the box stall. "Could I lead him to school, do you think—to show the kids?"

But Billy shook his head. "He's not even halter-broke yet. We had a time getting him here. Had to almost drag him. You better be starting for school though."

"I'll bring the kids to see him here this afternoon," Jody said.

Six boys came over the hill half an hour early that afternoon, running hard, their heads down, their forearms working, their breath whistling. They swept by the house and cut across the stubble-field to the barn. And then they stood self-consciously before the pony, and then they looked at Jody with eyes in which there was a new admiration and a new respect. Before today Jody had been a boy, dressed in overalls and a blue shirt—quieter than most, even suspected of being a little cowardly. And now he was different. Out of a thousand centuries they drew the ancient admiration of the footman for the horseman. They knew instinctively that a man on a horse is spiritually as well as physically bigger than a man on foot. They knew that Jody had been miraculously lifted out of equality with them, and had been placed over them. Gabilan put his head out of the stall and sniffed them.

"Why'n't you ride him?" the boys cried. "Why'n't you braid his tail with ribbons like in the fair?" "When you going to ride him?"

Jody's courage was up. He too felt the superiority of the horseman. "He's not old enough. Nobody can ride him for a long time. I'm going to train him on the long halter. Billy Buck is going to show me how."

"Well, can't we even lead him around a little?"

"He isn't even halter-broke," Jody said. He wanted to be completely alone when he took the pony out the first time. "Come and see the saddle."

They were speechless at the red morocco saddle, completely shocked out of comment. "It isn't much use in the brush," Jody explained. "It'll look pretty on him though. Maybe I'll ride bareback when I go into the brush."

"How you going to rope a cow without a saddle horn?"

"Maybe I'll get another saddle for every day. My father might want me to help him with the stock." He let them feel the red saddle, and showed them the brass chain throat-latch on the bridle and the big brass buttons at each temple where the headstall and brow band crossed. The whole thing was too wonderful. They had to go away after a little while, and each boy, in his mind, searched among his possessions for a bribe worthy of offering in return for a ride on the red pony when the time should come.

Jody was glad when they had gone. He took brush and currycomb from the wall, took down the barrier of the box stall and stepped cautiously in. The pony's eyes glittered, and he edged around into kicking position. But Jody touched him on the shoulder and rubbed his high arched neck as he had always seen Billy Buck do, and he crooned, "So-o-o Boy," in a deep voice. The pony gradually relaxed his tenseness. Jody curried and brushed until a pile of dead hair lay in the stall and until the pony's coat had taken on a deep red shine. Each time he finished he thought it might have been done better. He braided the mane into a dozen little pigtails, and he braided the forelock, and then he undid them and brushed the hair out straight again.

Jody did not hear his mother enter the barn. She was angry when she came, but when she looked in at the pony and at Jody working over him, she felt a curious pride rise up in her. "Have you forgot the wood-box?" she asked gently. "It's not far off from dark and there's not a stick of wood in the house, and the chickens aren't fed."

Jody quickly put up his tools. "I forgot, ma'am."

"Well, after this do your chores first. Then you won't forget. I expect you'll forget lots of things now if I don't keep an eye on you."

"Can I have carrots from the garden for him, ma'am?"

She had to think about that. "Oh—I guess so, if you only take the big tough ones."

"Carrots keep the coat good," he said, and again she felt the curious rush of pride.

Jody never waited for the triangle to get him out of bed after the coming of the pony. It became his habit to creep out of bed even before his mother was awake, to slip into his clothes and to go quietly down to the barn to see Gabilan. In the gray quiet mornings when the land and the brush and the houses and the trees were silver-gray and black like a photograph negative, he stole toward the barn, past the sleeping stones and the sleeping cypress tree. The turkeys, roosting in the tree out of coyotes' reach, clicked drowsily. The fields glowed with a gray frost-like light and in the dew the tracks of rabbits and of field mice stood out sharply. The good dogs came stiffly out of their little houses, hackles up and deep growls in their throats. Then they caught Jody's scent, and their stiff tails rose up and waved a greeting—Doubletree Mutt with the big thick tail, and Smasher, the incipient shepherd—then went lazily back to their warm beds.

It was a strange time and a mysterious journey, to Jody—an extension of a dream. When he first had the pony he liked to torture himself during the trip by thinking Gabilan would not be in his stall, and worse, would never have been there. And he had other delicious little self-induced pains. He thought how the rats had gnawed ragged holes in the red saddle, and how the mice had nibbled Gabilan's tail until it was stringy and thin. He usually ran the last little way to the barn. He unlatched the rusty hasp of the barn door and stepped in, and no matter how quietly he opened the door, Gabilan was always looking at him over the barrier of the box stall and Gabilan whinnied softly and stamped his front foot, and his eyes had big sparks of red fire in them like oakwood embers.

Sometimes, if the work horses were to be used that day, Jody found Billy Buck in the barn harnessing and currying. Billy stood with him and looked long at Gabilan and he told Jody a great many things about horses. He explained that they were terribly afraid for their feet, so that one must make a practice of lifting the legs and patting the hoofs and ankles to remove their terror. He told Jody how horses love conversation. He must talk to the pony all the time, and tell him the reasons for everything. Billy wasn't sure a horse could understand everything that was said to him, but it was impossible to say how much was understood. A horse never kicked up a fuss if some one he liked explained things to him. Billy could give examples, too. He had known, for instance, a horse nearly dead beat with fatigue to perk up when told it was only a little farther to his destination. And he had known a horse paralyzed with fright to come out of it when his rider told him what it was that was frightening him. While he talked in the mornings, Billy Buck cut twenty or thirty straws into neat three-inch lengths and stuck them into his hatband. Then during the whole day, if he wanted to pick his teeth or merely to chew on something, he had only to reach up for one of them.

Jody listened carefully, for he knew and the whole country knew that Billy Buck was a fine hand with horses. Billy's own horse was a stringy cayuse with a hammer head, but he nearly always won the first prizes at the stock trials. Billy could rope a steer, take a double half-hitch about the horn with his riata, and dismount, and his horse would play the steer as an angler plays a fish, keeping a tight rope until the steer was down or beaten.

Every morning, after Jody had curried and brushed the pony, he let down the barrier of the stall, and Gabilan thrust past him and raced down the barn and into the corral. Around and around he galloped, and sometimes he jumped forward and landed on stiff legs. He stood quivering, stiff ears forward, eyes rolling so that the whites showed, pretending to be frightened. At last he walked snorting to the water-trough and buried his nose in the water up to the nostrils. Jody was proud then, for he knew that was the way to judge a horse. Poor horses only touched their lips to the water, but a fine spirited beast put his whole nose and mouth under, and only left room to breathe.

Then Jody stood and watched the pony, and he saw things he had never noticed about any other horse, the sleek, sliding flank muscles and the cords of the buttocks, which flexed like a closing fist, and the shine the sun put on the red coat. Having seen horses all his life, Jody had never looked at them very closely before. But now he noticed the moving ears which gave expression and even inflection of expression to the face. The pony talked with his ears. You could tell exactly how he felt about everything by the way his ears pointed. Sometimes they were stiff and upright and sometimes lax and sagging. They went back when he was angry or fearful, and forward when he was anxious and curious and pleased; and their exact position indicated which emotion he had.

Billy Buck kept his word. In the early fall the training began. First there was the halter-breaking, and that was the hardest because it was the first thing. Jody held a carrot and coaxed and promised and pulled on the rope. The pony set his feet like a burro when he felt the strain. But before long he learned. Jody walked all over the ranch leading him. Gradually he took to dropping the rope until the pony followed him unled wherever he went.

And then came the training on the long halter. That was slower work. Jody stood in the middle of a circle, holding the long halter. He clucked with his tongue and the pony started to walk in a big circle, held in by the long rope. He clucked again to make the pony trot, and again to make him gallop. Around and around Gabilan went thunder-ing and enjoying it immensely. Then he called, "Whoa," and the pony stopped. It was not long until Gabilan was perfect at it. But in many ways he was a bad pony. He bit Jody in the pants and stomped on Jody's feet. Now and then his ears went back and he aimed a tremen-dous kick at the boy. Every time he did one of these bad things, Gabilan settled back and seemed to laugh to himself.

Billy Buck worked at the hair rope in the evenings before the fire-place. Jody collected tail hair in a bag, and he sat and watched Billy slowly constructing the rope, twisting a few hairs to make a string and rolling two strings together for a cord, and then braiding a number of cords to make the rope. Billy rolled the finished rope on the floor under his foot to make it round and hard.

The long halter work rapidly approached perfection. Jody's father, watching the pony stop and start and trot and gallop, was a little bothered by it.

"He's getting to be almost a trick pony," he complained. "I don't like trick horses. It takes all the—dignity out of a horse to make him do tricks. Why, a trick horse is kind of like an actor—no dignity, no character of his own." And his father said, "I guess you better be getting him used to the saddle pretty soon."

Jody rushed for the harness-room. For some time he had been riding the saddle on a sawhorse. He changed the stirrup length over and over, and could never get it just right. Sometimes, mounted on the sawhorse in the harness-room, with collars and hames and tugs hung all about him, Jody rode out beyond the room. He carried his rifle across the pommel. He saw the fields go flying by, and he heard the beat of the galloping hoofs.

It was a ticklish job, saddling the pony the first time. Gabilan hunched and reared and threw the saddle off before the cinch could be tightened. It had to be replaced again and again until at last the pony let it stay. And the cinching was difficult, too. Day by day Jody tightened the girth a little more until at last the pony didn't mind the saddle at all.

Then there was the bridle. Billy explained how to use a stick of licorice for a bit until Gabilan was used to having something in his mouth. Billy explained, "Of course we could force-break him to everything, but he wouldn't be as good a horse if we did. He'd always be a little bit afraid, and he wouldn't mind because he wanted to."

The first time the pony wore the bridle he whipped his head about and worked his tongue against the bit until the blood oozed from the corners of his mouth. He tried to rub the headstall off on the manger. His ears pivoted about and his eyes turned red with fear and with general rambunctiousness. Jody rejoiced, for he knew that only a mean-souled horse does not resent training.

And Jody trembled when he thought of the time when he would first sit in the saddle. The pony would probably throw him off. There was no disgrace in that. The disgrace would come if he did not get right up and mount again. Sometimes he dreamed that he lay in the dirt and cried and couldn't make himself mount again. The shame of the dream lasted until the middle of the day.

Gabilan was growing fast. Already he had lost the long-leggedness of the colt; his mane was getting longer and blacker. Under the constant currying and brushing his coat lay as smooth and gleaming as orange-red lacquer. Jody oiled the hoofs and kept them carefully trimmed so they would not crack.

The hair rope was nearly finished. Jody's father gave him an old pair of spurs and bent in the side bars and cut down the strap and took up the chainlets until they fitted. And then one day Carl Tiflin said:

"The pony's growing faster than I thought. I guess you can ride him by Thanksgiving. Think you can stick on?"

"I don't know," Jody said shyly. Thanksgiving was only three weeks off. He hoped it wouldn't rain, for rain would spot the red saddle.

Gabilan knew and liked Jody by now. He nickered when Jody came across the stubble-field, and in the pasture he came running when his master whistled for him. There was always a carrot for him every time.

Billy Buck gave him riding instructions over and over. "Now when you get up there, just grab tight with your knees and keep your hands away from the saddle, and if you get throwed, don't let that stop you. No matter how good a man is, there's always some horse can pitch him. You just climb up again before he gets to feeling smart about it. Pretty soon, he won't throw you no more, and pretty soon he *can't* throw you no more. That's the way to do it."

"I hope it don't rain before," Jody said.

"Why not? Don't want to get throwed in the mud?"

That was partly it, and also he was afraid that in the flurry of bucking Gabilan might slip and fall on him and break his leg or his hip. He had seen that happen to men before, had seen how they writhed on the ground like squashed bugs, and he was afraid of it.

He practiced on the sawhorse how he would hold the reins in his left hand and a hat in his right hand. If he kept his hands thus busy, he couldn't grab the horn if he felt himself going off. He didn't like to think of what would happen if he did grab the horn. Perhaps his father and Billy Buck would never speak to him again, they would be so ashamed. The news would get about and his mother would be ashamed too. And in the school yard—it was too awful to contemplate.

He began putting his weight in a stirrup when Gabilan was saddled, but he didn't throw his leg over the pony's back. That was forbidden until Thanksgiving.

Every afternoon he put the red saddle on the pony and cinched it tight. The pony was learning already to fill his stomach out unnaturally large while the cinching was going on. and then to let it down when the straps were fixed. Sometimes Jody led him up to the brush line and let him drink from the round green tub, and sometimes he led him up through the stubble-field to the hilltop from which it was possible to see the white town of Salinas and the geometric fields of the great valley, and the oak trees clipped by the sheep. Now and then they broke through the brush and came to little cleared circles so hedged in that the world was gone and only the sky and the circle of brush were left from the old life. Gabilan liked these trips and showed it by keeping his head very high and by quivering his nostrils with interest. When the two came back from an expedition they smelled of the sweet sage they had forced through.

Time dragged on toward Thanksgiving, but winter came fast. The clouds swept down and hung all day over the land and brushed the hilltops, and the winds blew shrilly at night. All day the dry oak leaves drifted down from the trees until they covered the ground, and yet the trees were unchanged.

Jody had wished it might not rain before Thanksgiving, but it did. The brown earth turned dark and the trees glistened. The cut ends of the stubble turned black with mildew; the haystacks grayed from exposure to the damp, and on the roofs the moss, which had been all summer as gray as lizards, turned a brilliant yellow-green. During the week of rain, Jody kept the pony in the box stall out of the dampness, except for a little time after school when he took him out for exercise and to drink at the water-trough in the upper corral. Not once did Gabilan get wet.

The wet weather continued until little new grass appeared. Jody walked to school dressed in a slicker and short rubber boots. At length one morning the sun came out brightly. Jody, at his work in the box stall, said to Billy Buck, "Maybe I'll leave Gabilan in the corral when I go to school today."

"Be good for him to be out in the sun," Billy assured him. "No animal likes to be cooped up too long. Your father and me are going back on the hill to clean the leaves out of the spring." Billy nodded and picked his teeth with one of his little straws.

"If the rain comes, though—" Jody suggested.

"Not likely to rain today. She's rained herself out." Billy pulled up his sleeves and snapped his arm bands. "If it comes on to rain—why a little rain don't hurt a horse."

"Well, if it does come on to rain, you put him in, will you, Billy? I'm scared he might get cold so I couldn't ride him when the time comes."

"Oh sure! I'll watch out for him if we get back in time. But it won't rain today."

And so Jody, when he went to school, left Gabilan standing out in the corral.

Billy Buck wasn't wrong about many things. He couldn't be. But he was wrong about the weather that day, for a little after noon the clouds pushed over the hills and the rain began to pour down. Jody heard it start on the schoolhouse roof. He considered holding up one finger for permission to go to the outhouse and, once outside, running for home to put the pony in. Punishment would be prompt both at school and at home. He gave it up and took ease from Billy's assurance that rain couldn't hurt a horse. When school was finally out, he hurried home through the dark rain. The banks at the sides of the road spouted little jets of muddy water. The rain slanted and swirled under a cold and gusty wind. Jody dog-trotted home, slopping through the gravelly mud of the road.

From the top of the ridge he could see Gabilan standing miserably in the corral. The red coat was almost black, and streaked with water. He stood head down with his rump to the rain and wind. Jody arrived running and threw open the barn door and led the wet pony in by his forelock. Then he found a gunny sack and rubbed the soaked hair and rubbed the legs and ankles. Gabilan stood patiently, but he trembled in gusts like the wind.

When he had dried the pony as well as he could, Jody went up to the horse and brought hot water down to the barn and soaked the grain in it. Gabilan was not very hungry. He nibbled at the hot mash, but he was not very much interested in it, and he still shivered now and then. A little steam rose from his damp back.

It was almost dark when Billy Buck and Carl Tiflin came home. "When the rain started we put up at Ben Herche's place, and the rain never let up all afternoon," Carl Tiflin explained. Jody looked reproachfully at Billy Buck and Billy felt guilty.

"You said it wouldn't rain," Jody accused him.

Billy looked away. "It's hard to tell, this time of year," he said, but his excuse was lame. He had no right to be fallible, and he knew it.

"The pony got wet, got soaked through."

"Did you dry him off?"

"I rubbed him with a sack and I gave him hot grain."

Billy nodded in agreement.

"Do you think he'll take cold, Billy?"

"A little rain never hurt anything," Billy assured him.

Jody's father joined the conversation then and lectured the boy a little. "A horse," he said, "isn't any lap-dog kind of thing." Carl Tiflin hated weakness and sickness, and he held a violent contempt for help-lessness.

Jody's mother put a platter of steaks on the table and boiled potatoes and boiled squash, which clouded the room with their steam. They sat down to eat. Carl Tiflin still grumbled about weakness put into animals and men by too much coddling.

Billy Buck felt bad about his mistake. "Did you blanket him?" he asked.

"No. I couldn't find any blanket. I laid some sacks over his back."

"We'll go down and cover him up after we eat, then." Billy felt better about it then. When Jody's father had gone in to the fire and his mother was washing dishes, Billy found and lighted a lantern. He and Jody walked through the mud to the barn. The barn was dark and warm and sweet. The horses still munched their evening hay. "You hold the lantern!" Billy ordered. And he felt the pony's legs and tested the heat of the flanks. He put his cheek against the pony's gray muzzle and then he rolled up the eyelids to look at the eyeballs and he lifted the lips to see the gums, and he put his fingers inside the ears. "He don't seem so chipper," Billy said. "I'll give him a rub-down."

Then Billy found a sack and rubbed the pony's legs violently and he rubbed the chest and the withers. Gabilan was strangely spiritless. He submitted patiently to the rubbing. At last Billy brought an old cotton comforter from the saddle-room, and threw it over the pony's back and tied it at neck and chest with string.

"Now he'll be all right in the morning," Billy said.

Jody's mother looked up when he got back to the house. "You're late up from bed," she said. She held his chin in her hard hand and brushed the tangled hair out of his eyes and she said, "Don't worry about the pony. He'll be all right. Billy's as good as any horse doctor in the country."

Jody hadn't known she could see his worry. He pulled gently away from her and knelt down in front of the fireplace until it burned his stomach. He scorched himself through and then went in to bed, but it was a hard thing to go to sleep. He awakened after what seemed a long time. The room was dark but there was a grayness in the window like that which precedes the dawn. He got up and found his overalls and searched for the legs, and then the clock in the other room struck two. He laid his clothes down and got back into bed. It was broad daylight when he awakened again. For the first time he had slept through the ringing of the triangle. He leaped up, flung on his clothes and went out of the door still buttoning his shirt. His mother looked after him for a moment and then went quietly back to her work. Her eyes were brooding and kind. Now and then her mouth smiled a little but without changing her eyes at all.

Jody ran on toward the barn. Halfway there he heard the sound he dreaded, the hollow rasping cough of a horse. He broke into a sprint then. In the barn he found Billy Buck with the pony. Billy was rubbing its legs with his strong thick hands. He looked up and smiled gaily. "He just took a little cold," Billy said. "We'll have him out of it in a couple of days."

Jody looked at the pony's face. The eyes were half closed and the lids thick and dry. In the eye corners a crust of hard mucus stuck. Gabilan's ears hung loosely sideways and his head was low. Jody put out his hand, but the pony did not move close to it. He coughed again and his whole body constricted with the effort. A little stream of thin fluid ran from his nostrils.

Jody looked back at Billy Buck. "He's awful sick, Billy."

"Just a little cold, like I said," Billy insisted. "You go get some breakfast and then go back to school. I'll take care of him."

"But you might have to do something else. You might leave him."

"No, I won't. I won't leave him at all. Tomorrow's Saturday. Then you can stay with him all day." Billy had failed again, and he felt bad about it. He had to cure the pony now.

Jody walked up to the house and took his place listlessly at the table. The eggs and bacon were cold and greasy, but he didn't notice it. He ate his usual amount. He didn't even ask to stay home from school. His mother pushed his hair back when she took his plate. "Billy'll take care of the pony," she assured him.

He moped through the whole day at school. He couldn't answer any questions nor read any words. He couldn't even tell anyone the pony was sick, for that might make him sicker. And when school was finally out he started home in dread. He walked slowly and let the other boys leave him. He wished he might continue walking and never arrive at the ranch.

Billy was in the barn, as he had promised, and the pony was worse. His eyes were almost closed now, and his breath whistled shrilly past an obstruction in his nose. A film covered that part of the eyes that was visible at all. It was doubtful whether the pony could see any more. Now and then he snorted, to clear his nose, and by the action seemed to plug it tighter. Jody looked dispiritedly at the pony's coat. The hair lay rough and unkempt and seemed to have lost all of its old luster. Bill stood quietly beside the stall. Jody hated to ask, but he had to know.

"Billy, is he—is he going to get well?"

Billy put his fingers between the bars under the pony's jaw and felt about. "Feel here," he said and he guided Jody's fingers to a large lump under the jaw. "When that gets bigger, I'll open it up and then he'll get better."

Jody looked quickly away, for he had heard about that lump. "What is the matter with him?"

Billy didn't want to answer, but he had to. He couldn't be wrong three times. "Strangles," he said shortly, "but don't you worry about that. I'll pull him out of it. I've seen them get well when they were worse than Gabilan is. I'm going to steam him now. You can help."

"Yes," Jody said miserably. He followed Billy into the grain room and watched him make the steaming bag ready. It was a long canvas nose bag with straps to go over a horse's ears. Billy filled it one-third full of bran and then he added a couple of handfuls of dried hops. On top of the dry substance he poured a little carbolic acid and a little turpentine. "I'll be mixing it all up while you run to the house for a kettle of boiling water," Billy said.

When Jody came back with the steaming kettle, Billy buckled the straps over Gabilan's head and fitted the bag tightly around his nose. Then through a little hole in the side of the bag he poured the boiling water on the mixture. The pony started away as a cloud of strong steam rose up, but then the soothing fumes crept through his nose and into his lungs, and the sharp steam began to clear out the nasal passages. He breathed loudly. His legs trembled in an ague, and his eyes closed against the biting cloud. Billy poured in more water and kept the steam rising for fifteen minutes. At last he set down the kettle and took the bag from Gabilan's nose. The pony looked better. He breathed freely, and his eyes were open wider than they had been.

"See how good it makes him feel," Billy said. "Now we'll wrap him up in the blanket again. Maybe he'll be nearly well by morning."

"I'll stay with him tonight," Jody suggested.

"No. Don't you do it. I'll bring my blankets down here and put them in the hay. You can stay tomorrow and steam him if he needs it."

The evening was falling when they went to the house for their supper. Jody didn't even realize that someone else had fed the chickens and filled the wood-box. He walked up past the house to the dark brush line and took a drink of water from the tub. The spring water was so cold that it stung his mouth and drove a shiver through him. The sky above the hills was still light. He saw a hawk flying so high that it caught the sun on its breast and shone like a spark. Two blackbirds were driving him down the sky, glittering as they attacked their enemy. In the west, the clouds were moving in to rain again.

Jody's father didn't speak at all while the family ate supper, but after Billy Buck had taken his blankets and gone to sleep in the barn, Carl Tiflin built a high fire in the fireplace and told stories. He told about the wild man who ran naked through the country and had a tail and ears like a horse, and he told about the rabbit-cats of Moro Cojo that hopped into the trees for birds. He revived the famous Maxwell brothers who found a vein of gold and hid the traces of it so carefully that they could never find it again.

Jody sat with his chin in his hands; his mouth worked nervously, and his father gradually became aware that he wasn't listening very carefully. "Isn't that funny?" he asked.

Jody laughed politely and said, "Yes, sir." His father was angry and hurt, then. He didn't tell any more stories. After a while, Jody took a lantern and went down to the barn. Billy Buck was asleep in the hay, and, except that his breath rasped a little in his lungs, the pony seemed to be much better. Jody stayed a little while, running his fingers over the red rough coat, and then he took up the lantern and went back to the house. When he was in bed, his mother came into the room.

"Have you enough covers on? It's getting winter."

"Yes, ma'am."

"Well, get some rest tonight." She hesitated to go out, stood uncertainly. "The pony will be all right," she said.

Jody was tired. He went to sleep quickly and didn't awaken until dawn. The triangle sounded, and Billy Buck came up from the barn before Jody could get out of the house.

"How is he?" Jody demanded.

Billy always wolfed his breakfast. "Pretty good. I'm going to open that lump this morning. Then he'll be better maybe."

After breakfast, Billy got out his best knife, one with a needle point. He whetted the shining blade a long time on a little carborundum stone. He tried the point and the blade again and again on his calloused thumb-ball, and at last he tried it on his upper lip.

On the way to the barn, Jody noticed how the young grass was up and how the stubble was melting day by day into the new green crop of volunteer. It was a cold sunny morning.

As soon as he saw the pony, Jody knew he was worse. His eyes were closed and sealed shut with dried mucus. His head hung so low that his nose almost touched the straw of his bed. There was a little groan in each breath, a deep seated, patient groan.

Billy lifted the weak head and made a quick slash with the knife. Jody saw the yellow pus run out. He held up the head while Billy swabbed out the wound with weak carbolic acid salve.

"Now he'll feel better," Billy assured him. "That yellow poison is what makes him sick."

Jody looked unbelieving at Billy Buck. "He's awful sick."

Billy thought a long time what to say. He nearly tossed off a careless assurance, but he saved himself in time. "Yes, he's pretty sick," he said at last. "I've seen worse ones get well. If he doesn't get pneumonia, we'll pull him through. You stay with him. If he gets worse, you can come and get me."

For a long time after Billy went away, Jody stood beside the pony, stroking him behind the ears. The pony didn't flip his head the way he had done when he was well. The groaning in his breathing was becoming more hollow.

Doubletree Mutt looked into the barn, his big tail waving provocatively, and Jody was so incensed at his health that he found a hard black clod on the floor and deliberately threw it. Doubletree Mutt went yelping away to nurse a bruised paw.

In the middle of the morning, Billy Buck came back and made another steam bag. Jody watched to see whether the pony improved this time as he had before. His breathing eased a little, but he did not raise his head.

The Saturday dragged on. Late in the afternoon Jody went to the house and brought his bedding down and made up a place to sleep in the hay. He didn't ask permission. He knew from the way his mother looked at him that she would let him do almost anything. That night he left a lantern burning on a wire over the box stall. Billy had told him to rub the pony's legs every little while.

At nine o'clock the wind sprang up and howled around the barn. And in spite of his worry, Jody grew sleepy. He got into his blankets and went to sleep, but the breathy groans of the pony sounded in his dreams. And in his sleep he heard a crashing noise which went on and on until it awakened him. The wind was rushing through the barn. He sprang up and looked down the lane of stalls. The barn door had blown open, and the pony was gone.

He caught the lantern and ran outside into the gale, and he saw Gabilan weakly shambling away into the darkness, head down, legs working slowly and mechanically. When Jody ran up and caught him by the forelock, he allowed himself to be led back and put into his stall. His groans were louder, and a fierce whistling came from his nose. Jody didn't sleep any more then. The hissing of the pony's breath grew louder and sharper.

He was glad when Billy Buck came in at dawn. Billy looked for a time at the pony as though he had never seen him before. He felt the ears and flanks. "Jody," he said, "I've got to do something you won't want to see. You run up to the house for a while."

Jody grabbed him fiercely by the forearm. "You're not going to shoot him?"

Billy patted his hand. "No. I'm going to open a little hole in his windpipe so he can breathe. His nose is filled up. When he gets well, we'll put a little brass button in the hole for him to breath through."

Jody couldn't have gone away if he had wanted to. It was awful to see the red hide cut, but infinitely more terrible to know it was being cut and not to see it. "I'll stay right here," he said bitterly. "You sure you got to?"

"Yes. I'm sure. If you stay, you can hold his head. If it doesn't make you sick, that is."

The fine knife came out again and was whetted again just as carefully as it had been the first time. Jody held the pony's head up and the throat taut, while Billy felt up and down for the right place. Jody sobbed once as the bright knife point disappeared into the throat. The pony plunged weakly away and then stood still, trembling violently. The blood ran thickly out and up the knife and across Billy's hand and into his shirtsleeve. The sure square hand sawed out a round hole in the flesh, and the breath came bursting out of the hole, throwing a fine spray of blood. With the rush of oxygen, the pony took a sudden strength. He lashed out with his hind feet and tried to rear, but Jody held his head down while Billy mopped the new wound with carbolic salve. It was a good job. The blood stopped flowing and the air puffed out the hole and sucked it in regularly with a little bubbling noise.

The rain brought in by the night wind began to fall on the barn roof. Then the triangle rang for breakfast. "You go up and eat while I wait," Billy said. "We've got to keep this hole from plugging up."

Jody walked slowly out of the barn. He was too dispirited to tell Billy how the barn door had blown open and let the pony out. He emerged into the wet gray morning and sloshed up to the house, taking a perverse pleasure in splashing through all the puddles. His mother fed him and put dry clothes on. She didn't question him. She seemed to know he couldn't answer questions. But when he was ready to go back to the barn she brought him a pan of steaming meal. "Give him this," she said.

But Jody did not take the pan. He said. "He won't eat anything," and ran out of the house. At the barn, Billy showed him how to fix a ball of cotton on a stick, with which to swab out the breathing hole when it became clogged with mucus.

Jody's father walked into the barn and stood with them in front of the stall. At length he turned to the boy. "Hadn't you better come with me? I'm going to drive over the hill." Jody shook his head. "You better come on, out of this," his father insisted.

Billy turned on him angrily. "Let him alone. It's his pony, isn't it?"

Carl Tiflin walked away without saying another word. His feelings were badly hurt.

All morning Jody kept the wound open and the air passing in and out freely. At noon the pony lay wearily down on his side and stretched his nose out.

Billy came back. "If you're going to stay with him tonight, you better take a little nap," he said. Jody went absently out of the barn. The sky had cleared to a hard thin blue. Everywhere the birds were busy with worms that had come to the damp surface of the ground.

Jody walked to the brush line and sat on the edge of the mossy tub. He looked down at the house and at the old bunkhouse and at the dark cypress tree. The place was familiar, but curiously changed. It wasn't itself any more, but a frame for things that were happening. A cold wind blew out of the east now, signifying that the rain was over for a little while. At his feet Jody could see the little arms of new weeds spreading out over the ground. In the mud about the spring were thousands of quail tracks.

Doubletree Mutt came sideways and embarrassed up through the vegetable patch, and Jody, remembering how he had thrown the clod, put his arm about the dog's neck and kissed him on his wide black nose. Doubletree Mutt sat still, as though he knew some solemn thing was happening. His big tail slapped the ground gravely. Jody pulled a swollen tick out of Mutt's neck and popped it dead between his thumb-nails. It was a nasty thing. He washed his hands in the cold spring water.

Except for the steady swish of the wind, the farm was very quiet. Jody knew his mother wouldn't mind if he didn't go in to eat his lunch. After a little while he went slowly back to the barn. Mutt crept into his own little house and whined softly to himself for a long time.

Billy Buck stood up from the box and surrendered the cotton swab. The pony still lay on his side and the wound in his throat bellowsed in and out. When Jody saw how dry and dead the hair looked, he knew at last that there was no hope for the pony. He had seen the dead 'hair before on dogs and on cows, and it was a sure sign. He sat heavily on the box and let down the barrier of the box stall. For a long time he kept his eyes on the moving wound, and at last he dozed, and the afternoon passed quickly. Just before dark his mother brought a deep dish of stew and left it for him and went away. Jody ate a little of it, and, when it was dark, he set the lantern on the floor by the pony's head so he could watch the wound and keep it open. And he dozed again until the night chill awakened him. The wind was blowing fiercely, bringing the north cold with it. Jody brought a blanket from his bed in the hay and wrapped himself in it. Gabilan's breathing was quiet at last; the hole in his throat moved gently. The owls flew through the hayloft, shrieking and looking for mice. Jody put his hands down on his head and slept. In his sleep he was aware that the wind had increased. He heard it slamming about the barn.

It was daylight when he awakened. The barn door had swung open. The pony was gone. He sprang up and ran out into the morning light.

The pony's tracks were plain enough, dragging through the frost-like dew on the young grass, tired tracks with little lines between them where the hoofs had dragged. They headed for the brush line halfway up the ridge. Jody broke into a run and followed them. The sun shone on the sharp white quartz that stuck through the ground here and there. As he followed the plain trail, a shadow cut across in front of him. He looked up and saw a high circle of black buzzards, and the slowly revolving circle dropped lower and lower. The solemn birds soon disappeared over the ridge. Jody ran faster then, forced on by panic and rage. The trail entered the brush at last and followed a winding route among the tall sage bushes.

At the top of the ridge Jody was winded. He paused, puffing noisily. The blood pounded in his ears. Then he saw what he was looking for. Below, in one of the little clearings in the brush, lay the red pony. In the distance, Jody could see the legs moving slowly and convulsively. And in a circle around him stood the buzzards, waiting for the moment of death they know so well.

Jody leaped forward and plunged down the hill. The wet ground muffled his steps and the brush hid him. When he arrived, it was all over. The first buzzard sat on the pony's head and its beak had just risen dripping with dark eye fluid. Jody plunged into the circle like a cat. The black brotherhood arose in a cloud, but the big one on the pony's head was too late. As it hopped along to take off, Jody caught its wing tip and pulled it down. It was nearly as big as he was. The free wing crashed into his face with the force of a club, but he hung on. The claws fastened on his leg and the wing elbows battered his head on either side. Jody groped blindly with his free hand. His fingers found the neck of the struggling bird. The red eyes looked into his face, calm and fearless and fierce; the naked head turned from side to side. Then the beak opened and vomited a stream of putrefied fluid. Jody brought up his knee and fell on the great bird. He held the neck to the ground with one hand while his other found a piece of sharp white quartz. The first blow broke the beak sideways and black blood spurted from the twisted, leathery mouth corners. He struck again and missed. The red fearless eyes still looked at him, impersonal and unafraid and detached. He struck again and again, until the buzzard lay dead, until its head was a red pulp. He was still beating the dead bird when Billy Buck pulled him off and held him tightly to calm his shaking.

Carl Tiflin wiped the blood from the boy's face with a red bandana. Jody was limp and quiet now. His father moved the buzzard with his toe. "Jody," he explained, "the buzzard didn't kill the pony. Don't you know that?"

"I know it," Jody said wearily.

It was Billy Buck who was angry. He had lifted Jody in his arms, and had turned to carry him home. But he turned back on Carl Tiflin. " 'Course he knows it," Billy said furiously, "Jesus Christ! man, can't you see how he'd feel about it?"

II. THE GREAT MOUNTAINS

In the humming heat of a midsummer afternoon the little boy Jody listlessly looked about the ranch for something to do. He had been to the barn, had thrown rocks at the swallows' nests under the eaves until every one of the little mud houses broke open and dropped its lining of straw and dirty feathers. Then at the ranch house he baited a rat trap with stale cheese and set it where Doubletree Mutt, that good big dog, would get his nose snapped. Jody was not moved by an impulse of cruelty; he was bored with the long hot afternoon. Doubletree Mutt put his stupid nose in the trap and got it smacked, and shrieked with agony and limped away with blood on his nostrils. No matter where he was hurt, Mutt limped. It was just a way he had. Once when he was young, Mutt got caught in a coyote trap, and always after that he limped, even when he was scolded.

When Mutt yelped, Jody's mother called from inside the house, "Jody! Stop torturing that dog and find something to do."

Jody felt mean then, so he threw a rock at Mutt. Then he took his slingshot from the porch and walked up toward the brush line to try to kill a bird. It was a good slingshot, with store-bought rubbers, but while Jody had often shot at birds, he had never hit one. He walked up through the vegetable patch, kicking his bare toes into the dust. And on the way he found the perfect slingshot stone, round and slightly flattened and heavy enough to carry through the air. He fitted it into the leather pouch of his weapon and proceeded to the brush line. His eyes narrowed, his mouth worked strenuously; for the first time that afternoon he was intent. In the shade of the sagebrush the little birds were working, scratching in the leaves, flying restlessly a few feet and scratching again. Jody pulled back the rubbers of the sling and advanced cautiously. One little thrush paused and looked at him and crouched, ready to fly. Jody sidled nearer, moving one foot slowly after the other. When he was twenty feet away, he carefully raised the sling and aimed. The stone whizzed; the thrush started up and flew right into it. And down the little bird went with a broken head. Jody ran to it and picked it up.

"Well, I got you," he said.

The bird looked much smaller dead than it had alive. Jody felt a little mean pain in his stomach, so he took out his pocket-knife and cut off the bird's head. Then he disemboweled it, and took off its wings, and finally he threw all the pieces into the brush. He didn't care about the bird, or its life, but he knew what older people would say if they had seen him kill it; he was ashamed because of their potential opinion. He decided to forget the whole thing as quickly as he could, and never to mention it.

The hills were dry at this season, and the wild grass was golden, but where the spring-pipe filled the round tub and the tub spilled over, there lay a stretch of fine green grass, deep and sweet and moist. Jody drank from the mossy tub and washed the bird's blood from his hands in cold water. Then he lay on his back in the grass and looked up at the dumpling summer clouds. By closing one eye and destroying perspective he brought them down within reach so that he could put up his fingers and stroke them. He helped the gentle wind push them down the sky; it seemed to him that they went faster for his help. One fat white cloud he helped clear to the mountain rims and pressed it firmly over, out of sight. Jody wondered what it was seeing, then. He sat up, the better to look at the great mountains where they went piling back, growing darker and more savage until they finished with one jagged ridge, high up against the west. Curious secret mountains; he thought of the little he knew about them.

"What's on the other side?" he asked his father once.

"More mountains, I guess. Why?"

"And on the other side of them?"

"More mountains. Why?"

"More mountains on and on?"

"Well, no. At last you come to the ocean."

"But what's in the mountains?"

"Just cliffs and brush and rocks and dry . ."

"Were you ever there?"

"No."

"Has anybody ever been there?"

"A few people, I guess. It's dangerous, with cliffs and things. Why, I've read there's more unexplored country in the mountains of Monterey County than any place in the United States." His father seemed proud that this should be so.

"And at last the ocean?"

"At last the ocean."

"But," the boy insisted, "but in between? No one knows?"

"Oh, a few people do, I guess. But there's nothing there to get. And not much water. Just rocks and cliffs and greasewood. Why?"

"It would be good to go."

"What for? There's nothing there."

Jody knew something was there, something very wonderful because it wasn't known, something secret and mysterious. He could feel within himself that this was so. He said to his mother, "Do you know what's in the big mountains?"

She looked at him and then back at the ferocious range, and she said, "Only the bear, I guess."

"What bear?"

"Why the one that went over the mountain to see what he could see."

Jody questioned Billy Buck, the ranch hand, about the possibility of ancient cities lost in the mountains, but Billy agreed with Jody's father.

"It ain't likely," Billy said. "There'd be nothing to eat unless a kind of people that can eat rocks live there."

That was all the information Jody ever got, and it made the mountains dear to him, and terrible. He thought often of the miles of ridge after ridge until at last there was the sea. When the peaks were pink in the morning they invited him among them: and when the sun had gone over the edge in the evening and the mountains were a purple-like despair, then Jody was afraid of them; then they were so impersonal and aloof that their very imperturbability was a threat.

Now he turned his head toward the mountains of the east, the Gabilans, and they were jolly mountains, with hill ranches in their greases, and with pine trees growing on the crests. People lived there, and battles had been fought against the Mexicans on the slopes. He looked back for an instant at the Great Ones and shivered a little at the contrast. The foothill cup of the home ranch below him was sunny and safe. The house gleamed with white light and the barn was brown and warm. The red cows on the farther hill ate their way slowly toward the north. Even the dark cypress tree by the bunkhouse was usual and safe. The chickens scratched about in the dust of the farmyard with quick waltzing steps.

Then a moving figure caught Jody's eye. A man walked slowly over the brow of the hill, on the road from Salinas, and he was headed toward the house. Jody stood up and moved down toward the house too, for if someone was coming, he wanted to be there to see. By the time the boy had got to the house the walking man was only halfway down the road, a lean man, very straight in the shoulders. Jody could tell he was old only because his heels struck the ground with hard jerks. As he approached nearer, Jody saw that he was dressed in blue jeans and in a coat of the same material. He wore clodhopper shoes and an old flat-brimmed Stetson hat. Over his shoulder he carried a gunny sack, lumpy and full. In a few moments he had trudged close enough so that his face could be seen. And his face was as dark as dried beef. A mustache, blue-white against the dark skin, hovered over his mouth, and his hair was white, too, where it showed at his neck. The skin of his face had shrunk back against the skull until it defined bone, not flesh, and made the nose and chin seem sharp and fragile. The eyes were large and deep and dark, with eyelids stretched tightly over them. Irises and pupils were one, and very black, but the eyeballs were brown. There were no wrinkles in the face at all. This old man wore a blue denim coat buttoned to the throat with brass buttons, as all men do who wear no shirts. Out of the sleeves came strong bony wrists and hands gnarled and knotted and hard as peach branches. The nails were flat and blunt and shiny.

The old man drew close to the gate and swung down his sack when he confronted Jody. His lips fluttered a little and a soft impersonal voice came from between them.

"Do you live here?"

Jody was embarrassed. He turned and looked at the house, and he turned back and looked toward the barn where his father and Billy Buck were. "Yes," he said, when no help came from either direction.

"I have come back," the old man said. "I am Gitano, and I have come back."

Jody could not take all this responsibility. He turned abruptly, and ran into the house for help, and the screen door banged after him. His mother was in the kitchen poking out the clogged holes of a colander with a hairpin, and biting her lower lip with concentration.

"It's an old man," Jody cried excitedly. "It's an old *paisano* man, and he says he's come back."

His mother put down the colander and stuck the hairpin behind the sink board. "What's the matter now?" she asked patiently.

"It's an old man outside. Come on out."

"Well, what does he want?" She untied the strings of her apron and smoothed her hair with her fingers.

"I don't know. He came walking."

His mother smoothed down her dress and went out, and Jody followed her. Gitano had not moved.

"Yes?" Mrs. Tiflin asked.

Gitano took off his old black hat and held it with both hands in front of him. He repeated, "I am Gitano, and I have come back."

"Come back? Back where?"

Gitano's whole straight body leaned forward a little. His right hand described the circle of the hills, the sloping fields and the mountains, and ended at his hat again. "Back to the rancho. I was born here, and my father, too."

"Here?" she demanded. "This isn't an old place."

"No, there," he said, pointing to the western ridge. "On the other side there, in a house that is gone."

At last she understood. "The old 'dobe that's washed almost away, you mean?"

"Yes, *señora*. When the rancho broke up they put no more lime on the 'dobe, and the rains washed it down."

Jody's mother was silent for a little, and curious homesick thoughts ran through her mind, but quickly she cleared them out. "And what do you want here now, Gitano?"

"I will stay here," he said quietly, "until I die."

"But we don't need an extra man here."

"I cannot work hard any more, *señora*. I can milk a cow, feed chickens, cut a little wood; no more. I will stay here." He indicated the sack on the ground beside him. "Here are my things."

She turned to Jody. "Run down to the barn and call your father."

Jody dashed away, and he returned with Carl Tiflin and Billy Buck behind him. The old man was standing as he had been, but he was resting now. His whole body had sagged into a timeless repose.

"What is it?" Carl Tiflin asked. "What's Jody so excited about?"

Mrs. Tiflin motioned to the old man. "He wants to stay here. He wants to do a little work and stay here."

"Well, we can't have him. We don't need any more men. He's too old. Billy does everything we need."

They had been talking over him as though he did not exist, and now, suddenly, they both hesitated and looked at Gitano and were embarrassed.

He cleared his throat. "I am too old to work. I come back where I was born."

"You weren't born here," Carl said sharply.

"No. In the 'dobe house over the hill. It was all one rancho before you came."

"In the mud house that's all melted down?"

"Yes. I and my father. I will stay here now on the rancho."

"I tell you you won't stay," Carl said angrily. "I don't need an old man. This isn't a big ranch. I can't afford food and doctor bills for an old man. You must have relatives and friends. Go to them. It is like begging to come to strangers."

"I was born here," Gitano said patiently and inflexibly.

Carl Tiflin didn't like to be cruel, but he felt he must. "You can eat here tonight," he said. "You can sleep in the little room of the old bunkhouse. We'll give you your breakfast in the morning, and then you'll have to go along. Go to your friends. Don't come to die with strangers."

Gitano put on his black hat and stooped for the sack. "Here are my things," he said.

Carl turned away. "Come on, Billy, we'll finish down at the barn. Jody, show him the little room in the bunkhouse."

He and Billy turned back toward the barn. Mrs. Tiflin went into the house, saying over her shoulder, "I'll send some blankets down."

Gitano looked questioningly at Jody. "I'll show you where it is," Jody said.

There was a cot with a shuck mattress, an apple box holding a tin lantern, and a backless rocking-chair in the little room of the bunkhouse. Gitano laid his sack carefully on the floor and sat down on the bed. Jody stood shyly in the room, hesitating to go. At last he said,

"Did you come out of the big mountains?"

Gitano shook his head slowly. "No, I worked down the Salinas Valley."

The afternoon thought would not let Jody go. "Did you ever go into the big mountains back there?"

The old dark eyes grew fixed, and their light turned inward on the years that were living in Gitano's head. "Once—when I was a little boy. I went with my father."

"Way back, clear into the mountains?"

"Yes."

"What was there?" Jody cried. "Did you see any people or any houses?"

"No."

"Well, what was there?"

Gitano's eyes remained inward. A little wrinkled strain came between his brows.

"What did you see in there?" Jody repeated.

"I don't know," Gitano said. "I don't remember."

"Was it terrible and dry?"

"I don't remember."

In his excitement, Jody had lost his shyness. "Don't you remember anything about it?"

Gitano's mouth opened for a word, and remained open while his brain sought the word. "I think it was quiet—I think it was nice."

Gitano's eyes seemed to have found something back in the years, for they grew soft and a little smile seemed to come and go in them.

"Didn't you ever go back in the mountains again?" Jody insisted.

"No."

"Didn't you ever want to?"

But now Gitano's face became impatient. "No," he said in a tone that told Jody he didn't want to talk about it any more. The boy was held by a curious fascination. He didn't want to go away from Gitano. His shyness returned.

"Would you like to come down to the barn and see the stock?" he asked.

Gitano stood up and put on his hat and prepared to follow.

It was almost evening now. They stood near the watering trough while the horses sauntered in from the hillsides for an evening drink. Gitano rested his big twisted hands on the top rail of the fence. Five horses came down and drank, and then stood about, nibbling at the dirt or rubbing their sides against the polished wood of the fence. Long after they had finished drinking an old horse appeared over the brow of the hill and came painfully down. It had long yellow teeth; its hoofs were flat and sharp as spades, and its ribs and hip-bones jutted out under its skin. It hobbled up to the trough and drank water with a loud sucking noise.

"That's old Easter," Jody explained. "That's the first horse my father ever had. He's thirty years old." He looked up into Gitano's old eyes for some response.

"No good any more," Gitano said.

Jody's father and Billy Buck came out of the barn and walked over.
"Too old to work," Gitano repeated. "Just eats and pretty soon dies."

Carl Tiflin caught the last words. He hated his brutality toward old
Gitano, and so he became brutal again.

"It's a shame not to shoot Easter," he said. "It'd save him a lot of
pains and rheumatism." He looked secretly at Gitano, to see whether
he noticed the parallel, but the big bony hands did not move, nor did
the dark eyes turn from the horse. "Old things ought to be put out of
their misery," Jody's father went on. "One shot, a big noise, one big
pain in the head maybe, and that's all. That's better than stiffness and
sore teeth."

Billy Buck broke in. "They got a right to rest after they worked all
of their life. Maybe they like to just walk around."

Carl had been looking steadily at the skinny horse. "You can't imagine now what Easter used to look like," he said softly. "High neck,
deep chest, fine barrel. He could jump a five-bar gate in stride. I won
a flat race on him when I was fifteen years old. I could of got two hundred dollars for him any time. You wouldn't think how pretty he
was." He checked himself, for he hated softness. "But he ought to be
shot now," he said.

"He's got a right to rest," Billy Buck insisted.

Jody's father had a humorous thought. He turned to Gitano. "If
ham and eggs grew on a side-hill I'd turn you out to pasture too," he
said. "But I can't afford to pasture you in my kitchen."

He laughed to Billy Buck about it as they went on toward the house.
"Be a good thing for all of us if ham and eggs grew on the side-hills."

Jody knew how his father was probing for a place to hurt in
Gitano. He had been probed often. His father knew every place in the
boy where a word would fester.

"He's only talking," Jody said. "He didn't mean it about shooting
Easter. He likes Easter. That was the first horse he ever owned."

The sun sank behind the high mountains as they stood there, and
the ranch was hushed. Gitano seemed to be more at home in the evening. He made a curious sharp sound with his lips and stretched one
of his hands over the fence. Old Easter moved stiffly to him, and
Gitano rubbed the lean neck under the mane.

"You like him?" Jody asked softly.

"Yes—but he's no damn good."

The triangle sounded at the ranch house. "That's supper," Jody
cried. "Come on up to supper."

As they walked up toward the house Jody noticed again that Gitano's
body was as straight as that of a young man. Only by a jerkiness in

his movements and by the scuffling of his heels could it be seen that he was old.

The turkeys were flying heavily into the lower branches of the cypress tree by the bunkhouse. A fat sleek ranch cat walked across the road carrying a rat so large that its tail dragged on the ground. The quail on the side-hills were still sounding the clear water call.

Jody and Gitano came to the back steps and Mrs. Tiflin looked out through the screen door at them.

"Come running, Jody. Come in to supper, Gitano."

Carl and Billy Buck had started to eat at the long oilcloth-covered table. Jody slipped into his chair without moving it, but Gitano stood holding his hat until Carl looked up and said, "Sit down, sit down. You might as well get your belly full before you go on." Carl was afraid he might relent and let the old man stay, and so he continued to remind himself that this couldn't be.

Gitano laid his hat on the floor and diffidently sat down. He wouldn't reach for food. Carl had to pass it to him. "Here, fill yourself up." Gitano ate very slowly, cutting tiny pieces of meat and arranging little pats of mashed potato on his plate.

The situation would not stop worrying Carl Tiflin. "Haven't you got any relatives in this part of the country?" he asked.

Gitano answered with some pride, "My brother-in-law is in Monterey. I have cousins there, too."

"Well, you can go and live there, then."

"I was born here," Gitano said in gentle rebuke.

Jody's mother came in from the kitchen, carrying a large bowl of tapioca pudding.

Carl chuckled to her, "Did I tell you what I said to him? I said if ham and eggs grew on the side-hills I'd put him out to pasture, like old Easter."

Gitano stared unmoved at his plate.

"It's too bad he can't stay," said Mrs. Tiflin.

"Now don't you start anything," Carl said crossly.

When they had finished eating, Carl and Billy Buck and Jody went into the living room to sit for a while, but Gitano, without a word of farewell or thanks, walked through the kitchen and out the back door. Jody sat and secretly watched his father. He knew how mean his father felt.

"This country's full of these old *paisanos*," Carl said to Billy Buck.

"They're damn good men," Billy defended them. "They can work older than white men. I saw one of them a hundred and five years old, and he could still ride a horse. You don't see any white men as old as Gitano walking twenty or thirty miles."

"Oh, they're tough, all right." Carl agreed. "Say, are you standing up for him too? Listen, Billy," he explained, "I'm having a hard enough time keeping this ranch out of the Bank of Italy without taking on anybody else to feed. You know that, Billy."

"Sure, I know," said Billy. "If you was rich, it'd be different."

"That's right, and it isn't like he didn't have relatives to go to. A brother-in-law and cousins right in Monterey. Why should I worry about him?"

Jody sat quietly listening, and he seemed to hear Gitano's gentle voice and its unanswerable, "But I was born here." Gitano was mysterious like the mountains. There were ranges back as far as you could see, but behind the last range piled up against the sky there was a great unknown country. And Gitano was an old man, until you got to the dull dark eyes. And in behind them was some unknown thing. He didn't ever say enough to let you guess what was inside, under the eyes. Jody felt himself irresistibly drawn toward the bunkhouse. He slipped from his chair while his father was talking and he went out the door without making a sound.

The night was very dark and far-off noises carried in clearly. The hamebells of a wood team sounded from way over the hill on the country road. Jody picked his way across the dark yard. He could see a light through the window of the little room of the bunkhouse. Because the night was secret he walked quietly up to the window and peered in. Gitano sat in the rocking-chair and his back was toward the window. His right arm moved slowly back and forth in front of him. Jody pushed the door open and walked in. Gitano jerked upright and, seizing a piece of deerskin, he tried to throw it over the thing in his lap, but the skin slipped away. Jody stood overwhelmed by the thing in Gitano's hand, a lean and lovely rapier with a golden basket hilt. The blade was like a thin ray of dark light. The hilt was pierced and intricately carved.

"What is it?" Jody demanded.

Gitano only looked at him with resentful eyes, and he picked up the fallen deerskin and firmly wrapped the beautiful blade in it.

Jody put out his hand. "Can't I see it?"

Gitano's eyes smoldered angrily and he shook his head.

"Where'd you get it? Where'd it come from?"

Now Gitano regarded him profoundly, as though he pondered. "I got it from my father."

"Well, where'd he get it?"

Gitano looked down at the long deerskin parcel in his hand. "I don' know."

"Didn't he ever tell you?"

"No."

"What do you do with it?"

Gitano looked slightly surprised. "Nothing. I just keep it."

"Can't I see it again?"

The old man slowly unwrapped the shining blade and let the lamp light slip along it for a moment. Then he wrapped it up again. "You go now. I want to go to bed." He blew out the lamp almost before Jody had closed the door.

As he went back toward the house, Jody knew one thing more sharply than he had ever known anything. He must never tell anyone about the rapier. It would be a dreadful thing to tell anyone about it, for it would destroy some fragile structure of truth. It was a truth that might be shattered by division.

On the way across the dark yard Jody passed Billy Buck. "They're wondering where you are," Billy said.

Jody slipped into the living room, and his father turned to him. "Where have you been?"

"I just went out to see if I caught any rats in my new trap."

"It's time you went to bed," his father said.

Jody was first at the breakfast table in the morning. Then his father came in, and last, Billy Buck. Mrs. Tiflin looked in from the kitchen.

"Where's the old man, Billy?" she asked.

"I guess he's out walking," Billy said. "I looked in his room and he wasn't there."

"Maybe he started early to Monterey," said Carl. "It's a long walk."

"No," Billy explained. "His sack is in the little room."

After breakfast Jody walked down to the bunkhouse. Flies were flashing about in the sunshine. The ranch seemed especially quiet this morning. When he was sure no one was watching him, Jody went into the little room, and looked into Gitano's sack. An extra pair of long cotton underwear was there, an extra pair of jeans and three pairs of worn socks. Nothing else was in the sack. A sharp loneliness fell on Jody. He walked slowly back toward the house. His father stood on the porch talking to Mrs. Tiflin.

"I guess old Easter's dead at last," he said. "I didn't see him come down to water with the other horses."

In the middle of the morning Jess Taylor from the ridge ranch rode down.

"You didn't sell that old gray crowbait of yours, did you, Carl?"

"No, of course not. Why?"

"Well," Jess said. "I was out this morning early, and I saw a funny thing. I saw an old man on an old horse, no saddle, only a piece of rope for a bridle. He wasn't on the road at all. He was cutting right up straight through the brush. I think he had a gun. At least I saw something shine in his hand."

"That's old Gitano," Carl Tiflin said. "I'll see if any of my guns are missing." He stepped into the house for a second. "Nope, all here. Which way was he heading, Jess?"

"Well, that's the funny thing. He was heading straight back into the mountains."

Carl laughed. "They never get too old to steal," he said. "I guess he just stole old Easter."

"Want to go after him, Carl?"

"Hell, no, just save me burying that horse. I wonder where he got the gun. I wonder what he wants back there."

Jody walked up through the vegetable patch, toward the brush line. He looked searchingly at the towering mountains—ridge after ridge after ridge until at last there was the ocean. For a moment he thought he could see a black speck crawling up the farthest ridge. Jody thought of the rapier and of Gitano. And he thought of the great mountains. A longing caressed him, and it was so sharp that he wanted to cry to get it out of his breast. He lay down in the green grass near the round tub at the brush line. He covered his eyes with his crossed arms and lay there a long time, and he was full of a nameless sorrow.

III. THE PROMISE

In a mid-afternoon of spring, the little boy Jody walked martially along the brush-lined road toward his home ranch. Banging his knee against the golden lard bucket he used for school lunch, he contrived a good bass drum, while his tongue fluttered sharply against his teeth to fill in snare drums and occasional trumpets. Some time back the other members of the squad that walked so smartly from the school had turned into the various little canyons and taken the wagon roads to their own home ranches. Now Jody marched seemingly alone, with high-lifted knees and pounding feet; but behind him there was a phantom army with great flags and swords, silent but deadly.

The afternoon was green and gold with spring. Underneath the spread branches of the oaks the plants grew pale and tall, and on the hills the feed was smooth and thick. The sagebrushes shone with new silver leaves and the oaks wore hoods of golden green. Over the hills there hung such a green odor that the horses on the flats galloped madly, and then stopped, wondering; lambs, and even old sheep jumped in the air unexpectedly and landed on stiff legs, and went on eating; young clumsy calves butted their heads together and drew back and butted again.

As the gray and silent army marched past, led by Jody, the animals stopped their feeding and their play and watched it go by.

Suddenly Jody stopped. The gray army halted, bewildered and nervous. Jody went down on his knees. The army stood in long uneasy ranks for a moment, and then, with a soft sigh of sorrow, rose up in a faint gray mist and disappeared. Jody had seen the thorny crown of a horny-toad moving under the dust of the road. His grimy hand went out and grasped the spiked halo and held firmly while the little beast struggled. Then Jody turned the horny-toad over, exposing its pale gold stomach. With a gentle forefinger he stroked the throat and chest until the horny-toad relaxed, until its eyes closed and it lay languorous and asleep.

Jody opened his lunch pail and deposited the first game inside. He moved on now, his knees bent slightly, his shoulders crouched; his bare feet were wise and silent. In his right hand there was a long gray rifle. The brush along the road stirred restively under a new and unexpected population of gray tigers and gray bears. The hunting was very good, for by the time Jody reached the fork of the road where the mail box stood on a post, he had captured two more horny-toads, four little grass lizards, a blue snake, sixteen yellow-winged grasshoppers and a brown damp newt from under a rock. This assortment scrabbled unhappily against the tin of the lunch bucket.

At the road fork the rifle evaporated and the tigers and bears melted from the hillsides. Even the moist and uncomfortable creatures in the lunch pail ceased to exist, for the little red metal flag was up on the mail box, signifying that some postal matter was inside. Jody set his pail on the ground and opened the letter box. There was a Montgomery Ward catalogue and a copy of the *Salinas Weekly Journal*. He slammed the box, picked up his lunch pail and trotted over the ridge and down into the cup of the ranch. Past the barn he ran, and past the used-up haystack and the bunkhouse and the cypress tree. He banged through the front screen door of the ranch house calling, "Ma'am, ma'am, there's a catalogue."

Mrs. Tiflin was in the kitchen spooning clabbered milk into a cotton bag. She put down her work and rinsed her hands under the tap. "Here in the kitchen, Jody. Here I am."

He ran in and clattered his lunch pail on the sink. "Here it is. Can I open the catalogue, ma'am?"

Mrs. Tiflin took up the spoon again and went back to her cottage cheese. "Don't lose it, Jody. Your father will want to see it." She scraped the last of the milk into the bag. "Oh, Jody, your father wants to see you before you go to your chores." She waved a cruising fly from the cheese bag.

Jody closed the new catalogue in alarm. "Ma'am?"

"Why don't you ever listen? I say your father wants to see you."

The boy laid the catalogue gently on the sink board. "Do you—is it something I did?"

Mrs. Tiflin laughed. "Always a bad conscience. What did you do?"

"Nothing, ma'am," he said lamely. But he couldn't remember, and besides it was impossible to know what action might later be construed as a crime.

His mother hung the full bag on a nail where it could drip into the sink. "He just said he wanted to see you when you got home. He's somewhere down by the barn."

Jody turned and went out the back door. Hearing his mother open the lunch pail and then gasp with rage, a memory stabbed him and he trotted away toward the barn, conscientiously not hearing the angry voice that called him from the house.

Carl Tiflin and Billy Buck, the ranch hand, stood against the lower pasture fence. Each man rested one foot on the lowest bar and both elbows on the top bar. They were talking slowly and aimlessly. In the pasture half a dozen horses nibbled contentedly at the sweet grass. The mare, Nellie, stood backed up against the gate, rubbing her buttocks on the heavy post.

Jody sidled uneasily near. He dragged one foot to give an impression of great innocence and nonchalance. When he arrived beside the men he put one foot on the lowest fence rail, rested his elbows on the second bar and looked into the pasture too. The two men glanced sideways at him.

"I wanted to see you," Carl said in the stern tone he reserved for children and animals.

"Yes, sir," said Jody guiltily.

"Billy, here, says you took good care of the pony before it died."

No punishment was in the air. Jody grew bolder. "Yes, sir, I did."

"Billy says you have a good patient hand with horses."

Jody felt a sudden warm friendliness for the ranch hand.

Billy put in, "He trained that pony as good as anybody I ever seen."

Then Carl Tiflin came gradually to the point. "If you could have another horse would you work for it?"

Jody shivered. "Yes, sir."

"Well, look here, then. Billy says the best way for you to be a good hand with horses is to raise a colt."

"It's the *only* good way," Billy interrupted.

"Now, look here, Jody," continued Carl. "Jess Taylor, up to the ridge ranch, has a fair stallion, but it'll cost five dollars. I'll put up the money, but you'll have to work it out all summer. Will you do that?"

Jody felt that his insides were shriveling. "Yes, sir," he said softly.

"And no complaining? And no forgetting when you're told to do something?"

"Yes, sir."

"Well, all right, then. Tomorrow morning you take Nellie up to the ridge ranch and get her bred. You'll have to take care of her, too, till she throws the colt."

"Yes, sir."

"You better get to the chickens and the wood now."

Jody slid away. In passing behind Billy Buck he very nearly put out his hand to touch the blue-jeaned legs. His shoulders swayed a little with maturity and importance.

He went to his work with unprecedented seriousness. This night he did not dump the can of grain to the chickens so that they had to leap over each other and struggle to get it. No, he spread the wheat so far and so carefully that the hens couldn't find some of it at all. And in the house, after listening to his mother's despair over boys who filled their lunch pails with slimy, suffocated reptiles, and bugs, he promised never to do it again. Indeed, Jody felt that all such foolishness was lost in the past. He was far too grown up ever to put horny-toads in his lunch pail any more. He carried in so much wood and built such a high structure with it that his mother walked in fear of an avalanche of oak. When he was done, when he had gathered eggs that had remained hidden for weeks, Jody walked down again past the cypress tree, and past the bunkhouse toward the pasture. A fat warty toad that looked out at him from under the watering trough had no emotional effect on him at all.

Carl Tiflin and Billy Buck were not in sight, but from a metallic ringing on the other side of the barn Jody knew that Billy Buck was just starting to milk a cow.

The other horses were eating toward the upper end of the pasture, but Nellie continued to rub herself nervously against the post. Jody walked slowly near, saying, "So, girl, so-o, Nellie." The mare's ears went back naughtily and her lips drew away from her yellow teeth. She turned her head around; her eyes were glazed and mad. Jody climbed to the top of the fence and hung his feet over and looked paternally down on the mare.

The evening hovered while he sat there. Bats and nighthawks flicked about. Billy Buck, walking toward the house carrying a full milk bucket, saw Jody and stopped. "It's a long time to wait," he said gently. "You'll get awful tired waiting."

"No, I won't, Billy. How long will it be?"

"Nearly a year."

"Well, I won't get tired."

The triangle at the house rang stridently. Jody climbed down from the fence and walked to supper beside Billy Buck. He even put out his hand and took hold of the milk bucket to help carry it.

The next morning after breakfast Carl Tiflin folded a five-dollar bill in a piece of newspaper and pinned the package in the bib pocket of Jody's overalls. Billy Buck haltered the mare Nellie and led her out of the pasture.

"Be careful now," he warned. "Hold her up short here so she can't bite you. She's crazy as a coot."

Jody took hold of the halter leather itself and started up the hill toward the ridge ranch with Nellie skittering and jerking behind him. In the pasturage along the road the wild oat heads were just clearing their scabbards. The warm morning sun shone on Jody's back so sweetly that he was forced to take a serious stiff-legged hop now and then in spite of his maturity. On the fences the shiny blackbirds with red epaulets clicked their dry call. The meadowlarks sang like water, and the wild doves, concealed among the bursting leaves of the oaks, made a sound of restrained grieving. In the fields the rabbits sat sunning themselves, with only their forked ears showing above the grass heads.

After an hour of steady uphill walking, Jody turned into a narrow road that led up a steeper hill to the ridge ranch. He could see the red roof of the barn sticking up above the oak trees, and he could hear a dog barking unemotionally near the house.

Suddenly Nellie jerked back and nearly freed herself. From the direction of the barn Jody heard a shrill whistling scream and a splintering of wood, and then a man's voice shouting. Nellie reared and whinnied. When Jody held to the halter rope she ran at him with bared teeth. He dropped his hold and scuttled out of the way, into the brush. The high scream came from the oaks again, and Nellie answered it. With hoofs battering the ground the stallion appeared and charged down the hill trailing a broken halter rope. His eyes glittered feverishly. His stiff, erected nostrils were as red as flame. His black, sleek hide shone in the sunlight. The stallion came on so fast that he couldn't stop when he reached the mare. Nellie's ears went back; she whirled and kicked at him as he went by. The stallion spun around and reared. He struck the mare with his front hoof, and while she staggered under the blow, his teeth raked her neck and drew an ooze of blood.

Instantly Nellie's mood changed. She became coquettishly feminine. She nibbled his arched neck with her lips. She edged around and rubbed her shoulder against his shoulder. Jody stood half-hidden in the brush and watched. He heard the step of a horse behind him, but before he could turn, a hand caught him by the overall straps and lifted him off the ground. Jess Taylor sat the boy behind him on the horse.

"You might have got killed," he said. "Sundog's a mean devil sometimes. He busted his rope and went right through a gate."

Jody sat quietly, but in a moment he cried, "He'll hurt her, he'll kill her. Get him away!"

Jess chuckled. "She'll be all right. Maybe you'd better climb off and go up to the house for a little. You could get maybe a piece of pie up there."

But Jody shook his head. "She's mine, and the colt's going to be mine. I'm going to raise it up."

Jess nodded. "Yes, that's a good thing. Carl has good sense sometimes."

In a little while the danger was over. Jess lifted Jody down and then caught the stallion by its broken halter rope. And he rode ahead, while Jody followed, leading Nellie.

It was only after he had unpinned and handed over the five dollars, and after he had eaten two pieces of pie, that Jody started for home again. And Nellie followed docilely after him. She was so quiet that Jody climbed on a stump and rode her most of the way home.

The five dollars his father had advanced reduced Jody to peonage for the whole late spring and summer. When the hay was cut he drove a rake. He led the horse that pulled on the Jackson-fork tackle, and when the baler came he drove the circling horse that put pressure on the bales. In addition, Carl Tiflin taught him to milk and put a cow under his care, so that a new chore was added night and morning.

The bay mare Nellie quickly grew complacent. As she walked about the yellowing hillsides or worked at easy tasks, her lips were curled in a perpetual fatuous smile. She moved slowly, with the calm importance of an empress. When she was put to a team, she pulled steadily and unemotionally. Jody went to see her every day. He studied her with critical eyes and saw no change whatever.

One afternoon Billy Buck leaned the many-tined manure fork against the barn wall. He loosened his belt and tucked in his shirt-tail and tightened the belt again. He picked one of the little straws from his hat-band and put it in the corner of his mouth. Jody, who was helping Doubletree Mutt, the big serious dog, to dig out a gopher, straightened up as the ranch hand sauntered out of the barn.

"Let's go up and have a look at Nellie," Billy suggested.

Instantly Jody fell into step with him. Doubletree Mutt watched them over his shoulder; then he dug furiously, growled, sounded little sharp yelps to indicate that the gopher was practically caught. When he looked over his shoulder again, and saw that neither Jody nor Billy was interested, he climbed reluctantly out of the hole and followed them up the hill.

The wild oats were ripening. Every head bent sharply under its load of grain, and the grass was dry enough so that it made a swishing sound as Jody and Billy stepped through it. Halfway up the hill they could see Nellie and the iron-gray gelding, Pete, nibbling the heads from the wild oats. When they approached, Nellie looked at them and backed her ears and bobbed her head up and down rebelliously. Billy walked to her and put his hand under her mane and patted her neck, until her ears came forward again and she nibbled delicately at his shirt.

Jody asked, "Do you think she's really going to have a colt?"

Billy rolled the lids back from the mare's eyes with his thumb and forefinger. He felt the lower lip and fingered the black, leathery teats. "I wouldn't be surprised," he said.

"Well, she isn't changed at all. It's three months gone."

Billy rubbed the mare's flat forehead with his knuckle while she grunted with pleasure. "I told you you'd get tired waiting. It'll be five months more before you can even see a sign, and it'll be at least eight months more before she throws the colt, about next January."

Jody sighed deeply. "It's a long time, isn't it?"

"And then it'll be about two years more before you can ride."

Jody cried out in despair, "I'll be grown up."

"Yep, you'll be an old man," said Billy.

"What color do you think the colt'll be?"

"Why, you can't ever tell. The stud is black and the dam is bay. Colt might be black or bay or gray or dappled. You can't tell. Sometimes a black dam might have a white colt."

"Well. I hope it's black, and a stallion."

"If it's a stallion, we'll have to geld it. Your father wouldn't let you have a stallion."

"Maybe he would," Jody said. "I could train him not to be mean."

Billy pursed his lips, and the little straw that had been in the corner of his mouth rolled down to the center. "You can't ever trust a stallion," he said critically. "They're mostly fighting and making trouble. Sometimes when they're feeling funny they won't work. They make the mares uneasy and kick hell out of the geldings. Your father wouldn't let you keep a stallion."

Nellie sauntered away, nibbling the drying grass. Jody skinned the grain from a grass stem and threw the handful into the air, so that each pointed, feathered seed sailed out like a dart. "Tell me how it'll be, Billy. Is it like when the cows have calves?"

"Just about. Mares are a little more sensitive. Sometimes you have to be there to help the mare. And sometimes if it's wrong you have to——" he paused.

"Have to what, Billy?"

"Have to tear the colt to pieces to get it out, or the mare'll die."

"But it won't be that way this time, will it, Billy?"

"Oh, no. Nellie's thrown good colts."

"Can I be there, Billy? Will you be certain to call me? It's my colt.'

"Sure, I'll call you. Of course I will."

"Tell me how it'll be."

"Why, you've seen the cows calving. It's almost the same. The mare starts groaning and stretching, and then, if it's a good right birth, the head and forefeet come out, and the front hoofs kick a hole just the way the calves do. And the colt starts to breathe. It's good to be there, 'cause if its feet aren't right maybe he can't break the sac, and then he might smother."

Jody whipped his leg with a bunch of grass. "We'll have to be there, then, won't we?"

"Oh, we'll be there, all right."

They turned and walked slowly down the hill toward the barn. Jody was tortured with a thing he had to say, although he didn't want to. "Billy," he began miserably, "Billy, you won't let anything happen to the colt, will you?"

And Billy knew he was thinking of the red pony, Gabilan, and of how it died of strangles. Billy knew he had been infallible before that, and now he was capable of failure. This knowledge made Billy much less sure of himself than he had been. "I can't tell," he said roughly. "All sorts of things might happen, and they wouldn't be my fault. I can't do everything." He felt bad about his lost prestige, and so he said, meanly, "I'll do everything I know, but I won't promise anything. Nellie's a good mare. She's thrown good colts before. She ought to this time." And he walked away from Jody and went into the saddle-room beside the barn, for his feelings were hurt.

Jody traveled often to the brushline behind the house. A rusty iron pipe ran a thin stream of spring water into an old green tub. Where the water spilled over and sank into the ground there was a patch of perpetually green grass. Even when the hills were brown and baked in the summer that little patch was green. The water whined softly into the trough all the year round. This place had grown to be a center-point for Jody. When he had been punished the cool green grass and the singing water soothed him. When he had been mean the biting acid of meanness left him at the brushline. When he sat in the grass and listened to the purling stream, the barriers set up in his mind by the stern day went down to ruin.

On the other hand, the black cypress tree by the bunkhouse was as repulsive as the water-tub was dear; for to this tree all the pigs came, sooner or later, to be slaughtered. Pig killing was fascinating, with the screaming and the blood, but it made Jody's heart beat so fast that it hurt him. After the pigs were scalded in the big iron tripod kettle and their skins were scraped and white, Jody had to go to the water-tub to sit in the grass until his heart grew quiet. The water-tub and the black cypress were opposites and enemies.

When Billy left him and walked angrily away, Jody turned up toward the house. He thought of Nellie as he walked, and of the little colt. Then suddenly he saw that he was under the black cypress, under the very singletree where the pigs were hung. He brushed his dry-grass hair off his forehead and hurried on. It seemed to him an unlucky thing to be thinking of his colt in the very slaughter place, especially after what Billy had said. To counteract any evil result of that bad conjunction he walked quickly past the ranch house, through the chicken yard, through the vegetable patch, until he came at last to the brushline.

He sat down in the green grass. The trilling water sounded in his ears. He looked over the farm buildings and across at the round hills, rich and yellow with grain. He could see Nellie feeding on the slope. As usual the water place eliminated time and distance. Jody saw a black, long-legged colt, butting against Nellie's flanks, demanding milk. And then he saw himself breaking a large colt to halter. All in a few moments the colt grew to be a magnificent animal, deep of chest, with a neck as high and arched as a sea-horse's neck, with a tail that

tongued and rippled like black flame. This horse was terrible to everyone but Jody. In the schoolyard the boys begged rides, and Jody smilingly agreed. But no sooner were they mounted than the black demon
pitched them off. Why, that was his name, Black Demon! For a
moment the trilling water and the grass and the sunshine came back,
and then . . .

Sometimes in the night the ranch people, safe in their beds, heard a
roar of hoofs go by. They said, "It's Jody, on Demon. He's helping out
the sheriff again." And then . . .

The golden dust filled the air in the arena at the Salinas Rodeo. The
announcer called the roping contests. When Jody rode the black horse
to the starting chute the other contestants shrugged and gave up first
place, for it was well known that Jody and Demon could rope and
throw and tie a steer a great deal quicker than any roping team of
twe men could. Jody was not a boy any more, and Demon was not a
horse. The two together were one glorious individual. And then . . .

The President wrote a letter and asked them to help catch a bandit
in Washington. Jody settled himself comfortably in the grass. The
little stream of water whined into the mossy tub.

The year passed slowly on. Time after time Jody gave up his colt
for lost. No change had taken place in Nellie. Carl Tiflin still drove her
to a light cart, and she pulled on a hay rake and worked the Jackson-
fork tackle when the hay was being put into the barn.

The summer passed, and the warm bright autumn. And then the
frantic morning winds began to twist along the ground, and a chill
came into the air, and the poison oak turned red. One morning in
September, when he had finished his breakfast, Jody's mother called
him into the kitchen. She was pouring boiling water into a bucket full
of dry midlings and stirring the materials to a steaming paste.

"Yes, ma'am?" Jody asked.

"Watch how I do it. You'll have to do it after this every other morning."

"Well, what is it?"

"Why, it's warm mash for Nellie. It'll keep her in good shape."

Jody rubbed his forehead with a knuckle. "Is she all right?" he asked
timidly.

Mrs. Tiflin put down the kettle and stirred the mash with a wooden
paddle. "Of course she's all right, only you've got to take better care
of her from now on. Here, take this breakfast out to her!"

Jody seized the bucket and ran, down past the bunkhouse, past the
barn, with the heavy bucket banging against his knees. He found Nellie

playing with the water in the trough, pushing waves and tossing her head so that the water slopped out on the ground.

Jody climbed the fence and set the bucket of steaming mash beside her. Then he stepped back to look at her. And she was changed. Her stomach was swollen. When she moved, her feet touched the ground gently. She buried her nose in the bucket and gobbled the hot breakfast. And when she had finished and had pushed the bucket around the ground with her nose a little, she stepped quietly over to Jody and rubbed her cheek against him.

Billy Buck came out of the saddle-room and walked over. "Starts fast when it starts, doesn't it?"

"Did it come all at once?"

"Oh, no, you just stopped looking for a while." He pulled her head around toward Jody. "She's goin' to be nice, too. See how nice her eyes are! Some mares get mean, but when they turn nice, they just love everything." Nellie slipped her head under Billy's arm and rubbed her neck up and down between his arm and his side. "You better treat her awful nice now," Billy said.

"How long will it be?" Jody demanded breathlessly.

The man counted in whispers on his fingers. "About three months," he said aloud. "You can't tell exactly. Sometimes it's eleven months to the day, but it might be two weeks early, or a month late, without hurting anything."

Jody looked hard at the ground. "Billy," he began nervously, "Billy, you'll call me when it's getting born, won't you? You'll let me be there, won't you?"

Billy bit the tip of Nellie's ear with his front teeth. "Carl says he wants you to start right at the start. That's the only way to learn. Nobody can tell you anything. Like my old man did with me about the saddle blanket. He was a government packer when I was your size, and I helped him some. One day I left a wrinkle in my saddle blanket and made a saddle-sore. My old man didn't give me hell at all. But the next morning he saddled me up with a forty-pound stock saddle. I had to lead my horse and carry that saddle over a whole damn mountain in the sun. It darn near killed me, but I never left no wrinkles in a blanket again. I couldn't. I never in my life since then put on a blanket but I felt that saddle on my back."

Jody reached up a hand and took hold of Nellie's mane. "You'll tell me what to do about everything, won't you? I guess you know everything about horses, don't you?"

Billy laughed. "Why, I'm half horse myself, you see," he said. "My ma died when I was born, and being my old man was a government packer in the mountains, and no cows around most of the time, why he just gave me mostly mare's milk." He continued seriously, "And horses know that. Don't you know it, Nellie?"

The mare turned her head and looked full into his eyes for a moment, and this is a thing horses practically never do. Billy was proud and sure of himself now. He boasted a little. "I'll see you get a good colt. I'll start you right. And if you do like I say, you'll have the best horse in the county."

That made Jody feel warm and proud, too; so proud that when he went back to the house he bowed his legs and swayed his shoulders as horsemen do. And he whispered, "Whoa, you Black Demon, you! Steady down there and keep your feet on the ground."

The winter fell sharply. A few preliminary gusty showers, and then a strong steady rain. The hills lost their straw color and blackened under the water, and the winter streams scrambled noisily down the canyons. The mushrooms and puffballs popped up and the new grass started before Christmas.

But this year Christmas was not the central day to Jody. Some undetermined time in January had become the axis day around which the months swung. When the rains fell, he put Nellie in a box stall and fed her warm food every morning and curried her and brushed her.

The mare was swelling so greatly that Jody became alarmed. "She'll pop wide open," he said to Billy.

Billy laid his strong square hand against Nellie's swollen abdomen. "Feel here," he said quietly. "You can feel it move. I guess it would surprise you if there were twin colts."

"You don't think so?" Jody cried. "You don't think it will be twins, do you, Billy?"

"No, I don't, but it does happen, sometimes."

During the first two weeks of January it rained steadily. Jody spent most of his time, when he wasn't in school, in the box stall with Nellie. Twenty times a day he put his hand on her stomach to feel the colt move. Nellie became more and more gentle and friendly to him. She rubbed her nose on him. She whinnied softly when he walked into the barn.

Carl Tiflin came to the barn with Jody one day. He looked admiringly at the groomed bay coat, and he felt the firm flesh over ribs and shoulders. "You've done a good job," he said to Jody. And this was the greatest praise he knew how to give. Jody was tight with pride for hours afterward.

The fifteenth of January came, and the colt was not born. And the twentieth came; a lump of fear began to form in Jody's stomach. "Is it all right?" he demanded of Billy.

"Oh, sure."

And again, "Are you sure it's going to be all right?"

Billy stroked the mare's neck. She swayed her head uneasily. "I told you it wasn't always the same time, Jody. You just have to wait."

When the end of the month arrived with no birth, Jody grew frantic. Nellie was so big that her breath came heavily, and her ears were close together and straight up, as though her head ached. Jody's sleep grew restless, and his dreams confused.

On the night of the second of February he awakened crying. His mother called to him, "Jody, you're dreaming. Wake up and start over again."

But Jody was filled with terror and desolation. He lay quietly a few moments, waiting for his mother to go back to sleep, and then he slipped his clothes on, and crept out in his bare feet.

The night was black and thick. A little misting rain fell. The cypress tree and the bunkhouse loomed and then dropped back into the mist. The barn door screeched as he opened it, a thing it never did in the daytime. Jody went to the rack and found a lantern and a tin box of matches. He lighted the wick and walked down the long straw-covered aisle to Nellie's stall. She was standing up. Her whole body weaved from side to side. Jody called to her, "So, Nellie, so-o, Nellie," but she did not stop her swaying nor look around. When he stepped into the stall and touched her on the shoulder she shivered under his hand. Then Billy Buck's voice came from the hayloft right above the stall.

"Jody, what are you doing?"

Jody started back and turned miserable eyes up toward the nest where Billy was lying in the hay. "Is she all right, do you think?"

"Why, sure, I think so."

"You won't let anything happen, Billy, you're sure you won't?"

Billy growled down at him, "I told you I'd call you, and I will. Now you get back to bed and stop worrying that mare. She's got enough to do without you worrying her."

Jody cringed, for he had never heard Billy speak in such a tone. "I only thought I'd come and see," he said. "I woke up."

Billy softened a little then. "Well, you get to bed. I don't want you bothering her. I told you I'd get you a good colt. Get along now."

Jody walked slowly out of the barn. He blew out the lantern and set it in the rack. The blackness of the night, and the chilled mist struck him and enfolded him. He wished he believed everything Billy said as he had before the pony died. It was a moment before his eyes, blinded by the feeble lantern-flame, could make any form of the darkness. The damp ground chilled his bare feet. At the cypress tree the roosting turkeys chattered a little in alarm, and the two good dogs responded to their duty and came charging out, barking to frighten away the coyotes they thought were prowling under the tree.

As he crept through the kitchen, Jody stumbled over a chair. Carl called from his bedroom, "Who's there? What's the matter there?"

And Mrs. Tiflin said sleepily, "What's the matter, Carl?"

The next second Carl came out of the bedroom carrying a candle, and found Jody before he could get into bed. "What are you doing out?"

Jody turned shyly away. "I was down to see the mare."

For a moment anger at being awakened fought with approval in Jody's father. "Listen," he said, finally, "there's not a man in this country that knows more about colts than Billy. You leave it to him."

Words burst out of Jody's mouth. "But the pony died——"

"Don't you go blaming that on him," Carl said sternly. "If Billy can't save a horse, it can't be saved."

Mrs. Tiflin called, "Make him clean his feet and go to bed, Carl. He'll be sleepy all day tomorrow."

It seemed to Jody that he had just closed his eyes to try to go to sleep when he was shaken violently by the shoulder. Billy Buck stood beside him, holding a lantern in his hand. "Get up," he said. "Hurry up." He turned and walked quickly out of the room.

Mrs. Tiflin called, "What's the matter? Is that you, Billy?"

"Yes, ma'am."

"Is Nellie ready?"

"Yes, ma'am."

"All right, I'll get up and heat some water in case you need it."

Jody jumped into his clothes so quickly that he was out the back door before Billy's swinging lantern was halfway to the barn. There was a rim of dawn on the mountain-tops, but no light had penetrated into the cup of the ranch yet. Jody ran frantically after the lantern and caught up to Billy just as he reached the barn. Billy hung the lantern to a nail on the stall-side and took off his blue denim coat. Jody saw that he wore only a sleeveless shirt under it.

Nellie was standing rigid and stiff. While they watched, she crouched. Her whole body was wrung with a spasm. The spasm passed. But in a few moments it started over again, and passed.

Billy muttered nervously, "There's something wrong." His bare hand disappeared. "Oh, Jesus," he said. "It's wrong."

The spasm came again, and this time Billy strained, and the muscles stood out on his arm and shoulder. He heaved strongly, his forehead beaded with perspiration. Nellie cried with pain. Billy was muttering, "It's wrong. I can't turn it. It's way wrong. It's turned all around wrong."

He glared wildly toward Jody. And then his fingers made a careful, careful diagnosis. His cheeks were growing tight and gray. He looked for a long questioning minute at Jody standing back of the stall. Then Billy stepped to the rack under the manure window and picked up a horseshoe hammer with his wet right hand.

"Go outside, Jody," he said.

The boy stood still and stared dully at him.

"Go outside, I tell you. It'll be too late."

Jody didn't move.

Then Billy walked quickly to Nellie's head. He cried, "Turn your face away, damn you, turn your face."

This time Jody obeyed. His head turned sideways. He heard Billy whispering hoarsely in the stall. And then he heard a hollow crunch of bone. Nellie chuckled shrilly. Jody looked back in time to see the hammer rise and fall again on the flat forehead. Then Nellie fell heavily to her side and quivered for a moment.

Billy jumped to the swollen stomach; his big pocket-knife was in his hand. He lifted the skin and drove the knife in. He sawed and ripped at the tough belly. The air filled with the sick odor of warm living entrails. The other horses reared back against their halter chains and squealed and kicked.

Billy dropped the knife. Both of his arms plunged into the terrible ragged hole and dragged out a big, white, dripping bundle. His teeth tore a hole in the covering. A little black head appeared through the tear, and little slick, wet ears. A gurgling breath was drawn, and then another. Bill shucked off the sac and found his knife and cut the string. For a moment he held the little black colt in his arms and looked at it. And then he walked slowly over and laid it in the straw at Jody's feet.

Billy's face and arms and chest were dripping red. His body shivered and his teeth chattered. His voice was gone; he spoke in a throaty whisper. "There's your colt. I promised. And there it is. I had to do it—had to." He stopped and looked over his shoulder into the box stall. "Go get hot water and a sponge," he whispered. "Wash him and dry him the way his mother would. You'll have to feed him by hand. But there's your colt, the way I promised."

Jody stared stupidly at the wet, panting foal. It stretched out its chin and tried to raise its head. Its blank eyes were navy blue.

"God damn you," Billy shouted, "will you go now for the water? *Will you go?*"

Then Jody turned and trotted out of the barn into the dawn. He ached from his throat to his stomach. His legs were stiff and heavy. He tried to be glad because of the colt, but the bloody face, and the haunted, tired eyes of Billy Buck hung in the air ahead of him.

64

A Portrait of Bascom Hawke

BY THOMAS WOLFE

URING the first twenty-five years of this century, business people who had their offices in or near State Street, Boston, no doubt grew very familiar with the cadaverous and extraordinary figure of my uncle, Bascom Hawke. Shortly before nine o'clock of every working day he would emerge from a subway exit near the head of the street and pause vaguely for a moment, making a craggy eddy in the tide of issuing workers that foamed swiftly about him while he stood with his enormous bony hands clutched comically before him at the waist, as if holding himself in, at the same time making the most horrible grimaces with his lean and amazingly flexible features. These grimaces were made by squinting his small sharp eyes together, widening his mouth in a ghastly travesty of a grin, and convolving his chin and cheek in a rapid series of pursed lips and horrible squints as he swiftly pressed his rubbery underlip against a few enormous horse teeth that decorated his upper jaw. Having completed these facial evolutions, he glanced quickly and, it must be supposed, blindly, in every direction; for he then plunged heedlessly across the street, sometimes choosing the moment when traffic had been halted, and pedestrians were hurrying across, sometimes diving into the midst of a roaring chaos of motor cars, trucks, and wagons, through which he sometimes made his way in safety, accompanied only by a scream of brake bands, a startled barking of horns, and the hearty curses of frightened drivers, or from which, howling with terror in the center of a web of traffic which he had snarled hopelessly and brought to a complete standstill, he was sometimes rescued by a red-faced and cursing young Irishman who was on point duty at that corner.

But Bascom was a fated man and he escaped. Once, it is true, a bright mindless beetle of machinery, which had no thought for fated men, had knocked him down and skinned and bruised him; again, an uninstructed wheel had passed across the soft toe-end of his shoe and held him prisoner, as if he were merely some average son of destiny—but he escaped. He escaped because he was a fated man and because the providence which guides the steps of children and the blind was kind to him; and because this same policeman whose simian upper lip had once been thick and twisted with its curses had long since run the scale from anger to wild fury, and thence to madness and despair and resignation, and had now come to have a motherly affection for this stray sheep, kept his eye peeled for its appearance every morning or, failing this, at once shrilled hard upon his whistle when he heard the well-known howl of terror and surprise, plunged to the center of the stalled traffic snarl, plucked Bascom out to safety under curse and shout and scream of brake, and marched him tenderly to the curb, gripping his brawny hand around my uncle's arm, feeling his joints, testing his bones, massaging anxiously his sinewy carcass, and calling him "bud" —although my uncle was old enough to be his grandfather. "Are you all right, bud? You're not hurt, are you, bud? Are you O. K.?"—to which Bascom if his shock and terror had been great, could make no answer for a moment save to pant hoarsely and to howl loudly and huskily from time to time "Ow! Ow! Ow! Ow!"

At length, becoming more coherent, if not more calm, he would launch into an ecclesiastical indictment of motor cars and their drivers delivered in a high, howling, and husky voice that suggested the pronouncements of a prophet from a mountain. This voice had a quality of strange remoteness and, once heard, would never be forgotten. It actually had a howling note in it, and carried to great distances, and yet it was not loud: it was very much as if Mr. Bascom Hawke were standing on a mountain and shouting to some one in a quiet valley below—the sounds came to one plainly but as if from a great distance, and it was full of husky, unearthly passion. It was really an ecclesiastical voice, the voice of a great preacher; one felt that it should be heard in churches, which was exactly where it once was heard, for my uncle Bascom had at various times and with great conviction, in the course of his long and remarkable life, professed and preached the faith of the Episcopalians, the Presbyterians, the Methodists, the Baptists, and the Unitarians.

Quite often, in fact, as now, when he had narrowly escaped disaster in the streets, Bascom Hawke still preached from the corner: as soon as he recovered somewhat from his shock, he would launch forth into a sermon of eloquent invective against any driver of motor cars within hearing, and if any of them entered the fray, as sometimes happened, a very interesting performance occurred.

"What happened to *you?*" the motorist might bitterly remark. "Do the keepers know you're out?"

Mr. Hawke would thereupon retort with an eloquent harangue, beginning with a few well-chosen quotations from the more violent prophets of the Old Testament, a few predictions of death, destruction and damnation for the owners of motor cars, and a few apt references to Days of Judgment and Reckoning, Chariots of Moloch, and Beasts of the Apocalypse.

"Oh, for God's sake!" the exasperated motorist might reply. "Are you *blind?* Where do you think you are? In a cow-pasture? Can't you read the signals? Didn't you see the cop put his hand up? Don't you know when it says to 'Stop' or 'Go'? Did you ever hear of the traffic law?"

"The *traffic* law!" my uncle Bascom sneeringly exclaimed, as if the mere use of the word by the motorist evoked his profoundest contempt. His voice now had a precise and meticulous way of speech, there was something sneering and pedantical in the way he pronounced each word, biting it off with a prim, nasal and heavily accented enunciation in the manner of certain pedants and purists who suggest by their pronunciation that language in the mouths of most people is vilely and carelessly treated, that each word has a precise, subtle, and careful meaning of its own, and that they—*they* alone—understand these matters. "The *traffic* law!" he repeated again: then he squinted his eyes together, pursed his rubbery lip against the big horsy upper teeth, and laughed down his nose in a forced, sneering manner, "The *traffic* law!" he said. "Why, you pit-i-ful ig-no-*ram*-us! You il-*lit*-er-ate ruffian! You dare to speak to me—to *me!*" he howled suddenly with an ecclesiastical lift of his voice, striking himself on his bony breast and glaring with a majestical fury as if the word of a mighty prophet had been contradicted by an upstart—"of the traffic law, when it is doubtful if you could *read* the law if you saw it,"—he sneered—"and it is obvious to any one with the perception of a schoolboy that you would not have intelligence enough to understand it, and"—here his voice rose to a howling emphasis and he held one huge bony finger up to command attention—"*and* to interpret it, if you could read."

"Is *that* so!" the motorist heavily remarked. "A *wise* guy, eh? One of these guys who knows it all, eh? You're a *pretty* wise guy, aren't you?" the motorist continued bitterly, as if caught up in the circle of his refrain and unable to change it. "Well, let me tell *you* something. You think you're pretty smaht, don't you? Well, you're not. See? It's wise guys like you who go around looking for a good bust on the nose. See? That's how smaht you are. If you wasn't an old guy I'd give you one, too," he said, getting a moody satisfaction from the thought.

"Ow-w! Ow-w! Ow-w!" Bascom howled in sudden terror.

"If you know so much, if you're so smaht as you think you are, what *is* the traffic law?"

Then, assuredly, if there was a traffic law, the unfortunate motorist was lost, for my uncle Bascom would deliver it to him verbatim, licking his lips with joy over all the technicalities of legal phrasing and pronouncing each phrase with a meticulous and pedantical enunciation.

"And furthermore!" he howled, holding up his big bony finger, "the Commonwealth of Massachusetts has decreed, by a statute that has been on the books since 1856, by a statute that is irrevocably, inexorably, ineluctably plain that any driver, director, governor, commander, manager, agent or conductor, or any other person who shall conduct or cause to be conducted any vehicular instrument, whether it be of two, four, six, eight or any number of wheels whatsoever, whether it be in the public service, or in the possession of a private individual, whether it be—" but by this time, the motorist, if he was wise, had had enough, and had escaped.

If, however, it had been one of his more fortunate mornings, if he had blindly but successfully threaded the peril of roaring traffic, my uncle Bascom proceeded rapidly down State Street, still clutching his raw bony hands across his meagre waist, still contorting his remarkable face in its endless series of pursed grimaces, and presently turned in to the entrance of a large somewhat dingy-looking building of blackened stone, one of those solid, unpretending, but very valuable properties which smells and looks like the early 1900's, and which belongs to that ancient and enormously wealthy corporation which lies across the river and is known as Harvard University.

Here, my uncle Bascom, still clutching himself together across the waist, mounted a flight of indented marble entry steps, lunged through revolving doors into a large marble corridor that was redolent with vibrating waves of hot steamy air, wet rubbers and galoshes, sanitary disinfectant, and serviceable but somewhat old-fashioned elevators and, entering one of the cars which had just plunged down abruptly, banged open its door, belched out two or three people and swallowed a dozen more, he was finally deposited with the same abruptness on the seventh floor, where he stepped out into a wide dark corridor, squinted and grimaced uncertainly to right and left as he had done for twenty-five years, and then went left along the corridor, past rows of lighted offices in which one could hear the preliminary clicking of typewriters, the rattling of crisp papers, and the sounds of people beginning their day's work. At the end of the corridor Bascom Hawke turned right along another corridor and at length paused before a door which bore this

inscription across the familiar glazed glass of American business offices:
The John T. Brill Realty Co.—Houses For Rent or Sale. Below this
bold legend in much smaller letters was printed: Bascom Hawke—
Att'y at Law—Conveyancer and Title Expert.

And now, before we enter this interesting office, let us give a closer and
more particular scrutiny to the appearance of this singular man.

The appearance of this strange figure in State Street, or anywhere
else, had always been sufficiently curious to attract attention and to
draw comment. Bascom Hawke, if he had straightened to his full
height, would have been six feet and three or four inches tall, but he
had always walked with a stoop and as he grew older, the stoop had
become confirmed: he presented a tall, gnarled, bony figure, cadaverous
and stringy, but tough as hickory. He was of that race of men who
seem never to wear out, or to grow old, or to die: they live with almost
undiminished vitality to great ages, and when they die they die suddenly. There is no slow wastage and decay because there is so little to
waste or decay: their mummied and stringy flesh has the durability of
granite.

Bascom Hawke clothed his angular figure with an assortment of odd
garments which seemed to have the same durability: they were immensely old and worn, but they also gave no signs of ever wearing out,
for by their cut and general appearance of age, it seemed that his frugal
soul had selected in the Nineties materials which it hoped would last
forever. His coat, which was originally of a dark dull pepper-and-salt
gray, had gone green at the seams and pockets, and moreover it was a
ridiculously short skimpy coat for a gaunt big-boned man like this:
it was hardly more than a jacket, his great wristy hands burst out of it
like lengths of cordwood, and the mark of his high humped narrow
shoulders cut into it with a knife-like sharpness. His trousers were
also tight and skimpy, of a lighter gray and of a rough woolly texture
from which all fuzz and fluff had long ago been rubbed, he wore
rough country brogans with raw-hide laces, and a funny little flat hat
of ancient black felt, which had also gone green along the band. One
understands now why the policeman called him "Bud": this great bony
figure seemed ruthlessly to have been crammed into garments in which a
country fledgling of the Eighties might have gone to see his girl, clutching a bag of gum drops in his large red hand. A stringy little necktie,
a clean but dilapidated collar which by its bluish and softly mottled look
Bascom Hawke must have laundered himself (a presumption which is
quite correct since my uncle did all his own laundry work, as well as
his mending, repairing, and cobbling)—this was his costume, winter
and summer, and it never changed, save that in winter he supplemented

it with an ancient blue sweater which he wore buttoned to the chin and whose frayed ends and cuffs projected inches below the scanty little jacket. He had never been known to wear an overcoat, not even on the coldest days of those long, raw, and formidable winters which Boston suffers.

The mark of my uncle's madness was plain upon him: intuitively men knew he was not a poor man, and the people who had seen him so many times in State Street would nudge one another, saying: "You see that old guy? You'd think he was waitin' for a handout from the Salvation Army, wouldn't you? Well, he's not. He's *got* it, brother. Believe me, he's *got* it good and plenty: he's *got* it salted away where no one ain't goin' to touch it. That guy's got a sock full of dough!"

"Jesus!" another remarks. "What good's it goin' to do an old guy like that? He can't take any of it with him, can he?"

"You said it, brother," and the conversation would become philosophical.

Bascom Hawke was himself conscious of his parsimony, and although he sometimes asserted that he was "only a poor man" he realized that his exaggerated economies could not be justified to his business associates on account of poverty: they taunted him slyly, saying, "Come on, Hawke, let's go to lunch. You can get a good meal at the Parker House for a couple of bucks." Or "Say, Hawke, I know a place where they're havin' a sale of winter overcoats: I saw one there that would just suit you—you can get it for sixty dollars." Or "Do you need a good laundry, Reverend? I know a couple of Chinks who do good work."

To which Bascom, with the characteristic evasiveness of parsimony, would reply, snuffling derisively down his nose: "No, sir! You won't catch me in any of their stinking restaurants. You never know what you're getting: if you could see the dirty, nasty, filthy kitchens where your food is prepared you'd lose your appetite quick enough." His parsimony had resulted in a compensating food mania: he declared that "in his young days" he "ruined his digestion by eating in restaurants," he painted the most revolting pictures of the filth of these establishments, laughing scornfully down his nose as he declared: "I suppose you think it tastes better after some dirty, nasty, stinking *nigger* has wiped his old hands all over it" (phuh-phuh-phuh-phuh-phuh!) –here he would contort his face and snuffle scornfully down his nose; and he was bitter in his denunciation of "rich foods," declaring they had "destroyed more lives than all the wars and all the armies since the beginning of time."

As he had grown older he had become more and more convinced

of the healthy purity of "raw foods," and he prepared for himself at home raw revolting messes of chopped-up carrots, onions, turnips, even raw potatoes, which he devoured at table, smacking his lips with an air of keen relish, and declaring to his wife: "You may poison *yourself* on your old roasts and oysters and turkeys if you please: you wouldn't catch *me* eating that stuff. No, sir! Not on your life! I think too much of my stomach!" But his use of the pronoun "you" was here universal rather than particular because if the lady's longevity had depended on her abstinence from "roasts and oysters and turkeys" there was no reason why she should not have lived forever.

Or again, if it were a matter of clothing, a matter of fencing in his bones and tallows against the frozen nail of Boston winter, he would howl derisively: "An overcoat! Not on your life! I wouldn't give two cents for all the old overcoats in the world! The only thing they're good for is to gather up germs and give you colds and pneumonia. I haven't worn an overcoat in thirty years, and I've never had the *vestige*—no! not the *semblance*—of a cold during all that time!"—an assertion that was not strictly accurate since he always complained bitterly of at least two or three during the course of a single winter, declaring at those times that no more hateful, treacherous, damnable climate than that of Boston had ever been known.

Similarly, if it were a question of laundries he would scornfully declare that he would not send *"his* shirts and collars to let some dirty old Chinaman spit and *hock* upon them—*yes!"* he would gleefully howl, as some new abomination of nastiness suggested itself to his teeming brain—"*Yes!* and iron it *in,* too, so you can walk around done up in old Chinaman's spit!"—(Phuh-phuh-phuh-phuh-phuh!)—here he would grimace, contort his rubbery lip, and laugh down his nose in forced snarls of gratification and triumph.

This was the old man who now stood clutching his raw bony hands across his waist, before entering his office.

This was his history:

Bascom Hawke had been the scholar of his amazing family: he was a man of powerful intelligence and disordered emotions. Even in his youth, his eccentricities of dress, speech, walk, manner had made him an object of ridicule to his Southern kinsmen, but their ridicule was streaked with pride, since they accepted the impact of his personality as another proof that theirs was an extraordinary family. "He's one of 'em, all right," they said exultantly, "queerer than any of us!"

Bascom's youth, following the war between the States, had been seared by a bitter poverty: at once enriched and warped by a life that clung to the earth with a root-like tenacity, that was manual, painful, spare and stricken, and that rebuilt itself—fiercely, cruelly, and richly—from the earth. And, because there burned and blazed in him from the first a hatred of human indignity, a passionate avowal of man's highness and repose, he felt more bitterly than the others the delinquencies of his father, and the multiplication of his father's offspring, who came regularly into a world of empty cupboards.

"As each of them made its unhappy entrance into the world," he would say later, his voice tremulous with passion, "I went out into the woods, striking my head against the trees, and blaspheming God in my anger. Yes, sir," he continued, pursing his long lip rapidly against his few loose upper teeth, and speaking with an exaggerated pedantry of enunciation, "I am not ashamed to confess that I did. For we were living in conditions un-*worthy—unworthy*"—his voice rising to an evangelical yell. "I had almost said—of the condition of animals. And —*say*—what do you think?"—he said, with a sudden shift in manner and tone, becoming, after his episcopal declaration, matter of fact and whispering confidential. "Why, do you know, my boy, at one time I had to take my *own* father aside, and point out to him we were living in no way becoming decent people."—Here his voice sank to a whisper, and he tapped me on the knee with his big stiff finger, grimacing horribly and pursing his lips against his dry upper teeth.

Poverty had been the mistress of his youth and Bascom Hawke had not forgotten: poverty had burned its way into his heart. He took what education he could find in a backwoods school, read everything he could, taught, for two or three years, in a country school and, at the age of twenty-one, borrowing enough money for railway fare, went to Boston to enroll himself at Harvard. And, somehow, because of the fire that burned in him, the fierce determination of his soul, he had been admitted, secured employment waiting on tables, tutoring, and pressing every one's trousers but his own, and lived in a room with two other starved wretches on $3.50 a week, cooking, eating, sleeping, washing, and studying in the one place.

At the end of seven years he had gone through the college and the school of theology, performing brilliantly in Greek, Hebrew, and metaphysics.

Poverty, fanatical study, the sexual meagerness of his surroundings, had made of him a gaunt zealot: at thirty he was a lean fanatic, a true Yankee madman, high-boned, with gray thirsty eyes and a thick flaring sheaf of oaken hair—six feet three inches of gangling and ludicrous height, gesticulating madly and obviously before a grinning world. But he had a grand lean head: he looked somewhat like the great Ralph Waldo Emerson—with the brakes off.

About this time, he married a young Southern woman of a good family: she was from Tennessee, her parents were both dead, in the Seventies she had come north and had lived for several years with an uncle in Providence, who had been constituted guardian of her estate, amounting probably to about seventy-five thousand dollars, although her romantic memory later multiplied the sum to two hundred thousand dollars. The man squandered part of her money and stole the rest: she came, therefore, to Bascom without much dowry, but she was pretty, bright, intelligent, and had a good figure. Bascom smote the walls of his room with bloody knuckles, and fell down before God.

When Bascom met her she was a music student in Boston: she had a deep full-toned contralto voice which was wrung from her somewhat tremulously when she sang. She was a small woman, birdlike and earnest, delicately fleshed and boned, quick and active in her movements and with a crisp tart speech which still bore, curiously, traces of a Southern accent. She was a brisk, serious, lady-like little person, without much humor, and she was very much in love with her gaunt suitor. They saw each other for two years: they went to concerts, lectures, sermons; they talked of music, poetry, philosophy and of God, but they never spoke of love. But one night Bascom met her in the parlor of her boarding house on Huntington Avenue, and with a voice vibrant and portentous with the importance of the words he had to utter, began as follows: "Miss Louise!" he said carefully, gazing thoughtfully over the apex of his hands. "There comes a time when a man, having reached an age of discretion and mature judgment must begin to consider one of the *gravest*—yes! by all means one of the most important events in human life. The event I refer to is—matrimony." He paused, a clock was beating out its punctual measured tock upon the mantel, and a horse went by with ringing hoofs upon the street. As for Louise, she sat quietly erect, with dignified and lady-like composure, but it seemed to her that the clock was beating in her own breast, and that it might cease to beat at any moment.

"For a minister of the gospel," Bascom continued, "the decision is particularly grave because, for him—once made it is *irrevocable,* once determined upon, it must be followed *inexorably, relentlessly*—aye! to the edge of the grave, to the *uttermost* gates of death, so that the possibility of an error in judgment is *fraught*," his voice sinking to a boding whisper—"is *fraught* with the most terrible consequences. Accordingly," Uncle Bascom said in a deliberate tone, "having decided to take this step, realizing to the *full*—to the *full,* mind you—its gravity, I have searched my soul, I have questioned my heart. I have gone up into the mount-ings and out into the desert and communed with my *Maker* until," his voice rose like a demon's howl, "there no longer remains an *atom* of doubt, a *particle* of uncertainty, a *vestige* of *disbelief!* Miss

Louise, I have decided that the young lady best fitted in every way to be my helpmate, the partner of my joys and griefs, the confidante of my dearest hopes, the in-*spir*-a-tion of my noblest endeavors, the companion of my declining years, and the *spirit* that shall accompany me along each step of life's vexed and troubled way, sharing with me whatever God in his *inscrutable* Providence shall will, whether of wealth or poverty, grief or happiness—I have decided, Miss Louise, that that lady must be—yourself!—and, therefore, I request," he said slowly and impressively, "the honor of your hand in mar-ri-age."

She loved him, she had hoped, prayed, and agonized for just such a moment, but now that it had come she rose immediately with lady-like dignity, and said: "Mistah Hawke: I am honuhed by this mahk of yoah esteem and affection, and I pwomise to give it my most *un*nest considahwation without delay. I wealize fully, Mistah Hawke, the gwavity of the wuhds you have just uttuhed. Foh my paht, I must tell you, Mistah Hawke, that if I accept youah pwoposal, I shall come to you without the fawchun which was *wight*fully mine, but of which I have been depwived and defwauded by the *wascality*—yes! the *wascality* of my gahdian. I shall come to you, theahfoh, without the dow'y I had hoped to be able to contwibute to my husband's fawchuns."

"Oh, my *dear* Miss Louise! My *dear* young lady!" Uncle Bascom cried, waving his great hand through the air with a dismissing gesture. "Do not suppose—do not for one instant suppose, I beg of you!—that consideration of a monetary nature could influence my decision. Oh, not in the slightest!" he cried. "Not at all, not at all!"

"Fawchnatly," Louise continued, "my inhewitance was not *wholly* dissipated by this scoundwel. A pohtion, a vewy small pohtion, remains."

"My dear girl! My dear young lady!" Uncle Bascom cried. "It is not of the *slightest* consequence. . . . How much did he leave?" he added.

Thus they were married.

Bascom immediately got a church in the Middle West: good pay and a house. But during the course of the next twenty years he was shifted from church to church, from sect to sect—to Brooklyn, then back to the Middle West, to the Dakotas, to Jersey City, to Western Massachusetts, and finally back to the small towns surrounding Boston.

When Bascom talked, you may be sure God listened: he preached magnificently, his gaunt face glowing from the pulpit, his rather high, enormously vibrant voice husky with emotion. His prayers were fierce solicitations of God, so mad with fervor that his audiences felt uncomfortably they came close to blasphemy. But, unhappily, on occasions my uncle's mad eloquence grew too much for him: his voice, always too near the heart of passion, would burst in splinters, and he would fall violently forward across his lectern, his face covered by his great gaunt fingers, sobbing horribly.

This, in the Middle West, where his first church had been, does not go down so well—yet it may be successful if one weeps mellowly, joyfully—smiling bravely through the tears—at a lovely aisle processional of repentant sinners; but Bascom, who chose uncomfortable titles for his sermons, would be overcome by his powerful feelings on these occasions when his topic was "Potiphar's Wife," "Ruth, the Girl in the Corn," "The Whores of Babylon," "The Woman on the Roof," and so on.

His head was too deeply engaged with his conscience—he was in turn Episcopal, Presbyterian, Unitarian, searching through the whole roaring confusion of Protestantism for a body of doctrine with which he could agree. And he was forever finding it, and later forever renouncing what he had found. At forty, the most liberal of Unitarians, the strains of agnosticism were piping madly through his sermons: he began to hint at his new faith in prose which he modelled on the mighty utterance of Carlyle, and in poetry, in what he deemed the manner of Matthew Arnold. His professional connection with the Unitarians, and indeed with the Baptists, Methodists, Holy Rollers, and Seventh Day Adventists, came to an abrupt ending after he read from his pulpit one morning a composition in verse entitled *The Agnostic,* which made up in concision what it lacked in melody, and which ended each stanza sadly, but very plainly, on this recurrence:

> "I do not know:
> It may be so."

Thus, when he was almost fifty Bascom Hawke stopped preaching in public. There was no question where he was going. He had his family's raging lust for property. He became a "conveyancer"; he acquired enough of the law of property to convey titles; but he began to buy pieces of land in the suburbs of Boston, and to build small cheap houses, using his own somewhat extraordinary designs to save the architect's fees and, wherever possible, doing such odd jobs as laying the foundations, installing the plumbing, and painting the structure.

He regarded the price of everything as exorbitant—his furious anguish over the wages of labor was marvellous to behold: it drove him raging home, where he stamped insanely upon the floors in his fury, declaring that the Italians, Irish, Belgians, Poles, Swiss, and Yankees —or whatever unfortunate race had been represented in the last bill of charges—were infamous scoundrels, foul and dishonest cutthroats, engaged in a conspiracy to empty both his purse and his cupboard. He called upon them the entire and plenteous artillery of his abuse, his high husky voice ascending to a scream, until his own powers failing

him, there flashed in him for a moment remembrance of one mightier
than he, the most terribly eloquent of all earth's thunderers—his obscene
and gargantuan partner, John T. Brill; and lifting his shaking hands
toward Heaven, he would invoke God and Brill at the same time.

Like others in his family seared with a terrible and minute memory
of war and hunger, he fled before the skeleton specter of poverty: he
was of that race which expects to avert starvation by eating sparingly.

Therefore, he mended his own shoes and wore historic clothing; he
fiercely sowed and reaped the produce of his stony garden, and contrived in countless other ways to thwart the forces of organized ex-
tortion.

The small houses that he—no, he did not build them!—he went
through the agonies of monstrous childbirth to produce them, he licked,
nursed, and fondled them into stunted growth, and he sold them on
long, but profitable terms to small Irish, Jewish, Negro, Belgian, Italian and Greek laborers and tradesmen. And at the conclusion of a
sale, or after receiving from one of these men the current payment,
Uncle Bascom went homeward in a delirium of joy, shouting in a
loud voice, to all who might be compelled to listen, the merits of the
Jews, Belgians, Irish, Swiss or Greeks.

"Finest people in the world! No question about it!"—this last being
his favorite exclamation in all moments of payment or conviction.

For when they paid, he loved them. Often on Sundays they would
come to pay him tramping over the frozen ground or the packed snow
through street after street of smutty gray-looking houses in the flat
weary-looking suburb where he lived. To this dismal heath, therefore,
they came, the swarthy children of a dozen races, clad in the hard and
decent blacks in which the poor pay debts and go to funerals. They
would advance across the barren lands, the harsh sere earth scarred with
its wastes of rust and rubbish, passing stolidly by below the blank board
fences of a brick yard, crunching doggedly through the lanes of dirty
rutted ice, passing before the gray besmutted fronts of wooden houses
which in their stark, desolate, and unspeakable ugliness seemed to
give a complete and final utterance to an architecture of weariness,
sterility and horror, so overwhelming in its absolute desolation that
it seemed as if the painful and indignant soul of man must sicken and
die at length before it, stricken, stupefied, and strangled without a
tongue to articulate the curse that once had blazed in him.

And at length they would pause before my uncle's little house—one
of a street of little houses which he had built there on the barren flat-
lands of the suburb, and to which he had given magnificently his own
name—Hawke Heights—although the only eminence in all that flat
and weary waste was a stunted and almost imperceptible rise a half

mile off. And here along this street which he had built, these little houses, warped, yet strong and hardy, seemed to burrow down solidly like moles for warmth into the ugly stony earth on which they were built and to cower and huddle doggedly below the immense and terrible desolation of the northern sky, with its rimy sun-hazed lights, its fierce and cruel rags and stripes of wintry red, its raw and savage harshness. And then, gripping their greasy little wads of money, as if the knowledge that all rewards below these fierce and cruel skies must be wrenched painfully and minutely from a stony earth, they went in to pay my uncle. He would come up to meet them from some lower cellar-depth, swearing, muttering, and banging doors; and he would come toward them howling greetings, buttoned to his chin in the frayed and faded sweater, gnarled, stooped and frosty-looking, clutching his great hands together at his waist. Then they would wait, stiffly, clumsily, fingering their hats, while with countless squints and grimaces and pursings of the lip, he scrawled out painfully their receipt—their fractional release from debt and labor, one more hard-won step toward the freedom of possession.

At length, having pocketed their money and finished the transaction, he would not permit them to depart at once, he would howl urgently at them an invitation to stay, he would offer long weedy-looking cigars to them, and they would sit uncomfortably, crouching on their buttock bones like stalled oxen, at the edges of chairs, shyly and dumbly staring at him, while he howled question, comment, and enthusiastic tribute at them.

"Why, my dear sir!" he would yell at Makropolos, the Greek. "You have a glorious past, a history of which any nation might well be proud!"

"Sure, sure!" said Makropolos, nodding vigorously. "Beeg heestory!"

" 'The isles of Greece, the isles of Greece!' " my uncle howled, " 'where burning Sappho loved and sung—' " (Phuh! phuh! phuh! phuh! phuh!)

"Sure, sure!" said Makropolos again, nodding good-naturedly but wrinkling his lowering finger-breadth of brow in a somewhat puzzled fashion. "Tha's right! You got it!"

"Why, my dear sir!" Uncle Bascom cried. "It has been the ambition of my lifetime to visit those hallowed scenes, to stand at sunrise on the Acropolis, to explore the glory that was Greece, to see the magnificent ruins of the noblest of ancient civ-i-*liz*-a-tions!"

For the first time a dark flush, a flush of outraged patriotism, began to burn upon the swarthy yellow of Mr. Makropolos' cheek: his manner became heavy and animated, and in a moment he said with passionate conviction:

"No, no, no! No ruin! Wat you t'ink, eh! Athens fine town! We got a million pipples dere!" He struggled for a word, then cupped his hairy paws indefinitely: "*You* know? *Beeg!* O, ni-ez!" he added greasily, with a smile. "Everyt'ing good! We got everyt'ing good dere as you got here! *You* know?" he said with a confiding and painful effort. "Everyt'ing ni-ez! Not old! No, no, no!" he cried with a rising and indignant vigor. "New! de same as here? Ni-ez! You get good and cheap—everyt'ing! Beeg place, new house, dumbwaiter, elevator—wat chew like!—oh, ni-ez!" he said earnestly. "Wat chew t'ink it cost, eh? Feefateen dollar a month! Sure, sure!" he nodded with a swarthy earnestness. "I wouldn't keed you!"

"Finest people on earth!" my uncle Bascom cried with an air of great conviction and satisfaction. "No question about it!"—and he would usher his visitor to the door howling farewells into the terrible desolation of those savage skies.

Meanwhile, my Aunt Louise, although she had not heard a word of what was said, although she had listened to nothing except the periods of Uncle Bascom's heavily accented and particular speech, kept up a constant snuffling laughter punctuated momently by faint whoops as she bent over her pots and pans in the kitchen, pausing from time to time as if to listen, and then snuffling to herself as she shook her head in pitying mirth which rose again up to the crisis of a faint crazy cackle as she scoured the pan; because, of course, during the forty-five years of her life with him thoroughly, imperceptibly, and completely, she had gone mad, and no longer knew or cared to know whether these words had just been spoken or were the echoes of lost voices long ago.

And again, she would pause to listen, with her small birdlike features uplifted gleefully in a kind of mad attentiveness as the door slammed and he stumped muttering back into the house, intent upon the secret designs of his own life, as remote and isolate from her as if they had each dwelt on separate planets, although the house they lived in was a small one.

The union of Bascom and Louise had been blessed by four childre—, all of whom had left their father's bed and board when they discovered how simple it is to secure an abundance of food, warmth, clothing, shelter and freedom in the generous world, whether by marriage, murder, or simply by hard labor. Of them, however, remarkable as their lives have been, it is not necessary to speak here, for he had forgotten them, they no longer touched his life: he had the power to forget, he belonged to a more ancient, a more lonely earth.

Such, briefly, had been the history of the old man who now stood before his dusty office. His life had come up from the wilderness, the buried past, the lost America. The potent mystery of old events and

moments had passed around him, and the magic light of dark time
fell across him.

Like all men in this land, he had been a wanderer, an exile on the
immortal earth. Like all of us he had no home. Wherever great wheels
carried him was home.

In the office which Bascom Hawke now entered there were two
rooms, one in front and one behind, L shaped, and set in the elbow
of the building, so that one might look out at the two projecting wings
of the building, and see lighted layers of offices, in which the actors of
a dozen enterprises "took" dictation, clattered at typewriters, walked
back and forth importantly, talked into telephones or, what they did
with amazing frequency, folded their palms behind their skulls, placed
their feet restfully on the nearest solid object, and gazed for long periods
dreamily and tenderly at the ceilings.

Through the broad and usually very dirty panes of the window in
the front office one could catch a glimpse of Faneuil Hall and the magnificent and exultant activity of the markets.

These dingy offices, however, from which a corner of this rich movement might be seen and felt, were merely the unlovely counterpart of
millions of others throughout the country and, in the telling phrase of
Baedeker, offered "little that need detain the tourist": a few chairs, two
scarred roll-top desks, a typist's table, a battered safe with a pile of
thumb-worn ledgers on top of it, a set of green filing cases, an enormous
green, greasy water-jar always half filled with a rusty liquid that no one
drank, and two spittoons, put there because Brill was a man who
chewed and spat widely in all directions—this, save for placards, each
bearing several photographs of houses with their prices written below
them—8 rooms, Dorchester, $6,500; 5 rooms and garage, Melrose, $4,500,
etc.—completed the furniture of the room, and the second room, save
for the disposition of objects, was similarly adorned.

To reach his own "office," as Bascom Hawke called the tiny cubicle
in which he worked and received his clients, the old man had to traverse
the inner room and open a door in a flimsy partition of varnished wood
and glazed glass at the other end. This was his office: it was really a
very narrow slice cut off from the larger room, and in it there was
barely space for one large dirty window, an ancient dilapidated desk
and swivel chair, a very small battered safe, buried under stacks of
yellowed newspapers, and a small bookcase with glass doors and two
small shelves on which there were a few worn volumes. An inspection
of these books would have revealed four or five tattered and musty
law books in their ponderous calf-skin bindings—one on *Contracts,*
one on *Real Property,* one on *Titles*—a two-volume edition of the poems

of Matthew Arnold, very dog-eared and thumbed over, a copy of *Sartor Resartus,* also much used, a volume of the essays of Ralph Waldo Emerson, the Iliad in Greek with minute yellow notations in the margins, a volume of the *World Almanac* several years old, and a very worn volume of the Holy Bible, greatly used and annotated in Bascom's small, stiffly laborious, and meticulous hand.

If the old man was a little late, as sometimes happened, he might find his colleagues there before him. Miss Muriel Brill, the typist, and the eldest daughter of Mr. John T. Brill, would be seated in her typist's chair, her heavy legs crossed as she bent over to undo the metal latches of the thick golashes she wore during the winter season. It is true there were also other seasons when Miss Brill did not wear galoshes, but so sharply and strongly do our memories connect people with certain gestures which, often for an inscrutable reason, seem characteristic of them, that any frequent visitor to these offices at this time of day would doubtless have remembered Miss Brill as always unfastening her galoshes. But the probable reason is that some people inevitably belong to seasons, and this girl's season was winter—not blizzards or howling winds, or the blind skirl and sweep of snow, but gray, grim, raw, thick, implacable winter: the endless successions of gray days and gray monotony. There was no spark of color in her, her body was somewhat thick and heavy, her face was white, dull, and thick-featured and instead of tapering downwards, it tapered up: it was small above, and thick and heavy below, and even in her speech, the words she uttered seemed to have been chosen by an automaton, and could only be remembered later by their desolate banality. One always remembered her as saying as one entered: ". . . Hello! . . . You're becoming quite a strangeh! . . . It's been some time since you was around, hasn't it? . . . I was thinkin' the otheh day it had been some time since you was around. . . . I'd begun to think you had forgotten us. . . . Well, how've you been? Lookin' the same as usual, I see. . . . Me? . . . Oh, can't complain. . . . Keepin' busy? *I'll* say! I manage to keep goin'. . . . Who you lookin' for? Father? He's in *there.* . . . Why, yeah! Go right on in."

This was Miss Brill, and at the moment that she bent to unfasten her galoshes, it is likely that Mr. Samuel Friedman would also be there in the act of rubbing his small dry hands briskly together, or of rubbing the back of one hand with the palm of the other in order to induce circulation. He was a small youngish man, a pale somewhat meager-looking little Jew with a sharp ferret face: he, too, was a person who goes to "fill in" those vast swarming masses of people along the pavements and in the subway—the mind cannot remember them or absorb the details of their individual appearance but they people the earth, they make up life. Mr. Friedman had none of the richness, color, and humor that some members of his race so abundantly possess, the succession of gray days, the grim weather seemed to have entered his soul as it enters the souls of many different races there—the Irish, the older New England stock, even the Jews—and it gives them a common touch that is prim, drab, careful, tight and sour. Mr. Friedman also wore galoshes, his clothes were neat, drab, a little worn and shiny, there was an odor of steamy thawing dampness and warm rubber about him as he rubbed his dry little hands saying: "Chee! How I hated to leave that good wahm bed this morning! When I got up I said, '*Holy* Chee!' My wife says, 'Whatsa mattah?' I says, 'Holy Chee! You step out heah a moment where I am an' you'll see whatsa mattah.' 'Is it cold?' she says. 'Is it cold! I'll tell the cock-eyed wuhld!' I says. Chee! You could have cut the frost with an ax: the wateh in the pitchehs was frozen hahd; an' she has the nuhve to ask me if it's cold! 'Is it cold!' I says. 'Do you know any more funny stories?' I says. Oh, how I do love my bed! Chee! I kept thinkin' of that guy in Braintree I got to go see today an' the more I thought about him, the less I liked him! I thought my feet would tu'n into two blocks of ice before I got the funniss stahted! 'Chee! I hope the ole bus is still workin', I says. 'If I've got to go thaw that damned thing out,' I says, 'I'm ready to quit.' Chee! Well, suh, I neveh had a bit of trouble: she stahted right up an' the way that ole moteh was workin' is nobody's business."

During the course of this monologue Miss Brill would give ear and assent from time to time by the simple interjection: "Uh!" It was a sound she uttered frequently, it had somewhat the same meaning as "Yes," but it was more noncommittal than "Yes." It seemed to render assent to the speaker, to let him know that he was being heard and understood, but it did not commit the auditor to any opinion, or to any real agreement.

The third member of this office staff, who was likely to be present at this time, was a gentleman named Stanley P. Ward. Mr. Stanley P. Ward was a neat middling figure of a man, aged fifty or thereabouts; he was plump and had a pink tender skin, a trim Vandyke, and a nice comfortable little pot of a belly which slipped snugly into the well-pressed and well-brushed garments that always fitted him so tidily. He was a bit of a fop, and it was at once evident that he was quietly but enormously pleased with himself. He carried himself very sprucely, he took short rapid steps and his neat little paunch gave his figure a movement not unlike that of a pouter pigeon. He was usually in quiet but excellent spirits, he laughed frequently and a smile—rather a subtly amused look—was generally playing about the edges of his mouth.

That smile and his laugh made some people vaguely uncomfortable: there was a kind of deliberate falseness in them, as if what he really thought and felt was not to be shared with other men. He seemed, in fact, to have discovered some vital and secret power, some superior knowledge and wisdom, from which the rest of mankind was excluded, a sense that he was "chosen" above other men, and this impression of Mr. Stanley Ward would have been correct, for he was a Christian Scientist, he was a pillar of the church, and a very big church at that —for Mr. Ward, dressed in fashionable striped trousers, rubber soles, and a cut-away coat might be found somewhere under the mighty dome of the Mother Church on Huntington Avenue every Sunday suavely, noiselessly, and expertly ushering the faithful to their pews.

This completes the personnel of the first office of the John T. Brill Realty Company, and if my uncle, Bascom Hawke, arrived late, if these three people were already present, if Mr. Bascom Hawke had not been defrauded of any part of his worldly goods by some contriving rascal, of whom the world has many, if his life had not been imperiled by some speed maniac, if the damnable New England weather was not too damnable, if, in short, Bascom Hawke was in fairly good spirits he would on entering immediately howl in a high, rapid, remote and perfectly monotonous tone: "Hello, Hello, Hello! Good-morning, Good-morning, Good-morning!"—after which he would close his eyes, grimace horribly, press his rubbery lip against his big horse teeth, and snuffle with laughter through his nose, as if pleased by a tremendous stroke of wit. At this demonstration the other members of the group would glance at one another with those knowing subtly supercilious nods and winks, that look of common self-congratulation and humor with which the more "normal" members of society greet the conduct of an eccentric, and Mr. Samuel Friedman would say: "What's the matteh with you, Pop? You look happy. Some one musta give you a shot in the ahm."

At which, a coarse powerful voice, deliberate and rich with its intimation of immense and earthly vulgarity, might roar out of the depth of the inner office: "No, I'll tell you what it is." Here the great figure of Mr. John T. Brill, the head of the business, would darken the doorway. "Don't you know what's wrong with the Reverend? It's that widder he's been takin' around." Here, the phlegmy burble that prefaced all of Mr. Brill's obscenities would appear in his voice, the shadow of a lewd smile would play around the corner of his mouth: "It's the widder. She's let him——"

At this delicate stroke of humor, the burble would burst open in Mr. Brill's great red throat, and he would roar with that high, choking,

phlegmy laughter that is frequent among big red-faced men. Mr.
Friedman would laugh dryly ("Heh, heh, heh, heh, heh!"), Mr. Stanley
Ward would laugh more heartily, but complacently, and Miss Brill
would snicker in a coy and subdued manner as became a modest young
girl. As for Bascom Hawke, if he was really in a good humor, he might
snuffle with nosey laughter, bend double at his meager waist, clutching his big hands together, and stamp at the floor violently several times
with one stringy leg; he might even go so far as to take a random
ecstatic kick at objects, still stamping and snuffling with laughter, and
prod Miss Brill stiffly with two enormous bony fingers, as if he did not
wish the full point and flavor of the jest to be lost on her.

My Uncle Bascom Hawke, however, was a very complicated person
with many moods, and if Mr. Brill's fooling did not catch him in a
receptive one, he might contort his face in a pucker of refined disgust,
and mutter his disapproval, as he shook his head rapidly from side to
side. Or he might rise to great heights of moral denunciation, beginning at first in a grave low voice that showed the seriousness of the
words he had to utter: "The lady to whom you refer," he would begin,
"the very charming and cultivated lady whose name, sir," here his voice
would rise on its howling note and he would wag his great bony forefinger, "whose name, sir, you have so foully traduced and blackened——"

"No, I wasn't, Reverend. I was only tryin' to whiten it," said Mr.
Brill, beginning to burble with laughter.

"—whose name, sir, you have so foully traduced and blackened with
your smutty suggestions," Bascom continued implacably, "—that lady
is known to me, as you very well know, sir," he howled, wagging his
great finger again, "solely and simply in a professional capacity."

"Why, hell, Reverend," said Mr. Brill innocently, "I never knew she
was a professional. I thought she was an amatoor."

At this conclusive stroke, Mr. Brill would make the whole place
tremble with his laughter, Mr. Friedman would laugh almost noiselessly, holding himself weakly at the stomach and bending across a
desk, Mr. Ward would have short bursts and fits of laughter, as he
gazed out of the window, shaking his head deprecatingly from time
to time, as if his more serious nature disapproved, and Miss Brill would
snicker, and turn to her machine, remarking: "This conversation is
getting too rough for me!"

And my uncle, if this jesting touched his complex soul at one of those
moments when such profanity shocked him, would walk away, confiding into vacancy, it seemed, with his powerful and mobile features
contorted in the most eloquent expression of disgust and loathing ever
seen on any face, the while he muttered, in a resonant whisper that

shuddered with passionate revulsion: "Oh, *bad!* Oh, *bad!* Oh, *bad, bad, bad!*"—shaking his head slightly from side to side with each word.

Yet there were other times, when Brill's swingeing vulgarity, the vast coarse sweep of his profanity not only found Uncle Bascom in a completely receptive mood, but they evoked from him gleeful responses, counter essays in swearing which he made slyly, craftily, snickering with pleasure and squinting around at his listeners at the sound of the words, and getting such stimulus from them as might a renegade clergyman, exulting in a feeling of depravity and abandonment for the first time.

To the other people in this office—that is, to Friedman, Ward and Muriel, the stenographer—my uncle was always an enigma; at first they had observed his peculiarities of speech and dress, his eccentricity of manner, and the sudden, violent, and complicated fluctuation of his temperament, with astonishment and wonder, then with laughter and ridicule, and now, with dull, uncomprehending acceptance. Nothing he did or said surprised them any more, they had no understanding and little curiosity, they accepted him as a fact in the gray schedule of their lives. Their relation to him was habitually touched by a kind of patronizing banter--"kidding the old boy along" they would have called it —by the communication of smug superior winks and the conspiracy of feeble jests, and in this there was something base and ignoble, for my uncle was a better man than any of them.

He did not notice any of this, it is not likely he would have cared if he had, for, like most eccentrics, his thoughts were usually buried in a world of his own creating to whose every fact and feeling and motion he was the central actor. Again, as much as any of his extraordinary family, he had carried with him throughout his life the sense that he was "fated"—a sense that was strong in all of them—that his life was pivotal to all the actions of providence, that, in short, the time might be out of joint, but not himself. Nothing but death could shake his powerful egotism, and his occasional storms of fury, his railing at the world, his tirades of invective at some motorist, pedestrian, or laborer occurred only when he discovered that these people were moving in a world at cross-purposes to his own and that some action of theirs had disturbed or shaken the logic of his universe.

It was curious that, of all the people in the office, the person who had the deepest understanding and respect for my uncle was John T. Brill. Mr. Brill was a huge creature of elemental desires and passions: a river of profanity rushed from his mouth with the relentless sweep and surge of the Mississippi, he could no more have spoken without swearing than a whale could swim in a frog-pond—he swore at every thing, at every one, and with every breath, casually and unconsciously, and yet when he addressed my uncle Bascom his oath was always impersonal, and tinged subtly by a feeling of respect.

Thus, he would speak to Uncle Bascom somewhat in this fashion: "Goddamn it, Hawke, did you ever look up the title for that stuff in Malden? That feller's been callin' up every day to find out about it."

"Which fellow?" my uncle Bascom asked precisely. "The man from Cambridge?"

"No," said Mr. Brill, "not him, the other — — — —, the Dorchester feller. How the hell am I goin' to tell him anything if there's no goddamn title for the stuff?"

Profane and typical as this speech was, it was always shaded nicely with impersonality toward my uncle Bascom—conscious to the full of the distinction between "damn *it*" and "damn *you*." Toward his other colleagues, however, Mr. Brill was neither nice nor delicate.

Brill was an enormous man physically: he was six feet two or three inches tall, and his weight was close to three hundred pounds. He was totally bald, his skull was a gleaming satiny pink; above his great red moon of face, with its ponderous and pendulous jowls, it looked almost egg-shaped. And in the heavy, deliberate, and powerful timbre of his voice there was always lurking this burble of exultant, gargantuan obscenity: it was so obviously part of the structure of his life, so obviously his only and natural means of expression, that it was impossible to condemn him. His epithet was limited and repetitive—but so, too, was Homer's, and, like Homer, he saw no reason for changing what had already been used and found good.

He was a lewd and innocent man. Like my uncle, by comparison with these other people, he seemed to belong to some earlier, richer and grander period of the earth, and perhaps this was why there was more actual kinship and understanding between them than between any of the other members of the office. These other people—Friedman, Brill's daughter, Muriel, and Ward—belonged to the myriads of the earth, to those numberless swarms that with ceaseless pullulation fill the streets of life with their gray immemorable tides. But Brill and my uncle Bascom were men in a thousand, a million: if one had seen them in a crowd he would have looked after them, if one had talked with them, he could never have forgotten them.

It is rare in modern life that one sees a man who can express himself with such complete and abundant certainty as Brill did—completely, and without doubt or confusion. It is true that his life expressed itself chiefly by two gestures—by profanity and by his great roar of full-throated, earth-shaking laughter, an explosive comment on existence which usually concluded and summarized his other means of expression.

Although the other people in the office laughed heartily at this soaring rhetoric of obscenity, it sometimes proved too much for Uncle Bascom. When this happened he would either leave the office immediately, or stump furiously into his own little cupboard that seemed silted over with the dust of twenty years, slamming the door behind him so violently that the thin partition rattled, and then stand for a moment pursing his lips, and convolving his features with incredible speed, and shaking his gaunt head slightly from side to side, until at length he whispered in a tone of passionate disgust and revulsion: "Oh, *bad! Bad! Bad!* By every *gesture,* by every *act,* he betrays the *boor,* the *vulgarian!* Can you imagine"—here his voice sunk even lower in its scale of passionate whispering repugnance—"can you for one *moment* imagine a man of *breeding* and the social graces talking in such a way publicly?—And before his own daughter. Oh, *bad! Bad! Bad! Bad!*"

And in the silence, while my uncle stood shaking his head in its movement of downcast and convulsive distaste, we could hear, suddenly, Brill's pungent answer to all the world—and his great bellow of throaty laughter. Later on, if my uncle had to consult him on any business, he would open his door abruptly, walk out into Brill's office clutching his hands together at the waist, and with disgust still carved upon his face, say: "Well, sir, . . . If you have concluded your morning devotions," here his voice sank to a bitter snarl, "we might get down to the transaction of some of the day's business."

"Why, Reverend!" Brill roared. "You ain't heard nothin' yet!"

And the great choking bellow of laughter would burst from him again, rattling the windows with its power as he hurled his great weight backward, with complete abandon, in his creaking swivel-chair.

It was obvious that he liked to tease my uncle, and never lost an opportunity of doing so: for example, if any one gave Uncle Bascom a cigar, Brill would exclaim with an air of innocent surprise: "Why, *Reverend,* you're not going to smoke that, are you?"

"Why, certainly," my Uncle Bascom said tartly. "That is the purpose for which it was intended, isn't it?"

"Why, yes," said Brill, "but you know how they make 'em, don't you? I didn't think you'd touch it after some dirty old Spaniard has wiped his old hands all over it—yes! an' *spit* upon it, too, because that's what they do!"

"Ah!" my uncle snarled contemptuously. "You don't know what

you're talking about! There is nothing cleaner than good tobacco! Finest and healthiest plant on earth! No question about it!"

"Well," said Brill, "I've learned something. We live and learn, Reverend. You've taught me somethin' worth knowing: when it's free it's clean; when you have to pay for it it stinks like hell!" He pondered heavily for a moment, and the burble began to play about in his great throat: "And by God!" he concluded, "tobacco's not the only thing that applies to, either. Not by a damned sight!"

Again, one morning, my uncle cleared his throat portentously, coughed, and suddenly said to me: "Now, David, my boy, you are going to have lunch with me today. There's no question about it whatever!" This was astonishing news, for he had never before invited me to eat with him when I came to his office, although I had been to his house for dinner many times. "Yes, sir!" he said, with an air of decision and satisfaction. "I have thought it all over. There is a splendid establishment in the basement of this building—small, of course, but everything clean and of the highest order! It is conducted by an Irish gentleman whom I have known for many years. Finest people on earth: no question about it!"

It was an astonishing and momentous occasion; I knew how infrequently he went to a restaurant. Having made his decision, Uncle Bascom immediately stepped into the outer offices, and began to discuss and publish his intentions with the greatest satisfaction.

"Yes, sir!" he said in a precise tone, smacking his lips in a ruminant fashion, and addressing himself to every one rather than to a particular person. "We shall go in and take our seats in the regular way, and I shall then give appropriate instructions, to one of the attendants—" again he smacked his lips as he pronounced this word with such an indescribable air of relish, that immediately my mouth began to water, and the delicious pangs of appetite and hunger began to gnaw my vitals—"I shall say: 'This is my nephew, a young man now enrolled at Harvard Un-i-ver-sit-tee!' "—here Bascom smacked his lips together again with that same maddening air of relish—" 'Yes, sir' (I shall say!) —'You are to fulfil his order without *stint,* without *delay,* and without *question,* and to the *utmost* of your ability' "—he howled, wagging his great bony forefinger through the air—"As for myself," he declared abruptly, "I shall take nothing. Good Lord, no!" he said with a scornful laugh. "I wouldn't touch a thing they had to offer. You couldn't pay me to: I shouldn't sleep for a month if I did. But you, my boy!" he howled, turning suddenly upon me, "—are to have everything your heart desires! Everything, everything, everything!" He made an inclusive gesture with his long arms; then closed his eyes, stamped at the floor, and began to snuffle with laughter.

Mr. Brill had listened to all this with his great-jowled face slack-jawed and agape with astonishment. Now, he said, heavily: "He's goin' to have everything, is he? Where are you goin' to take him to git it?"

"Why, sir!" my uncle said in an annoyed tone, "I have told you all along—we are going to the modest but excellent establishment in the basement of this very building."

"Why, Reverend," Brill said in a protesting tone. "You ain't goin' to take your nephew *there,* are you? I thought you said you was goin' to git somethin' to *eat.*"

"I had supposed," my uncle said with bitter sarcasm, "that one went there for that purpose. I had not supposed that one went there to get shaved."

"Well," said Brill, "if you go there you'll git shaved, all right. You'll not only git *shaved,* you'll git *skinned* alive. But you won't git anything to eat." And he hurled himself back again, roaring with laughter.

"Pay no attention to him!" my uncle said to me in a tone of bitter repugnance. "I have long known that his low and vulgar mind attempts to make a joke of everything, even the most sacred matters. I assure you, my boy, the place is excellent in every way:—do you suppose," he said now addressing Brill and all the others, with a howl of fury—"do you suppose, if it were not, that I should for a single moment *dream* of taking him there? Do you suppose that I would for an instant *contemplate* taking my own nephew, my sister's son, to any place in which I did not repose the fullest confidence? Not on your life!" he howled. "Not on your life!"

And we departed, followed by Brill's great bellow, and a farewell invitation which he shouted after me, "Don't worry, son! When you git through with that cockroach stew, come back an' I'll take you out to lunch with *me!*"

Although Brill delighted in teasing and baiting my uncle in this fashion, there was, at the bottom of his heart, a feeling of deep humility, of genuine respect and admiration for him: he respected Uncle Bascom's intelligence, he was secretly and profoundly impressed by the fact that my uncle had been a minister of the gospel and had preached in many churches.

Moreover, in the respect and awe with which Brill greeted these evidences of my uncle's superior education, in the eagerness he showed when he boasted to visitors, as he often did, of my uncle's learning, there was a quality of pride that was profoundly touching and paternal: it was as if my uncle had been his son, and as if he wanted at every opportunity to display his talents to the world. And this, in fact, was exactly what he did want to do. Much to my uncle's annoyance, Brill was con-

stantly speaking of his erudition to strangers who had come into the
office for the first time, and constantly urging my uncle to perform for
them, to "say some of them big words, Reverend." And even when my
uncle answered him, as he frequently did, in terms of scorn, anger, and
contempt, Brill was completely satisfied, if Uncle Bascom would only
use a few of the "big words" in doing it. Thus, one day, when one of his
boyhood friends, a New Hampshire man whom he had not seen in
thirty-five years, had come in to renew their acquaintance Brill, in describing the accomplishments of my uncle, said with an air of solemn
affirmation: "Why, hell yes, Jim! It'd take a college perfesser to know
what the Reverend is talkin' about half the time! No ordinary — —
— — is able to understand him! So help me God, it's true!" he swore
solemnly, as Jim looked incredulous. "The Reverend knows words the
average man ain't never heard. He knows words that ain't even in the
dictionary. Yes, sir!—an' uses 'em, too—all the time!" he concluded
triumphantly.

"Why, my dear sir!" my uncle answered in a tone of exacerbated contempt, "What on earth are you talking about? Such a man as you
describe would be a monstrosity, a heinous perversion of natural law!
A man so wise that no one could understand him:—so literate that he
could not communicate with his fellow creatures:—so erudite that he
led the inarticulate and incoherent life of a beast or a savage!"—here
Uncle Bascom squinted his eyes tightly shut, and laughed sneeringly
down his nose: "Phuh! phuh! phuh! phuh! phuh!—Why, you con-
sum-mate fool!" he sneered, "I have long known that your ignorance
was bottomless—but I had never hoped to see it equalled—Nay! Surpassed!" he howled, "by your asininity."

"There you are!" said Brill exultantly to his visitor, "What did I tell
you? There's one of them words, Jim: 'asserninity,' why, damn it, the
Reverend's the only one who knows what that word means—you won't
even find it in the dictionary!"

"Not find it in the dictionary!" my uncle yelled. "Almighty God, come
down and give this ass a tongue as Thou didst once before in Balaam's
time?"

Again, Brill was seated at his desk one day engaged with a client in
those intimate, cautious, and confidential preliminaries that mark the
consummation of a "deal" in real estate. On this occasion the prospective buyer was an Italian: the man sat awkwardly and nervously in a
chair beside Brill's desk while the great man bent his huge weight ponderously and persuasively toward him. From time to time the Italian's
voice, sullen, cautious, disparaging, interrupted Brill's ponderous and
coaxing drone. The Italian sat stiffly, his thick, clumsy body awkwardly

clad in his "good" clothes of heavy black, his thick, hairy, blunt-nailed hands cupped nervously upon his knees, his black eyes glittering with suspicion under his knitted inch of brow. At length, he shifted nervously, rubbed his paws tentatively across his knees and then, with a smile mixed of ingratiation and mistrust, said: "How mucha you want, eh?"

"How mucha we want?" Brill repeated vulgarly as the burble began to play about within his throat. "Why, how mucha you got? . . . You know we'll take every damn thing you got! It's not how mucha we want, it's how mucha you got!" And he hurled himself backward, bellowing with laughter. "By God, Reverend," he yelled as Uncle Bascom entered, "ain't that right? It's not how mucha we want, it's how mucha you got! 'od damn! We ought to take that as our motter. I've got a good mind to git it printed on our letterheads. What do you think, Reverend?"

"Hey?" howled Uncle Bascom absently, as he prepared to enter his own office.

"I say we ought to use it for our motter."

"Your *what?*" said Uncle Bascom scornfully, pausing as if he did not understand.

"Our motter," Brill said.

"Not your *motter,*" my uncle howled derisively. "The word is *not* motter," he said contemptuously. "Nobody of any refinement would say *motter. Motter* is *not* correct!" he howled finally. "Only an ig-no-*ram*-us would say *motter*. No!" he yelled with final conclusiveness. "That is *not* the way to pronounce it! That is ab-so-lute-ly and em-phat-ic-ally *not* the way to pronounce it!"

"All right, then, Reverend," said Brill, submissively. "You're the doctor. What is the word?"

"The word is *motto,*" Uncle Bascom snarled. "Of course! Any fool knows that!"

"Why, hell," Mr. Brill protested in a hurt tone. "That's what I said, ain't it?"

"No-o!" Uncle Bascom howled derisively. "No-o! By no means, by no means, by no means! You said *motter*. The word is *not* motter. The word is motto: m-o-t-t-o! M-O-T-T-O does *not* spell motter," he remarked with vicious decision.

"What does it spell?" said Mr. Brill.

"It spells *motto,*" Uncle Bascom howled. "It *has* always spelled motto! It *will* always spell motto! As it was in the beginning, is now, and ever shall be: A-a-men!" he howled huskily in his most evangelical fashion. Then, immensely pleased at his wit, he closed his eyes, stamped at the floor and snarled and snuffled down his nose with laughter.

"Well, anyway," said Brill, "no matter how you spell it, it's not how mucha we want, it's how mucha you got! That's the way we feel about it!"

And this, in fact, without concealment, without pretense, without evasion, was just how Brill did feel about it. He wanted everything that was his and, in addition, he wanted as much as he could get. And this rapacity, this brutal and unadorned gluttony, so far from making men wary of him, attracted them to him, inspired them with unshakable confidence in his integrity, his business honesty. Perhaps the reason for this was that concealment did not abide in the man: he published his intentions to the world with an oath and a roar of laughter—and the world, having seen and judged, went away with the confidence of this Italian—that Brill was "one fine-a man!" Even my uncle, who had so often turned upon his colleague the weapons of scorn, contempt, and mockery, had a curious respect for him, an acrid sunken affection: often, when we were alone, he would recall something Brill had said and his powerful and fluent features would suddenly be contorted in that familiar grimace, as he laughed his curious laugh which was forced out, with a deliberate and painful effort, through his powerful nose and his lips, barred with a few large teeth. "Phuh! phuh! phuh! phuh! phuh! . . . Of course!" he said, with a nasal rumination, as he stared over the apex of his great bony hands, clasped in meditation—"of course, he is just a poor ignorant fellow! I don't suppose—no, sir, I really do not suppose that Brill ever went to school over six months in his life!—say!" my uncle Bascom paused suddenly, turned to me abruptly with his strange fixed grin, and fastened his sharp old eyes keenly on me: in this sudden and abrupt change, this transference of his vision from his own secret and personal world, in which his thought and feeling was sunken, and which seemed to be so far away from the actual world about him, there was something impressive and disconcerting. His eyes were gray, sharp, and old, and one eyelid had a heavy droop or ptosis which, although it did not obscure his vision, gave his expression at times a sinister glint, a malevolent humor. "—Say!" here his voice sank to a deliberate and confiding whisper, "(Phuh! phuh! phuh! phuh! phuh!) Say—a man who would—he told me—Oh, vile! vile! vile! my boy!" my uncle whispered, shutting his eyes in a kind of shuddering ecstasy as if at the memory of things too gloriously obscene to be repeated. "Can you imagine, can you even dream of such a state of affairs if he had possessed an atom, a scintilla of delicacy and good breeding! Yes, sir!" he said with decision. "I suppose there's no doubt about it! His beginnings were very lowly, very poor and humble, indeed! . . . Not that that is in any sense to his discredit!" Uncle Bascom said hastily, as if it had occurred to him that his words might bear some taint of snobbishness.

"Oh, by no means, by no means, by no means!" he sang out, with a sweeping upward gesture of his long arm, as if he were clearing the air of wisps of smoke. "Some of our finest men—some of the nation's *leaders,* have come from just such surroundings as those. Beyond a doubt! Beyond a doubt! There's no question about it whatever! Say!"— here he turned suddenly upon me again with the ptotic and sinister intelligence of his eye. "Was *Lincoln* an aristocrat? Was he the issue of wealthy parents? Was he brought up with a silver spoon in his mouth? Was our *own* former governor, the Vice-President of the United States today, reared in the lap of luxury! Not on your life!" howled Uncle Bascom. "He came from frugal and thrifty Vermont farming stock, he has never deviated a *jot* from his early training, he remains today what he has always been—one of the simplest of men! Finest people on earth, no question about it whatever!"

Again, he meditated gravely with lost stare across the apex of his great joined hands, and I noticed again, as I had noticed so often, the great dignity of his head in thought—a head that was highbrowed, lean and lonely, a head that not only in its cast of thought but even in its physical contour, and in its profound and lonely earnestness, bore an astonishing resemblance to that of Emerson—it was, at times, like these, as grand a head as I had ever seen, and on it was legible the history of man's loneliness, his dignity, his grandeur and despair.

"Yes, sir!" he said, in a moment. "He is, of course, a vulgar fellow and some of the things he says at times are Oh! vile! vile! vile!" my uncle cried, closing his eyes and laughing. "Oh, vile! *most* vile! . . . but (phuh! phuh! phuh!) you can't help laughing at the fellow at times because he is so . . . Oh, I could tell you things, my boy! . . . Oh, *vile! vile!*" he cried, shaking his head downwards. "What coarseness! . . . What in-*vect*-ive!" he whispered, in a kind of ecstasy.

And this invective, I know, he cherished in his secret heart so dearly that on at least one notable occasion he had invoked it, and lamented that he did not have it by him as an aid. What Uncle Bascom had said on that occasion, lifting his arms to heaven, and crying out a confession of his own inadequacy in a tone of passionate supplication, was: "Oh, that J. T. were here at this moment!—or that I had his tongue!—that he might aid me with his *scathing* invective!"

The occasion was this: a few years before my uncle had taken his wife to Florida for the winter, and had rented there a cottage. The place he chose was small and modest, it was several miles away from one of the larger and more fashionable towns, it was not on the coast, but set a few miles inland, and it had the advantages of a river, or peninsular inlet which rose and fell with the recurrence of the tides. This modest winter colony was so small that it could afford only one small church and one minister, himself a member of the colony. During the winter this man was taken ill: he was unable to continue his services at the church, and his little following, in looking around for a substitute, learned that Uncle Bascom had formerly been a minister. They came to him, therefore, and asked if he would serve.

"Oh, *Lord,* no!" Bascom howled derisively. "Good *heavens,* no! I shouldn't *dream* of such a thing! I shouldn't for a moment *contemplate* such a thing! I am a *total*—for twenty years I have been a *complete*—agnostic."

The flock looked at him with a dazed expression. "Wal," said one of the leading parishioners, a lean Down-Easter, "most of us here are Presbyterians, but I don't know that that would make any difference. The way I see it, we're all met here to worship the Lord, and we need a preacher no matter what his denomination is. When all's said and done," he concluded comfortably, "I don't guess there's much difference between any of us in the long run."

"Why, my dear sir!" my uncle said, with a slight sneer. "If you think there is no difference between an agnostic and a Presbyterian you had better have your head examined by a doctor without further delay. No-o!" he howled faintly. "I cannot profess belief in what I do not know! I cannot simulate conviction when I have none! I cannot preach a faith I have not got! There, sir, you have my whole position in a nut-shell!"

Here, people in the group began to stir restlessly, to mutter uneasily, and to draw away: suddenly Uncle Bascom caught the muttered word "atheist."

"No-o!" he shouted, his ptotic eye beginning to glitter with the light of combat. "By no means! By no means! You only show your ignorance when you say a thing like that. They are not the same! They are ab-so-lute-ly and em-phat-i-cal-ly *not* the same! An atheist is *not* an agnostic and an agnostic is *not* an atheist! Why!" he yelled, "the mere sound of the words would teach you that if you had an atom of intelligence. An atheist is a man who does not believe in God!—it is composed of the Greek prefix 'a'—meaning *not,* and the noun 'the-os,' meaning God: an atheist therefore says there is no God! Now," he continued, licking his lips for joy, "we come to the word *agnostic.* Is the sound the same? No-o! Is the meaning the same? By no means! Are the parts the same? Not on your life! The word is *agnostic:* a-g-n-o-s-t-i-c! From what language is it derived? From Greek, of course—as any fool should know! From what words? From the vowel of negation 'a' again, and from 'gnostikos'—the word for *knowing.* An agnostic therefore is what?" he demanded, glaring around at their mute faces. "Why!" he said impatiently, as no one answered, "Any schoolboy knows that much! A not-knowing man! A man who does not know! Not a man who denies! Oh, by no means!"—his great hand rose impatiently—"An *atheist* is a man who denies! An *agnostic* is simply a man who does not know!"

"I can't see there's any difference," someone muttered. "They *both* sound like a couple of godless heathen to me!"

"No difference!" Bascom howled. "My dear sir, hold your tongue before you bring down lasting shame upon your progeny! . . . They are as different as night from day, as black from white, as the sneering irreverence of the cynic from the calm, temperate, and judicial spirit of the philosopher! Why!" he declared impressively, "Some of the finest spirits of our times have been agnostics. Yes, sir! Some of the grandest people that ever lived! . . . The *great* Matthew Arnold was an agnostic!" he yelled. "Does that sound as if there was no difference? Not on your life!"

He paused, and as there was no response from his involuntary congregation, he began, after a moment, to fumble at the inside pocket of his coat with his big fingers.

"I have here a poem," he said, taking it out of his pocket, "of my own composition"—here he coughed modestly—"although it may show traces, I admit, of the influence of the great man whose name I have just mentioned, and whom I am proud to call my master: Matthew Arnold. It will, I believe, illustrate my position better than anything I could say to you." He held up his great forefinger to command attention, and then began to read.

"The title of the poem," Uncle Bascom said, "is—'My Creed.'" After a short silence, he began:

> " 'Is there a land beyond the stars
> Where we may find eternal day,
> Life after death, peace after wars?
> Is there? I can not say.
>
> Shall we find there a happier life,
> All joy that here we never know,
> Love in all things, an end of strife?
> Perhaps: it may be so.' "

There were seventeen other stanzas which Uncle Bascom read to them deliberately and with telling enunciation, after which he folded the paper and looked about him with a sneer: "I think," he said, "that I have made my meaning clear. Now you know what an agnostic is."

They did. His meaning was so clear that they had no language to oppose to it: they turned, they went away like men who had been stunned. Among them, however, was one who did not yield so easily, a daughter of the Lord who had often won by persuasion and the soft violence of her beaming eye what others failed to win by harsher means. This lady was a widow, a Southern woman in her middle years: her charms were ripe, she had a gentle, loving touch, a soft and fruity unction in her voice. This lady had been able to resist few ministers and few ministers had been able to resist this lady. Now, as the others retreated, the lady advanced: she came forward with a practised sidling movement of her hips and Uncle Bascom, who was standing triumphantly in the midst of a receding host, suddenly found himself confronted by her gentle and importunate face.

"Oh, Mr. Hawke!" she crooned sweetly, with a kind of abdominal rapture in her voice (thus, the way she pronounced his name was—Mis-tah Haw-*uk!*). "I *jus'* know that you must've been a *won*-da-ful preach-ah! I can tell by yo' face that you'ah such a *g-o-o-d* man—" Again she grunted sweetly with this ecstatic abdominal expiration.

"Why, madame! Why—" Uncle Bascom began, decidedly in a confused tone, but taking her abundance in with a sharp appraising eye.

"I was *jus'* thrilled to death all the time that you was tawkin', Mistah Haw-*uk*," the widow said. "I was a-sittin' theah an' sittin' theah, just a-drinkin' it all in, just a-*baskin'* in the rays of yo' wisdom, Mistah Haw-uk! All the time you was readin' that wondaful poem, I was just a-sayin' to myse'f: What a wondaful thing it is that a man like this has been chosen fo' the Suvvice of the Lawd, what a wondaful thing it is to know that this man is one o' Gawd's Suvvants!"

"Why, madame!" Bascom cried, his gaunt face flushed with pleasure. "Why, madame, I assure you I am deeply grateful . . . deeply honored to think that a lady of your obvious . . . your *undoubted* intelligence . . . should feel that way about me! But, madame!——"

"Oh, Mistah Haw-*uk!*" the widow groaned. "I jus' *love* to heah you *tawk!* I jus' *love* the way you handle langwidge! You heah so much po' shoddy, good-fo'-nothin' tawk nowadays—all full o' slang an' bad grammah an' I don't know whatall: I don't know what folks ah *comin'* to—it's a real pleasuah—yes, suh! a real sho' nuff *treat*—to heah a man who can express himse'f the way you can. The minute I saw you I said to myse'f: I jus' *know* that that man can *tawk!* I *know* it! I *know* it! I *know* it!" the widow cried, shaking her head from side to side vigorously. "Theah's a man, I said," the widow continued, "theah's a man who kin do anything he likes with me—yes, suh! just anything!—I said that just as soon as you opened yo' mouf to speak!"

"Oh, madame, madame!" cried Bascom fervently, bowing with real dignity. "I thank you. I thank you sincerely and gratefully from the bottom of my heart!"

"Yes, suh! I could just enjoy myse'f—(I said)—just a-lookin' at his haid."

"At my what?" yelled Bascom, jumping as if he had received an electric shock.

"At yo' *haid*," the widow answered.

"Oh!" howled Bascom. "At my *head!* My *head!*"—and he began to laugh foolishly.

"Yes, suh, Mistah Haw-uk," the widow continued. "I jus' thought you had the *grandest* haid I evah saw. The moment you began to read that poem I said, 'Only a man with a haid like that could a-written that poem. Oh, thank Gawd! (I said) that he has dedicated his wondaful *haid* to the Lawd's wuk!"

"Why, madame," Bascom cried again. "You have paid me the greatest honor! I cannot sufficiently thank you! But I am afraid—in *justice*, in *fairness*, I must admit," he said with some difficulty, "that you may not have entirely understood—that you are not quite clear—that, perhaps I did not make the meaning, the general purpose of that poem—Oh! it's my own fault, I know! Beyond a doubt! Beyond a doubt!—but perhaps I did not make its meaning wholly plain!"

"Yes, you did!" the widow protested. "Every word of it was jus' as plain as day to me! I kep' sayin' to myse'f: That's *jus'* the way I've always felt, but I nevah could express myse'f befo': I nevah *met* anyone befo' that I could tawk to about it. An' now (I said), this wondaful man comes along an' puts the whole thing straight in my haid! Oh! (I said) if I could just sit at his feet, an' *listen* all day long, if I could jus' sit an' drink in all he had to say, if I could just *listen* to him tawk—I'd nevah ask fo' anything bettah!"

"Why, madame!" Bascom cried, deeply, genuinely moved. "I assure you I'd like nothing better! Yes, indeed! I assure you I'd be delighted! Oh, at any time! At any time!" he howled. "It is rare that one meets today—Oh, *most* rare!—a woman of your intelligence and perspicacity! We *must* have another talk!" he said. "Oh, by all means, by all means!"

"Uh-huh!" the widow grunted sweetly.

Bascom looked around craftily to see if my Aunt Louise was anywhere within sight or hearing. "Perhaps," he said, smacking his lips together, "we might meet and have a quiet walk together. Nothing is more conducive to contemplation than the tranquil peace of nature. There's no question about it."

"Uh-huh," the widow said.

"Tomorrow," Bascom whispered.

"Uh-huh," the widow crooned viscerally.

Thus, there began between Uncle Bascom and the widow a series of promenades, in which he expounded his views liberally, and in which she was able, by the harmonious adjustment of her nature, to find herself in complete agreement. Again and again, my Aunt Louise watched them depart, she peered after them through her bright mad eyes, snuffling with angry laughter, and muttering, as she had muttered many times before: "The old *fool!* . . . The *misable* old *skinflint!* . . . Too poor to buy his own wife a *dwess* . . . while he spends *faw*-chuns, *faw*-chuns on them! . . . It's in the blood . . . the blood!" she whispered hoarsely. "They're *mad* . . . *mad!* His family's *ovah-sexed,* all of them!"

One evening, as Bascom and the widow were returning from one of these walks, they found themselves toward sunset a mile or so from town. It was a desolate spot: their road wound on through fringes of scrub pine and stunted palm along the edges of the inlet: the tide was out, the water lay in shallow puddles across the bed of viscous mud, a few birds wheeled with creaking eery cries above this loneliness of earth and water, and there was the smell of shelled waste, sea-scum—the potent, magical, and exultant smell of the sea in harbors. The air and the sky were sweet with incomparable clarity, with an immense delicacy of light, and the sun, which now burned like a vast orange-colored ball, without violence or heat, was resting against the lonely and desolate space of the western horizon. The widow and Bascom paused for a moment to watch this scene, and then she said triumphantly: "Now, Mistah Haw-uk, you know that *Somebody* must've *done* all that. You know it jus' didn't go an' happen by itse'f. You know, when you see a beautiful sunset like that that nobody but Gawd himse'f could've made it. Now, you know you do, Mistah Haw-uk!"

"The question of its beauty," said my uncle precisely, "is debatable. The philosopher Hegel, for example, so far from seeing beauty in a sunset, remarked that it looked to him as if the sky had small-pox!" Here Bascom closed his eyes, and snuffled with laughter.

"Oh, Mistah Haw-uk!" the widow said reproachfully. "I know *you* don't feel that way about it. A man with a *haid* like yoah's could nevah believe a thing like that!"

"Oh!" Bascom shouted, immensely tickled for some reason. "By no means! By no means!" And he stamped violently at the earth, blind with his strange forced snarl of laughter.

For a moment they were silent: a vast and exuberant elation, an exultant vitality, was alive in Uncle Bascom. He looked at the shallow waters, he looked at the setting sun, he looked at the widow, and when he tried to speak, exultant mirth possessed him, and he could not.

"Shall we?—" he began at length inquiringly, but here a whimsy of humor seized him, he stopped short, contorted his face, stamped at the earth ecstatically, and snuffled down his nose—"shall we go in *wading?*" There was a deliberate, a luscious nasality in his precise enunciation of the last word.

"Oh, Mistah Haw-uk! Why-y!" the widow exclaimed fruitily. "Wading! For what?"

"For . . . oysters!" said Uncle Bascom lusciously and gently.

"For . . . *oysters!*" the widow cried. "But I didn't know there were any oysters!"

Bascom pondered this statement for a moment, and the more he considered it, the funnier it became to him. He bit his rubbery lip, closed his eyes, and began to snuffle down his nose with laughter. "Oh, yes!" he howled, "Oh, *my* yes! There are always . . . oysters! There are plenty of . . . oysters!"

So the widow, without much more than a half-hearted and decorous protest, and a cautious glance around to make sure that pine and palm gave shelter to no watchers, sat down beside my uncle and took off her shoes and stockings. Then, hand in hand, they advanced across the shallows and through water that rarely came above their knees, the widow tentatively, with a balancing movement and little abdominal cries of alarm, Uncle Bascom more boldly, and with confident assurances: "My dear girl!" he said, grasping her hand more tightly. "You are in no danger whatsoever! Oh, not the *slightest!*" he yelled. "You are as safe as you would be in your mother's arms. Yes, sir! You may rest assured on that score! There's no question of it!"

The widow held her skirts kilted up and knotted in one hand, midway along her milky thighs, while Uncle Bascom had rolled his trousers high above his bony knees and stringy calves, which now advanced through the shallow water with a storky and tentative step. At length, about the middle of the stream, they reached a bar of hard-packed sand, and here they stood for a while looking at the setting sun, pacing along their little beach, so absorbed in their contemplation of coming dark, of solitude, and of themselves that neither noticed that the tide was coming in.

And yet the tide came in. It came steadily, urgently, imperceptibly, feathering against the fringes of the inlet, advancing, retreating, advancing, retreating, but advancing always past its last retreat until suddenly Bascom felt the shock of water at his toes: he looked down and saw that their ledge of earth and safety was shrinking almost visibly below his glance: he yelled, first from alarm, and then for help: he shouted, but no one came: he seized the buxom widow and, by staggering effort lifted her, he tottered with her into the water. At the first step the water reached his knees, at the second, halfway up his shanks, at the third, he yelled, and dropped his cargo. She screamed, as a swirl of water caught her at the waist: she clutched him, she clung to him, she screamed, and suddenly Bascom began to curse. He shook a knotted fist at the imperturbable evening skies, he blasphemed against a deity in which he had no faith, and when a false step plunged him to his chin in water, he howled retraction of his blasphemy and begged for providential help. Neither could swim; perhaps neither was in the greatest danger, but both were terrified and shocked, the water wet their ears before they reached the shore, and when at length they tottered up on dry land again, the widow had reached the end and limit of her effort: for several moments she lay panting hoarsely, half out of water and half in, a battered half-emergent Phryne. As for Bascom, he stood on palsied limbs and with a chattering jaw for several moments: his long arms, his bony hands, his stooped shoulders, his stringy legs all bent in a common, constant drip—he was absolutely speechless, and stood there for some time chattering with fright, and dripping water. At length, the widow raised a portion of her charms, bedraggled but made undeniable by water, and moaned hoarsely, "Oh, Mistah Haw-uk! Mistah Haw-uk! Come an' git me, Mistah Haw-uk!"

At this moment Uncle Bascom's features were seized by a horrible convulsion, he opened his mouth to speak, but no words came, he raised two trembling fists toward heaven, but no words came. He tried to curse, but no words came. At length he mastered himself sufficiently to speak and, as if finding his own artillery too feeble for the occasion, he uttered slowly, with passionate conviction, the supplication already mentioned: "O that J. T. were here—that he might aid me with his *scathing* invective!

So ended romance between Uncle Bascom and the widow.

That year I was twenty, it had been my first year in New England, and the winter had seemed very long. In the man-swarm I felt alone and lost, a desolate atom in the streets of life. That year I went to see my uncle many times.

Some times I would find him in his dusty little cubicle, bent over the intricacy of a legal form, painfully and carefully, with compressed lips, filling in the blank spaces with his stiff angular and laborious hand. He would speak quietly, without looking up, as I came in: "Hello, my boy. Sit down, won't you? I'll be with you in a moment." And for a time the silence would be broken only by the heavy rumble of Brill's voice outside, by the minute scratching of my uncle's pen, and by the immense and murmurous sound of time, which rose above the city, which caught up in the upper air all of the city's million noises, and yet which seemed remote, essential, imperturbable and everlasting—fixed and unchanging, no matter what men lived or died.

Again, I would find him staring straight before him, with his great hands folded in a bony arch, his powerful gaunt face composed in rapt tranquillity of thought. At these times he seemed to have escaped from every particular and degrading thing in life—from the excess of absurd and eccentric speech and gesture, from all demeaning parsimonies, from niggling irascibilities, from everything that contorted his face and spirit away from its calmness and unity of thought. His face at such a time might well have been the mask of Thought, the visage of contemplation. Sometimes he would not speak for several minutes, his mind seemed to brood upon the lip and edge of time, to be remote from every dusty moment of the earth.

One day I went there and found him thus; after a few moments he lowered his great hands and, without turning toward me, sat for some time in an attitude of quiet relaxation. At length he said:

"What is man that thou art mindful of him?"

It was one of the first days of spring: the spring had come late, with a magical northern suddenness. It seemed to have burst out of the earth overnight, the air was lyrical and sang with it.

Spring came that year like a triumph and like a prophecy—it sang and shifted like a moth of light before me, but I was sure that it would bring me a glory and fulfilment I had never known.

My hunger and thirst had been immense: I was caught up for the first time in the midst of the Faustian web—there was no food that could feed me, no drink that could quench my thirst—like an insatiate and maddened animal I roamed the streets, trying to draw up mercy from the cobblestones, solace and wisdom from a million sights and faces, or prowled through endless shelves of high-piled books tortured by everything I could not see and could not know, and growing blind, weary, and desperate from what I read and saw. I wanted to know all, have all, be all—to be one and many, to have the whole riddle of this vast and swarming earth as legible, as tangible in my hand as a coin of minted gold.

Suddenly spring came, and I felt at once exultant certainty and joy. Outside my uncle's dirty window I could see the edge of Faneuil Hall, and hear the swarming and abundant activity of the markets. The deep roar of the markets came to us across the singing and lyrical air, and I drank into my lungs a thousand proud, potent, and mysterious odors which came to me like the breath of certainty, like the proof of magic, and like the revelation that all confusion had been banished—the world that I longed for won, the word that I sought for spoken, the hunger that devoured me fed and ended. And the markets, swarming with richness, joy, and abundance, thronged below me like a living evidence of fulfilment. For it seemed to me that nowhere more than here was the passionate enigma of New England felt: New England, with its harsh and stony soil, and its tragic and lonely beauty; its desolate rocky coasts and its swarming fisheries, the white, piled, frozen harshness of its winters with the magnificent jewelry of stars, the dark firwoods, and the warm little white houses at which it is impossible to look without thinking of groaning bins, hung bacon, hard cider, succulent bastings and love's warm, white, and opulent flesh.

There was the rustle of gingham by day and sober glances; then, under low eaves and starlight, the stir of the satiny thighs in feather beds, the white small bite and tigerish clasp of secret women—always the buried heart, the sunken passion, the frozen heat. And then, after the long, unendurably hard-locked harshness of the frozen winter, the coming of spring as now, like a lyrical cry, like a flicker of rain across a window glass, like the sudden and delicate noises of a spinet—the coming of spring and ecstasy, and overnight the thrum of wings, the burst of the tender buds, the ripple and dance of the roughened water, the light of flowers, the sudden, fleeting, almost captured, and exultant spring.

And here, within eighty yards of the dusty little room where my uncle Bascom had his desk, there was living evidence that this intuition was not false: the secret people, it was evident, did not subsist alone on codfish and a jug full of baked beans—they ate meat, and large chunks of it, for all day long, within the market district, the drivers of big wagons were standing to their chins in meat, boys dragged great baskets of raw meat along the pavements, red-faced butchers, aproned with gouts of blood, and wearing the battered straw hats that butchers wear, toiled through the streets below great loads of loin or haunch or rib and in chill shops with sawdust floors the beeves were hung in frozen regimental rows.

Right and left, around the central market, the old buildings stretched down to the harbor and the smell of ships: this was built-on land, in old days ships were anchored where these cobbles were, but the warehouses were also old—they had the musty, mellow, blackened air and smell of the Seventies, they looked like the Victorian prints, they reeked of ancient ledgers, of "counting houses," of proud monied merchants, and the soft-spoked rumble of victorias.

By day, this district was one snarled web of chaos: a *gewirr* of deep-bodied trucks, powerful dappled horses, cursing drivers, of loading, unloading, and shipping, of dispatch and order, of the million complicated weavings of life and business.

But if one came here at evening, after the work of the day was done, if one came here at evening on one of those delicate and sudden days of spring that New England knows, if one came here as many a lonely youth had come here in the past, some boy from the inland immensity of America, some homesick lad from the South, from the marvelous hills of Old Catawba, he might be pierced again by the bitter ecstasy of youth, the ecstasy that tears him apart with a cry that has no tongue, the ecstasy that is proud, lonely, and exultant, that is fierce with joy and blind with glory, but that yet carries in it a knowledge that is born in such a moment that the intangible cannot be touched, the ungraspable cannot be grasped—the imperial and magnificent minute is gone forever which, with all its promises, its million intuitions, he wishes to clothe with the living substance of beauty. He wishes to flesh the moment with the thighs and breast and belly of a wonderful mistress, he wishes to be great and glorious and triumphant, to distill the ether of this ecstasy in a liquor, and to drink strong joy forever; and at the heart of all this is the bitter knowledge of death—death of the moment, death of the day, death of one more infrequent spring.

Perhaps the thing that really makes New England wonderful is this sense of joy, this intuition of brooding and magic fulfilment that hovers like a delicate presence in the air of one of these days. Perhaps the answer is simple: perhaps it is only that this soft and sudden spring, with its darts and flicks of evanescent joy, its sprite-like presence that is only half-believed, its sound that is the sound of something lost and elfin, and half-dreamed, half-heard, seems wonderful after the grim frozen tenacity of the winter, the beautiful and terrible desolation, the assault of the frost and ice on living flesh which resists it finally as it would resist the cruel battering of a brute antagonist, so that the tart, stingy speech, the tight gestures, the withdrawn and suspicious air, the thin lips, red pointed noses and hard prying eyes of these people are really the actions of people who, having to defend themselves harshly against nature, harshly defend themselves against all the world.

At any rate, the thing the boy feels who comes here at the day's end is not completion, weariness, and sterility, but a sense of swelling ecstasy, a note of brooding fulfilment. The air will have in it the wonderful odors of the market and the smell of the sea: as he walks over the bare cobbled pavement under the corrugated tin awnings of the warehouses and produce stores a hundred smells of the rich fecundity of the earth will assail him: the clean sharp pungency of thin crated wood and the citric nostalgia of oranges, lemons and grapefruit, the stench of a decayed cabbage and the mashed pulp of a rotten orange. There will be also the warm coarse limey smell of chickens, the strong coddy smell of cold fish and oysters; and the crisp moist cleanliness of the garden

smells—of great lettuces, cabbages, new potatoes, with their delicate
skins loamy with sweet earth, the wonderful sweet crispness of crated
celery; and then the melons—the ripe golden melons bedded in fragrant
straw—and all the warm infusions of the tropics: the bananas, the pine-
apples and the alligator pears.

The delicate and subtle air of spring touches all these odors with a
new and delicious vitality; it draws the tar out of the pavements also,
and it draws slowly, subtly, from ancient warehouses, the compacted
perfumes of eighty years: the sweet thin piney scents of packing boxes,
the glutinous composts of half a century, that have thickly stained old
warehouse plankings, the smells of twine, tar, turpentine and hemp, and
of thick molasses, ginseng, pungent vines and roots and old piled sacking; the clean ground strength of fresh coffee, brown, sultry, pungent,
and exultantly fresh and clean; the smell of oats, baled hay and bran, of
crated eggs and cheese and butter; and particularly the smell of meat,
of frozen beeves, slick porks and veals, of brains and livers and kidneys,
of haunch, paunch and jowl; of meat that is raw and of meat that is
cooked, for upstairs in that richly dingy block of buildings there is a
room where the butchers, side by side with the bakers, the bankers, the
brokers and the Harvard boys, devour thick steaks of the best and
tenderest meat, smoking hot breads, and big jacketed potatoes.

And then there is always the sea. In dingy blocks, memoried with
time and money, the buildings stretch down to the docks, and there is
always the feeling that the sea was here, that this is built-on earth. A
single truck will rattle over the deserted stones, and then there is the
street that runs along the harbor, the dingy little clothing shops and
eating places, the powerful strings of freight cars, agape and empty,
odorous with their warm fatigued planking, and the smells of flanges
and axles that have rolled great distances.

And finally, by the edges of the water, there are great piers and store-
houses, calm and potent with their finished work: they lie there, immense, starkly ugly, yet touched with the powerful beauty of enormous
works and movements; they are what they are, they have been built
without a flourish for the work they do, their great sides rise in level
cliffs of brick, they are pierced with tracks and can engulf great trains;
and now that the day is done they breathe with the vitality of a tired
but living creature. A single footfall will make remote and lonely
echoes in their brooding depths, there will be the expiring clatter of a
single truck, the sound of a worker's voice as he says "Good-night," and
then the potent and magical silence.

And then there is the sea—the sea, beautiful and mysterious as it is
only when it meets the earth in harbors, the sea that bears in swell and
glut of tides the odorous savor of the earth, the sea that swings and slaps

against encrusted piles, the sea that is braided with long ropes of scummy weed, the sea that brings the mast and marly scent of shelled decay. There is the sea, and there are the great ships—the freighters, the fishing schooners, the clean white one-night boats that make the New York run, now also potent and silent, a glitter of bright lights, of gleaming brasses, of opulent saloons—a token of joy and splendor in dark waters, a hint of love and the velvet belly upon dark tides—and the sight of all these things, the fusion of all these odors by the sprite of May is freighted with unspeakable memories, with unutterable intuitions for the youth: he does not know what he could utter, but glory, love, power, wealth, flight and movement and the sight of new earth in the morning, and the living corporeal fulfilment of all his ecstasy is in his wish and his conviction.

Certainly, these things can be found in New England, but perhaps the person who finds this buried joy the most is this lonely visitor—and particularly the boy from the South, for in the heart of the Southerner alone, perhaps, is this true and secret knowledge of the North: it is there in his dreams and his childhood premonition, it is there like the dark Helen, and no matter what he sees to cheat it, he will always believe in it, he will always return to it. Certainly, this was true of the gnarled and miserly old man who now sat not far from all this glory in his dingy State Street office, for my uncle Bascom Hawke, although the stranger on seeing him might have said, "There goes the very image of a hard-bitten old Down-Easter," had come, as lonely and wretched a youth as ever lived, from the earth of Old Catawba, he had known and felt these things and, in spite of his frequent bitter attacks on the people, the climate, the life, New England was the place to which he had returned to live, and for which he felt the most affection.

—"What is man that thou art *mindful* of him?"—he said again, this time with that tell-tale pedantry of emphasis which foretold a seizure of his mouthing eccentricity. "What is *man* that thou art *mindful* of him?" he repeated with yet more emphasis. The word is *mindful, mindful, mindful!*—he made the word whine like the rasp of a saw. "M-I-N-D-F-U-L! (Phuh! phuh! phuh! phuh, phuh!)"

And again, his visage of calm and powerful thought was twisted by the disfiguring grimace, the inept and reasonless laughter. In a moment more, his face grew calm again, magnificently composed above his arched, gnarled hands; he spoke with eloquent deliberation. He became triumphant reasoning mind: he talked with superb and balanced judgment. And as the strange and lonely spirit of thought transformed his face, all the tumult and madness of his life was forgotten: no question of money or of self was involved.

"Beyond a doubt! Beyond a doubt!" he said deliberately. "The quality of the best writing in the books of the Old and New Testaments may take rank with the best writing that was ever done, but the amount of great writing is less than it is commonly supposed to be. There are passages—nay! *books!*"—his voice rising strangely to a husky howl—"of the vilest rubbish."

He paused a moment; then, in a remote voice—in the remote and passionate voice that had had such power to thrill men when it uttered poetry—he continued: "I am Alpha and Omega, the beginning and the end, the first and the last—the triumphant music of one of the mightiest of earth's poets, the sublime utterance of a man for whom God had opened the mysteries of heaven and hell, one of the mightiest lines, my dear boy, the most magnificent poetry that was ever written." And suddenly Bascom threw his gaunt hands before his face, and wept in strong, hoarse sobs: "Oh, my God! My God!—The beauty, the pity of it all! . . . You must excuse me," he whispered huskily after a moment, drawing his frayed and faded sleeve across his eyes. "You must excuse me. . . . It brought back . . . memories."

In spite of this ridiculous exhibition, and the absurd quality of these final words, there was something terrible and revolting about it, too: I was only twenty, and I shrank back for a moment and felt ashamed. In a moment more, however, Uncle Bascom was completely at his ease again: he acted as if nothing unusual had happened, and as if he had completely forgotten his outburst of a moment before.

After a pause, without looking at me, he said quietly, but with an unmistakable note of bitterness in his voice: "Have you seen any of my . . . children, recently?"

The question surprised me, because he rarely asked about them: most of the time he seemed to have forgotten their existence, to be wholly indifferent to them. I told him that I had seen one of his daughters the week before.

"My children—*basely* and *damnably, basely* and *damnably,* have deserted me!" he said with bitter passion. Then, quietly, indifferently, as if stating the fact more truthfully and temperately, he said: "I never see any of them any more. They never come to my house and I never go to theirs. I do not care. No, sir, I do not care. It makes no difference to me. Oh, not the slightest! None whatever!" and he dismissed it with his big-boned hand. In a moment he added: "Their *mother* visits them, I believe. . . . Their *mother* goes, of course, whenever she gets invited." —Here again, the note of bitterness and scorn was evident, as if he held his wife guilty of some treachery in visiting her own children; but indifference and contempt were also in his voice—he spoke of his wife and children as if they were all strangers to him, as if their lives touched only remotely the edges of the buried world—the world in which he lived and moved, in which his soul wrought out its fated destiny.

And this was true: like all of his family he had passed through a dozen lives in living his own, he was done with his children and done with his wife, he had forgotten them, he was indifferent to them, he did not need them. But they, two daughters and two sons, the youngest of whom was over thirty, the oldest more than forty, were neither able to forget him nor forgive him. He lived in their bitter memory; like men who are searching the causes for some fatal catastrophic flaw which has broken the back of a mighty bridge they went back through the painful annals of their childhood, the years of frustration and bitterness they had lived beneath his roof, the years they could not forget, escape, or deny. His shadow fell across them: they never saw him, and they always talked of him, aping his speech, his gesture, and his manner, mocking him with limber tongues, but living in his life again and secretly feeling the old fear, the old awe, because his life alone had done what it had wished to do—warped and twisted though it may have been, it had held the rails, it had kept its way, it had seen new lands. For them, it sometimes seemed, the years were passing like a bitter water on the wheel of life: the wheel turned and they got older.

And now, as if he, too, had seen them as he spoke of them, he said: "They can all look after themselves. Everyone must look after himself —say!" he paused suddenly, tapping his great finger on my knee, with the enquiring and combative glitter of his eye. "Does anyone *help* you to die? Does anyone go down into the grave with you? Can you *do* anything for anyone? No!" he said decisively, and in a moment he added, slowly and deliberately: "Is not my help in *me*?"

Then, ruminant and lost, he stared across the archway of his hands. In a moment, with what was only an apparent irrelevance, with what was really a part of the coherent past, a light plucked from dark adyts of the brain, he said: "Who knoweth the spirit of man that goeth upward, and the spirit of the beast that goeth downward to the earth?"

He was silent and thoughtful for a moment; then he added sadly: "I am an old man. I have lived a long time. I have seen so many things. Sometimes everything seems so long ago."

Then his eye went back into the wilderness, the lost earth, the buried men.

Presently he said, "I hope you will come out on Sunday. Oh, by all means! By all means! I believe your aunt is expecting you. Yes, sir, I believe she said something to that effect. Or perhaps she intends to pay a visit to one of her children. I do not know, I have not the *remotest*— not the *faintest* idea of what she proposes to do," he howled. "Of course," he said impatiently and scornfully, "I never have any notion what she has in mind. No, sir, I really could not tell you. I no longer pay any attention to what she says—Oh! not the slightest!" he waved his great hand through the air— "*Say!*" stiffly and harshly he tapped my knee, grinning at me with the combative glitter of his ptotic eye—"*Say!* did you ever find *one* of them with whom it was possible to carry on a coherent conversation? Did you ever find one of them who would respond to the processes of reason and ordered thought? My dear boy!" he cried, "You cannot talk to them. I assure you you cannot talk to them. You might as well whistle into the wind or spit into the waters of the Nile for all the good it will do you. In his youth man will bare the riches of his spirit to them, will exhaust the rich accumulations of his genius—his wisdom, his learning, his philosophy—in an effort to make them worthy of his companionship—and in the end, what does he *always* find? Why," said Uncle Bascom bitterly, "that he has spent his powers in talking to an imbecile"—and he snarled vengefully through his nose. In a moment more, he contorted his face, and nasally whined in a grotesque and mincing parody of a woman's voice, "Oh, I feel *so* sick! Oh, deary *me,* now! I think my *time* is coming on again! Oh, you don't *love* me any mo-o-ore! Oh, I *wish* I was dead! Oh, I can't get *up* today! Oh, I wish you'd bring me something *nice* from *ta-own!* Oh, if you loved me you'd buy me a *new* hat! Oh, I've got nothing to *we-e-ar!*" here his voice had an added snarl of bitterness—"I'm ashamed to go out on the street with all the other wim-men!"

Then he paused broodingly for a moment more, wheeled abruptly and tapped me on the knee again: "The proper study of mankind is— say!" he said with a horrible fixed grimace and in a kind of cunning whisper—"Does the poet say—*woman*? I want to ask you: *does* he, now? Not on your life!" yelled Uncle Bascom. "The word is *man, man, man!* Nothing else but *man!*"

Again he was silent: then, with an accent of heavy sarcasm, he went on: "Your aunt likes music. You may have observed your aunt is fond of music——"

It was, in fact, the solace of her life: on a tiny gramophone which one of her daughters had given her, she played constantly the records of the great composers, particularly of Wagner, lost in the enchanted forests of the music, her spirit wandering drunkenly down vast murky aisles of sound, through which the great hoarse throats of horns were baying faintly. And occasionally, on Sundays, on one of her infrequent excursions into the world, when her daughters bought her tickets for concerts at Symphony Hall—that great gray room lined on its sides with pallid plaster shells of Greece—she would sit perched high, a sparrow held by the hypnotic serpent's eye of music—following each motif, hearing minutely each subtle entry of the mellow flutes, the horns, the spinal ecstasy of violins—until her lonely and desolate life was spun out of her into aerial fabrics of bright sound.

"—Your aunt is fond of music," Bascom said deliberately. "Perhaps you may have thought—perhaps it seemed to you that she discovered it—perhaps you thought it was your aunt's own patent and invention—but there you would be wrong! Oh, yes! my boy!" he howled remotely, "You may have thought so, but you would be wrong— Say!" he turned slowly with a malevolent glint of interrogation, a controlled ironic power—"was the Fifth Symphony written by a woman? Was the object of your aunt's worship, Richard Wagner, a *female?*" he snarled. "By no means! Where are their great works—their mighty symphonies, their great paintings, their epic poetry? Was it in a woman's skull that the *Critique of Pure Reason* was conceived? Is the gigantic work upon the ceiling of the Sistine Chapel the product of a woman's genius?—Say! Did you ever hear of a lady by the name of William Shakespeare? Was it a female of that name who wrote *King Lear?* Are you familiar with the works of a nice young lady named John Milton? Or Fräulein Goethe, a sweet German girl?" he sneered. "Perhaps you have been edified by the writ-ings of Mademoiselle Voltaire or Miss Jonathan Swift! Phuh! Phuh! Phuh! Phuh! Phuh!"

He paused, stared deliberately across his hands, and in a moment repeated, slowly and distinctly: "The woman gave me of the tree and I did eat. Ah! that's it! There, my boy, you have it! There, in a nut-shell, you have the work for which they are best fitted." And he turned upon me suddenly with a blaze of passion, his voice husky and tremulous from the stress of his emotion. "The tempter! The Bringer of Forbidden Fruit! The devil's ambassador! Since the beginning of time that has been their office—to madden the brain, to turn man's spirit from its highest purposes, to corrupt, to seduce, and to destroy! To creep and crawl, to intrude into the lonely places of man's heart and brain, to wind herself into the core of his most secret life as a worm eats its way into a healthy fruit—to do all this with the guile of a serpent, the cunning of a fox—that, my boy, is what she's here for!—and she'll never change!" And, lowering his voice to an ominous and foreboding whisper, he said mysteriously, "Beware! Beware! Do not be deceived!"

In a moment more he had resumed his tone and manner of calm deliberation and, with an air of irrelevance, somewhat grudgingly, as if throwing a bone to a dog, he said, "Your aunt, of course, was a woman of considerable mentality—considerable, that is, for a female. Of course, her mind is no longer what it used to be. I never talk to her any more," he said indifferently. "I do not listen to her. I think she said something to me about your coming out on Sunday! But I do not know. No, sir,

I could not tell you what her plans are. I have my own interests, and I suppose she has hers. Of course, she has her music. . . . Yes, sir, she always has her music," he said indifferently and contemptuously, and, staring across the apex of his hands, he forgot her.

Yet, he had been young, and full of pain and madness. For a space he had known all the torments any lover ever knew. So much my aunt had told me, and so much he had not troubled to deny. For bending toward me swiftly, fiercely, and abruptly in the full rich progress of a meal, her eyes ablaze with a mad and earnest light, she had suddenly muttered this ominous warning: "Take care, Dave! Take care, boy! You're one of them! Don't brood! Don't brood! You mustn't be maw-bid," she whispered hoarsely, fixing the mad glitter of her bright old eyes even more intensely on me. "You're like all the rest of them—it's in the blood!" she muttered, hoarsely and fatally.

"Ah, what are you talk-ing about?" Bascom snarled in a tone of the profoundest contempt. "Scotch! English! Finest people on the face of the earth—no question about it!"

"Fugitive ideation! fugitive ideation!" she chattered like a monkey over a nut. "Mind goes off in all diwections—can't keep attention focused on anything foh five minutes! The modern decadents! Wead Nordau's book, Dave—you'll see, you'll see! You'ah all alike," she muttered. "You'ah ovah-sexed—all of you!"

"Ah," he snarled again, "You talk like a fool! Some more of your psychology, I suppose," he said with a heavy sneer. "The black magic of little minds."

He knew nothing about it, of course; occasionally he still read Kant, and he could be as deep in absolutes, categories, moments of negation, and definitions of a concept, as she with all of her complicated and extensive paraphernalia of phobias, complexes, fixations, and repressions.

Then, bending toward me once again, as if she had not heard him, she whispered: "Oh, yes! he's indifferent enough to me now—but there was a time, there was time, I tell you!—when he was mad about me! The old fool!" she cackled suddenly and bitterly with a seeming irrelevance. Then bending forward suddenly with a resumption of her former brooding intensity she whispered: "Yes! he was mad, mad, mad! Oh, he can't deny it!" she cried. "He couldn't keep his eyes off me for a minute! He went cwazy if any other man so much as looked at me!"

"Quite true, my dear! Quite true!" my uncle said without a trace of anger or denial in his voice, with one of his sudden and astonishing changes to a mood of tender and tranquil agreement. "Oh, yes," he said again, staring reminiscently across the apex of his great folded hands.

"It is all quite true—every word as she has spoken it—quite true, quite true. I had forgotten but it's all quite true." And he shook his gaunt head gently from side to side, turning his closed eyes downward, and snuffling gently, blindly, tenderly, with laughter, with a passive and indifferent memory.

For a year or two after his marriage he had been maddened by a black insanity of jealousy. It descended on his spirit like a choking and pestilence-laden cloud, it entered his veins with blackened tongues of poison, it crept along the conduits of his blood, sweltered venomously in his heart, it soaked into the convolutions of his brain until his brain was fanged with hatred, soaked in poison, stricken, maddened, and un-hinged. His gaunt figure wasted until he became the picture of skele-tonized emaciation, jealousy and fear ate like a vulture at his entrails, all of the vital energy, the power and intensity of his life, was fed into this poisonous and consuming fire and then, when it had almost wrecked his health, ruined his career, and destroyed his reason, it left him as suddenly as it came: his life reverted to its ancient and imbedded core of egotism, he grew weary of his wife, he thought of her indif-ferently, he forgot her.

And she, poor soul, was like a rabbit trapped before the fierce yellow eye, the hypnotic stare of a crouching tiger. She did not know whether he would spring, strike forth his paw to maul her, or walk off indif-ferently. She was dazed and stricken before the violence of his first passion, the unreasoning madness of his jealousy, and in the years that followed she was bewildered, resentful, and finally embittered by the abrupt indifference which succeeded it—an indifference so great that at times he seemed to forget her very existence for days at a time, to live with her in a little house as if he were scarcely conscious of her presence, stumping about the place in an intensity of self-absorption while he cursed and muttered to himself, banged open furnace doors, chopped up whatever combinations of raw foods his fantastic imagination might contrive, and answering her impatiently and contemptuously when she spoke to him: "What did you *say-y?* Oh, what are you talk-ing about?" —and he would stump away again, absorbed mysteriously with his own affairs. And sometimes, if he was the victim of conspiracy in the uni-verse—if God had forsaken him and man had tricked and cheated him, he would roll upon the floor, hammer his heels against the wall, and howl his curses at oblivious heaven.

Louise, meanwhile, her children having left her, played Wagner on the gramophone, kept her small house tidy, and learned to carry on involved and animated conversations with herself, or even with her pots and pans, for when she scrubbed and cleaned them, she would talk to them: if she dropped one, she would scold it, pick it from the floor, spank it across the bottom, saying: "No, you don't! Naughty, you bad thing, you!" And often, while he stumped through the house, these solitary conversations were interspersed by fits of laughter: she would bend double over her pots snuffling with soft laughter which was faintly broken at its climax, a long high "Who-o-op." Then she would shake her head pityingly, and be off again, but at what she was laughing she could not have said.

Suddenly one night, however, she interrupted one of Bascom's stamping and howling tirades by putting on her tiny gramophone *The Ride of the Valkyries,* as recorded by the Philadelphia Symphony Orchestra. Bascom, after the first paralysis of his surprise had passed, rushed furiously toward the offending instrument that was providing such melodious but mighty competition. Then Bascom halted; for suddenly he noticed that Louise was standing beside the instrument, that she was snuffling through her nose with laughter, and that from time to time she looked craftily toward him, and broke into a high piercing cackle. Bascom also noticed that she held a large carving knife in her hand. With a loud yell he turned and fled toward his room, where he locked the door, crying out strongly in an agony of terror: "Oh, momma! Momma! Save me!"

All this had amused Louise enormously. She played the record over time after time, forever snuffling with laughter and the high cackle: "Who-oo-oo!" She bent double with it.

The next morning after Bascom had gone furtively away to his office, Louise looked at her image in a mirror. She looked for a long time, and she said: "I wonder if I am going mad."

Her face at fifty was bloodless, bird-like, her bright eyes badly paunched and rimmed with red; her hair was dead white—all her delicate features were minutely carved with a fabric of tiny wrinkles. So she said: "I wonder if I'm going mad," and took up the study of psychology.

She read all the works of William James, and those of Professor William McDougall as often as they appeared. She subscribed to several magazines, and wrote a book herself. She called it "The Surgery of Psychic Analysis": the publishers rejected it.

"I'm a good hundred years ahead of my time," she said to one of her daughters.

Thus, Louise found the life of reason. She had found a curative for all disease: she became convinced very shortly that she was one of the very few perfectly balanced people in the world and, of course, that Bascom was utterly mad.

But sometimes, even now, the old resentment and bewilderment would return—she would remember the time of his passionate absorption in her, even the black insanity of his jealousy, with bitterness and regret.

What she had said was true. For two years after their marriage, before she had her first child, he had been like a man beset by furies. For the first time in his life his enormous egotism had been pulled away from its center: he went outside of himself, he became acutely sensitive to the world around him. Because of the fury of possession which raged in him, because the thing he possessed must be the best and dearest thing on earth, it suddenly seemed that men were united against him in an effort to take it from him. Louise was pretty and attractive: wherever she went men looked at her, and when Bascom noticed this, it almost drove him mad.

At this time he had his first church in a town in Illinois: sometimes in the middle of a sermon he would see her face below him and his own would grow livid; he would pause suddenly and lean forward gripping the edges of his lectern like a man stricken and foolish—he would recover himself and go on brokenly and indifferently, but his spirit would twist like a tortured animal, his entrails would get numb and sick, his heart seemed frozen in a ring of poison, and a thousand horrible and foolish doubts would torment him. There was no excess of fantastic possibility, no absurdity of suspicion that he did not know: his mind swarmed with poisonous fabrications, which in a second were translated into reality: he was unable to distinguish between cold fact and his delirious fancy—the moment he imagined anything he believed it to be true.

And what was the reason for this madness? He did not know, and yet he knew that he was mad. He could sit in a chair and watch the madness soak into his brain and crawl along his flesh as a man might watch the progress of a poison in his blood. It was a madness that his mind contested, that his reason knew was false, and yet it conquered him. It drove him brain-sick, heart-sick, cursing through the streets at night, it drove him stamping through the streets clutching his great hands together at the waist, and if he heard a burst of laughter in the dark, if he heard voices and the pronouns "he" and "she" he was sure the words had reference to his wife and him or to a rival, and he would turn and curse the people who had spoken. The interest of the earth and of the town he thought was fastened on his own life and his wife's: the earth was full of malevolent voices, evil whisperings—he saw himself at times as trapped, duped, tricked and mocked at by all men; he greeted his parishioners with a sick heart and a livid smile, and he searched their eyes, their faces, for a sly lurking humor, an evil and secret glee, or for some evidence that they knew the nature of his hurt, the ugly dishonor in his brain and heart, the foul color of his secret.

And it was not, it could no longer be, he felt, a secret; he felt as naked as an infant, he thought the reason for his grief was legible in every word and action, and when he went out in the streets, sometimes his spirit cowered in a dreadful kind of shame—he felt like shielding his face from sight. Shame pressed upon him from the skies, he could not escape it—and when it was not shame of his own dishonor, it was shame because he feared that he was being mocked and jeered at as a fool and cuckold by the world.

Great shapes of fear and cruelty were evoked out of immense and timeless skies, they hovered above him wherever he went, they darkened the wintry lights of desolate little towns like smears of blood: it seemed to him that there would never again be joy and confidence on earth, that the shapes of death and madness would walk in his brain forever and, having lost his faith in God, he now sought desperately for some faith in man: he dreamed of finding some earthly father, some man superior to himself in strength, wisdom, and age to whom he could confess the burden of his packed and overladen heart, from whom he might derive some wisdom, some medicine for the plague that was consuming him.

But he never found him, in his heart he knew that such a physician and confessor did not exist: he was caught in a trap, he could not confess the evil weight that lay upon his soul, he took the last full measure of man's loneliness. He could not add to his own dishonor by bringing dishonor on his wife, and always there was a censor in his brain, a core of sanity that in the darkest and evilest hours yet judged fairly, and told him he was mad.

Then it left him. When it seemed that life was no longer tolerable it left him. It guttered out as a fierce flame gutters out of the fuel it has fed upon, and it left him full of weariness, indifference, and a sense of completion: he turned from the hurt, bewildered woman into the orbit of his own remote and secret life, he went on into new lives, new places and projects, and he forgot her.

And now, as I looked at the old man, I had a sense of union with the past. It seemed to me if he would only speak, the living past, the voices of lost men, the pain, the pride, the madness and despair, the million scenes and faces of the buried life—all that an old man ever knew— would be revealed to me, would be delivered to me like a priceless treasure, as an inheritance which old men owed to young, and which should be the end and effort of all living. My savage humor was a kind of memory: I thought if he could speak, it would be fed.

And for a moment, it seemed, I saw the visages of time, dark time, the million lock-bolts shot back in man's memory, the faces of the lost Americans, and all the million casual moments of their lives, with Bascom blazing at them from a dozen pulpits, Bascom, tortured by love and madness, walking the streets of the nation, stumping the rutted roads, muttering through darkness with clasped bony hands, a gaunt and twisted figure reeling below immense and cruel skies across the continent. Light fell upon his face and darkness crossed it:—he came up from the wilderness, from derbied men and bustled women, from all of the memories of lavish brown, and from time, dark time—from a time that was further off than Saxon thanes, all of the knights, the spearheads, and the horses.

Was all this lost?

"It was so long ago," the old man said.

Bitterly, bitterly Boston one time more: the flying leaf, the broken cloud. Was no love crying in the wilderness?

"—So long ago. I have lived so long. I have seen so much. I could tell you so many things," my uncle said huskily, with weariness and indifference. His eye was lusterless and dead, he looked for a moment tired and old.

All at once, a strange and perplexing vision, which was to return many times in the years that followed, came to me. It was this: there were a company of old men and women at dinner, seated together around a table. All of them were very old, older than my uncle; the faces of the old men and women were fragile and delicate and like old yellowed china, their faces were frail and sexless, they had begun to look alike. In their youth all these people had known one another. The men had drunk, fought, whored, hated one another, and loved the women. Some had been devoured by the sterile and corrupt fear and envy that young men know. In secret their lips were twisted, their faces livid, and their hearts bitter; their eyes glittered with a reptilian hatred of another man—they dreaded his success, and they exulted in his failure, laughing with a delirious joy when they heard or read of his hurt, defeat or humiliation. They had been afraid to speak or confess what was in their hearts, they feared the mockery of their fellows; with one another their words were careful, picked, and disparaging. They gave the lie to passion and belief and they said what they knew was false. And yet along dark roads at night they had shouted out into the howling winds their great goat cries of joy, exultancy and power; they had smelled snow in thick brooding air at night, and they had watched it come, softly spitting at the window glass, numbing the footfalls of the earth with its soft silent fall, filling their hearts with a dark proud ecstasy, touching their entrails with impending prophecy. Each had a thousand dark desires and fantasies; each wanted wealth, power, fame and love; each saw himself as great, good and talented; each feared and hated rivals in business or in love—and in crowds they glared at one another with hard hostile eyes, they bristled up like crested cocks, they watched their women jealously, felt looks and glances through their shoulder blades, and hated men with white spermatic necks, amorous hair, and faces proud and insolent with female conquest.

They had been young and full of pain and combat, and now all this was dead in them: they smiled mildly, feebly, gently, they spoke in thin voices, and they looked at one another with eyes dead to desire, hostility, and passion.

As for the old women, they sat there on their yellowed and bony haunches. They were all beyond the bitter pain and ecstasy of youth— its frenzy, its hope, its sinew of bright blood and agony: they were beyond the pain and fear of anything save age and death. Here was a faithful wife, a fruitful mother; here was an adulterous and voluptuous woman, the potent mistress of a dozen men, here was her cuckold husband, who had screamed like a tortured animal when he had found her first in bed with another man, and here was the man he found her with; here was another man in whom the knowledge of his wife's infidelity had aroused only a corrupt inverted joy, he exulted in it, he urged her on into new love affairs, he besought her greedily to taunt him with it, he fed upon his pain—and now they were all old and meager and had the look of yellowed china. They turned their mild sunken faces toward one another with looks in which there was neither hate nor love nor desire nor passion, they laughed thinly, and their memory was of all things.

They no longer wanted to excel or to be first; they were no longer mad and jealous; they no longer hated rivals; they no longer wanted fame; they no longer cared for work or grew drunk on hope; they no longer turned into the dark and struck their bloody knuckles at the wall; they no longer writhed with shame upon their beds, cursed at the memory of defeat and desolation, or ripped the sheets between convulsive fingers. Could they not speak? Had they forgotten?

Why could not the old men speak? They had known pain, death and madness, yet all their words were stale and rusty. They had known the wilderness, the savage land, the blood of the murdered men ran down nto the earth that gave no answer; and they had seen it, they had shed it. Where were the passion, pain and pride, the million living moments of their lives? Was all this lost? Were they all tongueless? It seemed to me that there was something sly and evil in their glances as they sat together, as if they hoarded some cunning and malevolent wisdom in their brains, as if the medicine to all our grief and error was in them, but as if through the evil and conspirate communication of their glance, they had resolved to keep it from us. Or were they simply devoured with satiety, with weariness and indifference? Did they refuse to speak because they could not speak, because even memory had gone lifeless in them?

Yes. Words echoed in their throat but they were tongueless. For them the past was dead: they poured into our hands a handful of dry dust and ashes.

The dry bones, the bitter dust? The living wilderness, the silent waste? The barren land?

Have no lips trembled in the wilderness? No eyes sought seaward from the rock's sharp edge for men returning home? Has no pulse beat more hot with love or hate upon the river's edge? Or where the old wheel and the rusted stock lie stogged in desert sand: by the horsehead a woman's skull. No love?

No lonely footfalls in a million streets, no heart that beat its best and bloodiest cry out against the steel and stone, no aching brain, caught in its iron ring, groping among the labyrinthine canyons? Naught in that immense and lonely land but incessant growth and ripeness and pollution, the emptiness of forests and deserts, the unhearted, harsh and metal jangle of a million tongues, crying the belly-cry for bread, or the great cat's snarl for meat and honey? All, then, all? Birth and the twenty thousand days of snarl and jangle—and no love, no love? Was no love crying in the wilderness?

It was not true. The lovers lay below the lilac bush; the laurel leaves were trembling in the wood.

Suddenly it seemed to me, that if I could put my hand upon my uncle, if I could grip my fingers in his stringy arm, my strength and youth would go into him, and I could rekindle memory like a living flame in him, I could animate for an hour his ancient heart with the exultancy, the power, the joy that pulsed in me; I could make the old man speak.

I wanted to speak to him as people never speak to one another, I wanted to say and hear the things one never says and hears. I wanted to know what his own youth beyond its grim weather of poverty, loneliness, and desperation had been like. He had been over ten years old when the war had ended, he had seen the men plod home in wreaths of dust and heard their casual voices in a room, he had breathed the air of vanished summers, he had seen cloud shadows floating on the massed green of the wilderness, the twisting of a last lone leaf upon a bough; and he had heard the desolate and stricken voices in the South long,

long ago, the quiet and casual voices of lost men, a million vanished footsteps in the streets of life. And he had known the years of brown, dark lavish brown, the lost and hypocritic years, the thunder of the wheels and hooves upon the cobbles, the color of bright blood—the savagery, the hunger and the fear.

Was the memory of all this lost?

I touched him—I put my hand upon his shoulder, he did not move. Sunken in what lost world, buried in what incommunicable and tongueless past, he said—"So long ago."

Then I got up and left him and went out into the streets where the singing and lyrical air, the man-swarm passing in its million-footed weft, the glorious women and the girls compacted in a single music of belly and breasts and thighs, the sea, the earth, the proud, potent, clamorous city, all of the voices of time fused to a unity that was like a song, a token and a cry. Victoriously, I trod the neck of doubt as if it were a serpent: I was joined to the earth, a part of it, and I possessed it; I would be wasted and consumed, filled and renewed eternally; I would feel unceasingly alternate tides of life and dark oblivion; I would be emptied without weariness, replenished forever with strong joy. I had a tongue for agony, a food for hunger, a door for exile and a surfeit for insatiate desire: exultant certainty welled up in me, I thought I could possess it all, and I cried: "Yes! It will be mine!"

65

Night Club

BY KATHARINE BRUSH

P ROMPTLY at quarter of ten P. M.
Mrs. Brady descended the steps of the Elevated. She purchased
from the newsdealer in the cubbyhole beneath them a next month's
magazine and a tomorrow morning's paper and, with these tucked
under one plump arm, she walked. She walked two blocks north on
Sixth Avenue; turned and went west. But not far west. Westward half
a block only, to the place where the gay green awning marked "Club
Français" paints a stripe of shade across the glimmering sidewalk.
Under this awning Mrs. Brady halted briefly, to remark to the six-foot
doorman that it looked like rain and to await his performance of his
professional duty. When the small green door yawned open, she sighed
deeply and plodded in.

The foyer was a blackness, an airless velvet blackness like the inside
of a jeweler's box. Four drum-shaped lamps of golden silk suspended
from the ceiling gave it light (a very little) and formed the jewels:
gold signets, those, or cuff-links for a giant. At the far end of the foyer
there were black stairs, faintly dusty, rippling upward toward an amber
radiance. Mrs. Brady approached and ponderously mounted the stairs,
clinging with one fist to the mangy velvet rope that railed their edge.

From the top, Miss Lena Levin observed the ascent. Miss Levin was
the checkroom girl. She had dark-at-the-roots blonde hair and slender
hips upon which, in moments of leisure, she wore her hands, like
buckles of ivory loosely attached.

This was a moment of leisure. Miss Levin waited behind her counter.
Row upon row of hooks, empty as yet, and seeming to beckon—wee
curved fingers of iron—waited behind her.

"Late," said Miss Levin, "again."

"Go wan!" said Mrs. Brady. "It's only ten to ten. *Whew!* Them *stairs!*"

She leaned heavily, sideways, against Miss Levin's counter, and, applying one palm to the region of her heart, appeared at once to listen and to count. "Feel!" she cried then in a pleased voice.

Miss Levin obediently felt.

"Them stairs," continued Mrs. Brady darkly, "with my bad heart, will be the death of me. Whew! Well, dearie? What's the news?"

"You got a paper," Miss Levin languidly reminded her.

"Yeah!" agreed Mrs. Brady with sudden vehemence. "I got a paper!" She slapped it upon the counter. "An' a lot of time I'll get to *read* my paper, won't I now? On a Saturday night!" She moaned. "Other nights is bad enough, dear knows—but *Saturday* nights! How I dread 'em! Every Saturday night I say to my daughter, I say, 'Geraldine, I can't,' I say, 'I can't go through it again, an' that's all there is to it,' I say. 'I'll *quit!*' I say. An' I *will*, too!" added Mrs. Brady firmly, if indefinitely.

Miss Levin, in defense of Saturday nights, mumbled some vague something about tips.

"Tips!" Mrs. Brady hissed it. She almost spat it. Plainly money was nothing, nothing at all, to this lady. "I just wish," said Mrs. Brady, and glared at Miss Levin, "I just wish *you* had to spend one Saturday night, just one, in that dressing room! Bein' pushed an' stepped on and near knocked down by that gang of hussies, an' them orderin' an' bossin' you 'round like you was *black*, an' usin' your things an' then sayin' they're sorry, they got no change, they'll be back. Yeah! They *never* come back!"

"There's Mr. Costello," whispered Miss Levin through lips that, like a ventriloquist's, scarcely stirred.

"An' as I was sayin'," Mrs. Brady said at once brightly, "I got to leave you. Ten to ten, time I was on the job."

She smirked at Miss Levin, nodded, and right-about-faced. There, indeed, Mr. Costello was. Mr. Billy Costello, manager, proprietor, monarch of all he surveyed. From the doorway of the big room where the little tables herded in a ring around the waxen floor, he surveyed Mrs. Brady, and in such a way that Mrs. Brady, momentarily forgetting her bad heart, walked fast, scurried faster, almost ran.

The door of her domain was set politely in an alcove, beyond silken curtains looped up at the sides. Mrs. Brady reached it breathless, shouldered it open, and groped for the electric switch. Lights sprang up, a bright white blaze, intolerable for an instant to the eyes, like sun on snow. Blinking, Mrs. Brady shut the door.

The room was a spotless, white-tiled place, half beauty shop, half dressing-room. Along one wall stood washstands, sturdy triplets in a row, with pale-green liquid soap in glass balloons afloat above them. Against the opposite wall there was a couch. A third wall backed an elongated glass-topped dressing table; and over the dressing table and over the washstands long rectangular sheets of mirror reflected lights, doors, glossy tiles, lights multiplied. . . .

Mrs. Brady moved across this glitter like a thick dark cloud in a hurry. At the dressing table she came to a halt, and upon it she laid her newspaper, her magazine, and her purse—a black purse worn gray with much clutching. She divested herself of a rusty black coat and a hat of the mushroom persuasion, and hung both up in a corner cupboard which she opened by means of one of a quite preposterous bunch of keys. From a nook in the cupboard she took down a lace-edged handkerchief with long streamers. She untied the streamers and tied them again around her chunky black alpaca waist. The handkerchief became an apron's baby cousin.

Mrs. Brady relocked the cupboard door, fumbled her key-ring over, and unlocked a capacious drawer of the dressing table. She spread a fresh towel on the plate-glass top, in the geometrical center, and upon the towel she arranged with care a procession of things fished from the drawer. Things for the hair. Things for the complexion. Things for the eyes, the lashes, the brows, the lips, and the finger nails. Things in boxes and things in jars and things in tubes and tins. Also an ash tray, matches, pins, a tiny sewing kit, a pair of scissors. Last of all, a hand-printed sign, a nudging sort of sign:

NOTICE!

THESE ARTICLES, PLACED HERE FOR YOUR CONVENIENCE, ARE THE PROPERTY OF THE *MAID*.

And directly beneath the sign, propping it up against the looking-glass, a china saucer, in which Mrs. Brady now slyly laid decoy money: two quarters and two dimes, in four-leaf-clover formation.

Another drawer of the dressing table yielded a bottle of bromo-seltzer, a bottle of aromatic spirits of ammonia, a tin of sodium bicarbonate, and a teaspoon. These were lined up on a shelf above the couch.

Mrs. Brady was now ready for anything. And (from the grim, thin pucker of her mouth) expecting it.

Music came to her ears. Rather, the beat of music, muffled, rhythmic, remote. *Umpa-um, umpa-um, umpa-um-umm*——Mr. "Fiddle" Baer and his band, hard at work on the first fox-trot of the night. It was teasing, foot-tapping music; but the large solemn feet of Mrs. Brady were still. She sat on the couch and opened her newspaper; and for some moments she read uninterruptedly, with special attention to the murders, the divorces, the breaches of promise, the funnies.

Then the door swung inward, admitting a blast of Mr. Fiddle Baer's best, a whiff of perfume, and a girl.

Mrs. Brady put her paper away.

The girl was *petite* and darkly beautiful; wrapped in fur and mounted on tall jeweled heels. She entered humming the rag-time song the orchestra was playing, and while she stood near the dressing table, stripping off her gloves, she continued to hum it softly to herself:

> *"Oh, I know my baby loves me,*
> *I can tell my baby loves me."*

Here the dark little girl got the left glove off, and Mrs. Brady glimpsed a platinum wedding ring.

> *"'Cause there ain't no maybe*
> *In my baby's*
> *Eyes."*

The right glove came off. The dark little girl sat down in one of the chairs that faced the dressing table. She doffed her wrap, casting it carelessly over the chair back. It had a cloth-of-gold lining, and the name of a Paris house was embroidered in curlicues on the label. Mrs. Brady hovered solicitously near.

The dark little girl, still humming, looked over the articles, "placed here for your convenience," and picked up the scissors. Having cut off a very small hangnail with the air of one performing a perilous major operation, she seized and used the manicure buffer, and after that the eyebrow pencil. Mrs. Brady's mind, hopefully calculating the tip, jumped and jumped again like a taxi-meter.

> *"Oh, I know my baby loves me——"*

The dark little girl applied powder and lipstick belonging to herself. She examined the result searchingly in the mirror and sat back, satisfied. She cast some silver *Klink! Klink!* into Mrs. Brady's saucer, and half rose. Then, remembering something, she settled down again.

The ensuing thirty seconds were spent by her in pulling off her platinum wedding ring, tying it in a corner of a lace handkerchief, and tucking the handkerchief down the bodice of her tight white velvet gown.

"There!" she said.

She swooped up her wrap and trotted toward the door, jeweled heels merrily twinkling.

"'*Cause there ain't no maybe——*"

The door fell shut.

Almost instantly it opened again, and another girl came in. A blonde, this. She was pretty in a round-eyed, doll-like way; but Mrs. Brady, regarding her, mentally grabbed the spirits of ammonia bottle. For she looked terribly ill. The round eyes were dull, the pretty silly little face was drawn. The thin hands, picking at the fastenings of a specious beaded bag, trembled and twitched.

Mrs. Brady cleared her throat. "Can I do something for you, miss?"

Evidently the blonde girl had believed herself alone in the dressing room. She started violently and glanced up, panic in her eyes. Panic, and something else. Something very like murderous hate—but for an instant only, so that Mrs. Brady, whose perceptions were never quick, missed it altogether.

"A glass of water?" suggested Mrs. Brady.

"No," said the girl, "no." She had one hand in the beaded bag now. Mrs. Brady could see it moving, causing the bag to squirm like a live thing, and the fringe to shiver. "Yes!" she cried abruptly. "A glass of water—please—you get it for me."

She dropped on to the couch. Mrs. Brady scurried to the water cooler in the corner, pressed the spigot with a determined thumb. Water trickled out thinly. Mrs. Brady pressed harder, and scowled, and thought, "Something's wrong with this thing. I mustn't forget, next time I see Mr. Costello——"

When again she faced her patient, the patient was sitting erect. She was thrusting her clenched hand back into the beaded bag again.

She took only a sip of the water, but it seemed to help her quite miraculously. Almost at once color came to her cheeks, life to her eyes. She grew young again—as young as she was. She smiled up at Mrs. Brady.

"Well!" she exclaimed. "What do you know about that!" She shook her honey-colored head. "I can't imagine what came over me."

"Are you better now?" inquired Mrs. Brady.

"Yes. Oh, yes. I'm better now. You see," said the blonde girl confidentially, "we were at the theater, my boy friend and I, and it was hot and stuffy—I guess that must have been the trouble."

She paused, and the ghost of her recent distress crossed her face. "God! I thought that last act *never* would end!" she said.

While she attended to her hair and complexion, she chattered gayly to Mrs. Brady, chattered on with scarcely a stop for breath, and laughed much. She said, among other things, that she and her "boy friend" had not known one another very long, but that she was "ga-ga" about him. "He is about me, too," she confessed. "He thinks I'm grand."

She fell silent then, and in the looking-glass her eyes were shadowed, haunted. But Mrs. Brady, from where she stood, could not see the looking-glass; and half a minute later the blonde girl laughed and began again. When she went out she seemed to dance out on little winged feet; and Mrs. Brady, sighing, thought it must be nice to be young . . . and happy like that.

The next arrivals were two. A tall, extremely smart young woman in black chiffon entered first, and held the door open for her companion; and the instant the door was shut, she said, as though it had been on the tip of her tongue for hours, "Amy, what under the sun *happened*?"

Amy, who was brown-eyed, brown-bobbed-haired, and patently annoyed about something, crossed to the dressing table and flopped into a chair before she made reply.

"Nothing," she said wearily then.

"That's nonsense!" snorted the other. "Tell me. Was it something she said? She's a tactless ass, of course. Always was."

"No, not anything she said. It was——" Amy bit her lip. "All right! I'll tell you. Before we left your apartment I just happened to notice that Tom had disappeared. So I went to look for him—I wanted to ask him if he'd remembered to tell the maid where we were going—Skippy's subject to croup, you know, and we always leave word. Well, so I went into the kitchen, thinking Tom might be there mixing cocktails—and there he was—and there *she* was!"

The full red mouth of the other young woman pursed itself slightly. Her arched brows lifted. "Well?"

Her matter-of-factness appeared to infuriate Amy. "He was *kissing* her!" she flung out.

"Well?" said the other again. She chuckled softly and patted Amy's shoulder, as if it were the shoulder of a child. "You're surely not going to let *that* spoil your whole evening? Amy *dear*! Kissing may once have been serious and significant—but it isn't nowadays. Nowadays, it's like shaking hands. It means nothing."

But Amy was not consoled. "I hate her!" she cried desperately. "Redheaded *thing*! Calling me 'darling' and 'honey,' and s-sending me handkerchiefs for C-Christmas—and then sneaking off behind closed doors and k-kissing my h-h-husband——"

At this point Amy broke down, but she recovered herself sufficiently to add with venom, "I'd like to slap her!"

"Oh, oh, oh," smiled the tall young woman, "I wouldn't do that!"

Amy wiped her eyes with what might well have been one of the

Christmas handkerchiefs, and confronted her friend. "Well, what *would* you do, Vera? If you were I?"

"I'd forget it," said Vera, "and have a good time. I'd kiss somebody myself. You've no idea how much better you'd feel!"

"I don't do——" Amy began indignantly; but as the door behind her opened and a third young woman—red-headed, earringed, exquisite—lilted in, she changed her tone. "Oh, hello!" she called sweetly, beaming at the newcomer via the mirror. "We were wondering what had become of you!"

The red-headed girl, smiling easily back, dropped her cigarette on the floor and crushed it out with a silver-shod toe. "Tom and I were talking to Fiddle Baer," she explained. "He's going to play 'Clap Yo' Hands' next, because it's my favorite. Lend me a comb, will you?"

"There's a comb there," said Vera, indicating Mrs. Brady's business comb.

"But imagine using it!" murmured the red-headed girl. "Amy, darling, haven't you one?"

Amy produced a tiny comb from her rhinestone purse. "Don't forget to bring it when you come," she said, and stood up. "I'm going on out, I want to tell Tom something." She went.

The red-headed young woman and the tall black-chiffon one were alone, except for Mrs. Brady. The red-headed one beaded her incredible lashes. The tall one, the one called Vera, sat watching her. Presently she said, "Sylvia, look here." And Sylvia looked. Anybody, addressed in that tone, would have.

"There is one thing," Vera went on quietly, holding the other's eyes, "that I want understood. And that is, '*Hands off!*' Do you hear me?"

"I don't know what you mean."

"You do know what I mean!"

The red-headed girl shrugged her shoulders. "Amy told you she saw us, I suppose."

"Precisely. And," went on Vera, gathering up her possessions and rising, "as I said before, you're to keep away." Her eyes blazed sudden white-hot rage. "Because, as you very well know, he belongs to *me*," she said, and departed, slamming the door.

Between eleven o'clock and one Mrs. Brady was very busy indeed. Never for more than a moment during those two hours was the dressing room empty. Often it was jammed, full to overflowing with curled cropped heads, with ivory arms and shoulders, with silk and lace and chiffon, with legs. The door flapped in and back, in and back. The mirrors caught and held—and lost—a hundred different faces. Powder veiled the dressing table with a thin white dust; cigarette stubs, scarlet at

KATHARINE BRUSH

the tips, choked the ash-receiver. Dimes and quarters clattered into Mrs. Brady's saucer—and were transferred to Mrs. Brady's purse. The original seventy cents remained. That much, and no more, would Mrs. Brady gamble on the integrity of womankind.

She earned her money. She threaded needles and took stitches. She powdered the backs of necks. She supplied towels for soapy, dripping hands. She removed a speck from a teary blue eye and pounded the heel on a slipper. She curled the straggling ends of a black bob and a gray bob, pinned a velvet flower on a lithe round waist, mixed three doses of bicarbonate of soda, took charge of a shed pink-satin girdle, collected, on hands and knees, several dozen fake pearls that had wept from a broken string.

She served chorus girls and school girls, gay young matrons and gayer young mistresses, a lady who had divorced four husbands, and a lady who had poisoned one, the secret (more or less) sweetheart of a Most Distinguished Name, and the Brains of a bootleg gang. . . . She saw things. She saw a yellow check, with the ink hardly dry. She saw four tiny bruises, such as fingers might make, on an arm. She saw a girl strike another girl, not playfully. She saw a bundle of letters some man wished he had not written, safe and deep in a brocaded handbag.

About midnight the door flew open and at once was pushed shut, and a gray-eyed, lovely child stood backed against it, her palms flattened on the panels at her sides, the draperies of her white chiffon gown settling lightly to rest around her.

There were already five damsels of varying ages in the dressing room. The latest arrival marked their presence with a flick of her eyes and, standing just where she was, she called peremptorily, "Maid!"

Mrs. Brady, standing just where *she* was, said, "Yes, miss?"

"Please come here," said the girl.

Mrs. Brady, as slowly as she dared, did so.

The girl lowered her voice to a tense half-whisper. "Listen! Is there any way I can get out of here except through this door I came in?"

Mrs. Brady stared at her stupidly.

"Any window?" persisted the girl. "Or anything?"

Here they were interrupted by the exodus of two of the damsels-of-varying-ages. Mrs. Brady opened the door for them—and in so doing caught a glimpse of a man who waited in the hall outside, a debonair, old-young man with a girl's furry wrap hung over his arm, and his hat in his hand.

The door clicked. The gray-eyed girl moved out from the wall, against which she had flattened herself—for all the world like one eluding pursuit in a cinema.

"What about that window?" she demanded, pointing.

"That's all the farther it opens," said Mrs. Brady.

"Oh! And it's the only one—isn't it?"

"It is."

"Damn," said the girl. "Then there's *no* way out?"

"No way but the door," said Mrs. Brady testily.

The girl looked at the door. She seemed to look *through* the door, and to despise and to fear what she saw. Then she looked at Mrs. Brady. "Well," she said, "then I s'pose the only thing for me to do is to stay in here."

She stayed. Minutes ticked by. Jazz crooned distantly, stopped, struck up again. Other girls came and went. Still the gray-eyed girl sat on the couch, with her back to the wall and her shapely legs crossed, smoking cigarettes, one from the stub of another.

After a long while she said, "Maid!"

"Yes, miss?"

"Peek out that door, will you, and see if there's anyone standing there."

Mrs. Brady peeked, and reported that there was. There was a gentleman with a little bit of a black mustache standing there. The same gentleman, in fact, who was standing there "just after you came in."

"Oh, Lord," sighed the gray-eyed girl. "Well . . . I can't stay here all *night,* that's one sure thing."

She slid off the couch, and went listlessly to the dressing table. There she occupied herself for a minute or two. Suddenly, without a word, she darted out.

Thirty seconds later Mrs. Brady was elated to find two crumpled one-dollar bills lying in her saucer. Her joy, however, died a premature death. For she made an almost simultaneous second discovery. A saddening one. Above all, a puzzling one.

"Now what for," marveled Mrs. Brady, "did she want to walk off with them *scissors?*"

This at twelve twenty-five.

At twelve thirty a quartette of excited young things burst in, babbling madly. All of them had their evening wraps with them; all talked at once. One of them, a Dresden china girl with a heart-shaped face, was the center of attraction. Around her the rest fluttered like monstrous butterflies; to her they addressed their shrill exclamatory cries.

"Babe," they called her.

Mrs. Brady heard snatches: "Not in this state unless . . ." "Well, you can in Maryland, Jimmy says." "Oh, there must be some place nearer than . . ." "Isn't this marvelous?" "When did it happen, Babe? When did you decide?"

"Just now," the girl with the heart-shaped face sang softly, "when we were dancing."

The babble resumed, "But listen, Babe, what'll your mother and father . . . ?" "Oh, never mind, let's hurry." "Shall we be warm enough with just these thin wraps, do you think? Babe, will you be warm enough? Sure?"

Powder flew and little pocket combs marched through bright marcels. Flushed cheeks were painted pinker still.

"My pearls," said Babe, "are *old*. And my dress and my slippers are *new. Now*, let's see—what can I *borrow*?"

A lace handkerchief, a diamond bar pin, a pair of earrings were proffered. She chose the bar pin, and its owner unpinned it proudly, gladly.

"I've got blue garters!" exclaimed a shrill little girl in a silver dress.

"Give me one, then," directed Babe. "I'll trade with you. . . . There! That fixes that."

More babbling, "Hurry! Hurry up!" . . . "Listen, are you *sure* we'll be warm enough? Because we can stop at my house, there's nobody home." "Give me that puff, Babe, I'll powder your back." "And just to think a week ago you'd never even met each other!" "Oh, hurry *up*, let's get *started!*" "I'm ready." "So'm I." "Ready, Babe? You look adorable." "Come on, everybody."

They were gone again, and the dressing room seemed twice as still and vacant as before.

A minute of grace, during which Mrs. Brady wiped the spilled powder away with a damp gray rag. Then the door jumped open again. Two evening gowns appeared and made for the dressing table in a bee line. Slim tubular gowns they were, one green, one palest yellow. Yellow hair went with the green gown, brown hair with the yellow. The green-gowned, yellow-haired girl wore gardenias on her left shoulder, four of them, and a flashing bracelet on each fragile wrist. The other girl looked less prosperous; still, you would rather have looked at her.

Both ignored Mrs. Brady's cosmetic display as utterly as they ignored Mrs. Brady, producing full field equipment of their own.

"Well," said the girl with gardenias, rouging energetically, "how do you like him?"

"Oh-h—all right."

"Meaning, 'Not any,' hmm? I suspected as much!" The girl with gardenias turned in her chair and scanned her companion's profile with disapproval. "See here, Marilee," she drawled, "are you going to be a damn fool *all* your life?"

"He's fat," said Marilee dreamily. "Fat, and—greasy, sort of. I mean, greasy in his mind. Don't you know what I mean?"

"I know *one* thing," declared the other. "I know Who He Is! And if I were you, that's all I'd need to know. *Under the circumstances.*"

The last three words, stressed meaningly, affected the girl called Marilee curiously. She grew grave. Her lips and lashes drooped. For some seconds she sat frowning a little, breaking a black-sheathed lipstick in two and fitting it together again.

"She's worse," she said finally, low.

"Worse?"

Marilee nodded.

"Well," said the girl with gardenias, "there you are. It's the climate. She'll never be anything *but* worse, if she doesn't get away. Out West. Arizona or somewhere."

"I know," murmured Marilee.

The other girl opened a tin of eye shadow. "Of course," she said dryly, "suit yourself. She's not *my* sister."

Marilee said nothing. Quiet she sat, breaking the lipstick, mending it, breaking it.

"Oh, well," she breathed finally, wearily, and straightened up. She propped her elbows on the plate-glass dressing table top and leaned toward the mirror, and with the lipstick she began to make her coral-pink mouth very red and gay and reckless and alluring.

Nightly at one o'clock Vane and Moreno dance for the Club Français. They dance a tango, they dance a waltz; then, by way of encore, they do a Black Bottom, and a trick of their own called the Wheel. They dance for twenty, thirty minutes. And while they dance you do not leave your table—for this is what you came to see. Vane and Moreno. The new New York thrill. The sole justification for the five-dollar couvert extorted by Billy Costello.

From one until half-past, then, was Mrs. Brady's recess. She had been looking forward to it all the evening long. When it began—when the opening chords of the tango music sounded stirringly from the room outside—Mrs. Brady brightened. With a right good will she sped the parting guests.

Alone, she unlocked her cupboard and took out her magazine—the magazine she had bought three hours before. Heaving a great breath of relief and satisfaction, she plumped herself on the couch and fingered the pages.

Immediately she was absorbed, her eyes drinking up printed lines, her lips moving soundlessly.

The magazine was Mrs. Brady's favorite. Its stories were true stories. taken from life (so the editor said); and to Mrs. Brady they were live, vivid threads in the dull, drab pattern of her night.

66

Kneel to the Rising Sun

BY ERSKINE CALDWELL

A SHIVER went through Lonnie. He drew his hand away from his sharp chin, remembering what Clem had said. It made him feel now as if he were committing a crime by standing in Arch Gunnard's presence and allowing his face to be seen.

He and Clem had been walking up the road together that afternoon on their way to the filling station when he told Clem how much he needed rations. Clem stopped a moment to kick a rock out of the road, and said that if you worked for Arch Gunnard long enough, your face would be sharp enough to split the boards for your own coffin.

As Lonnie turned away to sit down on an empty box beside the gasoline pump, he could not help wishing that he could be as unafraid of Arch Gunnard as Clem was. Even if Clem was a Negro, he never hesitated to ask for rations when he needed something to eat; and when he and his family did not get enough, Clem came right out and told Arch so. Arch stood for that, but he swore that he was going to run Clem out of the country the first chance he got.

Lonnie knew without turning around that Clem was standing at the corner of the filling station with two or three other Negroes and looking at him, but for some reason he was unable to meet Clem's eyes.

Arch Gunnard was sitting in the sun, honing his jack-knife blade on his boot top. He glanced once or twice at Lonnie's hound, Nancy, who was lying in the middle of the road waiting for Lonnie to go home.

"That your dog, Lonnie?"

Jumping with fear, Lonnie's hand went to his chin to hide the lean face that would accuse Arch of short-rationing.

Arch snapped his fingers and the hound stood up, wagging her tail. She waited to be called.

"Mr. Arch, I——"

Arch called the dog. She began crawling toward them on her belly, wagging her tail a little faster each time Arch's fingers snapped. When she was several feet away, she turned over on her back and lay on the ground with her four paws in the air.

Dudley Smith and Jim Weaver, who were lounging around the filling station, laughed. They had been leaning against the side of the building, but they straightened up to see what Arch was up to.

Arch spat some more tobacco juice on his boot top and whetted the jack-knife blade some more.

"What kind of a hound dog is that, anyway, Lonnie?" Arch said. "Looks like to me it might be a ketch hound."

Lonnie could feel Clem Henry's eyes boring into the back of his head. He wondered what Clem would do if it had been his dog Arch Gunnard was snapping his fingers at and calling like that.

"His tail's way too long for a coon hound or a bird dog, ain't it, Arch?" somebody behind Lonnie said, laughing out loud.

Everybody laughed then, including Arch. They looked at Lonnie, waiting to hear what he was going to say to Arch.

"Is he a ketch hound, Lonnie?" Arch said, snapping his fingers again.

"Mr. Arch, I——"

"Don't be ashamed of him, Lonnie, if he don't show signs of turning out to be a bird dog or a fox hound. Everybody needs a hound around the house that can go out and catch pigs and rabbits when you are in a hurry for them. A ketch hound is a mighty respectable animal. I've known the time when I was mighty proud to own one."

Everybody laughed.

Arch Gunnard was getting ready to grab Nancy by the tail. Lonnie sat up, twisting his neck until he caught a glimpse of Clem Henry at the other corner of the filling station. Clem was staring at him with unmistakable meaning, with the same look in his eyes he had had that afternoon when he said that nobody who worked for Arch Gunnard ought to stand for short-rationing. Lonnie lowered his eyes. He could not figure out how a Negro could be braver than he was. There were a lot of times like that when he would have given anything he had to be able to jump into Clem's shoes and change places with him.

"The trouble with this hound of yours, Lonnie, is that he's too heavy on his feet. Don't you reckon it would be a pretty slick little trick to lighten the load some, being as how he's a ketch hound to begin with?"

Lonnie remembered then what Clem Henry had said he would do if Arch Gunnard ever tried to cut off his dog's tail. Lonnie knew, and Clem knew, and everybody else knew, that that would give Arch the chance he was waiting for. All Arch asked, he had said, was for Clem

Henry to overstep his place just one little half-inch, or to talk back to him with just one little short word, and he would do the rest. Everybody knew what Arch meant by that, especially if Clem did not turn and run. And Clem had not been known to run from anybody, after fifteen years in the country.

Arch reached down and grabbed Nancy's tail while Lonnie was wondering about Clem. Nancy acted as if she thought Arch were playing some kind of a game with her. She turned her head around until she could reach Arch's hand to lick it. He cracked her on the bridge of the nose with the end of the jack-knife.

"He's a mighty playful dog, Lonnie," Arch said, catching up a shorter grip on the tail, "but his wag-pole is way too long for a dog of his size, especially when he wants to be a ketch hound."

Lonnie swallowed hard.

"Mr. Arch, she's a mighty fine rabbit tracker. I——"

"Shucks, Lonnie," Arch said, whetting the knife blade on the dog's tail, "I ain't never seen a hound in all my life that needed a tail that long to hunt rabbits with. It's way too long for just a common, ordinary, everyday ketch hound."

Lonnie looked up hopefully at Dudley Smith and the others. None of them offered any help. It was useless for him to try to stop Arch, because Arch Gunnard would let nothing stand in his way when once he had set his head on what he wished to do. Lonnie knew that if he should let himself show any anger or resentment, Arch would drive him off the farm before sundown that night. Clem Henry was the only person there who would help him, but Clem . . .

The white men and the Negroes at both corners of the filling station waited to see what Lonnie was going to do about it. All of them hoped he would put up a fight for his hound. If anyone ever had the nerve to stop Arch Gunnard from cutting off a dog's tail, it might put an end to it. It was plain, though, that Lonnie, who was one of Arch's share-croppers, was afraid to speak up. Clem Henry might; Clem was the only one who might try to stop Arch, even if it meant trouble. And all of them knew that Arch would insist on running Clem out of the country, or filling him full of lead.

"I reckon it's all right with you, ain't it, Lonnie?" Arch said. "I don't seem to hear no objections."

Clem Henry stepped forward several paces, and stopped.

Arch laughed, watching Lonnie's face, and jerked Nancy to her feet. The hound cried out in pain and surprise, but Arch made her be quiet by kicking her in the belly.

Lonnie winced. He could hardly bear to see anybody kick his dog like that.

"Mr. Arch, I . . ."

A contraction in his throat almost choked him for several moments, and he had to open his mouth wide and fight for breath. The other white men around him were silent. Nobody liked to see a dog kicked in the belly like that.

Lonnie could see the other end of the filling station from the corner of his eye. He saw a couple of Negroes go up behind Clem and grasp his overalls. Clem spat on the ground, between outspread feet, but he did not try to break away from them.

"Being as how I don't hear no objections, I reckon it's all right to go ahead and cut it off," Arch said, spitting.

Lonnie's head went forward and all he could see of Nancy was her hind feet. He had come to ask for a slab of sowbelly and some molasses, or something. Now he did not know if he could ever bring himself to ask for rations, no matter how much hungrier they became at home.

"I always make it a habit of asking a man first," Arch said. "I wouldn't want to go ahead and cut off a tail if a man had any objections. That wouldn't be right. No, sir, it just wouldn't be fair and square."

Arch caught a shorter grip on the hound's tail and placed the knife blade on it two or three inches from the rump. It looked to those who were watching as if his mouth were watering, because tobacco juice began to trickle down the corners of his lips. He brought up the back of his hand and wiped his mouth.

A noisy automobile came plowing down the road through the deep red dust. Everyone looked up as it passed in order to see who was in it.

Lonnie glanced at it, but he could not keep his eyes raised. His head fell downward once more until he could feel his sharp chin cutting into his chest. He wondered then if Arch had noticed how lean his face was.

"I keep two or three ketch hounds around my place," Arch said, honing the blade on the tail of the dog as if it were a razor strop until his actions brought smiles to the faces of the men grouped around him, "but I never could see the sense of a ketch hound having a long tail. It only gets in their way when I send them out to catch a pig or a rabbit for my supper."

Pulling with his left hand and pushing with his right, Arch Gunnard docked the hound's tail as quickly and as easily as if he were cutting a willow switch in the pasture to drive the cows home with. The dog sprang forward with the release of her tail until she was far beyond Arch's reach, and began howling so loud she could be heard half a mile away. Nancy stopped once and looked back at Arch, and then she sprang to the middle of the road and began leaping and twisting in circles. All that time she was yelping and biting at the bleeding stub of her tail.

Arch leaned backward and twirled the severed tail in one hand while he wiped the jack-knife blade on his boot sole. He watched Lonnie's dog chasing herself around in circles in the red dust.

Nobody had anything to say then. Lonnie tried not to watch his dog's agony, and he forced himself to keep from looking at Clem Henry. Then, with his eyes shut, he wondered why he had remained on Arch Gunnard's plantation all those past years, share-cropping for a mere living on short-rations, and becoming leaner and leaner all the time. He knew then how true it was what Clem had said about Arch's share-croppers' faces becoming sharp enough to hew their own coffins. His hands went up to his chin before he knew what he was doing. His hand dropped when he had felt the bones of jaw and the exposed tendons of his cheeks.

As hungry as he was, he knew that even if Arch did give him some rations then, there would not be nearly enough for them to eat for the following week. Hatty, his wife, was already broken down from hunger and work in the fields, and his father, Mark Newsome, stone-deaf for the past twenty years, was always asking him why there was never enough food in the house for them to have a solid meal. Lonnie's head fell forward a little more, and he could feel his eyes becoming damp.

The pressure of his sharp chin against his chest made him so uncomfortable that he had to raise his head at last in order to ease the pain of it.

The first thing he saw when he looked up was Arch Gunnard twirling Nancy's tail in his left hand. Arch Gunnard had a trunk full of dogs' tails at home. He had been cutting off tails ever since anyone could remember, and during all those years he had accumulated a collection of which he was so proud that he kept the trunk locked and the key tied around his neck on a string. On Sunday afternoons when the preacher came to visit, or when a crowd was there to loll on the front porch and swap stories, Arch showed them off, naming each tail from memory just as well as if he had had a tag on it.

Clem Henry had left the filling station and was walking alone down the road toward the plantation. Clem Henry's house was in a cluster of Negro cabins below Arch's big house, and he had to pass Lonnie's house to get there. Lonnie was on the verge of getting up and leaving when he saw Arch looking at him. He did not know whether Arch was looking at his lean face, or whether he was watching to see if he were going to get up and go down the road with Clem.

The thought of leaving reminded him of his reason for being there. He had to have some rations before suppertime that night, no matter how short they were.

"Mr. Arch, I . . ."

Arch stared at him for a moment, appearing as if he had turned to listen to some strange sound unheard of before that moment.

Lonnie bit his lips, wondering if Arch was going to say anything about how lean and hungry he looked. But Arch was thinking about something else. He slapped his hand on his leg and laughed out loud.

"I sometimes wish niggers had tails," Arch said, coiling Nancy's tail into a ball and putting it into his pocket. "I'd a heap rather cut off nigger tails than dog tails. There'd be more to cut, for one thing."

Dudley Smith and somebody else behind them laughed for a brief moment. The laughter died out almost as suddenly as it had risen.

The Negroes who had heard Arch shuffled their feet in the dust and moved backwards. It was only a few minutes until not one was left at the filling station. They went up the road behind the red wooden building until they were out of sight.

Arch got up and stretched. The sun was getting low, and it was no longer comfortable in the October air. "Well, I reckon I'll be getting on home to get me some supper," he said.

He walked slowly to the middle of the road and stopped to look at Nancy retreating along the ditch.

"Nobody going my way?" he asked. "What's wrong with you, Lonnie? Going home to supper, ain't you?"

"Mr. Arch, I . . ."

Lonnie found himself jumping to his feet. His first thought was to ask for the sowbelly and molasses, and maybe some corn meal; but when he opened his mouth, the words refused to come out. He took several steps forward and shook his head. He did not know what Arch might say or do if he said "no."

"Hatty'll be looking for you," Arch said, turning his back and walking off.

He reached into his hip pocket and took out Nancy's tail. He began twirling it as he walked down the road toward the big house in the distance.

Dudley Smith went inside the filling station, and the others walked away.

After Arch had gone several hundred yards, Lonnie sat down heavily on the box beside the gas pump from which he had got up when Arch spoke to him. He sat down heavily, his shoulders drooping, his arms falling between his outspread legs.

Lonnie did not know how long his eyes had been closed, but when he opened them, he saw Nancy lying between his feet, licking the docked tail. While he watched her, he felt the sharp point of his chin cutting into his chest again. Presently the door behind him was slammed shut, and a minute later he could hear Dudley Smith walking away from the filling station on his way home.

II

Lonnie had been sleeping fitfully for several hours when he suddenly found himself wide awake. Hatty shook him again. He raised himself on his elbow and tried to see into the darkness of the room. Without knowing what time it was, he was able to determine that it was still nearly two hours until sunrise.

"Lonnie," Hatty said again, trembling in the cold night air, 'Lonnie, your pa aint in the house."

Lonnie sat upright in bed.

"How do you know he aint?" he said.

"I've been lying here wide awake ever since I got in bed, and I heard him when he went out. He's been gone all that time."

"Maybe he just stepped out for a while," Lonnie said, turning and trying to see through the bedroom window.

"I know what I'm saying, Lonnie," Hatty insisted. "Your pa's been gone a heap too long."

Both of them sat without a sound for several minutes while they listened for Mark Newsome.

Lonnie got up and lit a lamp. He shivered while he was putting on his shirt, overalls, and shoes. He tied his shoelaces in hard knots because he couldn't see in the faint light. Outside the window it was almost pitch-dark, and Lonnie could feel the damp October air blowing against his face.

"I'll go help look," Hatty said, throwing the covers off and starting to get up.

Lonnie went to the bed and drew the covers back over her and pushed her back into place.

"You try to get some sleep, Hatty," he said; "you can't stay awake the whole night. I'll go bring Pa back."

He left Hatty, blowing out the lamp, and stumbled through the dark hall, feeling his way to the front porch by touching the wall with his hands. When he got to the porch, he could still barely see any distance ahead, but his eyes were becoming more accustomed to the darkness. He waited a minute, listening.

Feeling his way down the steps into the yard, he walked around the corner of the house and stopped to listen again before calling his father.

"Oh, Pa!" he said loudly. "Oh, Pa!"

He stopped under the bedroom window when he realized what he had been doing.

"Now that's a fool thing for me to be out here doing," he said, scolding himself. "Pa couldn't hear it thunder."

He heard a rustling of the bed.

"He's been gone long enough to get clear to the crossroads, or more," Hatty said, calling through the window.

"Now you lay down and try to get a little sleep, Hatty," Lonnie told her. "I'll bring him back in no time."

He could hear Nancy scratching fleas under the house, but he knew she was in no condition to help look for Mark. It would be several days before she recovered from the shock of losing her tail.

"He's been gone a long time," Hatty said, unable to keep still.

"That don't make no difference," Lonnie said. "I'll find him sooner or later. Now you go on to sleep like I told you, Hatty."

Lonnie walked toward the barn, listening for some sound. Over at the big house he could hear the hogs grunting and squealing, and he wished they would be quiet so he could hear other sounds. Arch Gunnard's dogs were howling occasionally, but they were not making any more noise than they usually did at night, and he was accustomed to their howling.

Lonnie went to the barn, looking inside and out. After walking around the barn, he went into the field as far as the cotton shed. He knew it was useless, but he could not keep from calling his father time after time.

"Oh, Pa!" he said, trying to penetrate the darkness.

He went further into the field.

"Now, what in the world could have become of Pa?" he said, stopping and wondering where to look next.

After he had gone back to the front yard, he began to feel uneasy for the first time. Mark had not acted any more strangely during the past week than he ordinarily did, but Lonnie knew he was upset over the way Arch Gunnard was giving out short-rations. Mark had even said that, at the rate they were being fed, all of them would starve to death inside another three months.

Lonnie left the yard and went down the road toward the Negro cabins. When he got to Clem's house, he turned in and walked up the path to the door. He knocked several times and waited. There was no answer, and he rapped louder.

"Who's that?" he heard Clem say from bed.

"It's me," Lonnie said. "I've got to see you a minute, Clem. I'm out in the front yard."

He sat down and waited for Clem to dress and come outside. While he waited, he strained his ears to catch any sound that might be in the air. Over the fields toward the big house he could hear the fattening hogs grunt and squeal.

Clem came out and shut the door. He stood on the doorsill a moment speaking to his wife in bed, telling her he would be back and not to worry.

"Who's that?" Clem said, coming down into the yard.

Lonnie got up and met Clem half-way.

"What's the trouble?" Clem asked then, buttoning up his overall jumper.

"Pa's not in his bed," Lonnie said, "and Hatty says he's been gone from the house most all night. I went out in the field, and all around the barn, but I couldn't find a trace of him anywhere."

Clem then finished buttoning his jumper and began rolling a cigarette. He walked slowly down the path to the road. It was still dark, and it would be at least an hour before dawn made it any lighter.

"Maybe he was too hungry to stay in the bed any longer," Clem said. "When I saw him yesterday, he said he was so shrunk up and weak he didn't know if he could last much longer. He looked like his skin and bones couldn't shrivel much more."

"I asked Arch last night after suppertime for some rations—just a little piece of sowbelly and some molasses. He said he'd get around to letting me have some the first thing this morning."

"Why don't you tell him to give you full rations or none?" Clem said. "If you knew you wasn't going to get none at all, you could move away and find a better man to share-crop for, couldn't you?"

"I've been loyal to Arch Gunnard for a long time now," Lonnie said. "I'd hate to haul off and leave him like that."

Clem looked at Lonnie, but he did not say anything more just then. They turned up the road toward the driveway that led up to the big house. The fattening hogs were still grunting and squealing in the pen, and one of Arch's hounds came down a cotton row beside the driveway to smell their shoes.

"Them fattening hogs always get enough to eat," Clem said. "There's not a one of them that don't weigh seven hundred pounds right now, and they're getting bigger every day. Besides taking all that's thrown to them, they make a lot of meals off the chickens that get in there to peck around."

Lonnie listened to the grunting of the hogs as they walked up the driveway toward the big house.

"Reckon we'd better get Arch up to help look for Pa?" Lonnie said. "I'd hate to wake him up, but I'm scared Pa might stray off into the swamp and get lost for good. He couldn't hear it thunder, even. I never could find him back there in all that tangle if he got into it."

Clem said something under his breath and went on toward the barn and hog pen. He reached the pen before Lonnie got there.

"You'd better come here quick," Clem said, turning around to see where Lonnie was.

Lonnie ran to the hog pen. He stopped and climbed half-way up the wooden-and-wire sides of the fence. At first he could see nothing, but gradually he was able to see the moving mass of black fattening hogs on the other side of the pen. They were biting and snarling at each other like a pack of hungry hounds turned loose on a dead rabbit.

Lonnie scrambled to the top of the fence, but Clem caught him and pulled him back.

"Don't go in that hog pen that way," he said. "Them hogs will tear you to pieces, they're that wild. They're fighting over something."

Both of them ran around the corner of the pen and got to the side where the hogs were. Down under their feet on the ground Lonnie caught a glimpse of a dark mass splotched with white. He was able to see it for a moment only, because one of the hogs trampled over it.

Clem opened and closed his mouth several times before he was able to say anything at all. He clutched at Lonnie's arm, shaking him.

"That looks like it might be your pa," he said. "I swear before goodness, Lonnie, it does look like it."

Lonnie still could not believe it. He climbed to the top of the fence and began kicking his feet at the hogs, trying to drive them away. They paid no attention to him.

While Lonnie was perched there, Clem had gone to the wagon shed, and he ran back with two singletrees he had somehow managed to find there in the dark. He handed one to Lonnie, poking it at him until Lonnie's attention was drawn from the hogs long enough to take it.

Clem leaped over the fence and began swinging the singletree at the hogs. Lonnie slid down beside him, yelling at them. One hog turned on Lonnie and snapped at him, and Clem struck it over the back of the neck with enough force to drive it off momentarily.

By then Lonnie was able to realize what had happened. He ran to the mass of hogs, kicking them with his heavy stiff shoes and striking them on their heads with the iron-tipped singletree. Once he felt a stinging sensation, and looked down to see one of the hogs biting the calf of his leg. He had just enough time to hit the hog and drive it away before his leg was torn. He knew most of his overall leg had been ripped away, because he could feel the night air on his bare wet calf.

Clem had gone ahead and had driven the hogs back. There was no other way to do anything. They were in a snarling circle around them, and both of them had to keep the singletrees swinging back and forth all the time to keep the hogs off. Finally Lonnie reached down and got a grip on Mark's leg. With Clem helping, Lonnie carried his father to the fence and lifted him over to the other side.

They were too much out of breath for a while to say anything, or to do anything else. The snarling, fattening hogs were at the fence, biting the wood and wire, and making more noise than ever.

While Lonnie was searching in his pockets for a match, Clem struck one. He held the flame close to Mark Newsome's head.

They both stared unbelievingly, and then Clem blew out the match. There was nothing said as they stared at each other in the darkness.

Clem walked several steps away, and turned and came back beside Lonnie.

"It's him, though," Clem said, sitting down on the ground. "It's him, all right."

"I reckon so," Lonnie said. He could think of nothing else to say then.

They sat on the ground, one on each side of Mark, looking at the body. There had been no sign of life in the body beside them since they had first touched it. The face, throat, and stomach had been completely devoured.

"You'd better go wake up Arch Gunnard," Clem said after a while.

"What for?" Lonnie said. "He can't help none now. It's too late for help."

"Makes no difference," Clem insisted. "You'd better go wake him up and let him see what there is to see. If you wait till morning, he might take it into his head to say the hogs didn't do it. Right now is the time to get him up so he can see what his hogs did."

Clem turned around and looked at the big house. The dark outline against the dark sky made him hesitate.

"A man who short-rations tenants ought to have to sit and look at that till it's buried."

Lonnie looked at Clem fearfully. He knew Clem was right, but he was scared to hear a Negro say anything like that about a white man.

"You oughtn't talk like that about Arch," Lonnie said. "He's in bed asleep. He didn't have a thing to do with it. He didn't have no more to do with it than I did."

Clem laughed a little, and threw the singletree on the ground between his feet. After letting it lie there a little while, he picked it up and began beating the ground with it.

Lonnie got to his feet slowly. He had never seen Clem act like that before, and he did not know what to think about it. He left without saying anything and walked stiffly to the house in the darkness to wake up Arch Gunnard.

III

Arch was hard to wake up. And even after he was awake, he was in no hurry to get up. Lonnie was standing outside the bedroom window, and Arch was lying in bed six or eight feet away. Lonnie could hear him toss and grumble.

"Who told you to come and wake me up in the middle of the night?" Arch said.

"Well, Clem Henry's out here, and he said maybe you'd like to know about it."

Arch tossed around on his bed, flailing the pillow with his fists.

"You tell Clem Henry I said that one of these days he's going to find himself turned inside out, like a coat-sleeve."

Lonnie waited doggedly. He knew Clem was right in insisting that Arch ought to wake up and come out there to see what had happened. Lonnie was afraid to go back to the barnyard and tell Clem that Arch was not coming. He did not know, but he had a feeling that Clem might go into the bedroom and drag Arch out of bed. He did not like to think of anything like that taking place.

"Are you still out there, Lonnie?" Arch shouted.

"I'm right here, Mr. Arch. I——"

"If I wasn't so sleepy, I'd come out there and take a stick and—I don't know what I wouldn't do!"

Lonnie met Arch at the back step. On the way out to the hog pen Arch did not speak to him. Arch walked heavily ahead, not even waiting to see if Lonnie was coming. The lantern that Arch was carrying cast long flat beams of yellow light over the ground; and when they got to where Clem was waiting beside Mark's body, the Negro's face shone in the night like a highly polished plowshare.

"What was Mark doing in my hog pen at night, anyway?" Arch said, shouting at them both.

Neither Clem nor Lonnie replied. Arch glared at them for not answering. But no matter how many times he looked at them, his eyes turned each time to stare at the torn body of Mark Newsome on the ground at his feet.

"There's nothing to be done now," Arch said finally. "We'll just have to wait till daylight and send for the undertaker." He walked a few steps away. "Looks like you could have waited till morning in the first place. There wasn't no sense in getting me up."

He turned his back and looked sideways at Clem. Clem stood up and looked him straight in the eyes.

"What do you want, Clem Henry?" he said. "Who told you to be

coming around my house in the middle of the night? I don't want niggers coming here except when I send for them."

"I couldn't stand to see anybody eaten up by the hogs, and not do
anything about it," Clem said.

"You mind your own business," Arch told him. "And when you talk
to me, take off your hat, or you'll be sorry for it. It wouldn't take much
to make me do you up the way you belong."

Lonnie backed away. There was a feeling of uneasiness around
them. That was how trouble between Clem and Arch always began.
He had seen it start that way dozens of times before. As long as Clem
turned and went away, nothing happened, but sometimes he stayed
right where he was and talked up to Arch just as if he had been a white
man, too.

Lonnie hoped it would not happen this time. Arch was already mad
enough about being waked up in the middle of the night, and Lonnie
knew there was no limit to what Arch would do when he got good and
mad at a Negro. Nobody had ever seen him kill a Negro, but he had
said he had, and he told people that he was not scared to do it again.

"I reckon you know how he came to get eaten up by the hogs like
that," Clem said, looking straight at Arch.

Arch whirled around.

"Are you talking to me . . . ?"

"I asked you that," Clem stated.

"God damn you, yellow-blooded . . ." Arch yelled.

He swung the lantern at Clem's head. Clem dodged, but the bottom
of it hit his shoulder, and it was smashed to pieces. The oil splattered on
the ground, igniting in the air from the flaming wick. Clem was lucky
not to have it splash on his face and overalls.

"Now, look here . . ." Clem said.

"You yellow-blooded nigger," Arch said, rushing at him. "I'll teach
you to talk back to me. You've got too big for your place for the last
time. I've been taking too much from you, but I aint doing it no more."

"Mr. Arch, I . . ." Lonnie said, stepping forward partly between
them. No one heard him.

Arch stood back and watched the kerosene flicker out on the ground.

"You know good and well why he got eaten up by the fattening
hogs," Clem said, standing his ground. "He was so hungry he had to
get up out of bed in the middle of the night and come up here in the
dark trying to find something to eat. Maybe he was trying to find the
smokehouse. It makes no difference, either way. He's been on short-
rations like everybody else working on your place, and he was so old he
didn't know where else to look for food except in your smokehouse.

You know good and well that's how he got lost up here in the dark and fell in the hog pen."

The kerosene had died out completely. In the last faint flare, Arch had reached down and grabbed up the singletree that had been lying on the ground where Lonnie had dropped it.

Arch raised the singletree over his head and struck with all his might at Clem. Clem dodged, but Arch drew back again quickly and landed a blow on his arm just above the elbow before Clem could dodge it. Clem's arm dropped to his side, dangling lifelessly.

"You Goddamn yellow-blooded nigger!" Arch shouted. "Now's your time, you black bastard. I've been waiting for the chance to teach you your lesson. And this's going to be one you won't never forget."

Clem felt the ground with his feet until he had located the other singletree. He stooped down and got it. Raising it, he did not try to hit Arch, but held it in front of him so he could ward off Arch's blows at his head. He continued to stand his ground, not giving Arch an inch.

"Drop that singletree," Arch said.

"I won't stand here and let you beat me like that," Clem protested.

"By God, that's all I want to hear," Arch said, his mouth curling. "Nigger, your time has come, by God!"

He swung once more at Clem, but Clem turned and ran toward the barn. Arch went after him a few steps and stopped. He threw aside the singletree and turned and ran back to the house.

Lonnie went to the fence and tried to think what was best for him to do. He knew he could not take sides with a Negro, in the open, even if Clem had helped him, and especially after Clem had talked to Arch in the way he wished he could himself. He was a white man, and to save his life he could not stand to think of turning against Arch, no matter what happened.

Presently a light burst through one of the windows of the house, and he heard Arch shouting at his wife to wake her up.

When he saw Arch's wife go to the telephone, Lonnie realized what was going to happen. She was calling up the neighbors and Arch's friends. They would not mind getting up in the night when they found out what was going to take place.

Out behind the barn he could hear Clem calling him. Leaving the yard, Lonnie felt his way out there in the dark.

"What's the trouble, Clem?" he said.

"I reckon my time has come," Clem said. "Arch Gunnard talks that way when he's good and mad. He talked just like he did that time he carried Jim Moffin off to the swamp—and Jim never came back."

"Arch wouldn't do anything like that to you, Clem," Lonnie said excitedly, but he knew better.

Clem said nothing.

"Maybe you'd better strike out for the swamps till he changes his mind and cools off some," Lonnie said. "You might be right, Clem."

Lonnie could feel Clem's eyes burning into him.

"Wouldn't be no sense in that, if you'd help me," Clem said. "Wouldn't you stand by me?"

Lonnie trembled as the meaning of Clem's suggestion became clear to him. His back was to the side of the barn, and he leaned against it while sheets of black and white passed before his eyes.

"Wouldn't you stand by me?" Clem asked again.

"I don't know what Arch would say to that," Lonnie told him haltingly.

Clem walked away several paces. He stood with his back to Lonnie while he looked across the field toward the quarter where his home was.

"I could go in that little patch of woods out there and stay till they get tired of looking for me," Clem said, turning around to see Lonnie.

"You'd better go somewhere," Lonnie said uneasily. "I know Arch Gunnard. He's hard to handle when he makes up his mind to do something he wants to do. I couldn't stop him an inch. Maybe you'd better get clear out of the country, Clem."

"I couldn't do that, and leave my family down there across the field," Clem said.

"He's going to get you if you don't."

"If you'd only sort of help me out a little, he wouldn't. I would only have to go and hide out in that little patch of woods over there a while. Looks like you could do that for me, being as how I helped you find your pa when he was in the hog pen."

Lonnie nodded, listening for sounds from the big house. He continued to nod at Clem while Clem was waiting to be assured.

"If you're going to stand up for me," Clem said, "I can just go over there in the woods and wait till they get it off their minds. You won't be telling them where I'm at, and you could say I struck out for the swamp. They wouldn't ever find me without bloodhounds."

"That's right," Lonnie said, listening for sounds of Arch's coming out of the house. He did not wish to be found back there behind the barn where Arch could accuse him of talking to Clem.

The moment Lonnie replied, Clem turned and ran off into the night. Lonnie went after him a few steps, as if he had suddenly changed his mind about helping him, but Clem was lost in the darkness by then.

Lonnie waited for a few minutes, listening to Clem crashing through the underbrush in the patch of woods a quarter of a mile away. When he could hear Clem no longer, he went around the barn to meet Arch.

Arch came out of the house carrying his double-barreled shotgun and the lantern he had picked up in the house. His pockets were bulging with shells.

"Where is that damn nigger, Lonnie?" Arch asked him. "Where he go to?"

Lonnie opened his mouth, but no words came out.

"You know which way he went, don't you?"

Lonnie again tried to say something, but there were no sounds. He jumped when he found himself nodding his head to Arch.

"Mr. Arch, I——"

"That's all right, then," Arch said. "That's all I need to know now. Dudley Smith and Tom Hawkins and Frank and Dave Howard and the rest will be here in a minute, and you can stay right here so you can show us where he's hiding out."

Frantically Lonnie tried to say something. Then he reached for Arch's sleeve to stop him, but Arch had gone.

Arch ran around the house to the front yard. Soon a car came racing down the road, its headlights lighting up the whole place, hog pen and all. Lonnie knew it was probably Dudley Smith because his was the first house in that direction, only half a mile away. While he was turning into the driveway, several other automobiles came into sight, both up the road and down it.

Lonnie trembled. He was afraid Arch was going to tell him to point out where Clem had gone to hide. Then he knew Arch would tell him. He had promised Clem he would not do that. But try as he might, he could not make himself believe that Arch Gunnard would do anything more than whip Clem.

Clem had not done anything that called for lynching. He had not raped a white woman, he had not shot at a white man; he had only talked back to Arch, with his hat on. But Arch was mad enough to do anything; he was mad enough at Clem not to stop at anything short of lynching.

The whole crowd of men was swarming around him before he realized it. And there was Arch clutching his arm and shouting into his face.

"Mr. Arch, I . . ."

Lonnie recognized every man in the feeble dawn. They were excited, and they looked like men on the last lap of an all-night foxhunting party. Their shotguns and pistols were held at their waist, ready for the kill.

"What's the matter with you, Lonnie?" Arch said, shouting into his ear. "Wake up and say where Clem Henry went to hide out. We're ready to go get him."

Lonnie remembered looking up and seeing Frank Howard dropping yellow twelve-gauge shells into the breech of his gun. Frank bent forward so he could hear Lonnie tell Arch where Clem was hiding.

"You aint going to kill Clem this time, are you, Mr. Arch?" Lonnie asked.

"Kill him?" Dudley Smith repeated. "What do you reckon I've been waiting all this time for if it wasn't for a chance to get Clem? That nigger has had it coming to him ever since he came to this county. He's a bad nigger, and it's coming to him."

"It wasn't exactly Clem's fault," Lonnie said. "If Pa hadn't come up here and fell in the hog pen, Clem wouldn't have had a thing to do with it. He was helping me, that's all."

"Shut up, Lonnie," somebody shouted at him. "You're so excited you don't know what you're saying. You're taking up for a nigger when you talk like that."

People were crowding around him so tightly he felt as if he were being squeezed to death. He had to get some air, get his breath, get out of the crowd.

"That's right," Lonnie said.

He heard himself speak, but he did not know what he was saying.

"But Clem helped me find Pa when he got lost looking around for something to eat."

"Shut up, Lonnie," somebody said again. "You damn fool, shut up!"

Arch grabbed his shoulder and shook him until his teeth rattled. Then Lonnie realized what he had been saying.

"Now, look here, Lonnie," Arch shouted. "You must be out of your head, because you know good and well you wouldn't talk like a nigger-lover in your right mind."

"That's right," Lonnie said, trembling all over. "I sure wouldn't want to talk like that."

He could still feel the grip on his shoulder where Arch's strong fingers had hurt him.

"Did Clem go to the swamp, Lonnie?" Dudley Smith said. "Is that right, Lonnie?"

Lonnie tried to shake his head; he tried to nod his head. Then Arch's fingers squeezed his thin neck. Lonnie looked at the men wild-eyed.

"Where's Clem hiding, Lonnie?" Arch demanded, squeezing.

Lonnie went three or four steps toward the barn. When he stopped, the men behind him pushed forward again. He found himself being rushed behind the barn and beyond it.

"All right, Lonnie," Arch said. "Now which way?"

Lonnie pointed toward the patch of woods where the creek was. The swamp was in the other direction.

"He said he was going to hide out in that little patch of woods along the creek over there, Mr. Arch," Lonnie said. "I reckon he's over there now."

Lonnie felt himself being swept forward, and he stumbled over the rough ground trying to keep from being knocked down and trampled upon. Nobody was talking, and everyone seemed to be walking on tip-toes. The gray light of early dawn was increasing enough both to hide them and to show the way ahead.

Just before they reached the fringe of the woods, the men separated, and Lonnie found himself a part of the circle that was closing in on Clem.

Lonnie was alone, and there was nobody to stop him, but he was unable to move forward or backward. It began to be clear to him what he had done.

Clem was probably up a tree somewhere in the woods ahead, but by that time he had been surrounded on all sides. If he should attempt to break and run, he would be shot down like a rabbit.

Lonnie sat down on a log and tried to think what to do. The sun would be up in a few more minutes, and as soon as it came up, the men would close in on the creek and Clem. He would have no chance at all among all those shot guns and pistols.

Once or twice he saw the flare of a match through the underbrush where some of the men were lying in wait. A whiff of cigarette smoke struck his nostrils, and he found himself wondering if Clem could smell it wherever he was in the woods.

There was still no sound anywhere around him, and he knew that Arch Gunnard and the rest of the men were waiting for the sun, which would in a few minutes come up behind him in the east.

It was light enough by that time to see plainly the rough ground and the tangled underbrush and the curling bark on the pine trees.

The men had already begun to creep forward, guns raised as if stalking a deer. The woods were not large, and the circle of men would be able to cover it in a few minutes at the rate they were going forward. There was still a chance that Clem had slipped through the circle before dawn broke, but Lonnie felt that he was still there. He began to feel then that Clem was there because he himself had placed him there for the men to find more easily.

Lonnie found himself moving forward, drawn into the narrowing circle. Presently he could see the men all around him in dim outline. Their eyes were searching the heavy green pine tops as they went forward from tree to tree.

"Oh, Pa!" he said in a hoarse whisper. "Oh, Pa!"

He went forward a few steps, looking into the bushes and up into the tree tops. When he saw the other men again, he realized that it was not Mark Newsome being sought. He did not know what had made him forget like that.

The creeping forward began to work into the movement of Lonnie's body. He found himself springing forward on his toes, and his body was leaning in that direction. It was like creeping up on a rabbit when you did not have a gun to hunt with.

He forgot again what he was doing there. The springing motion in his legs seemed to be growing stronger with each step. He bent forward so far he could almost touch the ground with his fingertips. He could not stop now. He was keeping up with the circle of men.

The fifteen men were drawing closer and closer together. The dawn had broken enough to show the time on the face of a watch. The sun was beginning to color the sky above.

Lonnie was far in advance of anyone else by then. He could not hold himself back. The strength in his legs was more than he could hold in check.

He had for so long been unable to buy shells for his gun that he had forgotten how much he liked to hunt.

The sound of the men's steady creeping had become a rhythm in his ears.

"Here's the bastard!" somebody shouted, and there was a concerted crashing through the dry underbrush. Lonnie dashed forward, reaching the tree almost as quickly as anyone else.

He could see everybody with guns raised, and far into the sky above the sharply outlined face of Clem Henry gleamed in the rising sun. His body was hugging the slender top of the pine.

Lonnie did not know who was the first to fire, but the rest of the men did not hesitate. There was a deafening roar as the shot guns and revolvers flared and smoked around the trunk of the tree.

He closed his eyes; he was afraid to look again at the face above. The firing continued without break. Clem hugged the tree with all his might, and then, with the far-away sound of splintering wood, the top of the tree and Clem came crashing through the lower limbs to the ground. The body, sprawling and torn, landed on the ground with a thud that stopped Lonnie's heart for a moment.

He turned, clutching for the support of a tree, as the firing began once more. The crumpled body was tossed time after time, like a sackful of kittens being killed with an automatic shotgun, as charges of lead were fired into it from all sides. A cloud of dust rose from the ground and drifted overhead with the choking odor of burned powder.

Lonnie did not remember how long the shooting lasted. He found himself running from tree to tree, clutching at the rough pine bark, stumbling wildly toward the cleared ground. The sky had turned from gray to red when he emerged in the open, and as he ran, falling over the hard clods in the plowed field, he tried to keep his eyes on the house ahead.

Once he fell and found it almost impossible to rise again to his feet. He struggled to his knees, facing the round red sun. The warmth gave him strength to rise to his feet, and he muttered unintelligibly to himself. He tried to say things he had never thought to say before.

When he got home, Hatty was waiting for him in the yard. She had heard the shots in the woods, and she had seen him stumbling over the hard clods in the field, and she had seen him kneeling there looking straight into the face of the sun. Hatty was trembling as she ran to Lonnie to find out what the matter was.

Once in his own yard, Lonnie turned and looked for a second over his shoulder. He saw the men climbing over the fence at Arch Gunnard's. Arch's wife was standing on the back porch, and she was speaking to them.

"Where's your pa, Lonnie?" Hatty said. "And what in the world was all that shooting in the woods for?" Lonnie stumbled forward until he had reached the front porch. He fell upon the steps.

"Lonnie, Lonnie!" Hatty was saying. "Wake up and tell me what in the world is the matter. I've never seen the like of all that's going on."

"Nothing," Lonnie said. "Nothing."

"Well, if there's nothing the matter, can't you go up to the big house and ask for a little piece of streak-of-lean? We aint got a thing to cook for breakfast. Your pa's going to be hungrier than ever after being up walking around all night."

"What?" Lonnie said, his voice rising to a shout as he jumped to his feet.

"Why, I only said go up to the big house and get a little piece of streak-of-lean, Lonnie. That's all I said."

He grabbed his wife about the shoulders.

"Meat?" he yelled, shaking her roughly.

"Yes," she said, pulling away from him in surprise. "Couldn't you go ask Arch Gunnard for a little bit of streak-of-lean?"

Lonnie slumped down again on the steps, his hands falling between his outspread legs and his chin falling on his chest.

"No," he said almost inaudibly. "No, I aint hungry."

67

Do You Like It Here?

BY JOHN O'HARA

THE door was open. The door had to be kept open during study period, so there was no knock, and Roberts was startled when a voice he knew and hated said, "Hey, Roberts. Wanted in Van Ness's office." The voice was Hughes'.

"What for?" said Roberts.

"Why don't you go and find out what for, Dopey?" said Hughes.

"Phooey on you," said Roberts.

"Phooey on *you*," said Hughes, and left.

Roberts got up from the desk. He took off his eye-shade and put on a tie and coat. He left the light burning.

Van Ness's office, which was *en suite* with his bedroom, was on the ground floor of the dormitory, and on the way down Roberts wondered what he had done. It got so after a while, after going to so many schools, that you recognized the difference between being "wanted in Somebody's office" and "Somebody wants to see you." If a master wanted to see you on some minor matter, it didn't always mean that you had to go to his office; but if it was serious, they always said, "You're wanted in Somebody's office." That meant Somebody would be in his office, waiting for you, waiting specially for you. Roberts didn't know why this difference existed, but it did, all right. Well, all he could think of was that he had been smoking in the shower room, but Van Ness never paid much attention to that. Everybody smoked in the shower room, and Van Ness never did anything about it unless he just happened to catch you.

For minor offenses Van Ness would speak to you when he made his rounds of the rooms during study period. He would walk slowly down the corridor, looking in at each room to see that the proper occupant, and no one else, was there; and when he had something to bawl you out about, something unimportant, he would consult a list he carried, and he would stop in and bawl you out about it and tell you what punishment went with it. That was another detail that made the summons to the office a little scary.

Roberts knocked on Van Ness's half-open door and a voice said, "Come in."

Van Ness was sitting at his typewriter, which was on a small desk beside the large desk. He was in a swivel chair and when he saw Roberts he swung around, putting himself behind the large desk, like a damn judge.

He had his pipe in his mouth and he seemed to look over the steel rims of his spectacles. The light caught his Phi Beta Kappa key, which momentarily gleamed as though it had diamonds in it.

"Hughes said you wanted me to report here," said Roberts.

"I did," said Van Ness. He took his pipe out of his mouth and began slowly to knock the bowl empty as he repeated, "I did." He finished emptying his pipe before he again spoke. He took a long time about it, and Roberts, from his years of experience, recognized that as torture tactics. They always made you wait to scare you. It was sort of like the third degree. The horrible damn thing was that it always did scare you a little, even when you were used to it.

Van Ness leaned back in his chair and stared through his glasses at Roberts. He cleared his throat. "You can sit down," he said.

"Yes, sir," said Roberts. He sat down and again Van Ness made him wait.

"Roberts, you've been here now how long—five weeks?"

"A little over. About six."

"About six weeks," said Van Ness. "Since the seventh of January. Six weeks. Strange. Strange. Six weeks, and I really don't know a thing about you. Not much, at any rate. Roberts, tell me a little about yourself."

"How do you mean, Mister?"

"How do I mean? Well—about your life, before you decided to honor us with your presence. Where you came from, what you did, why you went to so many schools, so on."

"Well, I don't know."

"Oh, now. Now, Roberts. Don't let your natural modesty overcome the autobiographical urge. Shut the door."

Roberts got up and closed the door.

"Good," said Van Ness. "Now, proceed with this—uh—dossier. Give me the—huh—huh—*lowdown* on Roberts, Humphrey, Second Form, McAllister Memorial Hall, et cetera."

Roberts, Humphrey, sat down and felt the knot of his tie. "Well, I don't know. I was born at West Point, New York. My father was a first lieutenant then and he's a major now. My father and mother and I lived in a lot of places because he was in the Army and they transferred him. Is that the kind of stuff you want, Mister?"

"Proceed, proceed. I'll tell you when I want you to—uh—halt." Van Ness seemed to think that was funny, that "halt."

"Well, I didn't go to a regular school till I was ten. My mother got a divorce from my father and I went to school in San Francisco. I only stayed there a year because my mother got married again and we moved to Chicago, Illinois."

"Chicago, Illinois! Well, a little geography thrown in, eh, Roberts? Gratuitously. Thank you. Proceed."

"Well, so then we stayed there about two years and then we moved back East, and my stepfather is a certified public accountant and we moved around a lot."

"Peripatetic, eh, Roberts?"

"I guess so. I don't exactly know what that means." Roberts paused. "Go on, go on."

"Well, so I just went to a lot of schools, some day and some boarding. All that's written down on my application blank here. I had to put it all down on account of my credits."

"Correct. A very imposing list it is, too, Roberts, a very imposing list. Ah, to travel as you have. Switzerland. How I've regretted not having gone to school in Switzerland. Did you like it there?"

"I was only there about three months. I liked it all right, I guess."

"And do you like it here, Roberts?"

"Sure."

"You do? You're sure of that? You wouldn't want to change anything?"

"Oh, I wouldn't say that, not about any school."

"Indeed," said Van Ness. "With your vast experience, naturally you would be quite an authority on matters educational. I suppose you have many theories as to the strength and weaknesses inherent in the modern educational systems."

"I don't know. I just—I don't know. Some schools are better than others. At least I like some better than others."

"Of course. Of course." Van Ness seemed to be thinking about something. He leaned back in his swivel chair and gazed at the ceiling. He put his hands in his pants pockets and then suddenly he leaned forward. The chair came down and Van Ness's belly was hard against the desk and his arm was stretched out on the desk, full length, fist closed.

"Roberts! Did you ever see this before? Answer me!" Van Ness's voice was hard. He opened his fist, and in it was a wristwatch.

Roberts looked down at the watch. "No, I don't think so," he said. He was glad to be able to say it truthfully.

Van Ness continued to hold out his hand, with the wristwatch lying in the palm. He held out his hand a long time, fifteen seconds at least, without saying anything. Then he turned his hand over and allowed the watch to slip onto the desk. He resumed his normal position in the chair. He picked up his pipe, slowly filled it, and lit it. He shook the match back and forth long after the flame had gone. He swung around a little in his chair and looked at the wall, away from Roberts. "As a boy I spent six years at this school. My brothers, my two brothers, went to this school. My *father* went to this school. I have a deep and abiding and lasting affection for this school. I have been a member of the faculty of this school for more than a decade. I like to think that I am part of this school, that in some small measure I have assisted in its progress. I like to think of it as more than a mere stepping-stone to higher education. At this very moment there are in this school the sons of men who were my classmates. I have not been without my opportunities to take a post at this and that college or university, but I choose to remain here. Why? Why? Because I love this place. I love this place, Roberts. I cherish its traditions. I cherish its good name." He paused, and turned to Roberts. "Roberts, there is no room here for a thief!"

Roberts did not speak.

"There is no room here for a thief, I said!"

"Yes, sir."

Van Ness picked up the watch without looking at it. He held it a few inches above the desk. "This miserable watch was stolen last Friday afternoon, more than likely during the basketball game. As soon as the theft was reported to me I immediately instituted a search for it. My search was unsuccessful. Sometime Monday afternoon the watch was put here, here in my rooms. When I returned here after classes Monday afternoon, this watch was lying on my desk. Why? Because the contemptible rat who stole it knew that I had instituted the search, and like the rat he is, he turned yellow and returned the watch to me. Whoever it is, he kept an entire dormitory under a loathsome suspicion. I say to you, I do not know who stole this watch or who returned it to my rooms. But by God, Roberts, I'm going to find out, if it's the last thing I do. If it's the last thing I do. That's all, Roberts. You may go." Van Ness sat back, almost breathless.

Roberts stood up. "I give you my word of honor, I—"

"I said you may go!" said Van Ness.

Roberts was not sure whether to leave the door open or to close it, but he did not ask. He left it open.

He went up the stairs to his room. He went in and took off his coat and tie, and sat on the bed. Over and over again, first violently, then weakly, he said it, "The bastard, the dirty bastard."

68

The Daring Young Man on the Flying Trapeze

BY WILLIAM SAROYAN

I. SLEEP

HORIZONTALLY wakeful amid universal widths, practicing laughter and mirth, satire, the end of all, of Rome and yes of Babylon, clenched teeth, remembrance, much warmth volcanic, the streets of Paris, the plains of Jericho, much gliding as of reptile in abstraction, a gallery of watercolors, the sea and the fish with eyes, symphony, a table in the corner of the Eiffel Tower, jazz at the opera house, alarm clock and the tap-dancing of doom, conversation with a tree, the river Nile, Cadillac coupé to Kansas, the roar of Dostoyevsky, and the dark sun.

This earth, the face of one who lived, the form without the weight, weeping upon snow, white music, the magnified flower twice the size of the universe, black clouds, the caged panther staring, deathless space, Mr. Eliot with rolled sleeves baking bread, Flaubert and Guy de Maupassant, a wordless rhyme of early meaning, Finlandia, mathematics highly polished and slick as a green onion to the teeth, Jerusalem, the path to paradox.

The deep song of man, the sly whisper of someone unseen but vaguely known, hurricane in the cornfield, a game of chess, hush the queen, the king, Karl Franz, black Titanic, Mr. Chaplin weeping, Stalin, Hitler, a multitude of Jews, tomorrow is Monday, no dancing in the streets.

O swift moment of life: it is ended, the earth is again now.

II. WAKEFULNESS

He (the living) dressed and shaved, grinning at himself in the mirror. Very unhandsome, he said; where is my tie? (He had but one.) Coffee and a gray sky, Pacific Ocean fog, the drone of a passing streetcar, people going to the city, time again, the day, prose and poetry. He moved swiftly down the stairs to the street and began to walk, thinking suddenly, *It is only in sleep that we may know that we live. There only, in that living death, do we meet ourselves and the far earth, God and the saints, the names of our fathers, the substance of remote moments; it is there that the centuries merge in the moment, that the vast becomes the tiny, tangible atom of eternity.*

He walked into the day as alertly as might be, making a definite noise with his heels, perceiving with his eyes the superficial truth of streets and structures, the trivial truth of reality. Helplessly his mind sang, *He flies through the air with the greatest of ease; the daring young man on the flying trapeze;* then laughed with all the might of his being. It was really a splendid morning: gray, cold, and cheerless, a morning for inward vigor; ah, Edgar Guest, he said, how I long for your music.

In the gutter he saw a coin which proved to be a penny dated 1923, and placing it in the palm of his hand he examined it closely, remembering that year and thinking of Lincoln whose profile was stamped upon the coin. There was almost nothing a man could do with a penny. I will purchase a motorcar, he thought. I will dress myself in the fashion of a fop, visit the hotel strumpets, drink and dine, and then return to the quiet. Or I will drop the coin into a slot and weigh myself.

It was good to be poor, and the Communists—but it was dreadful to be hungry. What appetites they had, how fond they were of food! Empty stomachs. He remembered how greatly he needed food. Every meal was bread and coffee and cigarettes, and now he had no more bread. Coffee without bread could never honestly serve as supper, and there were no weeds in the park that could be cooked as spinach is cooked.

If the truth were known, he was half starved, and yet there was still no end of books he ought to read before he died. He remembered the young Italian in a Brooklyn hospital, a small sick clerk named Mollica, who had said desperately, I would like to see California once before I die. And he thought earnestly, I ought at least to read Hamlet once again; or perhaps Huckleberry Finn.

It was then that he became thoroughly awake: at the thought of dying. Now wakefulness was a state in the nature of a sustained shock. A young man could perish rather unostentatiously, he thought; and already he was very nearly starved. Water and prose were fine, they filled much inorganic space, but they were inadequate. If there were only some

work he might do for money, some trivial labor in the name of commerce. If they would only allow him to sit at a desk all day and add
trade figures, subtract and multiply and divide, then perhaps he would
not die. He would buy food, all sorts of it: untasted delicacies from
Norway, Italy, and France; all manner of beef, lamb, fish, cheese; grapes,
figs, pears, apples, melons, which he would worship when he had satisfied his hunger. He would place a bunch of red grapes on a dish beside
two black figs, a large yellow pear, and a green apple. He would hold a
cut melon to his nostrils for hours. He would buy great brown loaves of
French bread, vegetables of all sorts, meat; he would buy life.

From a hill he saw the city standing majestically in the east, great
towers, dense with his kind, and there he was suddenly outside of it all,
almost definitely certain that he should never gain admittance, almost
positive that somehow he had ventured upon the wrong earth, or perhaps
into the wrong age, and now a young man of twenty-two was to be permanently ejected from it. This thought was not saddening. He said to
himself, sometime soon I must write *An Application For Permission To
Live*. He accepted the thought of dying without pity for himself or for
man, believing that he would at least sleep another night. His rent for
another day was paid; there was yet another tomorrow. And after that
he might go where other homeless men went. He might even visit the
Salvation Army—sing to God and Jesus (unlover of my soul), be saved,
eat and sleep. But he knew that he would not. His life was a private life.
He did not wish to destroy this fact. Any other alternative would be
better.

Through the air on the flying trapeze, his mind hummed. Amusing
it was, astoundingly funny. A trapeze to God, or to nothing, a flying
trapeze to some sort of eternity; he prayed objectively for the strength
to make the flight with grace.

I have one cent, he said. It is an American coin. In the evening I shall
polish it until it glows like a sun and I shall study the words.

He was now walking in the city itself, among living men. There were
one or two places to go. He saw his reflection in the plate-glass windows
of stores and was disappointed with his appearance. He seemed not at
all as strong as he felt; he seemed, in fact, a trifle infirm in every part of
his body, in his neck, his shoulders, arms, trunk, and knees. This will
never do, he said, and with an effort he assembled all his disjointed parts
and became tensely, artificially erect and solid.

He passed numerous restaurants with magnificent discipline, refusing
even to glance into them, and at last reached a building, which he entered. He rose in an elevator to the seventh floor, moved down a hall,
and, opening a door, walked into the office of an employment agency.
Already there were two dozen young men in the place; he found a

corner where he stood waiting his turn to be interviewed. At length he was granted this great privilege and was questioned by a thin, scatter-brained miss of fifty.

Now tell me, she said; what can you do?

He was embarrassed. I can write, he said pathetically.

You mean your penmanship is good? Is that it? said the elderly maiden.

Well, yes, he replied. But I mean that I can write.

Write what? said the miss, almost with anger.

Prose, he said simply.

There was a pause. At last the lady said:

Can you use a typewriter?

Of course, said the young man.

All right, went on the miss, we have your address; we will get in touch with you. There is nothing this morning, nothing at all.

It was much the same at the other agency, except that he was questioned by a conceited young man who closely resembled a pig. From the agencies he went to the large department stores: there was a good deal of pomposity, some humiliation on his part, and finally the report that work was not available. He did not feel displeased, and strangely did not even feel that he was personally involved in all the foolishness. He was a living young man who was in need of money with which to go on being one, and there was no way of getting it except by working for it; and there was no work. It was purely an abstract problem which he wished for the last time to attempt to solve. Now he was pleased that the matter was closed.

He began to perceive the definiteness of the course of his life. Except for moments, it had been largely artless, but now at the last minute he was determined that there should be as little imprecision as possible.

He passed countless stores and restaurants on his way to the Y. M. C. A., where he helped himself to paper and ink and began to compose his *Application*. For an hour he worked on this document, then suddenly, owing to the bad air in the place and to hunger, he became faint. He seemed to be swimming away from himself with great strokes, and hurriedly left the building. In the Civic Center Park, across from the Public Library Building, he drank almost a quart of water and felt himself refreshed. An old man was standing in the center of the brick boulevard surrounded by sea gulls, pigeons, and robins. He was taking handfuls of bread crumbs from a large paper sack and tossing them to the birds with a gallant gesture.

Dimly he felt impelled to ask the old man for a portion of the crumbs, but he did not allow the thought even nearly to reach consciousness; he entered the Public Library and for an hour read Proust, then, feeling himself to be swimming away again, he rushed outdoors. He drank more water at the fountain in the park and began the long walk to his room.

I'll go and sleep some more, he said; there is nothing else to do. He knew now that he was much too tired and weak to deceive himself about being all right, and yet his mind seemed somehow still lithe and alert. It, as if it were a separate entity, persisted in articulating impertinent pleasantries about his very real physical suffering. He reached his room early in the afternoon and immediately prepared coffee on the small gas range. There was no milk in the can and the half pound of sugar he had purchased a week before was all gone; he drank a cup of the hot black fluid, sitting on his bed and smiling.

From the Y. M. C. A. he had stolen a dozen sheets of letter paper upon which he hoped to complete his document, but now the very notion of writing was unpleasant to him. There was nothing to say. He began to polish the penny he had found in the morning, and this absurd act somehow afforded him great enjoyment. No American coin can be made to shine so brilliantly as a penny. How many pennies would he need to go on living? Wasn't there something more he might sell? He looked about the bare room. No. His watch was gone; also his books. All those fine books; nine of them for eighty-five cents. He felt ill and ashamed for having parted with his books. His best suit he had sold for two dollars, but that was all right. He didn't mind at all about clothes. But the books. That was different. It made him very angry to think that there was no respect for men who wrote.

He placed the shining penny on the table, looking upon it with the delight of a miser. How prettily it smiles, he said. Without reading them he looked at the words, *E Pluribus Unum One Cent United States Of America,* and turning the penny over, he saw Lincoln and the words, *In God We Trust Liberty 1923.* How beautiful it is, he said.

He became drowsy and felt a ghastly illness coming over his blood, a feeling of nausea and disintegration. Bewildered, he stood beside his bed, thinking that there *is nothing to do but sleep.* Already he felt himself making great strides through the fluid of the earth, swimming away to the beginning. He fell face down upon the bed, saying, I ought first at least to give the coin to some child. A child could buy any number of things with a penny.

Then swiftly, neatly, with the grace of the young man on the trapeze, he was gone from his body. For an eternal moment he was all things at once: the bird, the fish, the rodent, the reptile, and man. An ocean of print undulated endlessly and darkly before him. The city burned. The herded crowd rioted. The earth circled away, and knowing that he did so, he turned his lost face to the empty sky and became dreamless, unalive, perfect.

69

The Hitch-Hikers

BY EUDORA WELTY

TOM HARRIS, a thirty-year-old salesman traveling in office supplies, got out of Victory a little after noon and saw people in Midnight and Louise, but went on toward Memphis. It was a base, and he was thinking he would like to do something that night.

Toward evening, somewhere in the middle of the Delta, he slowed down to pick up two hitch-hikers. One of them stood still by the side of the pavement, with his foot stuck out like an old root, but the other was playing a yellow guitar which caught the late sun as it came in a long straight bar across the fields.

Harris would get sleepy driving. On the road he did some things rather out of a dream. And the recurring sight of hitch-hikers waiting against the sky gave him the flash of a sensation he had known as a child: standing still, with nothing to touch him, feeling tall and having the world come all at once into its round shape underfoot and rush and turn through space and make his stand very precarious and lonely. He opened the car door.

"How you do?"

"How you do?"

Harris spoke to hitch-hikers almost formally. Now resuming his speed, he moved over a little in the seat. There was no room in the back for anybody. The man with the guitar was riding with it between his legs. Harris reached over and flicked on the radio.

"Well, music!" said the man with the guitar. Presently he began to smile. "Well, we been there a whole day in that one spot," he said softly. "Seen the sun go clear over. Course, part of the time we laid down under that one tree and taken our ease."

They rode without talking while the sun went down in red clouds and the radio program changed a few times. Harris switched on his lights. Once the man with the guitar started to sing "The One Rose That's Left in My Heart," which came over the air, played by the Aloha Boys. Then in shyness he stopped, but made a streak on the radio dial with his blackly calloused finger tip.

"I 'preciate them big 'lectric gittars some have," he said.

"Where are you going?"

"Looks like north."

"It's north," said Harris. "Smoke?"

The other man held out his hand.

"Well . . . rarely," said the man with the guitar.

At the use of the unexpected word, Harris's cheek twitched, and he handed over his pack of cigarettes. All three lighted up. The silent man held his cigarette in front of him like a piece of money, between his thumb and forefinger. Harris realized that he wasn't smoking it, but was watching it burn.

"My! gittin' night agin," said the man with the guitar in a voice that could assume any social surprise.

"Anything to eat?" asked Harris.

The man gave a pluck to a low string and glanced at him.

"Dewberries," said the other man. It was his only remark, and it was delivered in a slow and pondering voice.

"Some nice little rabbit come skinnin' by," said the man with the guitar, nudging Harris with a slight punch in his side, "but it run off the way it come."

The other man was so bogged in inarticulate anger that Harris could imagine him running down a cotton row after the rabbit. He smiled but did not look around.

"Now to look out for a place to sleep—is that it?" he remarked doggedly.

A pluck of the strings again, and the man yawned.

There was a little town coming up; the lights showed for twenty miles in the flat land.

"Is that Dulcie?" Harris yawned too.

"I bet you ain't got no idea where all I've slep'," the man said, turning around in his seat and speaking directly to Harris, with laughter in his face that in the light of a road sign appeared strangely teasing.

"I could eat a hamburger," said Harris, swinging out of the road under the sign in some automatic gesture of evasion. He looked out of the window, and a girl in red pants leaped onto the running board.

"Three and three beers?" she asked, smiling, with her head poked in. "Hi," she said to Harris.

"How are you?" said Harris. "That's right."

"My," said the man with the guitar. "Red sailor-boy britches." Harris listened for the guitar note, but it did not come. "But not purty," he said.

The screen door of the joint whined, and a man's voice called, "Come on in, boys, we got girls."

Harris cut off the radio, and they listened to the nickelodeon which was playing inside the joint and turning the window blue, red and green in turn.

"Hi," said the car-hop again as she came out with the tray. "Looks like rain."

They ate the hamburgers rapidly, without talking. A girl came and looked out of the window of the joint, leaning on her hand. The same couple kept dancing by behind her. There was something brassy playing, a swing record of "Love, Oh Love, Oh Careless Love."

"Same songs ever'where," said the man with the guitar softly. "I come down from the hills. . . . We had us owls for chickens and fox for yard dogs but we sung true."

Nearly every time the man spoke Harris's cheek twitched. He was easily amused. Also, he recognized at once any sort of attempt to confide, and then its certain and hasty retreat. And the more anyone said, the further he was drawn into a willingness to listen. I'll hear him play his guitar yet, he thought. It had got to be a pattern in his days and nights, it was almost automatic, his listening, like the way his hand went to his pocket for money.

"That'n's most the same as a ballat," said the man, licking mustard off his finger. "My ma, she was the one for ballats. Little in the waist as a dirt-dauber, but her voice carried. Had her a whole lot of tunes. Long ago dead an' gone. Pa'd come home from the courthouse drunk as a wheelbarrow, and she'd just pick up an' go sit on the front step facin' the hill an' sing. Ever'thing she knowed, she'd sing. Dead an' gone, an' the house burned down." He gulped at his beer. His foot was patting.

"This," said Harris, touching one of the keys on the guitar. "Couldn't you stop somewhere along here and make money playing this?"

Of course it was by the guitar that he had known at once that they were not mere hitch-hikers. They were tramps. They were full blown, abandoned to this. Both of them were. But when he touched it he knew obscurely that it was the yellow guitar, that bold and gay burden in the tramp's arms, that had caused him to stop and pick them up.

The man hit it flat with the palm of his hand.

"This box? Just play it for myself."

Harris laughed delightedly, but somehow he had a desire to tease him, to make him swear to his freedom.

"You wouldn't stop and play somewhere like this? For them to dance? When you know all the songs?"

Now the fellow laughed out loud. He turned and spoke completely as if the other man could not hear him. "Well, but right now I got *him*."

"Him?" Harris stared ahead.

"He'd gripe. He don't like foolin' around. He wants to git on. You always git a partner got notions."

The other tramp belched. Harris laid his hand on the horn.

"Hurry back," said the car-hop, opening a heart-shaped pocket over her heart and dropping the tip courteously within.

"Aw river!" sang out the man with the guitar.

As they pulled out into the road again, the other man began to lift a beer bottle, and stared beseechingly, with his mouth full, at the man with the guitar.

"Drive back, mister. Sobby forgot to give her back her bottle. Drive back."

"Too late," said Harris rather firmly, speeding on into Dulcie, thinking, I was about to take directions from him.

Harris stopped the car in front of the Dulcie Hotel on the square.

" 'Preciated it," said the man, taking up his guitar.

"Wait here."

They stood on the walk, one lighted by the street light, the other in the shadow of the statue of the Confederate soldier, both caved in and giving out an odor of dust, both sighing with obedience.

Harris went across the yard and up the one step into the hotel.

Mr. Gene, the proprietor, a white-haired man with little dark freckles all over his face and hands, looked up and shoved out his arm at the same time.

"If he ain't back." He grinned. "Been about a month to the day—I was just remarking."

"Mr. Gene, I ought to go on, but I got two fellows out front. O.K., but they've just got nowhere to sleep tonight, and you know that little back porch."

"Why, it's a beautiful night out!" bellowed Mr. Gene, and he laughed silently.

"They'd get fleas in your bed," said Harris, showing the back of his hand. "But you know that old porch. It's not so bad. I slept out there once, I forget how."

The proprietor let his laugh out like a flood. Then he sobered abruptly.

"Sure. O.K.," he said. "Wait a minute—Mike's sick. Come here, Mike, it's just old Harris passin' through."

Mike was an ancient collie dog. He rose from a quilt near the door and moved over the square brown rug, stiffly, like a table walking, and shoved himself between the men, swinging his long head from Mr. Gene's hand to Harris's and bearing down motionless with his jaw in Harris's palm.

"You sick, Mike?" asked Harris.

"Dyin' of old age, that's what he's doin'!" blurted the proprietor as if in anger.

Harris began to stroke the dog, but the familiarity in his hands changed to slowness and hesitancy. Mike looked up out of his eyes.

"His spirit's gone. You see?" said Mr. Gene pleadingly.

"Say, look," said a voice at the front door.

"Come in, Cato, and see poor old Mike," said Mr. Gene.

"I knew that was your car, Mr. Harris," said the boy. He was nervously trying to tuck a Bing Crosby cretonne shirt into his pants like a real shirt. Then he looked up and said, "They was tryin' to take your car, and down the street one of 'em like to bust the other one's head wide op'm with a bottle. Looks like you would 'a' heard the commotion. Everybody's out there. I said, 'That's Mr. Tom Harris's car, look at the out-of-town license and look at all the stuff he all time carries around with him, all bloody.'"

"He's not dead though," said Harris, kneeling on the seat of his car.

It was the man with the guitar. The little ceiling light had been turned on. With blood streaming from his broken head, he was slumped down upon the guitar, his legs bowed around it, his arms at either side, his whole body limp in the posture of a bareback rider. Harris was aware of the other face not a yard away: the man the guitar player had called Sobby was standing on the curb, with two men unnecessarily holding him. He looked more like a bystander than any of the rest, except that he still held the beer bottle in his right hand.

"Looks like if he was fixin' to hit him, *he* would of hit *him* with that gittar," said a voice. "That'd be a real good thing to hit somebody with. Whang!"

"The way I figure this thing out is," said a penetrating voice, as if a woman were explaining it all to her husband, "the men was left to 'emselves. So—that 'n' yonder wanted to make off with the car—he's the bad one. So the good one says, 'Naw, that ain't right.'"

Or was it the other way around? thought Harris dreamily.

"So the other one says bam! bam! He whacked him over the head. And so dumb—right where the movie was letting out."

"Who's got my car keys!" Harris kept shouting. He had, without realizing it, kicked away the prop, the guitar; and he had stopped the blood with something.

Nobody had to tell him where the ramshackle little hospital was—

he had been there once before, on a Delta trip. With the constable scuttling along after and then riding on the running board, glasses held tenderly in one fist, the handcuffed Sobby dragged alongside by the other, with a long line of little boys in flowered shirts accompanying him on bicycles, riding in and out of the headlight beam, with the rain falling in front of him and with Mr. Gene shouting in a sort of plea from the hotel behind and Mike beginning to echo the barking of the rest of the dogs, Harris drove in all carefulness down the long tree-dark street, with his wet hand pressed on the horn.

The old doctor came down the walk and, joining them in the car, slowly took the guitar player by the shoulders.

"I 'spec' he gonna die though," said a colored child's voice mournfully. "Wonder who goin' to git his box?"

In a room on the second floor of the two-story hotel Harris put on clean clothes, while Mr. Gene lay on the bed with Mike across his stomach.

"Ruined that Christmas tie you came in." The proprietor was talking in short breaths. "It took it out of Mike, I'm tellin' you." He sighed. "First time he's barked since Bud Milton shot up that Chinese." He lifted his head and took a long swallow of the hotel whisky, and tears appeared in his warm brown eyes. "Suppose they'd done it on the porch."

The phone rang.

"See, everybody knows you're here," said Mr. Gene.

"Ruth?" he said, lifting the receiver, his voice almost contrite.

But it was for the proprietor.

When he had hung up he said, "That little peanut—he ain't ever goin' to learn which end is up. The constable. Got a nigger already in the jail, so he's runnin' round to find a place to put this fella of yours with the bottle, and damned if all he can think of ain't the hotel!"

"Hell, is he going to spend the night with me?"

"Well, the same thing. Across the hall. The other fella may die. Only place in town with a key but the bank, he says."

"What time is it?" asked Harris all at once.

"Oh, it ain't *late*," said Mr. Gene.

He opened the door for Mike, and the two men followed the dog slowly down the stairs. The light was out on the landing. Harris looked out of the old half-open stained-glass window.

"Is that rain?"

"It's been rainin' since dark, but you don't ever know a thing like that —it's proverbial." At the desk he held up a brown package. "Here. I sent Cato after some Memphis whisky for you. He had to do something."

"Thanks."

"I'll see you. I don't guess you're goin' to get away very shortly in the mornin'. I'm real sorry they did it in your car if they were goin' to do it."

"That's all right," said Harris. "You'd better have a little of this."

"That? It'd kill me," said Mr. Gene.

In a drugstore Harris phoned Ruth, a woman he knew in town, and found her at home having a party.

"Tom Harris! Sent by heaven!" she cried. "I was wondering what I'd do about Carol—this *baby!*"

"What's the matter with her?"

"No date."

Some other people wanted to say hello from the party. He listened awhile and said he'd be out.

This had postponed the call to the hospital. He put in another nickel. ... There was nothing new about the guitar player.

"Like I told you," the doctor said, "we don't have the facilities for giving transfusions, and he's been moved plenty without you taking him to Memphis."

Walking over to the party, so as not to use his car, making the only sounds in the dark wet street, and only partly aware of the indeterminate shapes of houses with their soft-shining fanlights marking them off, there with the rain falling mist-like through the trees, he almost forgot what town he was in and which house he was bound for.

Ruth, in a long dark dress, leaned against an open door, laughing. From inside came the sounds of at least two people playing a duet on the piano.

"He would come like this and get all wet!" she cried over her shoulder into the room. She was leaning back on her hands. "What's the matter with your little blue car? I hope you brought us a present."

He went in with her and began shaking hands, and set the bottle wrapped in the paper sack on a table.

"He never forgets!" cried Ruth.

"Drinkin' whisky!" Everybody was noisy again.

"So this is the famous 'he' that everybody talks about all the time," pouted a girl in a white dress. "Is he one of your cousins, Ruth?"

"No kin of mine, he's nothing but a vagabond," said Ruth, and led Harris off to the kitchen by the hand.

I wish they'd call me "you" when I've got here, he thought tiredly.

"More has gone on than a little bit," she said, and told him the news while he poured fresh drinks into the glasses. When she accused him of nothing, of no carelessness or disregard of her feelings, he was fairly sure she had not heard about the assault in his car.

She was looking at him closely. "Where did you get that sunburn?"
"Well, I had to go to the Coast last week," he said.
"What did you do?"
"Same old thing." He laughed; he had started to tell her about something funny in Bay St. Louis, where an eloping couple had flagged him down in the residential section and threatened to break up if he would not carry them to the next town. Then he remembered how Ruth looked when he mentioned other places where he stopped on trips.

Somewhere in the house the phone rang and rang, and he caught himself jumping. Nobody was answering it.

"I thought you'd quit drinking," she said, picking up the bottle.

"I start and quit," he said, taking it from her and pouring his drink. "Where's my date?"

"Oh, she's in Leland," said Ruth.

They all drove over in two cars to get her.

She was a slight little thing, with her nightgown in some sort of little bag. She came out when they blew the horn, before he could go in after her. . . .

"Let's go holler off the bridge," said somebody in the car ahead.

They drove over a little gravel road, miles through the misty fields, and came to the bridge out in the middle of nowhere.

"Let's dance," said one of the boys. He grabbed Carol around the waist, and they began to tango over the boards.

"Did you miss me?" asked Ruth. She stayed by him, standing in the road.

"Woo-hoo!" they cried.

"I wish I knew what makes it holler back," said one girl. "There's nothing anywhere. Some of my kinfolks can't even hear it."

"Yes, it's funny," said Harris, with a cigarette in his mouth.

"Some people say it's an old steamboat got lost once."

"Might be."

They drove around and waited to see if it would stop raining.

Back in the lighted rooms at Ruth's he saw Carol, his date, give him a strange little glance. At the moment he was serving her with a drink from the tray.

"Are you the one everybody's 'miratin' and gyratin' over?" she said, before she would put her hand out.

"Yes," he said, "I come from afar." He placed the strongest drink from the tray in her hand, with a little flourish.

"Hurry back!" called Ruth.

In the pantry Ruth came over and stood by him while he set more glasses on the tray and then followed him out to the kitchen. Was she at all curious about him? he wondered. For a moment, when they were simply close together, her lips parted, and she stared off at nothing; her jealousy seemed to let her go free. The rainy wind from the back porch stirred her hair.

As if under some illusion, he set the tray down and told her about the two hitch-hikers.

Her eyes flashed.

"What a—stupid thing!" Furiously she seized the tray when he reached for it.

The phone was ringing again. Ruth glared at him.

It was as though he had made a previous engagement with the hitch-hikers.

Everybody was meeting them at the kitchen door.

"Aha!" cried one of the men, Jackson. "He tries to put one over on you, girls. Somebody just called up, Ruth, about the murder in Tom's car."

"Did he die?" asked Harris, without moving.

"I knew all about it!" cried Ruth, her cheeks flaming. "He told me all about it. It practically ruined his car. Didn't it!"

"Wouldn't he get into something crazy like that?"

"It's because he's an angel," said the girl named Carol, his date, speaking in a hollow voice from her highball glass.

"Who phoned?" asked Harris.

"Old Mrs. Daggett, that old lady about a million years old that's always calling up. She was right there."

Harris phoned the doctor's home and woke the doctor's wife. The guitar player was still the same.

"This is so exciting, tell us all," said a fat boy. Harris knew he lived fifty miles up the river and had driven down under the impression that there would be a bridge game.

"It was just a fight."

"Oh, he wouldn't tell you, he never talks. I'll tell you," said Ruth. "Get your drinks, for goodness' sake."

So the incident became a story. Harris grew very tired of it.

"It's marvelous the way he always gets in with somebody and then something happens," said Ruth, her eyes completely black.

"Oh, he's my hero," said Carol, and she went out and stood on the back porch.

"Maybe you'll still be here tomorrow," Ruth said to Harris, taking his arm. "Will you be detained, maybe?"

"If he dies," said Harris.

He told them all good-bye.

"Let's all go to Greenville and get a Coke," said Ruth.

"No," he said. "Good night."

"'Aw river,'" said the girl in the white dress. "Isn't that what the little man said?"

"Yes," said Harris, the rain falling on him, and he refused to spend the night or to be taken in a car back to the hotel.

In the antlered lobby, Mr. Gene bent over asleep under a lamp by the desk phone. His freckles seemed to come out darker when he was asleep.

Harris woke him. "Go to bed," he said. "What was the idea? Anything happened?"

"I just wanted to tell you that little buzzard's up in 202. Locked and double-locked, handcuffed to the bed, but I wanted to tell you."

"Oh. Much obliged."

"All a gentleman could do," said Mr. Gene. He was drunk. "Warn you what's sleepin' under your roof."

"Thanks," said Harris. "It's almost morning. Look."

"Poor Mike can't sleep," said Mr. Gene. "He scrapes somethin' when he breathes. Did the other fella poop out?"

"Still unconscious. No change," said Harris. He took the bunch of keys which the proprietor was handing him.

"You keep 'em," said Mr. Gene.

In the next moment Harris saw his hand tremble and he took hold of it.

"A murderer!" whispered Mr. Gene. All his freckles stood out. "Here he came . . . with not a word to say . . ."

"Not a murderer yet," said Harris, starting to grin.

When he passed 202 and heard no sound, he remembered what old Sobby had said, standing handcuffed in front of the hospital, with nobody listening to him. "I was jist tired of him always uppin' an' makin' a noise about ever'thing."

In his room, Harris lay down on the bed without undressing or turning out the light. He was too tired to sleep. Half blinded by the unshaded bulb he stared at the bare plaster walls and the equally white surface of the mirror above the empty dresser. Presently he got up and turned on the ceiling fan, to create some motion and sound in the room. It was a defective fan which clicked with each revolution, on and on. He lay perfectly still beneath it, with his clothes on, unconsciously breathing in a rhythm related to the beat of the fan.

He shut his eyes suddenly. When they were closed, in the red darkness he felt all patience leave him. It was like the beginning of desire. He remembered the girl dropping money into her heart-shaped pocket, and remembered a disturbing possessiveness, which meant nothing, Ruth leaning on her hands. He knew he would not be held by any of it. It was for relief, almost, that his thoughts turned to pity, to wonder about the two tramps, their conflict, the sudden brutality when his back was turned. How would it turn out? It was in this suspense that it was more acceptable to him to feel the helplessness of his life.

He could forgive nothing in this evening. But it was too like other evenings, this town was too like other towns, for him to move out of this lying still clothed on the bed, even into comfort or despair. Even the rain —there was often rain, there was often a party, and there had been other violence not of his doing—other fights, not quite so pointless, but fights in his car; fights, unheralded confessions, sudden love-making—none of any of this his, not his to keep, but belonging to the people of these towns he passed through, coming out of their rooted pasts and their mock rambles, coming out of their time. He himself had no time. He was free; helpless. We wished he knew how the guitar player was, if he was still unconscious, if he felt pain.

He sat up on the bed and then got up and walked to the window.

"Tom!" said a voice outside in the dark.

Automatically he answered and listened. It was a girl. He could not see her, but she must have been standing on the little plot of grass that ran around the side of the hotel. Wet feet, pneumonia, he thought. And he was so tired he thought of a girl from the wrong town.

He went down and unlocked the door. She ran in as far as the middle of the lobby as though from impetus. It was Carol, from the party.

"You're wet," he said. He touched her.

"Always raining." She looked up at him, stepping back. "How are you?"

"O.K., fine," he said.

"I was wondering," she said nervously. "I knew the light would be you. I hope I didn't wake up anybody." Was old Sobby asleep? he wondered.

"Would you like a drink? Or do you want to go to the All-Nite and get a Coca-Cola?" he said.

"It's open," she said, making a gesture with her hand. "The All-Nite's open—I just passed it."

They went out into the mist, and she put his coat on with silent protest, in the dark street not drunken but womanly.

"You didn't remember me at the party," she said, and did not look up when he made his exclamation. "They say you never forget anybody, so I found out they were wrong about that anyway."

"They're often wrong," he said, and then hurriedly, "Who are you?"

"We used to stay at the Manning Hotel on the Coast every summer—

I wasn't grown. Carol Thames. Just dances and all, but you had just started to travel then, it was on your trips, and you—you talked at intermission."

He laughed shortly, but she added:

"You talked about yourself."

They walked past the tall wet church, and their steps echoed.

"Oh, it wasn't so long ago—five years," she said. Under a magnolia tree she put her hand out and stopped him, looking up at him with her child's face. "But when I saw you again tonight I wanted to know how you were getting along."

He said nothing, and she went on.

"You used to play the piano."

They passed under a street light, and she glanced up as if to look for the little tic in his cheek.

"Out on the big porch where they danced," she said, walking on. "Paper lanterns . . ."

"I'd forgotten that, is one thing sure," he said. "Maybe you've got the wrong man. I've got cousins galore who all play the piano."

"You'd put your hands down on the keyboard like you'd say, 'Now this is how it really is!' " she cried, and turned her head away. "I guess I was crazy about you, though."

"Crazy about me then?" He struck a match and held a cigarette between his teeth.

"No—yes, and now too!" she cried sharply, as if driven to deny him.

They came to the little depot where a restless switch engine was hissing, and crossed the black street. The past and present joined like this, he thought, it never happened often to me, and it probably won't happen again. He took her arm and led her through the dirty screen door of the All-Nite.

He waited at the counter while she sat down by the wall table and wiped her face all over with her handkerchief. He carried the black coffees over to the table himself, smiling at her from a little distance. They sat under a calendar with some picture of giant trees being cut down.

They said little. A fly bothered her. When the coffee was all gone he put her into the old Cadillac taxi that always stood in front of the depot.

Before he shut the taxi door he said, frowning, "I appreciate it. . . . You're sweet."

Now she had torn her handkerchief. She held it up and began to cry. "What's sweet about me?" It was the look of bewilderment in her face that he would remember.

"To come out, like this—in the rain—to be here. . . ." He shut the door, partly from weariness.

She was holding her breath. "I hope your friend doesn't die," she said. "All I hope is your friend gets well."

But when he woke up the next morning and phoned the hospital, the guitar player was dead. He had been dying while Harris was sitting in the All-Nite.

"It *was* a murderer," said Mr. Gene, pulling Mike's ears. "That was just plain murder. No way anybody could call that an affair of honor."

The man called Sobby did not oppose an invitation to confess. He stood erect and turning his head about a little, and almost smiled at all the men who had come to see him. After one look at him Mr. Gene, who had come with Harris, went out and slammed the door behind him.

All the same, Sobby had found little in the night, asleep or awake, to say about it. "I done it, sure," he said. "Didn't ever'body see me, or was they blind?"

They asked him about the man he had killed.

"Name Sanford," he said, standing still, with his foot out, as if he were trying to recall something particular and minute. "But he didn't have nothing and he didn't have no folks. No more'n me. Him and me, we took up together two weeks back." He looked up at their faces as if for support. "He was uppity, though. He bragged. He carried a gittar around." He whimpered. "It was his notion to run off with the car."

Harris, fresh from the barbershop, was standing in the filling station where his car was being polished.

A ring of little boys in bright shirt-tails surrounded him and the car, with some colored boys waiting behind them.

"Could they git all the blood off the seat and the steerin' wheel, Mr. Harris?"

He nodded. They ran away.

"Mr. Harris," said a little colored boy who stayed. "Does you want the box?"

"The what?"

He pointed, to where it lay in the back seat with the sample cases. "The po' kilt man's gittar. Even the policemans didn't want it."

"No," said Harris, and handed it over.

70

The Portable Phonograph

BY WALTER VAN TILBURG CLARK

THE red sunset, with narrow, black cloud strips like threats across it, lay on the curved horizon of the prairie. The air was still and cold, and in it settled the mute darkness and greater cold of night. High in the air there was wind, for through the veil of the dusk the clouds could be seen gliding rapidly south and changing shapes. A sensation of torment, of two-sided, unpredictable nature, arose from the stillness of the earth air beneath the violence of the upper air. Out of the sunset, through the dead, matted grass and isolated weed stalks of the prairie, crept the narrow and deeply rutted remains of a road. In the road, in places, there were crusts of shallow, brittle ice. There were little islands of an old oiled pavement in the road too, but most of it was mud, now frozen rigid. The frozen mud still bore the toothed impress of great tanks, and a wanderer on the neighboring undulations might have stumbled, in this light, into large, partially filled-in and weed-grown cavities, their banks channeled and beginning to spread into badlands. These pits were such as might have been made by falling meteors, but they were not. They were the scars of gigantic bombs, their rawness already made a little natural by rain, seed and time. Along the road there were rakish remnants of fence. There was also, just visible, one portion of tangled and multiple barbed wire still erect, behind which was a shelving ditch with small caves, now very quiet and empty, at intervals in its back wall. Otherwise there was no structure or remnant of a structure visible over the dome of the darkling earth, but only, in sheltered hollows, the darker shadows of young trees trying again.

Under the wuthering arch of the high wind a V of wild geese fled south. The rush of their pinions sounded briefly, and the faint, plaintive notes of their expeditionary talk. Then they left a still greater vacancy.

There was the smell and expectation of snow, as there is likely to be when the wild geese fly south. From the remote distance, toward the red sky, came faintly the protracted howl and quick yap-yap of a prairie wolf.

North of the road, perhaps a hundred yards, lay the parallel and deeply intrenched course of a small creek, lined with leafless alders and willows. The creek was already silent under ice. Into the bank above it was dug a sort of cell, with a single opening, like the mouth of a mine tunnel. Within the cell there was a little red of fire, which showed dully through the opening, like a reflection or a deception of the imagination. The light came from the chary burning of four blocks of poorly aged peat, which gave off a petty warmth and much acrid smoke. But the precious remnants of wood, old fence posts and timbers from the long-deserted dugouts, had to be saved for the real cold, for the time when a man's breath blew white, the moisture in his nostrils stiffened at once when he stepped out, and the expansive blizzards paraded for days over the vast open, swirling and settling and thickening, till the dawn of the cleared day when the sky was a thin blue-green and the terrible cold, in which a man could not live for three hours unwarmed, lay over the uniformly drifted swell of the plain.

Around the smoldering peat four men were seated cross-legged. Behind them, traversed by their shadows, was the earth bench, with two old and dirty army blankets, where the owner of the cell slept. In a niche in the opposite wall were a few tin utensils which caught the glint of the coals. The host was rewrapping in a piece of daubed burlap, four fine, leather-bound books. He worked slowly and very carefully, and at last tied the bundle securely with a piece of grass-woven cord. The other three looked intently upon the process, as if a great significance lay in it. As the host tied the cord, he spoke. He was an old man, his long, matted beard and hair gray to nearly white. The shadows made his brows and cheekbones appear gnarled, his eyes and cheeks deeply sunken. His big hands, rough with frost and swollen by rheumatism, were awkward but gentle at their task. He was like a prehistoric priest performing a fateful ceremonial rite. Also his voice had in it a suitable quality of deep, reverent despair, yet perhaps, at the moment, a sharpness of selfish satisfaction.

"When I perceived what was happening," he said, "I told myself, 'It is the end. I cannot take much; I will take these.'

"Perhaps I was impractical," he continued. "But for myself, I do not regret, and what do we know of those who will come after us? We are the doddering remnant of a race of mechanical fools. I have saved what I love; the soul of what was good in us here; perhaps the new ones will make a strong enough beginning not to fall behind when they become clever."

He rose with slow pain and placed the wrapped volumes in the niche with his utensils. The others watched him with the same ritualistic gaze.

"Shakespeare, the Bible, *Moby Dick, The Divine Comedy,*" one of them said softly. "You might have done worse; much worse."

"You will have a little soul left until you die," said another harshly. "That is more than is true of us. My brain becomes thick, like my hands." He held the big, battered hands, with their black nails, in the glow to be seen.

"I want paper to write on," he said. "And there is none."

The fourth man said nothing. He sat in the shadow farthest from the fire, and sometimes his body jerked in its rags from the cold. Although he was still young, he was sick, and coughed often. Writing implied a greater future than he now felt able to consider.

The old man seated himself laboriously, and reached out, groaning at the movement, to put another block of peat on the fire. With bowed heads and averted eyes, his three guests acknowledged his magnanimity.

"We thank you, Doctor Jenkins, for the reading," said the man who had named the books.

They seemed then to be waiting for something. Doctor Jenkins understood, but was loath to comply. In an ordinary moment he would have said nothing. But the words of *The Tempest,* which he had been reading, and the religious attention of the three, made this an unusual occasion.

"You wish to hear the phonograph," he said grudgingly.

The two middle-aged men stared into the fire, unable to formulate and expose the enormity of their desire.

The young man, however, said anxiously, between suppressed coughs, "Oh, please," like an excited child.

The old man rose again in his difficult way, and went to the back of the cell. He returned and placed tenderly upon the packed floor, where the firelight might fall upon it, an old, portable phonograph in a black case. He smoothed the top with his hand, and then opened it. The lovely green-felt-covered disk became visible.

"I have been using thorns as needles," he said. "But tonight, because we have a musician among us"—he bent his head to the young man, almost invisible in the shadow—"I will use a steel needle. There are only three left."

The two middle-aged men stared at him in speechless adoration. The one with the big hands, who wanted to write, moved his lips, but the whisper was not audible.

"Oh, don't," cried the young man, as if he were hurt. "The thorns will do beautifully."

"No," the old man said. "I have become accustomed to the thorns, but they are not really good. For you, my young friend, we will have good music tonight.

"After all," he added generously, and beginning to wind the phonograph, which creaked, "they can't last forever."

"No, nor we," the man who needed to write said harshly. "The needle, by all means."

"Oh, thanks," said the young man. "Thanks," he said again, in a low, excited voice, and then stifled his coughing with a bowed head.

"The records, though," said the old man when he had finished winding, "are a different matter. Already they are very worn. I do not play them more than once a week. One, once a week, that is what I allow myself.

"More than a week I cannot stand it; not to hear them," he apologized.

"No, how could you?" cried the young man. "And with them here like this."

"A man can stand anything," said the man who wanted to write, in his harsh, antagonistic voice.

"Please, the music," said the young man.

"Only the one," said the old man. "In the long run we will remember more that way."

He had a dozen records with luxuriant gold and red seals. Even in that light the others could see that the threads of the records were becoming worn. Slowly he read out the titles, and the tremendous, dead names of the composers and the artists and the orchestras. The three worked upon the names in their minds, carefully. It was difficult to select from such a wealth what they would at once most like to remember. Finally the man who wanted to write named Gershwin's "New York."

"Oh, no," cried the sick young man, and then could say nothing more because he had to cough. The others understood him, and the harsh man withdrew his selection and waited for the musician to choose.

The musician begged Doctor Jenkins to read the titles again, very slowly, so that he could remember the sounds. While they were read, he lay back against the wall, his eyes closed, his thin, horny hand pulling at his light beard, and listened to the voices and the orchestras and the single instruments in his mind.

When the reading was done he spoke despairingly. "I have forgotten," he complained. "I cannot hear them clearly.

"There are things missing," he explained.

"I know," said Doctor Jenkins. "I thought that I knew all of Shelley by heart. I should have brought Shelley."

"That's more soul than we can use," said the harsh man. "*Moby Dick* is better.

"By God, we can understand that," he emphasized.

The doctor nodded.

"Still," said the man who had admired the books, "we need the absolute if we are to keep a grasp on anything.

"Anything but these sticks and peat clods and rabbit snares," he said bitterly.

"Shelley desired an ultimate absolute," said the harsh man. "It's too much," he said. "It's no good; no earthly good."

The musician selected a Debussy nocturne. The others considered and approved. They rose to their knees to watch the doctor prepare for the playing, so that they appeared to be actually in an attitude of worship. The peat glow showed the thinness of their bearded faces, and the deep lines in them, and revealed the condition of their garments. The other two continued to kneel as the old man carefully lowered the needle onto the spinning disk, but the musician suddenly drew back against the wall again, with his knees up, and buried his face in his hands.

At the first notes of the piano the listeners were startled. They stared at each other. Even the musician lifted his head in amazement, but then quickly bowed it again, strainingly, as if he were suffering from a pain he might not be able to endure. They were all listening deeply, without movement. The wet, blue-green notes tinkled forth from the old machine, and were individual, delectable presences in the cell. The individual, delectable presences swept into a sudden tide of unbearably beautiful dissonance, and then continued fully the swelling and ebbing of that tide, the dissonant inpourings, and the resolutions, and the diminishments, and the little, quiet wavelets of interlude lapping between. Every sound was piercing and singularly sweet. In all the men except the musician, there occurred rapid sequences of tragically heightened recollection. He heard nothing but what was there. At the final, whispering disappearance, but moving quietly, so that the others would not hear him and look at him, he let his head fall back in agony, as if it were drawn there by the hair, and clenched the fingers of one hand over his teeth. He sat that way while the others were silent, and until they began to breathe again normally. His drawn-up legs were trembling violently.

Quickly Doctor Jenkins lifted the needle off, to save it, and not to spoil the recollection with scraping. When he had stopped the whirling of the sacred disk, he courteously left the phonograph open and by the fire, in sight.

The others, however, understood. The musician rose last, but then abruptly, and went quickly out at the door without saying anything. The others stopped at the door and gave their thanks in low voices. The doctor nodded magnificently.

"Come again," he invited, "in a week. We will have the 'New York.'"

When the two had gone together, out toward the rimmed road, he stood in the entrance, peering and listening. At first there was only the resonant boom of the wind overhead, and then, far over the dome of the dead, dark plain, the wolf cry lamenting. In the rifts of clouds the doctor saw four stars flying. It impressed the doctor that one of them had just been obscured by the beginning of a flying cloud at the very moment he heard what he had been listening for, a sound of suppressed coughing. It was not near by, however. He believed that down against the pale alders he could see the moving shadow.

With nervous hands he lowered the piece of canvas which served as his door, and pegged it at the bottom. Then quickly and quietly, looking at the piece of canvas frequently, he slipped the records into the case, snapped the lid shut, and carried the phonograph to his couch. There, pausing often to stare at the canvas and listen, he dug earth from the wall and disclosed a piece of board. Behind this there was a deep hole in the wall, into which he put the phonograph. After a moment's consideration, he went over and reached down his bundle of books and inserted it also. Then, guardedly, he once more sealed up the hole with the board and the earth. He also changed his blankets, and the grass-stuffed sack which served as a pillow, so that he could lie facing the entrance. After carefully placing two more blocks of peat on the fire, he stood for a long time watching the stretched canvas, but it seemed to billow naturally with the first gusts of a lowering wind. At last he prayed, and got in under his blankets, and closed his smoke-smarting eyes. On the inside of the bed, next the wall, he could feel with his hand, the comfortable piece of lead pipe.

71

Act of Faith

BY IRWIN SHAW

PRESENT it in a pitiful light,"
Olson was saying, as they picked their way through the mud toward
the orderly room tent. "Three combat-scarred veterans, who fought
their way from Omaha Beach to—what was the name of the town we
fought our way to?"

"Konigstein," Seeger said.

"Konigstein." Olson lifted his right foot heavily out of a puddle and
stared admiringly at the three pounds of mud clinging to his overshoe.
"The backbone of the army. The noncommissioned officer. We deserve
better of our country. Mention our decorations in passing."

"What decorations should I mention?" Seeger asked. "The marks-
man's medal?"

"Never quite made it," Olson said. "I had a cross-eyed scorer at the
butts. Mention the bronze star, the silver star, the Croix de Guerre, with
palms, the unit citation, the Congressional Medal of Honor."

"I'll mention them all." Seeger grinned. "You don't think the CO'll
notice that we haven't won most of them, do you?"

"Gad, sir," Olson said with dignity, "do you think that one Southern
military gentleman will dare doubt the word of another Southern military gentleman in the hour of victory?"

"I come from Ohio," Seeger said.

"Welch comes from Kansas," Olsen said, coolly staring down a
second lieutenant who was passing. The lieutenant made a nervous little
jerk with his hand as though he expected a salute, then kept it rigid, as a
slight superior smile of scorn twisted at the corner of Olson's mouth.
The lieutenant dropped his eyes and splashed on through the mud.
"You've heard of Kansas," Olson said. "Magnolia-scented Kansas."

"Of course," said Seeger. "I'm no fool."

"Do your duty by your men, Sergeant." Olson stopped to wipe the rain off his face and lectured him. "Highest ranking noncom present took the initiative and saved his comrades, at great personal risk, above and beyond the call of you-know-what, in the best traditions of the American army."

"I will throw myself in the breach," Seeger said.

"Welch and I can't ask more," said Olson, approvingly.

They walked heavily through the mud on the streets between the rows of tents. The camp stretched drearily over the Rheims plain, with the rain beating on the sagging tents. The division had been there over three weeks by now, waiting to be shipped home, and all the meager diversions of the neighborhood had been sampled and exhausted, and there was an air of watchful suspicion and impatience with the military life hanging over the camp now, and there was even reputed to be a staff sergeant in C Company who was laying odds they would not get back to America before July Fourth.

"I'm redeployable," Olson sang. "It's so enjoyable . . ." It was a jingle he had composed to no recognizable melody in the early days after the victory in Europe, when he had added up his points and found they only came to 63. "Tokyo, wait for me . . ."

They were going to be discharged as soon as they got back to the States, but Olson persisted in singing the song, occasionally adding a mournful stanza about dengue fever and brown girls with venereal disease. He was a short, round boy who had been flunked out of air cadets' school and transferred to the infantry, but whose spirits had not been damaged in the process. He had a high, childish voice and a pretty baby face. He was very good-natured, and had a girl waiting for him at the University of California, where he intended to finish his course at government expense when he got out of the army, and he was just the type who is killed off early and predictably and sadly in motion pictures about the war, but he had gone through four campaigns and six major battles without a scratch.

Seeger was a large, lanky boy, with a big nose, who had been wounded at Saint Lô, but had come back to his outfit in the Siegfried Line, quite unchanged. He was cheerful and dependable, and he knew his business and had broken in five or six second lieutenants who had been killed or wounded and the CO had tried to get him commissioned in the field, but the war had ended while the paperwork was being fumbled over at headquarters.

"They reached the door of the orderly tent and stopped. "Be brave, Sergeant," Olson said. "Welch and I are depending on you."

"O.K.," Seeger said, and went in.

The tent had the dank, army-canvas smell that had been so much a part of Seeger's life in the past three years. The company clerk was reading a July, 1945, issue of the *Buffalo Courier-Express*, which had just reached him, and Captain Taney, the company CO, was seated at a sawbuck table he used as a desk, writing a letter to his wife, his lips pursed with effort. He was a small, fussy man, with sandy hair that was falling out. While the fighting had been going on, he had been lean and tense and his small voice had been cold and full of authority. But now he had relaxed, and a little pot belly was creeping up under his belt and he kept the top button of his trousers open when he could do it without too public loss of dignity. During the war Seeger had thought of him as a natural soldier, tireless, fanatic about detail, aggressive, severely anxious to kill Germans. But in the past few months Seeger had seen him relapsing gradually and pleasantly into a small-town wholesale hardware merchant, which he had been before the war, sedentary and a little shy, and, as he had once told Seeger, worried, here in the bleak champagne fields of France, about his daughter, who had just turned twelve and had a tendency to go after the boys and had been caught by her mother kissing a fifteen-year-old neighbor in the hammock after school.

"Hello, Seeger," he said, returning the salute in a mild, offhand gesture. "What's on your mind?"

"Am I disturbing you, sir?"

"Oh, no. Just writing a letter to my wife. You married, Seeger?" He peered at the tall boy standing before him.

"No, sir."

"It's very difficult," Taney sighed, pushing dissatisfiedly at the letter before him. "My wife complains I don't tell her I love her often enough. Been married fifteen years. You'd think she'd know by now." He smiled at Seeger. "I thought you were going to Paris," he said. "I signed the passes yesterday."

"That's what I came to see you about, sir."

"I suppose something's wrong with the passes." Taney spoke resignedly, like a man who has never quite got the hang of army regulations and has had requisitions, furloughs, requests for court-martial returned for correction in a baffling flood.

"No, sir," Seeger said. "The passes're fine. They start tomorrow. Well, it's just . . ." He looked around at the company clerk, who was on the sports page.

"This confidential?" Taney asked.

"If you don't mind, sir."

"Johnny," Taney said to the clerk, "go stand in the rain some place."

"Yes, sir," the clerk said, and slowly got up and walked out.

Taney looked shrewdly at Seeger, spoke in a secret whisper. "You pick up anything?" he asked.

Seeger grinned. "No, sir, haven't had my hands on a girl since Strasbourg."

"Ah, that's good." Taney leaned back, relieved, happy he didn't have to cope with the disapproval of the Medical Corps.

"It's—well," said Seeger, embarrassed, "it's hard to say—but it's money."

Taney shook his head sadly. "I know."

"We haven't been paid for three months, sir, and . . ."

"Damn it!" Taney stood up and shouted furiously. "I would like to take every bloody chair-warming old lady in the Finance Department and wring their necks."

The clerk stuck his head into the tent. "Anything wrong? You call for me, sir?"

"No," Taney shouted. "Get out of here."

The clerk ducked out.

Taney sat down again. "I suppose," he said, in a more normal voice, "they have their problems. Outfits being broken up, being moved all over the place. But it is rugged."

"It wouldn't be so bad," Seeger said. "But we're going to Paris tomorrow. Olson, Welch and myself. And you need money in Paris."

"Don't I know it." Taney wagged his head. "Do you know what I paid for a bottle of champagne on the Place Pigalle in September . . . ?" He paused significantly. "I won't tell you. You won't have any respect for me the rest of your life."

Seeger laughed. "Hanging," he said, "is too good for the guy who thought up the rate of exchange."

"I don't care if I never see another franc as long as I live." Taney waved his letter in the air, although it had been dry for a long time.

There was silence in the tent and Seeger swallowed a little embarrassedly, watching the CO wave the flimsy sheet of paper in regular sweeping movements. "Sir," he said, "the truth is, I've come to borrow some money for Welch, Olson and myself. We'll pay it back out of the first pay we get, and that can't be too long from now. If you don't want to give it to us, just tell me and I'll understand and get the hell out of here. We don't like to ask, but you might just as well be dead as be in Paris broke."

Taney stopped waving his letter and put it down thoughtfully. He peered at it, wrinkling his brow, looking like an aged bookkeeper in the single gloomy light that hung in the middle of the tent.

"Just say the word, Captain," Seeger said, "and I'll blow . . ."

"Stay where you are, son," said Taney. He dug in his shirt pocket and took out a worn, sweat-stained wallet. He looked at it for a moment. "Alligator," he said, with automatic, absent pride. "My wife sent it to me when we were in England. Pounds don't fit in it. However . . ." He opened it and took out all the contents. There was a small pile of francs on the table in front of him. He counted them. "Four hundred francs," he said. "Eight bucks."

"Excuse me," Seeger said humbly. "I shouldn't have asked."

"Delighted," Taney said vigorously. "Absolutely delighted." He started dividing the francs into two piles. "Truth is, Seeger, most of my money goes home in allotments. And the truth is, I lost eleven hundred francs in a poker game three nights ago, and I ought to be ashamed of myself. Here . . ." he shoved one pile toward Seeger. "Two hundred francs."

Seeger looked down at the frayed, meretricious paper, which always seemed to him like stage money, anyway. "No, sir," he said, "I can't take it."

"Take it," Taney said. "That's a direct order."

Seeger slowly picked up the money, not looking at Taney. "Some time, sir," he said, "after we get out, you have to come over to my house and you and my father and my brother and I'll go on a real drunk."

"I regard that," Taney said, gravely, "as a solemn commitment."

They smiled at each other and Seeger started out.

"Have a drink for me," said Taney, "at the Café de la Paix. A small drink." He was sitting down to write his wife he loved her when Seeger went out of the tent.

Olson fell into step with Seeger and they walked silently through the mud between the tents.

"Well, *mon vieux?*" Olson said finally.

"Two hundred francs," said Seeger.

Olson groaned. "Two hundred francs! We won't be able to pinch a whore's behind on the Boulevard des Capucines for two hundred francs. That miserable, penny-loving Yankee!"

"He only had four hundred," Seeger said.

"I revise my opinion," said Olson.

They walked disconsolately and heavily back toward their tent.

Olson spoke only once before they got there. "These raincoats," he said, patting his. "Most ingenious invention of the war. Highest saturation point of any modern fabric. Collect more water per square inch, and hold it, than any material known to man. All hail the quartermaster!"

Welch was waiting at the entrance of their tent. He was standing there peering excitedly and short-sightedly out at the rain through his glasses, looking angry and tough, like a big-city hack-driver, individual and incorruptible even in the ten-million colored uniforms. Every time Seeger came upon Welch unexpectedly, he couldn't help smiling at the belligerent stance, the harsh stare through the steel-rimmed GI glasses, which had nothing at all to do with the way Welch really was. "It's a family inheritance," Welch had once explained. "My whole family stands as though we were getting ready to rap a drunk with a beer glass. Even my old lady." Welch had six brothers, all devout, according to Welch, and Seeger from time to time idly pictured them standing in a row, on Sunday mornings in church, seemingly on the verge of general violence, amid the hushed Latin and Sabbath millinery.

"How much?" Welch asked loudly.

"Don't make us laugh," Olson said, pushing past him into the tent.

"What do you think I could get from the French for my combat jacket?" Seeger said. He went into the tent and lay down on his cot.

Welch followed them in and stood between the two of them, a superior smile on his face. "Boys," he said, "on a man's errand."

"I can just see us now," Olson murmured, lying on his cot with his hands clasped behind his head, "painting Montmartre red. Please bring on the naked dancing girls. Four bucks worth."

"I am not worried," Welch announced.

"Get out of here." Olson turned over on his stomach.

"I know where we can put our hands on sixty-five bucks." Welch looked triumphantly first at Olson, then at Seeger.

Olson turned over slowly and sat up. "I'll kill you," he said, "if you're kidding."

"While you guys are wasting your time," Welch said, "fooling around with the infantry, I used my head. I went into Reems and used my head."

"Rance," Olson said automatically. He had had two years of French in college and he felt, now that the war was over, that he had to introduce his friends to some of his culture.

"I got to talking to a captain in the air force," Welch said eagerly. "A little fat old paddle-footed captain that never got higher off the ground than the second floor of Com Z headquarters, and he told me that what he would admire to do more than anything else is take a nice shiny German Luger pistol with him to show to the boys back in Pacific Grove, California."

Silence fell on the tent and Welch and Olson looked tentatively at Seeger.

"Sixty-five bucks for a Luger, these days," Olson said, "is a very good figure."

"They've been sellin' for as low as thirty-five," said Welch hesitantly.

"I'll bet," he said to Seeger, "you could sell yours now and buy another one back when you get some dough, and make a clear twenty-five on the deal."

Seeger didn't say anything. He had killed the owner of the Luger, an enormous SS major, in Coblenz, behind some paper bales in a warehouse, and the major had fired at Seeger three times with it, once nicking his helmet, before Seeger hit him in the face at twenty feet. Seeger had kept the Luger, a long, heavy, well-balanced gun, very carefully since then, lugging it with him, hiding it at the bottom of his bedroll, oiling it three times a week, avoiding all opportunities of selling it, although he had been offered as much as a hundred dollars for it and several times eighty and ninety, while the war was still on, before German weapons became a glut on the market.

"Well," said Welch, "there's no hurry. I told the captain I'd see him tonight around 8 o'clock in front of the Lion D'Or Hotel. You got five hours to make up your mind. Plenty of time."

"Me," said Olson, after a pause. "I won't say anything."

Seeger looked reflectively at his feet and the other two men avoided looking at him. Welch dug in his pocket. "I forgot," he said. "I picked up a letter for you." He handed it to Seeger.

"Thanks," Seeger said. He opened it absently, thinking about the Luger.

"Me," said Olson, "I won't say a bloody word. I'm just going to lie here and think about that nice fat air force captain."

Seeger grinned a little at him and went to the tent opening to read the letter in the light. The letter was from his father, and even from one glance at the handwriting, scrawly and hurried and spotted, so different from his father's usual steady, handsome, professorial script, he knew that something was wrong.

"Dear Norman," it read, "sometime in the future, you must forgive me for writing this letter. But I have been holding this in so long, and there is no one here I can talk to, and because of your brother's condition I must pretend to be cheerful and optimistic all the time at home, both with him and your mother, who has never been the same since Leonard was killed. You're the oldest now, and although I know we've never talked very seriously about anything before, you have been through a great deal by now, and I imagine you must have matured considerably, and you've seen so many different places and people. . . . Norman, I need help. While the war was on and you were fighting, I kept this to myself. It wouldn't have been fair to burden you with this. But now the war is over, and I no longer feel I can stand up under this alone. And you will have to face it some time when you get home, if you haven't faced it already, and perhaps we can help each other by facing it together...."

"I'm redeployable," Olson was singing softly, on his cot. "It's so enjoyable, In the Pelilu mud, With the tropical crud ..." He fell silent after his burst of song.

Seeger blinked his eyes, at the entrance of the tent, in the wan rainy light, and went on reading his father's letter, on the stiff white stationery with the University letterhead in polite engraving at the top of each page.

"I've been feeling this coming on for a long time," the letter continued, "but it wasn't until last Sunday morning that something happened to make me feel it in its full force. I don't know how much you've guessed about the reason for Jacob's discharge from the Army. It's true he was pretty badly wounded in the leg at Metz, but I've asked around, and I know that men with worse wounds were returned to duty after hospitalization. Jacob got a medical discharge, but I don't think it was for the shrapnel wound in his thigh. He is suffering now from what I suppose you call combat fatigue, and he is subject to fits of depression and hallucinations. Your mother and I thought that as time went by and the war and the army receded, he would grow better. Instead, he is growing worse. Last Sunday morning when I came down into the living room from upstairs he was crouched in his old uniform, next to the window, peering out ..."

"What the hell," Olson was saying, "if we don't get the sixty-five bucks we can always go to the Louvre. I understand the Mona Lisa is back."

"I asked Jacob what he was doing," the letter went on. "He didn't turn around. 'I'm observing,' he said. 'V-1's and V-2's. Buzz-bombs and rockets. They're coming in by the hundreds.' I tried to reason with him and he told me to crouch and save myself from flying glass. To humor him I got down on the floor beside him and tried to tell him the war was over, that we were in Ohio, 4,000 miles away from the nearest spot where bombs had fallen, that America had never been touched. He wouldn't listen. 'These're the new rocket bombs,' he said, 'for the Jews.' "

"Did you ever hear of the Pantheon?" Olson asked loudly.

"No," said Welch.

"It's free."

"I'll go," said Welch.

Seeger shook his head a little and blinked his eyes before he went back to the letter.

"After that," his father went on, "Jacob seemed to forget about the bombs from time to time, but he kept saying that the mobs were coming up the street armed with bazookas and Browning automatic rifles. He mumbled incoherently a good deal of the time and kept walking back and forth saying, 'What's the situation? Do you know what the situation is?' And he told me he wasn't worried about himself, he was a soldier and he expected to be killed, but he was worried about Mother and myself and Leonard and you. He seemed to forget that Leonard was dead. I tried to calm him and get him back to bed before your mother came down, but he refused and wanted to set out immediately to rejoin his division. It was all terribly disjointed and at one time he took the ribbon he got for winning the Bronze star and threw it in the fireplace, then he got down on his hands and knees and picked it out of the ashes and made me pin it on him again, and he kept repeating, 'This is when they are coming for the Jews.' "

"The next war I'm in," said Olson, "they don't get me under the rank of colonel."

It had stopped raining by now and Seeger folded the unfinished letter and went outside. He walked slowly down to the end of the company street, and facing out across the empty, soaked French fields, scarred and neglected by various armies, he stopped and opened the letter again.

"I don't know what Jacob went through in the army," his father wrote, "that has done this to him. He never talks to me about the war and he refuses to go to a psychoanalyst, and from time to time he is his own bouncing, cheerful self, playing in tennis tournaments, and going around with a large group of girls. But he has devoured all the concentration camp reports, and I have found him weeping when the newspapers reported that a hundred Jews were killed in Tripoli some time ago.

"The terrible thing is, Norman, that I find myself coming to believe that it is not neurotic for a Jew to behave like this today. Perhaps Jacob is the normal one, and I, going about my business, teaching economics in a quiet classroom, pretending to understand that the world is comprehensible and orderly, am really the mad one. I ask you once more to forgive me for writing you a letter like this, so different from any letter or any conversation I've ever had with you. But it is crowding me, too. I do not see rockets and bombs, but I see other things.

"Wherever you go these days—restaurants, hotels, clubs, trains—you seem to hear talk about the Jews, mean, hateful, murderous talk. Whatever page you turn to in the newspapers you seem to find an article about Jews being killed somewhere on the face of the globe. And there are large, influential newspapers and well-known columnists who each day are growing more and more outspoken and more popular. The day that Roosevelt died I heard a drunken man yelling outside a bar, 'Finally, they got the Jew out of the White House.' And some of the people who heard him merely laughed and nobody stopped him. And on V-E Day, in celebration, hoodlums in Los Angeles savagely beat a Jewish writer. It's difficult to know what to do, whom to fight, where to look for allies.

"Three months ago, for example, I stopped my Thursday night poker game, after playing with the same men for over ten years. John Reilly happened to say that the Jews were getting rich out of this war, and when I demanded an apology, he refused, and when I looked around at the faces of the men who had been my friends for so long, I could see they were not with me. And when I left the house no one said good night to me. I know the poison was spreading from Germany before the war and during it, but I had not realized it had come so close.

"And in my economics class, I find myself idiotically hedging in my lectures. I discover that I am loath to praise any liberal writer or any liberal act and find myself somehow annoyed and frightened to see an article of criticism of existing abuses signed by a Jewish name. And I hate to see Jewish names on important committees, and hate to read of Jews fighting for the poor, the oppressed, the cheated and hungry. Somehow, even in a country where my family has lived a hundred years, the enemy has won this subtle victory over me—he has made me disfranchise myself from honest causes by calling them foreign, Communist, using Jewish names connected with them as ammunition against them.

"And, most hateful of all, I find myself looking for Jewish names in the casualty lists and secretly being glad when I discover them there, to prove that there at least, among the dead and wounded, we belong. Three times, thanks to you and your brothers, I have found our name there, and, may God forgive me, at the expense of your blood and your brother's life, through my tears, I have felt that same twitch of satisfaction. . . .

"When I read the newspapers and see another story that Jews are still being killed in Poland, or Jews are requesting that they be given back their homes in France, or that they be allowed to enter some country where they will not be murdered, I am annoyed with them, I feel they are boring the rest of the world with their problems, they are making demands upon the rest of the world by being killed, they are disturbing everyone by being hungry and asking for the return of their property. If we could all fall through the crust of the earth and vanish in one hour, with our heroes and poets and prophets and martyrs, perhaps we would be doing the memory of the Jewish race a service. . . .

"This is how I feel today, son. I need some help. You've been to the war, you've fought and killed men, you've seen the people of other countries. Maybe you understand things that I don't understand. Maybe you see some hope somewhere. Help me. Your loving father."

Seeger folded the letter slowly, not seeing what he was doing because the tears were burning his eyes. He walked slowly and aimlessly across the dead autumn grass of the empty field, away from the camp.

He tried to wipe away his tears, because with his eyes full and dark, he kept seeing his father and brother crouched in the old-fashioned living room in Ohio and hearing his brother, dressed in the old, discarded uniform, saying, "These're the new rocket bombs. For the Jews."

He sighed, looking out over the bleak, wasted land. Now, he thought, now I have to think about it. He felt a slight, unreasonable twinge of anger at his father for presenting him with the necessity of thinking about it. The army was good about serious problems. While you were fighting, you were too busy and frightened and weary to think about anything, and at other times you were relaxing, putting your brain on a shelf, postponing everything to that impossible time of clarity and beauty after the war. Well, now, here was the impossible, clear, beautiful time, and here was his father, demanding that he think. There are all sorts of Jews, he thought, there are the sort whose every waking moment is ridden by the knowledge of Jewishness, who see signs against the Jew in every smile on a streetcar, every whisper, who see pogroms in every newspaper article, threats in every change of the weather, scorn in every handshake, death behind each closed door. He had not been like that. He was young, he was big and healthy and easy-going and people of all kinds had seemed to like him all his life, in the army and out. In America, especially, what was going on in Europe had seemed remote, unreal, unrelated to him. The chanting, bearded old men burning in the Nazi furnaces, and the dark-eyed women screaming prayers in Polish and Russian and German as they were pushed naked into the gas chambers had seemed as shadowy and almost as unrelated to him as he trotted out onto the Stadium field for a football game, as they must have been to the men named O'Dwyer and Wickersham and Poole who played in the line beside him.

They had seemed more related in Europe. Again and again in the towns that had been taken back from the Germans, gaunt, gray-faced men had stopped him humbly, looking searchingly at him, and had asked, peering at his long, lined, grimy face, under the anonymous helmet, "Are you a Jew?" Sometimes they asked it in English, sometimes French, or Yiddish. He didn't know French or Yiddish, but he learned to recognize the phrase. He had never understood exactly why they had asked the question, since they never demanded anything from him, rarely even could speak to him, until, one day in Strasbourg, a little bent old man and a small, shapeless woman had stopped him, and asked, in English, if he was Jewish.

"Yes," he said, smiling at them.

The two old people had smiled widely, like children. "Look," the old man had said to his wife. "A young American soldier. A Jew. And so large and strong." He had touched Seeger's arm reverently with the tips of his fingers, then had touched the Garand he was carrying. "And such a beautiful rifle . . ."

And there, for a moment, although he was not particularly sensitive, Seeger got an inkling of why he had been stopped and questioned by so many before. Here, to these bent, exhausted old people, ravaged of their families, familiar with flight and death for so many years, was a symbol of continuing life. A large young man in the uniform of the liberator, blood, as they thought, of their blood, but not in hiding, not quivering in fear and helplessness, but striding secure and victorious down the street, armed and capable of inflicting terrible destruction on his enemies.

Seeger had kissed the old lady on the cheek and she had wept and the old man had scolded her for it, while shaking Seeger's hand fervently and thankfully before saying good-bye.

And, thinking back on it, it was silly to pretend that, even before his father's letter, he had been like any other American soldier going through the war. When he had stood over the huge dead SS major with the face blown in by his bullets in the warehouse in Coblenz, and taken the pistol from the dead hand, he had tasted a strange little extra flavor of triumph. How many Jews, he'd thought, has this man killed, how fitting it is that I've killed him. Neither Olson nor Welch, who were like his brothers, would have felt that in picking up the Luger, its barrel still hot from the last shots its owner had fired before dying. And he had resolved that he was going to make sure to take this gun back with him to America, and plug it and keep it on his desk at home, as a kind of vague, half-understood sign to himself that justice had once been done and he had been its instrument.

Maybe, he thought, maybe I'd better take it back with me, but not as a memento. Not plugged, but loaded. America by now was a strange country for him. He had been away a long time and he wasn't sure what was waiting for him when he got home. If the mobs were coming down the street toward his house, he was not going to die singing and praying.

When he was taking basic training he'd heard a scrawny, clerklike-looking soldier from Boston talking at the other end of the PX bar, over the watered beer. "The boys at the office," the scratchy voice was saying, "gave me a party before I left. And they told me one thing. 'Charlie,' they said, 'hold onto your bayonet. We're going to be able to use it when you get back. On the Yids.' "

He hadn't said anything then, because he'd felt it was neither possible nor desirable to fight against every random overheard voice raised against the Jews from one end of the world to another. But again and again, at odd moments, lying on a barracks cot, or stretched out trying to sleep on the floor of a ruined French farmhouse, he had heard that voice, harsh, satisfied, heavy with hate and ignorance, saying above the beery grumble of apprentice soldiers at the bar, "Hold onto your bayonet. . . ."

And the other stories—Jews collected stories of hatred and injustice and inklings of doom like a special, lunatic kind of miser. The story of the naval officer, commander of a small vessel off the Aleutians, who, in the officers' wardroom, had complained that he hated the Jews because it was the Jews who had demanded that the Germans be beaten first and the forces in the Pacific had been starved in consequence. And when one of his junior officers, who had just come aboard, had objected and told the commander that he was a Jew, the commander had risen from the table and said, "Mister, the Constitution of the United States says I have to serve in the same navy with Jews, but it doesn't say I have to eat at the same table with them." In the fogs and the cold, swelling Arctic seas off the Aleutians, in a small boat, subject to sudden, mortal attack at any moment . . .

And the two young combat engineers in an attached company on D Day, when they were lying off the coast right before climbing down into the landing barges. "There's France," one of them had said.

"What's it like?" the second one had asked, peering out across the miles of water toward the smoking coast.

"Like every place else," the first one had answered. "The Jews've made all the dough during the war."

"Shut up!" Seeger had said, helplessly thinking of the dead, destroyed, wandering, starving Jews of France. The engineers had shut up, and they'd climbed down together into the heaving boat, and gone into the beach together.

And the million other stories. Jews, even the most normal and best adjusted of them, became living treasuries of them, scraps of malice and bloodthirstiness, clever and confusing and cunningly twisted so that every act by every Jew became suspect and blameworthy and hateful. Seeger had heard the stories, and had made an almost conscious effort to forget them. Now, holding his father's letter in his hand, he remembered them all.

He stared unseeingly out in front of him. Maybe, he thought, maybe it would've been better to have been killed in the war, like Leonard. Simpler. Leonard would never have to face a crowd coming for his mother and father. Leonard would not have to listen and collect these hideous, fascinating little stories that made of every Jew a stranger in any town, on any field, on the face of the earth. He had come so close to being killed so many times, it would have been so easy, so neat and final.

Seeger shook his head. It was ridiculous to feel like that, and he was ashamed of himself for the weak moment. At the age of twenty-one, death was not an answer.

"Seeger!" It was Olson's voice. He and Welch had sloshed silently up behind Seeger, standing in the open field. "Seeger, *mon vieux,* what're you doing—grazing?"

Seeger turned slowly to them. "I wanted to read my letter," he said.

Olson looked closely at him. They had been together so long, through so many things, that flickers and hints of expression on each other's faces were recognized and acted upon. "Anything wrong?" Olson asked.

"No," said Seeger. "Nothing much."

"Norman," Welch said, his voice young and solemn. "Norman, we've been talking, Olson and me. We decided—you're pretty attached to that Luger, and maybe—if you—well . . ."

"What he's trying to say," said Olson, "is we withdraw the request. If you want to sell it, O.K. If you don't, don't do it for our sake. Honest."

Seeger looked at them, standing there, disreputable and tough and familiar. "I haven't made up my mind yet," he said.

"Anything you decide," Welch said oratorically, "is perfectly all right with us. Perfectly."

They walked aimlessly and silently across the field, away from camp. As they walked, their shoes making a wet, sliding sound in the damp, dead grass, Seeger thought of the time Olson had covered him in the little town outside Cherbourg, when Seeger had been caught going down the side of a street by four Germans with a machine gun on the second story of a house on the corner and Olson had had to stand out in the middle of the street with no cover at all for more than a minute, firing continuously, so that Seeger could get away alive. And he thought of the time outside Saint Lô when he had been wounded and had lain in a minefield for three hours and Welch and Captain Taney had come looking for him in the darkness and had found him and picked him up and run for it, all of them expecting to get blown up any second.

And he thought of all the drinks they'd had together and the long marches and the cold winter together, and all the girls they'd gone out with together, and he thought of his father and brother crouching behind the window in Ohio waiting for the rockets and the crowds armed with Browning automatic rifles.

"Say," he stopped and stood facing them. "Say, what do you guys think of the Jews?"

Welch and Olson looked at each other, and Olson glanced down at the letter in Seeger's hand.

"Jews?" Olson said finally. "What're they? Welch, you ever hear of the Jews?"

Welch looked thoughtfully at the gray sky. "No," he said. "But remember, I'm an uneducated fellow."

"Sorry, Bud," Olson said, turning to Seeger. "We can't help you. Ask us another question. Maybe we'll do better."

Seeger peered at the faces of his friends. He would have to rely upon them, later on, out of uniform, on their native streets, more than he had ever relied on them on the bullet-swept street and in the dark minefield in France. Welch and Olson stared back at him, troubled, their faces candid and tough and dependable.

"What time," Seeger asked, "did you tell that captain you'd meet him?"

"Eight o'clock," Welch said. "But we don't have to go. If you have any feeling about that gun . . ."

"We'll meet him," Seeger said. "We can use that sixty-five bucks."

"Listen," Olson said, "I know how much you like that gun and I'll feel like a heel if you sell it."

"Forget it," Seeger said, starting to walk again. "What could I use it for in America?"

72

My Christmas Carol

BY BUDD SCHULBERG

WHEN I was a little boy, I lived with my parents in what was then a small suburb of Los Angeles called Hollywood. My father was general manager in charge of production for Firmament-Famous Artists-Lewin. It was a mouthful, but I used to have to remember the whole thing for the your-father-my-father arguments I was always having with a kid down the block whose old man was only an associate producer at Warner Brothers.

One of the things I remember most about Firmament-Famous Artists-Lewin was the way that studio and Christmas were all mixed up together in my mind. My earliest memory of the Christmas season is associated with a large studio truck, bearing the company's trademark, that always drove up to the house just before supper on Christmas Eve. I would stand outside the kitchen door with my little sister and watch the driver and his helper carry into our house armload after armload of wonderful red and green packages—all for us. Sometimes the gleaming handlebars of a tricycle or the shiny wheels of a miniature fire engine would break through their bright wrappers, and I'd shout, "I know what that is!" until my mother would lead me away. Santa Claus still had so many houses to visit, she'd say, that I mustn't get in the way of these two helpers of his. Then I'd go down the street to argue the respective merits of our two studios with the Warner Brothers kid, or pass the time tormenting my little sister, perfectly content in the thought that the Firmament-Famous Artists-Lewin truck was the standard vehicle of transportation for Santa Claus in semitropical climates like Southern California.

On Christmas morning I had the unfortunate habit of rising at five o'clock, rushing across the hallway to my sister's room in annual disobedience of my mother's request to rise quietly, and shouting, "Merry

Christmas, Sandra! Let's wake Mommy and Daddy and open our presents."

We ran down the hall into the master bedroom with its canopied twin beds. "Merry Christmas!" we shouted together. My father groaned, rolled over and pulled the covers further up over his head. He was suffering the after-effects of the studio's annual all-day Christmas party from which he hadn't returned until after we had gone to sleep. I climbed up on the bed, crawling over him, and bounced up and down, chanting, "Merry Christmas, Merry Christmas. . . ."

"Oh-h-h . . ." Father said, and flipped over on his belly. Mother shook his shoulder gently. "Sol, I hate to wake you, but the children won't go down without you."

Father sat up slowly, muttering something about its being still dark outside and demanding to know who had taken his bathrobe. Mother picked it up where he had dropped it and brought it to him. It was black and white silk with an elegant embroidered monogram.

"The kids'll be opening presents for the next twelve hours," my father said. "It seems God-damn silly to start opening them at five o'clock in the morning."

Downstairs there were enough toys, it seemed, to fill all the windows of a department store. The red car was a perfect model of a Pierce-Arrow, and probably only slightly less expensive, with a green leather seat wide enough for Sandra to sit beside me, and real headlights that turned on and off. There was a German electric train that passed through an elaborate Bavarian village in miniature. And a big scooter with rubber wheels and a gear shift just like our Cadillac's. And dozens more that I've forgotten. Sandra had a doll that was a life-size replica of Baby Peggy, which was Early Twenties for Margaret O'Brien, an imported silk Hungarian peasant costume from Lord & Taylor, a six-ounce bottle of French toilet water, and so many other things that we all had to help her unwrap them.

Just when we were reaching the end of this supply, people started arriving with more presents. That's the way it had been every Christmas since I could remember, men and women all dressed up dropping in all day long with packages containing wonderful things that they'd wait for us to unwrap. They'd sit around a while, laughing with my mother and father and lifting from James the butler's tray a cold yellow drink that I wasn't allowed to have, and then they'd pick us up and kiss us and tell us we were as pretty as my mother or as intelligent as my father and then there would be more laughing and hugging and hand-shaking and God bless you and then they'd be gone, and others would arrive to take their place. Sometimes there must have been ten or twenty all there at once and Sandra and I would be sort of sorry in a way because Mother and Father would be too busy with their guests to play with us. But it was nice to get all those presents.

I remember one tall dark man with a little pointed mustache who kissed Mother's hand when he came in. His present was wrapped in beautiful silvery paper and the blue ribbon around it felt thick and soft like one of Mother's evening dresses. Inside was a second layer of thin white tissue paper and inside of that was a handsome silver comb-and-brush set, just like my father's. Tied to it was a little card that I could read because it was printed and I could read almost anything then as long as it wasn't handwriting: "Merry Christmas to my future boss from Uncle Norman."

"Mommy," I said, "is Uncle Norman my uncle? You never told me I had an Uncle Norman. I have an Uncle Dave and an Uncle Joe and an Uncle Sam, but I never knew I had an Uncle Norman."

I can still remember how white and even Norman's teeth looked when he smiled at me. "I'm a new uncle," he said. "Don't you remember the day your daddy brought you on my set and I signed your autograph book and I told you to call me Uncle Norman?"

I combed my hair with his silver comb suspiciously. "Did you give me this comb and brush . . . Uncle Norman?"

Norman drank down the last of the foamy yellow stuff and carefully wiped off his mustaches with his pale-blue breast-pocket handkerchief. "Yes, I did, sonny," he said.

I turned on my mother accusingly. "But you said Santa Claus gives us all these presents."

This all took place, as I found out later, at a crucial moment in my relationship with S. Claus, when a child's faith was beginning to crumble under the pressure of suspicions. Mother was trying to keep Santa Claus alive for us as long as possible, I learned subsequently, so that Christmas would mean something more to us than a display of sycophancy on the part of Father's stars, directors, writers and job-seekers.

"Norman signed his name to your comb and brush because he is one of Santa Claus's helpers," Mother said. "Santa has so much work to do taking care of all the good little children in the world that he needs lots and lots of helpers."

My father offered one of his long, fat cigars to "Uncle" Norman and bit off the end of another one for himself.

"Daddy, is that true, what Mommy says?" I asked.

"You must always believe your mother, boy," my father said.

"I've got twenty-eleven presents already," Sandra said.

"You mean thirty-one," I said. "I've got thirty-two."

Sandra tore open a box that held an exquisite little gold ring, inlaid with amethyst, her birthstone.

"Let me read the card," I said. " 'Merry Chirstmas, Sandra darling, from your biggest fan, Aunt Ruth.' "

Ruth was the pretty lady who played opposite Uncle Norman in one of my father's recent pictures. I hadn't been allowed to see it, but I used to boast to that Warner Brothers kid about how much better it was than anything Warners' could make.

Sandra, being very young, tossed Aunt Ruth's gold ring away and turned slowly in her hand the little box it had come in. "Look, it says numbers on it," she said. "Why are the numbers, Chris?"

I studied it carefully. "Ninety-five. That looks like dollars," I said. "Ninety-five dollars. Where does Santa Claus get all his money, Daddy?"

My father gave my mother a questioning look. "Er . . . what's that, son?" I had to repeat the question. "Oh . . . those aren't dollars, no . . . That's just the number Santa puts on his toys to keep them from getting all mixed up before he sends them down from the North Pole," my father said, and then he took a deep breath and another gulp of that yellow drink.

More people kept coming in all afternoon. More presents. More uncles and aunts. More Santa Claus's helpers. I never realized he had so many helpers. All afternoon the phone kept ringing, too. "Sol, you might as well answer it, it must be for you," my mother would say, and then I could hear my father laughing on the phone: "Thanks, L.B., and a merry Christmas to you . . . Thanks, Joe . . . Thanks, Mary . . . Thanks, Doug . . . Merry Christmas, Pola . . ." Gifts kept arriving late into the day, sometimes in big limousines and town cars, carried in by chauffeurs in snappy uniforms. No matter how my father explained it, it seemed to me that Santa must be as rich as Mr. Zukor.

Just before supper, one of the biggest stars in Father's pictures drove up in a Rolls Royce roadster, the first one I had ever seen. She came in with a tall, broad-shouldered, sunburned man who laughed at anything anybody said. She was a very small lady and she wore her hair tight around her head like a boy's. She had on a tight yellow dress that only came down to the top of her knees. She and the man she was with had three presents for me and four for Sandra. She looked down at me and said, "Merry Christmas, you little darling," and before I could get away, she had picked me up and was kissing me. She smelled all funny, with perfumy sweetness mixed up with the way Father smelled when he came home from that Christmas party at the studio and leaned over my bed to kiss me when I was half asleep.

I didn't like people to kiss me, especially strangers. "Lemme go," I said.

"That's no way to act, Sonny," the strange man said. "Why, right this minute every man in America would like to be in your shoes."

All the grownups laughed, but I kept squirming, trying to get away. "Aw, don't be that way, honey," the movie star said. "Why, I love men!"

They all laughed again. I didn't understand it so I started to cry. Then she put me down. "All right for you," she said, "if you don't want to be my boy friend."

After she left, when I was unwrapping her presents, I asked my father, "Who is she? Is she one of Santa Claus's helpers, too?" Father winked at Mother, turned his head away, put his hand to his mouth and laughed into it, but I saw him. Mother looked at him the way she did when she caught me taking a piece of candy just before supper. "Her name is Clara, dear," she said. "She's one of Santa Claus's helpers, too."

And that's the way Christmas was, until one Christmas when a funny thing happened. The big Firmament-Famous Artists-Lewin truck never showed up. I kept looking for it all afternoon, but it never came. When it got dark and it was time for me to have my supper and go to bed and still no truck, I got pretty worried. My mind ran back through the year trying to remember some bad thing I might have done that Santa was going to punish me for. I had done lots of bad things, like slapping my sister and breaking my father's fountain pen, but they were no worse than the stuff I had pulled the year before. Yet what other reason could there possibly be for that truck not showing up?

Another thing that seemed funny about that Christmas Eve was that my father didn't bother to go to his studio Christmas party. He stayed home all morning and read aloud to me from a Christmas present he let me open a day early, a big blue book called *Typee*. And late that night when I tiptoed halfway down the stairs to watch my mother trim the tree that Santa was supposed to decorate, my father was helping her string the colored lights. Another thing different about that Christmas was that when Sandra and I ran in shouting and laughing at five, as we always did, my father got up just as soon as my mother.

When we went downstairs, we found almost as many presents as on other Christmas mornings. There was a nice fire engine from Uncle Norman, a cowboy suit from Aunt Ruth, a Meccano set from Uncle Adolph, something, in fact, from every one of Santa Claus's helpers. No, it wasn't the presents that made this Christmas seem so different, it was how quiet every thing was. Pierce-Arrows and Packards and Cadillacs didn't keep stopping by all day long with new presents for us. And none of the people like Norman and Ruth and Uncle Edgar, the famous director, and Aunt Betty, the rising ingenue, and Uncle Dick, the young star, and the scenario writer, Uncle Bill, none of them dropped in at all. James the butler was gone, too. For the first Christmas since I could remember, we had Father all to ourselves. Even the phone was quiet for a change. Except for a couple of real relatives, the only one who showed up at all was Clara. She came in around supper time with an old man whose hair was yellow at the temples and gray on top. Her face was very red and when she picked me up to kiss me, her breath reminded me of the Christmas before, only stronger. My father poured her and her friend the foamy yellow drink I wasn't allowed to have.

She held up her drink and said, "Merry Christmas, Sol. And may next Christmas be even merrier."

My father's voice sounded kind of funny, not laughing as he usually did. "Thanks, Clara," he said. "You're a pal."

"Nerts," Clara said. "Just because I don't wanna be a fair-weather friend like some of these other Hollywood bas—"

"Shhh, the children," my mother reminded her.

"Oh hell, I'm sorry," Clara said. "But anyway, you know what I mean."

My mother looked from us to Clara and back to us again. "Chris, Sandra," she said. "Why don't you take your toys up to your own room and play? We'll be up later."

In three trips I carried up to my room all the important presents. I also took up a box full of cards that had been attached to the presents. As a bit of holiday homework, our penmanship teacher Miss Whitehead had suggested that we separate all Christmas-card signatures into those of Spencerian grace and those of cramp-fingered illegibility. I played with my Meccano set for a while, I practiced twirling my lasso and I made believe Sandra was an Indian, captured her and tied her to the bedstead as my hero Art Acord did in the movies. I captured Sandra three or four times and then I didn't know what to do with myself, so I spread all the Christmas cards out on the floor and began sorting them just as Miss Whitehead had asked.

I sorted half a dozen, all quite definitely non-Spencerian, but it wasn't until I had sorted ten or twelve that I began to notice something funny. It was all the same handwriting. Then I came to a card of my father's. I was just beginning to learn how to read handwriting, and I wasn't very good at it yet, but I could recognize the three little bunched-together letters that spelled *Dad*. I held my father's card close to my eyes and compared it with the one from Uncle Norman. It was the same handwriting. Then I compared them with the one from Uncle Adolph. All the same handwriting. Then I picked up one of Sandra's cards, from

Aunt Ruth, and held that one up against my father's. I couldn't understand it. My father seemed to have written them all.

I didn't say anything to Sandra about this, or to the nurse when she gave us our supper and put us to bed. But when my mother came in to kiss me good night I asked her why my father's handwriting was on all the cards. My mother turned on the light and sat on the edge of the bed.

"You don't really believe in Santa Claus any more, do you?" she asked.

"No," I said. "Fred and Clyde told me all about it at school."

"Then I don't think it will hurt you to know the rest," my mother said. "Sooner or later you will have to know these things."

Then she told me what had happened. Between last Christmas and this one, my father had lost his job. He was trying to start his own company now. Lots of stars and directors had promised to go with him. But when the time had come to make good on their promises, they had backed out. Though I didn't fully understand it at the time, even in the simplified way my mother tried to explain it, I would say now that for most of those people the security of a major-company payroll had outweighed an adventure on Poverty Row—the name for the group of little studios where the independent producers struggled to survive.

So this had been a lean year for my father. We had sold one of the cars, let the butler go, and lived on a budget. As Christmas approached, Mother had cut our presents to a minimum.

"Anyway, the children will be taken care of," my father said. "The old gang will see to that."

The afternoon of Christmas Eve my father had had a business appointment, to see a banker about more financing for his program of pictures. When he came home, Sandra and I had just gone to bed, and Mother was arranging the presents around the tree. There weren't many presents to arrange, just the few they themselves had bought. There were no presents at all from my so-called aunts and uncles.

"My pals," Father said. "My admirers. My loyal employees."

Even though he had the intelligence to understand why these people had always sent us those expensive presents, his vanity, or perhaps I can call it his good nature, had led him to believe they did it because they liked him and because they genuinely were fond of Sandra and me.

"I'm afraid the kids will wonder what happened to all those Santa Claus's helpers," my mother said.

"Wait a minute," my father said. "I've got an idea. Those bastards are going to be Santa Claus's helpers whether they know it or not."

Then he had rushed out to a toy store on Hollywood Boulevard and brought a gift for every one of the aunts and uncles who were so conspicuously absent.

I remember, when my mother finished explaining, how I bawled. I don't know whether it was out of belated gratitude to my old man or whether I was feeling sorry for myself because all those famous people didn't like me as much as I thought they did. Maybe I was only crying because that first, wonderful and ridiculous part of childhood was over. From now on I would have to face a world in which there was not only no Santa Claus, but very, very few on-the-level Santa Claus's helpers.

73

Pretty Mouth and Green My Eyes

BY J. D. SALINGER

WHEN the phone rang, the gray-haired man asked the girl, with quite some little deference, if she would rather for any reason he didn't answer it. The girl heard him as if from a distance, and turned her face toward him, one eye—on the side of the light—closed tight, her open eye very, however disingenuously, large, and so blue as to appear almost violet. The gray-haired man asked her to hurry up, and she raised up on her right forearm just quickly enough so that the movement didn't quite look perfunctory. She cleared her hair back from her forehead with her left hand and said, "God. I don't know. I mean what do you think?" The gray-haired man said he didn't see that it made a helluva lot of difference one way or the other, and slipped his left hand under the girl's supporting arm, above the elbow, working his fingers up, making room for them between the warm surfaces of her upper arm and chest wall. He reached for the phone with his right hand. To reach it without groping, he had to raise himself somewhat higher, which caused the back of his head to graze a corner of the lampshade. In that instant, the light was particularly, if rather vividly, flattering to his gray, mostly white, hair. Though in disarrangement at that moment, it had obviously been freshly cut—or, rather, freshly maintained. The neckline and temples had been trimmed conventionally close, but the sides and top had been left rather more than just longish, and were, in fact, a trifle "distinguished-looking." "Hello?" he said resonantly into the phone. The girl stayed propped up on her forearm and watched him. Her eyes, more just open than alert or speculative, reflected chiefly their own size and color.

A man's voice—stone dead, yet somehow rudely, almost obscenely quickened for the occasion—came through at the other end: "Lee? I wake you?"

The gray-haired man glanced briefly left, at the girl. "Who's that?" he asked. "Arthur?"

"Yeah—I wake you?"

"No, no. I'm in bed, reading. Anything wrong?"

"You sure I didn't wake you? Honest to God?"

"No, no—absolutely," the gray-haired man said. "As a matter of fact, I've been averaging about four lousy hours—"

"The reason I called, Lee, did you happen to notice when Joanie was leaving? Did you happen to notice if she left with the Ellenbogens, by any chance?"

The gray-haired man looked left again, but high this time, way from the girl, who was now watching him rather like a young, blue-eyed Irish policeman. "No, I didn't, Arthur," he said, his eyes on the far, dim end of the room, where the wall met the ceiling. "Didn't she leave with you?"

"No. Christ, no. You didn't see her leave at all, then?"

"Well, no, as a matter of fact, I didn't, Arthur," the gray-haired man said. "Actually, as a matter of fact, I didn't see a bloody thing all evening. The minute I got in the door, I got myself involved in one long Jesus of a session with that French poop, Viennese poop—whatever the hell he was. Every bloody one of these foreign guys keep an eye open for a little free legal advice. Why? What's up? Joanie lost?"

"Oh, Christ. Who knows? I don't know. You know her when she gets all tanked up and rarin' to go. *I* don't know. She *may* have just—"

"You call the Ellenbogens?" the gray-haired man asked.

"Yeah. They're not home yet. I don't know. Christ, I'm not even sure she *left* with them. I know one thing. I know one goddam thing. I'm through beating my brains out. I mean it. I really mean it this time. I'm through. Five years. Christ."

"All right, try to take it a little easy, now, Arthur," the gray-haired man said. "In the first place, if I know the Ellenbogens, they probably all hopped in a cab and went down to the Village for a couple of hours. All three of 'em'll probably barge—"

"I have a feeling she went to work on some bastard in the kitchen. I just have a feeling. She always starts necking some bastard in the kitchen when she gets tanked up. I'm through. I swear to God I mean it this time. Five goddam—"

"Where are you now, Arthur?" the gray-haired man asked. "Home?"

"Yeah. Home. Home sweet home. Christ."

"Well, just try to take it a little—What are ya—drunk, or what?"

"I don't know. How the hell do I know?"

"All right, now, listen. Relax. Just relax," the gray-haired man said. "You know the Ellenbogens, for Chrissake. What probably happened, they probably missed their last train. All three of 'em'll probably barge in on you any minute, full of witty, night-club—"

"They drove in."

"How do you know?"

"Their baby-sitter. We've had some scintillating goddam conversations. We're close as hell. We're like two goddam peas in a pod."

"All right. All right. So what? Will ya sit tight and relax, now?" said the gray-haired man. "All three of 'em'll probably waltz in on you any minute. Take my word. You know Leona. I don't know what the hell it is—They all get this god-awful Connecticut *gai*ety when they get in to New York. You know that."

"Yeah. I know. I know. I don't know, though."

"Certainly you do. Use your imagination. The two of 'em probably dragged Joanie bodily—"

"Listen. Nobody ever has to *drag* Joanie *anywhere*. Don't gimmie any of that dragging stuff."

"Nobody's giving you any dragging stuff, Arthur," the gray-haired man said quietly.

"I know, I know! Excuse me. Christ, I'm losing my mind. Honest to God, you sure I didn't wake you?"

"I'd tell you if you had, Arthur," the gray-haired man said. Absently, he took his left hand out from between the girl's upper arm and chest wall. "Look, Arthur. You want my advice?" he said. He took the telephone cord between his fingers, just under the transmitter. "I mean this, now. You want some advice?"

"Yeah. I don't know. Christ, I'm keeping you up. Why don't I just go cut my—"

"Listen to me a minute," the gray-haired man said. "First—I mean this, now—get in bed and relax. Make yourself a nice, big nightcap, and get under the—"

"*Night*cap! Are you kidding? Christ, I've killed about a quart in the last two goddam hours. *Night*cap! I'm so plastered now I can hardly—"

"All right. All right. Get in bed, then," the gray-haired man said. "And relax—ya hear me? Tell the truth. Is it going to do any good to sit around and stew?"

"Yeah, I know. I wouldn't even worry, for Chrissake, but you can't trust her! I swear to God. I swear to God you can't. You can trust her about as far as you can throw a—I don't know *what*. Aaah, what's the use? I'm losing my goddam mind."

"All right. Forget it, now. Forget it, now. Will ya do me a favor and try to put the whole thing out of your mind?" the gray-haired man said. "For all you know, you're making—I honestly think you're making a mountain—"

"You know what I do? *You know what I do?* I'm ashameda tell ya, but you know what I very nearly goddam do every night? When I get home? You want to know?"

"Arthur, listen, this isn't—"

"*Wait* a second—I'll *tell* ya, God damn it. I practically have to keep myself from opening every goddam closet door in the apartment—I swear to God. Every night I come home, I half expect to find a bunch of bastards hiding all over the place. *Ele*vator boys. *Deliv*ery boys. *Cops*—"

"All right. All right. Let's try to take it a little easy, Arthur," the gray-haired man said. He glanced abruptly to his right, where a cigarette, lighted some time earlier in the evening, was balanced on an ashtray. It obviously had gone out, though, and he didn't pick it up. "In the first place," he said into the phone, "I've told you many, many times, Arthur, that's ex*actly* where you make your biggest mistake. You know what you do? Would you like me to tell you what you do? You go out of your way—I mean this, now—You actually go out of your way to torture yourself. As a matter of fact, you actually in*spire* Joanie—" He broke off. "You're bloody lucky she's a wonderful kid. I mean it. You give that kid absolutely no credit for having any good taste—or *brains*, for Chrissake, for that matter—"

"Brains! Are you kidding? She hasn't got any goddam brains! She's an animal!"

The gray-haired man, his nostrils dilating, appeared to take a fairly deep breath. "We're all animals," he said. "Basically, we're all animals."

"Like hell we are. I'm no goddam animal. I may be a stupid, fouled-up twentieth-century son of a bitch, but I'm no animal. Don't gimme that. I'm no animal."

"Look, Arthur. This isn't getting us—"

"*Brains.* Jesus, if you knew how funny that was. She thinks she's a goddam intellectual. That's the funny part, that's the hilarious part. She reads the theatrical page, and she watches television till she's practically blind—so she's an intellectual. You know who I'm married to? You want to know who I'm married to? I'm married to the *greatest living undeveloped, undiscovered act*ress, *nov*elist, psych*oan*alyst, and all-around goddam unappreciated celebrity-genius in New York. You didn't know that, didja? Christ, it's so funny I could cut my throat. Madame Bovary at Columbia Extension School. Madame—"

"Who?" asked the gray-haired man, sounding annoyed.

"Madame Bovary takes a course in Television Appreciation. God, if you knew how—"

"All right, all right. You realize this isn't getting us anyplace," the gray-haired man said. He turned and gave the girl a sign, with two fingers near his mouth, that he wanted a cigarette. "In the first place," he said, into the phone, "for a helluvan intelligent guy, you're about as tactless as it's humanly possible to be." He straightened his back so that the girl could reach behind him for the cigarettes. "I mean that. It shows up in your private life, it shows up in your—"

"*Brains*. Oh, God, that kills me! Christ almighty! Did you ever hear her describe anybody—some man, I mean? Sometime when you haven't anything to do, do me a favor and get her to describe some man for you. She describes every man she sees as 'terribly attractive.' It can be the oldest, crummiest, greasiest—"

"All right, Arthur," the gray-haired man said sharply. "This is getting us nowhere. But nowhere." He took a lighted cigarette from the girl. She had lit two. "Just incidentally," he said, exhaling smoke through his nostrils, "how'd you make out today?"

"What?"

"How'd you make out today?" the gray-haired man repeated. "How'd the case go?"

"Oh, Christ! I don't know. Lousy. About two minutes before I'm all set to start my summation, the attorney for the plaintiff, Lissberg, trots in this crazy chambermaid with a bunch of bedsheets as evidence—bedbug stains all over them. Christ!"

"So what happened? You lose?" asked the gray-haired man, taking another drag on his cigarette.

"You know who was on the bench? Mother Vittorio. What the hell that guy has against me, I'll never know. I can't even open my mouth and he jumps all over me. You can't reason with a guy like that. It's impossible."

The gray-haired man turned his head to see what the girl was doing. She had picked up the ashtray and was putting it between them. "You lose, then, or what?" he said into the phone.

"What?"

"I said, Did you lose?"

"Yeah. I was gonna tell you about it. I didn't get a chance at the party, with all the ruckus. You think Junior'll hit the ceiling? Not that I give a good goddam, but what do you think? Think he will?"

With his left hand, the gray-haired man shaped the ash of his cigarette on the rim of the ashtray. "I don't think he'll necessarily hit the *ceiling,* Arthur," he said quietly. "Chances are very much in favor, though, that he's not going to be overjoyed about it. You know how long we've handled those three bloody hotels? Old man Shanley himself started the whole—"

"I know, I know. Junior's told me about it at least fifty times. It's one of the most beautiful stories I ever heard in my life. All right, so I lost the goddam case. In the first place, it wasn't my fault. First, this lunatic Vittorio baits me all through the trial. Then this moron chambermaid starts passing out sheets full of bedbug—"

"Nobody's saying it's your fault, Arthur," the gray-haired man said. "You asked me if I thought Junior would hit the ceiling. I simply gave you an honest—"

"I know—I know that. . . . I don't know. What the hell. I may go back in the Army anyway. I tell you about that?"

The gray-haired man turned his head again toward the girl, perhaps to show her how forbearing, even stoic, his countenance was. But the girl missed seeing it. She had just overturned the ashtray with her knee and was rapidly, with her fingers, brushing the spilled ashes into a little pick-up pile; her eyes looked up at him a second too late. "No, you didn't, Arthur," he said into the phone.

"Yeah. I may. I don't know yet. I'm not crazy about the idea, naturally, and I won't go if I can possibly avoid it. But I may have to. I don't know. At least, it's oblivion. If they gimme back my little helmet and my big, fat desk and my nice, big mosquito net, it might not—" "I'd like to beat some sense into that head of yours, boy, that's what *I'd* like to do," the gray-haired man said. "For a helluvan—For a supposedly intelligent guy, you talk like an absolute child. And I say that in all sincerity. You let a bunch of minor little things snowball to an extent that they get so bloody paramount in your mind that you're absolutely unfit for any—"

"I shoulda left her. You know that? I should've gone through with it last summer, when I really had the ball rolling—you know that? You know why I didn't? You want to know why I didn't?"

"Arthur. For Chris*sake*. This is getting us exactly nowhere."

"Wait a second. Lemme tellya why! You want to know why I didn't? I can tellya exactly why. Because I felt sorry for her. That's the whole simple truth. I felt sorry for her."

"Well, I don't know. I mean that's out of my jurisdiction," the gray-haired man said. "It seems to me, though, that the one thing you seem to forget is that Joanie's a grown woman. I don't know, but it seems to me—"

"Grown woman! You crazy? She's a grown *child*, for Chrissake! Listen, I'll be shaving—listen to this—I'll be shaving, and all of a sudden she'll call me from way the hell the other end of the apartment. I'll go see what's the matter—right in the middle of shaving, lather all over my goddam face. You know what she'll want? She'll want to ask me if I think she has a good mind. I swear to God. She's *pathetic*, I tellya. I watch her when she's asleep, and I know what I'm talkin' about. Believe me."

"Well, that's something you know better than—I mean that's out of my jurisdiction," the gray-haired man said. "The point is, God damn it, you don't do anything at all constructive to—"

"We're mis*mat*ed, that's all. That's the whole simple story. We're just mismated as hell. You know what she needs? She needs some big silent bastard to just walk over once in a while and knock her out cold —then go back and finish reading his paper. That's what she needs. I'm too goddam weak for her. I knew it when we got married—I swear to God I did. I mean you're a smart bastard, you've never been married, but every now and then, before anybody gets married, they get these *flash*es of what it's going to be like after they're married. I ignored 'em. I ignored all my goddam flashes. I'm weak. That's the whole thing in a nutshell."

"You're not weak. You just don't use your head," the gray-haired man said, accepting a freshly lighted cigarette from the girl.

"Certainly I'm weak! Certainly I'm weak! God damn it, I know whether I'm weak or not! If I weren't weak, you don't think I'd've let everything get all—Aah, what's the usea talking? Certainly I'm weak . . . God, I'm keeping you awake all night. Why don't you hang the hell up on me? I mean it. Hang up on me."

"I'm not going to hang up on you, Arthur. I'd like to help you, if it's humanly possible," the gray-haired man said. "Actually, you're your own worst—"

"She doesn't respect me. She doesn't even love me, for God's sake. *Basi*cally—in the last analysis—I don't love her any more, either. I don't know. I do and I don't. It varies. It fluctuates. Christ! Every time I get all set to put my foot down, we have dinner out, for some reason, and I meet her somewhere and she comes in with these goddam white *gloves* on or something. I don't know. Or I start thinking about the first time we drove up to New Haven for the Princeton game. We had a flat right after we got off the Parkway, and it was cold as hell, and she held the flashlight while I fixed the goddam thing—You know what I mean. I don't know. Or I start thinking about—Christ, it's embarrassing—I start thinking about this goddam poem I sent her when we first started goin' around together. 'Rose my color is and white, Pretty mouth and green my eyes.' Christ, it's em*bar*rassing—it used to *remind* me of her. She doesn't have green eyes—she has eyes like goddam *sea* shells, for Chrissake—but it reminded me anyway . . . I don't know. What's the usea talking? I'm losing my mind. Hang up on me, why don't you? I mean it."

The gray-haired man cleared his throat and said, "I have no intention of hanging up on you, Arthur. There's just one—"

"She bought me a suit once. With her own money. I tell you about that?"

"No, I—"

"She just went into I think Tripler's and bought it. I didn't even go with her. I mean she has some goddam nice traits. The funny thing was it wasn't a bad fit. I just had to have it taken in a little bit around the seat —the pants—and the length. I mean she has some goddam nice traits."

The gray-haired man listened another moment. Then, abruptly, he turned toward the girl. The look he gave her, though only glancing, fully informed her what was suddenly going on at the other end of the phone. "Now, Arthur. Listen. That isn't going to do any good," he said into the phone. "That isn't going to do any good. I mean it. Now, listen. I say this in all sincerity. Willya get undressed and get in bed, like a good guy? And relax? Joanie'll probably *be* there in about *two minutes*. You don't want her to see you like that, do ya? The bloody Ellenbogens'll probably barge in with her. You don't want the whole bunch of 'em to see you like that, do ya?" He listened. "Arthur? You hear me?"

"God, I'm keeping you awake all night. Everything I do, I—"

"You're *not* keeping me awake all night," the gray-haired man said. "Don't even think of that. I've already told you, I've been averaging about four hours' sleep a night. What I *would* like to do, though, if it's at all humanly possible, I'd like to help you, boy." He listened. "Arthur? You there?"

"Yeah. I'm here. Listen. I've kept you awake all night anyway. Could I come over to your place for a drink? Wouldja mind?"

The gray-haired man straightened his back and placed the flat of his free hand on the top of his head, and said, "Now, do you mean?"

"Yeah. I mean if it's all right with you. I'll only stay a minute. I'd just like to sit down somewhere and—I don't know. Would it be all right?"

"Yeah, but the point is I don't think you should, Arthur," the gray-haired man said, lowering his hand from his head. "I mean you're more than welcome to come, but I honestly think you should just sit tight and relax till Joanie waltzes in. I honestly do. What *you* want to be, you want to be right there on the spot when she waltzes in. Am I right, or not?"

"Yeah. I don't know. I swear to God, I don't know."

"Well, I do, I honestly do," the gray-haired man said. "Look. Why don't you hop in bed now, and relax, and then later, if you feel like it, give me a ring. I mean if you feel like talking. And *don't worry*. That's the main thing. Hear me? Willya do that now?"

"All right."

The gray-haired man continued for a moment to hold the phone to his ear, then lowered it into its cradle.

"What did he say?" the girl immediately asked him.

He picked his cigarette out of the ashtray—that is, selected it from an accumulation of smoked and half-smoked cigarettes. He dragged on it and said, "He wanted to come over here for a drink."

"God! What'd you say?" said the girl.

"You heard me," the gray-haired man said, and looked at her. "You could hear me. Couldn't you?" He squashed out his cigarette.

"You were wonderful. Absolutely marvellous," the girl said, watching him. "God, I feel like a dog!"

"Well," the gray-haired man said, "it's a tough situation. I don't know how marvellous I was."

"You were. You were wonderful," the girl said. "I'm *limp*. I'm absolutely *limp*. Look at me!"

The gray-haired man looked at her. "Well, actually, it's an impossible situation," he said. "I mean the whole thing's so fantastic it isn't even—"

"Darling—Excuse me," the girl said quickly, and leaned forward. "I think you're on *fire*." She gave the back of his hand a short, brisk, brushing stroke with the flats of her fingers. "No. It was just an ash." She leaned back. "No, you were marvellous," she said. "God, I feel like an absolute *dog!*"

"Well, it's a very, very tough situation. The guy's obviously going through absolute—"

The phone suddenly rang.

The gray-haired man said "Christ!" but picked it up before the second ring. "Hello?" he said into it.

"Lee? Were you asleep?"

"No, no."

"Listen, I just thought you'd want to know. Joanie just barged in."

"What?" said the gray-haired man, and bridged his left hand over his eyes, though the light was behind him.

"Yeah. She just barged in. About ten seconds after I spoke to you. I just thought I'd give you a ring while she's in the john. Listen, thanks a million, Lee. I mean it—you know what I mean. You weren't asleep, were ya?"

"No, no. I was just—No, no," the gray-haired man said, leaving his fingers bridged over his eyes. He cleared his throat.

"Yeah. What happened was, apparently Leona got stinking and then had a goddam crying jag, and Bob wanted Joanie to go out and grab a drink with them somewhere and iron the thing out. I don't know. You know. Very involved. Anyway, so she's home. What a rat race. Honest to God, I think it's this goddam New York. What I think maybe we'll do, if everything goes along all right, we'll get ourselves a little place in Connecticut maybe. Not too far out, necessarily, but far enough that we can lead a normal goddam life. I mean she's crazy about plants and all that stuff. She'd probably go mad if she had her own goddam garden and stuff. Know what I mean? I mean—except you—who do we know in New York except a bunch of neurotics? It's bound to undermine even a normal person sooner or later. Know what I mean?"

The gray-haired man didn't give an answer. His eyes, behind the bridge of his hand, were closed.

"Anyway, I'm gonna talk to her about it tonight. Or tomorrow, maybe. She's still a little under the weather. I mean she's a helluva good kid basically, and if we *have* a chance to straighten ourselves out a little bit, we'd be goddam stupid not to at least have a go at it. While I'm at it, I'm also gonna try to straighten out this lousy bedbug mess, too. I've been thinking. I was just wondering, Lee. You think if I went in and talked to Junior personally, I could—"

"Arthur, if you don't mind, I'd appreciate—"

"I mean I don't want you to think I just called you back or anything because I'm *worried* about my goddam job or anything. I'm not. I mean basically, for Chrissake, I couldn't care less. I just thought if I could straighten Junior out without beating my brains out, I'd be a goddam fool—"

"Listen, Arthur," the gray-haired man interrupted, taking his hand away from his face, "I have a helluva headache all of a sudden. I don't know where I got the bloody thing from. You mind if we cut this short? I'll talk to you in the morning—all right?" He listened for another moment, then hung up.

Again the girl immediately spoke to him, but he didn't answer her. He picked a burning cigarette—the girl's out of the ashtray and started to bring it to his mouth, but it slipped out of his fingers. The girl tried to help him retrieve it before anything was burned, but he told her to just *sit still,* for Chrissake, and she pulled back her hand.

Biographical Notes

Biographical Notes

WASHINGTON IRVING
(1783–1859)

WASHINGTON IRVING was the first American man of letters—the first to adopt literature as a life work and to support himself successfully by his pen. Though Irving was born and died in New York, he was a "Knickerbocker" who spent many years abroad. In Italy he had met Coleridge and Washington Allston, and under the spell of the latter momentarily debated with himself whether to stake his career upon writing or painting. In 1842, as biographer of Columbus, he was appointed Minister to Spain. Particularly he loved England, and upon his death Thackeray pronounced him "the first ambassador whom the New World of Letters sent to the Old." In the history of the short story Irving holds a distinguished place. *Rip Van Winkle* and *The Legend of Sleepy Hollow* were tales of a kind till then unknown in English literature—though Walter Map, in his tale of King Herla in *De Nugis Curialium,* had centuries before told in Latin a no less beautiful version of the ancient folk-tale of Rip Van Winkle. Of himself Irving wrote to a friend: "I consider a story merely as a frame on which to sketch my materials; it is the play of thought and sentiment, and language; the weaving in of character, lightly yet expressively delineated; the familiar and faithful exhibition of scenes of common life; and the half-concealed vein of humor that is often playing through the whole; these are among what I aim at."

NATHANIEL HAWTHORNE
(1804–1864)

UNTIL his forty-sixth year, when he produced *The Scarlet Letter* in 1850, Nathaniel Hawthorne was, as he once called himself, "the obscurest man of letters in America." Before that time he published stories and sketches, many anonymously; he had married Sophia Peabody; he had for three years been surveyor of the port of Salem. With *The Scarlet Letter* came quick and lasting recognition, followed two years later by a long-delayed pilgrimage to the Old World. Hawthorne was absent seven years, the first four of which he spent as Consul to Liverpool, one of the best-paid offices under the Government. In 1860, **as a result** of a year and a half spent in Italy, he published *The Marble Faun*. Four years of life remained to him, but he accomplished little. The Civil War came on, his health was breaking, the labor of writing wearied and depressed him.

At intervals since his death all the writings he left behind have been published—his private letters, his note-books. While these have not added to his fame, they give further confirmation of the extraordinary depth and luminosity of his consciousness and the fine seriousness of his craftsmanship.

The Great Stone Face and *Rappaccini's Daughter,* with their deep moral insight and their skillful narrative power, are among the very best of Hawthorne's shorter pieces.

EDGAR ALLAN POE
(1809–1849)

INTERNATIONALLY the most famous of all American writers, Edgar Allan Poe suffered during his short lifetime the deepest bitterness and humiliation in his native land. The victim of an acrimonious biography by Rufus Griswold, and, more disastrously, the victim of his own dark demon and an incurable alcoholism, his genius surmounts all the vicissitudes of his life. Brander Matthews contrasts the "honorable longevity" of all the other classical American writers with the exceptional Poe who "died young and alone and poor and in ill repute."

He was admitted to West Point in 1830 and was expelled in 1831. At the age of 22 he published his first volume of poems, and from 1833 until his death had a phenomenal career as an editor on a succession of periodicals. As a critic the fierce vehemence of his philippics made for him many enemies. But it is as a writer of short stories that Poe achieved his highest distinction. To him belongs the credit, with the publication of *The Murders in the Rue Morgue*, of the invention of the detective story. Subsequently, he originated the story based on ratiocination with *The Gold Bug*. There followed *The Mystery of Marie Roget, The Purloined Letter* and many notable tales of the macabre. Charles Cestre has said of him: "His work owes much to the drift of romanticism (of which he is a late heir) towards the occult and the satanic. It owes much also to his own feverish dreams, to which he applied a strange power of logic and a rare faculty of shaping plausible fabrics out of impalpable materials."

HERMAN MELVILLE
(1819–1891)

HERMAN MELVILLE is one of the very few writers to achieve great posthumous fame. During his lifetime, as a result of his South-Sea adventures as recorded in *Typee* and *Omoo,* he enjoyed a kind of minor popularity as "the man who lived with the cannibals." His masterpiece, *Moby Dick,* published when he was forty-three, was a total fiasco. This was his sixth book; and its failure to sell was final and sufficient demonstration to Melville that he could not support himself and his wife and four children by his pen. For twenty years (between 1866 and 1886) he was Inspector of Customs in New York. He resigned this post when his wife came into an inheritance that allowed him an ultimate serenity in his closing years: It was then that he wrote *Billy Budd, Foretopman,* finished only a few months before his death, and first published in 1924.

EDWARD EVERETT HALE
(1822–1909)

EDWARD EVERETT HALE was descended from a distinguished and public-minded family; his father was the proprietor of a Boston daily, an uncle was notable as orator and statesman, and his great-uncle, Nathan Hale, was the martyr spy. In 1842 Hale began to preach, and in 1903 he was named chaplain of the United States Senate. He first came into notice as a writer in 1859 with the appearance of *My Double and How He Undid Me* in the *Atlantic Monthly.* He published other stories in the same periodical. Of these, the best known is *The Man Without a Country* (1863), which did much to strengthen the Union cause.

FITZ–JAMES O'BRIEN
(1828?–1862)

ABOUT the year 1828 Fitz-James O'Brien was born in Ireland. He was educated at Dublin University, received a patrimony, proceeded to London, as did many of the young Irishmen of his day, spent his patrimony, and was left stranded. He followed the example of other of his countrymen, and emigrated to America in 1852, settling in New York. He was a great favorite among the Bohemians for his wit and his gayety; and he found an audience very soon for his gifts as a writer. He wrote poems, plays, essays, and stories for a period of ten years. When the Civil War broke out, he was given a commission. Fatally wounded in February of 1862, he died two months later.

O'Brien has often been compared to Poe in his choice of bizarre material. But he is very different from Poe in that he attempts to relate his subject matter to the everyday world of reality. He was of course strongly under the spell of the current Gothic romanticism, which made an especial appeal to O'Brien's Gaelic temperament. He was, moreover, particularly adroit in fictionizing current discoveries in the realm of fact. His best-known stories are *What Was It?* and *The Diamond Lens.*

FRANK R. STOCKTON
(1834–1902)

The Lady, or the Tiger? is not only the most famous of Frank R. Stockton's stories; it is one of the most famous of all short stories. The author wrote many others that are amusing, clever, whimsical or richly humorous. But this particular one is perhaps the most skillful of "trick" stories, and it gained for its author an undue amount of publicity.

Stockton was born in Philadelphia, and it was not until he was nearly forty that he published his first fiction for adults. About that time he moved to New York, where for a number of years he held editorial positions, all the time turning out his sketches and stories and tales. He was an exceedingly popular author in his time.

MARK TWAIN
(*Samuel Langhorne Clemens*)
(1835–1910)

MARK TWAIN is perhaps the most widely read and the most deeply loved of all American writers. He escaped being born in New England, nor could the literary provincialities of the other side of the Mason and Dixon line claim him. He was not the mouthpiece of any "literary" locale. As Ludwig Lewisohn has said of him (in contrast with Whitman): "It was a younger man from the Mississippi Valley, a normal, busy, humorous, kind-hearted American, a newspaper man, a prospector, pioneer, publisher, gainer and loser of fortunes, perfect husband, devoted father, pal of millionaires and clergyman and right-thinking men of letters, of lords and dukes and sovereigns too, later on—it was Samuel Clemens, eternal adolescent and hence creator of the finest picaresque novel composed for centuries—it was he whom the American people chose as their great spokesman and literary hero." Of Mark Twain's humor Mr. Lewisohn has said: "It is directed against preten-

tiousness and falseness, against all 'putting on' of 'airs'. . . . His sketches
and stories are well written about a practical joke of some kind. But
he is careful, unlike his predecessors, to be sure that the objects of the
practical joke have justly lost the reader's moral sympathy. *The Man
That Corrupted Hadleyburg* is an excellent illustration of this method."

THOMAS BAILEY ALDRICH
(1836–1907)

THOMAS BAILEY ALDRICH was born in the historic town of Portsmouth,
New Hampshire. From Portsmouth he was taken as a boy to New
Orleans, and that city with its French charm and exotic flavor left a
deep impression upon him.

While he was preparing for Harvard, his father died; there was
no money, and young Aldrich had to go to work. He served for
several years as a clerk in his uncle's office in New York. His first
book of verse, *The Bells,* was a success, and he left the business world to
become literary critic on the *Evening Mirror.* For the remainder of his
life, except for time spent as a war correspondent, he wrote verse and
stories and served in one editorial capacity or another. He was for years
known for the extraordinary skill and felicity of his light verse. Of
Aldrich, Brander Matthews wrote: "He was a story-teller as well as a
lyrist, carrying into fiction the ingenious fantasy which characterized
his verse. He is best known by his exquisite short story, *Marjorie Daw,*
and by his vivacious *Story of a Bad Boy,* which is almost autobiographic."

WILLIAM DEAN HOWELLS
(1837–1920)

SON of an Ohio printer-journalist, Howells spent his early life as
type-setter, reporter and editor in the offices of various newspapers. And
throughout his distinguished life he was never far from a printing-press,
unless exception be made of the five years ensuing upon 1860 when he
was Consul at Venice. In 1865 he joined the staff of the *Atlantic
Monthly,* and from 1872 to 1881 he was its editor-in-chief. He was extraordinarily prolific as a writer-novelist, poet, dramatist, essayist, critic.
The unusual charm of his personality won him a host of friends. He
was long considered the foremost representative of the realistic school
of indigenous fiction. Despite his sojourn in Italy and his mastery of
several European tongues, he insisted upon seeing and portraying American life under its own skies and in its own vocabulary.

FRANCIS BRET HARTE
(1839–1902)

AN EASTERNER by birth, Bret Harte migrated to California when he was nineteen, after a childhood of hardship and ill health. For a time he taught school; he was a druggist's clerk, a tutor and an express messenger on a California stage. The romance and the picturesqueness of the gold rush held him under its spell. It was the "Argonauts of '49" whom he recorded in *The Luck of Roaring Camp*. These stories, with *The Outcasts of Poker Flat*, are Harte's earliest work. He never surpassed them. Their freshness and vigor capture the flavor of an epoch.

AMBROSE BIERCE
(1842–1914)

AMBROSE BIERCE was born in Meiggs County, Ohio. He served throughout the Civil War, was brevetted major for distinguished services. After the war, he went to San Francisco, where he held editorial positions on several San Francisco weeklies. In 1872, he went to London and there for four years he continued his journalistic career. His first literary work appeared while he was abroad. He returned in 1876 to San Francisco and for nearly all of the next twenty-one years he worked for newspapers. Mr. George Sterling says of Bierce: "By far the greater part of this work was polemical in its nature. . . . Bierce's pen was dipped in wormwood and acid, and . . . his assaults were more dreaded than the bowie knife and revolver. . . ."

The two stories by Bierce represented here are taken from his volume *Tales of Soldiers and Civilians,* and it is interesting to see what the author wrote as a prefatory note. "Denied existence by the chief publishing houses of the country, this book owes itself to Mr. E. L. G. Steele, merchant, of this city. In attesting Mr. Steele's faith in his judgment and his friend, it will serve its author's main and best ambition. A. B., San Francisco, Sept. 4, 1891."

His stories deal with the horrible and the gruesome or the supernatural. We may hate his stories, as Mr. Sterling says, but we cannot forget them. "His heroes, or rather victims, are lonely men, passing to unpredictable dooms, and hearing, from inaccessible crypts of space, the voices of unseen malevolences."

In November, 1913, Bierce left San Francisco and went to Mexico. For a number of years there was no word whatever about him. But it now seems clearly certain that he was shot in 1914 by one or another of the revolutionary factions in Mexico.

HENRY JAMES
(1843–1916)

FOR a number of years after the World War, Henry James's reputation suffered an eclipse. Mr. H. G. Wells wrote a triumphant last word when he had one of his characters compare the labored intensity of Henry James's efforts to explore the deepest recesses of the human heart to "a magnificent but painful hippopotamus resolved at any cost, even at the cost of its dignity, upon picking up a pea which has got into a corner of its den." But the values that Henry James lived for have again emerged from eclipse.

The Dial Press has published a collection of his novelettes, Henry Seidel Canby is writing his definitive biography, and Clifton Fadiman has edited for Random House a bumper volume of his best short stories.

Rebecca West closes her beautiful little book on Henry James thus: "In July, 1915, he took the great step, fraught for him with the deepest emotions, of renouncing his American citizenship and becoming a naturalized British subject; and in January, 1916, he did England the further honor of accepting the Order of Merit. And on 28th February, 1916, he died, leaving the white light of his genius to shine out for the eternal comfort of the mind of man."

JOEL CHANDLER HARRIS
(1848–1908)

HARRIS was a Georgian who wrote many sketches and stories of Southern life. Although he had earlier established himself as a brilliant newspaper man, it was through his delineation of a Negro, the shrewd and masterful Uncle Remus who told tales to a little boy, that he won for himself a secure fame.

Speaking of the generation of American writers during the last decades of the nineteenth century, Carl Van Doren says: "Outside of Mark Twain the generation left hardly a single lasting folk-hero except Uncle Remus and the animals of his bestiary."

SARAH ORNE JEWETT
(1849–1909)

THE advice that Sarah Orne Jewett gave to Willa Cather—to write truthfully about the things she knew—might well describe what Miss Jewett herself did for her own New England people. She disclaimed all commerce with those writers who were given to "prettify." She looked out on her New England scene, and she recorded what she saw. And though her stories seem not to be very much read nowadays, few of us realize how important her influence has been upon many writers who followed after her.

She was born at South Berwick, Maine, of a family that had for generations known the advantages of culture. Her first book, *Deephaven,* was published in 1887. It is a very careful study of her New England people in the form of an autobiography. From that date, she continued to publish novels and stories, and in all of her work she never got far from the characters and lives of the New Englanders she knew so intimately.

The Courting of Sister Wisby appeared in 1888 in the volume *The King of Folly Island and Other People.*

LAFCADIO HEARN
(1850–1904)

LEUCADIA (pronounced Lefcadia) is famous as the Ionian island from which Sappho is reputed to have leapt to suicide. Hearn's father was an Irish Surgeon-major stationed in the Aegean, his mother a Greek. He gleaned a casual education at a Catholic college in Durham, and he died a Buddhist. At the age of 19, thrown upon his own resources, he migrated to America to try his hand at journalism. Though he was practically blind, he was pulled up the spire of Saint Patrick's Cathedral, New York, to record for the reading public the view from that height. He was for some time in New Orleans, writing for the *Times Democrat,* and was sent by that paper for two years as correspondent to the West Indies. In 1891, as journalist, he was sent to Japan. There he promptly broke with journalism, became a teacher of English at the University of Tokio, had children that were half Japanese, and, in order that these children might be entered in the Japanese public schools, became a naturalized Japanese under the name of Yakumo Koizumi. The realistic Japanese thereupon promptly reduced his salary to the native scale (foreign teachers were then paid much more than natives). Hearn then returned to America, hating the Orient, to write several volumes of short stories, and to furnish copy for Dr. G. M. Gould's informative volume, *Concerning Lafcadio Hearn.*

GERTRUDE ATHERTON
(1857–1948)

Mrs. Gertrude Atherton, a native of San Francisco, California, spent most of her life in her own state. The early history of California was a dominant theme in her writings, and the story, "The Pearls of Loreto" is an excellent example of the manner in which she reconstructed a past age, and seized a dramatic situation for illuminating a tale. Indeed, Mrs. Atherton was most successful in transforming the facts of history into vivid fiction. Her fine novel, *The Conqueror,* deals with the life and times of Alexander Hamilton and Aaron Burr; her *Rezanov* is another instance of her power of imaginative reconstruction. With Mrs. Atherton's novels of her declining years, the editors of this anthology have little patience.

HAMLIN GARLAND
(1860–1940)

Hamlin Garland was born in West Salem, Wisconsin. In 1881 he was graduated from Cedar Valley Seminary, Osage, Iowa, where he devoted himself to the study of literature. When he was not in school, he worked on a farm. Later he taught school in Illinois. Then he migrated to South Dakota and took up a claim. But soon thereafter we find him in Boston, writing stories.

There had been a good deal of romanticizing of the West, and Hamlin Garland, who knew at first hand the hardships and privations of the lives of the settlers, was the first writer to give us the truth about conditions of pioneer life. He did for the West what Mary E. Wilkins Freeman was doing for New England. Mr. Garland has been the chief interpreter of the Middle Border in the United States during the nineteenth century. His work is marked by a realism that accents the more somber aspects of life. But this must be said: Mr. Garland was always true to his own vision. Like Hardy, he was more preoccupied with tragic than with light themes.

MARY E. WILKINS FREEMAN
(1862-1930)

MARY E. WILKINS was born in Randolph, Massachusetts, and lived there and in Brattleboro, Vermont, until she married Dr. C. M. Freeman in 1902. The remainder of her life was spent in New Jersey. Before her marriage, Mary E. Wilkins had established for herself a reputation for her vivid and true delineations of New England characters. For the most part, she delighted in revealing the lives of New England farmers, their wives—particularly their wives—and their children. While her work sometimes makes concessions to the romantic demands of the last two decades of the nineteenth century, her stories are noted for their realistic treatment. Her name has been for a long time associated with the New England of the latter part of the last century, much as Hawthorne's name is associated with the New England of an earlier day.

A New England Nun is the title story of her first volume of stories, and although for more than thirty years Mrs. Freeman produced volume after volume, and was regarded as the foremost interpreter of New England life, none of her volumes has transcended this one, and few of her stories indeed surpass it.

EDITH WHARTON
(1862-1937)

No BETTER estimate of what Edith Wharton represents in the field of American literature has been made than Robert Morss Lovett's, in discussing the tendency of America to lag behind the literary movements of England and the Continent. The decadence of the nineties was remote from American writers. What emerged in America during this decade was a healthy local realism. Robert Morss Lovett writes: "American realism was not continental naturalism. The Puritan inheritance of morality and the new spirit of culture combined to insist upon the claims of significance of subject matter (a significance which is necessarily in the large sense moral) and of beauty of form, as opposed to the requirement of sheer fidelity to the objective world. Into this America of the 1890's came Edith Wharton, and in it she has steadily remained. The most superficial reading of her work brings evidence of her absorption in the somewhat mechanical operations of culture, her preoccupation with the upper class, and her loyalty to the theory of the art of fiction set forth by Henry James, of which the basis was a recognition of moral values. If one were to equip himself with a set of pigeon holes in which to collect the results of an analysis of Edith Wharton's work, they would be labelled: Culture, Class, Morality." Miss Wharton's *Ethan Frome* is one of America's masterpieces of fiction. Perhaps her most typical work, however, is *The Age of Innocence*. The 1935 Pulitzer Prize Play, *The Old Maid*, was based on a story by Edith Wharton.

O. HENRY
(*William Sydney Porter*)
(1862–1910)

BORN at Greensboro, North Carolina, William Sydney Porter—known throughout the world as O. Henry—received little formal education. As a young man, he went to Texas, where he worked in the General Land Office, and later in a bank. He became unfortunately involved in a mysterious business deal, and served a short prison sentence as a result thereof. This fact of his life is mentioned because it was from prison that he sent out his first stories. Immediately his work found a very responsive public, and for years he was kept hard at work by editors. His name is now given to a certain kind of story, one in which the whole emphasis is so placed that the sudden or reversal ending will shock or surprise the reader. Many writers have tried to imitate him, but few have had anything like the success of O. Henry. He is perhaps one of the most inventive of short story writers; but in his best work he is more than inventive: he is creative in the truest sense. No two O. Henry enthusiasts can agree on which of his tales best deserve reprinting in an anthology. The three that we have chosen are *our* favorites. The sadly overworked *Gift of the Magi* was omitted purposely.

RICHARD HARDING DAVIS
(1864–1916)

DURING his life Richard Harding Davis contributed much to the entertainment of the American people. A handsome man with a flair for romantic fiction and with a real gift for journalism, he became the first of our globe-trotting, highly personalized war correspondents. He was born in Philadelphia, the son of Lemuel Clark Davis, editorial writer, and Rebecca Harding Davis who was a well-known author. He attended Swarthmore, Lehigh, and Johns Hopkins, but sports and social events were more interesting to him than studies, and he gave up the academic world at the age of twenty-two to launch into journalism. In spite of his contacts he had difficulty in placing his story *Gallagher,* but in 1890 it appeared in *Scribner's Magazine,* and made the author famous. "Here with," says Thomas Beer, "Davis mounted into celebrity as gracefully as he might have swung his fine body in its handsome dress to the cushion of a waiting cab." His Van Bibber stories, charming but superficial studies of New York society of his day, made him a fortune.

The Bar Sinister was such a valuable literary property that its original publishers are here permitting its reproduction in an anthology for the first time.

GEORGE ADE
(1866–1944)

PERHAPS it is true, as Professor Fred L. Pattee says, that "In the evolution of a native literature, original humor is the last element to come. It arrives only with independence grown habitual, with national uniqueness achieved, with localized individuality become as ingrained as the fundamentals of race." In the history of American letters, these requisites seem to have been met within twenty or thirty years after the close of the Civil War. George Ade, born in Indiana, graduated from Purdue University, belongs in the best tradition of American humor. But one must distinguish between earlier American humor and the gracious wit and urbanity of the writings of George Ade.

When he left college, he went into journalism. He is best known for his stories in the American vernacular, antedating by some years the work of Ring Lardner, and chiefly for his *Fables in Slang* (1899). He has written musical comedy librettos, plays and film scenarios. "My early story stuff," he says, "was intended to be 'realistic,' and I believed firmly in short words and short sentences. By a queer twist of circumstances I have become known to the general public as a 'humorist' and a writer of 'slang.' I never wanted to be a comic or tried to be one. The playful vernacular and idiomatic talk of the street and the fanciful figures of speech which came out for years under the heading *Fables in Slang* had no relation whatever to the cryptic language of the underworld or the patois of the criminal element. Always I wrote for the 'family trade' and I used no word or phrase which might give offense to mother and the girls or a professor of English."

BOOTH TARKINGTON
(1869–1946)

BOOTH TARKINGTON, born in Indianapolis, Indiana, was educated at Princeton. His first work was in the romantic vein that was decidedly in the taste of the day. His little novelette, *Monsieur Beaucaire*, had a tremendous vogue. But Booth Tarkington responded to the changes of the American scene throughout his career, and he soon began to look with a more realistic eye at the life about him. Though he wrote several interesting novels with profound themes, his most important contribution to American letters, perhaps, is his work dealing with adolescents. His Penrod books are those to which one constantly returns. Even though his novels mirror their particular period with truth, they are often "dated." The stories about Penrod and the other young people remain as fresh as youth itself and interest in them recurs generation after generation.

FRANK NORRIS
(1870–1902)

THE brief thirty-two years of Frank Norris's life were crowded with ambitious projects. At the age of seventeen he left his native Chicago to enroll as an art student in Paris. After two years at Julian's Academy, he returned to America to attend the University of California and Harvard. The college records do not show that he achieved scholastic prominence, nor do they reveal that one of the first American naturalistic novels was begun within their walls. At the outbreak of the Boer War, Frank Norris was sent to South Africa as a war correspondent for the San Francisco *Chronicle*. On his return, he became associate editor of the San Francisco *Wave* and began his career as a novelist in earnest. The Spanish-American War found him in Cuba as a correspondent for *McClure's Magazine*. He had also been a publishers' reader in New York. He went back to California to launch on what was to have been his *magnum opus: The Epic of Wheat*, a trilogy, the first two volumes of which, *The Octopus* and *The Pit*, created a national furor. The final volume, *The Wolf*, had not been begun when an operation for appendicitis proved fatal. The story *A Deal in Wheat* might well serve as a microcosm of the great epic he had in mind.

STEPHEN CRANE
(1871–1900)

STEPHEN CRANE's place in American literature was made secure by one book—*The Red Badge of Courage*—that superb story of the Civil War whose breath-taking descriptions of actual battle scenes are all the more remarkable in light of the fact that their author never saw as much as a skirmish in his whole life. *The Red Badge* stands by itself, but other works, notably *Maggie, A Girl of the Streets,* and *The Open Boat* contributed to the gradual acceptance of Crane as one of America's truly important writers. Thomas Beer's admirable biography sent present-day readers scurrying for his books.

Stephen Crane was born in Newark, New Jersey. His short life was full of sickness and trouble. His record as a journalist and war correspondent is studded with discouragements and failures. He had very pronounced—and for his time, advanced—ideas about writing, with which most of his editors emphatically disagreed. He died abroad, where he had gone for his health.

The Open Boat was a favorite story of Joseph Conrad's. "The deep and simple humanity of the presentation of that story of four men in a very small boat," he wrote, "seems somehow to illustrate the essentials of life itself."

THEODORE DREISER
(1871–1945)

FROM the time *Sister Carrie* was published in 1900, Theodore Dreiser hewed to his own line as a realistic writer. His has been perhaps the most invigorating and inspiriting influence in American letters. Sherwood Anderson has said of Dreiser: "Something gray and bleak and hurtful, that has been in the world perhaps forever, is personified in him." He goes on to say that after Dreiser many young men will write books, and their books will have qualities, it may be, that Dreiser's have not; they will have humor and "grace, lightness of touch, a dream of beauty breaking through the husks of life." But Theodore Dreiser was the pioneer; he was the man who had fought always for the truth. And that, Mr. Anderson felt, was one of the great merits of this author. "The feet of Theodore are making a path, the heavy brutal feet. They are tramping through the wilderness of lies, making a path . . . The prose writers in America who follow Dreiser will have much to do that he has never done. Their road is a long one, but, because of him, those who follow will never have to face the road through the wilderness of Puritan denial, the road that Dreiser faced alone."

For those who are given to carping about the unpolished style of Theodore Dreiser, this story *The Lost Phœbe,* with its ease and grace and beauty, is sufficient evidence that he could, and often did, write beautifully.

GERTRUDE STEIN
(1874–1946)

About 1922, Sherwood Anderson returned from a trip to France, and published in *The New Republic* an article on Gertrude Stein, extolling her literary gifts, and explaining that her *Tender Buttons* had made a deep impression upon him. But this eulogy was more than twelve years after Miss Stein had published her *Three Lives* (1909). One cannot help but feel that what Sherwood Anderson had accomplished in fiction, with no conscious awareness of what he was actually doing, Miss Stein had as early as 1909 done with a very deep artistic awareness indeed. To read any of the three stories in *Three Lives,* remembering when they were written, is to realize that Miss Stein stands within the tradition of American realism fostered with such fanatic devotion by Frank Norris and Stephen Crane. There are, to be sure, the tricks of repetitive prose in these stories that Miss Stein later carried toward a conclusion that some people might call logical. The fact remains that these early stories are readable and clearly understandable, whereas much of Miss Stein's later work, interestingly experimental though it may be, is unintelligible to a great many readers.

Gertrude Stein was born in Allegheny, Pennsylvania, educated at Radcliffe and at Johns Hopkins University in Baltimore. About forty-five years ago she went to Europe, and lived in France, chiefly in Paris, continuously until her visit to her own country in the Winter of 1934–1935. She died in Paris in 1946. For details about Miss Stein the reader is referred to her own autobiography, perhaps the most interesting of all her experiments, entitled *The Autobiography of Alice B. Toklas.*

WILLA CATHER
(1875–1947)

Willa Cather was born in Virginia, and moved in the 1880's to Nebraska. She attended the University of Nebraska, then she taught in Pittsburgh, and came to New York later to do editorial work with *McClure's Magazine.* The impressions of the early years of her life in Nebraska are beautifully recorded in the novel *My Antonia.* Her first novel, *Alexander's Bridge,* was an attempt to manage material with which she was not familiar at first hand. Very early in Miss Cather's career, Sarah Orne Jewett advised her to write "truthfully and simply" about her own subject matter. And Miss Cather followed that admonition conscientiously. Thus. in all of her books, when she went back to the scenes and the people of her earlier life in the Middle West, she was most successful. She enriched American literature with her novels of these pioneering people.

Miss Cather wrote few short stories. Those that are collected, notably the volume *Youth and the Bright Medusa,* though well written, are not as consistently fine as her novels. But a few of them stand out—*A Wagner Matinee, The Sculptor's Funeral,* and *Paul's Case.* And perhaps one should also mention *Death in the Desert.*

In the story *Paul's Case,* Miss Cather recorded what must have been, in essence, an experience encountered while she was teaching English in Pittsburgh. The subject matter is pathological, and it would be merely another case history, except for the creative imagination that took the facts and fused them into a story that is illuminating and sympathetic and profound.

JACK LONDON
(1876–1916)

JACK LONDON was born in Oakland, California. His life is more extraordinary than his books. He himself must have felt this, because he has written much that is of an autobiographical nature. One of his most interesting books, particularly from this viewpoint, is *Martin Eden.* Due to poverty in childhood and the terrible struggles of early manhood, his sympathies were always with the downtrodden. In book after book, he champions the cause of the unfortunate and dispossessed. His intense interest in propaganda often mars the artistry of his work.

The violent struggles in the world of nature, he believed, were little less violent than the struggles between man and man. His most successful book *The Call of the Wild* has a kind of allegorical parallelism: as the animals behave, so, really, do men behave.

In some of his very finest short stories the struggle depicted is between man and the external world of nature. *To Build a Fire* belongs in this group.

HARVEY O'HIGGINS
(1876–1928)

MR. O'HIGGINS was born in London, Ontario, attended the University of Toronto for a few years, left without taking his degree, and came to New York to make his way as a writer. He served his apprenticeship in journalism—that school, or training place of so many American writers —and indeed he never got quite completely away from newspaper work.

During the years when "muck-raking" was the fashion, Mr. O'Higgins was constantly engaged to write up the findings of the investigators. He had a great gift for journalism. But he was always deeply concerned with the art of fiction, and his best work in that field was undoubtedly in the short story. He came to be much interested in the findings of the new psychologists—Freud and Jung—and believed that their discoveries were fruitful fields for the fiction writer. In one of his justly famous stories, *Sir Watson Tyler,* he chooses a certain significant moment in the life of the eminent man who is the hero, to show how the man's whole success in life was based upon his choice of alternatives during one dramatic moment. It is a psycho-analytical story, but its art lies in the fact that Mr. O'Higgins has so beautifully subdued the analysis. Written about the same time, his *Big Dan Reilly,* based on the model of an actual political "boss" that he knew well, and understood deeply, deserves a place in an American anthology of short stories.

Mr. O'Higgins died at the too early age of fifty-two.

SHERWOOD ANDERSON
(1876–1941)

CHEKHOV once wrote in a letter to a friend that he thought it would be a good thing for short story writers to cut off the beginnings and the ends of their stories, for "that is where we are most inclined to lie." Since the Russian writer is often accused of writing formless stories, that is, stories that are not like those of Poe and O. Henry, and since Sherwood Anderson is accused of the same thing, it is not remarkable that some critics felt, when Mr. Anderson's stories appeared, that he had been influenced by the Russian. Mr. Anderson humorously meets this challenge in an episode in his *The Story Teller's Story,* where he explains: "This I found, that in Russian novels the characters are always eating cabbage soup and I have no doubt Russian writers eat it too. This was a revelation to me. Many of the Russian tales are concerned with the lives of peasants and a Boston critic once said I had brought the American peasant into literature; and it is likely that Russian writers, like all the other writers who have ever lived and have not pandered to the popular demand for sentimental romances, were fortunate if they could live as well as a peasant. 'What the critics say is no doubt true,' I told myself; for, like so many of the Russian writers, I was raised largely on cabbage soup!"

Mr. Anderson was born in Ohio, moved to Chicago, then to New York, and later to Virginia. He never subscribed to the "pattern" story; he was a born teller of tales; and his chief gift was his depth of insight into his character, and, in his best work, the simplicity and clarity of his prose.

OWEN JOHNSON
(1878–1952)

OWEN JOHNSON was born in New York City, and when his affluent parents selected Lawrenceville as his "prep" school they little realized what a fortunate choice they were making for both their son and the school. For Johnson's series of books about Lawrenceville (*The Prodigious Hickey, The Tennessee Shad, The Varmint,* etc., etc.) are among the finest stories of adolescent boyhood in our literature, and if present-day youngsters aren't as familiar with them as they should be, that's their loss!

Stover at Yale was published in 1911. Thereafter Mr. Johnson abruptly abandoned this type of book, and, until his death, devoted himself to the writing of novels of the highly sophisticated, "best-seller" variety. In 1926 he married for the fifth time. He lived in New York and Stockbridge.

JAMES BRANCH CABELL
(1879–   )

JAMES BRANCH CABELL is one of the few American writers living through an age given over almost wholly to the more relentless and violent forms of realism who has chosen quite deliberately to be the spokesman for romanticism. Mr. Cabell, born in Richmond, Virginia, educated at William and Mary, for a while instructor in Latin and Greek, returned to live his life quietly and charmingly in the city of his birth. With his equipment, then, and in such a setting, one might well expect to find in his romantic books and stories both scholarship and a very urbane outlook on life. And these are precisely what one does find. There are also to be found wit and irony, and often profound reflections on manners and morals. From his own account, in *These Restless Heads,* he tells us that in most of his books he has steadily praised the conventional and tried virtues, "in praise of monogamy in *Jurgen,* and of keeping up appearances in *Figures of Earth,* and of chastity in *Something About Eve . . .*" But even this statement may contain its own irony.

The story, called for convenience *Porcelain Cups,* is one part of a book of stories that are held together by a common line of interest. The full title is *The Episode called Porcelain Cups, from The Line of Love: Dizain des mariages.*

JOSEPH HERGESHEIMER
(1880–   )

ALTHOUGH born in Philadelphia, Joseph Hergesheimer has for a number of years lived a life of pleasant retirement in West Chester, Pennsylvania—as everyone knows who has read much of his fiction, or his essays. But his retirement has been one filled with work, for he set himself years ago the long task of learning to write—an apprenticeship almost as arduous as that of Maupassant. The result was that when Mr. Hergesheimer began to publish there was a finish and an authority about his craftsmanship that few will deny. He gained his first popular success with his novels *The Three Black Pennys* and *Java Head*. It is perhaps not unfair to say that Mr. Hergesheimer is usually more successful in dealing with the romantic or romanticized past than he is when confronted by the immediate and realistic present—life in Palm Beach, for example! With his passions for collecting and his deep interest in antiquarianism, he manages to reconstruct other times and other places with a fidelity of detail that aids much in establishing the characters as authentic individuals in their various scenes. In his creation of character he follows in the steps of Galsworthy and Arnold Bennett rather, let us say, than in the technical experimentations of James Joyce or Virginia Woolf. *Wild Oranges* is deservedly one of the most popular of his stories.

SUSAN GLASPELL
(1882–1948)

SUSAN GLASPELL and her husband, George Cram Cook, were the leaders of that discerning and enterprising group of writers who established the Provincetown Players on an old wharf on the tip of Cape Cod in the summer of 1913. It was they who were responsible for the first production of a play by a then unknown youngster just back from a stretch of sailing and adventuring around the world. His name is Eugene O'Neill.

Later Miss Glaspell and Mr. Cook moved to Greece, and, after his death there in 1923, she wrote *The Road to the Temple,* a moving and most successful story of his life. Among her numerous plays and novels is *Alison's House,* the Pulitzer Prize Play for 1931.

Miss Glaspell was a native of Davenport, Iowa. She lived, until her death, in Truro, Massachusetts.

RING LARDNER
(1885–1933)

RING LARDNER was born in 1885 at Niles, Michigan. He was educated at the Armour Institute in Chicago; was a reporter on the South Bend, Ind. *Times* for two years; and for four years he did newspaper work in Chicago, St. Louis and New York. During this period he gained for himself a wide audience as a gifted and original writer on sports. But with the publication of his *You Know Me, Al* about the time of the War, it was evident that this sports writer was more than a sports reporter—that there was a creative imagination at work. With the appearance of further stories he gained steadily in reputation, until even the "highbrow" critics acclaimed him a master in his own *genre*.

More perhaps than any contemporary American writer he caught the flavor of American speech and of various American types of character. Some of his stories dealing with baseball players are masterpieces of their kind. At his best he is a humorist of the highest order. And like other humorous writers—notably Mark Twain and Chekhov—there is a deep undercurrent of sadness and satire as well as a sense of tragedy underlying some of his work. His stories *Haircut* and *Champion* exemplify this. These two stories, however, usual nominations of anthologists, were never among Lardner's personal favorites. The two he preferred above all others were *The Golden Honeymoon* and *Some Like Them Cold,* and they are the two you will find in this collection.

WILBUR DANIEL STEELE
(1886–   )

WILBUR DANIEL STEELE has won the O. Henry Memorial Award four times. His stories are characterized by originality of theme and by skillful dramatic presentation. Often his themes are morbid or melodramatic, but Mr. Steele stands with the few contemporary writers who can, by their art, give plausibility to their material. The story *The Man Who Saw Through Heaven,* printed first in *Harper's Magazine,* is often regarded as one of his best stories.

Born in Greensboro, North Carolina, Mr. Steele as a child was educated in Berlin. He was reared in Denver, where he attended the university. His education continued with the study of painting in Paris, etching in Italy. He has traveled a great deal—in Europe, North Africa, the West Indies. For a number of years he made his home in Provincetown or Nantucket, and many of his stories deal with the people he has known on Cape Cod. He now lives either in Charleston, South Carolina, or in Connecticut.

EDNA FERBER
(1887–)

BENEATH the perfect urbanity and *savoir faire* of Miss Edna Ferber's present-day manner there beats still the heart of a simple, eager country girl, born in Kalamazoo, Michigan, and educated in Appleton, Wisconsin. The blend gives her every story just the right warmth and just the right sophistication to send it catapulting to the top of the national best-seller list. These, however, are best sellers that we may be proud of. Edna Ferber's *Show Boat, Cimarron, So Big* and *Giant* possess genuine literary quality; they are real pictures of American life.

Miss Ferber's training as a writer began on the *Milwaukee Journal.* Her first fictional work appeared in 1911. Today she lives on a fabulous Westchester estate, makes fabulous sums from her plays, short stories and novels, and is constantly surrounded by all the most fabulously clever people in New York. Some of her other books: *A Peculiar Treasure, Saratoga Trunk, Great Man, Giant.*

THOMAS BEER
(1889–1940)

THOMAS BEER was a native of Ohio, educated at Yale, but lived most of his life in or near New York and was identified with the writers of that section. He spent much time in Nantucket, and many of his stories have their locale there. He was successful in creating a number of characters and using them in story after story, so that for one who has followed his work, his men and women become as familiar as people in a novel. His story, *Tact,* is one of the first to introduce Mrs. Egg and her son Dammy.

There is a lightness of touch in Mr. Beer's stories, but very often it is a lightness of touch that deceives, because if you examine his work closely, there is always some very human trait involved—vicious and wicked and designing people are exposed, or very human follies revealed, or decent human behavior extolled.

Mr. Beer is the author of several novels, of a life of Stephen Crane, of a sensitive and discerning book, *The Mauve Decade.*

CONRAD AIKEN
(1889–   )

BORN in Savannah, Georgia, Conrad Aiken was left an orphan when a small child and was brought up in New Bedford, Massachusetts. He was graduated from Harvard, where, as a student, he distinguished himself in poetry. In 1930 Mr. Aiken was awarded the Pulitzer Prize for his *Selected Poems*. Mr. Aiken is primarily a poet, and in the forms of poetry, an experimenter. But his experimentations usually show the hand of a master technician. When he turned to prose, his gifts served him in that form with equal distinction. His novel *Blue Voyage* is a *tour de force* in the manipulation of the "stream of consciousness" technique.

The story here reprinted, *Silent Snow, Secret Snow,* is Conrad Aiken at his very best. He handles one of the most difficult of all themes; he reproduces the workings of the mind of a twelve-year-old boy—a mind hovering on the brink of madness.

CHRISTOPHER MORLEY
(1890–   )

BORN into the academic world, at Haverford, Pennsylvania, Christopher Morley was brought up in that atmosphere. His father moved from Haverford to become Professor of Mathematics at Johns Hopkins University, in Baltimore. Mr. Morley went back to Haverford for his undergraduate work. He was appointed a Rhodes Scholar to Oxford. When he returned to America, he went into newspaper work, and for a number of years he conducted a "column" on the old *New York Evening Post*. His gifts are peculiarly adapted to this kind of journalistic work. Each issue of his old column was something of an intimate and personal essay. His work has in fact been largely in the essay. But he has contributed as well to American letters longer pieces of fiction. In *The Arrow* there are brought together Mr. Morley's various talents—the wit, the urbanity, and the penchant for telling a story that have made him one of the most eagerly "collected" authors in America, as well as New York's most indefatigable and indispensable after-dinner speakers. When he is not writing or speaking, Mr. Morley serves as judge for the Book-of-the-Month Club, publishes a book himself ever so often, and holds down six or seven other jobs we cannot recall offhand.

DOROTHY PARKER
(1893–   )

On the basis of three slim volumes of verse, two books of short stories, and countless (usually scandalous) anecdotes, Dorothy Parker has become a myth to the entire country. Behind a mask of childlike innocence there lurks in her a ruthless malice, a devastating humor, that lays bare in a trice the foibles of humanity. Mr. Chesterton said of Jane Austen "that though she might have been protected from life, there was very little of life that was protected from Jane Austen." Dorothy Parker is the Jane Austen of her day.

Dorothy Parker is a native of New York, where she spends most of her time, unless called to Hollywood for a writing stint for the movies. Her public, however, longs for her to resume the literary life, and write more stories like *Big Blonde*.

THYRA SAMTER WINSLOW
(1893–   )

Thyra Samter Winslow was born in Fort Smith, Arkansas, was educated in Little Rock and the University of Missouri, and proceeded to Chicago, where for a number of years she worked in journalism. Then she came to New York and has lived there for the last fifteen years. She brought with her to her newspaper work, as well as to her fiction, her very sharp powers of observation. Unlike Ruth Suckow, Mrs. Winslow has written more of city people than of people on the land or in the small towns and cities of the Middle West. It is for city people of all kinds that she has the most sensitive appreciation—of their petty and circumscribed lives, of their struggles, their aspirations, and their achievements and defeats. Her work is for the most part impersonal, detached; she records faithfully and lets the facts speak for themselves. Mrs. Winslow's outlook is one of trenchant irony. *A Cycle of Manhattan* is a characteristic story, and one of her best.

KATHERINE ANNE PORTER
(1894–   )

Because Katherine Anne Porter is one of the most meticulous and discriminating of our contemporary writers, her books of short novels and stories have appeared after long intervals of preparation and revision. Her first, *Flowering Judas,* was published in 1930. It was not until 1939 that *Pale Horse, Pale Rider,* a collection of three short novels, was issued, and, after five years, *The Leaning Tower and Other Stories* made its appearance in 1944. Her most recent book, *The Days Before,* was published in 1952. Born in Texas and brought up in New Orleans, Miss Porter has lived in many parts of the United States, Mexico and Europe. She has been awarded two Guggenheim grants, a Book-of-the-Month Club fellowship and the honorary degree of Litt.D. by the Women's College of the University of North Carolina. She has been a vice-president of the National Institute of Arts and Letters and a fellow of the Library of Congress. Her tales, exquisitely wrought, have earned for her a world-wide reputation as an artist in the medium of the short story.

JAMES THURBER
(1894–   )

COLUMBUS, Ohio, James Thurber's birthplace, has been lovingly celebrated by its most tolerant yet critical son. But it is through the world of his own making—in memoirs, fables, satires, fantasies, stories and drawings—that James Thurber wanders restlessly and, in passing, becomes its recording angel. His imagination has given life to many quaint and hitherto obscure characters and has caricatured ambiguous fears into simple and not-at-all-frightening realities. Thurber, virtually blind, sees life in all its direct manifestations and fantasies and sets it down in simplified line and in crystal prose. The short story by which he is represented in this collection is, in our opinion, Thurber at his inimitable best.

F. SCOTT FITZGERALD
(1896–1940)

F. SCOTT FITZGERALD, bright, glittering star of the jazz age in American fiction, was born in Saint Paul, Minnesota, educated at Princeton, and as a handsome, popular young officer in the A. E. F., rounded off a preliminary training that equipped him to perfection for the sort of books he was destined to write. *This Side of Paradise* in 1920 and *The Beautiful and Damned* in 1922 not only enjoyed an enormous vogue, but set a new fashion for stories of the younger generation. And all the while, Fitzgerald and his beautiful wife, Zelda, were the toast of the smart set in New York, perfect counterparts of the characters he was writing about.

With maturity came adventures and misadventures of many descriptions. Fitzgerald's writing took a more serious turn. In 1925 he produced his finest book: *The Great Gatsby*. And then, after an eight-year silence, he produced another memorable novel, in 1933, called *Tender Is the Night*.

Fitzgerald (a direct descendant of the author of "The Star-Spangled Banner") spent the best years of his life in Baltimore. Then he went to Hollywood, where, when his heart gave way at forty-four, he was working on an unfinished novel about the fantastic motion-picture world, called *The Last Tycoon*. *The Rich Boy* is a typical Fitzgerald creation.

JOHN DOS PASSOS
(1896–   )

For a few years after the close of the War in 1918 American fiction maintained a silence about the events of the conflict, or treated the subject sentimentally. But with the publication in 1921 of John Dos Passos' *Three Soldiers* a new voice arose with the ring of truth about what really happened to young men engaged in the brutal conflict. And in every other book that followed, Dos Passos has maintained a high level of reality. Few authors have been as sensitive to the constantly changing American scene of the past thirty years. He has attempted to evolve new technical devices in writing that will most truly and adequately record that scene. His book, *1919*, records, episodically, the impression upon a sensitive man of the swift kaleidoscope of American life. *The Body of an American* is taken from this book because it forms a complete story.

Dos Passos was born in Chicago and educated at Harvard. When he was very young he went to France as an ambulance driver, at the very outset of the World War. Today he is engaged in the writing of novels and many articles on the American social and political scene.

WILLIAM FAULKNER
(1897–   )

The value and significance of William Faulkner's work has aroused more controversy than that of any other contemporary writer. On the one hand he has been completely damned, and on the other very highly praised. His damnation derives from his preoccupation with the lives of decadent and neurotic and even insane people in the South. Nevertheless, many modern critics are unanimous in their recognition of Faulkner's unusual power to impose upon his characters a vivid reality. More than any modern writer he can create moods and atmosphere.

He was born in Ripley, Mississippi; but since childhood he has lived in Oxford, in that State. He left the University of Mississippi when he was very young to join the Canadian Flying Corps. Wounded in an airplane crash, he returned to the United States, went to New Orleans, shared an apartment with Sherwood Anderson, did some sketches for newspapers, and settled down to write. In 1951 Faulkner was awarded the Nobel Prize for Literature.

Mr. Harlan Hatcher says of his work: "In an age inured to horror and indifferent through repetition to the cruelty and the crudity of decadent people, he has succeeded in extending their potency for shock. . . . And he defines the farthest limits to which the innovations and revolts that were at one time necessary to the continued well-being of our literature can be carried without final self-defeat."

ERNEST HEMINGWAY
(1898-   )

ERNEST HEMINGWAY's reputation as the leading American writer of the post-war generation rests squarely on his two fine novels, *The Sun Also Rises* and *A Farewell to Arms,* but his short stories have also contributed to his fame. The two stories reprinted in this anthology, or *The Undefeated,* or *Fifty Grand,* have been analyzed and discussed in probably every short story class in American colleges.

Hemingway himself has become an almost mythical character. He was born in Illinois. His father was a country doctor, and Hemingway accompanied him on many of his rounds (see his first book of stories, *In Our Time*). Just before the First World War, he served as a reporter on the *Kansas City Star,* but soon after the outbreak of hostilities, he enlisted in an American ambulance unit. He served with conspicuous bravery on the Italian front, where he was seriously wounded. After the Armistice, he became foreign correspondent for the *Toronto Star,* and later moved to Paris for the Hearst Syndicate. These Paris days marked the beginning of Hemingway's fame. His brusque, highly individual style of writing became the model for a horde of imitators; publishers began hailing one new hopeful after another as "another Ernest Hemingway!"

Hemingway's visit to the front in the Spanish Civil War furnished the material for one of his best novels, *For Whom the Bell Tolls.* At home, he usually can be found fishing off the Florida keys or in Cuba. His most recent work, *The Old Man and the Sea,* has reaffirmed his greatness as a story-teller. An avid outdoors man, he sedulously avoids the so-called literary set, particularly book critics.

JOHN STEINBECK
(1900–   )

JOHN STEINBECK is generally recognized today as one of the four greatest writers in America. *The Grapes of Wrath* is his outstanding novel, but *Tortilla Flat, Of Mice and Men,* and *The Moon Is Down* follow close behind. The best of his short stories are contained in a volume called *The Long Valley,* which includes "The Red Pony," reprinted here. Steinbeck was born in Salinas, California, and his close association with the bunkhouses and workingmen he describes so graphically began while he was in school. After intermittent attendance at Stanford University, he headed for New York. One of his jobs there was carrying bricks for the construction of Madison Square Garden. His first novel, *Cup of Gold,* published in 1929, was written while he was laboring as a watchman on a job seven thousand feet up in the High Sierras. In 1952 *East of Eden,* perhaps his most ambitious work of fiction, became a national best-seller and again confirmed the reputation he has maintained for more than twenty years as one of the foremost novelists of America.

THOMAS WOLFE
(1900–1938)

WE HAVE more information about Mr. Wolfe than about any contemporary writer, because Mr. Wolfe had, under a thin veil of autobiography, written about himself in two very long and revealing novels: *Look Homeward, Angel* and *Of Time and the River.* In them, one feels, all is set down. If one were trying to evaluate the defects and the virtues of this writer, one would have first to speak of the amazing prolificity of the man, and of his equally amazing treatment of scene after scene of the most restrained and telling realism. Then one would have to speak of the pages overladen with rhapsodic paeans, and of the repetitions that often weary. In *A Portrait of Bascom Hawke* are to be discovered his best qualities.

Mr. Wolfe was a "born" writer, but even with his unusual natural gifts he was tormented by his own despair and his lack of self-confidence before he had arrived. Like other young men aspiring to authorship, he was always thinking that he would go to Paris, or to Oxford, or some little place in Spain or Switzerland, "to settle down and write." And then he discovered finally that the place to write was anywhere, "so long as the heart, the power, the faith, the desperation, the bitter and unendurable necessity, and the naked courage were there inside him all the time." These references are to the hero Eugene Gant who is, however, often indistinguishable from Thomas Wolfe himself.

His untimely death in 1938 cut short a career that gave promise of a rich and permanent contribution to Amercian fiction.

KATHARINE BRUSH
(1902–1952)

THE work of this writer, particularly in *Night Club,* the story here included, exemplifies the statement that the very effective short story "comes nearer to the domain of the dramatist than the novelist; for it is in the truest sense a dramatic moment, which seizes on us by its intensity, its swift dynamic, its direct appeal." Instead of there being one such moment, there are a series of such moments in this story, each involving separate stories, yet all whirling ironically about the life of the very prosaic Mrs. Brady.

Katharine Brush, born in Middletown, Connecticut, was the daughter of the headmaster of a boys' school in New England. When she was confronted with the choice of going to college or to work, she preferred the latter, and began her career in the newspaper world. She lived for a while in Ohio, and then came to New York, and later went to California. Her work is characterized by keen observation and penetrating insight—all recorded in a swift and sophisticated style. Her best and most popular novels are *Young Man of Manhattan* and *Red-Headed Woman.*

ERSKINE CALDWELL
(1903–   )

MR. CALDWELL is best known for his novel *Tobacco Road* and for the play that was made from that book. His fame was of course enhanced by attempts to suppress his second novel, *God's Little Acre,* but his reputation as an artist did not need that artificial stimulant. He writes of the poor white trash of the Southern mountains, of the people of Georgia, chiefly. Where William Faulkner, dealing with some of the same people, casts his own spell upon them, and creates compelling moods, Mr. Caldwell, with much greater detachment from his people, merely records them; they create their own moods. And the result is that the characters in Mr. Caldwell's world—though difficult for most people to accept—are nevertheless made plausible on their own account.

It is as if the author said: Believe it or not, but this is what they are like. Mr. Caldwell is the son of a Presbyterian pastor. The migratory life of his family made formal schooling difficult. The son finally attended the University of Virginia for a while and then the University of Pennsylvania, but after three years "of effort to educate myself on university grounds, I gave the whole thing up," Mr. Caldwell writes, "and got a job in a newspaper office." He wrote for seven years before anything was published.

JOHN O'HARA
(1905–   )

FOR ten years after his graduation from prep school in 1924, John O'Hara wandered from one casual job to another as ship steward, railway freight clerk, gas-meter reader, amusement-park guard, soda clerk and secretary to the late Heywood Broun. Then, in 1934, the publication of his first novel, *Appointment in Samarra,* won for him a startlingly immediate and then a more lasting literary reputation. Subsequent novels and collections of short stories confirmed the first generous praise of critics and his early readers. His novel, *A Rage to Live,* was an enormous success and the musical comedy, *Pal Joey,* based on his short stories, became one of the all-time Broadway hits when it was revived eleven years after its original production. John O'Hara's short stories are notable for their accuracy in significant detail, for the acute ear which catches the most subtle distinctions of speech and the suggested, but never underlined, tensions of human conflict.

WILLIAM SAROYAN
(1908–   )

WILLIAM SAROYAN, an American of Armenian parentage, burst into the limelight with the publication in *Story Magazine* early in 1934 of his story *The Daring Young Man on the Flying Trapeze.* His first volume, bearing the same title, was published a few months later, and evoked critical hoop-las from many high places. He is one of the young contemporary writers who has breathed new life into the American short story. And he has managed to do this in part by completely disregarding all formulae for the conventionally constructed short story. Let him speak for himself in the following words, quoted from a letter written to a friend: "I cannot understand why you should be so excited about the violation of a number of rules of writing . . . inasmuch as rules, actually, are valuable and necessary only when they emerge from the immediate and specific needs of a work. . . . It is wise to presume, I think, that rules, by themselves, do not exist at all. They come into being when material for a work of art comes into being, and their function is to give the work grace and liveliness, meaning, finality, wholeness. . . . What I write is not a story; very good. It doesn't matter in the slightest. I dislike dickering. Whatever it is, it is not dead. . . . I am very much interested in the potentialities of our literature, and my notion is that if we monkey with rules too much our best writing is never going to get into print."

His play, *The Time of Your Life*, won the Pulitzer Prize in 1940, but the unpredictable Saroyan disdained to accept it. The Book-of-the-Month Club chose both *My Name Is Aram* and *The Human Comedy*, which more than offset the failure on Broadway of his last two plays. During the Second World War he enlisted in the Signal Corps and since then has written several novels, many plays, innumerable short stories and even a very popular song.

EUDORA WELTY
(1909–   )

To MISSISSIPPI Eudora Welty owes the memories and impressions of her childhood and early womanhood which later she fashioned into novels and stories of imagination and insight. She was born in the Delta State and, except for absences to complete her education at the University of Wisconsin and Columbia University, has lived there all her life. While an undergraduate at the Mississippi State College for Women she began to write stories and soon they made their appearance in national magazines. Author of five books—*A Curtain of Green* (1941), *The Robber Bridegroom* (1942), *The Wide Net* (1943), *Delta Wedding* (1946) and *The Golden Apples* (1949)—Miss Welty received the O. Henry Memorial Prize for the short story in 1942 and 1943 and was awarded $1000 by the American Academy of Arts and Letters "in recognition of her skill in the short story and her artistry in the subtle portrayal of character."

WALTER VAN TILBURG CLARK
(1909–   )

ALTHOUGH he was born in East Oreland, Maine, virtually all of Walter Van Tilburg Clark's life has been identified with the Rocky Mountain

West. His father was President of the University of Nevada in Reno and it was there that the author of "The Portable Phonograph" spent his undergraduate days. He became a teacher of English, a lecturer and a basketball coach. When his first novel, *The Ox-Bow Incident,* was published it was acclaimed as the greatest "Western" since Owen Wister's *The Virginian* and in its motion-picture incarnation became a film classic. Two other novels— *The City of Trembling Leaves* (1945) and *The Track of the Cat* (1949)—and many short stories, notably the collection, *The Watchful Gods and Other Stories* (1950), have added to his stature as a writer of scrupulous and uncompromising devotion to his craft and art.

IRWIN SHAW
(1913-   )

IRWIN SHAW's progress from his apprenticeship as a writer of countless radio serials to his present position as one of America's foremost novelists and short-story writers did not lack for color and excitement on its own account. At college he was a star football player, a prolific undergraduate dramatist, columnist and ghost writer. On the side, he amplified his income by tutoring, typing and anonymously collaborating on doctoral theses. In 1936, his first play, *Bury the Dead,* earned for him a national reputation, and when he went to Hollywood he became a top-flight screen writer. In the meantime, he wrote several plays which achieved Broadway production and a very considerable success. During the Second World War he saw service, as enlisted man and then as officer, in Africa, England, France and Germany. His first novel, *The Young Lions,* immediately became a national best-seller and his second, *The Troubled Air,* stirred up a tempest of controversy. But Irwin Shaw is best known for his short stories, the last collection of which—*Mixed Company*—was received with unmixed praise from critics and readers alike.

BUDD SCHULBERG
(1914-   )

AFTER a childhood and youth in Hollywood, Budd Schulberg reversed the direction in Horace Greeley's advice and came East to try his fortunes as a novelist. He was brought up, virtually, on a motion-picture lot; for many years his father was production chief of Paramount Studios. After graduation from Dartmouth, where he was a frequent contributor to the college literary journal, Budd Schulberg tried his hand at short stories, many of which were published in national magazines. One of these was called "What Makes Sammy Run?" Subsequently it was developed into the novel of that name and immediately after publication in 1941 aroused a whirlwind of praise and blame. Its title soon became a phrase incorporated into our language and its central character, Sammy Glick, came to personify the All-American heel. In 1947, Schulberg's second novel, *The Harder They Fall,* written after many years' association with prize fighters and the ring, gained what is known among followers of the manly art as a split decision. But it was in 1950, with the publication of *The Disenchanted,* the novel of a golden figure in the glittering decade of the Twenties, a Book-of-the-Month Club choice and a national best-seller, that Budd Schulberg won a place in the very first rank of American writers. His collection of short stories, *Some Faces in the Crowd,* made its appearance in the Spring of 1953.

J. D. SALINGER
(1919–   )

THE wonder and pleasure and pain of the world to a boy of sixteen, set down with imagination and compassion in *The Catcher in the Rye,* called nationwide attention to a new and unmistakably original voice in American fiction. Before his impressive debut as a novelist, J. D. Salinger had been writing short stories, most of which appeared in *The New Yorker.* He was born in New York City and attended its public schools until he entered a military academy in Pennsylvania. Exposure to three colleges, none of which granted him a degree, completed his formal education. After one footloose year in Europe and four as a foot soldier in the Army during World War Two, Salinger established non-military headquarters in Westport, Connecticut, where he is devoting himself to the writing of a novel and more short stories.

These biographical sketches have been revised in August, 1953. As further changes become necessary, they will be made in future editions.

THE EDITORS

MODERN LIBRARY GIANTS

*A series of full-sized library editions of books that formerly
were available only in cumbersome and expensive sets.*
THE MODERN LIBRARY GIANTS REPRESENT A
SELECTION OF THE WORLD'S GREATEST BOOKS

These volumes contain from 600 to 1,400 pages each

G1. TOLSTOY, LEO. War and Peace.
G2. BOSWELL, JAMES. Life of Samuel Johnson.
G3. HUGO, VICTOR. Les Miserables.
G4. THE COMPLETE POEMS OF KEATS AND SHELLEY.
G5. PLUTARCH'S LIVES (The Dryden Translation).
G6.
G7. } GIBBON, EDWARD. The Decline and Fall of the Roman
G8.   Empire (Complete in three volumes).
G9. GREAT VOICES OF THE REFORMATION.
G10. TWELVE FAMOUS RESTORATION PLAYS (1660-1820)
     (Congreve, Wycherley, Gay, Goldsmith, Sheridan, etc.)
G11. JAMES, HENRY. The Short Stories of
G12. THE MOST POPULAR NOVELS OF SIR WALTER
     SCOTT (Quentin Durward, Ivanhoe and Kenilworth).
G13. CARLYLE, THOMAS. The French Revolution.
G14. BULFINCH'S MYTHOLOGY (Illustrated).
G15. CERVANTES. Don Quixote (Illustrated).
G16. THE EUROPEAN PHILOSOPHERS FROM DESCARTES TO
     NIETZSCHE.
G17. THE POEMS AND PLAYS OF ROBERT BROWNING.
G18. ELEVEN PLAYS OF HENRIK IBSEN.
G19. THE COMPLETE WORKS OF HOMER.
G20. THE LIFE AND WRITINGS OF ABRAHAM LINCOLN.
G21. SIXTEEN FAMOUS AMERICAN PLAYS.
G22. THIRTY FAMOUS ONE-ACT PLAYS.
G23. TOLSTOY, LEO. Anna Karenina.
G24. LAMB, CHARLES. The Complete Works and Letters of
G25. THE COMPLETE PLAYS OF GILBERT AND SULLIVAN.
G26. MARX, KARL. Capital.
G27. DARWIN, CHARLES. Origin of Species & The Descent of Man.
G28. THE COMPLETE WORKS OF LEWIS CARROLL.
G29. PRESCOTT, WILLIAM H. The Conquest of Mexico and
     The Conquest of Peru.
G30. MYERS, GUSTAVUS. History of the Great American
     Fortunes.
G31. FAMOUS SCIENCE-FICTION STORIES: ADVENTURES IN
     TIME AND SPACE
G32. SMITH, ADAM. The Wealth of Nations.
G33. COLLINS, WILKIE. The Moonstone and The Woman in White.
G34. NIETZSCHE, FRIEDRICH. The Philosophy of Nietzsche.
G35. BURY, J. B. A History of Greece.
G36. DOSTOYEVSKY, FYODOR. The Brothers Karamazov.
G37. THE COMPLETE NOVELS AND SELECTED TALES OF
     NATHANIEL HAWTHORNE.
G38. MURASAKA, LADY, The Tale of Genji.